JONATHAN STRANGE

&

Mr NORRELL

JONATHAN STRANGE

Mr NORRELL

Susanna Clarke

Illustrations by Portia Rosenberg

BLOOMSBURY

First published 2004
This paperback edition published 2005

Copyright © 2004 by Susanna Clarke

The moral right of the author has been asserted

Illustrations copyright © 2004 by Portia Rosenberg

Bloomsbury Publishing Plc, 38 Soho Square, London WID 3HB

A CIP catalogue for this book is available from the British Library

ISBN 0 7475 8069 3
9780747580690

10 9 8 7 6 5 4 3 2 1

Typeset by Hewer Text UK Ltd, Edinburgh
Printed in the United States of America
by Quebecor World Buffalo

All papers used by Bloomsbury Publishing are natural,
recyclable products made from wood grown in well-managed
forests. The manufacturing processes conform to the
environmental regulations of the country of origin.

www.jonathanstrange.com

In memory of my brother,
Paul Frederick Gunn Clarke, 1961–2000

CONTENTS

Volume II: Jonathan Strange

Volume III: John Uskglass

Volume I

Mr NORRELL

He hardly ever spoke of magic, and when he
did it was like a history lesson and no one
could bear to listen to him.

1

The library at Hurtfew

Autumn 1806–January 1807

SOME YEARS AGO there was in the city of York a society of
magicians. They met upon the third Wednesday of every
month and read each other long, dull papers upon the
story of English magic.

They were gentleman-magicians, which is to say they had never
armed any one by magic – nor ever done any one the slightest
ood. In fact, to own the truth, not one of these magicians had ever
ast the smallest spell, nor by magic caused one leaf to tremble
pon a tree, made one mote of dust to alter its course or changed a
ngle hair upon any one's head. But, with this one minor reserva-
on, they enjoyed a reputation as some of the wisest and most
agical gentlemen in Yorkshire.

A great magician has said of his profession that its practitioners
. . must pound and rack their brains to make the least learning
in, but quarrelling always comes very naturally to them,"[1] and
e York magicians had proved the truth of this for a number of
ears.

In the autumn of 1806 they received an addition in a gentleman
lled John Segundus. At the first meeting that he attended Mr
egundus rose and addressed the society. He began by compli-

The History and Practice of English Magic, by Jonathan Strange, vol. I, chap. 2,
ub. John Murray, London, 1816.

menting the gentlemen upon their distinguished history; he liste
the many celebrated magicians and historians that had at one tin
or another belonged to the York society. He hinted that it ha
been no small inducement to him in coming to York to know of th
existence of such a society. Northern magicians, he reminded h
audience, had always been better respected than southern one
Mr Segundus said that he had studied magic for many years ar
knew the histories of all the great magicians of long ago. He rea
the new publications upon the subject and had even made
modest contribution to their number, but recently he had begun
wonder why the great feats of magic that he read about remaine
on the pages of his book and were no longer seen in the street
written about in the newspapers. Mr Segundus wished to know, l
said, why modern magicians were unable to work the magic the
wrote about. In short, he wished to know why there was no mo
magic done in England.

It was the most commonplace question in the world. It was th
question which, sooner or later, every child in the kingdom asks h
governess or his schoolmaster or his parent. Yet the learne
members of the York society did not at all like hearing it aske
and the reason was this: they were no more able to answer it tha
any one else.

The President of the York society (whose name was Dr Fo
castle) turned to John Segundus and explained that the questio
was a wrong one. "It presupposes that magicians have some sort
duty to do magic – which is clearly nonsense. You would not,
imagine, suggest that it is the task of botanists to devise mor
flowers? Or that astronomers should labour to rearrange the star
Magicians, Mr Segundus, study magic which was done long ag
Why should any one expect more?"

An elderly gentleman with faint blue eyes and faintly-coloure
clothes (called either Hart or Hunt – Mr Segundus could neve
quite catch the name) faintly said that it did not matter in the lea
whether any body expected it or not. A gentleman could not d

4

agic. Magic was what street sorcerers pretended to do in order to
b children of their pennies. Magic (in the practical sense) was
uch fallen off. It had low connexions. It was the bosom compan-
n of unshaven faces, gypsies, house-breakers; the frequenter of
ngy rooms with dirty yellow curtains. Oh no! A gentleman could
t do magic. A gentleman might study the history of magic
othing could be nobler) but he could not do any. The elderly
ntleman looked with faint, fatherly eyes at Mr Segundus and
d that he hoped Mr Segundus had not been trying to cast spells.
Mr Segundus blushed.

But the famous magician's maxim held true: two magicians – in
is case Dr Foxcastle and Mr Hunt or Hart – could not agree
thout two more thinking the exact opposite. Several of the
ntlemen began to discover that they were entirely of Mr
gundus's opinion and that no question in all of magical scholar-
ip could be so important as this one. Chief among Mr Segun-
us's supporters was a gentleman called Honeyfoot, a pleasant,
endly sort of man of fifty-five, with a red face and grey hair. As
e exchanges became more bitter and Dr Foxcastle grew in
rcasm towards Mr Segundus, Mr Honeyfoot turned to him
veral times and whispered such comfort as, "Do not mind them,
. I am entirely of your opinion;" and "You are quite right, sir,
) not let them sway you;" and "You have hit upon it! Indeed you
ve, sir! It was the want of the right question which held us back
fore. Now that you are come we shall do great things."

Such kind words as these did not fail to find a grateful listener in
hn Segundus, whose shock shewed clearly in his face. "I fear that
iave made myself disagreeable," he whispered to Mr Honeyfoot.
That was not my intention. I had hoped for these gentlemen's
od opinion."

At first Mr Segundus was inclined to be downcast but a
rticularly spiteful outburst from Dr Foxcastle roused him to
little indignation. "That gentleman," said Dr Foxcastle, fixing
r Segundus with a cold stare, "seems determined that we should

5

share in the unhappy fate of the Society of Manchester Magicians!"

Mr Segundus inclined his head towards Mr Honeyfoot and said "I had not expected to find the magicians of Yorkshire quite obstinate. If magic does not have friends in Yorkshire where must we find them?"

Mr Honeyfoot's kindness to Mr Segundus did not end with the evening. He invited Mr Segundus to his house in High-Petergate to eat a good dinner in company with Mrs Honeyfoot and her three pretty daughters, which Mr Segundus, who was a single gentleman and not rich, was glad to do. After dinner Mr Honeyfoot played the pianoforte and Miss Jane sang in Italian. The next day Mrs Honeyfoot told her husband that John Segundus was exactly what a gentleman should be, but she feared he would never profit by it for it was not the fashion to be modest and quiet and kind-hearted.

The intimacy between the two gentlemen advanced very rapidly. Soon Mr Segundus was spending two or three evenings out of every seven at the house in High-Petergate. Once there was quite a crowd of young people present which naturally led to dancing. It was all very delightful but often Mr Honeyfoot and Mr Segundus would slip away to discuss the one thing which really interested both them – why was there no more magic done in England? But talk they would (often till two or three in the morning) they came no nearer to an answer; and perhaps this was not so very remarkable for all sorts of magicians and antiquarians and scholars had been asking the same question for rather more than two hundred years.

Mr Honeyfoot was a tall, cheerful, smiling gentleman with a great deal of energy, who always liked to be doing or planning something, rarely thinking to inquire whether that something were to the purpose. The present task put him very much in mind of the great mediaeval magicians,[2] who, whenever they had some seeming

---

[2] More properly called *Aureate* or Golden Age magicians.

impossible problem to solve, would ride away for a year and a day with only a fairy-servant or two to guide them and at the end of this time never failed to find the answer. Mr Honeyfoot told Mr Segundus that in his opinion they could not do better than emulate these great men, some of whom had gone to the most retired parts of England and Scotland and Ireland (where magic was strongest) while others had ridden out of this world entirely and no one nowadays was quite clear about where they had gone or what they had done when they got there. Mr Honeyfoot did not propose going quite so far – indeed he did not wish to go far at all because it was winter and the roads were very shocking. Nevertheless he was strongly persuaded that they should go *somewhere* and consult *someone*. He told Mr Segundus that he thought they were both growing stale; the advantage of a fresh opinion would be immense. But no destination, no object presented itself. Mr Honeyfoot was in despair: and then he thought of the other magician.

Some years before, the York society had heard rumours that there was another magician in Yorkshire. This gentleman lived in a very retired part of the country where (it was said) he passed his days and nights studying rare magical texts in his wonderful library. Dr Foxcastle had found out the other magician's name and where he might be found, and had written a polite letter inviting the other magician to become a member of the York society. The other magician had written back, expressing his sense of the honour done him and his deep regret: he was quite unable – the long distance between York and Hurtfew Abbey – the indifferent roads – the work that he could on no account neglect – etc., etc.

The York magicians had all looked over the letter and expressed their doubts that any body with such small handwriting could ever make a tolerable magician. Then – with some slight regret for the wonderful library they would never see – they had dismissed the other magician from their thoughts. But Mr Honeyfoot said to Mr

Segundus that the importance of the question, "Why was there no more magic done in England?" was such that it would be very wrong of them to neglect any opening. Who could say? – the other magician's opinion might be worth having. And so he wrote a letter proposing that he and Mr Segundus give themselves the satisfaction of waiting on the other magician on the third Tuesday after Christmas at half past two. A reply came very promptly; Mr Honeyfoot with his customary good nature and good fellowship immediately sent for Mr Segundus and shewed him the letter. The other magician wrote in his small handwriting that he would be very happy in the acquaintance. This was enough. Mr Honeyfoot was very well pleased and instantly strode off to tell Waters, the coachman, when he would be needed.

Mr Segundus was left alone in the room with the letter in his hand. He read: ". . . I am, I confess, somewhat at a loss to account for the sudden honour done to me. It is scarcely conceivable that the magicians of York with all the happiness of each other's society and the incalculable benefit of each other's wisdom should feel any necessity to consult a solitary scholar such as myself . . ."

There was an air of subtle sarcasm about the letter; the writer seemed to mock Mr Honeyfoot with every word. Mr Segundus was glad to reflect that Mr Honeyfoot could scarcely have noticed or he would not have gone with such elated spirits to speak to Waters. It was such a *very* unfriendly letter that Mr Segundus found that all his desire to look upon the other magician had quite evaporated. Well, no matter, he thought, I must go because Mr Honeyfoot wishes it – and what, after all, is the worst that can happen? We will see him and be disappointed and that will be an end of it.

The day of the visit was preceded by stormy weather; rain had made long ragged pools in the bare, brown fields; wet roofs were like cold stone mirrors; and Mr Honeyfoot's post-chaise travelled through a world that seemed to contain a much higher proportion of chill grey sky and a much smaller one of solid comfortable earth than was usually the case.

Ever since the first evening Mr Segundus had been intending to ask Mr Honeyfoot about the Learned Society of Magicians of Manchester which Dr Foxcastle had mentioned. He did so now.

"It was a society of quite recent foundation," said Mr Honeyfoot, "and its members were clergymen of the poorer sort, respectable ex-tradesmen, apothecaries, lawyers, retired mill owners who had got up a little Latin and so forth, such people as might be termed half-gentlemen. I believe Dr Foxcastle was glad when they disbanded – he does not think that people of that sort have any business becoming magicians. And yet, you know, there were several clever men among them. They began, as you did, with the aim of bringing back practical magic to the world. They were practical men and wished to apply the principles of reason and science to magic as they had done to the manufacturing arts. They called it 'Rational Thaumaturgy'. When it did not work they became discouraged. Well, they cannot be blamed for that. But they let their disillusionment lead them into all sorts of difficulties. They began to think that there was not now nor ever had been magic in the world. They said that the *Aureate* magicians were all deceivers or were themselves deceived. And that the Raven King was an invention of the northern English to keep themselves from the tyranny of the south (being north-country men themselves they had some sympathy with that). Oh, their arguments were very ingenious – I forget how they explained fairies. They disbanded, as I told you, and one of them, whose name was Aubrey I think, meant to write it all down and publish it. But when it came to the point he found that a sort of fixed melancholy had settled on him and he was not able to rouse himself enough to begin."

"Poor gentleman," said Mr Segundus. "Perhaps it is the age. It is not an age for magic or scholarship, is it sir? Tradesmen prosper, sailors, politicians, but not magicians. Our time is past." He thought for a moment. "Three years ago," he said, "I was in London and I met with a street magician, a vagabonding, yellow-curtain sort of fellow with a strange disfiguration. This man

9

persuaded me to part with quite a high sum of money – in return for which he promised to tell me a great secret. When I had paid him the money he told me that one day magic would be restored to England by two magicians. Now I do not at all believe in prophecies, yet it is thinking on what he said that has determined me to discover the truth of our fallen state – is not that strange?"

"You were entirely right – prophecies are great nonsense," said Mr Honeyfoot, laughing. And then, as if struck by a thought, he said, "We are two magicians. Honeyfoot and Segundus," he said, trying it out, as if thinking how it would look in the newspapers and history books, "Honeyfoot and Segundus – it sounds very well."

Mr Segundus shook his head. "The fellow knew my profession and it was only to be expected that he should pretend to me that I was one of the two men. But in the end he told me quite plainly that I was not. At first it seemed as if he was not sure of it. There was something about me . . . He made me write down my name and looked at it a good long while."

"I expect he could see there was no more money to be got out of you," said Mr Honeyfoot.

Hurtfew Abbey was some fourteen miles north-west of York. The antiquity was all in the name. There had been an abbey but that was long ago; the present house had been built in the reign of Anne. It was very handsome and square and solid-looking in a fine park full of ghostly-looking wet trees (for the day was becoming rather misty). A river (called the Hurt) ran through the park and a fine classical-looking bridge led across it.

The other magician (whose name was Norrell) was in the hall to receive his guests. He was small, like his handwriting, and his voice when he welcomed them to Hurtfew was rather quiet as if he were not used to speaking his thoughts out loud. Mr Honeyfoot who was a little deaf did not catch what he said; "I get old, sir – a common failing. I hope you will bear with me."

Mr Norrell led his guests to a handsome drawing-room with a

ood fire burning in the hearth. No candles had been lit; two fine
windows gave plenty of light to see by – although it was a grey sort
of light and not at all cheerful. Yet the idea of a second fire, or
candles, burning somewhere in the room kept occurring to Mr
Segundus, so that he continually turned in his chair and looked
about him to discover where they might be. But there never was
any thing – only perhaps a mirror or an antique clock.

Mr Norrell said that he had read Mr Segundus's account of the
careers of Martin Pale's fairy-servants.[3] "A creditable piece of
work, sir, but you left out Master Fallowthought. A very minor
spirit certainly, whose usefulness to the great Dr Pale was ques-
tionable.[4] Nevertheless your little history was incomplete without
him."

There was a pause. "A fairy-spirit called Fallowthought, sir?"
said Mr Segundus, "I . . . that is . . . that is to say I never heard of
any such creature – in this world or any other."

Mr Norrell smiled for the first time – but it was an inward sort of
smile. "Of course," he said, "I am forgetting. It is all in Holgarth
and Pickle's history of their own dealings with Master Fallowthought, which you could scarcely have read. I congratulate
you – they were an unsavoury pair – more criminal than magical:
the less one knows of them the better."

"Ah, sir!" cried Mr Honeyfoot, suspecting that Mr Norrell was
speaking of one of his books. "We hear marvellous things of your
library. All the magicians in Yorkshire fell into fits of jealousy
when they heard of the great number of books you had got!"

"Indeed?" said Mr Norrell coldly. "You surprize me. I had no
idea my affairs were so commonly known . . . I expect it is

---

[3] *A Complete Description of Dr Pale's fairy-servants, their Names, Histories, Characters
and the Services they performed for Him* by John Segundus, pub. by Thomas
Burnham, Bookseller, Northampton, 1799.
[4] Dr Martin Pale (1485–1567) was the son of a Warwick leather-tanner. He
was the last of the *Aureate* or Golden Age magicians. Other magicians followed
him (c.f. Gregory Absalom) but their reputations are debatable. Pale was
certainly the last English magician to venture into Faerie.

11

Thoroughgood," he said thoughtfully, naming a man who sol
books and curiosities in Coffee-yard in York. "Childermass ha
warned me several times that Thoroughgood is a chatterer."

Mr Honeyfoot did not quite understand this. If *he* had had suc
quantities of magical books he would have loved to talk of them, b
complimented on them, and have them admired; and he could no
believe that Mr Norrell was not the same. Meaning therefore to b
kind and to set Mr Norrell at his ease (for he had taken it into h
head that the gentleman was shy) he persisted: "Might I b
permitted to express a wish, sir, that we might see your wonderfu
library?"

Mr Segundus was certain that Norrell would refuse, bu
instead Mr Norrell regarded them steadily for some momen
(he had small blue eyes and seemed to peep out at them fror
some secret place inside himself) and then, almost graciously, h
granted Mr Honeyfoot's request. Mr Honeyfoot was all grati
tude, happy in the belief that he had pleased Mr Norrell as muc
as himself.

Mr Norrell led the other two gentlemen along a passage – a ver
ordinary passage, thought Mr Segundus, panelled and floore
with well-polished oak, and smelling of beeswax; then there was
staircase, or perhaps only three or four steps; and then anothe
passage where the air was somewhat colder and the floor was goo
York stone: all entirely unremarkable. (Unless the second passag
had come before the staircase or steps? Or had there in truth bee
a staircase at all?) Mr Segundus was one of those happy gentleme
who can always say whether they face north or south, east or west
It was not a talent he took any particular pride in – it was a
natural to him as knowing that his head still stood upon hi
shoulders – but in Mr Norrell's house his gift deserted him. H
could never afterwards picture the sequence of passageways an
rooms through which they had passed, nor quite decide how lon
they had taken to reach the library. And he could not tell th
direction; it seemed to him as if Mr Norrell had discovered som

ifth point of the compass – not east, nor south, nor west, nor north, but somewhere quite different and this was the direction in which he led them. Mr Honeyfoot, on the other hand, did not appear to notice any thing odd.

The library was perhaps a little smaller than the drawing-room they had just quitted. There was a noble fire in the hearth and all was comfort and quiet. Yet once again the light within the room did not seem to accord with the three tall twelve-paned windows, so that once again Mr Segundus was made uncomfortable by a persistent feeling that there ought to have been other candles in the room, other windows or another fire to account for the light. What windows there were looked out upon a wide expanse of dusky English rain so that Mr Segundus could not make out the view nor guess where in the house they stood.

The room was not empty; there was a man sitting at a table who rose as they entered, and whom Mr Norrell briefly declared to be Childermass, his man of business.

Mr Honeyfoot and Mr Segundus, being magicians themselves, had not needed to be told that the library of Hurtfew Abbey was dearer to its possessor than all his other riches; and they were not surprized to discover that Mr Norrell had constructed a beautiful jewel box to house his heart's treasure. The bookcases which lined the walls of the room were built of English woods and resembled Gothic arches laden with carvings. There were carvings of leaves (dried and twisted leaves, as if the season the artist had intended to represent were autumn), carvings of intertwining roots and branches, carvings of berries and ivy – all wonderfully done. But the wonder of the bookcases was nothing to the wonder of the books.

The first thing a student of magic learns is that there are books *about* magic and books *of* magic. And the second thing he learns is that a perfectly respectable example of the former may be had for two or three guineas at a good bookseller, and that the value of the latter is above rubies.[5] The collection of the York society wa reckoned very fine – almost remarkable; among its many volume were five works written between 1550 and 1700 and which migh reasonably be claimed as books of magic (though one was no mor than a couple of ragged pages). Books of magic are rare an neither Mr Segundus nor Mr Honeyfoot had ever seen more tha two or three in a private library. At Hurtfew all the walls wer lined with bookshelves and all the shelves were filled with book And the books were all, or almost all, old books; books of magic Oh! to be sure many had clean modern bindings, but clearly thes were volumes which Mr Norrell had had rebound (he favoured, seemed, plain calf with the titles stamped in neat silver capitals But many had bindings that were old, old, old, with crumblin spines and corners.

Mr Segundus glanced at the spines of the books on a nearb shelf; the first title he read was *How to putte Questiones to the Dark an understand its Answeres*.

---

[5] Magicians, as we know from Jonathan Strange's maxim, will quarrel abou any thing and many years and much learning has been applied to the vexe question of whether such and such a volume qualifies as a book of magic. Bu most laymen find they are served well enough by this simple rule: book written before magic ended in England are books of magic, books writte later are books about magic. The principle, from which the layman's rule thumb derives, is that a book of magic should be written by a practising magician, rather than a theoretical magician or a historian of magic. Wha could be more reasonable? And yet already we are in difficulties. The grea masters of magic, those we term the Golden Age or *Aureate* magician (Thomas Godbless, Ralph Stokesey, Catherine of Winchester, the Rave King) wrote little, or little has survived. It is probable that Thomas Godbles could not write. Stokesey learnt Latin at a little grammar school in his nativ Devonshire, but all that we know of him comes from other writers.

Magicians only applied themselves to writing books when magic wa already in decline. Darkness was already approaching to quench the glor of English magic; those men we call the Silver Age or *Argentine* magician (Thomas Lanchester, 1518–90; Jacques Belasis, 1526–1604; Nicholas Gou bert, 1535–78; Gregory Absalom, 1507–99) were flickering candles in th twilight; they were scholars first and magicians second. Certainly the claimed to do magic, some even had a fairy-servant or two, but they seen to have accomplished very little in this way and some modern scholars hav doubted whether they could do magic at all.

"A foolish work," said Mr Norrell. Mr Segundus started – he had not known his host was so close by. Mr Norrell continued, "I would advise you not to waste a moment's thought upon it."

So Mr Segundus looked at the next book which was Belasis's *Instructions.*

"You know Belasis, I dare say?" asked Mr Norrell.

"Only by reputation, sir," said Mr Segundus, "I have often heard that he held the key to a good many things, but I have also heard – indeed all the authorities agree – that every copy of *The Instructions* was destroyed long ago. Yet now here it is! Why, sir, it is extraordinary! It is wonderful!"

"You expect a great deal of Belasis," remarked Norrell, "and once upon a time I was entirely of your mind. I remember that for many months I devoted eight hours out of every twenty-four to studying his work; a compliment, I may say, that I have never paid any other author. But ultimately he is disappointing. He is mystical where he ought to be intelligible – and intelligible where he ought to be obscure. There are some things which have no business being put into books for all the world to read. For myself I no longer have any very great opinion of Belasis."

"Here is a book I never even heard of, sir," said Mr Segundus, "*The Excellences of Christo-Judaic Magick.* What can you tell me of this?"

"Ha!" cried Mr Norrell. "It dates from the seventeenth century, but I have no great opinion of it. Its author was a liar, a drunkard, an adulterer and a rogue. I am glad he has been so completely forgot."

It seemed that it was not only live magicians which Mr Norrell despised. He had taken the measure of all the dead ones too and found them wanting.

Mr Honeyfoot meanwhile, his hands in the air like a Methodist praising God, was walking rapidly from bookcase to bookcase; he could scarcely stop long enough to read the title of one book before his eye was caught by another on the other side of the room. "Oh, Mr Norrell!" he cried. "Such a quantity of books! Surely we shall find the answers to all our questions here!"

"I doubt it, sir," was Mr Norrell's dry reply.

The man of business gave a short laugh – laughter which was clearly directed at Mr Honeyfoot, yet Mr Norrell did not reprimand him either by look or word, and Mr Segundus wondered what sort of business it could be that Mr Norrell entrusted to this person. With his long hair as ragged as rain and as black as thunder, he would have looked quite at home upon a windswept moor, or lurking in some pitch-black alleyway, or perhaps in a novel by Mrs Radcliffe.

Mr Segundus took down *The Instructions* of Jacques Belasis and, despite Mr Norrell's poor opinion of it, instantly hit upon two extraordinary passages.[6] Then, conscious of time passing and of

---

[6] The first passage which Mr Segundus read concerned England, Faerie (which magicians sometimes call "the Other Lands") and a strange country that is reputed to lie on the far side of Hell. Mr Segundus had heard something of the symbolic and magical bond which links these three lands, yet never had he read so clear an explanation of it as was put forward here.

The second extract concerned one of England's greatest magicians, Martin Pale. In Gregory Absalom's *The Tree of Learning* there is a famous passage which relates how, while journeying through Faerie, the last of the great *Aureate* magicians, Martin Pale, paid a visit to a fairy-prince. Like most of his race the fairy had a great multitude of names, honorifics, titles and pseudonyms; but usually he was known as Cold Henry. Cold Henry made a long and deferential speech to his guest. The speech was full of metaphors and obscure allusions, but what Cold Henry seemed to be saying was that fairies were naturally wicked creatures who did not always know when they were going wrong. To this Martin Pale briefly and somewhat enigmatically replied that not all Englishmen have the same size feet.

For several centuries no one had the faintest idea what any of this might mean, though several theories were advanced – and John Segundus was familiar with all of them. The most popular was that developed by William Pantler in the early eighteenth century. Pantler said that Cold Henry and Pale were speaking of theology. Fairies (as everybody knows) are beyond the reach of the Church; no Christ has come to them, nor ever will – and what is to become of them on Judgement Day no one knows. According to Pantler Cold Henry meant to enquire of Pale if there was any hope that fairies, like men, might receive Eternal Salvation. Pale's reply – that Englishmen's feet are different sizes – was his way of saying that not all Englishmen will be saved. Based on this Pantler goes on to attribute to Pale a rather odd belief that Heaven is large enough to hold only a finite number of the Blessed; for every Englishmen who is damned, a place opens up in Heaven for a fairy.

the queer, dark eye of the man of business upon him, he opened *The Excellences of Christo-Judaic Magick*. This was not (as he had supposed) a printed book, but a manuscript scribbled down very hurriedly upon the backs of all kinds of bits of paper, most of them old ale-house bills. Here Mr Segundus read of wonderful adventures. The seventeenth-century magician had used his scanty magic to battle against great and powerful enemies: battles which no human magician ought to have attempted. He had scribbled down the history of his patchwork victories just as those enemies were closing around him. The author had known very well that, as he wrote, time was running out for him and death was the best that he could hope for.

The room was becoming darker; the antique scrawl was growing dim on the page. Two footmen came into the room and, watched by the unbusinesslike man of business, lit candles, drew window curtains and heaped fresh coals upon the fire. Mr Segundus thought it best to remind Mr Honeyfoot that they had not yet explained to Mr Norrell the reason for their visit.

As they were leaving the library Mr Segundus noticed something he thought odd. A chair was drawn up to the fire and by the chair stood a little table. Upon the table lay the boards and leather bindings of a very old book, a pair of scissars and a strong, cruel-looking knife, such as a gardener might use for pruning. But the pages of the book were nowhere to be seen. Perhaps, thought Mr

---

[6] *cont'd* Pantler's reputation as a theoretical magician rests entirely on the book he wrote on the subject

In Jacques Belasis's *Instructions* Mr Segundus read a very different explanation. Three centuries before Martin Pale set foot in Cold Henry's castle Cold Henry had had another human visitor, an English magician even greater than Pale – Ralph Stokesey – who had left behind him a pair of boots. The boots, said Belasis, were old, which is probably why Stokesey did not take them with him, but their presence in the castle caused great consternation to all its fairy-inhabitants who held English magicians in great veneration. In particular Cold Henry was in a pickle because he feared that in some devious, incomprehensible way, Christian morality might hold him responsible for the loss of the boots. So he was trying to rid himself of the terrible objects by passing them on to Pale who did not want them.

Segundus, he has sent it away to be bound anew. Yet the old binding still looked strong and why should Mr Norrell trouble himself to remove the pages and risk damaging them? A skilled bookbinder was the proper person to do such work.

When they were seated in the drawing-room again, Mr Honey-foot addressed Mr Norrell. "What I have seen here today, sir, convinces me that you are the best person to help us. Mr Segundus and I are of the opinion that modern magicians are on the wrong path; they waste their energies upon trifles. Do not you agree, sir?"

"Oh! certainly," said Mr Norrell.

"Our question," continued Mr Honeyfoot, "is why magic has fallen from its once-great state in our great nation. Our question is, sir, why is no more magic done in England?"

Mr Norrell's small blue eyes grew harder and brighter and his lips tightened as if he were seeking to suppress a great and secret delight within him. It was as if, thought Mr Segundus, he had waited a long time for someone to ask him this question and had had his answer ready for years. Mr Norrell said, "I cannot help you with your question, sir, for I do not understand it. It is a wrong question, sir. Magic is not ended in England. I myself am quite a tolerable practical magician."

2

The Old Starre Inn

January–February 1807

A s THE CARRIAGE passed out of Mr Norrell's sweep-gate Mr Honeyfoot exclaimed; "A practical magician in England! And in Yorkshire too! We have had the most extraordinary good luck! Ah, Mr Segundus, we have you to thank for this. You were awake, when the rest of us had fallen asleep. Had it not been for your encouragement, we might never have discovered Mr Norrell. And I am quite certain that he would never have sought us out; he is a little reserved. He gave us no particulars of his achievements in practical magic, nothing beyond the simple fact of his success. That, I fancy, is the sign of a modest nature. Mr Segundus, I think you will agree that our task is clear. It falls to us, sir, to overcome Norrell's natural timidity and aversion to praise, and lead him triumphantly before a wider public!"

"Perhaps," said Mr Segundus doubtfully.

"I do not say it will be easy," said Mr Honeyfoot. "He is a little reticent and not fond of company. But he must see that such knowledge as he possesses must be shared with others for the Nation's good. He is a gentleman: he knows his duty and will do it, I am sure. Ah, Mr Segundus! You deserve the grateful thanks of every magician in the country for this."

But whatever Mr Segundus deserved, the sad fact is that

magicians in England are a peculiarly ungrateful set of men. Mr Honeyfoot and Mr Segundus might well have made the most significant discovery in magical scholarship for three centuries – what of it? There was scarcely a member of the York society who, when he learnt of it, was not entirely confident that he could have done it much better – and, upon the following Tuesday when an extraordinary meeting of the Learned Society of York Magicians was held, there were very few members who were not prepared to say so.

At seven o'clock upon the Tuesday evening the upper room of the Old Starre Inn in Stonegate was crowded. The news which Mr Honeyfoot and Mr Segundus had brought seemed to have drawn out all the gentlemen in the city who had ever peeped into a book of magic – and York was still, after its own fashion, one of the most magical cities in England; perhaps only the King's city of Newcastle could boast more magicians.

There was such a crush of magicians in the room that, for the present, a great many were obliged to stand, though the waiters were continually bringing more chairs up the stairs. Dr Foxcastle had got himself an excellent chair, tall and black and curiously carved – and this chair (which rather resembled a throne), and the sweep of the red velvet curtains behind him and the way in which he sat with his hands clasped over his large round stomach, all combined to give him a deeply magisterial air.

The servants at the Old Starre Inn had prepared an excellent fire to keep off the chills of a January evening and around it were seated some ancient magicians – apparently from the reign of George II or thereabouts – all wrapped in plaid shawls, with yellowing spider's-web faces, and accompanied by equally ancient footmen with bottles of medicine in their pockets. Mr Honeyfoot greeted them with: 'How do you do, Mr Aptree? How do you do, Mr Greyshippe? I hope you are in good health, Mr Tunstall? I am very glad to see you here, gentlemen! I hope you have all come to rejoice with us? All our years in the dusty wilderness are at an end. Ah! no one knows better than you, Mr Aptree and you, Mr Greyshippe what years they have been, for you have lived through a great many of them. But now we shall see magic once more Britain's counsellor and protector! And the French, Mr Tunstall! What will be the feelings of the French when they hear about it? Why! I should not be surprized if it were to bring on an immediate surrender.''

Mr Honeyfoot had a great deal more to say of the same sort; he had prepared a speech in which he intended to lay before them all the wonderful advantages that were to accrue to Britain from this discovery. But he was never allowed to deliver more than a few sentences of it, for it seemed that each and every gentleman in the room was bursting with opinions of his own on the subject, all of which required to be communicated urgently to every other gentleman. Dr Foxcastle was the first to interrupt Mr Honeyfoot. From his large, black throne he addressed Mr Honeyfoot thus: ''I am very sorry to see you, sir, bringing magic – for which I know you have a genuine regard – into disrepute with impossible tales and wild inventions. Mr Segundus,'' he said, turning to the gentleman whom he regarded as the source of all the trouble, ''I do not know what is customary where you come from, but in Yorkshire we do not care for men who build their reputations at the expence of other men's peace of mind.''

This was as far as Dr Foxcastle got before he was drowned by the loud, angry exclamations of Mr Honeyfoot and Mr Segundus's supporters. The next gentleman to make himself heard wondered that Mr Segundus and Mr Honeyfoot should have been so taken in. Clearly Norrell was mad – no different from any stark-eyed madman who stood upon the street corner screaming out that he was the Raven King.

A sandy-haired gentleman in a state of great excitement thought that Mr Honeyfoot and Mr Segundus should have insisted on Mr Norrell leaving his house upon the instant and coming straightway in an open carriage (though it was January) in triumph to York, so that the sandy-haired gentleman might

22

rew ivy leaves in his path;[1] and one of the very old men by the fire as in a great passion about something or other, but being so old is voice was rather weak and no one had leisure just then to iscover what he was saying.

There was a tall, sensible man in the room called Thorpe, a entleman with very little magical learning, but a degree of ommon sense rare in a magician. He had always thought that Ir Segundus deserved encouragement in his quest to find where ractical English magic had disappeared to – though like everyone lse Mr Thorpe had not expected Mr Segundus to discover the nswer quite so soon. But now that they had an answer Mr Thorpe as of the opinion that they should not simply dismiss it: "Gentle-en, Mr Norrell has said he can do magic. Very well. We know a ttle of Norrell – we have all heard of the rare texts he is supposed have and for this reason alone we would be wrong to dismiss his laims without careful consideration. But the stronger arguments Norrell's favour are these: that two of our own number – sober cholars both – have seen Norrell and come away convinced." He urned to Mr Honeyfoot. "You believe in this man – any one may e by your face that you do. You have seen something that onvinced you – will you not tell us what it was?"

Now Mr Honeyfoot's reaction to this question was perhaps a little trange. At first he smiled gratefully at Mr Thorpe as if this was xactly what he could have wished for: a chance to broadcast the xcellent reasons he had for believing that Mr Norrell could do nagic; and he opened his mouth to begin. Then he stopped; he aused; he looked about him, as if those excellent reasons which had eemed so substantial a moment ago were all turning to mist and othingness in his mouth, and his tongue and teeth could not catch old of even one of them to frame it into a rational English sentence. Ie muttered something of Mr Norrell's honest countenance.

The conquerors of Imperial Rome may have been honoured with wreaths of aurel leaves; lovers and fortune's favourites have, we are told, roses strewn in heir paths; but English magicians were always only ever given common ivy.

The York society did not think this very satisfactory (and ha
they actually been privileged to see Mr Norrell's countenance the
might have thought it even less so). So Thorpe turned to M
Segundus and said, "Mr Segundus, you have seen Norrell to
What is your opinion?"

For the first time the York society noticed how pale M
Segundus was and it occurred to some of the gentlemen that h
had not answered them when they had greeted him, as if he coul
not quite collect his thoughts to reply. "Are you unwell, sir?" aske
Mr Thorpe gently. "No, no," murmured Mr Segundus, "it i
nothing. I thank you." But he looked so lost that one gentlema
offered him his chair and another went off to fetch a glass c
Canary-wine, and the excitable sandy-haired gentleman who ha
wished to strew ivy leaves in Mr Norrell's path nurtured a secre
hope that Mr Segundus might be enchanted and that they migh
see something extraordinary!

Mr Segundus sighed and said, "I thank you. I am not ill, bu
this last week I have felt very heavy and stupid. Mrs Pleasance ha
given me arrowroot and hot concoctions of liquorice root, but the
have not helped – which does not surprize me for I think th
confusion is in my head. I am not so bad as I was. If you were t
ask me now, gentlemen, why it is that I believe that magic ha
come back to England, I should say it is because I have seen magi
done. The impression of having seen magic done is most vivid her
and here . . ." (Mr Segundus touched his brow and his heart.
"And yet I know that I have seen none. Norrell did none while w
were with him. And so I suppose that I have dreamt it."

Fresh outbreak of the gentlemen of the York society. The fain
gentleman smiled faintly and inquired if any one could make an
thing of this. Then Mr Thorpe cried, "Good God! It is ver
nonsensical for us all to sit here and assert that Norrell can o
cannot do this or can or cannot do that. We are all rational being
I think, and the answer, surely, is quite simple – we will ask him t
do some magic for us in proof of his claims."

This was such good sense that for a moment the magicians were ent – though this is not to say that the proposal was universally pular – not at all. Several of the magicians (Dr Foxcastle was ie) did not care for it. If they asked Norrell to do magic, there as always the danger that he might indeed do some. They did not ant to see magic done; they only wished to read about it in books. thers were of the opinion that the York society was making itself ry ridiculous by doing even so little as this. But in the end most of e magicians agreed with Mr Thorpe that: "As scholars, gentle-en, the least we can do is to offer Mr Norrell the opportunity to nvince us." And so it was decided that someone should write other letter to Mr Norrell.

It was quite clear to all the magicians that Mr Honeyfoot and r Segundus had handled the thing very ill and upon one subject least – that of Mr Norrell's wonderful library – they did seem markably stupid, for they were not able to give any intelligible port of it. What had they seen? Oh, books, many books. A markable number of books? Yes, they believed they had thought remarkable at the time. Rare books? Ah, probably. Had they en permitted to take them down and look inside them? Oh no! r Norrell had not gone so far as to invite them to do that. But ey had read the titles? Yes, indeed. Well then, what were the les of the books they had seen? They did not know; they could ot remember. Mr Segundus said that one of the books had a title at began with a 'B', but that was the beginning and end of his formation. It was very odd.

Mr Thorpe had always intended to write the letter to Mr orrell himself, but there were a great many magicians in the om whose chief idea was to give offence to Mr Norrell in return r his impudence and these gentlemen thought quite rightly that eir best means of insulting Norrell was to allow Dr Foxcastle to rite the letter. And so this was carried. In due time it brought rth an angry letter of reply.

Hurtfew Abbey, Yorkshire,
Feb. 1st, 1807

Sir—

Twice in recent years I have been honoured by a letter from the
gentlemen of the Learned Society of York Magicians soliciting
my acquaintance. Now comes a third letter informing me of the
society's displeasure. The good opinion of the York society seems
as easily lost as it is gained and a man may never know how he
came to do either. In answer to the particular charge contained in
your letter that I have exaggerated my abilities and laid claim to
powers I cannot possibly possess I have only this to say: other men
may fondly attribute their lack of success to a fault in the world
rather than to their own poor scholarship, but the truth is that
magic is as achievable in this Age as in any other; as I have proved
to my own complete satisfaction any number of times within the
last twenty years. But what is my reward for loving my art better
than other men have done? – for studying harder to perfect it? – it
is now circulated abroad that I am a fabulist; my professional
abilities are slighted and my word doubted. You will not, I dare
say, be much surprized to learn that under such circumstances as
these I do not feel much inclined to oblige the York society in any
thing – least of all a request for a display of magic. The Learned
Society of York Magicians meets upon Wednesday next and
upon that day I shall inform you of my intentions.

Your servant
Gilbert Norrell

This was all rather disagreeably mysterious. The theoretica
magicians waited somewhat nervously to see what the practica
magician would send them next. What Mr Norrell sent them nex
was nothing more alarming than an attorney, a smiling, bobbing
bowing attorney, a quite commonplace attorney called Robinso
with neat black clothes and neat kid gloves, with a document, th

26

ke of which the gentlemen of the York society had never seen efore; a draft of an agreement, drawn up in accordance with England's long-forgotten codes of magical law.

Mr Robinson arrived in the upper room at the Old Starre promptly at eight and seemed to suppose himself expected. He had place of business and two clerks in Coney-street. His face was well known to many of the gentlemen.

"I will confess to you, sirs," smiled Mr Robinson, "that this paper is largely the work of my principal, Mr Norrell. I am no expert upon thaumaturgic law. Who is nowadays? Still, I dare say that if I go wrong, you will be so kind as to put me right again."

Several of the York magicians nodded wisely.

Mr Robinson was a polished sort of person. He was so clean and healthy and pleased about everything that he positively shone – which is only to be expected in a fairy or an angel, but is somewhat disconcerting in an attorney. He was most deferential to the gentlemen of the York society for he knew nothing of magic, but he thought it must be difficult and require great concentration of mind. But to professional humility and a genuine admiration of the York society Mr Robinson added a happy vanity that these monumental brains must now cease their pondering on esoteric matters for a time and listen to him. He put golden spectacles upon his nose, adding another small glitter to his shining person.

Mr Robinson said that Mr Norrell undertook to do a piece of magic in a certain place at a certain time. "You have no objection I hope, gentlemen, to my principal settling the time and place?"

The gentlemen had none.

"Then it shall be the Cathedral, Friday fortnight."[2]

_____
The great church at York is both a *cathedral* (meaning the church where the throne of the bishop or archbishop is housed) and a *minster* (meaning a church founded by a missionary in ancient times). It has borne both these names at different periods. In earlier centuries it was more usually called the *Minster*, but nowadays the people of York prefer the term *Cathedral* as one which elevates their church above those of the nearby towns of Ripon and Beverley. Ripon and Beverley have minsters, but no cathedrals.

Mr Robinson said that if Mr Norrell failed to do the magic the he would publicly withdraw his claims to be a practical magician indeed to be any sort of magician at all, and he would give his oat never to make any such claims again.

"He need not go so far," said Mr Thorpe. "We have no desire punish him; we merely wished to put his claims to the test."

Mr Robinson's shining smile dimmed a little, as if he ha something rather disagreeable to communicate and was not qui sure how to begin.

"Wait," said Mr Segundus, "we have not heard the other side the bargain yet. We have not heard what he expects of us."

Mr Robinson nodded. Mr Norrell intended it seemed to exac the same promise from each and every magician of the Yor society as he made himself. In other words if he succeeded, the they must without further ado disband the Society of Yor Magicians and none of them claim the title "magician" eve again. And after all, said Mr Robinson, this would be only fai since Mr Norrell would then have proved himself the only tru magician in Yorkshire.

"And shall we have some third person, some independent part to decide if the magic has been accomplished?" asked Mr Thorpe

This question seemed to puzzle Mr Robinson. He hoped the would excuse him if he had taken up a wrong idea he said, h would not offend for the world, but he had thought that all th gentlemen present were magicians.

Oh, yes, nodded the York society, they were all magicians.

Then surely, said Mr Robinson, they would recognize magi when they saw it? Surely there were none better qualified to do so

Another gentleman asked what magic Norrell intended to do Mr Robinson was full of polite apologies and elaborate explana tions; he could not enlighten them, he did not know.

It would tire my reader's patience to rehearse the many windin arguments by which the gentlemen of the York society came t sign Mr Norrell's agreement. Many did so out of vanity; they ha ublicly declared that they did not believe Norrell could do magic, hey had publicly challenged Norrell to perform some – under uch circumstances as these it would have looked peculiarly foolish o change their minds – or so they thought.

Mr Honeyfoot, on the other hand, signed precisely *because* he believed in Norrell's magic. Mr Honeyfoot hoped that Mr Norrell would gain public recognition by this demonstration of his powers and go on to employ his magic for the good of the nation.

Some of the gentlemen were provoked to sign by the suggestion (originating with Norrell and somehow conveyed by Robinson) that hey would not shew themselves true magicians unless they did so.

So one by one and there and then, the magicians of York signed he document that Mr Robinson had brought. The last magician was Mr Segundus.

"I will not sign," he said. "For magic is my life and though Mr Norrell is quite right to say I am a poor scholar, what shall I do when it is taken from me?"

A silence.

"Oh!" said Mr Robinson. "Well, that is . . . Are you quite sure, sir, that you should not like to sign the document? You see how all your friends have done it? You will be quite alone."

"I am quite sure," said Mr Segundus, "thank you."

"Oh!" said Mr Robinson. "Well, in that case I must confess that I do not know quite how to proceed. My principal gave me no instruction what to do if only *some* of the gentlemen signed. I shall consult with my principal in the morning."

Dr Foxcastle was heard to remark to Mr Hart or Hunt that once again it was the newcomer who brought a world of trouble upon everyone's heads.

But two days later Mr Robinson waited upon Dr Foxcastle with a message to say that on this particular occasion Mr Norrell would be happy to overlook Mr Segundus's refusal to sign; he would consider that his contract was with all the members of the York society *except* for Mr Segundus.

The night before Mr Norrell was due to perform the magic, snow fell on York and in the morning the dirt and mud of the city had disappeared, all replaced by flawless white. The sounds of hooves and footsteps were muffled, and the very voices of York citizens were altered by a white silence that swallowed up every sound. Mr Norrell had named a very early hour in the day. In their separate homes the York magicians breakfasted alone. They watched in silence as a servant poured their coffee, broke the warm white-bread rolls, fetched the butter. The wife, the sister, the daughter, the daughter-in-law, or the niece who usually performed these little offices was still in bed; and the pleasant female domestic chat, which the gentlemen of the York society affected to despise so much, and which was in truth the sweet and mild refrain in the music of their ordinary lives, was absent. And the breakfast rooms where these gentlemen sat were changed from what they had been yesterday. The winter gloom was quite gone and in its place was a fearful light – the winter sun reflected many times over by the snowy earth. There was a dazzle of light upon the white linen tablecloth. The rosebuds that patterned the daughter's pretty coffee-cups seemed almost to dance in it. Sunbeams were struck from the niece's silver coffee-pot, and the daughter-in-law's smiling china shepherdesses were all become shining angels. It was as if the table were laid with fairy silver and crystal.

Mr Segundus, putting his head out of a third-storey window in Lady-Peckitt's-yard, thought that perhaps Norrell had already done the magic and this was it. There was an ominous rumble above him and he drew in his head quickly to avoid a sudden fall of snow from the roof. Mr Segundus had no servant any more than he had a wife, sister, daughter, daughter-in-law, or niece, but Mrs Pleasance, his landlady, was an early riser. Many times in the last fortnight she had heard him sigh over his books and she hoped to cheer him up with a breakfast of two freshly grilled herrings, tea and fresh milk, and white bread and butter on a blue-and-white china plate. With the same generous aim she had sat down to talk o him. On seeing how despondent he looked she cried, "Oh! I have no patience with this old man!"

Mr Segundus had not told Mrs Pleasance that Mr Norrell was old and yet she fancied that he must be. From what Mr Segundus had told her she thought of him as a sort of miser who hoarded magic instead of gold, and as our narrative progresses, I will allow the reader to judge the justice of this portrait of Mr Norrell's character. Like Mrs Pleasance I always fancy that misers are old. I cannot tell why this should be since I am sure that there are as many young misers as old. As to whether or not Mr Norrell was in fact old, he was the sort of man who had been old at seventeen.

Mrs Pleasance continued, "When Mr Pleasance was alive, he used to say that no one in York, man or woman, could bake a loaf to rival mine, and other people as well have been kind enough to say that they never in their lives tasted bread so good. But I have always kept a good table for love of doing a thing well and if one of those queer spirits from the Arabian fables came out of this very teapot now and gave me three wishes I hope I would not be so ill-natured as to try to stop other folk from baking bread – and should their bread be as good as mine then I do not see that it hurts me, but rather is so much the better for them. Come, sir, try a bit," she said, pushing a plateful of the celebrated bread towards her lodger. "I do not like to see you get so thin. People will say that Hettie Pleasance has lost all her skill at housekeeping. I wish you would not be so downcast, sir. You have not signed this perfidious document and when the other gentlemen are forced to give up, you will still continue and I very much hope, Mr Segundus, that you may make great discoveries and perhaps then this Mr Norrell who thinks himself so clever will be glad to take you into partnership and so be brought to regret his foolish pride."

Mr Segundus smiled and thanked her. "But I do not think that will happen. My chief difficulty will be lack of materials. I have very little of my own, and when the society is disbanded, – well I cannot tell what will happen to its books, but I doubt that they will come to me."

31

Mr Segundus ate his bread (which was just as good as the lat[e] Mr Pleasance and his friends had said it was) and his herrings an[d] drank some tea. Their power to soothe a troubled heart must hav[e] been greater than he had supposed for he found that he felt a littl[e] better and, fortified in this manner, he put on his greatcoat and h[is] hat and his muffler and his gloves and stamped off through th[e] snowy streets to the place that Mr Norrell had appointed for th[e] day's wonders – the Cathedral of York.

And I hope that all my readers are acquainted with an ol[d] English Cathedral town or I fear that the significance of M[r] Norrell's chusing that particular place will be lost upon them[.] They must understand that in an old Cathedral town the great ol[d] church is not one building among many; it is *the* building different from all others in scale, beauty and solemnity. Even i[n] modern times when an old Cathedral town may have provide[d] itself with all the elegant appurtenances of civic buildings, assem[-] bly and meeting rooms (and York was well-stocked with these) th[e] Cathedral rises above them – a witness to the devotion of ou[r] forefathers. It is as if the town contains within itself somethin[g] larger than itself. When going about one's business in the muddl[e] of narrow streets one is sure to lose sight of the Cathedral, but the[n] the town will open out and suddenly it is there, many times talle[r] and many times larger than any other building, and one realize[s] that one has reached the heart of the town and that all streets an[d] lanes have in some way led here, to a place of mysteries muc[h] deeper than any Mr Norrell knew of. Such were Mr Segundus['] thoughts as he entered the Close and stood before the grea[t] brooding blue shadow of the Cathedral's west face. Now cam[e] Dr Foxcastle, sailing magisterially around the corner like a fa[t] black ship. Spying Mr Segundus there he steered himself toward[s] that gentleman and bid him good morning.

"Perhaps, sir," said Dr Foxcastle, "you would be so kind as t[o] introduce me to Mr Norrell? He is a gentleman I very much wis[h] to know."

"I shall be only too happy, sir." said Mr Segundus and looked bout him. The weather had kept most people within doors and here were only a few dark figures scuttling over the white field hat lay before the great grey Church. When scrutinized these vere discovered to be gentlemen of the York society, or clergymen nd Cathedral attendants – vergers and beadles, sub-choirmasters, provosts, transept-sweepers and such-like persons – who had been ent by their superiors out into the snow to see to the Church's ousiness.

"I should like nothing better, sir," said Mr Segundus, "than to oblige you, but I do not see Mr Norrell."

Yet there was someone.

Someone was standing in the snow alone directly in front of the Minster. He was a dark sort of someone, a not-quite-respectable omeone who was regarding Mr Segundus and Dr Foxcastle with n air of great interest. His ragged hair hung about his shoulders ike a fall of black water; he had a strong, thin face with something wisted in it, like a tree root; and a long, thin nose; and, though his kin was very pale, something made it seem a dark face – perhaps it vas the darkness of his eyes, or the proximity of that long, black greasy hair. After a moment this person walked up to the two nagicians, gave them a sketchy bow and said that he hoped they would forgive his intruding upon them but they had been pointed out to him as gentlemen who were there upon the same business as imself. He said that his name was John Childermass, and that he vas Mr Norrell's steward in certain matters (though he did not say what these were).

"It seems to me," said Mr Segundus thoughtfully, "that I know your face. I have seen you before, I think?"

Something shifted in Childermass's dark face, but it was gone in a moment and whether it had been a frown or laughter it was mpossible to say. "I am often in York upon business for Mr Norrell, sir. Perhaps you have seen me in one of the city book-elling establishments?"

"No," said Mr Segundus, "I have seen you . . . I can pictur
you . . . Where? . . . Oh! I shall have it in a moment!"

Childermass raised an eyebrow as if to say he very muc
doubted it.

"But surely Mr Norrell is coming himself?" said Dr Foxcastl

Childermass begged Dr Foxcastle's pardon, but he did not thin
Mr Norrell would come; he did not think Mr Norrell saw an
reason to come.

"Ah!" cried Dr Foxcastle. "then he concedes, does he? We
well, well. Poor gentleman. He feels very foolish, I dare say. We
indeed. It was a noble attempt at any rate. We bear him no ill-wi
for having made the attempt." Dr Foxcastle was much relieve
that he would see no magic and it made him generous.

Childermass begged Dr Foxcastle's pardon once more; he feare
that Dr Foxcastle had mistaken his meaning. Mr Norrell woul
certainly do magic; he would do it in Hurtfew Abbey and th
results would be seen in York. "Gentlemen," said Childermass
Dr Foxcastle, "do not like to leave their comfortable fireside
unless they must. I dare say if you, sir, could have managed th
seeing part of the business from your own drawing-room yo
would not be here in the cold and wet."

Dr Foxcastle drew in his breath sharply and bestowed on Joh
Childermass a look that said that he thought John Childerma
very insolent.

Childermass did not seem much dismayed by Dr Foxcastle
opinion of him, indeed he looked rather entertained by it. He saic
"It is time, sirs. You should take your stations within the Churcl
You would be sorry, I am sure, to miss anything when so muc
hangs upon it."

It was twenty minutes past the hour and gentlemen of the Yor
society were already filing into the Cathedral by the door in th
south transept. Several looked about them before going inside, as
taking a last fond farewell of a world they were not quite sure o
seeing again.

3

The stones of York

February 1807

A GREAT OLD CHURCH in the depths of winter is a discouraging place at the best of times; the cold of a hundred winters seems to have been preserved in its stones and to seep out of them. In the cold, dank, twilight interior of the Cathedral the gentlemen of the York society were obliged to stand and wait to be astonished, without any assurance that the surprize when it came would be a pleasant one.

Mr Honeyfoot tried to smile cheerfully at his companions, but for a gentleman so practised in the art of a friendly smile it was a very poor attempt.

Upon the instant bells began to toll. Now these were nothing more than the bells of St Michael-le-Belfrey telling the half hour, but inside the Cathedral they had an odd, far-away sound like the bells of another country. It was not at all a cheerful sound. The gentlemen of the York society knew very well how bells often went with magic and in particular with the magic of those unearthly beings, *fairies*; they knew how, in the old days, silvery bells would often sound just as some Englishman or Englishwoman of particular virtue or beauty was about to be stolen away by fairies to live in strange, ghostly lands for ever. Even the Raven King – who was not a fairy, but an Englishman – had a somewhat regrettable habit of abducting men and women and taking them to live with him in his castle in the Other Lands.[1] Now, had you and I the power to seize by magic any human being that took our fancy and the power to keep that person by our side through all eternity, and had we all the world to chuse from, then I dare say our choice might fall on someone a little more captivating than a member of the Learned Society of York Magicians, but this comforting thought did not occur to the gentlemen inside York Cathedral and several of them began to wonder how angry Dr Foxcastle's letter had made Mr Norrell and they began to be seriously frightened.

As the sounds of the bells died away a voice began to speak from somewhere high up in the gloomy shadows above their heads. The magicians strained their ears to hear it. Many of them were now in such a state of highly-strung nervousness that they imagined that instructions were being given to them as in a fairy-tale. They

---

[1] The well-known ballad "The Raven King" describes just such an abduction

Not long, not long my father said
Not long shall you be ours
The Raven King knows all too well
Which are the fairest flowers

The priest was all too worldly
Though he prayed and rang his bell
The Raven King three candles lit
The priest said it was well

Her arms were all too feeble
Though she claimed to love me so
The Raven King stretched out his hand
She sighed and let me go

This land is all too shallow
It is painted on the sky
And trembles like the wind-shook rain
When the Raven King goes by

For always and for always
I pray remember me
Upon the moors, beneath the stars
With the King's wild company

ought that perhaps mysterious prohibitions were being related
them. Such instructions and prohibitions, the magicians knew
om the fairy-tales, are usually a little queer, but not very difficult
conform to – or so it seems at first sight. They generally follow
e style of: "Do not eat the last candied plum in the blue jar in the
rner cupboard," or "Do not beat your wife with a stick made
om wormwood." And yet, as all fairy-tales relate, circumstances
ways conspire against the person who receives the instructions
d they find themselves in the middle of doing the very thing that
as forbidden to them and a horrible fate is thereby brought upon
eir heads.

At the very least the magicians supposed that their doom was
ing slowly recited to them. But it was not at all clear what
nguage the voice was speaking. Once Mr Segundus thought he
ard a word that sounded like "*maleficient*" and another time
nterficere" a Latin word meaning "to kill". The voice itself was
t easy to understand; it bore not the slightest resemblance to a
man voice – which only served to increase the gentlemen's fear
at fairies were about to appear. It was extraordinarily harsh,
ep and rasping; it was like two rough stones being scraped
gether and yet the sounds that were produced were clearly
tended to be speech – indeed *were* speech. The gentlemen peered
into the gloom in fearful expectation, but all that could be seen
as the small, dim shape of a stone figure that sprang out from one
the shafts of a great pillar and jutted into the gloomy void. As
ey became accustomed to the queer sound they recognized more
d more words; old English words and old Latin words all mixed
together as if the speaker had no conception of these being two
stinct languages. Fortunately, this abominable muddle pre-
nted few difficulties to the magicians, most of whom were
customed to unravelling the ramblings and writings of the
holars of long ago. When translated into clear, comprehensible
nglish it was something like this: *Long, long ago*, (said the voice),
ve hundred years ago or more, on a winter's day at twilight, a young man

entered the Church with a young girl with ivy leaves in her hair. There was
one else there but the stones. No one to see him strangle her but the stones. H
let her fall dead upon the stones and no one saw but the stones. He was nev
punished for his sin because there were no witnesses but the stones. The yea
went by and whenever the man entered the Church and stood among th
congregation the stones cried out that this was the man who had murdered th
girl with the ivy leaves wound into her hair, but no one ever heard us. But it
not too late! We know where he is buried! In the corner of the south transep
Quick! Quick! Fetch picks! Fetch shovels! Pull up the paving stones. Dig u
his bones! Let them be smashed with the shovel! Dash his skull against th
pillars and break it! Let the stones have vengeance too! It is not too late! It
not too late!

Hardly had the magicians had time to digest this and to wonde
some more who it was that spoke, when another stony voice begar
This time the voice seemed to issue from the chancel and it spoke onl
English; yet it was a queer sort of English full of ancient and forgotte
words. This voice complained of some soldiers who had entered th
Church and broken some windows. A hundred years later they ha
come again and smashed a rood screen, erased the faces of the saint
carried off plate. Once they had sharpened their arrowheads on th
brim of the font; three hundred years later they had fired their pisto
in the chapter house. The second voice did not appear to understan
that, while a great Church may stand for millennia, men cannot liv
so long. "They delight in destruction!" it cried. "And they them
selves deserve only to be destroyed!" Like the first, this speake
seemed to have stood in the Church for countless years and had
presumably, heard a great many sermons and prayers, yet th
sweetest of Christian virtues – mercy, love, meekness – were ur
known to him. And all the while the first voice continued to lamer
the dead girl with ivy leaves in her hair and the two gritty voice
clashed together in a manner that was very disagreeable.

Mr Thorpe, who was a valiant gentleman, peeped into th
chancel alone, to discover who it was that spoke. "It is a statue,
he said.

And then the gentlemen of the York society peered up again into the gloom above their heads in the direction of the first unearthly voice. And this time very few of them had any doubts that it was the little stone figure that spoke, for as they watched they could perceive its stubby stone arms that it waved about in its distress.

Then all the other statues and monuments in the Cathedral began to speak and to say in their stony voices all that they had seen in their stony lives and the noise was, as Mr Segundus later told Mrs Pleasance, beyond description. For York Cathedral had many little carved people and strange animals that flapped their wings.

Many complained of their neighbours and perhaps this is not so surprising since they had been obliged to stand together for so many hundreds of years. There were fifteen stone kings that stood each upon a stone pedestal in a great stone screen. Their hair was tightly curled as if it had been put into curl papers and never brushed out – and Mrs Honeyfoot could never see them without declaring that she longed to take a hairbrush to each of their royal heads. From the first moment of their being able to speak the kings began quarrelling and scolding each other – for the pedestals were all of a height, and kings – even stone ones – dislike above all things to be made equal to others. There was besides a little group of queer figures with linked arms that looked out with stone eyes from atop an ancient column. As soon as the spell took effect each of these tried to push the others away from him, as if even stone arms begin to ache after a century or so and stone people begin to tire of being shackled to each other.

One statue spoke what seemed to be Italian. No one knew why this should be, though Mr Segundus discovered later that it was a copy of a work by Michael Angel. It seemed to be describing an entirely different church, one where vivid black shadows contrasted sharply with brilliant light. In other words it was describing what the parent-statue in Rome could see.

Mr Segundus was pleased to observe that the magicians, though very frightened, remained within the walls of the Church. Some were so amazed by what they saw that they soon forgot their fear entirely and ran about to discover more and more miracles, making observations, writing down notes with pencils in little memorandum books as if they had forgotten the perfidious document which from today would prevent them studying magic. For a long time the magicians of York (soon, alas, to be magicians no more!) wandered through the aisles and saw marvels. And at every moment their ears were assaulted by the hideous cacophony of a thousand stone voices all speaking together.

In the chapter house there were stone canopies with many little stone heads with strange headgear that all chattered and cackled together. Here were marvellous stone carvings of a hundred English trees: hawthorn, oak, blackthorn, wormwood, cherry and bryony. Mr Segundus found two stone dragons no longer than his forearm, which slipped one after the other, over and under and between stone hawthorn branches, stone hawthorn leaves, stone hawthorn roots and stone hawthorn tendrils. They moved, it seemed, with as much ease as any other creature and yet the sound of so many stone muscles moving together under a stone skin, that scraped stone ribs, that clashed against a heart made of stone – and the sound of stone claws rattling over stone branches – was quite intolerable and Mr Segundus wondered that they could bear it. He observed a little cloud of gritty dust, such as attends the work of a stonecutter, that surrounded them and rose up in the air; and he believed that if the spell allowed them to remain in motion for any length of time they would wear themselves away to a sliver of limestone.

Stone leaves and herbs quivered and shook as if tossed in the breeze and some of them so far emulated their vegetable counterparts as to grow. Later, when the spell had broken, strands of stone ivy and stone rose briars would be discovered wound around chairs and lecterns and prayer-books where no stone ivy or briars had been before.

But it was not only the magicians of the York society who saw wonders that day. Whether he had intended it or not Mr Norrell's magic had spread beyond the Cathedral close and into the city. Three statues from the west front of the Cathedral had been taken to Mr Taylor's workshops to be mended. Centuries of Yorkshire rain had worn down these images and no one knew any longer what great personages they were intended to represent. At half past ten one of Mr Taylor's masons had just raised his chisel to the face of one of these statues intending to fashion it into the likeness of a pretty saintess; at that moment the statue cried out aloud and raised its arm to ward off the chisel, causing the poor workman to fall down in a swoon. The statues were later returned to the exterior of the Cathedral untouched, their faces worn as flat as biscuits and as bland as butter.

Then all at once there seemed a change in the sound and one by one the voices stopped until the magicians heard the bells of St Michael-le-Belfrey ring for the half hour again. The first voice (the voice of the little figure high up in the darkness) continued for some time after the others had fallen silent, upon its old theme of the undiscovered murderer (*It is not too late! It is not too late!*) until it too fell silent.

The world had changed while the magicians had been inside the Church. Magic had returned to England whether the magicians wished it to or not. Other changes of a more prosaic nature had also occurred: the sky had filled with heavy, snow-laden clouds. These were scarcely grey at all, but a queer mixture of slate-blue and sea-green. This curious coloration made a kind of twilight such as one imagines is the usual illumination in fabled kingdoms under the sea.

Mr Segundus felt very tired by his adventure. Other gentlemen had been more frightened than he; he had seen magic and thought it wonderful beyond any thing he had imagined, and yet now that it was over his spirits were greatly agitated and he wished very much to be allowed to go quietly home without speaking to any

41

one. While he was in this susceptible condition he found himself halted and addressed by Mr Norrell's man of business.

"I believe, sir," said Mr Childermass, "that the society must now be broken up. I am sorry for it."

Now it may have been due entirely to Mr Segundus's lowness of spirits, but he suspected that, in spite of Childermass's manner which was very respectful, in some other part of Childermass's person he was laughing at the York magicians. Childermass was one of that uncomfortable class of men whose birth is lowly and who are destined all their lives to serve their betters, but whose clever brains and quick abilities make them wish for recognition and rewards far beyond their reach. Sometimes, by some strange combination of happy circumstances, these men find their own path to greatness, but more often the thought of what might have been turns them sour; they become unwilling servants and perform their tasks no better – or worse – than their less able fellows. They become insolent, lose their places and end badly.

"I beg your pardon, sir," said Childermass, "but I have a question to put to you. I hope you will not think it impertinent, but I would like to know if you ever look into a London paper?"

Mr Segundus replied that he did.

"Indeed? That is most interesting. I myself am fond of a newspaper. But I have little leisure for reading – except such books as come my way in the course of my duties for Mr Norrell. And what sort of thing does one find in a London paper nowadays? – you will excuse my asking, sir, only Mr Norrell, who never looks at a paper of any sort, put the question to me yesterday and I did not think myself qualified to answer it."

"Well," said Mr Segundus, a little puzzled, "there are all sorts of things. What did you wish to know? There are accounts of the actions of His Majesty's Navy against the French; speeches of the Government; reports of scandals and divorces. Is this what you meant?"

"Oh yes!" said Childermass. "You explain it very well, sir. I wonder," he continued, growing thoughtful, "whether provincial news is ever reported in the London papers? – whether (for example) today's remarkable occurrences might merit a paragraph?"

"I do not know," said Mr Segundus. "It seems to me quite possible but then, you know, Yorkshire is so far from London – perhaps the London editors will never get to hear of what has happened."

"Ah," said Mr Childermass; and then was silent.

Snow began to fall; a few flakes at first – then rather more than a few; until a million little flakes were drifting down from a soft, heavy greenish-grey sky. All the buildings of York became a little fainter, a little greyer in the snow; the people all seemed a little smaller; the cries and shouts, the footsteps and hoofsteps, the creaks of carriages and the slammings of doors were all a little more distant. And all these things became somehow less important until all the world contained was the falling snow, the sea-green sky, the dim, grey ghost of York Cathedral – and Childermass.

And all this time Childermass said nothing. Mr Segundus wondered what more he required – all his questions had been answered. But Childermass waited and watched Mr Segundus with his queer black eyes, as if he were waiting for Mr Segundus to say one thing more – as if he fully expected that Mr Segundus would say it – indeed as if nothing in the world were more certain.

"If you wish," said Mr Segundus, shaking the snow from his cape, "I can remove all the uncertainty from the business. I can write a letter to the editor of *The Times* informing him of Mr Norrell's extraordinary feats."

"Ah! That is generous indeed!" said Childermass. "Believe me, sir, I know very well that not every gentleman would be so magnanimous in defeat. But it is no more than I expected. For I told Mr Norrell that I did not think there could be a more obliging gentleman than Mr Segundus."

"Not at all," said Mr Segundus, "it is nothing."

The Learned Society of York Magicians was disbanded and its members were obliged to give up magic (all except Mr Segundus) – and, though some of them were foolish and not all of them were entirely amiable, I do not think that they deserved such a fate. For what is a magician to do who, in accordance with a pernicious agreement, is not allowed to study magic? He idles about his house day after day, disturbs his niece (or wife, or daughter) at her needlework and pesters the servants with questions about matters in which he never took an interest before – all for the sake of having someone to talk to, until the servants complain of him to their mistress. He picks up a book and begins to read, but he is not attending to what he reads and he has got to page 22 before he discovers it is a *novel* – the sort of work which above all others he most despises – and he puts it down in disgust. He asks his niece (or wife, or daughter) ten times a day what o'clock it is, for he cannot believe that time can go so slowly – and he falls out with his pocket watch for the same reason.

Mr Honeyfoot, I am glad to say, fared a little better than the others. He, kind-hearted soul, had been very much affected by the story that the little stone figure high up in the dimness had related. It had carried the knowledge of the horrid murder in its small stone heart for centuries, it remembered the dead girl with the ivy leaves in her hair when no one else did, and Mr Honeyfoot thought that its faithfulness ought to be rewarded. So he wrote to the Dean and to the Canons and to the Archbishop, and he made himself very troublesome until these important personages agreed to allow Mr Honeyfoot to dig up the paving stones of the south transept. And when this was done Mr Honeyfoot and the men he had employed uncovered some bones in a leaden coffin, just as the little stone figure had said they would. But then the Dean said that he could not authorize the removal of the bones from the Cathedral (which was what Mr Honeyfoot wanted) on the evidence of the little stone figure; there was no precedent for such a thing. Ah! said Mr Honeyfoot but there was, you know; and the argument raged for a number of years and, as a consequence, Mr Honeyfoot really had no leisure to repent signing Mr Norrell's document.[2]

The library of the Learned Society of York Magicians was sold to Mr Thoroughgood of Coffee-yard. But somehow no one thought to mention this to Mr Segundus and he only learnt about it in a round-about fashion when Mr Thoroughgood's shopboy told a friend (that was a clerk in Priestley's linen-drapers) and the friend chanced to mention it to Mrs Cockcroft of the George Inn and she told Mrs Pleasance who was Mr Segundus's landlady. As soon as Mr Segundus heard of it he ran down through the snowy streets to Mr Thoroughgood's shop without troubling to put on his hat or his coat or his boots. But the books were already gone. He inquired of Mr Thoroughgood who had bought them. Mr Thoroughgood begged Mr Segundus's pardon but he feared he could not divulge the name of the gentleman; he did not think the

---

[2] The example cited by Mr Honeyfoot was of a murder that had taken place in 1279 in the grim moor town of Alston. The body of a young boy was found in the churchyard hanging from a thorn-tree that stood before the church-door. Above the door was a statue of the Virgin and Child. So the people of Alston sent to Newcastle, to the Castle of the Raven King and the Raven King sent two magicians to make the Virgin and the Jesus-Child speak and say how they had seen a stranger kill the boy, but for what reason they did not know. And after that, whenever a stranger came to the town, the people of Alston would drag him before the church-door and ask "Is this him?" but always the Virgin and Child replied that it was not. Beneath the Virgin's feet were a lion and a dragon who curled around each other in a most puzzling manner and bit each other's necks. These creatures had been carved by someone who had never seen a lion or a dragon, but who had seen a great many dogs and sheep and something of the character of a dog and a sheep had got into his carving. Whenever some poor fellow was brought before the Virgin and Child to be examined the lion and the dragon would cease biting each other and look up like the Virgin's strange watchdogs and the lion would bark and the dragon would bleat angrily.

Years went by and the townspeople who remembered the boy were all dead, and the likelihood was that the murderer was too. But the Virgin and Child had somehow got into the habit of speaking and whenever some unfortunate stranger passed within the compass of their gaze they would still turn their stone heads and say, "It is not him." And Alston acquired the reputation of an eerie place and people would not go there if they could help it.

45

gentleman wished his name to be generally known. Mr Segundus, hatless and coatless and breathless, with water-logged shoes and mud-splashes on his stockings and the eyes of everybody in the shop upon him, had some satisfaction in telling Mr Thoroughgood that it did not signify whether Mr Thoroughgood told him or not, for he believed he knew the gentleman anyway.

Mr Segundus did not lack curiosity about Mr Norrell. He thought about him a great deal and often talked of him with Mr Honeyfoot.[3] Mr Honeyfoot was certain that everything that had happened could be explained by an earnest wish on Mr Norrell's part to bring back magic to England. Mr Segundus was more doubtful and began to look about him to try if he could discover any acquaintance of Norrell's that might be able to tell him something more.

A gentleman in Mr Norrell's position with a fine house and a large estate will always be of interest to his neighbours and, unless those neighbours are very stupid, they will always contrive to know a little of what he does. Mr Segundus discovered a family in Stonegate who were cousins to some people that had a farm five miles from Hurtfew Abbey – and he befriended the Stonegate family and persuaded them to hold a dinner-party and to invite their cousins to come to it. (Mr Segundus grew quite shocked at his own skill in thinking up these little stratagems.) The cousins duly arrived and were all most ready to talk about their rich and peculiar neighbour who had bewitched York Cathedral, but the

---

[3] To aid his better understanding of Mr Norrell's character and of Mr Norrell's magical powers Mr Segundus wrote a careful description of the visit to Hurtfew Abbey. Unfortunately he found his memory on this point peculiarly unclear. Whenever he returned to read what he had written he discovered that he now remembered things differently. Each time he began by crossing out words and phrases and putting in new ones, and he ended by re-writing completely. After four or five months he was obliged to admit to himself that he no longer knew what Mr Honeyfoot had said to Mr Norrell, or what Mr Norrell had said in reply, or what he – Mr Segundus – had seen in the house. He concluded that to attempt to write any thing upon the subject was futile, and he threw what he had written into the fire.

46

beginning and the end of their information was that Mr Norrell was about to leave Yorkshire and go to London.

Mr Segundus was surprized to hear this, but more than that he was surprized at the effect this news had upon his own spirits. He felt oddly discomfited by it – which was very ridiculous, he told himself; Norrell had never shewn any interest in him or done him the least kindness. Yet Norrell was Mr Segundus's only colleague now. When he was gone Mr Segundus would be the only magician, the last magician in Yorkshire.

4

The Friends of English Magic

Early spring 1807

CONSIDER, IF YOU WILL, a man who sits in his library day after day; a small man of no particular personal attractions. His book is on the table before him. A fresh supply of pens, a knife to cut new nibs, ink, paper, notebooks – all conveniently to hand. There is always a fire in the room – he cannot do without a fire, he feels the cold. The room changes with the season: he does not. Three tall windows open on a view of English countryside which is tranquil in spring, cheerful in summer, melancholy in autumn and gloomy in winter – just as English landscape should be. But the changing seasons excite no interest in him – he scarcely raises his eyes from the pages of his book. He takes his exercise as all gentlemen do; in dry weather his long walk crosses the park and skirts a little wood; in wet weather there is his short walk in the shrubbery. But he knows very little of shrubbery or park or wood. There is a book waiting for him upon the library table; his eyes fancy they still follow its lines of type, his head still runs upon its argument, his fingers itch to take it up again. He meets his neighbours twice or thrice a quarter – for this is England where a man's neighbours will never suffer him to live entirely bereft of society, let him be as dry and sour-faced as he may. They pay him visits, leave their cards with his servants, invite him to dine or to dance at assembly-balls. Their intentions are largely

48

charitable – they have a notion that it is bad for a man to be always alone – but they also have some curiosity to discover whether he has changed at all since they last saw him. He has not. He has nothing to say to them and is considered the dullest man in Yorkshire.

Yet within Mr Norrell's dry little heart there was as lively an ambition to bring back magic to England as would have satisfied even Mr Honeyfoot, and it was with the intention of bringing that ambition to a long-postponed fulfilment that Mr Norrell now proposed to go to London.

Childermass assured him that the time was propitious and Childermass knew the world. Childermass knew what games the children on street-corners are playing – games that all other grown-ups have long since forgotten. Childermass knew what old people by firesides are thinking of, though no one has asked them in years. Childermass knew what young men hear in the rattling of the drums and the tooting of the pipes that makes them leave their homes and go to be soldiers – and he knew the half-eggcupful of glory and the barrelful of misery that await them. Childermass could look at a smart attorney in the street and tell you what he had in his coat-tail pockets. And all that Childermass knew made him smile; and some of what he knew made him laugh out loud; and none of what he knew wrung from him so much as ha'pennyworth of pity.

So when Childermass told his master, "Go to London. Go now," Mr Norrell believed him.

"The only thing I do not quite like," said Mr Norrell, "is your plan to have Segundus write to one of the London newspapers upon our behalf. He is certain to make errors in what he writes – have you thought of that? I dare say he will try his hand at interpretation. These third-rate scholars can never resist putting in something of themselves. He will make guesses – wrong guesses – at the sorts of magic I employed at York. Surely there is enough confusion surrounding magic without our adding to it. Must we make use of Segundus?"

Childermass bent his dark gaze upon his master and his even darker smile, and replied that he believed they must. "I wonder sir," he said, "if you have lately heard of a naval gentleman of the name of Baines?"

"I believe I know the man you mean," said Mr Norrell.

"Ah!" said Childermass. "And how did you come to hear of him?"

A short silence.

"Well then," said Mr Norrell reluctantly, "I suppose that I have seen Captain Baines's name in one of the newspapers."

"Lieutenant Hector Baines served on *The King of the North*, a frigate," said Childermass. "At twenty-one years of age he lost a leg and two or three fingers in an action in the West Indies. In the same battle the Captain of *The King of the North* and many of the seamen died. Reports that Lieutenant Baines continued to command the ship and issue orders to his crew while the ship's doctor was actually sawing at his leg are, I dare say, a good deal exaggerated, but he certainly brought a fearfully damaged ship out of the Indies, attacked a Spanish ship full of bounty, gained a fortune and came home a hero. He jilted the young lady to whom he was engaged and married another. This, sir, is the Captain's history as it appeared in *The Morning Post*. And now I shall tell you what followed. Baines is a northerner like you, sir, a man of obscure birth with no great friends to make life easy for him. Shortly after his marriage he and his bride went to London to stay at the house of some friends in Seacoal-lane, and while they were there they were visited by people of all ranks and stations. They ate their dinner at viscountesses' tables, were toasted by Members of Parliament, and all that influence and patronage can do for Captain Baines was promised to him. This success, sir, I attribute to the general approbation and esteem which the report in the newspaper gained for him. But perhaps you have friends in London who will perform the same services for you without troubling the editors of the newspapers?"

"You know very well that I do not," said Mr Norrell impatiently.

In the meantime, Mr Segundus laboured very long over his letter and it grieved him that he could not be more warm in his praise of Mr Norrell. It seemed to him that the readers of the London newspaper would expect him to say something of Mr Norrell's personal virtues and would wonder why he did not.

In due course the letter appeared in *The Times* entitled: "EXTRAORDINARY OCCURRENCES IN YORK: AN APPEAL TO THE FRIENDS OF ENGLISH MAGIC." Mr Segundus ended his description of the magic at York by saying that the Friends of English Magic must surely bless that love of extreme retirement which marked Mr Norrell's character – for it had fostered his studies and had at last borne fruit in the shape of the wonderful magic at York Cathedral – but, said Mr Segundus, he appealed to the Friends of English Magic to join him in begging Mr Norrell not to return to a life of solitary study but to take his place upon the wider stage of the Nation's affairs and so begin a new chapter in the History of English Magic.

AN APPEAL TO THE FRIENDS OF ENGLISH MAGIC had a most sensational effect, particularly in London. The readers of *The Times* were quite thunderstruck by Mr Norrell's achievements. There was a general desire to see Mr Norrell; young ladies pitied the poor old gentlemen of York who had been so frightened by him, and wished very much to be as terrified themselves. Clearly such an opportunity as this was scarcely likely to come again; Mr Norrell determined to establish himself in London with all possible haste. "You must get me a house, Childermass," he said. "Get me a house that says to those that visit it that magic is a respectable profession – no less than Law and a great deal more so than Medicine."

Childermass inquired drily if Mr Norrell wished him to seek out architecture expressive of the proposition that magic was as respectable as the Church?

51

Mr Norrell (who knew there were such things as jokes in the world or people would not write about them in books, but who had never actually been introduced to a joke or shaken its hand) considered a while before replying at last that no, he did not think they could quite claim that.

So Childermass (perhaps thinking that nothing in the world is so respectable as money) directed his master to a house in Hanover-square among the abodes of the rich and prosperous. Now I do not know what may be your opinion yet to say the truth I do not much care for the south side of Hanover-square; the houses are so tall and thin – four storeys at least – and all the tall, gloomy windows are so regular, and every house so exactly resembles its neighbours that they have something of the appearance of a high wall blocking out the light. Be that as it may, Mr Norrell (a less fanciful person than I) was satisfied with his new house, or at least as satisfied as any gentleman could be who for more than thirty years has lived in a large country-house surrounded by a park of mature timber, which is in its turn surrounded by a good estate of farms and woods – a gentleman, in other words, whose eye has never been offended by the sight of any other man's property whenever he looked out of the window.

"It is certainly a small house, Childermass," he said, "but I do not complain. My own comfort, as you know, I do not regard."

Childermass replied that the house was larger than most.

"Indeed?" said Mr Norrell, much surprized. Mr Norrell was particularly shocked by the smallness of the library, which could not be made to accommodate one third of the books he considered indispensable; he asked Childermass how people in London housed their books? Perhaps they did not read?

Mr Norrell had been in London not above three weeks when he received a letter from a Mrs Godesdone, a lady of whom he had never heard before.

". . . I know it is very *shoking* that I should write to you upon no acquaintance whatsoever & no doubt you say to yourself who is

ais impertinent creachure? I did not now there was such a person
a existence! and consider me shokingly bold etc. etc. but Draw-
ght is a dear freind of mine and assures me that you are the
weetest-natured creachure in the world and will not mind it. I am
aost impatient for the pleasure of your acquaintance and would
onsider it the greatest honour in the world if you would consent to
ive us the pleasure of your company at an evening-party on
hursday se'night. Do not let the apprehension of meeting with a
roud prevent you from coming – I detest a croud of all things and
nly my most intimate freinds will be invited to meet you . . ."

It was not the sort of letter to make any very favourable
npression upon Mr Norrell. He read it through very rapidly,
ut it aside with an exclamation of disgust and took up his book
gain. A short while later Childermass arrived to attend to the
norning's business. He read Mrs Godesdone's letter and inquired
vhat answer Mr Norrell intended to return to it?

"A refusal," said Mr Norrell.

"Indeed? And shall I say that you have a prior engagement?"
sked Childermass.

"Certainly, if you wish," said Mr Norrell.

"And *do* you have a prior engagement?" asked Childermass.

"No," said Mr Norrell.

"Ah!" said Childermass. "Then perhaps it is the overabundance
f your engagements on other days that makes you refuse this one?
'ou fear to be too tired?"

"I have no engagements. You know very well that I do not." Mr
Jorrell read for another minute or two before remarking (appar-
ntly to his book), "You are still here."

"I am," said Childermass.

"Well then," said Mr Norrell, "what is it? What is the matter?"

"I had thought you were come to London to shew people what a
nodern magician looked like. It will be a slow business if you are to
tay at home all the time."

Mr Norrell said nothing. He picked up the letter and looked at it. "Drawlight," he said at last. "What does she mean by that? know no one of that name."

"I do not know what she means," said Childermass, "but I d know this: at present it will not do to be too nice."

At eight o'clock on the evening of Mrs Godesdone's party M Norrell in his best grey coat was seated in his carriage, wonderin about Mrs Godesdone's dear friend, Drawlight, when he wa roused to a realization that the carriage was no longer moving Looking out of the window he saw a great lamp-lit chaos of peopl carriages and horses. Thinking that everyone else must find th London streets as confusing as he did, he naturally fell into th supposition that his coachman and footman had lost their wa and, banging on the roof of the carriage with his stick, he cried "Davey! Lucas! Did not you hear me say Manchester-street? Wh did you not make sure of the way before we set off?"

Lucas, on the box-seat, called down that they were already i Manchester-street, but must wait their turn – there was a long lin of carriages that were to stop at the house before them.

"Which house?" cried Mr Norrell.

The house they were going to, said Lucas.

"No, no! You are mistaken," said Mr Norrell. "It is to be a smal gathering."

But on his arrival at Mrs Godesdone's house Mr Norrell foun himself instantly plunged into the midst of a hundred or so of Mr Godesdone's most intimate friends. The hall and reception room were crowded with people and more were arriving at ever moment. Mr Norrell was very much astonished, yet what i the world was there to be surprized at? It was a fashionabl London party, no different from any other that might be held a any of half a dozen houses across Town every day of the week.

And how to describe a London party? Candles in lustres of cut glass are placed everywhere about the house in dazzling profusion elegant mirrors triple and quadruple the light until night outshine day; many-coloured hot-house fruits are piled up in stately

yramids upon white-clothed tables; divine creatures, resplendent
vith jewels, go about the room in pairs, arm in arm, admired by all
vho see them. Yet the heat is over-powering, the pressure and
oise almost as bad; there is nowhere to sit and scarce anywhere to
tand. You may see your dearest friend in another part of the
oom; you may have a world of things to tell him – but how in the
vorld will you ever reach him? If you are fortunate then perhaps
ou will discover him later in the crush and shake his hand as you
re both hurried past each other. Surrounded by cross, hot
trangers, your chance of rational conversation is equal to what
: would be in an African desert. Your only wish is to preserve your
avourite gown from the worst ravages of the crowd. Every body
omplains of the heat and the suffocation. Every body declares it to
e entirely insufferable. But if it is all misery for the guests, then
vhat of the wretchedness of those who have not been invited? Our
ufferings are nothing to theirs! And we may tell each other
omorrow that it was a delightful party.

It so happened that Mr Norrell arrived at the same moment as a
ery old lady. Though small and disagreeable-looking she was
learly someone of importance (she was all over diamonds). The
ervants clustered round her and Mr Norrell proceeded into the
ouse, unobserved by any of them. He entered a room full of
eople where he discovered a cup of punch upon a little table.
Vhile he was drinking the punch it occurred to him that he had
old no one his name and consequently no one knew he was here.
Ie found himself in some perplexity as to how to proceed. His
ellow-guests were occupied in greeting their friends, and as for
pproaching one of the servants and announcing himself, Mr
Norrell felt quite unequal to the task; their proud faces and air
f indescribable superiority unnerved him. It was a great pity that
ne or two of the late members of the Society of York Magicians
vere not there to see him looking so all forlorn and ill at ease; it
night have cheered them up immeasurably. But it is the same with
ll of us. In familiar surroundings our manners are cheerful and

easy, but only transport us to places where we know no one and no one knows us, and Lord! how uncomfortable we become!

Mr Norrell was wandering from room to room, wishing only to go away again, when he was stopped in mid-perambulation by the sound of his own name and the following enigmatic words: ". . . assures me that he is never to be seen without a mystic robe of midnight blue, adorned with otherlandish symbols! But Drawlight – who knows this Norrell very well – says that . . ."

The noise of the room was such that it is to be marvelled at that Mr Norrell heard anything at all. The words had been spoken by a young woman and Mr Norrell looked frantically about him to try and discover her, but without success. He began to wonder what else was being said about him.

He found himself standing near to a lady and a gentleman. She was unremarkable enough – a sensible-looking woman of forty or fifty – he, however, was a style of man not commonly seen in Yorkshire. He was rather small and was dressed very carefully in a good black coat and linen of a most exquisite whiteness. He had a little pair of silver spectacles that swung from a black velvet ribbon around his neck. His features were very regular and rather good; he had short, dark hair and his skin was very clean and white – except that about his cheeks there was the faintest suggestion of rouge. But it was his eyes that were remarkable: large, well-shaped, dark and so very brilliant as to have an almost liquid appearance. They were fringed with the longest, darkest eyelashes. There were many little feminine touches about him that he had contrived for himself, but his eyes and eyelashes were the only ones which nature had given him.

Mr Norrell paid good attention to their conversation to discover if they were talking about him.

". . . the advice that I gave Lady Duncombe about her own daughter," said the small man. "Lady Duncombe had found a most unexceptional husband for her daughter, a gentleman with nine hundred a year! But the silly girl had set her heart upon a

56

enniless Captain in the Dragoons, and poor Lady Duncombe was most frantic. 'Oh, your ladyship!' I cried the instant that I heard about it, 'Make yourself easy! Leave everything to me. I do not set up as any very extraordinary genius, as your ladyship knows, but my odd talents are exactly suited to this sort of thing.' Oh, madam! you will laugh when you hear how I contrived matters! I dare say no one else in the world would have thought of such a ridiculous scheme! I took Miss Susan to Gray's in Bond-street where we both spent a very agreeable morning in trying on necklaces and ear-rings. She has passed most of her life in Derbyshire and has not been accustomed to really *remarkable* jewels. I do not think she had ever thought *seriously* upon such things before. Then Lady Duncombe and I dropt one or two hints that in marrying Captain Hurst she would put it quite out of her power to make such delightful purchases ever again, whereas if she married Mr Watts she might make her choice of the best of them. I next took pains to get acquainted with Captain Hurst and persuaded him to accompany me to Boodle's where – well I will not deceive you, madam – where there is gambling!" The small man giggled. "I lent him a little money to try his luck – it was not my own money you understand. Lady Duncombe had given it to me for the purpose. We went three or four times and in a remarkably short space of time the Captain's debts were – well, madam, *I* cannot see how he will ever get clear of them! Lady Duncombe and I represented to him that it is one thing to expect a young woman to marry upon a small income, but quite another to expect her to take a man encumbered with debts. He was not inclined to listen to us at first. At first he made use of – what shall I say? – some rather *military* expressions. But in the end he was obliged to admit the justice of all we said."

Mr Norrell saw the sensible-looking woman of forty or fifty give the small man a look of some dislike. Then she bowed, very slightly and coldly, and passed without a word away into the crowd; the small man turned in the other direction and immediately hailed a friend.

Mr Norrell's eye was next caught by an excessively pretty youn woman in a white-and-silver gown. A tall, handsome-looking ma was talking to her and she was laughing very heartily at everythin he said.

". . . and what if he should discover two dragons – one red an one white – beneath the foundations of the house, locked in etern struggle and symbolizing the future destruction of Mr Godesdon I dare say," said the man slyly, "you would not mind it if he did.

She laughed again, even more merrily than before, and M Norrell was surprized to hear in the next instant someone addre her as "Mrs Godesdone".

Upon reflection Mr Norrell thought that he ought to have spoke to her but by then she was nowhere to be seen. He was sick of th noise and sight of so many people and determined to go quietl away, but it so happened that just at that moment the crowds abou the door were particularly impenetrable; he was caught up in th current of people and carried away to quite another part of th room. Round and round he went like a dry leaf caught up in a drai in one of these turns around the room he discovered a quiet corn near a window. A tall screen of carved ebony inlaid with mother-o pearl half-hid – ah! what bliss was this! – a bookcase. Mr Norre slipped behind the screen, took down John Napier's *A Plai Discouverie of the Whole Revelation of St John* and began to read.

He had not been there very long when, happening to glance u he saw the tall, handsome man who had been speaking to M Godesdone and the small, dark man who had gone to such troubl to destroy the matrimonial hopes of Captain Hurst. They wer discoursing energetically, but the press and flow of people aroun them was so great that, without any ceremony, the tall man g hold of the small man's sleeve and pulled him behind the scree and into the corner which Mr Norrell occupied.

"He is not here," said the tall man, giving each word a emphasis with a poke of his finger in the other's shoulder. "Wher are the fiercely burning eyes that you promised us? Where th

ances that none of us can explain? Has any one been cursed? – I
o not think so. You have called him up like a spirit from the vasty
eep, and he has not come."

"I was with him only this morning," said the small man
efiantly, "to hear of the wonderful magic that he has been doing
cently and he said then that he would come."

"It is past midnight. He will not come now." The tall man
niled a very superior smile. "Confess, you do not know him."

Then the small man smiled in rivalry of the other's smile (these
vo gentlemen positively jousted in smiles) and said, "No one in
ondon knows him better. I shall confess that I am a little – a very
ttle – disappointed."

"Ha!" cried the tall man. "It is the opinion of the room that we
ave all been most abominably imposed upon. We came here in
ie expectation of seeing something very extraordinary, and
istead we have been obliged to provide our own amusement."
Iis eye happening to light upon Mr Norrell, he said, "*That*
entleman is reading a book."

The small man glanced behind him and in doing so happened to
nock his elbow against *A Plaine Discouverie of the Whole Revelation of
t John*. He gave Mr Norrell a cool look for filling up so very small
space with so very large a book.

"I have said that I am disappointed," continued the small man,
but I am not at all surprised. You do not know him as I do. Oh! I
an assure you he has a pretty shrewd notion of his value. No one
an have a better. A man who buys a house in Hanover-square
nows the style in which things ought to be done. Oh, yes! He has
ought a house in Hanover-square! You had not heard that, I dare
ay? He is as rich as a Jew. He had an old uncle called
Iaythornthwaite who died and left him a world of money. He
as – among other trifles – a good house and a large estate – that of
Iurtfew Abbey in Yorkshire."

"Ha!" said the tall man drily. "He was in high luck. Rich old
ncles who die are in shockingly short supply."

"Oh, indeed!" cried the small man. "Some friends of mine, th Griffins, have an amazingly rich old uncle to whom they have pai all sorts of attentions for years and years – but though he was least a hundred years old when they began, he is not dead yet an it seems he intends to live for ever to spite them, and all the Griffi are growing old themselves and dying one by one in a state of th most bitter disappointment. Yet I am sure that *you*, my dea Lascelles, need not concern yourself with any such vexatious ol persons – your fortune is comfortable enough, is it not?"

The tall man chose to disregard this particular piece of im pertinence and instead remarked coolly, "I believe that gentlema wishes to speak to you."

The gentleman in question was Mr Norrell who, quite amazed hear his fortune and property discussed so openly, had been waitin to speak for some minutes past. "I beg your pardon," he said.

"Yes?" said the small man sharply.

"I am Mr Norrell."

The tall man and the small man gave Mr Norrell two ver broad stares.

After a silence of some moments the small gentleman, who ha begun by looking offended, had passed through a stage of lookin blank and was beginning to look puzzled, asked Mr Norrell repeat his name.

This Mr Norrell did, whereupon the small gentleman said, ' do beg your pardon, but . . . Which is to say . . . I hope you wi excuse my asking so impertinent a question, but is there at yo house in Hanover-square someone all dressed in black, with a thi face like a twisted hedge-root?"

Mr Norrell thought for a moment and then he said, "Child ermass. You mean Childermass."

"Oh, Childermass!" cried the small man, as if all was no perfectly plain. "Yes, of course! How stupid of me! That is Chil ermass! Oh, Mr Norrell! I can hardly begin to express my delight i making your acquaintance. My name, sir, is Drawlight."

"Do you know Childermass?" asked Mr Norrell, puzzled.

"I . . ." Mr Drawlight paused. "I have seen such a person as I described coming out of your house and I . . . Oh, Mr Norrell! Such a noodle I am upon occasion! I mistook him for you! Pray do not be offended, sir! For now that I behold you, I plainly see that whereas *he* has the wild, romantic looks one associates with magicians, *you* have the meditative air of a scholar. Lascelles, does not Mr Norrell have the grave and sober bearing of a scholar?"

The tall man said, without much enthusiasm, that he supposed so.

"Mr Norrell, my friend, Mr Lascelles," said Drawlight.

Mr Lascelles made the slightest of bows.

"Oh, Mr Norrell!" cried Mr Drawlight. "You cannot imagine the torments I have suffered tonight, in wondering whether or not you would come! At seven o'clock my anxieties upon this point were so acute that I could not help myself! I actually went down to the Glasshouse-street boiling-cellar expressly to inquire of Davey and Lucas to know their opinions! Davey was certain that you would not come, which threw me, as you may imagine, into the utmost despair!"

"Davey and Lucas!" said Mr Norrell in tones of the greatest astonishment. (These, it may be remembered, were the names of Mr Norrell's coachman and footman.)

"Oh, yes!" said Mr Drawlight. "The Glasshouse-street boiling-cellar is where Davey and Lucas occasionally take their mutton, as I dare say you know." Mr Drawlight paused in his flow of chatter, just long enough for Mr Norrell to murmur that he had not known that.

"I have been most industriously talking up your extraordinary powers to all my wide acquaintance," continued Mr Drawlight. "I have been your John the Baptist, sir, preparing the way for you! – and I felt no hesitation in declaring that you and I were great friends for I had a presentiment from the first, my dear Mr Norrell, that we would be; and as you see I was quite right, for now here we are, chatting so comfortably to one another!"

5

Drawlight

Spring to autumn 1807

EARLY NEXT MORNING Mr Norrell's man of business, Childermass, answered a summons to attend his master in the breakfast-room. He found Mr Norrell pale-faced and in a state of some nervous agitation.

"What is the matter?" asked Childermass.

"Oh!" cried Mr Norrell, looking up. "You dare to ask me that? You, who have so neglected your duties that any scoundrel may put a watch upon my house and question my servants without fear of disturbance! Aye, and get answers to those questions, too! What do I employ you for, I should like to know, if not to protect me from such impertinence as this?"

Childermass shrugged. "You mean Drawlight, I suppose."

A short, astonished silence.

"You knew of it?" cried Mr Norrell. "Good God, man! What were you thinking of? Have you not told me a hundred times that in order to secure my privacy, the servants must be kept from gossiping?"

"Oh! certainly!" said Childermass. "But I am very much afraid, sir, that you must give up some of your habits of privacy. Retirement and seclusion are all very well in Yorkshire, but we are not in Yorkshire any more."

"Yes, yes!" said Mr Norrell irritably. "I know that we are not

But that is not the question. The question is: what does this Drawlight want?"

"To have the distinction of being the first gentleman in London to make the acquaintance of a magician. That is all."

But Mr Norrell was not to be reasoned out of his fears. He rubbed his yellow-white hands nervously together, and directed fearful glances into the shadowy corners of the room as though suspecting them of harbouring other Drawlights, all spying upon him. "He did not look like a scholar in those clothes," he said, "but that is no guarantee of any thing. He wore no rings of power or allegiance but still . . ."

"I do not well understand you," said Childermass. "Speak plainly."

"Might he not have some *skill* of his own, do you suppose?" said Mr Norrell. "Or perhaps he has friends who are jealous of my success! Who are his associates? What is his education?"

Childermass smiled a long smile that went all up one side of his face. "Oh! You have talked yourself into a belief that he is the agent of some other magician. Well, sir, he is not. You may depend upon me for that. Far from neglecting your interests, after we received Mrs Godesdone's letter I made some inquiries about the gentleman – as many, I dare say, as he has made about you. It would be an odd sort of magician, I think, that employed such a creature as he is. Besides, if such a magician had existed you would have long since found him out, would not you? – and discovered the means to part him from his books and put an end to his scholarship? You have done it before, you know."

"You know no harm of this Drawlight then?"

Childermass raised an eyebrow and smiled his sideways smile. "Upon the contrary," he said.

"Ah!" cried Mr Norrell, "I knew it! Well then, I shall certainly make a point of avoiding his society."

"Why?" asked Childermass. "I did not say so. Have I not just told you that he is no threat to you? What is it to you that he is a bad man? Take my advice, sir, make use of the tool which is to hand."

Then Childermass related to Mr Norrell what he had discovered about Drawlight: how he belonged to a certain breed of gentlemen, only to be met with in London, whose main occupation is the wearing of expensive and fashionable clothes; how they pass their lives in ostentatious idleness, gambling and drinking to excess and spending months at a time in Brighton and other fashionable watering places; how in recent years this breed seemed to have reached a sort of perfection in Christopher Drawlight. Even his dearest friends would have admitted that he possessed not a single good quality.[1]

Despite Mr Norrell's tuttings and suckings-in of air at every new revelation, there is no doubt that this conversation did him good. When Lucas entered the room ten minutes later with a pot of chocolate, he was composedly eating toast and preserves and appeared entirely different from the anxious, fretful creature he had been earlier that morning.

A loud rap was heard at the door and Lucas went to answer it. A light tread was next heard upon the stairs and Lucas re-appeared to announce, "Mr Drawlight!"

"Ah, Mr Norrell! How do you do, sir?" Mr Drawlight entered the room. He wore a dark blue coat, and carried an ebony stick with a silver knob. He appeared to be in excellent spirits, and bowed and smiled and walked to and fro so much that five minutes later there was scarcely an inch of carpet in the room that he had not stood upon, a table or chair he had not lightly and caressingly

---

[1] He had once found himself in a room with Lady Bessborough's long-haired white cat. He happened to be dressed in an immaculate black coat and trousers, and was therefore thoroughly alarmed by the cat's stalking round and round and making motions as if it proposed to sit upon him. He waited until he believed himself to be unobserved, then he picked it up, opened a window and tossed it out. Despite falling three storeys to the ground, the cat survived, but one of its legs was never quite right afterwards and it always evinced the greatest dislike to gentlemen in black clothes.

touched, a mirror he had not danced across, a painting that he had not for a moment smiled upon.

Mr Norrell, though confident now that his guest was no great magician or great magician's servant, was still not much inclined to take Childermass's advice. His invitation to Mr Drawlight to sit down at the breakfast-table and take some chocolate was of the coldest sort. But sulky silences and black looks had no effect upon Mr Drawlight whatsoever, since he filled up the silences with his own chatter and was too accustomed to black looks to mind them.

"Do you not agree with me, sir, that the party last night was the most charming in the world? Though, if I may say so, I think you were quite right to leave when you did. I was able to go round afterwards and tell everyone that the gentleman that they had just espied walking out of the room was indeed Mr Norrell! Oh! believe me, sir, your departure was not unobserved. The Honourable Mr Masham was quite certain he had just caught sight of your esteemed shoulder, Lady Barclay thought she had seen a neat grey curl of your venerable wig, and Miss Fiskerton was quite ecstatic to think that her gaze had rested momentarily upon the tip of your scholarly nose! And the little that they have seen of you, sir, has made them desire more. They long to view the complete man!"

"Ah!" said Mr Norrell, with some satisfaction.

Mr Drawlight's repeated assurances that the ladies and gentlemen at Mrs Godesdone's party had been utterly enchanted by Mr Norrell went some way to diminish Mr Norrell's prejudices against his guest. According to Mr Drawlight, Mr Norrell's company was like seasoning: the smallest pinch of it could add a relish to the entire dish. Mr Drawlight made himself so agreeable that Mr Norrell grew by degrees more communicative.

"And to what fortunate circumstance, sir," asked Mr Drawlight, "do we owe the happiness of your society? What brings you to London?"

"I have come to London in order to further the cause of modern magic. I intend, sir, to bring back magic to Britain," answered Mr Norrell gravely. "I have a great deal to communicate to the Great Men of our Age. There are many ways in which I may be of service to them."

Mr Drawlight murmured politely that he was sure of it.

"I may tell you, sir," said Mr Norrell, "that I heartily wish this duty had fallen to the lot of some other magician." Mr Norrell sighed and looked as noble as his small, pinched features would allow. It is an extraordinary thing that a man such as Mr Norrell - a man who had destroyed the careers of so many of his fellow-magicians - should be able to convince himself that he would rather all the glory of his profession belonged to one of them, but there is no doubt that Mr Norrell believed it when he said it.

Mr Drawlight murmured sympathetically. Mr Drawlight was sure that Mr Norrell was too modest. Mr Drawlight could not suppose for a moment that anyone could be better suited to the task of bringing back magic to Britain than Mr Norrell.

"But I labour under a disadvantage, sir," said Mr Norrell.

Mr Drawlight was surprized to hear it.

"I do not know the world, sir. I know that I do not. I have a scholar's love of silence and solitude. To sit and pass hour after hour in idle chatter with a roomful of strangers is to me the worst sort of torment - but I dare say there will be a good deal of that sort of thing. Childermass assures me that there will be." Mr Norrell looked wistfully at Drawlight as if hopeful that Drawlight might contradict him.

"Ah!" Mr Drawlight considered a moment. "And that is exactly why I am so happy that you and I have become friends! I do not pretend to be a scholar, sir; I know next to nothing of magicians or magical history, and I dare say that, from time to time, you may find my society irksome, but you must set any little irritations of that nature against the great good that I may do you in taking you about and shewing you to people. Oh, Mr Norrell, sir! You cannot imagine how useful I may be to you!"

Mr Norrell declined to give his word there and then to accompany Mr Drawlight to all the places that Mr Drawlight said were so delightful and to meet all those people whose friendship, Mr Drawlight said, would add a new sweetness to Mr Norrell's existence, but he did consent to go with Mr Drawlight that evening to a dinner at Lady Rawtenstall's house in Bedford-square.

Mr Norrell got through the dinner with less fatigue than he expected, and so agreed to meet Mr Drawlight upon the morrow at Mr Plumtree's house. With Mr Drawlight as his guide, Mr Norrell entered society with greater confidence than before. His engagements became numerous; he was busy from eleven o'clock in the morning to past midnight. He paid morning-visits; he ate his dinner in dining-parlours all over the Town; he attended evening-parties, balls and concerts of Italian music; he met baronets, viscounts, viscountesses, and honourable thises and thats; he was to be met with walking down Bond-street, arm-in-arm with Mr Drawlight; he was observed taking the air in a carriage in Hyde-park with Mr Drawlight and Mr Drawlight's dear friend, Mr Lascelles.

On days when Mr Norrell did not dine abroad Mr Drawlight took his mutton at Mr Norrell's house in Hanover-square – which Mr Norrell imagined Mr Drawlight must be very glad to do, for Childermass had told him that Mr Drawlight had scarcely any money. Childermass said that Drawlight lived upon his wits and his debts; none of his great friends had ever been invited to visit him at home, because home was a lodging above a shoemaker's in Little Ryder-street.

Like every new house, the house in Hanover-square – which had seemed perfection at first – was soon discovered to be in need of every sort of improvement. Naturally, Mr Norrell was impatient to have it all accomplished as soon as possible, but when he appealed to Drawlight to agree with him that the London workmen were extraordinarily slow, Drawlight took the opportunity to ascertain all Mr Norrell's plans for colours, wallpapers, carpets, furniture and ornaments, and to find fault with all of them. They argued the point for a quarter of an hour and then Mr Drawlight ordered Mr Norrell's carriage to be got ready and directed Davey to take him and Mr Norrell straight to Mr Ackermann's shop in the Strand. There Mr Drawlight shewed Mr Norrell a book which contained a picture by Mr Repton of an empty, old-fashioned parlour, where a stony-faced old person from the time of Queen Elizabeth stared out of a painting on the wall and the empty chairs all gaped at each other like guests at a party who discover they have nothing to say to one another. But on the next page, ah! what changes had been wrought by the noble arts of joinery, paper-hanging and upholstery! Here was a picture of the same parlour new-furnished and improved beyond all recognition! A dozen or so fashionably-dressed ladies and gentlemen had been enticed into the smart new apartment by the prospect of refreshing their spirits by reclining in elegant postures upon the chairs, or walking in the vine-clad conservatory which had mysteriously appeared on the other side of a pair of French windows. The moral, as Mr Drawlight explained it, was that if Mr Norrell hoped to win friends for the cause of modern magic, he must insert a great many more French windows into his house.

Under Mr Drawlight's tutelage Mr Norrell learnt to prefer picture-gallery reds to the respectable dull greens of his youth. In the interests of modern magic, the honest materials of Mr Norrell's house were dressed up with paint and varnish, and made to represent things they were not – like actors upon a stage. Plaster was painted to resemble wood, and wood was painted to resemble different sorts of wood. By the time it came to select the appointments for the dining-parlour, Mr Norrell's confidence in Drawlight's taste was so complete that Drawlight was commissioned to chuse the dinner-service without reference to any one else.

"You will not regret it, my dear sir!" cried Drawlight, "for three weeks ago I chose a set for the Duchess of B—— and she declared e moment she saw it that she never in her life saw anything half charming!"

On a bright May morning Mr Norrell was seated in a drawing-om in Wimpole-street at the house of a Mrs Littleworth. Among e people gathered there were Mr Drawlight and Mr Lascelles. Ir Lascelles was exceedingly fond of Mr Norrell's society, indeed e came second only to Mr Drawlight in this respect, but his easons for courting Mr Norrell's notice were quite different. Mr ,ascelles was a clever, cynical man who thought it the most diculous thing in the world that a scholarly old gentleman ould have talked himself into the belief that he could perform agic. Consequently, Mr Lascelles took great pleasure in asking Ir Norrell questions about magic whenever the opportunity arose ） that he might amuse himself with the answers.

"And how do you like London, sir?" he asked.

"Not at all," said Mr Norrell.

"I am sorry to hear it," said Mr Lascelles. "Have you dis-overed any brother-magicians to talk to?"

Mr Norrell frowned and said he did not believe there were any agicians in London, or if so, then all his researches had not been ble to uncover them.

"Ah, sir!" cried Mr Drawlight. "There you are mistaken! You ave been most abominably misinformed! We have magicians in ondon – Oh! forty at least. Lascelles, would not you agree that we ave hundreds of magicians in London? One may see them upon ractically every street corner. Mr Lascelles and I will be very appy to make you acquainted with them. They have a sort of ing whom they call Vinculus – a tall, ragged scarecrow of a man ho has a little booth just outside St Christopher Le Stocks, all lashed with mud, with a dirty yellow curtain and, if you give im two pennies, he will prophesy."

"Vinculus's fortunes are nothing but calamities," observed Mr ,ascelles, laughing. "Thus far he has promised me drowning, adness, the destruction by fire of all my property and a natural

69

daughter who will do me great injury in my old age by he spitefulness."

"I shall be glad to take you, sir," said Drawlight to Mr Norrel "I am as fond as any thing of Vinculus."

"Take care if you do go, sir," advised Mrs Littleworth. "Some of these men can put one in a dreadful fright. The Cruickshank brought a magician – a very dirty fellow – to the house to shew their friends some tricks, but when he got there it seemed he di not know any – and so they would not pay him. In a great rage h swore that he would turn the baby into a coal scuttle; and the they were in great confusion because the baby was nowhere to b found – though no new coal scuttles had appeared, just the ol familiar ones. They searched the house from top to bottom an Mrs Cruickshank was half-dead with anxiety and the physician wa sent for – until the nursemaid appeared with the baby at the doc and it came out that she had taken it to shew her mother in Jame street."

Despite such enticements as these, Mr Norrell declined M Drawlight's kind offer to take him to see Vinculus in his yellov booth.

"And what is your opinion of the Raven King, Mr Norrell? asked Mrs Littleworth eagerly.

"I have none. He is a person I never think of."

"Indeed?" remarked Mr Lascelles. "You will excuse my sayin so, Mr Norrell, but that is rather an extraordinary statement. never met a magician yet who did not declare that the Black Kin was the greatest of them all – the magician *par excellence*! A ma who could, had he so desired, have wrested Merlin from the tre spun the old gentleman on his head and put him back in again.""

Mr Norrell said nothing.

"But surely," continued Mr Lascelles, "none of the othe *Aureates* could rival his achievements? Kingdoms in all the world

---

[2] Merlin is presumed to have been imprisoned in a hawthorn tree by th sorceress, Nimue.

70

that ever were.[3] Bands of human knights and fairy knights to carry out his bidding. Magic woods that walked about. To say nothing of his longevity – a three-hundred-year reign – and at the end of it we are told that he was still, in appearance at least, a young man."

Mr Norrell said nothing.

"But perhaps you think that the histories lie? I have frequently heard it suggested that the Raven King never existed – that he was not one magician at all, but a long train of magicians, all looking much the same. Perhaps that is what you think?"

Mr Norrell looked as if he would prefer to remain silent, but the directness of Mr Lascelles's question obliged him to give a reply. "No," he said at last, "I am quite certain that he existed. But I cannot consider his influence upon English magic as any thing other than deplorable. His magic was of a particularly pernicious sort and nothing would please me more than that he should be forgot as completely as he deserves."

"And what of your fairy-servants, sir?" said Mr Lascelles. "Are they visible only to yourself? Or may other people perceive them?"

Mr Norrell sniffed and said he had none.

"What none?" exclaimed a lady in a carnation-pink gown, much surprised.

"You are wise, Mr Norrell," said Mr Lascelles. "Tubbs *versus* Starhouse must stand as a warning to all magicians."[4]

---

[3] Mr Lascelles exaggerates. The Raven King's kingdoms were never more than three in number.

[4] Tubbs *versus* Starhouse: a famous case brought before the Quarter Sessions at Nottingham a few years ago.

A Nottinghamshire man called Tubbs wished very much to see a fairy and, from thinking of fairies day and night, and from reading all sorts of odd books about them, he took it into his head that his coachman was a fairy.

The coachman (whose name was Jack Starhouse) was dark and tall and scarcely ever said a word which discomfited his fellow-servants and made them think him proud. He had only recently entered Mr Tubbs's household, and said that previously he had been coachman to an old man called Browne at a place called Coldmicklehill in the north. He had one great talent: he could make any creature love him. The horses were always very willing when he had the reins and never cross or fidgety at all, and he could command cats

"Mr Tubbs was no magician," said Mr Norrell. "Nor did I ever hear that he claimed to be one. But had he been the greatest magician in Christendom, he would still have been wrong to wish for the company of fairies. A more poisonous race or one more

[4] *cont'd* in a way that the people of Nottinghamshire had never seen before. He had a whispering way of talking to them; any cat he spoke to would stay quite still with an expression of faint surprize on its face as if it had never heard such good sense in all its life nor ever expected to again. He could also make them dance. The cats that belonged to Mr Tubbs's household were as grave and mindful of their dignity as any other set of cats, but Jack Starhouse could make them dance wild dances, leaping about upon their hind legs and casting themselves from side to side. This he did by strange sighs and whistlings and hissings.

One of the other servants observed that if only cats had been good for any thing – which they were not – then all this might have had some point to it. But Starhouse's wonderful mastery was not useful, nor did it entertain his fellow-servants; it only made them uncomfortable.

Whether it were this or his handsome face with the eyes a little too wide apart that made Mr Tubbs so certain he was a fairy I do not know, but Mr Tubbs began to make inquiries about the coachman in secret.

One day Mr Tubbs called Starhouse to his study. Mr Tubbs said that he had learnt that Mr Browne was very ill – had been ill for all the time Starhouse had claimed to work for him – and had not gone out for years and years. So Mr Tubbs was curious to know what he had needed a coachman for.

For a little while Jack Starhouse said nothing. Then he admitted that he had not been in Mr Browne's employ. He said he had worked for another family in the neighbourhood. He had worked hard, it had been a good place, he had been happy; but the other servants had not liked him, he did not know why, it had happened to him before. One of the other servants (a woman) had told lies about him and he had been dismissed. He had seen Mr Browne once years ago. He said he was very sorry that he had lied to Mr Tubbs, but he had not known what else to do.

Mr Tubbs explained that there was no need to invent further stories. He knew that Starhouse was a fairy and said he was not to fear; he would not betray him; he only wished to talk to him about his home and people.

At first Starhouse did not at all understand what Mr Tubbs meant, and when finally he did understand, it was in vain that he protested that he was a human being and an Englishman, Mr Tubbs did not believe him.

After this, whatever Starhouse was doing, wherever he went, he would find Mr Tubbs waiting for him with a hundred questions about fairies and Faerie. Starhouse was made so unhappy by this treatment (though Mr Tubbs was always kind and courteous), that he was obliged to give up his place. While yet unemployed, he met with a man in an ale-house in Southwell who persuaded him to bring an action against his former master for defamation of character. In a famous ruling Jack Starhouse became the first man to be declared human under English law.

inimical to England has never existed. There have been far too many magicians too idle or ignorant to pursue a proper course of study, who instead bent all their energies upon acquiring a fairy-servant – and when they had got such a servant they depended upon him to complete all their business for them. English history is full of such men and some, I am glad to say, were punished for it as they deserved. Look at Bloodworth."[5]

---

[4] *cont'd* But this curious episode ended unhappily for both Tubbs and Starhouse. Tubbs was punished for his harmless ambition to see a fairy by being made an object of ridicule everywhere. Unflattering caricatures of him were printed in the London, Nottingham, Derby and Sheffield papers, and neighbours with whom he had been on terms of the greatest goodwill and intimacy for years declined to know him any more. While Starhouse quickly discovered that no one wished to employ a coachman who had brought an action against his master; he was forced to accept work of a most degrading nature and very soon fell into great poverty.

The case of Tubbs *versus* Starhouse is interesting not least because it serves as an illustration of the widely-held belief that fairies have not left England completely. Many Englishmen and women think that we are surrounded by fairies every day of our lives. Some are invisible and some masquerade as Christians and may in fact be known to us. Scholars have debated the matter for centuries but without reaching any conclusion.

[5] Simon Bloodworth's fairy-servant came to him quite out of the blue offering his services and saying he wished to be known as "Buckler". As every English schoolchild nowadays can tell you, Bloodworth would have done better to have inquired further and to have probed a little deeper into who, precisely, Buckler was, and why, exactly, he had come out of Faerie with no other aim than to become the servant of a third-rate English magician.

Buckler was very quick at all sorts of magic and Bloodworth's business in the little wool-town of Bradford on Avon grew and prospered. Only once did Buckler cause any sort of difficulty when, in a sudden fit of rage, he destroyed a little book belonging to Lord Lovel's chaplain.

The longer Buckler remained with Bloodworth the stronger he became and the first thing that Buckler did when he became stronger was to change his appearance: his dusty rags became a suit of good clothes; a rusty pair of scissars that he had stolen from a locksmith in the town became a sword; his thin, piebald fox-face became a pale and handsome human one; and he grew very suddenly two or three feet taller. This, he was quick to impress on Mrs Bloodworth and her daughters, was his true appearance – the other merely being an enchantment he had been under.

On a fine May morning in 1310 when Bloodworth was away from home Mrs Bloodworth discovered a tall cupboard standing in the corner of her kitchen where no cupboard had ever been before. When she asked Buckler about it, he said immediately that it was a magical cupboard and that he had

Mr Norrell made many new acquaintances, but kindled no pure flame of friendship in the hearts of any. In general, London found him disappointing. He did no magic, cursed no one, foretold nothing. Once at Mrs Godesdone's house he was heard to remark that he thought it might rain, but this, if a prophecy, was a disappointing one, for it did not rain – indeed no rain fell until the

---

[5] *cont'd* brought it there. He said that he had always thought that it was a pity that magic was not more commonly used in England; he said it pained him to see Mrs Bloodworth and her daughters washing and sweeping and cooking and cleaning from dawn to dusk when they ought, in his opinion, to be sitting on cushions in jewel–spangled gowns eating comfits. This, thought Mrs Bloodworth, was very good sense. Buckler said how he had often reproved her husband for his failure to make Mrs Bloodworth's life pleasant and easy, but Bloodworth had not paid him any attention. Mrs Bloodworth said that she was not a bit surprized.

Buckler said that if she stepped inside the cupboard she would find herself in a magical place where she could learn spells that would make any work finished in an instant, make her appear beautiful in the eyes of all who beheld her, make large piles of gold appear whenever she wished it, make her husband obey her in all things, etc., etc.

How many spells were there? asked Mrs Bloodworth.

About three, thought Buckler.

Were they hard to learn?

Oh no! Very easy.

Would it take long?

No, not long, she would be back in time for Mass.

Seventeen people entered Buckler's cupboard that morning and were never seen again in England; among them were Mrs Bloodworth, her two youngest daughters, her two maids and two manservants, Mrs Bloodworth's uncle and six neighbours. Only Margaret Bloodworth, Bloodworth's eldest daughter, refused to go.

The Raven King sent two magicians from Newcastle to investigate the matter and it is from their written accounts that we have this tale. The chief witness was Margaret who told how, on his return, "my poor father went purposely into the cupboard to try if he could rescue them, tho' I begged him not to. He has not come out again."

Two hundred years later Dr Martin Pale was journeying through Faerie. At the castle of John Hollyshoes (an ancient and powerful fairy-prince) he discovered a human child, about seven or eight years old, very pale and starved-looking. She said her name was Anne Bloodworth and she had been in Faerie, she thought, about two weeks. She had been given work to do washing a great pile of dirty pots. She said she had been washing them steadily since she arrived and when she was finished she would go home to see her parents and sisters. She thought she would be finished in a day or two.

following Saturday. He hardly ever spoke of magic, and when he did it was like a history lesson and no one could bear to listen to him. He rarely had a good word to say for any other magician, except once when he praised a magician of the last century, Francis Sutton-Grove.[6]

"But I thought, sir," said Mr Lascelles, "that Sutton-Grove was unreadable. I have always heard that *De Generibus Artium* was entirely unreadable."

"Oh!" said Mr Norrell, "how it fares as an amusement for ladies and gentlemen I do not know, but I do not think that the serious student of magic can value Sutton-Grove too highly. In Sutton-Grove he will find the first attempt to define those areas of magic that the modern magician ought to study, all laid out in lists and tables. To be sure, Sutton-Grove's system of classification is often erroneous – perhaps that is what you mean by 'unreadable'? – nevertheless I know of no more pleasant sight in the world than a dozen or so of his lists; the student may run his eye over them and think 'I know this,' or, 'I have this still to do,' and there before him is work enough for four, perhaps five years."

The tale of the statues in the Cathedral of York grew so stale in

---

[6] Francis Sutton-Grove (1682–1765), theoretical magician. He wrote two books *De Generibus Artium Magicarum Anglorum*, 1741, and *Prescriptions and Descriptions*, 1749. Even Mr Norrell, Sutton-Grove's greatest (and indeed only) admirer, thought that *Prescriptions and Descriptions* (wherein he attempted to lay down rules for practical magic) was abominably bad, and Mr Norrell's pupil, Jonathan Strange, loathed it so much that he tore his copy into pieces and fed it to a tinker's donkey (see *Life of Jonathan Strange* by John Segundus, 1820, pub. John Murray).

De Generibus Artium Magicarum Anglorum was reputed to be the dreariest book in the canon of English magic (which contains many tedious works). It was the first attempt by an Englishman to define the areas of magic that the modern magician ought to study; according to Sutton-Grove these numbered thirty-eight thousand, nine hundred and forty-five and he listed them all under different heads. Sutton-Grove foreshadows the great Mr Norrell in one other way: none of his lists make any mention of the magic traditionally ascribed to birds or wild animals, and Sutton-Grove purposely excludes those kinds of magic for which it is customary to employ fairies, e.g. bringing back the dead.

the retelling that people began to wonder if Mr Norrell had ever done anything else and Mr Drawlight was obliged to invent some new examples.

"But what can this magician do, Drawlight?" asked Mrs Godesdone one evening when Mr Norrell was not present.

"Oh, madam!" cried Drawlight. "What can he not do? Why! It was only a winter or so ago that in York – which as you may know, madam, is Mr Norrell's native city – a great storm came out of the north and blew everybody's washing into the mud and the snow – and so the aldermen, thinking to spare the ladies of the town the labour of washing everything again, applied to Mr Norrell – and he sent a troop of fairies to wash it all anew – and all the holes in people's shirts and nightcaps and petticoats were mended and all the frayed edges were made whole and good again and everybody said that they had never seen such a dazzling whiteness in all their days!"

This particular story became very popular and raised Mr Norrell in everyone's estimation for several weeks that summer, and consequently when Mr Norrell spoke, as he sometimes did, of modern magic, most of his audience supposed that this was the sort of thing he must mean.

But if the ladies and gentlemen whom Mr Norrell met in London's drawing-rooms and dining-parlours were generally disappointed in *him*, then he was becoming equally dissatisfied with *them*. He complained constantly to Mr Drawlight of the frivolous questions that they put to him, and said that the cause of English magic had not been furthered one whit by the hours he had spent in their company.

One dull Wednesday morning at the end of September Mr Norrell and Mr Drawlight were seated together in the library in Hanover-square. Mr Drawlight was in the middle of a long tale of something that Mr F. had said in order to insult Lord S., and what Lady D. had thought about it all, when Mr Norrell suddenly said, "I would be grateful, Mr Drawlight, if you could advise me on the following important point: has any body informed the Duke of Portland of my arrival in London?"[7]

"Ah! sir," cried Drawlight, "only you, with your modest nature, could suppose it possible. I assure you *all* the Ministers have heard of the extraordinary Mr Norrell by now."

"But if that is the case," said Mr Norrell, "then why has his Grace sent me no message? No, I begin to think that they must be entirely ignorant of my existence – and so, Mr Drawlight, I would be grateful if you could inform me of any connexions in Government that you may have to whom I could apply."

"The Government, sir?" replied Mr Drawlight.

"I came here to be useful," said Mr Norrell, plaintively. "I had hoped by now to play some distinguished part in the struggle against the French."

"If you feel yourself neglected, sir, then I am heartily sorry for it!" cried Drawlight. "But there is no need, I do assure you. There are ladies and gentlemen all over Town who would be happy to see any little tricks or illusions you might like to shew us one evening after dinner. You must not be afraid of overwhelming us – our nerves are all pretty strong."

Mr Norrell said nothing.

"Well, sir," said Mr Drawlight, with a smooth smile of his white teeth and a conciliatory look in his dark, liquid eyes, "we must not argue about it. I only wish I were able to oblige you but, as you see, it is entirely out of my power. The Government has its sphere. I have mine."

In fact Mr Drawlight knew several gentlemen in various Government posts who might be very glad to meet Mr Drawlight's friend and to listen to what that friend might have to say, in return for a promise from Mr Drawlight never to tell one or two curious things he knew about them. But the truth was that Mr Drawlight could see no advantage to himself in introducing Mr Norrell to any

---

[7] Duke of Portland, Prime Minister and First Lord of the Treasury 1807–09.

of these gentlemen; he preferred to keep Mr Norrell in the drawing-rooms and dining-parlours of London where he hoped, in time, to persuade him to perform those little tricks and what-not that Mr Drawlight's acquaintance longed to see.

Mr Norrell began writing urgent letters to gentlemen in Government, which he shewed to Mr Drawlight before giving them to Childermass to deliver, but the gentlemen in Government did not reply. Mr Drawlight had warned Mr Norrell that they would not. Gentlemen in Government are generally kept pretty busy.

A week or so later Mr Drawlight was invited to a house in Soho-square to hear a famous Italian soprano, newly arrived from Rome. Naturally, Mr Norrell was invited too. But on arriving at the house Drawlight could not find the magician among the crowd. Lascelles was leaning upon the mantelpiece in conversation with some other gentlemen. Drawlight went up to him and inquired if he knew where Mr Norrell was.

"Oh!" said Mr Lascelles. "He is gone to pay a visit to Sir Walter Pole. Mr Norrell has important information which he wishes conveyed to the Duke of Portland immediately. And Sir Walter Pole is the man that Mr Norrell intends to honour with the message."

"Portland?" cried another gentleman. "What? Are the Ministers got so desperate as that? Are they consulting magicians?"

"You have run away with a wrong idea," smiled Mr Lascelles. "It is all Norrell's own doing. He intends to offer his services to the Government. It seems he has a plan to defeat the French by magic. But I think it highly improbable that he will persuade the Ministers to listen to him. What with the French at their throats on the Continent, and everybody else at their throats in Parliament – I doubt if a more harassed set of gentlemen is to be found anywhere, or one with less attention to spare for a Yorkshire gentleman's eccentricities."

Like the hero of a fairy-tale Mr Norrell had discovered that the power to do what he wished had been his own all along. Even a magician must have relations, and it so happened that there was a distant connexion of Mr Norrell (on his mother's side) who had once made himself highly disagreeable to Mr Norrell by writing him a letter. To prevent such a thing ever occurring again Mr Norrell had made this man a present of eight hundred pounds (which was what the man wanted), but I am sorry to say that this failed to suppress Mr Norrell's mother's relative, who was steeped in villainy, and he had written a *second* letter to Mr Norrell in which he heaped thanks and praise upon his benefactor and declared that, ". . . henceforth I shall consider myself and my friends as belonging to your interest and we hold ourselves ready to vote at the next election in accordance with your noble wishes, and if, in time to come, it should appear that any service of mine might be useful to you, your commands will only honour, and elevate in the opinion of the World, your humble and devoted servant, Wendell Markworthy."

Thus far Mr Norrell had never found it necessary to elevate Mr Markworthy in the opinion of the world by honouring him with any commands, but it now appeared (it was Childermass that had found it out) that Mr Markworthy had used the money to secure for himself and his brother clerkships in the East India Company. They had gone to India and ten years later had returned very rich men. Having never received any instructions from Mr Norrell, his first patron, as to which way to vote, Mr Markworthy had followed the lead of Mr Bonnell, his superior at the East India Company, and had encouraged all his friends to do the same. He had made himself very useful to Mr Bonnell, who was in turn a great friend of the politician, Sir Walter Pole. In the busy worlds of trade and government this gentleman owes that one a favour, while he in his turn is owed a favour by someone else, and so on until a chain is formed of promises and obligations. In this case the chain extended all the way from Mr Norrell to Sir Walter Pole and Sir Walter Pole was now a Minister.

6

"Magic is not respectable, sir."

October 1807

I T WAS A difficult time to be a Minister.

The war went from bad to worse and the Government was universally detested. As each fresh catastrophe came to the public's notice some small share of blame might attach itself to this or that person, but in general everyone united in blaming the Ministers, and they, poor things, had no one to blame but each other – which they did more and more frequently.

It was not that the Ministers were dull-witted – upon the contrary there were some brilliant men among them. Nor were they, upon the whole, bad men; several led quite blameless domestic lives and were remarkably fond of children, music, dogs, landscape painting. Yet so unpopular was the Government that, had it not been for the careful speeches of the Foreign Secretary, it would have been almost impossible to get any piece of business through the House of Commons.

The Foreign Secretary was a quite peerless orator. No matter how low the Government stood in the estimation of everyone, when the Foreign Secretary stood up and spoke – ah! how different everything seemed then! How quickly was every bad thing discovered to be the fault of the previous administration (an evil set of men who wedded general stupidity to wickedness of purpose). As for the present Ministry, the Foreign Secretary said that not since the days of Antiquity had the world seen gentlemen so virtuous, so misunderstood and so horribly misrepresented by their enemies. They were all as wise as Solomon, as noble as Caesar and as courageous as Mark Antony; and no one in the world so much resembled Socrates in point of honesty as the Chancellor of the Exchequer. But in spite of all these virtues and abilities none of the Ministers' plans to defeat the French ever seemed to come to anything and even their cleverness was complained of. Country gentlemen who read in their newspapers the speeches of this or that Minister would mutter to themselves that he was certainly a clever fellow. But the country gentlemen were not made comfortable by this thought. The country gentlemen had a strong suspicion that cleverness was somehow unBritish. That sort of restless, unpredictable brilliance belonged most of all to Britain's arch-enemy, the Emperor Napoleon Buonaparte; the country gentlemen could not approve it.

Sir Walter Pole was forty-two and, I am sorry to say, quite as clever as any one else in the Cabinet. He had quarrelled with most of the great politicians of the age at one time or another and once, when they were both very drunk, had been struck over the head with a bottle of madeira by Richard Brinsley Sheridan. Afterwards Sheridan remarked to the Duke of York, "Pole accepted my apologies in a handsome, gentleman-like fashion. Happily he is such a plain man that one scar more or less can make no significant difference."

To my mind he was not so very plain. True, his features were all extremely bad; he had a great face half as long again as other faces, with a great nose (quite sharp at the end) stuck into it, two dark eyes like clever bits of coal and two little stubby eyebrows like very small fish swimming bravely in a great sea of face. Yet, taken together, all these ugly parts made a rather pleasing whole. If you had seen that face in repose (proud and not a little melancholy), you would have imagined that it must always look so, that no face in existence could be so ill-adapted to express feeling. But you could not have been more wrong.

81

Nothing was more characteristic of Sir Walter Pole than *Surprize*. His eyes grew large, his eyebrows rose half an inch upon his face and he leant suddenly backwards and altogether he resembled nothing so much as a figure in the engravings of Mr Rowlandson or Mr Gillray. In public life *Surprize* served Sir Walter very well. "But, surely," he cried, "You cannot mean to say —!" And, always supposing that the gentleman who was so foolish as to suggest — in Sir Walter's hearing was no friend or yours, or if you have that sort of mischief in you that likes to see blunt wits confounded by sharp ones, you would be entertained. On days when he was full of cheerful malice Sir Walter was better than a play in Drury-lane. Dull gentlemen in both Houses grew perplexed, and avoided him when they could. (Old Lord So-and-so waves his stick at Sir Walter as he trots down the little stone passage that connects the House of Commons to the Horse-Guards, and cries over his shoulder, "I will not speak to you, sir! You twist my words! You give me meanings I never intended!")

Once, while making a speech to a mob in the City, Sir Walter had memorably likened England and her politicians to an orphaned young lady left in the care of a pack of lecherous, avaricious old men. These scoundrels, far from offering the young lady protection from the wicked world, stole her inheritance and plundered her house. And if Sir Walter's audience stumbled on some of his vocabulary (the product of an excellent classical education) it did not much matter. All of them were capable of imagining the poor young lady standing on her bed in her petticoats while the leading Whig politicians of the day ransacked her closets and sold off all her bits of things to the rag man. And all the young gentlemen found themselves pleasantly shocked by the picture.

Sir Walter had a generous spirit and was often kind-hearted. He told someone once that he hoped his enemies all had reason to fear him and his friends reason to love him – and I think that upon the whole they did. His cheerful manner, his kindness and cleverness, the great station he now held in the world – these were even more to his credit as he maintained them in the face of problems that would almost certainly have brought down a lesser man. Sir Walter was distressed for money. I do not mean that he merely lacked for cash. Poverty is one thing, Sir Walter's debts quite another. Miserable situation! – and all the more bitter since it was no fault of his: *he* had never been extravagant and he had certainly never been foolish, but he was the son of one imprudent man and the grandson of another. Sir Walter had been born in debt. Had he been a different sort of man, then all might have been well. Had he been at all inclined to the Navy then he might have made his fortune in prize money; had he loved farming he might have improved his lands and made his money with corn. Had he even been a Minister fifty years before he might have lent out Treasury-money at twenty per cent interest and pocketed the profit. But what can a modern politician do? – he is more likely to spend money than make it.

Some years ago his friends in Government had got him the position of Secretary-in-Ordinary to the Office of Supplication, for which he received a special hat, a small piece of ivory and seven hundred pounds a year. There were no duties attached to the place because no one could remember what the Office of Supplication was supposed to do or what the small piece of ivory was for. But then Sir Walter's friends went out and new Ministers came in, declaring that they were going to abolish sinecures, and among the many offices and places which they pruned from the tree of Government was the Office of Supplication.

By the spring of 1807 it seemed as if Sir Walter's political career must be pretty much at an end (the last election had cost him almost two thousand pounds). His friends were almost frantic. One of those friends, Lady Winsell, went to Bath where, at a concert of Italian music, she made the acquaintance of some people called Wintertowne, a widow and her daughter. A week later Lady Winsell wrote to Sir Walter: "It is exactly what I have always wished for you. Her mother is all for a great marriage and will make no difficulties – or at least if she does then I rely upon *you* to charm them away. As for the money! I tell you, my dear friend, when they named the sum that is to be hers, tears sprang into my eyes! What would you say to one thousand a year? I will say nothing of the young person herself – when you have seen her you shall praise her to me much more ably than ever I could to you."

At about three o'clock upon the same day that Mr Drawlight attended the recital by the Italian lady, Lucas, Mr Norrell's footman, knocked upon the door of a house in Brunswick-square where Mr Norrell had been summoned to meet Sir Walter. Mr Norrell was admitted to the house and was shown to a very fine room upon the first floor.

The walls were hung with a series of gigantic paintings in gilded frames of great complexity, all depicting the city of Venice, but the day was overcast, a cold stormy rain had set in, and Venice – that city built of equal parts of sunlit marble and sunlit sea – was drowned in a London gloom. Its aquamarine-blues and cloud-whites and glints of gold were dulled to the greys and greens of drowned things. From time to time the wind flung a little sharp rain against the window (a melancholy sound) and in the grey light the well-polished surfaces of tulipwood *chiffoniers* and walnut writing-tables had all become black mirrors, darkly reflecting one another. For all its splendour, the room was peculiarly comfortless; there were no candles to light the gloom and no fire to take off the chill. It was as if the housekeeping was under the direction of someone with excellent eyesight who never felt the cold.

Sir Walter Pole rose to receive Mr Norrell and begged the honour of presenting Mrs Wintertowne and her daughter, Miss Wintertowne. Though Sir Walter spoke of *two* ladies, Mr Norrell could perceive only *one*, a lady of mature years, great dignity and magisterial aspect. This puzzled Mr Norrell. He thought Sir Walter must be mistaken, and yet it would be rude to contradict

Sir Walter so early in the interview. In a state of some confusion, Mr Norrell bowed to the magisterial lady.

"I am very glad to meet you, sir," said Sir Walter. "I have heard a great deal about you. It seems to me that London talks of very little else but the extraordinary Mr Norrell," and, turning to the magisterial lady, Sir Walter said, "Mr Norrell is a magician, ma'am, a person of great reputation in his native county of Yorkshire."

The magisterial lady stared at Mr Norrell.

"You are not at all what I expected, Mr Norrell," remarked Sir Walter. "I had been told you were a *practical* magician – I hope you are not offended, sir – it is merely what I was told, and I must say that it is a relief to me to see that you are nothing of the sort. London is plagued with a great number of mock-sorcerers who trick the people out of their money by promising them all sorts of unlikely things. I wonder, have you seen Vinculus, who has a little booth outside St Christopher Le Stocks? He is the worst of them. You are a *theoretical* magician, I imagine?" Sir Walter smiled encouragingly. "But they tell me that you have something to ask me, sir."

Mr Norrell begged Sir Walter's pardon but said that he was indeed a practical magician; Sir Walter looked surprized. Mr Norrell hoped very earnestly that he would not by this admission lose Sir Walter's good opinion.

"No, no. By no means," murmured Sir Walter politely.

"The misapprehension under which you labour," said Mr Norrell, "by which I mean, of course, the belief that all practical magicians must be charlatans – arises from the shocking idleness of English magicians in the last two hundred years. I have performed one small feat of magic – which the people in York were kind enough to say they found astounding – and yet I tell you, Sir Walter, any magician of modest talent might have done as much. This general lethargy has deprived our great nation of its best support and left us defenceless. It is this deficiency which I hope to supply. Other magicians may be able to neglect their duty, but I cannot; I am come, Sir Walter, to offer you my help in our present difficulties."

"Our present difficulties?" said Sir Walter. "You mean the war?" He opened his small black eyes very wide. "My dear Mr Norrell! What has the war to do with magic? Or magic to do with the war? I believe I have heard what you did in York, and I hope the housewives were grateful, but I scarcely see how we can apply such magic to the war! True, the soldiers get very dirty, but then, you know," and he began to laugh, "they have other things of think of."

Poor Mr Norrell! He had not heard Drawlight's story of how the fairies had washed the people's clothes and it came as a great shock to him. He assured Sir Walter that he had never in his life washed linen – not by magic nor by any other means – and he told Sir Walter what he had really done. But, curiously, though Mr Norrell was able to work feats of the most breath-taking wonder, he was only able to describe them in his usual dry manner, so that Sir Walter was left with the impression that the spectacle of half a thousand stone figures in York Cathedral all speaking together had been rather a dull affair and that he had been fortunate in being elsewhere at the time. "Indeed?" he said. "Well, that is most interesting. But I still do not quite understand how . . ."

Just at that moment someone coughed, and the moment that Sir Walter heard the cough he stopped speaking as if to listen.

Mr Norrell looked round. In the furthest, most shadowy corner of the room a young woman in a white gown lay upon a sopha, with a white shawl wrapped tightly around her. She lay quite still. One hand pressed a handkerchief to her mouth. Her posture, her stillness, everything about her conveyed the strongest impression of pain and ill-health.

So certain had Mr Norrell been that the corner was unoccupied, that he was almost as startled by her sudden appearance as if she had come there by someone else's magic. As he watched she was seized by a fit of coughing that continued for some moments, and during that time Sir Walter appeared most uncomfortable. He did not look at the young woman (though he looked everywhere else in the room). He picked up a gilt ornament from a little table by his side, turned it over, looked at its underneath, put it down again. Finally he coughed – a brief clearing of the throat as though to suggest that everyone coughed – coughing was the most natural thing in the world – coughing could never, under any circumstances, be cause for alarm. The young woman upon the sopha came at last to the end of her own coughing fit, and lay quite still and quiet, though her breathing did not seem to come easily.

Mr Norrell's gaze travelled from the young lady to the great, gloomy painting that hung above her and he tried to recollect what he had been speaking of.

"It is a marriage," said the majestic lady.

"I beg your pardon, madam?" said Mr Norrell.

But the lady only nodded in the direction of the painting and bestowed a stately smile upon Mr Norrell.

The painting which hung above the young lady shewed, like every other picture in the room, Venice. English cities are, for the most part, built upon hills; their streets rise and fall, and it occurred to Mr Norrell that Venice, being built upon the sea, must be the flattest, as well as the queerest, city in the world. It was the flatness which made the painting look so much like an exercise in perspective; statues, columns, domes, palaces, and cathedrals stretched away to where they met a vast and melancholy sky, while the sea that lapped at the walls of those buildings was crowded with ornately carved and gilded barges, and those strange black Venetian vessels that so much resemble the slippers of ladies in mourning.

"It depicts the symbolic marriage of Venice to the Adriatic," said the lady (whom we must now presume to be Mrs Wintertowne), "a curious Italian ceremony. The paintings which you see in this room were all bought by the late Mr Wintertowne during his travels on the Continent; and when he and I were married they were his wedding-gift to me. The artist – an Italian – was then quite unknown in England. Later, emboldened by the patronage he received from Mr Wintertowne, he came to London."

Her manner of speech was as stately as her person. After each sentence she paused to give Mr Norrell time to be impressed by the information it contained.

"And when my dear Emma is married," she continued, "these paintings shall be my wedding-present to her and Sir Walter."

Mr Norrell inquired if Miss Wintertowne and Sir Walter were to be married soon.

"In ten days' time!" answered Mrs Wintertowne triumphantly.

Mr Norrell offered his congratulations.

"You are a magician, sir?" said Mrs Wintertowne. "I am sorry to hear it. It is a profession I have a particular dislike to." She looked keenly at him as she said so, as though her disapproval might in itself be enough to make him renounce magic instantly and take up some other occupation.

When he did not she turned to her prospective son-in-law. "My own stepmother, Sir Walter, placed great faith in a magician. After my father's death he was always in the house. One could enter a room one was quite sure was empty and find him in a corner half hidden by a curtain. Or asleep upon the sopha with his dirty boots on. He was the son of a leather tanner and his low origins were frankly displayed in all he did. He had long, dirty hair and a face like a dog, but he sat at our table like a gentleman. My stepmother deferred to him in all she did and for seven years he governed our lives completely."

"And your own opinion was disregarded, ma'am?" said Sir Walter. "I am surprized at that!"

Mrs Wintertowne laughed. "I was only a child of eight or nine when it began, Sir Walter. His name was Dreamditch and he told us constantly how happy he was to be our friend, though my

brother and I were equally constant in assuring him that we considered him no friend of ours. But he only smiled at us like a dog that has learned how to smile and does not know how to leave off. Do not misunderstand me, Sir Walter. My stepmother was in many ways an excellent woman. My father's esteem for her was such that he left her six hundred a year and the care of his three children. Her only weakness was foolishly to doubt her own capabilities. My father believed that, in understanding and in knowledge of right and wrong and in many other things, women are men's equals and I am entirely of his opinion. My stepmother should not have shrunk from the charge. When Mr Wintertowne died *I* did not."

"No, indeed, ma'am," murmured Sir Walter.

"Instead," continued Mrs Wintertowne, "she placed all her faith in the magician, Dreamditch. He had not an ounce of magic in him and was consequently obliged to invent some. He made rules for my brother, my sister and me, which, he assured my stepmother, would keep us safe. We wore purple ribbons tied tightly round our chests. In our room six places were laid at the table, one for each of us and one for each of the spirits which Dreamditch said looked after us. He told us their names. What do you suppose they were, Sir Walter?"

"I have not the least idea in the world, ma'am."

Mrs Wintertowne laughed. "Meadowlace, Robin Summerfly and Buttercup. My brother, Sir Walter, who resembled myself in independence of spirit, would often say in my stepmother's hearing, 'Damn Meadowlace! Damn Robin Summerfly! Damn Buttercup!' and she, poor silly woman, would plead very piteously with him to stop. They did us no good those fairy spirits. My sister became ill. Often I went to her room and found Dreamditch there, stroking her pale cheeks and unresisting hand with his long yellow unclean fingernails. He was almost weeping, the fool. He would have saved her if he could. He made spells, but she died. A beautiful child, Sir Walter. For years I hated my stepmother's magician. For years I thought him a wicked man, but in the end, Sir Walter, I knew him to be nothing but a sad and pitiful fool."

Sir Walter turned in his chair. "Miss Wintertowne!" he said. "You spoke – but I did not hear what it was you said."

"Emma! What is it?" cried Mrs Wintertowne.

There was a soft sigh from the sopha. Then a quiet, clear voice said, "I said that you were quite wrong, Mama."

"Am I, my love?" Mrs Wintertowne, whose character was so forceful and whose opinions were handed down to people in the manner of Moses distributing the commandments, did not appear in the least offended when her daughter contradicted her. Indeed she seemed almost pleased about it.

"Of course," said Miss Wintertowne, "we must have magicians. Who else can interpret England's history to us and in particular her northern history, her black northern King? Our common historians cannot." There was silence for a moment. "I am fond of history," she said.

"I did not know that," said Sir Walter.

"Ah, Sir Walter!" cried Mrs Wintertowne. "Dear Emma does not waste her energies upon novels like other young women. Her reading has been extensive; she knows more of biography and poetry than any young woman I know."

"Yet I hope," said Sir Walter eagerly, leaning over the back of his chair to speak to his betrothed, "that you like novels as well, and then, you know, we could read to each other. What is your opinion of Mrs Radcliffe? Of Madame d'Arblay?"

But what Miss Wintertowne thought of these distinguished ladies Sir Walter did not discover for she was seized by a second fit of coughing which obliged her to struggle – with an appearance of great effort – into a sitting position. He waited some moments for an answer, but when her coughing had subsided she lay back on the sopha as before, with looks of pain and exhaustion, and closed her eyes.

Mr Norrell wondered that no one thought to go to her assistance. There seemed to be a sort of conspiracy in the room to deny that the poor young woman was ill. No one asked if they could bring her anything. No one suggested that she go to bed, which Mr Norrell – who was often ill himself – imagined would be by far the best thing for her.

"Mr Norrell," said Sir Walter, "I cannot claim to understand what this help is that you offer us . . ."

"Oh! As to particulars," Mr Norrell said, "I know as little of warfare as the generals and the admirals do of magic, and yet . . ."

". . . but whatever it is," continued Sir Walter, "I am sorry to say that it will not do. Magic is not respectable, sir. It is not," Sir Walter searched for a word, "serious. The Government cannot meddle with such things. Even this innocent little chat that you and I have had today, is likely to cause us a little embarrassment when people get to hear of it. Frankly, Mr Norrell, had I understood better what you were intending to propose today, I would not have agreed to meet you."

Sir Walter's manner as he said all this was far from unkind, but, oh, poor Mr Norrell! To be told that magic was not serious was a very heavy blow. To find himself classed with the Dreamditches and the Vinculuses of this world was a crushing one. In vain he protested that he had thought long and hard about how to make magic respected once more; in vain he offered to shew Sir Walter a long list of recommendations concerning the regulation of magic in England. Sir Walter did not wish to see them. He shook his head and smiled, but all he said was: "I am afraid, Mr Norrell, that I can do nothing for you."

When Mr Drawlight arrived at Hanover-square that evening he was obliged to listen to Mr Norrell lamenting the failure of all his hopes of succeeding with Sir Walter Pole.

"Well, sir, what did I tell you?" cried Drawlight. "But, oh! Poor Mr Norrell! How unkind they were to you! I am very sorry for it. But I am not in the least surprised! I have always heard that those Wintertownes were stuffed full of pride!"

But there was, I regret to say, a little duplicity in Mr Drawlight's nature and it must be said that he was not quite as sorry as he professed to be. This display of independence had provoked him and he was determined to punish Mr Norrell for it. For the next week Mr Norrell and Mr Drawlight attended only the quietest dinners and, without quite arranging matters so that Mr Norrell would find himself the guest of Mr Drawlight's shoe-maker or the old lady who dusts the monuments in Westminster Abbey, Mr Drawlight took care that their hosts were people of as little consequence, influence, or fashion, as possible. In this way Drawlight hoped to create in Mr Norrell the impression that not only the Poles and Wintertownes slighted him, but the whole world, so that Mr Norrell might be brought to understand who was his true friend, and might become a little more accommodating when it came to performing those small tricks of magic that Drawlight had been promising for many months now.

Such were the hopes and schemes that animated the heart of Mr Norrell's dearest friend but, unfortunately for Mr Drawlight, so cast down was Mr Norrell by Sir Walter's rejection that he scarcely noticed the change in the style of entertainments and Drawlight succeeded in punishing no one but himself.

Now that Sir Walter was quite beyond Mr Norrell's reach, Mr Norrell became more and more convinced that Sir Walter was exactly the patron he wished for. A cheerful, energetic man, with pleasant, easy manners, Sir Walter Pole was everything that Mr Norrell was not. Therefore, reasoned Mr Norrell, Sir Walter Pole would have achieved everything that he *could* not. The influential men of the Age would have listened to Sir Walter.

"If only he had listened to me," sighed Mr Norrell one evening as he and Drawlight dined alone. "But I could not find the words to convince him. Of course I wish now that I had asked you or Mr Lascelles to come with me. Men of the world prefer to be talked to by other men of the world. I know that now. Perhaps I should have done some magic to shew him – turned the teacups into rabbits or the teaspoons into goldfish. At least then he would have believed me. But I do not think the old lady would have been pleased if I had done that. I do not know. What is your opinion?"

But Drawlight, who had begun to believe that if anyone had ever died of boredom then he was almost certain to expire within the next quarter of an hour, found that he had lost the will to speak and the best he could manage was a withering smile.

7

An opportunity unlikely to occur again

October 1807

"WELL, SIR! YOU have your revenge!" cried Mr Drawlight appearing quite suddenly in the library in Hanover-square.

"My revenge!" said Mr Norrell. "What do you mean?"

"Oh!" said Mr Drawlight. "Sir Walter's bride, Miss Wintertowne, is dead. She died this very afternoon. They were to be married in two days' time, but, poor thing, she is quite dead. A thousand pounds a year! – Imagine his despair! Had she only contrived to remain alive until the end of the week, what a difference it would have made! His need of the money is quite desperate – he is all to pieces. I should not be at all surprized if we were to hear tomorrow that he has cut his throat."

Mr Drawlight leant for a moment upon the back of a good, comfortable chair by the fire and, looking down, discovered a friend. "Ah, Lascelles, I declare. There you are behind the newspaper I see. How do you do?"

Meanwhile Mr Norrell stared at Mr Drawlight. "The young woman is dead, you say?" he said in amazement. "The young woman that I saw in that room? I can scarcely believe it. This is very unexpected."

"Oh! Upon the contrary," said Drawlight, "nothing was more probable."

"But the wedding!" said Mr Norrell. "All the necessary arrangements! They could not have known how ill she was."

"But I assure you," said Drawlight, "they did know. Everyone knew. Why! there was a fellow called Drummond, who saw her at Christmas at a private ball in Leamington Spa, and wagered Lord Carlisle fifty pounds that she would be dead within a month."

Mr Lascelles tutted in annoyance and put down his newspaper. "No, no," he said, "that was not Miss Wintertowne. You are thinking of Miss Hookham-Nix, whose brother has threatened to shoot her, should she bring disgrace upon the family – which everyone supposes she must do sooner or later. But it happened at Worthing – and it was not Lord Carlisle who took the bet but the Duke of Exmoor."

Drawlight considered this a moment. "I believe you are right," he said at last. "But it does not matter, for everyone *did* know that Miss Wintertowne was ill. Except of course the old lady. *She* thought her daughter perfection – and what can Perfection have to say to ill-health? Perfection is only to be admired; Perfection has only to make a great marriage. But the old lady has never allowed that Perfection might be ill – she could never bear to hear the subject mentioned. For all Miss Wintertowne's coughs and swoonings upon the ground and lyings-down upon the sopha, I never heard that any physician ever came near her."

"Sir Walter would have taken better care of her," said Lascelles, shaking out his newspaper before he began once more to read it. "One may say what one likes about his politics, but he is a sensible man. It is a pity she could not have lasted till Thursday."

"But, Mr Norrell," said Drawlight turning to their friend, "you look quite pale and sick! You are shocked, I dare say, at the spectacle of a young and innocent life cut off. Your good feelings, as ever, do you credit, sir – and I am entirely of your opinion – the thought of the poor young lady crushed out of existence like a lovely flower beneath someone's boot – well, sir, it cuts my heart like a knife – I can hardly bear to think of it. But then, you know, she was very ill and must have died at some time or other – and by your own account she was not very kind to *you*. I know it is not the fashion to say so, but I am the sternest advocate in the world for young people giving respectful attention to scholarly old persons such as yourself. Impudence, and sauciness, and everything of that sort I hate."

But Mr Norrell did not appear to hear the comfort his friend was so kind as to give him and when at last he spoke his words seemed chiefly addressed to himself, for he sighed deeply and murmured, "I never thought to find magic so little regarded here." He paused and then said in a quick, low voice, "It is a very dangerous thing to bring someone back from the dead. It has not been done in three hundred years. I could not attempt it!"

This was rather extraordinary and Mr Drawlight and Mr Lascelles looked round at their friend in some surprise.

"Indeed, sir," said Mr Drawlight, "and no one proposes that you should."

"Of course I know the form of it," continued Mr Norrell as if Drawlight had not spoken, "but it is precisely the sort of magic that I have set my face against! – It relies so much upon . . . It relies so much . . . That is to say the outcome must be entirely unpredictable. – Quite out of the magician's power to determine. No! I shall not attempt it. I shall not even think of it."

There was a short silence. But despite the magician's resolve to think no more about the dangerous magic, he still fidgeted in his chair and bit his finger-ends and breathed very quick and exhibited other such signs of nervous agitation.

"My dear Mr Norrell," said Drawlight slowly, "I believe I begin to perceive your meaning. And I must confess that I think the idea an excellent one! You have in mind a great act of magic, a testimony to your extraordinary powers! Why, sir! Should you succeed all the Wintertownes and Poles in England will be on your doorstep soliciting the acquaintance of the wonderful Mr Norrell!"

"And if he should fail," observed Mr Lascelles, drily, "every one else in England will be shutting his door against the notorious Mr Norrell."

"My dear Lascelles," cried Drawlight, "what nonsense you talk! Upon my word, there is nothing in the world so easy to explain as failure – it is, after all, what every body does all the time."

Mr Lascelles said that that did not follow at all, and they were just beginning to argue about it when an anguished cry burst from the lips of their friend, Mr Norrell.

"Oh, God! What shall I do? What shall I do? I have laboured all these months to make my profession acceptable in the eyes of men and still they despise me! Mr Lascelles, you know the world, tell me . . ."

"Alas, sir," interrupted Mr Lascelles quickly, "I make a great point of never giving advice to any one." And he went back to his newspaper.

"My dear Mr Norrell!" said Drawlight (who did not wait to be asked for *his* opinion). "Such an opportunity is hardly likely to occur again . . ." (A potent argument this, and one which caused Mr Norrell to sigh very deeply.) ". . . and I must say I do not think that I could forgive myself if I allowed you to pass it by. With one stroke you return to us that sweet young woman – whose death no one can hear of without shedding a tear; you restore a fortune to a worthy gentleman; *and* you re-establish magic as a power in the realm for generations to come! Once you have proved the virtue of your skills – their utility and so forth – who will be able to deny magicians their dues of veneration and praise? They will be quite as much respected as admirals, a great deal more than generals, and probably as much as archbishops and lord chancellors! I should not be at all surprized if His Majesty did not immediately set up a convenient arrangement of degrees with magicians-in-ordinary and magicians-canonical, non-stipendiary magicians and all that sort of thing. And you, Mr Norrell, at the top as Arch-Magician! And all this with one stroke, sir! With one stroke!"

Drawlight was pleased with this speech; Lascelles, rustling the paper in his irritation, clearly had a great many things to say in contradiction of Drawlight, but had put it out of his power to say any of them by his declaration that he never gave advice.

"There is scarcely any form of magic more dangerous!" said Mr Norrell in a sort of horrified whisper. "It is dangerous to the magician and dangerous to the subject."

"Well, sir," said Drawlight reasonably, "I suppose you are the best judge of the danger as it applies to yourself, but the subject, as you term her, is dead. What worse can befall her?"

Drawlight waited a moment for a reply to this interesting question, but Mr Norrell made none.

"I shall now ring for the carriage," Drawlight declared and did so. "I shall go immediately to Brunswick-square. Have no fear, Mr Norrell, I have every expectation that all our proposals will meet with most ready acquiesence on all sides. I shall return within the hour!"

After Drawlight had hurried away, Mr Norrell sat for a quarter of an hour or so simply staring in front of him and though Lascelles did not believe in the magic that Mr Norrell said would be done (nor, therefore, in the danger that Mr Norrell said would be braved) he was glad that he could not see what Mr Norrell seemed to see.

Then Mr Norrell roused himself and took down five or six books in a great hurry and opened them up – presumably searching out those passages which were full of advice for magicians who wished to awaken dead young ladies. This occupied him until another three-quarters of an hour had passed, when a little bustle could be heard outside the library, and Mr Drawlight's voice preceded him into the room.

". . . the greatest favour in the world! So very much obliged to you . . ." Mr Drawlight danced through the library-door, his face one immense smile. "All is well, sir! Sir Walter did hold back a little at first, but all is well! He asked me to convey to you his gratitude for your kind attention, but he did not think that it could do any good. *I* said that if he were thinking of the thing getting out afterwards and being talked about, then he need not fear at all, for we had no wish to see him embarrassed – and that Mr Norrell's one desire was to be of service to him and that Lascelles and I were discretion itself – but he said he did not mind about that, for people would always laugh at a Minister, only he had rather Miss Wintertowne were left sleeping now – which he thought more respectful of her present situation. My dear Sir Walter! cried I, how can you say so? You cannot mean that a rich and beautiful young lady would gladly quit this life on the very eve of her marriage – when you yourself were to be the happy man! Oh! Sir Walter! – I said – *you* may not believe in Mr Norrell's magic, but what can it hurt to try? Which the old lady saw the sense of immediately and added her arguments to mine – and she told me of a magician she had known in her childhood, a most talented person and a devoted friend to all her family, who had prolonged her sister's life several years beyond what any one had expected. I tell you, Mr Norrell, nothing can express the gratitude Mrs Wintertowne feels at your goodness and she begs me to say to you that you are to come immediately – and Sir Walter himself says that he can see no sense in putting it off – so I told Davey to wait at the door and on no account to go anywhere else. Oh! Mr Norrell, it is to be a night of reconciliations! All misunderstandings, all unfortunate constructions which may have been placed on one or two ill-chosen words – all, all are to be swept away! It is to be quite like a play by Shakespeare!"

Mr Norrell's greatcoat was fetched and he got into the carriage; and from the expression of surprize upon his face when the carriage-doors opened and Mr Drawlight jumped in one side and Mr Lascelles jumped in the other I am tempted to suppose that he had not originally intended that those two gentlemen should accompany him to Brunswick-square.

Lascelles threw himself into the carriage, snorting with laughter and saying that he had never in his life heard of anything so ridiculous and comparing their snug drive through the London streets in Mr Norrell's carriage to ancient French and Italian fables in which fools set sail in milk-pails to fetch the moon's reflection from the bottom of a duckpond – all of which might well have offended Mr Norrell had Mr Norrell been in spirits to attend to him.

When they arrived at Brunswick-square they found, gathered upon the steps, a little crowd of people. Two men ran out to catch the horses' heads and the light from the oil-lamp above the steps shewed the crowd to be a dozen or so of Mrs Wintertowne's servants all on the look-out for the magician who was to bring back their young lady. Human nature being what it is, I dare say there may have been a few among them who were merely curious to see what such a man might look like. But many shewed in their pale faces signs that they had been grieving and these were, I think, prompted by some nobler sentiment to keep their silent vigil in the cold midnight street.

One of them took a candle and went before Mr Norrell and his friends to shew them the way, for the house was very dark and cold. They were upon the staircase when they heard Mrs Wintertowne's voice calling out from above, "Robert! Robert! Is it Mr Norrell? Oh! Thank God, sir!" She appeared before them very suddenly in a doorway. "I thought you would never come!" And then, much to Mr Norrell's consternation, she took both his hands in her own and, pressing them hard, entreated him to use his most potent spells to bring Miss Wintertowne back to life. Money was not to be thought of. He might name his price! Only say that he would return her darling child to her. He must promise her that he would!

Mr Norrell cleared his throat and was perhaps about to embark upon one of his long, uninteresting expositions of the philosophy of modern magic, when Mr Drawlight glided forward, took Mrs Wintertowne's hands and rescued them both.

"Now I beg of you, my dear madam," cried Drawlight, "to be

more tranquil! Mr Norrell is come, as you see, and we must try what his power may do. He begs that you will not mention payment again. Whatever he does tonight will be done for friendship's sake . . ." And here Mr Drawlight stood upon tiptoes and lifted his chin to look over Mrs Wintertowne's shoulder to where Sir Walter Pole was standing within the room. Sir Walter had just risen from his chair and stood a little way off, regarding the newcomers. In the candlelight he was pale and hollow-eyed and there was about him a kind of gauntness which had not been there before. Mere common courtesy said that he ought to have come forward to speak to them, but he did not do so.

It was curious to observe how Mr Norrell hesitated in the doorway and exhibited great unwillingness to be conducted further into the house until he had spoken to Sir Walter. "But I must just speak to Sir Walter! Just a few words with Sir Walter! – I shall do my utmost for you, Sir Walter!" he called out from the door. "Since the young lady is, ahem!, not long gone from us, I may say that the situation is promising. Yes, I think I may go so far as to say that the situation is a promising one. I shall go now, Sir Walter, and do my work. I hope, in due course, I shall have the honour of bringing you good news!"

All the assurances that Mrs Wintertowne begged for – and did not get – from Mr Norrell, Mr Norrell was now anxious to bestow upon Sir Walter who clearly did not want them. From his sanctuary in the drawing-room Sir Walter nodded and then, when Mr Norrell still lingered, he called out hoarsely, "Thank you, sir. Thank you!" And his mouth stretched out in a curious way. It was, perhaps, meant for a smile.

"I wish with all my heart, Sir Walter," called out Mr Norrell, "that I might invite you to come up with me and to see what it is I do, but the curious nature of this particular magic demands solitude. I will, I hope, have the honour of shewing you some magic upon another occasion."

Sir Walter bowed slightly and turned away.

Mrs Wintertowne was at that moment speaking to her servant, Robert, and Drawlight took advantage of this slight distraction to pull Mr Norrell to one side and whisper frantically in his ear: "No, no, sir! Do not send them away! My advice is to gather as many of them around the bed as can be persuaded to come. It is, I assure you, the best guarantee of our night's exploits being generally broadcast in the morning. And do not be afraid of making a little bustle to impress the servants – your best incantations if you please! Oh! What a noodle-head I am! Had only I thought to bring some Chinese powders to throw in the fire! I don't suppose that you have any about you?"

Mr Norrell made no reply to this but asked to be brought without delay to where Miss Wintertowne was.

But though the magician particularly asked to be taken there alone, his dear friends, Mr Drawlight and Mr Lascelles, were not so unkind as to leave him to face this great crisis of his career alone and consequently the three of them together were conducted by Robert to a chamber upon the second floor.

8

A gentleman with thistle-down hair

October 1807

THERE WAS NO one there.

Which is to say there was someone there. Miss Wintertowne lay upon the bed, but it would have puzzled
philosophy to say now whether she were someone or no one at all.

They had dressed her in a white gown and hung a silver chain
about her neck; they had combed and dressed her beautiful hair
and put pearl-and-garnet earrings in her ears. But it was extremely
doubtful whether Miss Wintertowne cared about such things any
more. They had lit candles and laid a good fire in the hearth, they
had put roses about the room, which filled it with a sweet perfume,
but Miss Wintertowne could have lain now with equal composure
in the foulest-smelling garret in the city.

"And she was quite tolerable to look at, you say?" said Mr
Lascelles.

"You never saw her?" said Drawlight. "Oh! she was a heavenly
creature. Quite divine. An angel."

"Indeed? And such a pinched-looking ruin of a thing now! I
shall advise all the good-looking women of my acquaintance not to
die," said Mr Lascelles. He leaned closer. "They have closed her
eyes," he said.

"Her eyes were perfection," said Drawlight, "a clear dark grey,
with long, dark eye-lashes and dark eye-brows. It is a pity you

never saw her – she was exactly the sort of creature you would have admired." Drawlight turned to Mr Norrell. "Well, sir, are you ready to begin?"

Mr Norrell was seated in a chair next to the fire. The resolute, businesslike manner, which he had adopted on his arrival at the house, had disappeared; instead he sat with neck bowed, sighing heavily, his gaze fixed upon the carpet. Mr Lascelles and Mr Drawlight looked at him with that degree of interest appropriate to the character of each – which is to say that Mr Drawlight was all fidgets and bright-eyed anticipation, and Mr Lascelles all cool, smiling scepticism. Mr Drawlight took a few respectful steps back from the bed so that Mr Norrell might more conveniently approach it and Mr Lascelles leant against a wall and crossed his arms (an attitude he often adopted in the theatre).

Mr Norrell sighed again. "Mr Drawlight, I have already said that this particular magic demands complete solitude. I must ask you to wait downstairs."

"Oh, but, sir!" protested Drawlight. "Surely such intimate friends as Lascelles and I can be no inconvenience to you? We are the quietest creatures in the world! In two minutes' time you will have quite forgotten that we are here. And I must say that I consider our presence as absolutely essential! For who will broadcast the news of your achievement tomorrow morning if not Lascelles and myself? Who will describe the ineffable grandeur of the moment when your magicianship triumphs and the young woman rises from the dead? Or the unbearable pathos of the moment when you are forced to admit defeat? You will not do it half so well yourself, sir. You know that you will not."

"Perhaps," said Mr Norrell. "But what you suggest is entirely impossible. I will not, *cannot* begin until you leave the room."

Poor Drawlight! He could not force the magician to begin the magic against his will, but to have waited so long to see some magic and then to be excluded! It was almost more than he could bear. Even Mr Lascelles was a little disappointed for he had hoped to witness something very ridiculous that he could laugh at.

When they had gone Mr Norrell rose wearily from his seat and took up a book that he had brought with him. He opened it at a place he had marked with a folded letter and placed it upon a little table so that it would be to hand if he needed to consult it. Then he began to recite a spell.

It took effect almost immediately because suddenly there was something green where nothing green had been before and a fresh, sweet smell as of woods and fields wafted through the room. Mr Norrell stopped speaking.

Someone was standing in the middle of the room: a tall, handsome person with pale, perfect skin and an immense amount of hair, as pale and shining as thistle-down. His cold, blue eyes glittered and he had long dark eye-brows, which terminated in an upward flourish. He was dressed exactly like any other gentleman, except that his coat was of the brightest green imaginable – the colour of leaves in early summer.

"*O Lar!*" began Mr Norrell in a quavering voice. "*O Lar! Magnum opus est mihi tuo auxilio. Haec virgo mortua est et familia eius eam ad vitam redire vult.*"[1] Mr Norrell pointed to the figure on the bed.

At the sight of Miss Wintertowne the gentleman with the thistle-down hair suddenly became very excited. He spread wide his hands in a gesture of surprized delight and began to speak Latin very rapidly. Mr Norrell, who was more accustomed to seeing Latin written down or printed in books, found that he could not follow the language when it was spoken so fast, though he did recognize a few words here and there, words such as "*formosa*" and "*venusta*" which are descriptive of feminine beauty.

Mr Norrell waited until the gentleman's rapture had subsided and then he directed the gentleman's attention to the mirror above

---

[1] "O Fairy. I have great need of your help. This virgin is dead and her family wish her to be returned to life."

the mantelpiece. A vision appeared of Miss Wintertowne walking along a narrow rocky path, through a mountainous and gloomy landscape. "*Ecce mortua inter terram et caelum!*" declared Mr Norrell. "*Scito igitur, O Lar, me ad hanc magnam operam te elegisse quia . . .*"[2]

"Yes, yes!" cried the gentleman suddenly breaking into English. "You elected to summon *me* because my genius for magic exceeds that of all the rest of my race. Because I have been the servant and confidential friend of Thomas Godbless, Ralph Stokesey, Martin Pale *and* of the Raven King. Because I am valorous, chivalrous, generous and as handsome as the day is long! That is all quite understood! It would have been madness to summon anyone else! We both know who *I* am. The question is: who in the world are *you*?"

"I?" said Mr Norrell, startled. "I am the greatest magician of the Age!"

The gentleman raised one perfect eye-brow as if to say he was surprized to hear it. He walked around Mr Norrell slowly, considering him from every angle. Then, most disconcerting of all, he plucked Mr Norrell's wig from his head and looked underneath, as if Mr Norrell were a cooking pot on the fire and he wished to know what was for dinner.

"I . . . I am the man who is destined to restore magic to England!" stammered Mr Norrell, grabbing back his wig and replacing it, slightly askew, upon his head.

"Well, obviously you are *that*!" said the gentleman. "Or I should not be here! You do not imagine that I would waste my time upon a three-penny hedge-sorcerer, do you? But *who* are you? That is what I wish to know. What magic have you done? Who was your master? What magical lands have you visited? What enemies have you defeated? Who are your allies?"

Mr Norrell was extremely surprized to be asked so many questions and he was not at all prepared to answer them. He

[2] "Here is the dead woman between earth and heaven! Know then, O Fairy, that I have chosen you for this great task because . . ."

wavered and hesitated before finally fixing upon the only one to which he had a sensible answer. "I had no master. I taught myself."

"How?"

"From books."

"Books!" (This in a tone of the utmost contempt.)

"Yes, indeed. There is a great deal of magic in books nowadays. Of course, most of it is nonsense. No one knows as well as I how much nonsense is printed in books. But there is a great deal of useful information too and it is surprizing how, after one has learnt a little, one begins to see . . ."

Mr Norrell was beginning to warm to his subject, but the gentleman with the thistle-down hair had no patience to listen to other people talk and so he interrupted him.

"Am I the first of my race that you have seen?"

"Oh, yes!"

This answer seemed to please the gentleman with the thistle-down hair and he smiled. "So! Should I agree to restore this young woman to life, what would be my reward?"

Mr Norrell cleared his throat. "What sort of thing . . . ?" he said, a little hoarsely.

"Oh! That is easily agreed!" cried the gentleman with the thistle-down hair. "My wishes are the most moderate things in the world. Fortunately I am utterly free from greed and sordid ambition. Indeed, you will find that my proposal is much more to your advantage than mine – such is my unselfish nature! I simply wish to be allowed to aid you in all your endeavours, to advise you upon all matters and to guide you in your studies. Oh! and you must take care to let all the world know that your greatest achievements are due in larger part to me!"

Mr Norrell looked a little ill. He coughed and muttered something about the gentleman's generosity. "Were I the sort of magician who is eager to entrust all his business to another person, then your offer would be most welcome. But unfortunately . . . I fear . . . In short I have no notion of employing you – or indeed any other member of your race – ever again."

A long silence.

"Well, this is ungrateful indeed!" declared the gentleman, coldly. "I have put myself to the trouble of paying you this visit. I have listened with the greatest good nature to your dreary conversation. I have borne patiently with your ignorance of the proper forms and etiquette of magic. And now you scorn my offer of assistance. Other magicians, I may say, have endured all sorts of torments to gain my help. Perhaps I would do better to speak to the other one. Perhaps he understands better than you how to address persons of high rank and estate?" The gentleman glanced about the room. "I do not see him. Where is he?"

"Where is who?"

"The other one."

"The other what?"

"Magician!"

"Magici . . ." Mr Norrell began to form the word but it died upon his lips. "No, no! There is no other magician! I am the only one. I assure you I am the only one. Why should you think that . . . ?"

"*Of course* there is another magician!" declared the gentleman, as if it were perfectly ridiculous to deny anything quite so obvious. "He is your dearest friend in all the world!"

"I have no friends," said Mr Norrell.

He was utterly perplexed. Whom might the fairy mean? Childermass? Lascelles? *Drawlight?*

"He has red hair and a long nose. And he is very conceited – as are all Englishmen!" declared the gentleman with the thistle-down hair.

This was no help. Childermass, Lascelles and Drawlight were all very conceited in their ways, Childermass and Lascelles both had long noses, but none of them had red hair. Mr Norrell could make nothing of it and so he returned, with a heavy sigh, to the matter in hand. "You will not help me?" he said. "You will not bring the young woman back from the dead?"

"I did not say so!" said the gentleman with the thistle-down hair, in a tone which suggested that he wondered why Mr Norrell should think *that*. "I must confess," he continued, "that in recent centuries I have grown somewhat bored of the society of my family and servants. My sisters and cousins have many virtues to recommend them, but they are not without faults. They are, I am sorry to say, somewhat boastful, conceited and proud. This young woman," he indicated Miss Wintertowne, "she had, I dare say, all the usual accomplishments and virtues? She was graceful? Witty? Vivacious? Capricious? Danced like sunlight? Rode like the wind? Sang like an angel? Embroidered like Penelope? Spoke French, Italian, German, Breton, Welsh and many other languages?"

Mr Norrell said he supposed so. He believed that those were the sorts of things young ladies did nowadays.

"Then she will be a charming companion for me!" declared the gentleman with the thistle-down hair, clapping his hands together.

Mr Norrell licked his lips nervously. "What exactly are you proposing?"

"Grant me half the lady's life and the deal is done."

"Half her life?" echoed Mr Norrell.

"Half," said the gentleman with the thistle-down hair.

"But what would her friends say if they learnt I had bargained away half her life?" asked Mr Norrell.

"Oh! They will never know any thing of it. You may rely upon me for that," said the gentleman. "Besides, she has no life now. Half a life is better than none."

Half a life did indeed seem a great deal better than none. With half a life Miss Wintertowne might marry Sir Walter and save him from bankruptcy. Then Sir Walter might continue in office and lend his support to all Mr Norrell's plans for reviving English magic. But Mr Norrell had read a great many books in which were described the dealings of other English magicians with persons of this race and he knew very well how deceitful they could be. He thought he saw how the gentleman intended to trick him.

"How long is a life?" he asked.

The gentleman with the thistle-down hair spread his hands in a gesture of the utmost candour. "How long would you like?"

Mr Norrell considered. "Let us suppose she had lived until she was ninety-four. Ninety-four would have been a good age. She is nineteen now. That would be another seventy-five years. If you were to bestow upon her another seventy-five years, then I see no reason why you should not have half of it."

"Seventy-five years then," agreed the gentleman with the thistle-down hair, "exactly half of which belongs to me."

Mr Norrell regarded him nervously. "Is there any thing more we must do?" he asked. "Shall we sign something?"

"No, but I should take something of the lady's to signify my claim upon her."

"Take one of these rings," suggested Mr Norrell, "or this necklace about her neck. I am sure I can explain away a missing ring or necklace."

"No," said the gentleman with the thistle-down hair. "It ought to be something . . . Ah! I know!"

Drawlight and Lascelles were seated in the drawing-room where Mr Norrell and Sir Walter Pole had first met. It was a gloomy enough spot. The fire burnt low in the grate and the candles were almost out. The curtains were undrawn and no one had put up the shutters. The rattle of the rain upon the windows was very melancholy.

"It is certainly a night for raising the dead," remarked Mr Lascelles. "Rain and trees lash the window-panes and the wind moans in the chimney – all the appropriate stage effects, in fact. I am frequently struck with the play-writing fit and I do not know that tonight's proceedings might not inspire me to try again – a tragi-comedy, telling of an impoverished minister's desperate attempts to gain money by any means, beginning with a mercenary marriage and ending with sorcery. I should think it might be received very well. I believe I shall call it, *'Tis Pity She's a Corpse.*"

Lascelles paused for Drawlight to laugh at this witticism, but Drawlight had been put out of humour by the magician's refusal to allow him to stay and witness the magic, and all he said was: "Where do you suppose they have all gone?"

"I do not know."

"Well, considering all that you and I have done for them, I think we have deserved better than this! It is scarcely half an hour since they were so full of their gratitude to us. To have forgotten us so soon is very bad! And we have not been offered so much as a bit of cake since we arrived. I dare say it is rather too late for dinner – though I for one am famished to death!" He was silent a moment. "The fire is going out too," he remarked.

"Then put some more coals on," suggested Lascelles.

"What! And make myself all dirty?"

One by one all the candles went out and the light from the fire grew less and less until the Venetian paintings upon the walls became nothing but great squares of deepest black hung upon walls of a black that was slightly less profound. For a long time they sat in silence.

"That was the clock striking half-past one o'clock!" said Drawlight suddenly. "How lonely it sounds! Ugh! All the horrid things one reads of in novels always happen just as the church bell tolls or the clock strikes some hour or other in a dark house!"

"I cannot recall an instance of any thing very dreadful happening at half-past one," said Lascelles.

At that moment they heard footsteps on the stairs – which quickly became footsteps in the passageway. The drawing-room door was pushed open and someone stood there, candle in hand.

Drawlight grasped for the poker.

But it was Mr Norrell.

"Do not be alarmed, Mr Drawlight. There is nothing to be afraid of."

Yet Mr Norrell's face, as he raised up his candlestick, seemed to tell a different story; he was very pale and his eyes were wide and not yet emptied, it seemed, of the dregs of fear. "Where is Sir Walter?" he asked. "Where are the others? Miss Wintertowne is asking for her mama."

Mr Norrell was obliged to repeat the last sentence twice before the other two gentlemen could be made to understand him.

Lascelles blinked two or three times and opened his mouth as if in surprize, but then, recovering himself, he shut his mouth again and assumed a supercilious expression; this he wore for the remainder of the night, as if he regularly attended houses where young ladies were raised from the dead and considered this particular example to have been, upon the whole, a rather dull affair. Drawlight, in the meantime, had a thousand things to say and I dare say he said all of them, but unfortunately no one had attention to spare just then to discover what they were.

Drawlight and Lascelles were sent to find Sir Walter. Then Sir Walter fetched Mrs Wintertowne, and Mr Norrell led that lady, tearful and trembling, to her daughter's room. Meanwhile the news of Miss Wintertowne's return to life began to penetrate other parts of the house; the servants learnt of it and were overjoyed and full of gratitude to Mr Norrell, Mr Drawlight and Mr Lascelles. A butler and two manservants approached Mr Drawlight and Mr Lascelles and begged to be allowed to say that if ever Mr Drawlight or Mr Lascelles could benefit from any small service that the butler or the manservants might be able to render them, they had only to speak.

Mr Lascelles whispered to Mr Drawlight that he had not realized before that doing kind actions would lead to his being addressed in such familiar terms by so many low people – it was most unpleasant – he would take care to do no more. Fortunately the low people were in such glad spirits that they never knew they had offended him.

It was soon learnt that Miss Wintertowne had left her bed and, leaning upon Mr Norrell's arm, had gone to her own sitting-room where she was now established in a chair by her fire and that she had asked for a cup of tea.

Drawlight and Lascelles were summoned upstairs to a pretty little sitting-room where they found Miss Wintertowne, her mother, Sir Walter, Mr Norrell and some of the servants.

One would have thought from their looks that it had been Mrs Wintertowne and Sir Walter who had journeyed across several supernatural worlds during the night, they were so grey-faced and drawn; Mrs Wintertowne was weeping and Sir Walter passed his hand across his pale brow from time to time like someone who had seen horrors.

Miss Wintertowne, on the other hand, appeared quite calm and collected, like a young lady who had spent a quiet, uneventful evening at home. She was sitting in a chair in the same elegant gown that she had been wearing when Drawlight and Lascelles had seen her last. She rose and smiled at Drawlight. "I think, sir, that you and I scarcely ever met before, yet I have been told how much I owe to you. But I fear it is a debt quite beyond any repaying. That I am here at all is in a large part due to your energy and insistence. Thank you, sir. Many, many thanks."

And she held out both her hands to him and he took them.

"Oh! Madam!" he cried, all bows and smiles. "It was, I do assure you, the greatest hon . . ."

And then he stopped and was silent a moment. "Madam?" he said. He gave a short, embarrassed laugh (which was odd enough in itself – Drawlight was not easily embarrassed). He did not let go of her hands, but looked around the room as if in search of someone to help him out of a difficulty. Then he lifted one of her own hands and shewed it to her. She did not appear in any way alarmed by what she saw, but she did look surprized; she raised the hand so that her mother could see it.

The little finger of her left hand was gone.

9

Lady Pole

October 1807

I T HAS BEEN remarked (by a lady infinitely cleverer than the present author) how kindly disposed the world in general feels to young people who either die or marry. Imagine then the interest that surrounded Miss Wintertowne! No young lady ever had such advantages before: for she died upon the Tuesday, was raised to life in the early hours of Wednesday morning, and was married upon the Thursday; which some people thought too much excitement for one week.

The desire to see her was quite universal. The full stretch of most people's information was that she had lost a finger in her passage from one world to the next and back again. This was most tantalizing; was she changed in any other way? No one knew.

On Wednesday morning (which was the morning that followed her happy revival) the principals in this marvellous adventure seemed all in a conspiracy to deprive the Town of news; morning-callers at Brunswick-square learnt only that Miss Wintertowne and her mother were resting; in Hanover-square it was exactly the same – Mr Norrell was very much fatigued – it was entirely impossible that he see any body; and as for Sir Walter Pole, no body was quite certain where to find him (though it was strongly suspected that he was at Mrs Wintertowne's house in Brunswick-square). Had it not been for Mr Drawlight and Mr Lascelles (benevolent souls!) the Town would have been starved of information of any sort, but they drove diligently about London making their appearance in a quite impossible number of drawing-rooms, morning-rooms, dining-rooms and card-rooms. It is impossible to say how many dinners Drawlight was invited to sit down to that day – and it is fortunate that he was never at any time much of an eater or he might have done some lasting damage to his digestion. Fifty times or more he must have described how, after Miss Wintertowne's restoration, Mrs Wintertowne and he had wept together; how Sir Walter Pole and he had clasped each other's hand; how Sir Walter had thanked him most gratefully and how he had begged Sir Walter not to think of it; and how Mrs Wintertowne had insisted that Mr Lascelles and he both be driven home in her very own carriage.

Sir Walter Pole had left Mrs Wintertowne's house at about seven o'clock and had gone back to his lodgings to sleep for a few hours, but at about midday he returned to Brunswick-square just as the Town had supposed. (How our neighbours find us out!) By this time it had become apparent to Mrs Wintertowne that her daughter now enjoyed a certain celebrity; that she had, as it were, risen to public eminence overnight. As well as the people who left their cards at the door, great numbers of letters and messages of congratulation were arriving every hour for Miss Wintertowne, many of them from people of whom Mrs Wintertowne had never heard. "Permit me, madam," wrote one, "to entreat you to shake off the oppression of that shadowy vale which has been revealed to you."

That unknown persons should think themselves entitled to comment upon so private a matter as a death and a resurrection, that they should vent their curiosity in letters to her daughter was a circumstance to excite Mrs Wintertowne's utmost displeasure; she had a great deal to say in censure of such vulgar, ill-bred beings, and upon his arrival at Brunswick-square Sir Walter was obliged to listen to all of it.

"My advice, ma'am," he said, "is to think no more about it. As we politicians well know a policy of dignity and silence is our best defence against this sort of impertinence."

"Ah! Sir Walter!" cried his mother-in-law to be. "It is very gratifying to me to discover how frequently our opinions agree! Dignity and silence. Quite. I do not think we can ever be too discreet upon the subject of poor, dear Emma's sufferings. After tomorrow I for one am determined never to speak of it again."

"Perhaps," said Sir Walter, "I did not mean to go so far. Because, you know, we must not forget Mr Norrell. We shall always have a standing reminder of what has happened in Mr Norrell. I fear he must often be with us – after the service he has done us we can scarcely ever shew him consideration enough." He paused and then added with a wry twist of his ugly face, "Happily Mr Norrell himself has been so good as to indicate how he thinks *my* share of the obligation might best be discharged." This was a reference to a conversation which Sir Walter and Mr Norrell had had at four o'clock that morning, when Mr Norrell had waylaid Sir Walter upon the stairs and talked to him at great length about his plans to baffle the French by magic.

Mrs Wintertowne said that she would, of course, be glad to distinguish Mr Norrell with marks of special respect and consideration; any one might know how highly she regarded him. Quite apart from his great magicianship – which, said Mrs Wintertowne, there was no need to mention when he came to the house – he seemed a very good sort of old gentleman.

"Indeed," said Sir Walter. "But for now our most pressing concern must be that Miss Wintertowne should not undertake more than she is equal to – and it was of this that I particularly wished to speak to you. I do not know what may be your opinion but it seems to me that it would be as well to put off the wedding for a week or two."

Mrs Wintertowne could not approve of such a plan; all the arrangements were made and so much of the wedding-dinner ooked. Soup, jellies, boiled meats, pickled sturgeon and so forth were all ready; what was the good of letting it all spoil now, only to ave it all to do over again in a week or so? Sir Walter had nothing o say to arguments of domestic economy, and so he suggested that hey ask Miss Wintertowne to say whether or not she felt strong nough.

And so they rose from their seats in the icy drawing-room where this conversation had taken place) and went up to Miss Vintertowne's sitting-room on the second-floor where they put the uestion to her.

"Oh!" said she. "I never felt better in my life. I feel very strong nd well. Thank you. I have been out already this morning. I do ot often walk. I rarely feel equal to exercise, but this morning I elt as if the house were a prison. I longed to be outside."

Sir Walter looked very concerned. "Was that wise?" He turned o Mrs Wintertowne. "Was that well done?"

Mrs Wintertowne opened her mouth to protest but her daughter only laughed and exclaimed, "Oh! Mama knew nothing of it, I ssure you. I went out while she was asleep in her room. Barnard vent with me. And I walked round Brunswick-square twenty imes. Twenty! – is not that the most ridiculous thing you ever eard? But I was possessed of such a desire to walk! Indeed I would ave run, I think, if it were at all possible, but in London, you now . . ." She laughed again. "I wanted to go further but arnard would not let me. Barnard was in a great flutter and vorry lest I should faint away in the road. She would not let me go ut of sight of the house."

They stared at her. It was – apart from anything else – probably he longest speech Sir Walter had ever heard her utter. She was tting very straight with a bright eye and blooming complexion – he very picture of health and beauty. She spoke so rapidly and vith such expression; she looked so cheerful and was so exceed- gly animated. It was as if Mr Norrell had not only restored her to fe, but to twice or thrice the amount of life she had had before.

It was very odd.

"Of course," said Sir Walter, "if you feel well enough to tak exercise, then I am sure that no one would wish to prevent you nothing is so likely to make you strong, and to ensure you continuing health, as regular exercise. But perhaps, for the pre ent, it would be as well not to go out without telling any one. Yo should have someone more than Barnard to guard you. Fron tomorrow, you know, I may claim that honour for myself."

"But you will be busy, Sir Walter," she reminded him. "Yo will have all your Government business to attend to."

"Indeed, but . . ."

"Oh! I know that you will be pretty constantly engaged wit business affairs. I know I must not expect anything else."

She seemed so cheerfully resigned to his neglecting her that h could not help opening his mouth to protest – but the justice c what she said prevented him from saying a word. Ever since h had first seen her at Lady Winsell's house in Bath he had bee greatly struck by her beauty and elegance – and had quickl concluded that it would be a very good thing, not only to marr her as soon as it could conveniently be contrived, but also to ge better acquainted with her – for he had begun to suspect tha setting aside the money, she might suit him very well as a wife. H thought that an hour or so of conversation might accomplish great deal towards setting them upon that footing of perfec unreserve and confidence which was so much to be desire between husband and wife. He had high hopes that such tête-à-tête would soon provide ample proofs of their mutu; sympathies and tastes. Several things she had said had encourage him to hope that it might be so. And being a man – and a clevc one – and forty-two years old, he naturally had a great deal c information and a great many opinions upon almost every subjec you care to mention, which he was eager to communicate to lovely woman of nineteen – all of which, he thought, she could nc fail but to find quite enthralling. But, what with *his* great pr ccupation with business and *her* poor health they had yet to have his interesting conversation; and now she told him that she expected things to continue much the same after they were married. She did not appear to resent it. Instead, with her new, lively spirits, she seemed quite entertained that he should ever have deceived himself that matters could be otherwise.

Unfortunately he was already late for an appointment with the Foreign Secretary so he took Miss Wintertowne's hand (her whole, right hand) and kissed it very gallantly; told her how much he looked forward to the morrow that would make him the happiest of men; attended politely – hat in hand – to a short speech by Mrs Wintertowne upon the subject; and left the house resolving to consider the problem further – just as soon, in fact, as he could find the time.

Upon the following morning the wedding did indeed take place at St George's Hanover-square. It was attended by almost all of his Majesty's Ministers, two or three of the Royal Dukes, half a dozen admirals, a bishop and several generals. But I am sorry to say that, vital as such great men must always be to a Nation's peace and prosperity, on the day that Miss Wintertowne married Sir Walter Pole, no body cared tuppence for any of them. The man who drew most eyes, the man whom every body whispered to his neighbour to point out to him, was the magician, Mr Norrell.

10

The difficulty of finding employment for a magician

October 1807

SIR WALTER INTENDED to introduce the subject of magi among the other Ministers by degrees, allowing them grow gradually accustomed to the idea before proposin that they make trial of Mr Norrell in the war. He was afraid tha they would oppose him; he was sure that Mr Canning would b sarcastic, that Lord Castlereagh would be uncooperative, and th Earl of Chatham merely bemused.

But all of these fears were entirely unfounded. The Ministers, he soo discovered, were quite as alive to the novelty of the situation as any on else in London. The next time the cabinet met at Burlington Hous

[1] Burlington House in Piccadilly was the London residence of the Duke Portland, the First Minister of the Treasury (whom many people nowada like to call the *Prime Minister* in the French style). It had been erected in a Age when English noblemen were not afraid to rival their Monarch displays of power and wealth and it had no equal for beauty anywhere the capital. As for the Duke himself, he was a most respectable old perso but, poor man, he did not accord with any body's idea of what a Prin Minister ought to be. He was very old and sick. Just at present he lay in curtained room somewhere in a remote part of the house, stupefied laudanum and dying by degrees. He was of no utility whatsoever to h country and not much to his fellow Ministers. The only advantage of h leadership as far as they could see was that it allowed them to use magnificent house as their meeting-place and to employ his magnifice servants to fetch them any little thing they might fancy out of his cellar. (Th generally found that governing Great Britain was a thirsty business.)

hey declared themselves eager to employ England's only magician. But it was by no means clear what ought to be done with im. It had been two hundred years since the English Government ad last commissioned a magician and they were a little out of the abit of it.

"*My* chief problem," explained Lord Castlereagh, "is in finding nen for the Army – a quite impossible task, I assure you; the British are a peculiarly unmilitary race. But I have my eye on Lincolnshire; I am told that the pigs in Lincolnshire are particularly fine and by eating them the population grows very stout and strong. Now what would suit me best would be a general spell cast ver Lincolnshire so that three or four thousand young men would ll at once be filled with a lively desire to become soldiers and fight he French." He looked at Sir Walter rather wistfully. "Would our friend know of such a spell, Sir Walter, do you think?"

Sir Walter did not know but he said he would ask Mr Norrell.

Later that same day Sir Walter called upon Mr Norrell and put he question to him. Mr Norrell was delighted. He did not believe hat anyone had ever proposed such a piece of magic before and begged Sir Walter to convey his compliments to Lord Castlereagh s the possessor of a most original brain. As to whether or not it vere possible; "The difficulty lies in confining the application of he spell to Lincolnshire – and to young men. There is a danger hat if we were successful – which I flatter myself we would be – hen Lincolnshire – and several of the neighbouring counties – night be entirely emptied of people."

Sir Walter went back to Lord Castlereagh and told him no.

The next magic which the Ministers proposed pleased Mr Norrell a great deal less. The resurrection of Lady Pole engrossed he thoughts of everyone in London and the Ministers were by no neans exempt from the general fascination. Lord Castlereagh egan it when he asked the other Ministers who was it that Napoleon Buonaparte had feared most in all the world? Who ad always seemed to know what the wicked French emperor would do next? Who had inflicted so resounding a defeat upon th French that they dare not stick their French noses out of thei ports? Who had united in one person all the virtues that make u an Englishman? Who else, said Lord Castlereagh, but Lor Nelson? Clearly the first thing to be done was to bring back Lor Nelson from the dead. Lord Castlereagh begged Sir Walter' pardon – perhaps he had not understood something – but wh they were wasting time talking about it?

Whereupon Mr Canning, an energetic and quarrelsome person replied quickly that of course Lord Nelson was sadly missed Nelson had been the Nation's hero, Nelson had done everythin Lord Castlereagh said he did. But when all was said and done and Mr Canning meant no disrespect to the Navy, that mos glorious of British institutions – Nelson had only been a sailo whereas the late Mr Pitt had been everything.[2] If anyone dead wa going to be brought back to life then really there was no choice – i must be Pitt.

Lord Chatham (who was also the late Mr Pitt's brother naturally seconded this proposal but he wondered why the had to make a choice – why not resurrect both Pitt and Nelson It would only be a question of paying the magician twice and ther could not be any objection to that, he supposed?

Then other Ministers proposed other dead gentlemen as can didates for restoration until it seemed that half the vaults i England might be emptied. Very soon they had quite a long li and were, as usual, starting to argue about it.

"This will not do," said Sir Walter. "We must begin somewher and it seems to me that every one of us was helped to his presen position by the friendship of Mr Pitt. We would do very wrong t give some other gentleman the preference."

---

[2] William Pitt the Younger (1759–1806). It is very doubtful that we will ev see his like again, for he became Prime Minister at the age of twenty-four an led the country from that day forth, with just one brief interval of three year until his death.

A messenger was sent to fetch Mr Norrell from Hanover-square to Burlington House. Mr Norrell was led into the magnificent painted saloon where the Ministers were sitting. Sir Walter told him that they were contemplating another resurrection.

Mr Norrell turned very pale and muttered something of how his special regard for Sir Walter had compelled him to undertake a sort of magic which otherwise he would not have attempted – he really had no wish to make a second attempt – the Ministers did not know what they were asking.

But when Mr Norrell understood better *who* it was that they proposed as a candidate, he looked a great deal relieved and was heard to say something about the condition of the *body*.

Then the Ministers thought how Mr Pitt had been dead for almost two years, and that, devoted as they had been to Pitt in his life, they really had very little desire to see him in his present condition. Lord Chatham (Mr Pitt's brother) remarked sadly that poor William would certainly have come a good deal unravelled by now.

The subject was not mentioned again.

A week or so later Lord Castlereagh proposed sending Mr Norrell to the Netherlands or possibly Portugal – places where the Ministers entertained faint hopes of gaining some foothold against Buonaparte – where Mr Norrell might do magic under the direction of the generals and the admirals. So Admiral Paycocke, an ancient red-faced seaman, and Captain Harcourt-Bruce of the 20th Light Dragoons were dispatched as a joint military and naval expedition to Hanover-square to take an observation of Mr Norrell.

Captain Harcourt-Bruce was not only dashing, handsome and brave, he was also rather romantic. The reappearance of magic in England thrilled him immensely. He was a great reader of the more exciting sort of history – and his head was full of ancient battles in which the English were outnumbered by the French and doomed to die, when all at once would be heard the sound of strange, unearthly music, and upon a hilltop would appear the Raven King in his tall, black helmet with its mantling of raven feathers streaming in the wind; and he would gallop down the hillside on his tall, black horse with a hundred human knights and a hundred fairy knights at his back, and he would defeat the French by magic.

That was Captain Harcourt-Bruce's idea of a magician. *That* was the sort of thing which he now expected to see reproduced on every battlefield on the Continent. So when he saw Mr Norrell in his drawing-room in Hanover-square, and after he had sat and watched Mr Norrell peevishly complain to his footman, first that the cream in his tea was too creamy, and next that it was too watery – well, I shall not surprize you when I say he was somewhat disappointed. In fact he was so downcast by the whole under taking that Admiral Paycocke, a bluff old gentleman, felt rather sorry for him and only had the heart to laugh at him and tease him very moderately about it.

Admiral Paycocke and Captain Harcourt-Bruce went back to the Ministers and said it was absolutely out of the question to send Mr Norrell anywhere; the admirals and the generals would never forgive the Government if they did it. For some weeks that autumn it seemed the Ministers would never be able to find employment for their only magician.

11

Brest

November 1807

IN THE FIRST week of November a squadron of French ships was preparing to leave the port of Brest which lies on the west coast of Brittany in France. The intention of the French was to cruise about the Bay of Biscay looking for British ships to capture or, if they were unable to do that, to prevent the British from doing any thing which they appeared to want to do.

The wind blew steadily off the land. The French sailors made their preparations quickly and efficiently and the ships were almost ready when heavy black clouds appeared suddenly and a rain began to fall.

Now it was only natural that such an important port as Brest should contain a great number of people who studied the winds and the weather. Just as the ships were about to set sail several of these persons hurried down to the docks in great excitement to warn the sailors that there was something very queer about the rain: the clouds, they said, had come from the north, whereas the wind was blowing from the east. The thing was impossible, but it had happened. The captains of the ships just had time to be astonished, incredulous or unnerved – as their characters dictated – when another piece of news reached them.

Brest harbour consists of an inner bay and an outer, the inner bay being separated from the open sea by a long thin peninsula. As the rain grew heavier the French officers in charge of the ships learnt that a great fleet of British ships had appeared in the outer bay.

How many ships were there? The officers' informants did not know. More than could be easily counted – perhaps as many as a hundred. Like the rain, the ships had seemingly arrived in a single instant out of an empty sea. What sort of ships were they? Ah! That was the strangest thing of all! The ships were all ships of the line, heavily armed two- and three-decked warships.

This was astonishing news. The ships' great number and their great size was, in truth, more puzzling than their sudden appearance. The British Navy blockaded Brest continually, but never with more than twenty-five ships at a time, of which only ten or twelve were ships of the line, the remainder being agile little frigates, sloops and brigs.

So peculiar was this tale of a hundred ships that the French captains did not believe it until they had ridden or rowed to Lochrist or Camaret Saint-Julien or other places where they could stand upon the clifftops and see the ships for themselves.

Days went by. The sky was the colour of lead and the rain continued to fall. The British ships remained stubbornly where they were. The people of Brest were in great dread lest some of the ships might attempt to come up to the town and bombard it. But the British ships did nothing.

Stranger still was the news that came from other ports in the French Empire, from Rochefort, Toulon, Marseilles, Genoa, Venice, Flushing, Lorient, Antwerp and a hundred other towns of lesser importance. They too were blockaded by British fleets of a hundred or so warships. It was impossible to comprehend. Added together these fleets contained more warships than the British possessed. Indeed they contained more warships than there were upon the face of the earth.

The most senior officer at Brest at that time was Admiral Desmoulins. He had a servant, a very small man no bigger than an eight-year-old child, and as dark as a European can be. He looked as if he had been put into the oven and baked for too long and was now rather overdone. His skin was the colour of a coffee-bean and the texture of a dried-up rice-pudding. His hair was black, twisted and greasy like the spines and quills you may observe on the less succulent parts of roasted chickens. His name was Perroquet (which means parrot). Admiral Desmoulins was very proud of Perroquet; proud of his size, proud of his cleverness, proud of his agility and most of all, proud of his colour. Admiral Desmoulins often boasted that he had seen blacks who would appear fair next to Perroquet.

It was Perroquet who sat in the rain for four days studying the ships through his eye-glass. Rain spurted from his child-size bicorn hat as if from two little rainspouts; it sank into the capes of his child-size coat, making the coat fearfully heavy and turning the wool into felt; and it ran in little streams down his baked, greasy skin; but he paid it not the slightest attention.

After four days Perroquet sighed, jumped to his feet, stretched himself, took off his hat, gave his head a good scratch, yawned and said, "Well, my Admiral, they are the queerest ships I have ever seen and I do not understand them."

"In what way, Perroquet?" asked the Admiral.

Gathered on the cliffs near Camaret Saint-Julien with Perroquet were Admiral Desmoulins and Captain Jumeau, and rain spurted from *their* bicorn hats and turned the wool of *their* coats into felt and filled their boots with half an inch of water.

"Well," said Perroquet, "the ships sit upon the sea as if they were becalmed and yet they are not becalmed. There is a strong westerly wind which ought by rights to blow them on to these rocks, but does it? No. Do the ships beat off? No. Do they reduce sail? No. I cannot count the number of times the wind has changed since I have sat here, but what have the men on those ships done? Nothing."

Captain Jumeau, who disliked Perroquet and was jealous of his influence with the Admiral, laughed. "He is mad, my Admiral. If the British were really as idle or ignorant as he says, their ships would all be heaps of broken spars by now."

"They are more like pictures of ships," mused Perroquet, paying the Captain no attention, "than the ships themselves. But a queerer thing still, my Admiral, is that ship, the three-decker at the northernmost tip of the line. On Monday it was just like the others but now its sails are all in tatters, its mizzen mast is gone and there is a ragged hole in its side."

"Huzza!" cried Captain Jumeau. "Some brave French crew has inflicted this damage while we stand here talking."

Perroquet grinned. "And do you think, Captain, that the British would permit one French ship to go up to their hundred ships and blow one of them to bits and then sail calmly away again? Ha! I should like to see you do it, Captain, in your little boat. No, my Admiral, it is my opinion that the British ship is melting."

"Melting!" declared the Admiral in surprize.

"The hull bulges like an old woman's knitting bag," said Perroquet. "And the bowsprit and the spritsail yard are drooping into the water."

"What idiotic nonsense!" declared Captain Jumeau. "How can a ship melt?"

"I do not know," said Perroquet, thoughtfully. "It depends upon what it is made of."

"Jumeau, Perroquet," said Admiral Desmoulins, "I believe that our best course will be to sail out and examine those ships. If the British fleet seems likely to attack, we will turn back, but in the meantime perhaps we may learn something."

So Perroquet and the Admiral and Captain Jumeau set sail in the rain with a few brave men; for sailors, though they face hardship with equanimity, are superstitious, and Perroquet was not the only person in Brest who had noticed the queerness of the British ships.

After they had gone some way, our adventurers could see that the strange ships were entirely grey and that they glittered; even under that dark sky, even in all that drenching rain they shone. Once, for a moment, the clouds parted and a ray of sunlight struck the sea. The ships disappeared. Then the clouds closed and the ships were there again.

"Dear God!" cried the Admiral. "What does all this mean?"

"Perhaps," said Perroquet uneasily, "the British ships have all been sunk and these are their ghosts."

Still the strange ships glittered and shone, and this led to some discussion as to what they might be made of. The Admiral thought perhaps iron or steel. (Metal ships indeed! The French are, as I have often supposed, a very whimsical nation.)

Captain Jumeau wondered if they might not be of silver paper.

"Silver paper!" exclaimed the Admiral.

"Oh, yes!" said Captain Jumeau. "Ladies, you know, take silver paper and roll it into quills and make little baskets of it, which they then decorate with flowers and fill with sugar plums."

The Admiral and Perroquet were surprized to hear this, but Captain Jumeau was a handsome man, and clearly knew more of the ways of ladies than they did.

But if it took one lady an evening to make a basket, how many ladies would it take to make a fleet? The Admiral said it made his head hurt to think of it.

The sun came out again. This time, since they were closer to ships, they could see how the sunlight shone *through* them and made them colourless until they were just a faint sparkle upon the water.

"Glass," said the Admiral, and he was near to the mark, but it was clever Perroquet who finally hit upon the truth.

"No, my Admiral, it is the rain. They are made of rain."

As the rain fell from the heavens the drops were made to flow together to form solid masses – pillars and beams and sheets, which someone had shaped into the likeness of a hundred ships.

Perroquet and the Admiral and Captain Jumeau were consumed with curiosity to know who could have made such a thing and they agreed he must be a master-rainsmith.

"But not only a master-rainsmith!" exclaimed the Admiral, "A master-puppeteer! See how they bob up and down upon the water! How the sails billow and fall!"

"They are certainly the prettiest things that ever I saw, my Admiral," agreed Perroquet, "but I repeat what I said before; he knows nothing of sailing or seamanship, whoever he is."

For two hours the Admiral's wooden ship sailed in and out of the rain-ships. Being ships of rain they made no sound at all – no creaking of timber, no slap of sail in the wind, no call of sailor to his mate. Several times groups of smooth-faced men of rain came to the ship's rail to gaze out at the wooden ship with its crew of flesh-and-blood men, but what the rain-sailors were thinking, no one could tell. Yet the Admiral, the Captain and Perroquet felt themselves to be perfectly safe, for, as Perroquet remarked, "Even if the rain-sailors wish to fire upon us, they only have rain-cannonballs to do it with and we will only get wet."

Perroquet and the Admiral and Captain Jumeau were lost in admiration. They forgot that they had been tricked, forgot that they had wasted a week and that for a week the British had been slipping into ports on the Baltic coast and ports on the Portuguese coast and all sorts of other ports where the Emperor Napoleon Buonaparte did not want them to go. But the spell which held the ships in place appeared to be weakening (which presumably explained the melting ship at the northernmost point of the fleet). After two hours it stopped raining and in the same moment the spell broke, which Perroquet and the Admiral and Captain Jumeau knew by a curious twist of their senses, as if they had tasted a string quartet, or been, for a moment, deafened by the sight of the colour blue. For the merest instant the rain-ships became mist-ships and then the breeze gently blew them apart.

The Frenchmen were alone upon the empty Atlantic.

12

The Spirit of English Magic urges Mr Norrell to the Aid of Britannia

December 1807

O N A DAY in December two great draycarts happened to collide in Cheapside. One, which was loaded with barrels of sherry-wine, overturned. While the draymen argued about which of them was to blame, some passers-by observed that sherry-wine was leaking from one of the barrels. Soon a crowd of drinkers gathered with glasses and pint-pots to catch the sherry, and hooks and bars to make holes in those casks which were still undamaged. The draycarts and crowd had soon so effectively stopt up Cheapside that queues of carriages formed in all the neighbouring streets, Poultry, Threadneedle-street, Bartholomew-lane and, in the other direction, Aldersgate, Newgate and Paternoster-row. It became impossible to imagine how the knot of carriages, horses and people would ever get undone again.

Of the two draymen one was handsome and the other was fat and, having made up their quarrel, they became a sort of Bacchus and Silenus to the revel. They decided to entertain both themselves and their followers by opening all the carriage-doors to see what the rich people were doing inside. Coachmen and footmen tried to prevent this impertinence but the crowd were too many to be held off and too drunk to mind the blows of the whip which the crosser sort of coachmen gave them. In one of these carriages the fat drayman discovered Mr Norrell and cried, "What! Old Norrell!" The draymen both climbed into the carriage to shake Mr Norrell's hand and breathe sherry fumes all over him and assure him that they would lose no time in moving everything out of the way so that he – the hero of the French Blockade – might pass. Which promise they kept and respectable people found their horses unhitched and their carriages pushed and shoved into tanners' yards and other nasty places, or backed into dirty brick-lanes where they got stuck fast and all the varnish was scraped off; and when the draymen and their friends had made this triumphal path for Mr Norrell they escorted him and his carriage along it, as far as Hanover-square, cheering all the way, flinging their hats in the air and making up songs about him.

Everyone, it seemed, was delighted with what Mr Norrell had done. A large part of the French Navy had been tricked into remaining in its ports for eleven days and during that time the British had been at liberty to sail about the Bay of Biscay, the English Channel and the German Sea, just as it pleased and a great many things had been accomplished. Spies had been deposited in various parts of the French Empire and other spies brought back to England with news about what Buonaparte was doing. British merchant ships had unloaded their cargoes of coffee and cotton and spices in Dutch and Baltic ports without any interference.

Napoleon Buonaparte, it was said, was scouring France to find a magician of his own – but with no success. In London the Ministers were quite astonished to find that, for once, they had done something the Nation approved.

Mr Norrell was invited to the Admiralty, where he drank madeira-wine in the Board Room. He sat in a chair close to the fire and had a long comfortable chat with the First Lord of the Admiralty, Lord Mulgrave, and the First Secretary to the Admiralty, Mr Horrocks. Above the fireplace there were carvings of nautical instruments and garlands of flowers which Mr Norrell greatly admired. He described the beautiful carvings in the library at Hurtfew Abbey; "And yet," said Mr Norrell, "I envy you, my lord. Indeed I do. Such a fine representation of the instruments of your profession! I wish that I might have done the same. Nothing looks so striking. Nothing, I believe, inspires a man with such eagerness to begin his day's work as the sight of his instruments neatly laid out – or their images in good English oak as we have here. But really a magician has need of so few tools. I will tell you a little trick, my lord, the more apparatus a magician carries about with him – coloured powders, stuffed cats, magical hats and so forth – the greater the fraud you will eventually discover him to be!"

And what, inquired Mr Horrocks politely, were the few tools that a magician did require?

"Why! Nothing really," said Mr Norrell. "Nothing but a silver basin for seeing visions in."

"Oh!" cried Mr Horrocks. "I believe I would give almost any thing to see *that* magic done – would not you, my lord? Oh, Mr Norrell, might we prevail upon you to shew us a vision in a silver basin?"

Usually Mr Norrell was the last man in the world to satisfy such idle curiosity, but he had been so pleased with his reception at the Admiralty (for the two gentlemen paid him a world of compliments) that he agreed almost immediately and a servant was dispatched to find a silver basin; "A silver basin about a foot in diameter," said Mr Norrell, "which you must fill with clean water."

The Admiralty had lately sent out orders for three ships to rendezvous south of Gibraltar and Lord Mulgrave had a great curiosity to know whether or not this had occurred; would Mr Norrell be able to find it out? Mr Norrell did not know, but promised to try. When the basin was brought and Mr Norrell bent over it, Lord Mulgrave and Mr Horrocks felt as if nothing else could have so conjured up the ancient glories of English magic;

they felt as if they were living in the Age of Stokesey, Godbless and the Raven King.

A picture appeared upon the surface of the water in the silver basin, a picture of three ships riding the waves of a blue sea. The strong, clear light of the Mediterranean shone out into the gloomy December room and lit up the faces of the three gentlemen who peered into the bowl.

"It moves!" cried Lord Mulgrave in astonishment.

It did indeed. The sweetest white clouds imaginable were gliding across the blue sky, the ships rode the waves and tiny people could be seen moving about them. Lord Mulgrave and Mr Horrocks had no difficulty in recognizing HMS *Catherine of Winchester*, HMS *Laurel* and HMS *Centaur*.

"Oh, Mr Norrell!" cried Mr Horrocks. "The *Centaur* is my cousin's ship. Can you shew me Captain Barry?"

Mr Norrell fidgeted about and drew in his breath with a sharp hiss and stared fiercely at the silver basin, and by and by appeared a vision of a pink-faced, gold-haired, overgrown cherub of a man walking about a quarterdeck. This, Mr Horrocks assured them, was his cousin, Captain Barry.

"He looks very well, does he not?" cried Mr Horrocks. "I am glad to know he is in such good health."

"Where are they? Can you tell?" Lord Mulgrave asked Mr Norrell.

"Alas," said Mr Norrell, "this art of making pictures is the most imprecise in the world.[1] I am delighted to have had the honour of shewing your lordship some of His Majesty's ships. I am yet more pleased that they are the ones you want – which is frankly more than I expected – but I fear I can tell you nothing further."

So delighted was the Admiralty with all that Mr Norrell had accomplished that Lord Mulgrave and Mr Horrocks soon looked about them to see what other tasks they could find for the

---

[1] Four years later during the Peninsular War Mr Norrell's pupil, Jonathan Strange, had similar criticisms to make about this form of magic.

magician. His Majesty's Navy had recently captured a French ship of the line with a very fine figurehead in the shape of a mermaid with bright blue eyes, coral-pink lips, a great mass of sumptuous golden curls artistically strewn with wooden representations of starfish and crabs, and a tail that was covered all over with silver-gilt as if it might be made of gingerbread inside. It was known that before it had been captured, the ship had been at Toulon, Cherbourg, Antwerp, Rotterdam and Genoa, and so the mermaid had seen a great deal of enemy defences and of the Emperor Napoleon Buonaparte's great scheme of ship-building which was going forward at that time. Mr Horrocks asked Mr Norrell to put a spell on her so that she might tell all she knew. This Mr Norrell did. But though the mermaid could be made to speak she could not at first be brought to answer any questions. She considered herself the implacable enemy of the British and was highly delighted to be given powers of speech so that she could express her hatred of them. Having passed all her existence among sailors she knew a great many insults and bestowed them very readily on anyone who came near her in a voice that sounded like the creaking of masts and timbers in a high wind. Nor did she confine herself to abusing Englishmen with words. There were three seamen that had work to do about the ship, but the moment that they got within reach of the mermaid's wooden arms she picked them up in her great wooden hands and threw them in the water.

Mr Horrocks who had gone down to Portsmouth to talk to her, grew tired of her and told her that he would have her chopped up and made a bonfire of. But, though French, she was also very brave and said she would like to see the man that would try to burn her. And she lashed her tail and waved her arms menacingly; and all the wooden starfish and crabs in her hair bristled.

The situation was resolved when the handsome young Captain who had captured her ship was sent to reason with her. He was able to explain to her in clear, comprehensible French the rightness of the British cause and the terrible wrongness of the French one, and whether it were the persuasiveness of his words or the handsomeness of his face that convinced her I do not know, but she told Mr Horrocks all he wished to know.

Mr Norrell rose every day to new heights of public greatness and an enterprising printmaker called Holland who had a print-shop in St Paul's Churchyard was inspired to commission an engraving of him to be sold in the shop. The engraving shewed Mr Norrell in the company of a young lady, scantily dressed in a loose smock. A great quantity of stiff, dark material swirled and coiled about the young lady's body without ever actually touching it and, for the further embellishment of her person, she wore a crescent moon tucked in among the tumbling locks of her hair. She had taken Mr Norrell (who appeared entirely astonished by the proceedings) by the arm and was energetically pulling him up a flight of stairs and pointing in most emphatic manner towards a lady of mature years who sat at the top. The lady of mature years was attired like the young lady in smock and draperies, with the handsome addition of a Roman helmet on her head; she appeared to be weeping in the most uninhibited fashion, while an elderly lion, her only companion, lay at her feet with a gloomy expression upon his countenance. This engraving, entitled *The Spirit of English Magic urges Mr Norrell to the Aid of Britannia*, was an immense success and Mr Holland sold almost seven hundred copies in a month.

Mr Norrell did not go out so much as formerly; instead he stayed at home and received respectful visits from all sorts of great people. It was not uncommon for five or six coronet-coaches to stop at his house in Hanover-square in the space of one morning. He was the still same silent, nervous little man he had always been and, had it not been for Mr Drawlight and Mr Lascelles, the occupants of those carriages must have found their visits dull indeed. Upon such occasions Mr Drawlight and Mr Lascelles supplied all the conversation. Indeed Mr Norrell's dependence upon these two gentlemen increased daily. Childermass had once said that it would be

an odd sort of magician that would employ Drawlight, yet Mr
Norrell now employed him constantly; Drawlight was forever
being driven about in Mr Norrell's carriage upon Mr Norrell's
business. Every day he came early to Hanover-square to tell Mr
Norrell what was being said about the Town, who was rising, who
falling, who was in debt, who in love, until Mr Norrell, sitting
alone in his library, began to know as much of the Town's business
as any City matron.

More surprizing, perhaps, was Mr Lascelles's devotion to the
cause of English magic. The explanation, however, was quite
simple. Mr Lascelles was one of that uncomfortable breed of
men who despise steady employment of any sort. Though perfectly
conscious of his own superior understanding, he had never
troubled to acquire any particular skills or knowledge, and had
arrived at the age of thirty-nine entirely unfitted for any office or
occupation. He had looked about him and seen men, who had
worked diligently all the years of their youth, risen to positions of
power and influence; and there is no doubt that he envied them.
Consequently it was highly agreeable to Mr Lascelles to become
counsellor-in-chief to the greatest magician of the Age, and have
respectful questions put to him by the King's Ministers. Naturally,
he made a great shew of being the same careless, indifferent
gentleman as before, but in truth he was extremely jealous of
his new-found importance. He and Drawlight had come to an
understanding one night in the Bedford over a bottle of port. Two
friends, they had agreed, were quite sufficient for a quiet gentleman such as Mr Norrell, and they had formed an alliance to guard
each other's interest and to prevent any other person from gaining
any influence over the magician.

It was Mr Lascelles who first encouraged Mr Norrell to think of
publication. Poor Mr Norrell was constantly affronted by people's
misconceptions concerning magic and was forever lamenting the
general ignorance upon the subject. "They ask me to shew them
fairy-spirits," he complained, "and unicorns and manticores and

things of that sort. The *utility* of the magic I have done is entirely lost on them. It is only the most frivolous sorts of magic that excite their interest."

Mr Lascelles said, "Feats of magic will make your *name* known everywhere, sir, but they will never make your *opinions* understood. For that you must publish."

"Yes, indeed," cried Mr Norrell, eagerly, "and I have every intention of writing a book – just as you advise – only I fear it will be many years before I have leisure enough to undertake it."

"Oh! I quite agree – a book would mean a world of work," said Mr Lascelles, languidly, "but I had no notion of a book. Two or three articles was what I had in mind. I dare say there is not an editor in London or Edinburgh who would not be delighted to publish any little thing you cared to send him – you may make your choice of the periodicals, but if you take my advice, sir, you will chuse *The Edinburgh Review*. There is scarcely a household in the kingdom with any pretensions to gentility that does not take it. There is no quicker way of making your views more widely understood."

Mr Lascelles was so persuasive upon the subject and conjured up such visions of Mr Norrell's articles upon every library-table and Mr Norrell's opinions discussed in every drawing-room that, had it not been for the great dislike that Mr Norrell had to *The Edinburgh Review*, he would have sat down there and then to begin writing. Unfortunately, *The Edinburgh Review* was a publication renowned chiefly for radical opinions, criticism of the Government and opposition to the war with France – none of which Mr Norrell could approve.

"Besides," said Mr Norrell, "I really have no desire to write reviews of other people's books. Modern publications upon magic are the most pernicious things in the world, full of misinformation and wrong opinions."

"Then sir, you may say so. The ruder you are, the more the editors will be delighted."

"But it is my own opinions which I wish to make better known, not other people's."

"Ah, but, sir," said Lascelles, "it is precisely by passing judgements upon other people's work and pointing out their errors that readers can be made to understand your own opinions better. It is the easiest thing in the world to turn a review to one's own ends. One only need mention the book once or twice and for the rest of the article one may develop one's theme just as one chuses. It is, I assure you, what every body else does."

"Hmm," said Mr Norrell thoughtfully, "you may be right. But no. It would seem as if I were lending support to what ought never to have been published in the first place."

And upon this point Mr Norrell proved unpersuadable.

Lascelles was disappointed; *The Edinburgh Review* far surpassed its rivals in brilliance and wit. Its articles were devoured by everyone in the kingdom from the meanest curate to the Prime Minister. Other publications were very dull in comparison.

He was inclined to abandon the notion altogether and had almost forgotten all about it when he happened to receive a letter from a young bookseller named Murray. Mr Murray respectfully requested that Mr Lascelles and Mr Drawlight would do him the honour of permitting him to wait upon them at any hour and upon any day to suit them. He had, he said, a proposal to put before them, a proposal which concerned Mr Norrell.

Lascelles and Drawlight met the bookseller at Mr Lascelles's house in Bruton-street a few days later. His manner was energetic and businesslike and he laid his proposal before them immediately.

"Like every other inhabitant of these isles, gentlemen, I have been amazed and delighted at the recent extraordinary revival of English magic. And I have been equally struck by the enthusiasm with which the British Public has greeted this reappearance of an art long thought dead. I am convinced that a periodical devoted to magic would achieve a wide circulation. Literature, politics, religion and travel are all very well – they will always be popular,

142

subjects for a periodical, but magic – real, practical magic like Mr Norrell's – has the advantage of complete novelty. I wonder, gentlemen, if you could tell me whether Mr Norrell would look favourably upon my proposal? I have heard that Mr Norrell has a great deal to say upon the subject. I have heard that Mr Norrell's opinions are quite surprizing! Of course we all learnt a little of the history and theory of magic in our schoolrooms, but it is so long since any magic was practised in these islands that I dare say what we have been taught is full of errors and misconceptions."

"Ah!" cried Mr Drawlight. "How perceptive of you, Mr Murray! How happy it would make Mr Norrell to hear you say so! Errors and misconceptions – exactly so! Whenever, my dear sir, you are privileged to enjoy Mr Norrell's conversation – as I have been upon many occasions – you will learn that such is the exact state of affairs!"

"It has long been the dearest wish of Mr Norrell's heart," said Lascelles, "to bring a more precise understanding of modern magic before a wider audience, but alas, sir, private wishes are often frustrated by public duties, and the Admiralty and the War Office keep him so busy."

Mr Murray replied politely that of course all other considerations must give way before the great consideration of the war and Mr Norrell was a National Treasure. "But I hope that some way might be found to arrange matters so that the chief burden did not fall upon Mr Norrell's shoulders. We would employ an editor to plan each issue, solicit articles and reviews, make changes – all under Mr Norrell's guidance, naturally."

"Ah, yes!" said Lascelles. "Quite. All under Mr Norrell's guidance. We would insist upon that."

The interview ended very cordially upon both sides with Lascelles and Drawlight promising to speak to Mr Norrell immediately.

Drawlight watched Mr Murray leave the room. "A Scotchman," he said as soon as the door was closed.

"Oh, quite!" agreed Lascelles. "But I do not mind that. The Scotch are often very able, very canny in business. I believe this might do very well."

"He seemed quite a respectable person – almost a gentleman in fact. Except that he has a queer trick of fixing his right eye upon one while his other eye travels the room. I found that a little disconcerting."

"He is blind in his right eye."

"Indeed?"

"Yes. Canning told me. One of his schoolmasters stuck a pen-knife in it when he was boy."

"Dear me! But, just imagine, my dear Lascelles! A whole periodical devoted to one person's opinions! I would never have believed it possible! The magician will be astonished when we tell him."

Mr Lascelles laughed. "He will consider it the most natural thing in the world. His vanity is beyond any thing."

As Lascelles had predicted, Mr Norrell found nothing extraordinary in the proposal, but straightaway he began to make difficulties. "It is an excellent plan," he said, "but unfortunately completely impracticable. I have no time to edit a periodical and I could scarcely entrust so important a task to any one else."

"I was quite of the same mind, sir," said Mr Lascelles, "until I thought of Portishead."

"Portishead? Who is Portishead?" asked Mr Norrell.

"Well," said Lascelles, "He *was* a theoretical magician, but . . ."

"A theoretical magician?" interrupted Mr Norrell in alarm. "You know what I think of that!"

"Ah, but you have not heard what follows," said Lascelles. "So great is his admiration of *you*, sir, that on being told you did not approve of theoretical magicians he immediately gave up his studies."

"Did he indeed?" said Mr Norrell, somewhat placated by this information.

"He has published one or two books. I forget what exactly – a history of sixteenth-century magic for children or something of that sort.[2] I really feel that you might safely entrust the periodical to Lord Portishead, sir. There is no danger of him publishing any thing of which you disapprove; he is known as one of most honourable men in the kingdom. His first wish will be to please you, I am quite certain."[3]

Somewhat reluctantly Mr Norrell agreed to meet Lord Portishead and Mr Drawlight wrote a letter summoning him to Hanover-square.

Lord Portishead was about thirty-eight years of age. He was very tall and thin with long, thin hands and feet. He habitually wore a whitish coat and light-coloured breeches. He was a gentle soul whom everything made uncomfortable: his excessive height made him uncomfortable; his status as a former theoretical magician made him uncomfortable (being an intelligent man he knew that Mr Norrell disapproved of him); meeting such polished men of the world as Drawlight and Lascelles made him uncomfortable and meeting Mr Norrell – who was his great hero – made him most uncomfortable of all. At one point he became so agitated that he began to sway backwards and forwards – which, taken in conjunction with his height and whitish clothes, gave him the appearance of a silver-birch tree in a high wind.

---

[2] In this speech Mr Lascelles has managed to combine all Lord Portishead's books into one. By the time Lord Portishead gave up the study of magic in early 1808 he had published three books: *The Life of Jacques Belasis*, pub. Longman, London, 1801, *The Life of Nicholas Goubert*, pub. Longman, London, 1805, and *A Child's History of the Raven King*, pub. Longman, London, 1807, engravings by Thomas Bewick. The first two were scholarly discussions of two sixteenth-century magicians. Mr Norrell had no great opinion of them, but he had a particular dislike of *A Child's History*. Jonathan Strange, on the other hand, thought this an excellent little book.

[3] "It was odd that so wealthy a man – for Lord Portishead counted large portions of England among his possessions – should have been so very self-effacing, but such was the case. He was besides a devoted husband and the father of ten children. Mr Strange told me that to see Lord Portishead play with his children was the most delightful thing in the world. And indeed he was a little like a child himself. For all his great learning he could no more recognize evil than he could spontaneously understand Chinese. He was the gentlest lord in all of the British aristocracy."

The Life of Jonathan Strange by John Segundus, pub. John Murray, London, 1820.

Despite his nervousness he managed to convey his great sense of the honour done to him in being summoned to meet Mr Norrell. Indeed so gratified was Mr Norrell by Lord Portishead's extreme deference towards him that he graciously gave his permission for Lord Portishead to study magic again.

Naturally Lord Portishead was delighted, but when he heard that Mr Norrell desired him to sit for long periods of time in a corner of Mr Norrell's own drawing-room, soaking up Mr Norrell's opinions upon modern magic, and then to edit, under Mr Norrell's direction, Mr Murray's new periodical, it seemed that he could conceive of no greater happiness.

The new periodical was named *The Friends of English Magic*, the title being taken from Mr Segundus's letter to *The Times* in the previous spring. Curiously none of the articles which appeared in *The Friends of English Magic* were written by Mr Norrell, who was found to be entirely incapable of finishing a piece of writing; he was never satisfied with what he had written. He could never be sure that he had not said too much or too little.[4]

---

[4] *The Friends of English Magic* was first published in February 1808 and was an immediate success. By 1812 Norrell and Lascelles were boasting of a circulation in excess of 13,000, though how reliable this figure may be is uncertain.

From 1808 until 1810 the editor was nominally Lord Portishead but there is little doubt that both Mr Norrell and Lascelles interfered a great deal. There was a certain amount of disagreement between Norrell and Lascelles as to the general aims of the periodical. Mr Norrell wished *The Friends of English Magic* first to impress upon the British Public the great importance of English modern magic, secondly to correct erroneous views of magical history and thirdly to vilify those magicians and classes of magicians whom he hated. He did not desire to explain the procedures of English magic within its pages – in other words he had no intention of making it in the least informative. Lord Portishead, whose admiration of Mr Norrell knew no bounds, considered it his first duty as editor to follow Norrell's numerous instructions. As a result the early issues of *The Friends of English Magic* are rather dull and often puzzling – full of odd omissions, contradictions and evasions. Lascelles, on the other hand, understood very well how the periodical might be used to gain support for the revival of English magic and he was anxious to make it lighter in tone. He grew more and more irritated at Portishead's cautious approach. He manoeuvred and from 1810 he and Lord Portishead were joint editors.

John Murray was the publisher of *The Friends of English Magic* until early

146

There is not much to interest the serious student of magic in the early issues and the only entertainment to be got from them is contained in several articles in which Portishead attacks on Mr Norrell's behalf: gentleman-magicians; lady-magicians; street-magicians; vagabond-magicians; child-prodigy-magicians; the Learned Society of York Magicians; the Learned Society of Manchester Magicians; learned societies of magicians in general; any other magicians whatsoever.

[4] *cont'd*   1815 when he and Norrell quarrelled. Deprived of Norrell's support, Murray was obliged to sell the periodical to Thomas Norton Longman, another publisher. In 1816 Murray and Strange planned to set up a rival periodical to *The Friends of English Magic*, entitled *The Famulus*, but only one issue was ever published.

13

The magician of Threadneedle-street

December 1807

THE MOST FAMOUS street-magician in London was undoubtedly Vinculus. His magician's booth stood before the church of St Christopher Le Stocks in Threadneedle-street opposite the Bank of England, and it would have been difficult to say whether the bank or the booth were the more famous.

Yet the reason for Vinculus's celebrity – or notoriety – was a little mysterious. He was no better a magician than any of the other charlatans with lank hair and a dirty yellow curtain. His spells did not work, his prophecies did not come true and his trances had been proven false beyond a doubt.

For many years he was much addicted to holding deep and weighty conference with the Spirit of the River Thames. He would fall into a trance and ask the Spirit questions and the voice of the Spirit would issue forth from his mouth in accents deep, watery and windy. On a winter's day in 1805 a woman paid him a shilling to ask the Spirit to tell her where she might find her runaway husband. The Spirit provided a great deal of quite surprizing information and a crowd began to gather around the booth to listen to it. Some of the bystanders believed in Vinculus's ability and were duly impressed by the Spirit's oration, but others began to taunt the magician and his client. One such jeerer (a most ingenious fellow) actually managed to set Vinculus's shoes on fire while Vinculus was speaking. Vinculus came out of his trance immediately: he leapt about, howling and attempting to pull off his shoes and stamp out the fire at one and the same time. He was throwing himself about and the crowd were all enjoying the sight immensely, when something popt out of his mouth. Two men picked it up and examined it: it was a little metal contraption not more than an inch and a half long. It was something like a mouth-organ and when one of the men placed it in his own mouth he too was able to produce the voice of the Spirit of the River Thames.

Despite such public humiliations Vinculus retained a certain authority, a certain native dignity which meant that he, among all the street-magicians of London, was treated with a measure of respect. Mr Norrell's friends and admirers were continually urging him to pay a visit to Vinculus and were surprized that he shewed no inclination to do it.

On a day in late December when storm clouds made Alpine landscapes in the sky above London, when the wind played such havoc in the heavens that the city was one moment plunged in gloom and the next illuminated by sunlight, when rain rattled upon the windowpane, Mr Norrell was seated comfortably in his library before a cheerful fire. The tea table spread with a quantity of good things stood before him and in his hand was Thomas Lanchester's *The Language of Birds*. He was turning the pages in search of a favourite passage when he was nearly frightened out of his wits by a voice suddenly saying very loudly and contemptuously, "Magician! You think that you have amazed everyone by your deeds!"

Mr Norrell looked up and was astonished to find that there was someone else in the room, a person he had never seen before, a thin, shabby, ragged hawk of a man. His face was the colour of three-day-old milk; his hair was the colour of a coal-smoke-and-ashes London sky; and his clothes were the colour of the Thames at dirty Wapping. Nothing about him – face, hair, clothes – was particularly clean, but in all other points he corresponded to the common notion of what a magician should look like (which Mr Norrell most certainly did not). He stood very erect and the expression of his fierce grey eyes was naturally imperious.

"Oh, yes!" continued this person, glaring furiously at Mr Norrell. "You think yourself a very fine fellow! Well, know this, Magician! Your coming was foretold long ago. I have been expecting you these past twenty years! Where have you been hiding yourself?"

Mr Norrell sat in amazed silence, staring at his accuser with open mouth. It was as if this man had reached into his breast, plucked out his secret thought and held it up to the light. Ever since his arrival in the capital Mr Norrell had realized that he had indeed been ready long ago; he could have been doing magic for England's benefit years before; the French might have been defeated and English magic raised to that lofty position in the Nation's regard which Mr Norrell believed it ought to occupy. He was tormented with the idea that he had betrayed English magic by his dilatoriness. Now it was as if his own conscience had taken concrete form and started to reproach him. This put him somewhat at a disadvantage in dealing with the mysterious stranger. He stammered out an inquiry as to who the person might be.

"I am Vinculus, magician of Threadneedle-street!"

"Oh!" cried Mr Norrell, relieved to find that at least he was no supernatural apparition. "And you have come here to beg I suppose? Well, you may take yourself off again! I do not recognize you as a brother-magician and I shall not give you any thing! Not money. Not promises of help. Not recommendations to other people. Indeed I may tell you that I intend . . ."

"Wrong again, Magician! I want nothing for myself. I have come to explain your destiny to you, as I was born to do."

"Destiny? Oh, it's prophecies, is it?" cried Mr Norrell contemptuously. He rose from his chair and tugged violently at the bell pull, but no servant appeared. "Well, now I really have nothing to say to people who pretend to do prophecies. *Lucas!* Prophecies are without a doubt one of the most villainous tricks which rascals like you play upon honest men. Magic cannot see into the future and magicians who claimed otherwise were liars. *Lucas!*"

Vinculus looked round. "I hear you have all the books that were ever written upon magic," he said, "and it is commonly reported that you have even got back the ones that were lost when the library of Alexandria burnt – and know them all by heart, I dare say!"

"Books and papers are the basis of good scholarship and sound knowledge," declared Mr Norrell primly. "Magic is to be put on the same footing as the other disciplines."

Vinculus leaned suddenly forward and bent over Mr Norrell with a look of the most intense, burning concentration. Without quite meaning to, Mr Norrell fell silent and he leaned towards Vinculus to hear whatever Vinculus was about to confide to him.

"*I reached out my hand,*" whispered Vinculus, "*England's rivers turned and flowed the other way . . .*"

"I beg your pardon?"

"*I reached out my hand,*" said Vinculus, a little louder, "*my enemies's blood stopt in their veins . . .*" He straightened himself, opened wide his arms and closed his eyes as if in a religious ecstasy of some sort. In a strong, clear voice full of passion he continued:

"*I reached out my hand; thought and memory flew out of my enemies' heads like a flock of starlings;*
My enemies crumpled like empty sacks.
I came to them out of mists and rain;
I came to them in dreams at midnight;
I came to them in a flock of ravens that filled a northern sky at dawn;
When they thought themselves safe I came to them in a cry that broke the silence of a winter wood . . ."

"Yes, yes!" interrupted Mr Norrell. "Do you really suppose that this sort of nonsense is new to me? Every madman on every street-corner screams out the same threadbare gibberish and every vagabond with a yellow curtain tries to make himself mysterious by reciting something of the sort. It is in every third-rate book on magic published in the last two hundred years! 'I came to them in a flock of ravens!' What does that *mean*, I should like to know? Who came to whom in a flock of ravens? *Lucas!*"

Vinculus ignored him. His strong voice overpowered Mr Norrell's weak, shrill one.

> "*The rain made a door for me and I went through it;*
> *The stones made a throne for me and I sat upon it;*
> *Three kingdoms were given to me to be mine forever;*
> *England was given to me to be mine forever.*
> *The nameless slave wore a silver crown;*
> *The nameless slave was a king in a strange country . . .*"

"Three kingdoms!" exclaimed Mr Norrell. "Ha! Now I understand what this nonsense pretends to be! A prophecy of the Raven King! Well, I am sorry to tell you that if you hope to impress me by recounting tales of that gentleman you will be disappointed. Oh, yes, you are entirely mistaken! There is no magician whom I detest more!"[1]

> "*The weapons that my enemies raised against me are venerated in Hell as holy relics;*
> *Plans that my enemies made against me are preserved as holy texts;*
> *Blood that I shed upon ancient battlefields is scraped from the stained earth by Hell's sacristans and placed in a vessel of silver and ivory.*
> *I gave magic to England, a valuable inheritance*

---

[1] The Raven King was traditionally held to have possessed three kingdoms: one in England, one in Faerie and one, a strange country on the far side of Hell.

But Englishmen have despised my gift

Magic shall be written upon the sky by the rain but they shall not be able to read it;

Magic shall be written on the faces of the stony hills but their minds shall not be able to contain it;

In winter the barren trees shall be a black writing but they shall not understand it . . ."

"It is every Englishman's birthright to be served by competent and well-educated magicians," interrupted Mr Norrell. "What do you offer them instead? Mystical ramblings about stones and rain and trees! This is like Godbless who told us that we should learn magic from wild beasts in the forest. Why not pigs in the sty? Or stray dogs, I wonder? This is not the sort of magic which civilized men wish to see practised in England nowadays!" He glared furiously at Vinculus and, as he did so, something caught his eye.

Vinculus had dressed himself with no particular care. His dirty neckcloth had been negligently wound about his neck and a little gap of unclean skin shewed between neckcloth and shirt. In that space was a curious curving mark of a vivid blue, not unlike the upward stroke of a pen. It might have been a scar – the relic of a street brawl perhaps – but what it most resembled was that barbaric painting of the skin which is practised by the natives of the South Sea islands. Curiously Vinculus, who was able to stand entirely at his ease in another man's house railing at him, seemed embarrassed by this mark and when he saw that Mr Norrell had observed it he put his hand to his throat and plucked at the cloth to hide it.

"Two magicians shall appear in England . . ."

A sort of exclamation broke from Mr Norrell, an exclamation that began as a cry and ended as a soft, unhappy sigh.

"The first shall fear me; the second shall long to behold me;
The first shall be governed by thieves and murderers; the second shall conspire at his own destruction;

The first shall bury his heart in a dark wood beneath the snow, yet still feel its ache;
The second shall see his dearest possession in his enemy's hand . . ."

"Oh! Now I know that you have come here with no other aim but to wound me! False Magician, you are jealous of my success! You cannot destroy my magic and so you are determined to blacken my name and destroy my peace . . ."

"The first shall pass his life alone; he shall be his own gaoler;
The second shall tread lonely roads, the storm above his head, seeking a dark tower upon a high hillside . . ."

Just then the door opened and two men ran in.

"Lucas! Davey!" screeched Mr Norrell, hysterically. "Where have you been?"

Lucas began to explain something about the bell-cord.

"What? Seize hold of him! Quickly!"

Davey, Mr Norrell's coachman, was built on the same generous scale as others of his profession and had the strength that comes from daily opposing his will to that of four high-bred coach-horses in the prime of life. He took hold of Vinculus around his body and his throat. Vinculus struggled energetically. He did not neglect in the meantime to continue berating Mr Norrell:

"I sit upon a black throne in the shadows but they shall not see me.
The rain shall make a door for me and I shall pass through it;
The stones shall make a throne for me and I shall sit upon it . . ."

Davey and Vinculus careered against a little table upsetting a pile of books that stood upon it.

"Aaaah! Be careful!" exclaimed Mr Norrell, "For God's sake be careful! He will knock over that ink pot! He will damage my books!"

Lucas joined Davey in endeavouring to pinion Vinculus's wild, windmilling arms, while Mr Norrell scampered round the library a great deal faster than any one had seen him move for many years, gathering up books and putting them out of harm's way.

"*The nameless slave shall wear a silver crown,*" gasped Vinculus – Davey's arm tightening about his throat rendered his oration decidedly less impressive than before. Vinculus made one last effort and pulled the upper part of his body free of Davey's grasp and shouted, "*The nameless slave shall be a king in a strange country . . .*" Then Lucas and Davey half-pulled, half-carried him out of the room.

Mr Norrell went and sat down in the chair by the fire. He picked up his book again but he found that he was a great deal too agitated to return to his reading. He fidgeted about, bit his fingernails, walked about the room, returned constantly to those volumes which had been displaced in the struggle and examined them for signs of damage (there were none), but most of all he went to the windows and peered out anxiously to see if any one was watching the house. At three o'clock the room began to grow dusky. Lucas returned to light the candles and mend the fire and just behind him was Childermass.

"Ah!" cried Mr Norrell. "At last! Have you heard what happened? I am betrayed on all sides! Other magicians keep watch upon me and plot my downfall! My idle servants forget their duties. It is a matter of complete indifference to them whether my throat is cut or not! And as for you, you villain, you are the very worst of all! I tell you this man appeared so suddenly in the room – *as if by magic!* And when I rang the bell and cried out *no one came!* You must put aside all your other work. Your only task now is to discover what spells this man employed to gain entry to the house! Where did he learn his magic? What does he know?"

Childermass gave his master an ironical look. "Well, if that is my only task, it is done already. There was no magic. One of the kitchenmaids left the pantry window open and the sorcerer climbed in and crept about the house until he found you. That is all. No one came because he had cut the bell-cord and Lucas and the others did not hear you shout. They heard nothing until he started to rant and then they came immediately. Is that not so, Lucas?"

Lucas, kneeling at the hearth with the poker in his hand, agreed that that was exactly how it had been. "And so I tried to tell you, sir. Only you would not listen."

But Mr Norrell had worked himself up into such a frenzy of anxiety over Vinculus's supposed magical powers that this explanation had at first little power to soothe him. "Oh!" he said. "But still I am certain he means me harm. Indeed he has done me great harm already."

"Yes," agreed Childermass, "very great harm! For while he was in the pantry he ate three meat-pies."

"And two cream cheeses," added Lucas.

Mr Norrell was forced to admit to himself that this did not seem much like the actions of a great magician, but still he could not be entirely easy until he had vented his anger upon someone. Childermass and Lucas being most conveniently to hand, he began with them and treated them to a long speech, full of invective against Vinculus as the greatest villain who ever lived and ending with several strong hints about the bad ends that impudent and neglectful servants came to.

Childermass and Lucas, who had been obliged to listen to something of this sort practically every week since they had entered Mr Norrell's service, felt no particular alarm, but merely waited until their master had talked out his displeasure, whereupon Childermass said: "Leaving aside the pies and cheeses, he has put himself to a great deal of trouble and risked a hanging to pay you this visit. What did he want?"

"Oh! To deliver a prophecy of the Raven King's. Hardly an original idea. It was quite as impenetrable as such ramblings generally are. There was something about a battlefield and something about a throne and something about a silver crown, but the chief burden of what he had to say was to boast of another magician – by which I suppose he meant himself."

Now that Mr Norrell was reassured that Vinculus was not a terrible rival he began to regret that he had ever been led on to argue with him. It would have been far better, he thought, to maintain a lofty and magisterial silence. He comforted himself with the reflection that Vinculus had looked a great deal less imposing when Lucas and Davey were dragging him from the room. Gradually this thought and the consciousness of his own infinitely superior education and abilities began to make him feel comfortable again. But alas! such comfort was short-lived. For, on taking up *The Language of Birds* again, he came upon the following passage:

> . . . *There is nothing else in magic but the wild thought of the bird as it casts itself into the void. There is no creature upon the earth with such potential for magic. Even the least of them may fly straight out of this world and come by chance to the Other Lands. Where does the wind come from that blows upon your face, that fans the pages of your book? Where the harum-scarum magic of small wild creatures meets the magic of Man, where the language of the wind and the rain and the trees can be understood, there we will find the Raven King* . . . [2]

The next time that Mr Norrell saw Lord Portishead (which happened two days later) he immediately went up to his lordship and addressed him with the following words: "I hope, my lord, that you will have some very sharp things to say about Thomas Lanchester in the periodical. For years I have admired *The Language of Birds* as a valiant attempt to place before the reader a clear and comprehensive description of the magic of the *Aureate* magicians, but upon closer examination I find his writing is tainted with their worst characteristics . . . He is mystical, my lord! He is mystical!"

---

[2] Thomas Lanchester, *Treatise concerning the Language of Birds*, Chapter 6.

14

Heart-break Farm

January 1808

SOME THIRTY YEARS before Mr Norrell arrived in London with a plan to astonish the world by restoring English magic, a gentleman named Laurence Strange came into his inheritance. This comprised a house in an almost ruinous state, some barren lands and a mountain of debts and mortgages. These were grave ills indeed, but, thought Laurence Strange, they were nothing that the acquisition of a large sum of money might not cure; and so like many other gentlemen before and after him, he made it his business to be particularly agreeable to heiresses whenever he met with any, and, being a handsome man with elegant manners and a clever way of talking, in no time at all he had captivated a Miss Erquistoune, a young Scottish lady with £900 a year.

With the money Miss Erquistoune brought him, Laurence Strange repaired his house, improved his lands and repaid his debts. Soon he began to make money instead of owing it. He extended his estate and lent out money at fifteen per cent. In these and other similar pursuits he found occupation for every waking hour. He could no longer be at the trouble of shewing his bride much attention. Indeed he made it quite plain that her society and conversation were irksome to him; and she, poor thing, had a very hard time of it. Laurence Strange's estate was in Shropshire, in a retired part of the country near the Welsh border. Mrs Strange knew no one there. She was accustomed to city life, to Edinburgh balls and Edinburgh shops and the clever conversation of her Edinburgh friends; the sight of the high, gloomy hills forever shrouded in Welsh rain was very dispiriting. She bore with this lonely existence for five years, before dying of a chill she had caught while taking a solitary walk on those same hills in a storm.

Mr and Mrs Strange had one child who was, at the time of his mother's death, about four years of age. Mrs Strange had not been buried more than a few days when this child became the subject of a violent quarrel between Laurence Strange and his late wife's family. The Erquistounes maintained that in accordance with the terms of the marriage settlement a large part of Mrs Strange's fortune must now be put aside for her son for him to inherit at his majority. Laurence Strange – to no one's very great surprize – claimed that every penny of his wife's money was his to do with as he liked. Both parties consulted lawyers and two separate lawsuits were started, one in the Doctors Commons in London and one in the Scottish courts. The two lawsuits, Strange *versus* Erquistoune and Erquistoune *versus* Strange, went on for years and years and during this time the very sight of his son became displeasing to Laurence Strange. It seemed to him that the boy was like a boggy field or a copse full of diseased trees – worth money on paper but failing to yield a good annual return. If English law had entitled Laurence Strange to sell his son and buy a better one, he probably would have done it.[1]

Meanwhile the Erquistounes realized that Laurence Strange had it in his power to make his son every bit as unhappy as his wife had been, so Mrs Strange's brother wrote urgently to Laurence Strange suggesting that the boy spend some part of every year at his own house in Edinburgh. To Mr Erquistoune's great surprize, Mr Strange made no objection.[2]

---

[1] Eventually, both lawsuits were decided in favour of Laurence Strange's son.
[2] Upon the contrary Laurence Strange congratulated himself on avoiding paying for the boy's food and clothes for months at a time. So may a love of money make an intelligent man small-minded and ridiculous.

So it was that Jonathan Strange spent half of every year of his childhood at Mr Erquistoune's house in Charlotte-square in Edinburgh, where, it is to be presumed, he learnt to hold no very high opinion of his father. There he received his early education in the company of his three cousins, Margaret, Maria and Georgiana Erquistoune.[3] Edinburgh is certainly one of the most civilized cities in the world and the inhabitants are full as clever and as fond of pleasure as those of London. Whenever he was with them Mr and Mrs Erquistoune did everything they could to make him happy, hoping in this way to make up for the neglect and coldness he met with at his father's house. And so it is not to be wondered at if he grew up a little spoilt, a little fond of his own way and a little inclined to think well of himself.

Laurence Strange grew older and richer, but no better.

A few days before Mr Norrell's interview with Vinculus, a new manservant came to work at Laurence Strange's house. The other servants were very ready with help and advice: they told the new manservant that Laurence Strange was proud and full of malice, that everybody hated him, that he loved money beyond any thing, and that he and his son had barely spoken to each other for years and years. They also said that he had a temper like the devil and that upon no account whatsoever must the new manservant do any thing to offend him, or things would go the worse for him.

The new manservant thanked them for the information and promised to remember what they had said. But what the other servants did not know was that the new manservant had a temper to rival Mr Strange's own; that he was sometimes sarcastic, often rude, and that he had a very high opinion of his own abilities and a correspondingly low one of other people's. The new manservant did not mention his failings to the other servants for the simple

---

[3] Strange's biographer, John Segundus, observed on several occasions how Strange preferred the society of clever women to that of men. *Life of Jonathan Strange*, pub. John Murray, London, 1820.

reason that he knew nothing of them. Though he often found himself quarrelling with his friends and neighbours, he was always puzzled to discover the reason and always supposed that it must be their fault. But in case you should imagine that this chapter will treat of none but disagreeable persons, it ought to be stated at once that, whereas malice was the beginning and end of Laurence Strange's character, the new manservant was a more natural blend of light and shade. He possessed a great deal of good sense and was as energetic in defending others from real injury as he was in revenging imaginary insults to himself.

Laurence Strange was old and rarely slept much. Indeed it would often happen that he found himself more lively at night than during the day and he would sit up at his desk, writing letters and conducting his business. Naturally one of the servants always sat up as well, and a few days after he had first entered the household, this duty fell to the new manservant.

All went well until a little after two o'clock in the morning when Mr Strange summoned the new manservant and asked him to fetch a small glass of sherry-wine. Unremarkable as this request was, the new manservant did not find it at all easy to accomplish. Having searched for the sherry-wine in the usual places, he was obliged to wake first the maid, and ask her where the butler's bedroom might be, and next the butler and ask him where the sherry-wine was kept. Even then the new manservant had to wait some moments more while the butler talked out his surprize that Mr Strange should ask for sherry-wine, a thing he hardly ever took. Mr Strange's son, Mr Jonathan Strange – added the butler for the new manservant's better understanding of the household – was very fond of sherry-wine and generally kept a bottle or two in his dressing-room.

In accordance with the butler's instructions the new manservant fetched the sherry-wine from the cellars – a task which involved much lighting of candles, much walking down long stretches of dark, cold passage-ways, much brushing dirty old

162

cobwebs from his clothes, much knocking of his head against rusty old implements hanging from musty old ceilings, and much wiping of blood and dirt from his face afterwards. He brought the glass to Mr Strange who drank it straight down and asked for another.

The new manservant felt that he had seen enough of the cellars for one night and so, remembering what the butler had said, he went upstairs to the dressing-room of Mr Jonathan Strange. Entering cautiously he found the room apparently unoccupied, but with candles still burning. This did not particularly surprize the new manservant who knew that conspicuous among the many vices peculiar to rich, unmarried gentlemen is wastefulness of candles. He began to open drawers and cupboards, pick up chamber-pots and look into them, look under tables and chairs, and peer into flower-vases. (And if you are at all surprized by all the places into which the new manservant looked, then all I can say is that he had more experience of rich, unmarried gentlemen than you do, and knew that their management of household affairs is often characterized by a certain eccentricity.) He found the bottle of sherry-wine, much as he had expected, performing the office of a boot-jack inside one of its owner's boots.

As the new manservant poured the wine into the glass, he happened to glance into a mirror that was hanging on the wall and discovered that the room was was not, after all, empty. Jonathan Strange was seated in a high-backed, high-shouldered chair watching every thing that the new manservant did with a look of great astonishment upon his face. The new manservant said not a word in explanation – for what explanation could he have given that a gentleman would have listened to? A servant would have understood him in an instant. The new manservant left the room.

Since his arrival in the house the new manservant had entertained certain hopes of rising to a position of authority over the other servants. It seemed to him that his superior intellects and greater experience of the world made him a natural lieutenant for the two Mr Stranges in any difficult business they might have; in his fancy they already said to him such things as: "As you know, Jeremy, these are serious matters, and I dare not trust any one but you with their execution." It would be going too far to say that he immediately abandoned these hopes, but he could not disguise from himself that Jonathan Strange had not seemed greatly pleased to discover someone in his private apartment pouring wine from his private supply.

Thus the new manservant entered Laurence Strange's writing-room with fledgling ambition frustrated and spirits dangerously irritated. Mr Strange drank the second glass of sherry straight down and remarked that he thought he would have another. At this the new manservant gave a sort of strangled shout, pulled his own hair and cried out, "Then why in God's name, you old fool, did you not say so in the first place? I could have brought you the bottle!"

Mr Strange looked at him in surprize and said mildly that of course there was no need to bring another glass if it was such a world of trouble to him.

The new manservant went back to the kitchen (wondering as he did so, if in fact he had been a little curt). A few minutes later the bell sounded again. Mr Strange was sitting at his desk with a letter in his hand, looking out through the window at the pitch-black, rainy night. "There is a man that lives up on the hill opposite," he said, "and this letter, Jeremy, must be delivered to him before break of day."

Ah! thought the new manservant, how quickly it begins! An urgent piece of business that must be conducted under the cover of night! What can it mean? – except that already he has begun to prefer *my* assistance to that of the others. Greatly flattered he declared eagerly that he would go straightaway and took the letter which bore only the enigmatic legend, "Wyvern". He inquired if the house had a name, so that he might ask someone if he missed his way.

Mr Strange began to say that the house had no name, but then he stopt himself and laughed. "You must ask for Wyvern of Heart-break Farm," he said. He told the new manservant that he must leave the high-road by a broken wicket that stood opposite Blackstock's ale-house; behind the wicket he would find a path that would take him straight to Heart-break Farm.

So the new manservant fetched a horse and a stout lantern and rode out on to the high-road. It was a dismal night. The air was a great confusion of noisy wind and bitter, driving rain which got into all the gaps in his clothing so that he was very soon chilled to death.

The path that began opposite Blackstock's ale-house and wound up the hill was fearfully overgrown. Indeed it scarcely deserved the name of "path", for young saplings grew in the middle of it, which the strong wind took and turned into rods to lash the new manservant as he struggled past. By the time he had travelled half a mile he felt as if he had fought several strong men one after the other (and being a hot-headed sort of person who was always getting into quarrels in public places it was a sensation perfectly familiar to him). He cursed Wyvern for a negligent, idle fellow who could not even keep his hedges in order. It was only after an hour or so that he reached a place which might have been a field once, but which was now a wilderness of briars and brambles and he began to regret that he had not brought an axe with him. He left the horse tied to a tree and tried to push his way through. The thorns were large, sharp and plentiful; several times he found himself pinned into the briar-bushes in so many places and in such an elaborate fashion (an arm up here, a leg twisted behind him) that he began to despair of ever getting out again. It seemed odd that any one could live behind such a high hedge of thorns, and he began to think that it would be no great surprize to discover that Mr Wyvern had been asleep for a hundred years or so. Well, I shall not mind *that* so much, he thought, so long as I am not expected to kiss him.

As a sad, grey dawn broke over the hillside he came upon a

ruined cottage which did not so much seem to have broken its heart, as its neck. The chimney wall sagged outwards in a great bow and the chimney tottered above it. A landslide of stone tiles from the roof had left holes where the timbers shewed like ribs. Elder-trees and thorn-bushes filled the interior and, in the vigour of their growth, had broken all the windows and pushed the doors out of the door-frames.

The new manservant stood in the rain for some time contemplating this dismal sight. On looking up he saw someone striding down the hillside towards him; a fairy-tale figure with a large and curious hat upon his head and a staff in his hand. As the figure drew closer it proved to be a yeoman-farmer, a sensible-looking man whose fantastic appearance was entirely due to his having folded a piece of canvas about his head to keep the rain off.

He greeted the new manservant thus: "Man! What have you done to yourself? You are all over blood and your good clothes are in tatters!"

The new manservant looked down at himself and discovered this was true. He explained that the path was overgrown and full of thorns.

The farmer looked at him in amazement. "But there is a good road," he cried, "not a quarter of a mile to the west that you could have walked in half the time! Who in the world directed you to come by that old path?"

The new manservant did not answer but instead asked if the farmer knew where Mr Wyvern of Heart-break Farm might be found?

"That is Wyvern's cottage, but he has been dead five years. Heart-break Farm, you say? Who told you it was called that? Someone has been playing tricks upon you. Old paths, Heart-break Farm indeed! But then I dare say it is as good a name as any; Wyvern did indeed break his heart here. He had the misfortune, poor fellow, to own some land which a gentleman in the valley took a fancy to and when Wyvern would not sell it, the gentleman sent ruffians in the middle of the night to dig up all the beans and carrots and cabbages that Wyvern had planted and when that did not work he put lawsuits upon him – poor Wyvern knew nothing of the law and could not make head or tail of it."

The new manservant thought about this for a moment. "And I fancy," he said at last, "that I could tell you the name of that gentleman."

"Oh!" said the farmer. "Anyone could do that." He looked a little closer at the new manservant. "Man," he said, "you are white as a milk pudding and shivering fit to break yourself in pieces!"

"I am cold," said the new manservant.

Then the farmer (who said his name was Bullbridge) was very pressing with the new manservant to return with him to his own fireside where he could warm himself and take something to eat and drink, and perhaps lie down a spell. The new manservant thanked him but said he was cold, that was all.

So Bullbridge led the new manservant back to his horse (by a way which avoided the thorns) and shewed him the proper way to the road and then the new manservant went back to Mr Strange's house.

A bleak, white sun rose in a bleak, white sky like an allegorical picture of despair and, as he rode, it seemed to the new manservant that the sun was poor Wyvern and that the sky was Hell, and that Wyvern had been put there by Mr Strange to be tormented for ever.

Upon his return the other servants gathered about him. "Ah, lad!" cried the butler in his concern. "What a sight you are! Was it the sherry-wine, Jeremy? Did you make him angry over the sherry-wine?"

The new manservant toppled off the horse on to the ground. He grasped the butler's coat and begged the butler to bring him a fishing-rod, explaining that he needed it to fish poor Wyvern out of Hell.

From this and other such coherent speeches the other servants quickly deduced that he had taken a cold and was feverish. They put him to bed and sent a man for the physician. But Laurence Strange got to hear about it and he sent a second messenger after the first to tell the physician he was not wanted. Next Laurence Strange said that he thought he would take some gruel and told the butler that he wanted the new manservant to bring it to him. This prompted the butler to go in search of Mr Jonathan Strange, to beg him to do something, but Jonathan Strange had, it seemed, got up early to ride to Shrewsbury and was not expected back until the following day. So the servants were obliged to get the new manservant out of bed, dress him, put the tray of gruel into his unresisting hand, and push him through the door. All day long Mr Strange maintained a steady succession of minor requests, each of which – and Mr Strange was most particular about this – was for the new manservant to carry out.

By nightfall the new manservant was as hot to the touch as a iron kettle and talked wildly of oyster-barrels. But Mr Strange declared his intention of sitting up another night and said that the new manservant should wait upon him in the writing-room.

The butler pleaded bravely with his master to let him sit up instead.

"Ah! but you cannot conceive what a fancy I have taken to this fellow," said Mr Strange, his eyes all bright with dislike, "and how I wish to have him always near me. You think he does not look well? In *my* opinion he only wants fresh air." And so saying he unfastened the window above his writing-table. Instantly the room became bitter-cold and a handful of snow flakes blew in from outside.

The butler sighed, and propped the new manservant (who had begun to fall down again) more securely against the wall, and secretly put hand-warmers in his pockets.

At midnight the maid went in to take Mr Strange some gruel. When she returned to the kitchen she reported that Mr Strange had found the hand-warmers and taken them out and put them on the table. The servants went sorrowfully to bed, convinced that the new manservant would be dead by morning.

Morning came. The door to Mr Strange's writing-room was closed. Seven o'clock came and no one rang the bell for the servant; no one appeared. Eight o'clock came. Nine o'clock. Ten. The servants wrung their hands in despair.

But what they had forgot – what, indeed, Laurence Strange had forgot – was that the new manservant was a young, strong man, whereas Laurence Strange was an old one – and some of what the new manservant had been made to suffer that night, Laurence Strange had been forced to share. At seven minutes past ten the butler and the coachman ventured in together and found the new manservant upon the floor fast asleep, his fever gone. On the other side of the room, seated at his writing-table was Laurence Strange, frozen to death.

When the events of those two nights became more generally known there was a great curiosity to see the new manservant, such as there might be to see a dragonslayer or a man who had toppled a giant. Of course the new manservant was glad to be thought remarkable, and as he told and re-told the story he discovered that what he had *actually* said to Mr Strange when he asked for the third glass of sherry-wine was: "Oh! it may suit you very well now, you wicked old sinner, to abuse honest men and drive them into their graves, but a day is coming – and not far off either – when you shall have to answer for every sigh you have forced from an honest man's breast, every tear you have wrung from a widow's eye!" Likewise it was soon well known in the neighbourhood that when Mr Strange had opened the window with the kind intention of starving the new manservant to death with cold the new manservant had cried out, "Cold at first, Laurence Strange, but hot at last! Cold at first, hot at last!" – a prophetic reference to Mr Strange's present situation.

15

"How is Lady Pole?"

January 1808

"How is Lady Pole?"

In every part of the Town and among all stations and degrees of citizen the question was to be heard. In Covent-garden at break of dawn, costermongers asked flower-girls, "How is Lady Pole?". In Ackermann's in the Strand, Mr Ackermann himself inquired of his customers (members of the nobility and persons of distinction) whether they had any news of Lady Pole. In the House of Commons during dull speeches, Members of Parliament whispered the question to their neighbours (each regarding Sir Walter out of the corner of his eye as he did so). In Mayfair dressing-rooms in the early hours of the morning, maids begged their mistresses' pardons, ". . . but was Lady Pole at the party tonight? And how is her ladyship?"

And so the question went round and round; "How is Lady Pole?"

And, "Oh!" (came back the reply), "her ladyship is very well, exceedingly well."

Which demonstrates the sad poverty of the English language, for her ladyship was a great deal more than well. Next to her ladyship every other person in the world looked pale, tired, half-dead. The extraordinary energy she had exhibited the morning after her resurrection had never left her; when she took her walk people stared to see a lady get on so fast. And as for the footman who was meant to attend her, he, poor fellow, was generally many yards in the rear, red-faced and breathless. The Secretary of War, coming out of Drummond's in Charing Cross one morning, was brought into sudden and unexpected conjunction with her ladyship walking rapidly along the street and was quite overturned. She helped him to his feet, said she hoped she had not hurt him and was gone before he could think of a reply.

Like every other young lady of nineteen Lady Pole was wild for dancing. She would dance every dance at a ball without ever once losing her breath and was dismayed that everyone went away so soon. "It is ridiculous to call such a half-hearted affair a ball!" she told Sir Walter. "We have had scarcely three hours dancing!" And she marvelled too at the frailty of the other dancers. "Poor things! I pity them."

Her health was drunk by the Army, the Navy and the Church. Sir Walter Pole was regularly named as the most fortunate man in the Kingdom and Sir Walter himself was quite of the same opinion. Miss Wintertowne – poor, pale, sick Miss Wintertowne – had excited his compassion, but Lady Pole, in a constant glow of extraordinary good health and happy spirits, was the object of his admiration. When she accidentally knocked the Secretary of War to the ground he thought it the best joke in the world and spoke of it to everyone he met. He privately confided to Lady Winsell, his particular friend, that her ladyship was exactly the wife to suit him – so clever, so lively, so everything he could have wished for. He was particularly struck by her independent opinions.

"She advised me last week that the Government ought not to send money and troops to the King of Sweden – which is what we have decided – but instead to lend our support to the Governments of Portugal and Spain and make these countries the bases of our operations against Buonaparte. At nineteen, to have thought so deeply upon all manner of things and to have come to so many conclusions about them! At nineteen, to contradict all the Government so boldly! Of course I told her that she ought to be in Parliament!"

Lady Pole united in one person all the different fascinations of Beauty, Politics, Wealth and *Magic*. The fashionable world had no doubt but that she was destined to become one of its most brilliant leaders. She had been married almost three months now; it was time to embark upon the course that Destiny and the fashionable world had marked out for her. Cards were sent out for a magnificent dinner-party to be held in the second week of January.

The first dinner-party of a bride's career is a momentous occasion, entailing a world of small anxieties. The accomplishments which have won her acclaim in the three years since she left the schoolroom are no longer enough. It is no longer enough to dress exquisitely, to chuse jewels exactly appropriate to the occasion, to converse in French, to play the pianoforte and sing. Now she must turn her attention to French cooking and French wines. Though other people may advise her upon these important matters, her own taste and inclinations must guide her. She is sure to despise her mother's style of entertaining and wish to do things differently. In London fashionable people dine out four, five times a week. However will a new bride – nineteen years old and scarcely ever in a kitchen before – think of a meal to astonish and delight such jaded palates?

Then there are the servants. In the new bride's new house the footmen are all new to their business. If something is needed quickly – candles, a different sort of fork, a heavy cloth in which to carry a hot soup tureen – will they be able to find it? In the case of Lady Pole's establishment at no. 9 Harley-street the problems were multiplied threefold. Half of the servants were from Northamptonshire – from her ladyship's estate at Great Hitherden – and half were newly hired in London; and as everybody knows there is a world of difference between country servants and London servants. It is not a matter of duties exactly. Servants must cook and clean and fetch and carry in Northamptonshire just as in

London. No, the distinction lies more in the manner in which those duties are carried out. Say a country squire in Northamptonshire visits his neighbour. The visit over, the footman fetches the squire's greatcoat and helps the squire on with it. While he is doing so it is only natural for the footman to inquire respectfully after the squire's wife. The squire is not in the least offended and responds with some inquiries of his own. Perhaps the squire has heard that the footman's grandmother fell over and hurt herself while cutting cabbages in her garden and he wishes to know if she is recovered. The squire and the footman inhabit a very small world and have known each other from childhood. But in London this will never do. A London footman must not address his master's guests. He must look as if he did not know there were such things as grand-mothers and cabbages in the world.

At no. 9 Harley-street Lady Pole's country servants were continually ill at ease, afraid of going wrong and never sure of what was right. Even their speech was found fault with and mocked. Their Northamptonshire accent was not always intelligible to the London servants (who, it must be said, made no very great efforts to understand them) and they used words like goosegogs, sparrow-grass, betty-cat and battle-twigs, when they should have said gooseberries, asparagus, she-cat and earwigs.

The London servants delighted in playing tricks on the country servants. They gave Alfred, a young footman, plates of nasty, dirty water and told him it was French soup and bade him serve it up to the other servants at dinner. Often they gave the country servants messages to pass on to the butcher's boy, the baker and the lamplighter. The messages were full of London slang and the country servants could make neither head nor tail of them, but to the butcher's boy, the baker and the lamplighter, who understood them very well, they were both vulgar and insulting. The butcher's boy punched Alfred in the eye on account of what was said to him, while the London servants hid in the larder, to listen and laugh.

Naturally, the country servants complained vigorously to Lady Pole (whom they had known all their lives) about the manner in which they were persecuted and Lady Pole was shocked to find that all her old friends were unhappy in their new home. But she was inexperienced and uncertain how to proceed. She did not doubt the truth of what the country servants said for a moment, but she feared making matters worse.

"What ought I to do, Sir Walter?" she asked.

"Do?" said Sir Walter in surprise. "Do nothing. Leave it all to Stephen Black. By the time Stephen has finished with them they will all be as meek as lambs and as harmonious as blackbirds."

Before his marriage Sir Walter had had only one servant, Stephen Black, and Sir Walter's confidence in this person knew scarcely any bounds. At no. 9 Harley-street he was called "butler", but his duties and responsibilities extended far beyond the range of any ordinary butler: he dealt with bankers and lawyers on Sir Walter's behalf; he studied the accounts of Lady Pole's estates and reported to Sir Walter upon what he found there; he hired servants and workmen without reference to any one else; he directed their work and paid bills and wages.

Of course in many households there is a servant who by virtue of his exceptional intelligence and abilities is given authority beyond what is customary. But in Stephen's case it was all the more extraordinary since Stephen was a negro. I say "extraordinary", for is it not generally the case that a negro servant is the least-regarded person in a household? No matter how hardworking he or she may be? No matter how clever? Yet somehow Stephen Black had found a way to thwart this universal principle. He had, it is true, certain natural advantages: a handsome face and a tall, well-made figure. It certainly did him no harm that his master was a politician who was pleased to advertise his liberal principles to the world by entrusting the management of his house and business to a black servant.

The other servants were a little surprized to find they were put under a black man – a sort of person that many of them had never even seen before. Some were inclined to be indignant at first and told each other that if he dared to give them an order they would return him a very rude answer. But whatever their intentions, they discovered that when they were actually in Stephen's presence they did nothing of the sort. His grave looks, air of authority and reasonable instructions made it very natural to do whatever he told them.

The butcher's boy, the baker, the lamplighter and other similar new acquaintances of the Harley-street servants shewed great interest in Stephen from the first. They asked the Harley-street servants questions about Stephen's mode of life. What did he eat and drink? Who were his friends? Where did he like to go whenever he should happen to be at liberty to go anywhere? When the Harley-street servants replied that Stephen had had three boiled eggs for breakfast, the Secretary at War's Welsh valet was a great friend of his and that he had attended a servants' ball in Wapping the night before, the butcher's boy, the baker and the lamplighter were most grateful for the information. The Harley-street servants asked them why they wished to know. The butcher's boy, the baker and the lamplighter were entirely astonished. Did the Harley-street servants really not know? The Harley-street servants really did not. The butcher's boy, the baker and the lamplighter explained that a rumour had been circulating London for years to the effect that Stephen Black was not really a butler at all. Secretly he was an African prince, the heir to a vast kingdom, and it was well known that as soon as he grew tired of being a butler he would return there and marry a princess as black as himself.

After this revelation the Harley-street servants watched Stephen out of the corners of their eyes and agreed among themselves that nothing was more likely. In fact, was not their own obedience to Stephen the best proof of it? For it was hardly likely that such independent, proud-spirited Englishmen and women would have submitted to the authority of a *black man*, had they not instinctively felt that respect and reverence which a commoner feels for a king!

Meanwhile Stephen Black knew nothing of these curious speculations. He performed his duties diligently as he had always done. He continued to polish silver, train the footmen in the duties of *service à la française*, admonish the cooks, order flowers, linen, knives and forks and do all the thousand and one things necessary to prepare house and servants for the important evening of the magnificent dinner-party. When it finally came, everything was as splendid as his ingenuity could make it. Vases of hot-house roses filled the drawing-room and dining-room and lined the staircase. The dining-table was laid with a heavy white damask cloth and shone with all the separate glitters that silver, glass and candlelight can provide. Two great Venetian mirrors hung upon the wall and on Stephen's instructions these had been made to face each other, so that the reflections doubled and tripled and twice-tripled the silver and the glasses and the candles, and when the guests finally sat down to dinner they appeared to be gently dissolving in a dazzling, golden light like a company of the blessed in glory.

Chief among the guests was Mr Norrell. What a contrast now with that period when he had first arrived in London! Then he had been disregarded – a Nobody. Now he sat among the highest in the land and was courted by them! The other guests continually directed remarks and questions to him and seemed quite delighted by his short, ungracious replies: "I do not know whom you mean," or "I have not the pleasure of that gentleman's acquaintance," or "I have never been to the place you mention."

Some of Mr Norrell's conversation – the more entertaining part – was supplied by Mr Drawlight and Mr Lascelles. They sat upon either side of him, busily conveying his opinions upon modern magic about the table. Magic was a favourite subject that evening. Finding themselves at one and the same time in the presence of England's only magician and of the most famous subject of his magic, the guests could neither think nor talk of any thing else.

Very soon they fell to discussing the numerous claims of successful spells which had sprung up all over the country following Lady Pole's resurrection.

"Every provincial newspaper seems to have two or three reports," agreed Lord Castlereagh. "In the *Bath Chronicle* the other day I read about a man called Gibbons in Milsom-street who awoke in the night because he heard thieves breaking into his house. It seems that this man has a large library of magical books. He tried a spell he knew and turned the housebreakers into mice."

"Really?" said Mr Canning. "And what happened to the mice?"

"They all ran away into holes in the wainscotting."

"Ha!" said Mr Lascelles. "Believe me, my lord, there was no magic. Gibbons heard a noise, feared a housebreaker, said a spell, opened a door and found – not housebreakers, but mice. The truth is, it was mice all along. All of these stories prove false in the end. There is an unmarried clergyman and his sister in Lincoln called Malpas who have made it their business to look into supposed instances of magical occurrences and they have found no truth in any of them."

"They are such admirers of Mr Norrell, this clergyman and his sister!" added Mr Drawlight, enthusiastically. "They are so delighted that such a man has arisen to restore the noble art of English magic! They cannot bear that other people should tell falsehoods and claim to imitate his great deeds! They hate it that other people should make themselves seem important at Mr Norrell's expense! They feel it as a personal affront! Mr Norrell has been so kind as to supply them with certain infallible means of establishing beyond a doubt the falsity of all such claims and Mr Malpas and Miss Malpas drive about the country in their phaeton confounding these imposters!"

"I believe you are too generous to Gibbons, Mr Lascelles," said Mr Norrell in his pedantic fashion. "It is not at all certain that he did not have some malicious purpose in making his false claim. At the very least he lied about his library. I sent Childermass to see it and Childermass says there is not a book earlier than 1760. Worthless! Quite worthless!"

"Yet we must hope," said Lady Pole to Mr Norrell, "that the clergyman and his sister will soon uncover a magician of genuine ability – someone to help you, sir."

"Oh! But there is no one!" exclaimed Drawlight. "No one at all! You see, in order to accomplish his extraordinary deeds Mr Norrell shut himself away for years and years reading books. Alas, such devotion to the interests of one's country is very rare! I assure you there is no one else!"

"But the clergyman and his sister must not give up their search," urged her ladyship. "I know from my own example how much labour is involved in one solitary act of magic. Think how desirable it would be if Mr Norrell were provided with an assistant."

"Desirable yet hardly likely," said Mr Lascelles. "The Malpases have found nothing to suggest that any such person is in existence."

"But by your own account, Mr Lascelles, they have not been looking!" said Lady Pole. "Their object has been to expose false magic, not find new magicians. It would be very easy for them, as they drive about in their phaeton, to make some inquiries as to who does magic and who has a library. I am certain they will not mind the extra trouble. They will be glad to do what they can to help you, sir." (This to Mr Norrell.) "And we shall all hope that they soon succeed, because I think you must feel a little lonely."

In due course a suitable proportion of the fifty or so dishes was deemed to have been eaten and the footmen took away what was left. The ladies withdrew and the gentlemen were left to their wine. But the gentlemen found they had less pleasure in each other's society than usual. They had got to the end of all they had to say about magic. They had no relish for gossiping about their acquaintance and even politics seemed a little dull. In short they felt that they should like to have the pleasure of looking at Lady Pole again, and so they told Sir Walter – rather than asked him – that he missed his wife. He replied that he did not. But this was not allowed to be possible; it was well known that newly married gentlemen were never happy apart from their wives; the briefest of absences could depress a new husband's spirits and interfere with his digestion. Sir Walter's guests asked each other if they thought he looked bilious and they agreed that he did. He denied it. Ah, he was putting a brave face on it, was he? Very good. But clearly it was a desperate case. They would have mercy on him and go and join the ladies.

In the corner by the sideboard Stephen Black watched the gentlemen leave. Three footmen – Alfred, Geoffrey and Robert – remained in the room.

"Are we to go and serve the tea, Mr Black?" inquired Alfred, innocently.

Stephen Black raised one thin finger as a sign they were to stay where they were and he frowned slightly to shew they were to be silent. He waited until he was sure the gentlemen were out of hearing and then he exlaimed, "What in the world was the matter with everyone tonight? Alfred! I know that you have not often been in such company as we have tonight, but that is no reason to forget all your training! I was astonished at your stupidity!"

Alfred mumbled his apologies.

"Lord Castlereagh asked you to bring him *partridges with truffles*. I heard him most distinctly! Yet you brought him a *strawberry jelly*! What were you thinking of?"

Alfred said something rather indistinct in which only the word "fright" was distinguishable.

"You had a fright? What fright?"

"I thought I saw a queer figure standing behind her ladyship's chair."

"Alfred, what are you talking about?"

"A tall person with a head of shining silver hair and a green coat. He was leaning down to look at her ladyship. But the next moment there was no one at all."

"Alfred, look to that end of the room."

"Yes, Mr Black."

"What do you see?"

"A curtain, Mr Black."

"And what else?"

"A chandelier."

"A green velvet curtain and a chandelier ablaze with candles. That is your green-coated, silver-headed person, Alfred. Now go and help Cissie put away the china and do not be so foolish in future." Stephen Black turned to the next footman. "Geoffrey! Your behaviour was every bit as bad as Alfred's. I swear your thoughts were somewhere else entirely. What have you to say for yourself?"

Poor Geoffrey did not answer immediately. He was blinking his eyes and pressing his lips together and generally doing all those things that a man will do when he is trying not to cry. "I am sorry, Mr Black, but it was the music that distracted me."

"What music?" asked Stephen. "There was no music. There! Listen! That is the string quartet just starting up in the drawing-room. They have not played until now."

"Oh, no, Mr Black! I mean the pipe and fiddle that were playing in the next room all the time the ladies and gentlemen were at dinner. Oh, Mr Black! It was the saddest music that I ever heard. I thought it would break my heart!"

Stephen stared at him in perplexity. "I do not understand you," he said. "There was no pipe and fiddle." He turned to the last footman, a solid-looking, dark-haired man of forty or so. "And Robert! I scarcely know what to say to you! Did we not talk yesterday?"

"We did, Mr Black."

"Did I not tell you how much I relied upon you to set an example to the others?"

"Yes, Mr Black."

"Yet half a dozen times this evening you went to the window! What were you thinking of? Lady Winsell was looking round for someone to bring her a clean glass. Your business was at the table, attending to her ladyship's guests, not at the window."

"I am sorry, Mr Black, but I heard a knocking at the window."

"A knocking? What knocking?"

"Branches beating against the glass, Mr Black."

Stephen Black made a little gesture of impatience. "But, Robert, there is no tree near the house! You know very well there is not."

"I thought a wood had grown up around the house," said Robert.

"What?" cried Stephen.

16

Lost-hope

January 1808

T HE SERVANTS IN Harley-street continued to believe that they were haunted by eerie sights and mournful sounds. The cook, John Longridge, and the kitchenmaids were troubled by a sad bell. The effect of the bell, explained John Longridge to Stephen Black, was to bring vividly to mind every-one they had ever known who had died, all the good things they had ever lost and every bad thing which had ever happened to them. Consequently, they had become dejected and low and their lives were not worth living.

Geoffrey and Alfred, the two youngest footmen, were tormented by the sound of the fife and violin which Geoffrey had first heard on the night of the dinner-party. The music always appeared to come from the next room. Stephen had taken them all over the house and proved that nowhere was any one playing any such instruments, but it did no good; they continued afraid and un-happy.

Most bewildering of all, in Stephen's opinion, was the behaviour of Robert, the eldest footman. Robert had struck Stephen from the first as a sensible man, conscientious, reliable – in short the last person in the world to fall prey to imaginary fears. Yet Robert still insisted that he could hear an invisible wood growing up around the house. Whenever he paused in his work, he heard ghostly branches scraping at the walls and tapping upon the windows, and tree-roots slyly extending themselves beneath the foundations and prising apart the bricks. The wood was old, said Robert, and full of malice. A traveller in the wood would have as much to fear from the trees as from another person hiding there.

But, argued Stephen, the nearest wood of any size was four miles away upon Hampstead Heath and even there the trees were quite domesticated. They did not crowd around people's houses and try to destroy them. Stephen could say what he liked; Robert only shook his head and shivered.

Stephen's only consolation was that this peculiar mania had erased all the servants' other differences. The London servants no longer cared that the country servants were slow of speech and had old-fashioned manners. The country servants no longer complained to Stephen that the London servants played tricks upon them and sent them on imaginary errands. All the servants were united by the belief that the house was haunted. They sat in the kitchen after their work was done and told stories of all the other houses that they had ever heard of where there were ghosts and horrors, and of the horrible fates that had befallen the people who lived there.

One evening, about a fortnight after Lady Pole's dinner-party, they were gathered about the kitchen fire, engaged in this favourite occupation. Stephen soon grew tired of listening to them and retired to his own little room to read a newspaper. He had not been there more than a few minutes when he heard a bell ringing. So he put down his newspaper, put on his black coat and went to see where he was wanted.

In the little passage-way that connected the kitchen to the butler's room was a little row of bells and beneath the bells the names of various rooms were neatly inscribed in brown paint: *The Venetian Drawing-room*; *The Yellow Drawing-room*; *The Dining-room*; *Lady Pole's Sitting-room*; *Lady Pole's Bed-chamber*; *Lady Pole's Dressing-room*; *Sir Walter's Study*; *Sir Walter's Bed-chamber*; *Sir Walter's Dressing-room*; *Lost-hope*.

"Lost-hope?" thought Stephen. "What in the world is that?"

He had paid the carpenter that very morning for the work in putting up the bells and he had entered the amount in his account-book: *To Amos Judd, for putting up 9 bells in the kitchen passageway and painting the names of the rooms beneath, 4 shillings.* But now there were ten bells. And the bell for Lost-hope was ringing violently.

"Perhaps," thought Stephen, "Judd means it as a joke. Well, he shall be fetched back tomorrow and made to put it right."

Not knowing quite what else to do, Stephen went up to the ground floor and looked in every room; all were empty. And so he climbed the staircase to the first floor.

At the top of the staircase was a door which he had never seen before.

"Who's there?" whispered a voice from behind the door. It was not a voice Stephen knew and, though it was only a whisper, it was curiously penetrating. It seemed to get into Stephen's head by some other means than his ears.

"There is someone upon stairs!" insisted the whispering voice. "Is it the servant? Come here, if you please! I need you!"

Stephen knocked and went in.

The room was every bit as mysterious as the door. If anyone had asked Stephen to describe it, he would have said it was decorated in the Gothic style – this being the only explanation he could think of to account for its extraordinary appearance. But it had none of the usual Gothic embellishments such as one might see depicted in the pages of Mr Ackermann's *Repository of the Arts*. There were no pointed mediaeval arches, no intricately carved wood, no eccle-siastical motifs. The walls and floor of the room were of plain grey stone, very worn and uneven in places. The ceiling was of vaulted stone. One small window looked out upon a starlit sky. The window had not so much as a scrap of glass in it and the winter wind blew into the room.

A pale gentleman with an extraordinary quantity of silvery, thistle-down hair was looking at his reflection in an old cracked mirror with an air of deep dissatisfaction. "Oh, there you are!" he said, glancing sourly at Stephen. "A person may call and call in this house, but no one comes!"

"I am very sorry, sir," said Stephen, "but no one told me you were here." He supposed the gentleman must be a guest of Sir Walter's or Lady Pole's – which explained the gentleman, but not the room. Gentlemen are often invited to stay in other people's houses. Rooms hardly ever are.

"In what way may I serve you, sir?" asked Stephen.

"How stupid you are!" cried the gentleman with the thistle-down hair. "Don't you know that Lady Pole is to attend a ball tonight at my house? My own servant has run off and hidden himself somewhere. How can I appear by the side of the beautiful Lady Pole in this condition?"

The gentleman had cause for complaint: his face was unshaven, his curious hair was a mass of tangles and he was not dressed, but only wrapped in an old-fashioned powdering gown.

"I shall be with you in an instant, sir," Stephen assured him. "But first I must find the means to shave you. You do not happen to know what your servant has done with the razor, I suppose?"

The gentleman shrugged.

There was no dressing-table in the room. Indeed there was very little furniture of any description. There was the mirror, an old three-legged milking stool and a queer carved chair that appeared to be made of bones. Stephen did not quite believe that they were human bones, although they did look remarkably like it.

Atop the milking stool, next to a pretty little box, Stephen found a delicate silver razor. A battered pewter basin full of water stood upon the floor.

Curiously there was no fireplace in the room, but only a rusting iron brazier full of hot coals, that spilt its dirty ashes on the floor. So Stephen heated the basin of water on the brazier and then he shaved the gentleman. When he had finished, the gentleman inspected his face and pronounced himself excessively pleased.

He removed his gown and stood patiently in his dressing-trousers while Stephen massaged his skin with a bristle-brush. Stephen could not help but observe that, whereas other gentlemen grow red as lobsters under such treatment, this gentleman remained as pale as ever and the only difference was that his skin took on a whitish glow as of moonlight or mother-of-pearl.

His clothes were the finest Stephen had ever seen; his shirt was exquisitely laundered and his boots shone like black mirrors. But best of all were a dozen or so white muslin neckcloths, each as thin as a cobweb and as stiff as music paper.

It took two hours to complete the gentleman's toilet, for he was, Stephen found, extremely vain. During this time the gentleman became more and more delighted with Stephen. "I tell you that my own ignorant fellow has not got half your skill at dressing hair," he declared, "and when it comes to the delicate art of tying a muslin neckcloth, why! he cannot be made to understand it at all!"

"Well, sir, it is exactly the sort of task I like," said Stephen. "I wish I could persuade Sir Walter to take more care of his clothes, but political gentlemen have no leisure for thinking of such things."

Stephen helped the gentleman on with his leaf-green coat (which was of the very best quality and most fashionable cut), then the gentleman went over to the milking stool and picked up the little box that lay there. It was made of porcelain and silver, and was about the size of a snuff box but a little longer than snuff boxes generally are. Stephen made some admiring remark about the colour which was not exactly pale blue and not exactly grey, not precisely lavender and not precisely lilac.

"Yes, indeed! It is beautiful," agreed the gentleman enthusiastically. "And very hard to make. The pigment must be mixed with the tears of spinsters of good family, who must live long lives of impeccable virtue and die without ever having had a day of true happiness!"

"Poor ladies!" said Stephen. "I am glad it is so rare."

"Oh! It is not the tears that make it rare – I have bottles full of those – it is the skill to mix the colour."

The gentleman had by now become so affable, so willing to talk that Stephen had no hesitation in asking him, "And what do you keep in such a pretty little box, sir? Snuff?"

"Oh, no! It is a great treasure of mine that I wish Lady Pole to wear at my ball tonight!" He opened the box and shewed Stephen a small, white finger.

At first this struck Stephen as a little unusual, but his surprize faded in a moment and if any one had questioned him about it just then, he would have replied that gentlemen often carried fingers about with them in little boxes and that this was just one of many examples he had seen.

"Has it been in your family long, sir?" he asked, politely.

"No, not long."

The gentleman snapped shut the box and put it in his pocket.

Together, he and Stephen admired his reflection in the mirror. Stephen could not help but notice how they perfectly complemented each other: gleaming black skin next to opalescent white skin, each a perfect example of a particular type of masculine beauty. Exactly the same thought seemed to strike the gentleman.

"How handsome we are!" he said in a wondering tone. "But I see now that I have made a horrible blunder! I took you for a servant in this house! But that is quite impossible! Your dignity and handsomeness proclaim you to be of noble, perhaps kingly birth! You are a visitor here, I suppose, as I am. I must beg your pardon for imposing upon you and thank you for the great service you have done me in making me ready to meet the beautiful Lady Pole."

Stephen smiled. "No, sir. I am a servant. I am Sir Walter's servant."

The gentleman with the thistle-down hair raised his eye-brow in astonishment. "A man as talented and handsome as yourself ought not be a servant!" he said in a shocked tone. "He ought to be the ruler of a vast estate! What is beauty for, I should like to know, if not to stand as a visible sign of one's superiority to everyone else? But I see how it is! Your enemies have conspired together to deprive you of all your possessions and to cast you down among the ignorant and lowly!"

"No, sir. You are mistaken. I have always been a servant."

"Well, I do not understand it," declared the gentleman with the thistle-down hair, with a puzzled shake of his head. "There is some mystery here and I shall certainly look into it just as soon as I am at liberty. But, in the meantime, as a reward for dressing my hair so well and all the other services you have done me, you shall attend my ball tonight."

This was such a very extraordinary proposal that for a moment Stephen did not know quite what to say. "Either he is mad," he thought, "or else he is some sort of radical politician who wishes to destroy all distinctions of rank."

Aloud he said, "I am very sensible of the honour you do me, sir, but only consider. Your other guests will come to your house expecting to meet ladies and gentlemen of their own rank. When they discover that they are consorting with a servant I am sure they will feel the insult very keenly. I thank you for your kindness, but I should not wish to embarrass you or offend your friends."

This seemed to astonish the gentleman with the thistle-down hair even more. "What nobility of feeling!" he cried. "To sacrifice your own pleasure to preserve the comfort of others! Well, it is a thing, I confess, that would never occur to me. And it only increases my determination to make you my friend and do everything in my power to aid you. But you do not quite understand. These guests of mine on whose account you are so scrupulous, they are all my vassals and subjects. There is not one of them who would dare to criticize *me* or any one I chose to call my friend. And if they did, why! we could always kill them! But really," he added as if he were suddenly growing bored of this conversation, "there is very little use debating the point since you are already here!"

With that the gentleman walked away and Stephen found that he was standing in a great hall where a crowd of people were dancing to sad music.

Once again he was a little surprized but, as before, he grew accustomed to the idea in a moment and began to look about him. Despite all that the gentleman with the thistle-down hair had said upon the point, he was a little apprehensive at first that he would be recognized. A few glances about the room were enough to reassure him that there were no friends of Sir Walter present – indeed there was no one Stephen had ever seen before and in his neat black clothes and clean white linen he believed he might very easily pass for a gentleman. He was glad that Sir Walter had never required him to wear livery or a powdered wig, which would have marked him out as a servant in an instant.

Everyone was dressed in the very height of fashion. The ladies wore gowns of the most exquisite colours (though, to own the truth, very few of them were colours that Stephen could remember having seen before). The gentlemen wore knee breeches and white stockings and coats of brown, green, blue and black, their linen was a sparkling, shining white and their kid gloves had not so much as a stain or mark upon them.

But in spite of all the fine clothes and gaiety of the guests, there were signs that the house was not so prosperous as once it had been. The room was dimly lit by an insufficient number of tallow candles, and there was just one viol and one fife to provide the music.

"That must be the music that Geoffrey and Alfred spoke of," thought Stephen. "How odd that I could not hear it before! It is every bit as melancholy as they said."

He made his way to a narrow unglazed window and looked out upon a dark, tangled wood under starlight. "And this must be the wood which Robert talks about. How malevolent it looks! And is there a bell, I wonder?"

"Oh, yes!" said a lady who was standing close by. She wore a gown the colour of storms, shadows and rain and a necklace of broken promises and regrets. He was surprized to find himself addressed by her since he was quite certain that he had not spoken his thoughts out loud.

"There is indeed a bell!" she told him, "It is high up in one of the towers."

She was smiling and regarding him with such frank admiration that Stephen thought it only polite to say something.

"This is certainly a most elegant assembly, madam. I do not know when I last saw so many handsome faces and graceful figures gathered together in one place. And every one of them in the utmost bloom of youth. I confess that I am surprised to see no older people in the room. Have these ladies and gentlemen no mothers and fathers? No aunts or uncles?"

"What an odd remark!" she replied, laughing. "Why should the Master of Lost-hope House invite aged and unsightly persons to his ball? Who would want to look at them? Besides we are not so young as you suppose. England was nothing but dreary wood and barren moor when last we saw our sires and dams. But wait! See! There is Lady Pole!"

Between the dancers Stephen caught a glimpse of her ladyship. She was wearing a blue velvet gown and the gentleman with the thistle-down hair was leading her to the top of the dance.

Then the lady in the gown the colour of storms, shadows and rain inquired if he would like to dance with her.

"Gladly," he said.

When the other ladies saw how well Stephen danced, he found he could have any partner he wished for. After the lady in the gown the colour of storms, shadows and rain he danced with a young woman who had no hair, but who wore a wig of shining beetles that swarmed and seethed upon her head. His third partner complained bitterly whenever Stephen's hand happened to brush against her gown; she said it put her gown off its singing; and, when Stephen looked down, he saw that her gown was indeed covered with tiny mouths which opened and sang a little tune in a series of high, eerie notes.

Although in general the dancers followed the usual custom and changed partners at the end of two dances, Stephen observed that the gentleman with the thistle-down hair danced with Lady Pole the whole night long and that he scarcely spoke to any other person in the room. But he had not forgotten Stephen. Whenever Stephen chanced to catch his eye, the gentleman with the thistle-down hair smiled and bowed his head and gave every sign of wishing to convey that, of all the delightful circumstances of the ball, what pleased him most was to see Stephen Black there.

17

The unaccountable appearance
of twenty-five guineas

January 1808

THE BEST GROCER's in Town is Brandy's in St James's-street. I am not alone in that opinion; Sir Walter Pole's grandfather, Sir William Pole, declined to purchase coffee, chocolate or tea from any other establishment, declaring that in comparison with Mr Brandy's Superfine High Roasted Turkey Coffee, all other coffees had a mealy flavour. It must be said, however, that Sir William Pole's patronage was a somewhat mixed blessing. Though liberal in his praise and always courteous and condescending to the shop-people, he was scarcely ever known to pay a bill and when he died, the amount of money owing to Brandy's was considerable. Mr Brandy, a short-tempered, pinched-faced, cross little old man, was beside himself with rage about it. He died shortly afterwards, and was presumed by many people to have done so on purpose and to have gone in pursuit of his noble debtor.

At Mr Brandy's death, the business came into the possession of his widow. Mr Brandy had married rather late in life and my readers will not be much surprized, I dare say, to learn that Mrs Brandy had not been entirely happy in her marriage. She had quickly discovered that Mr Brandy loved to look at guineas and shillings more than he had ever loved to look at her – though *I* say it must have been a strange sort of man that did not love to look at her, for she was everything that was delightful and amiable, all soft brown curls, light blue eyes and a sweet expression. It would seem to me that an old man, such as Mr Brandy, with nothing to recommend him but his money, ought to have treasured a young, pretty wife, and studied hard to please her in everything he could; but he did not. He had even denied her a house of her own to live in – which was something he could have afforded very easily. So loath had he been to part with a sixpence that he declared they should live in the little room above the shop in St. James's Street, and for the twelve years of her marriage this apartment served Mrs Brandy as parlour, bedroom, dining-parlour and kitchen. But Mr Brandy had not been dead three weeks when she bought a house in Islington, near the Angel, and acquired three maids, whose names were Sukey, Dafney and Delphina.

She also employed two men to attend the customers in the shop. John Upchurch was a steady soul, hard-working and capable. Toby Smith was a red-haired, nervous man whose behaviour often puzzled Mrs Brandy. Sometimes he would be silent and unhappy and at other times he would be suddenly cheerful and full of unexpected confidences. From certain discrepancies in the accounts (such as may occur in any business) and from the circumstances of Toby looking miserable and ill at ease whenever she questioned him about it, Mrs Brandy had begun to fear that he might be pocketing the difference. One January evening her dilemma took a strange turn. She was sitting in her little parlour above the shop when there was a knock upon the door and Toby Smith came shuffling in, quite unable to meet her eye.

"What's the matter, Toby?"

"If you please, ma'am," said Toby looking this way and that, "the money won't come right. John and me have counted it out again and again, ma'am, and cast up the sums a dozen times or more, but we cannot make head or tail of it."

Mrs Brandy tutted and sighed and asked by how much they were out.

"Twenty-five guineas, ma'am."

"Twenty-five guineas!" cried Mrs Brandy in horror. "Twenty-five guineas! How could we possibly have lost so much? Oh! I hope you are mistaken, Toby. Twenty-five guineas! I would not have supposed there to be so much money in the shop! Oh, Toby!" she cried, as another thought struck her. "We must have been robbed!"

"No, ma'am," said Toby. "Beg your pardon, ma'am, but you mistake. I did not mean to say we are twenty-five guineas short. We are over, ma'am. By that amount."

Mrs Brandy stared at him.

"Which you may see for yourself, ma'am," said Toby, "if you will just come down to the shop," and he held the door open for her with an anxious, pleading expression upon his face. So Mrs Brandy ran downstairs into the shop and Toby followed after her.

It was about nine o'clock on a moonless night. The shutters were all put up and John and Toby had extinguished the lamps. The shop ought to have been as dark as the inside of a tea-caddy, but instead it was filled with a soft, golden light which appeared to emanate from something golden which lay upon the counter-top.

A heap of shining guineas was lying there. Mrs Brandy picked up one of the coins and examined it. It was as if she held a ball of soft yellow light with a coin at the bottom of it. The light was odd. It made Mrs Brandy, John and Toby look quite unlike themselves: Mrs Brandy appeared proud and haughty, John looked sly and deceitful and Toby wore an expression of great ferocity. Needless to say, all of these were qualities quite foreign to their characters. But stranger still was the transformation that the light worked upon the dozens of small mahogany drawers that formed one wall of the shop. Upon other evenings the gilt lettering upon the drawers proclaimed the contents to be such things as: *Mace (Blades)*, *Mustard (Unhusked)*, *Nutmegs*, *Ground Fennel*, *Bay Leaves*,

Pepper of Jamaica, *Essence of Ginger*, *Caraway*, *Peppercorns* and *Vinegar* and all the other stock of a fashionable and prosperous grocery business. But now the words appeared to read: *Mercy (Deserved)*, *Mercy (Undeserved)*, *Nightmares*, *Good Fortune*, *Bad Fortune*, *Persecution by Families*, *Ingratitude of Children*, *Confusion*, *Perspicacity* and *Veracity*. It was as well that none of them noticed this odd change. Mrs Brandy would have been most distressed by it had she known. She would not have had the least notion what to charge for these new commodities.

"Well," said Mrs Brandy, "they must have come from somewhere. Has any one sent today to pay their bill?"

John shook his head. So did Toby. "And, besides," added Toby, "no one owes so much, excepting, of course, the Duchess of Worksop and frankly, ma'am, in that case . . ."

"Yes, yes, Toby, that will do," interrupted Mrs Brandy. She thought for a moment. "Perhaps," she said, "some gentleman, wishing to wipe the rain from his face, pulled out his handkerchief, and so caused the money to tumble out of his pocket on to the floor."

"But we did not find it upon the floor," said John, "it was here in the cash-box with all the rest."

"Well," said Mrs Brandy, "I do not know what to say. Did anyone pay with a guinea today?"

No, said Toby and John, no one had paid today with a guinea, let alone twenty-five such guineas or twenty-five such persons.

"And such yellow guineas, ma'am," remarked John, "each one the very twin of all the others, without a spot of tarnish upon any of them."

"Should I run and fetch Mr Black, ma'am?" asked Toby.

"Oh, yes!" said Mrs Brandy, eagerly. "But then again, perhaps no. We ought not to trouble Mr Black unless there is any thing very wrong. And nothing is wrong, is it, Toby? Or perhaps it is. I cannot tell."

The sudden and unaccountable arrival of large sums of money is such a very rare thing in our Modern Age that neither Toby nor John was able to help their mistress decide whether it were a wrong thing or a right.

"But, then," continued Mrs Brandy, "Mr Black is so clever. I dare say he will understand this puzzle in an instant. Go to Harley-street, Toby. Present my compliments to Mr Black and say that if he is at liberty I should be glad of a few moments' conversation with him. No, wait! Do not say that, it sounds so presumptuous. You must apologize for disturbing him and say that whenever he should happen to be at liberty I should be grateful – no, honoured – no, grateful – I should be grateful for a few moments' conversation with him."

Mrs Brandy's acquaintance with Stephen Black had begun when Sir Walter had inherited his grandfather's debts and Mrs Brandy had inherited her husband's business. Every week or so Stephen had come with a guinea or two to help pay off the debt. Yet, curiously, Mrs Brandy was often reluctant to accept the money. "Oh! Mr Black!" she would say, "Pray put the money away again! I am certain that Sir Walter has greater need of it than I. We did such excellent business last week! We have got some carracca chocolate in the shop just at present, which people have been kind enough to say is the best to be had any where in London – infinitely superior to other chocolate in both flavour and texture! – and they have been sending for it from all over Town. Will not you take a cup, Mr Black?"

Then Mrs Brandy would bring the chocolate in a pretty blue-and-white china chocolate-pot, and pour Stephen a cup, and anxiously inquire how he liked it; for it seemed that, even though people had been sending for it from all over Town, Mrs Brandy could not feel quite convinced of its virtues until she knew Stephen's opinion. Nor did her care of him end with making him chocolate. She was solicitous for his health. If it happened to be a cold day, she would be concerned that he was not warm enough; if it were raining she would worry that he might catch a cold; if it were a hot, dry day she would insist that he sit by a window overlooking a little green garden to refresh himself.

When it was time for him to go, she would revive the question of the guinea. "But as to next week, Mr Black, I cannot say. Next week I may need a guinea very badly – people do not always pay their bills – and so I will be so bold as to ask you to bring it again on Wednesday. Wednesday at about three o'clock. I shall be quite disengaged at three o'clock and I shall be sure to have a pot of chocolate ready, as you are so kind as to say you like it very much."

The gentlemen among my readers will smile to themselves and say that women never did understand business, but the ladies may agree with me that Mrs Brandy understood her business very well, for the chief business of Mrs Brandy's life was to make Stephen Black as much in love with her as she was with him.

In due course Toby returned, not with a message from Stephen Black, but with Stephen himself and Mrs Brandy's anxiety about the coins was swept away by a new and altogether more pleasant agitation. "Oh, Mr Black! We did not expect to see you so soon! I did not imagine you would be at liberty!"

Stephen stood in the darkness outside the radiance cast by the strange coins. "It does not matter where I am tonight," he said in a dull tone quite unlike his usual voice. "The house is all at sixes and sevens. Her ladyship is not well."

Mrs Brandy, John and Toby were shocked to hear this. Like every other citizen of London they took a close interest in everything that concerned her ladyship. They prided themselves upon their connexion with all sorts of aristocratic persons, but it was the patronage of Lady Pole which gave them the greatest satisfaction. Nothing pleased them so much as being able to assure people that when Lady Pole sat down to breakfast, her ladyship's roll was spread with Mrs Brandy's preserves and her coffee cup was filled with coffee made with Mrs Brandy's beans.

Mrs Brandy was suddenly struck with a most unpleasant idea.

"I hope her ladyship did not eat something which disagreed with her?" she asked.

"No," said Stephen with a sigh, "it is nothing of that sort. She complains of aches in all her limbs, odd dreams and feeling cold. But mostly she is silent and out of spirits. Her skin is icy to the touch."

Stephen stepped into the queer light.

The strange alterations which it had made to the appearance of Toby, John and Mrs Brandy were nothing to the changes it worked upon Stephen: his native handsomeness increased five-, seven-, tenfold; he acquired an expression of almost supernatural nobility; and, most extraordinary of all, the light somehow seemed to concentrate in a band around his brow so that he appeared to have been crowned with a diadem. Yet, just as before, none of those present noticed anything out of the common.

He turned the coins over in his thin black fingers. "Where were they, John?"

"Here in the cash-box with all the rest of the money. Where in the world can they have come from, Mr Black?"

"I am as puzzled as you are. I have no explanation to offer." Stephen turned to Mrs Brandy. "My chief concern, ma'am, is that you should protect yourself from any suspicion that you have come by the money dishonestly. I think you must give the money to a lawyer. Instruct him to advertise in *The Times* and *The Morning Chronicle* to discover if any one lost twenty-five guineas in Mrs Brandy's shop."

"A lawyer, Mr Black!" cried Mrs Brandy, horrified. "Oh, but that will cost a world of money!"

"Lawyers always do, ma'am."

At that moment a gentleman in St. James's-street passed Mrs Brandy's shop and, discerning a golden radiance shining out of the chinks in the shutters, realized that someone was within. He happened to be in need of tea and sugar and so he knocked upon the door.

"Customer, Toby!" cried Mrs Brandy.

Toby hurried to open the door and John put the money away. The instant that he closed the lid of the cash-box, the room became dark and for the first time they realized that they had been seeing each other by the light of the eerie coins. So John ran around, re-lighting the lamps and making the place look cheerful and Toby weighed out the things which the customer wanted.

Stephen Black sank into a chair and passed his hand across his forehead. He looked grey-faced and tired to death.

Mrs Brandy sat down in the chair next to his and touched his hand very gently. "You are not well, my dear Mr Black."

"It is just that I ache all over – as a man does who has been dancing all night." He sighed again and rested his head upon his hand.

Mrs Brandy withdrew her hand. "I did not know there was a ball last night," she said. There was a tinge of jealousy to her words. "I hope you had a most delightful time. Who were your partners?"

"No, no. There was no ball. I seem to have all the pains of dancing, without having had any of the pleasure." He raised his head suddenly. "Do you hear that?" he asked.

"What, Mr Black?"

"That bell. Tolling for the dead."

She listened a moment. "No, I do not hear any thing. I hope you will stay to supper, my dear Mr Black? It would do us so much honour. I fear it will not be a very elegant meal. There is very little. Hardly anything at all. Just some steamed oysters and a pigeon-pie and a harrico of mutton. But an old friend like you will make allowances, I am sure. Toby can fetch some . . ."

"Are you certain you do not hear it?"

"No."

"I cannot stay." He looked as if he meant to say something more – indeed he opened his mouth to say it, but the bell seemed to intrude itself upon his attention again and he was silent. "Good evening to you!" He rose and, with a rapid half-bow, he walked out.

In St James's-street the bell continued to toll. He walked like a man in a fog. He had just reached Piccadilly when an aproned porter carrying a basket full of fish came very suddenly out of a little alleyway. In trying to get out of the porter's way, Stephen collided with a stout gentleman in a blue coat and a Bedford hat who was standing on the corner of Albemarle-street.

The stout gentleman turned and saw Stephen. Instantly he was all alarm; he saw a black face close to his own face and black hands near his pockets and valuables. He paid no attention to Stephen's expensive clothes and respectable air but, immediately concluding that he was about to be robbed or knocked down, he raised his umbrella to strike a blow in his own defence.

It was the moment that Stephen had dreaded all his life. He supposed that constables would be called and he would be dragged before the magistrates and it was probable that even the patronage and friendship of Sir Walter Pole would not save him. Would an English jury be able to conceive of a black man who did not steal and lie? A black man who was a respectable person? It did not seem very likely. Yet now that his fate had come upon him, Stephen found he did not care very much about it and he watched events unfold as though he were watching a play through thick glass or a scene at the bottom of a pond.

The stout gentleman opened his eyes wide in fright, anger and indignation. He opened his mouth wide to begin accusing Stephen but in that moment he began to change. His body became the trunk of a tree; he suddenly sprouted arms in all directions and all the arms became branches; his face became a bole and he shot up twenty feet; where his hat and umbrella had been there was a thick crown of ivy.

"An oak tree in Piccadilly," thought Stephen, not much interested. "That is unusual."

Piccadilly was changing too. A carriage happened to be passing.

It clearly belonged to someone of importance for as well as the coachman upon his box, two footmen rode behind; there was a coat of arms upon the door and it was drawn by four matched greys. As Stephen watched the horses grew taller and thinner until they seemed about to disappear entirely and at that point they were suddenly transformed into a grove of delicate silver birches. The carriage became a holly bush and the coachman and the footmen became an owl and two nightingales which promptly flew away. A lady and gentleman walking along together suddenly sprouted twigs in every direction and became an elder-bush, a dog became a shaggy clump of dry bracken. The gas lamps that hung above the street were sucked up into the sky and became stars in a fretwork of winter trees and Piccadilly itself dwindled to a barely discernible path through a dark winter wood.

But just as in a dream where the most extraordinary events arrive complete with their own explanation and become reasonable in an instant, Stephen found nothing to be surprised at. Rather, it seemed to him that he had always known that Piccadilly stood in close proximity to a magical wood.

He began to walk along the path.

The wood was very dark and quiet. Above his head the stars were the brightest he had ever seen and the trees were nothing more than black shapes, mere absences of stars.

The thick grey misery and stupidity which had enveloped his mind and spirit all day disappeared and he began to muse upon the curious dream he had the night before about meeting a strange green-coated person with thistle-down hair who had taken him to a house where he had danced all night with the queerest people.

The sad bell sounded much clearer in the wood than it had in London and Stephen followed the sound along the path. In a very short while he came to an immense stone house with a thousand windows. A feeble light shone out of some of these openings. A high wall surrounded the house. Stephen passed through (though he did not quite understand how, for he saw no sign of a gate) and found himself in a wide and dreary courtyard where skulls, broken bones, and rusting weapons were scattered about, as if they had lain there for centuries. Despite the size and grandeur of the house its only entrance was a mean little door and Stephen had to bend low to pass through. Immediately he beheld a vast crowd of people all dressed in the finest clothes.

Two gentlemen stood just inside the door. They wore fine dark coats, spotless white stockings and gloves and dancing pumps. They were talking together, but the moment Stephen appeared, one turned and smiled.

"Ah, Stephen Black!" he said. "We have been waiting for you!"

At that moment the viol and pipe started up again.

18

Sir Walter consults
gentlemen in several professions

February 1808

L ADY POLE SAT by the window, pale and unsmiling. She
said very little and whenever she did say any thing her
remarks were odd and not at all to the point. When her
husband and friends anxiously inquired what the matter was, she
replied that she was sick of dancing and wished to dance no more.
As for music, it was the most detestable thing in the world – she
wondered that she had never realized it before.

Sir Walter regarded this lapse into silence and indifference as
highly alarming. It was altogether too like that illness which had
caused her ladyship so much suffering before her marriage and
ended so tragically in her early death. Had she not been pale
before? Well, she was pale now. Had she not been cold before? She
was so again.

During her ladyship's previous illness no doctor had ever
attended her and naturally doctors everywhere resented this as
an insult to their profession. "Oh!" they cried whenever Lady
Pole's name was mentioned, "the magic which brought her back
to life was no doubt very wonderful, but if only the proper
medicines had been administered in time then there would have
been no need for the magic in the first place."

Mr Lascelles had been right when he declared the fault to be entirely Mrs Wintertowne's. She detested doctors and had never allowed one to come near her daughter. Sir Walter, however, was hindered by no such prejudice; he sent immediately for Mr Baillie.

Mr Baillie was a Scottish gentleman who had long been considered the foremost practitioner of his profession in London. He had written a great many books with important-sounding titles and he was Physician Extraordinary to the King. He had a sensible face and carried a gold-topped stick as a symbol of his pre-eminence. He answered Sir Walter's summons swiftly, eager to prove the superiority of medicine to magic. The examination done, he came out again. Her ladyship was in excellent health, he said. She had not got so much as a cold.

Sir Walter explained again how different she was today from what she had been only a few days ago.

Mr Baillie regarded Sir Walter thoughtfully. He said he believed he understood the problem. Sir Walter and her ladyship had not been married long, had they? Well, Sir Walter must forgive him, but doctors were often obliged to say things which other people would not. Sir Walter was not accustomed to married life. He would soon discover that married people often quarrelled. It was nothing to be ashamed of – even the most devoted couples disagreed sometimes, and when they did it was not uncommon for one partner to pretend an indisposition. Nor was it always the lady that did so. Was there perhaps something that Lady Pole had set her heart upon? Well, if it were a small thing, like a new gown or a bonnet, why not let her have it since she wanted it so much? If it were a large thing like a house or a visit to Scotland, then perhaps it would be best to talk to her about it. Mr Baillie was sure that her ladyship was not an unreasonable person.

There was a pause during which Sir Walter stared at Mr Baillie down his long nose. "Her ladyship and I have not quarrelled," he said at last.

Ah, said Mr Baillie in a kindly fashion. It might well appear to Sir Walter that there had been no quarrel. It was often the case that gentlemen did not observe the signs. Mr Baillie advised Sir Walter to think carefully. Might he not have said something to vex her ladyship? Mr Baillie did not speak of blame. It was all part of the little accommodations that married people must make in beginning their life together.

"But it is not Lady Pole's character to behave like a spoilt child!"

No doubt, no doubt, said Mr Baillie. But her ladyship was very young and young persons ought always be permitted some licence for folly. Old heads did not sit upon young shoulders. Sir Walter ought not to expect it. Mr Baillie was rather warming to his subject. He had examples to hand (drawn from history and literature) of sober-minded, clever men and women who had all done foolish things in their youth, however a glance at Sir Walter's face persuaded him that he should press the point no further.

Sir Walter was in a similar situation. He too had several things to say and a great mind to say some of them, but he felt himself on uncertain ground. A man who marries for the first time at the age of forty-two knows only too well that almost all his acquaintance are better qualified to manage his domestic affairs than him. So Sir Walter contented himself with frowning at Mr Baillie and then, since it was almost eleven o'clock, he called for his carriage and his secretary and drove to Burlington House where he had an appointment to meet the other Ministers.

At Burlington House he walked through pillared courtyards and gilded ante-rooms. He mounted great marble staircases that were overhung by painted ceilings in which impossible numbers of painted gods, goddesses, heroes and nymphs tumbled out of blue skies or reclined on fluffy white clouds. He was bowed at by a whole host of powdered, liveried footmen until he came to the room where the Ministers were looking at papers and arguing with one another.

"But why do you not send for Mr Norrell, Sir Walter?" asked

Mr Canning, the moment he heard what the matter was. "I am astonished that you have not already done so. I am sure that her ladyship's indisposition will prove to be nothing more than some slight irregularity in the magic which brought her back to life. Mr Norrell can make some small adjustment to a spell and her ladyship will be well again."

"Oh, quite!" agreed Lord Castlereagh. "It seems to me that Lady Pole has gone beyond physicians. You and I, Sir Walter, are set upon this earth by the Grace of God, but her ladyship is here by the grace of Mr Norrell. Her hold upon life is different from the rest of us – theologically and, I dare say, medically as well."

"Whenever Mrs Perceval is unwell," interjected Mr Perceval, a small, precise lawyer of unremarkable aspect and manners who held the exalted position of Chancellor of the Exchequer, "the first person I apply to is her maid. After all, who knows a lady's state of health better than her maid? What does Lady Pole's maid say?"

Sir Walter shook his head. "Pampisford is as mystified as I am. She agreed with me that her ladyship was in excellent health two days ago and now she is cold, pale, listless and unhappy. That is the beginning and end of Pampisford's information. That and a great deal of nonsense about the house being haunted. I do not know what is the matter with the servants just now. They are all in an odd, nervous condition. One of the footmen came to me this morning with a tale of meeting someone upon the stairs at midnight. A person with a green coat and a great quantity of pale, silvery hair."

"What? A ghost? An apparition?" asked Lord Hawkesbury.

"I believe that is what he meant, yes."

"How very extraordinary! Did it speak?" asked Mr Canning.

"No. Geoffrey said it gave him a cold, disdainful look and passed on."

"Oh! Your footman was dreaming, Sir Walter. He was certainly dreaming," said Mr Perceval.

"Or drunk," offered Mr Canning.

"Yes, that occurred to me too. So naturally I asked Stephen Black," said Sir Walter, "but Stephen is as foolish as the rest of them. I can scarcely get him to speak to me."

"Well," said Mr Canning, "you will not, I think, attempt to deny that there is something here that suggests magic? And is it not Mr Norrell's business to explain what other people cannot? Send for Mr Norrell, Sir Walter!"

This was so reasonable that Sir Walter began to wonder why he had not thought of it himself. He had the highest opinion of his own abilities and did not think he would generally miss so obvious a connection. The truth was, he realized, that he did not really *like* magic. He had never liked it – not at the beginning when he had supposed it to be false and not now that it had proved to be real. But he could hardly explain this to the other Ministers – he who had persuaded them to employ a magician for the first time in two hundred years!

At half-past three he returned to Harley-street. It was the eeriest part of a winter day. Twilight was turning all the buildings and people to blurred, black nothingnesses while, above, the sky remained a dizzying silver-blue and was full of cold light. A winter sunset was painting a swathe of rose-colour and blood-colour at the end of all the streets – pleasing to the eyes but somehow chilling to the heart. As Sir Walter gazed from his carriage-window, he thought it fortunate that he was not in any way a fanciful person. Someone else might have been quite unsettled by the combination of the disagreeable task of consulting a magician and this queer, black-and-bloody dissolution of the London streets.

Geoffrey opened the door of no. 9 Harley-street and Sir Walter rapidly mounted the stairs. On the first floor he passed the Venetian drawing-room where her ladyship had been sitting that morning. A sort of presentiment made him look inside. At first it did not seem as though any body could be there. The fire was low in the grate, creating a sort of second twilight within the room. No body had lit a lamp or candle yet. And then he saw her.

She was sitting very upright in a chair by the window. Her back was towards him. Everything about her – chair, posture, even the folds of her gown and shawl – was precisely the same as when he had left her that morning.

The moment he reached his study, he sat down and wrote an urgent message to Mr Norrell.

Mr Norrell did not come immediately. An hour or two passed. At last he arrived with an expression of fixed calm upon his face. Sir Walter met him in the hall and described what had happened. He then proposed that they go upstairs to the Venetian drawing-room.

"Oh!" said Mr Norrell, quickly. "From what you tell me, Sir Walter, I am quite certain there is no need to trouble Lady Pole because, you see, I fear I can do nothing for her. Much as it pains me to say this to you, my dear Sir Walter – for as you know I should always wish to serve you when I can – but whatever it is that has distressed her ladyship I do not believe that it is in the power of magic to remedy."

Sir Walter sighed. He ran his hand through his hair and looked unhappy. "Mr Baillie found nothing wrong and so I thought . . ."

"Oh! But it is precisely that circumstance which makes me so certain that I cannot help you. Magic and medicine are not always so distinct from one another as you seem to imagine. Their spheres often overlap. An illness may have both a medical cure and a magical one. If her ladyship were truly ill or if, God forbid!, she were to die again, then certainly there is magic to cure or restore her. But forgive me, Sir Walter, what you have described seems more a spiritual ailment than a physical one and as such belongs neither to magic nor medicine. I am no expert in these matters but perhaps a clergyman might be found to answer better?"

"But Lord Castlereagh thought – I do not know if it is true – Lord Castlereagh thought that since Lady Pole owes her life to magic – I confess that I did not understand him very well, but I believe he meant to say that since her ladyship's life is founded upon magic, she would only be susceptible to cure by magic."

"Indeed? Lord Castlereagh said that? Oh! He is quite mistaken, but I am most intrigued that he should have thought of it. That is what used to be called the Meraudian Heresy.[1] A twelfth-century abbot of Rievaulx dedicated himself to its destruction and was later made a saint. Of course the theology of magic has never been a favourite subject of mine, but I believe I am correct in saying that in the sixty-ninth chapter of William Pantler's *Three Perfectible States of Being* . . ."[2]

Mr Norrell seemed about to embark upon one of his long, dull speeches upon the history of English magic, full of references to books no one had ever heard of. Sir Walter interrupted him with, "Yes, yes! But do you have any notion who the person with the green coat and the silver hair might be?"

"Oh!" said Mr Norrell. "You think there was somebody then? But that seems to me most unlikely. Might it not be something more in the nature of a dressing gown left hanging on a hook by a negligent servant? Just where one does not expect to see it? I myself have often been badly startled by this wig which you see now upon my head. Lucas ought to put it away each night – he knows he ought – but several times now he has left it on its wig stand on the mantelpiece where it is reflected in the mirror above the fireplace

---

[1] This theory was first expounded by a Cornish magician called Meraud in the twelfth century and there were many variants. In its most extreme form it involves the belief that any one who has been cured, saved or raised to life by magic is no longer subject to God and His Church, though they may owe all sorts of allegiance to the magician or fairy who has helped them.

Meraud was arrested and brought before Stephen, King of Southern England, and his bishops at a Council in Winchester. Meraud was branded, beaten and stripped half-naked. Then he was cast out. The bishops ordered that no one should help him. Meraud tried to walk from Winchester to Newcastle, where the Raven King's castle was. He died on the way.

The Northern English belief that certain sorts of murderers belong not to God or to the Devil but to the Raven King is another form of the Meraudian Heresy.

[2] *Three Perfectible States of Being* by William Pantler, pub. Henry Lintot, London, 1735. The three perfectible beings are angels, men and fairies.

and resembles nothing so much in the world as two gentlemen with their heads together, whispering about me."

Mr Norrell blinked his small eyes rapidly at Sir Walter. Then, having declared that he could do nothing, he wished Sir Walter good evening and left the house.

Mr Norrell went straight home. As soon as he arrived at his house in Hanover-square he immediately went up to a little study upon the second floor. This was a quiet room at the back of the house, overlooking the garden. The servants never entered when he was working in this room and even Childermass needed some unusually pressing reason to disturb him there. Though Mr Norrell rarely gave warning of when he intended to use this little study, it was one of the rules of the household that it was always kept in readiness for him. Just now a fire was burning brightly in the grate and all the lamps were lit, but someone had neglected to draw the curtains and consequently the window had become a black mirror, in which the room was reflected.

Mr Norrell sat down at the desk which faced the window. He opened a large volume, one of many upon the desk, and began to murmur a spell to himself.

A coal falling from the grate, a shadow moving in the room, caused him to look up. He saw his own alarmed reflection in the dark window and he saw someone standing behind him – a pale, silvery face with a mass of shining hair around it.

Mr Norrell did not turn but instead addressed the reflection in the window in a bitter, angry tone. "When you said that you would take half the young lady's life, I thought you would permit her to remain with her friends and family for half seventy-five years. I thought it would appear as if she had simply died!"

"I never said so."

"You cheated me! You have not helped me at all! You risk undoing everything by your tricks!" cried Mr Norrell.

The person in the window made a sound of disapproval. "I had hoped that I would find you more reasonable at our second meeting. Instead you are full of arrogance and unreasonable anger against me! *I* have kept to the terms of our agreement! I have done what you asked and taken nothing that was not mine to take! If you were truly concerned for the happiness of Lady Pole, you would rejoice that she is now placed among friends who truly admire and esteem her!"

"Oh! As to that," said Mr Norrell, scornfully, "I do not care one way or the other. What is the fate of one young woman compared to the success of English magic? No, it is her husband that concerns me – the man for whom I did all this! He is brought quite low by your treachery. Supposing he should not recover! Supposing he were to resign from Government! I might never find another ally so willing to help me.[3] I shall certainly never again have a Minister so much in my debt!"

"Her husband, is it? Well, then I shall raise him up to some lofty position! I shall make him much greater than any thing he could achieve by his own efforts. He shall be Prime Minister. Or Emperor of Great Britain perhaps? Will that suit you?"

"No, no!" cried Mr Norrell. "You do not understand! I merely want him to be pleased with me and to talk to the other Ministers and to persuade them of the great good that my magic can do the country!"

"It is entirely mysterious to me," declared the person in the window, haughtily, "why you should prefer the help of this person to mine! What does he know of magic? Nothing! *I* can teach you to raise up mountains and crush your enemies beneath them! I can make the clouds sing at your approach. I can make it spring when you arrive and winter when you leave. I can . . ."

"Oh, yes! And all you want in return is to shackle English magic to your whims! You will steal Englishmen and women away from

---

[3] It is clear from this remark that Mr Norrell did not yet comprehend how highly the Ministers in general regarded him nor how eager they were to make use of him in the war.

their homes and make England a place fit only for your degenerate race! The price of your help is too high for me!"

The person in the window did not reply directly to these accusations. Instead a candlestick suddenly leapt from its place on a little table and flew across the room, shattering a mirror on the opposite wall and a little china bust of Thomas Lanchester.

Then all was quiet.

Mr Norrell sat in a state of fright and trembling. He looked down at the books spread out upon his desk, but if he read, then it was in a fashion known only to magicians, for his eye did not travel over the page. After an interval of several minutes he looked up again. The person reflected in the window was gone.

Everyone's plans concerning Lady Pole came to nothing. The marriage – which for a few short weeks had seemed to promise so much to both partners – lapsed into indifference and silence upon her part and into anxiety and misery upon his. Far from becoming a leader of the fashionable world, she declined to go any where. No one visited her and the fashionable world very soon forgot her.

The servants at Harley-street grew reluctant to enter the room where she sat, though none of them could have said why. The truth was that there hung about her the faintest echo of a bell. A chill wind seemed to blow upon her from far away and caused any one who came near her to shiver. So she sat, hour after hour, wrapped in her shawl, neither moving nor speaking, and bad dreams and shadows gathered about her.

19

The Peep-O'Day-Boys

February 1808

CURIOUSLY, NO ONE noticed that the strange malady that afflicted her ladyship was to a precision the same as that which afflicted Stephen Black. He too complained of feeling tired and cold, and on the rare occasions that either of them said any thing, they both spoke in a low, exhausted manner.

But perhaps it was not so curious. The different styles of life of a lady and a butler tend to obscure any similarities in their situations. A butler has his work and must do it. Unlike Lady Pole, Stephen was not suffered to sit idly by the window, hour after hour, without speaking. Symptoms that were raised to the dignity of an illness in Lady Pole were dismissed as mere low spirits in Stephen.

John Longridge, the cook at Harley-street, had suffered from low spirits for more than thirty years, and he was quick to welcome Stephen as a newcomer to the freemasonry of melancholy. He seemed glad, poor fellow, of a companion in woe. In the evenings when Stephen would sit at the kitchen table with his head buried in his hands, John Longridge would come and sit down on the other side of the table, and begin commiserating with him.

"I condole with you, sir, indeed I do. Low spirits, Mr Black, are the very worst torment that a man can be afflicted with. Sometimes it seems to me that all of London resembles nothing so much as cold pease porridge, both in colour and consistency. I see people with cold-pease-porridge faces and cold-pease-porridge hands walking down cold-pease-porridge streets. Ah, me! How bad I feel then! The very sun up in the sky is cold and grey and porridge-y, and has no power to warm me. Do you often feel chilled, sir?" John Longridge would lay his hand upon Stephen's hand. "Ah, Mr Black, sir," he would say, "you are cold as the tomb."

Stephen felt he was like a person sleepwalking. He did not live any more; he only dreamed. He dreamed of the house in Harley-street and of the other servants. He dreamed of his work and his friends and of Mrs Brandy. Sometimes he dreamed of things that were very strange – things that he knew, in some small, chilly, far-off part of himself, ought not to be. He might be walking along a hallway or up the stairs in the house in Harley-street and he would turn and see other hallways and staircases leading off into the distance – hallways and staircases which did not belong there. It would be as if the house in Harley-street had accidentally got lodged inside a much larger and more ancient edifice. The passageways would be stone-vaulted and full of dust and shadows. The stairs and floors would be so worn and uneven that they would more resemble stones found in nature than architecture. But the strangest thing of all about these ghostly halls was that they would be quite familiar to Stephen. He did not understand why or how, but he would catch himself thinking, "Yes, just beyond that corner is the Eastern Armoury." Or, "Those stairs lead to the Disembroweller's Tower."

Whenever he saw these passageways or, as he sometimes did, sensed their presence without actually perceiving them, then he would feel a little more lively, a little more like his old self. Whatever part of him it was that had frozen up (his soul? his heart?) unfroze itself the merest hair's breadth and thought, curiosity and feeling began to pulse again within him. But for the rest nothing amused him; nothing satisfied him. All was shadows, emptiness, echoes and dust.

Sometimes his restless spirit would cause him to go on long, solitary wanders through the dark winter streets around Mayfair and Piccadilly. On one such evening in late February he found himself outside Mr Wharton's coffee-house in Oxford-street. It was a place he knew well. The upper-room was home to the Peep-O'Day-Boys, a club for the grander sort of male servants in London's grand houses. Lord Castlereagh's valet was a notable member; the Duke of Portland's coachman was another and so was Stephen. The Peep-O'Day-Boys met upon the third Tuesday of every month and enjoyed the same pleasures as the members of any other London club – they drank and ate, gambled, talked politics and gossiped about their mistresses. On other evenings of the month it was the habit of Peep-O'Day-Boys who happened to find themselves disengaged to repair to the upper-room of Mr Wharton's coffee-house, there to refresh their spirits with the society of their fellows. Stephen went inside and mounted the stairs to the upper-room.

This apartment was much like the corresponding part of any similar establishment in the city. It was as full of tobacco smoke as such resorts of the masculine half of society usually are. It was panelled in dark wood. Partitions of the same wood divided off the room into boxes so that customers were able to enjoy being in a little wooden world all their own. The bare floor was kept pleasant with fresh sawdust everyday. White cloths covered the tables and oil-lamps were kept clean and their wicks trimmed. Stephen sat down in one of the boxes and ordered a glass of port which he then proceeded to stare at gloomily.

Whenever one of the Peep-O'Day-Boys passed Stephen's box, they would stop for a word with Stephen and he would raise a hand to them in half-hearted salutation, but tonight he did not trouble himself to answer them. This had happened, Oh!, two or three times, when suddenly Stephen heard someone say in a vivid whisper, "You are quite right to pay them no attention! For, when all is said and done, what are they but servants and drudges? And when, with my assistance, you are elevated to your rightful place at the very pinnacle of nobility and greatness, it will be a great comfort to you to remember that you spurned their friendship!" It was only a whisper, yet Stephen heard it most distinctly above the voices and laughter of the Peep-O'Days and other gentlemen. He had the odd idea that, though only a whisper, it could have passed through stone or iron or brass. It could have spoken to you from a thousand feet beneath the earth and you would have still heard it. It could have shattered precious stones and brought on madness.

This was so very extraordinary that for a moment he was roused from his lethargy. A lively curiosity to discover who had spoken took hold of him and he looked around the room but saw no one he did not know. So he stuck his head round the partition and looked into the next box. It contained one person of very striking appearance. He appeared very much at his ease. His arms were resting on the tops of the partition and his booted feet were resting on the table. He had several remarkable features, but the chief among them was a mass of silvery hair, as bright and soft and shining as thistle-down. He winked at Stephen. Then he rose from his own box and came and sat in Stephen's.

"I may as well tell you," he said, speaking in a highly confidential manner, "that this city has not the hundredth part of its former splendour! I have been gravely disappointed since my return. Once upon a time, to look upon London was to look upon a forest of towers and pinnacles and spires. The many-coloured flags and banners that flew from each and every one dazzled the eye! Upon every side one saw stone carvings as delicate as fingerbones and as intricate as flowing water! There were houses ornamented with stone dragons, griffins and lions, symbolizing the wisdom, courage and ferocity of the occupants, while in the gardens of those same houses might be found flesh-and-blood dragons, griffins and lions, locked in strong cages. Their roars, which could be clearly heard in the street, terrified the faint-of-heart. In every church a blessed saint lay, performing miracles hourly at the behest of the populace. Each saint was confined within an ivory casket, which was secreted in a jewel-studded coffin, which in turn was displayed in a magnificent shrine of gold and silver that shone night and day with the light of a thousand wax candles! Every day there was a splendid procession to celebrate one or other of these blessed saints, and London's fame passed from world to world! Of course in those days the citizens of London were wont to come to *me* for advice about the construction of their churches, the arrangement of their gardens, the decoration of their houses. If they were properly respectful in their petitions I would generally give them good counsel. Oh, yes! When London owed its appearance to *me* it was beautiful, noble, peerless. But now . . ."

He made an eloquent gesture, as if he had crumpled London into a ball in his hand and thrown it away. "But how stupid you look when you stare at me so! I have put myself to any amount of trouble to pay you this visit – and you sit there silent and sullen, with your mouth hanging open! You are surprized to see me, I dare say, but that is no reason to forget all your good manners. Of course," he remarked in the manner of someone making a great concession, "Englishmen are often all amazement in my presence – *that* is the most natural thing in the world – but you and I are such friends that I think I have deserved a better welcome than this!"

"Have we met before, sir?" asked Stephen in astonishment. "I have certainly dreamt of you. I dreamt that you and I were together in an immense mansion with endless, dusty corridors!"

" 'Have we met before, sir?' " mocked the gentleman with the thistle-down hair. "Why! What nonsense you talk! As if we had not attended the same feasts and balls and parties every night for weeks and weeks!"

"Certainly in my dreams . . ."

"I had not thought you could be so dull-witted!" cried the gentleman. "Lost-hope is not a *dream*! It is the oldest and most beautiful of my mansions – which are numerous – and it is quite as real as Carlton House.[1] In fact it is a great deal more so! Much of

---

[1] The London home of the Prince of Wales in Pall Mall.

218

the future is known to me and I tell you that Carlton House will be levelled to the ground in twenty years' time and the city of London itself will endure, oh!, scarcely another two thousand years, whereas Lost-hope will stand until the next age of the World!" He looked ridiculously pleased with this thought, and indeed it must be said that his natural manner seemed to be one of extreme self-congratulation. "No, it is no dream. You are merely under an enchantment which brings you each night to Lost-hope to join our fairy revels!"

Stephen stared at the gentleman uncomprehendingly. Then, remembering that he must speak or lay himself open to accusations of sullenness and bad manners, he gathered his wits and stammered out, "And . . . And is the enchantment yours, sir?"

"But of course!"

It was clear from the pleased air with which he spoke that the gentleman with the thistle-down hair considered that he had bestowed the greatest of favours upon Stephen by enchanting him. Stephen thanked him politely for it. ". . . although," he added, "I cannot imagine what I have done to deserve such kindness from you. Indeed, I am sure I have done nothing at all."

"Ah!" cried the gentleman, delighted. "Yours are excellent manners, Stephen Black! You could teach the proud English a thing or two about the proper respect that is due to persons of quality. *Your* manners will bring you good luck in the end!"

"And those golden guineas in Mrs Brandy's cash box," said Stephen, "were they yours too?"

"Oh! Have you only just guessed it? But only observe how clever I have been! Remembering all that you told me about how you are surrounded night and day by enemies who wish you harm, I conveyed the money to a friend of yours. Then when you and she marry, the money will be yours."

"How did . . ." began Stephen and stopt. Clearly there was no part of his life that the gentleman did not know about and nothing with which the gentleman did not feel entitled to interfere. "But you are mistaken about my enemies, sir," he said, "I do not have any."

"My dear Stephen!" cried the gentleman, greatly amused, "*Of course* you have enemies! And the chief among them is that wicked man who is your master and Lady Pole's husband! He forces you to be his servant and do his bidding night and day. He sets tasks before you that are entirely unsuited to a person of your beauty and nobility. And why does he do these things?"

"I suppose because . . ." began Stephen.

"Precisely!" declared the gentleman triumphantly. "Because in the fulsomeness of his wickedness he has captured you and girded you with chains and now he triumphs over you, dancing about and howling with wicked laughter to see you in such straits!"

Stephen opened his mouth to protest that Sir Walter Pole had never done any of those things; that he had always treated Stephen with great kindness and affection; that when Sir Walter was younger he had paid money he could ill afford so that Stephen could go to school; and that later, when Sir Walter was poorer still, they had often eaten the same food and shared the same fire. As for triumphing over his enemies, Stephen had often seen Sir Walter wear a very self-satisfied smirk when he believed he had scored a point against his political opponents, but he had never seen him dance about or howl with wicked laughter. Stephen was about to say these things, when the mention of the word "chains" seemed to send a sort of silent thunderbolt through him. Suddenly in his fancy he saw a dark place – a terrible place – a place full of horror – a hot, rank, closed-in place. There were shadows in the darkness and the slither and clank of heavy iron chains. What this image meant or where it had come from he had not the least idea. He did not think it could be a memory. Surely he had never been in such a place?

". . . If he ever were to discover that every night you and she escape from him to be happy in my house, why! he would be thrown instantly into fits of jealousy and would, I dare say, try to kill you both. But fear not, my dear, dear Stephen! I will take good care he never finds out. Oh! How I detest such selfish people! *I* know what it is to be scorned and slighted by the proud English and put to perform tasks that are beneath one's dignity. I cannot bear to see the same fate befall you!" The gentleman paused to caress Stephen's cheek and brow with his icy white fingers, which produced a queer tingling sensation in Stephen's skin. "You cannot conceive what a warm interest I feel in you and how anxious I am to do you some lasting service! – which is why I have conceived a plan to make you the king of some fairy kingdom!"

"I . . . I beg your pardon, sir. I was thinking of something else. A king, you say? No, sir. I could not be a king. It is only your great kindness to me that makes you think it possible. Besides I am very much afraid that fairyland does not quite agree with me. Ever since I first visited your house I have been stupid and heavy. I am tired morning, noon and night and my life is a burden to me. I dare say the fault is all mine, but perhaps mortals are not formed for fairy bliss?"

"Oh! That is simply the sadness you feel at the dreariness of England compared to the delightful life you lead at my house where there is always dancing and feasting and everyone is dressed in their finest clothes!"

"I dare say you are right, sir, yet if you were to find it in your heart to release me from this enchantment, I should be very grateful to you."

"Oh! But that is impossible!" declared the gentleman. "Do you not know that my beautiful sisters and cousins – for each of whom, I may say, kings have killed each other and great empires fallen into decay – all quarrel over who will be your next dancing-partner? And what would they say if I told them you would come to Lost-hope no more? For amongst my many other virtues I am a most attentive brother and cousin and always try to please the females in my household when I can. And as for declining to become a king, there is nothing, I assure you, more agreeable than having everyone bow before one and call one by all sorts of noble titles."

He resumed his extravagant praises of Stephen's beauty, dignified countenance and elegant dancing – all of which he seemed to consider the chief qualifications for the ruler of a vast kingdom in Faerie – and he began to speculate upon which kingdom would suit Stephen best. "Untold-Blessings is a fine place, with dark, impenetrable forests, lonely mountains and uncrossable seas. It has the advantage of being without a ruler at present – but then it has the disadvantage that there are twenty-six other claimants already and you would be plunged straightaway into the middle of a bloody civil war – which perhaps you would not care for? Then there is the Dukedom of Pity-Me. The present Duke has no friends to speak of. Oh, but I could not bear to see any friend of mine ruler of such a miserable little place as Pity-Me!"

20

The unlikely milliner

February 1808

THOSE PEOPLE WHO had expected the war to be over now that the magician had appeared upon the scene were soon disappointed. "Magic!" said Mr Canning, the Foreign Secretary. "Do not speak to me of magic! It is just like everything else, full of setbacks and disappointments."

There was some justice in this, and Mr Norrell was always happy to give long, difficult explanations of why something was not possible. Once, in making one of these explanations, he said something which he later regretted. It was at Burlington House and Mr Norrell was explaining to Lord Hawkesbury, the Home Secretary,[1] that something or other could not be attempted since it would take, oh!, at least a dozen magicians working day and night. He made a long, tedious speech about the pitiful state of English magic, ending, "I would it were otherwise but, as your lordship is aware, our talented young men look to the Army, the Navy and the Church for their careers. My own poor profession is sadly neglected." And he gave a great sigh.

Mr Norrell meant nothing much by this, except perhaps to draw attention to his own extraordinary talent, but unfortunately Lord Hawkesbury took up quite another idea.

---

[1] Robert Banks Jenkinson, Lord Hawkesbury (1770–1828). On the death of his father in December 1808 he became the Earl of Liverpool. For the next nine years he would prove to be one of Mr Norrell's most steady supporters.

"Oh!" he cried. "You mean we need more magicians? Oh, yes! I quite see that. Quite. A school perhaps? Or a Royal Society under His Majesty's patronage? Well, Mr Norrell, I really think we will leave the details to you. If you will be so good as to draw up a memorandum upon the subject I shall be glad to read it and submit its proposals to the other Ministers. We all know your skill at drawing up such things, so clear and so detailed and your handwriting so good. I dare say, sir, we shall find you a little money from somewhere. When you have time, sir. There is no hurry. I know how busy you are."

Poor Mr Norrell! Nothing could be less to his taste than the creation of other magicians. He comforted himself with the thought that Lord Hawkesbury was an exemplary Minister, devoted to business, with a thousand and one things to think about. Doubtless he would soon forget all about it.

But the very next time that Mr Norrell was at Burlington House Lord Hawkesbury came hurrying up to him, crying out, "Ah! Mr Norrell! I have spoken to the King about your plan for making new magicians. His Majesty was very pleased, thought the idea an excellent one and asked me to tell you that he will be glad to extend his patronage to the scheme."

It was fortunate that before Mr Norrell could reply, the sudden arrival of the Swedish Ambassador in the room obliged his lordship to hurry away again.

But a week or so later Mr Norrell met Lord Hawkesbury again, this time at a special dinner given by the Prince of Wales in honour of Mr Norrell at Carlton House. "Ah! Mr Norrell, there you are! I don't suppose that you have the recommendations for the Magicians School about you? Only I have just been speaking to the Duke of Devonshire and he is most interested – thinks he has a house in Leamington Spa which would be just the thing and has asked me questions about the curriculum and whether there would be prayers and where the magicians would sleep – all sorts of things I have not the least idea about. I wonder – would you be so kind as to speak to him? He is just over there by the mantelpiece – he has seen us – he is coming this way. Your Grace, here is Mr Norrell ready to tell you all about it!"

It was with some difficulty that Mr Norrell was able to convince Lord Hawkesbury and the Duke of Devonshire that a school would take up far too much time and moreover he had yet to see any young men with sufficient talent to make the attempt worthwhile. Reluctantly his Grace and his lordship were obliged to agree and Mr Norrell was able to turn his attention to a far more agreeable project: that of destroying the magicians already in existence.

The street-sorcerers of the City of London had long constituted a standing irritation of his spirits. While he was still unknown and unregarded, he had begun to petition members of the Government and other eminent gentlemen for the removal of these vagabond magicians. Naturally, the moment that he attained public eminence he doubled and tripled his efforts. His first idea was that magic ought to be regulated by the Government and magicians ought to be licensed (though naturally he had no idea of any one being licensed but himself). He proposed that a proper regulatory Board of Magic be established, but in this he was too ambitious.

As Lord Hawkesbury said to Sir Walter; "We have no wish to offend a man who has done the country such service, but in the middle of a long and difficult war to demand that a Board be set up with Privy Councillors and Secretaries and Lord knows what else! And for what? To listen to Mr Norrell talk and to pay Mr Norrell compliments! It is quite out of the question. My dear Sir Walter, persuade him to some other course, I beg you."

So the next time that Sir Walter and Mr Norrell met (which was at Mr Norrell's house in Hanover-square) Sir Walter addressed his friend with the following words.

"It is an admirable purpose, sir, and no one quarrels with it, but a Board is precisely the wrong way of going about it. Within the City of London – which is where the problem chiefly lies – the

Board would have no authority. I tell you what we shall do; tomorrow you and I shall go to the Mansion House to wait upon the Lord Mayor and one or two of the aldermen. I think we shall soon find some friends for our cause."

"But, my dear Sir Walter!" cried Mr Norrell. "It will not do. The problem is not confined to London. I have looked into it since I left Yorkshire . . ." (Here he delved about in a pile of papers upon a little table at his elbow to fetch out a list.) "There are twelve street-sorcerers in Norwich, two in Yarmouth, two in Gloucester, six in Winchester, *forty-two* in Penzance! Why! Only the other day, one – a dirty female – came to my house and would not be satisfied without seeing me, whereupon she demanded that I give her a paper – a certificate of competence, no less! – testifying to my belief that she could do magic. I was never more astonished in my life! I said to her, 'Woman . . .'"

"As to the other places that you mention," said Sir Walter, interrupting hastily. "I think you will find that once London rids itself of this nuisance then the others will be quick to follow. They none of them like to feel themselves left behind."

Mr Norrell soon found that it was just as Sir Walter had predicted. The Lord Mayor and the aldermen were eager to be part of the glorious revival of English magic. They persuaded the Court of Common Council to set up a Committee for Magical Acts and the Committee decreed that only Mr Norrell was permitted to do magic within the City boundaries and that other persons who "set up booths or shops, or otherwise molested the citizens of London with claims to do magic" were to be expelled forthwith.

The street-sorcerers packed up their little stalls, loaded their shabby possessions into handcarts and trudged out of the City. Some took the trouble to curse London as they left, but by and large they bore the change in their fortunes with admirable philosophy. Most had simply settled it in their own minds that henceforth they would give up magic and become instead beggars and thieves and, since they had indulged in beggary and thievery in an amateur way for years, the wrench was not so great as you might imagine.

But one did not go. Vinculus, the magician of Threadneedle-street, stayed in his booth and continued to foretell unhappy futures and to sell petty revenges to slighted lovers and resentful apprentices. Naturally, Mr Norrell complained very vigorously to the Committee for Magical Acts about this state of affairs since Vinculus was the sorcerer whom he hated most. The Committee for Magical Acts dispatched beadles and constables to threaten Vinculus with the stocks but Vinculus paid them no attention, and he was so popular among London's citizens that the Committee feared a riot if he was removed by force.

On a bleak February day Vinculus was in his magician's booth beside the church of St Christopher Le Stocks. In case there are any readers who do not remember the magicians' booths of our child-hood, it ought to be stated that in shape the booth rather resembled a Punch and Judy theatre or a shopkeeper's stall at a fair and that it was built of wood and canvas. A yellow curtain, ornamented to half its height with a thick crust of dirt, served both as a door and as a sign to advertise the services that were offered within.

On this particular day Vinculus had no customers and very little hope of getting any. The City streets were practically deserted. A bitter grey fog that tasted of smoke and tar hung over London. The City shopkeepers had heaped coals upon their fires and lit every lamp they possessed in a vain attempt to dispel the dark and the cold, but today their bow windows cast no cheerful glow into the streets: the light could not penetrate the fog. Consequently no one was enticed into the shops to spend money and the shopmen in their long white aprons and powdered wigs stood about at their ease, chatting to each other or warming themselves at the fire. It was a day when any one with something to do indoors stayed indoors to do it, and any one who was obliged to go outside did so quickly and got back inside again as soon as he could.

Vinculus sat gloomily behind his curtain half frozen to death, turning over in his mind the names of the two or three ale-house-keepers who might be persuaded to sell him a glass or two of hot spiced wine on credit. He had almost made up his mind which of them to try first when the sounds of someone stamping their feet and blowing upon their fingers seemed to suggest that a customer stood without. Vinculus raised the curtain and stepped outside.

"Are you the magician?"

Vinculus agreed a little suspiciously that he was (the man had the air of a bailiff).

"Excellent. I have a commission for you."

"It is two shillings for the first consultation."

The man put his hand in his pocket, pulled out his purse and put two shillings into Vinculus's hand.

Then he began to describe the problem that he wished Vinculus to magic away. His explanation was very clear and he knew exactly what it was that he wished Vinculus to do. The only problem was that the more the man talked, the less Vinculus believed him. The man said that he had come from Windsor. That was perfectly possible. True, he spoke with a northern accent, but there was nothing odd in that; people often came down from the northern counties to make their fortunes. The man also said he was the owner of a successful millinery business – now that seemed a good deal less likely, for any one less like a milliner it was difficult to imagine. Vinculus knew little enough about milliners but he did know that they generally dress in the very height of fashion. This fellow wore an ancient black coat that had been patched and mended a dozen times. His linen, though clean and of a good quality, would have been old-fashioned twenty years ago. Vinculus did not know the names of the hundred and one little fancy articles that milliners make, but he knew that milliners know them. This man did not; he called them "fol-de-lols".

In the freezing weather the ground had become an unhappy compound of ice and frozen mud and as Vinculus was writing down the particulars in a greasy little book, he somehow missed his footing and fell against the unlikely milliner. He tried to stand but so treacherous was the icy ground that he was obliged to use the other man as a sort of ladder to climb up. The unlikely milliner looked rather appalled to have strong fumes of ale and cabbage breathed in his face and bony fingers grabbing him all over, but he said nothing.

"Beg pardon," muttered Vinculus, when at last he was in an upright position again.

"Granted," said the unlikely milliner politely, brushing from his coat the stale crumbs, gobbets of matted grease and dirt and other little signs of Vinculus having been there.

Vinculus too was adjusting his clothes which had got somewhat disarranged in his tumble.

The unlikely milliner continued with his tale.

"So, as I say, my business thrives and my bonnets are the most sought-after in all of Windsor and scarcely a week goes by but one of the Princesses up at the Castle comes to order a new bonnet or fol-de-lol. I have put a great golden plaster image of the Royal Arms above my door to advertise the royal patronage I enjoy. Yet still I cannot help but think that millinery is a great deal of work. Sitting up late at night sewing bonnets, counting my money and so forth. It seems to me that my life might be a great deal easier if one of the Princesses were to fall in love with me and marry me. Do you have such a spell, Magician?"

"A love spell? Certainly. But it will be expensive. I generally charge four shillings for a spell to catch a milkmaid, ten shillings for a seamstress and six guineas for a widow with her own business. A Princess . . . Hmm." Vinculus scratched his unshaven cheek with his dirty fingernails. "Forty guineas," he hazarded.

"Very well."

"And which is it?" asked Vinculus.

"Which what is what?" asked the unlikely milliner.

"Which Princess?"

"They are all pretty much the same, aren't they? Does the price vary with the Princess?"

"No, not really. I will give you the spell written upon a piece of paper. Tear the paper in two and sew half inside the breast of your coat. You need to place the other half in a secret place inside the garments of whichever Princess you decide upon."

The unlikely milliner looked astonished. "And how in the world can I do that?"

Vinculus looked at the man. "I thought you just said that you sewed their bonnets?"

The unlikely milliner laughed. "Oh yes! Of course."

Vinculus stared at the man suspiciously. "You are no more a milliner than I am a . . . a . . ."

"A magician?" suggested the unlikely milliner. "You must certainly admit that it is not your only profession. After all you just picked my pockets."

"Only because I wished to know what sort of villain you are," retorted Vinculus, and he shook his arm until the articles he had taken from the pockets of the unlikely milliner fell out of his sleeve. There were a handful of silver coins, two golden guineas and three or four folded sheets of paper. He picked up the papers.

The sheets were small and thick and of excellent quality. They were all covered in close lines of small, neat handwriting. At the top of the first sheet was written, *Two Spells to Make an Obstinate Man leave London and One Spell to Discover what My Enemy is doing Presently.*

"The magician of Hanover-square!" declared Vinculus.

Childermass (for it was he) nodded.

Vinculus read through the spells. The first was intended to make the subject believe that every London churchyard was haunted by the people who were buried there and that every bridge was haunted by the suicides who had thrown themselves from it. The subject would see the ghosts as they had appeared at their deaths with all the marks of violence, disease and extreme old age upon

230

them. In this way he would become more and more terrified until he dared not pass either a bridge or a church – which in London is a serious inconvenience as the bridges are not more than a hundred yards apart and the churches considerably less. The second spell was intended to persuade the subject that he would find his one true love and all sorts of happiness in the country and the third spell – the one to discover what your enemy was doing – involved a mirror and had presumably been intended by Norrell to enable Childermass to spy upon Vinculus.

Vinculus sneered. "You may tell the Mayfair magician that his spells have no effect upon me!"

"Indeed?" said Childermass, sarcastically. "Well, that is probably because I have not cast them."

Vinculus flung the papers down upon the ground. "Cast them now!" He folded his arms in an attitude of defiance and made his eyes flash as he did whenever he conjured the Spirit of the River Thames.

"Thank you, but no."

"And why not?"

"Because, like you, I do not care to be told how to conduct my business. My master has ordered me to make sure that you leave London. But I intend to do it in my way, not his. Come, I think it will be best if you and I have a talk, Vinculus."

Vinculus thought about this. "And could this talk take place somewhere warmer? An ale-house perhaps?"

"Certainly if you wish."

The papers with Norrell's spells upon them were blowing about their feet. Vinculus stooped down, gathered them together and, paying no regard to the bits of straw and mud sticking to them, put them in the breast of his coat.

21

The cards of Marseilles

February 1808

THE ALE-HOUSE WAS called the Pineapple and had once
been the refuge and hiding-place of a notorious thief and
murderer. This thief had had an enemy, a man as bad as
himself. The thief and his enemy had been partners in some
dreadful crime, but the thief had kept both shares of the spoils
and sent a message to the magistrates telling them where his enemy
might be found. As soon as the enemy had escaped from Newgate,
he had come to the Pineapple in the dead of night with thirty men.
He had set them to tear the slates off the roof and unpick the very
bricks of walls until he could reach inside and pluck out the thief.
No one had seen what happened next but many had heard the
dreadful screams issuing from the pitch-black street. The landlord
had discovered that the Pineapple's dark reputation was good for
business and consequently he had never troubled to mend his
house, other than by applying timber and pitch to the holes, which
gave it the appearance of wearing bandages as if it had been
fighting with its neighbours.

Three greasy steps led down from the street-door into a gloomy
parlour. The Pineapple had its own particular perfume, compounded of ale, tobacco, the natural fragrance of the customers
and the unholy stink of the Fleet River, which had been used as a
sewer for countless years. The Fleet ran beneath the Pineapple's

foundations and the Pineapple was generally supposed to be sinking into it. The walls of the parlour were ornamented with cheap engravings – portraits of famous criminals of the last century who had all been hanged and portraits of the King's dissolute sons who had not been hanged yet.

Childermass and Vinculus sat down at a table in a corner. A shadowy girl brought a cheap tallow candle and two pewter tankards of hot spiced ale. Childermass paid.

They drank in silence a while and then Vinculus looked up at Childermass. "What was all that nonsense about bonnets and princesses?"

Childermass laughed. "Oh, that was just a notion I had. Ever since the day you appeared in his library my master has been petitioning all his great friends to help him destroy you. He asked Lord Hawkesbury and Sir Walter Pole to complain to the King on his behalf. I believe he had an idea that His Majesty might send the Army to make war upon you, but Lord Hawkesbury and Sir Walter said that the King was unlikely to put himself to a great deal of trouble over one yellow-curtained, ragged-arsed sorcerer. But it occurred to me that if His Majesty were to learn that you had somehow threatened the virgin state of his daughters, he might take a different view of the matter."[1] Childermass took another draught of his spiced ale. "But tell me, Vinculus, don't you tire of fake spells and pretend oracles? Half your customers come to laugh at you. They no more believe in your magic than you do. Your day is over. There is a real magician in England now."

Vinculus gave a little snort of disgust. "The magician of Hanover-square! All the great men in London sit telling one another that they never saw a man so honest. But I know magicians and I

---

[1] The King was a most loving and devoted father to his six daughters, but his affection was such that it led him to act almost as if he were their jailer. He could not bear the thought that any of them might marry and leave him. They were required to lead lives of quite intolerable dullness with the ill-tempered Queen at Windsor Castle. Out of the six only one contrived to get married before she was forty.

know magic and I say this: all magicians lie and this one more than most."

Childermass shrugged as if he would not trouble to deny it.

Vinculus leaned forward across the table. "*Magic shall be written on the faces of the stony hills, but their minds shall not be able to contain it. In winter the barren trees shall be a black writing but they shall not understand it.*"

"Trees and hills, Vinculus? When did you last see a tree or a hill? Why don't you say that magic is written on the faces of the dirty houses or that the smoke writes magic in the sky?"

"It is not my prophecy!"

"Ah, yes. Of course. You claim it as a prophecy of the Raven King. Well there is nothing unusual in that. Every charlatan I ever met was the bearer of a message from the Raven King."

"*I sit upon a black throne in the shadows,*" muttered Vinculus, "*but they shall not see me. The rain shall make a door for me and I shall pass through it.*"

"Quite. So, since you did not write this prophecy yourself, where did you find it?"

For a moment Vinculus looked as if he would not answer, but then he said, "It is written in a book."

"A book? What book? My master's library is extensive. He knows of no such prophecy."

Vinculus said nothing.

"Is it your book?" asked Childermass.

"It is in my keeping."

"And where did *you* get a book? Where did you steal it?"

"I did not steal it. It is my inheritance. It is the greatest glory and the greatest burden that has been given to any man in this Age."

"If it is really valuable then you can sell it to Norrell. He has paid great prices for books before now."

"The magician of Hanover-square will never own this book. He will never even see it."

"And where do you keep such a great treasure?"

Vinculus laughed coldly as if to say it was not very likely that he would tell that to the servant of his enemy.

Childermass called to the girl to bring them some more ale. She brought it and they drank for a while longer in silence. Then Childermass took a pack of cards from the breast of his coat and shewed them to Vinculus. "The cards of Marseilles. Did you ever see their like before?"

"Often," said Vinculus, "but yours are different."

"They are copies of a set belonging to a sailor I met in Whitby. He bought them in Genoa with the intention of using them to discover the hiding places of pirates' gold, but when he came to look at them, he found that he could not understand them. He offered to sell them to me, but I was poor and could not pay the price he asked. So we struck a bargain: I would tell him his fortune and in return he would lend me the cards long enough to make copies. Unfortunately his ship set sail before I was able to complete the drawings and so half are done from memory."

"And what fortune did you tell him?"

"His true one. That he would be drowned dead before the year was out."

Vinculus laughed approvingly.

It seemed that when Childermass had made the bargain with the dead sailor he had been too poor even to afford paper and so the cards were drawn upon the backs of ale-house bills, laundry lists, letters, old accounts and playbills. At a later date he had pasted the papers on to coloured cardboard, but in several instances the printing or writing on the other side shewed through, giving them an odd look.

Childermass laid out nine cards in a line. He turned over the first card.

Beneath the picture was a number and a name: *VIIII. L'Ermite.* It shewed an old man in a monkish robe with a monkish hood. He carried a lantern and walked with a stick as if he had come near to losing the use of his limbs through too much sitting and studying. His face was pinched and suspicious. A dry atmosphere seemed to rise up and envelop the observer as if the card itself were peppery with dust.

"Hmm!" said Childermass . "For the present your actions are governed by a hermit. Well, we knew that already."

The next card was *Le Mat*, which is the only picture card to remain numberless, as if the character it depicts is in some sense outside the story. Childermass's card shewed a man walking along a road beneath a summer tree. He had a stick to lean upon and another stick over his shoulder with a handkerchief bundle hanging from it. A little dog skipped after him. The figure was intended to represent the fool or jester of ancient times. He had a bell in his hat and ribbons at his knees which Childermass had coloured red and green. It appeared that Childermass did not know quite how to interpret this card. He considered a while and then turned over the next two cards: *VIII. La Justice*, a crowned woman holding a sword and a pair of scales; and *The Two of Wands*. The wands were crossed and might among other things be thought to represent a crossroads.

Childermass let out a brief burst of laughter. "Well, well!" he said, crossing his arms and regarding Vinculus with some amusement. "This card here," he tapped *La Justice*, "tells me you have weighed your choices and come to a decision. And this one," he indicated *The Two of Wands*. "tells me what your decision is: you are going wandering. It seems I have wasted my time. You have already made up your mind to leave London. So many protestations, Vinculus, and yet you always intended to go!"

Vinculus shrugged, as if to say, what did Childermass expect?

The fifth card was the *Valet de Coupe*, the Page of Cups. One naturally thinks of a page as being a youthful person, but the picture shewed a mature man with bowed head. His hair was shaggy and his beard was thick. In his left hand he carried a heavy cup, yet it could not be that which gave such an odd, strained expression to his countenance – not unless it were the heaviest cup in the world. No, it must be some other burden, not immediately apparent. Owing to the materials which Childermass had been compelled to use to construct his cards this picture had a most peculiar look. It had been drawn upon the back of a letter and the writing shewed through the paper. The man's clothes were a mass of scribble and even his face and hands bore parts of letters.

Vinculus laughed when he saw it as though he recognized it. He gave the card three taps in friendly greeting. Perhaps it was this that made Childermass less certain than he had been before. "You have a message to deliver to someone," he said in an uncertain tone.

Vinculus nodded. "And will the next card shew me this person?" he asked.

"Yes."

"Ah!" exclaimed Vinculus and turned over the sixth card himself.

The sixth card was the *Cavalier de Baton*. The Knight of Wands. A man in a broad-brimmed hat sat upon a horse of a pale colour. The countryside through which he rode was indicated by a few rocks and tufts of grass at his horse's hooves. His clothes were well-made and expensive-looking, but for some inexplicable reason he was carrying a heavy club. Even to call it a club was to make it sounder grander than it was. It was scarcely more than a thick branch torn from a tree or hedge; there were still twigs and leaves protruding from it.

Vinculus picked up the card and studied it carefully.

The seventh card was *The Two of Swords*. Childermass said nothing but immediately turned over the eighth card – *Le Pendv*, The Hanged Man. The ninth card was *Le Monde*, The World. It shewed a naked female figure dancing; in the four corners of the card were an angel, an eagle, a winged bull and a winged lion – the symbols of the evangelists.

"You may expect a meeting," said Childermass, "leading to an ordeal of some sort, perhaps even death. The cards do not say whether you survive or not, but whatever happens, this," he touched the last card, "says that you will achieve your purpose."

237

"And do you know what I am now?" asked Vinculus.

"Not exactly, but I know more of you than I did."

"You see that I am not like the others," said Vinculus.

"There is nothing here that says you are anything more than a charlatan," said Childermass and he began to collect his cards.

"Wait," said Vinculus, "I will tell your fortune."

Vinculus took the cards and laid out nine. Then he turned them over one by one: *XVIII La Lune, XVI La Maison Dieu* reversed, *The Nine of Swords, Valet de Baton, The Ten of Batons* reversed, *II La Papesse, X La Rove de Fortvne, The Two of Coins, The King of Cups.* Vinculus looked at them. He picked up *La Maison Dieu* and examined it, but he said nothing at all.

Childermass laughed. "You are right, Vinculus. You are not like the others. That is my life – there on the table. But you cannot read it. You are a strange creature – the very reverse of all the magicians of the last centuries. They were full of learning but had no talent. You have talent and no knowledge. You cannot profit by what you see."

Vinculus scratched his long, sallow cheek with his unclean fingernails.

Childermass began again to gather up his cards, but once again Vinculus prevented him and indicated that they should lay out the cards again.

"What?" asked Childermass in surprize. "I have told you your fortune. You have failed to tell me mine. What more is there?"

"I am going to tell his fortune."

"Whose? Norrell's? But you will not understand it."

"Shuffle the cards," said Vinculus, stubbornly.

So Childermass shuffled the cards and Vinculus took nine and laid them out. Then he turned over the first card. *IIII. L'Emperevr.* It shewed a king seated upon a throne in the open air with all the customary kingly accoutrements of crown and sceptre. Childermass leaned forward and examined it.

"What is it?" asked Vinculus.

"I do not seem to have copied this card very well. I never noticed before. The inking is badly done. The lines are thick and smudged so that the Emperor's hair and robe appear almost black. And someone has left a dirty thumbprint over the eagle. The Emperor should be an older man than this. I have drawn a young man. Are you going to hazard an interpretation?"

"No," said Vinculus and indicated by a contemptuous thrust of his chin that Childermass should turn the next card.

IIII. L'Emperevr.

There was a short silence.

"That is not possible," said Childermass. "There are not two Emperors in this pack. I know there are not."

If anything the king was younger and fiercer than before. His hair and robes were black and the crown upon his head had become a thin band of pale metal. There was no trace of the thumbprint upon the card, but the great bird in the corner was now decidedly black and it had cast off its eagle-like aspects and settled itself into a shape altogether more English: it had become a raven.

Childermass turned over the third card. *IIII. L'Emperevr.* And the fourth. *IIII. L'Emperevr.* By the fifth the number and name of the card had disappeared, but the picture remained the same: a young, dark-haired king at whose feet strutted a great, black bird. Childermass turned over each and every card. He even examined the remainder of the pack, but in his anxiety to see he fumbled and the cards somehow fell everywhere. Black Kings crowded about Childermass, spinning in the cold, grey air. Upon each card was the same figure with the same pale, unforgiving gaze.

"There!" said Vinculus softly. "That is what you may tell the magician of Hanover-square! That is his past and his present and his future!"

Needless to say when Childermass returned to Hanover-square and told Mr Norrell what had occurred, Mr Norrell was very angry. That Vinculus should continue to defy Mr Norrell was bad

enough; that he should claim to have a book and Mr Norrell not be able read it was considerably worse; but that he should pretend to tell Mr Norrell's fortune and threaten him with pictures of Black Kings was absolutely unbearable.

"He tricked you!" declared Mr Norrell, angrily. "He hid your own cards and supplanted them with a deck of his own. I am amazed you were so taken in!"

"Quite," agreed Mr Lascelles, regarding Childermass coldly.

"Oh, to be sure, Vinculus is nothing but conjuring tricks," agreed Drawlight. "But still I should have liked to have seen it. I am as fond as any thing of Vinculus. I wish you had told me, Mr Childermass, that you were going to see him. I would have come with you."

Childermass ignored Lascelles and Drawlight and addressed Mr Norrell. "Even supposing that he is an able enough conjuror to perform such a trick – which I am very far from allowing – how was he to know I possessed such a thing as a pack of Marseilles cards? How was he to know when you did not?"

"Aye, and it was as well for you that I did not know! Telling fortunes with picture cards – it is everything I despise! Oh, it has been a very ill-managed business from start to finish!"

"And what of this book that the sorcerer claims to have?" asked Lascelles.

"Yes, indeed," said Mr Norrell. "That odd prophecy. I dare say it is nothing, yet there were one or two expressions which suggested great antiquity. I believe it would be best if I examined that book."

"Well, Mr Childermass?" asked Lascelles.

"I do not know where he keeps it."

"Then we suggest you find out."

So Childermass set spies to follow Vinculus and the first and most surprizing discovery they made was that Vinculus was married. Indeed he was a great deal more married than most people. His wives were five in number and they were scattered throughout the various parishes of London and the surrounding towns and villages. The eldest was forty-five and the youngest fifteen and each was entirely ignorant of the existence of the other four. Childermass contrived to meet with each of them in turn. To two of them he appeared in the character of the unlikely milliner; to another he presented himself as a customs officer; for the benefit of the fourth he became a drunken, gambling rogue; and he told the fifth that, though he appeared to the world to be a servant of the great Mr Norrell of Hanover-square, he was in secret a magician himself. Two tried to rob him; one said she would tell him any thing he wanted to know as long as he paid for her gin; one tried to make him go with her to a Methodist prayer meeting; and the fifth, much to everyone's surprize, fell in love with him. But in the end all his playacting was for nothing because none of them were even aware that Vinculus possessed such a thing as a book, let alone where he kept it.

Mr Norrell refused to believe this and in his private study on the second floor he cast spells and peered into a silver dish of water, examining the lodgings of Vinculus's five wives, but nowhere was there any thing resembling a book.

Meanwhile on the floor above, in a little room set aside for his own particular use, Childermass laid out his cards. The cards had all returned to their original form, except for *The Emperevr* who had not shaken off his Raven-Kingish look. Certain cards appeared over and over again, among them *The Ace of Cups* – an ecclesiastical-looking chalice of such elaborate design that it more resembled a walled city on a stalk – and *II. La Papesse*. According to Childermass's way of thinking both these cards stood for something hidden. The suit of Wands also appeared with quite unwonted frequency, but they were always in the higher numbers, the Seven, the Eight, the Nine and Ten. The more Childermass gazed at these rows of wands the more they appeared to him to be lines of writing. Yet at the same time they were a barrier, an obstacle to understanding, and so Childermass came to believe that Vinculus's book, whatever it was, was in an unknown language.

22

The Knight of Wands

February 1808

JONATHAN STRANGE WAS a very different sort of person from his father. He was not avaricious; he was not proud; he was not ill-tempered and disagreeable. But though he had no striking vices, his virtues were perhaps almost as hard to define. At the pleasure parties of Weymouth and in the drawing-rooms of Bath he was regularly declared to be "the most charming man in the world" by the fashionable people he met there, but all that they meant by this was that he talked well, danced well, and hunted and gambled as much as a gentleman should.

In person he was rather tall and his figure was considered good. Some people thought him handsome, but this was not by any means the universal opinion. His face had two faults: a long nose and an ironic expression. It is also true that his hair had a reddish tinge and, as everybody knows, no one with red hair can ever truly be said to be handsome.

At the time of his father's death he was much taken up with a scheme to persuade a certain young lady to marry him. When he arrived home from Shrewsbury on the day of his father's death and the servants told him the news, his first thoughts were to wonder how his suit would be affected. Was she more likely to say yes now? Or less?

This marriage ought to have been the easiest matter in the world to arrange. Their friends all approved the match and the lady's brother – her only relation – was scarcely less ardent in wishing for it than Jonathan Strange himself. True, Laurence Strange had objected strongly to the lady's poverty, but he had put it out of his power to make any serious difficulty when he froze himself to death.

But, though Jonathan Strange had been the acknowledged suitor of this young lady for some months, the engagement – hourly expected by all their acquaintance – did not follow. It was not that she did not love him; he was quite certain that she did, but sometimes it seemed as if she had fallen in love with him for the sole purpose of quarrelling with him. He was quite at a loss to account for it. He believed that he had done everything she wanted in the way of reforming his behaviour. His card-playing and other sorts of gambling had dwindled away almost to nothing and he drank very little now – scarcely more than a bottle a day. He had told her that he had no objection to going to church more if that would please her – as often, say, as once a week – twice, if she would like it better – but she said that she would leave such matters to his own conscience, that they were not the sort of thing that could be dictated by another person. He knew that she disliked his frequent visits to Bath, Brighton, Weymouth and Cheltenham and he assured her that she had nothing to fear from the women in those places – doubtless they were very charming, but they were nothing to him. She said that was not what concerned her. *That* had not even occurred to her. It was just that she wished he could find a better way to occupy his time. She did not mean to moralize and no one loved a holiday better than her, but perpetual holidays! Was that really what he wanted? Did that make him happy?

He told her that he quite agreed with her and in the past year he had continually been forming plans to take up this or that profession or regular train of study. The plans themselves were very good. He thought he might seek out a destitute poetic genius and become his patron; he thought he would study law; look for fossils on the beach at Lyme Regis; buy an ironworks; study iron-founding; ask a fellow he knew about new methods of agriculture; study theology; and finish reading a fascinating work on engineering which he was almost certain he had put down on a little table at the furthest corner of his father's library two or three years ago. But to each of these projected courses some formidable obstacle was found to exist. Destitute poetic geniuses were harder to come by than he had imagined;[1] lawbooks were dull; he could not remember the name of the fellow who knew about agriculture; and the day that he intended to start for Lyme Regis it was raining heavily.

And so on and so on. He told the young lady that he heartily wished that he had gone into the Navy years ago. Nothing in the world would have suited him so well! But his father would never have agreed to it and he was twenty-eight now. It was far too late to take up a naval career.

The name of this curiously dissatisfied young woman was Arabella Woodhope and she was the daughter of the late curate

---

[1] It appears that Strange did not abandon the notion of a poetical career easily. In *The Life of Jonathan Strange*, pub. John Murray, London, 1820, John Segundus describes how, having been disappointed in his search for a poet, Strange decided to write the poems himself. "Things went very well upon the first day; from breakfast to dinner he sat in his dressing gown at the little writing table in his dressing room and scribbled very fast upon several dozen sheets of quarto. He was very delighted with everything he wrote and so was his valet, who was a literary man himself and who gave advice upon the knotty questions of metaphor and rhetoric, and who ran about gathering up the papers as they flew about the room and putting them in order and then running downstairs to read the most exhilarating parts to his friend, the under-gardener. It really was astonishing how quickly Strange wrote; indeed the valet declared that when he put his hand close to Strange's head he could feel a heat coming off it because of the immense creative energies within. On the second day Strange sat down to write another fifty or so pages and immediately got into difficulties because he could not think of a rhyme for " 'let love suffice'. 'Sunk in vice' was not promising; 'a pair of mice' was nonsense, and 'what's the price?' merely vulgar. He struggled for an hour, could think of nothing, went for a ride to loosen his brains and never looked at his poem again."

of St Swithin's in Clunbury.[2] At the time of Laurence Strange's death she was paying an extended visit to some friends in the Gloucestershire village where her brother was a curate. Her letter of condolence reached Strange on the morning of the funeral. It expressed everything that was proper – sympathy for his loss tempered by an understanding of the elder Mr Strange's many failings as a parent. But there was something more besides. She was concerned about him. She regretted her absence from Shropshire. She did not like him being alone and friendless at such a time.

His mind was made up upon the instant. He could not imagine that he was ever likely to find himself in a more advantageous situation. She would never be more full of anxious tenderness than she was at this moment and he would never be richer. (He could not quite believe that she was as indifferent to his wealth as she claimed.) He supposed he ought to allow a proper interval between his father's funeral and his proposal of marriage. Three days seemed about right, so on the morning of the fourth day he ordered his valet to pack his clothes and his groom to make his horse ready and he set off for Gloucestershire.

He took with him the new manservant. He had spoken at length to this man and had found him to be energetic, resourceful and able. The new manservant was delighted to be chosen (though his vain spirit told him that this was the most natural thing in the world). But now that the new manservant has passed the giant-toppling stage of his career – now that he has, as it were, stepped out of myth and into the workaday world, it will perhaps be found more convenient to give him his name like an ordinary mortal. His name was Jeremy Johns.

Upon the first day they endured nothing but the commonplace adventures which befall any traveller: they quarrelled with a man who set his dog to bark at them for no reason and there was an

---

[2] A village five or six miles from Strange's home.

alarm about Strange's horse which began to shew signs of being sickly and which then, upon further investigation, was discovered to be in perfect health. On the morning of the second day they were riding through a pretty landscape of gently sloping hills, winter woods and prosperous-looking, tidy farms. Jeremy Johns was occupied in practising the correct degree of haughtiness for the servant of a gentleman newly come into an extensive property and Jonathan Strange was thinking about Miss Woodhope.

Now that the day had arrived when he was to see her again he began to have some doubts of his reception. He was glad to think she was with her brother – dear, good Henry who saw nothing but good in the match and who, Strange was quite certain, never failed to encourage his sister to think favourably of it. But he had some doubts about the friends with whom she was staying. They were a clergyman and his wife. He knew nothing of them, but he had the natural distrust that a young, rich, self-indulgent man feels for members of the clergy. Who could say what notions of extra- ordinary virtue and unnecessary self-sacrifice they might be daily imparting to her?

The low sun cast immense shadows. Ice and frost sparkled upon the branches of the trees and in hollows of the fields. Catching sight of a man ploughing a field, he was reminded of the families who lived upon his land and whose welfare had always been cause for concern to Miss Woodhope. An ideal conversation began to develop in his head. *And what are your intentions regarding your tenants?* she would ask – *Intentions?* he would say – *Yes*, she would say. *How will you ease their burdens? Your father took every penny he could from them. He made their lives miserable – I know he did,* Strange would say, *I have never defended my father's actions – Have you lowered the rents yet?* she would say. *Have you talked to the parish council? Have you thought about almshouses for the old people and a school for the children?*

"It is really quite unreasonable for her to be talking of rents, almhouses and a school," thought Strange gloomily. "After all, my father only died last Tuesday."

"Well, that is odd!" remarked Jeremy Johns.

"Hmmm?" said Strange. He discovered that they had halted at a white gate. At the side of the road was a neat little white-painted cottage. It was newly built and had six sides and Gothic windows.

"Where is the toll-keeper?" asked Jeremy Johns.

"Hmmm?" said Strange.

"It is a tollhouse, sir. See, there is the board with the list of money to pay. But there is no one about. Shall I leave them sixpence?"

"Yes, yes. As you wish."

So Jeremy Johns left the toll upon the doorstep of the cottage and opened the gate so that Strange and he could pass through. A hundred yards further on they entered a village. There was an ancient stone church with winter's golden light upon it, an avenue of ancient, twisted hornbeams that led somewhere or other, and twenty or so neat stone cottages with smoke rising up from their chimneys. A stream ran by the side of the road. It was bordered by dry, yellow grasses with pendants of ice hanging from them.

"Where are all the people?" said Jeremy.

"What?" said Strange. He looked around and saw two little girls looking out of a cottage window. "There," he said.

"No, sir. Those are children. I meant grown-ups. I do not see any."

This was true; there were none to be seen. There were some chickens strutting about, a cat sitting on some straw in an ancient cart and some horses in a field, but no people. Yet as soon as Strange and Jeremy Johns left the village, the reason for this queer state of affairs became apparent. A hundred yards or so from the last house in the village a crowd was gathered round a winter hedge. They carried an assortment of weapons – billhooks, sickles, sticks and guns. It was a very odd picture, both sinister and a little ridiculous. Any one would have thought that the village had decided to make war upon hawthorn bushes and elder-trees. The low winter sun shone full upon the villagers, gilding their clothes and weapons and their strange, intent expressions. Long, blue shadows streamed behind them. They were completely silent and whenever one of them moved, he did so with great care as though afraid of making a noise.

As they rode by, Strange and Jeremy stood up in the stirrups and craned their necks to catch a glimpse of whatever it was that the villagers were looking at.

"Well, that is odd!" exclaimed Jeremy when they were past. "There was nothing there!"

"No," said Strange, "there was a man. I am not surprised you could not see him. At first I took him for a hedge-root, but it was definitely a man – a grey, gaunt, weather-worn man – a man remarkably like a hedge-root, but a man nevertheless."

The road led them into a dark winter wood. Jeremy John's curiosity had been excited and he wondered who the man could be and what the villagers were intending to do to him. Strange answered once or twice at random, but soon fell to thinking of Miss Woodhope.

"It will be best to avoid discussing the changes brought on by my father's death," he thought. "It is altogether too dangerous. I will begin with light, indifferent subjects – the adventures of this journey for example. Now, what has happened that will amuse her?" He looked up. Dark, dripping trees surrounded him. "There must have been something." He remembered a windmill he had seen near Hereford with a child's red cloak caught up on one of the sails. As the sails turned the cloak was one moment being dragged through the slush and the mud and the next flying through the air like a vivid scarlet flag. "Like an allegory of something or other. Then I can tell her about the empty village and the children at the window peeping out between the curtains, one with a doll in her hand and the other with a wooden horse. Next come the silent crowd with their weapons and the man beneath the hedge."

Oh! she was certain to say, *Poor man! What happened to him? – I do not know*, Strange would say. *But surely you stayed to help him*, she would say. *No*, Strange would say. *Oh!*, she would say . . .

"Wait!" cried Strange, reining in his horse. "This will not do at all! We must go back. I do not feel easy in my mind about the man under the hedge."

"Oh!" cried Jeremy Johns, in relief. "I am very glad to hear you say so, sir. Neither am I."

"I don't suppose you thought to bring a set of pistols, did you?" said Strange.

"No, sir."

"D—!" said Strange and then flinched a little, because Miss Woodhope did not approve of oaths. "What about a knife? Something of that sort?"

"No, nothing, sir. But do not fret." Jeremy jumped off his horse and went delving about in the undergrowth. "I can make us some clubs out of these branches which will do almost as well as pistols."

There were some stout branches which someone had cut from a coppice of trees and left lying on the ground. Jeremy picked one up and offered it to Strange. It was scarcely a club, more a branch with twigs growing out of it.

"Well," said Strange, doubtfully, "I suppose that it is better than nothing."

Jeremy equipped himself with another branch just the same, and, thus armed, they rode back to the village and the silent crowd of people.

"You there!" cried Strange, singling out a man dressed in a shepherd's smock with a number of knitted shawls tied over it and a wide-brimmed hat upon his head. He made a few flourishing gestures with his club in what he hoped was a threatening manner. "What . . . ?"

Upon the instant several of the crowd turned together and put their fingers to their lips.

Another man came up to Strange. He was dressed rather more respectably than the first in a coat of brown cord. He touched his fingers to his hat and said very softly, "Beg pardon, sir, but could not you take the horses further off? They stamp their feet and breathe very loud."

"But . . ." began Strange.

"Hush, sir!" whispered the man, "Your voice. It is too loud. You will wake him up!"

"Wake him up? Who?"

"The man under the hedge, sir. He is a magician. Did you never hear that if you wake a magician before his time, you risk bringing his dreams out of his head into the world?"

"And who knows what horrors he is dreaming of!" agreed another man, in a whisper.

"But how . . ." began Strange. Once again several people among the crowd turned and frowned indignantly at him and made signs that he was to speak more softly.

"But how do you know he is a magician?" he whispered.

"Oh! He has been in Monk Gretton for the past two days, sir. He tells everyone he is a magician. On the first day he tricked some of our children into stealing pies and beer from their mothers' larders, saying that they were for the Queen of the Fairies. Yesterday he was found wandering in the grounds of Farwater Hall, which is our great house here, sir. Mrs Morrow – whose property it is – hired him to tell her fortune, but all he said was that her son, Captain Morrow, has been shot dead by the French – and now, poor lady, she has lain down upon her bed and says she will lie there until she dies. And so, sir, we have had enough of this man. We mean to make him go. And if he will not, we shall send him to the workhouse."

"Well, that seems most reasonable," whispered Strange. "But what I do not understand is . . ."

Just at that moment the man under the hedge opened his eyes. The crowd gave a sort of soft, communal gasp and several people took a step or two backwards.

The man extracted himself from the hedge. This was no easy task because various parts of it – hawthorn twigs, elder branches, strands of ivy, mistletoe and witches' broom – had insinuated

251

themselves among his clothes, limbs and hair during the night or glued themselves to him with ice. He sat up. He did not seem in the least surprized to find he had an audience; indeed one would almost have supposed from his behaviour that he had been expecting it. He looked at them all and gave several disparaging sniffs and snorts.

He ran his fingers through his hair, removing dead leaves, bits of twig and half a dozen earwigs. "I reached out my hand," he muttered to no one in particular. "England's rivers turned and flowed the other way." He loosened his neckcloth and fished out some spiders which had taken up residence inside his shirt. In doing so, he revealed that his neck and throat were ornamented with an odd pattern of blue lines, dots, crosses and circles. Then he wrapped his neckcloth back about his neck and, having thus completed his toilet to his satisfaction, he rose to his feet.

"My name is Vinculus," he declared. Considering that he had just spent a night under a hedge his voice was remarkably loud and clear. "For ten days I have been walking westwards in search of a man who is destined to be a great magician. Ten days ago I was shewn a picture of this man and now by certain mystic signs I see that it is you!"

Everyone looked around to see who he meant.

The man in the shepherd's smock and the knitted shawls came up to Strange and plucked at his coat. "It is you, sir," he said.

"Me?" said Strange.

Vinculus approached Strange.

"Two magicians shall appear in England," he said.
"The first shall fear me; the second shall long to behold me;
The first shall be governed by thieves and murderers; the second shall conspire at his own destruction;
The first shall bury his heart in a dark wood beneath the snow, yet still feel its ache;
The second shall see his dearest possession in his enemy's hand . . ."

252

"I see," interrupted Strange. "And which am I, the first or the second? No, do not tell me. It does not matter. Both sound entirely dreadful. For someone who is anxious that I should become a magician, I must say you do not make the life sound very appealing. I hope to be married soon and a life spent in dark woods surrounded by thieves and murderers would be inconvenient to say the least. I suggest you chuse someone else."

"I did not chuse you, Magician! You were chosen long ago."

"Well, whoever it was, they will be disappointed."

Vinculus ignored this remark and took a firm grasp of the bridle of Strange's horse as a precaution against his riding off. He then proceeded to recite in its entirety the prophecy which he had already performed for the benefit of Mr Norrell in the library at Hanover-square.

Strange received it with a similar degree of enthusiasm and when it was done, he leant down from his horse and said very slowly and distinctly, "I do not know any magic!"

Vinculus paused. He looked as if he was prepared to concede that this might be a legitimate obstacle to Strange's becoming a great magician. Happily the solution occurred to him immediately; he stuck his hand into the breast of his coat and pulled out some sheets of paper with bits of straw sticking to them. "Now," he said, looking even more mysterious and impressive than before, "I have here some spells which . . . No, no! I cannot *give* them to you!" (Strange had reached out to take them.) "They are precious objects. I endured years of torment and suffered great ordeals in order to possess them."

"How much?" said Strange.

"Seven shillings and sixpence," said Vinculus.

"Very well."

"Surely you do not intend to give him any money, sir?" asked Jeremy Johns.

"If it will stop him talking to me, then, yes, certainly."

Meanwhile the crowd was regarding Strange and Jeremy Johns

in no very friendly manner. Their appearance had coincided more or less with Vinculus's waking and the villagers were starting to wonder if they might not be two apparitions from Vinculus's dreams. The villagers began to accuse one another of having woken Vinculus up. They were just starting to quarrel about it when an official-looking person in an important-looking hat arrived and informed Vinculus that he must go to the workhouse as a pauper. Vinculus retorted that he would do no such thing as he was not a pauper any longer – he had seven shillings and sixpence! And he dangled the money in the man's face in a very impertinent fashion. Just as a fight seemed certain to ensue from one cause or another, peace was suddenly restored to the village of Monk Gretton by the simple expedient of Vinculus turning and walking off one way and Strange and Jeremy Johns riding off another.

Towards five o'clock they arrived at an inn in the village of S— near Gloucester. So little hope had Strange that his meeting with Miss Woodhope would be productive of any thing but misery to them both that he thought he would put it off until the following morning. He ordered a good dinner and went and sat down by the fire in a comfortable chair with a newspaper. But he soon discovered that comfort and tranquillity were poor substitutes for Miss Woodhope's company and so he cancelled the dinner and went immediately to the house of Mr and Mrs Redmond in order to begin being unhappy as soon as possible. He found only the ladies at home, Mrs Redmond and Miss Woodhope.

Lovers are rarely the most rational beings in creation and so it will come as no surprize to my readers to discover that Strange's musings concerning Miss Woodhope had produced a most inexact portrait of her. Though his imaginary conversations might be said to describe her *opinions*, they were no guide at all to her *disposition* and *manners*. It was *not* her habit to harass recently bereaved persons with demands that they build schools and almshouses. Nor did she find fault with everything they said. She was not so unnatural.

She greeted him in a very different manner from the cross, scolding young lady of his imaginings. Far from demanding that he immediately undo every wrong his father had ever done, she behaved with particular kindness towards him and seemed altogether delighted to see him.

She was about twenty-two years of age. In repose her looks were only moderately pretty. There was very little about her face and figure that was in any way remarkable, but it was the sort of face which, when animated by conversation or laughter, is completely transformed. She had a lively disposition, a quick mind and a fondness for the comical. She was always very ready to smile and, since a smile is the most becoming ornament that any lady can wear, she had been known upon occasion to outshine women who were acknowledged beauties in three counties.

Her friend, Mrs Redmond, was a kindly, placid creature of forty-five. She was not rich, widely travelled or particularly clever. Under other circumstances she would have been puzzled to know what to say to a man of the world like Jonathan Strange, but happily his father had just died and that provided a subject.

"I dare say you are a great deal occupied just now, Mr Strange," she said. "I remember when my own father died, there was a world of things to do. He left so many bequests. There were some china jugs that used to stand upon the kitchen mantelpiece at home. My father wished a jug to be given to each of our old servants. But the descriptions of the jugs in his will were most confusing and no one could tell which jug was meant for which person. And then the servants quarrelled and they all desired to be given the yellow jug with pink roses. Oh! I thought I would never be done with those bequests. Did your father leave many bequests, Mr Strange?"

"No, madam. None. He hated everybody."

"Ah! That is fortunate, is it not? And what shall you do now?"

"Do?" echoed Strange.

"Miss Woodhope says your poor, dear father bought and sold things. Shall you do the same?"

"No, madam. If I have my way – and I believe I shall – my father's business will all be wound up as soon as possible."

"Oh! But then I dare say you will be a good deal taken up with farming? Miss Woodhope says your estate is a large one."

"It is, madam. But I have tried farming and I find it does not suit me."

"Ah!" said Mrs Redmond, wisely.

There was a silence. Mrs Redmond's clock ticked and the coals shifted in the grate. Mrs Redmond began to pull about some embroidery silks that lay in her lap and had got into a fearful knot. Then her black cat mistook this activity for a game and stalked along the sopha and tried to catch at the silks. Arabella laughed and caught up the cat and started to play with it. This was exactly the sort of tranquil domestic scene that Strange had set his heart upon (though he did not want Mrs Redmond and was undecided about the cat) and it was all the more desirable in his eyes since he had never met with anything other than coldness and disagreeableness in his childhood home. The question was: how to persuade Arabella that it was what she wanted too? A sort of inspiration came over him and he suddenly addressed Mrs Redmond again. "In short, madam, I do not think that I shall have the time. I am going to study magic."

"Magic!" exclaimed Arabella, looking at him in surprize.

She seemed about to question him further, but at this highly interesting moment Mr Redmond was heard in the hall. He was accompanied by his curate, Henry Woodhope – the same Henry Woodhope who was both brother to Arabella and childhood friend to Jonathan Strange. Naturally there were introductions and explanations to get through (Henry Woodhope had not known Strange was coming) and for the moment Strange's unexpected announcement was forgotten.

The gentlemen were just come from a parish meeting and as soon as everyone was seated again in the drawing-room, Mr Redmond and Henry imparted various items of parish news to

Mrs Redmond and Arabella. Then they inquired about Strange's journey, the state of the roads and how the farmers got on in Shropshire, Herefordshire and Gloucestershire (these being the counties Strange had travelled through). At seven o'clock the tea things were brought in. In the silence that followed, while they were all eating and drinking, Mrs Redmond remarked to her husband, "Mr Strange is going to be a magician, my love." She spoke as if it were the most natural thing in the world, because to her it was.

"A magician?" said Henry, quite astonished. "Why should you want to do that?"

Strange paused. He did not wish to tell his real reason – which was to impress Arabella with his determination to do something sober and scholarly – and so he fell back upon the only other explanation he could think of. "I met a man under a hedge at Monk Gretton who told me that I was a magician."

Mr Redmond laughed, approving the joke. "Excellent!" he said.

"Did you, indeed?" said Mrs Redmond.

"I do not understand," said Henry Woodhope.

"You do not believe me, I suppose?" said Strange to Arabella.

"Oh, on the contrary, Mr Strange!" said Arabella with an amused smile. "It is all of a piece with your usual way of doing things. It is quite as strong a foundation for a career as I should expect from you."

Henry said, "But if you are going to take up a profession – and I cannot see why you should want one at all, now that you have come into your property – surely you can chuse something better than magic! It has no practical application."

"Oh, but I think you are wrong!" said Mr Redmond. "There is that gentleman in London who confounds the French by sending them illusions! I forget his name. What is it that he calls his theory? Modern magic?"

"But how is that different from the old-fashioned sort?" wondered Mrs Redmond. "And which will you do, Mr Strange?"

"Yes, do tell us, Mr Strange," said Arabella, with an arch look. "Which will you do?"

"A little of both, Miss Woodhope. A little of both!" Turning to Mrs Redmond, he said, "I purchased three spells from the man under the hedge. Should you like to see one, madam?"

"Oh, yes, indeed!"

"Miss Woodhope?" asked Strange.

"What are they for?"

"I do not know. I have not read them yet." Jonathan Strange took the three spells Vinculus had given him out of his breast pocket and gave them to her to look at.

"They are very dirty," said Arabella.

"Oh! We magicians do not regard a little dirt. Besides I dare say they are very old. Ancient, mysterious spells such as these are often . . ."

"The date is written at the top of them. 2nd February 1808. That is two weeks ago."

"Indeed? I had not observed."

"*Two Spells to Make an Obstinate Man leave London*," read Arabella. "I wonder why the magician would want to make people leave London?"

"I do not know. There are certainly too many people in London, but it seems a great deal of work to make them leave one at a time."

"But these are horrible! Full of ghosts and horrors! Making them think that they are about to meet their one true love, when in truth the spell does nothing of the sort!"

"Let me see!" Strange snatched back the offending spells. He examined them rapidly and said, "I promise you I knew nothing of their content when I purchased them – nothing whatsoever. The truth is that the man I bought them from was a vagabond and quite destitute. With the money I gave him he was able to escape the workhouse."

"Well, I am glad of that. But his spells are still horrible and I hope you will not use them."

"But what of the last spell? *One Spell to Discover what My Enemy is doing Presently*. I think you can have no objection to that? Let me do the last spell."

"But will it work? You do not have any enemies, do you?"

"None that I know of. And so there can be no harm in attempting it, can there?"

The instructions called for a mirror and some dead flowers,[3] so Strange and Henry lifted a mirror off the wall and laid it upon the table. The flowers were more difficult; it was February and the only flowers Mrs Redmond possessed were some dried lavender, roses and thyme.

"Will these do?" she asked Strange.

He shrugged. "Who knows? Now . . ." He studied the instructions again. "The flowers must be placed around, like so. And then I draw a circle upon the mirror with my finger like this. And quarter the circle. Strike the mirror thrice and say these words . . ."

"Strange," said Henry Woodhope, "where did you get this nonsense?"

"From the man under the hedge. Henry, you do not listen."

"And he seemed honest, did he?"

"Honest? No, not particularly. He seemed, I would say, cold. Yes, 'cold' is a good word to describe him and 'hungry' another."

"And how much did you pay for these spells?"

"Henry!" said his sister. "Did you not just hear Mr Strange say that he bought them as an act of charity?"

Strange was absent-mindedly drawing circles upon the surface of the mirror and quartering them. Arabella, who was sitting next to him, gave a sudden start of surprize. Strange looked down.

"Good God!" he cried.

---

[3] Mr Norrell appears to have adapted it from a description of a Lancashire spell in Peter Watershippe's *Death's Library* (1448).

In the mirror was the image of a room, but it was not Mrs Redmond's drawing-room. It was a small room, furnished not extravagantly but very well. The ceiling – which was high – gave the idea of its being a small apartment within a large and perhaps rather grand house. There were bookcases full of books and other books lay about on tables. There was a good fire in the fireplace and candles on the desk. A man worked at a desk. He was perhaps fifty and was dressed very plainly in a grey coat. He was a quiet, unremarkable sort of man in an old-fashioned wig. Several books lay open on his desk and he read a little in some and wrote a little in others.

"Mrs Redmond! Henry!" cried Arabella. "Come quickly! See what Mr Strange has done!"

"But who in the world is he?" asked Strange, mystified. He lifted the mirror and looked under it, apparently with the idea that he might discover there a tiny gentleman in a grey coat, ready to be questioned. When the mirror was replaced upon the table the vision of the other room and the other man was still there. They could hear no sounds from the other room but the flames of the fire danced in the grate and the man, with his glinting spectacles on his nose, turned his head from one book to another.

"Why is he your enemy?" asked Arabella.

"I have not the least idea."

"Do you owe him money, perhaps?" asked Mr Redmond.

"I do not *think* so."

"He could be a banker. It looks a little like a counting house," suggested Arabella.

Strange began to laugh. "Well, Henry, you can cease frowning at me. If I am a magician, I am a very indifferent one. Other adepts summon up fairy-spirits and long-dead kings. I appear to have conjured the spirit of a banker."

Volume II

JONATHAN STRANGE

"Can a magician kill a man by magic?" Lord
Wellington asked Strange. Strange frowned.
He seemed to dislike the question. "I suppose
a magician might," he admitted, "but a
gentleman never could."

23

The Shadow House

July 1809

O N A SUMMER'S day in 1809 two riders were travelling
along a dusty country lane in Wiltshire. The sky was of a
deep, brilliant blue, and beneath it England lay sketched
in deep shadows and in hazy reflections of the sky's fierce light. A
great horse-chestnut leant over the road and made a pool of black
shadow, and when the two riders reached the shadow it swallowed
them up so that nothing remained of them except their voices.

". . . and how long will it be before you consider publication?"
said one. "For you must, you know. I have been considering the
matter and I believe it is the first duty of every modern magician to
publish. I am surprized Norrell does not publish."

"I dare say he will in time," said the other. "As to my publishing, who would wish to read what I have written? These days,
when Norrell performs a new miracle every week, I cannot
suppose that the work of a purely *theoretical* magician would be
of much interest to any body."

"Oh! You are too modest," said the first voice. "You must not
leave every thing to Norrell. Norrell cannot do every thing."

"But he can. He does," sighed the second voice.

How pleasant to meet old friends! For it is Mr Honeyfoot and
Mr Segundus. Yet why do we find them on horseback? – a kind of
exercise which agrees with neither of them and which neither takes

regularly, Mr Honeyfoot being too old and Mr Segundus too poor. And on such a day as this! So hot that it will make Mr Honeyfoot first sweat, and then itch, and then break out in red pimples; a day of such dazzling brightness that it is certain to bring on one of Mr Segundus's headachs. And what are they doing in Wiltshire?

It had so happened that, in the course of his labours on behalf of the little stone figure and the girl with the ivy-leaves in her hair, Mr Honeyfoot had discovered something. He believed that he had identified the murderer as an Avebury man. So he had come to Wiltshire to look at some old documents in Avebury parish church. "For," as he had explained to Mr Segundus, "if I discover *who* he was, then perhaps it may lead me to discover who was the girl and what dark impulse drove him to destroy her." Mr Segundus had gone with his friend and had looked at all the documents and helped him unpick the old Latin. But, though Mr Segundus loved old documents (no one loved them more) and though he put great faith in what they could achieve, he secretly doubted that seven Latin words five centuries old could explain a man's life. But Mr Honeyfoot was all optimism. Then it occurred to Mr Segundus that, as they were already in Wiltshire, they should take the opportunity to visit the Shadow House which stood in that county and which neither of them had ever seen.

Most of us remember hearing of the Shadow House in our school-rooms. The name conjures up vague notions of magic and ruins yet few of us have any very clear recollection of why it is so important. The truth is that historians of magic still argue over its significance – and some will be quick to tell you that it is of no significance whatsoever. No great events in English magical history took place there; furthermore, of the two magicians who lived in the house, one was a charlatan and the other was a woman – neither attribute likely to recommend its possessor to the gentleman-magicians and gentle-man-historians of recent years – and yet for two centuries the Shadow House has been known as one of the most magical places in England.

It was built in the sixteenth century by Gregory Absalom, court magician to King Henry VIII and to Queens Mary and Elizabeth. If we measure a magician's success by how much magic he does, then Absalom was no magician at all, for his spells hardly ever took effect. However, if instead we examine the amount of money a magician makes and allow that to be our yardstick, then Absalom was certainly one of the greatest English magicians who ever lived, for he was born in poverty and died a very rich man.

One of his boldest achievements was to persuade the King of Denmark to pay a great handful of diamonds for a spell which, Absalom claimed, would turn the flesh of the King of Sweden into water. Naturally the spell did nothing of the sort, but with the money he got for half these jewels Absalom built the Shadow House. He furnished it with Turkey carpets and Venetian mirrors and glass and a hundred other beautiful things; and, when the house was completed, a curious thing happened – or may have happened – or did not happen at all. Some scholars believe – and others do not – that the magic which Absalom had pretended to do for his clients began to appear of its own accord in the house.

On a moonlit night in 1610 two maids looked out of a window on an upper floor and saw twenty or thirty beautiful ladies and handsome gentlemen dancing in a circle on the lawn. In February 1666 Valentine Greatrakes, an Irishman, held a conversation in Hebrew with the prophets Moses and Aaron in a little passageway near the great linen press. In 1667 Mrs Penelope Chelmorton, a visitor to the house, looked in a mirror and saw a little girl of three or four years old looking out. As she watched, she saw the child grow up and grow older and she recognized herself. Mrs Chelmorton's reflection continued to age until there was nought but a dry, dead corpse in the mirror. The reputation of the Shadow House is based upon these and a hundred other such tales.

Absalom had one child, a daughter named Maria. She was born in the Shadow House and lived there all her life, scarcely ever leaving it for more than a day or two. In her youth the house was visited by kings and ambassadors, by scholars, soldiers and poets.

Even after the death of her father, people came to look upon the end of English magic, its last strange flowering on the eve of its long winter. Then, as the visitors became fewer, the house weakened and began to decay and the garden went to the wild. But Maria Absalom refused to repair her father's house. Even dishes that broke were left in cracked pieces on the floor.[1]

In her fiftieth year the ivy was grown so vigorous and had so far extended itself that it grew inside all the closets and made much of the floor slippery and unsafe to walk upon. Birds sang as much within the house as without. In her hundredth year the house and woman were ruinous together – though neither was at all extinguished. She continued another forty-nine years, before dying one summer morning in her bed with the leaf shadows of a great ash-tree and the broken sunlight falling all around her.

As Mr Honeyfoot and Mr Segundus hurried towards the Shadow House on this hot afternoon, they were a little nervous in case Mr Norrell should get to hear of their going (for, what with admirals and Ministers sending him respectful letters and paying him visits, Mr Norrell was growing greater by the hour). They feared lest he should consider that Mr Honeyfoot had broken the

---

[1] Some scholars (Jonathan Strange among them) have argued that Maria Absalom knew exactly what she was about when she permitted her house to go to rack and ruin. It is their contention that Miss Absalom did what she did in accordance with the commonly-held belief that all ruined buildings belong to the Raven King. This presumably would account for the fact that the magic at the Shadow House appeared to grow stronger *after* the house fell into ruin.

"All of Man's works, all his cities, all his empires, all his monuments will one day crumble to dust. Even the houses of my own dear readers must – though it be for just one day, one hour – be ruined and become houses where the stones are mortared with moonlight, windowed with starlight and furnished with the dusty wind. It is said that in that day, in that hour, our houses become the possessions of the Raven King. Though we bewail the end of English magic and say it is long gone from us and inquire of each other how it was possible that we came to lose something so precious, let us not forget that it also waits for us at England's end and one day we will no more be able to escape the Raven King than, in this present Age, we can bring him back." *The History and Practice of English Magic* by Jonathan Strange, pub. John Murray, London, 1816.

terms of his contract. So, in order that as few people as possible should know what they were about, they had told no one where they were going and had set off very early in the morning and had walked to a farm where they could hire horses and had come to the Shadow House by a very roundabout way.

At the end of the dusty, white lane they came to a pair of high gates. Mr Segundus got down from his horse to open them. The gates had been made of fine Castillian wrought iron, but were now rusted to a dark, vivid red and their original form was very much decayed and shrivelled. Mr Segundus's hand came away with dusty traces upon it as if a million dried and powdered roses had been compacted and formed into the dreamlike semblance of a gate. The curling iron had been further ornamented with little bas-reliefs of wicked, laughing faces, now ember-red and disintegrating, as if the part of Hell where these heathens were now resident was in the charge of an inattentive demon who had allowed his furnace to get too hot.

Beyond the gate were a thousand pale pink roses and high, nodding cliffs of sunlit elm and ash and chestnut and the blue, blue sky. There were four tall gables and a multitude of high grey chimneys and stone-latticed windows. But the Shadow House had been a ruined house for well over a century and was built as much of elder-trees and dog roses as of silvery limestone and had in its composition as much of summer-scented breezes as of iron and timber.

"It is like the Other Lands," said Mr Segundus, pressing his face into the gate in his enthusiasm, and receiving from it an impression of its shape apparently in powdered roses.[2] He pulled open the

---

[2] When people talk of "the Other Lands", they generally have in mind Faerie, or some such other vague notion. For the purposes of general conversation such definitions do very well, but a magician must learn to be more precise. It is well known that the Raven King ruled three kingdoms: the first was the Kingdom of Northern England that encompassed Cumberland, Northumberland, Durham, Yorkshire, Lancashire, Derbyshire and part of Nottinghamshire. The other two were called "the King's Other Lands". One was part of Faerie and the other was commonly supposed to be a country on the far side of Hell, sometimes called "the Bitter Lands". The King's enemies said that he leased it from Lucifer.

gate and led in his horse. Mr Honeyfoot followed. They tied up their horses by a stone basin and began to explore the gardens.

The grounds of the Shadow House did not perhaps deserve the name, "gardens". No one had tended them for over a hundred years. But nor were they a wood. Or a wilderness. There is no word in the English language for a magician's garden two hundred years after the magician is dead. It was richer and more disordered than any garden Mr Segundus and Mr Honeyfoot had ever seen before.

Mr Honeyfoot was highly delighted with everything he saw. He exclaimed over a great avenue of elms where the trees stood almost to their waists, as it were, in a sea of vivid pink foxgloves. He wondered aloud over a carving of a fox which carried a baby in its mouth. He spoke cheerfully of the remarkable magical atmosphere of the place, and declared that even Mr Norrell might learn something by coming here.

But Mr Honeyfoot was not really very susceptible to atmospheres; Mr Segundus, on the other hand, began to feel uneasy. It seemed to him that Absalom's garden was exerting a strange kind of influence on him. Several times, as Mr Honeyfoot and he walked about, he found himself on the point of speaking to someone he thought he knew. Or of recognizing a place he had known before. But each time, just as he was about to remember what he wanted to say, he realized that what he had taken for a friend was in fact only a shadow on the surface of a rose bush. The man's head was only a spray of pale roses and his hand another. The place that Mr Segundus thought he knew as well as the common scenes of childhood was only a chance conjunction of a yellow bush, some swaying elder branches and the sharp, sunlit corner of the house. Besides he could not think who was the friend or what was the place. This began to disturb him so much that, after half an hour, he proposed to Mr Honeyfoot that they sit for a while.

"My dear friend!" said Mr Honeyfoot, "What is the matter?

Are you ill? You are very pale – your hand is trembling. Why did you not speak sooner?"

Mr Segundus passed his hand across his head and said somewhat indistinctly that he believed that some magic was about to take place. He had a most definite impression that that was the case.

"Magic?" exclaimed Mr Honeyfoot. "But what magic could there be?" He looked about him nervously in case Mr Norrell should appear suddenly from behind a tree. "I dare say it is nothing more than the heat of the day which afflicts you. I myself am very hot. But we are blockheads to remain in this condition. For here is comfort! Here is refreshment! To sit in the shade of tall trees – such as these – by a sweet, chattering brook – such as this – is generally allowed to be the best restorative in the world. Come, Mr Segundus, let us sit down!"

They sat down upon the grassy bank of a brown stream. The warm, soft air and the scent of roses calmed and soothed Mr Segundus. His eyes closed once. Opened. Closed again. Opened slowly and heavily . . .

He began to dream almost immediately.

He saw a tall doorway in a dark place. It was carved from a silver-grey stone that shone a little, as if there was moonlight. The doorposts were made in the likeness of two men (or it might only be one man, for both were the same). The man seemed to stride out of the wall and John Segundus knew him at once for a magician. The face could not clearly be seen, only enough to know that it would be a young face and a handsome one. Upon his head he wore a cap with a sharp peak and raven wings upon each side.

John Segundus passed through the door and for a moment saw only the black sky and the stars and the wind. But then he saw that there was indeed a room, but that it was ruinous. Yet despite this, such walls as there were, were furnished with pictures, tapestries and mirrors. But the figures in the tapestries moved about and spoke to each other, and not all the mirrors gave faithful reproductions of the room; some seemed to reflect other places entirely.

At the far end of the room in an uncertain compound of moonlight and candlelight someone was sitting at a table. She wore a gown of a very ancient style and of a greater quantity of material than John Segundus could have supposed necessary, or even possible, in one garment. It was of a strange, old, rich blue; and about the gown, like other stars, the last of the King of Denmark's diamonds were shining still. She looked up at him as he approached – two curiously slanting eyes set farther apart than is generally considered correct for beauty and a long mouth curved into a smile, the meaning of which he could not guess at. Flickers of candlelight suggested hair as red as her dress was blue.

Suddenly another person arrived in John Segundus's dream – a gentleman, dressed in modern clothes. This gentleman did not appear at all surprized at the finely dressed (but somewhat outmoded) lady, but he did appear very astonished to find John Segundus there and he reached out his hand and took John Segundus by the shoulder and began to shake him . . .

Mr Segundus found that Mr Honeyfoot had grasped his shoulder and was gently shaking him.

"I beg your pardon!" said Mr Honeyfoot. "But you cried out in your sleep and I thought perhaps you would wish to be woken."

Mr Segundus looked at him in some perplexity. "I had a dream," he said. "A most curious dream!"

Mr Segundus told his dream to Mr Honeyfoot.

"What a remarkably magical spot!" said Mr Honeyfoot, approvingly. "Your dream – so full of odd symbols and portents – is yet another proof of it!"

"But what does it *mean*?" asked Mr Segundus.

"Oh!" said Mr Honeyfoot, and stopt to think a while. "Well, the lady wore blue, you say? Blue signifies – let me see – immortality, chastity and fidelity; it stands for Jupiter and can be represented by tin. Hmmph! Now where does that get us?"

"Nowhere, I think," sighed Mr Segundus. "Let us walk on."

Mr Honeyfoot, who was anxious to see more, quickly agreed to this proposal and suggested that they explore the interior of the Shadow House.

In the fierce sunlight the house was no more than a towering, green-blue haze against the sky. As they passed through the doorway to the Great Hall, "Oh!" cried Mr Segundus.

"Why! What is it now?" asked Mr Honeyfoot, startled.

Upon either side of the doorway stood a stone image of the Raven King. "I saw these in my dream," said Mr Segundus.

In the Great Hall Mr Segundus looked about him. The mirrors and the paintings that he had seen in his dream were long since gone. Lilac and elder trees filled up the broken walls. Horse-chestnuts and ash made a roof of green and silver that flowed and dappled against the blue sky. Fine gold grasses and ragged robin made a latticework for the empty stone windows.

At one end of the room there were two indistinct figures in a blaze of sunlight. A few odd items were scattered about the floor, a kind of magical debris: some pieces of paper with scraps of spells scribbled upon them, a silver basin full of water and a half-burnt candle in an ancient brass candlestick.

Mr Honeyfoot wished these two shadowy figures a good morning and one replied to him in grave and civil tones, but the other cried out upon the instant, "Henry, it is he! That is the fellow! That is the very man I described! Do you not see? A small man with hair and eyes so dark as to be almost Italian – though the hair has grey in it. But the expression so quiet and timid as to be English without a doubt! A shabby coat all dusty and patched, with frayed cuffs that he has tried to hide by snipping them close. Oh! Henry, this is certainly the man! You sir!" he cried, suddenly addressing Mr Segundus. "Explain yourself!"

Poor Mr Segundus was very much astonished to hear himself and his coat so minutely described by a complete stranger – and the description itself of such a peculiarly distressing sort! Not at all polite. As he stood, trying to collect his thoughts, his interlocutor moved into the shade of an ash-tree that formed part of the north wall of the hall and for the first time in the waking world Mr Segundus beheld Jonathan Strange.

Somewhat hesitantly (for he was aware as he said it how strangely it sounded) Mr Segundus said, "I have seen you, sir, in my dream, I think."

This only enraged Strange more. "The dream, sir, was mine! I lay down on purpose to dream it. I can bring proofs, witnesses that the dream was mine. Mr Woodhope," he indicated his companion, "saw me do it. Mr Woodhope is a clergyman – the rector of a parish in Gloucestershire – I cannot imagine that his word could be doubted! I am rather of the opinion that in England a gentleman's dreams are his own private concern. I fancy there is a law to that effect and, if there is not, why, Parliament should certainly be made to pass one immediately! It ill becomes another man to invite himself into them." Strange paused to take breath.

"Sir!" cried Mr Honeyfoot hotly. "I must beg you to speak to this gentleman with more respect. You have not the good fortune to know this gentleman as I do, but should you have that honour you will learn that nothing is further from his character than a wish to offend others."

Strange made a sort of exclamation of exasperation.

"It is certainly very odd that people should get into each other's dreams," said Henry Woodhope. "Surely it cannot really have been the same dream?"

"Oh! But I fear it is," said Mr Segundus with a sigh. "Ever since I entered this garden I have felt as if it were full of invisible doors and I have gone through them one after the other, until I fell asleep and dreamt the dream where I saw this gentleman. I was in a greatly confused state of mind. I knew it was not me that had set these doors ajar and made them to open, but I did not care. I only wanted to see what was at the end of them."

Henry Woodhope gazed at Mr Segundus as if he did not entirely understand this. "But I still think it cannot be the *same* dream, you know," he explained to Mr Segundus, as if to a rather stupid child. "What did you dream of?"

"Of a lady in a blue gown," said Mr Segundus. "I supposed that it was Miss Absalom."

"Well, *of course*, it was Miss Absalom!" cried Strange in great exasperation as if he could scarcely bear to hear any thing so obvious mentioned. "But unfortunately the lady's appointment was to meet one gentleman. She was naturally disturbed to find two and so she promptly disappeared." Strange shook his head. "There cannot be more than five men in England with any pretensions to magic, but one of them must come here and interrupt my meeting with Absalom's daughter. I can scarcely believe it. I am the unluckiest man in England. God knows I have laboured long enough to dream that dream. It has taken me three weeks – working night and day! – to prepare the spells of summoning, and as for the . . ."

"But this is marvellous!" interrupted Mr Honeyfoot. "This is wonderful! Why! Not even Mr Norrell himself could attempt such a thing!"

"Oh!" said Strange, turning to Mr Honeyfoot. "It is not so difficult as you imagine. First you must send out your invitation to the lady – any spell of summoning will do. I used Ormskirk.[3] Of course the troublesome part was to adapt Ormskirk so that both Miss Absalom and I arrived in my dream at the same time –

---

[3] Paris Ormskirk (1496–1587), a schoolmaster from the village of Clerkenwell near London. He wrote several treatises on magic. Though no very original thinker, he was a diligent worker who set himself the task of assembling and sifting through all the spells of summoning he could find, to try to uncover one reliable version. This took him twelve years, during which time his little house on Clerkenwell-green filled up with thousands of small pieces of paper with spells written on them. Mrs Ormskirk was not best pleased, and she, poor woman, became the original of the magician's wife in stock comedies and second-rate novels – a strident, scolding, unhappy person.

The spell that Ormskirk eventually produced became very popular and was widely used in his own century and the two following ones; but, until Jonathan Strange made his own alterations to the spell and brought forth Maria Absalom into his own dream and Mr Segundus's, I never heard of any one who had the least success with it – perhaps for the reasons that Jonathan Strange gives.

Ormskirk is so loose that the person one summons might go pretty well anywhere at any time and feel that they had fulfilled their obligations – *that*, I admit, was not an easy task. And yet, you know, I am not displeased with the results. Second I had to cast a spell upon myself to bring on a magic sleep. Of course I have heard of such spells but confess that I have never actually seen one, and so, you know, I was obliged to invent my own – I dare say it is feeble enough, but what can one do?"

"Good God!" cried Mr Honeyfoot. "Do you mean to say that practically all this magic was your own invention?"

"Oh! well," said Strange, "as to that . . . I had Ormskirk – I based everything on Ormskirk."

"Oh! But might not Hether-Gray be a better foundation than Ormskirk?" asked Mr Segundus.[4] "Forgive me. I am no practical magician but Hether-Gray has always seemed to me so much more reliable than Ormskirk."

"Indeed?" said Strange. "Of course I have heard of Hether-Gray. I have recently begun to correspond with a gentleman in Lincolnshire who says he has a copy of Hether-Gray's *The Anatomy of a Minotaur*. So Hether-Gray is really worth looking into, is he?"

Mr Honeyfoot declared that Hether-Gray was no such thing, that his book was the most thick-headed nonsense in the world; Mr Segundus disagreed and Strange grew more interested, and less mindful of the fact that he was supposed to be angry with Mr Segundus.

For who can remain angry with Mr Segundus? I dare say there are people in the world who are able to resent goodness and amiability, whose spirits are irritated by gentleness – but I am glad to say that Jonathan Strange was not of their number. Mr Segundus offered his apologies for spoiling the magic and Strange,

---

[4] Mr Segundus's good sense seems to have deserted him at this point. Charles Hether-Gray (1712–89) was another historio-magician who published a famous spell of summoning. His spell and Ormskirk's are equally bad; there is not a pin to chuse between them.

with a smile and a bow, said that Mr Segundus should think of it no more.

"I shall not ask, sir," said Strange to Mr Segundus, "if you are a magician. The ease with which you penetrate other people's dreams proclaims your power." Strange turned to Mr Honeyfoot, "But are you a magician also, sir?"

Poor Mr Honeyfoot! So blunt a question to be applied to so tender a spot! He was still a magician at heart and did not like to be reminded of his loss. He replied that he *had* been a magician not so many years before. But he had been obliged to give it up. Nothing could have been further from his own wishes. The study of magic – of good English magic – was, in his opinion, the most noble occupation in the world.

Strange regarded him with some surprise. "But I do not very well comprehend you. How could any one make you give up your studies if you did not wish it?"

Then Mr Segundus and Mr Honeyfoot described how they had been members of the Learned Society of York Magicians, and how the society had been destroyed by Mr Norrell.

Mr Honeyfoot asked Strange for his opinion of Mr Norrell.

"Oh!" said Strange with a smile. "Mr Norrell is the patron saint of English booksellers."

"Sir?" said Mr Honeyfoot.

"Oh!" said Strange. "One hears of Mr Norrell in every place where the book trade is perpetrated from Newcastle to Penzance. The bookseller smiles and bows and says, 'Ah sir, you are come too late! I *had* a great many books upon subjects magical and historical. But I sold them all to a very learned gentleman of Yorkshire.' It is always Norrell. One may buy, if one chuses, the books that Norrell has left behind. I generally find that the books that Mr Norrell leaves behind are really excellent things for lighting fires with."

Mr Segundus and Mr Honeyfoot were naturally all eagerness to be better acquainted with Jonathan Strange, and he seemed just as anxious to talk to them. Consequently, after each side had made and answered the usual inquiries ("Where are you staying?" "Oh! the George in Avebury." "Well, that is remarkable. So are we."), it was quickly decided that all four gentlemen should ride back to Avebury and dine together.

As they left the Shadow House Strange paused by the Raven King doorway and asked if either Mr Segundus or Mr Honeyfoot had visited the King's ancient capital of Newcastle in the north. Neither had. "This door is a copy of one you will find upon every corner there," said Strange. "The first in this fashion were made when the King was still in England. In that city it seems that everywhere you turn the King steps out of some dark, dusty archway and comes towards you." Strange smiled wryly. "But his face is always half hidden and he will never speak to you."

At five o'clock they sat down to dinner in the parlour of the George inn. Mr Honeyfoot and Mr Segundus found Strange to be a most agreeable companion, lively and talkative. Henry Wood-hope on the other hand ate diligently and when he was done eating, he looked out of the window. Mr Segundus feared that he might feel himself neglected, and so he turned to him and complimented him upon the magic that Strange had done at the Shadow House.

Henry Woodhope was surprized. "I had not supposed it was a matter for congratulation," he said. "Strange did not say it was anything remarkable."

"But, my dear sir!" exclaimed Mr Segundus. "Who knows when such a feat was last attempted in England?"

"Oh! I know nothing of magic. I believe it is quite the fashion-able thing – I have seen reports of magic in the London papers. But a clergyman has little leisure for reading. Besides I have known Strange since we were boys and he is of a most capricious character. I am surprized this magical fit has lasted so long. I dare say he will soon tire of it as he has of everything else." With that he rose from the table and said that he thought he would walk about the village for a while. He bade Mr Honeyfoot and Mr Segundus a good evening and left them.

"Poor Henry," said Strange, when Mr Woodhope had gone. "I suppose we must bore him horribly."

"It is most good-natured of your friend to accompany you on your journey, when he himself can have no interest in its object," said Mr Honeyfoot.

"Oh, certainly!" said Strange. "But then, you know, he was forced to come with me when he found it so quiet at home. Henry is paying us a visit of some weeks, but ours is a very retired neighbourhood and I believe I am a great deal taken up with my studies."

Mr Segundus asked Mr Strange when he began to study magic.

"In the spring of last year."

"But you have achieved so much!" cried Mr Honeyfoot. "And in less than two years! My dear Mr Strange, it is quite remark-able!"

"Oh! Do you think so? It seems to me that I have hardly done any thing. But then, I have not known where to turn for advice. You are the first of my brother-magicians that I ever met with, and I give you fair warning that I intend to make you sit up half the night answering questions."

"We shall be delighted to help you in any way we can," said Mr Segundus, "But I very much doubt that we can be of much service to you. We have only ever been *theoretical* magicians."

"You are much too modest," declared Strange. "Consider, for example, how much more extensive your reading has been than mine."

So Mr Segundus began to suggest authors whom Strange might not yet have heard of and Strange began to scribble down their names and works in a somewhat haphazard fashion, sometimes writing in a little memorandum book and other times writing upon the back of the dinner bill and once upon the back of his hand. Then he began to question Mr Segundus about the books.

Poor Mr Honeyfoot! How he longed to take part in this interesting conversation! How, in fact, he *did* take part in it, deceiving no one but himself by his little stratagems. "Tell him he must read Thomas Lanchester's *The Language of Birds*," he said, addressing Mr Segundus, rather than Strange. "Oh!" he said. "I know you have no opinion of it, but I think one may learn many things from Lanchester."

Whereupon Mr Strange told them how, to his certain knowledge, there had been four copies of *The Language of Birds* in England not more than five years ago: one in a Gloucester bookseller's; one in the private library of a gentleman-magician in Kendal; one the property of a blacksmith near Penzance who had taken it in part payment for mending an iron-gate; and one stopping a gap in a window of the boys' school in the close of Durham Cathedral.

"But where are they now?" cried Mr Honeyfoot. "Why did you not purchase a copy?"

"By the time that I came to each place Norrell had got there before me and bought them all," said Mr Strange. "I never laid eyes upon the man, and yet he thwarts me at every turn. That is why I hit upon this plan of summoning up some dead magician and asking him – or her – questions. I fancied a *lady* might be more sympathetic to my plight, and so I chose Miss Absalom."[5]

Mr Segundus shook his head. "As a means of getting knowledge, it strikes me as more dramatic than convenient. Can you not think of an easier way? After all, in the Golden Age of English magic, books were much rarer than they are now, yet men still became magicians."

"I have studied histories and biographies of the *Aureates* to discover how they began," said Strange, "but it seems that in those days, as soon as any one found out he had some aptitude for

---

[5] In mediaeval times conjuring the dead was a well-known sort of magic and there seems to have been a consensus that a dead magician was both the easiest spirit to raise and the most worth talking to.

magic, he immediately set off for the house of some other, older, more experienced magician and offered himself as a pupil."[6]

"Then you should apply to Mr Norrell for assistance!" cried Mr Honeyfoot, "Indeed you should. Oh! yes, I know," seeing that Mr Segundus was about to make some objection, "Norrell is a little reserved, but what is that? Mr Strange will know how to overcome his timidity I am sure. For all his faults of temper, Norrell is no fool and must see the very great advantages of having such an assistant!"

Mr Segundus had many objections to this scheme, in particular Mr Norrell's great aversion to other magicians; but Mr Honeyfoot, with all the enthusiasm of his eager disposition, had no sooner conceived the idea than it became a favourite wish and he could not suppose there would be any drawbacks. "Oh! I agree," he said, "that Norrell has never looked very favourably upon us *theoretical* magicians. But I dare say he will behave quite differently towards an *equal*."

Strange himself did not seem at all averse to the idea; he had a natural curiosity to see Mr Norrell. Indeed Mr Segundus could not help suspecting that he had already made up his mind upon the point and so Mr Segundus gradually allowed his doubts and objections to be argued down.

"This is a great day for Great Britain, sir!" cried Mr Honeyfoot.

---

[6] There have been very few magicians who did not learn magic from another practitioner. The Raven King was not the first British magician. There had been others before him – notably the seventh-century half-man, half-demon, Merlin – but at the time the Raven King came into England there were none. Little enough is known about the Raven King's early years, but it is reasonable to suppose that he learnt both magic and kingship at the court of a King of Faerie. Early magicians in mediaeval England learnt their art at the court of the Raven King and these magicians trained others.

One exception may be the Nottinghamshire magician, Thomas Godbless (1105?–82). Most of his life is entirely obscure to us. He certainly spent some time with the Raven King, but this seems to have been late in his life when he had already been a magician for years. He is perhaps one example that a magician may be self-created – as of course were both Gilbert Norrell and Jonathan Strange.

"Look at all that one magician has been able to accomplish! Only consider what two might do! Strange and Norrell! Oh, it sounds very well!" Then Mr Honeyfoot repeated "Strange and Norrell" several times over, in a highly delighted manner that made Strange laugh very much.

But like many gentle characters, Mr Segundus was much given to changes of mind. As long as Mr Strange stood before him, tall, smiling and assured, Mr Segundus had every confidence that Strange's genius must receive the recognition it deserved – whether it be with Mr Norrell's help, or in spite of Mr Norrell's hindrance; but the next morning, after Strange and Henry Woodhope had ridden off, his thoughts returned to all the magicians whom Mr Norrell had laboured to destroy, and he began to wonder if Mr Honeyfoot and he might not have misled Strange.

"I cannot help thinking," he said, "that we should have done a great deal better to warn Mr Strange to avoid Mr Norrell. Rather than encouraging him to seek out Norrell we should have advised him to hide himself!"

But Mr Honeyfoot did not understand this at all. "No gentleman likes to be told to hide," he said, "and if Mr Norrell should mean any harm to Mr Strange – which I am very far from allowing to be the case – then I am sure that Mr Strange will be the first to find it out."

24

Another magician

September 1809

M R DRAWLIGHT TURNED slightly in his chair, smiled, and said, "It seems, sir, that you have a rival."

Before Mr Norrell could think of a suitable reply, Lascelles asked what was the man's name.

"Strange," said Drawlight.

"I do not know him," said Lascelles.

"Oh!" cried Drawlight. "I think you must. Jonathan Strange of Shropshire. Two thousand pounds a year."

"I have not the least idea whom you mean. Oh, but wait! Is not this the man who, when an undergraduate at Cambridge, frightened a cat belonging to the Master of Corpus Christi?"

Drawlight agreed that this was the very man. Lascelles knew him instantly and they both laughed.

Meanwhile Mr Norrell sat silent as a stone. Drawlight's opening remark had been a terrible blow. He felt as if Drawlight had turned and struck him – as if a figure in a painting, or a table or a chair had turned and struck him. The shock of it had almost taken his breath away; he was quite certain he would be ill. What Drawlight might say next Mr Norrell dared not think – something of greater powers, perhaps – of wonders performed beside which Mr Norrell's own would appear pitiful indeed. And he had taken such pains to ensure there could be no rivals! He felt like the man who goes about his house at night, locking doors and barring windows, only to hear the certain sounds of someone walking about in an upstairs room.

But as the conversation progressed these unpleasant sensations lessened and Mr Norrell began to feel more comfortable. As Drawlight and Lascelles talked of Mr Strange's Brighton pleasure-trips and visits to Bath and Mr Strange's estate in Shropshire, Mr Norrell thought he understood the sort of man this Strange must be: a fashionable, shallow sort of man, a man not unlike Lascelles himself. That being so (said Mr Norrell to himself) was it not more probable that "You have a rival," was addressed, not to himself, but to Lascelles? This Strange (thought Mr Norrell) must be Lascelles's rival in some love affair or other. Norrell looked down at his hands clasped in his lap and smiled at his own folly.

"And so," said Lascelles, "Strange is now a magician?"

"Oh!" said Drawlight, turning to Mr Norrell. "I am sure that not even his greatest friends would compare his talents to those of the estimable Mr Norrell. But I believe he is well enough thought of in Bristol and Bath. He is in London at present. His friends hope that you will be kind enough to grant him an interview – and may I express a wish to be present when two such practitioners of the art meet?"

Mr Norrell lifted his eyes very slowly. "I shall be happy to meet Mr Strange," he said.

Mr Drawlight was not made to wait long before he witnessed the momentous interview between the two magicians (which was just as well for Mr Drawlight hated to wait). An invitation was issued and both Lascelles and Drawlight made it their business to be present when Mr Strange waited upon Mr Norrell.

He proved neither as young nor as handsome as Mr Norrell had feared. He was nearer thirty than twenty and, as far as another gentleman may be permitted to judge these things, not handsome at all. But what was very unexpected was that he brought with him a pretty young woman: Mrs Strange.

Mr Norrell began by asking Strange if he had brought his writing? He would, he said, very much like to read what Mr Strange had written.

"My writing?" said Strange and paused a moment. "I am afraid, sir, that I am at a loss to know what you mean. I have written nothing."

"Oh!" said Mr Norrell. "Mr Drawlight told me that you had been asked to write something for *The Gentleman's Magazine* but perhaps . . ."

"Oh, that!" said Strange. "I have scarcely thought about it. Nichols assured me he did not need it until the Friday after next."

"A week on Friday and not yet begun!" said Mr Norrell, very much astonished.

"Oh!" said Strange. "I think that the quicker one gets these things out of one's brain and on to the paper and off to the printers, the better. I dare say, sir," and he smiled at Mr Norrell in a friendly manner, "that you find the same."

Mr Norrell, who had never yet got any thing successfully out of his brain and off to the printers, whose every attempt was still at some stage or other of revision, said nothing.

"As to what I shall write," continued Strange, "I do not quite know yet, but it will most likely be a refutation of Portishead's article in *The Modern Magician*.[1] Did you see it, sir? It put me in a rage for a week. He sought to prove that modern magicians have no business dealing with fairies. It is one thing to admit that we have lost the power to raise such spirits – it is quite another to renounce all intention of ever employing them! I have no patience with any such squeamishness. But what is most extraordinary is that I have yet to see any criticism of Portishead's article anywhere. Now that we have something approaching a magical

---

[1] *The Modern Magician* was one of several magical periodicals set up following the first appearance of *The Friends of English Magic* in 1808. Though not appointed by Mr Norrell, the editors of these periodicals never dreamt of deviating from orthodox magical opinion as laid down by Mr Norrell.

community I think we would be very wrong to let such thick-headed nonsense pass unreproved."

Strange, apparently thinking that he had talked enough, waited for one of the other gentlemen to reply.

After a moment or two of silence Mr Lascelles remarked that Lord Portishead had written the article at Mr Norrell's express wish and with Mr Norrell's aid and approval.

"Indeed?" Strange looked very much astonished.

There was a silence of some moments and then Lascelles languidly inquired how one learnt magic these days?

"From books," said Strange.

"Ah, sir!" cried Mr Norrell. "How glad I am to hear you say so! Waste no time, I implore you, in pursuing any other course, but apply yourself constantly to reading! No sacrifice of time or pleasure can ever be too great!"

Strange regarded Mr Norrell somewhat ironically and then remarked, "Unfortunately lack of books has always been a great obstacle. I dare say you have no conception, sir, how few books of magic there are left in circulation in England. All the booksellers agree that a few years ago there were a great many, but now . . ."

"Indeed?" interrupted Mr Norrell, hurriedly. "Well, that is very odd to be sure."

The silence which followed was peculiarly awkward. Here sat the only two English magicians of the Modern Age. One confessed he had no books; the other, as was well known, had two great libraries stuffed with them. Mere common politeness seemed to dictate that Mr Norrell make some offer of help, however slight; but Mr Norrell said nothing.

"It must have been a very curious circumstance," said Mr Lascelles after a while, "that made you chuse to be a magician."

"It was," said Strange. "Most curious."

"Will you not tell us what that circumstance was?"

Strange smiled maliciously. "I am sure that it will give Mr Norrell great pleasure to know that he was the cause of my becoming a magician. One might say in fact that Mr Norrell made me a magician."

"I?" cried Mr Norrell, quite horrified.

"The truth is, sir," said Arabella Strange quickly, "that he had tried everything else – farming, poetry, iron-founding. In the course of a year he ran through a whole variety of occupations without settling to any of them. He was bound to come to magic sooner or later."

There was another silence, then Strange said, "I had not understood before that Lord Portishead wrote at your behest, sir. Perhaps you will be so good as to explain something to me. I have read all of his lordship's essays in *The Friends of English Magic* and *The Modern Magician* but have yet to see any mention of the Raven King. The omission is so striking that I am beginning to think it must be deliberate."

Mr Norrell nodded. "It is one of my ambitions to make that man as completely forgotten as he deserves," he said.

"But surely, sir, without the Raven King there would be no magic and no magicians?"

"That is the common opinion, certainly. But even it were true – which I am very far from allowing – he has long since forfeited any entitlement to our esteem. For what were his first actions upon coming into England? To make war upon England's lawful King and rob him of half his kingdom! And shall you and I, Mr Strange, let it be known that we have chosen such a man as our model? That we account *him* the first among us? Will that make our profession respected? Will that persuade the King's ministers to put their trust in us? I do not think so! No, Mr Strange, if we cannot make his name forgotten, then it is our duty – yours and mine – to broadcast our hatred of him! To let it be known everywhere our great abhorrence of his corrupt nature and evil deeds!"

It was clear that a great disparity of views and temper existed between the two magicians and Arabella Strange seemed to think that there was no occasion for them to continue any longer in the same room to irritate each other more. She and Strange left very shortly afterwards.

Naturally, Mr Drawlight was the first to pronounce upon the new magician. "Well!" he said rather *before* the door had closed upon Strange's back. "I do not know what may be your opinion, but I never was more astonished in my life! I was informed by several people that he was a handsome man. What could they have meant, do you suppose? With such a nose as he has got and that hair. Reddish-brown is such a fickle colour – there is no wear in it – I am quite certain I saw some grey in it. And yet he cannot be more than – what? – thirty? thirty-two perhaps? She, on the other hand, is quite delightful! So much animation! Those brown curls, so sweetly arranged! But I thought it a great pity that she had not taken more trouble to inform herself of the London fashions. The sprigged muslin she had on was certainly very pretty, but I should like to see her wear something altogether more stylish – say forest-green silk trimmed with black ribbons and black bugle-beads. That is only a first thought, you understand – I may be struck with quite a different idea when I see her again."

"Do you think that people will be curious about him?" asked Mr Norrell.

"Oh! certainly," said Mr Lascelles.

"Ah!" said Mr Norrell. "Then I am very much afraid – Mr Lascelles, I would be very glad if you could advise me – I am very much afraid that Lord Mulgrave may send for Mr Strange. His lordship's zeal for using magic in the war – excellent in itself, of course – has had the unfortunate effect of encouraging him to read all sorts of books on magical history and forming opinions about what he finds there. He has devised a plan to summon up witches to aid me in defeating the French – I believe he is thinking of those half-fairy, half-human women to whom malicious people were used to apply when they wished to harm their neighbours – the sort of witches, in short, that Shakespeare describes in *Macbeth*. He asked me to invoke three or four, and was not best pleased that I refused to do it. Modern magic can do many things, but summoning up witches could bring a world of trouble upon everyone's head. But now I fear he might send for Mr Strange instead. Mr Lascelles, do not you think that he might? And then Mr Strange might try it, not understanding any thing of the danger. Perhaps it would be as well to write to Sir Walter asking if he would be so good as to have a word in his lordship's ear to warn him against Mr Strange."

"Oh!" said Lascelles. "I see no occasion for that. If *you* think that Mr Strange's magic is not safe then it will soon get about."

Later in the day a dinner was given in Mr Norrell's honour at a house in Great Titchfield-street, at which Mr Drawlight and Mr Lascelles were also present. It was not long before Mr Norrell was asked to give his opinion of the Shropshire magician.

"Mr Strange," said Mr Norrell, "seems a very pleasant gentleman and a very talented magician who may yet be a most creditable addition to our profession, which has certainly been somewhat depleted of late."

"Mr Strange appears to entertain some very odd notions of magic," said Lascelles. "He has not troubled to inform himself of the modern ideas on the subject – by which I mean, of course, Mr Norrell's ideas, which have so astonished the world with their clarity and succinctness."

Mr Drawlight repeated his opinion that Mr Strange's red hair had no wear in it and that Mrs Strange's gown, though not exactly fashionable, had been of a very pretty muslin.

At about the same time that this conversation was taking place another set of people (among them Mr and Mrs Strange) was sitting down to dinner in a more modest dining-parlour in a house in Charterhouse-square. Mr and Mrs Strange's friends were naturally anxious to know their opinion of the great Mr Norrell.

"He says he hopes that the Raven King will soon be forgot," said Strange in amazement. "What do you make of that? A magician who hopes the Raven King will soon be forgot! If the Archbishop of Canterbury were discovered to be working secretly to suppress all knowledge of the Trinity, it would make as much sense to me."

"He is like a musician who wishes to conceal the music of Mr Handel," agreed a lady in a turban eating artichokes with almonds.

"Or a fishmonger who hopes to persuade people that the sea does not exist," said a gentleman helping himself to a large piece of mullet in a good wine sauce.

Then other people proposed similar examples of folly and everyone laughed except Strange who sat frowning at his dinner.

"I thought you meant to ask Mr Norrell to help you," said Arabella.

"How could I when we seemed to be quarrelling from the first moment we met?" cried Strange. "He does not like me. Nor I him."

"Not like you! No, perhaps he did not *like* you. But he did not so much as look at any other person the whole time we were there. It was as if he would eat you up with his eyes. I dare say he is lonely. He has studied all these years and never had any body he could explain his mind to. Certainly not to those disagreeable men – I forget their names. But now that he has seen you – and he knows that he could talk to you – well! it would be very odd if he did not invite you again."

In Great Titchfield-street Mr Norrell put down his fork and dabbed at his lips with his napkin. "Of course," he said, "he must apply himself. I urged him to apply himself."

Strange in Charterhouse-square said, "He told me to apply myself. – To what? I asked. – To reading he said. I was never more astonished in my life. I was very near asking him what I was supposed to read when he has all books."

The next day Strange told Arabella that they could go back to Shropshire any time she pleased – he did not think that there was any thing to keep them in London. He also said that he had resolved to think no more about Mr Norrell. In this he was not entirely successful for several times in the next few days Arabella found herself listening to a long recital of all Mr Norrell's faults, both professional and personal.

Meanwhile in Hanover-square Mr Norrell constantly inquired of Mr Drawlight what Mr Strange was doing, whom he visited, and what people thought of him.

Mr Lascelles and Mr Drawlight were a little alarmed at this development. For more than a year now they had enjoyed no small degree of influence over the magician and, as his friends, they were courted by admirals, generals, politicians, any one in fact who wished to know Mr Norrell's opinion upon this, or wished Mr Norrell to do that. The thought of another magician who might attach himself to Mr Norrell by closer ties than Drawlight or Lascelles could ever hope to forge, who might take upon himself the task of advising Mr Norrell was very disagreeable. Mr Drawlight told Mr Lascelles that Norrell should be discouraged from thinking of the Shropshire magician and, though Mr Lascelles's whimsical nature never permitted him to agree outright with any one, there is little doubt that he thought the same.

But three or four days after Mr Strange's visit, Mr Norrell said, "I have been considering the matter very carefully and I believe that something ought to be done for Mr Strange. He complained of his lack of materials. Well, of course, I can see that that might . . . In short I have decided to make him a present of a book."

"But, sir!" cried Drawlight. "Your precious books! You must not give them away to other people – especially to other magicians who may not use them as wisely as yourself!"

"Oh!" said Mr Norrell. "I do not mean one of my own books. I fear I could not spare a single one. No, I have purchased a volume from Edwards and Skittering to give Mr Strange. The choice was, I confess, a difficult one. There are many books which, to be perfectly frank, I would not be quite comfortable in recommending to Mr Strange yet; he is not ready for them. He would imbibe all sorts of wrong ideas from them. This book," Mr Norrell looked at it in an anxious sort of way, "has many faults – I fear it has a great many. Mr Strange will learn no actual magic from it. But it has a great deal to say on the subjects of diligent research and the perils of committing oneself to paper too soon – lessons which I hope Mr Strange may take to heart."

So Mr Norrell invited Strange to Hanover-square again and as on the previous occasion Drawlight and Lascelles were present, but Strange came alone.

The second meeting took place in the library at Hanover-square. Strange looked about him at the great quantities of books, but said not a word. Perhaps he had got to the end of his anger. There seemed to be a determination on both sides to speak and behave more cordially.

"You do me great honour, sir," said Strange when Mr Norrell gave him his present. "*English Magic* by Jeremy Tott." He turned the pages. "Not an author I have ever heard of."

"It is a biography of his brother, a theoretical magic-historian of the last century called Horace Tott," said Mr Norrell.[2] He explained about the lessons of diligent research and not committing oneself to paper that Strange was to learn. Strange smiled politely, bowed, and said he was sure it would be most interesting.

Mr Drawlight admired Strange's present.

Mr Norrell gazed at Strange with an odd expression upon his face as though he would have been glad of a little conversation with him, but had not the least idea how to begin.

Mr Lascelles reminded Mr Norrell that Lord Mulgrave of the Admiralty was expected within the hour.

---

[2] Horace Tott spent an uneventful life in Cheshire always intending to write a large book on English magic, but never quite beginning. And so he died at seventy-four, still imagining he might begin next week, or perhaps the week after that.

"You have business to conduct, sir," said Strange. "I must not intrude. Indeed I have business for Mrs Strange in Bond-street that must not be neglected."

"And perhaps one day," said Drawlight, "we shall have the honour of seeing a piece of magic worked by Mr Strange. I am excessively fond of seeing magic done."

"Perhaps," said Strange.

Mr Lascelles rang the bell for the servant. Suddenly Mr Norrell said, "I should be glad to see some of Mr Strange's magic now – if he would honour us with a demonstration."

"Oh!" said Strange. "But I do not . . ."

"It would do me great honour," insisted Mr Norrell.

"Very well," said Strange, "I shall be very glad to shew you something. It will be a little awkward, perhaps, compared to what you are accustomed to. I very much doubt, Mr Norrell, that I can match you in elegance of execution."

Mr Norrell bowed.

Strange glanced two or three times around the room in search of some magic to do. His glance fell upon a mirror that hung in the depths of a corner of the room where the light never penetrated. He placed *English Magic* by Jeremy Tott upon the library-table so that its reflection was clearly visible in the mirror. For some moments he stared at it and nothing happened. And then he made a curious gesture; he ran both hands through his hair, clasped the back of his neck and stretched his shoulders, as a man will do who eases himself of the cramps. Then he smiled and altogether looked exceedingly pleased with himself.

Which was odd because the book looked exactly as it had done before.

Lascelles and Drawlight, who were both accustomed to seeing – or hearing about – Mr Norrell's wonderful magic, were scarcely impressed by this; indeed it was a great deal less than a common conjuror might manage at a fairground. Lascelles opened his mouth – doubtless to say some scathing thing – but was forestalled by Mr Norrell suddenly crying out in a tone of wonder, "But that is remarkable! That is truly . . . My dear Mr Strange! I never even heard of such magic before! It is not listed in Sutton-Grove. I assure you, my dear sir, it is not in Sutton-Grove!"

Lascelles and Drawlight looked from one magician to the other in some confusion.

Lascelles approached the table and stared hard at the book. "It is a little longer than it was perhaps," he said.

"I do not think so," said Drawlight.

"It is tan leather now," said Lascelles. "Was it blue before?"

"No," said Drawlight, "it was always tan."

Mr Norrell laughed out loud; Mr Norrell, who rarely even smiled, laughed at them. "No, no, gentlemen! You have not guessed it! Indeed you have not! Oh! Mr Strange, I cannot tell how much . . . but they do not understand what it is you have done! Pick it up!" he cried. "Pick it up, Mr Lascelles!"

More puzzled than ever Lascelles put out his hand to grasp the book, but all he grasped was the empty air. The book lay there in appearance only.

"He has made the book and its reflection change places," said Mr Norrell. "The real book is over there, in the mirror." And he went to peer into the mirror with an appearance of great professional interest. "But how did you do it?"

"How indeed?" murmured Strange; he walked about the room, examining the reflection of the book upon the table from different angles like a billiards-player, closing one eye and then the other.

"Can you get it back?" asked Drawlight.

"Sadly, no," said Strange. "To own the truth," he said at last, "I have only the haziest notion of what I did. I dare say it is just the same with you, sir, one has a sensation like music playing at the back of one's head – one simply knows what the next note will be."

"Quite remarkable," said Mr Norrell.

What was perhaps rather more remarkable was that Mr Norrell, who had lived all his life in fear of one day discovering a rival, had finally seen another man's magic, and far from being crushed by the sight, found himself elated by it.

Mr Norrell and Mr Strange parted that afternoon on very cordial terms, and upon the following morning met again without Mr Lascelles or Mr Drawlight knowing any thing about it. This meeting ended in Mr Norrell's offering to take Mr Strange as a pupil. Mr Strange accepted.

"I only wish that he had not married," said Mr Norrell fretfully. "Magicians have no business marrying."

25

The education of a magician

September–December 1809

O N THE FIRST morning of Strange's education, he was invited to an early breakfast at Hanover-square. As the two magicians sat down at the breakfast-table, Mr Norrell said, "I have taken the liberty of drawing up a plan of study for you for the next three or four years."

Strange looked a little startled at the mention of three or four years, but he said nothing.

"Three or four years is such a very short time," continued Mr Norrell with a sigh, "that, try as I can, I cannot see that we will achieve very much."

He passed a dozen or so sheets of paper to Strange. Each sheet was covered in three columns of Mr Norrell's small, precise handwriting; each column contained a long list of different sorts of magic.[1]

Strange looked them over and said that there was more to learn than he had supposed.

"Ah! I envy you, sir," said Mr Norrell. "Indeed I do. The *practice* of magic is full of frustrations and disappointments, but the *study* is a continual delight! All of England's great magicians are one's companions and guides. Steady labour is rewarded by

---

[1] Naturally, Mr Norrell based his syllabus upon the classifications contained in *De Generibus Artium Magicarum Anglorum* by Francis Sutton-Grove.

increase of knowledge and, best of all, one need not so much as look upon another of one's fellow creatures from one month's end to the next if one does not wish it!"

For a few moments Mr Norrell seemed lost in contemplation of this happy state, then, rousing himself, he proposed that they deny themselves the pleasure of Strange's education no longer but go immediately into the library to begin.

Mr Norrell's library was on the first floor. It was a charming room in keeping with the tastes of its owner who would always chuse to come here for both solace and recreation. Mr Drawlight had persuaded Mr Norrell to adopt the fashion of setting small pieces of mirror into odd corners and angles. This meant that one was constantly meeting with a bright gleam of silver light or the sudden reflection of someone in the street where one least expected it. The walls were covered with a light green paper, with a pattern of green oak leaves and knobbly oak twigs, and there was a little dome set into the ceiling which was painted to represent the leafy canopy of a glade in spring. The books all had matching bindings of pale calf leather with their titles stamped in neat silver capitals on the spine. Among all this elegance and harmony it was somewhat surprizing to observe so many gaps among the books, and so many shelves entirely empty.

Strange and Mr Norrell seated themselves one on each side of the fire.

"If you will permit me, sir," said Strange, "I should like to begin by putting some questions to you. I confess that what I heard the other day concerning fairy-spirits entirely astonished me, and I wondered if I might prevail upon you to talk to me a little upon this subject? To what dangers does the magician expose himself in employing fairy-spirits? And what is your opinion of their utility?"

"Their utility has been greatly exaggerated, the danger much underestimated," said Mr Norrell.

"Oh! Is it your opinion that fairies are, as some people think, demons?" asked Strange.

"Upon the contrary. I am quite certain that the common view of them is the correct one. Do you know the writings of Chaston upon the subject? It would not surprize me if Chaston turned out to have come very near the truth of it.[2] No, no, my objection to fairies is quite another thing. Mr Strange, tell me, in your opinion why does so much English magic depend – or appear to depend – upon the aid of fairy-spirits?"

Strange thought a moment. "I suppose because all English magic comes from the Raven King who was educated at a fairy court and learnt his magic there."

"I agree that the Raven King has every thing to do with it," said Mr Norrell, "but not, I think, in the way you suppose. Consider, if you will, Mr Strange, that all the time the Raven King ruled Northern England, he also ruled a fairy kingdom. Consider, if you will, that no king ever had two such diverse races under his sway. Consider, if you will, that he was as great a king as he was a magician – a fact which almost all historians are prone to overlook. I think there can be little doubt that he was much preoccupied with the task of binding his two peoples together – a task which he accomplished, Mr Strange, *by deliberately exaggerating the role of fairies in magic.* In this way he increased his human subjects' esteem for fairies, he provided his fairy subjects with useful occupation, and made both peoples desire each other's company."

"Yes," said Strange, thoughtfully, "I see that."

"It seems to me," continued Mr Norrell, "that even the greatest of *Aureate* magicians miscalculated the extent to which fairies are necessary to human magic. Look at Pale! He considered his fairy-servants so essential to the pursuit of his art that he wrote that his greatest treasures were the three or four fairy-spirits living in his

---

[2] Richard Chaston (1620–95). Chaston wrote that men and fairies both contain within them a faculty of reason and a faculty of magic. In men reason is strong and magic is weak. With fairies it is the other way round: magic comes very naturally to them, but by human standards they are barely sane.

house! Yet my own example makes it plain that almost all *respectable* sorts of magic are perfectly achievable without assistance from any one! What have I ever done that has needed the help of a fairy?"

"I understand you," said Strange, who imagined that Mr Norrell's last question must be rhetorical. "And I must confess, sir, that this idea is quite new to me. I have never seen it in any book."

"Neither have I," said Mr Norrell. "Of course there are some sorts of magic which are entirely impossible without fairies. There may be times – and I sincerely hope that such occasions will be rare – when you and I shall have to treat with those pernicious creatures. Naturally we shall have to exercise the greatest caution. Any fairy we summon will almost certainly have dealt with English magicians before. He will be eager to recount for us all the names of the great magicians he has served and the services he has rendered to each. He will understand the forms and precedents of such dealings a great deal better than we do. It puts us – will put us – at a disadvantage. I assure you, Mr Strange, nowhere is the decline of English magic better understood than in the Other Lands."

"Yet fairy-spirits hold a great fascination for ordinary people," mused Strange, "and perhaps if you were occasionally to employ one in your work it might help make our art more popular. There is still a great deal of prejudice against using magic in the war."

"Oh! Indeed!" cried Mr Norrell, irritably. "People believe that magic begins and ends with fairies! They scarcely consider the skill and learning of the magician at all! No, Mr Strange, that is no argument with me for employing fairies! Rather the reverse! A hundred years ago the magio-historian, Valentine Munday, denied that the Other Lands existed. He thought that the men who claimed to have been there were all liars. In this he was quite wrong, but his position remains one with which I have a great deal of sympathy and I wish we could make it more generally believed. Of course," said Mr Norrell thoughtfully, "Munday went on to deny that America existed, and then France and so on. I believe that by the time he died he had long since given up Scotland and was beginning to entertain doubts of Carlisle . . . I have his book here."[3] Mr Norrell stood up and fetched it from the shelves. But he did not give it to Strange straightaway.

After a short silence Strange said, "You advise me to read this book?"

"Yes, indeed. I think you should read it," said Mr Norrell.

Strange waited, but Norrell continued to gaze at the book in his hand as though he were entirely at a loss as to how to proceed. "Then you must give it to me, sir," said Strange gently.

"Yes, indeed," said Mr Norrell. He approached Strange cautiously and held the book out for several moments, before suddenly tipping it up and off into Strange's hand with an odd gesture, as though it was not a book at all, but a small bird which clung to him and would on no account go to any one else, so that he was obliged to trick it into leaving his hand. He was so intent upon this manoeuvre that fortunately he did not look up at Strange who was trying not to laugh.

Mr Norrell remained a moment, looking wistfully at his book in another magician's hand.

But once he had parted with one book the painful part of his ordeal seemed to be over. Half an hour later he recommended another book to Strange and went and got it with scarcely any fuss. By midday he was pointing out books on the shelves to Strange and allowing him to fetch them down for himself. By the end of the day Mr Norrell had given Strange a quite extraordinary number of books to read, and said that he expected him to have read them by the end of the week.

---

[3] *The Blue Book: being an attempt to expose the most prevalent lies and common deceptions practised by English magicians upon the King's subjects and upon each other*, by Valentine Munday, pub. 1698.

A whole day of conversation and study was a luxury they could not often afford; generally they were obliged to spend some part of every day in attending to Mr Norrell's visitors – whether these were the fashionable people whom Mr Norrell still believed it essential to cultivate or gentlemen from the various Government departments.

By the end of a fortnight Mr Norrell's enthusiasm for his new pupil knew no bounds. "One has but to explain something to him once," Norrell told Sir Walter, "and he understands it immediately! I well remember how many weeks I laboured to comprehend Pale's Conjectures Concerning the Foreshadowing of Things To Come, yet Mr Strange was master of this exceptionally difficult theory in little more than four hours!"

Sir Walter smiled. "No doubt. But I think you rate your own achievements too low. Mr Strange has the advantage of a teacher to explain the difficult parts to him, whereas you had none – *you* have prepared the way for him and made everything smooth and easy."

"Ah!" cried Mr Norrell. "But when Mr Strange and I sat down to talk of the Conjectures some more, I realized that they had a much wider application than I had supposed. It was his questions, you see, which led me to a new understanding of Dr Pale's ideas!"

Sir Walter said, "Well, sir, I am glad that you have found a friend whose mind accords so well with your own – there is no greater comfort."

"I agree with you, Sir Walter!" cried Mr Norrell. "Indeed I do!"

Strange's admiration for Mr Norrell was of a more restrained nature. Norrell's dull conversation and oddities of behaviour continued to grate upon his nerves; and at about the same time as Mr Norrell was praising Strange to Sir Walter, Strange was complaining of Norrell to Arabella.

"Even now I scarcely know what to make of him. He is, at one and the same time, the most remarkable man of the Age and the most tedious. Twice this morning our conversation was inter-

302

rupted because he *thought* he heard a mouse in the room – mice are a particular aversion of his. Two footmen, two maids and I moved all the furniture about looking for the mouse, while he stood by the fireplace, rigid with fear."

"Has he a cat?" suggested Arabella. "He should get a cat."

"Oh, but that is quite impossible! He hates cats even more than mice. He told me that if he is ever so unlucky as to find himself in the same room as a cat, then he is sure to be all over red pimples within an hour."

It was Mr Norrell's sincere wish to educate his pupil thoroughly, but the habits of secrecy and dissimulation which he had cultivated all his life were not easily thrown off. On a day in December, when snow was falling in large, soft flakes from heavy, greenish-grey clouds, the two magicians were seated in Mr Norrell's library. The slow drifting motion of the snow outside the windows, the heat of the fire and the effects of a large glass of sherry-wine which he had been so ill-advised as to accept when Mr Norrell offered it, all combined to make Strange very heavy and sleepy. His head was supported upon his hand and his eyes were almost closing.

Mr Norrell was speaking. "Many magicians," he said, steepling his hands, "have attempted to confine magical powers in some physical object. It is not a difficult operation and the object can be any thing the magician wishes. Trees, jewels, books, bullets, hats have all been employed for this purpose at one time or another." Mr Norrell frowned hard at his fingertips. "By placing some of his power in whatever object he chuses, the magician hopes to make himself secure from those wanings of power, which are the inevitable result of illness and old age. I myself have often been severely tempted to do it; my own skills can be quite overturned by a heavy cold or a bad sore throat. Yet after careful consideration I have concluded that such divisions of power are most ill-advised. Let us examine the case of rings. Rings have long been considered peculiarly suitable for this sort of magic by virtue of their small size. A man may keep a ring continually upon his finger for years, without exciting the smallest comment – which would not be the case if he shewed the same attachment to a book or a pebble – and yet there is scarcely a magician in history who, having once committed some of his skill and power to a magic ring, did not somehow lose that ring and was put to a world of trouble to get it back again. Take for example, the twelfth-century Master of Nottingham, whose daughter mistook his ring of power for a common bauble, put it on her finger, and went to St Matthew's Fair. This negligent young woman . . ."

"What?" cried Strange, suddenly.

"What?" echoed Mr Norrell, startled.

Strange gave the other gentleman a sharp, questioning look. Mr Norrell gazed back at him, a little frightened.

"I beg your pardon, sir," said Strange, "but do I understand you aright? Are we speaking of magical powers that are got by some means into rings, stones, amulets – things of that sort?"

Mr Norrell nodded cautiously.

"But I thought you said," said Strange. "That is," he made some effort to speak more gently, "I *thought* that you told me some weeks ago that magic rings and stones were a fable."

Mr Norrell stared at his pupil in alarm.

"But perhaps I was mistaken?" said Strange.

Mr Norrell said nothing at all.

"I was mistaken," said Strange again. "I beg your pardon, sir, for interrupting you. Pray, continue."

But Mr Norrell, though he appeared greatly relieved that Strange had resolved the matter, was no longer equal to continuing and instead proposed that they have some tea; to which Mr Strange agreed very readily.[4]

That evening Strange told Arabella all that Mr Norrell had

---

[4] The story of the Master of Nottingham's daughter (to which Mr Norrell never returned) is worth recounting and so I set it down here.

The fair to which the young woman repaired was held on St Matthew's Feast in Nottingham. She spent a pleasant day, going about among the booths, making purchases of linens, laces and spices. Sometime during the

said and all that he, Strange, had said in reply.

"It was the queerest thing in the world! He was so frightened at having been found out, that he could think of nothing to say. It fell to me to think of fresh lies for him to tell me. I was

---

[4] *cont'd* afternoon she happened to turn suddenly to see some Italian tumblers who were behind her and the edge of her cloak flew out and struck a passing goose. This bad-tempered fowl ran at her, flapping its wings and screaming. In her surprize she dropt her father's ring, which fell into the goose's open gullet and the goose, in *its* surprize, swallowed it. But before the Master of Nottingham's daughter could say or do any thing the gooseherd drove the goose on and both disappeared into the crowd.

The goose was bought by a man called John Ford who took it back to his house in the village of Fiskerton and the next day his wife, Margaret Ford, killed the goose, plucked it and drew out its innards. In its stomach she found a heavy silver ring set with a crooked piece of yellow amber. She put it down on a table near three hens' eggs that had been gathered that morning.

Immediately the eggs began to shake and then to crack open and from each egg something marvellous appeared. From the first egg came a stringed instrument like a viol, except that it had little arms and legs, and played sweet music upon itself with a tiny bow. From the next egg emerged a ship of purest ivory with sails of fine white linen and a set of silver oars. And from the last egg hatched a chick with strange red-and-gold plumage. This last was the only wonder to survive beyond the day. After an hour or two the viol cracked like an eggshell and fell into pieces and by sunset the ivory ship had set sail and rowed away through the air; but the bird grew up and later started a fire which destroyed most of Grantham. During the conflagration it was observed bathing itself in the flames. From this circumstance it was presumed to be a phoenix.

When Margaret Ford realized that a magic ring had somehow fallen into her possession, she was determined to do magic with it. Unfortunately she was a thoroughly malicious woman, who tyrannized over her gentle husband, and spent long hours pondering how to revenge herself upon her enemies. John Ford held the manor of Fiskerton, and in the months that followed he was loaded with lands and riches by greater lords who feared his wife's wicked magic.

Word of the wonders performed by Margaret Ford soon reached Nottingham, where the Master of Nottingham lay in bed waiting to die. So much of his power had gone into the ring that the loss of it had made him first melancholy, then despairing and finally sick. When news of his ring finally came he was too ill to do any thing about it.

His daughter, on the other hand, was thoroughly sorry for bringing this misfortune on her family and thought it her duty to try and get the ring back; so without telling any one what she intended she set off along the riverbank to the village of Fiskerton.

She had only got as far as Gunthorpe when she came upon a very dreadful

obliged to conspire with him against myself."

"But I do not understand," said Arabella. "Why should he contradict himself in this odd way?"

"Oh! He is determined to keep some things to himself. That

---

[4] *cont'd*   sight. A little wood was burning steadily with fierce flames lapping every part of it. The black bitter smoke made her eyes sting and her throat ache, yet the wood was not consumed by the fire. A low moan issued from the trees as if they cried out at such unnatural torment. The Master's daughter looked round for someone to explain this wonder to her. A young woodsman, who was passing, told her, "Two weeks ago, Margaret Ford stopt in the wood on the road from Thurgarton. She rested under the shade of its branches, drank from its stream and ate its nuts and berries, but just as she was leaving a root caught her foot and made her fall, and when she rose from the ground a briar was so impertinent as to scratch her arm. So she cast a spell upon the wood and swore it would burn for ever."

The Master's daughter thanked him for the information and walked on for a while. She became thirsty and crouched down to scoop up some water from the river. All at once a woman – or something very like a woman – half-rose out of the water. There were fish-scales all over her body, her skin was as grey and spotted as a trout's and her hair had become an odd arrangement of spiny grey trout fins. She seemed to glare at the Master's daughter, but her round cold fish-eyes and stiff fishskin were not well adapted to reproduce human expressions and so it was hard to tell.

"Oh! I beg your pardon!" said the Master's daughter, startled.

The woman opened her mouth, shewing a fish throat and mouth full of ugly fish teeth, but she seemed unable to make a sound. Then she rolled over and plunged back into the water.

A woman who was washing clothes on the riverbank explained to the Master's daughter, "That is Joscelin Trent who is so unfortunate as to be the wife of a man that Margaret Ford likes. Out of jealousy Margaret Ford has cast a spell on her and she is forced, poor lady, to spend all her days and nights immersed in the shallows of the river to keep her enchanted skin and flesh from drying out, and as she cannot swim she lives in constant terror of drowning."

The Master's daughter thanked the woman for telling her this.

Next the Master's daughter came to the village of Hoveringham. A man and his wife who were both squeezed together atop a little pony advised her not to enter the village, but led her around it by narrow lanes and paths. From a little green knoll the Master's daughter looked down and saw that everyone in the village wore a thick blindfold round his eyes. They were not at all used to their self-created blindness and constantly banged their faces against walls, tripped over stools and carts, cut themselves on knives and tools and burnt themselves in the fire. As a consequence they were covered in gashes and wounds, yet not one of them removed his blindfold.

"Oh!" said the wife. "The priest of Hoveringham has been bold enough to

much is obvious – and I suppose he cannot always remember what is to be a secret and what is not. You remember that I told you there are gaps among the books in his library? Well, it seems that the very day he accepted me as his pupil, he ordered five shelves to

[4] cont'd denounce the wickedness of Margaret Ford from his pulpit. Bishops, abbots and canons have all been silent, but this frail old man defied her and so she has cursed the whole village. It is their fate to have vivid images of all their worst fears constantly before their eyes. These poor souls see their children starve, their parents go mad, their loved ones scorn and betray them. Wives and husbands see each other horribly murdered. And so, though these sights be nought but illusions, the villagers must blindfold themselves or else be driven mad by what they see."

Shaking her head over the appalling wickedness of Margaret Ford, the Master's daughter continued on her way to John Ford's manor, where she found Margaret and her maidservants, each with a wooden stick in her hand, driving the cows to their evening's milking.

The Master's daughter went boldly up to Margaret Ford. Upon the instant Margaret Ford turned and struck her with her stick. "Wicked girl!" she cried. "I know who you are! My ring has told me. I know that you plan to lie to me, who have never done you any harm at all, and ask to become my servant. I know that you plan to steal my ring. Well, know this! I have set strong spells upon my ring. If any thief were foolish enough to touch it, then within a very short space of time bees and wasps and all kinds of insects would fly up from the earth and sting him; eagles and hawks and all kinds of birds would fly down from the sky and peck at him; then bears and boars and all kinds of wild creatures would appear and tear and trample him to pieces!"

Then Margaret Ford beat the Master's daughter soundly, and told the maids to put her to work in the kitchen.

Margaret Ford's servants, a miserable, ill-treated lot, gave the Master's daughter the hardest work to do and whenever Margaret Ford beat them or raged at them – which happened very often – they relieved their feelings by doing the same to her. Yet the Master's daughter did not allow herself to become low-spirited. She stayed working in the kitchen for several months and thought very hard how she might trick Margaret Ford into dropping the ring or losing it.

Margaret Ford was a cruel woman, quick to take offence and her anger, once roused, could never be appeased. But for all that she adored little children; she took every opportunity to nurse babies and once she had a child in her arms she was gentleness itself. She had no child of her own and no one who knew her doubted that this was a source of great sorrow to her. It was widely supposed that she had expended a great deal of magic upon trying to conceive a child, but without success.

One day Margaret Ford was playing with a neighbour's little girl, and saying how if she ever were to have a child then she would rather it were a girl

be emptied and the books sent back to Yorkshire, because they were too dangerous for me to read."

"Good Lord! However did you find that out?" asked Arabella, much surprized.

---

[4] *cont'd* and how she would wish it to have a creamy white skin and green eyes and copper curls (this being Margaret Ford's own colouring).

"Oh!" said the Master's daughter innocently "The wife of the Reeve in Epperstone has a baby of exactly that description, the prettiest little creature that ever you saw."

Then Margaret Ford made the Master's daughter take her to Epperstone and shew her the Reeve's wife's baby, and when Margaret Ford saw that the baby was indeed the sweetest, prettiest child that ever there was (just as the Master's daughter had said) she announced to the horrified mother her intention of taking the child away with her.

As soon as she had possession of the Reeve's wife's baby Margaret Ford became almost a different person. She spent her days in looking after the baby, playing with her and singing to her. Margaret Ford became contented with her lot. She used her magic ring a great deal less than she had before and scarcely ever lost her temper.

So things went on until the Master of Nottingham's daughter had lived in Margaret Ford's house for almost a year. Then one summer's day Margaret Ford, the Master's daughter, the baby and the other maids took their midday meal upon the banks of the river. After eating, Margaret Ford rested in the shade of a rose-bush. It was a hot day and they were all very sleepy.

As soon as she was certain that Margaret Ford was asleep the Master's daughter took out a sugar-plum and shewed it to the baby. The baby, knowing only too well what should be done to sugar-plums, opened its mouth wide and the Master's daughter popped it in. Then, as quick as she could and making sure that none of the other maids saw what she did, she slipped the magic ring from Margaret Ford's finger.

Then, "Oh! Oh!" she cried. "Wake up, madam! The baby has taken your ring and put it in her mouth! Oh, for the dear child's sake, undo the spell. Undo the spell!"

Margaret Ford awoke and saw the baby with its cheek bulging out, but for the moment she was too sleepy and surprized to understand what was happening.

A bee flew past and the Master's daughter pointed at it and screamed. All the other maids screamed too. "Quickly, madam, I beg you!" cried the Master's daughter. " Oh!" She looked up. "Here are the eagles and hawks approaching! Oh!" She looked into the distance. "Here are the bears and boars running to tear the poor little thing to pieces!"

Margaret Ford cried out to the ring to stop the magic which it did immediately, and almost at the same moment the baby swallowed the sugar-plum. While Margaret Ford and the maids begged and coaxed the baby and shook it to make it cough up the magic ring, the Master of

"Drawlight and Lascelles told me. They took great pleasure in it."

"Ill-natured wretches!"

Mr Norrell was most disappointed to learn that Strange's education must be interrupted for a day or two while he and Arabella sought for a house to live in. "It is his wife that is the problem," Mr Norrell explained to Drawlight, with a sigh. "Had he been a single man, I dare say he would not have objected to coming and living here with me."

Drawlight was most alarmed to hear that Mr Norrell had entertained such a notion and, in case it were ever revived, he took the precaution of saying, "Oh, but sir! Think of your work for the Admiralty and the War Office, so important and so confid-

---

[4] *cont'd* Nottingham's daughter began to run along the riverbank towards Nottingham.

The rest of the story has all the usual devices. As soon as Margaret Ford discovered how she had been tricked she fetched horses and dogs to chase the Master's daughter. Upon several occasions the Master's daughter seemed lost for sure – the riders were almost upon her and the dogs just behind her. But the story tells how she was helped by all the victims of Margaret Ford's magic: how the villagers of Hoveringham tore off their blindfolds and, in spite of all the horrifying sights they saw, rushed to build barricades to prevent Margaret Ford from passing; how poor Joscelin Trent reached up out of the river and tried to pull Margaret Ford down into the muddy water; how the burning wood threw down flaming branches upon her.

The ring was returned to the Master of Nottingham who undid all the wrongs Margaret Ford had perpetrated and restored his own fortune and reputation.

There is another version of this story which contains no magic ring, no eternally-burning wood, no phoenix – no miracles at all, in fact. According to this version Margaret Ford and the Master of Nottingham's daughter (whose name was Donata Torel) were not enemies at all, but the leaders of a fellowship of female magicians that flourished in Nottinghamshire in the twelfth century. Hugh Torel, the Master of Nottingham, opposed the fellowship and took great pains to destroy it (though his own daughter was a member). He very nearly succeeded, until the women left their homes and fathers and husbands and went to live in the woods under the protection of Thomas Godbless, a much greater magician than Hugh Torel. This less colourful version of the story has never been as popular as the other but it is this version which Jonathan Strange said was the true one and which he included in *The History and Practice of English Magic*.

ential! The presence of another person in the house would impede it greatly."

"Oh, but Mr Strange is going help me with that!" said Mr Norrell. "It would be very wrong of me to deprive the country of Mr Strange's talents. Mr Strange and I went down to the Admiralty last Thursday to wait upon Lord Mulgrave. I believe that Lord Mulgrave was none too pleased at first to see that I had brought Mr Strange . . ."

"That is because his lordship is accustomed to your superior magic! I dare say he thinks that a mere *amateur* – however talented – has no business meddling with Admiralty matters."

". . . but when his lordship heard Mr Strange's ideas for defeating the French by magic he turned to me with a great smile upon his face and said, 'You and I, Mr Norrell, had grown stale. We wanted new blood to stir us up, did we not?'"

"Lord Mulgrave said *that*? To *you*?" said Drawlight. "That was abominably rude of him. I hope, sir, that you gave him one of your looks!"

"What?" Mr Norrell was engrossed in his own tale and had no attention to spare for whatever Mr Drawlight might be saying. "'Oh!' I said to him – I said, 'I am quite of your mind, my lord. But only wait until you have heard the rest of what Mr Strange has to say. You have not heard the half of it!'"

It was not only the Admiralty – the War Office and all the other departments of Government had reason to rejoice at the advent of Jonathan Strange. Suddenly a good many things which had been difficult before were made easy. The King's Ministers had long treasured a plan to send the enemies of Britain bad dreams. The Foreign Secretary had first proposed it in January 1808 and for over a year Mr Norrell had industriously sent the Emperor Napoleon Buonaparte a bad dream each night, as a result of which nothing had happened. Buonaparte's empire had not foundered and Buonaparte himself had ridden into battle as coolly as ever. And so eventually Mr Norrell was instructed to leave off. Privately Sir Walter and Mr Canning thought that the plan had failed because Mr Norrell had no talent for creating horrors. Mr Canning complained that the nightmares Mr Norrell had sent the Emperor (which chiefly concerned a captain of Dragoons hiding in Buonaparte's wardrobe) would scarcely frighten his children's governess let alone the conqueror of half of Europe. For a while he had tried to persuade the other Ministers that they should commission Mr Beckford, Mr Lewis and Mrs Radcliffe to create dreams of vivid horror that Mr Norrell could then pop into Buonaparte's head. But the other Ministers considered that to employ a magician was one thing, novelists were quite another and they would not stoop to it.

With Strange the plan was revived. Strange and Mr Canning suspected that the wicked French Emperor was proof against such insubstantial evils as dreams, and so they decided to begin this time with his ally, Alexander, the Emperor of Russia. They had the advantage of a great many friends at Alexander's court: Russian nobles who had made a great deal of money selling timber to Britain and were anxious to do so again, and a brave and ingenious Scottish lady who was the wife of Alexander's valet.

On learning that Alexander was a curiously impressionable person much given to mystical religion, Strange decided to send him a dream of eerie portents and symbols. For seven nights in succession Alexander dreamt a dream in which he sat down to a comfortable supper with Napoleon Buonaparte at which they were served some excellent venison soup. But no sooner had the Emperor tasted the soup, than he jumped up and cried, "J'ai une faim qui ne saurait se satisfaire de potage."[5] whereupon he turned into a she-wolf which ate first Alexander's cat, then his dog, then his horse, then his pretty Turkish mistress. And as the she-wolf set to work to eat up more of Alexander's friends and relations, her

---

[5] "I have a hunger which soup can never satisfy!"

womb opened and disgorged the cat, dog, horse, Turkish mistress, friends, relations, etc. again, but in horrible misshapen forms. And as she ate she grew; and when she was as big as the Kremlin, she turned, heavy teats swaying and maw all bloody, intent on devouring all of Moscow.

"There can be nothing dishonourable in sending him a dream which tells him that he is wrong to trust Buonaparte and that Buonaparte will betray him in the end," explained Strange to Arabella. "I might, after all, send him a letter to say as much. He *is* wrong and nothing is more certain than that Buonaparte *will* betray him in the end."

Word soon came from the Scottish lady that the Russian Emperor had been exceedingly troubled by the dreams and that, like King Nebuchadnezzar in the Bible, he had sent for astrologers and soothsayers to interpret it for him – which they very soon did.

Strange then sent more dreams to the Russian Emperor. "And," he told Mr Canning, "I have taken your advice and made them more obscure and difficult of interpretation that the Emperor's sorcerers may have something to do."

The indefatigable Mrs Janet Archibaldovna Barsukova was soon able to convey the satisfying news that Alexander neglected the business of government and war, and sat all day musing upon his dreams and discussing them with astrologers and sorcerers; and that whenever a letter came for him from the Emperor Napoleon Buonaparte he was seen to turn pale and shudder.

26

Orb, crown and sceptre

September 1809

EVERY NIGHT WITHOUT fail Lady Pole and Stephen Black were summoned by the sad bell to dance in Lost-hope's shadowy halls. For fashion and beauty these were, without a doubt, the most splendid balls Stephen had ever seen, but the fine clothes and smart appearance of the dancers made an odd contrast with the mansion itself which exhibited numerous signs of poverty and decay. The music never varied. The same handful of tunes were scraped out by a single violin, and tooted out by a single pipe. The greasy tallow-candles – Stephen could not help but observe with his butler's eye how there were far too few of them for such a vast hall – cast up strange shadows that spun across the walls as the dancers went through their figures.

On other occasions Lady Pole and Stephen took part in long processions in which banners were carried through dusty, ill-lit halls (the gentleman with the thistle-down hair having a great fondness for such ceremonies). Some of the banners were ancient and decaying pieces of dense embroidery; others represented the gentleman's victories over his enemies and were in fact made from the preserved skins of those enemies, their lips, eyes, hair and clothes having been embroidered on to their yellow skins by his female relations. The gentleman with the thistle-down hair never grew tired of these pleasures and he never appeared to entertain the slightest doubt that Stephen and Lady Pole were equally delighted with them.

Though changeable in all else, he remained constant in two things: his admiration of her ladyship and his affection for Stephen Black. The latter he continued to demonstrate by making Stephen extravagant gifts and by sending him strange pieces of good fortune. Some of the gifts were made, as before, to Mrs Brandy on Stephen's behalf and some were sent directly to Stephen for, as the gentleman told Stephen cheerfully, "Your wicked enemy will know nothing about it!" (He meant Sir Walter.) "I have very cleverly blinded him with my magic and it will never occur to him to wonder about it. Why! You could be made Archbishop of Canterbury tomorrow and he would think nothing of it! No one would." A thought appeared to strike him. "Would you like to be Archbishop of Canterbury tomorrow, Stephen?"

"No, thank you, sir."

"Are you quite certain? It is scarcely any trouble and if the Church has any attraction for you . . . ?"

"I promise you, sir, it has none."

"Your good taste as ever does you credit. A mitre is a wretchedly uncomfortable sort of thing to wear and not at all becoming."

Poor Stephen was assailed by miracles. Every few days something would occur to profit him in some way. Sometimes the actual value of what he gained was unremarkable – perhaps no more than a few shillings – but the means by which it came to him were always extraordinary. Once, for example, he received a visit from the overseer of a farm who insisted that, some years before, he had met Stephen at a cockfight near Richmond in the North Riding of Yorkshire and that Stephen had wagered him that the Prince of Wales would one day do something to bring disgrace upon the country. As this had now happened (the overseer cited the Prince's desertion of his wife as the shameful deed) the overseer had come to London by the stagecoach to bring Stephen twenty-seven shillings and sixpence – which, he said, was the amount of the wager. It was useless for Stephen to insist that he had never been to a cockfight or to Richmond in Yorkshire; the overseer would not be content until Stephen had taken the money.

A few days after the overseer's visit a large grey dog was discovered standing in the road opposite the house in Harley-street. The poor creature was drenched by the rain and splattered with mud and bore every sign of having travelled a great distance. More curious still, it had a document grasped between its jaws. The footmen, Robert and Geoffrey, and John Longridge, the cook, did their best to get rid of it by shouting and hurling bottles and stones at it, but the dog bore this treatment philosophically and declined to move until Stephen Black had come out in the rain and taken the document from its mouth. Then it went away with a quietly contented air, as if congratulating itself upon a difficult task well done. The document proved to be a map of a village in Derbyshire and shewed, among other surprizing things, a secret door let into the side of a hill.

Another time Stephen received a letter from the mayor and aldermen of Bath describing how, two months before, the Marquess of Wellesley had been in Bath and had done nothing during his stay but talk of Stephen Black and his remarkable honesty, intelligence and faithfulness to his master. So impressed had the mayor and the aldermen been by his lordship's report, that they had immediately ordered a medal, celebrating Stephen's life and virtues, to be struck. When five hundred medals had been made, the mayor and the aldermen had ordered them to be distributed to the chief householders of Bath amid general rejoicing. They enclosed a medal for Stephen, and begged that whenever he next found himself in Bath he would make himself known to them so that they might hold a magnificent dinner in his honour.

None of these miracles did any thing to raise poor Stephen's spirits. They only served to emphasize the eerie character of his present life. He knew that the overseer, dog and the mayor and the aldermen were all acting against their natures: overseers loved money – they did not give it away for no good reason; dogs did not patiently pursue strange quests for weeks on end; and mayors and aldermen did not suddenly develop a lively interest in negro servants they had never seen. Yet none of his friends seemed to think there was any thing remarkable about the course his life was taking. He was sick of the sight of gold and silver, and his little room at the top of the house in Harley-street was full of treasures he did not want.

He had been almost two years under the gentleman's enchantment. He had often pleaded with the gentleman to release him – or, if not him, then Lady Pole – but the gentleman would not hear of it. So Stephen had roused himself to try and tell someone about what he and Lady Pole suffered. He was anxious to discover if there were precedents for their case. He had faint hopes of finding someone who would help free them. The first person he had spoken to was Robert, the footman. He had warned Robert that he was about to hear a private revelation of a secret woe, and Robert had looked suitably solemn and interested. But, when Stephen began to speak, he found to his own astonishment that it was upon quite a different matter; he found himself delivering a very earnest and learned discourse upon the cultivation and uses of peas and beans – a subject he knew nothing about. Worse still, some of his information was of a most unusual nature and would have frankly astonished any farmer or gardener who had heard it. He explained the different properties of beans either planted or gathered by moonlight, by moondark, at Beltane or on Midsummer's Night, and how these properties were changed if you sowed or gathered the beans with a silver trowel or knife.

The next person to whom he attempted to describe his trouble was John Longridge. This time he found himself delivering an exact account of Julius Caesar's dealings and experiences in Britain. It was clearer and more detailed than any scholar could have managed, tho' he had studied the subject for twenty years or more. Once again it contained information that was not set down in any book.[1]

He made two more attempts to communicate his horrible situation. To Mrs Brandy he delivered an odd defence of Judas Iscariot in which he declared that in all Iscariot's last actions he was following the instructions of two men called John Copperhead and John Brassfoot whom Iscariot had believed to be angels; and to Toby Smith, Mrs Brandy's shopman, he gave a list of all the people in Ireland, Scotland, Wales and England who had been stolen away by fairies in the last two hundred years. None of them were people he had ever heard of.

Stephen was obliged to conclude that, try as he might, he *could not* speak of his enchantment.

The person who suffered most from his strange silences and dismal spirits was, without a doubt, Mrs Brandy. She did not

---

[1] Stephen described how, not long after Julius Caesar had arrived upon these shores, he had left his army and wandered into a little green wood. He had not gone far when he came upon two young men, sighing deeply and striking the ground in their frustration. Both were remarkably handsome and both were dressed in the finest linens dyed with the rarest dyes. Julius Caesar was so struck with the noble appearance of these young men that he asked them all sorts of questions and they answered him candidly and without the least diffidence. They explained how they were both plaintiffs at a court nearby. The court was held every Quarter Day to settle arguments and punish wrongdoers among their people, but unfortunately the race to which they belonged was a peculiarly wicked and quarrelsome one, and just at present no suits could be heard because they could not find an impartial judge; every venerable person among them either stood accused of a crime, or else had been found to have some other close connexion with one of the suits. On hearing this Caesar was struck with pity for them and immediately offered to be their judge himself – to which they eagerly agreed.

They led him a short way through the wood to a grassy hollow between smooth green hills. Here he found a thousand or so of the handsomest men and women that he had ever seen. He sat down upon the hillside and heard all their complaints and accusations; and when he had heard them he gave judgements so wise that everyone was delighted and no one went away feeling himself ill-used.

So pleased were they with Julius Caesar's judgements that they offered him any thing he liked as payment. Julius Caesar thought for a moment and said that he would like to rule the world. This they promised him.

understand that he had changed to the whole world, she only saw that he had changed towards *her*. One day at the beginning of September Stephen paid her a visit. They had not met for some weeks, which had made Mrs Brandy so unhappy that she had written to Robert Austin, and Robert had gone to Stephen and scolded him for his neglect. However once Stephen had arrived in the little parlour above the shop in St James's-street, no one could have blamed Mrs Brandy if she had wished him immediately away again. He sat with his head in his hand, sighing heavily, and had nothing to say to her. She offered him Constantia-wine, marmalade, an old-fashioned wigg bun – all sorts of delicacies – but he refused them all. He wanted nothing; and so she sat down on the opposite side of the fire and resumed her needlework – a nightcap which she was despondently embroidering for him.

"Perhaps," she said, "you are tired of London and of me, and you wish to return to Africa?"

"No," said Stephen.

"I dare say Africa is a remarkably charming place," said Mrs Brandy, who seemed determined to punish herself by sending Stephen immediately to Africa. "I have always heard that it is. With oranges and pineapples everywhere one looks, and sugar canes and chocolate trees." She had laboured fourteen years in the grocery trade and had mapped out her world in its stock. She laughed bitterly. "It seems that I would fare very ill in Africa. What need have people of shops when they have only to stretch out their hand and pluck the fruit of the nearest tree? Oh, yes! I should be ruined in no time in Africa." She snapped a thread between her teeth. "Not that I should not be glad to go tomorrow," She poked the thread viciously into the needle's innocent eye, "if any one were to ask me."

"Would you go to Africa for my sake?" asked Stephen in surprise.

She looked up. "I would go any where for your sake," she said. "I thought you knew that."

They regarded one another unhappily.

Stephen said that he must return and attend to his duties in Harley-street.

Outside in the street, the sky darkened and rain began to fall. People put up umbrellas. As Stephen walked up St James's-street, he saw a strange sight – a black ship sailing towards him through the grey rainy air above the heads of the crowd. It was a frigate, some two feet high, with dirty, ragged sails and peeling paint. It rose and fell, mimicking the motion of ships at sea. Stephen shivered a little to see it. A beggar emerged from the crowd, a negro with skin as dark and shining as Stephen's own. Fastened to his hat was this ship. As he walked he ducked and raised his head so that his ship could sail. As he went he performed his curious bobbing and swaying movements very slowly and carefully for fear of upsetting his enormous hat. The effect was of a man dancing amazingly slowly. The beggar's name was Johnson. He was a poor, crippled sailor who had been denied a pension. Having no other means of relief, he had taken to singing and begging to make a livelihood, in which he had been most successful and he was known throughout the Town for the curious hat he wore. Johnson held out his hand to Stephen, but Stephen looked away. He always took great care not to speak to, or in any way acknowledge, negroes of low station. He feared that if he were seen speaking to such people it might be supposed that he had some connexion with them.

He heard his name cried out, and he jumped as if he had been scalded, but it was only Toby Smith, Mrs Brandy's shopman.

"Oh! Mr Black!" cried Toby, hurrying up. "There you are! You generally walk so fast, sir! I was sure you would be in Harley-street by now. Mrs Brandy sends her compliments, sir, and says you left this by your chair."

Toby held out a silver diadem, a delicate band of metal of a size to fit Stephen's head exactly. It had no ornament other than a few odd signs and queer letters cut into its surface.

"But this is not mine!" said Stephen.

"Oh!" said Toby, blankly, but then he appeared to decide that Stephen was joking. "Oh, Mr Black, as if I have not seen it upon your head a hundred times!" Then he laughed and bowed and ran back to the shop, leaving Stephen with the diadem in his hand.

He crossed over Piccadilly into Bond-street. He had not gone far when he heard shouting, and a tiny figure came running down the street. In stature the figure appeared no more than four or five years old, but its dead-white, sharp-featured face belonged to a much older child. It was followed at a distance by two or three men, shouting "Thief!" and "Stop him!"

Stephen sprang into the thief's path. But though the young thief could not entirely escape Stephen (who was nimble), Stephen was not quite able to fasten on to the thief (who was slippery). The thief held a long bundle wrapped in a red cloth, which he somehow contrived to tip into Stephen's hands, before darting in among a crowd of people outside Hemmings's, the goldsmith. These people were but newly emerged from Hemmings's and knew nothing of the pursuit, so they did not spring apart when the thief arrived among them. It was impossible to say which way he went.

Stephen stood, holding the bundle. The cloth, which was a soft, old velvet, slipped away, revealing a long rod of silver.

The first of the pursuers to arrive was a dark, handsome gentleman sombrely, but elegantly dressed in black. "You had him for a moment," he said to Stephen.

"I am only sorry, sir," said Stephen, "that I could not hold him for you. But, as you see, I have your property." Stephen offered the man the rod of silver and the red velvet cloth but the man did not take them.

"It was my mother's fault!" said the gentleman, angrily. "Oh! How could she be so negligent? I have told her a thousand times that if she left the drawing-room window open, sooner or later a thief would come in by it. Have I not said so a hundred times,

Edward? Have I not said so, John?" The latter part of this speech was addressed to the gentleman's servants, who had come running up after their master. They lacked breath to reply, but were able to assure Stephen by emphatic nods that the gentleman had indeed said so.

"All the world knows that I keep many treasures at my house," continued the gentleman, "and yet she continues to open the window in spite of my entreaties! And now, of course, she sits weeping for the loss of this treasure which has been in my family for hundreds of years. For my mother takes great pride in our family and all its possessions. This sceptre, for example, is proof that we are descended from the ancient kings of Wessex, for it belonged to Edgar or Alfred or someone of that sort."

"Then you must take it back, sir," urged Stephen. "Your mother, I dare say, will be much relieved to see it safe and sound."

The gentleman reached out to take the sceptre, but suddenly drew back his hand. "No!" he cried. "I will not! I vow I will not. If I were to return this treasure to my mother's keeping, then she would never learn the evil consequences of her negligence! She would never learn to keep the window shut! And who knows what I might lose next? Why, I might come home tomorrow to an empty house! No, sir, you must keep the sceptre! It is a reward for the service you did me in trying to catch hold of the thief."

The gentleman's servants all nodded as if they saw the sense of this, and then a coach drew up and gentleman and servants all got into it and drove away.

Stephen stood in the rain with a diadem in one hand and a sceptre in the other. Ahead of him were the shops of Bond-street, the most fashionable shops in all the kingdom. In their windows were displayed silks and velvets, headdresses of pearl and peacock feathers, diamonds, rubies, jewels and every sort of gold and silver trinkets.

"Well," thought Stephen, "doubtless he will be able to make all sorts of eerie treasures for me out of the contents of those shops. But I shall be cleverer than him. I shall go home by another way."

He turned into a narrow alleyway between two buildings, crossed a little yard, passed through a gate, down another alleyway and emerged in a little street of modest houses. It was quite deserted here and strangely quiet. The only sound was the rain striking the cobblestones. Rain had darkened all the fronts of the houses until they appeared to be almost black. The occupants of the houses seemed a very frugal lot, for not one of them had lit a lamp or a candle despite the gloominess of the day. Yet the heavy cloud did not cover the sky completely and a watery white light shewed at the horizon, so that between the dark sky and the dark earth the rain fell in bright silver shafts.

A shining something rolled suddenly out of a dark alleyway and skittered unevenly over the wet cobblestones, coming to a stop directly in front of Stephen.

He looked at it and heaved a great sigh when he saw that it was, as he expected, a little silver ball. It was very battered and old-looking. At the top where there ought to have been a cross to signify that all the world belonged to God, there was a tiny open hand. One of the fingers was broken off. This symbol – the open hand – was one that Stephen knew well. It was one of those employed by the gentleman with the thistle-down hair. Only last night Stephen had taken part in a procession and carried a banner bearing this very emblem through dark, windswept courtyards and along avenues of immense oak-trees in whose unseen branches the wind soughed.

There was the sound of a window sash being raised. A woman poked her head out of a window at the top of the house. Her hair was all in curl papers. "Well, pick it up!" she cried, glaring furiously at Stephen.

"But it is not mine!" he called up to her.

"It is not his, he says!" This made her angrier still. "And I suppose I did not just see it fall out of your pocket and roll away! And I suppose my name is not Mariah Tompkins! And I suppose I do not labour night and day to keep Pepper-street clean and tidy, but you must come here a-purpose to throw away your rubbish!"

With a heavy sigh, Stephen picked up the orb. He found that, whatever Mariah Tompkins said or believed, if he put it in his pocket there was a very real danger of it tearing the cloth, it was so heavy. So he was obliged to walk through the rain, sceptre in one hand, orb in the other. The diadem he put on his head, as the most convenient place for it, and attired in this fashion he walked home.

On arriving at the house in Harley-street, he went down to the area and opened the kitchen door. He found himself, not in the kitchen as he had expected, but in a room he had never seen before. He sneezed three times.

A moment was enough to reassure him that he was not at Lost-hope. It was a quite commonplace sort of room – the sort of room, in fact, that one might find in any well-to-do house in London. It was, however, remarkably untidy. The inhabitants, who were presumably new to the house, appeared to be in the middle of unpacking. All the articles usually belonging to a sitting-room and study were present: card-tables, work-tables, reading-tables, fire-irons, chairs of varying degrees of comfortableness and usefulness, mirrors, tea-cups, sealing-wax, candle-sticks, pictures, books (a great number of these), sanders, ink-stands, pens, papers, clocks, balls of string, footstools, fire-screens and writing-desks. But they were all jumbled together and standing upon one another in new and surprizing combinations. Packing-cases and boxes and bundles were scattered about, some unpacked, some half-unpacked and some scarcely begun. The straw from the packing-cases had been pulled out and now lay scattered about the room and over the furniture, which had the effect of making everything dusty and causing Stephen to sneeze twice more. Some of the straw had even got into the fireplace so that there was a very real danger of the whole room going up in a conflagration at any moment.

The room contained two people: a man whom Stephen had never seen before and the gentleman with the thistle-down hair.

The man he had never seen before was seated at a little table in front of the window. Presumably he ought to have been unpacking his things and setting his room in order, but he had abandoned this task and was presently engaged in reading a book. He broke off every now and then to look things up in two or three other volumes that lay on the table; to mutter excitedly to himself; and to dash down a note or two in an ink-splashed little book.

Meanwhile the gentleman with the thistle-down hair sat in an arm-chair on the opposite side of the fireplace, directing at the other man a look of such extreme malevolence and irritation as made Stephen fear for the man's life. Yet the moment the gentleman with the thistle-down hair beheld Stephen, he became all delight, all affability. "Ah, there you are!" he cried. "How noble you look in your kingly accoutrements!"

There happened to be a large mirror standing opposite the door. For the first time Stephen saw himself with the crown, sceptre and orb. He looked every inch a king. He turned to look at the man at the table to discover how he bore with the sudden appearance of a black man in a crown.

"Oh! Do not concern yourself about *him*!" said the gentleman with the thistle-down hair. "He can neither see nor hear us. He has no more talent than the other one. Look!" He screwed up a piece of paper and threw it energetically at the man's head. The man did not flinch or look up or appear to know any thing about it.

"The other one, sir?" said Stephen. "What do you mean?"

"That is the younger magician. The one lately arrived in London."

"Is it indeed? I have heard of him, of course. Sir Walter thinks highly of him. But I confess I have forgotten his name."

"Oh! Who cares what his name is! What matters is that he is just as stupid as the other one and very near as ugly."

"What?" said the magician, suddenly. He turned away from his book and looked around the room with a slightly suspicious air. "Jeremy!" he called out very loudly.

A servant put his head around the door, but did not trouble himself so far as to come into the room. "Sir?" he said.

Stephen's eyes opened very wide at this lazy behaviour – it was a thing he would never have allowed in Harley-street. He made a point of staring very coldly at the man to shew him what he thought of him before he remembered that the man could not see him.

"These London houses are shockingly built," said the magician. "I can hear the people in the next house."

This was interesting enough to tempt the servant called Jeremy all the way into the room. He stood and listened.

"Are all the walls so thin?" continued the magician. "Do you suppose there can be something wrong with them?"

Jeremy knocked on the wall which divided the house from its neighbour. It responded with as dull and quiet a sound as any stout, well-built wall in the kingdom. Making nothing of this, he said, "I do not hear any thing, sir. What were they saying?"

"I believe I heard one of them call the other stupid and ugly."

"Are you sure, sir? It is two old ladies that live upon that side."

"Ha! That proves nothing. Age is no guarantee of any thing these days."

With this remark the magician appeared suddenly to grow tired of this conversation. He turned back to his book and started reading.

Jeremy waited a moment and then, since his master appeared to have forgotten all about him, he went away again.

"I have not thanked you yet, sir," said Stephen to the gentleman, "for these wonderful gifts."

"Ah, Stephen! I am glad I have pleased you. The diadem, I confess, is your own hat transformed by magic. I would have greatly preferred to give you a real crown, but I was entirely unable to lay my hand upon one at such short notice. You are disappointed, I dare say. Although now I come to think of it, the King of England has several crowns, and rarely makes use of any of them."

He raised his hands in the air and pointed upwards with two immensely long white fingers.

"Oh!" cried Stephen, suddenly realizing what the gentleman was about. "If you think of casting spells to bring the King of England here with one of his crowns – which I imagine you do, since you are all kindness – then I beg that you will spare yourself the trouble! I have no need of one at the moment, as you know, and the King of England is such an old gentleman – would it not perhaps be kinder to let him stay at home?"

"Oh, very well!" said the gentleman, lowering his hands.

For lack of any other occupation, he reassumed his abuse of the new magician. Nothing about the man pleased him. He ridiculed the book he was reading, found fault with the make of his boots, and was entirely unable to approve of his height (despite the fact that he was exactly the same height as the gentleman with the thistle-down hair – as was proved when they both happened to stand up at the same time.)

Stephen was anxious to return to his duties in Harley-street, but he feared that if he left them alone together then the gentleman might start throwing something more substantial than paper at the magician. "Shall you and I walk to Harley-street together, sir?" he asked. "Then you may tell me how your noble actions have moulded London and made it glorious. That is always so very entertaining. I never grow tired of hearing about it."

"Gladly, Stephen! Gladly!"

"Is it far, sir?"

"Is what far, Stephen?"

"Harley-street, sir. I do not know where we are."

"We are in Soho-square and no, it is not far at all!"

When they reached the house in Harley-street the gentleman took a most affectionate farewell of Stephen, urging him not to feel sad at this parting and reminding him that they would meet again that very night at Lost-hope. ". . . when a most charming cere-mony will be held in the belfry of the Easternmost Tower. It commemorates an occasion which happened – oh! five hundred years ago or so – when I cleverly contrived to capture the little children of my enemy and we pushed them out of the belfry to their deaths. Tonight we will re-enact this great triumph! We will dress straw dolls in the children's blood-stained clothes and fling them down on to the paving stones and then we will sing and dance and rejoice over their destruction!"

"And do you perform this ceremony every year, sir? I feel sure I would have remembered it if I had seen it before. It is so very . . . striking."

"I am glad you think so. I perform it whenever I think of it. Of course it was a great deal more striking when we used real children."

27

The magician's wife

December 1809–January 1810

THERE WERE NOW two magicians in London to be admired and made much of and I doubt if it will come as
much surprize to any one to learn that, of the two,
London preferred Mr Strange. Strange was everyone's idea of
what a magician ought to be. He was tall; he was charming; he
had a most ironical smile; and, unlike Mr Norrell, he talked a great
deal about magic and had no objection to answering any body's
questions on the subject. Mr and Mrs Strange attended a great
many evening- and dinner-parties, and at some point in the
proceedings Strange would generally oblige the company with
a shew of one of the minor sorts of magic. The most popular magic
he did was to cause visions to appear upon the surface of water.[1]

---

[1] On May 14th, 1810 Strange wrote to John Segundus:

". . . There is a great passion here for seeing visions, which I am always
glad to satisfy whenever I can. Whatever Norrell may say, it is very little
trouble and nothing delights the layman so much. My only complaint is that
people always end by asking me to shew them their relations. I was in
Tavistock-square on Tuesday at the house of a family called Fulcher. I spilt
some wine upon the table, did the magic and shewed them a sea-battle which
was at that moment raging in the Bahamas, a view of a ruined Neapolitan
monastery by moonlight and finally the Emperor Napoleon Buonaparte
drinking a cup of chocolate with his feet in a steaming bowl of water.

"The Fulchers were well-bred enough to seem interested in what I was
doing, but at the end of the evening they asked me if I might be able to shew
them their aunt who lives in Carlisle. For the next half an hour Arabella and I

Unlike Norrell, he did not use a silver basin which was the traditional vessel for seeing visions in. Strange said that really one could see so little in a basin that it was scarcely worth the trouble of casting the spells. He preferred instead to wait until the servants had cleared the dishes off the table and removed the cloth, then he would tip a glass of water or wine over the table and conjure visions into the pool. Fortunately his hosts were generally so delighted with the magic that they hardly ever complained of their stained, spoilt tables and carpets.

For their part Mr and Mrs Strange were settled in London much to their satisfaction. They had taken a house in Soho-square and Arabella was deep in all the pleasant cares connected with a new home: commissioning elegant new furniture from the cabinet-makers, entreating her friends to help her to some steady servants and going every day to the shops.

One morning in mid-December she received a message from one of the shopmen at Haig and Chippendale's Upholstery (a most attentive person) to say that a bronze silk with alternate satin and watered stripes had just arrived in the shop and he believed it might be the very thing for Mrs Strange's drawing-room curtains. This necessitated a little re-organization of Arabella's day.

"It appears from Mr Sumner's description to be very elegant," she told Strange at breakfast, "and I expect to like it very much. But if I chuse bronze-coloured silk for the curtains, then I believe I must give up any notion of having a wine-coloured velvet for the chaise-longue. I do not think bronze-colour and wine-colour will look well together. So I shall to go to Flint and Clark's to look at the wine-coloured velvet again, and see if I can bear to give it up. Then I will go to Haig and Chippendale's. But that means I will have no time to visit your aunt – which I really ought to do as she is leaving for Edinburgh this morning. I want to thank her for finding Mary for us."

"Mmm?" said Strange, who was eating hot rolls and preserves, and reading *Curiose Observations upon the Anatomie of Faeries* by Holgarth and Pickle.[2]

"Mary. The new maid. You saw her last night."

"Ah," said Strange, turning a page.

"She seems a nice, pleasant girl with quiet ways. I am sure we will be very happy with her. So, as I was saying, I would be very grateful, Jonathan, if you would call upon your aunt this morning. You can walk down to Henrietta-street after breakfast and thank her for Mary. Then you can come to Haig and Chippendale's and wait for me there. Oh! And could you look in at Wedgwood and Byerley's and ask the people when the new dinner-service will be ready? It will be scarcely any trouble. It is very nearly on your way." She looked at him doubtfully. "Jonathan, are you listening to me?"

"Mmm?" said Strange, looking up. "Oh, entirely!"

So Arabella, attended by one of the footmen, walked to Wigmore-street where Flint and Clark had their establishment. But on this second viewing of the wine-coloured velvet she concluded that, though very handsome, it was altogether too sombre. So then she walked on, all anticipation, to St Martin's-lane to behold the bronze-coloured silk. When she arrived at Haig and Chippendale's she found the shopman waiting for her, but not her husband. The shopman was most apologetic but Mr Strange had not been there all morning.

She went out into the street again.

"George, do you see your master anywhere?" she asked the footman.

"No, madam."

---

[2] One of Mr Norrell's books. Mr Norrell mentioned it, somewhat obliquely, when Mr Segundus and Mr Honeyfoot waited upon him in early January 1807.

A grey rain was beginning to fall. A sort of premonition inspired her to look in at the window of a bookseller's. There she discovered Strange, talking energetically to Sir Walter Pole. So she went into the shop, bid Sir Walter good morning and sweetly inquired of her husband if he had visited his aunt or looked in at Wedgwood and Byerley's.

Strange seemed somewhat perplexed by the question. He looked down and discovered that he had a large book in his hand. He frowned at it as if he could not imagine how it had got there. "I *would* have done so, my love, of course," he said, "only Sir Walter has been talking to me all this while which has quite prevented me from beginning."

"It has been entirely my fault," Sir Walter hastily assured Arabella. "We have a problem with our blockade. It is the usual sort of thing and I have been telling Mr Strange about it in the hope he and Mr Norrell will be able to help us."

"And can you help?" asked Arabella.

"Oh, I should think so," said Strange.

Sir Walter explained that the British Government had received intelligence that some French ships – possibly as many as ten – had slipped through the British blockade. No one knew where they had gone or what they intended to do when they got there. Nor did the Government know where to find Admiral Armingcroft who was supposed to prevent this sort of thing happening. The Admiral and his fleet of ten frigates and two ships of the line had quite disappeared – presumably he had gone in pursuit of the French. There was a promising young captain, presently stationed at Madeira, and if the Admiralty had only been able to discover what was happening and *where* it was happening, they would have gladly put Captain Lightwood in charge of four or five more ships and sent him there. Lord Mulgrave had asked Admiral Greenwax what he thought they ought to do and Admiral Greenwax had asked the Ministers and the Ministers said that the Admiralty ought to consult Mr Strange and Mr Norrell immediately.

"I would not have you think that the Admiralty is entirely helpless without Mr Strange," smiled Sir Walter. "They have done what they can. They sent one of the clerks, a Mr Petrofax, to Greenwich to seek out a childhood friend of Admiral Armingcroft's to ask him, with his superior knowledge of the Admiral's character, what he thought the Admiral would do under such circumstances. But when Mr Petrofax got to Greenwich the Admiral's childhood friend was drunk in bed, and Mr Petrofax was not sure that he understood the question."

"I dare say Norrell and I will be able to suggest something," said Strange, thoughtfully, "but I think I should like to see the problem on a map."

"I have all the necessary maps and papers at my house. One of our servants will bring them to Hanover-square later today and then perhaps you will be so kind as to talk to Norrell . . ."

"Oh! But we can do that now!" said Strange. "Arabella does not mind waiting a few moments! You do not mind, do you?" he said to his wife. "I am meeting Mr Norrell at two o'clock and I believe that if I can explain the problem to him straightaway then we may be able to return an answer to the Admiralty before dinner."

Arabella, like a sweet, compliant woman and good wife, put all thoughts of her new curtains aside for the moment and assured both gentlemen that in such a cause it was no trouble to her to wait. It was settled that Mr and Mrs Strange would accompany Sir Walter to his house in Harley-street.

Strange took out his watch and looked at it. "Twenty minutes to Harley-street. Three-quarters of an hour to examine the problem. Then another fifteen minutes to Soho-square. Yes, there is plenty of time."

Arabella laughed. "He is not always so scrupulous, I assure you," she said to Sir Walter, "but he was late on Tuesday for an appointment with Lord Liverpool and Mr Norrell was not best pleased."

"That was not my fault," said Strange. "I was ready to leave the

332

house in good time but I could not find my gloves." Arabella's teasing accusation of lateness continued to vex him and on the way to Harley-street he examined his watch as though in hopes of discovering something about the operation of Time which had hitherto gone unnoticed and which would vindicate him. When they reached Harley-street he thought he had it. "Ha!" he cried suddenly. "I know what it is. My watch is wrong!"

"I do not think so," said Sir Walter, taking out his own watch and shewing it to Strange. "It is precisely noon. Mine says the same."

"Then why do I hear no bells?" said Strange. "Do you hear bells?" he said to Arabella.

"No, I hear nothing."

Sir Walter reddened and muttered something about the bells in this parish and the neighbouring ones being no longer rung.

"Really?" asked Strange. "Why in the world not?"

Sir Walter looked as if he would have thanked Strange to keep his curiosity to himself, but all he said was, "Lady Pole's illness has left her nerves in a sad condition. The tolling of a bell is peculiarly distressing to her and I have asked the vestries of St Mary-le-bone and St Peter if they would, out of consideration for Lady Pole's nerves, forbear from ringing the church bells, and they have been so obliging as to agree."

This was rather extraordinary, but then it was generally agreed that Lady Pole's illness was a rather extraordinary thing with symptoms quite unlike any other. Neither Mr nor Mrs Strange had ever seen Lady Pole. No one had seen her for two years.

When they arrived at no. 9 Harley-street Strange was anxious to begin looking at Sir Walter's documents straightaway but he was obliged to curb his impatience while Sir Walter satisfied himself that Arabella would not lack for amusement in their absence. Sir Walter was a well-bred man and greatly disliked leaving any guest alone in his house. To abandon a lady was particularly bad. Strange on the other hand was anxious to be on time for his appointment with Mr Norrell, so as fast as Sir Walter could suggest diversions, Strange was endeavouring to prove that Arabella needed none of them.

Sir Walter shewed Arabella the novels in the bookcase, and recommended Mrs Edgeworth's *Belinda* in particular as being likely to amuse her. "Oh," said Strange, interrupting, "I read *Belinda* to Arabella two or three years ago. Besides, you know, I do not think we will be so long that she will have time to finish a *three-volume* novel."

"Then perhaps some tea and seed-cake . . . ?" Sir Walter said to Arabella.

"But Arabella does not care for seed-cake," interrupted Strange, absent-mindedly picking up *Belinda* himself and beginning to read the first volume, "It is a thing she particularly dislikes."

"A glass of madeira, then," said Sir Walter. "You will take some madeira, I am sure. Stephen! . . . Stephen, fetch Mrs Strange a glass of madeira."

In the eerie, silent fashion peculiar to high-trained London servants, a tall black servant appeared at Sir Walter's elbow. Mr Strange seemed quite startled by his sudden arrival and stared hard at him for several moments, before he said to his wife, "You do not want madeira, do you? You do not want any thing."

"No, Jonathan. I do not want any thing," agreed his wife, laughing at their odd argument. "Thank you, Sir Walter, but I am perfectly content to sit here quietly and read."

The black servant bowed and departed as silently as he had come, and Strange and Sir Walter went off to talk of the French fleet and the missing English ships.

But when she was left alone, Arabella found that she was not after all in a mood for reading. On looking round the room in search of amusement her eye was caught by a large painting. It was a landscape comprising woods and a ruined castle perched on top of a cliff. The trees were dark and the ruins and cliff were touched with gold by the light of a setting sun; the sky by contrast was full of light and glowed with pearly colour. A large portion of the foreground was occupied by a silvery pool in which a young woman appeared to be drowning; a second figure bent over her – whether man, woman, satyr or faun, it was impossible to determine and, though Arabella studied their postures carefully, she could not decide whether it was the intention of the second figure to save the young woman or murder her. When she had tired of looking at this painting Arabella wandered out into the passage to look at the pictures there but, as these were for the most part watercolour views of Brighton and Chelmsford, she found them very dull.

Sir Walter and Strange could be heard talking in another room.

". . . extraordinary thing! Yet he is an excellent fellow in his way," said Sir Walter's voice.

"Oh! I know who you mean! He has a brother who is the organist at Bath Cathedral," said Strange. "He has a black-and-white cat that walks about the Bath streets just ahead of him. Once, when I was in Milsom-street . . ."

A door stood open, through which Arabella could see a very elegant drawing-room with a great number of paintings that appeared to be more splendid and richly coloured than any she had yet seen. She went in.

The room seemed to be full of light, although the day was every bit as grey and forbidding as it had been before. "So where does all this light come from?" wondered Arabella. "It is almost as if it shines out of the paintings, but that is impossible." The paintings were all of Venice[3] and certainly the great quantities of sky and sea which they contained made the room seem somehow insubstantial.

---

[3] These were Venetian paintings which Mr Norrell had seen at Mrs Wintertowne's house two years before. Mrs Wintertowne had informed Mr Norrell at the time that she intended to give them to Sir Walter and Miss Wintertowne as a wedding-present.

When she had done examining the paintings upon one wall, she turned to cross to the opposite wall and immediately discovered – much to her mortification – that she was not alone. A young woman was sitting before the fire on a blue sopha, regarding her with some curiosity. The sopha had a rather high back, which was the reason Arabella had not observed her before.

"Oh! I do beg your pardon!"

The young woman said nothing.

She was a remarkably elegant woman with a pale, perfect skin and dark hair most gracefully arranged. She wore a gown of white muslin and an Indian shawl of ivory, silver and black. She seemed altogether too well dressed to be a governess and too much at home to be a lady's companion. Yet if she were a guest in the house, why had Sir Walter not introduced her?

Arabella curtsied to the young woman and, blushing slightly, said, "I thought there was no one here! I beg your pardon for intruding upon you." She turned to leave.

"Oh!" said the young woman. "I hope you do not think of going! I so rarely see any one – scarcely any one at all! And besides you wished to see the paintings! You cannot deny it, you know, for I saw you in that mirror as you entered the room and your intention was plain." A large Venetian mirror hung above the fireplace. It had a most elaborate frame which was also made of mirror-glass and it was decorated with the ugliest glass flowers and scrolls imaginable. "I hope," said the young woman, "that you will not allow me to prevent you."

"But I fear I disturb you," said Arabella.

"Oh, but you do not!" The young woman gestured towards the paintings, "Pray. Continue."

So, feeling it would be a still worse breach of manners to refuse, Arabella thanked the young woman and went and examined the other paintings, but she did it less minutely than before because she was conscious that the young woman watched her in the mirror the entire time.

When she had finished, the young woman asked Arabella to sit. "And how do they please you?" she asked.

"Well," said Arabella, "they are certainly very beautiful. I particularly like the pictures of processions and feasts – we have nothing like them in England. So many fluttering banners! So many gilded boats and exquisite costumes! But it seems to me that the artist loves buildings and blue skies more than people. He has made them so small, so insignificant! Among so many marble palaces and bridges they seem almost lost. Do not you think so?"

This seemed to amuse the young woman. She smiled a wry smile. "Lost?" she said. "Oh, I should think they are indeed lost, poor souls! For, when all is said and done, Venice is only a labyrinth – a vast and beautiful labyrinth to be sure, but a labyrinth nonetheless and none but its oldest inhabitants can be sure of finding their way about – or, at least, that is my understanding."

"Indeed?" said Arabella. "That must certainly be very inconvenient. But then the sensation of being lost in a labyrinth must be so delightful! Oh! I believe I should give almost any thing to go there!"

The young woman regarded her with an odd, melancholy smile. "If you had spent months, as I have done, wearily parading through endless dark passageways, you would think very differently. The pleasures of losing oneself in a maze pall very quickly. And as for curious ceremonies, processions and feasts, well . . ." She shrugged. "I quite detest them!"

Arabella did not very well comprehend her, but thought that it might help if she discovered who the young woman was, and so she inquired as to her name.

"I am Lady Pole."

"Oh! Of course!" said Arabella and wondered why she had not thought of this before. She told Lady Pole her own name and that her husband had business with Sir Walter, which was the reason of her being there.

A sudden burst of loud laughter was heard from the direction of the library.

"They are supposed to be talking of the war," Arabella observed to her ladyship, "but either the war has got a great deal more entertaining recently, or else – as I suspect – they have left business far behind and have got to gossiping about their acquaintance. Half an hour ago Mr Strange could think of nothing but his next appointment, but now I suppose Sir Walter has drawn him off to talk of other things and I dare say he has forgot all about it." She smiled to herself as wives do when they pretend to criticize their husbands, but are really boasting of them. "I really do believe he is the most easily distracted creature in the world. Mr Norrell's patience must be sorely tried sometimes."

"Mr Norrell?" said Lady Pole.

"Mr Strange has the honour to be Mr Norrell's pupil," said Arabella.

She expected her ladyship to reply with some praise for Mr Norrell's extraordinary magical ability or some words of gratitude for his kindness. But Lady Pole said nothing and so Arabella continued in an encouraging tone, "Of course we have heard a great deal of the wonderful magic which Mr Norrell performed on your ladyship's behalf."

"Mr Norrell has been no friend to me," said Lady Pole in a dry, matter-of-fact tone. "I had far better be dead than be as I am."

It was such a shocking thing to hear that for several moments Arabella could think of nothing to say. She had no reason to love Mr Norrell. He had never done her any kindness – indeed he had several times gone out of his way to shew how little he regarded her, but for all that he was the only other representative of her husband's profession. So, just as the wife of an admiral will always take the part of the Navy or the wife of a bishop will speak up in favour of the Church, Arabella felt obliged to say something in defence of the other magician. "Pain and suffering are the very worst of companions and no doubt your ladyship grows heartily sick of them. No one in the world could blame you for wishing to be rid of them . . ." (Yet even as Arabella spoke these words, she was thinking, "It is very odd but she does not look ill. Not in the least.") "But if what I hear be true, then your ladyship is not without solace in your suffering. I must confess that I have never heard your ladyship's name spoken without its being accompanied by some praise for your devoted husband. Surely you would not gladly leave him? Surely, your ladyship, you must feel a little grateful to Mr Norrell – if only for Sir Walter's sake."

Lady Pole did not reply to this; instead she began to question Arabella about her husband. How long had he practised magic? How long had he been Mr Norrell's pupil? Was his magic generally successful? Did he perform magic by himself or only under Norrell's direction?

Arabella did her best to answer all the questions adding, "If there is any thing your ladyship would like me to ask Mr Strange on your behalf, if there is any service he can do, then your ladyship has only to name it."

"Thank you. But what I have to tell you is as much for your husband's sake as mine. I think Mr Strange ought to hear how I was left to a horrible fate by Mr Norrell. Mr Strange should know what sort of man he has to deal with. Will you tell him?"

"Of course. I . . ."

"Promise me that you will."

"I will tell Mr Strange any thing your ladyship wishes."

"I should warn you that I have made many attempts to tell people of my misery and I have never yet succeeded."

As Lady Pole said this something happened which Arabella did not quite understand. It was as if something in one of the paintings had moved, or someone had passed behind one of the mirrors, and the conviction came over her once again that this room was no room at all, that the walls had no real solidity but instead the room were only a sort of crossroads where strange winds blew upon Lady Pole from faraway places.

"In 1607," began Lady Pole, "a gentleman named Redeshawe in Halifax, West Yorkshire inherited £10 from his aunt. He used the money to buy a Turkish carpet, which he then brought home and spread over the stone flags of his parlour. Then he drank some beer and fell asleep in a chair by the fire. He awoke at two in the morning to find the carpet covered with three or four hundred people, each about two or three inches high. Mr Redeshawe observed that the most important individuals among them, both men and women, were gorgeously attired in gold and silver armour and that they rode white rabbits – which were to them as elephants are to us. When he asked what they were doing, one brave soul among them climbed up to his shoulder and bellowed in his ear that they intended to fight a battle according to the rules of Honoré Bonet and Mr Redeshawe's carpet was exactly suited to their purpose because the regularity of the patterns helped the heralds determine that each army was positioned correctly and took no unfair advantage over the other. However Mr Redeshawe did not chuse that a battle should be fought upon his new carpet and so he took a broom and . . . No, wait!" Lady Pole stopt and suddenly covered her face with her hands. "That is not what I wished to say!"

She began again. This time she told a story of a man who had gone hunting in a wood. He had become separated from his friends. His horse had caught its hoof in a rabbit-hole and he had tumbled off. As he fell he had had the strangest impression that he was somehow falling into the rabbit-hole. When he picked himself up he found he was in a strange country lit by its own sun and nurtured by its own rain. In a wood very like the one he had just left, he found a mansion where a party of gentlemen – some of them rather odd – were all playing cards together.

Lady Pole had just got to the part where the gentlemen invited the lost huntsman to join them, when a slight sound – scarcely more than an indrawn breath – made Arabella turn. She discovered that Sir Walter had entered the room and was gazing down at his wife in dismay.

"You are tired," he said to her.

Lady Pole looked up at her husband. Her expression at that moment was curious. There was sadness in it and pity too and, oddly enough, a little amusement. It was as if she were saying to herself, "Look at us! What a sad pair we make!" Aloud she said, "I am only as tired as I usually am. I must have walked for miles and miles last night. And danced for hours too!"

"Then you must rest," he insisted. "Let me take you upstairs to Pampisford and she will take care of you."

At first her ladyship seemed inclined to resist him. She seized Arabella's hand and held it, as if to shew him that she would not consent to be parted from her. But then just as suddenly she gave it up and allowed him to lead her away.

At the door she turned. "Goodbye, Mrs Strange. I hope they will let you come again. I hope you will do me that honour. I see no one. Or rather, I see whole roomfuls of people, but not a Christian among them."

Arabella stepped forward, intending to shake Lady Pole's hand and to assure her that she would gladly come again, but Sir Walter had already removed her ladyship from the room. For the second time that day Arabella was left alone in the house in Harley-street.

A bell began to toll.

Naturally she was a little surprized after all that Sir Walter had said about the bells of Mary-le-bone standing silent out of deference to Lady Pole's illness. This bell sounded very sad and far-away and it brought before her imagination all sorts of melancholy scenes . . .

. . . bleak, wind-swept fens and moors; empty fields with broken walls and gates hanging off their hinges; a black, ruined church; an open grave; a suicide buried at a lonely crossroads; a fire of bones blazing in the twilit snow; a gallows with a man swinging from its arm; another man crucified upon a wheel; an ancient spear plunged into the mud with a strange talisman, like a little leather finger, hanging from it; a scarecrow whose black rags blew about so violently in the wind that he seemed about to leap into the grey air and fly towards you on vast black wings . . .

"I must beg your pardon if you have seen any thing here to disturb you," said Sir Walter, coming suddenly back into the room.

Arabella caught hold of a chair to steady herself.

"Mrs Strange? You are not well." He took hold of her arm and helped her sit down. "May I fetch someone? Your husband? Her ladyship's maid?"

"No, no," said Arabella, a little out of breath. "I want no one, nothing. I thought . . . I did not know you were here. That is all."

Sir Walter stared at her in great concern. She tried to smile at him, but she was not quite sure that the smile turned out well.

He put his hands in his pockets, took them out, ran his fingers through his hair, and sighed deeply. "I dare say her ladyship has been telling you all sorts of odd tales," he said, unhappily.

Arabella nodded.

"And hearing them has distressed you. I am very sorry for it."

"No, no. Not at all. Her ladyship did talk a little of . . . of what seemed rather odd, but I did not mind it. Not in the least! I felt a little faint. But do not connect the two, I beg you! It was nothing to do with her ladyship! I had a sort of foolish idea that there was a sort of mirror before me with all sorts of strange landscapes in it and I thought I was falling into it. I suppose I must have been about to faint and your coming in just then prevented it. But it is very odd. I never did such a thing before."

"Let me fetch Mr Strange."

Arabella laughed. "You may if you wish, but I assure you he will be a great deal less concerned about me than you are. Mr Strange has never been much interested in other people's indispositions. His own are quite another matter! But, there is no need to fetch any body. See! I am myself again. I am perfectly well."

There was a little pause.

"Lady Pole . . ." began Arabella and paused, not knowing quite how to continue.

"Her ladyship is generally calm enough," said Sir Walter, "not

342

exactly at peace, you understand, but calm enough. But on the rare occasions when any one new comes to the house, it always excites her to these outlandish speeches. I am sure you are too good to repeat any thing of what she has said."

"Oh! Of course! I would not repeat it for the world!"

"You are very kind."

"And may . . . may I come again? Her ladyship seems to wish it very much and I would be very happy in the acquaintance."

Sir Walter took a long moment to consider this proposal. Finally he nodded. Then he somehow turned his nod into a bow. "I shall consider that you do us both great honour," he said. "Thank you."

Strange and Arabella left the house in Harley-street and Strange was in high spirits. "I see the way to do it," he told her. "Nothing could be simpler. It is a pity that I must wait for Norrell's opinion before beginning or I believe I might solve the entire problem in the next half hour. As I see it, there are two crucial points. The first . . . Whatever is the matter?"

With a little "Oh!" Arabella had stopt.

It had suddenly occurred to her that she had given two entirely contradictory promises: one to Lady Pole to tell Strange about the gentleman in Yorkshire who had purchased a carpet; and the second to Sir Walter not to repeat any thing that Lady Pole had said. "It is nothing," she said.

"And which of the many occupations that Sir Walter was preparing for you did you fix upon?"

"None of them. I . . . I saw Lady Pole and we had some conversation together. That is all."

"Did you indeed? A pity I was not with you. I should have liked to see the woman who owes her life to Norrell's magic. But I have not told you what happened to me! You remember how the negro servant came in very suddenly? Well, just for a moment I had the distinct impression that there was a tall black king standing there, crowned with a silver diadem and holding a shining silver sceptre

343

and an orb – but when I looked again there was no one there but Sir Walter's negro servant. Is not that absurd?" Strange laughed.

Strange had gossiped so long with Sir Walter that he was almost an hour late for his appointment with Mr Norrell and Mr Norrell was very angry. Later the same day Strange sent a message to the Admiralty to say that Mr Norrell and he had looked into the problem of the missing French ships and that they believed they were in the Atlantic, on their way to the West Indies where they intended to cause some mischief. Furthermore the two magicians thought that Admiral Armingcroft had guessed correctly what the French were doing and had gone after them. The Admiralty, on the advice of Mr Strange and Mr Norrell, sent orders to Captain Lightwood to follow the Admiral westwards. In due course some of the French ships were captured and those that were not fled back to their French ports and stayed there.

Arabella's conscience was sorely racked over the two promises she had made. She put the problem to several matrons, friends of hers in whose good sense and careful judgement she reposed a great deal of confidence. Naturally she presented it in an ideal form without naming any one or mentioning any of the particular circumstances. Unfortunately this had the effect of making her dilemma entirely incomprehensible and the wise matrons were unable to help her. It distressed her that she could not confide in Strange, but clearly even to mention it would be to break her word to Sir Walter. After much deliberation she decided that a promise to a person *in* their senses ought to be more binding than a promise to someone *out of* their senses. For, after all, what was to be gained by repeating the nonsensical ramblings of a poor madwoman? So she never told Strange what Lady Pole had said.

A few days later, Mr and Mrs Strange were at a house in Bedford-square attending a concert of Italian music. Arabella found much to enjoy, but the room where they sat was not quite warm and so in a little pause that ensued when a new singer was joining the musicians, she slipped away without any fuss to fetch her shawl from where it lay in another room. She was just wrapping it around herself when there was a whisper of sound behind her and she looked up to see Drawlight, approaching her with the rapidity of a dream and crying out, "Mrs Strange! How glad I am to see you! And how is dear Lady Pole? I hear that you have seen her?"

Arabella agreed reluctantly that she had.

Drawlight drew her arm through his as a precaution against her running away, and said, "The trouble I have been at to procure an invitation to that house you would scarcely believe! None of my efforts have met with the least success! Sir Walter puts me off with one paltry excuse after another. It is always exactly the same – her ladyship is ill or she is a little better, but she is never well enough to see any body."

"Well, I suppose . . ." offered Arabella.

"Oh! Quite!" interrupted Drawlight. "*If* she is ill, then of course the rabble must be kept away. But that is no reason for excluding *me*. I saw her when she was a *corpse*! Oh, yes! You did not know that, I dare say? On the night he brought her back from the dead Mr Norrell came to me and pleaded with me to accompany him to the house. His words were, 'Come with me, my dear Drawlight, for I do not think that my spirits can support the sight of a lady, young, fair and innocent, cut off in the sweetest period of existence!' She stays in the house and sees no one. Some people think that her resurrection has made her proud and unwilling to mix with ordinary mortals. But I think the truth is quite different. I believe that her death and resurrection have bred in her a taste for odd experiences. Do not you think they might? It seems to me entirely possible that she takes something in order to see horrors! I suppose you saw no evidence of any thing of that sort? She took no sips from a glass of odd-coloured liquid? There was no folded paper pushed hurriedly into a pocket as you entered the room? – A paper such as might contain a teaspoon or two of powder? No? Laudanum generally comes in a little blue glass vial two or three inches high. In cases of addiction the family always believe that they can conceal the truth, but it is quite in vain. It is always found out in the end." He gave an affected laugh, "*I* always find it out."

Arabella gently removed her arm from his and begged his pardon. She was quite unable to supply him with the information he required. She knew nothing of any little bottles or powders.

She returned to the concert with much less agreeable feelings than she had taken away.

"Odious, odious little man!"

28

The Duke of Roxburghe's library

November 1810–January 1811

A T THE END of 1810 the Government's situation was about as bad as it could possibly be. Bad news met the Ministers at every turn. The French were everywhere triumphant; the other great European powers who had once combined with Britain to fight the Emperor Napoleon Buonaparte (and who had subsequently been defeated by him) now discovered their mistake and became instead his allies. At home, trade was destroyed by the war and men in every part of the kingdom were bankrupted; the harvest failed two years together. The King's youngest daughter fell ill and died, and the King went mad from grief.

The war destroyed every present comfort and cast a deep gloom over the future. Soldiers, merchants, politicians and farmers all cursed the hour that they were born, but magicians (a contrary breed of men if ever there was one) were entirely delighted by the course events were taking. Not for many hundreds of years had their art been held in such high regard. Many attempts to win the war had ended in disaster and magic now seemed the greatest hope Britain had. There were gentlemen from the War Office and all the various boards and offices of the navy who were most anxious to employ Mr Norrell and Mr Strange. The press of business at Mr Norrell's house in Hanover-square was often so great that visitors were obliged to wait until three or four in the morning before Mr Strange and Mr Norrell were able to attend to them. This was no very great trial as long as there was a crowd of gentlemen in Mr Norrell's drawing-room, but woe to the one who was last, for it is never a pleasant thing to have to wait in the middle of night outside a closed door and know that behind the door are two magicians doing magic.[1]

A story which was circulating at the time (one heard it everywhere one went) was the tale of the Emperor Napoleon Buonaparte's bungled attempts to find a magician of his own. Lord Liverpool's spies[2] reported that the Emperor was so jealous of the success of English magicians that he had sent out officers to search through all his Empire for some person or persons with magical abilities. Thus far, however, all that they had discovered was a Dutchman called Witloof who had a magic wardrobe. The wardrobe had been taken to Paris in a barouche-landau. At Versailles, Witloof had promised the Emperor that he could find the answer to any question inside the wardrobe.

According to the spies, Buonaparte had asked the wardrobe the following three questions: "Would the baby the Empress was expecting be male?"; "Would the Czar of Russia change sides again?"; "When would the English be defeated?"

Witloof had gone inside the wardrobe and come out with the

---

[1] Among the forms of magic which Strange and Norrell performed in 1810 were: causing an area of sea in the Bay of Biscay to silt up and a vast wood of monstrous trees to appear there (thus destroying twenty French ships); causing unusual tides and winds to baffle French ships and destroy French crops and livestock; the fashioning of rain into fleets of ships, walled cities, gigantic figures, flights of angels, etc., etc., in order to frighten, confuse or charm French soldiers and sailors; bringing on night when the French were expecting day and vice versa.

All the above are listed in *De Generibus Artium Magicarum Anglorum* by Francis Sutton-Grove.

[2] The previous Secretary of War, Lord Castlereagh, had quarrelled violently with Mr Canning in late 1809. The two gentlemen had fought a duel, after which both had been obliged to resign from the Government. The present Secretary of War, Lord Liverpool, was in fact the same person as Lord Hawkesbury, who has been mentioned before in these pages. He had left off one title and assumed another when his father died in December 1808.

following answers: "Yes," "No," and "In four weeks time". Every time Witloof entered the wardrobe there was the most hideous noise as if half the demons in Hell were screaming inside it, clouds of little silver stars issued from the cracks and hinges and the wardrobe rocked slightly upon its ball-and-claw feet. After the three questions had been answered, Buonaparte regarded the wardrobe silently for some moments, and then he strode over and pulled open the doors. Inside he found a goose (to make the noises) and some saltpetre (to produce the silver stars) and a dwarf (to ignite the saltpetre and prod the goose). No one knew for certain what had happened to Witloof and the dwarf, but the Emperor had eaten the goose for dinner the following day.

In the middle of November the Admiralty invited Mr Norrell and Mr Strange to Portsmouth to review the Channel Fleet, an honour usually reserved for admirals, heroes and kings. The two magicians and Arabella went down to Portsmouth in Mr Norrell's carriage. Their entrance into the town was marked by a salute of guns from all the ships in the harbour and all the arsenals and forts that surrounded it. They were rowed about among the ships at Spithead, accompanied by a whole array of admirals, flag officers and captains in their several barges. Other less official boats went too, full of the good citizens of Portsmouth come to look at the two magicians and wave and cheer. On returning to Portsmouth Mr Norrell and Mr and Mrs Strange looked over the dock-yard and in the evening a grand ball was given in their honour at the Assembly Rooms and all the town was illuminated.

The ball was generally reckoned a very delightful affair. There was one slight annoyance early on when some of the guests were foolish enough to make some remarks to Mr Norrell upon the pleasantness of the occasion and the beauty of the ballroom. Mr Norrell's rude reply immediately convinced them that he was a cross, disagreeable man, unwilling to talk to any one below the rank of admiral. However they found ample compensation for this disappointment in the lively, unreserved manners of Mr and Mrs

Strange. *They* were happy to be introduced to Portsmouth's principal inhabitants and they spoke admiringly of Portsmouth, of the ships they had seen and of things naval and nautical in general. Mr Strange danced every dance without exception, Mrs Strange only sat out for two and they did not return to their rooms at the Crown until after two o'clock in the morning.

Having got to bed a little before three, Strange was not best pleased to be woken again at seven by a knock on the door. He got up and found one of the inn-servants standing in the hallway.

"Beg pardon, sir," said the man, "but the port-admiral has sent to say the *False Prelate* is run upon Horse Sand. He has sent Captain Gilbey to fetch one of the magicians but the other magician has the headach and will not go."

This was not perhaps as perfectly comprehensible as the man intended, and Strange suspected that, even if he had been rather more awake, he would not have understood it. Nevertheless it was clear that *something* had occurred and that he was required to go *somewhere*. "Tell Captain Whatever-it-is to wait," he said with a sigh. "I am coming."

He dressed and went downstairs. In the coffee-room he found a handsome young man in a captain's uniform who was pacing up and down. This was Captain Gilbey. Strange remembered him from the ballroom – an intelligent-seeming man with pleasant manners. He looked greatly relieved to see Strange and explained that a ship, the *False Prelate*, had run upon one of the shoals at Spithead. It was an awkward situation. The *False Prelate* might be got off without serious damage or she might not. In the meantime the port-admiral sent his compliments to Mr Norrell and Mr Strange and begged that one or both of them go with Captain Gilbey to see if there was any thing that they could do.

A gig stood outside the Crown with one of the inn-servants at the horse's head. Strange and Captain Gilbey got into it and Captain Gilbey drove them briskly through the town. The town was beginning to stir with a certain air of hurry and alarm.

Windows were opening; heads in nightcaps were poking out of them and shouting down questions; people in the street were shouting back answers. A great many people seemed to be hurrying in the same direction as Captain Gilbey's carriage.

When they reached the ramparts, Captain Gilbey halted. The air was cold and damp and there was a fresh breeze blowing off the sea. A little way out a huge ship was lying on her side. Sailors very small and black and far away could be seen clinging to the rail and clambering down the side of the ship. A dozen or so rowing boats and small sailing vessels were crowded around her. Some of the occupants of these boats appeared to be holding energetic conversations with the sailors on the ship.

To Strange's unnautical eye, it looked very much as if the ship had simply lain down and gone to sleep. He felt that if he had been the Captain he would have spoken to her sternly and made her get up again.

"But surely," he said, "dozens of ships go in and out of Portsmouth all the time. How could such a thing happen?"

Captain Gilbey shrugged. "I am afraid it is not so remarkable as you suppose. The master might not be familiar with the channels of Spithead, or he might be drunk."

A large crowd was assembling. In Portsmouth every inhabitant has some connexion with the sea and ships, and some interest of his own to preserve. The daily talk about the place is of the ships going in and out of the harbour and the ships that lie at anchor at Spithead. An event such as this was of almost universal concern. It drew not only the regular loungers of the place (who were numerous enough), but also the steadier citizens and tradesmen, and of course every naval gentleman who had leisure to go and see. A vigorous argument was already taking place over what the master of the ship had done wrong, and what the port admiral must do to put it right. As soon as the crowd understood who Strange was and what he had come to do, it was glad to transfer the benefit of its many opinions to him. Unfortunately a great deal of nautical language was employed and Strange had at best an indistinct impression of his informants' meaning. After one explanation he made the mistake of inquiring what "beating off" and "heaving to" meant, which led to such a very perplexing explanation of the principles of sailing that he understood a great deal less at the end of it than he had at the beginning.

"Well!" he said. "The chief problem is surely that she is on her side. Shall I simply turn her upright? That would be quite easy to accomplish."

"Good Lord! No!" cried Captain Gilbey. "That will not do at all! Unless it is done in the most careful manner imaginable her keel would almost certainly snap in two. Everybody would drown."

"Oh!" said Strange.

His next attempt to help fared even worse. Something somebody said about a fresher breeze blowing the ship off the sandbank at high water caused him to think that a strong wind might help. He raised his hands to begin conjuring one up.

"What are you doing?" asked Captain Gilbey.

Strange told him.

"No! No! No!" cried the Captain, appalled.

Several people seized Strange bodily. One man started shaking him vigorously, as though he thought that he might in this way dispel any magic before it took effect.

"The wind is the from south-west," explained Captain Gilbey. "If it grows stronger, it will batter the ship against the sands and almost certainly break her up. Everybody will drown!"

Someone else was heard to remark that he could not for the life of him understand why the Admiralty thought so highly of this fellow whose ignorance was so astonishing.

A second man replied sarcastically that he might not be much of a magician but at least he danced very well.

A third person laughed.

"What is the sand called?" asked Strange.

Captain Gilbey shook his head in an exasperated fashion to convey that he had not the least idea what Strange was talking about.

"The . . . the place . . . the thing on which the ship is caught," urged Strange. "Something about horses?"

"The shoal is called Horse Sand," said Captain Gilbey coldly and turned away to speak to someone else.

For the next minute or two no one paid any attention to the magician. They watched the progress of the sloops and brigs and barges around the *False Prelate* and they looked to the skies and talked of how the weather was changing and where the wind would be at high water.

Suddenly several people called attention to the water. Something odd had appeared there. It was a large, silvery something with a long, oddly-shaped head and hair like long pale weeds waving behind it. It seemed to be swimming towards the *False Prelate*. No sooner had the crowd begun to exclaim and wonder about this mysterious object than several more appeared. The next moment there were a whole host of silvery shapes – more than a man could count – all swimming towards the ship with great ease and speed.

"What in the world are they?" asked a man in the crowd.

They were much too large to be men and not at all like fish or dolphins.

"They are horses," said Strange.

"Where did they come from?" asked another man.

"I made them," said Strange, "out of the sand. Out of Horse Sand, to be precise."

"But will they not dissolve?" asked one of the crowd.

"And what are they for?" asked Captain Gilbey.

Strange said, "They are made of sand and sea-water and magic, and they will last as long as there is work for them to do. Captain Gilbey, get one of the boats to take a message to the Captain of the *False Prelate* to say that his men should lash the horses to the ship,

353

as many of them as they can. The horses will pull the ship off the shoal."

"Oh!" said Captain Gilbey. "Very well. Yes, of course."

Within half an hour of the message reaching the *False Prelate*, the ship was clear of the shoal and the sailors were busy putting the sails to rights and doing the thousand and one things which sailors do (things which are quite as mysterious in their way as the actions of magicians). However, it ought to be said that the magic did not work quite as Strange intended. He had not imagined there would be much difficulty in capturing the horses. He supposed that the ship would have plenty of ropes to make the halters and he had tried to regulate the magic so that the horses would be as biddable as possible. But sailors in general do not know much of horses. They know the sea and that is all. Some of the sailors did their best to catch hold of the horses and harness them, but many had not the least idea how to begin or they were too afraid of the silvery, ghostly creatures to go anywhere near them. Of the hundred horses that Strange created only about twenty were eventually harnessed to the ship. These twenty were certainly instrumental in pulling the *False Prelate* off the sand, but equally useful was the great trough in the sandbank which appeared as more and more horses were created out of it.

In Portsmouth opinion was divided over whether Strange had done something glorious in saving the *False Prelate* or whether he had merely used the disaster to improve his own career. Many of the captains and officers about the place said that the magic he had done had been of a very showy sort and was obviously intended more to draw attention to his own talent and impress the Admiralty than to save the ship. Nor were they best pleased about the sand-horses. These did not just disappear when their work was done, as Strange had said they would; instead they swam about Spithead for a day and a half, after which they lay down and became sandbanks in new and entirely unexpected places. The masters and pilots of Portsmouth complained to the port-admiral that Strange had permanently altered the channels and shoals in Spithead so that the Navy would now have all the expense and trouble of taking soundings and surveying the anchorage again.

However, in London, where the Ministers knew as little of ships and seamanship as Strange, only one thing was clear: Strange had saved a ship, the loss of which would have cost the Admiralty a vast amount of money.

"One thing that the rescue of the *False Prelate* demonstrates," remarked Sir Walter Pole to Lord Liverpool, "is the very great advantage of having a magician upon the spot, able to deal with a crisis as it occurs. I know that we considered sending Norrell somewhere and were forced to give it up, but what of Strange?"

Lord Liverpool considered this. "I think," he said, "we could only justify sending Mr Strange to serve with one of the generals if we were reasonably confident of that general shortly achieving some sort of success against the French. Anything else would be an unforgivable waste of Mr Strange's talents which, God knows, we need badly enough in London. Frankly the choice is not great. Really there is no one but Lord Wellington."

"Oh, quite!"

Lord Wellington was in Portugal with his army and so his opinion could not be easily ascertained, but by an odd coincidence his wife lived at no. 11 Harley-street, just opposite Sir Walter's own house. When Sir Walter went home that evening he knocked at Lady Wellington's door and asked her ladyship what she thought Lord Wellington would say to the idea of a magician. But Lady Wellington, a small, unhappy person whose opinion was not much valued by her husband, did not know.

Strange, on the other hand, was delighted with the proposal. Arabella, though somewhat less delighted, gave her assent very readily. The greatest obstacle to Strange's going proved to be, to no one's great surprize, Norrell. In the past year Mr Norrell had grown to rely a great deal upon his pupil. He consulted Strange upon all those matters which in bygone days had been referred to

Drawlight and Lascelles. Mr Norrell talked of nothing but Mr Strange when Strange was away, and talked to no one *but* Strange when Strange was present. His feelings of attachment seemed all the stronger for being entirely new; he had never felt truly comfortable in any one's society before. If, in a crowded drawing-room or ballroom, Strange contrived to escape for a quarter of an hour, Mr Norrell would send Drawlight after him to discover where he had gone and whom he was talking to. Consequently, when Mr Norrell learnt there was a plan to send his only pupil and friend to the war he was shocked. "I am astonished, Sir Walter," he said, "that you should even suggest such a thing!"

"But every man must be prepared to make sacrifices for the sake of his country during a war," said Sir Walter with some irritation, "and thousands have already done so, you know."

"But they were *soldiers*!" cried Mr Norrell. "Oh! I dare say a soldier is very valuable in his way but that is nothing to the loss the Nation would sustain if any thing were to happen to Mr Strange! There is, I understand, a school at High Wycombe where 300 officers are trained every year. I would to God that I were so fortunate as to have 300 magicians to educate! If I had, then English magic might be in a much more promising situation than it is at present!"

After Sir Walter had tried and failed, Lord Liverpool and the Duke of York undertook to speak to Mr Norrell on the subject, but Mr Norrell could not be persuaded by any of them to view Strange's proposed departure with any thing other than horror.

"Have you considered, sir," said Strange, "the great respect that it will win for English magic?"

"Oh, I dare say it might," said Mr Norrell peevishly, "but nothing is so likely to evoke the Raven King and all that wild, mischievous sort of magic as the sight of an English magician upon a battlefield! People will begin to think that we raise fairy-spirits and consult with owls and bears. Whereas it is my hope for English magic that it should be regarded as a quiet, respectable sort of profession – the sort of profession in fact . . ."

"But, sir," said Strange, hastily interrupting a speech he had heard a hundred times before, "I shall have no company of fairy knights at my back. And there are other considerations which we would do very wrong to ignore. You and I have often lamented that we are continually asked to do the same sorts of magic over and over again. I dare say the exigencies of the war will require me to do magic that I have not done before – and, as we have often observed to each other, sir, the practice of magic makes the theory so much easier to understand."

But the two magicians were too different in temperament ever to come to an agreement upon such a point. Strange spoke of braving the danger in order to win glory for English magic. His language and metaphors were all drawn from games of chance and from war and were scarcely likely to find favour with Mr Norrell. Mr Norrell assured Mr Strange that he would find war very disagreeable. "One is often wet and cold upon a battlefield. You will like it a great deal less than you suppose."

For several weeks in January and February 1811 it seemed as if Mr Norrell's opposition would prevent Strange's going to war. The mistake that Sir Walter, Lord Liverpool, the Duke of York and Strange had all made was to appeal to Mr Norrell's nobility, patriotism and sense of duty. There is no doubt that Mr Norrell possessed these virtues, but there were other principles which were stronger in him and which would always counter any higher faculty.

Fortunately there were two gentlemen at hand who knew how to manage matters rather better. Lascelles and Drawlight were as anxious as every body else that Strange should go to Portugal and in their opinion the best method to achieve it was to play upon Mr Norrell's anxiety over the fate of the Duke of Roxburghe's library.

This library had long been a thorn in Mr Norrell's side. It was one of the most important private libraries in the kingdom – second only to Mr Norrell's own. It had a curious, poignant history. Some fifty years before, the Duke of Roxburghe, a most intelligent, civilized and respectable gentleman, had chanced to fall in love with the Queen's sister and had applied to the King for permission to marry her. For various reasons to do with court etiquette, form and precedence the King had refused. Heartbroken, the Duke and the Queen's sister made a solemn promise to love each other for ever and never upon any inducement to marry any one else. Whether the Queen's sister kept her side of the bargain I do not know, but the Duke retired to his castle in the Scottish borders and, to fill his lonely days, he began to collect rare books: exquisite illuminated mediaeval manuscripts and editions of the very first printed books produced in the workshops of men of such genius as William Caxton of London and Valdarfer of Venice. By the early years of the century the Duke's library was one of the wonders of the world. His Grace was fond of poetry, chivalry, history and theology. He had no particular interest in magic, but all old books delighted him and it would have been very odd if one or two magical texts had not found their way into his library.

Mr Norrell had written to the Duke a number of times begging to be allowed to examine and perhaps purchase any books of magic which the Duke possessed. The Duke, however, felt no inclination to satisfy Mr Norrell's curiosity and, being immensely wealthy, he did not want Mr Norrell's money. Having been true to his promise to the Queen's sister through many a long year, the Duke had no children and no obvious heir. When he died a large number of his male relatives were seized by a strong conviction that they were the next Duke of Roxburghe. These gentlemen took their claims before the Committee of Privileges of the House of Lords. The Committee considered and came to the conclusion that the new Duke was either Major-General Ker or Sir James Innes, but as to which of them it might be the Committee was not quite certain and it settled itself to consider the matter further. By early 1811 it had still not come to a decision.

On a cold, wet Tuesday morning Mr Norrell was seated with

Mr Lascelles and Mr Drawlight in the library at Hanover-square. Childermass was also in the room, writing letters to various Government departments upon Mr Norrell's behalf. Strange had gone to Twickenham with Mrs Strange to visit a friend.

Lascelles and Drawlight were speaking of the lawsuit between Ker and Innes. One or two seemingly random allusions upon Lascelles's part to the famous library caught Mr Norrell's attention.

"What do we know of these men?" he asked Lascelles. "Have they any interest in the practice of magic?"

Lascelles smiled. "You may be easy on that score, sir. I assure you the only thing that Innes or Ker cares for is to be Duke. I do not think I have ever seen either of them so much as open a book."

"Indeed? They do not care for books? Well, that is most reassuring." Mr Norrell thought for a moment. "But supposing one of them were to come into possession of the Duke's library and chanced to find some rare magical text upon a shelf and become curious about it. People are curious about magic, you know. That has been one of the more regrettable consequences of my own success. This man might read a little and find himself inspired to try a spell or two. It is, after all, exactly how I began myself when as a boy of twelve I opened a book from my uncle's library and found inside a single page torn from a much older volume. The instant I read it, the conviction took hold of me that I must be a magician!"

"Indeed? That is most interesting," said Lascelles, in tones of complete boredom. "But it is hardly, I think, likely to happen to Innes or Ker. Innes must be in his seventies and Ker about the same. Neither man is in search of a new career."

"Oh! But have they no young relatives? Relatives who are perhaps avid readers of *The Friends of English Magic* and *The Modern Magician*? Relatives who would seize upon any books of magic the instant they laid eyes upon them! No, forgive me, Mr Lascelles, but I cannot regard the advanced age of the two gentlemen as any security at all!"

"Very well. But I doubt, sir, if these young thaumatomanes[3] whom you describe so vividly will have any opportunity to view the library. In order to pursue their claim to the dukedom, both Ker and Innes have incurred vast legal expenses. The first concern of the new Duke, whoever he may be, will be to pay off his lawyers. His first act upon entering Floors Castle will be to look around for something to sell.[4] I shall be very much surprized if the library is not put up for sale within a week of the Committee giving its decision."

"A book sale!" exclaimed Mr Norrell in alarm.

"What are you afraid of now?" asked Childermass, looking up from his writing. "A book sale is generally the thing most calculated to please you."

"Oh! but that was before," said Mr Norrell, "when no one in the kingdom had the least interest in books of magic except me, but now I fear a great many people might try to buy them. I dare say there might be accounts in *The Times*."

"Oh!" cried Drawlight. "If the books are bought by someone else you may complain to the Ministers! You may complain to the Prince of Wales! It is not in the interests of the Nation that books of magic should be in any one's possession but your own, Mr Norrell."

"Except Strange," said Lascelles. "I do not think the Prince of Wales or the Ministers would have any objections to Strange's owning the books."

"That is true," agreed Drawlight. "I had forgot Strange."

Mr Norrell looked more alarmed than ever. "But Mr Strange will understand that it is proper for the books to be mine," he said. "They should be collected together in one library. They ought not to be separated." He looked about hopefully for someone to agree with him. "Naturally," he continued, "I shall have no objection to

---

[3] Thaumatomane: a person possessed of a passion for magic and wonders, *Dictionary of the English Language* by Samuel Johnson.

[4] Floors Castle is the home of the Dukes of Roxburghe.

Mr Strange reading them. Everyone knows how many of my books – my own precious books – I have lent to Mr Strange. That is . . . I mean, it would depend upon the subject."

Drawlight, Lascelles and Childermass said nothing. They did indeed know how many books Mr Norrell had lent Mr Strange. They also knew how many he had withheld.

"Strange is a gentleman," said Lascelles. "He will behave as a gentleman and expect you to do the same. If the books are offered privately to you and you alone, then I think you may buy them, but if they are auctioned, he will feel entitled to bid against you."

Mr Norrell paused, looked at Lascelles and licked his lips nervously. "And how do you suppose the books will be sold? By auction or by private transaction?"

"Auction," said Lascelles, Drawlight and Childermass together.

Mr Norrell covered his face with his hands.

"Of course," said Lascelles, slowly as if the idea were just occurring to him at that moment, "if Strange were abroad, he would not be able to bid." He took a sip of his coffee. "Would he?"

Mr Norrell looked up with new hope in his face.

Suddenly it became highly desirable that Mr Strange should go to Portugal for a year or so.[5]

---

[5] The Committee of Privileges eventually decided in favour of Sir James Innes and, just as Mr Lascelles had predicted, the new Duke immediately put the library up for sale.

The auction in the summer of 1812 (while Strange was in the Peninsula) was possibly the most notable bibliographic event since the burning of the library at Alexandria. It lasted for forty-one days and was the cause of at least two duels.

Among the Duke's books there were found seven magical texts, all of them extraordinary.

Rosa et Fons was a mystical meditation upon magic by an unknown fourteenth-century magician.

Thomas de Dundelle, a hitherto undiscovered poem by Chrétien de Troyes, was a colourful version of the life of Thomas Dundale, the Raven King's first human servant.

[5] *cont'd*   *The Book of Loveday Ingham* was an account of the day-to-day occupations of a fifteenth-century magician in Cambridge.

Exercitatio Magica Nobilissima was a seventeenth-century attempt to describe all of English magic.

The History of Seven was a very muddled work, partly in English, partly in Latin and partly in an unknown fairy language. Its age could not be guessed at, the author could not be identified and the purpose of the said author in writing the book was entirely obscure. It appeared to be, upon the whole, the history of a city in Faerie, called "Seven", but the information was presented in a very confusing style and the author would frequently break off from his narrative to accuse some unspecified person of having injured him in some mysterious way. These parts of the text more resembled an indignant letter than any thing else.

The Parliament of Women was an allegorical sixteenth-century description of the wisdom and magic that belongs particularly to women.

But by far the most wonderful was *The Mirrour of the Lyf of Ralph Stokesie*, which along with a first edition of Boccaccio's *Decameron* was put up for auction on the last day. Even Mr Norrell had been entirely ignorant of the existence of this book until that day. It appeared to have been written by two authors, one a fifteenth-century magician called William Thorpe, the other Ralph Stokesey's fairy servant, Col Tom Blue. For this treasure Mr Norrell paid the quite unheard-of sum of 2,100 guineas.

Such was the general respect for Mr Norrell that not a single gentleman in the room bid against him. But a lady bid against him for every book. In the weeks before the auction Arabella Strange had been very busy. She had written numerous letters to Strange's relations and paid visits to all her friends

^{5} cont'd
in London in attempt to borrow enough money to buy some of the books for her husband, but Norrell outbid her for every one.

Sir Walter Scott, the author, was present and he described the end of the auction. "Such was Mrs Strange's disappointment at losing *The Life of Ralph Stokesey* that she sat in tears. At that moment Mr Norrell walked by with the book in his hand. Not a word, not a glance did this man have for his pupil's wife. I do not know when I last saw behaviour so little to my liking. Several people observed this treatment and I have heard some harsh things said of Norrell. Even Lord Portishead, whose admiration of the magician knows no bounds, admits that he thinks Norrell has behaved remarkably ill towards Mrs Strange."

But it was not only Mr Norrell's treatment of Mrs Strange that drew unfavourable comment. In the weeks that followed the auction scholars and historians waited to hear what new knowledge was to be found in the seven wonderful books. In particular they were in high hopes that *The Mirrour of the Lyf of Ralph Stokesey* would provide answers to some of the most puzzling mysteries in English magic. It was commonly supposed that Mr Norrell would reveal his new discoveries in the pages of *The Friends of English Magic* or that he would cause copies of the books to be printed. He did neither of these things. One or two people wrote him letters asking him specific questions. He did not reply. When letters appeared in the newspapers complaining of this behaviour he was most indignant. After all he was simply acting as he had always done – acquiring valuable books and then hiding them away where no man else could see them. The difference was that in the days when he was an unknown gentleman no one had thought any thing of it, but now the eyes of the world were upon him. His silence was wondered at and people began to remember other occasions when Mr Norrell had acted in a rude or arrogant manner.

29

At the house of José Estoril

January–March 1811

"I HAVE BEEN THINKING, sir, that my leaving for the Peninsula will be the cause of many changes in your dealings with the War Office," said Strange. "I am afraid that when I am gone you will not find it so convenient to have people knocking at the door at all hours of the day and night, asking for this or that piece of magic to be performed forthwith. There will be no one but you to attend to them. When will you sleep? I think we must persuade them to some other way of doing things. If I can be of any assistance in arranging matters, I should be glad to do so. Perhaps we should invite Lord Liverpool to dine one evening this week?"

"Oh, yes indeed!" said Mr Norrell in high good humour with this proof of Strange's considerateness. "You must be there. You explain everything so well! You have only to say a thing and Lord Liverpool understands immediately!"

"Then shall I write to his lordship?"

"Yes, do! Do!"

It was the first week of January. The date of Strange's departure was not yet fixed, but was likely to be soon. Strange sat down and wrote the invitation. Lord Liverpool replied very promptly and the next day but one saw him at Hanover-square.

It was the habit of Mr Norrell and Jonathan Strange to spend the hour before dinner in Mr Norrell's library and it was in this room that they received his lordship. Childermass was also present, ready to act as clerk, counsellor, messenger or servant just as circumstances should require.

Lord Liverpool had never seen Mr Norrell's library and before he sat down he took a little turn about the room. "I had been told, sir," he said, "that your library was one of the Wonders of the Modern World, but I never imagined any thing half so extensive."

Mr Norrell was very well pleased. Lord Liverpool was exactly the sort of guest he liked – one who admired the books but shewed no inclination to take them down from the shelves and read them.

Then Strange said, addressing Mr Norrell, "We have not spoken yet, sir, about the books I should take to the Peninsula. I have made a list of forty titles, but if you think it can be improved upon I should be glad of your advice." He pulled a folded sheet from a jumble of papers on a table and handed it to Mr Norrell.

It was not a list to delight Mr Norrell's soul. It was full of first thoughts crossed-out, second thoughts crossed-out and third thoughts put in at angles and made to wriggle around other words that were in the way. There were ink blots, titles misspellt, authors misnamed and, most confusing of all, three lines of a riddle-poem that Strange had begun composing as a farewell-present for Arabella. Nevertheless it was not this that made Mr Norrell grow pale. It had never occurred to him before that Strange would need books in Portugal. The idea of forty precious volumes being taken into a country in a state of war where they might get burnt, blown up, drowned or dusty was almost too horrible to contemplate. Mr Norrell did not know a great deal about war, but he suspected that soldiers are not generally your great respecters of books. They might put their dirty fingers on them. They might tear them! They might – horror of horrors! – read them and try the spells! Could soldiers read? Mr Norrell did not know. But with the fate of the entire Continent at stake and Lord Liverpool in the room, he realized how very difficult it would be – impossible in fact – to refuse to lend them.

He turned with a look of desperate appeal to Childermass. Childermass shrugged.

Lord Liverpool continued to gaze about him in a calm manner. He appeared to be thinking that the temporary absence of forty books or so would scarcely be noticed among so many thousands.

"I should not wish to take more than forty," continued Strange in a matter-of-fact tone.

"Very wise, sir," said Lord Liverpool. "Very wise. Do not take more than you can conveniently carry about."

"Carry about!" exclaimed Mr Norrell, more shocked than ever. "But surely you do not intend to take them from place to place? You must put them in a library the moment you arrive. A library in a castle will be best. A stout, well-defended castle . . ."

"But I fear they will do me little good in a library," said Strange with infuriating calmness. "I shall be in camps and on battlefields. And so must they."

"Then you must place them in a box!" said Mr Norrell. "A very sturdy wooden box or perhaps an iron chest! Yes, iron will be best. We can have one made specially. And then . . ."

"Ah, forgive me, Mr Norrell," interrupted Lord Liverpool, "but I strongly advise Mr Strange against the iron chest. He must not trust to any provision being made for him in the carts. The soldiers need the carts for their equipment, maps, food, ammunition and so on. Mr Strange will occasion the Army the least inconvenience if he carries all his possessions on a mule or donkey as the officers do." He turned to Strange. "You will need a good, strong mule for your baggage and your servant. Purchase some saddlebags at Hewley and Ratt's and place the books in them. Military saddlebags are most capacious. Besides, on a cart the books would almost certainly be stolen. Soldiers, I am sorry to say, steal everything." He thought for a moment and then added, "Or at least ours do."

How the dinner went after that Mr Norrell knew very little. He was dimly aware that Strange and his lordship talked a great deal and laughed a great deal. Several times he heard Strange say, "Well, that is decided then!" And he heard his lordship reply, "Oh, certainly!" But what they were talking about, Mr Norrell neither knew nor cared. He wished he had never come to London. He wished he had never undertaken to revive English magic. He wished he had stayed at Hurtfew Abbey, reading and doing magic for his own pleasure. None of it, he thought, was worth the loss of forty books.

After Lord Liverpool and Strange had gone he went to the library to look at the forty books and hold them and treasure them while he could.

Childermass was still there. He had taken his dinner at one of the tables and was now doing the household accounts. As Mr Norrell entered, he looked up and grinned. "I believe Mr Strange will do very well in the war, sir. He has already out-manoeuvred you."

On a bright, moonlit night in early February a British ship called *St Serlo's Blessing*[1] sailed up the Tagus and landed at Black-horse square in the middle of the city of Lisbon. Among the first to disembark were Strange and his servant, Jeremy Johns. Strange had never been in a foreign country before and he found that the consciousness of being so now and the important military and naval bustle that was going on all around him was quite exhilarating. He was eager to begin doing magic.

"I wonder where Lord Wellington is," he said to Jeremy Johns. "Do you suppose any of these fellows will know?" He looked with some curiosity at a vast, half-built arch at one end of the square. It had a very military appearance and he would not have been at all surprized to learn that Wellington was somewhere at the rear of it.

---

[1] *St Serlo's Blessing* had been captured from the French. Its French name was *Le Temple Foudroyé*. Saint Serlo's Blessing was, of course, the name of one of the four magical woods which surrounded and protected the Raven King's capital city, Newcastle.

"But it is two o'clock in the morning, sir," said Jeremy. "His lordship will be asleep."

"Oh, do you think so? With the fate of all Europe in his hands? I suppose you may be right."

Reluctantly, Strange agreed that it would be better to go to the hotel now and look for Lord Wellington in the morning.

They had been recommended to a hotel in Shoemaker-street which belonged to a Mr Prideaux, a Cornishman. Mr Prideaux's guests were almost all British officers who had just returned to Portugal from England or who were waiting for ships to take them on leave of absence. It was Mr Prideaux's intention that during their stay at his hotel the officers should feel as much at home as possible. In this he was only partly successful. Do whatsoever he might, Mr Prideaux found that Portugal continually intruded itself upon the notice of his guests. The wallpaper and furnishings of the hotel might all have been brought originally from London, but a Portuguese sun had shone on them for five years and faded them in a peculiarly Portuguese manner. Mr Prideaux might instruct the cook to prepare an English bill of fare but the cook was Portuguese and there was always more pepper and oil in the dishes than the guests expected. Even the guests' boots had a faintly Portuguese air after the Portuguese bootboy had blacked them.

The next morning Strange rose rather late. He ate a large breakfast and then strolled about for an hour or so. Lisbon proved to be a city well provided with arcaded squares, elegant modern buildings, statues, theatres and shops. He began to think that war could not be so very dreadful after all.

As he returned to the hotel he saw four or five British officers, gathered in the doorway, conversing eagerly together. This was just the opportunity he had hoped for. He went up to them, begged their pardon for interrupting, explained who he was and asked where in Lisbon Lord Wellington might be found.

The officers turned and gave him a rather surprised look as if they thought the question a wrong one, though he could not tell why it should be. "Lord Wellington is not in Lisbon," said one, a man in the blue jacket and white breeches of the Hussars.

"Oh! When is he coming back?" asked Strange.

"Back?" said the officer. "Not for weeks – months, I expect. Perhaps never."

"Then where will I find him?"

"Good God!" said the officer. "He might be anywhere."

"Don't you know where he is?" asked Strange.

The officer looked at him rather severely. "Lord Wellington does not stay in one place," he said. "Lord Wellington goes wherever he is needed. And Lord Wellington," he added for Strange's better understanding, "is needed *everywhere*."

Another officer who wore a bright scarlet jacket liberally adorned with silver lace, said in a rather more kindly tone, "Lord Wellington is in the Lines."

"In the Lines?" said Strange.

"Yes."

Unfortunately this was not quite the clear and helpful explanation that the officer intended it to be. But Strange felt that he had demonstrated his ignorance long enough. His desire to ask questions had quite evaporated.

"Lord Wellington is in the Lines." It was a very curious phrase and if Strange had been obliged to hazard a guess at its meaning he believed he would have said it was some sort of slang for being drunk.

He went back into the hotel and told the porter to find Jeremy Johns. If any one was going to appear ignorant and foolish in front of the British Army he had much rather it was Jeremy.

"There you are!" he said when Jeremy appeared. "Go and find a soldier or officer and ask him where I shall find Lord Wellington."

"Certainly, sir. But don't you want to ask him yourself?"

"Quite impossible. I have magic to do."

So Jeremy went out and after a very brief interval he returned.

"Have you found it out?" asked Strange.

"Oh yes, sir!" said Jeremy, cheerfully. "There is no great secret about it. Lord Wellington is in the Lines."

"Yes, but what does that mean?"

"Oh, I beg your pardon, sir! The gentleman said it so naturally. As if it were the most commonplace thing in the world. I thought you would know."

"Well, I do not. Perhaps I had better ask Prideaux."

Mr Prideaux was delighted to be of assistance. There was nothing simpler in the world. Mr Strange must go to the Army's Headquarters. He was certain to find his lordship there. It was a half day's ride from the city. Perhaps a little more. "As far as from Tyburn to Godalming, sir, if you can picture it."

"Well, if you would be so good as to shew me on a map . . ."

"Lord bless you, sir!" said Mr Prideaux, much amused. "You would never find it on your own. I must find a man to take you."

The person whom Mr Prideaux found was an Assistant Commissary with business in Torres Vedras, a town four or five miles further on than Headquarters. The Assistant Commissary declared himself very happy to ride with Strange and shew him the way.

"Now, at last," thought Strange, "I am making progress."

The first part of the journey was through a pleasant landscape of fields and vineyards scattered here and there with pretty little white-painted farms and stone-built windmills with brown canvas sails. Large numbers of Portuguese soldiers in brown uniforms were continually going to and fro along the road and there were also a few British officers whose brighter uniforms of scarlet or blue appeared – to Strange's patriotic eye at any rate – more manly and warlike. After they had been riding for three hours they saw a line of mountains rising up from the plain like a wall.

As they entered a narrow valley between two of the highest mountains the Assistant Commissary said, "This is the beginning of the Lines. You see that fort there high up on one side of the pass?" He pointed to the right. The "fort" appeared to have started out life as a windmill, but had recently received all sorts of additions in the way of bastions, battlements and gun embrasures. "And the other fort on the other side of the pass?" added the Assistant Commissary. He pointed to the left. "And then on the next rocky outcrop another little fort? And then – though you can't see it, since today is dull and cloudy – there is another beyond that. And so on and so on. A whole line of forts from the Tagus to the sea! But that is not all! There are two more lines to the north of us. Three lines in all!"

"It is certainly impressive. And did the Portuguese do this?"

"No, sir. Lord Wellington did it. The French mayn't pass here. Why, sir! a beetle mayn't pass unless that beetle has a paper with Lord Wellington's writing on it! And that, sir, is why the French Army sits at Santarem and can get no further, while you and I sleep safe in our beds at Lisbon!"

Very soon they left the road and took a steep and winding lane that led up the hillside to the tiny village of Pero Negro. Strange was struck by the difference between war, as he had imagined it, and war, as it actually was. He had pictured Lord Wellington sitting in some grand building in Lisbon, issuing orders. Instead he found him in a place so small that it barely would have qualified as a village in England.

The Army's Headquarters proved to be an entirely unremarkable house in a plain cobbled yard. Strange was informed that Lord Wellington had gone out to inspect the Lines. No one knew when he would return – probably not until dinner. No one had any objection to Strange's waiting – providing he did not get in their way.

But from the first moment of his entering the house Strange found himself subject to that peculiarly uncomfortable Natural Law which states that whenever a person arrives at a place where he is not known, then wherever he stands he is sure to be in the way. He could not sit because the room he had been placed in contained no chairs – presumably in case the French should somehow penetrate the house and hide behind them – so he took up a position in front of a window. But then two officers came in and one of them wished to demonstrate some important military characteristic of the Portuguese landscape, for which purpose it was necessary to look out of the window. They glared at Strange who moved to stand in front of a half-curtained arch.

Meanwhile a voice was calling every moment from the passageway for someone named Winespill to bring the gunpowder barrels and to do it quickly. A soldier of very small stature and with a slight hunchback entered the room. He had a vivid purple birthmark on his face and appeared to be wearing part of the uniform of every regiment in the British Army. This, presumably, was Winespill. Winespill was unhappy. He could not find the gunpowder. He hunted in cupboards, under staircases and on balconies. He called back every now and then "One moment!" – until the moment came when he thought to look behind Strange, behind the curtain and under the arch. Immediately he shouted out that he had found the casks of gunpowder now and he would have seen them earlier only Someone – here he gave Strange a very black look – was standing in front of them.

The hours passed slowly. Strange was back at his station by the window and almost falling asleep, when he realized from certain sounds of bustle and disruption that Someone of Importance had just entered the house. The next moment three men swept into the room and Strange found himself at last in the presence of Lord Wellington.

How to describe Lord Wellington? How can such a thing be necessary or even possible? His face is everywhere one looks – a cheap print upon the wall of the coaching inn – a much more elaborate one, embellished with flags and drums, at the top of the Assembly-room staircase. Nowadays no young lady of average romantic feeling will reach the age of seventeen without purchasing at least one picture of him. She will think a long, aquiline nose infinitely preferable to a short, stubby one and consider it the worst misfortune of her life that he is married already. To make up for it she fully intends to name her first-born son, Arthur. Nor is she alone in her devotion. Her younger brothers and sisters are every bit as fanatical. The handsomest toy soldier in an English nursery is always called Wellington and has more adventures than the rest of the toy box put together. Every schoolboy impersonates Wellington at least once a week, and so do his younger sisters. Wellington embodies every English virtue. He is Englishness carried to perfection. If the French carry Napoleon in their bellies (which apparently they do), then we carry Wellington in our hearts.[2]

Just at present Lord Wellington was none too pleased about something.

"My orders were perfectly clear, I think!" he said to the other two officers. "The Portuguese were to destroy all the corn that they could not carry away, so that it should not fall into the hands of the French. But I have just spent half the day watching the French soldiers going into the caves at Cartaxo and bringing out sacks again."

"It was very hard for the Portuguese farmers to destroy their corn. They feared to be hungry," explained one of the officers.

The other officer made the hopeful suggestion that perhaps it was not corn that the French had found in the sacks, but something else altogether less useful. Gold or silver, perhaps?

Lord Wellington eyed him coolly. "The French soldiers took the sacks to the windmills. The sails were going round in plain view! Perhaps you think they were milling gold? Dalziel, complain to the Portuguese authorities, if you please!" His gaze, darting angrily about the room, came to rest upon Strange. "Who is that?" he asked.

The officer called Dalziel murmured something in his lordship's ear.

---

[2] Of course it may be objected that Wellington himself was *Irish*, but a patriotic English pen does not stoop to answer such quibbling.

"Oh!" said Lord Wellington and then, addressing Strange, he said, "You are the magician." The faintest note of inquiry pervaded his remark.

"Yes," said Strange.

"Mr Norrell?"

"Ah, no. Mr Norrell is in England. I am Mr Strange."

Lord Wellington looked blank.

"The other magician," explained Strange.

"I see," said Lord Wellington.

The officer called Dalziel stared at Strange with an expression of surprize, as if he thought that once Lord Wellington had told Strange who he was, it was rather ill-bred of him to insist on being someone else.

"Well, Mr Strange," said Lord Wellington, "I fear you have had a wasted journey. I must tell you frankly that if I had been able to prevent your coming I would have done so. But now that you are here I shall take the opportunity to explain to you the great nuisance which you and the other gentleman have been to the Army."

"Nuisance?" said Strange.

"Nuisance," repeated Lord Wellington. "The visions you have shewn the Ministers have encouraged them to believe that they understand how matters stand in Portugal. They have sent me a great many more orders and interfered to a far greater extent than they would have done otherwise. Only I know what needs to be done in Portugal, Mr Strange, since only I am acquainted with all the circumstances. I do not say that you and the other gentleman may not have done some good elsewhere – the Navy seem pleased – I know nothing of that – but what I *do* say is that I need no magician here in Portugal."

"But surely, my lord, here in Portugal magic is liable to no such misuse, since I shall be wholly at your service and under your direction."

Lord Wellington gave Strange a sharp look. "What I chiefly need is men. Can you make more?"

"Men? Well, that depends on what your lordship means. It is an interesting question . . ." To Strange's great discomfort, he found he sounded exactly like Mr Norrell.

"Can you make more?" interrupted his lordship.

"No."

"Can you make the bullets fly any quicker to strike the French? They fly very quickly as it is. Can you perhaps upturn the earth and move the stones to build my Redoubts, Lunettes and Other Defensive Works?"

"No, my lord. But, my lord . . ."

"The name of the chaplain to the Headquarters is Mr Briscall. The name of the chief medical officer is Dr McGrigor. Should you decide to stay in Portugal then I suggest you make yourself known to these gentlemen. Perhaps you may be of some use to them. You are none to me." Lord Wellington turned away and immediately shouted for someone named Thornton to get dinner ready. In this way Strange was given to understand that the interview was at an end.

Strange was used to deferential treatment from Government Ministers. He was accustomed to being addressed as an equal by some of the highest in the land. To find himself suddenly classed with the chaplains and doctors of the Army – mere supernumeraries – was very bad indeed.

He spent the night – very uncomfortably – at Pero Negro's only inn and as soon as it was light he rode back to Lisbon. When he arrived back at the hotel in Shoemaker-street, he sat down and wrote a long letter to Arabella describing in great detail the shocking way he was treated. Then, feeling a little better, he decided that it was unmanly to complain and so he tore the letter up.

He next made a list of all the sorts of magic which Norrell and he had done for the Admiralty and tried to decide which would suit Lord Wellington best. After careful consideration he concluded that there were few better ways of adding to the misery of the

French Army than by sending it storms of thunder and drenching rain. He immediately determined upon writing his lordship a letter offering to do this magic. A definite course of action is always a cheering thing and Strange's spirits rose immediately – until, that is, he happened to glance out of the window. The skies were black, the rain was coming down in torrents and a fierce wind was blowing. It looked as if it might very well thunder in a short while. He went in search of Mr Prideaux. Prideaux confirmed that it had been raining like this for weeks – that the Portuguese thought it would continue for a good long while – and, yes, the French were indeed very unhappy.

Strange pondered this for a while. He was tempted to send Lord Wellington a note offering to make it *stop* raining, on the principle that it must be very uncomfortable for the British soldiers as well – but in the end he decided that the whole question of weather-magic was too vexed until he understood the war and Lord Wellington better. In the meantime he settled upon a plague of frogs as the best thing to drop on the heads of the French soldiers. It was highly Biblical and what, thought Strange, could be more respectable than that?

The next morning he was sitting gloomily in his hotel room, pretending to read one of Norrell's books but actually watching the rain, when there was a knock at the door. It was a Scottish officer in the uniform of the Hussars who looked inquiringly at Strange and said, "Mr Norrell?"

"I am not . . . Oh, never mind! What can I do for you?"

"Message for you from Headquarters, Mr Norrell." The young officer presented Strange with a piece of paper.

It was his own letter to Wellington. Someone had scrawled over it in thick, blue pencil the single word, "Denied".

"Whose writing is that?" asked Strange.

"Lord Wellington's, Mr Norrell."

"Ah."

The next day Strange wrote Wellington another note, offering to make the waters of the River Tagus rise up and overwhelm the French. This at least provoked Wellington into writing a rather longer reply explaining that at present the entire British Army and most of the Portuguese Army were *between* the Tagus and the French and consequently Mr Strange's suggestion was not found to be at all convenient.

Strange refused to be deterred. He continued to send Wellington one proposal every day. All were rejected.

On a particularly gloomy day at the end of February he was passing through the hallway of Mr Prideaux's hotel on his way to a solitary dinner when he almost collided with a fresh-faced young man in English clothes. The young man begged his pardon and asked if he knew where Mr Strange was to be found.

"I am Strange. Who are you?"

"My name is Briscall. I am Chaplain to the Headquarters."

"Mr Briscall. Yes. Of course."

"Lord Wellington has asked me to pay you a visit," explained Mr Briscall. "He said something about your aiding me by magic?" Mr Briscall smiled. "But I believe his real reason is that he hopes I may be able to dissuade you from writing to him every day."

"Oh!" said Strange. "I shall not stop until he gives me something to do."

Mr Briscall laughed. "Very well, I shall tell him."

"Thank you. And is there any thing I can do for you? I have never done magic for the Church before. I will be frank with you, Mr Briscall. My knowledge of ecclesiastical magic is very slight, but I should be glad to be of use to someone."

"Hmm. I will be equally frank with you, Mr Strange. My duties are really very simple. I visit the sick and wounded. I read the soldiers the services and try and get them a decent burial when they are killed, poor fellows. I do not see what you could do to help."

"Neither does any one else," said Strange with a sigh. "But come, have dinner with me? At least I shall not have to eat alone."

This was quickly agreed to and the two men sat down in the hotel dining-parlour. Strange found Mr Briscall to be a pleasant dinner companion who was happy to tell all he knew of Lord Wellington and the Army.

"Soldiers are not in general religious men," he said, "but then I never expected that they would be and I have been greatly helped by the circumstance that all the chaplains before me went on leave almost as soon as they arrived. I am the first to stay – and the men are grateful to me for that. They look very kindly on any one who is prepared to share their hard life."

Strange said he was sure of it.

"And what of you, Mr Strange? How do you get on?"

"I? I do not get on at all. No one wants me here. I am addressed – on the rare occasions when any one speaks to me at all – quite indiscriminately as Mr Strange or Mr Norrell. No one seems to have any notion that these might be *distinct* persons."

Briscall laughed.

"And Lord Wellington rejects all my offers of help as soon as I make them."

"Why? What have you offered him?"

Strange told him about his first proposal to send a plague of frogs to fall on the French from the sky.

"Well, I am really not at all surprized he refused *that*!" said Briscall, contemptuously. "The French cook frogs and eat them, do they not? It is a vital part of Lord Wellington's plan that the French should starve. You might as well have offered to drop roast chickens on their heads or pork pies!"

"It is not my fault," said Strange, a little stung. "I would be only too glad to take Lord Wellington's plans into consideration – only I do not know what they are. In London the Admiralty told us their intentions and we shaped our magic accordingly."

"I see," said Briscall. "Forgive me, Mr Strange – perhaps I have not understood very well – but it seems to me that you have a great advantage here. In London you were obliged to rely upon the

Admiralty's opinion as to what might be happening hundreds of miles away – and I dare say the Admiralty was quite often mistaken. Here you can go and see for yourself. Your experience is no different from my own. When I first arrived no one took the least notice of me either. I drifted from one regiment to another. No one wanted me."

"And yet now you are a part of Wellington's Staff. How did you do it?"

"It took time, but in the end I was able to prove my usefulness to his lordship – and I am sure you will do the same."

Strange sighed. "I try. But all I seem to do is demonstrate my superfluousness. Over and over again!"

"Nonsense! As far as I can see you have only made one real mistake – and that is in remaining here in Lisbon. If you take my advice, you will leave as soon as you can. Go and sleep on the mountains with the men and the officers! You will not understand them until you do. Talk to them. Spend your days with them in the deserted villages beyond the Lines. They will soon love you for it. They are the best fellows in the world."

"Really? It was reported in London that Wellington had called them the scum of the earth."

Briscall laughed as if being the scum of the earth were a very minor sort of indiscretion and indeed a large part of the Army's charm. This was, thought Strange, an odd position for a clergy-man to take.

"Which are they?" he asked.

"They are both, Mr Strange. They are both. Well, what do you say? Will you go?"

Strange frowned. "I do not know. It is not that I fear hardship and discomfort, you understand. I believe I can endure as much of that sort of thing as most men. But I know no one there. I seem to have been in every body's way since I arrived and without friends to go to . . ."

"Oh! That is easily remedied! This is not London or Bath where one needs letters of introduction. Take a barrel of brandy – and a case or two of Champagne if your servant can carry them. You will soon have a very wide acquaintance among the officers if you have brandy and Champagne to spare."

"Really? It is as simple as that, is it?"

"Oh, to be sure! But do not trouble to take any red wine. They have plenty of that already."

A few days later Strange and Jeremy Johns left Lisbon for the country beyond the Lines. The British officers and men were a little surprized to find a magician in their midst. They wrote letters home to their friends describing him in a variety of uncomplimentary ways and wondering what in the world he was doing there. But Strange did as Mr Briscall had advised. Every officer he met was invited to come and drink Champagne with him that evening after dinner. They soon excused him the eccentricity of his profession. What mattered was that one could always meet with some very jolly fellows at Strange's bivouack and something decent to drink.

Strange also took up smoking. It had never really appealed to him as a pastime before, but he discovered that a ready supply of tobacco was quite invaluable for striking up conversations with the enlisted men.

It was an odd sort of life and an eerie sort of landscape. The villages beyond the Lines had all been emptied of inhabitants on Lord Wellington's instructions and the crops burnt. The soldiers of both armies went down to the deserted villages and helped themselves to whatever looked useful. On the British side it was not unusual to come upon sophas, wardrobes, beds, chairs and tables standing on a hillside or in a woodland glade. Occasionally one would find whole bed-chambers or drawing-rooms, complete with shaving equipment, books and lamps, but minus the impediment of walls and ceiling.

But if the British Army suffered inconvenience from the wind and the rain, then the plight of the French Army was far, far worse.

Their clothes were in rags and they had nothing to eat. They had been staring at Lord Wellington's Lines since the previous October. They could not attack the British Army – it had three lines of impregnable forts behind which to retreat at any moment it chose. Nor did Lord Wellington trouble to attack the French. Why should he, when Hunger and Disease were killing his enemies faster than he could? On the 5th of March the French struck camp and turned north. Within a very few hours Lord Wellington and the British Army were in pursuit. Jonathan Strange went with them.

One very rainy morning about the middle of the month Strange was riding at the side of a road along which the 95th Rifles were marching. He happened to spy some particular friends of his a little way ahead. Urging his horse to a canter, he soon caught up with them.

"Good morning, Ned," he said, addressing a man he had reason to regard as a thoughtful, sensible sort of person.

"Good morning, sir," said Ned, cheerfully.

"Ned?"

"Yes, sir?"

"What is it that you chiefly desire? I know it is an odd question, Ned, and you will excuse my asking it. But I really need to know."

Ned did not answer immediately. He sucked in his breath and furrowed his brow and exhibited other signs of deep thinking. Meanwhile his comrades helpfully told Strange what they chiefly desired – things such as magic pots of gold that would never be empty and houses carved out of a single diamond. One, a Welshman, sang out dolefully, "Toasted cheese! Toasted cheese!" several times – which caused the others to laugh a good deal, Welshmen being naturally humorous.

Meanwhile Ned had got to the end of his ruminations. "New boots," he said.

"Really?" said Strange in surprize.

"Yes, sir," answered Ned. "New boots. It is these d—d Portuguese roads." He gestured ahead at the collection of stones and pot-holes that the Portuguese were pleased to call a road. "They tear a man's boots to ribbons and at night his bones ache from walking over them. But if I had new boots, oh! wouldn't I be fresh after a day's march? Couldn't I just fight the French then? Couldn't I just make Johnny sweat for it?"

"Your appetite for the fray does you great credit, Ned," said Strange. "Thank you. You have given me an excellent answer." He rode off, followed by a great many shouts of "When will Ned be getting his boots, then?" and "Where's Ned's boots?"

That evening Lord Wellington's headquarters were set up in a once-splendid mansion in the village of Lousão. The house had once belonged to a wealthy and patriotic Portuguese nobleman, José Estoril, but he and his sons had all been tortured and killed by the French. His wife had died of a fever, and various stories were in circulation concerning the sad fate of his daughters. For many months it had been a very melancholy place, but now Wellington's Staff had arrived to fill it with the sound of their noisy jokes and arguments, and the gloomy rooms were made almost cheerful by the officers in their coats of red and blue passing in and out.

The hour before dinner was one of the busiest of the day and the room was crowded with officers bringing reports or collecting orders, or simply gathering gossip. At one end of the room was a very venerable, ornate and crumbling stone staircase which led to a pair of ancient doors. Behind the doors, it was said, Lord Wellington was hard at work devising new plans to defeat the French, and it was a curious fact that everyone who came into the room was sure to cast a respectful glance up to the top of that staircase. Two of Wellington's senior staff, the Quartermaster-General, Colonel George Murray, and the Adjutant-General, General Charles Stewart, were seated one upon either side of a large table, both busily engaged in making arrangements for the disposal of the Army upon the following day. And I pause here merely to observe that if, upon reading the words "Colonel" and "General", you fancy these are two *old* men sitting at the table, you could not be more wrong. It is true that when the French war had begun eighteen years before, the British Army had been commanded by some very venerable old persons many of whom had passed their whole careers without glimpsing a battlefield. But the years had gone by and these old generals were all retired or dead and it had been found more convenient to replace them with younger, more energetic men. Wellington himself was only a little more than forty and most of his senior officers were younger still. The room in José Estoril's house was a room of young men, all fond of a fight, all fond of dancing, all quite devoted to Lord Wellington.

The March evening, though rainy, was mild – as mild as May in England. Since his death, José Estoril's garden had grown wild and in particular a great number of lilac trees had appeared, crowding against the walls of the house. These trees were now all in flower and the windows and shutters of the house stood open to let in the damp, lilac-scented air. Suddenly Colonel Murray and General Stewart found that both they and their important papers were being comprehensively showered with drops of water. On looking up in some indignation they saw Strange, outside on the verandah unconcernedly shaking the water off his umbrella.

He entered the room and bid good evening to various officers with whom he had some acquaintance. He approached the table and inquired if he might possibly speak to Lord Wellington. General Stewart, a proud, handsome man, made no reply other than to shake his head vigorously. Colonel Murray, who was a gentler and more courteous soul, said he feared it would not be possible.

Strange glanced up the venerable staircase to the great carved doors behind which his lordship sat. (Curious how everyone who entered knew instinctively where he was to be found. Such is the fascination that great men exert!) Strange shewed no inclination to go. Colonel Murray supposed that he must be feeling lonely.

A tall man with vivid black eyebrows and long black mustaches to match approached the table. He wore the dark blue jacket and gold braid of the Light Dragoons. "Where have you put the French prisoners?" he demanded of Colonel Murray.

"In the belfry," said Colonel Murray.

"That will do," said the man. "I only ask because last night Colonel Pursey put three Frenchmen in a little shed, thinking they could do no harm there. But it seems some lads of the 52nd had previously put some chickens in the shed and during the night the Frenchmen ate the chickens. Colonel Pursey said that this morning several of his lads were eyeing the Frenchmen in a very particular manner as if they were wondering how much of the flavour of the chickens had got into the Frenchmen and whether it might not be worth cooking one of them to find out."

"Oh!" said Colonel Murray. "There is no danger of any thing like that happening tonight. The only other creatures in the belfry are the rats and I should think that if any one is going to eat any one else, the rats will eat the Frenchmen."

Colonel Murray, General Stewart and the man with black mustaches began to laugh, when suddenly they were interrupted by the magician saying, "The road between Espinhal and Lousão is abominably bad." (This was the road along which a substantial part of the British Army had come that day.)

Colonel Murray agreed that the road was very bad indeed.

Strange continued, "I cannot tell how many times today my horse stumbled into pot-holes and slipped in the mud. I was certain she would fall lame. Yet it was no worse than any of the other roads that I have seen since I arrived here, and tomorrow I understand some of us must go where there are no roads whatsoever."

"Yes," said Colonel Murray, wishing very heartily that the magician would go away.

"Through flooded rivers and stony plains, and through woods and thickets, I suppose," said Strange. "That will be very bad for all of us. I dare say we shall make very poor progress. I dare say we shall not get on at all."

"It is one of the disadvantages of waging war in such a backward, out-of-the-way place as Portugal," said Colonel Murray.

General Stewart said nothing but the angry look he gave the magician expressed quite clearly his opinion that perhaps Mr Strange would make better progress if he and his horse took themselves back to London.

"To take forty-five thousand men and all their horses and carts and equipment, across such an abominable country! No one in England would believe it possible." Strange laughed. "It is a pity that his lordship cannot spare a moment to talk to me, but perhaps you will be so good as to give him a message. Say this: Mr Strange presents his compliments to Lord Wellington and says that if it is of any interest to his lordship to have a nice, well-made road for the Army to march along tomorrow, then Mr Strange will be glad to conjure one up for him. Oh! And if he wishes he may have bridges too, to replace the ones the French have blown up. Good evening to you." With that Strange bowed to both gentlemen, picked up his umbrella and left.

Strange and Jeremy Johns had been unable to find anywhere to stay in Lousão. None of the gentlemen who found quarters for the generals and told the rest of the soldiers which damp field they were to sleep in, had made any provision for the magician and his servant. Strange had eventually agreed terms for a tiny upstairs room with a man who kept a little wine shop a few miles down the road to Miranda de Corvo.

Strange and Jeremy ate the supper the wine-shop owner had provided for them. It was a stew and their evening's entertainment chiefly consisted in trying to guess what had gone into it.

"What the devil is that?" asked Strange, holding up his fork. On the end of it was something whitish and glistening that curled over and under itself.

"A fish perhaps?" ventured Jeremy.

"It looks more like a snail," said Strange.

"Or part of someone's ear," added Jeremy.

Strange stared at it a moment longer. "Would you like it?" he asked.

"No, thank you, sir," said Jeremy with a resigned glance into his own cracked plate, "I have several of my own."

When they had finished supper and when the last candle had burnt out there seemed nothing else to do but go to bed – and so they did. Jeremy curled up upon one side of the room and Strange lay down upon the other. Each had devised his own bed from whatever materials had taken his fancy. Jeremy had a mattress fashioned out of his spare clothes and Strange had a pillow formed chiefly of books from Mr Norrell's library.

All at once there came the sound of someone's horse galloping up the road to the little wine-shop. This was quickly followed by the sound of someone's boots pounding up the rickety stairs, which in turn was followed by the sound of someone's fist pounding on the ramshackle door. The door opened and a smart young man in the uniform of the Hussars half-tumbled into the room. The smart young man was somewhat out of breath but managed to convey, between gulps of air, that Lord Wellington presented his compliments to Mr Strange and that if it was at all convenient to Mr Strange Lord Wellington would like to speak to him immediately.

At José Estoril's house Wellington was at dinner with a number of his staff officers and other gentlemen. Strange could have sworn that the gentlemen at the table had all been engaged in the liveliest conversation up to the moment when he entered the room, but now all fell silent. This rather suggested that they had been talking about him.

"Ah, Strange!" cried Lord Wellington, raising a glass in greeting. "There you are! I have had three *aides-de-camp* looking for you all evening. I wished to invite you to dinner, but my boys could not find you. Sit down anyway and have some Champagne and dessert."

Strange looked rather wistfully at the remains of the dinner which the servants were clearing away. Among other good things Strange believed he recognized were the remains of some roast geese, the shells from buttered prawns, half a ragoo of celery, and the ends of some spicy Portuguese sausages. He thanked his lordship and sat down. A servant brought him a glass of Champagne and he helped himself to almond-tart and dried cherries.

"And how do you like the war, Mr Strange?" asked a fox-haired, fox-faced gentleman at the other end of the table.

"Oh, it is a little confusing at first, like most things," said Strange, "but having now experienced many of the adventures a war affords, I grow used to it. I have been robbed – once. I have been shot at – once. Once I found a Frenchman in the kitchen and had to chase him out, and once the house I was sleeping in was set on fire."

"By the French?" inquired General Stewart.

"No, no. By the English. There was a company of the 43rd who were apparently very cold that night and so they set fire to the house to warm themselves."

"Oh, that always happens!" said General Stewart.

There was a little pause and then another gentleman in a cavalry uniform said, "We have been talking – arguing rather – about magic and how it is done. Strathclyde says that you and the other magician have given every word in the Bible a number, and you look for the words to make up the spell and then you add the numbers together and then you do something else and then . . ."

"*That* was not what I said!" complained another person, presumably Strathclyde. "You have not understood at all!"

"I am afraid I have never done any thing remotely resembling what you describe," said Strange. "It seems rather complicated and I do not think it would work. As to how I do magic, there are many, many procedures. As many, I dare say, as for making war."

"I should like to do magic," said the fox-haired, fox-faced

gentleman at the other end of the table. "I should have a ball every night with fairy music and fairy fireworks and I would summon all the most beautiful women out of history to attend. Helen of Troy, Cleopatra, Lucrezia Borgia, Maid Marian and Madame Pompadour. I should bring them all here to dance with you fellows. And when the French appeared on the horizon, I would just," he waved his arm vaguely, "do something, you know, and they would all fall down dead."

"Can a magician kill a man by magic?" Lord Wellington asked Strange.

Strange frowned. He seemed to dislike the question. "I suppose a magician might," he admitted, "but a gentleman never could."

Lord Wellington nodded as if this was just as he would have expected. And then he said, "This road, Mr Strange, which you have been so good as to offer us, what sort of road would it be?"

"Oh! The details are the easiest thing in the world to arrange, my lord. What sort of road would you like?"

The officers and gentlemen around Lord Wellington's dinner-table looked at each other; they had not given the matter any thought.

"A chalk road, perhaps?" said Strange, helpfully. "A chalk road is pretty."

"Too dusty in the dry and a river of mud in the rain," said Lord Wellington. "No, no. A chalk road will never do. A chalk road is scarcely better than no road at all."

"What about a cobbled road?" suggested Colonel Murray.

"Cobbles will make the men's boots wear out," said Wellington.

"And besides the artillery will not like it," said the fox-haired, fox-faced gentleman, "They will have a devil of a time dragging the guns along a cobbled road."

Someone else suggested a gravel road. But that, thought Wellington, was liable to the same objection as a chalk road: it would become a river of mud in the rain – and the Portuguese *did* seem to think that it would rain again tomorrow.

"No," said his lordship, "I believe, Mr Strange, that what would suit us best would be a road along the Roman pattern, with a nice ditch upon either side to drain off the water and good flat stones well fitted together on top."

"Very well," said Strange.

"We set off at daybreak," said Wellington.

"Then, my lord, if someone would be good enough to shew me where the road ought to go, I shall see to it immediately."

By morning the road was in place and Lord Wellington rode along it on Copenhagen – his favourite horse – and Strange rode beside him on Egyptian – who was *his* favourite horse. In his customary decisive manner Wellington pointed out those things which he particularly liked about the road and those things which he did not like; ". . . But really I have hardly any criticisms to make. It is an excellent road! Only make it a little wider tomorrow, if you please."

Lord Wellington and Strange agreed that as a general rule the road should be in place a couple of hours before the first regiment stepped on to it and disappear an hour after the last soldier had passed along it. This was to prevent the French Army from gaining any benefit from the roads. The success of this plan depended on Wellington's Staff providing Strange with accurate information as to when the Army was likely to begin and end marching. Obviously these calculations were not always correct. A week or so after the first appearance of the road Colonel Mackenzie of the 11th Foot came to see Lord Wellington in a great temper and complained that the magician had allowed the road to disappear before his regiment could reach it.

"By the time we got to Celorico, my lord, it was disappearing under our feet! An hour after that it had vanished entirely. Could not the magician summon up visions to find out what the different regiments are doing? I understand that this is something he can do very easily! Then he could make sure that the roads do not disappear until everyone has finished with them."

Lord Wellington said sharply, "The magician has a great deal to do. Beresford needs roads.[3] I need roads. I really cannot ask Mr Strange to be forever peering into mirrors and bowls of water to discover where every stray regiment has got to. You and your lads must keep up, Colonel Mackenzie. That is all."

Shortly after this the British Headquarters received intelligence of something that had befallen a large part of the French Army as it was marching from Guarda to Sabugal. A patrol had been sent out to look at the road between the two towns, but some Portuguese had come along and told the patrol that this was one of the English magician's roads and was certain to disappear in an hour or two taking everyone upon it to Hell – or possibly England. As soon as this rumour reached the ears of the soldiers they declined absolutely to walk along the road – which was in fact perfectly real and had existed for almost a thousand years. Instead the French followed some serpentine route over mountains and through rocky valleys that wore out their boots and tore their clothes and delayed them for several days.

Lord Wellington could not have been more delighted.

---

[3] There were three great fortresses which guarded the border into Spain: Almeida, Badajoz and Ciudad Rodriguez. In the early months of 1811 all three were held by the French. While Wellington advanced upon the Almeida he despatched General Beresford with the Portuguese Army to besiege the fortress of Badajoz further south.

30

The book of Robert Findhelm

January–February 1812

A MAGICIAN'S HOUSE IS expected to have certain peculiarities, but the most peculiar feature of Mr Norrell's house was, without a doubt, Childermass. In no other household in London was there any servant like him. One day he might be observed removing a dirty cup and wiping crumbs from a table like a common footman. The next day he would interrupt a room full of admirals, generals and noblemen to tell them in what particulars he considered them mistaken. Mr Norrell had once publicly reprimanded the Duke of Devonshire for speaking at the same time as Childermass.

On a misty day at the end of January 1812 Childermass entered the library at Hanover-square where Mr Norrell was working and briefly informed him that he was obliged to go away upon business and did not know when he would return. Then, having given the other servants various instructions about the work they were to do in his absence, he mounted his horse and rode away.

In the three weeks that followed Mr Norrell received four letters from him: one from Newark in Nottinghamshire, one from York in the East Riding of Yorkshire, one from Richmond in the North Riding of Yorkshire and one from Sheffield in the West Riding of Yorkshire. But the letters were only about business matters and threw no light upon his mysterious journey.

He returned one night in the second half of February. Lascelles and Drawlight had dined at Hanover-square and were in the drawing-room with Mr Norrell when Childermass entered. He came directly from the stables; his boots and breeches were splashed with mud and his coat was still damp with rain.

"Where in the world have you been?" demanded Mr Norrell.

"In Yorkshire," said Childermass, "making inquiries about Vinculus."

"Did you see Vinculus?" asked Drawlight, eagerly.

"No, I did not."

"Do you know where he is?" asked Mr Norrell.

"No, I do not."

"Have you found Vinculus's book?" asked Lascelles.

"No, I have not."

"Tut," said Lascelles. He eyed Childermass disapprovingly. "If you take my advice, Mr Norrell, you will not permit Mr Childermass to waste any more time upon Vinculus. No one has heard or seen any thing of him for years. He is probably dead."

Childermass sat down upon the sopha like a man who had a perfect right to do so and said, "The cards say he is not dead. The cards say he is still alive and still has the book."

"The cards! The cards!" cried Mr Norrell. "I have told you a thousand times how I detest any mention of those objects! You will oblige me by removing them from my house and never speaking of them again!"

Childermass threw his master a cool look. "Do you wish to hear what I have learnt or not?" he asked.

Mr Norrell nodded sullenly.

"Good," said Childermass. "In your interest, Mr Norrell, I have taken care to improve my acquaintance with all Vinculus's wives. It has always seemed to me nigh on impossible that one of them did not know something that would help us. It seemed to me that all I had to do was to go with them to enough gin-houses, buy them enough gin, and let them talk, and eventually one of them would reveal it to me. Well, I was right. Three weeks ago Nan Purvis told me a story which finally put me on the track of Vinculus's book."

"Which one is Nan Purvis?" inquired Lascelles.

"The first. She told me something that happened twenty or thirty years ago when Vinculus and she were first married. They had been drinking at a gin-house. They had spent their money and exhausted their credit and it was time to return to their lodgings. They staggered along the street and in the gutter they saw a creature even worse for drink than themselves. An old man was lying there, dead drunk. The filthy water flowed around him and over his face, and it was only by chance that he did not drown. Something about this wretch caught Vinculus's eye. It seemed that he recognized him. He went and peered at him. Then he laughed and gave the old man a vicious kick. Nan asked Vinculus who the old man was. Vinculus said his name was Clegg. She asked how he knew him. Vinculus replied angrily that he did not know Clegg. He said he had never known Clegg! What was more, he told her, he was determined never to know him! In short there was no one in the world whom he despised more than Clegg! When Nan complained that this was not a very full explanation, Vinculus grudgingly said that the man was his father. After this he refused to say any more."

"But what has this to do with any thing?" interrupted Mr Norrell. "Why do you not ask these wives of Vinculus's about the *book*?"

Childermass looked annoyed. "I did so, sir. Four years ago. You may remember I told you. None of them knew any thing about it."

With an exasperated wave of his hand Mr Norrell indicated that Childermass was to continue.

"Some months later Nan was in a tavern, listening to an account of a hanging at York that someone was reading from a newspaper. Nan loved to hear of a good hanging and this report particularly impressed her because the name of the man who had been executed was Clegg. It stuck in her mind and that evening she told Vinculus. To her surprize, she found that he already knew all about it and that it was indeed his father. Vinculus was delighted Clegg had been hanged. He said Clegg richly deserved it. He said Clegg had been guilty of a terrible crime – the worst crime committed in England in the last hundred years."

"What crime?" asked Lascelles.

"At first Nan could not bring it to mind," said Childermass. "But with a little persistent questioning and the promise of more gin she remembered. He had stolen a book."

"A book!" exclaimed Mr Norrell.

"Oh, Mr Norrell!" cried Drawlight. "It must be the same book. It must be Vinculus's book!"

"Is it?" asked Mr Norrell.

"I believe so," said Childermass.

"But did this woman know what the book was?" said Mr Norrell.

"No, that was the end of Nan's information. So I rode north to York, where Clegg had been tried and executed, and I examined the records of the Quarter Sessions. The first thing I discovered was that Clegg was originally from Richmond in Yorkshire. Oh yes!" Here Childermass glanced meaningfully at Mr Norrell. "Vinculus is, by descent at least, a Yorkshireman.[1] Clegg began life as a tightrope walker at the northern fairs, but as tightrope-walking is not a trade that combines well with drinking – and Clegg was a famous drinker – he was obliged to give it up. He returned to Richmond and hired himself out as a servant on a prosperous farm. He did well there and impressed the farmer with his cleverness, so that he began to be entrusted with more and more business. From time to time he would go drinking with bad companions and on these occasions he never stopped at one bottle

---

[1] Yorkshire was part of the Raven King's kingdom of Northern England. Childermass and Norrell's respect for Vinculus would have increased a little, knowing that he was, like them, a Northerner.

or two. He drank until the spigots gave out and the cellars were emptied. He was mad-drunk for days and in that time he got up to all sorts of mischief – thieving, gambling, fighting, destruction of property – but he always made sure that these wild adventures took place far away from the farm and he always had some plausible excuse to explain his absence so that his master, the farmer, never suspected any thing was amiss, though the other servants knew all about it. The farmer's name was Robert Findhelm. He was a quiet, kindly, respectable sort of man – the sort of man easily deceived by a rogue like Clegg. The farm had been in his family for generations, but once, long ago, it had been one of the granges of the Abbey of Easby . . ."

Mr Norrell drew in his breath sharply and fidgeted in his chair. Lascelles looked inquiringly at him.

"Easby Abbey was one of the foundations of the Raven King," explained Mr Norrell.

"As was Hurtfew," added Childermass.

"Indeed!" said Lascelles in surprize.[2] "I confess that after all you have said about him, I am surprized that you live in a house so closely connected to him."

"You do not understand," said Mr Norrell, irritably. "We are speaking of Yorkshire, of John Uskglass's Kingdom of Northern England where he lived and ruled for three hundred years. There is scarcely a village, scarcely a field even, that does not have some close connexion with him."

Childermass continued. "Findhelm's family possessed something else that had once belonged to the Abbey – a treasure that had been given into their keeping by the last Abbot and which was handed down from father to son with the land."

"A book of magic?" asked Norrell, eagerly.

---

[2] Many people besides Lascelles remarked upon the odd circumstance that Mr Norrell who hated any mention of the Raven King should have lived in a house built of stones quarried upon the King's instruction, and upon land which the King had once owned and knew well.

"If what they told me in Yorkshire is true, it was more than a book of magic. It was The Book of Magic. A book written by the Raven King and set down in his own hand."

There was a silence.

"Is this possible?" Lascelles asked Mr Norrell.

Mr Norrell did not answer. He was sitting deep in thought, wholly taken up with this new, and not altogether pleasant, idea.

At last he spoke, but it was more as if he were speaking his thoughts out loud, rather than answering Lascelles's question. "A book belonging to Raven King or written by him is one of the great follies of English magic. Several people have imagined that they have found it or that they know where it is hidden. Some of them were clever men who might have written important works of scholarship but instead wasted their lives in pursuit of the King's book. But that is not to say that such a book might not exist somewhere . . ."

"And if it did exist," urged Lascelles, "and if it were found — what then?"

Mr Norrell shook his head and would not reply.

Childermass answered for him. "Then all of English magic would have to be reinterpreted in the light of what was found there."

Lascelles raised an eyebrow. "Is this true?" he asked.

Mr Norrell hesitated and looked very much as if he would like to say that it was not.

"Do *you* believe that this was the King's book?" Lascelles asked Childermass.

Childermass shrugged. "Findhelm certainly believed it. In Richmond I discovered two old people who had been servants in Findhelm's house in their youth. They said that the King's book was the pride of his existence. He was Guardian of The Book first, and all else — husband, parent, farmer — second." Childermass paused. "The greatest glory and the greatest burden given to any man in this Age," he mused. "Findhelm seems to have been a theoretical magician himself in a small way. He bought books about magic and paid a magician in Northallerton to teach him. But one thing struck me as very curious – both these old servants insisted that Findhelm never read the King's book and had only the vaguest notion of what it contained."

"Ah!" exclaimed Mr Norrell, softly.

Lascelles and Childermass looked at him.

"So he could not read it," said Mr Norrell. "Well, that is very . . ." He fell silent, and began to chew on his fingernails.

"Perhaps it was in Latin," suggested Lascelles.

"And why do you assume that Findhelm did not know Latin?" replied Childermass with some irritation. "Just because he was a farmer . . ."

"Oh! I meant no disrespect to farmers in general, I assure you," laughed Lascelles. "The occupation has its utility. But farmers are not in general known for their classical scholarship. Would this person even have recognized Latin when he saw it?"

Childermass retorted that of course Findhelm would have recognized Latin. He was not a fool.

To which Lascelles coldly replied that he had never said he was. The quarrel was becoming heated when they were both suddenly silenced by Mr Norrell saying slowly and thoughtfully, "When the Raven King first came into England, he could not read and write. Few people could in those days – even kings. And the Raven King had been brought up in a fairy house where there was no writing. He had never even seen writing before. His new human servants shewed it to him and explained its purpose. But he was a young man then, a very young man, perhaps no more than fourteen or fifteen years of age. He had already conquered kingdoms in two different worlds and he had all the magic a magician could desire. He was full of arrogance and pride. He had no wish to read other men's thoughts. What were other men's thoughts compared to his own? So he refused to learn to read and write Latin – which was what his servants wanted – and instead he invented a writing of his own to preserve his thoughts for later times. Presumably this writing mirrored the workings of his own mind more closely than Latin could have done. That was at the very beginning. But the longer he remained in England, the more he changed, becoming less silent, less solitary – less like a fairy and more like a man. Eventually he consented to learn to read and write as other men did. But he did not forget his own writing – the King's Letters, as it is called – and he taught it to certain favoured magicians so that they might understand his magic more perfectly. Martin Pale mentions the King's Letters and so does Belasis, but neither of them had ever seen so much as a single penstroke of it. If a piece of it has survived and in the King's own hand, then certainly . . ." Mr Norrell fell silent again.

"Well, Mr Norrell," said Lascelles, "you are full of surprizes tonight! So much admiration for a man you have always claimed to hate and despise!"

"My admiration does not lessen my hatred one whit!" said Mr Norrell, sharply. "I said he was a great magician. I did not say he was a good man or that I welcomed his influence upon English magic. Besides what you have just heard was my private opinion and not for public circulation. Childermass knows. Childermass understands."

Mr Norrell glanced nervously at Drawlight, but Drawlight had stopped listening some time ago – just as soon as he discovered that Childermass's story concerned no one in the fashionable world, but only Yorkshire farmers and drunk servants. At present he was busy polishing his snuff box with his handkerchief.

"So Clegg stole this book?" said Lascelles to Childermass. "Is that what you are going to tell us?"

"In a manner of speaking. In the autumn of 1754 Findhelm gave the book to Clegg and told him to deliver it to a man in the village of Bretton in the Derbyshire Peak. Why, I do not know. Clegg set off and on the second or third day of his journey he reached Sheffield. He stopped at a tavern, and there he fell in with a man, a blacksmith by trade, whose reputation as a drinker was almost as extraordinary as his own. They began a drinking contest that lasted two days and two nights. At first they simply drank to see which of them could drink the most, but on the second day they began to set each other mad, drunken challenges. There was a barrel of salted herrings in the corner. Clegg challenged the blacksmith to walk across a floor of herrings. An audience had gathered by this time and all the lookers-on and the loungers-about emptied out the herrings and paved the floor with fish. Then the blacksmith walked from one end of the room to the other till the floor was a stinking mess of pulped fish and the blacksmith was bloody from head to foot with all the falls he had taken. Then the blacksmith challenged Clegg to walk along the edge of the tavern roof. Clegg had been drunk for a whole day by this time. Time after time the onlookers thought he was about to fall and break his worthless neck, but he never did. Then Clegg challenged the blacksmith to roast and eat his shoes – which the blacksmith did – and finally, the blacksmith challenged Clegg to eat Robert Find-helm's book. Clegg tore it into strips and ate it piece by piece.''

Mr Norrell gave a cry of horror. Even Lascelles blinked in surprise.

"Days later," said Childermass, "when Clegg awoke he realized what he had done. He made his way down to London and four years after that he tumbled a serving girl in a Wapping tavern, who was Vinculus's mother."

"But surely the explanation is clear!" cried Mr Norrell. "The book is not lost at all! The story of the drinking contest was a mere invention of Clegg's to blind Findhelm to the truth! In reality he kept the book and gave it to his son! Now if we can only discover . . ."

"But why?" said Childermass. "Why should he go to all this trouble in order to procure the book for a son he had never seen and did not care about? Besides Vinculus was not even born when Clegg set off on the road to Derbyshire."

Lascelles cleared his throat. "For once, Mr Norrell, I agree with Mr Childermass. If Clegg still had the book or knew where it was to be found, then surely he would have produced it at his trial or tried to use it to bargain for his life."

"And if Vinculus had profited so much from his father's crime," added Childermass, "why did he hate his father? Why did he rejoice when his father was hanged? Robert Findhelm was quite sure that the book was destroyed – that is plain. Nan told me Clegg had been hanged for stealing a book, but the charge Robert Findhelm brought against him was not theft. The charge Findhelm brought against him was book-murder. Clegg was the last man in England to be hanged for book-murder."[3]

"So why does Vinculus claim to have this book if his father ate it?' said Lascelles in a wondering tone. "The thing is not possible."

"Somehow Robert Findhelm's inheritance has passed to Vinculus, but how it happened I do not pretend to understand," said Childermass.

"What of the man in Derbyshire?" asked Mr Norrell, suddenly. "You said that Findhelm was sending the book to a man in Derbyshire."

Childermass sighed. "I passed through Derbyshire on my way back to London. I went to the village of Bretton. Three houses and an inn high on a bleak hill. Whoever the man was that Clegg was sent to seek out, he is long dead. I could discover nothing there."

Stephen Black and the gentleman with the thistle-down hair were seated in the upper room of Mr Wharton's coffee-house in Oxford-street where the Peep-O'Day-Boys met.

The gentleman was speaking, as he often did, of his great affection for Stephen. "Which reminds me," he said; "I have been meaning for many months to offer you an apology and an explanation."

---

[3] Book-murder was a late addition to English magical law. The wilful destruction of a book of magic merited the same punishment as the murder of a Christian.

"An apology to me, sir?"

"Yes, Stephen. You and I wish for nothing in the world so much as Lady Pole's happiness, yet I am bound by the terms of the magician's wicked agreement to return her to her husband's house each morning where she must while away the long day until evening. But, clever as you are, you must surely have observed that there are no such constraints upon you and I dare say you are wondering why I do not take you away to Lost-hope House to be happy for ever and for ever."

"I have wondered about that, sir," agreed Stephen. He paused because his whole future seemed to depend upon the next question. "Is there something which prevents you?"

"Yes, Stephen. In a way there is."

"I see," said Stephen. "Well, that is most unfortunate."

"Would not you like to know what it is?" asked the gentleman.

"Oh yes, sir! Indeed, sir!"

"Know then," said the gentleman, putting on grave and important looks quite unlike his usual expression, "that we fairy-spirits know something of the future. Often Fate chuses us as her vessels for prophecy. In the past we have lent our aid to Christians to allow them to achieve great and noble destinies – Julius Caesar, Alexander the Great, Charlemagne, William Shakespeare, John Wesley and so forth.[4] But often our knowledge of things to come is misty and . . ." The gentleman gestured furiously as if he were brushing away thick cobwebs from in front of his face. ". . . imperfect. Out of my dear love for you, Stephen, I have traced the smoke of burning cities and battlefields and prised dripping, bloody guts out of dying men to discover your future. You are indeed destined to be a king! I must say that I am not in the least surprised! I felt strongly from the first that you should be a king and it was most unlikely that I should be wrong. But more than

---

[4] Not all the Worthies referred to by the gentleman are Christian. Just as we refer to a great many diverse tribes and races as "fairies", so they commonly name us "Christians" regardless of our religion, race or era.

this, I believe I know which kingdom is to be yours. The smoke and guts and all the other signs state quite clearly that it is to be a kingdom where you have already been! A kingdom with which you are already closely connected."

Stephen waited.

"But do you not see?" cried the gentleman, impatiently. "It must be England! I cannot tell you how delighted I was when I learnt this important news!"

"England!" exclaimed Stephen.

"Yes, indeed! Nothing could be more beneficial for England herself than that you should be her King. The present King is old and blind and as for his sons, they are all fat and drunk! So now you see why I cannot take you away to Lost-hope. It would be wholly wrong of me to remove you from your rightful kingdom!"

Stephen sat for a moment, trying to comprehend. "But might not the kingdom be somewhere in Africa?" he said at last. "Perhaps I am destined to find my way back there and perhaps by some strange portent the people will recognize me as the descendant of one of their kings?"

"Perhaps," said the gentleman, doubtfully. "But, no! That cannot be. For you see it is a kingdom where *you have already been*. And you never were in Africa. Oh, Stephen! How I long for your wonderful destiny to be accomplished. On that day I shall ally my many kingdoms to Great Britain – and you and I shall live in perfect amity and brotherhood. Think how our enemies will be confounded! Think how eaten up with rage the magicians will be! How they will curse themselves that they did not treat us with more respect!"

"But I think that you must be mistaken, sir. I cannot rule England. Not with this . . ." He spread out his hands in front of him. *Black skin*, he thought. Aloud he continued, "Only you, sir, with your partiality for me, could think such a thing possible. Slaves do not become kings, sir."

"Slave, Stephen? Whatever do you mean?"

"I was born into slavery, sir. As are many of my race. My mother was a slave on an estate in Jamaica that Sir Walter's grandfather owned. When his debts grew too great Sir William went to Jamaica to sell the estate – and one of the possessions which he brought back with him was my mother. Or rather he intended to bring her back to be a servant in his house, but during the voyage she gave birth to me and died."

"Ha!" exclaimed the gentleman in triumph. "Then it is exactly as I have said! You and your estimable mother were enslaved by the wicked English and brought low by their machinations!"

"Well, yes, sir. That is true in a sense. But I am not a slave now. No one who stands on British soil can be a slave. The air of England is the air of liberty. It is a great boast of Englishmen that this is so." *And yet*, he thought, *they own slaves in other countries*. Out loud he said, "From the moment that Sir William's valet carried me as a tiny infant from the ship I was free."

"Nevertheless we should punish them!" cried the gentleman. "We can easily kill Lady Pole's husband, and then I will descend into Hell and find his grandfather, and then . . ."

"But it was not Sir William and Sir Walter who did the enslaving," protested Stephen. "Sir Walter has always been very much opposed to the slave trade. And Sir William was kind to me. He had me christened and educated."

"Christened? What? Even your name is an imposition of your enemies? Signifying slavery? Then I strongly advise you to cast it off and chuse another when you ascend the throne of England! What was the name your mother called you?"

"I do not know, sir. I am not sure that she called me any thing."

The gentleman narrowed his eyes as a sign that he was thinking hard. "It would be a strange sort of mother," he mused, "that did not name her child. Yes, there will be a name that belongs to you. Truly belongs to you. That much is clear to me. The name your mother called you in her heart during those precious moments when she held you in her arms. Are you not curious to know what it was?"

"Certainly, sir. But my mother is long dead. She may never have told that name to another soul. Her own name is lost. Once when I was a boy I asked Sir William, but he could not remember it."

"Doubtless he knew it well, but in his malice would not tell it to you. It would need someone very remarkable to recover your name, Stephen – someone of rare perspicacity, with extraordinary talents and incomparable nobility of character. Me, in fact. Yes, that is what I will do. As a token of the love I bear you, I will find your true name!"

31

Seventeen dead Neapolitans

April 1812–June 1814

THERE WERE IN the British Army at that time a number of
"exploring officers" whose business it was to talk to the
local people, to steal the French Army's letters and always to know the whereabouts of the French troops. Let your
notions of war be as romantic as they may, Wellington's exploring
officers would always exceed them. They forded rivers by moonlight and crossed mountain ranges under the searing sun. They
lived more behind French lines than English ones and knew
everyone favourable to the British cause.

The greatest of these exploring officers was, without a doubt,
Major Colquhoun Grant of the 11th Foot. Often the French would
look up from whatever they were doing and see Major Grant on
horseback, observing them from atop a far-off hill. He would peer
at them through his telescope and then make notes about them in
his little notebook. It made them most uncomfortable.

One morning in April 1812, quite by chance, Major Grant
found himself caught between two French cavalry patrols. When it
became clear that he could not outride them he abandoned his
horse and hid in a little wood. Major Grant always considered
himself to be a soldier rather than a spy, and, as a soldier, he made
it a point of honour to wear his uniform at all times. Unfortunately
the uniform of the 11th Foot (as of almost all infantry regiments)

was bright scarlet and as he hid amongst the budding spring leaves the French had no difficulty whatsoever in perceiving him.

For the British the capture of Grant was a calamity akin to losing a whole brigade of ordinary men. Lord Wellington immediately sent out urgent messages – some to the French generals proposing an exchange of prisoners and some to the *guerrilla* commanders,[1] promising them silver dollars and weapons aplenty if they could effect Grant's rescue. When neither of these proposals produced any results Lord Wellington was obliged to try a different plan. He hired one of the most notorious and ferocious of all the *guerrilla* chieftains, Jeronimo Saornil, to convey Jonathan Strange to Major Grant.

"You will find that Saornil is rather a formidable person," Lord Wellington informed Strange before he set off, "but I have no fears upon that account, because frankly, Mr Strange, so are you."

Saornil and his men were indeed as murderous a set of villains as you could wish to see. They were dirty, evil-smelling and unshaven. They had sabres and knives stuck into their belts and rifles slung over their shoulders. Their clothes and saddle-blankets were covered with cruel and deadly images: skulls and crossbones; hearts impaled upon knives; gallows; crucifixions upon cartwheels; ravens pecking at hearts and eyes; and other such pleasant devices. These images were formed out of what appeared at first to be pearl buttons but which, on closer examination, proved to be the teeth of all the Frenchmen they had killed. Saornil, in particular, had so many teeth attached to his person that he rattled whenever he moved, rather as if all the dead Frenchmen were still chattering with fear.

---

[1] *Guerrilla* – a Spanish word meaning "little war". *Guerrilla* bands were groups of Spaniards numbering between dozens and thousands who fought and harassed the French armies. Some were led by ex-soldiers and maintained an impressive degree of military discipline. Others were little more than bandits and devoted as much of their energies to terrifying their own unfortunate countrymen as they did to fighting the French.

Surrounded as they were by the symbols and accoutrements of death, Saornil and his men were confident of striking terror into everyone they met. They were therefore a little disconcerted to find that the English magician had outdone them in this respect – he had brought a coffin with him. Like many violent men they were also rather superstitious. One of them asked Strange what was inside the coffin. He replied carelessly that it contained a man.

After several days of hard riding the *guerrilla* band brought Strange to a hill which overlooked the principal road leading out of Spain and into France. Along this road, they assured Strange, Major Grant and his captors were sure to pass.

Saornil's men set up camp nearby and settled themselves to wait. On the third day they saw a large party of French soldiers coming along the road and, riding in the middle of them, in his scarlet uniform, was Major Grant. Immediately Strange gave instructions for his coffin to be opened. Three of the *guerrilleros* took crowbars and prised off the lid. Inside they found a pottery person – a sort of mannikin made from the same rough red clay which the Spanish use to make their colourful plates and jugs. It was life-size, but very crudely made. It had two holes for eyes and no nose to speak of. It was, however, carefully dressed in the uniform of an officer of the 11th Foot.

"Now," said Strange to Jeronimo Saornil, "when the French outriders reach that rock there, take your men and attack them."

Saornil took a moment to digest this, not least because Strange's Spanish had several eccentricities of grammar and pronunciation.

When he had understood he asked, "Shall we try to free *El Bueno Granto*?" (*El Bueno Granto* was the Spaniards' name for Major Grant.)

"Certainly not!" replied Strange. "Leave *El Bueno Granto* to me!"

Saornil and his men went halfway down the hill to a place where thin trees made a screen that hid them from the road. From here they opened fire. The French were taken entirely by surprize. Some were killed; many others wounded. There were no rocks and very few bushes – scarcely any where to hide – but the road was still before them, offering a good chance of outrunning their attackers. After a few minutes of panic and confusion the French gathered up their wits and their wounded and sped away.

As the *guerrilleros* climbed back up the hill, they were very doubtful that any thing had been accomplished; after all, the figure in the scarlet uniform had still been among the Frenchmen as they rode off. They reached the place where they had left the magician and were amazed to find he was no longer alone. Major Grant was with him. The two men were sitting sociably on a rock, eating cold chicken and drinking claret.

". . . Brighton is all very well," Major Grant was saying, "but I prefer Weymouth."

"You amaze me," replied Strange. "I detest Weymouth. I spent one of the most miserable weeks of my life there. I was horribly in love with a girl called Marianne and she snubbed me for a fellow with an estate in Jamaica and a glass eye."

"That is not Weymouth's fault," said Major Grant. "Ah! Capitán Saornil!" He waved a chicken leg at the chieftain by way of greeting. "Buenos Días!"

Meanwhile the officers and soldiers of the French escort continued on their way to France and when they reached Bayonne they delivered their prisoner into the keeping of the Head of Bayonne's Secret Police. The Head of the Secret Police came forward to greet what he confidently believed to be Major Grant. He was somewhat disconcerted when, on reaching out to shake the Major's hand, the entire arm came away in his hand. So surprized was he that he dropped it on the ground where it shattered into a thousand pieces. He turned to make his apologies to Major Grant and was even more appalled to discover large black cracks appearing all over the Major's face. Next, part of the Major's head fell off – by which means he was discovered to be completely hollow inside – and a moment later he fell to bits like the Humpty-Dumpty person in *Mother Goose's Melody*.

On July 22nd Wellington fought the French outside the ancient university city of Salamanca. It was the most decisive victory for any British Army in recent years.

That night the French Army fled through the woods that lay to the south of Salamanca. As they ran, the soldiers looked up and were amazed to see flights of angels descending through the dark trees. The angels shone with a blinding light. Their wings were as white as swans' wings and their robes were the shifting colours of mother-of-pearl, fish scales or skies before thunder. In their hands they held flaming lances and their eyes blazed with a divine fury. They flew through the trees with astonishing rapidity and brandished their lances in the faces of the French.

Many of the soldiers were stricken with such terror that they turned and ran back towards the city – towards the pursuing British Army. Most were too amazed to do any thing but stand and stare. One man, braver and more resolute than the rest, tried to understand what was happening. It seemed to him highly unlikely that Heaven should suddenly have allied itself with France's enemies; after all such a thing had not been heard of since Old Testament times. He noticed that though the angels threatened the soldiers with their lances, they did not attack them. He waited until one of the angels swooped down towards him and then he plunged his sabre into it. The sabre encountered no resistance – nothing but empty air. Nor did the angel exhibit any signs of hurt or shock. Immediately the Frenchman called out to his compatriots that there was no reason to be afraid; these were nothing but illusions produced by Wellington's magician; they could not harm them.

The French soldiers continued along the road, pursued by the phantom angels. As they came out of the trees they found themselves on the bank of the River Tormes. An ancient bridge crossed the river, leading into the town of Alba de Tormes. By an error on the part of one of Lord Wellington's allies this bridge had been left entirely unguarded. The French crossed over and escaped through the town.

Some hours later, shortly after dawn, Lord Wellington rode wearily across the bridge at Alba de Tormes. With him were three other gentlemen: Lieutenant-Colonel De Lancey who was the Army's Deputy Quartermaster; a handsome young man called Fitzroy Somerset who was Lord Wellington's Military Secretary; and Jonathan Strange. All of them were dusty and battle-stained and none of them had been to bed for some days. Nor was there much likelihood of their doing so soon since Wellington was determined to continue his pursuit of the fleeing French.

The town with its churches, convents and mediaeval buildings stood out with perfect clarity against an opalescent sky. Despite the hour (it was not much after half past five) the town was already up. Bells were already being rung to celebrate the defeat of the French. Regiments of weary British and Portuguese soldiers were filing through the streets and the townspeople were coming out of their houses to press gifts of bread, fruit and flowers on them. Carts bearing wounded men were lined up against a wall while the officer in charge sent men to seek out the hospital and other places to receive them. Meanwhile five or six plain-faced, capable-looking nuns had arrived from one of the convents and were going about among the wounded men giving them draughts of fresh milk from a tin cup. Small boys whom nobody could persuade to stay in bed were excitedly cheering every soldier they saw and forming impromptu victory parades behind any that did not seem to mind it.

Lord Wellington looked about him. "Watkins!" he cried, hailing a soldier in an artillery uniform.

"Yes, my lord?" said the man.

"I am in search of my breakfast, Watkins. I don't suppose you have seen my cook?"

"Sergeant Jefford said he saw your people going up to the castle, my lord."

"Thank you, Watkins," said his lordship and rode on with his party.

The Castle of Alba de Tormes was not much of a castle. Many years ago at the start of the war the French had laid siege to it and with the exception of one tower it was all in ruins. Birds and wild creatures now made nests and holes where once the Dukes of Alba had lived in unimaginable luxury. The fine Italian murals for which the castle had once been famous were a great deal less impressive now that the ceilings were all gone and they had been subjected to the rough caresses of rain, hail, sleet and snow. The dining-parlour lacked some of the convenience that other dining-parlours have; it was open to the sky and there was a young birch tree growing in the middle of it. But this troubled Lord Wellington's servants not one whit; they were accustomed to serve his lordship his meals in far stranger places. They had set a table beneath the birch tree and spread it with a white cloth. As Wellington and his companions rode up to the castle they had just begun to lay it with plates of bread rolls, slices of Spanish ham, bowls of apricots and dishes of fresh butter. Wellington's cook went off to fry fish, devil kidneys and make coffee.

The four gentlemen sat down. Colonel De Lancey remarked that he did not believe he could remember when his last meal had been. Somebody else agreed and then they all silently applied themselves to the serious business of eating and drinking.

They were just beginning to feel a little more like their usual selves and grow a little more conversational when Major Grant arrived.

"Ah! Grant," said Lord Wellington. "Good Morning. Sit down. Have some breakfast."

"I will in a moment, my lord. But first I have some news for you. Of rather a surprizing sort. It seems the French have lost six cannon."

412

"Cannon?" said his lordship, not much interested. He helped himself to a bread roll and some devilled kidneys. "Of course they have lost cannon. Somerset!" he said, addressing his Military Secretary. "How many pieces of French cannon did I capture yesterday?"

"Eleven, my lord."

"No, no, my lord," said Major Grant. "I beg your pardon, but you misunderstand. I am not speaking of the cannon that were captured during the battle. These cannon were never in the battle. They were on their way from General Caffarelli in the north to the French Army. But they did not arrive in time for the battle. In fact they never arrived at all. Knowing that you were in the vicinity, my lord, and pressing the French hard, General Caffarelli was anxious to deliver them with all dispatch. He made up his escort out of the first thirty soldiers that came to hand. Well, my lord, he acted in haste and has repented at leisure for it seems that ten out of thirty were Neapolitan."

"Neapolitan! Were they indeed?" said his lordship.

De Lancey and Somerset exchanged pleased looks with one another and even Jonathan Strange smiled.

The truth was that, although Naples was part of the French Empire, the Neapolitans hated the French. The young men of Naples were forced to fight in the French Army but they took every opportunity they could to desert, often running away to the enemy.

"But what of the other soldiers?" asked Somerset. "Surely we must assume that they will prevent the Neapolitans doing much mischief?"

"It is too late for the other soldiers to do any thing," said Major Grant. "They are all dead. Twenty pairs of French boots and twenty French uniforms are, at this very moment, hanging in the shop of an old clothes dealer in Salamanca. The coats all have long slits in the back, such as might be made by an Italian stiletto, and they are all over blood stains."

"So, the cannon are in the hands of a pack of Italian deserters, are they?" said Strange. "What will they do? Start a war of their own?"

"No, no!" said Grant. "They will sell them to the highest bidder. Either to you, my lord or to General Castanos." (This was the name of the General in charge of the Spanish Army.)

"Somerset!" said his lordship. "What ought I to give for six French cannon? Four hundred dollars?"

"Oh! It is certainly worth four hundred dollars to make the French feel the consequences of their foolishness, my lord. But what I do not understand is why we have not heard something from the Neapolitans already. What can they be waiting for?"

"I believe I know the answer to that," said Major Grant. "Four nights ago two men met secretly in a little graveyard upon a hillside not far from Castrejon. They wore ragged French uniforms and spoke a sort of Italian. They conferred a while and when they parted one went south towards the French Army at Cantalapiedra, the other went north towards the Duero. My lord, it is my belief that the Neapolitan deserters are sending messages to their countrymen to come and join them. I dare say they believe that with the money that you or General Castanos will give them for the guns, they will all be able to sail back to Naples in a golden ship. There is probably not a man among them who does not have a brother or cousin in some other French regiment. They do not wish to return home and face their mothers and grandmothers without bringing their relations with them."

"I have always heard that Italian women are rather fierce," agreed Colonel De Lancey.

"All we need to do, my lord," continued Major Grant, "is find some Neapolitans and question them. I am certain we will find that they know where the thieves are and where the guns are."

"Are there any Neapolitans among yesterday's prisoners?" asked Wellington.

Colonel De Lancey sent a man to find out.

"Of course," continued Wellington, thoughtfully, "it would suit me much better to pay nothing at all. Merlin!" (This was his name for Jonathan Strange.) "If you will be so good as to conjure up a vision of the Neapolitans, perhaps we will gain some clue as to where they and the guns are to be found and then we can simply go and get them!"

"Perhaps," said Strange.

"I dare say there will be an oddly shaped mountain in the background," said his lordship cheerfully, "or a village with a distinctive church tower. One of the Spanish guides will soon recognize the place."

"I dare say," said Strange.

"You do not seem very sure of it."

"Forgive me, my lord, but – as I think I have said before – visions are precisely the wrong sort of magic for this sort of thing."[2]

"Well, have you any thing better to suggest?" asked his lordship.

---

[2] *Jonathan Strange to John Segundus*, Madrid, Aug. 20th, 1812.
"Whenever someone or something needs to be found, Lord Wellington is sure to ask me to conjure up a vision. It never works. The Raven King and the other *Aureates* had a sort of magic for finding things and persons. As I understand it they began with a silver basin of water. They divided the surface of the water into quarters with glittering lines of light. (By the by, John, I really cannot believe that you are having as much difficulty as you say in creating these lines. I *cannot* describe the magic any more clearly. They are the simplest things in the world!) The quarters represent Heaven, Hell, Earth and Faerie. It seems that you employ a spell of election to establish in which of these realms the person or thing you seek is to be found – but how it goes on from there I have not the least idea, and neither does Norrell. If I only had this magic! Wellington or his staff is forever giving me tasks which I cannot do or which I must leave half-completed because I do not have it. I feel the lack of it almost daily. Yet I have no time for experiment. And so, John, I would be infinitely obliged to you if you could spend a little time attempting this spell and let me know *immediately* if you have the least success."

There is nothing in any of John Segundus's surviving papers to suggest that he had any success in his attempts to retrieve this magic. However in the autumn of 1814 Strange realised that a passage in Paris Ormskirk's *Revelations of Thirty-Six Other Worlds* – long thought to be a description of a shepherd's counting rhyme – was in fact a somewhat garbled version of precisely this spell. By late 1814 both Strange and Mr Norrell were performing this magic with confidence.

"No, my lord. Not at present."

"Then it is decided!" said Lord Wellington. "Mr Strange, Colonel De Lancey and Major Grant can turn their attention to the discovery of these guns. Somerset and I will go and annoy the French." The brisk manner in which his lordship spoke suggested that he expected all of these things to start happening very soon. Strange and the gentlemen of the Staff swallowed the rest of their breakfast and went to their various tasks.

At about midday Lord Wellington and Fitzroy Somerset were seated upon their horses on a slight ridge near the village of Garcia Hernandez. On the stony plain below several brigades of British Dragoons were preparing to charge some squadrons of cavalry which formed the rearguard of the French Army.

Just then Colonel De Lancey rode up.

"Ah, Colonel!" said Lord Wellington. "Have you found me any Neapolitans?"

"There are no Neapolitans among the prisoners, my lord," said De Lancey. "But Mr Strange suggested we look among the dead upon yesterday's battlefield. By magical means he has identified seventeen corpses as Neapolitan."

"Corpses!" said Lord Wellington, putting down his telescope in surprise. "What in the world does he want corpses for?"

"We asked him that, my lord, but he grew evasive and would not answer. However he has asked that the dead men be put somewhere safe where they will be neither lost nor molested."

"Well, I suppose one ought not to employ a magician and then complain that he does not behave like other people," said Wellington.

At that moment an officer standing close by cried out that the Dragoons had increased their pace to a gallop and would soon be upon the French. Instantly the eccentricities of the magician were forgotten; Lord Wellington put his telescope to his eye and every man present turned his attention to the battle.

Strange meanwhile had returned from the battlefield to the castle at Alba de Tormes. In the Armoury Tower (the only part of the castle still standing) he had found a room that no one was using and had appropriated it. Scattered about the room were Norrell's forty books. They were all still more or less in one piece, though some were decidedly battered-looking. The floor was covered with Strange's notebooks and pieces of paper with scraps of spells and magical calculations scribbled on them. On a table in the centre of the room stood a wide and shallow silver bowl, filled with water. The shutters had been pulled tight and the only light in the room came from the silver bowl. All in all it was a veritable magician's cave and the pretty Spanish maid who brought coffee and almond biscuits at regular intervals was quite terrified and ran out again as soon as she had put down her trays.

An officer of the 18th Hussars called Whyte had arrived to assist Strange. Captain Whyte had lived for a time at the house of the British Envoy in Naples. He was adept at languages and understood the Neapolitan dialect perfectly.

Strange had no difficulty in conjuring up the visions but, just as he had predicted, the visions gave very little clue as to where the men were. The guns, he discovered, were half hidden behind some pale yellow rocks – the sort of rocks which were scattered liberally throughout the Peninsula – and the men were camped in a sparse woodland of olive and pine trees – the sort of woodland in fact that one might discover by casting one's glance in any direction.

Captain Whyte stood at Strange's side and translated everything the Neapolitans said into clear, concise English. But, though they stared into the silver bowl all day they learnt very little. When a man has been hungry for eighteen months, when he has not seen his wife or sweetheart for two years, when he has spent the last four months sleeping upon mud and stones his powers of conversation tend to be somewhat dulled. The Neapolitans had very little to say to each other and what they did say chiefly concerned the food they wished they were eating, the charms of the absent wives and

417

sweethearts they wished they were enjoying, and the soft feather mattresses they wished they were sleeping upon.

For half the night and most of the following day Strange and Captain Whyte remained in the Armoury Tower, engaged in the dull work of watching the Neapolitans. Towards the evening of the second day an *aide-de-camp* brought a message from Wellington. His lordship had set up his Headquarters at a place called Flores de Avila and Strange and Captain Whyte were summoned to attend him there. So they packed up Strange's books and the silver bowl and gathered their other possessions and set off along the hot, dusty roads.

Flores de Avila proved to be rather an obscure place; none of the Spanish men and women whom Captain Whyte accosted had heard of it. But when two of Europe's greatest armies have recently travelled along a road, they cannot help but leave some signs of their passing; Strange and Captain Whyte found that their best plan was to follow the trail of discarded baggage, broken carts, corpses and feasting black birds. Against a background of empty, stone-strewn plains these sights resembled nothing so much as images from a mediaeval painting of Hell and they provoked Strange to make a great many gloomy remarks upon the Horror and Futility of War. Ordinarily Captain Whyte, a professional soldier, would have felt inclined to argue, but he too was affected by the sombre character of their surroundings and only answered, "Very true, sir. Very true."

But a soldier ought not to dwell too long on such matters. His life is full of hardship and he must take his pleasure where he can. Though he may take time to reflect upon the cruelties that he sees, place him among his comrades and it is almost impossible for his spirits not to rise. Strange and Captain Whyte reached Flores de Avila at about nine o'clock and within five minutes they were greeting their friends cheerfully, listening to the latest gossip about Lord Wellington and making a great many inquiries about the previous day's battle – another defeat for the French. One would scarcely suppose they had seen any thing to distress them within the last twelvemonth.

The Headquarters had been set up in a ruined church on a hillside above the village and there Lord Wellington, Fitzroy Somerset, Colonel De Lancey and Major Grant were waiting to meet them.

For all that he had won two battles in as many days Lord Wellington was not in the best of tempers. The French Army, famed throughout Europe for the rapidity of its marches, had got away from him and was now well on the way to Valladolid and safety. "It is a perfect mystery to me how they get on so fast," he complained, "and I would give a great deal to catch up with them and destroy them. But this is the only army I have and if I wear it out I cannot get another."

"We have heard from the Neapolitans with the guns," Major Grant informed Strange and Captain Whyte. "They are asking a hundred dollars a piece for them. Six hundred dollars in all."

"Which is too much," said his lordship briefly. "Mr Strange, Captain Whyte, I hope you have good news for me?"

"Hardly, my lord," said Strange. "The Neapolitans are in a wood. But as to where that wood might be I have not the least idea. I am not sure how to progress. I have exhausted everything I know."

"Then you must quickly learn something else!"

For a moment Strange looked as if he was going to return his lordship an angry reply, but thinking better of it he sighed and inquired whether the seventeen dead Neapolitans were being kept safe.

"They have been put in the bell tower," said Colonel De Lancey. "Sergeant Nash has charge of them. Whatever you want them for, I advise you to use them soon. I doubt they will last much longer in this heat."

"They will last another night," said Strange. "The nights are cold." Then he turned and went out of the church.

Wellington's Staff watched him go with some curiosity. "You know," said Fitzroy Somerset, "I really cannot help wondering what he is going to do with seventeen corpses."

"Whatever it is," said Wellington, dipping his quill in the ink and beginning a letter to the Ministers in London, "he does not relish the thought of it. He is doing everything he can to avoid it."

That night Strange did a sort of magic he had never done before. He attempted to penetrate the dreams of the Neapolitan company. In this he was perfectly successful.

One man dreamt that he was chased up a tree by a vicious Roast Leg of Lamb. He sat in the tree weeping with hunger while the Leg of Lamb ran round and round and thrust its knob of bone at him in a menacing way. Shortly afterwards the Leg of Lamb was joined by five or six spiteful Boiled Eggs who whispered the most dreadful lies about him.

Another man dreamt that, as he was walking through a little wood, he met his dead mother. She told him that she had just looked down a rabbit hole and seen Napoleon Buonaparte, the King of England, the Pope and the Czar of Russia at the bottom. The man went down the rabbit hole to see, but when he arrived at the bottom he discovered that Napoleon Buonaparte, the King of England, the Pope and the Czar of Russia were in fact all the same person, a huge blubbering great man as big as a church with rusty iron teeth and burning cartwheels for eyes. "Ha!" sneered this ogre. "You did not think we were really different people, did you?" And it reached into a bubbling cauldron that stood nearby and pulled out the dreamer's little son and ate him. In short the Neapolitans' dreams, though interesting, were not very illuminating.

Next morning at about ten o'clock Lord Wellington was sitting at a makeshift desk in the chancel of the ruined church. He looked up and saw Strange entering the church. "Well?" he asked.

Strange sighed and said, "Where is Sergeant Nash? I need him to bring out the dead bodies. With your permission, my lord, I will try some magic that I heard of once."[3]

News quickly got about Headquarters that the magician was going to do something to the dead Neapolitans. Flores de Avila was a tiny place, scarcely more than a hundred dwellings. The previous evening had proved very dull for an army of young men who had just won a great victory and who felt inclined to celebrate and it was considered highly probable that Strange's magic would prove the best entertainment of the day. A small crowd of officers and men soon gathered to see it.

---

[3] Strange knew of it as a piece of magic done by the Raven King. Most of the King's magic was mysterious, beautiful, subtle, and so it comes as some surprize to us to learn that he should have employed any spell so brutal.

In the mid-thirteenth century several of the King's enemies were attempting to form an alliance against him. Most of its members were known to him: the King of France was one, the King of Scotland another, and there were several disaffected fairies who gave themselves grandiose titles and who may, or may not, have governed the vast territories they claimed. There were also other personages more mysterious, but even greater. The King had for most of his reign been on good terms with most angels and demons, but now it was rumoured that he had quarrelled with two: Zadkiel who governs mercy and Alrinach who governs shipwreck.

The King does not seem to have been greatly worried by the activities of the alliance. But he became more interested when certain magical portents seemed to shew that one of his own noblemen had joined with them and was plotting against him. The man he suspected was Robert Barbatus, Earl of Wharfdale, a man so known for his cunning and manipulative ways that he was nicknamed the Fox. In the King's eyes there was no greater crime than betrayal.

When the Fox's eldest son, Henry Barbatus, died of a fever, the Raven King had his body taken out of its grave and he brought him back to life to tell what he knew. Thomas of Dundale and William Lanchester both had a deep disgust for this particular sort of magic and pleaded with the King to employ some other means. But the King was bitterly angry and they could not dissuade him. There were a hundred other forms of magic he could have used, but none were so quick or so direct and, like most great magicians, the Raven King was nothing if not practical.

It was said that in his fury the Raven King beat Henry Barbatus. In life Henry had been a splendid young man, much admired for his handsome face and graceful manners, much feared for his knightly prowess. That such a noble knight should have been reduced to a cowering, whimpering doll by the King's magic made William Lanchester very angry and was the cause of a bitter quarrel between the two of them which lasted several years.

The church had a stone terrace which overlooked a narrow valley and a prospect of pale, towering mountains. Vineyards and olive groves clothed the slopes. Sergeant Nash and his men fetched the seventeen corpses from the bell tower and propped them up in a sitting position against a low wall that marked the edge of the terrace.

Strange walked along, looking at each in turn. "I thought I told you," he said to Sergeant Nash, "that I particularly did not want any one interfering with the corpses."

Sergeant Nash looked indignant. "I am sure, sir," he said, "that none of our lads has touched them. But my lord," he said, appealing to Lord Wellington, "there was scarcely a corpse on the battlefield that those Spanish irregulars had not done something to . . ." He expatiated on the various national failings of the Spanish and concluded that if a man so much as went to sleep where the Spanish could find him he would be sorry for it when he woke up.

Lord Wellington waved impatiently at the man to make him be quiet. "I do not see that they are very much mutilated," he said to Strange. "Does it matter if they are?"

Strange muttered blackly that he supposed it did not except that he had to look at them.

Indeed, most of the wounds that the Neapolitans bore appeared to have been the ones that killed them, but all of them had been stripped naked and several had had their fingers cut off – the better to remove their rings. One had been a handsome young man, but his beauty was very much marred now that someone had plucked out his teeth (to make false teeth) and cut off most of his black hair (to make wigs).

Strange told a man to fetch a sharp knife and a clean bandage. When the knife was brought he took off his coat and rolled up the sleeve of his shirt. Then he began muttering to himself in Latin. He next made a long, deep cut in his arm, and when he had got a good strong spurt of blood, he let it splash over the heads of the corpses, taking care to anoint the eyes, tongue and nostrils of each. After a moment the first corpse roused itself. There was a horrible rasping

sound as its dried-out lungs filled with air and its limbs shook in a way that was very dreadful to behold. Then one by one the corpses revived and began to speak in a guttural language which contained a much higher proportion of screams than any language known to the onlookers.

Even Wellington looked a little pale. Only Strange continued apparently without emotion.

"Dear God!" cried Fitzroy Somerset, "What language is that?"

"I believe it is one of the dialects of Hell," said Strange.

"Is it indeed?" said Somerset. "Well, that is remarkable."

"They have learnt it very quickly," said Lord Wellington, "They have only been dead three days." He approved of people doing things promptly and in a businesslike fashion. "But do you speak this language?" he asked Strange.

"No, my lord."

"Then how are we to talk to them?"

For answer Strange grasped the head of the first corpse, pulled open its jabbering jaws and spat inside its mouth. Instantly it began to speak in its native, *earthly* language – a thick Neapolitan dialect of Italian, which to most people was quite as impenetrable and almost as horrible as the language it had been speaking before. It had the advantage, however, of being perfectly comprehensible to Captain Whyte.

With Captain Whyte's help Major Grant and Colonel De Lancey interrogated the dead Neapolitans and were highly pleased by the answers they returned. Being dead, the Neapolitans were infinitely more anxious to please their questioners than any living informer could have been. It seemed that shortly before their deaths at the battle of Salamanca, these wretches had each received a secret message from their countrymen hidden in the woods, informing them of the capture of the cannon and telling them to make their way to a village a few leagues north of the city of Salamanca, from where they would easily be able to find the wood by following secret signs chalked on trees and boulders.

Major Grant took a small detachment of cavalry and within a few days he returned with both guns and deserters. Wellington was delighted.

Unfortunately, Strange was entirely unable to discover the spell for sending the dead Neapolitans back to their bitter sleep.[4] He made several attempts, but these had very little effect except that once he made all seventeen corpses suddenly shoot up until they were twenty feet tall and strangely transparent, like huge water-colour paintings of themselves done on thin muslin banners. When Strange had returned them to their normal size, the problem of what should be done with them remained.

At first they were placed with the other French prisoners. But the other prisoners protested loudly about being confined with such shambling, shuffling horrors. ("And really," observed Lord Wellington as he eyed the corpses with distaste, "one cannot blame them.")

So when the prisoners were sent back to England the dead Neapolitans remained with the Army. All that summer they travelled in a bullock cart and on Lord Wellington's orders they were shackled. The shackles were intended to restrict their move-ments and keep them in one place, but the dead Neapolitans were not afraid of pain – indeed they did not seem to feel it – so it was very little trouble to them to extricate themselves from their shackles, sometimes leaving pieces of themselves behind. As soon as they were free they would go in search of Strange and begin pleading with him in the most pitiful manner imaginable to restore them to the fullness of life. They had seen Hell and were not anxious to return there.

In Madrid the Spanish artist, Francisco Goya, made a sketch in red chalk of Jonathan Strange surrounded by the dead Neapo-litans. In the picture Strange is seated on the ground. His gaze is cast down and his arms hang limp at his sides and his whole

---

[4] To end the "lives" of the corpses you cut out their eyes, tongues and hearts.

attitude speaks of helplessness and despair. The Neapolitans crowd around him; some are regarding him hungrily; others have expressions of supplication on their faces; one is putting out a tentative finger to stroke the back of his hair. It is, needless to say, quite different from any other portrait of Strange.

On the 25th of August Lord Wellington gave an order for the dead Neapolitans to be destroyed.[5]

Strange was in some anxiety lest Mr Norrell get to hear of the magic he had done at the ruined church at Flores de Avila. He made no mention of it in his own letters and he begged Lord Wellington to leave it out of his Dispatches.

"Oh, very well!" said his lordship. Lord Wellington was not in any case particularly fond of writing about magic. He disliked having to deal with any thing he did not understand extremely well. "But it will do very little good," he pointed out. "Every man that has written a letter home in the last five days will have given his friends a very full account of it."

"I know," said Strange, uncomfortably, "but the men always exaggerate what I do and perhaps by the time people in England have made allowances for the usual embellishments it will not appear so very remarkable. They will merely imagine that I healed some Neapolitans that were wounded or something of that sort."

The raising of the seventeen dead Neapolitans was a good example of the sort of problem faced by Strange in the latter half of the war. Like the Ministers before him, Lord Wellington was becoming more accustomed to using magic to achieve his ends and

---

[5] "Concerning the dead Italian soldiers I can only say that we greatly regretted such cruelty to men who had already suffered a great deal. But we were obliged to act as we did. They could not be persuaded to leave the magician alone. If they had not killed him, then they would have certainly driven him mad. We were obliged to set two men to watch him while he slept to keep the dead men from touching him and waking him up. They had been so battered about since their deaths. They were not, poor fellows, a sight any one wished to see upon waking. In the end we made a bonfire and threw them on it."

Lord Fitzroy Somerset to his brother, 2nd Sept., 1812.

he demanded increasingly elaborate spells from his magician. However, unlike the Ministers, Wellington had very little time or inclination for listening to long explanations of why a thing was not possible. After all, he regularly demanded the impossible of his engineers, his generals and his officers and he saw no reason to make an exception of his magician. "Find another way!" was all he would say, as Strange tried to explain that such-and-such a piece of magic had not been attempted since 1302 – or that the spell had been lost – or that it had never existed in the first place. As in the early days of his magicianship, before he had met Norrell, Strange was obliged to invent most of the magic he did, working from general principles and half-remembered stories from old books.

In the early summer of 1813 Strange again performed a sort of magic the like of which had not been done since the days of the Raven King: he moved a river. It happened like this. The war that summer was going well and everything Lord Wellington did was crowned with success. However it so happened that one particular morning in June the French found themselves in a more advantageous position than had been the case for some time. His lordship and the other generals immediately gathered together to discuss what could be done to correct this highly undesirable situation. Strange was summoned to join them in Lord Wellington's tent. He found them gathered round a table upon which was spread a large map.

His lordship was in really excellent spirits that summer and he greeted Strange almost affectionately. "Ah, Merlin! There you are! Here is our problem! We are on this side of the river and the French are on the other side, and it would suit me much better if the positions were reversed."

One of the generals began to explain that if they marched the Army west *here*, and then built a bridge across the river *here*, and then engaged the French *here* . . .

"It will take too long!" declared Lord Wellington. "Far too long! Merlin, could not you arrange for the Army to grow wings and fly over the French? Could you do that, do you think?" His lordship was perhaps half-joking, but only half. "It is only a matter of supplying each man with a little pair of wings. Take Captain Macpherson for example," he said, eyeing an enormous Scotsman. "I have a great fancy to see Macpherson sprout wings and flutter about."

Strange regarded Captain Macpherson thoughtfully. "No," he said at last, "but I would be grateful, my lord, if you would permit me to borrow him – and the map – for an hour or two."

Strange and Captain Macpherson peered at the map for some time, and then Strange went back to Lord Wellington and said it would take too long for every man in the army to sprout wings, but it would take no time at all to move the river and would that do? "At the moment," said Strange, "the river flows south here and then twists northwards here. If upon the other hand it flowed north instead of south and twisted southwards here, then, you see, we would be on the north bank and the French on the south."

"Oh!" said his lordship. "Very well."

The new position of the river so baffled the French that several French companies, when ordered to march north, went in entirely the wrong direction, so convinced were they that the direction *away* from the river must be north. These particular companies were never seen again and so it was widely supposed that they had been killed by the Spanish *guerrilleros*.

Lord Wellington later remarked cheerfully to General Picton that there was nothing so wearying for troops and horses as constant marching about and that in future he thought it would be better to keep them all standing still, while Mr Strange moved Spain about like a carpet beneath their feet.

Meanwhile the Spanish Regency Council in Cadiz became rather alarmed at this development and began to wonder whether, when they finally regained their country from the French, they would recognize it. They complained to the Foreign Secretary (which many people thought ungrateful). The Foreign Secretary persuaded Strange to write the Regency Council a letter promising that after the war he would replace the river in its original position and also ". . . any thing else which Lord Wellington requires to be moved during the prosecution of the war." Among the many things which Strange moved were: a wood of olive trees and pines in Navarra;[6] the city of Pamplona;[7] and two churches in the town of St Jean de Luz in France.[8]

On the 6th April 1814 the Emperor Napoleon Buonaparte abdicated. It is said that when Lord Wellington was told he performed a little dance. When Strange heard the news he laughed aloud, and then suddenly stopped and murmured, "Dear God! What will

---

[6] Colonel Vickery had reconnoitred the wood and discovered it to be full of French soldiers waiting to shoot at the British Army. His officers were just discussing what to do about it when Lord Wellington rode up. "We could go round it, I suppose," said Wellington, "but that will take time and I am in a hurry. Where is the magician?"

Someone went and fetched Strange.

"Mr Strange!" said Lord Wellington. "I can scarcely believe that it will be much trouble to you to move these trees! A great deal less, I am sure, than to make four thousand men walk seven miles out of their way. Move the wood, if you please!"

So Strange did as he was asked and moved the wood to the opposite side of the valley. The French soldiers were left cowering on a barren hillside and very quickly surrendered to the British.

[7] Owing to a mistake in Wellington's maps of Spain the city of Pamplona was not exactly where the British had supposed it to be. Wellington was deeply disappointed when, after the Army had marched twenty miles in one day, they did *not* reach Pamplona which was discovered to be ten miles further north. After swift discussion of the problem it was found to be more convenient to have Mr Strange move the city, rather than change all the maps.

[8] The churches in St Jean de Luz were something of an embarrassment. There was no reason whatsoever to move them. The fact of the matter was that one Sunday morning Strange was drinking brandy for breakfast at a hotel in St Jean de Luz with three Captains and two lieutenants of the 16th Light Dragoons. He was explaining to these gentlemen the theory behind the magical transportation of various objects. It was an entirely futile undertaking: they would not have understood him very well had they been sober and neither they nor Strange had been entirely sober for two days. By way of an illustration Strange swapped the positions of the two churches with the congregations still inside them. He fully intended to change them round again before the people came out, but shortly afterwards he was called away to a game of billiards and never thought of it again. Indeed despite Strange's many assurances he never found the time or inclination to replace river, wood, city, or indeed any thing at all in its original position.

they do with us now?" It was presumed at the time that this somewhat enigmatic remark referred to the Army, but afterwards several people wondered if he might perhaps have been talking about himself and the other magician.

The map of Europe was created anew: Buonaparte's new kingdoms were dismantled and the old ones put back in their place; some kings were deposed; other were restored to their thrones. The peoples of Europe congratulated themselves on finally vanquishing the Great Interloper. But to the inhabitants of Great Britain it suddenly appeared that the war had had an entirely different purpose: it had made Great Britain the Greatest Nation in the World. In London Mr Norrell had the satisfaction of hearing from everyone that magic – his magic and Mr Strange's – had been of vital importance in achieving this.

One evening towards the end of May Arabella returned home from a Victory Dinner at Carlton House. She had heard her husband spoken of in terms of the warmest praise, toasts had been made in his honour and the Prince Regent had said a great many complimentary things to her. Now it was just after midnight and she was sitting in the drawing-room reflecting that all she needed to complete her happiness was her husband home again, when one of the maids burst in and cried out, "Oh, madam! The master is here!"

Someone came into the room.

He was a thinner, browner person than she remembered. His hair had more grey in it and there was a whitish scar above his left eyebrow. The scar was not recent, but she had never seen it before. His features were what they had always been, but somehow his air was different. This scarcely seemed to be the person she had been thinking of only a moment ago. But before she could be disappointed, or awkward, or any of the things she had feared she would be when he at last came home, he looked around the room with a quick, half-ironic glance that she knew in an instant. Then he looked at her with the most familiar smile in the world and said, "I'm home."

* * *

The next morning they still had not said a hundredth part of all they had to tell each other.

"Sit there," said Strange to Arabella.

"In this chair?"

"Yes."

"Why?"

"So that I may look at you. I have not looked at you for three years and I have long felt the lack of it. I must supply the deficiency."

She sat down, but after a moment or two she began to smile. "Jonathan, I cannot keep my countenance if you stare at me like that. At this rate you will have supplied the deficiency in half an hour. I am sorry to disappoint you, but you never did look at me so very often. You always had your nose in some dusty old book."

"Untrue. I had entirely forgotten how quarrelsome you are. Hand me that piece of paper. I shall make a note of it."

"I shall do no such thing," said Arabella, laughing.

"Do you know what my first thought upon waking this morning was? I thought I ought to get up and shave and breakfast before some other fellow's servant took all the hot water and all the bread rolls. Then I remembered that all the servants in the house were mine and all the hot water in the house was mine and all the bread rolls were mine too. I do not think I was ever so happy in my life."

"Were you never comfortable in Spain?"

"In a war one is either living like a prince or a vagabond. I have seen Lord Wellington – his Grace, I should say[9] – sleeping under a tree with only a rock for a pillow. At other times I have seen thieves

---

[9] The British Government made Lord Wellington a Duke. At the same time there was a great deal of talk of ennobling Strange. "A baronetcy is the least he will expect," said Lord Liverpool to Sir Walter, "and we would be perfectly justified in doing something more – what would you say to a viscountcy?" The reason that none of this ever happened was because, as Sir Walter pointed out, it was entirely impossible to bestow a title on Strange without doing something for Norrell and somehow no one in the Government liked Norrell well enough to wish to do it. The thought of having to address Mr Norrell as "Sir Gilbert" or "my lord" was somehow rather depressing.

and beggars snoring upon feather-beds in palace bed-chambers. War is a very topsy-turvy business."

"Well, I hope you will not find it dull in London. The gentleman with the thistle-down hair said that once you had tasted war, you were sure to be bored at home."

"Ha! No, indeed! What, with everything clean, and just so? And all one's books and possessions so close to hand and one's wife just before one whenever one looks up? What does . . . ? Who did you say it was? The gentleman with what sort of hair?"

"Thistle-down. I am sure you must know the person I mean. He lives with Sir Walter and Lady Pole. At least, I am not sure he lives there, but I see him whenever I go to the house."

Strange frowned. "I do not know him. What is his name?"

But Arabella did not know. "I have always supposed him to be a relation of Sir Walter or Lady Pole. How queer it is that I never thought to ask him his name. I have had, oh! hours of conversation with him!"

"Have you indeed? I am not sure that I approve of that. Is he handsome?"

"Oh, yes! Very! How odd that I do not know his name! He is very entertaining. Quite unlike most people one meets."

"And what do you talk of?"

"Oh, everything! But it always ends in him wishing to give me presents. On Monday last he wanted to fetch me a tiger from Bengal. On Wednesday he wished to bring me the Queen of Naples – because, he said, she and I are so much alike that we were sure to be the best of friends and on Friday he wished to send a servant to bring me a music-tree . . ."

"A music-tree?"

Arabella laughed. "A music-tree! He says that somewhere on a mountain with a storybook name there grows a tree which bears sheet music instead of fruit and the music is far superior to any other. I can never quite tell whether he believes his own tales or not. Indeed, there have been occasions when I have wondered if he is mad. I always make some excuse or other for not accepting his presents."

"I am glad. I should not at all have cared to come home and find the house full of tigers and queens and music-trees. Have you heard from Mr Norrell recently?"

"Not recently, no."

"Why are you smiling?" asked Strange.

"Was I? I did not know. Well then, I will tell you. He once sent me a message and that is all."

"Once? In three years?"

"Yes. About a year ago there was a rumour that you had been killed at Vitoria and Mr Norrell sent Childermass to ask if it was true. I knew no more than he did. But that evening Captain Moulthrop arrived. He had landed at Portsmouth not two days before and had come straight here to tell me that there was not a word of truth in it. I shall never forget his kindness! Poor young man! His arm had been amputated only a month or so before and he was still suffering very much. But there is a letter for you from Mr Norrell on the table. Childermass brought it yesterday."

Strange got up and went to the table. He picked up the letter and turned it over in his hands. "Well, I suppose I shall have to go," he said doubtfully.

The truth was that he was not looking forward to meeting his old tutor with any very great enthusiasm. He had become accustomed to independence of thought and action. In Spain he had had his instructions from the Duke of Wellington but what magic he did to fulfil those instructions had been entirely his own decision. The prospect of doing magic under Mr Norrell's direction again was not an appealing one; and after months spent in the company of Wellington's bold, dashing young officers, the thought of long hours with only Mr Norrell to talk to was a little grim.

Yet in spite of his misgivings it was a very cordial meeting. Mr Norrell was so delighted to see him, so full of questions about the precise nature of the spells he had employed in Spain, so full of praise for all that had been achieved, that Strange almost began to feel he had misjudged his tutor.

Naturally enough Mr Norrell would not hear of Strange's giving up his role as Mr Norrell's pupil. "No, no, no! You must return here! We have a great deal to do. Now the war is over, all the real work is ahead of us. We must establish magic for the Modern Age! I have had the most gratifying assurances from several Ministers who were anxious to assure me of the utter impossibility of their continuing to govern the country without the aid of our magic! And despite everything that you and I have done there are misconceptions! Why! Only the other day I overheard Lord Castlereagh tell someone that you had, at the Duke of Wellington's insistence, employed Black Magic in Spain! I was swift to assure his lordship that you had employed nothing but the most modern methods."

Strange paused and then inclined his head slightly in a manner which Mr Norrell certainly took for acquiescence. "But we were speaking of whether or not I should continue as your pupil. I have mastered all the sorts of magic on the list you made four years ago. You told me, sir, before I went to the Peninsula, that you were entirely delighted with my progress – as I dare say you remember."

"Oh! But that was barely a beginning. I have made another list while you were in Spain. I shall ring for Lucas to fetch it from the library. Besides, there are *other books*, you know, which I wish you to read." He blinked his little blue eyes nervously at Strange.

Strange hesitated. This was a reference to the library at Hurtfew Abbey which Strange had still not seen.

"Oh, Mr Strange!" exclaimed Mr Norrell. "I am very glad that you have come home, sir. I am very glad to see you! I hope we may have many hours of conversation. Mr Lascelles and Mr Drawlight have been here a great deal . . ."

Strange said he was sure of it.

". . . but there is no talking to them about magic. Come back tomorrow. Come early. Come to breakfast!"

32

The King

November 1814

EARLY IN NOVEMBER 1814 Mr Norrell was honoured by a visit from some very noble gentlemen – an earl, a duke and two baronets – who came, they said, to speak to him upon a matter of the utmost delicacy and were so discreet themselves that half an hour after they had begun talking Mr Norrell was still entirely ignorant of what they wished him to do.

It emerged that, elevated as these gentlemen were, they were the representatives of one still greater – the Duke of York – and they had come to speak to Mr Norrell about the madness of the King. The King's sons had recently paid a visit to their father and had been very shocked by his sad condition; and, though all of them were selfish and some of them were dissolute and none of them were much given to making sacrifices of any sort, they had all told each other how they would give any amount of money and cut off any number of limbs to make the King a little more comfortable.

But, just as the King's children quarrelled amongst themselves as to which doctor their father should have, so they now quarrelled as to whether or not a magician should attend the King. Chief in opposition to the idea was the Prince Regent. Many years before, during the life of the great Mr Pitt, the King had suffered a severe bout of madness and the Prince had ruled in his place, but then the King had recovered and the Prince had found his powers and privileges stripped away from him. Of all the tiresome situations in the world, thought the Prince Regent, the most tiresome was to rise from one's bed in a state of uncertainty as to whether or not one was the ruler of Great Britain. So perhaps the Prince might be forgiven for wishing that the King remain mad or, at least, only gain such relief as Death would supply.

Mr Norrell, who had no wish to offend the Prince Regent, declined to offer his assistance, adding that he doubted very much whether the King's illness were susceptible of treatment by magic. So the King's second son, the Duke of York, who was a military gentleman, asked the Duke of Wellington if he thought that Mr Strange might be persuaded to visit the King.

"Oh! I am certain of it!" replied the Duke of Wellington. "Mr Strange is always glad of an opportunity to do magic. Nothing pleases him more. The tasks I set him in Spain posed all sorts of difficulties and, though he made a great shew of complaining, the truth was he could not have been more delighted. I have a great opinion of Mr Strange's abilities. Spain is, as your Royal Highness knows, one of the most uncivilized places in the world, with scarcely any thoroughfare superior to a goat track from one end of the country to the other. But thanks to Mr Strange my men had good English roads to take them wherever they were needed and if there was a mountain or a forest or a city in our way, why! Mr Strange simply moved it somewhere else."

The Duke of York remarked that King Ferdinand of Spain had sent a letter to the Prince Regent complaining that many parts of his kingdom had been rendered entirely unrecognizable by the English magician and demanding that Mr Strange return and restore the country to its original form.

"Oh," said the Duke of Wellington, not much interested, "they are still complaining about that, are they?"

As a consequence of this conversation Arabella Strange came downstairs one Thursday morning to find her drawing-room full of the King's male offspring. There were five of them; their Royal

Highnesses the Dukes of York, Clarence, Sussex, Kent and Cambridge. They were all between forty and fifty years of age. All had been handsome once, but all were rather fond of eating and drinking, and consequently all were growing rather stout.

Mr Strange was standing with his elbow on the mantelpiece, one of Mr Norrell's books in his hand and a polite look of interest upon his face, while their Royal Highnesses all talked at the same time and interrupted one another in their eagerness to describe the terrible pathos of the King's situation.

"Were you to see how His Majesty dribbles his bread and milk when he eats," said the Duke of Clarence to Arabella with tears in his eyes, "how full of imaginary fears he is and how he holds long conversations with Mr Pitt who has been dead this age . . . well, my dear, you could not help but be brought very low by the sight." The Duke took Arabella's hand and began to stroke it, apparently under the impression that she was the parlour-maid.

"All of His Majesty's subjects are very sorry that he is ill," said Arabella. "None of us can think of his suffering with indifference."

"Oh, my dear!" cried the Duke delighted, "How it touches my heart to hear you say so!" and he planted a large wet royal kiss upon her hand and looked at her very tenderly.

"If Mr Norrell does not consider it a subject capable of treatment by magic then frankly I do not think the chances are good," said Strange. "But I will gladly wait upon His Majesty."

"In that case," said the Duke of York, "there is only the problem of the Willises."

"The Willises?" said Strange.

"Oh, indeed!" cried the Duke of Cambridge. "The Willises are more impertinent than any one can imagine."

"We must be careful not to vex the Willises too much," warned the Duke of Clarence, "or they are sure to revenge themselves upon His Majesty."

"The Willises will have a great many objections to Mr Strange visiting the King," sighed the Duke of Kent.

The Willises were two brothers who owned a madhouse in Lincolnshire. For many years now they had attended the King whenever His Majesty had happened to become mad. And whenever he had happened to be in his right mind the King had repeatedly told everyone how much he hated the Willises and how deeply he resented their cruel treatment of him. He had extracted promises from the Queen and the Dukes and the Princesses that, should he ever become mad again, they would not surrender him to the Willises. But it had done no good. At the first sign of delirium the Willises had been sent for, and they had come immediately and locked the King in a room and clapped him in a strait waistcoat and given him strong, purging medicines.

I believe it will puzzle my readers (for it puzzled everyone else) that a king should be so little able to command his own fate. But consider with what alarm the rumour of madness is greeted in private families. Consider then how much greater the alarm when the sufferer is the King of Great Britain! If you or I go mad, it is a misfortune for ourselves, our friends and family. When a king goes mad, it is a disaster for the whole Nation. Frequently in the past King George's illness had left it entirely uncertain who should govern the country. There were no precedents. No one had known what to do. It was not that the Willises were liked or respected – they were not. It was not that their treatments granted the King any relief from his torments – they did not. The secret of the Willises' success was that they were cool when everyone else was in a panic. They embraced a responsibility which everyone else was most anxious to avoid. In return they demanded absolute control of the King's person. No one was permitted to speak to the King without a Willis being present. Not the Queen, not the Prime Minister. Not even the King's thirteen sons and daughters.

"Well, said Strange when all this had been explained to him, "I admit that I would much rather speak to His Majesty without the encumbrance of other people – particularly people unfavourable to my purpose. However, I have upon occasion baffled the entire French Army. I dare say I can manage two doctors. Leave the Willises to me."

Strange refused to discuss the matter of a fee until he had seen the King. He would make no charge for visiting His Majesty, which the Dukes – who all had gambling debts to pay and houses full of illegitimate children to feed and educate – thought very handsome of him.

Early the next day Strange rode out to Windsor Castle to see the King. It was a sharp, cold morning and a thick, white mist lay everywhere. On the way he cast three small spells. The first ensured that the Willises would sleep long past their customary hour; the second spell caused the wives and servants of the Willises to forget to wake them; and the third made sure that when the Willises finally woke, none of their clothes or boots would be in the places where they had left them. Two years earlier Strange would have scrupled to play even so slight a trick as this upon two strangers, but now he did not give it a second thought. Like many other gentlemen who had been in Spain with the Duke of Wellington, he had begun unconsciously to imitate his Grace, part of whose character it was always to act in the most direct way possible.[1]

Towards ten o'clock he crossed the River Thames by the little wooden bridge at the village of Datchet. He passed along the lane between the river and the Castle wall and entered the town of Windsor. At the Castle-gate he told the sentry who he was and his business with the King. A servant in a blue uniform appeared to escort him to the King's apartments. The servant was a civil, intelligent sort of man and, as often happens with servants in grand places, he was excessively proud of the Castle and every thing to do with it. His chief pleasure in life laying in shewing people around the Castle and in fancying them astonished, awed

---

[1] In *The Life of Jonathan Strange*, John Segundus discusses other ways in which he believes Strange's later actions were influenced by the Duke of Wellington.

and amazed. "Surely this cannot be your first visit to the Castle, sir?" was his first question to Strange.

"Upon the contrary. I was never here in my life."

The man looked shocked. "Then, sir, you have missed one of the noblest sights that England has to offer!"

"Indeed? Well, I am here now."

"But you are here on business, sir," answered the servant in a reproving tone, "and will not, I dare say, have leisure to examine everything properly. You must come again, sir. In summer. And in case you should be a married gentleman, I take the liberty of observing that ladies are always particularly delighted with the Castle."

He led Strange through a courtyard of impressive size. Long ago, in times of war it must have provided a refuge for a large number of people and their livestock and there were still a few ancient buildings in a very simple style that bore witness to the military character which the Castle had originally possessed. But as time had gone on the desire for kingly pomp and splendour had begun to outweigh more utilitarian considerations and a magnificent church had been built which filled up most of the space. This church (called the Chapel, but in truth more like a Cathedral) displayed all the complexity and elaborateness of which the Gothic style is capable. It was hedged about with prickly stone buttresses, crowned with stone pinnacles and it bulged with chapels, oratories and vestries.

The servant took Strange past a steep mound with smooth sides, surmounted by the round tower which is the most easily recognizable part of the Castle when viewed from a distance. Passing through a mediaeval gateway, they entered another courtyard. This was almost as magnificently proportioned as the first courtyard, but whereas the other had been peopled with servants, soldiers and household officials, this was silent and empty.

"It is a great pity that you did not come here a few years ago, sir," said the servant. "At that time it was possible to visit the King and Queen's Apartments upon application to the housekeeper, but His Majesty's illness has made that impossible."

He led Strange to an imposing Gothic entrance in the middle of a long range of stone buildings. As they mounted a flight of stone stairs he continued to bemoan the many obstacles which stood in the way of Strange's seeing the Castle. He could not help but suppose Strange's disappointment to be very great. "I have it!" he declared suddenly. "I will shew you St George's Hall! Oh, it is not a hundredth part of what you ought to see, sir, but still it will give you a notion of the sublimity of which Windsor Castle is capable!"

At the top of the stairs he turned to the right and went swiftly through a hall with arrangements of swords and pistols upon the walls. Strange followed. They entered a long and lofty hall, some two or three hundred feet long.

"There!" said the servant with as much satisfaction as if he had built and decorated it himself.

Tall, arched windows along the south wall let in the cold, misty light. The lower part of the walls was panelled with pearwood and the panels all had carved and gilded borders. The upper part of the walls and the ceiling were covered with paintings of gods and goddesses, kings and queens. The ceiling shewed Charles II in the process of being carried up to eternal glory upon a white and blue cloud, surrounded by fat, pink cherubs. Generals and diplomats laid trophies at his feet, while Julius Caesar, Mars, Hercules and various important personages stood about in some embarrassment, having been suddenly struck with a mortifying conscious-ness of their inferiority to the British King.

All of this was most magnificent, but the painting which caught Strange's eye was a huge mural that stretched the entire length of the north wall. In the middle were two kings seated upon two thrones. On each side stood or knelt knights, ladies, courtiers, pages, gods and goddesses. The left-hand part of the painting was steeped in sunlight. The king upon this side was a strong, hand-some man who displayed all the vigour of youth. He was dressed in a pale robe and his hair was golden and curling. There was a laurel wreath upon his brow and a sceptre in his hand. The people and gods who attended him were all equipped with helmets, breast-plates, spears and swords, as if the artist wished to suggest that this king only attracted the most warlike of men and gods to be his friends. In the right-hand part of the painting the light grew dim and dusky, as if the artist meant to depict a summer's twilight. Stars shone above and around the figures. The king on this side was pale-skinned and dark-haired. He wore a black robe and his expression was unfathomable. He had a crown of dark ivy leaves and in his left hand he held a slim ivory wand. His entourage was composed largely of magical creatures: a phoenix, a unicorn, a manticore, fauns and satyrs. But there were also some mysterious persons: a male figure in a monklike robe with his hood pulled down over his face, a female figure in a dark, starry mantle with her arm thrown over her eyes. Between the two thrones stood a young woman in a loose white robe with a golden helmet upon her head. The warlike king had placed his left hand protectively upon her shoulder; the dark king held out his right hand towards her and she had extended her hand to his so that their fingertips lightly touched.

"The work of Antonio Verrio, an Italian gentleman," said the servant. He pointed to the king upon the left. "That is Edward the Third of Southern England." He pointed to the king upon the right, "And that is the Magician-King of Northern England, John Uskglass."

"Is it though?" said Strange, greatly interested. "I have seen statues of him of course. And engravings in books. But I do not think I ever saw a painting before. And the lady between the two kings, who is she?"

"That is Mrs Gwynn, one of the mistresses of Charles II. She is meant to represent Britannia."

"I see. It is something, I suppose, that he still has a place of honour in the King's house. But then they put him in Roman dress

442

and make him hold hands with an actress. I wonder what he would say to that?"

The servant led Strange back through the weapon-lined room to a black door of imposing size overtopped with a great jutting marble pediment.

"I can take you no further than this, sir. My business ends here and the Dr Willises' begins. You will find the King behind that door." He bowed and went back down the stairs.

Strange knocked on the door. From somewhere inside came the sound of a harpsichord and someone singing.

The door opened to reveal a tall, broad fellow of thirty or forty. His face was round, white, pockmarked and bedabbled with sweat like a Cheshire cheese. All in all he bore a striking resemblance to the man in the moon who is reputed to be made of cheese. He had shaved himself with no very high degree of skill and here and there on his white face two or three coarse black hairs appeared – rather as if a family of flies had drowned in the milk before the cheese was made and their legs were poking out of it. His coat was of rough brown drugget and his shirt and neckcloth were of the coarsest linen. None of his clothes were particularly clean.

"Yes?" he said, keeping his hand upon the door as if he intended to shut it again at the least provocation. He had very little of the character of a palace servant and a great deal of the character of a madhouse attendant, which was what he was.

Strange raised his eyebrow at this rude behaviour. He gave his name rather coldly and said he had come to see the King.

The man sighed. "Well, sir, I cannot deny that we were expecting you. But, you see, you cannot come in. Dr John and Dr Robert . . ." (These were the names of the two Willis brothers) ". . . are not here. We have been expecting them every minute for the past hour and a half. We do not understand where they can have got to."

"That is most unfortunate," said Strange. "But it is none of my concern. I have no desire to see the gentlemen you mention. My business is with the King. I have a letter signed by the Archbishops of Canterbury and York granting me permission to visit His Majesty today." Strange waved the letter in the man's face.

"But you must wait, sir, until Dr John and Dr Robert come. They will not allow any one to interfere with their system of managing the King. Silence and seclusion are what suits the King best. Conversation is the very worst thing for him. You can scarcely imagine, sir, what terrible harm you might do to the King merely by speaking to him. Say you were to mention that it is raining. I dare say you would consider that the most innocent remark in the world. But it might set the King a-thinking, you see, and in his madness his mind runs on from one thing to another, enraging him to a most dangerous degree. He might think of times in the past when it rained and his servants brought him news of battles that were lost, and daughters that were dead, and sons that had disgraced him. Why! It might be enough to kill the King outright! Do you want to kill the King, sir?"

"No," said Strange.

"Well, then," said the man coaxingly, "do you not see, sir, that it would be far better to wait for Dr John and Dr Robert?"

"Thank you, but I think I will take my chances. Conduct me to the King if you please."

"Dr John and Dr Robert will be very angry," warned the man.

"I do not care if they are," replied Strange coolly.

The man looked entirely astonished at this.

"Now," said Strange, with a most determined look and another flourish of his letter, "will you let me see the King or will you defy the authority of two Archbishops? That is a very grave matter, punishable by . . . well, I do not exactly know what, but something rather severe, I should imagine."

The man sighed. He called to another man (as rough and dirty as himself) and told him to go immediately to the houses of Dr John and Dr Robert to fetch them. Then with great reluctance he stood aside for Strange to enter.

The proportions of the room were lofty. The walls were panelled in oak and there was a great deal of fine carving. More royal and symbolic personages lounged about upon clouds on the ceiling. But it was a dreary place. There was no covering upon the floor and it was very cold. A chair and a battered-looking harpsichord were the only furniture. An old man was seated at the harpsichord with his back to them. He was dressed in a dressing-gown of ancient purple brocade. There was a crumpled nightcap of scarlet velvet on his head and dirty broken slippers on his feet. He was playing with great vigour and singing loudly in German. When he heard the sound of approaching footsteps he stopped.

"Who's there?" he demanded. "Who is it?"

"The magician, Your Majesty," said the madhouse attendant.

The old man seemed to consider this a moment and then he said in a loud voice, "It is a profession to which I have a particular dislike!" He struck the keys of his harpsichord again and resumed his loud singing.

This was rather a discouraging beginning. The madhouse attendant gave an impertinent snigger and walked off, leaving Strange and the King alone. Strange took a few paces further into the room and placed himself where he might observe the King's face.

It was a face in which all the misery of madness was compounded by the misery of blindness. The eyes had irises of clouded blue and whites as discoloured as rotten milk. Long locks of whitish hair streaked with grey hung down on either side of cheeks patched with broken veins. As the King sang, spittle flew from his slack red lips. His beard was almost as long and white as his hair. He was nothing at all like the pictures Strange had seen of him, for they had been made when he was in his right mind. With his long hair, long beard and long, purple robe, what he chiefly resembled was someone very tragic and ancient out of Shakespeare – or, rather, two very tragic and ancient persons out of Shakespeare. In his madness and his blindness he was Lear and Gloucester combined.

Strange had been cautioned by the Royal Dukes that it was contrary to Court etiquette to speak to the King unless the King addressed him first. However there seemed little hope of this since the King disliked magicians so much. So when the King ceased his playing and singing again, he said, "I am Your Majesty's humble servant, Jonathan Strange of Ashfair in Shropshire. I was Magician-in-Ordinary to the Army during the late war in Spain where, I am happy to say, I was able to do Your Majesty some service. It is the hope of Your Majesty's sons and daughters that my magic might afford Your Majesty some relief from your illness."

"Tell the magician I do not see him!" said the King airily.

Strange did not trouble to make any reply to this nonsensical remark. Of course the King could not see him, the King was blind.

"But I see his companion *very well!*" continued His Majesty in an approving tone. He turned his head as though to gaze at a point two or three feet to the left of Strange. "With such silver hair as he has got, I think I ought to be able to see him! He looks a very wild fellow."

So convincing was this speech that Strange actually turned to look. Of course there was no one.

In the past few days he had searched Norrell's books for something pertinent to the King's condition. There were remarkably few spells for curing madness. Indeed he had found only one, and even then he was not sure that was what it was meant for. It was a prescription in Ormskirk's *Revelations of Thirty-Six Other Worlds*. Ormskirk said that it would dispel illusions and correct wrong ideas. Strange took out the book and read through the spell again. It was a peculiarly obscure piece of magic, consisting only of the following words:

Place the moon at his eyes and her whiteness shall devour the false sights the deceiver has placed there.
Place a swarm of bees at his ears. Bees love truth and will destroy the deceiver's lies.

Place salt in his mouth lest the deceiver attempt to delight him with the taste of honey or disgust him with the taste of ashes.

Nail his hand with an iron nail so that he shall not raise it to do the deceiver's bidding.

Place his heart in a secret place so that all his desires shall be his own and the deceiver shall find no hold there.

Memorandum. The colour red may be found beneficial.

However, as Strange read it through, he was forced to admit that he had not the least idea what it meant.[2] How was the magician supposed to fetch the moon to the afflicted person? And if the second part were correct, then the Dukes would have done better to employ a beekeeper instead of a magician. Nor could Strange believe that their Royal Highnesses would be best pleased if he began piercing the King's hands with iron nails. The note about the colour red was odd too. He thought he remembered hearing or reading something about red but he could not at present recall what it was.

The King, meanwhile, had fallen into conversation with the imaginary silver-haired person. "I beg your pardon for mistaking you for a common person," he said. "You may be a king just as you say, but I merely take the liberty of observing that I have never heard of any of your kingdoms. Where is Lost-hope? Where are the Blue Castles? Where is the City of Iron Angels? I, on the other hand, am King of *Great Britain*, a place everyone knows and which is clearly marked on all the maps!" His Majesty paused, presumably to attend to the silver-haired person's reply for he suddenly cried out, "Oh, do not be angry! Pray, do not be angry! You are a king and I am a king! We shall all be kings together!

[2] The likelihood was that neither did Ormskirk. He had simply written down a spell that someone else had told him or that he had found in another book. This is a perennial problem with the writings of the *Argentine* magicians. In their anxiety to preserve any scrap of magical knowledge, they were often obliged to set down what they themselves did not understand.

And there is really no need for either of us to be angry! I shall play and sing for you!" He drew a flute from the pocket of his dressing-gown and began to play a melancholy air.

As an experiment Strange reached forward and plucked off His Majesty's scarlet nightcap. He watched closely to see if the King grew any more mad without it, but after several minutes of observation he was forced to admit that he could see no difference. He put the nightcap back on.

For the next hour and a half he tried all the magic he could think of. He cast spells of remembering, spells of finding, spells of awakening, spells to concentrate the mind, spells to dispel night-mares and evil thoughts, spells to find patterns in chaos, spells to find a path when one was lost, spells of demystification, spells of discernment, spells to increase intelligence, spells to cure sickness and spells to repair a limb that is shattered. Some of the spells were long and complicated. Some were a single word. Some had to be said out loud. Some had only to be thought. Some had no words at all but consisted of a single gesture. Some were spells that Strange and Norrell had employed in some form or other every day for the last five years. Some had probably not been used for centuries. Some used a mirror; two used a tiny bead of blood from the magician's finger; and one used a candle and a piece of ribbon. But they all had this in common: they had no effect upon the King whatsoever.

At the end of this time: "Oh, I give up!" thought Strange.

His Majesty, who had been happily unconscious of the magic directed at him, was chatting confidentially to the person with the silver hair that only he could see. "Have you been sent here for ever or can you go away again? Oh, do not stay to be caught! This is a bad place for kings! They put us in strait waistcoats! The last time I was permitted to go out of these rooms was on a Monday in 1811. They tell me that was three years ago, but they lie! By my calculation, it will be two hundred and forty-six years on Saturday fortnight!"

"Poor, unhappy gentleman!" thought Strange. "Shut away in

449

this cold, melancholy place without friends or amusements! Small wonder time passes so slowly for him. Small wonder he is mad!"

Out loud he said, "I shall be very happy to take you outside, Your Majesty, if you wish it."

The King paused in his chatter and turned his head slightly. "Who said that?" he demanded.

"I did, Your Majesty. Jonathan Strange, the magician." Strange made the King a respectful bow, before recollecting that His Majesty could not see it.

"Great Britain! My dear Kingdom!" cried the King. "How I should love to see her again – especially now that it is summertime. The trees and meadows are all decked in their brightest finery and the air is sweet as cherry-tart!"

Strange glanced out of the window at the white, icy mist and the skeletal winter trees. "Quite so. And I would account it a great honour if Your Majesty would accompany me outside."

The King seemed to consider this proposal. He took off one of his slippers and attempted to balance it upon his head. When this did not work, he put the slipper back on, took a tassel that hung from the end of his dressing-gown cord and sucked upon it thoughtfully. "But how do I know that you are not a wicked demon come to tempt me?" he asked at last in a tone of the most complete reasonableness.

Strange was somewhat lost for an answer to this question. While he was considering what to say, the King continued, "Of course if you are a wicked demon, then you should know that I am Eternal and cannot die. If I discover that you are my Enemy, I shall stamp my foot and send you straight back to Hell!"

"Really? Your Majesty must teach me the trick of that. I should like to know something so useful. But permit me to observe that, with such powerful magic at your command, Your Majesty has nothing to fear from accompanying me outside. We should leave as quickly and discreetly as we can. The Willises are sure to be here soon. Your Majesty must be very quiet!"

The King said nothing, but he tapped his nose and looked very sly.

Strange's next task was to discover a way out without alerting the madhouse attendants. The King was no help at all in this regard. When asked where the various doors led to, he gave it as his opinion that one door led to America, another to Everlasting Perdition and a third might possibly be the way to next Friday. So Strange picked one – the one the King thought led to America – and quickly escorted His Majesty through several rooms. All had painted ceilings in which English monarchs were depicted as dashing about the sky in fiery chariots, vanquishing persons who symbolized Envy, Sin and Sedition, and establishing Temples of Virtue, Palaces of Eternal Justice and other useful institutions of that sort. But though the ceilings were full of the most intense activity, the rooms beneath them were forlorn, threadbare and full of dust and spiders. The furniture was all covered up with sheets so that it appeared as if these chairs and tables must have died some time ago and these were their gravestones.

They came to a sort of back-staircase. The King, who had taken Strange's warning to be quiet very much to heart, insisted upon tip-toeing down the stairs in the highly exaggerated manner of a small child. This took some time.

"Well, Your Majesty," said Strange, cheerfully, when at last they reached the bottom, "I think we managed that rather well. I do not hear any sounds of pursuit. The Duke of Wellington would be glad to employ either of us as Intelligence Officers. I do not believe that Captain Somers-Cocks or Colquhoun Grant himself could have crossed enemy territory with more . . ."

He was interrupted by the King playing a very loud, very triumphant blare upon his flute.

"D—!" said Strange and listened for sounds of the madhouse attendants coming or, worse still, the Willises.

But nothing happened. Somewhere close at hand there was an odd, irregular thumping and clattering, accompanied by screams and wailing – rather as if someone were being beaten by a whole cupboardful of brooms at once. Apart from that, all was quiet.

A door opened on to a broad stone terrace. From here the land descended steeply and at the foot of the slope lay a Park. On the right a long, double line of winter trees could be just seen.

Arm in arm the King and Strange walked along the terrace to the corner of the Castle. Here Strange found a path leading down the slope and into the Park. They descended this path and had not walked far into the Park when they came upon an ornamental pool, bounded by a low stone rim.[3] At its centre stood a little stone pavilion decorated with carved creatures. Some resembled dogs – except that their bodies were long and low like lizards and each had a row of spines along its back. Others were meant to represent curved stone dolphins which had somehow contrived to fasten themselves to the walls. On the roof half a dozen classical ladies and gentlemen were sitting in classical attitudes, holding vases. It had clearly been the architect's intention that fountains of water should gush out of the mouths of all these strange animals and out of the vases on the roof and tumble decoratively into the pool, but just now all was frozen and silent.

Strange was about to make some remark on the melancholy sight which this frozen pool presented, when he heard several shouts. He looked back and saw that a group of people was descending the slope of the Castle very rapidly. As they drew nearer he saw that they were four in number: two gentlemen he had never seen before and the two madhouse attendants – the one with the face like a Cheshire cheese and the one who had been sent to fetch the Willises. They all looked angry.

The gentlemen hurried up, frowning in an important, offended sort of manner. They shewed every symptom of having dressed in a

---

[3] This pool and the line of trees were all that remained of a vast ornamental garden planned by King William III which had been begun, but never completed. It had been abandoned when the cost proved far too great. The land had been allowed to return to its former state of Park and meadow.

great hurry. One was attempting to fasten the buttons of his coat, but without much success. As soon as he did up the buttons, they flew open again. He was about Mr Norrell's age and wore an old-fashioned wig (rather like Mr Norrell's) which from time to time made a little jump and spun round on his head. But he differed from Mr Norrell in that he was rather tall, rather handsome and had an imposing, decisive manner. The other gentleman (who was several years younger) was plagued by his boots, which seemed to have developed opinions of their own. While he was struggling to walk forwards, they were attempting to carry him off in an entirely different direction. Strange could only suppose that his earlier magic had been rather more successful than he had expected and had made the clothes themselves difficult to manage.

The tallest gentleman (the one who wore the playful wig) gave Strange a furious stare. "Upon whose authority is the King outside?" he demanded.

Strange shrugged. "Mine, I suppose."

"You! Who are you?"

Not liking the manner in which he was addressed, Strange retorted, "Who are you?"

"I am Dr John Willis. This is my brother, Dr Robert Darling Willis. We are the King's physicians. We have charge of the King's person by order of the Queen's Council. No one is allowed to see His Majesty without our permission. I ask you again: who are you?"

"I am Jonathan Strange. I have come at the request of their Royal Highnesses the Dukes of York, Clarence, Sussex, Kent and Cambridge to see whether or not His Majesty might be cured by magic."

"Ha!" cried Dr John contemptuously. "Magic! That is chiefly used for killing Frenchmen, is it not?"

Dr Robert laughed in a sarcastic manner. But the effect of cold, scientific disdain was rather spoilt when his boots suddenly carried him off with such force that he banged his nose against a tree.

"Well, Magician!" said Dr John. "You mistake your man if you think you may mistreat me and my servants with impunity. You will admit, I dare say, that you glued the doors of the Castle shut by magic, so that my men could not prevent you leaving?"

"Certainly not!" declared Strange. "I did nothing of the sort! I *might* have done it," he conceded, "if there had been any need. But your men are as idle as they are impertinent! When His Majesty and I left the Castle they were nowhere to be seen!"

The first madhouse attendant (the one with a face like a Cheshire cheese) almost exploded upon hearing this. "That is not true!" he cried. "Dr John, Dr Robert, I beg that you will not listen to these lies! Martin here," he indicated the other madhouse attendant, "has had his voice entirely taken from him. He could not make a sound to raise the alarm!" The other madhouse attendant mouthed and gestured furiously in confirmation. "As for me, sir, I was in the passageway at the bottom of the stairs, when the door opened at the top. I was just readying myself to speak to this magician – and some strong words I was going to give him too, sir, on your behalf – when I was pulled by magic into a broom cupboard and the door shut fast upon me . . ."

"What nonsense!" cried Strange.

"Nonsense, is it?" cried the man. "And I suppose you did not make the brooms in the cupboard beat me! I am all over bruises."

This, at least, was perfectly true. His face and hands were covered in red marks.

"There, Magician!" cried Dr John, triumphantly. "What do you say now? Now that all your tricks are exposed?"

"Oh, really!" said Strange. "He has done that to himself to make his story more convincing!"

The King blew a vulgar noise on his flute.

"Be assured," said Dr John, "that the Queen's Council will soon hear of your impudence!" Then, turning away from Strange, he cried out, "Your Majesty! Come here!"

The King skipped nimbly behind Strange.

"You will oblige me by returning the King to my care," said Dr John.

"I will do no such thing," declared Strange.

"And you know how lunatics should be treated, do you?" said Dr Robert with a sneer. "You have studied the matter?"

"I know that to keep a man without companionship, to deny him exercise and a change of air cannot possibly cure any thing," said Strange. "It is barbaric! I would not keep a dog so."

"In speaking as you do," added Dr Robert, "you merely betray your ignorance. The solitude and tranquility of which you complain so vigorously are the cornerstones of our whole system of treating the King."

"Oh!" said Strange. "You call it a system, do you? And what does it consist of, this system?"

"There are three main principles," declared Dr Robert. "Intimidation . . ."

The King played a few sad notes upon his flute . . .

". . . isolation . . ."

. . . which became a lonely little tune . . .

". . . and restraint."

. . . ending in a long note like a sigh.

"In this way," continued Dr Robert, "all possible sources of excitement are suppressed and the patient is denied material with which to construct his fantasies and improper notions."

"But in the end," added Dr John, "it is by the imposition of his will upon his patient that the doctor effects his cure. It is the forcefulness of the doctor's own character which determines his success or failure. It was observed by many people that our father could subdue lunatics merely by fixing them with his eye."

"Really?" said Strange, becoming interested in spite of himself. "I had never thought of it before, but something of the sort is certainly true of magic. There are all sorts of occasions when the success of a piece of magic depends upon the forcefulness of the magician's character."

"Indeed?" said Dr John, glancing briefly to his left.

"Yes. Take Martin Pale for example. Now he . . ." Strange's eyes involuntarily followed where Dr John had looked. One of the madhouse attendants – the one who could not speak – was creeping around the ornamental pool towards the King with a pale-coloured something in his hands. Strange could not think at first what it could be. And then he recognized it. It was a strait waistcoat.

Several things happened at once. Strange shouted something – he did not know what – the other madhouse attendant lunged towards the King – both Willises attempted to grab Strange – the King blew piercing shrieks of alarm on his flute – and there was an odd noise as if a hundred or so people had all cleared their throats at once.

Everyone stopped and looked about them. The sound appeared to have come from the little stone pavilion at the centre of the frozen pool. Suddenly out of the mouths of each stone creature a dense white cloud appeared, as if they had all exhaled at once. The breath-clouds glittered and sparkled in the thin, misty light, and then fell upon the ice with a faint tinkling sound.

There was a silence, followed immediately by a horrible sound like blocks of marble being ripped apart. Then the stone creatures tore themselves from the walls of the pavilion and began to crawl and waddle down and across the ice towards the Willises. Their blank stone eyes rolled in their sockets. They opened their stone mouths and from every stone throat came a plume of water. Stone tails snaked from side to side and stone legs went stiffly up and down. The lead pipes which conducted water to their mouths extended magically behind them.

The Willises and the madhouse attendants stared, quite unable to comprehend what was happening. The grotesque creatures crawled, dragging their pipes behind them and dousing the Willises with water. The Willises shrieked and leapt about, more from fright than because of any real hurt they had sustained.

The madhouse attendants ran away and as to the Willises remaining any longer with the King, there could be no question of it. In the cold air their drenched clothes were turning icy.

"Magician!" cried Dr John, as he turned to run back to the Castle. "Why! It is just another name for liar! Lord Liverpool shall know of it, Magician! He shall know how you use the King's physicians! Ow! Ow!" He would have said more but the stone figures on the roof of the pavilion had stood up and begun pelting him with stones.

Strange merely bestowed a contemptuous smile on both Willises. But he was acting more confident than he felt. The truth was he was beginning to feel decidedly uncomfortable. Whatever magic had just been done, had not been done by him.

33

Place the moon at my eyes

November 1814

IT WAS MOST mysterious. Could someone in the Castle be a magician? One of the servants perhaps? Or one of the Princesses? It did not seem likely. Could it be Mr Norrell's doing? Strange pictured his tutor sitting in his little room upon the second floor at Hanover-square peering into his silver dish, watching all that had happened and finally driving away the Willises with magic. It was possible, he supposed. Bringing statues to life was, after all, something of a speciality of Mr Norrell's. It had been the first magic to bring him to the public notice. And yet, and yet . . . Why would Mr Norrell suddenly decide to help him? Out of the kindness of his heart? Hardly. Besides there had been a dark humour in the magic which was not like Norrell at all. The magician had not merely wanted to frighten the Willises; he had wanted to make them ridiculous. No, it could not be Norrell. But who then?

The King did not seem in the least fatigued. In fact he was more inclined to dance and skip about and generally rejoice over the defeat of the Willises. So, thinking that further exercise would certainly do His Majesty no harm, Strange walked on.

The white mist had erased all detail and colour from the landscape and left it ghostly. Earth and sky were blended together in the same insubstantial grey element.

The King took Strange's arm in a most affectionate manner and seemed to have quite forgot that he disliked magicians. He began to talk about the things that preoccupied him in his madness. He was convinced that a great many disasters had befallen Great Britain since he had become mad. He seemed to imagine that the wreck of his own reason must be matched by a corresponding wreck of the kingdom. Chief among these delusions was the belief that London had been drowned in a great flood. ". . . and when they came to me and said that the cold, grey waters had closed over the dome of St Paul's Cathedral and that London was become a domain of fishes and sea-monsters, my feelings are not to be described! I believe I wept for three weeks together! Now the buildings are all covered in barnacles and the markets sell nothing but oysters and sea-urchins! Mr Fox told me that three Sundays ago he went to St Vedast in Foster-lane where he heard an excellent sermon preached by a turbot.[1] But I have a plan for my kingdom's restoration! I have dispatched ambassadors to the King of the Fishes with proposals that I should marry a mermaid and so end the strife between our two great Nations! . . ."

The other subject which preoccupied His Majesty was that of the silver-haired person whom only he could see. "He says he is a king," he whispered eagerly, "but I believe he is an angel! With all that silver hair I think it very likely. And those two Evil Spirits – the ones you were talking to – he has been abusing them most horribly. It is my belief he has come to smite them and cast them into a fiery pit! Then, no doubt, he will carry you and me away to glory in Hanover!"

"Heaven," said Strange. "Your Majesty means Heaven."

They walked on. Snow began to fall, a slow tumble of white over a pale grey world. It was very quiet.

---

[1] Charles James Fox, a radical politician who had died some eight years before. This remark proves how far the King's wits were deranged: Mr Fox was a celebrated atheist who would never upon any inducement have entered a church.

Suddenly the sound of a flute was heard. The music was unutterably lonely and mournful, but at the same time full of nobility.

Thinking that it must be the King who was playing, Strange turned to watch. But the King was standing with his hands at his side and his flute in his pocket. Strange looked around. The mist was not dense enough to hide anyone who might have been standing near them. There was no one. The Park was empty.

"Ah, listen!" cried the King. "He is describing the tragedy of the King of Great Britain. That run of notes there! That is for past powers all gone! That melancholy phrase! That is for his Reason destroyed by deceitful politicians and the wicked behaviour of his sons. That little tune fit to break your heart – that is for the beautiful young creature whom he adored when he was a boy and was forced by his friends to give up. Ah, God! How he wept then!"

Tears rolled down the King's face. He began to perform a slow, grave dance, waving his body and his arms from side to side and spinning slowly over the ground. The music moved away, deeper into the Park and the King danced after it.

Strange was mystified. The music seemed to be leading the King in the direction of a grove of trees. At least Strange had supposed it was a grove. He was almost certain that a moment ago he had seen a dozen trees – probably fewer. But now the grove had become a thicket – no, a wood – a deep, dark wood where the trees were ancient and wild. Their great branches resembled twisted limbs and their roots tumbling nests of snakes. They were twined about thickly with ivy and mistletoe. There was a little path between the trees; it was pitted with deep, ice-rimmed hollows and fringed with frost-stiffened weeds. Pale pinpricks of light deep within the wood suggested a house where no house ought to be.

"Your Majesty!" cried Strange. He ran after the King and caught him by the hands. "Your Majesty must forgive me, but I do not quite like the look of those trees. I think perhaps that we would be as well to return to the Castle."

The King was quite enraptured by the music and did not wish to leave. He grumbled and pulled his arm away from Strange's grasp. Strange caught him again and half-led, half-dragged him back towards the gate.

But the invisible flute-player did not seem inclined to give them up so easily. The music suddenly grew louder; it was all around them. Another tune crept in almost imperceptibly and blended sweetly with the first.

"Ah! Listen! Oh, listen!" cried the King, spinning round. "He is playing for you now! That harsh melody is for your wicked tutor who will not teach you what you have every right to learn. Those discordant notes describe your anger at being prevented from making new discoveries. That slow, sad march is for the great library he is too selfish to shew you."

"How in the world . . ." began Strange and then stopped. He heard it too – the music that described his whole life. He realized for the first time how full of sadness his existence was. He was surrounded by mean-spirited men and women who hated him and were secretly jealous of his talent. He knew now that every angry thought he had ever had was justified and that every generous thought was misplaced. His enemies were despicable and his friends were treacherous. Norrell (naturally) was worst of all, but even Arabella was weak and unworthy of his love.

"Ah!" sighed His Majesty, "So you have been betrayed too."

"Yes," said Strange, sadly.

They were facing the wood again. The lights among the trees – tiny as they were – conveyed to Strange a strong idea of the house and its comforts. He could almost see the soft candlelight falling upon the comfortable chairs, the ancient hearths where cheerful fires blazed, the glasses of hot spiced wine which would be provided to warm them after their walk through the dark wood. The lights suggested other ideas too. "I think there is a library," he said.

"Oh, certainly!" declared the King, clapping his hands together in his enthusiasm. "You shall read the books and when your eyes grow tired, I shall read them to you! But we must hurry! Listen to the music! He grows impatient for us to follow him!"

His Majesty reached out to take Strange's left arm. In order to accommodate him, Strange found that he must move something he was holding in his left hand. It was Ormskirk's *Revelations of Thirty-Six Other Worlds*.

"Oh, *that*!" he thought. "Well, I do not need that any longer. There are sure to be better books at the house in the wood!" He opened his hand and let *Revelations* fall upon the snowy ground.

The snow fell thicker. The flute-player played. They hurried towards the wood. As they ran, the King's scarlet nightcap fell over his eyes. Strange reached up and straightened it. As he did so, he suddenly remembered what it was that he knew about the colour red: it was powerful protection against enchantment.

"Hurry! Hurry!" cried the King.

The flute-player played a series of rapid notes which rose and fell to mimic the sound of the wind. A real wind appeared out of nowhere and half-lifted, half-pushed them over the ground towards the wood. When it set them down again they were a great deal nearer to the wood.

"Excellent!" cried the King.

The nightcap caught Strange's eye again.

. . . *Protection against enchantment* . . .

The flute-player conjured up another wind. This one blew the King's nightcap off.

"No matter! No matter!" cried the King cheerfully. "He has promised me nightcaps a-plenty when we get to his house."

But Strange let go of the King's arm and staggered back through the snow and the wind to fetch it. It lay in the snow, bright scarlet among all the misty shades of white and grey.

. . . *Protection against enchantment* . . .

He remembered saying to one of the Willises that in order to practise magic successfully a magician must employ the forcefulness of his own character; why should he think of that now?

Place the moon at my eyes (he thought) *and her whiteness shall devour the false sights the deceiver has placed there.*

The moon's scarred white disc appeared suddenly – not in the sky, but somewhere else. If he had been obliged to say exactly where, he would have said that it was inside his own head. The sensation was not a pleasant one. All he could think of, all he could see was the moon's face, like a sliver of ancient bone. He forgot about the King. He forgot he was a magician. He forgot Mr Norrell. He forgot his own name.

He forgot everything except the moon . . .

The moon vanished. Strange looked up and found himself in a snowy place a little distance from a dark wood. Between him and the wood stood the blind King in his dressing-gown. The King must have walked on when he stopped. But without his guide to lean on, the King felt lost and afraid. He was crying out, "Magician! Magician! Where are you?"

The wood no longer struck Strange as a welcoming place. It appeared to him now as it had at first – sinister, unknowable, *unEnglish*. As for the lights, he could barely see them; they were the merest pricks of white in the darkness and suggested nothing except that the inhabitants of the house could not afford many candles.

"Magician!" cried the King.

"I am here, Your Majesty."

Place a swarm of bees at my ears (he thought). *Bees love truth and will destroy the deceiver's lies.*

A low murmuring noise filled his ears, blocking out the music of the flute-player. It was very like language and Strange thought that in a little while he would understand it. It grew, filling his head and his chest to the very tips of his fingers and toes. Even his hair seemed electrified and his skin buzzed and shook with the noise. For one horrible moment he thought that his mouth was full of bees and that there were bees buzzing and flying under his skin, in his guts and his ears.

The buzzing stopped. Strange heard the flute-player's music again but it did not sound as sweet as before and it no longer seemed to be describing his life.

Place salt in my mouth (he thought) *lest the deceiver attempt to delight me with the taste of honey or disgust me with the taste of ashes.*

This part of the spell had no effect whatsoever.[2]

Nail my hand with an iron nail so that I shall not raise it to do the deceiver's bidding.

"Aaaghh! Dear God!" screamed Strange. There was an excruciating pain in the palm of his left hand. When it ceased (as suddenly as it had begun) he no longer felt compelled to hurry towards the wood.

Place my heart in a secret place so that all my desires shall be my own and the deceiver shall find no hold there.

He pictured Arabella, as he had seen her a thousand times, prettily dressed and seated in a drawing-room among a crowd of people who were all laughing and talking. He gave her his heart. She took it and placed it quietly in the pocket of her gown. No one observed what she did.

Strange next applied the spell to the King and at the last step he gave the King's heart to Arabella to keep in her pocket. It was interesting to observe the magic from the outside. There had been so many unusual occurrences in the King's poor head that the moon's sudden appearance there seemed to occasion him no surprise. But he did not care for the bees; he was brushing them away for some time afterwards.

When the spell was finished, the flute-player abruptly ceased playing.

"And now, Your Majesty," said Strange, "I think it is time we returned to the Castle. You and I, Your Majesty, are a British King and a British magician. Though Great Britain may desert us,

---

[2] When Strange reviewed the morning's events afterwards he could only suppose that the flute-player had made no attempt to deceive him by his sense of taste.

we have no right to desert Great Britain. She may have need of us yet."

"True, true! I swore an oath at my coronation always to serve her! Oh, my poor country!" The King turned and waved in the direction he supposed the mysterious flute-player to be. "Goodbye! Goodbye, dear sir! God bless you for your kindness to George III!"

Revelations of Thirty-Six Other Worlds lay half-covered up by the snow. Strange picked it up and brushed off the snow. He looked back. The dark wood had gone. In its place was a most innocent clump of five leafless beech trees.

On the ride back to London Strange was deep in thought. He was aware that he ought to have been disturbed by his experience at Windsor, perhaps even frightened. But his curiosity and excitement far exceeded his uneasiness. Besides, whatever, or whoever, had done the magic, he had defeated them and imposed his will upon theirs. They had been strong, but he had been stronger. The whole adventure had confirmed something he had long suspected: that there was more magic in England than Mr Norrell admitted.

Consider the matter from whichever point of view he would, he continually came back to the silver-haired person whom only the King could see. He tried to recall what exactly the King had said about this person, but he could recall nothing beyond the simple fact of his silver hair.

He reached London at about half past four. The city was growing dark. Lights were glowing in all the shops, and the lamplighters were out in the streets. When he got to the corner of Oxford-street and New Bond-street he turned aside and rode to Hanover-square. He found Mr Norrell in his library, drinking tea.

Mr Norrell was, as ever, delighted to see the other magician and he was eager to hear all about Strange's visit to the King.

Strange told him how the King was kept a solitary prisoner in his own palace, and he listed the spells he had done. But of the drenching of the Willises, the enchanted wood and the invisible flute-player he said not a word.

"I am not at all surprized that you could not help His Majesty," said Mr Norrell. "I do not believe that even the *Aureate* magicians could cure madness. In fact I am not sure that they tried. They seem to have considered madness in quite a different light. They held madmen in a sort of reverence and thought they knew things sane men did not – things which might be useful to a magician. There are stories of both Ralph Stokesey and Catherine of Winchester consulting with madmen."

"But it was not only magicians, surely?" said Strange. "Fairies too had a strong interest in madmen. I am sure I remember reading that somewhere."

"Yes, indeed! Some of our most important writers have remarked upon the strong resemblance between madmen and fairies. Both are well known for talking without sense or connexion – I dare say you noticed something of the sort with the King. But there are other similarities. Chaston, as I remember, has several things to say upon the subject. He gives the example of a lunatic in Bristol who each morning told his family of his intention to take his walk in company with one of the dining chairs. The man was quite devoted to this article of furniture, considered it one of his closest friends, and held imaginary conversations with it in which they discussed the walk they would take and the likelihood of meeting other tables and chairs. Apparently, the man became quite distressed whenever any one proposed sitting upon the chair. Clearly the man was mad, but Chaston says that fairies would not consider his behaviour as ridiculous as we do. Fairies do not make a strong distinction between the animate and the inanimate. They believe that stones, doors, trees, fire, clouds and so forth all have souls and desires, and are either masculine or feminine. Perhaps this explains the extraordinary sympathy for madness which fairies exhibit. For example, it used to be well known that when fairies hid themselves from general sight, lunatics were often able to perceive them. The most celebrated instance which I can recall was of a mad boy called Duffy in Chesterfield in Derbyshire in the fourteenth century, who was the favourite of a mischievous fairy-spirit which had tormented the town for years. The fairy took a great fancy to this boy and made him extravagant presents – most of which would have scarcely been of any use to him in his right mind and were certainly no use to him in his madness – a sailing boat encrusted with diamonds, a pair of silver boots, a singing pig . . ."

"But why did the fairy pay Duffy all these attentions?"

"Oh! He told Duffy they were brothers in adversity. I do not know why. Chaston wrote that a great many fairies harboured a vague sense of having been treated badly by the English. Though it was a mystery to Chaston – as it is to me – why they should have thought so. In the houses of the great English magicians fairies were the first among the servants and sat in the best places after the magician and his lady. Chaston has a great many interesting things to say upon the subject. His best work is the *Liber Novus*." Mr Norrell frowned at his pupil. "I am sure I have recommended it to you half a dozen times," he said. "Have you not read it yet?"

Unfortunately, Mr Norrell did not always recall with absolute precision which books he wished Strange to read and which books he had sent to Yorkshire for the express purpose of keeping them out of Strange's reach. The *Liber Novus* was safe on a shelf in the library at Hurtfew Abbey. Strange sighed and remarked that the moment Mr Norrell put the book into his hand he would be very glad to read it. "But in the meantime, sir, perhaps you would be so good as to finish the tale of the fairy of Chesterfield."

"Oh, yes! Now where was I? Well, for a number of years nothing went wrong for Duffy and nothing went right for the town. A wood grew up in the market square and the townspeople could not conduct their business. Their goats and swine grew wings and flew away. The fairy turned the stones of the half-built parish church into sugar loaves. The sugar grew hot and sticky under the sun and part of the church melted. The town smelt like a giant pastry-cook's. Worse still dogs and cats came and licked at the church, and birds, rats and mice came and nibbled at it. So the towns-people were left with a half-eaten, misshapen church – which was not at all the effect that they had in mind. They were obliged to apply to Duffy and beg him to plead with the fairy on their behalf. But he was sullen and would not help them because he remem-bered how they had mocked him in the past. So they were obliged to pay the poor, mad wretch all sorts of compliments on his cleverness and handsomeness. So then Duffy pleaded with the fairy and, ah!, what a difference then! The fairy stopped torment-ing them and he turned the sugar church back into stone. The townspeople cut down the wood in the market place and bought new animals. But they could never get the church quite right again. Even today there is something odd about the church in Chesterfield. It is not quite like other churches."

Strange was silent a moment. Then he said, "Is it your opinion, Mr Norrell, that fairies have left England completely?"

"I do not know. There are many stories of Englishmen and women meeting with fairies in out-of-the-way places in the last three or four hundred years, but as none of these people were scholars or magicians their evidence cannot be said to be worth a great deal. When you and I summon fairies – I mean," he added hastily, "if we were so ill-advised as to do such a thing – then, providing we cast our spells correctly, the fairies will appear promptly. But where they come from or by what paths they travel is uncertain. In John Uskglass's day very plain roads were built that led out of England into Faerie – wide green roads between high green hedges or stone walls. Those roads still exist, but I do not think fairies use them nowadays any more than Christians. The roads are all overgrown and ruined. They have a lonely look and I am told that people avoid them."

"People believe that fairy roads are unlucky," said Strange.

468

"They are foolish," said Norrell. "Fairy roads cannot hurt them. Fairy roads lead nowhere at all."[3]

"And what of the half-human descendants of fairies? Do they inherit their forefathers' knowledge and powers?" asked Strange.

"Oh! That is quite another question. Many people nowadays have surnames that reveal their ancestors' fairy origins. Otherlander and Fairchild are two. Elfick is another. And Fairey, obviously. I remember there was a Tom Otherlander who worked upon one of our farms when I was a child. But it is quite rare for any of these descendants of fairies to exhibit the least magical talent. Indeed more often than not they have a reputation for malice, pride and laziness – all vices for which their fairy-ancestors were well known."

---

[3] Whether Mr Norrell was right to say that fairy roads can do no harm is debatable. They are eerie places and there are dozens of tales of the strange adventures which befell people who attempted to travel along them. The following is one of the better known. It is hard to say what precisely was the fate suffered by the people in the road – certainly it is not a fate you or I would wish to share.

In Yorkshire in the late sixteenth century there was a man who had a farm. Early one morning in summer he went out with two or three of his men to begin the hay-making. A white mist lay upon the land and the air was cool. Along one side of the field there was an ancient fairy road bounded by high hawthorn hedges. Tall grass and young saplings grew in the road and even on the brightest day it was dim and shadowy. The farmer had never seen any one on the fairy road, but that morning he and his men looked up and saw a group of people coming along it. Their faces were strange and they were outlandishly dressed. One among them – a man – strode ahead of the others. He left the road and came into the field. He was dressed in black and was young and handsome; and though they had never seen him before, the farmer and his men knew him immediately – it was the Magician King, John Uskglass. They knelt before him and he raised them up. He told them that he was on a journey and they brought him a horse, and some food and drink. They went and fetched their wives and children, and John Uskglass blessed them and gave them good fortune.

The farmer looked doubtfully at the strange people who remained in the fairy road; but John Uskglass told the farmer not to be afraid. He promised him that the people could do him no harm. Then he rode away.

The strange people in the ancient road lingered a little while, but when the first rays of the strong summer sun touched them they disappeared with the mist.

The next day Strange met with the Royal Dukes and told them how much he regretted that he had been unable to alleviate the King's madness. Their Royal Highnesses were sorry to hear it, but they were not at all surprized. It was the outcome they had expected and they assured Strange that they did not blame him in the least. In fact they were pleased with all he had done and they particularly liked that he had not charged them a fee. As a reward they granted him their Royal Warrants. This meant that he could, if he wished, put gilt and plaster images of all their five coats of arms above his door in Soho-square, and he was at liberty to tell any one he liked that he was Magician to the Royal Dukes by appointment.

Strange did not tell the Dukes that he deserved their gratitude more than they knew. He was quite certain he had saved the King from some horrible fate or other. He simply did not know what it was.

34

On the edge of the desert

November 1814

STEPHEN AND THE gentleman with the thistle-down hair were walking through the streets of a strange town.

"Are you not growing weary, sir?" asked Stephen. "I know that I am. We have been walking here for hours."

The gentleman let out a burst of high-pitched laughter. "My dear Stephen! You have only just this instant arrived! A moment ago you were at Lady Pole's house, being forced to perform some menial task at the bidding of her wicked husband!"

"Oh!" said Stephen. He realized that the last thing he remembered was cleaning the silver in his little room near the kitchen, but that seemed like, oh!, years ago.

He looked around him. There was nothing here he recognized. Even the smell of the place, a mixture of spices, coffee, rotting vegetables and roasting meats, was new to him.

He sighed. "It is this magic, sir. It is so very confusing."

The gentleman squeezed his arm affectionately.

The town appeared to be built upon a steep hillside. There did not seem to be any proper streets, but only narrow alleyways composed mainly of steps that wound up and down between the houses. The houses themselves were of the utmost simplicity; one might say severity. The walls were made of earth or clay, painted white, the doorways had plain wooden doors and the windows had plain wooden shutters. The steps of the alleys were also painted white. In all the town there did not seem to be so much as a spot of colour anywhere to relieve the eye: no flower in a flowerpot upon a windowsill, no painted toy left where a child had abandoned it in a doorway. Walking through these narrow streets was, thought Stephen, rather like losing oneself in the folds of an enormous linen napkin.

It was eerily silent. As they went up and down the narrow steps they heard the murmur of grave conversation coming from the houses, but there was no laughter, no song, no child's voice raised in excitement. From time to time they met an inhabitant of the town; a solemn, dark-faced man dressed in a white robe and pantaloons with a white turban upon his head. All carried walking-sticks – even the young men – though in truth none of them seemed to be very young; the inhabitants of this town had been born old.

They saw only one woman (at least the gentleman with the thistle-down hair said it was a woman). She stood at her husband's side robed from the crown of her head to the tip of her toe in a single garment the colour of shadows. When Stephen first saw her she had her back to him and it seemed in keeping with the dream-like atmosphere of the place that as she turned slowly towards him, he saw that her face was not a face at all, but a panel of densely embroidered cloth of the same dusky hue as the rest of her garment.

"These people are very strange," whispered Stephen. "But they do not appear to be surprized to find us here."

"Oh!" said the gentleman. "It is part of the magic I have done that you and I should appear to them as two of their number. They are quite convinced that they have known us since child-hood. Moreover you will find that you understand them perfectly and they will understand you – in spite of the obscurity of their language which is scarcely comprehensible to their own country-men twenty-five miles away!"

Presumably, Stephen thought, it was also part of the magic that the town's inhabitants should not notice how loud the gentleman spoke and how his words echoed from every white-washed corner.

The street they were descending turned a corner and ended abruptly at a low wall that had been put there to prevent unwary pedestrians from tumbling off the hill. From this spot the surrounding country could be viewed. A desolate valley of white rock lay before them under a cloudless sky. A hot wind blew across it. It was a world from which all flesh had been stripped, leaving only the bones.

Stephen would have supposed that this place was a dream or part of his enchantment, had not the gentleman with the thistledown hair informed him excitedly that this was, ". . . Africa! Your ancestral soil, my dear Stephen!"

"But," thought Stephen, "my ancestors did not live here, I am sure. These people are darker than Englishmen, but they are far fairer than me. They are Arabs, I suppose." Out loud he said, "Are we going anywhere in particular, sir?"

"To see the market, Stephen!"

Stephen was glad to hear it. The silence and emptiness were oppressive. The market presumably would have some noise, some bustle.

But the market of this town proved to be of a very curious character. It was situated close to the high town walls just by a great wooden gate. There were no stalls, no crowds of eager people going about to view the wares. Instead everyone who felt at all inclined to buy any thing sat silently upon the ground with his hands folded while a market official – a sort of auctioneer – carried the goods about and shewed them to the prospective buyers. The auctioneer named the last price he had been offered and the buyer either shook his head or offered a higher one. There was not a great deal of variety in the goods – there were some bales of fine cloth and some embroidered articles, but mostly it was carpets. When Stephen remarked upon this to his companion, the gentleman replied, "Their religion is of the strictest sort, Stephen. Almost everything is forbidden to them except carpets."

Stephen watched them as they went mournfully about the market, these men whose mouths were perpetually closed lest they spoke some forbidden word, whose eyes were perpetually averted from forbidden sights, whose hands refrained at every moment from some forbidden act. It seemed to him that they did little more than half-exist. They might as well have been dreams or ghosts. In the silent town and the silent countryside only the hot wind seemed to have any real substance. Stephen felt he would not be surprized if one day the wind blew the town and its inhabitants entirely away.

Stephen and the gentleman seated themselves in a corner of the market beneath a tattered brown awning.

"Why are we here, sir?" asked Stephen.

"So that we may have some quiet conversation, Stephen. A most serious matter has arisen. I am sorry to have to tell you that all our wonderful plans have been rudely overturned and once again it is the magicians who thwart us! Never was there such a rascally pair of men! Their only pleasure, I think, is in demonstrating their contempt of us! But one day, I believe . . ."

The gentleman was a great deal more interested in abusing the magicians than he was in making his meaning clear and so it was some time before Stephen was able to understand what had happened. It seemed that Jonathan Strange had paid a visit to the King of England – for what reason the gentleman did not explain – and the gentleman had gone too with the idea first of seeing what the magician did and secondly of looking at the King of England.

". . . and I do not know how it is, but for some reason I never paid my respects to His Majesty before. I discovered him to be a most delightful old person! Very respectful to me! We had a great deal of conversation! He has suffered much from the cruel treatment of his subjects. The English take great pleasure in humbling the great and the noble. A great many Worthies throughout history have suffered from their vicious persecutions – people such as Charles I, Julius Caesar and, above all, you and me!"

"I beg your pardon, sir. But you mentioned plans. What plans are these?"

"Why, our plans to make you King of England, of course! You had not forgotten?"

"No, indeed! But . . ."

"Well! I do not know what may be your opinion, dearest Stephen," declared the gentleman, not waiting to find out, "but I confess I grow weary of waiting for your wonderful destiny to happen of its own accord. I am very much inclined to anticipate the tardy Fates and make you King myself. Who knows? Perhaps I am meant to be the noble instrument that raises you to the lofty position that is yours by right! Nothing seems so likely! Well! While the King and I were talking, it occurred to me that the first step to making you King was to get rid of him! Observe! I meant the old man no harm. Upon the contrary! I wrapped his soul in sweetness and made him happier than he has been in many a long year. But this would not do for the magician! I had barely begun to weave an enchantment when the magician began to work against me. He employed ancient fairy magic of immense power. I was never more surprised in my life! Who could have supposed that he would have known how to do such a thing?"

The gentleman paused in his tirade long enough for Stephen to say, "Grateful as I am for your care of me, sir, I feel obliged to observe that the present King has thirteen sons and daughters, the eldest of whom is already governing the country. Even if the King were dead, the Crown would certainly pass to one of them."

"Yes, yes! But the King's children are all fat and stupid. Who wishes to be governed by such frights? When the people of England understand that they might instead be governed by you, Stephen – who are all elegance and charm and whose noble countenance would look so well upon a coin – why! they must be very dull indeed if they are not immediately delighted and rush to support your cause!"

The gentleman, thought Stephen, understood the character of Englishmen a great deal less than he supposed.

At that moment their conversation was interrupted by a most barbaric sound – a great horn was being blown. A number of men rushed forward and heaved the great town gates shut. Thinking that perhaps some danger threatened the town, Stephen looked round in alarm. "Sir, what is happening?"

"Oh, it is these people's custom to shut the gate every night against the wicked heathen," said the gentleman, languidly, "by which they mean everyone except themselves. But tell me your opinion, Stephen? What should we do?"

"Do, sir? About what?"

"The magicians, Stephen! The magicians! It is clear to me now that as soon as your wonderful destiny begins to unfold, they are certain to interfere. Though why it should matter to them who is King of England, I cannot tell. I suppose being ugly and stupid themselves, they prefer to have a king the same. No, they are our enemies and consequently it behoves us to seek a way to destroy them utterly. Poison? Knives? Pistols? . . ."

The auctioneer approached, holding out yet another carpet. "Twenty silver pennies," he said in a slow, deliberate tone as if he were pronouncing a righteous doom upon all the world.

The gentleman with the thistle-down hair regarded the carpet thoughtfully. "It is possible, of course," he said, "to imprison someone within the pattern of a carpet for a thousand years or so. That is a particularly horrible fate which I always reserve for people who have offended me deeply – as have these magicians! The endless repetition of colour and pattern – not to mention the irritation of the dust and the humiliation of stains – never fails to render the prisoner completely mad! The prisoner always emerges from the carpet determined to wreak revenge upon all the world and then the magicians and heroes of that Age must join together to kill him or, more usually, imprison him a second time for yet more thousands of years in some even more ghastly prison. And so he goes on growing in madness and evil as the millennia pass. Yes, carpets! Perhaps . . ."

"Thank you," said Stephen to the auctioneer, quickly, "but we have no wish to buy this carpet. Pray, sir, pass on."

"You are right, Stephen," said the gentleman. "Whatever their faults these magicians have proved themselves most adept at avoiding enchantments. We must find some other way to crush their spirits so that they no longer have the will to oppose us! We must make them wish they had never taken up the practice of magic!"

35

The Nottinghamshire gentleman

November 1814

URING STRANGE'S THREE-YEAR absence Mr Drawlight and Mr Lascelles had enjoyed a little revival of their influence over Mr Norrell. Any one wishing to talk to Mr Norrell or ask for Mr Norrell's assistance had been obliged to apply first to them. They had advised Mr Norrell upon the best way of managing the Ministers and the Ministers upon the best way of managing Mr Norrell. As friends and counsellors of England's most eminent magician their acquaintance had been solicited by all the wealthiest and most fashionable people in the kingdom.

After Strange's return they continued to wait upon Mr Norrell as assiduously as ever, but now it was Strange's opinion which Mr Norrell most wished to hear and Strange's advice which he sought before any other. Naturally, this was not a state of affairs to please them and Drawlight, in particular, did all that was in his power to increase those little annoyances and resentments which each magician occasionally felt at the behaviour of the other.

"I cannot believe that I do not know something that would harm him," he said to Lascelles. "There are some very odd stories about what he did in Spain. Several people have told me that he raised a whole army of dead soldiers to fight the French. Corpses with shattered limbs and eyes hanging by a thread and every sort of horror that you can imagine! What do you suppose Norrell would say if he heard that?"

Lascelles sighed. "I wish I could convince you of the futility of trying to manufacture a quarrel between them. They will do that themselves sooner or later."

A few days after Strange's visit to the King a crowd of Mr Norrell's friends and admirers gathered in the library at Hanover-square with the object of admiring a new portrait of the two magicians by Mr Lawrence.[1] Mr Lascelles and Mr Drawlight

---

[1] This portrait, now lost, hung in Mr Norrell's library from November 1814 until the summer of the following year when it was removed. It has not been seen since.

The following extract from a volume of memoirs describes the difficulties experienced by Mr Lawrence (later Sir Thomas Lawrence) in painting the portrait. It is also of interest for the light it sheds upon the relationship of Norrell and Strange in late 1814. It seems that, in spite of many provocations, Strange was still struggling to bear patiently with the older magician and to encourage others to do the same.

"The two magicians sat for the picture in Mr Norrell's library. Mr Lawrence found Mr Strange to be a most agreeable man and Strange's part of the portrait progressed very well. Mr Norrell, on the other hand, was very restless from the start. He would shift about in his chair and crane his neck as if he were trying to catch sight of Mr Lawrence's hands – a futile endeavour as the easel stood between them. Mr Lawrence supposed he must be anxious about the picture and assured him it went well. Mr Lawrence added that Mr Norrell might look if he wished, but this did nothing to cure Mr Norrell's fidgets.

All at once Mr Norrell addressed Mr Strange, who was in the room and busy writing a letter to one of the Ministers. 'Mr Strange, I feel a draught! I do believe that the window behind Mr Lawrence is open! Pray, Mr Strange, go and see if the window is open!' Without looking up, Strange replied, 'No, the window is not open. You are mistaken.' A few minutes later Mr Norrell thought he heard a pie-seller in the square and begged Mr Strange to go to the window and look out, but once again Mr Strange refused. Next it was a duchess's coach that Mr Norrell heard. He tried everything that he could think of to make Mr Strange go to the window, but Mr Strange would not go. This was very odd, and Mr Lawrence began to suspect that all Mr Norrell's agitation had nothing to with imaginary draughts or pie-sellers or duchesses but that it had something to do with the painting.

So when Mr Norrell went out of the room Mr Lawrence asked Mr Strange what the matter was. At first Mr Strange insisted that nothing was wrong, but Mr Lawrence was determined to find out and pressed Mr Strange to tell him the truth. Mr Strange sighed. 'Oh, very well! He has got it into his head that you are copying spells out of his books behind your easel.'

were there, as were Mr and Mrs Strange and several of the King's Ministers.

The portrait shewed Mr Norrell in his plain grey coat and his old-fashioned wig. Both coat and wig seemed a little too large for him. He appeared to have withdrawn inside them and his small, blue eyes looked out at the world with a curious mixture of fearfulness and arrogance that put Sir Walter Pole in mind of his valet's cat. Most people, it seemed, were having to put themselves to a little effort to find any thing flattering to say of Mr Norrell's half of the picture, but everyone was happy to admire Strange's half. Strange was painted behind Mr Norrell, half-sitting, half-leaning against a little table, entirely at his ease, with his mocking half-smile and his eyes full of smiles and secrets and spells – just as magicians' eyes should be.

"Oh! it is an excellent thing," enthused a lady. "See how the darkness of the mirror behind the figures sets off Mr Strange's head."

"People always imagine that magicians and mirrors go together," complained Mr Norrell. "There is no mirror in that part of my library."

"Artists are tricky fellows, sir, forever reshaping the world according to some design of their own," said Strange. "Indeed they are not unlike magicians in that. And yet he has made a curious piece of work of it. It is more like a door than a mirror – it is

---

[1] *cont'd*   Mr Lawrence was shocked. He had painted the greatest in the land and never before been suspected of stealing. This was not the sort of treatment he expected.

'Come,' said Mr Strange, gently, 'do not be angry. If any man in England deserves our patience, it is Mr Norrell. All the future of English magic is on his shoulders and I assure you he feels it very keenly. It makes him a little eccentric. What would be your sensations, I wonder, Mr Lawrence, if you woke one morning and found yourself the only artist in Europe? Would not you feel a little lonely? Would you not feel the watchful gaze of Michelangelo and Raphael and Rembrandt and all the rest of them upon you, as if they both defied and implored you to equal their achievements? Would you not sometimes be out of spirits and out of temper?' "

From *Recollections of Sir Thomas Lawrence during an intimacy of nearly thirty years* by Miss Croft

so dark. I can almost feel a draught coming from it. I do not like to see myself sitting so close to it – I am afraid that I may catch cold."

One of the Ministers, who had never been in Mr Norrell's library before, made some admiring remark about its harmonious proportions and style of fitting up, which led other people to say how beautiful they thought it.

"It is certainly a very fine room," agreed Drawlight, "but it is really nothing in comparison with the library at Hurtfew Abbey! That is truly a charming room. I never in my life saw any thing so delightful, so complete. There are little pointed arches and a dome with pillars in the Gothic style and the carvings of leaves – dried and twisted leaves, as if withered by some horrid winter blast, all done in good English oak and ash and elm – are the most perfect things I ever saw. 'Mr Norrell,' I said, when I saw them, 'there are depths in you that we have not suspected. You are quite a Romantic, sir.' "

Mr Norrell looked as if he did not much like to hear the library at Hurtfew talked about so much, but Mr Drawlight continued regardless: "It is like being in a wood, a pretty little wood, late in the year, and the bindings of the books, being all tan and brown and dry with age, compound that impression. Indeed there are as many books, it seems, as the leaves in a wood." Mr Drawlight paused. "And were you ever at Hurtfew, Mr Strange?"

Strange replied that he had not yet had that pleasure.

"Oh, you should go," Drawlight smiled spitefully. "Indeed you should. It is truly wonderful."

Norrell looked anxiously at Strange but Strange did not reply. He had turned his back on them all and was gazing intently at his own portrait.

As the others moved away and began to speak of something else, Sir Walter murmured, "You must not mind his malice."

"Mmmm?" said Strange. "Oh, it is not that. It is the mirror. Does it not look as if one could just walk into it? It would not be so difficult I think. One could use a spell of revelation. No, of

481

unravelling. Or perhaps both. The way would be clear before one. One step forward and away." He looked around him and said, "And there are days when I would be away."

"Where?" Sir Walter was surprised; there was no place he found so much to his liking as London with its gaslights and its shops, its coffee-houses and clubs, its thousand pretty women and its thousand varieties of gossip and he imagined it must be the same for every one.

"Oh, wherever men of my sort used to go, long ago. Wandering on paths that other men have not seen. Behind the sky. On the other side of the rain."

Strange sighed again and his right foot tapped impatiently on Mr Norrell's carpet, suggesting that, if he did not make up his mind soon to go to the forgotten paths, then his feet would carry him there of their own accord.

By two o'clock the visitors had gone and Mr Norrell, who was rather anxious to avoid any conversation with Strange, went upstairs and hid himself away in his little room at the back of the house on the second floor. He sat down at his table and began to work. Very soon he had forgot all about Strange and the library at Hurtfew and all the disagreeable sensations which Drawlight's speech had produced. He was therefore somewhat dismayed when a few minutes later there was a knock at the door and Strange walked in.

"I beg your pardon for disturbing you, sir," he said, "but there is something I wish to ask you."

"Oh!" said Mr Norrell nervously. "Well, of course I am always very happy to answer any questions you may have, but just now there is a piece of business which I fear I cannot neglect. I have spoken to Lord Liverpool about our plan to secure the coast of Great Britain from storms by magic and he is quite delighted with it. Lord Liverpool says that every year property to the value of many hundreds of thousands of pounds is destroyed by the sea. Lord Liverpool says that he considers the preservation of property to be the first task of magic in peacetime. As always his lordship wishes it done immediately and it is a great deal of work. The county of Cornwall alone will take a week. I fear we must postpone our conversation until some other time."

Strange smiled. "If the magic is as urgent as that, sir, then I had better assist you and we can talk while we work. Where do you begin?"

"At Yarmouth."

"And what are you using? Belasis?"

"No, not Belasis. There is a reconstruction of Stokesey's magic for calming stormy waters in Lanchester's *Language of Birds*. I am not so foolish as to suppose that Lanchester greatly resembles Stokesey but he is the best we have. I have made some revisions to Lanchester and I am adding Pevensey's spells of Ward and Watch."[2] Mr Norrell pushed some papers towards Strange. Strange studied the papers and then he too began to work.

After a while Strange said, "I recently found a reference in Ormskirk's *Revelations of Thirty-Six Other Worlds* to the kingdom

---

[2] Francis Pevensey, sixteenth-century magician. Wrote *Eighteen Wonders to be found in the House of Albion*. We know that Pevensey was trained by Martin Pale. The *Eighteen Wonders* has all the characteristics of Pale's magic, including his fondness for complicated diagrams and intricate magical apparatus.

For many years Francis Pevensey occupied a minor but respectable place in English magical history as a follower of Martin Pale and it was a great surprize to everyone when he suddenly became the subject of one of the bitterest controversies in eighteenth-century magical theory.

It began in 1754 with the discovery of a number of letters in the library of a gentleman in Stamford in Lincolnshire. They were all in an antique hand and signed by Martin Pale. The magical scholars of the period were besides themselves with joy.

But upon closer examination the letters proved to be *love letters* with no word of magic in them from beginning to end. They were of the most passionate description imaginable: Pale compared his beloved to a sweet shower of rain falling upon him, to a fire at which he warmed himself, to a torment that he preferred to any comfort. There were various references to milk-white breasts and perfumed legs and long soft, brown hair in which stars became entangled, and other things not at all interesting to the magical scholars who had hoped for magic spells.

Pale was much addicted to writing his beloved's name – which was Francis – and in one letter he made a sort of punning poem or riddle upon her surname: Pevensey. At first the eighteenth-century magical scholars were inclined to argue that Pale's mistress must have been the sister or wife of the

---

that lies behind mirrors, a kingdom which is apparently full of the most convenient roads by which a traveller may get from one place to another."

This would not ordinarily have been a subject to please Mr Norrell, but he was so relieved to discover that Strange did not intend to quarrel with him about the library at Hurtfew that he grew quite communicative. "Oh yes, indeed! There is indeed a path which joins all the mirrors of the world. It was well-known to the Great Mediaevals. No doubt they trod it often. I fear I cannot give you any more precise information. The writers I have seen all describe it in different ways. Ormskirk says it is a road across a wide, dark moor, whereas Hickman calls it a vast house with many dark passages and great staircases.[3] Hickman says that within this house there are stone bridges spanning deep chasms and canals of black water flowing between stone walls – to what destination or for what purpose no one knows." Suddenly Mr Norrell was in an

---

[2] *cont'd* other Francis Pevensey. In the sixteenth century Francis had been a common name for both men and women. Then Charles Hether-Gray published seven different extracts from the letters which mentioned *Eighteen Wonders in the House of Albion* and shewed plainly that Pale's mistress and the author of the book were one and the same person.

William Pantler argued that the letters were forgeries. The letters had been found in the library of a Mr Whittlesea. Mr Whittlesea had a wife who had written several plays, two of which had been performed at the Drury Lane Theatre. Clearly, said Pantler, a woman who would stoop to writing plays would stoop to any thing and he suggested that Mrs Whittlesea had forged the letters ". . . in order to elevate her Sex above the natural place that God had ordained for it . . ." Mr Whittlesea challenged William Pantler to a duel and Pantler, who was a scholar through and through and knew nothing of weapons, apologized and published a formal retraction of his accusations against Mrs Whittlesea.

Mr Norrell was quite happy to employ Pevensey's magic, since he had settled it in his own mind long ago that Pevensey was a man. As to the letters – since they contained no word of magic he did not concern himself with them. Jonathan Strange took a different view. According to him only one question needed to be asked and answered in order to settle the matter: would Martin Pale have taught a woman magic? The answer was, again according to Strange, yes. After all Martin Pale claimed to have been taught by a woman – Catherine of Winchester.

[3] Thaddeus Hickman (1700–38), author of a life of Martin Pale.

484

excellent humour. To sit quietly doing magic with Mr Strange was to him the very height of enjoyment. "And how does the article for the next *Gentleman's Magazine* come along?" he asked.

Strange thought for a moment. "I have not quite completed it," he said.

"What is it about? No, do not tell me! I greatly look forward to reading it! Perhaps you will bring it with you tomorrow?"

"Oh! Tomorrow certainly."

That evening Arabella entered the drawing-room of her house in Soho-square and was somewhat surprized to discover that the carpet was now covered with small pieces of paper upon which were written spells and notes and fragments of Norrell's conversation. Strange was standing in the middle of the room, staring down at the papers and pulling his hair.

"What in the world can I put in the next article for the *Gentleman's Magazine*?" he demanded.

"I do not know, my love. Has Mr Norrell made no suggestion?"

Strange frowned. "For some reason he thinks it is already done."

"Well, what about trees and magic?" suggested Arabella. "You were only saying the other day how interesting the subject is and very much neglected."

Strange took a clean sheet of paper and began rapidly scribbling notes upon it. "Oak trees can be befriended and will aid you against your enemies if they think your cause is just. Birch woods are well known for providing doors into Faerie. Ash-trees will never cease to mourn until the Raven King comes home again.[4]

---

[4] The ivy promised to bind England's enemies
Briars and thorns promised to whip them
The hawthorn said he would answer any question
The birch said he would make doors to other countries
The yew brought us weapons
The raven punished our enemies
The oak watched the distant hills
The rain washed away all sorrow
This traditional English saying supposedly lists the various contracts which John Uskglass, the Raven King, made on England's behalf with the forests.

No, no! That will never do. I cannot say that. Norrell would have a fit." He crumpled up the paper and threw it in the fire.

"Oh! Then perhaps you will listen for a moment to what I have to say," said Arabella. "I paid a visit to Lady Westby's house today, where I met a very odd young lady who seems to be under the impression that you are teaching her magic."

Strange looked up briefly. "I am not teaching any one magic," he said.

"No, my love," said Arabella patiently, "I know that you are not. That is what makes it so extraordinary."

"And what is the name of this confused young person?"

"Miss Gray."

"I do not know her."

"A smart, stylish girl, but not handsome. She is apparently very rich and absolutely wild for magic. Everybody says so. She has a fan decorated with your pictures – yours and Mr Norrell's – and she has read every word that you and Lord Portishead have ever published."

Strange stared thoughtfully at her for several seconds, so that Arabella mistakenly supposed he must be considering what she had just said. But when he spoke it was only to say in a tone of gentle reproof, "My love, you are standing on my papers." He took her arm and moved her gently aside.

"She told me that she has paid you four hundred guineas for the privilege of being your pupil. She says that in return you have sent her letters with descriptions of spells and recommendations of books to read."

"Four hundred guineas! Well, that is odd. I might forget a young lady, but I do not think I could forget four hundred guineas." A piece of paper caught Strange's eye and he picked it up and began to read it.

"I thought at first that she might have invented this story in order to make me jealous and cause a quarrel between us, but her mania does not seem to be of that sort. It is not your person she

486

admires, it is your profession. I cannot make head nor tail of it. What can these letters be? Who can have written them?"

Strange picked up a little memorandum book (it happened to be Arabella's housekeeping book and nothing to do with him at all) and began to scribble notes in it.

"Jonathan!"

"Mmm?"

"What should I say to Miss Gray when I see her next?"

"Ask her about the four hundred guineas. Tell her I have not received it yet."

"Jonathan! This is a serious matter."

"Oh! I quite agree. There are few things as serious as four hundred guineas."

Arabella said again that it was the oddest thing in the world. She told Strange that she was quite concerned upon Miss Gray's account and she said she wished he would speak to Miss Gray so that the mystery might be resolved. But she said all this for her own satisfaction, since she knew perfectly well that he was no longer attending to her.

A few days later Strange and Sir Walter Pole were playing at billiards at the Bedford in Covent-garden. The game had come to an *impasse* as Sir Walter had begun, as usual, to accuse Strange of transporting billiard balls about the table by magic.

Strange declared that he had done no such thing.

"I saw you touch your nose," complained Sir Walter.

"Good God!" cried Strange. "A man may sneeze, mayn't he? I have a cold."

Two other friends of Strange and Sir Walter, Lieutenant-Colonel Colquhoun Grant and Colonel Manningham, who were watching the game, said that if Strange and Sir Walter merely wished to quarrel then was it entirely necessary for them to occupy the billiards table to do it? Colquhoun Grant and Colonel Manningham hinted that there were other people – more interested in the game itself – who were waiting to play. This, developing into a more general argument, unfortunately led two country gentlemen to put their heads round the door and inquire when the table might be free for a game, unaware that on Thursday evenings the billiards room at the Bedford was generally considered to be the personal property of Sir Walter Pole and Jonathan Strange and their particular friends.

"Upon my word," said Colquhoun Grant, "I do not know. But probably not for a very long while."

The first of the two country gentlemen was a thick-set, solid-looking person with a coat of heavy brown cloth and boots which would have appeared more to advantage at some provincial market than in the fashionable surroundings of the Bedford. The second country gentleman was a limp little man with an expression of perpetual astonishment.

"But, sir," said the first man, addressing Strange in tones of the utmost reasonableness, "you are talking, not playing. Mr Tantony and I are from Nottinghamshire. We have ordered our dinner but are told we must wait another hour before it is ready. Let us play while you have your chat and then we will be only too glad to give up the table to you again."

His manner as he said this was perfectly polite, yet it rather rankled with Strange's party. Everything about him plainly spoke him to be a farmer or a tradesman and they were not best pleased that he took it upon himself to order them about.

"If you examine the table," said Strange, "you will see that we have just begun. To ask a gentleman to break off before his game is ended – well, sir, it is a thing that is never done at the Bedford."

"Ah! Is it not?" said the Nottinghamshire gentleman pleasantly. "Then I beg your pardon. But perhaps you will not object to telling me whether you think it will be a short game or a long one?"

"We have already told you," said Grant. "We do not know." He gave Strange a look which plainly said, "This fellow is very stupid."

It was at this point that the Nottinghamshire gentleman began to suspect that Strange's party were not merely unhelpful, but that they intended to be rude to him. He frowned and indicated the limp little man with the astonished expression who stood at his side. "It is Mr Tantony's first visit to London and he does not desire to come again. I particularly wished to shew him the Bedford Coffee-house, but I did not think to find the people so very disobliging."

"Well, if you do not like it here," said Strange, angrily, "then I can only suggest that you go back home to wherever it is . . . Nothing-shire, I think you said?"

Colquhoun Grant gave the Nottinghamshire gentleman a very cool look and remarked to nobody in particular, "It is no wonder to me that farming is in such a parlous condition. Farmers nowadays are always upon the gad. One meets with them at all the idlest haunts in the kingdom. They consult nothing but their own pleasure. Is there no wheat to be sown in Nottingham-shire, I wonder? No pigs to be fed?"

"Mr Tantony and I are not farmers, sir!" exclaimed the Nottinghamshire gentleman indignantly. "We are brewers. Gat-combe and Tantony's Entire Stout is our most celebrated beer and it is famed throughout three counties!"

"Thank you, but we have beer and brewers enough in London already," remarked Colonel Manningham. "Pray, do not stay upon our account."

"But we are not here to sell beer! We have come for a far nobler purpose than that! Mr Tantony and I are enthusiasts for magic! We consider that it is every patriotic Englishman's duty to interest himself in the subject. London is no longer merely the capital of Great Britain – it is the centre of our magical scholarship. For many years it was Mr Tantony's dearest wish that he might learn magic, but the art was in such a wretched condition that it made him despair. His friends bade him be more cheerful. We told him that it is when things are at their worst that they start to mend.

And we were right, for almost immediately there appeared two of the greatest magicians that England has ever known. I refer of course to Mr Norrell and Mr Strange! The wonders which they have performed have given Englishmen cause to bless the country of their birth again and encouraged Mr Tantony to hope that he might one day be of their number."

"Indeed? Well, it is my belief that he will be disappointed," observed Strange.

"Then, sir, you could not be more wrong!" cried the Nottinghamshire gentleman triumphantly. "Mr Tantony is being instructed in the magical arts by Mr Strange himself!"

Unfortunately, Strange happened at that moment to be leaning across the table, balanced upon one foot to take aim at a billiard ball. So surprized was he at what he heard that he missed the shot entirely, struck his cue against the side of the table and promptly fell over.

"I think there must be some mistake," said Colquhoun Grant.

"No, sir. No mistake," said the Nottinghamshire gentleman with an air of infuriating calmness.

Strange, getting up from the floor, asked, "What does he look like, this Mr Strange?"

"Alas," said the Nottinghamshire gentleman, "I cannot give you any precise information upon that point. Mr Tantony has never met Mr Strange. Mr Tantony's education is conducted entirely by letters. But we have great hopes of seeing Mr Strange in the street. We go to Soho-square tomorrow expressly for the purpose of looking at his house."

"Letters!" exclaimed Strange.

"I would think an education by correspondence must of a very inferior sort," said Sir Walter.

"Not at all!" cried the Nottinghamshire gentleman. "Mr Strange's letters are full of sage advice and remarkable insights into the condition of English magic. Why, only the other day Mr Tantony wrote and asked Mr Strange for a spell to make it stop raining – we get a great deal of rain in our part of Nottingham-shire. The very next day Mr Strange wrote back and said that, though there were indeed spells that could move rain and sunshine about, like pieces on a chessboard, he would never employ them except in the direst need, and he advised Mr Tantony to follow his example. English magic, said Mr Strange, had grown up upon English soil and had in a sense been nurtured by English rain. Mr Strange said that in meddling with English weather, we meddled with England, and in meddling with England we risked destroying the very foundations of English magic. We thought that a very striking instance of Mr Strange's genius, did we not, Mr Tant-ony?" The Nottinghamshire man gave his friend a little shake which made him blink several times.

"Did you ever say that?" murmured Sir Walter.

"Why! I think I did," answered Strange. "I believe I said something of the sort . . . when would it have been? Last Friday, I suppose."

"And to whom did you say it?"

"To Norrell, of course."

"And was there any other person in the room?"

Strange paused. "Drawlight," he said slowly.

"Ah!"

"Sir," said Strange to the Nottinghamshire gentleman. "I beg your pardon if I offended you before. But you must admit that there was something about the way in which you spoke to me which was not quite . . . In short I have a temper and you piqued me. I am Jonathan Strange and I am sorry to tell you that I never heard of you or Mr Tantony until today. I suspect that Mr Tantony and I are both the dupes of an unscrupulous man. I presume that Mr Tantony pays me for his education? Might I ask where he sends the money? If it is to Little Ryder-street then I shall have the proof I need."

Unfortunately the Nottinghamshire gentleman and Mr Tant-ony had formed an idea of Strange as a tall, deep-chested man with a long white beard, a ponderous way of speaking and an antiquated mode of dress. As the Mr Strange who stood before them was slender, clean-shaven, quick of speech and dressed exactly like every other rich, fashionable gentleman in London, they could not at first be persuaded that this was the right person.

"Well, that is easily resolved," said Colquhoun Grant.

"Of course," said Sir Walter, "I will summon a waiter. Perhaps the word of a servant will do what the word of a gentleman cannot. John! Come here! We want you!"

"No, no, no!" cried Grant, "That was not what I meant at all. John, you may go away again. We do not want you. There are any number of things which Mr Strange could do which would prove his incomparable magicianship far better than any mere assurances. He is after all the Greatest Magician of the Age."

"Surely," said the Nottinghamshire man with a frown, "that title belongs to Mr Norrell?"

Colquhoun Grant smiled. "Colonel Manningham and I had the honour, sir, to fight with his Grace the Duke of Wellington in Spain. I assure you we knew nothing of Mr Norrell there. It was Mr Strange – this gentleman here – whom we trusted. Now, if he were to perform some startling act of magic then I do not think you could doubt any longer and then I am sure your great respect for English magic and English magicians would not allow you to remain silent a moment longer. I am sure you would wish to tell him all you know about these forged letters." Grant looked at the Nottinghamshire gentleman inquiringly.

"Well," said the Nottinghamshire gentleman, "you are a very queer set of gentlemen, I must say, and what you can mean by spinning me such a tale as this, I do not know. For I tell you plainly I will be very much surprised if the letters prove to be forgeries when every line, every word breathes good English magic!"

"But," said Grant, "if, as we suppose, this scoundrel made use of Mr Strange's own words to concoct his lies, then that would explain it, would it not? Now, in order to prove that he is who we say he is, Mr Strange shall now shew you something that no man living has ever seen!"

"Why?" said the Nottinghamshire man. "What will he do?"

Grant smiled broadly and turned to Strange, as if he too were suddenly struck with curiosity. "Yes, Strange, tell us. What will you do?"

But it was Sir Walter who answered. He nodded in the direction of a large Venetian mirror which took up most of one wall and was at that moment reflecting only darkness, and he declared, "He will walk into that mirror and he will not come out again."

36

All the mirrors of the world

November 1814

THE VILLAGE OF Hampstead is situated five miles north of London. In our grandfathers' day it was an entirely unremarkable collection of farmhouses and cottages, but the existence of so rustic a spot close to London attracted large numbers of people to go there to enjoy the sweet air and verdure. A racecourse and bowling-green were built for their amusement. Bun shops and tea-gardens provided refreshment. Rich people bought summer cottages there and Hampstead soon became what it is today: one of the favourite resorts of fashionable London society. In a very short space of time it has grown from a country village to a place of quite respectable size – almost a little town.

Two hours after Sir Walter, Colonel Grant, Colonel Manningham and Jonathan Strange had quarrelled with the Nottinghamshire gentleman a carriage entered Hampstead on the London road and turned into a dark lane which was overhung with elder bushes, lilacs and hawthorns. The carriage drove to a house at the end of the lane where it stopped and Mr Drawlight got out.

The house had once been a farmhouse, but it had been much improved in recent years. Its small country windows – more useful for keeping out the cold than letting in the light – had all been made large and regular; a pillared portico had replaced the mean country doorway; the farm-yard had been entirely swept away and a flower garden and shrubbery established in its place.

Mr Drawlight knocked upon the door. A maidservant answered his knock and immediately conducted him to a drawing-room. The room must once have been the farmhouse-parlour, but all signs of its original character had disappeared beneath costly French wallpapers, Persian carpets and English furniture of the newest make and style.

Drawlight had not waited there more than a few minutes when a lady entered the room. She was tall, well-formed and beautiful. Her gown was of scarlet velvet and her white neck was set off by an intricate necklace of jet beads.

Through an open door across the passageway could be glimpsed a dining-parlour, as expensively got up as the drawing-room. The remains of a meal upon the table shewed that the lady had dined alone. It seemed that she had put on the red gown and black necklace for her own amusement.

"Ah, madam!" cried Drawlight leaping up. "I hope you are well?"

She made a little gesture of dismissal. "I suppose I am well. As well as I can be with scarcely any society and no variety of occupation."

"What!" cried Drawlight in a shocked voice. "Are you all alone here?"

"I have one companion – an old aunt. She urges religion upon me."

"Oh, madam!" cried Drawlight. "Do not waste your energies upon prayers and sermons. You will get no comfort there. Instead, fix your thoughts upon *revenge*."

"I shall. I do," she said simply. She sat down upon the sopha opposite the window. "And how are Mr Strange and Mr Norrell?"

"Oh, busy, madam! Busy, busy, busy! I could wish for their sakes, as well as yours, that they were less occupied. Only yesterday Mr Strange inquired most particularly after you. He wished to know if you were in good spirits. 'Oh! Tolerable,' I told him, 'merely tolerable.' Mr Strange is shocked, madam, frankly shocked at the heartless behaviour of your relations."

"Indeed? I wish that his indignation might shew itself in more practical ways," she said coolly. "I have paid him more than a hundred guineas and he has done nothing. I am tired of trying to arrange matters through an intermediary, Mr Drawlight. Convey to Mr Strange my compliments. Tell him I am ready to meet him wherever he chuses at any hour of the day or night. All times are alike to me. I have no engagements."

"Ah, madam! How I wish I could do as you ask. How Mr Strange wishes it! But I fear it is quite impossible."

"So you say, but I have heard no reason – at least none that satisfies me. I suppose Mr Strange is nervous of what people will say if we are seen together. But our meeting may be quite private. No one need know."

"Oh, madam! You have quite misunderstood Mr Strange's character! Nothing in the world would please him so much as an opportunity to shew the world how he despises your persecutors. It is entirely upon your account that he is so circumspect. He fears . . ."

But what Mr Strange feared the lady never learnt, for at that moment Drawlight stopt suddenly and looked about him with an expression of the utmost perplexity upon his face. "What in the world was that?" he asked.

It was as if a door had opened somewhere. Or possibly a series of doors. There was a sensation as of a breeze blowing into the house and bringing with it the half-remembered scents of childhood. There was a shift in the light which seemed to cause all the shadows in the room to fall differently. There was nothing more definite than that, and yet, as often happens when some magic is occurring, both Drawlight and the lady had the strongest impression that nothing in the visible world could be relied upon any more. It was as if one might put out one's hand to touch any thing in the room and discover it was no longer there.

A tall mirror hung upon the wall above the sopha where the lady sat. It shewed a second great white moon in a second tall dark window and a second dim mirror-room. But Drawlight and the lady did not appear in the mirror-room at all. Instead there was a kind of an indistinctness, which became a sort of shadow, which became the dark shape of someone coming towards them. From the path which this person took, it could clearly be seen that the mirror-room was not like the original at all and that it was only by odd tricks of lighting and perspective − such as one might meet with in the theatre − that they appeared to be the same. It seemed that the mirror-room was actually a long corridor. The hair and coat of the mysterious figure were stirred by a wind which could not be felt in their own room and, though he walked briskly towards the glass which separated the two rooms, it was taking him some time to reach it. But finally he reached the glass and then there was a moment when his dark shape loomed very large behind it and his face was still in shadow.

Then Strange hopped down from the mirror very neatly, smiled his most charming smile and bid both Drawlight and the lady, "Good evening."

He waited a moment, as if allowing someone else time to speak and then, when no one did, he said, "I hope you will be so kind, madam, as to forgive the lateness of my visit. To say the truth the way was a little more meandering than I had anticipated. I took a wrong turning and very nearly arrived in . . . well, I do not quite know where."

He paused again, as if waiting for someone to invite him to sit down. When no one did, he sat down anyway.

Drawlight and the lady in the red gown stared at him. He smiled back at them.

"I have been getting acquainted with Mr Tantony," he told Drawlight. "A most pleasant gentleman, though not very talkative. His friend, Mr Gatcombe, however, told me all I wished to know."

"You are Mr Strange?" asked the lady in the red gown.

"I am, madam."

"This is most fortunate. Mr Drawlight was just explaining to me why you and I could never meet."

"It is true, madam, that until tonight circumstances did not favour our meeting. Mr Drawlight, pray make the introductions."

Drawlight muttered that the lady in the red gown was Mrs Bullworth.

Strange rose, bowed to Mrs Bullworth and sat down again.

"Mr Drawlight has, I believe, told you of my horrible situation?" said Mrs Bullworth.

Strange made a small gesture with his head which might have meant one thing or might have meant another thing or might have meant nothing at all. He said, "A narration by an unconnected person can never match the tale told by someone intimately concerned with the events. There may be vital points which Mr Drawlight has, for one reason or another, omitted. Indulge me, madam. Let me it hear from you."

"All?"

"All."

"Very well. I am, as you know, the daughter of a gentleman in Northamptonshire. My father's property is extensive. His house and income are large. We are among the first people in that county. But my family have always encouraged me to believe that with my beauty and accomplishments I might occupy an even higher position in the world. Two years ago I made a very advantageous marriage. Mr Bullworth is rich and we moved in the most fashionable circles. But still I was not happy. In the summer of last year I had the misfortune to meet a man who is everything Mr Bullworth is not: handsome, clever, amusing. A few short weeks were enough to convince me that I preferred this man to any one I had ever seen." She gave a little shrug of her shoulders. "Two days before Christmas I left my husband's house in his company. I hoped – indeed expected – to divorce Mr

Bullworth and marry him. But that was not his intention. By the end of January we had quarrelled and my friend had deserted me. He returned to his house and all his usual pursuits, but there was to be no such revival of a former life for me. My husband cast me off. My friends refused to receive me. I was forced back upon the mercy of my father. He told me that he would provide for me for the rest of my life, but in return I must live in perfect retirement. No more balls for me, no more parties, no more friends. No more any thing." She gazed into the distance for a moment, as if in contemplation of all that she had lost, but just as quickly she shook off her melancholy and declared, "And now to business!" She went to a little writing-table, opened a drawer and drew out a paper which she offered to Strange. "I have, as you suggested, made a list of all the people who have betrayed me," she said.

"Ah, I told you to make a list, did I?" said Strange, taking the paper. "How businesslike I am! It is quite a long list."

"Oh!" said Mrs Bullworth. "Every name will be considered a separate commission and you shall have your fee for each. I have taken the liberty of writing by each name the punishment which I believe ought to be theirs. But your superior knowledge of magic may suggest other, more appropriate fates for my enemies. I should be glad of your recommendations."

" 'Sir James Southwell. Gout,' " read Strange.

"My father," explained Mrs Bullworth. "He wearied me to death with speeches upon my wicked character and exiled me for ever from my home. In many ways it is he who is the author of all my miseries. I wish I could harden my heart enough to decree some more serious illness for him. But I cannot. I suppose that is what is meant by the weakness of women."

"Gout is exceedingly painful," observed Strange. "Or so I am told."

Mrs Bullworth made a gesture of impatience.

" 'Miss Elizabeth Church,' " continued Strange. " 'To have her engagement broken off.' Who is Miss Elizabeth Church?"

"A cousin of mine – a tedious, embroidering sort of girl. No one ever paid her the least attention until I married Mr Bullworth. Yet now I hear she is to be married to a clergyman and my father has given her a banker's draft to pay for wedding clothes and new furniture. My father has promised Lizzie and the clergyman that he will use his interest to get them all sorts of preferments. Their way is to be made easy. They are to live in York where they will attend dinners and parties and balls, and enjoy all those pleasures which ought to have been mine. Mr Strange," she cried, growing more energetic, "surely there must be spells to make the clergyman hate the very sight of Lizzie? To make him shudder at the sound of her voice?"

"I do not know," said Strange. "I never considered the matter before. I suppose there must be." He returned to the list. " 'Mr Bullworth' . . ."

"My husband," she said.

". . . 'To be bitten by dogs.' "

"He has seven great black brutes and thinks more of them than of any human creature."

" 'Mrs Bullworth senior' – your husband's mother, I suppose – 'To be drowned in a laundry tub. To be choked to death on her own apricot preserves. To be baked accidentally in a bread oven.' That is three deaths for one woman. Forgive me, Mrs Bullworth, but the greatest magician that ever lived could not kill the same person three different ways."

"Do as much as you can manage," said Mrs Bullworth stubbornly. "The old woman is so insufferably proud of her housekeeping. She bored me to death upon the subject."

"I see. Well, this is all very Shakespearian. And so we come to the last name. 'Henry Lascelles.' I know this gentleman." Strange looked inquiringly at Drawlight.

Mrs Bullworth said, "That is the person under whose protection I left my husband's house."

"Ah! And what shall his fate be?"

"Bankruptcy," she said in a fierce, low voice. "Lunacy. Fire. A disfiguring disease. A horse to trample upon him! A villain to lie in wait for him and cut his face with a knife! A vision of horror to haunt him and drive away sleep night after night!" She rose and began to pace about the room. "Let every mean and dishonourable action he ever did be published in the newspaper! Let everyone in London shun him! Let him seduce some country girl who will go mad for love of him. Let her follow him wherever he goes for years and years. Let him become an object of ridicule because of her. Let her never leave him in peace. Let some mistake upon the part of an honest man lead to his being accused of a crime. Let him suffer all the indignities of trial and imprisonment. Let him be branded! Let him be beaten! Let him be whipped! And let him be executed!"

"Mrs Bullworth," said Strange, "pray, calm yourself."

Mrs Bullworth stopped pacing. She ceased calling down horrible fates upon Mr Lascelles's head, but still she could hardly have been said to be calm. Her breath came rapidly, she trembled all over and her face still worked furiously.

Strange watched until he judged her enough in command of herself to understand what he wanted to say and then he began, "I am sorry, Mrs Bullworth, but you have been the victim of a cruel deception. This," he glanced at Drawlight, "person has lied to you. Mr Norrell and I have never undertaken commissions for private individuals. We have never employed this person as an agent to find business for us. I never even heard your name until tonight."

Mrs Bullworth stared at him a moment and then turning upon Drawlight. "Is this true?"

Drawlight fixed his miserable gaze upon the carpet and mumbled some sort of speech in which only the words "madam" and "peculiar situation" were discernible.

Mrs Bullworth reached up and rang the bellpull.

The maid who had let Drawlight into the house reappeared.

"Haverhill," said Mrs Bullworth, "remove Mr Drawlight."

Unlike the majority of maids in fashionable households who are chosen mainly for their pretty faces, Haverhill was a competent-looking person of the middle age with strong arms and an unforgiving expression. But on this occasion she was required to do very little since Mr Drawlight was only too grateful for the opportunity to remove himself. He picked up his stick and scuttled out of the room the moment Haverhill opened the door.

Mrs Bullworth turned to Strange. "Will you help me? Will you do what I ask? If the money is not sufficient . . ."

"Oh, the money!" Strange made a dismissive gesture. "I am sorry, but as I have just told you, I do not undertake private commissions."

She stared at him, and then said in a wondering tone, "Can it be that you are entirely unmoved by the misery of my situation?"

"Upon the contrary, Mrs Bullworth, a system of morality which punishes the woman and leaves no share of blame to the man seems to me quite detestable. But beyond that I will not go. I will not hurt innocent people."

"Innocent!" she cried. "Innocent! Who is innocent? No one!"

"Mrs Bullworth, there is nothing to be said. I can do nothing for you. I am sorry."

She regarded him sourly. "Hmm, well. At least you have the grace to refrain from recommending repentance or good works or needlework or whatever it is the other fools hold up as a cure for a blank life and a broken heart. Nevertheless I think it will be best for both of us if this interview is brought to a conclusion. Good night, Mr Strange."

Strange bowed. As he left the room he gave a wistful glance at the mirror above the sopha, as if he would have preferred to depart by that means, but Haverhill held the door open and common politeness obliged him to go through it.

Having neither horse nor carriage, he walked the five miles from Hampstead to Soho-square. On arriving at his own front door he discovered that although it was almost two o'clock in the morning there was a light in every window of the house. Before he could even fish in his pocket for his doorkey, the door was flung open by Colquhoun Grant.

"Good heavens! What are you doing here?" cried Strange.

Grant did not trouble to answer him, but instead turned back into the house and called, "He is here, ma'am! He is quite safe."

Arabella came running, almost tumbling, out of the drawing-room, followed a moment later by Sir Walter. Then Jeremy Johns and several of the servants appeared in the passageway leading to the kitchen.

"Has something happened? Is something wrong?" asked Strange, gazing at them all in surprize.

"Blockhead!" laughed Grant, striking him affectionately on the head. "We were concerned about you! Where in the world have you been?"

"Hampstead."

"Hampstead!" exclaimed Sir Walter. "Well, we are very glad to see you!" He glanced at Arabella and added nervously, "I fear we have made Mrs Strange anxious for no good reason."

"Oh!" said Strange to his wife. "You were not afraid, were you? I was perfectly well. I always am."

"There, ma'am!" declared Colonel Grant cheerfully. "It is just as I told you. In Spain Mr Strange was often in great peril, but we were never in the least concerned about him. He is too clever to come to any harm."

"Must we stand in the hallway?" asked Strange. On the way from Hampstead he had been thinking about magic and he had intended to continue doing so at home. Instead, he found a house full of people all talking together. It put him out of humour.

He led the way into the drawing-room and asked Jeremy to bring him some wine and something to eat. When they were all seated he said, "It was just as we supposed. Drawlight has been arranging for Norrell and I to perform every sort of Black Magic you can think of. I found him with a most excitable young woman who wanted me to inflict torments upon her relations."

"How horrible!" said Colonel Grant.

"And what did Drawlight say?" asked Sir Walter. "How did he explain himself?"

"Ha!" Strange let out a short burst of uncheerful laughter. "He did not say any thing. He simply ran away – which was a pity, as I had a great mind to challenge him to a duel."

"Oh!" said Arabella suddenly. "It is duels now, is it?"

Sir Walter and Grant both looked at her in alarm, but Strange was too absorbed in what he was saying to notice her angry expression. "Not that I suppose he would have accepted, but I should have liked to frighten him a little. God knows he deserves it."

"But you have not said any thing about this kingdom, path – whatever it is – behind the mirror," said Colonel Grant. "Did it answer your expectations?"

Strange shook his head. "I do not have the words to describe it. All that Norrell and I have done is as nothing in comparison! And yet we have the audacity to call ourselves magicians! I wish I could give you an idea of its grandeur! Of its size and complexity! Of the great stone halls that lead off in every direction! I tried at first to judge their length and number, but soon gave up. There seemed no end to them. There were canals of still water in stone embankments. The water appeared black in the gloomy light. I saw staircases that rose up so high I could not see the top of them, and others that descended into utter blackness. Then suddenly I passed under an arch and found myself upon a stone bridge that crossed a dark, empty landscape. The bridge was so vast that I could not see the end of it. Imagine a bridge that joined Islington to Twickenham! Or York to Newcastle! And everywhere in the halls and on the bridge I saw his likeness."

"Whose likeness?" asked Sir Walter.

"The man that Norrell and I have slandered in almost everything we have written. The man whose name Norrell can hardly bear to hear mentioned. The man who built the halls, canals, bridge, everything! John Uskglass, the Raven King! Of course, the structure has fallen into disrepair over the centuries. Whatever John Uskglass once used these roads for, it seems he no longer needs them. Statues and masonry have collapsed. Shafts of light break in from God-knows-where. Some halls are blocked, while others are flooded. And I will tell you something else very curious. There were a great number of discarded shoes everywhere I went. Presumably they belonged to other travellers. They were of a very ancient style and much decayed. From which I conclude that these passages have been little frequented in recent years. In all the time I was walking I only saw one other person."

"You saw someone else?" said Sir Walter.

"Oh, yes! At least I think it was a person. I saw a shadow moving along a white road that crossed the dark moor. You must understand that I was upon the bridge at the time and it was much higher than any bridge I have ever seen in this world. The ground appeared to be several thousand feet beneath me. I looked down and saw someone. If I had not been so set upon finding Drawlight, I would certainly have found a way down and followed him or her, for it seems to me that there could be no better way for a magician to spend his time than in conversation with such a person."

"But would such a person be safe?" asked Arabella.

"Safe?" said Strange, contemptuously. "Oh, no. I do not think so. But then I flatter myself that neither am I particularly *safe*. I hope I have not missed my chance. I hope that when I return tomorrow I will find some clue as to where the mysterious figure went."

"Return!" exclaimed Sir Walter. "But are you sure . . . ?"

"Oh!" cried Arabella, interrupting. "I see how it is to be! You will be walking these paths every moment Mr Norrell can spare you, while I remain here in a condition of the most miserable suspense, wondering if I am ever to see you again!"

Strange looked at her in surprize. "Arabella? Whatever is the matter?"

"The matter! You are set upon putting yourself in the most horrible danger and you expect me to say nothing about it!"

Strange made a sort of gesture of combined appeal and help-lessness, as if he were calling upon Sir Walter and Grant to bear witness how exceedingly unreasonable this was. He said, "But when I told you I was going to Spain, you were perfectly composed, even though a vicious war was raging there at the time. This, on the other hand, is quite . . ."

"Perfectly composed? I assure you I was nothing of the kind! I was horribly afraid for you – as were all the wives and mothers and sisters of the men in Spain. But you and I agreed that you had a duty to go. And besides, in Spain you had the entire British Army with you, whereas there you will be perfectly alone. I say 'there', but none of us knows where 'there' is!"

"I beg your pardon, but I know exactly where it is! It is the King's Roads. Really, Arabella, I think it is a little late in the day to decide you do not like my profession!"

"Oh, that is not fair! I have never said a word against your profession. I think it one of the noblest in the world. I am proud beyond measure of what you and Mr Norrell have done and I have never objected in the least to your learning whatever new magic you saw fit – but until today you have always been content to make your discoveries in books."

"Well, no longer. To confine a magician's researches to the books in his library, well, you might just as well tell an explorer that you approve his plan to search for the source of, of – whatever it is those African rivers are called – on the condition that he never steps outside Tunbridge Wells!"

Arabella gave an exclamation of exasperation. "I thought you meant to be a magician not an explorer!"

"It is the same thing. An explorer cannot stay at home reading maps other men have made. A magician cannot increase the stock of magic by reading other men's books. It is quite obvious to me that sooner or later Norrell and I must look beyond our books!"

"Indeed? That is obvious to you, is it? Well, Jonathan, I very much doubt that it is obvious to Mr Norrell."

Throughout this exchange Sir Walter and Lieutenant-Colonel Grant looked as uncomfortable as any two people can who inadvertently find themselves witnesses to a little outburst of marital disharmony. Nor was their situation improved by the consciousness that just at present neither Arabella nor Strange was feeling particularly well disposed towards them. They had already had to endure some sharp words from Arabella when they had confessed their part in encouraging Strange to perform the dangerous magic. Now Strange was directing angry glances at them, as if he wondered by what right they had come to his house in the middle of the night and put his usually sweet-tempered wife out of temper. As soon as there was any thing like a pause in the conversation, Colonel Grant muttered something incoherent about the lateness of the hour and about their kind hospitality being more than he deserved and about wishing them all good night. But then, as no one paid the slightest attention to his speech, he was obliged to continue where he was.

Sir Walter, however, was of a more resolute character. He concluded that he had been wrong in sending Strange upon the mirror-path and he was determined to do what he could to put matters right. Being a politician, he was never dissuaded from giving any body his opinion by the mere fact that they were not inclined to hear it. "Have you read every book upon magic?" he demanded of Strange.

"What? No, of course not! You know very well I have not!" said Strange. (He was thinking of the books in the library at Hurtfew.)

"These halls that you saw tonight, do you know where they all lead?" asked Sir Walter.

"No," said Strange.

"Do you know what the dark land is that the bridge crosses?"

"No, but . . ."

"Then, surely it would be better to do as Mrs Strange suggests and read all you can about these roads, before returning to them," said Sir Walter.

"But the information in books is inaccurate and contradictory! Even Norrell says so and he has read everything there is to read about them. You may be certain of that!"

Arabella, Strange and Sir Walter continued to argue for another half hour until everyone was cross and wretched and longing to go to bed. Only Strange seemed at all comfortable with these descriptions of eerie, silent halls, unending pathways and vast, dark landscapes. Arabella was genuinely frightened by what she had heard and even Sir Walter and Colonel Grant felt decidedly unsettled. Magic, which had seemed so familiar just hours before, so *English*, had suddenly become inhuman, unearthly, *otherlandish*.

As for Strange, it was his decided opinion that they were the most incomprehensible and infuriating set of people in the country. They did not appear to comprehend that he had done something entirely *remarkable*. It would not be going too far (he thought) to say that this had been the most extraordinary achievement of his career so far. No English magician since Martin Pale had been on the King's Roads. But instead of congratulating him and praising his skill – which any one else would have done – all they did was complain in a Norrellish sort of way.

The following morning he awoke determined to return to the King's Roads. He greeted Arabella cheerfully, talked to her upon indifferent subjects and generally tried to pretend that the quarrel had been due to her tiredness and overwrought state the previous evening. But long before he could take advantage of this convenient fiction (and slip away to the Roads by the nearest large mirror) Arabella told him very plainly that she felt just the same as she had last night.

In the end is it not futile to try and follow the course of a quarrel between husband and wife? Such a conversation is sure to meander more than any other. It draws in tributary arguments and grievances from years before – all quite incomprehensible to any but the two people they concern most nearly. Neither party is ever proved right or wrong in such a case, or, if they are, what does it signify?

The desire to live in harmony and friendship with one's spouse is very strong, and Strange and Arabella were no different from other people in this respect. Finally, after two days arguing the point back and forth, they made each other a promise. He promised her not to go upon the King's Roads again until she said that he might. In return she promised him to grant him that permission just as soon as he convinced her that it was safe to do so.

37

The Cinque Dragownes

November 1814

SEVEN YEARS AGO Mr Lascelles's house in Bruton-street was generally reckoned to be one of the best in London. It had the sort of perfection that can only be achieved by a very rich, very idle man who devotes the greater part of his time to collecting pictures and sculpture and the greater part of his mental energies to chusing furniture and wallpapers. His taste was remarkably good and he had a talent for combining colours in new and quite striking ways. He was particularly fond of blues, greys and a sort of darkish, metallic bronze. Yet he never became sentimentally attached to his possessions. He sold paintings as frequently as he bought them and his house never deteriorated into that picture-gallery confusion which besets the homes of some collectors. Each of Lascelles's rooms contained only a handful of pictures and *objets d'art*, but that handful included some of the most beautiful and remarkable objects in all of London.

In the last seven years however the perfection of Mr Lascelles's house had become somewhat diminished. The colours were as exquisite as ever, but they had not been changed for seven years. The furnishings were expensive, but they represented what had been most fashionable seven years ago. In the last seven years no new paintings had been added to Lascelles's collection. In the last seven years remarkable antique sculptures had arrived in London from Italy, Egypt and Greece but other gentlemen had bought them.

What is more, there were signs that the owner of the house had been engaged in useful occupation, that he had, in short, been *working*. Reports, manuscripts, letters and Government papers lay upon every table and chair, and copies of *The Friends of English Magic* and books on magic were to be found in every room.

The truth was that, though Lascelles still affected to despise work, in the seven years since Mr Norrell had first arrived in London he had been busier than ever before. Though it had been his suggestion to appoint Lord Portishead editor of *The Friends of English Magic*, the manner in which his lordship had carried on his editorial duties had exasperated Lascelles to a degree scarcely to be borne. Lord Portishead had deferred to Mr Norrell in all things – had instantly executed all of Mr Norrell's unnecessary amendments – and, as a result, *The Friends of English Magic* had grown duller and more circumlocutious with every issue. In the autumn of 1810 Lascelles had contrived to have himself appointed joint editor. *The Friends of English Magic* had one of the largest subscriptions of any periodical in the kingdom; the work was not inconsiderable. In addition Lascelles wrote upon modern magic for other periodicals and newspapers; he advised the Government upon magical policy; he visited Mr Norrell almost every day and in his spare time he studied the history and theory of magic.

On the third day after Strange had paid his visit to Mrs Bullworth, Lascelles happened to be working hard in his library upon the next issue of *The Friends of English Magic*. Though it was a little after noon he had not yet found the time to shave and dress and was sitting in his dressing-gown amid a litter of books, papers, breakfast plates and coffee cups. A letter he wanted was missing and so he went to look for it. On entering the drawing-room he was surprized to find someone there.

"Oh!" he said. "It's you."

The wretched-looking creature who drooped in a chair by the fire raised his head. He said, "Your servant has gone to find you and tell you I am here."

"Ah!" said Lascelles and paused, apparently at a loss for something to say next. He sat down in the opposite chair, rested his head upon his hand and regarded Drawlight thoughtfully.

Drawlight's face was pale and his eyes were sunk in his head. His coat was dusty, his boots were but indifferently polished and even his linen had a wilted look.

"I think it most unkind of you," said Lascelles at last, "to accept money for arranging to have me ruined, crippled and driven mad. And from Maria Bullworth of all people! Why she should be so angry is quite beyond me! It was quite as much her doing as mine. I did not force her to marry Bullworth. I merely offered her an escape when she could no longer bear the sight of him. Is it true that she wanted Strange to inflict leprosy upon me?"

"Oh, probably," sighed Drawlight. "I really do not know. There was never the least danger in the world that any thing would happen to you. You sit there, every bit as rich, healthy and comfortable as ever you were, whereas I am the wretchedest being in London. I have not slept in three days. This morning my hands were shaking so much I could scarcely tie my cravat. No one knows what mortification it is to me to appear in this scarecrow condition. Not that any one will see me, so what does it matter? I have been turned away from every door in London. Yours is the only house where I am admitted." He paused. "I ought not to have told you that."

Lascelles shrugged. "What I do not understand," he said, "is how you expected to succeed with such a perfectly absurd scheme."

"It was not in the least absurd! Upon the contrary I was

scrupulous in my choice of . . . of *clients*. Maria Bullworth lives in perfect retirement from society. Gatcombe and Tantony are brewers! From Nottinghamshire! Who could have predicted that they and Strange would ever meet?"

"And what of Miss Gray? Arabella Strange met her at Lady Westby's house in Bedford-square."

Drawlight sighed. "Miss Gray was eighteen years old and lived with her guardians in Whitby. According to the terms of her father's will she was obliged to consult their wishes in everything she did until she was thirty-six. They detested London and were determined never to leave Whitby. Unfortunately they both caught colds and died very suddenly two months ago and the wretched girl immediately set off for the capital." Drawlight paused and licked his lips nervously. "Is Norrell very angry?"

"Beyond any thing I ever saw," said Lascelles softly.

Drawlight retreated a little further into his chair. "What will they do?"

"I do not know. Since your little adventure became known I have thought it best to absent myself from Hanover-square for a while. I heard from Admiral Summerhayes that Strange wished to call you out . . ." (Drawlight gave a sort of yelp of fright.) ". . . but Arabella disapproves of duelling and so nothing came of it."

"Norrell has no right to be angry with me!" declared Drawlight suddenly. "He owes everything to me! Magicianship is all very well, but had it not been for me taking him about and shewing him to people, no one would ever have heard of him. He could not do without me then, and he cannot do without me now."

"You think so?"

Drawlight's dark eyes grew larger than ever and he put a finger in his mouth as though to gnaw a fingernail for comfort, but finding that he was still wearing his gloves, he took it out again quickly. "I shall call again this evening," he said. "Shall you be at home?"

"Oh, probably! I have half-promised Lady Blessington to go to her salon, but I doubt that I shall go. We are horribly behind with the *Friends*. Norrell keeps plaguing us with contradictory instructions."

"So much work! My poor Lascelles! That will not suit you at all! What a slavedriver the old man is!"

After Drawlight had gone Lascelles rang for his servant. "I shall go out in an hour, Emerson. Tell Wallis to get my clothes ready . . . Oh, and Emerson! Mr Drawlight has expressed an intention of returning here later this evening. When he comes, do not upon any consideration admit him."

At the same time that the above conversation was taking place Mr Norrell, Mr Strange and John Childermass were gathered in the library at Hanover-square to discuss Drawlight's treachery. Mr Norrell sat in silence, staring into the fire while Childermass described to Strange how he had discovered another of Drawlight's dupes, an elderly gentleman in Twickenham called Palgrave who had given Drawlight two hundred guineas to have his life prolonged by another eighty years and his youth returned to him.

"I am not sure," continued Childermass, "that we will ever know for certain how many people have paid Drawlight in the belief that they were commissioning you to perform Black Magic. Both Mr Tantony and Miss Gray have received promises of some future position in a hierarchy of magicians, which Drawlight told them will soon exist and which I do not pretend to understand very well."

Strange sighed. "How we shall ever convince people that we had no part in it, I do not know. We should do something, but I confess that I have not the least idea what."

Suddenly Mr Norrell said, "I have been considering the matter very carefully during the last two days – indeed I may say that I have thought of little else – and I have come to the conclusion that we must revive the Cinque Dragownes!"[1]

There was a short silence and then Strange said, "I beg your pardon, sir. Did you say the Cinque Dragownes?"

Mr Norrell nodded. "It is quite clear to me that this villain should be tried by the Cinque Dragownes. He is guilty of False Magic and Evil Tendings. Happily the old mediaeval law has never been revoked."

"Old mediaeval law," said Childermass, with a short laugh, "required twelve magicians to sit in judgement in the Court of

---

[1] Les Cinque Dragownes (The Five Dragons). This court took its name not, as is generally supposed, from the ferocity of its judges, but from a chamber in the house of John Uskglass, the Raven King, in Newcastle where the judgements were originally given. This chamber was said to be twelve-sided and to be decorated by wonderful carvings, some of them the work of men and some of them the work of fairies. The most marvellous of all were the carvings of five dragons.

Crimes tried by the Cinque Dragownes included: "Evil Tendings" – magic with an inherently malevolent purpose; "False Magic" – pretending to do magic or promising to do magic which one either could not or did not intend to do; selling magic rings, hats, shoes, coats, belts, shovels, beans, musical instruments etc., etc. to people who could not be expected to control those powerful articles; pretending to be a magician or pretending to act on behalf of a magician; teaching magic to unsuitable persons, e.g. drunkards, mad-men, children, persons of vicious habits and inclinations; and many other magical crimes committed by trained magicians and other Christians. Crimes against the person of John Uskglass were also tried by the Cinque Dragownes. The only category of magical crimes with which the Cinque Dragownes had nothing to do was crimes by fairies. These were dealt with by the separate court of Folflures.

In England in the twelfth, thirteenth and fourteenth centuries a thriving community of magicians and fairies was continually performing magic. Magic is notoriously difficult to regulate and, naturally enough, not all the magic that was done was well intentioned. John Uskglass seems to have devoted a great deal of time and energy to the creation of a body of law to govern magic and magicians. When the practice of magic spread throughout England, the southern English kings were only too grateful to borrow the wisdom of their northern neighbour. It is a peculiarity of that time that though England was divided into two countries with separate judiciary systems, the body of law which governed magic was the same for both. The southern English equivalent of the Cinque Dragownes was called the Petty Dragownes of London and was situated near Blackfriars.

Cinque Dragownes. There are not twelve magicians in England. You know very well there are not. There are two."

"We could find others," said Mr Norrell.

Strange and Childermass looked at him in astonishment.

Mr Norrell had the grace to appear a little embarrassed at contradicting all that he had maintained for seven years, but nevertheless he continued, "There is Lord Portishead and that dark little man in York who would not sign the agreement. That is two and I dare say," here he looked at Childermass, "you will find some more if you put your mind to it."

Childermass opened his mouth, presumably to say something of all the magicians he had already found for Mr Norrell – magicians who were magicians no longer now that Mr Norrell had their books, or had turned them out of their businesses or made them sign pernicious agreements or, in some other way, destroyed them.

"Forgive me, Mr Norrell," interrupted Strange, "but when I spoke of something being done, I meant an advertisement in the newspaper or something of that sort. I very much doubt that Lord Liverpool and the Ministers would allow us, for the sake of punishing one man, to revive a branch of English law that has been defunct for more than two hundred years. And even if they were so obliging as to permit it, I think we must assume that twelve magicians means twelve *practising* magicians. Lord Portishead and John Segundus are both theoretical magicians. Besides it is very likely that Drawlight will soon be prosecuted for fraud, forgery, theft and I do not know what else. I fail to see what advantage the Cinque Dragownes has over the common-law courts."

"The justice of the common-law courts is entirely unpredictable! The judge will know nothing of magic. The magnitude of this man's crimes will be entirely lost upon him. I am speaking of his crimes against English magic, his crimes against *me*. The Cinque Dragownes was renowned for its severity. I consider it our best security that he will be hanged."

"Hanged!"

"Oh, yes. I am quite determined to see him hanged! I thought that was what we were talking about." Mr Norrell blinked his small eyes rapidly.

"Mr Norrell," said Strange, "I am quite as angry with this man as you are. He is unprincipled. He is deceitful. He is everything I despise. But I will not be the cause of any one's death. I was in the Peninsula, sir. I have seen enough men die."

"But two days ago you wished to challenge him to a duel!"

Strange gave him an angry look. "That is quite another thing!"

"In any case," continued Mr Norrell, "I scarcely think Drawlight more to blame than you!"

"Me?" cried Strange, startled. "Why? What have I done?"

"Oh, you know very well what I mean! What in the world possessed you to go upon the King's Roads? Alone and entirely without preparation! You could hardly suppose that I would approve such a wild adventure! Your actions that night will do as much to bring magic into disrepute as anything that man has done. Indeed they will probably do more! No one ever did think well of Christopher Drawlight. It is no surprize to any one that he turns out a villain. But you are known everywhere as my pupil! You are the Second Magician in the land! People will think that I approved what you did. People will think that this is part of my plan for the restoration of English magic!"

Strange stared at his master. "God forbid, Mr Norrell, that you should feel compromised by any action of mine. Nothing, I assure you, could be further from my wishes. But it is easily remedied. If you and I part company, sir, then each of us may act independently. The world will judge each of us without reference to the other."

Mr Norrell looked very shocked. He glanced at Strange, glanced away again and muttered in a low voice that he had not meant *that*. He hoped Mr Strange knew he had not meant *that*. He cleared his throat. "I hope Mr Strange will make some allowance for the irritation of my spirits. I hope Mr Strange cares enough for English magic to bear with my fretfulness. He knows how important it is that he and I speak and act together for the good of English magic. It is altogether too soon for English magic to be exposed to the buffeting of contrary winds. If Mr Strange and I begin to contradict each other upon important matters of magical policy, then I do not believe that English magic will survive."

A silence.

Strange rose from his chair and made Mr Norrell a stiff, formal bow.

The next few moments were awkward. Mr Norrell looked as if he would have been glad to say something but was at a loss for a subject.

It so happened that Lord Portishead's new book, the *Essay on the Extraordinary Revival of English Magic, &c.*, had just arrived from the printer and was lying to hand upon a little table. Mr Norrell seized upon it. "What an excellent little work this is! And how devoted to our cause is Lord Portishead! After such a crisis one does not feel much inclined to trust any body – and yet I think we may always rely upon Lord Portishead!"

He handed Strange the book.

Strange turned the pages, thoughtfully. "He has certainly done everything we asked. Two long chapters attacking the Raven King and scarcely a mention of fairies at all. As I remember, his original manuscript had a long description of the Raven King's magic."

"Yes, indeed," said Mr Norrell. "Until you made those corrections, it was worthless. Worse than worthless – dangerous! But the long hours you spent with him, guiding his opinions, have all borne fruit! I am excessively pleased with it."

By the time Lucas brought in the tray with the tea-things the two magicians seemed like their natural selves again (though Strange was perhaps a little quieter than usual). The quarrel seemed mended.

Just before Strange left he asked if he might borrow Lord Portishead's book.

"Certainly!" cried Mr Norrell. "Keep it as your own! I have several other copies."

Despite all that Strange and Childermass had said against it Mr Norrell was unable to give up his plan to revive the Cinque Dragownes. The more he thought of it, the more it seemed to him that he would never enjoy peace again until there was a proper court of magical law in England. He felt that no punishment that might be meted out to Drawlight from any other quarter could ever satisfy him. So later that same day he sent Childermass to Lord Liverpool's house to beg the favour of a few minutes' conversation with his lordship. Lord Liverpool sent back a message that he would see Mr Norrell upon the following day.

At the appointed hour Mr Norrell waited upon the Prime Minister and explained his plan. When he had finished Lord Liverpool frowned.

"But magical law has fallen into disuse in England," said his lordship. "There are no lawyers trained to practise in such a court. Who would take the cases? Who would judge them?"

"Ah!" exclaimed Mr Norrell, producing a thick sheaf of papers. "I am glad your lordship asks such pertinent questions. I have drawn up a document describing the workings of the Cinque Dragownes. Sadly there are many lacunae in our knowledge, but I have suggested ways in which we might restore what has been lost. I have taken as my model the ecclesiastical courts of the Doctors Commons. As your lordship will see, we have a great deal of work before us."

Lord Liverpool glanced at the papers. "Too much work by far, Mr Norrell," he declared flatly.

"Oh, but it is very necessary I assure you! Very necessary indeed! How else will we regulate magic? How else will we guard against wicked magicians and their servants?"

"What wicked magicians? There is only Mr Strange and you."

"Well, that is true, but . . ."

"Do you feel particularly wicked at present, Mr Norrell? Is there some pressing reason that the British Government should establish a separate body of law to control your vicious tendencies?"

"No, I . . ."

"Or perhaps Mr Strange is exhibiting a strong inclination to murder, maim and steal?"

"No, but . . ."

"Then all we are left with is this Mr Drawlight – who, as far as I can tell, is not a magician at all."

"But his crimes are specifically magical crimes. Under English law he ought to be tried by the court of Cinque Dragownes – it is the proper place for him. These are the names of his crimes." Mr Norrell placed yet another list before the Prime Minister. "There! False Magic, Evil Tendings and Malevolent Pedagogy. No ordinary court is competent to deal with them."

"No doubt. But, as I have already observed, there is no one who can try the case."

"If your lordship will only cast your eye over page forty-two of my notes, I propose employing judges, advocates and proctors from the Doctors Commons. I could explain the principles of thaumaturgic law to them – it will take no more than a week or so. And I could lend them my servant, John Childermass, for as long as the trial lasts. He is a very knowledgeable man and could easily tell them when they were going wrong."

"What! The judge and lawyers to be coached in their duties by the plaintiff and his servant! Certainly not! Justice recoils from the idea!"

Mr Norrell blinked. "But what other security do I have that other magicians might not arise to challenge my authority and contradict me?"

"Mr Norrell, it is not the duty of the court – any court – to exalt one person's opinions above others! Not in magic nor in any other sphere of life. If other magicians think differently from you, then you must battle it out with them. You must prove the superiority of your opinions, as I do in politics. You must argue and publish and practise your magic and you must learn to live as I do – in the face of constant criticism, opposition and censure. That, sir, is the English way."

"But . . ."

"I am sorry, Mr Norrell. I will hear no more. That is an end of it. The Government of Great Britain is grateful to you. You have done your country immeasurable service. Any one may know how highly we prize you, but what you ask is quite impossible."

Drawlight's deception soon became common knowledge and, as Strange had predicted, a certain amount of blame attached to the two magicians. Drawlight was, after all, the bosom companion of one of them. It made an excellent subject for the caricaturists and several quite startling examples were published. One by George Cruikshank shewed Mr Norrell making a long speech to a group of his admirers about the nobility of English magic, while in a backroom Strange dictated a sort of bill of fare to a servant who chalked it upon a blackboard; "For killing a slight acquaintance by magic – twenty guineas. For killing a close friend – forty guineas. For killing a relation – one hundred guineas. For killing a spouse – four hundred guineas." In another caricature by Rowlandson a fashionable lady was walking in the street leading a fluffy little dog upon a leash. She was met by some of her acquaintance who began exclaiming over her dog: "La! Mrs Foulkes, what a sweet little pug!" "Yes," replied Mrs Foulkes, "it is Mr Foulkes. I paid Mr Strange and Mr Norrell fifty guineas to make my husband obedient to my every desire and this is the result."

There is no doubt that the caricatures and malicious paragraphs in the newspapers did the cause of English magic considerable damage. It was now possible for magic to be considered in quite a different light – not as the Nation's Greatest Defence, but as the tool of Malice and Envy.

And what of the people whom Drawlight had harmed? How did they view matters? There is no doubt that Mr Palgrave – the ancient, sick and disagreeable person who had hoped to live for ever – intended to prosecute Drawlight for fraud, but he was prevented from doing so by the circumstance of his dying suddenly the next day. His children and heirs (who all hated him) were rather pleased than otherwise to discover that his last days had been characterized by frustration, misery and disappointment. Nor did Drawlight have any thing to fear from Miss Gray or Mrs Bullworth. Miss Gray's friends and relations would not allow her to become embroiled in a vulgar court case and Mrs Bullworth's instructions to Drawlight had been so malicious as to make her culpable herself; she was powerless to strike at him. That left Gatcombe and Tantony, the Nottinghamshire brewers. As a practical man of business Mr Gatcombe was chiefly concerned to recover the money and sent bailiffs to London to fetch it. Unfortunately, Drawlight was unable to oblige Mr Gatcombe in this small particular, as he had spent it all long ago.

And so we come to Drawlight's real downfall, for no sooner had he escaped the gallows than his true Nemesis appeared in the already-cloudy sky of his existence, whirling through the air upon black wings to crush him. He had never been rich, indeed quite the reverse. He lived chiefly upon credit and by borrowing from his friends. Sometimes he won money at gambling clubs, but more often he encouraged foolish young Toms and Jerrys to gamble, and when they lost (which they invariably did) he would take them by the arm and, talking all the while, would lead them to this or that money-lender of his acquaintance. "I could not honestly recommend you to any other money-lender," he would tell them solicitously, "they require such monstrous amounts of interest – but Mr Buzzard is quite another sort. He is such a kindly old gentleman. He cannot bear to see any body denied a pleasure when he has the means of obtaining it for them. I truly think that he considers the lending of small sums of money more in the light of a work of charity than a business venture!"

For this small but important role in luring young men into debt, vice and ruination, Drawlight received payment from the money-lenders – generally four per cent of the first year's interest for the son of a commoner, six per cent for the son of a viscount or baronet and ten per cent for the son of an earl or duke.

News of his disgrace began to circulate. Tailors, hatters and glovemakers to whom he owed money became anxious and began to clamour for payment. Debts which he had confidently supposed might be put off for another four or five years were suddenly revived and made matters of urgency. Rough-faced men with sticks in their hands came pounding upon his door. He was advised by several people to go abroad immediately, but he could not quite believe that he was so entirely forsaken by his friends. He thought Mr Norrell would relent; he thought Lascelles, his dear, dear Lascelles, would help him. He sent them both respectful letters requesting the immediate loan of four hundred guineas. But Mr Norrell never replied and Lascelles only wrote to say that he made it a rule never to lend money to any one. Drawlight was arrested for debt upon the Tuesday morning and by the following Friday he was a prisoner in the King's Bench Prison.

On an evening towards the end of November, a week or so after these events, Strange and Arabella were sitting in the drawing-room at Soho-square. Arabella was writing a letter and Strange was plucking absent-mindedly at his hair and staring straight ahead of him. Suddenly he got up and went out of the room.

He reappeared an hour later with a dozen sheets of paper covered in writing.

Arabella looked up. "I thought the article for *The Friends of English Magic* was done," she said.

"This is not the article for *The Friends of English Magic*. It is a review of Portishead's book."

Arabella frowned. "But you cannot review a book which you yourself helped write."

"I believe I might. Under certain circumstances."

"Indeed! And what circumstances are those?"

"If I say it is an abominable book, a wicked fraud perpetrated upon the British public."

Arabella stared at him. "Jonathan!" she said at last.

"Well, it *is* an abominable book."

He handed her the sheaf of papers and she began to read them. The mantelpiece clock struck nine and Jeremy brought in the tea-things. When she had finished, she sighed. "What are you going to do?"

"I do not know. Publish it, I suppose."

"But what of poor Lord Portishead? If he has written things in his book that are wrong, then of course someone ought to say so. But you know very well that he only wrote them because you told him to. He will feel himself very ill used."

"Oh, quite! It is a wretched business from start to finish," said Strange unconcernedly. He sipped his tea and ate a piece of toast. "But that is not the point. Ought I to allow my regard for Portishead to prevent me from saying what I think is true? I do not think so. Do you?"

"But must it be you?" said Arabella with a miserable look. "Poor man, he will feel it so much more coming from you."

Strange frowned. "Of course it must be me. Who else is there? But, come. I promise you I will make him a very handsome apology just as soon as the occasion arises."

And with that Arabella was obliged to be content.

In the meantime Strange considered where he should send his review. His choice fell upon Mr Jeffrey, the editor of *The Edinburgh Review* in Scotland. *The Edinburgh Review*, it may be remembered, was a radical publication in favour of political reform, emancipation of Catholics and Jews, and all sorts of other things Mr Norrell did not approve. As a consequence, in recent years Mr Jeffrey had seen reviews and articles upon the Revival of English Magic appear in rival publications, while he, poor fellow, had none.

Naturally he was delighted to receive Strange's review. He was not in the least concerned about its astonishing and revolutionary content, since that was the sort of thing that he liked best. He wrote Strange a letter immediately, assuring him that he would publish it as soon as possible, and a couple of days later he sent Strange a haggis (a sort of Scotch pudding) as a present.

38

From *The Edinburgh Review*

January 1815

ART. XIII. *Essay on the Extraordinary Revival of English Magic, &c.* By JOHN WATERBURY, Lord PORTISHEAD, with an Account of the Magic done in the late Peninsular War: By JONATHAN STRANGE, Magician-in-Ordinary to His Grace the Duke of WELLINGTON. London, 1814. John Murray.

As the valued aide and confidant of Mr NORRELL and the friend of Mr STRANGE, Lord PORTISHEAD is admirably fitted to write the history of recent magical events, for he has been at the centre of many of them. Each of Mr NORRELL and Mr STRANGE's achievements has been widely discussed in the newspapers and reviews, but Lord PORTISHEAD's readers will have their understanding much improved by having the tale set out for them in its entirety.

Mr NORRELL's more enthusiastic admirers would have us believe that he arrived in London in the Spring of 1807 fully formed as England's Greatest Magician and the First Phenomenon of the Age, but it is clear from PORTISHEAD's account that both he and STRANGE have grown in confidence and skill from very tentative beginnings. PORTISHEAD does not neglect to mention their failures as well as their successes. Chapter Five contains a tragi-comic account of their long-running argument with the HORSE GUARDS which began in 1810 when one of the generals had the original notion of replacing the Cavalry's horses with unicorns. In this way it was hoped to grant the soldiers the power of goring Frenchmen through their hearts. Unfortunately, this excellent plan was never implemented since, far from finding unicorns in sufficient number for the Cavalry's use, Mr NORRELL and Mr STRANGE have yet to discover a single one.

Of more dubious value is the second half of his lordship's book, wherein he leaves description behind and begins to lay down rules to determine what is, and is not, respectable English magic – in other words what shall be called White Magic and what Black. There is nothing new here. Were the reader to cast his eye over the offerings of the recent commentators upon Magic, he would begin to perceive a curious uniformity of opinion. All recite the same history and all use the same arguments to establish their conclusions.

Perhaps the time has come to ask why this should be so. In every other branch of Knowledge our understanding is enlarged by rational opposition and debate. Law, Theology, History and Science have their various factions. Why then, in Magic, do we hear nothing but the same tired arguments? One begins to wonder why any one troubles to argue at all, since everyone appears to be convinced of the same truths. This dreary monotone is particularly evident in recent accounts of ENGLISH MAGICAL HISTORY which are growing more eccentric with each retelling.

Eight years ago this very author published *A Child's History of the Raven King*, one of the most perfect things of its kind. It conveys to the reader a vivid sense of the eeriness and wonder of JOHN USKGLASS's magic. So why does he now pretend to believe that true English Magic began in the sixteenth century with MARTIN PALE? In Chapter 6 of the *Essay on the Extraordinary Revival of English Magic, &c.*, he declares that PALE consciously set out to purge English Magic of its darker elements. He does not attempt to present any evidence for this extraordinary claim – which is just as well, since no evidence exists.

According to PORTISHEAD's present view, the tradition which began with PALE was more perfectly elaborated by HICKMAN, LANCHESTER, GOUBERT, BELASIS *et al* (those we term the ARGENTINE magicians), and has now reached its glorious apogee with Mr NORRELL and Mr STRANGE. It is certainly a view that Mr STRANGE and Mr NORRELL have worked hard to perpetrate. But it simply will not do. MARTIN PALE and the ARGENTINE magicians never intended to lay the foundations of English Magic. In every spell they recorded, in every word they wrote, they were trying to re-create the glorious Magic of their predecessors (those we term the Golden Age or AUREATE magicians): THOMAS GODBLESS, RALPH DE STOKESEY, CATHERINE OF WINCHESTER and, above all, JOHN USKGLASS. MARTIN PALE was the devoted follower of these magicians. He never ceased to regret that he had been born two hundred years out of his proper time.

One of the most extraordinary characteristics of the revival of English Magic has been its treatment of JOHN USKGLASS. Nowadays it seems that his name is only spoken in order to revile him. It is as if Mr DAVY and Mr FARADAY and our other Great Men of Science felt obliged to begin their lectures by expressing their contempt and loathing of ISAAC NEWTON. Or as if our eminent Physicians prefaced every announcement of a new discovery in Medicine with a description of the wickedness of WILLIAM HARVEY.

Lord PORTISHEAD devotes a long chapter of his book to trying to prove that JOHN USKGLASS is not, as is commonly supposed, the founder of English Magic since there were magicians in these islands before his time. I do not deny it. But what I do most vehemently deny is that there was any *tradition of Magic* in England before JOHN USKGLASS.

Let us examine these earlier magicians that PORTISHEAD

makes so much of. Who were they? JOSEPH OF ARIMATHEA was one, a magician who came from the Holy Lands and planted a magic tree to protect England from harm – but I never heard that he stayed long enough to teach any of the inhabitants his skills. MERLIN was another but, as he was upon his mother's side *Welsh* and upon his father's *Infernal*, he will scarcely do for that pattern of respectable English Magic upon which PORTISHEAD, NOR-RELL and STRANGE have set their hearts. And who were MERLIN's pupils and followers? We cannot name a single one. No, for once the common view is the correct one: Magic had been long extinct in these islands until JOHN USKGLASS came out of Faerie and established his Kingdom of Northern England.

PORTISHEAD seems to have had some doubts upon this point himself and in case his arguments have failed to convince his readers he sets about proving that JOHN USKGLASS's magic was inherently wicked. But it is far from clear that the examples he chuses support this conclusion. Let us examine one of them. Everyone has heard of the four magical woods that surrounded JOHN USKGLASS's capital city of Newcastle. Their names were Great Tom, Asmody's Citadel, Petty Egypt and Serlo's Blessing. They moved from place to place and were known, upon occasion, to swallow up people who approached the city intending harm to the inhabitants. Certainly the notion of man-eating woods strikes us as eerie and horrible, but there is no evidence that JOHN USKGLASS's contemporaries found it so. It was a violent Age; JOHN USKGLASS was a mediaeval king and he acted as a mediaeval king should, to protect his city and his citizens.

Often it is difficult to decide upon the morality of USKGLASS's actions because his motives are so obscure. Of all the AUREATE magicians he is the most mysterious. No one knows why in 1138 he caused the moon to disappear from the sky and made it travel through all the lakes and rivers of England. We do not know why in 1202 he quarrelled with Winter and banished it from his kingdom, so that for four years Northern England enjoyed continual Summer. Nor do we know why for thirty consecutive nights in May and June of 1345 every man, woman and child in the kingdom dreamt that they had been gathered together upon a dark red plain beneath a pale golden sky to build a tall black tower. Each night they laboured, waking in the morning in their own beds completely exhausted. The dream only ceased to trouble them when, on the thirtieth night, the tower and its fortifications were completed. In all these stories – but particularly in the last – we have a sense of great events going on, but what they might be we cannot tell. Several scholars have speculated that the tall black tower was situated in that part of Hell which USKGLASS was reputed to lease from LUCIFER and that USKGLASS was building a fortress in order to prosecute a war against his enemies in Hell. However, MARTIN PALE thought otherwise. He believed that there was a connexion between the construction of the tower and the appearance in England three years later of the Black Death. JOHN USKGLASS's kingdom of Northern England suffered a good deal less from the disease than its southern neighbour and PALE believed that this was because USKGLASS had constructed some sort of defence against it.

But according to the *Essay on the Extraordinary Revival of English Magic* we have no business even to wonder about such things. According to Mr NORRELL and Lord PORTISHEAD the Modern Magician ought not to meddle with things only half-understood. But *I* say that it is precisely because these things are only half-understood that we must study them.

English Magic is the strange house we magicians inhabit. It is built upon foundations that JOHN USKGLASS made and we ignore those foundations at our peril. They should be studied and their nature understood so that we can learn what they will support and what they will not. Otherwise cracks will appear, letting in winds from God-knows-where. The corridors will lead us to places we never intended to go.

In conclusion PORTISHEAD's book – though containing many excellent things – is a fine example of the mad contradiction at the heart of Modern English Magic: our foremost magicians continually declare their intention of erasing every hint and trace of JOHN USKGLASS from English Magic, but how is this even possible? It is JOHN USKGLASS's magic that we do.

39

The two magicians

February 1815

OF ALL THE CONTROVERSIAL pieces ever published in *The Edinburgh Review*, this was the most controversial by far. By the end of January there scarcely seemed to be an educated man or woman from one end of the country to the other who had not read it and formed an opinion upon it. Though it was unsigned, everyone knew who the author was – Strange. Oh, certainly at the beginning some people hesitated and pointed to the fact that Strange was as much criticized as Norrell – perhaps more. But these people were judged very stupid by their friends. Was not Jonathan Strange known to be precisely the sort of whimsical, contradictory person who *would* publish against himself? And did not the author declare himself to be a magician? Who else could it possibly be? Who else could speak with so much authority?

When Mr Norrell had first come to London, his opinions had seemed very new and not a little eccentric. But since then people had grown accustomed to them and he had seemed no more than the Mirror of the Times when he said that magic, like the oceans themselves, should agree to be governed by Englishmen. Its boundaries were to be drawn up and all that was not easily comprehensible to modern ladies and gentlemen – John Uskglass's three-hundred-year reign, the strange, uneasy history of our dealings with fairies – might be conveniently done away with. Now Strange had turned the Norrellite view of magic on its head. Suddenly it seemed that all that had been learnt in every English childhood of the wildness of English magic might still be true, and even now on some long-forgotten paths, behind the sky, on the other side of the rain, John Uskglass might be riding still, with his company of men and fairies.

Most people thought the partnership between the two magicians must be broken up. In London there was a rumour that Strange had been to Hanover-square and the servants had turned him away. And there was another, contradictory rumour to the effect that Strange had *not* been to Hanover-square, but that Mr Norrell was sitting night and day in his library, waiting for his pupil, pestering the servants every five minutes to go and look out of the window to see if he were coming.

On a Sunday evening in early February Strange did at last call upon Mr Norrell. This much was certain because two gentlemen on their way to St George's, Hanover-square saw him standing on the steps of the house; saw the door opened; saw Strange speak to the servant; and saw him instantly admitted as one who had been long expected. The two gentlemen continued on their way to church where they immediately told their friends in the neighbouring pews what they had seen. Five minutes later a thin, saintly-looking young man arrived at the church. Under the pretext of saying his prayers, he whispered that he had just spoken to someone who was leaning out of the first-floor window of the house next door to Mr Norrell's and this person believed he could hear Mr Strange ranting and haranguing his master. Two minutes later it was being reported throughout the church that both magicians had threatened each other with a kind of magical excommunication. The service began and several of the congregation were seen to gaze longingly at the windows, as if wondering why those apertures were always placed so high in ecclesiastical buildings. An anthem was sung to the accompaniment of the organ and some people said later that above the sound of the music they had heard great rolls of thunder – a sure sign of magical disturbances. But other people said that they had imagined it.

All of which would have greatly astonished the two magicians who were at that moment standing silently in Mr Norrell's library, regarding each other warily. Strange, who had not seen his tutor for some days, was shocked at his appearance. His face was haggard and his body shrunken – he looked ten years older.

"Shall we sit down, sir?" said Strange. He moved towards a chair and Mr Norrell flinched at the suddenness of the movement. It was almost as if he were expecting Strange to hit him. The next moment, however, he had recovered himself enough to sit down.

Strange was not much more comfortable. In the last few days he had asked himself over and over again if he had been right to publish the review, and repeatedly he had come to the conclusion that he had been. He had decided that the correct attitude to take was one of dignified moral superiority softened by a very moderate amount of apology. But now that he was actually sitting in Mr Norrell's library again, he did not find it easy to meet his tutor's eye. His gaze fixed itself upon an odd succession of objects – a small porcelain figure of Dr Martin Pale; the doorknob; his own thumbnail; Mr Norrell's left shoe.

Mr Norrell, on the other hand, never once took his eyes from Strange's face.

After several moments' silence both men spoke at once.

"After all your kindness to me . . ." began Strange.

"You think that I am angry," began Mr Norrell.

Both paused and then Strange indicated that Mr Norrell should continue.

"You think that I am angry," said Mr Norrell, "but I am not. You think I do not know why you have done what you have done, but I do. You think you have put all your heart into that writing and that every one in England now understands you. What do they understand? Nothing. I understood you before you wrote a word." He paused and his face worked as if he were struggling to say something that lay very deep inside him. "What you wrote, you wrote for me. For me alone."

Strange opened his mouth to protest at this surprizing conclusion. But upon consideration he realized it was probably true. He was silent.

Mr Norrell continued. "Do you really believe that I have never felt the same . . . the same *longing* you feel? *It is John Uskglass's magic that we do.* Of course it is. What else should it be? I tell you, there were times when I was young when I would have done any thing, endured any thing, to find him and throw myself at his feet. I tried to conjure him up – Ha! That was the act of a very young, very foolish man – to treat a king like a footman and summon him to come and talk to me. I consider it one of the most fortunate circumstances of my life that I was unsuccessful! Then I tried to find him using the old spells of election. I could not even make the spells work. All the magic of my youth was wasted in trying to find him. For ten years I thought of nothing else."

"You never said any of this before, sir."

Mr Norrell sighed. "I wished to prevent you from falling into my error." He raised his hands in a gesture of helplessness.

"But by your own account, Mr Norrell, this was long ago when you were young and inexperienced. You are a very different magician now, and I flatter myself that I am no ordinary assistant. Perhaps if we were to try again?"

"One cannot find so powerful a magician unless he wishes to be found," declared Mr Norrell, flatly. "It is useless to make the attempt. Do you think he cares what happens to England? I tell you he does not. He abandoned us long ago."

"Abandoned?" said Strange, frowning. "That is rather a harsh word. I suppose years of disappointment would naturally incline one towards a conclusion of that sort. But there are many accounts of people who saw John Uskglass long after he had supposedly left England. The glovemaker's child in Newcastle,[1]

---

[1] In the late seventeenth century there was a glovemaker in the King's city of Newcastle who had a daughter – a bold little thing. One day this child, whom everyone supposed to be playing in some corner of her father's house, was missed. Her mother and father and brothers searched for her. The neighbours searched, but she was nowhere to be found. Then in the late afternoon they looked up and saw her coming down the muddy, cobbled hill. Some of them thought for a moment that they saw someone beside her in the dark winter street, but she came on alone. She was quite unharmed and her story, when they had pieced it together, was this:

She had left her father's house to go wandering in the city and had quickly come upon a street she had never seen before. This street was wide and well-paved and led her straight up, higher than she had ever been before, to the gate and courtyard of a great stone house. She had gone into the house and looked into many rooms, but all were silent, empty, full of dust and spiders. On one side of the house there was a suite of rooms where the shadows of leaves fell ceaselessly over walls and floor as if there were summer trees outside the windows, but there were no trees (and it was, in any case, winter). One room contained nothing but a high mirror. Room and mirror seemed to have quarrelled at some time for the mirror shewed the room to be filled with birds but the room was empty. Yet the glovemaker's child could hear birdsong all around her. There was a long dark corridor with a sound of rushing water as if some dark sea or river lay at the end of it. From the windows of some rooms she saw the city of Newcastle, but from others she saw a different city entirely and others shewed only high, wild moors and a cold blue sky.

She saw many staircases winding up inside the house, great staircases at first, which grew rapidly narrower and more twisting as she mounted higher in the house, until at the top they were only such chinks and gaps in the masonry that a child might notice and a child could slip through. The last of these led to a little door of plain wood.

Having no reason to fear she pushed it open but what she found on the other side made her cry out. It seemed to her that a thousand, thousand birds thronged the air, so that there was neither daylight nor darkness but only a great confusion of black wings. A wind seemed to come to her from far away and she had the impression of immense space as if she had climbed up to the sky and found it full of ravens. The glovemaker's child began to be very much afraid, but then she heard someone say her name. Instantly the birds disappeared and she found herself in a small room with bare stone walls and a bare stone floor. There was no furniture of any kind but, seated upon the floor, was a man who beckoned to her and called her by her name again and told her not to be afraid. He had long, ragged black hair and strange, ragged black clothes. There was nothing about him that suggested a king and

the Yorkshire farmer,[2] the Basque sailor . . ."[3]

Mr Norrell made a small sound of irritation. "Hearsay and superstition! Even if those stories are true – which I am very far from allowing – I have never understood how any of them knew

---

[1] *cont'd*   the only symbol of his magicianship was the great silver dish of water at his side. The glovemaker's daughter stayed by the man's side for some hours until dusk, when he led her down through the house into the city to her home.

[2] See Chapter 33, footnote 3.

[3] Perhaps the eeriest tale told of John Uskglass's return was that told by a Basque sailor, a survivor of the Spanish king's great Armada. After his ship was destroyed by storms on the far northern coasts of England, the sailor and two companions had fled inland. They dared not go near villages, but it was winter and the frost was thick upon the ground; they feared they would die of the cold. As night came on they found an empty stone building on a high hillside of bare frozen earth. It was almost dark inside, but there were openings high in the wall that let in starlight. They lay down upon the earth floor and slept.

The Basque sailor dreamt that there was a king who watched him.

He woke. Above him dim shafts of grey light pierced the winter dark. In the shadows at the farthest end of the building he thought he saw a raised stone dais. As the light grew he saw something upon the dais: a chair or throne. A man sat upon the throne; a pale man with long black hair, wrapped in a black robe. Terrified, the man woke his fellows and shewed them the uncanny sight of the man who sat upon the throne. He seemed to watch them but he never moved, not so much as a finger; yet it did not occur to them to doubt that he was a living man. They stumbled to the door and ran away across the frozen fields.

The Basque sailor soon lost his companions: one man died of cold and heartbreak within the week; the other, determined to try and make his way back to the Bay of Biscay, began to walk south, and what became of him no one knows. But the Basque sailor stayed in Cumbria and was taken in by some farm people. He became a servant at that same farm and married a young girl from a neighbouring farm. All his life he told the story of the stone barn upon the high hills, and he was taught by his new friends and neighbours to believe that the man upon the black throne was the Raven King. The Basque sailor never found the stone barn again, and neither did his friends nor any of his children.

And all his life whenever he went into dark places he said, "I greet thee, Lord, and bid thee welcome to my heart" – in case the pale king with the long black hair should be seated in the darkness waiting for him. Across the expanses of northern England a thousand, thousand darknesses, a thousand, thousand places for the King to be. "I greet thee, Lord, and bid thee welcome to my heart."

that the person they had seen was John Uskglass. No portraits of him exist. Two of your examples – the glovemaker's child and the Basque sailor – did not in fact identify him as Uskglass. They saw a man in black clothes and other people *told* them later that it was John Uskglass. But it is really of very little consequence whether or not he returned at this or that time or was seen by this or that person. The fact remains that when he abandoned his throne and rode out of England he took the best part of English magic with him. From that day forth it began to decline. Surely that is enough in itself to mark him as our enemy? You are familiar, I dare say, with Watershippe's *A Faire Wood Withering*?"[4]

"No, I do not know it," said Strange. He gave Mr Norrell a sharp look that seemed to say he had not read it for the usual reason. "But I cannot help wishing, sir, that you had said some of this before."

"Perhaps I have been wrong to keep so much of my mind from you," said Mr Norrell, knotting his fingers together. "I am almost certain now that I have been wrong. But I decided long ago that Great Britain's best interests were served by absolute silence on these subjects and old habits are hard to break. But surely you see the task before us, Mr Strange? Yours and mine? Magic cannot wait upon the pleasure of a King who no longer cares what happens to England. We must break English magicians of their dependence on him. We must make them forget John Uskglass as completely as he has forgotten us."

---

[4] *A Faire Wood Withering* (1444) by Peter Watershippe. This is a remarkably detailed description by a contemporary magician of how English magic declined after John Uskglass left England. In 1434 (the year of Uskglass's departure) Watershippe was twenty-five, a young man just beginning to practise magic in Norwich. *A Faire Wood Withering* contains precise accounts of spells which were perfectly practicable as long as Uskglass and his fairy subjects remained in England but which no longer had any effect after their departure. Indeed it is remarkable how much of our knowledge of *Aureate* English magic comes from Watershippe. *A Faire Wood Withering* seems an angry book until one compares it with two of Watershippe's later books: *A Defence of my Deeds Written while Wrongly Imprisoned by my Enemies in Newark Castle* (1459/60) and *Crimes of the False King* (written 1461?, published 1697, Penzance).

Strange shook his head, frowning. "No. In spite of all you say, it still seems to me that John Uskglass stands at the very heart of English magic and that we ignore him at our peril. Perhaps I will be proved wrong in the end. Nothing is more likely. But on a matter of such vital importance to English magic I need to understand for myself. Do not think that I am ungrateful, sir, but I believe the period of our collaboration is over. It seems to me that we are too different . . ."

"Oh!" cried Mr Norrell. "I know that in character . . ." He made a gesture of dismissal. "But what does that matter? We are magicians. That is the beginning and end of me and the beginning and end of you. It is all that either of us cares about. If you leave this house today and pursue your own course, who will you talk to? – as we are talking now? –there is no one. You will be quite alone." In a tone almost of pleading, he whispered, "Do not do this!"

Strange stared in perplexity at his master. This was by no means what he had expected. Far from being driven into a passion of fury by Strange's review, Mr Norrell seemed only to have been provoked into an outburst of honesty and humility. At that moment it seemed to Strange both reasonable and desirable to return to Mr Norrell's tutelage. It was only pride and the consciousness that he was certain to feel differently in an hour or two which prompted him to say, "I am sorry, Mr Norrell, but ever since I returned from the Peninsula it has not felt right to me to call myself your pupil. I have felt as if I was acting a part. To submit my writings for your approval so that you can make changes in any way that you see fit – it is what I can no longer do. It is making me say what I no longer believe."

"All, all is to be done in public," sighed Mr Norrell. He leaned forward and said with more energy, "Be guided by me. Promise me that you will publish nothing, speak nothing, do nothing until you are quite decided upon these matters. Believe me when I tell you that ten, twenty, even fifty years of silence is worth the satisfaction of knowing at the end that you have said what you ought – no more, no less. Silence and inaction will not suit you – I know that. But I promise to make what amends I can. You will not lose by it. If you have ever had cause to consider me ungrateful, you shall not find me so in future. I shall tell everyone how highly I prize you. We shall no longer be tutor and pupil. Let it be a partnership of equals! Have I not in any case learnt almost as much from you as you have from me? The most lucrative business shall all be yours! The books . . ." He swallowed slightly. "The books which I ought to have lent you and which I have kept from you, you shall read them! We will go to Yorkshire, you and I together – tonight if you wish it! – and I will give you the key to the library and you shall read whatever you desire. I . . ." Mr Norrell passed his hand across his brow, as if in surprize at his own words. "I shall not even ask for a retraction of the review. Let it stand. Let it stand. And in time, you and I, together, will answer all the questions you raise in it."

There was a long silence. Mr Norrell watched the other magician's face eagerly. His offer to shew Strange the library at Hurtfew was not without effect. For some moments Strange was clearly wavering in his determination to part with his master, but at last he said, "I am honoured, sir. You are not usually a man for a compromise, I know. But I think I must follow my own course now. I think we must part."

Mr Norrell closed his eyes.

At that moment the door opened. Lucas and one of the other footmen entered with the tea-tray.

"Come, sir," said Strange.

He touched his master's arm to rouse him a little and England's only two magicians took tea together for the last time.

Strange left Hanover-square at half past eight. Several people, lingering by their downstairs windows, saw him go. Other people, who scorned to watch themselves, had sent their maids and

541

footmen to stand about the square. Whether Lascelles had made some arrangement of this sort is not known, but ten minutes after Strange had turned the corner into Oxford-street Lascelles knocked upon Mr Norrell's door.

Mr Norrell was still in the library, still in the chair he had been sitting in when Strange had left. He was staring fixedly at the carpet.

"Is he gone?" asked Lascelles.

Mr Norrell did not answer.

Lascelles sat down. "Our conditions? How did he receive them?"

Still no reply.

"Mr Norrell? You told him what we agreed? You told him that unless he publishes a retraction we shall be forced to reveal what we know of the Black Magic done in Spain? You told him that under no circumstances would you accept him any longer as a pupil?"

"No," said Mr Norrell. "I said none of those things."

"But . . ."

Mr Norrell sighed deeply. "It does not matter what I said to him. He is gone."

Lascelles was silent a moment and looked with some displeasure at the magician. Mr Norrell, still lost in his own thoughts, did not observe this.

Finally, Lascelles shrugged. "You were right in the beginning, sir," he said. "There can be only one magician in England."

"What do you mean?"

"I mean that *two* of any thing is a most uncomfortable number. *One* may do as he pleases. *Six* may get along well enough. But *two* must always struggle for mastery. *Two* must always watch each other. The eyes of all the world will be on *two*, uncertain which of them to follow. You sigh, Mr Norrell. You know that I am right. Henceforth we must consider Strange in all our plans – what he will say, what he will do, how to counter him. You have often told

542

me that he is a remarkable magician. His brilliance was a great advantage when it was employed in your service. But that is all over now. Sooner or later he is sure to turn his talents against you. We cannot begin to guard against him too soon. I am speaking quite literally. His genius for magic is so great and his materials so poor and the end of it will be that he comes to believe that all things are permitted to a magician – be they house-breaking, theft or deception." Lascelles leant forward. "I do not mean that he is so depraved as to steal from you at this moment, but if a day ever comes when he is in great need, then it will appear to his undisciplined mind that any breach of trust, any violation of private property is justified." He paused. "You have made provision against thieves at Hurtfew? Spells of concealment?"

"Spells of concealment would be no protection against Strange!" declared Mr Norrell, angrily. "They would only serve to attract his eye! It would bring him straight to my most precious volumes! No, no, you are right." He sighed. "Something more is needed here. I must think."

Two hours after Strange's departure Mr Norrell and Lascelles left Hanover-square in Mr Norrell's carriage. Three servants accompanied them and they had every appearance on embarking on a long journey.

The following day, Strange, as whimsical and contradictory as ever, was inclined to regret his break with Mr Norrell. Mr Norrell's prediction that he would never again have any one to talk to about magic continually presented itself to his mind. He had been rehearsing their conversation. He was almost certain that all Norrell's conclusions concerning John Uskglass were wrong. As a consequence of what Mr Norrell had said he had developed a great many new ideas about John Uskglass, and now he was suffering all the misery of having no one to tell them to.

In the absence of a more suitable listener he went and complained to Sir Walter Pole in Harley-street.

"Since last night I have thought of fifty things I ought to have said to him. Now I suppose I shall have to put them in an article or a review – which will not be published until April at the earliest – and then he will have to instruct Lascelles or Portishead to write a repudiation – which will not appear until June or July. Five or six months to know what he would say to me! It is a very cumbersome way of conducting an argument, particularly when you consider that until yesterday I could simply have walked to Hanover-square and asked him what he thought. And I am certain now to get no sight nor smell of the books which matter! How is a magician to exist without books? Let someone explain *that* to me. It is like asking a politician to achieve high office without the benefit of bribes or patronage."

Sir Walter took no offence at this peculiarly uncivil remark, but charitably made allowances for the irritation of Strange's spirits. As a schoolboy at Harrow he had been forced to study magical history (which he had loathed) and he now cast his mind back to discover if he remembered any thing which might be useful. He found that he did not remember much – as much, he thought wryly, as might half-fill a very small wine-glass.

He thought for a moment or two and at last offered the following. "It is my understanding that the Raven King learnt all there is to know of English magic without the aid of any books – since there were none at that time in England – and so perhaps you could do the same?"

Strange gave him a very cool look. "And it is *my* understanding that the Raven King was the favourite foster-child of King Auberon, which, among other trifles, secured him an excellent magical education and a large kingdom of his own. I suppose that I could take to loitering in out-of-the-way copses and mossy glades in the hopes of being adopted by some fairy royalty but I rather think that they might find me a little tall for the purpose."

Sir Walter laughed. "And what shall you do now, without Mr Norrell to fill your days for you? Shall I tell Robson at the Foreign

Office to send you some magic to do? Only last week he was complaining that he is obliged to wait until all the work for the Admiralty and the Treasury is done before Mr Norrell has any time to spare for him."

"By all means. But tell him it cannot be for two or three months. We are going home to Shropshire. Both Arabella and I have a great desire to be in our own country and now that we need not consult the convenience of Mr Norrell, nothing remains to prevent our going."

"Oh!" said Sir Walter. "But you are not going immediately?"

"In two days' time."

"So soon?"

"Do not look so stricken! Really, Pole, I had no idea you were so fond of my company!"

"I am not. I was thinking of Lady Pole. It will be a sad change for her. She will miss her friend."

"Oh! Oh, yes!" said Strange, a little discomfited. "Of course!"

Later that morning Arabella made her parting visit to Lady Pole. Five years had made very little difference to her ladyship's beauty and none at all to her sad condition. She was as silent as ever and as indifferent to every pain or pleasure. Kindness or coldness left her equally unmoved. She passed her days sitting by the window in the Venetian drawing-room in the house in Harley-street. She never exhibited the least inclination for any occupation and Arabella was her only visitor.

"I wish you were not going," said her ladyship, when Arabella told her the news. "What sort of a place is Shropshire?"

"Oh! I fear I am a very partial judge. I believe that most people would agree that it is a pretty place with green hills and woods and sweet country lanes. Of course we shall have to wait for spring to enjoy it completely. But even in winter the views can be very striking. It is a peculiarly romantic county with a noble history. There are ruined castles and stones planted on the hilltops by who-knows-what people – and being so close to Wales it has often been fought over – there are ancient battlefields in almost every valley."

"Battlefields!" said Lady Pole. "I know only too well what that is like. To glance out of a window and see nothing but broken bones and rusting armour everywhere one looks! It is a very melancholy sight. I hope you will not find it too distressing."

"Broken bones and armour?" echoed Arabella. "No, indeed. Your ladyship misunderstands me. The battles were all long ago. There is nothing to see – certainly nothing to distress one."

"And yet, you know," continued Lady Pole, scarcely attending to her, "battles have been fought at some time or other almost everywhere. I remember learning in my schoolroom how London was once the scene of a particularly fierce battle. The people were put to death in horrible ways and the city was burnt to the ground. We are surrounded by the shadows of violence and misery all the days of our life and it seems to me that it matters very little whether any material sign remains or not."

Something changed in the room. It was as if cold, grey, beating wings had passed over their heads or as if someone had walked through the mirrors and cast a shadow into the room. It was an odd trick of the light which Arabella had often observed when she sat with Lady Pole. Not knowing what else to attribute it to, she supposed it must be because there were so many mirrors in the room.

Lady Pole shivered and pulled her shawl tighter round her. Arabella leaned forward and took her hand. "Come! Fix your thoughts upon more cheerful objects."

Lady Pole looked at her blankly. She had no more idea how to be cheerful than to fly.

So Arabella began to talk, hoping to distract her for a time from thinking of horrors. She spoke of new shops and new fashions. She described a very pretty ivory-coloured sarsenet she had seen in a window in Friday-street and a trimming of turquoise-coloured bugle beads she had seen somewhere else which would match the ivory sarsenet beautifully. She went on to relate what her dressmaker had said about bugle beads, and then to describe an extraordinary plant that the dressmaker possessed which stood in a pot on a little iron balcony outside the window and which had grown so tall in the space of a year that it had entirely blocked up a window on the floor above belonging to a candlestick-maker. Next came other surprizingly tall plants – Jack and his beanstalk – the giant at the top of the beanstalk – giants and giant-killers in general – Napoleon Buonaparte and the Duke of Wellington – the Duke's merits in every sphere of life except in one – the great unhappiness of the Duchess.

"Happily, it is what you and I have never known any thing of," she finished up, a little breathless, "to have one's peace continually cut up by the sight of one's husband paying attentions to other women."

"I suppose so," answered Lady Pole, somewhat doubtfully.

This annoyed Arabella. She tried to make allowances for all Lady Pole's oddities, but she found it rather hard to forgive her her habitual coolness towards her husband. Arabella could not visit at Harley-street as often as she did without being aware of how very devoted Sir Walter was to Lady Pole. If he ever thought that any thing might bring her pleasure or ease her sufferings in the slightest, then that thing was done in an instant, and Arabella could never observe without a pang the very meagre return he got for his pains. It was not that Lady Pole shewed any dislike towards him; but sometimes she scarcely seemed to know that he was there.

"Oh! But you do not consider what a blessing it is," said Arabella. "One of the best blessings of existence."

"What is?"

"Your husband's love."

Lady Pole looked surprized. "Yes, he does love me," she said at last. "Or at least he tells me that he does. But what good is that to me? It has never warmed me when I was cold – and I always am cold, you know. It has never shortened a long, dreary ball by so

547

much as a minute or stopped a procession through long, dark, ghostly corridors. It has never saved me from any misery at all. Has the love of your husband ever saved you from any thing?"

"Mr Strange?" smiled Arabella. "No, never. I am more in the habit of saving him! I mean," she added quickly, since it was clear that Lady Pole did not understand her, "that he often meets with people who wish him to do magic on their behalf. – Or they have a great-nephew who wishes to learn magic from him. – Or they believe they have discovered a magic shoe or fork or some such nonsense. They mean no harm. Indeed they are generally most respectful. But Mr Strange is not the most patient of men and so I am obliged to go in and rescue him before he says something that he had much better not."

It was time for Arabella to be thinking of leaving and she began upon her goodbyes. Now that they might not meet again for many months she was particularly anxious to say something cheerful. "And I hope, my dear Lady Pole," she said, "that when you and I next meet you will be a great deal better and perhaps able to go out into society again. It is my dearest wish that one day we shall see each other at a theatre or in a ballroom . . ."

"A ballroom!" exclaimed Lady Pole in horror. "What in the world should make you say that? God forbid that you and I should ever meet in a ballroom!"

"Hush! Hush! I never meant to distress you. I forgot how you hate dancing. Come, do not weep! Do not think of it, if it makes you unhappy!"

She did her best to soothe her friend. She embraced her, kissed her cheek and her hair, stroked her hand, offered her lavender-water. Nothing did any good. For several minutes Lady Pole was entirely given over to a fit of weeping. Arabella could not quite understand what the matter was. But then again, what understanding could there be? It was part of her ladyship's complaint to be put in a fright by trifles, to be made unhappy by nothing at all. Arabella rang the bell to summon the maid.

Only when the maid appeared, did her ladyship at last make an effort to compose herself. "You do not understand what you have said!" she cried. "And God forbid that you should ever find out as I have. I shall try to warn you – I know it is hopeless, but I shall try! Listen to me, my dear, dear Mrs Strange. Listen as if your hopes of eternal salvation depended upon it!"

So Arabella looked as attentive as she possibly could.

But it was all to no end. This occasion proved no different from any other when her ladyship had claimed to have something of great importance to communicate to Arabella. She looked pale, took several deep breaths – and then proceeded to relate a very odd story about the owner of a Derbyshire leadmine who fell in love with a milkmaid. The milkmaid was everything the mine-owner had ever hoped for, except that her reflection always came several minutes too late into a mirror, her eyes changed colour at sunset and her shadow was often seen dancing wild dances when she herself was still.

After Lady Pole had gone upstairs, Arabella sat alone. "How stupid of me!" she thought. "When I know very well that any mention of dancing distresses her beyond measure! How can I have been so unguarded? I wonder what it was that she wished to tell me? I wonder if she knows herself? Poor thing! Without the blessing of health and reason, riches and beauty are worthless indeed!"

She was moralizing to herself in this strain, when a slight noise behind her caused her to look round. Immediately she rose from her seat and walked rapidly towards the door with hands out-stretched.

"It is you! How glad I am to see you! Come! Shake hands with me. This will be our last meeting for a long time."

That evening she said to Strange, "One person at least is delighted that you have turned your attention to the study of John Uskglass and his fairy-subjects."

"Oh? And who is that?"

"The gentleman with the thistle-down hair."

"Who?"

"The gentleman who lives with Sir Walter and Lady Pole. I told you before."

"Oh, yes! I remember." There was a silence of some moments while Strange considered this. "Arabella!" he suddenly exclaimed. "Do you mean to tell me that you have still not learnt his name?" He began to laugh.

Arabella looked annoyed. "It is not my fault," she said. "He has never said his name and I have never remembered to ask him. But I am glad you take it so lightly. I thought at one time that you were inclined to be jealous."

"I do not remember that I was."

"How odd! I remember it quite distinctly."

"I beg your pardon, Arabella, but it is difficult to be jealous of a man whose acquaintance you made a number of years ago and whose name you have yet to discover. So he approves of my work, does he?"

"Yes, he has often told me that you will never get anywhere until you begin to study fairies. He says that that is what true magic is – the study of fairies and fairy magic."

"Indeed? He seems to have very decided views upon the subject! And what, pray, does he know about it? Is he a magician?"

"I do not think so. He once declared that he had never read a book upon the subject in his life."

"Oh! He is one of those, is he?" said Strange, contemptuously. "He has not studied the subject at all, but has managed to devise a great many theories about it. I meet with that sort very often. Well, if he is not a magician, what is he? Can you at least tell me that?"

"I think I can," said Arabella in the pleased manner of someone who has made a very clever discovery.

Strange sat expectantly.

"No," said Arabella, "I will not tell you. You will only laugh at me again."

"Probably."

"Well, then," said Arabella after a moment, "I believe he is a prince. Or a king. He is certainly of royal blood."

"What in the world should make you think that?"

"Because he has told me a great deal of his kingdoms and his castles and his mansions – though I confess they all have very odd names and I never heard of a single one before. I think he must be one of the princes that Buonaparte deposed in Germany or Swisserland."

"Indeed?" said Strange, with some irritation. "Well, now that Buonaparte has been defeated, perhaps he would like to go home again."

None of these half-explanations and guesses concerning the gentleman with the thistle-down hair quite satisfied him and he continued to wonder about Arabella's friend. The following day (which was to be the Stranges' last in London) he walked to Sir Walter's office in Whitehall with the express intention of discovering who the fellow was.

But when Strange arrived, he found only Sir Walter's private secretary hard at work.

"Oh! Moorcock! Good morning! Has Sir Walter gone?"

"He has just gone to Fife House,[5] Mr Strange. Is there any thing I can do for you?"

"No, I do not . . . Well, perhaps. There is something I always mean to ask Sir Walter and I never remember. I don't suppose that you are at all acquainted with the gentleman who lives at his house?"

"Whose house, sir?"

"Sir Walter's."

Mr Moorcock frowned. "A gentleman at Sir Walter's house? I cannot think whom you mean. What is his name?"

---

[5] Lord Liverpool's London home, a quaint, old, rambling mansion which stood by the Thames.

"That is what I wish to know. I have never seen the fellow, but Mrs Strange always seems to meet him the moment she steps out of the house. She has known him for years yet she has never been able to discover his name. He must be a very eccentric sort of person to make such a secret of it. Mrs Strange always calls him the gentleman with the silvery nose or the gentleman with the snow-white complexion. Or some odd name of that sort."

But Mr Moorcock only looked even more bewildered at this information. "I am very sorry, sir. I do not think I can ever have seen him."

40

"Depend upon it; there is no such place."

June 1815

THE EMPEROR NAPOLEON Buonaparte had been banished to the island of Elba. However His Imperial Majesty had some doubts whether a quiet island life would suit him – he was, after all, accustomed to governing a large proportion of the known world. And so before he left France he told several people that when violets bloomed again in spring he would return. This promise he kept.

The moment he arrived upon French soil he gathered an army and marched north to Paris in further pursuit of his destiny, which was to make war upon all the peoples of the world. Naturally he was eager to re-establish himself as *Emperor*, but it was not yet known where he would chuse to be Emperor *of*. He had always yearned to emulate Alexander the Great and so it was thought that he might go east. He had invaded Egypt once before and had some success there. Or he might go west: there were rumours of a fleet of ships at Cherbourg ready and waiting to take him to America to begin the conquest of a fresh, new world.

But wherever he chose, everyone agreed that he was sure to begin by invading Belgium and so the Duke of Wellington went to Brussels to await the arrival of Europe's Great Enemy.

The English newspapers were full of rumours: Buonaparte had assembled his army; he was advancing with appalling swiftness upon Belgium; he was there; he was victorious! Then the next day it would appear that he was still in his palace in Paris, never having stirred from there in the first place.

At the end of May, Jonathan Strange followed Wellington and the Army to Brussels. He had spent the past three months quietly in Shropshire thinking about magic and so it was hardly surprizing that he should feel a little bewildered at first. However after he had walked about for an hour or two he came to the conclusion that the fault was not in him, but in Brussels itself. He knew what a city at war looked like, and this was not it. There ought to have been companies of soldiers passing up and down, carts with supplies, anxious-looking faces. Instead he saw fashionable-looking shops and ladies lounging in smart carriages. True, there were groups of officers everywhere, but none of them appeared to have any idea of pursuing military business (one was expending a great deal of concentration and effort in mending a toy parasol for a little girl). There was a great deal more laughter and gaiety than seemed quite consistent with an imminent invasion by Napoleon Buonaparte.

A voice called out his name. He turned and found Colonel Manningham, an acquaintance of his, who immediately invited Strange to go with him to Lady Charlotte Greville's house. (This was an English lady who was living in Brussels.) Strange protested that he had no invitation and anyway he ought to go and look for the Duke. But Manningham declared that the lack of an invitation could not possibly matter – he was sure to be welcome – and the Duke was just as likely to be in Lady Charlotte Greville's drawing-room as anywhere else.

Ten minutes later Strange found himself in a luxurious apartment filled with people, many of whom he already knew. There were officers; beautiful ladies; fashionable gentlemen; British politicians; and representatives, so it seemed, of every rank and degree of British peer. All of them were loudly discussing the war and making jokes about it. It was quite a new idea to Strange:

war as a fashionable amusement. In Spain and Portugal it had been customary for the soldiers to regard themselves as martyred, maligned and forgotten. Reports in the British newspapers had always endeavoured to make the situation sound as gloomy as possible. But here in Brussels it was the noblest thing in the world to be one of his Grace's officers – and the second noblest to be his Grace's magician.

"Does Wellington really want all these people here?" whispered Strange to Manningham in amazement. "What will happen if the French attack? I wish I had not come. Someone is sure to begin asking me about my disagreement with Norrell, and I really do not want to talk about it."

"Nonsense!" Manningham whispered back. "No one cares about that here! And anyway here is the Duke!"

There was a little bustle and the Duke appeared. "Ah, Merlin!" he cried as his eye lighted upon Strange. "I am very glad to see you! Shake hands with me! You are acquainted with the Duke of Richmond, of course. No? Then allow me to make the introduction!"

If the assembly had been lively before, how much more spirited it became now his Grace was here! All eyes turned in his direction to discover whom he was talking to and (more interesting still) whom he was flirting with. One would not have supposed to look at him that he had come to Brussels for any other reason than to enjoy himself. But every time Strange tried to move away, the Duke fixed him with a look, as if to say, "No, *you* must stay. I have need of you!" Eventually, still smiling, he inclined his head and murmured in Strange's ear, "There, I believe that will do. Come! There is a conservatory at the other end of the room. We will be out of the crowd there."

They took their seats amid the palms and other exotic plants.

"A word of warning," said the Duke. "This is not Spain. In Spain the French were the detested enemy of every man, woman and child in the country. But here matters stand quite differently.

Buonaparte has friends in every street and in a great many parts of the Army. The city is full of spies. And so it is our job – yours and mine – to look as if nothing in the world were more certain than his defeat! Smile, Merlin! Take some tea. It will steady your nerves."

Strange tried a careless smile, but it immediately turned itself into an anxious frown and so, to draw his Grace's attention away from the deficiencies of his face, he inquired how his Grace liked the Army.

"Oh! It is a bad army at best. The most miscellaneous Army I ever commanded. British, Belgians, Dutch and Germans all mixed up together. It is like trying to build a wall out of half a dozen materials. Each material may be excellent in its way, but one cannot help wondering if the thing will hold together. But the Prussian Army has promised to fight with us. And Blücher is an excellent old fellow. Loves a fight." (This was the Prussian General.) "Unfortunately, he is also mad. He believes he is pregnant."

"Ah!"

"With a baby elephant."

"Ah!"

"But we must put you to work straightaway! Have you your books? Your silver dish? A place to work? I have a strong presentiment that Buonaparte will appear first in the west, from the direction of Lille. It is certainly the way I would chuse and I have letters from our friends in that city assuring me that he is hourly expected there. That is your task. Watch the western border for signs of his approach and tell me the instant you catch a glimpse of French troops."

For the next fortnight Strange summoned up visions of places where the Duke thought the French might appear. The Duke provided him with two things to help him: a large map and a young officer called William Hadley-Bright.

Hadley-Bright was one of those happy men for whom Fortune reserves her choicest gifts. Everything came easily to him. He was the adored only child of a rich widow. He had wanted a military career; his friends had got him a commission in a fashionable regiment. He had wanted excitement and adventure; the Duke of Wellington had chosen him to be one of his *aides-de-camp*. Then, just as he had decided that the one thing he loved more than soldiering was English magic, the Duke had appointed him to assist the sublime and mysterious Jonathan Strange. But only persons of a particularly sour disposition could resent Hadley-Bright's success; everyone else was disarmed by his cheerfulness and good nature.

Day after day Strange and Hadley-Bright examined ancient fortified cities in the west of Belgium; they peered at dull village streets; they watched vast, empty vistas of fields beneath even vaster prospects of watercolour clouds. But the French did not appear.

On a hot, sticky day in the middle of June they were seated at this interminable task. It was about three o'clock. The waiter had neglected to remove some dirty coffee-cups and a fly buzzed around them. From the open window came the mingled odours of horse-sweat, peaches and sour milk. Hadley-Bright, perched on a dining-chair, was demonstrating to perfection one of the most important skills of a soldier – that of falling asleep under any circumstances and at any time.

Strange glanced at his map and chose a spot at random. In the water of his silver dish a quiet crossroads appeared; nearby was a farm and two or three houses. He watched for a moment. Nothing happened. His eyes closed and he was on the point of dozing off when some soldiers dragged a gun into position beneath some elm-trees. They had a rather businesslike air. He kicked Hadley-Bright to wake him up. "Who are those fellows?" he asked.

Hadley-Bright blinked at the silver dish.

The soldiers at the crossroads wore green coats with red facings. There suddenly seemed to be a great many of them.

"Nassauers," said Hadley-Bright, naming some of Wellington's

German troops. "The Prince of Orange's boys. Nothing to worry about. What are you looking at?"

"A crossroads twenty miles south of the city. A place called Quatre Bras."

"Oh! There is no need to spend time on that!" declared Hadley-Bright with a yawn. "That is on the road to Charleroi. The Prussian Army is at the other end of it – or so I am told. I wonder if those fellows are supposed to be there?" He began to leaf through some papers describing the disposition of the various Allied armies. "No, I really don't think . . ."

"And what is *that*?" interrupted Strange, pointing at a soldier in a blue coat who had appeared suddenly over the opposite rise with his musket at the ready.

There was the merest pause. "A Frenchman," said Hadley-Bright.

"Is *he* supposed to be there?" asked Strange.

The one Frenchman had been joined by another. Then fifty more appeared. The fifty became two hundred – three hundred – a thousand! The hillside seemed to be breeding Frenchmen as a cheese breeds maggots. The next moment they all began to discharge their muskets upon the Nassauers at the crossroads. The engagement did not last long. The Nassauers fired their cannons. The Frenchmen, who appeared to have no cannons of their own, retreated over the hill.

"Ha!" cried Strange, delighted. "They are beaten! They have run away!"

"Yes, but where did they come from in the first place," muttered Hadley-Bright. "Can you look over that hill?"

Strange tapped the water and made a sort of twisting gesture above the surface. The crossroads vanished and in its place appeared an excellent view of the French Army – or, if not the whole Army, a very substantial part of it.

Hadley-Bright sat down like a marionette whose strings have been cut. Strange swore in Spanish (a language he naturally associated with warfare). The Allied armies were in entirely the wrong place. Wellington's divisions were in the west, ready to defend to the death all sorts of places that Buonaparte had no intention of attacking. General Blücher and the Prussian army were too far east. And here was the French Army suddenly popping up in the south. As matters stood at present, these Nassauers (who amounted to perhaps three or four thousand men) were all that lay between Brussels and the French.

"Mr Strange! Do something, I implore you!" cried Hadley-Bright.

Strange took a deep breath and opened wide his arms, as though he were gathering up all the magic he had ever learnt.

"Hurry, Mr Strange! Hurry!"

"I could move the city!" said Strange. "I could move Brussels! I could put it somewhere where the French will not find it."

"Put it where?" cried Hadley-Bright, grabbing Strange's hands and forcing them down again. "We are surrounded by armies. Our own armies! If you move Brussels you are liable to crush some of our regiments under the buildings and the paving stones. The Duke will not be pleased. He needs every man."

Strange thought some more. "I have it!" he cried.

A sort of breeze rushed by. It was not unpleasant – indeed it had the refreshing fragrance of the ocean. Hadley-Bright looked out of the windows. Beyond the houses, churches, palaces and parks were mountain-ridges that had not been there a moment ago. They were black, as if covered with pine trees. The air was much fresher – like air that had never been breathed before.

"Where are we?" asked Hadley-Bright.

"America," said Strange. And then by way of an explanation he added, "It always looks so empty on the maps."

"Dear God! But this is no better than before! Have you forgotten that we have only just signed a peace treaty with America? Nothing will excite the Americans' displeasure so much as the appearance of a European city on their soil!"

"Oh, probably! But there is no need for concern, I assure you. We are a long way from Washington or New Orleans or any of those places where the battles were. Hundreds of miles I expect. At least . . . That is to say I am not sure where exactly. Do you think it matters?"[1]

<hr>

[1] The citizens of Brussels and the various armies occupying the city were intrigued to learn that they were now situated in a far-away country. Unfortunately they were much occupied in preparing for the coming battle (or in the case of the richer and more frivolous part of the population in preparing for the Duchess of Richmond's ball that evening) and hardly any one had leisure just then to go and discover what the country was like or who its inhabitants were. Consequently for a long time it was unclear where precisely Strange had put Brussels on that June afternoon.

In 1830 a trader and trapper named Pearson Denby was travelling through the Plains country. He was approached by a Lakota chief of his acquaintance, Man-afraid-of-the-Water. Man-afraid-of-the-Water asked if Denby could acquire for him some black lightning balls. Man-afraid-of-the-Water explained that he was intending to make war upon his enemies and had urgent need of the balls. He said that at one time he had had about fifty of the balls and he had always used them sparingly, but now they were all gone. Denby did not understand. He asked if Man-afraid-of-the-Water meant ammunition. No, said Man-afraid-of-the-Water. Like ammunition, but much bigger. He took Denby back to his camp and showed him a brass 5½-inch howitzer made by the Carron Company of Falkirk in Scotland. Denby was astonished and asked how Man-afraid-of-the-Water had acquired the gun in the first place. Man-afraid-of-the-Water explained that in some nearby hills lived a tribe called the Half-Finished People. They had been created very suddenly one summer, but their Creator had only given them one of the skills men need to live: that of fighting. All other skills they lacked; they did not know how to hunt buffalo or antelope, how to tame horses or how to make houses for themselves. They could not even understand each other since their crazy Creator had given them four or five different languages. But they had had this gun, which they had traded to Man-afraid-of-the-Water in exchange for food.

Intrigued, Denby sought out the tribe of Half-Finished People. At first they seemed like any other tribe, but then Denby noticed that the older men had an oddly European look and some of them spoke English. Some of their customs were the same as the Lakota tribes' but others seemed to be founded upon European military practice. Their language was like Lakota but contained a great many English, Dutch and German words.

A man called Robert Heath (otherwise Little-man-talks-too-much) told Denby that they had all deserted from several different armies and regiments on the afternoon of 15th June 1815 because a great battle was going to be fought the next day and they had all had a strong presentiment that they would die if they remained. Did Denby know if the Duke of Wellington or Napoleon Buonaparte was now King of France? Denby could not say. "Well, sir," said Heath philosophically, "Whichever of 'em it is, I dare say life goes on just the same for the likes of you and me."

Hadley-Bright dashed outside to find the Duke and tell him that, contrary to what he might have supposed, the French were now in Belgium, but he, the Duke, was not.

His Grace (who happened to be taking tea with some British politicians and Belgian countesses) received the news in his customary imperturbable fashion. But half an hour later he appeared in Strange's hotel with the Quartermaster General, Colonel De Lancey. He stared down at the vision in the silver dish with a grim expression. "Napoleon has humbugged me, by God!" he exclaimed. "De Lancey, you must write the orders as quickly as you can. We must gather the Army at Quatre Bras."

Poor Colonel De Lancey looked most alarmed. "But how do we deliver the orders to the officers with all the Atlantic between us?" he asked.

"Oh," said his Grace, "Mr Strange will take care of that." His eye was caught by something outside the window. Four horsemen were passing by. They had the bearing of kings and the expressions of emperors. Their skin was the colour of mahogany; their long hair was the shiny jet-black of a raven's wing. They were dressed in skins decorated with porcupine quills. Each was equipped with a rifle in a leather case, a fearsome-looking spear (as feathered as their heads) and a bow. "Oh, and De Lancey! Find someone to ask those fellows if they would like to fight tomorrow, would you? They look as if they could do the business."

An hour or so later, in the town of Ath twenty miles from Brussels (or, rather, twenty miles from where Brussels usually stood) a *pâtissier* took a batch of little cakes from the oven. After the cakes had cooled he drew a letter upon each one in pink icing – a thing he had never in his life done before. His wife (who knew not a word of English) laid the cakes in a wooden tray and gave the tray to the *sous-pâtissier*. The *sous-pâtissier* carried it to the Head-quarters of the Allied Army in the town, where Sir Henry Clinton was issuing orders to his officers. The *sous-pâtissier* presented the cakes to Sir Henry. Sir Henry took one and was about to carry it to his mouth when Major Norcott of the 95th Rifles gave a cry of surprize. There in front of them, written in pink icing on little cakes, was a dispatch from Wellington instructing Sir Henry to move the 2nd Division of Infantry towards Quatre Bras with as little delay as possible. Sir Henry looked up in amazement. The *sous-pâtissier* beamed at him.

At about the same time the general in charge of the 3rd Division – a Hanoverian gentleman called Sir Charles Alten – was hard at work in a château twenty-five miles south-west of Brussels. He happened to look out of the window and observed a very small and oddly behaved rainstorm in the courtyard. It shed its rain in the centre of the courtyard and touched the walls not at all. Sir Charles was curious enough to go outside and look more closely. There, written in the dust with raindrops, was the following missive:

> *Bruxelles, 15th June, 1815*
> *The 3rd Division to move upon Quatre Bras immediately.*
> *Wellington*

Meanwhile some Dutch and Belgian generals in Wellington's Army had discovered for themselves that the French were at Quatre Bras and were on their way there with the 2nd Netherlands Division. Consequently these generals (whose names were Rebecq and Perponcher) were more annoyed than enlightened when a great mass of songbirds alighted in the trees all around and began to sing:

> *The Duke's ideas let us expound*
> *At Quatre Bras the French are found*
> *All his troops must gather round*
> *To the crossroads all are bound*

"Yes, yes! We know!" cried General Perponcher, gesturing at the birds to shoo them away. "Be off, d— you!" But the birds only flew closer and some actually settled upon his shoulders and horse. They continued singing in the most officious manner possible:

> There reputations will be made
> The Duke commands: be not afraid!
> All the army's plans are laid
> Go quickly now with your brigade!

The birds accompanied the soldiers for all the remainder of the day, never ceasing for a moment to twitter and cheep the same aggravating song. General Rebecq – whose English was excellent – managed to catch hold of one of them and tried to teach it a new song, in the hopes that it might return to Jonathan Strange and sing it to him:

> The Duke's magician must be kicked
> From Bruxelles to Maastricht
> For playing tricks on honest men
> To Maastricht and back again[2]

At six o'clock Strange returned Brussels to European soil. Immediately those regiments which had been quartered inside the city marched out of the Namur Gate and down the road that led to Quatre Bras. That done, Strange was able to make his own preparations for war. He collected together his silver dish; half a dozen books of magic; a pair of pistols; a light summer coat with a number of unusually deep pockets; a dozen hard-boiled eggs; three flasks of brandy; some pieces of pork pie wrapped in paper; and a very large silk umbrella.

The next morning, with these necessaries stowed in various

---

[2] General Rebecq also made up a Dutch version of his jingle which was sung by his soldiers on the way to Quatre Bras. They taught it to their English comrades and it later became a child's skipping rhyme, both in England and the Netherlands.

places about his person and his horse, he rode with the Duke and his staff up to the crossroads at Quatre Bras. Several thousand Allied troops were assembled there now, but the French had yet to shew themselves. From time to time there was the sound of a musket, but it was scarcely more than you would hear in any English wood where gentlemen are shooting.

Strange was looking about him when a songthrush alighted upon his shoulder and began to chirrup:

> The Duke's ideas let us expound
> At Quatre Bras the French are found . . .

"What?" muttered Strange. "What are you doing here? You were supposed to have disappeared hours ago!" He made Ormskirk's sign to disperse a magic spell and the bird flew off. In fact, rather to his consternation, a whole flock of birds took flight at the same moment. He glanced round nervously to see if any one had noticed that he had bungled the magic; but everyone seemed busy with military concerns and he concluded they had not.

He found a position to his liking – in a ditch directly in front of Quatre Bras farmhouse. The crossroads was on his immediate right and the 92nd Foot, the Highland Regiment were on his left. He took the hard-boiled eggs out of his pockets and gave them to such of the Highlanders as thought they might like to eat them. (In peacetime some sort of introduction is generally required to make a person's acquaintance; in war a small eatable will perform the same office.) The Highlanders gave him some sweet, milky tea in return and soon they were chatting very companionably together.

The day was intensely hot. The road went down between the fields of rye, which seemed, under that bright sun, to glow with an almost supernatural brilliance. Three miles away the Prussian Army had already engaged with the French and there were faint sounds of guns booming and men shouting, like the ghosts of things to come. Just before noon drums and fierce singing were heard in the distance. The ground began to shake with the stamping of tens of thousands of feet, and through the rye towards them came the thick, dark columns of French infantry.

The Duke had given Strange no particular orders and so, when the fighting began, he set about performing all the magic he used to do on Spanish battlefields. He sent fiery angels to menace the French and dragons to breathe flames over them. These illusions were larger and brighter than any thing he had managed in Spain. Several times he climbed out of the ditch to admire the effect – in spite of the warnings of the Highlanders that he was liable to be shot at any moment.

He had been diligently casting such spells for three or four hours when something happened. Out on the battlefield, a sudden assault by the French Chasseurs threatened to envelop the Duke and his staff. These gentlemen were obliged to wheel round and ride pell-mell back to the Allied lines. The nearest troops happened to be the 92nd Foot.

"92nd!" cried the Duke. "Lie down!"

The Highlanders immediately lay down. Strange looked up from the ditch to see the Duke upon Copenhagen[3] skimming over their heads. His Grace was quite unharmed and indeed appeared more invigorated than alarmed by his adventure. He looked around to see what everyone was doing. His eye alighted upon Strange.

"Mr Strange! What are you doing? When I want a display of Vauxhall-Gardens magic I shall ask for it![4] The French saw plenty of this sort of thing in Spain – they are not in the least disturbed by it. But it is entirely new to the Belgians, Dutch and Germans in *my*

---

[3] Copenhagen, the Duke's famous chestnut horse, 1808–36.

[4] In 1810 Messrs George and Jonathan Barratt, the proprietors of Vauxhall Gardens, had offered Strange and Norrell a vast sum of money to stage displays of magic every night in the gardens. The magic which the Barratts were proposing was of exactly this sort – illusions of magical creatures, famous persons from the Bible and history etc., etc. Naturally enough, Mr Norrell had refused.

Army. I have just seen one of your dragons menace a company of Brunswickers in that wood. Four of them fell over. It will not do, Mr Strange! It simply will not do!" He galloped off.

Strange stared after him. He had half a mind to make some pointed remarks about the Duke's ingratitude to his friends, the Highlanders; but they seemed a little busy at the moment, being shot at by cannons and hacked at by sabres. So he picked up his map, climbed out of the ditch and made his way to the crossroads where the Duke's military secretary, Lord Fitzroy Somerset, was looking about him with an anxious air.

"My lord?" said Strange. "I need to ask you something. How is the battle going?"

Somerset sighed. "All will be well in the end. Of course it will. But half the Army is not here yet. We have scarcely any cavalry to speak of. I know you sent the divisions their orders very promptly but some of them were simply too far away. If the French get reinforcements before we get ours, then . . ." He shrugged.

"And if French reinforcements do come, which direction will they come from? The south, I suppose?"

"The south and south-east."

Strange did not return to the battle. Instead, he walked to Quatre Bras farm, just behind the British lines. The farm was quite deserted. Doors stood open; curtains billowed out of windows; a scythe and hoe had been thrown down in the dust in the haste to get away. In the milk-smelling gloom of the dairy he found a cat with some newborn kittens. Whenever the guns sounded (which was often) the cat trembled. He fetched her some water and spoke to her gently. Then he sat down upon the cool flagstones and placed his map before him.

He began to move the roads, lanes and villages to the south and east of the battlefield. First he changed the positions of two villages. Then he made all the roads that went east to west, run north to south. He waited ten minutes and then he put it all back the way it was. He made all the woods in the vicinity turn round and face the other way. Next he made the brooks flow in the wrong direction. Hour after hour he continued to change the landscape. It was intricate, tedious work – quite as dull as any thing he had done with Norrell. At half-past six he heard the Allied bugles sound the advance. At eight o'clock he stood up and stretched his cramped limbs. "Well," he remarked to the cat, "I have not the least idea whether that achieved any thing or not."[5]

Black smoke hung over the fields. Those dismal attendants of any battle, the crows and ravens, had arrived in their hundreds. Strange found his friends, the Highlanders, in a most forlorn condition. They had captured a house next to the road, but in doing so they had lost half their men and twenty-five of their thirty-six officers, including their colonel – a man whom many of them had regarded as a father. More than one grizzled-looking veteran was sitting with his head in his hands, weeping.

The French had apparently returned to Frasnes – the town they had come from that morning. Strange asked several people if this meant the Allies had won, but no one seemed to have any precise information upon this point.

He slept that night in Genappe, a village three miles up the road to Brussels. He was at breakfast when Captain Hadley-Bright appeared, bearing news: the Duke's Allies, the Prussian Army had received a terrible beating in the fighting of previous day.

-----

[5] The accepted magical technique for creating confusion within roads, landscapes, rooms and other physical spaces is to make a labyrinth within them. But Strange did not learn this magic until February 1817.

Nevertheless this was arguably the decisive action of the campaign. Unknown to Strange, the French general, D'Erlon, was trying to reach the battlefield with 20,000 men. Instead he spent those crucial hours marching through a landscape which changed inexplicably every few minutes. Had he and his men succeeded in reaching Quatre Bras it is probable the French would have won and Waterloo would never have happened. Strange was piqued by the Duke's abruptness earlier in the day and did not mention to any one what he had done. Later he told John Segundus and Thomas Levy. Consequently historians of Quatre Bras were perplexed to account for D'Erlon's failure until John Segundus's *The Life of Jonathan Strange* was published in 1820.

"Are they defeated?" asked Strange.

"No, but they have retreated and so the Duke says we must do the same. His Grace has chosen somewhere to fight and the Prussians will meet us there. A place called Waterloo."

"Waterloo? What a ridiculously odd name!" said Strange.

"It is odd, is it not? I could not find it on the map."

"Oh!" said Strange. "This was continually happening in Spain! No doubt the fellow who told you got the name wrong. Depend upon it, there is no such place as Waterloo!"

A little after noon they mounted their horses and were about to follow the Army out of the village, when a message arrived from Wellington: a squadron of French lancers was approaching and could Mr Strange do something to annoy them? Strange, anxious to avoid another accusation of Vauxhall-Gardens magic, asked Hadley-Bright's advice. "What do cavalry hate the most?"

Hadley-Bright thought for a moment. "Mud," he said.

"Mud? Really? Yes, I suppose you are right. Well, there are few things more plain and workman-like than weather magic!"

The skies darkened. An inky thundercloud appeared; it was as large as all Belgium and so full and heavy that its ragged skirts seemed to brush the tops of the trees. There was a flash and the world turned bone-white for an instant. There was a deafening crack and the next moment the rain came down in such torrents that the earth boiled and hissed.

Within minutes the surrounding fields had turned to a quagmire. The French lancers were quite unable to indulge in their favourite sport of fast and dextrous riding; Wellington's rearguard got safely away.

An hour later Strange and Hadley-Bright were surprized to discover that there was indeed a place called Waterloo and that they had arrived at it. The Duke was sitting on his horse in the rain, gazing in high good humour at the filthy men, horses and carts. "Excellent mud, Merlin!" he called out cheerfully. "Very sticky and slippery. The French will not like it at all. More rain,

568

if you please! Now, you see that tree where the road dips down?"

"The elm, your Grace?"

"The very one. If you will stand there during the battle tomorrow, I will be much obliged to you. I will be there some of the time, but probably not very often. My boys will bring you your instructions."

That evening the various divisions of the Allied Army took up positions along a shallow ridge south of Waterloo. Above them the thunder roared and the rain came down in torrents. From time to time deputations of bedraggled men approached the elm-tree and begged Strange to make it stop, but he only shook his head and said, "When the Duke tells me to stop, I shall."

But the veterans of the Peninsular War remarked approvingly that rain was always an Englishman's friend in times of war. They told their comrades: "There is nothing so comforting or familiar to us, you see – whereas other nations it baffles. It rained on the nights before Fuentes, Salamanca and Vitoria." (These were the names of some of Wellington's great victories in the Peninsula.)

In the shelter of his umbrella Strange mused on the battle to come. Ever since the end of the Peninsular War he had been studying the magic that the *Aureates* used in times of war. Very little was known about it; there were rumours – nothing more – of a spell which John Uskglass had used before his own battles. It foretold the outcome of present events. Just before nightfall Strange had a sudden inspiration. "There is no way of finding out what Uskglass did, but there is always Pale's Conjectures Concerning the Foreshadowing of Things To Come. That is very likely a watered-down version of the same thing. I could use that."

For a moment or two before the spell took effect, he was aware of all the sounds around him: rain splashing on metal and leather, and running down canvas; horses shuffling and snorting; Englishmen singing and Scotsmen playing bagpipes; two Welsh soldiers arguing over the proper interpretation of a Bible passage; the Scottish captain, John Kincaid, entertaining the American savages and teaching them to drink tea (presumably with the idea that once a man had learnt to drink tea, the other habits and qualities that make up a Briton would naturally follow).

Then silence. Men and horses began to disappear, few by few at first, and then more quickly – hundreds, thousands of them vanishing from sight. Great gaps appeared among the close-packed soldiers. A little further to the east an entire regiment was gone, leaving a hole the size of Hanover-square. Where, moments before, all had been life, conversation and activity, there was now nothing but the rain and the twilight and the waving stalks of rye. Strange wiped his mouth because he felt sick. "Ha!" he thought. "That will teach me to meddle with magic meant for kings! Norrell is right. Some magic is not meant for ordinary magicians. Presumably John Uskglass knew what to do with this horrible knowledge. I do not. Should I tell someone? The Duke? He will not thank me for it."

Someone was looking down at him; someone was speaking to him – a captain in the Horse Artillery. Strange saw the man's mouth move but he heard not a sound. He snapped his fingers to dismiss the spell. The captain was inviting him to come and share some brandy and cigars. Strange shivered and declined.

For the rest of the night he sat by himself under the elm-tree. Until this moment it had never seemed to him that his magician-ship set him apart from other men. But now he had glimpsed the wrong side of something. He had the eeriest feeling – as if the world were growing older around him, and the best part of existence – laughter, love and innocence – were slipping irrevocably into the past.

At about half past eleven the next morning the French guns began to fire. The Allied artillery replied. The clear summer air between the two armies was filled with drifting veils of bitter, black smoke.

The French attack was chiefly directed at the Château of Hougoumont, an Allied outpost in the valley, whose woods and buildings were defended by the 3rd Foot Guards, Coldstream Guards, Nassauers and Hanoverians. Strange summoned vision after vision into his silver dish so that he could watch the bloody engagements in the woods around the château. He was in half a mind to move the trees to give the Allied soldiers a better shot at their attackers, but this sort of close hand-to-hand fighting was the very worst subject for magic. He reminded himself that in war a soldier may do more harm by acting too soon or too impetuously than by never acting at all. He waited.

The cannonade grew fiercer. British veterans told their friends that they had never known shot fall so fast and thick. Men saw comrades cut in half, smashed to pieces or beheaded by cannon-balls. The very air shook with the guns' reverberations. "Hard pounding this," remarked the Duke coolly, and ordered the front ranks to withdraw behind the crest of the ridge and lie down. When it was over, the Allies lifted their heads to see the French infantry advancing through the smoke-filled valley: sixteen thousand men shoulder to shoulder in immense columns, all shouting and stamping together.

More than one soldier wondered if, at last, the French had found a magician of their own; the French infantrymen appeared much taller than ordinary men and the light in their eyes as they drew closer burnt with an almost supernatural fury. But this was only the magic of Napoleon Buonaparte, who knew better than any one how to dress his soldiers so they would terrify the enemy, and how to deploy them so that any onlooker would think them indestructible.

Now Strange knew exactly what to do. The thick, clogging mud was already proving a decided hindrance to the advancing soldiers. To hamper them further he set about enchanting the stalks of rye. He made them wind themselves around the Frenchmen's feet. The stalks were as tough as wires; the soldiers staggered and fell over. With luck, the mud would hold them down and they would be trampled by their comrades – or by the French cavalry who soon appeared behind them. But it was painstaking work and, in spite of all his efforts, this first magic of Strange's probably did no more harm against the French than the firing of a skilful British musketeer or rifleman.

An *aide-de-camp* flew up with impossible velocity and thrust a strip of goatskin into Strange's hand with a shout of, "Message from his Grace!" In an instant he was off again.

> *French shells have set the Château of Hougoumont on fire. Put out the flames.*
>
> *Wellington*

Strange summoned another vision of Hougoumont. The men there had suffered greatly since he had last seen the château. The wounded of both sides lay in every room. The haystack, outbuildings and château were all on fire. Black, choking smoke was everywhere. Horses screamed and wounded men tried to crawl away – but there was hardly anywhere to go. Meanwhile the battle raged on around them. In the chapel Strange found half a dozen images of saints painted on the walls. They were seven or eight feet tall and oddly proportioned – the work, it seemed, of an enthusiastic *amateur*. They had long, brown beards and large, melancholy eyes.

"They'll do!" he muttered. At his command the saints stepped down from the walls. They moved in a series of jerks, like marionettes, but they had a certain lightness and grace. They stalked through the ranks of wounded men to a well in one of the courtyards. Here they drew buckets of water which they carried to the flames. All seemed to be going well until two of them (possibly Saint Peter and Saint Jerome) caught fire and burnt up – being composed of nothing but paint and magic they burnt rather easily. Strange was trying to think how to remedy this situation when part of an exploded French shell hit the side of his silver dish, sending it spinning fifty yards to the right. By the time he had retrieved it, knocked out a large dent in its side and set it to rights, all the painted saints had succumbed to the flames. Wounded men and horses were burning. There were no more paintings upon the walls. Almost brought to tears by his frustration, Strange cursed the unknown artist for his idleness.

What else was there? What else did he know? He thought hard. Long ago John Uskglass would sometimes make a champion for himself out of ravens – birds would flock together to become a black, bristling, shifting giant who could perform any task with ease. On other occasions Uskglass would make servants out of earth.

Strange conjured a vision of Hougoumont's well. He drew the water out of the well in a sort of fountain; and then, before the fountain could spill on the ground, he forced it to take on the clumsy semblance of a man. Next he commanded the water-man to hurry to the flames and cast himself down upon them. In this way a stall in the stables was successfully doused and three men were saved. Strange made more as quickly as he could, but water is not an element that holds a coherent form easily; after an hour or so of this labour his head was spinning and his hands were shaking uncontroulably.

Between four and five o'clock something entirely unexpected happened. Strange looked up to see a brilliant mass of French cavalry approaching. Five hundred abreast they rode and twelve deep – yet the thunder of the guns was such that they made no sound that any one could hear; they seemed to come silently. "Surely," thought Strange, "they must realize that Wellington's infantry is unbroken. They will be cut to pieces." Behind him the infantry regiments were forming squares; some of the men called to Strange to come and shelter inside their square. This seemed like good advice and so he went.

From the relative safety of the square Strange watched the

cavalry's approach; the cuirassiers wore shining breast-plates and tall crested helmets; the lancers' weapons were embellished with fluttering pennants of red and white. They seemed scarcely to belong to this dull age. Theirs was the glory of ancient days – but Strange was determined to match it with an ancient glory of his own. The images of John Uskglass's servants burnt in his mind – servants made of ravens, servants made of earth. Beneath the French horsemen the mud began to swell and bubble. It shaped itself into gigantic hands; the hands reached up and pulled down men and horses. The ones who fell were trampled by their comrades. The rest endured a storm of musket-fire from the Allied infantry. Strange watched impassively.

When the French had been beaten back, he returned to his silver dish.

"Are you the magician?" said someone.

He spun round and was astonished to find a little, round, soft-looking person in civilian clothes who smiled at him. "Who in God's name are you?" he demanded.

"My name is Pink," explained the man. "I am a commercial traveller for Welbeck's Superior Buttons of Birmingham. I have a message from the Duke for you."

Strange, who was covered in mud and more tired than he had ever been in his life, took a moment to comprehend this. "Where are all the Duke's *aides-de-camp*?"

"He says that they are dead."

"What? Hadley-Bright is dead? What about Colonel Canning?"

"Alas," smiled Mr Pink, "I can offer no precise information. I came out from Antwerp yesterday to see the battle and when I espied the Duke I took the opportunity to introduce myself and to mention in passing the excellent qualities of Welbeck's Superior Buttons. He asked me as a particular favour to come and tell you that the Prussian army is on their way here and have reached Paris Wood, but, says his Grace, they are having the devil of a time . . ." (Mr Pink smiled and blinked to hear himself say such a soldierly

word.) ". . . the devil of a time in the little lanes and the mud, and would you be so good as to make a road for them between the wood and the battlefield?"

"Certainly," said Strange, rubbing some of the mud from his face.

"I will tell his Grace." He paused and asked wistfully, "Do you think his Grace would like to order some buttons?"

"I do not see why not. He is as fond of buttons as most men."

"Then, you know, we could put 'Supplier of Buttons to his Grace the Duke of Wellington' in all our advertisements." Mr Pink beamed happily. "Off I go then!"

"Yes, yes. Off you go." Strange created the road for the Prussians, but in later times he was always inclined to suppose he must have dreamt Mr Pink of Welbeck's Superior Buttons.[6]

Events seemed to repeat themselves. Again and again the French cavalry charged and Strange took refuge within the infantry square. Again the deadly horsemen swirled against the sides of the square like waves. Again Strange drew monstrous hands from the earth to pull them down. Whenever the cavalry withdrew the cannonade began again; he returned to his silver dish and made men out of water to put out the flames and succour the dying in ruined, desperate Hougoumont. Everything happened over and over, again and again; it was inconceivable that the fighting would ever end. He began to think it had always been like this.

"There must come a time when the musket-balls and cannon-shot run out," he thought. "And what will we do then? Hack at each other with sabres and bayonets? And if we all die, every one of us, who will they say has won?"

The smoke rolled back revealing frozen moments like tableaux in a ghostly theatre: at the farmhouse called La Haye Sainte the

---

[6] In actual fact Mr Pink was only one of the civilians whom the Duke pressed into service as unofficial *aides-de-camp* that day. Others included a young Swiss gentleman and another commercial traveller, this time from London.

French were climbing a mountain of their own dead to get over the wall and kill the German defenders.

Once Strange was caught outside the square when the French arrived. Suddenly, directly in front of him, was an enormous French cuirassier upon an equally enormous horse. His first thought was to wonder if the fellow knew who he was. (He had been told the entire French Army hated the English magician with a vivid, Latin passion.) His second thought was that he had left his pistols inside the infantry square.

The cuirassier raised his sabre. Without thinking, Strange muttered Stokesey's *Animam Evocare*. Something like a bee flew out of the breast of the cuirassier and settled in the palm of Strange's hand. But it was not a bee; it was a bead of pearly blue light. A second light flew out of the cuirassier's horse. The horse screamed and reared up. The cuirassier stared, puzzled.

Strange raised his other hand to smash horse and horseman out of existence. Then he froze.

"And can a magician kill a man by magic?" the Duke had asked.

And he had answered, "A magician might, but a gentleman never could."

While he was hesitating a British cavalry officer – a Scots Grey – swung round out of nowhere. He slashed the cuirassier's head open, from his chin, upwards through his teeth. The man toppled like a tree. The Scots Grey rode on.

Strange could never quite remember what happened after this. He believed that he wandered about in a dazed condition. He did not know for how long.

The sound of cheering brought him to himself. He looked up and saw Wellington upon Copenhagen. He was waving his hat – the signal that the Allies were to advance upon the French. But the smoke wreathed itself so thickly about the Duke that only the soldiers nearest to him could share in this moment of victory.

So Strange whispered a word and a little gap appeared in the billows. A single ray of evening sunlight shone down upon Well-

577

ington. All along the ridge the faces of the soldiers turned towards him. The cheering grew louder.

"There," thought Strange, "that is the proper use of English magic."

He followed the soldiers and the retreating French down through the battlefield. Scattered about among the dead and the dying were the great earthen hands he had created. They seemed frozen in gestures of outrage and horror as if the land itself despaired. When he came level with the French guns that had done the Allied soldiers such profound injury, he did one last act of magic. He drew more hands out of the earth. The hands grasped the cannons and pulled them under.

At the Inn of Belle Alliance on the far side of the battlefield, he found the Duke with the Prussian General, Prince Blücher. The Duke nodded to him and said, "Come to dinner with me."

Prince Blücher shook his hand warmly and said a great many things in German (none of which Strange understood). Then the old gentleman pointed to his stomach wherein lay the illusory elephant and made a wry face as if to say, "What can one do?"

Strange stepped outside and immediately he almost walked into Captain Hadley-Bright. "I was told you were dead!" he cried.

"I was sure you would be," replied Hadley-Bright.

There was a pause. Both men felt faintly embarrassed. The ranks of dead and wounded stretched away upon all sides as far as the eye could see. Simply being alive at that moment seemed, in some indefinable way, ungentlemanly.

"Who else survived? Do you know?" asked Hadley-Bright.

Strange shook his head. "No."

They parted.

At Wellington's Headquarters in Waterloo that night the table was laid for forty or fifty people. But when the dinner-hour came, only three men were there: the Duke, General Alava (his Spanish attaché) and Strange. Whenever the door opened the Duke turned his head to see if it was one of his friends, alive and well; but no one came.

Many places at that table had been laid for gentlemen who were either dead or dying: Colonel Canning, Lieutenant-Colonel Gordon, Major-General Picton, Colonel De Lancey. The list would grow longer as the night progressed.

The Duke, General Alava and Mr Strange sat down in silence.

41

Starecross

Late September–December 1815

FORTUNE, IT SEEMED, could not be persuaded to smile upon Mr Segundus. He had come to live in York with the aim of enjoying the society and conversation of the city's many magicians. But no sooner had he got there than all the other magicians were deprived of their profession by Mr Norrell, and he was left alone. His little stock of money had dwindled considerably and in the autumn of 1815 he was forced to seek employment.

"And it is not to be supposed," he remarked to Mr Honeyfoot with a sigh, "that I shall be able to earn very much. What am I qualified to do?"

Mr Honeyfoot could not allow this. "Write to Mr Strange!" he advised. "He may be in need of a secretary."

Nothing would have pleased Mr Segundus better than to work for Jonathan Strange, but his natural modesty would not allow him to propose it. It would be a shocking thing to put himself forward in such a way. Mr Strange might be embarrassed to know how to answer him. It might even look as if he, John Segundus, considered himself Mr Strange's equal!

Mr and Mrs Honeyfoot assured him that if Mr Strange did not like the idea he would very soon say so – and so there could be no possible harm in asking him. But upon this point Mr Segundus proved unpersuadable.

Their next proposal, however, pleased him better. "Why not see if there are any little boys in the town who wish to learn magic?" asked Mrs Honeyfoot. Her grandsons – stout little fellows of five and seven – were just now of an age to begin their education and so the subject rather occupied her mind.

So Mr Segundus became a tutor in magic. As well as little boys, he also discovered some young ladies whose studies would have more usually been confined to French, German and music, but who were now anxious to be instructed in theoretical magic. Soon he was asked to give lessons to the young ladies' older brothers, many of whom began to picture themselves as magicians. To young men of a studious turn of mind, who did not desire to go into the Church or the Law, magic was very appealing, particularly since Strange had triumphed on the battlefields of Europe. It is, after all, many centuries since clergymen distinguished themselves on the field of war, and lawyers never have.

In the early autumn of 1815 Mr Segundus was engaged by the father of one of his pupils upon an errand. This gentleman, whose name was Palmer, had heard of a house in the north of the county that was being sold. Mr Palmer did not wish to buy the house, but a friend had told him that there was a library there worth examining. Mr Palmer was not at leisure just then to go and see for himself. Though he trusted his servants in many other matters, their talents did not quite run to scholarship, so he asked Mr Segundus to go in his place, to find out how many books there were and what their condition might be and whether they were worth purchasing.

Starecross Hall was the principal building in a village which otherwise comprised a handful of stone cottages and farmhouses. Starecross itself stood in a most isolated spot, surrounded on all sides by brown, empty moors. Tall trees sheltered it from storms and winds – yet at the same time they made it dark and solemn. The village was amply provided with tumbledown stone walls and tumbledown stone barns. It was very quiet; it felt like the end of the world.

There was a very ancient and worn-looking packhorse bridge that crossed a deep beck of fast-running water. Bright yellow leaves flowed swiftly upon the dark, almost-black water, making patterns as they went. To Mr Segundus the patterns looked a little like magical writing. "But then," he thought, "so many things do."

The house itself was a long, low, rambling building, constructed of the same dark stone as the rest of the village. Its neglected gardens, garths and courts were filled with deep drifts of autumn leaves. It was hard to know who would wish to buy such a house. It was much too large for a farmhouse, yet altogether too gloomy and remote for a gentleman's residence. It might have done for a parsonage except that there was no church. It might have done for an inn, except that the old pack-road that had once passed through the village had fallen into disuse and the bridge was all that remained of it.

No one came in answer to Mr Segundus's knock. He observed that the front door was ajar. It seemed rather impertinent simply to go inside, but after four or five minutes of fruitless knocking he did so.

Houses, like people, are apt to become rather eccentric if left too much on their own; this house was the architectural equivalent of an old gentleman in a worn dressing-gown and torn slippers, who got up and went to bed at odd times of day, and who kept up a continual conversation with friends no one else could see. As Mr Segundus wandered about in search of whoever was in charge, he found a room which contained nothing but china cheese-moulds, all stacked one upon another. Another room had heaps of queer red clothes, the like of which he had never seen before – something between labourers' smocks and clergymen's robes. The kitchen had very few of those articles that usually belong to kitchens, but it did have the skull of an alligator in a glass case; the skull had a great grin and seemed very pleased with itself, though Mr Segundus did not know why it should be. There was one room that could only be reached by a queer arrangement of steps and staircases, where the pictures all seemed to have been chosen by someone with an inordinate love of fighting; there were pictures of men fighting, boys fighting, cocks fighting, bulls fighting, dogs fighting, centaurs fighting and even a startling depiction of two beetles locked in combat. Another room was almost empty except for a doll's house standing on a table in the middle of the floor; the doll's house was an exact copy of the real house – except that inside the doll's house a number of smartly dressed dolls were enjoying a peaceful and rational existence together: making doll-sized cakes and loaves of bread, entertaining their friends with a diminutive harpsichord, playing casino with tiny cards, educating miniature children, and dining upon roast turkeys the size of Mr Segundus's thumbnail. It formed a strange contrast with the bleak, echoing reality.

He seemed to have looked in every room, but he still had not found the library and he still had not found any people. He came to a small door half-hidden by a staircase. Behind it was a tiny room – scarcely more than a closet. A man in a dirty white coat with his boots propped up on the table was drinking brandy and staring at the ceiling. After a little persuasion this person agreed to shew him where the library was.

The first ten books Mr Segundus looked at were worthless – books of sermons and moralizing from the last century, or descriptions of persons whom no one living cared about. The next fifty were very much the same. He began to think his task would soon be done. But then he stumbled upon some very interesting and unusual works of geology, philosophy and medicine. He began to feel more sanguine.

He worked steadily for two or three hours. Once he thought he heard a carriage arrive at the house, but he paid it no attention. At the end of that time he was suddenly aware that he was extremely hungry. He had no idea whether any arrangements had been made for his dinner or not, and the house was a long way from the nearest inn. He went off in search of the negligent man in the tiny room to ask him what could be done. In the labyrinth of rooms and corridors he was lost immediately. He wandered about opening every door, feeling more and more hungry, and more and more out of temper with the negligent man.

He found himself in an old-fashioned parlour with dark oak panelling and a mantelpiece the size of a young triumphal arch. Directly before him a lovely young woman was sitting in a deep window-seat, gazing out at the trees and the high, bare hills beyond. He had just time enough to notice that her left hand lacked a little finger, when suddenly she was not there at all – or perhaps it was more accurate to say she changed. In her place was a much older, stouter woman, a woman about Mr Segundus's own age, dressed in a violet silk gown, with an Indian shawl about her shoulders and a little dog in her lap. This lady sat in exactly the same attitude as the other, gazing out of the window with the same wistful expression.

All these details took but a moment to apprehend, yet the impression made upon Mr Segundus by the two ladies was unusually vivid – almost supernaturally so – like images in a delirium. A queer shock thrilled through his whole being, his senses were overwhelmed and he fainted away.

When he came to himself he was lying on the floor and two ladies were leaning over him, with exclamations of dismay and concern. Despite his confusion he quickly comprehended that neither lady was the beautiful young woman with the missing finger whom he had seen first. One was the lady with the little dog whom he had seen *second*, and the other was a thin, fair-haired, equally mature lady of unremarkable face and figure. It appeared that she had been in the room all along, but she had been seated *behind* the door and so he had not observed her.

The two ladies would not permit him to stand up or attempt any movement of his limbs. They would scarcely allow him to speak; they warned him sternly it would bring on another fainting fit.

They fetched cushions for his head, and blankets to keep him warm (he protested he was perfectly warm to begin with, but they would not listen to him). They dispensed lavender water and *sal volatile*. They stopt a draught they thought might be coming from under one of the doors. Mr Segundus began to suspect that they had had an uneventful morning, and that when a strange gentleman had walked into the room and dropt down in a swoon, they were rather pleased than otherwise.

After quarter of an hour of this treatment he was permitted to sit in a chair and sip weak tea unaided.

"The fault is entirely mine," said the lady with the little dog. "Fellowes told me that the gentleman had come from York to see the books. I ought to have made myself known to you before. It was too great a shock coming upon us like that!"

The name of this lady was Mrs Lennox. The other was Mrs Blake, her companion. They generally resided in Bath and they had come to Starecross so that Mrs Lennox might see the house one more time before it was sold.

"Foolish, is it not?" said Mrs Lennox to Mr Segundus. "The house has stood vacant for years and years. I ought to have sold it long ago, but when I was a child I spent several summers here which were particularly happy."

"You are still very pale, sir," offered Mrs Blake. "Have you eaten any thing today?"

Mr Segundus confessed that he was very hungry.

"Did not Fellowes offer to fetch your dinner?" asked Mrs Lennox in surprize.

Fellowes was presumably the negligent servant in the tiny room. Mr Segundus did not like to say that he had barely been able to rouse Fellowes to speak to him.

Fortunately, Mrs Lennox and Mrs Blake had brought an ample dinner with them and Fellowes was, at that moment, preparing it. Half an hour later the two ladies and Mr Segundus sat down to dine in an oak-panelled room with a melancholy view of autumn trees. The only slight inconvenience was that the two ladies wished Mr Segundus, in his invalid character, to eat light, easily digestible foods, whereas in truth he was very hungry and wanted fried beefsteaks and hot pudding.

The two ladies were glad of a companion and asked him a great many questions about himself. They were most interested to learn that he was a magician; they had never met one before.

"And have you found any magical texts in my library?" asked Mrs Lennox.

"None, madam," said Mr Segundus. "But magical books, valuable ones, are very rare indeed. I would have been most surprized to find any."

"Now that I think of it," mused Mrs Lennox, "I believe there were a few. But I sold them all years ago to a gentleman who lived near York. Just between ourselves I thought him a little foolish to pay me such a great sum for books no one wanted. But perhaps he was wise after all."

Mr Segundus knew that "the gentleman who lived near York" had probably not paid Mrs Lennox one quarter the proper value of the books, but it does no good to say such things out loud and so he smiled politely, and kept his reflections to himself.

He told them about his pupils, both male and female, and how clever they were and how eager to learn.

"And since you encourage them with such praise," said Mrs Blake, kindly, "they are sure to fare better under your tutelage than they would with any other master."

"Oh! I do not know about that," said Mr Segundus.

"I had not quite understood before," said Mrs Lennox, with a thoughtful air, "how universally popular the study of magic has become. I had thought that it was confined to those two men in London. What are their names? Presumably, Mr Segundus, the next step is a school for magicians? Doubtless that is where you will direct your energies?"

"A school!" said Mr Segundus. "Oh! But that would require –

well, I do not know what exactly – but a great deal of money and a house."

"Perhaps there would be difficulty in acquiring pupils?" said Mrs Lennox.

"No, indeed! I can think of four young men immediately."

"And if you were to advertise . . ."

"Oh! But I would never do that!" said Mr Segundus, rather shocked. "Magic is the noblest profession in the world – well, the second noblest perhaps, after the Church. One ought not to soil it with commercial practices. No, I would only take young men upon private recommendation."

"Then all that remains is for someone to find you a little money and a house. Nothing could be easier. But I dare say your friend, Mr Honeyfoot, of whom you speak with such regard, would wish to lend you the money. I dare say he would want to claim that honour for his own."

"Oh, no! Mr Honeyfoot has three daughters – the dearest girls in the world. One of them is married and another is engaged and the third cannot make up her mind. No, Mr Honeyfoot must think of his family. His money is quite tied up."

"Then I can tell you my hope with a clear conscience! Why should I not lend you the money?"

Mr Segundus was all amazement and for several moments quite at a loss for an answer. "You are very kind, madam!" he stammered at last.

Mrs Lennox smiled. "No, sir. I am not. If magic is as popular as you say – and I shall, of course, ascertain the opinion of other people upon this point – then I believe the profits will be handsome."

"But my experience of business is woefully small," said Mr Segundus. "I should fear to make a mistake and lose you your money. No, you are very kind and I thank you with all my heart, but I must decline."

"Well, if you dislike the notion of becoming a borrower of

money – and I know it does not suit everyone – then that is easily solved. The school shall be mine – mine alone. I will bear the expence and the risk. You will be master of the school and our names will appear upon the prospectus together. After all, what better purpose for this house could there be than as a school for magicians? As a residence it has many drawbacks, but its advantages as a school are considerable. It is a very isolated situation. There is no shooting to speak of. There would be little opportunity for the young men to gamble or hunt. Their pleasures will be quite restricted and so they will apply themselves to their studies."

"I would not chuse young men who gamble!" said Mr Segundus, rather shocked.

She smiled again. "I do not believe you have ever given your friends a moment's anxiety – except for worrying that this wicked world would quickly take advantage of someone so honest."

After dinner Mr Segundus dutifully returned to the library and in the early evening he took his leave of the two ladies. They parted in a most friendly manner and with a promise on Mrs Lennox's side that she would soon invite him to Bath.

On the way back he gave himself stern warnings not to place any reliance on these wonderful plans for Future Usefulness and Happiness, but he could not help indulging in ideal pictures of teaching the young men and of their extraordinary progress; of Jonathan Strange coming to visit the school; of his pupils being delighted to discover that their master was a friend and intimate of the most famous magician of the Modern Age; of Strange saying to him, "It is all excellent, Segundus. I could not be better pleased. Well done!"

It was after midnight when he got home, and it took all his resolve not to run to Mr Honeyfoot's house immediately to tell them the news. But the following morning when he arrived at the house at a very early hour, their raptures were scarcely to be described. They were full of the happiness he had hardly dare allow himself to feel. Mrs Honeyfoot still had a great deal of the schoolgirl in her and she caught up her husband's hands and danced around the breakfast-table with him as the only possible means of expressing what she felt. Then she took Mr Segundus's hands and danced around the table with *him*, and when both magicians protested against any more dancing, she continued by herself. Mr Segundus's only regret (and it was a very slight one) was that Mr and Mrs Honeyfoot did not feel the *surprize* of the thing quite as he intended they should; their opinion of him was so high that they found nothing particularly remarkable in great ladies wishing to establish schools solely for his benefit.

"She may consider herself very lucky to have found you!" declared Mr Honeyfoot. "For who is better fitted to direct a school for magicians? No one!"

"And after all," reasoned Mrs Honeyfoot, "what else has she to do with her money? Poor, childless lady!"

Mr Honeyfoot was convinced that Mr Segundus's fortune was now made. His sanguine temper would not permit him to expect less. Yet he had not lived so long in the world without acquiring some sober habits of business and he told Mr Segundus that they would make some inquiries about Mrs Lennox, who she was and whether she was as rich as she seemed.

They wrote to a friend of Mr Honeyfoot's who lived in Bath. Fortunately Mrs Lennox was well known as a great lady, even in Bath, a city beloved by the rich and the elevated. She had been born rich and married an even richer husband. This husband had died young and not much regretted, leaving her at liberty to indulge her active temperament and clever mind. She had increased her fortune with good investments and careful management of her lands and estates. She was famed for her bold, decisive temper, her many charitable activities and the warmth of her friendship. She had houses in every part of the kingdom, but resided chiefly at Bath with Mrs Blake.

Meanwhile Mrs Lennox had been asking the same sort of questions about Mr Segundus, and she must have been pleased with the answers because she soon invited him up to Bath where every detail of the projected school was quickly decided.

The next months were spent in repairing and fitting up Stare-cross Hall. The roof leaked, two chimneys were blocked and part of the kitchen had actually fallen down. Mr Segundus was shocked to discover how much everything would cost. He calculated that if he did not clear the second chimney, made do with old country settles and wooden chairs instead of buying new furniture, and confined the number of servants to three, he could save £60. His letter to this effect produced an immediate reply from Mrs Lennox; she informed him he was not spending enough. His pupils would all be from good families; they would expect good fires and comfort. She advised him to engage nine servants, in addition to a butler and a French cook. He must completely refurnish the house and purchase a cellar of good French wines. The cutlery, she said, must all be silver and the dining-service Wedgwood.

In early December Mr Segundus received a letter of congrat-ulation from Jonathan Strange, who promised to visit the school the following spring. But in spite of everyone's good wishes and everyone's endeavours, Mr Segundus could not get rid of the feeling that the school would never actually come into being; something would occur to prevent it. This idea was constantly at the back of his thoughts, do what he would to suppress it.

One morning around the middle of December he arrived at the Hall and found a man seated, quite at his ease, upon the steps. Though he did not believe he had ever seen the man before, he knew him instantly: he was Bad Fortune personified; he was the Ruin of Mr Segundus's Hopes and Dreams. The man was dressed in a black coat of an old-fashioned cut, as worn and shabby as Mr Segundus's own, and he had mud on his boots. With his long, ragged dark hair he looked like the portent of doom in a bad play.

"Mr Segundus, you cannot do this!" he said in a Yorkshire accent.

"I beg your pardon?" said Mr Segundus.

"The school, sir. You must give up this notion of a school!"

"What?" cried Mr Segundus, bravely pretending that he did not know the man spoke an inevitable truth.

"Now, sir," continued the dark man, "you know me and you know that when I say a thing is so, that thing will be so – however much you and I might privately regret it."

"But you are quite mistaken," said Mr Segundus. "I do not know you. At least I do not believe I ever saw you before."

"I am John Childermass, Mr Norrell's servant. We last talked nine years ago, outside the Cathedral in York. When you confined yourself to a few pupils, Mr Segundus, I was able to turn a blind eye. I said nothing and Mr Norrell remained in ignorance of what you were doing. But a regular school for grown-up magicians, that is a different matter. You have been too ambitious, sir. He knows, Mr Segundus. He knows and it is his desire that you wind up the business immediately."

"But what has Mr Norrell or Mr Norrell's desires to do with me? *I* did not sign the agreement. You should know that I am not alone in this undertaking. I have friends now."

"That is true," said Childermass, mildly amused. "And Mrs Lennox is a very rich woman, and an excellent woman for business. But does she have the friendship of every Minister in the Cabinet like Mr Norrell? Does she have his influence? Remember the Society of Learned Magicians, Mr Segundus! Remember how he crushed them!"

Childermass waited a moment and then, since the conversation appeared to be at an end, he strode off in the direction of the stables.

Five minutes later he reappeared on a big, brown horse. Mr Segundus was standing, just as before, with his arms crossed, glaring at the paving-stones.

Childermass looked down at him. "I am sorry it ends like this, sir. Yet, surely all is not lost? This house is just as suited to another kind of school as it is for a magical one. You would not think it to look at me, but I am a very fine fellow with a wide acquaintance among great people. Chuse some other sort of school and the next time I hear that a lord or lady has need of such an establishment for their little lordlings, I will send them your way."

"I do not want another kind of school!" said Mr Segundus, peevishly.

Childermass smiled his sideways smile and rode away.

Mr Segundus travelled to Bath and informed his patroness of their dismal situation. She was full of indignation that some gentleman she had never even met should presume to instruct her in what she could and could not do. She wrote Mr Norrell an angry letter. She got no reply, but her bankers, lawyers and partners in other business ventures suddenly found themselves in receipt of odd letters from great people of their acquaintance, all complaining in an oblique fashion of Mr Segundus's school. One of the bankers – an argumentative and obdurate old person – was unwise enough to wonder publicly (in the lobby of the House of Commons) what a school for magicians in Yorkshire could possibly have to do with him. The result was that several ladies and gentlemen – friends of Mr Norrell – withdrew their patronage from his bank.

In Mrs Honeyfoot's drawing-room in York a few evenings later Mr Segundus sat with his head in his hands, lamenting. "It is as if some evil fortune is determined to torment me, holding out great prizes in front of me, only to snatch them away again."

Mrs Honeyfoot clucked sympathetically, patted his shoulder and offered the same damning censure of Mr Norrell with which she had consoled both Mr Segundus and Mr Honeyfoot for the past nine years: to wit, that Mr Norrell seemed a very odd gentleman, full of queer fancies, and that she would never understand him.

"Why not write to Mr Strange?" said Mr Honeyfoot, suddenly. "He will know what to do!"

Mr Segundus looked up. "Oh! I know that Mr Strange and Mr

Norrell have parted, but still I should not like to be a cause of argument between them."

"Nonsense!" cried Mr Honeyfoot. "Have you not read the recent issues of *The Modern Magician*? This is the very thing Strange wants! – some principle of Norrellite magic that he can attack openly and so bring the whole edifice tumbling down. Believe me, he will consider himself obliged to you for the opportunity. You know, Segundus, the more I think of it, the more I like this plan!"

Mr Segundus thought so too. "Let me only consult Mrs Lennox and if she is in agreement, then I shall certainly do as you suggest!"

Mrs Lennox's ignorance concerning recent magical events was extensive. She knew very little of Jonathan Strange other than his name and that he had some vague connexion to the Duke of Wellington. But she was quick to assure Mr Segundus that if Mr Strange disliked Mr Norrell, then she was very much in his favour. So on the 20th December Mr Segundus sent Strange a letter informing him of Gilbert Norrell's actions in regard to the school at Starecross Hall.

Unfortunately, far from leaping to Mr Segundus's defence, Strange never even replied.

42

Strange decides to write a book

June–December 1815

IT MAY VERY easily be imagined with what pleasure Mr Norrell received the news that on his return to England Mr Strange had gone straight to Shropshire.

"And the best part of it is," Mr Norrell told Lascelles, "that in the country he is unlikely to publish any more of those mischievous articles upon the magic of the Raven King."

"No indeed, sir," said Lascelles, "for I very much doubt that he will have time to write them."

Mr Norrell took a moment to consider what this might mean.

"Oh! Have you not heard, sir?" continued Lascelles. "Strange is writing a book. He writes to his friends of nothing else. He began very suddenly about two weeks ago and is, by his own account, making very rapid progress. But then we all know with what ease Strange writes. He has sworn to put the entirety of English magic into his book. He told Sir Walter that he would be greatly astonished if he could cram it all into two volumes. He rather thinks that it will need three. It is to be called *The History and Practice of English Magic* and Murray has promised to publish it when it is done."

There could scarcely have been worse news. Mr Norrell had always intended to write a book himself. He intended to call it *Precepts for the Education of a Magician* and he had begun it when he had first become tutor to Mr Strange. His notes already filled two shelves of the little book-lined room on the second floor. Yet he had always spoken of his book as something for the distant future. He had a quite unreasonable terror of committing himself to paper which eight years of London adulation had not cured. All his volumes of private notes and histories and journals had yet to be seen by anyone (except, in a few instances, by Strange and Childermass). Mr Norrell could never believe himself ready to publish: he could never be sure that he had got at the truth; he did not believe he had thought long enough upon the matter; he did not know if it were a fit subject to place before the public.

As soon as Mr Lascelles had gone, Mr Norrell called for a silver dish of clear water to be brought to him in his room on the second floor.

In Shropshire, Strange was working upon his book. He did not look up, but suddenly he smiled a little wryly and wagged his finger at the empty air as if to tell some unseen person *No*. All the mirrors in the room had been turned to face the wall and, though Mr Norrell spent several hours bent over his silver dish, by the end of the evening he was no wiser.

On an evening at the beginning of December Stephen Black was polishing silver in his room at the end of the kitchen-passage. He looked down and discovered that the strings of his polishing-apron were untying themselves. It was not that the bow had come loose (Stephen had never tied a lazy bow in his life), but rather that the strings were snaking about in a bold, decisive way like apron-strings that knew what they were about. Next his polishing-sleeves and polishing-gloves slipped off his arms and hands and folded themselves up neatly upon the table. Then his coat leapt from the chairback where he had hung it. It took firm hold of him and helped him on with itself. Finally the butler's room itself disappeared.

Suddenly he was standing in a small apartment panelled in dark wood. A table took up most of the space. The table was laid with a cloth of scarlet linen with a deep and ornate border of gold and silver. It was crowded with gold and silver dishes and the dishes were heaped with food. Jewelled ewers were filled with wine. Wax candles in gold candlesticks made a blaze of light and incense burnt in two golden censers. Besides the table the only other furniture were two carved wooden chairs draped with cloth of gold and made luxurious with embroidered cushions. In one of these chairs the gentleman with the thistle-down hair was sitting.

"Good evening, Stephen!"

"Good evening, sir."

"You look a little pale tonight, Stephen. I hope you are not unwell."

"I am merely a little out of breath, sir. I find these sudden removals to other countries and continents a little perplexing."

"Oh! But we are still in London, Stephen. This is the Jerusalem Coffee-house in Cowper's-court. Do you not know it?"

"Oh, yes indeed, sir. Sir Walter would often sup here with his rich friends when he was a bachelor. It is just that it was never so magnificent before. As for this banquet, there are hardly any dishes here I recognize."

"Oh! That is because I have ordered an exact copy of a meal I ate in this very house four or five hundred years ago! Here is a haunch of roasted wyvern and a pie of honeyed hummingbirds. Here is roasted salamander with a relish of pomegranates; here a delicate fricassee of the combs of cockatrices spiced with saffron and powdered rainbows and ornamented with gold stars! Now sit you down and eat! That will be the best cure for your dizziness. What will you take?"

"It is all very wonderful, sir, but I believe I see some plain pork steaks which look very good indeed."

"Ah, Stephen! As ever your noble instincts have led you to pick the choicest dish of all! Though the pork steaks are indeed quite plain, they have been fried in fat that was rendered down from the

596

exorcised ghosts of black Welsh pigs that wander through the hills of Wales at night terrifying the inhabitants of that deplorable country! The ghostliness and ferocity of the pigs lends the steaks a wonderful flavour which is quite unlike any other! And the sauce which accompanies them is made from cherries that were grown in a centaur's orchard!"

Taking up a jewelled and gilded ewer, the gentleman poured Stephen a glass of ruby-red wine. "This wine is one of the vintages of Hell – but do not allow yourself to be dissuaded from tasting it upon that account! I dare say you have heard of Tantalus? The wicked king who baked his little son in a pie and ate him? He has been condemned to stand up to his chin in a pool of water he cannot drink, beneath a vine laden with grapes he cannot eat. This wine is made from those grapes. And, since the vine was planted there for the sole purpose of tormenting Tantalus, you may be sure the grapes have an excellent flavour and aroma – and so does the wine. The pomegranates too are from Persephone's own orchard."

Stephen tasted the wine and the pork steaks. "It is altogether excellent, sir. What was the occasion when you dined here before?"

"Oh! I and my friends were celebrating our departure for the Crusades. William of Lanchester[1] was here and Tom Dundell[2] and many other noble lords and knights, both Christian and fairy. Of course it was not a coffee-house then. It was an inn. From where we sat we looked out over a wide courtyard surrounded by carved and gilded pillars. Our servants, pages and squires went to and fro, making everything ready for us to wreak a terrible vengeance upon our wicked enemies! On the other side of the courtyard were the stables where were housed not only the most beautiful horses in England, but three unicorns that another fairy – a cousin of mine –

---

[1] William of Lanchester was John Uskglass's seneschal and favourite servant, and consequently one of the most important men in England.
[2] Thomas of Dundale, John Uskglass's first human servant. See footnote 2, Chapter 45.

was taking to the Holy Lands to pierce our enemies through and through. Several talented magicians were seated at the table with us. They in no way resembled the horrors that pass for magicians nowadays. They were as handsome in their persons as they were accomplished in their art! The birds of the air stooped to hear their commands. The rains and the rivers were their servants. The north wind, the south wind, etc., etc., only existed to do their bidding. They spread their hands and cities crumbled – or sprang up whole again! What a contrast to that horrible old man who sits in a dusty room, muttering to himself and turning the pages of some ancient volume!" The gentlemen ate some cockatrice fricassee thought-fully. "The other one is writing a book," he said.

"So I have heard, sir. Have you been to look at him recently?"

The gentleman frowned. "I? Did you just not hear me say that I consider these magicians the stupidest, most abominable men in England? No, I have not seen him above twice or three times a week since he left London. When he writes, he cuts his nibs rather square with a old pen-knife. *I* should be ashamed to use so battered and ugly an old knife, but these magicians endure all sorts of nastiness that you and I would shudder at! Sometimes he gets so lost in what he is writing that he forgets to mend his nib and then the ink splatters on to his paper and into his coffee and he pays it no attention at all."

Stephen reflected how odd it was that the gentleman, who lived in a partly ruinous house surrounded by the grisly bones of bygone battles, should be so sensitive to disorder in other people's houses. "And what of the subject of the book, sir?" he asked. "What is your opinion of that?"

"It is most peculiar! He describes all the most important appearances of my race in this country. There are accounts of how we have intervened in Britain's affairs for Britain's good and the greater glory of the inhabitants. He continually gives it as his opinion that nothing is so desirable as that the magicians of this Age should immediately summon us up and beg for our assistance.

Can you make any thing of this, Stephen? I cannot. When I wished to bring the King of England to my house and shew him all sorts of polite attentions, this same magician thwarted me. His behaviour upon that occasion seemed calculated to insult me!"

"But I think, sir," said Stephen, gently, "that perhaps he did not quite understand who or what you were."

"Oh! who can tell what these Englishmen understand? Their minds are so peculiar! It is impossible to know what they are thinking! I fear you will find it so, Stephen, when you are their King!"

"I really have no wish to be King of anywhere, sir."

"You will feel very differently when you are King. It is just that you are cast down at the thought of being excluded from Lost-hope and all your friends. Be easy upon that score! I too would be miserable if I thought that your elevation would be the means of parting us. But I see no necessity for you to reside permanently in England merely because you are its monarch. A week is the utmost any person of taste could be expected to linger in such a dull country. A week is more than enough!"

"But what of my duties, sir? It is my understanding that kings have a great deal of business, and as little as I want to be King, I should not wish . . ."

"My dear Stephen!" cried the gentleman in affectionate but amused delight. "That is what seneschals are for! They can perform all the dull business of government, while you remain with me at Lost-hope to enjoy our usual pleasures. You will return here every so often to collect your taxes and the tribute of conquered nations and put them into a bank. Oh, I suppose that once in a while it will be prudent to stay in England long enough to have your portrait painted so that the populace may adore you all the more. Sometimes you may graciously permit all the most beautiful ladies in the land to wait in line to kiss your hands and fall in love with you. Then, all your duties performed to perfection, you can return to Lady Pole and me with a good conscience!" The gentleman paused and grew unusually thoughtful. "Though I must confess," he said at last, "that my delight in the beautiful Lady Pole is not so overpowering as once it was. There is another lady whom I like much more. She is only moderately pretty, but the deficiency in beauty is more than compensated for by her lively spirits and sweet conversation. And this other lady has one great advantage over Lady Pole. As you and I both know, Stephen, however often Lady Pole visits my house, she must always go away again in accordance with the magician's agreement. But in the case of this lady, there will be no need for any such foolish agreement. Once I have obtained her, I shall be able to keep her always at my side!"

Stephen sighed. The thought of some other poor lady held prisoner at Lost-hope for ever and a day was melancholy indeed! Yet it would be foolish to suppose that he could do any thing to prevent it and it might be that he could turn it to Lady Pole's advantage. "Perhaps, sir," he said, respectfully, "in that case you would consider releasing her ladyship from her enchantment? I know her husband and friends would be glad to have her restored to them."

"Oh! But I shall always regard Lady Pole as a most desirable addition to all our entertainments. A beautiful woman is always good company and I doubt if her ladyship has her equal for beauty in England. There are not many to equal her in Faerie. No, what you suggest is entirely impossible. But to return to the subject in hand. We must decide upon a scheme to pluck this other lady from her home and carry her off to Lost-hope. I know, Stephen, that you will be all the more eager to help me when I tell you that I consider the removal of this lady from England as quite essential to our noble aim of making you King. It will be a terrible blow to our enemies! It will cast them down into utter despair! It will produce strife and dissension amongst them. Oh, yes! It will be all good things to us and all bad to them! We would fail in our lofty duties if we did any thing less!"

Stephen could make very little of this. Was the gentleman speaking of one of the Princesses at Windsor Castle? It was well known that the King had gone mad when his youngest and favourite daughter died. Perhaps the gentleman with the thistle-down hair supposed that the loss of another Princess might actually kill him, or loosen the wits of some other members of the Royal Family.

"Now, my dear Stephen," said the gentleman. "The question before us is: how may we fetch the lady away without any one noticing – particularly the magicians!" He considered a moment. "I have it! Fetch me a piece of moss-oak!"

"Sir?"

"It must be about your own girth and as tall as my collar bone."

"I would gladly fetch it for you immediately, sir. But I do not know what moss-oak is."

"Ancient wood that has been sunk in peat bogs for countless centuries!"

"Then, sir, I fear we are not very likely to find any in London. There are no peat bogs here."

"True, true." The gentleman flung himself back in his chair and stared at the ceiling while he considered this tricky problem.

"Would any other sort of wood suit your purposes, sir?" asked Stephen, "There is a timber merchant in Gracechurch-street, who I dare say . . ."

"No, no," said the gentleman, "This must be done . . ."

At that instant Stephen experienced the queerest sensation: he was plucked out of his chair and stood upon his feet. At the same moment the coffee-house disappeared and was replaced by a pitch-black, ice-cold nothingness. Though he could see nothing at all, Stephen had the sense that he was in a wide, open place. A bitter wind howled about his ears and a thick rain seemed to be falling upon him from all directions at once.

". . . properly," continued the gentleman in exactly the same tone as before. "There is a very fine piece of moss-oak hereabouts.

At least I think I remember . . ." His voice, which had been somewhere near Stephen's right ear, moved away. "Stephen!" he cried, "Have you brought a flaughter, a rutter and a tusker?"

"What, sir? Which, sir? No, sir. I have not brought any of those things. To own the truth, I did not quite understand that we were going any where." Stephen found that his feet and ancles were deep in cold water. He tried to step aside. Immediately the ground lurched most alarmingly and he sank suddenly into it up to the middle of his calves. He screamed.

"Mmm?" inquired the gentleman.

"I . . . I would never presume to interrupt you, sir. But the ground appears to be swallowing me up."

"It is a bog," said the gentleman, helpfully.

"It is certainly a most terrifying substance." Stephen attempted to mimic the gentleman's calm, uninterested tone. He knew only too well that the gentleman set a great value upon dignity in every situation and he feared that if he let the gentleman hear how terrified he was, there was every possibility that the gentleman would grow disgusted with him and wander off, leaving him to be sucked into the bog. He tried to move, but found nothing solid beneath his feet. He flailed about, almost fell and the only result was that his feet and legs slipped a little further into the watery mud. He screamed again. The bog made a series of most unpleasant sucking noises.

"Ah, God! I take the liberty of observing, sir, that I am sinking by degrees. Ah!" He began to slip sideways. "You have often been so kind as to express an affection for me, sir, and to say how much you prefer my society to that of any other person. If it would not inconvenience you in any way, perhaps I might prevail upon you to rescue me from this horrible bog?"

The gentleman did not trouble to reply. Instead Stephen found himself plucked by magic out of the bog and stood upon his feet. He was quite weak with fright and would have liked to lie down, but dared not move. The ground here seemed solid enough, but it was unpleasantly wet and he had no idea where the bog was.

"I would gladly help you, sir," he called into the darkness, "but I dare not move for fear of falling into the bog again!"

"Oh, it does not matter!" said the gentleman. "In truth, there is nothing to do but wait. Moss-oak is most easily discovered at dawn."

"But dawn is not for another nine hours!" exclaimed Stephen in horror.

"No, indeed! Let us sit down and wait."

"Here, sir? But this is a dreadful place. Black and cold and awful!"

"Oh, quite! It is most disagreeable!" agreed the gentleman with aggravating calmness. He fell silent then and Stephen could only suppose that he was pursuing this mad plan of waiting for the dawn.

The icy wind blew upon Stephen; the damp seeped up into every part of his being; the blackness pressed down upon him; and the long hours passed with excruciating slowness. He had no expectation of being able to sleep, but at some time during the night he experienced a little relief from the misery of his situation. It was not that he fell asleep exactly, but he did fall to dreaming.

In his dream he had gone to the pantry to fetch someone a slice of a magnificent pork pie. But when he cut the pie open he found that there was very little pork inside it. Most of the interior was taken up by the city of Birmingham. Within the pie-crust forges and smithies smoked and engines pounded. One of the citizens, a civil-looking person, happened to stroll out from the cut that Stephen had made and when his glance fell upon Stephen, he said . . .

Just then a high, mournful sound broke in upon Stephen's dream – a slow, sad song in an unknown language and Stephen understood without ever actually waking that the gentleman with the thistle-down hair was singing.

It may be laid down as a general rule that if a man begins to sing, no one will take any notice of his song except his fellow human beings. This is true even if his song is surpassingly beautiful. Other men may be in raptures at his skill, but the rest of creation is, by and large, unmoved. Perhaps a cat or a dog may look at him; his horse, if it is an exceptionally intelligent beast, may pause in cropping the grass, but that is the extent of it. But when the fairy sang, the whole world listened to him. Stephen felt clouds pause in their passing; he felt sleeping hills shift and murmur; he felt cold mists dance. He understood for the first time that the world is not dumb at all, but merely waiting for someone to speak to it in a language it understands. In the fairy's song the earth recognized the names by which it called itself.

Stephen began to dream again. This time he dreamt that hills walked and the sky wept. Trees came and spoke to him and told him their secrets and also whether or not he might regard them as friends or enemies. Important destinies were hidden inside pebbles and crumpled leaves. He dreamt that everything in the world – stones and rivers, leaves and fire – had a purpose which it was determined to carry out with the utmost rigour, but he also understood that it was possible sometimes to persuade things to a different purpose.

When he awoke it was dawn. Or something like dawn. The light was watery, dim and incomparably sad. Vast, grey, gloomy hills rose up all around them and in between the hills there was a wide expanse of black bog. Stephen had never seen a landscape so calculated to reduce the onlooker to utter despair in an instant.

"This is one of your kingdoms, I suppose, sir?" he said.

"My kingdoms?" exclaimed the gentleman in surprise. "Oh, no! This is Scotland!"

The gentleman disappeared suddenly – and reappeared a moment later with an armful of tools. There was an axe and a spit and three things Stephen had never seen before. One was a little like a hoe, one was a little like a spade and the last was a very strange object, something between a spade and a scythe. He handed all of them to Stephen, who examined them with a puzzled air. "Are they new, sir? They shine so brightly."

"Well, obviously one cannot employ tools of ordinary metal for such a magical undertaking as I am proposing. These are made of a compound of quicksilver and starshine. Now, Stephen, we must look for a patch of ground where the dew has not settled and if we dig there we are sure to find moss-oak!"

All through the glen all the grasses and tiny coloured bog-plants were covered with dew. Stephen's clothes, hands, hair and skin had a velvety, grey bloom, and the gentleman's hair – which was always extraordinary – had added the sparkle of a million tiny spheres of water to its customary brilliance. He appeared to be wearing a jewelled halo.

The gentleman walked slowly across the glen, his eyes fixed upon the ground. Stephen followed.

"Ah!" cried the gentleman. "Here we are!"

How the gentleman knew this, Stephen could not tell.

They were standing in the middle of a boggy expanse, exactly like every other part of the glen. There was no distinguishing tree or rock nearby to mark the spot. But the gentleman strode on with a confident air until he came to a shallow depression. In the middle of the depression was a long, broad stripe where there was no dew at all.

"Dig here, Stephen!"

The gentleman proved surprizingly knowledgeable about the art of peat cutting. And though he did none of the actual work himself he carefully instructed Stephen how to cut away the uppermost layer of grasses and moss with one tool, how to cut the peat with another tool and how to lift out the pieces with a third.

Stephen was unaccustomed to hard labour and he was soon out of breath and every part of him ached. Fortunately, he had not cut down very far when he struck something much harder than the peat.

"Ah!" cried the gentleman, very well pleased. "That is the moss oak. Excellent! Now, Stephen, cut around it!"

This was easier said than done. Even when Stephen had cut away enough of the peat to expose the moss-oak to the air it was still very difficult to see what was oak and what was peat – both were black, wet and oozing. He dug some more and he began to suspect that, though the gentleman called it a log, this was in fact an entire tree.

"Could you not lift it out by magic, sir?" he asked.

"Oh, no! No, indeed! I shall ask a great deal of this wood and therefore it is incumbent upon us to make its passage from the bog into the wider world as easy as we can! Now, do you take this axe, Stephen, and cut me a piece as tall as my collar-bone. Then with the spit and the tusker we will prise it out!"

It took them three more hours to accomplish the task. Stephen chopped the wood to the size the gentleman had asked for, but the task of manoeuvring it out of the bog was more than one man could manage and the gentleman was obliged to descend into the muddy, stinking hole with him and they strained and pulled and heaved together.

When at last they had finished, Stephen threw himself upon the ground in a condition of the utmost exhaustion, while the gentleman stood, regarding his log with delight.

"Well," he said, "that was a great deal easier than I had imagined."

Stephen suddenly found himself once more in the upper room of the Jerusalem Coffee-house. He looked at himself and at the gentleman. Their good clothes were in tatters and they were covered from head to foot with bog-mud.

For the first time he was able to see the log of moss-oak properly. It was as black as sin, extremely fine-grained, and it oozed black water.

"We must dry it out before it will be fit for any thing," he said.

"Oh, no!" said the gentleman with a brilliant smile. "For my purposes it will do very well as it is!"

43

The curious adventure of Mr Hyde

December 1815

ONE MORNING IN the first week of December Jeremy knocked upon the door of Strange's library at Ashfair House and said that Mr Hyde begged the favour of a few minutes' conversation with him.

Strange was not best pleased to be interrupted. Since he had been in the country he had grown almost as fond of quiet and solitude as Norrell. "Oh, very well!" he muttered.

Delaying only to write another paragraph, look up three or four things in a biography of Valentine Greatrakes, blot his paper, correct some spellings and blot his paper again, he went immediately to the drawing-room.

A gentleman was sitting alone by the fire, staring pensively into the flames. He was a vigorous-looking, active sort of man of fifty or so years, dressed in the stout clothes and boots of a gentleman-farmer. On a table at his side there was a little glass of wine and a small plate of biscuits. Clearly Jeremy had decided that the visitor had sat alone long enough to require some refreshment.

Mr Hyde and Jonathan Strange had been neighbours all their lives, but the marked differences in their fortunes and tastes had meant that they had never been more than common acquaintances. This was in fact the first time they had met since Strange had become a magician.

They shook hands.

"I dare say, sir," began Mr Hyde, "you are wondering what can bring me to your door in such weather."

"Weather?"

"Yes, sir. It is very bad."

Strange looked out of the window. The high hills surrounding Ashfair were sheathed in snow. Every branch, every twig bore its burden of snow. The very air seemed white with frost and mist.

"So it is. I had not observed. I have not been out of the house since Sunday."

"Your servant tells me that you are very much occupied with your studies. I beg your pardon for interrupting you, but I have something to tell you which can wait no longer."

"Oh! There is no explanation necessary. And how is your . . ." Strange paused and tried to remember whether Mr Hyde had a wife, any children, brothers, sisters or friends. He found he was entirely without information upon the subject. "Farm," he finished. "I recollect it is at Aston."

"It is nearer to Clunbury."

"Clunbury. Yes."

"All is well with me, Mr Strange, except for something rather . . . unsettling which happened to me three days ago. I have been debating with myself ever since whether I ought to come and speak to you about it. I have asked the advice of my friends and my wife and all are agreed that I ought to tell you what I have seen. Three days ago I had business on the Welsh side of the border, with David Evans – I dare say you know him, sir?"

"I know him by sight. I have never spoken to him. Ford knows him, I believe." (Ford was the agent who managed all the business of Strange's estate.)

"Well, sir, David Evans and I had finished our business by two o'clock and I was very anxious to get home. There was a thick snow lying everywhere and the roads between here and Llanfair Waterdine were very bad. I dare say you do not know it, sir, but

David Evans's house is high up on a hill with a long view westwards and the moment he and I stepped outside we saw great grey clouds full of snow coming towards us. Mrs Evans, Davey's mother, pressed me to stay with them and come home the next day, but Evans and I talked it over and we both agreed that all would be well providing I left instantly and came home by the most direct way possible – in other words I should ride up to the Dyke and cross over into England before the storm was upon me."[1]

"The Dyke?" said Strange, frowning, "That is a steep ride – even in summer – and a very lonely place if any thing were to happen to you. I do not think I would have attempted it. But I dare say you know these hills and their temper better than I."

"Perhaps you are wiser than I was, sir. As I rode up to the Dyke a hard, high wind began to blow and it caught up the snow that had already fallen and carried it up into the air. The snow stuck to my horse's coat and to my own greatcoat so that when I looked down we were as white as the hillside, as white as the air. As white as everything. The wind made eerie shapes with the snow so that I seemed to be surrounded by spinning ghosts and the kind of evil spirits and bad angels that are in the Arabian lady's stories. My poor horse – who is not generally a nervous beast – seemed to be seeing all manner of things to frighten him. As you may imagine, I was beginning to wish very heartily that I had accepted Mrs Evans's hospitality when I heard the sound of a bell tolling."

"A bell?" said Strange.

"Yes, sir."

"But what bell could there have been?"

"Well, none at all, sir, in that lonely place. Indeed it is a wonder to me that I could have heard any thing at all what with the horse snorting and the wind howling."

---

[1] The Dyke is a great wall of earth and stones, now much decayed, which divides Wales from England – the work of Offa, an eighth-century Mercian king, who had learnt by experience to distrust his Welsh neighbours.

Strange, who imagined that Mr Hyde must have come in order to have this queer bell explained to him, began to talk of the magical significance of bells: how bells were used as a protection against fairies and other evil spirits and how a bad fairy might sometimes be frightened away by the sound of a church bell. And yet, at the same time, it was well known that fairies loved bells; fairy magic was often accompanied by the tolling of a bell; and bells often sounded when fairies appeared. "I cannot explain this odd contradiction," he said. "Theoretical magicians have puzzled over it for centuries."

Mr Hyde listened to this speech with every appearance of politeness and attentiveness. When Strange had finished, Mr Hyde said, "But the bell was just the beginning, sir."

"Oh!" said Strange, a little annoyed. "Very well. Continue."

"I got so far up the hill that I could see the Dyke where it runs along the top. There were a few bent trees, some broken-down walls of loose stones. I looked to the south and I saw a lady walking very fast along the Dyke towards me . . ."

"A lady!"

"I saw her very clearly. Her hair was loose and the wind was setting it on end and making it writhe about her head." Mr Hyde gestured with his hands to shew how the lady's hair had danced in the snowy air. "I think I called out to her. I know that she turned her head and looked at me, but she did not stop or slow her pace. She turned away again and walked on along the Dyke with all the snowy wraiths around her. She wore only a black gown. No shawl. No pelisse. And that made me very afraid for her. I thought that some dreadful accident must have befallen her. So I urged my horse up the hill, as fast as the poor creature could go. I tried to keep her in sight the whole time, but the wind kept carrying the snow into my eyes. I reached the Dyke and she was nowhere to be seen. So I rode back and forth along the Dyke. I searched and cried myself hoarse – I was sure she must have fallen down behind a heap of stones or snow, or tripped in some rabbit-hole. Or

perhaps been carried away by the person who had done her the evil in the first place."

"The evil?"

"Well, sir, I supposed that she must have been carried to the Dyke by someone who meant her harm. One hears such terrible things nowadays."

"You knew the lady?"

"Yes, sir."

"Who was it?"

"Mrs Strange."

There was a moment's silence.

"But it could not have been," said Strange, perplexed. "Mr Hyde, if any thing of a distressing nature had happened to Mrs Strange, I think someone would have told me. I am not so shut up with my books as that. I am sorry, Mr Hyde, but you are mistaken. Whoever this poor woman was, it was not Mrs Strange."

Mr Hyde shook his head. "If I saw you, sir, in Shrewsbury or Ludlow, I might not know you immediately. But Mrs Strange's father was curate of my parish for forty-seven years. I have known Mrs Strange – Miss Woodhope as she was then – since she was an infant taking her first steps in Clunbury churchyard. Even if she had not looked at me I would have known her. I would have known her by her figure, by her way of walking, by her everything."

"What did you do after you had lost sight of the woman?"

"I rode straight here – but your servant would not let me in."

"Jeremy? The man you spoke to just now?"

"Yes. He told me that Mrs Strange was safe within. I confess that I did not believe him and so I walked around your house and looked in at all the windows, until I saw her seated upon a sofa in this very room." Mr Hyde pointed to the sofa in question. "She was wearing a pale blue gown – not black at all."

"Well, there is nothing remarkable in that. Mrs Strange never wears black. It is not a colour I like to see a young woman wear."

Mr Hyde shook his head and frowned. "I wish I could convince you, sir, of what I saw. But I see that I cannot."

"And I wish I could explain it to you. But I cannot."

They shook hands at parting. Mr Hyde looked solemnly at Strange and said, "I never wished her harm, Mr Strange. Nobody could be more thankful that she is safe."

Strange bowed slightly. "And we intend to keep her so."

The door closed upon Mr Hyde's back.

Strange waited a moment and then went to find Jeremy. "Why did not you tell me that he had been here before?"

Jeremy made a sort of snorting noise of derision. "I believe I know better, sir, than to trouble you with such nonsense! Ladies in black dresses walking about in snow-storms!"

"I hope you did not speak too harshly to him."

"Me, sir? No, indeed!"

"Perhaps he was drunk. Yes, I expect that was it. I dare say he and David Evans were celebrating the successful conclusion of their business."

Jeremy frowned. "I do not think so, sir. David Evans is a Methodist preacher."

"Oh! Well, yes. I suppose you are right. And indeed it is not much like a hallucination brought on by drunkenness. It is more the sort of thing one might imagine if one took opium after reading one of Mrs Radcliffe's novels."

Strange found himself unsettled by Mr Hyde's visit. The thought of Arabella – even an ideal, imaginary Arabella – lost in the snow, wandering upon the hilltops, was disturbing. He could not help but be reminded of his own mother, who had taken to walking those same hills alone to escape the miseries of an unhappy marriage and who had caught a chill in a rainstorm and died.

That evening at dinner he said to Arabella, "I saw John Hyde today. He thought he saw you walking upon the Dyke last Tuesday in the middle of a snow-storm."

"No!"

"Yes."

"Poor man! He must have been a good deal startled."

"I believe he was."

"I shall certainly visit Mr and Mrs Hyde when Henry is here."

"You seem intent upon visiting every body in Shropshire when Henry is here," said Strange. "I hope you will not be disappointed."

"Disappointed! What do you mean?"

"Only that the weather is bad."

"Then we will tell Harris to drive slowly and carefully. But he would do that anyway. And Starling is a very steady horse. It takes a great deal of snow and ice to frighten Starling. He is not easily daunted. Besides, you know, there are people whom Henry *must* visit – people who would be most unhappy if he did not. Jenny and Alwen – my father's two old servants. They talk of nothing but Henry's coming. It is five years since they saw him last and they are scarcely likely to last another five years, poor things."

"Very well! Very well! I only said that the weather would be bad. That is all."

But that was not quite all. Strange was aware that Arabella had high hopes of this visit. She had seen her brother only rarely since her marriage. He had not come to Soho-square as often as she would have liked and, once there, he had never stayed as long as she wished. But this Christmas visit would restore all their old intimacy. They would be together among all the scenes of their childhood and Henry had promised to stay almost a month.

Henry arrived and at first it seemed that Arabella's dearest wishes would all be answered. The conversation at dinner that evening was very animated. Henry had a great deal of news to relate about Great Hitherden, the Northamptonshire village where he was Rector.[2]

Great Hitherden was a large and prosperous village. There were several gentlemen's families in the neighbourhood. Henry was highly pleased with the respectable place he occupied in its society. After a long description of his friends and their dinner-parties and balls, he ended by saying, "But I would not have you think that we neglect charitable works. We are a very active neighbourhood. There is much to do and many distressed persons. The day before yesterday I paid a visit to a poor, sick family and I found Miss Watkins already at the cottage, dispensing money and good advice. Miss Watkins is a very compassionate young lady." Here he paused as if expecting someone to say something.

Strange looked blank; then, suddenly, a thought seemed to strike him. "Why, Henry, I do beg your pardon. You will think us very remiss. You have now mentioned Miss Watkins five times in ten minutes and neither Bell nor I have made the least inquiry about her. We are both a little slow tonight – it is this cold Welsh air – it chills the brain – but now that I have awoken to your meaning I shall be happy to quiz you about her quite as much as you could wish for. Is she fair or dark? A brown complexion or a pale one? Does she favour the piano or the harp? What are her favourite books?"

Henry, who suspected he was being teased, frowned and seemed inclined to say no more about the lady.

Arabella, with a cool look at her husband, took up the inquiries in a gentler style and soon got out of Henry the following

---

[2] At the time of Strange and Arabella's marriage Henry had been Rector of Grace Adieu in Gloucestershire. While there he had conceived a wish to marry a young lady of the village, a Miss Parbringer. But Strange had not approved the young lady or her friends. The living of Great Hitherden had happened to fall vacant at this time and so Strange persuaded Sir Walter Pole, in whose gift it lay, to appoint Henry. Henry had been delighted. Great Hitherden was a much larger place than Grace Adieu and he soon forgot the unsuitable young lady.

information – that Miss Watkins had only lately removed to the neighbourhood of Great Hitherden – that her Christian name was Sophronia – that she lived with her guardians, Mr and Mrs Swoonfirst (persons to whom she was distantly related) – that she was fond of reading (though Henry could not say precisely what) – that her favourite colour was yellow – and that she had a particular dislike of pineapples.

"And her looks? Is she pretty?" asked Strange.

The question seemed to embarrass Henry.

"Miss Watkins is not generally considered one of the first in beauty, no. But then upon further acquaintance, you know – that is worth a great deal. People of both sexes, whose looks are very indifferent at the beginning, may appear almost handsome on further acquaintance. A well-informed mind, nice manners and a gentle nature – all of these are much more likely to contribute to a husband's happiness than mere transient beauty."

Strange and Arabella were a little surprized at this speech. There was a pause and then Strange asked, "Money?"

Henry looked quietly triumphant. "Ten thousand pounds," he said.

"My dear Henry!" cried Strange.

Later, when they were alone, Strange said to Arabella, "As I understand it, Henry is to be congratulated upon his cleverness. It seems that he has found the lady before any one else could. I take it that she has not been overpowered by offers – there is something in her face or figure that protects her from a too universal admiration."

"But I do not think that it can be only the money," said Arabella, who was inclined to defend her brother. "I think there must be some liking too. Or Henry would not have thought of it."

"Oh, I dare say," said Strange. "Henry is a very good fellow. And, besides, I never interfere, as you know."

"You are smiling," said Arabella, "which you have no right to do. *I* was just as clever as Henry in my time. I do not believe that

616

any one had thought of marrying you, with your long nose and unamiable disposition, until it occurred to me to do so."

"That is true," said Strange thoughtfully. "I had forgotten that. It is a family failing."

The next day Strange stayed in the library while Arabella and Henry drove out to visit Jenny and Alwen. But the enjoyment of the first few days did not last long. Arabella soon discovered that she no longer had a great deal in common with her brother. Henry had passed the last seven years in a small country village. She, on the other hand, had been in London where she had observed at close hand some of the most important events of recent years. She had the friendship of more than one Cabinet Minister. She was acquainted with the Prime Minister and had danced several times with the Duke of Wellington. She had met the Royal Dukes, curtsied to the Princesses and could always rely upon a smile and a word from the Prince Regent whenever she happened to be at Carlton House. As for her large acquaintance with every one connected with the glorious revival of English magic, *that* went without saying.

But, while she was greatly interested in all her brother's news, he had next to no interest in hers. Her descriptions of London life drew no more than a polite, "Ah, indeed?" from him. Once when she was speaking of something the Duke of Wellington had said to her and relating what she had said in reply, Henry turned and looked at her with a raised eye-brow and a bland smile – a look and smile which said very plainly, "I do not believe you." Such behaviour wounded her. She did not believe she was boasting – such encounters had been part of the daily tenor of her London life. She realized with a little pang that whereas his letters had always delighted her, he must have found her replies tedious and affected.

Meanwhile, poor Henry had dissatisfactions of his own. When he had been a boy he had greatly admired Ashfair House. Its size, its situation and the great importance of its owner in the neighbourhood of Clun, had all seemed equally wonderful to him. He had always looked forward to the day when Jonathan Strange would inherit and he could visit Ashfair in the important character of Friend of The Master. Now that all of this had come to pass he discovered that he did not really enjoy being there. Ashfair was inferior to many houses that he had seen in the intervening years. It had almost as many gables as windows. Its rooms were all low-ceilinged and oddly shaped. The many generations of inhabitants had placed the windows in the walls just as it had pleased them – without any thought to the general appearance of the house – and the windows themselves were darkened, every one, by the roses and ivy growing up the walls. It was an old-fashioned house – the sort of house in fact, as Strange expressed it, which a lady in a novel might like to be persecuted in.

Several houses in the neighbourhood of Great Hitherden had recently been improved and elegant new cottages built for ladies and gentlemen with rustic inclinations and so – partly because it was impossible for Henry to keep any thing connected to his parish to himself – and partly because he was intending to be married soon and so his mind rather ran upon domestic improvements – he was quite unable to refrain from giving Strange advice upon the matter. He was particularly distressed by the position of the stable yard which, as he told Strange, "One is obliged to walk through to get to the southerly part of the pleasure-grounds and the orchard. You could very easily pull it down and build it again somewhere else."

Strange did not exactly reply to this, but instead suddenly addressed his wife. "My love, I hope you like this house? I am very much afraid that I never thought to ask you before. Say if you do not and we shall instantly remove elsewhere!"

Arabella laughed and said that she was quite satisfied with the house. "And I am sorry, Henry, but I am just as satisfied with the stable-yard as with everything else."

Henry tried again. "Well, surely, you will agree that a great improvement could be made simply by cutting down those trees that crowd about the house so much and darken every room? They grow just as they please – just where the acorn or seed fell, I suppose."

"What?" asked Strange, whose eyes had wandered back to his book during the latter part of the conversation.

"The trees," said Henry.

"Which trees?"

"Those," said Henry, pointing out of the window to a whole host of ancient and magnificent oaks, ashes and beech trees.

"As far as neighbours go, those trees are quite exemplary. They mind their own affairs and have never troubled me. I rather think that I will return the compliment."

"But they are blocking the light."

"So are you, Henry, but I have not yet taken an axe to you."

The truth was that, though Henry saw much to criticize in the grounds and position of Ashfair, this was not his real complaint. What really disturbed him about the house was the all-pervading air of magic. When Strange had first taken up the profession of magic, Henry had not thought any thing of it. At that time news of Mr Norrell's wonderful achievements was only just beginning to spread throughout the kingdom. Magic had seemed little more than an esoteric branch of history, an amusement for rich, idle gentlemen; and Henry still somehow contrived to regard it in that light. He prided himself upon Strange's wealth, his estate, his important pedigree, but not upon his magic. He was always a little surprized whenever any one congratulated him on his close connexion with the Second Greatest Magician of the Age.

Strange was a long way from Henry's ideal of a rich English gentleman. He had pretty well abandoned those pursuits with which gentlemen in the English countryside customarily occupy their time. He took no interest in farming or hunting. His neighbours went shooting – Henry heard their shots echoing in the snowy woods and fields and the barking of their dogs – but

Strange never picked up a gun. It took all Arabella's persuasion to make him go outside and walk about for half an hour. In the library the books that had belonged to Strange's father and grandfather – those works in English, Greek and Latin which every gentleman has upon his shelves – had all been removed and piled up upon the floor to make room for Strange's own books and notebooks.[3] Periodicals concerned with the practice of magic, such as *The Friends of English Magic* and *The Modern Magician*, were everywhere scattered about the house. Upon one of the tables in the library there stood a great silver dish, which was sometimes full of water. Strange would often sit for half an hour peering into the water, tapping the surface and making odd gestures and writing down notes of what he saw there. On another table amid a jumble of books there lay a map of England upon which Strange was marking the old fairy roads which once led out of England to who-knows-where.

There were other things too which Henry only half-understood but which he disliked even more. He knew for instance that Ashfair's rooms often had an odd look, but he did not see that this was because the mirrors in Strange's house were as likely as not to be reflecting the light of half an hour ago, or a hundred years ago. And in the morning, when he awoke, and at night, just before he fell asleep, he heard the sound of a distant bell – a sad sound, like the bell of a drowned city heard across a waste of ocean. He never really thought of the bell, or indeed remembered any thing about it, but its melancholy influence stayed with him through the day.

He found relief for all his various disappointments and dissatisfactions in drawing numerous comparisons between the way things were done in Great Hitherden and the way they were done in Shropshire (much to the detriment of Shropshire), and in

---

[3] The books Strange possessed were, of course, books *about* magic, not books *of* magic. The latter were all in the possession of Mr Norrell. *C.f.* Chapter 1, footnote 5.

wondering aloud that Strange should study so hard – "quite as if he had no estate of his own and all his fortune was still to make." These remarks were generally addressed to Arabella, but Strange was often in earshot and pretty soon Arabella found herself in the unenviable position of trying to keep the peace between the two of them.

"When I want Henry's advice," said Strange, "I shall ask for it. What business is it of his, I should like to know, where I chuse to build my stables? Or how I spend my time?"

"It is very aggravating, my love," agreed Arabella, "and no one should wonder if it put you out of temper, but only consider . . ."

"My temper! It is he who keeps quarrelling with me!"

"Hush! Hush! He will hear you. You have been very sorely tried and any one would say that you have borne it like an angel. But, you know, I think he means to be kind. It is just that he does not express himself very well, and for all his faults we shall miss him greatly when he is gone."

Upon this last point Strange did not perhaps look as convinced as she could have wished. So she added, "Be kind to Henry? For my sake?"

"Of course! Of course! I am patience itself. You know that! There used to be a proverb – quite defunct now – something about priests sowing wheat and magicians sowing rye, all in the same field. The meaning is that priests and magicians will never agree.[4]

---

[4] The meaning was perhaps a little more than this. As early as the twelfth century it was recognized that priests and magicians are in some sense rivals. Both believe that the universe is inhabited by a wide variety of supernatural beings and subject to supernatural forces. Both believe that these beings can be petitioned through spells or prayers and so be persuaded to help or hinder mankind. In many ways the two cosmologies are remarkably similar, but priests and magicians draw very different conclusions from this understanding.

Magicians are chiefly interested in the usefulness of these supernatural beings; they wish to know under what circumstances and by what means angels, demons and fairies can be brought to lend their aid in magical practices. For their purposes it is almost irrelevant that the first class of beings is divinely good, the second infernally wicked and the third morally suspect.

I never found it so until now. I believe I was on friendly terms with the London clergy. The Dean of Westminster Abbey and the Prince Regent's chaplain are excellent fellows. But Henry irks me."

On Christmas-day the snow fell thick and fast. Whether from the vexations of recent days or from some other cause, Arabella awoke in the morning quite sick and wretched with a headach, and unable to rise from her bed. Strange and Henry were obliged to keep each other company the whole day. Henry talked a great deal about Great Hitherden and in the evening they played ecarte. This was a game they were both rather fond of. It might perhaps have produced a more natural state of enjoyment, but halfway through the second game Strange turned over the nine of spades and was immediately struck by several new ideas concerning the magical significance of this card. He abandoned the game, abandoned Henry and took the card with him to the library to study it. Henry was left to his own devices.

Sometime in the early hours of the following morning he woke – or half-woke. There was a faint silvery radiance in the room which might easily have been a reflection of the moonlight on the snow

---

[4] *cont'd*   Priests on the other hand are scarcely interested in any thing else.

In mediaeval England attempts to reconcile the two cosmologies were doomed to failure. The Church was quick to identify a whole host of different heresies of which an unsuspecting magician might be guilty. The Meraudian Heresy has already been mentioned.

Alexander of Whitby (1230s?-1302) taught that the universe is like a tapestry only parts of which are visible to us at a time. After we are dead we will see the whole and then it will be clear to us how the different parts relate to each other. Alexander was forced to issue a retraction of his thesis and priests were henceforth on the lookout for the Whitbyian Heresy. Even the humblest of village magicians was obliged to become a cunning politician if he or she wished to avoid accusations of heresy.

This is not to say that all magicians avoided confusing religion and magic. Many "spells" which have come down to us exhort such-and-such a saint or holy person to help the magician. Surprizingly the source of the confusion was often the magicians' fairy-servants. Most fairies were forcibly baptized as soon as they entered England and they soon began to incorporate references to Saints and Apostles into their magic.

outside. He thought he saw Arabella, dressed and seated on the foot of the bed with her back towards him. She was brushing her hair. He said something to her – or at least thought he said something.

Then he went back to sleep.

At about seven o'clock he woke properly, anxious to get to the library and work for an hour or two before Henry appeared. He rose quickly, went to his dressing-room and rang for Jeremy Johns to come and shave him.

At eight o'clock Arabella's maid, Janet Hughes, knocked on the bed-chamber door. There was no reply and Janet, thinking her mistress might still have the headach, went away again.

At ten o'clock Strange and Henry breakfasted together. Henry had decided to spend the day shooting and was at some pains to persuade Strange to go with him.

"No, no. I have work to do, but that need not prevent your going. After all you know these fields and woods as well as I. I can lend you a gun and dogs can be found from somewhere, I am sure."

Jeremy Johns appeared and said that Mr Hyde had returned. He was in the hall and had asked to speak to Strange on a matter of urgency.

"Oh, what does the fellow want this time?" muttered Strange.

Mr Hyde entered hurriedly, his face grey with anxiety.

Suddenly Henry exclaimed, "What in the world does that fellow think he is doing? He is neither in the room nor out of it!" One of Henry's several sources of vexation at Ashfair was the servants who rarely behaved with that degree of ceremony that Henry considered proper for members of such an important household. On this occasion Jeremy Johns had begun to leave the room but had only got as far as the doorway, where, half-hidden by the door, he and another servant were conducting a conversation in urgent whispers.

Strange glanced at the doorway, sighed and said, "Henry, it really does not matter. Mr Hyde, I . . ."

Meanwhile Mr Hyde, whose agitation appeared to have been increased by this delay, burst out, "An hour ago I saw Mrs Strange again upon the Welsh hills!"

Henry gave a start and looked at Strange.

Strange gave Mr Hyde a very cool look and said, "It is nothing, Henry. Really it is nothing."

Mr Hyde flinched a little at this, but there was a sort of stubbornness in him that helped him bear it. "It was upon Castle Idris and just as before, Mrs Strange was walking away from me and I did not see her face. I tried to follow her and catch up with her, but, just as before, I lost sight of her. I know that the last time it was accounted no more than a delusion – a phantom made by my own brain out of the snow and wind – but today is clear and calm and I know that I saw Mrs Strange – as clearly, sir, as I now see you."

"The last time?" said Henry in confusion.

Strange, somewhat impatiently, began to thank Mr Hyde for his great good nature in bringing them this . . . (He was not quite able to find the word he wanted.) "But as I know Mrs Strange to be safe within my own house, I dare say you will not be surprized, if I . . ."

Jeremy came back into the room rather suddenly. He went immediately to Strange and bent and whispered in his ear.

"Well, speak, man! Tell us what is the matter!" said Henry.

Jeremy looked rather doubtfully at Strange, but Strange said nothing. He covered his mouth with his hand and his eyes went this way and that, as if he were suddenly taken up with some new, and not very pleasant, idea.

Jeremy said, "Mrs Strange is no longer in the house, sir. We do not know where she is."

Henry was questioning Mr Hyde about what he had seen on the hills and barely giving him time to answer one question before asking another. Jeremy Johns was frowning at them both. Strange, meanwhile, sat silently, staring in front of him. Suddenly he stood up and went rapidly out of the room.

"Mr Strange!" called Mr Hyde. "Where are you going?"

"Strange!" cried Henry.

As nothing could be done or decided without him, they had no choice but to follow him. Strange mounted the stairs to his library on the first floor and went immediately to the great silver dish that stood upon one of the tables.

"Bring water," he said to Jeremy Johns.

Jeremy Johns fetched a jug of water and filled the dish.

Strange spoke a single word and the room seemed to grow twilit and shadowy. In the same moment the water in the dish darkened and became slightly opaque.

The lessening of the light terrified Henry.

"Strange!" he cried. "What are we doing here? The light is failing! My sister is outside. We ought not to remain in the house a moment longer!" He turned to Jeremy Johns as the only person present likely to have any influence with Strange. "Tell him to stop! We must start to search!"

"Be quiet, Henry," said Strange.

He drew his finger over the surface of the water twice. Two glittering lines of light appeared, quartering the water. He made a gesture above one of the quarters. Stars appeared in it and more lines, veinings and webs of light. He stared at this for some moments. Then he made a gesture above the next quarter. A different pattern of light appeared. He repeated the process for the third and fourth quarters. The patterns did not remain the same. They shifted and sparkled, sometimes appearing like writing, at other times like the lines of a map and at other times like constellations of stars.

"What is all this meant to do?" asked Mr Hyde, in a wondering tone.

"Find her," said Strange. "At least, that is what it is supposed to do."

He tapped one of the quarters. Instantly the other three patterns disappeared. The remaining pattern grew until it filled the surface

625

of the water. Strange divided it into quarters, studied it for a while and then tapped one of the quarters. He repeated this process several times. The patterns grew denser and began more and more to resemble a map. But the further Strange got, the more doubting his expression grew and the less sure he seemed of what the dish was shewing him.

After several minutes Henry could bear it no longer. "For God's sake, this is no time for magic! Arabella is lost! Strange, I beg you! Leave this nonsense and let us look for her!"

Strange said nothing in reply but he looked angry and struck the water. Instantly the lines and stars disappeared. He took a deep breath and began again. This time he proceeded in a more confident manner and quickly reached a pattern he seemed to consider relevant. But far from drawing any useful information from it, he sat instead regarding it with a mixture of dismay and perplexity.

"What is it?" asked Mr Hyde in alarm. "Mr Strange, do you see your wife?"

"I can make no sense of what the spell is telling me! It says she is not in England. Not in Wales. Not in Scotland. Not in France. I cannot get the magic right. You are right, Henry. I am wasting time here. Jeremy, fetch my boots and coat!"

A vision blossomed suddenly on the face of the water. In an ancient, shadowy hall a crowd of handsome men and lovely women were dancing. But as this could have no conceivable connexion with Arabella, Strange struck the surface of the water again. The vision vanished.

Outside, the snow lay thick upon everything. All was frozen, still and silent. The grounds of Ashfair were the first places to be searched. When these proved to contain hardly so much as a wren or a robin, Strange, Henry, Mr Hyde and the servants began to search the roads.

Three of the maidservants went back to the house where they went into attics that had scarcely been disturbed since Strange had been a boy. They took an axe and a hammer and broke open chests that had been locked fifty years before. They looked into closets and drawers, some of which could hardly have contained the body of an infant, let alone that of a grown woman.

Some of the servants ran to houses in Clun. Others took horses and rode to Clunton, Purslow, Clunbury and Whitcott. Soon there was not a house in the neighbourhood that did not know Mrs Strange was missing and not a house that did not send someone to join the search. Meanwhile the women of these houses kept up their fires and made all manner of preparations so that should Mrs Strange be brought to *that* house, she should instantly have as much warmth, nourishment, and comfort as one human being can benefit from at a time.

The first hour brought them Captain John Ayrton of the 12th Light Dragoons, who had been with Wellington and Strange in the Peninsula and at Waterloo. His lands adjoined those of Strange. They were the same age and had been neighbours all their lives, but Captain Ayrton was so shy and reserved a gentleman that they had rarely exchanged more than twenty words in the course of a year. In this crisis he arrived with maps and a quiet, solemn promise to Strange and Henry to give them all the assistance that was in his power.

It was soon discovered that Mr Hyde was not the only person to have seen Arabella. Two farm labourers, Martin Oakley and Owen Bullbridge, had also seen her. Jeremy Johns learnt this from some friends of the two men, whereupon he instantly took the first horse he could lay his hands upon and rode to the snowy fields on the banks of the Clun river where Oakley and Bullbridge had joined the general search. Jeremy half-escorted them, half-herded them back to Clun to appear before Captain Ayrton, Mr Hyde, Henry Woodhope and Strange.

They discovered that Oakley and Bullbridge's account contradicted Mr Hyde's in odd ways. Mr Hyde had seen Arabella on the bare snowy hillsides of Castle Idris. She had been walking northwards. He had seen her at precisely nine o'clock and, just as before, he had heard bells ringing.

Oakley and Bullbridge, on the other hand, had seen her hurrying through the dark winter trees some five miles east of Castle Idris, yet they too claimed to have seen her at precisely nine o'clock.

Captain Ayrton frowned and asked Oakley and Bullbridge to explain how they had known it was nine o'clock, since, unlike Mr Hyde, neither of them possessed a pocket-watch. Oakley replied that they had thought it must be nine o'clock because they had heard bells ringing. The bells, Oakley thought, belonged to St George's in Clun. But Bullbridge said that they were *not* the bells of St George's – that the bells he had heard were many, and that St George's had but one. He had said that the bells he had heard were sad bells – funeral bells, he thought – but, when asked to explain what he meant by this, he could not.

The two accounts agreed in all other details. In neither was there any nonsense about black gowns. All three men said she had been wearing a white gown and all agreed that she had been walking rather fast. None of them had seen her face.

Captain Ayrton set the men to search the dark winter woods in groups of four and five. He set women to find lanterns and warm clothing and he set riders to cover the high, open hills around Castle Idris. He put Mr Hyde – who would be satisfied with nothing else – in charge of them. Ten minutes after Oakley and Bullbridge had finished speaking, all were gone. As long as daylight lasted they searched, but daylight could not last long. They were only five days from the Winter Solstice: by three o'clock the light was fading; by four it was gone altogether.

The searchers returned to Strange's house, where Captain Ayrton intended to review what had been done so far and hoped to determine what ought to be done next. Several of the ladies of the neighbourhood were also present. They had tried waiting in their own houses for news of Mrs Strange's fate and found it a lonely, anxious business. They had come to Ashfair partly in case they were needed, but chiefly so that they might take comfort in each other's society.

The last to arrive were Strange and Jeremy Johns. They came, booted and muddy, direct from the stables. Strange was ashen-faced and hollow-eyed. He looked and moved like a man in dream. He would probably not even have sat down, had Jeremy Johns not pushed him into a chair.

Captain Ayrton laid out his maps upon the table and began to question each of the search parties about where they had been and what they had found – which was nothing at all.

Every man and woman present thought how the neatly drawn lines and words upon the maps were in truth ice-covered pools and rivers, silent woods, frozen ditches and high, bare hills and every one of them thought how many sheep and cattle and wild creatures died in this season.

"I think I woke last night . . ." said a hoarse voice, suddenly. They looked round.

Strange was still seated in the chair where Jeremy had placed him. His arms hung at his sides and he was staring at the floor. "I think I woke last night. I do not know when exactly. Arabella was sitting at the foot of the bed. She was dressed."

"You did not say this before," said Mr Hyde.

"I did not remember before. I thought I had dreamt it."

"I do not understand," said Captain Ayrton. "Do you mean to say that Mrs Strange may have left your house during the night?"

Strange seemed to cast about for an answer to this highly reasonable question, but without success.

"But surely," said Mr Hyde, "you must know if she was there or not in the morning?"

"She was there. Of course she was there. It is ridiculous to suggest . . . At least . . ." Strange paused. "That is to say I was thinking about my book when I rose and the room was dark."

Several people present began to think that as a husband

629

Jonathan Strange, if not absolutely neglectful, was at least curiously unobservant of his wife, and some of them were led to eye him doubtingly and run through in their minds the many reasons why an apparently devoted wife might suddenly run away into the snow. Cruel words? A violent temper? The dreadful sights attendant on a magician's work – ghosts, demons, horrors? The sudden discovery that he had a mistress somewhere and half a dozen natural children?

Suddenly there was a shout from outside in the hall. Afterwards no one could say whose voice it had been. Several of Strange's neighbours who were standing nearest the door went to see what the matter was. Then the exclamations of those people drew out the rest.

The hall was dark at first, but in a moment candles were brought and they could see that someone was standing at the foot of the stairs.

It was Arabella.

Henry rushed forward and embraced her; Mr Hyde and Mrs Ayrton told her how glad they were to see her safe and sound; other people began to express their amazement and to inform any one who would listen that they had not had the least idea of her being there. Several of the ladies and maids gathered around her, asking her questions. Was she hurt? Where had she been? Had she got lost? Had something happened to distress her?

Then, as sometimes will happen, several people became aware at the same time of something rather odd: Strange had said nothing, made no movement towards her – nor, for that matter, had she spoken to him or made any movement towards him.

The magician stood, staring silently at his wife. Suddenly he exclaimed, "Good God, Arabella! What have you got on?"

Even by the candles' uncertain, flickering light it was quite plain that she was wearing a black gown.

44

Arabella

December 1815

"Y OU MUST BE chilled to the bone!" declared Mrs Ayrton, taking one of Arabella's hands. "Oh, my dear! You are as cold as the grave!"

Another lady ran and fetched one of Arabella's shawls from the drawing-room. She returned carrying a blue Indian cashmere with a delicate border of gold and pink threads, but when Mrs Ayrton wrapped it around her, the black gown seemed to extinguish all its prettiness.

Arabella, with her hands folded in front of her, looked at them all with a calm, indifferent expression upon her face. She did not trouble to answer any of their kind inquiries. She seemed neither surprized nor embarrassed to find them there.

"Where in the world have you been?" demanded Strange.

"Walking," she said. Her voice was just as it had always been.

"Walking! Arabella, are you quite mad? In three feet of snow? Where?"

"In the dark woods," she said, "among my soft-sleeping brothers and sisters. Across the high moors among the sweet-scented ghosts of my brothers and sisters long dead. Under the grey sky through the dreams and murmurs of my brothers and sisters yet to come."

Strange stared at her. "What?"

With such gentle questioning as this to encourage her, it surprized no one that she said no more and at least one of the ladies began to think that it was her husband's harshness that made her so quiet and made her answer in such odd strain.

Mrs Ayrton put her arm around Arabella and gently turned her towards the stairs. "Mrs Strange is tired," she said firmly. "Come, my dear, let you and I go up to . . ."

"Oh, no!" declared Strange. "Not yet! I wish to know where that gown came from. I beg your pardon, Mrs Ayrton, but I am quite determined to . . ."

He advanced towards them, but then stopt suddenly and stared down at the floor in puzzlement. Then he carefully stepped out of the way of something. "Jeremy! Where did this water come from? Just where Mrs Strange was standing."

Jeremy Johns brought a candelabra to the foot of the stairs. There was a large pool. Then he and Strange peered at the ceiling and the walls. The other manservants became interested in the problem and so did the gentlemen.

While the men were thus distracted, Mrs Ayrton and the ladies led Arabella quietly away.

The hall at Ashfair was as old-fashioned as the rest of the house. It was panelled in cream-painted elmwood. The floor was well-swept stone flags. One of the manservants thought that the water must have seeped up from under the stones and so he went and fetched an iron rod to poke about at them to prove that one of them was loose. But he could not make them move. Nowhere was there any sign of where the water could have crept in. Someone else thought that perhaps Captain Ayrton's two dogs might have shed the water. The dogs were carefully examined. They were not in the least wet.

Finally they examined the water itself.

"It is black and there are tiny scraps of something in it," pointed out Strange.

"It looks like moss," said Jeremy Johns.

They continued to wonder and exclaim for some time until a complete lack of any success obliged them to abandon the matter. Shortly afterwards the gentlemen left, taking their wives with them.

At five o'clock Janet Hughes went up to her mistress's bed-chamber and found her lying upon the bed. She had not even troubled to take off the black dress. When Janet asked her if she felt unwell, Arabella replied that she had a pain in her hands. So Janet helped her mistress undress and then went and told Strange.

On the second day Arabella complained of a pain which went from the top of her head all down her right side to her feet (or at least that was what they supposed she meant when she said, "from my crown to the tips of my roots"). This was sufficiently alarming for Strange to send for Mr Newton, the physician at Church Stretton. Mr Newton rode over to Clun in the afternoon, but apart from the pain he could find nothing wrong and he went away cheerfully, telling Strange that he would return in a day or two.

On the third day she died.

Volume III

JOHN USKGLASS

It is the contention of Mr Norrell of Hanover-
square that everything belonging to John
Uskglass must be shaken out of modern magic,
as one would shake moths and dust out of an
old coat. What does he imagine he will have
left? If you get rid of John Uskglass you will
be left holding the empty air.

Jonathan Strange, Prologue to *The History and
Practice of English Magic*, pub. John Murray,
London, 1816

45

Prologue to
The History and Practice of English Magic

by Jonathan Strange

I N THE LAST months of 1110 a strange army appeared in Northern England. It was first heard of near a place called Penlaw some twenty or thirty miles north-west of Newcastle. No one could say where it had come from – it was generally supposed to be an invasion of Scots or Danes or perhaps even of French.

By early December the army had taken Newcastle and Durham and was riding west. It came to Allendale, a small stone settlement that stands high among the hills of Northumbria, and camped one night on the edge of a moor outside the town. The people of Allendale were sheep-farmers, not soldiers. The town had no walls to protect it and the nearest soldiers were thirty-five miles away, preparing to defend the castle of Carlisle. Consequently, the townspeople thought it best to lose no time in making friends with the strange army. With this aim in mind several pretty young women set off, a company of brave Judiths determined to save themselves and their neighbours if they could. But when they arrived at the place where the army had their camp the women became fearful and hung back.

The camp was a dreary, silent place. A thick snow was falling and the strange soldiers lay, wrapped in their black cloaks, upon the snowy ground. At first the young women thought the soldiers must be dead – an impression which was strengthened by the great multitude of ravens and other black birds which had settled over the camp, and indeed upon the prostrate forms of the soldiers themselves – yet the soldiers were not dead; from time to time one would stir himself and go attend to his horse, or brush a bird away if it tried to peck at his face.

At the approach of the young women a soldier got to his feet. One of the women shook off her fears and went up to him and kissed him on the mouth.

His skin was very pale (it shone like moonlight) and entirely without blemish. His hair was long and straight like a fall of dark brown water. The bones of his face were unnaturally fine and strong. The expression of the face was solemn. His blue eyes were long and slanting and his brows were as fine and dark as pen-strokes with a curious flourish at the end. None of this worried the girl in the least. For all she knew every Dane, Scot and Frenchman ever born is eerily beautiful.

He took well enough to the kiss and allowed her to kiss him again. Then he paid her back in kind. Another soldier rose from the ground and opened his mouth. Out of it came a sad, wailing sort of music. The first soldier – the one the girl had kissed – began to coax her to dance with him, pushing her this way and that with his long white fingers until she was dancing in a fashion to suit him.

This went on for some time until she became heated with the dance and paused for a moment to take off her cloak. Then her companions saw that drops of blood, like beads of sweat, were forming on her arms, face and legs, and falling on to the snow. This sight terrified them and so they ran away.

The strange army never entered Allendale. It rode on in the night towards Carlisle. The next day the townspeople went cautiously up to the fields where the army had camped. There they found the girl, her body entirely white and drained of blood while the snow around her was stained bright red.

By these signs they recognized the *Daoine Sidhe* – the Fairy Host.

Battles were fought and the English lost every one. By Christmas the Fairy Host was at York. They held Newcastle, Durham, Carlisle and Lancaster. Aside from the exsanguination of the maid of Allendale the fairies displayed very little of the cruelty for which their race is famed. Of all the towns and fortifications which they took, only Lancaster was burnt to the ground. At Thirsk, north of York, a pig offended a member of the Host by running out under the feet of his horse and causing it to rear up and fall and break its back. The fairy and his companions hunted the pig and when they had caught it they put its eyes out. Generally, however, the arrival of the Host at any new place was a cause of great rejoicing among animals both wild and domesticated as if they recognized in the fairies an ally against their common foe, Man.

At Christmas, King Henry summoned his earls, bishops, abbots and the great men of his realm to his house in Westminster to discuss the matter. Fairies were not unknown in England in those days. There were long-established fairy settlements in many places, some hidden by magic, some merely avoided by their Christian neighbours. King Henry's counsellors agreed that fairies were naturally wicked. They were lascivious, mendacious and thieving; they seduced young men and women, confused travellers, and stole children, cattle and corn. They were astonishingly indolent: they had mastered the arts of masonry, carpentry and carving thousands of years ago but, rather than take the trouble to build themselves houses, most still preferred to live in places which they were pleased to call castles but which were in fact *brugh* – earth barrows of great antiquity. They spent their days drinking and dancing while their barley and beans rotted in the fields, and their beasts shivered and died on the cold hillside. Indeed, all King Henry's advisers agreed that, had it not been for their extraordinary magic and near immortality, the entire fairy race would have long since perished from hunger and thirst. Yet this feckless, improvident people had invaded a well-defended Christian kingdom, won every battle they had fought and had ridden from place to place securing each stronghold as they came to it. All this spoke of a measure of purposefulness which no fairy had ever been known to possess.

No one knew what to make of it.

In January the Fairy Host left York and rode south. At the Trent they halted. So it was at Newark on the banks of the Trent that King Henry and his army met the *Daoine Sidhe* in battle.

Before the battle a magic wind blew through the ranks of King Henry's army and a sweet sound of pipe music was heard, which caused a great number of the horses to break free and flee to the fairy side, many taking their unlucky riders with them. Next, every man heard the voices of his loved ones – mothers, fathers, children, lovers – call out to him to come home. A host of ravens descended from the sky, pecking at the faces of the English and blinding them with a chaos of black wings. The English soldiers not only had the skill and ferocity of the *Sidhe* to contend with, but also their own fear in the face of such eerie magic. It is scarcely to be wondered at that the battle was short and that King Henry lost. At the moment when all fell silent and it became clear beyond any doubt that King Henry had been defeated the birds for miles around began singing as if for joy.

The King and his counsellors waited for some chieftain or king to step forward. The ranks of the *Daoine Sidhe* parted and someone appeared.

He was rather less than fifteen years old. Like the *Daoine Sidhe* he was dressed in ragged clothes of coarse black wool. Like them his dark hair was long and straight. Like them, he spoke neither English nor French – the two languages current in England at that time – but only a dialect of Faerie.[1] He was pale and handsome

---

[1] No one in England nowadays knows this language and all we have left of it is a handful of borrowed words describing various obscure magical techniques. Martin Pale wrote in *De Tractatu Magicarum Linguarum* that it was related to the ancient Celtic languages.

and solemn-faced, yet it was clear to everyone present that he was human, not fairy.

By the standards of the Norman and English earls and knights, who saw him that day for the first time, he was scarcely civilized. He had never seen a spoon before, nor a chair, nor an iron kettle, nor a silver penny, nor a wax candle. No fairy clan or kingdom of the period possessed any such fine things. When King Henry and the boy met to divide England between them, Henry sat upon a wooden bench and drank wine from a silver goblet, the boy sat upon the floor and drank ewe's milk from a stone cup. The chronicler, Orderic Vitalis, writing some thirty years later, describes the shock felt by King Henry's court when they saw, in the midst of all these important proceedings, a *Daoine Sidhe* warrior lean across and begin solicitously plucking lice out of the boy's filthy hair.

There was among the Fairy Host a young Norman knight called Thomas of Dundale.[2] Though he had been a captive in Faerie for many years he remembered enough of his own language (French) to make the boy and King Henry understand each other.

King Henry asked the boy his name.

The boy replied that he had none.[3]

King Henry asked him why he made war on England.

The boy said that he was the only surviving member of an aristocratic Norman family who had been granted lands in the north of England by King Henry's father, William the Conqueror.

---

[2] Variously Thomas de Dundelle or Thomas de Donvil. It seems that several of Henry's noblemen recognized Thomas as the younger son of a powerful Norman magnate who had disappeared one Christmas fourteen years before. Given the circumstances of his return it is doubtful whether they felt particularly pleased to have him back.

[3] When he was a child in Faerie the *Sidhe* had called him a word in their own language which, we are told, meant "Starling", but he had already abandoned that name by the time he entered England. Later he took to calling himself by his father's name – John d'Uskglass – but in the early part of his reign he was known simply by one of the many titles his friends or enemies gave him: the King; the Raven King; the Black King; the King in the North.

The men of the family had been deprived of their lands and their lives by a wicked enemy named Hubert de Cotentin. The boy said that some years before his father had appealed to William II (King Henry's brother and predecessor) for justice, but had received none. Shortly afterwards his father had been murdered. The boy said that he himself had been taken by Hubert's men while still a baby and abandoned in the forest. But the *Daoine Sidhe* had found him and taken him to live with them in Faerie. Now he had returned.

He had a very young man's belief in the absolute rightness of his own cause and the absolute wrongness of everyone else's. He had settled it in his own mind that the stretch of England which lay between the Tweed and the Trent was a just recompense for the failure of the Norman kings to avenge the murders of his family. For this reason and no other King Henry was suffered to retain the southern half of his kingdom.

The boy said that he was already a king in Faerie. He named the fairy king who was his overlord. No one understood.[4]

That day he began his unbroken reign of more than three hundred years.

At the age of fourteen he had already created the system of magic that we employ today. Or rather that we would employ if we could; most of what he knew we have forgotten. His was a perfect blending of fairy magic and human organization – their powers were wedded to his own terrifying purposefulness. There is no reason that we know of to explain why one stolen Christian child should suddenly emerge the greatest magician of any age. Other children, both before and since, have been held captive in the borderlands of Faerie, but none other ever profited from the experience in the way he did. By comparison with his achievements all our efforts seem trivial, insignificant.

It is the contention of Mr Norrell of Hanover-square that

---

[4] The name of this *Daoine Sidhe* King was particularly long and difficult. Traditionally he has always been known as Oberon.

everything belonging to John Uskglass must be shaken out of modern magic, as one would shake moths and dust out of an old coat. What does he imagine he will have left? If you get rid of John Uskglass you will be left holding the empty air.

From *The History and Practice of English Magic*, volume I, by Jonathan Strange, published by John Murray, 1816

46

"The sky spoke to me . . ."

January 1816

I T WAS A dark day. A chill wind blew snowflakes against the windows of Mr Norrell's library where Childermass sat writing business letters. Though it was only ten o'clock in the morning the candles were already lit. The only sounds were the coals being consumed in the grate and the scratch of Childermass's pen against the paper.

Hanover-square
To Lord Sidmouth, the Home Secretary   Jan. 8th, 1816.

My lord,
Mr Norrell desires me to inform you that the spells to prevent flooding of the rivers in the County of Suffolk are now complete. The bill will be sent to Mr Wynne at the Treasury today . . .

Somewhere a bell was tolling, a mournful sound. It was very far away. Childermass barely noticed it and yet, under the influence of the bell, the room around him grew darker and lonelier.

. . . The magic will keep the waters within the confines of the rivers' customary courses. However Mr Leeves, the young engineer employed by the Lord Lieutenant of Suffolk to assess

the strength of the present bridges and other structures adjacent
to the rivers, has expressed some doubts . . .

*The image of a dreary landscape was before him. He saw it very vividly as if
it were somewhere he knew well or a painting that he had seen every day for
years and years. A wide landscape of brown, empty fields and ruined
buildings beneath a bleak, grey sky . . .*

. . . whether the bridges over the Stour and the Orwell are
capable of withstanding the more violent flow of water which
will certainly ensue at times of heavy rains. Mr Leeves recom-
mends an immediate and thorough examination of the bridges,
mills and fords in Suffolk, beginning with the Stour and Orwell.
I am told that he has already written to your lordship about this
matter . . .

*He was no longer merely thinking of the landscape. It seemed to him that he
was actually there. He was standing in an old road, rutted and ancient, that
wound up a black hill towards the sky where a great flock of black birds was
gathering . . .*

. . . Mr Norrell has declined to put a period to the magic. It is
his private opinion that it will last as long as the rivers
themselves, however he begs leave to recommend to your
lordship that the spells be re-examined in twenty years. On
Tuesday next Mr Norrell will begin to put in place the same
magic for the County of Norfolk . . .

*The birds were like black letters against the grey of the sky. He thought that
in a moment he would understand what the writing meant. The stones in the
ancient road were symbols foretelling the traveller's journey.*

Childermass came to himself with a start. The pen jerked from his
hand and the ink splattered over the letter.

He looked around in confusion. He did not appear to be dreaming. All the old, familiar objects were there: the shelves of books, the mirror, the ink pot, the fire-irons, the porcelain figure of Martin Pale. But his confidence in his own senses was shaken. He no longer trusted that the books, the mirrors, the porcelain figure were really there. It was as if everything he could see was simply a skin that he could tear with one fingernail and find the cold, desolate landscape behind it.

The brown fields were partly flooded; they were strung with chains of chill, grey pools. The pattern of the pools had meaning. The pools had been written on to the fields by the rain. The pools were a magic worked by the rain, just as the tumbling of the black birds against the grey was a spell that the sky was working and the motion of grey-brown grasses was a spell that the wind made. Everything had meaning.

Childermass leapt up away from the desk and shook himself. He took a hurried turn around the room and rang the bell for the servant. But even as he waited the magic began to reassert itself. By the time Lucas appeared he was no longer certain if he were in Mr Norrell's library or standing upon an ancient road . . .

He shook his head violently and blinked several times. "Where is my master?" he said, "Something is wrong."

Lucas gazed at him in some concern. "Mr Childermass? Are you ill, sir?"

"Never mind that. Where is Mr Norrell?"

"He is at the Admiralty, sir. I thought you knew. The carriage came for him over an hour ago. I dare say he will be back shortly."

"No," said Childermass, "that cannot be. He cannot have gone. Are you sure that he is not upstairs doing magic?"

"Quite sure, sir. I saw the carriage leave with the master inside it. Let me send Matthew for a physician, Mr Childermass. You look very ill."

Childermass opened his mouth to protest that he was not ill at all, but just at that moment . . .

. . . the sky looked at him. He felt the earth shrug because it felt him upon its back.

The sky spoke to him.

It was a language he had never heard before. He was not even certain there were words. Perhaps it only spoke to him in the black writing the birds made. He was small and unprotected and there was no escape. He was caught between earth and sky as if cupped between two hands. They could crush him if they chose.

The sky spoke to him again.

"I do not understand," he said.

He blinked and found that Lucas was bending over him. His breath was coming in gasps. He put out his hand and his hand brushed something at his side. He turned to look at it and was puzzled to discover that it was a chair-leg. He was lying on the floor. "What . . . ?" he asked.

"You are in the library, sir," said Lucas. "I think you fainted."

"Help me up. I need to talk to Norrell."

"But I told you already, sir . . ."

"No," said Childermass. "You are wrong. He must be here. He must be. Take me upstairs."

Lucas helped him up and out of the room, but when they reached the stairs he very nearly collapsed again. So Lucas called for Matthew, the other footman, and together they half-supported, half-carried Childermass to the little study upon the second floor where Mr Norrell performed his most private magic.

Lucas opened the door. Inside, a fire was burning in the grate. Pens, pen-knives, pen-holders and pencils were placed neatly in a little tray. The inkwell was filled and the silver cap placed on it. Books and notebooks stood stacked neatly or tidied away. Everything was dusted and polished and in perfect order. Clearly Mr Norrell had not been there that morning.

Childermass pushed the footmen away from him. He stood and gazed at the room in some perplexity.

"You see, sir?" said Lucas. "It is just as I told you. The master is at the Admiralty."

"Yes," said Childermass.

But it made no sense to him. If the eerie magic was not Norrell's, then whose could it be? "Has Strange been here?" he asked.

"No, indeed!" Lucas was indignant. "I hope I know my duties better than to let Mr Strange in the house. You still look queer, sir. Let me send for a physician."

"No, no. I am better. I am a great deal better. Here, help me to a chair." Childermass collapsed into a chair with a sigh. "What in God's name are you both staring at?" He waved them both away. "Matthew, have you no work to do? Lucas, fetch me a glass of water!"

He was still dazed and dizzy, but the sick feeling in his stomach had lessened. He could picture the landscape in every detail. The image of it was fixed in his head. He could taste its desolation, its otherworldliness, but he no longer felt in danger of losing himself in it. He could think.

Lucas returned with a tray with a wine-glass and a decanter full of water. He poured a glass of water and Childermass drank it off.

There was a spell Childermass knew. It was a spell to detect magic. It could not tell you what the magic was or who was performing it; it simply told you whether there was any magic occurring or not. At least that was what it was supposed to do. Childermass had only ever tried it once and there had been nothing. He had no way of knowing whether or not it worked.

"Fill the glass again," he told Lucas.

Lucas did so.

This time Childermass did not drink from the glass. Instead he muttered some words at it. Then he held it up to the light and peered through it, turning slowly until he had surveyed every part of the room through the glass.

There was nothing.

"I am not even sure what I am looking for," he murmured. To Lucas he said, "Come. I need your help."

They returned to the library. Childermass held up the glass again and said the words and looked through it.

Nothing.

He approached the window. For a moment he thought he saw something at the bottom of the glass like a pearl of white light.

"It is in the square," he said.

"What is in the square?" asked Lucas.

Childermass did not answer. Instead, he looked out of the window. Snow covered the muddy cobbles of Hanover-square. The black railings that surrounded the enclosure in the centre shewed sharply against the whiteness. Snow was still falling and there was a sharp wind. Despite this there were several people in the square. It was well known that Mr Norrell lived in Hanover-square and people came here, hoping to catch a glimpse of him. Just now a gentleman and two young ladies (all, doubtless, fanatics for magic) were standing in front of the house, gazing at it in some excitement. A little further off a dark young man was lounging against the railings. Near him was an ink-seller with a ragged coat and a little barrel of ink upon his back. On the right there was another lady. She had turned away from the house and was walking slowly in the direction of Hanover-street, but Childermass had the notion that she had been among the onlookers only a moment before. She was fashionably and expensively dressed in a dark green pelisse trimmed with ermine, and she carried a large ermine muff.

Childermass knew the ink-seller well – he had often bought ink from him. The others were, he thought, all strangers. "Do you recognize anyone?" he asked.

"That dark-haired fellow." Lucas pointed to the young man

leaning against the railings. "That is Frederick Marston. He has been here several times to ask Mr Norrell to take him as a pupil, but Mr Norrell has always refused to see him."

"Yes. I think you told me about him." Childermass studied the people in the square a moment longer and then he said, "Unlikely as it seems, one of them must be performing some sort of magic. I need to go down and see. Come. I cannot do this without you."

In the square the magic was stronger than ever. The sad bell tolled inside Childermass's head. Behind the curtain of snow the two worlds flickered back and forth, like images in a magic lantern – one moment Hanover-square, one moment dreary fields and a black writing upon the sky.

Childermass held up the wine-glass in preparation to saying the words of the spell, but there was no need. It blazed with a soft white light. It was the brightest thing in the whole of that dark winter's day, its light clearer and purer than any lamp could be and it threw curious shadows upon the faces of Childermass and Lucas.

The sky spoke to him again. This time he thought it was a question. Great consequences hung upon his answer. If he could just understand what was being asked and find the correct words in which to frame his reply, then something would be revealed – something that would change English magic for ever, something that Strange and Norrell had not even guessed at yet.

For a long moment he struggled to understand. The language or spell seemed tantalizingly familiar now. In a moment, he thought, he would grasp it. After all, the world had been speaking these words to him every day of his life – it was just that he had not noticed it before . . .

Lucas was saying something. Childermass must have begun to fall again because he now found that Lucas was grasping him under the arms and dragging him upright. The wine-glass lay shattered upon the cobbles and the white light was split across the snow.

". . . the queerest thing," said Lucas. "That's it, Mr Childermass. Up you come. I have never known you taken like this. Are you sure, sir, that you don't want to go inside? But, here is Mr Norrell. He will know what to do.''

Childermass looked to the right. Mr Norrell's carriage was turning into the square from George-street.

The ink-seller saw it too. Immediately he approached the gentleman and two young ladies. He made them a respectful bow and spoke to the gentleman. All three turned their heads and looked at the carriage. The gentleman reached into a pocket and gave the ink-seller a coin. The ink-seller bowed again and withdrew.

Mr Marston, the dark young man, did not need any one to tell him that this was Mr Norrell's carriage. As soon as he observed its approach, he stood away from the railings and moved forward.

Even the fashionably dressed lady had turned and was walking back towards the house, apparently with the intention of looking at England's Foremost Magician.

The carriage stopped in front of the house. The footman descended from the box and opened the door. Mr Norrell stepped out. He was so wrapped up in mufflers that his shrunken little form appeared almost stout. Immediately Mr Marston hailed him and began to say something to him. Mr Norrell shook his head impatiently and waved Mr Marston away.

The fashionably dressed lady passed Childermass and Lucas. She was very pale and solemn-looking. It occurred to Childermass that she would probably have been considered handsome by the people who cared about such things. Now that he looked at her properly he began to think that he knew her. "Lucas," he murmured, "who is that woman?"

"I am sorry, sir. I don't think I ever saw her before."

At the foot of the carriage steps Mr Marston was growing more insistent and Mr Norrell was growing angrier. Mr Norrell looked around; he saw Lucas and Childermass close at hand and beckoned to them.

Just then the fashionably dressed lady took a step towards him. For a moment it seemed that she too was going to address him, but that was not her intention. She took a pistol from her muff and, with all the calm in the world, aimed it at his heart.

Mr Norrell and Mr Marston both stared at her.

Several things happened at once. Lucas loosed his hold of Childermass – who dropt like a stone to the ground – and ran to help his master. Mr Marston seized hold of the lady around her waist. Davey, Mr Norrell's coachman, jumped down from his box and grabbed the arm which held the pistol.

Childermass lay amid the snow and shards of glass. He saw the woman shrug herself free of Mr Marston's grasp with what seemed like remarkable ease. She pushed him to the ground with such force that he did not get up again. She put one small, gloved hand to Davey's chest and Davey was flung several yards backwards. Mr Norrell's footman – the one who had opened the carriage door – tried to knock her down, but his blow had not the least effect upon her. She put her hand upon his face – it looked like the lightest touch in the world – he crumpled to the ground. Lucas she simply struck with the pistol.

Childermass could make very little sense of what was happening. He dragged himself upright and stumbled forward for half a dozen yards, scarcely knowing whether he was walking upon the cobblestones of Hanover-square or an ancient road in Faerie.

Mr Norrell stared at the lady in the utmost horror, too frightened to cry out or run away. Childermass put up his hands to her in a gesture of conciliation. "Madam . . ." he began.

She did not even look at him.

The dizzying fall of white flakes confused him. Try as he might, he could not keep his hold upon Hanover-square. The eerie landscape was claiming him; Mr Norrell would be killed and there was nothing he could do to prevent it.

Then something strange happened.

Something strange happened. Hanover-square disappeared. Mr Norrell,
Lucas and all the rest of them disappeared.

But the lady remained.

She stood facing him, upon the ancient road, beneath the sky with its
tumble and seethe of black birds. She raised her pistol and aimed it out of
Faerie and into England at Mr Norrell's heart.

"Madam," said Childermass again.

She looked at him with a cold, burning fury. There was nothing in the
world he could say to deter her. Nothing in this world nor any other. And so he
did the only thing he could think of. He seized hold of the barrel of the pistol.

There was a shot, an intolerably loud sound.

It was the force of the noise, Childermass supposed, which pushed
him back into England.

Suddenly he was half-sitting, half-lying in Hanover-square with
his back to the carriage-steps. He wondered where Norrell was and
whether he was dead. He supposed he ought to go and find out,
but he found he did not much care about it and so he stayed where
he was.

It was not until a surgeon arrived that he understood that the
lady had indeed shot someone and that the someone was himself.

The rest of that day and most of the following one passed in a
confusion of pain and laudanum-dreams. Sometimes Childermass
thought he was standing on the ancient road under the speaking
sky, but now Lucas was with him talking of maids-of-honour and
coal-scuttles. A tight-rope was strung across the sky and a great
many people were walking on it. Strange was there and so was
Norrell. They both had piles of books in their hands. There was
John Murray, the publisher, and Vinculus and many others.
Sometimes the pain in Childermass's shoulder escaped from
him and ran about the room and hid. When this happened he
thought it became a small animal. No one else knew it was there.
He supposed he ought to tell them so that they could chase it out.

Once he caught sight of it; it had flame-coloured fur, brighter than a fox . . .

On the evening of the second day he was lying in bed with a much clearer notion of who he was, and where he was, and what had happened. At about seven o'clock Lucas entered the room, carrying one of the dining-chairs. He placed it by the bed. A moment later Mr Norrell entered the room and sat upon it.

For some moments Mr Norrell did nothing but stare at the counterpane with an anxious expression. Then he muttered a question.

Childermass did not hear what was said, but he naturally supposed that Mr Norrell must be inquiring about his health, so he began to say that he hoped he would be better in a day or two.

Mr Norrell interrupted him and said again more sharply, "Why were you performing Belasis's Scopus?"

"What?" asked Childermass.

"Lucas said that you were doing magic," said Mr Norrell. "I made him describe it to me. Naturally I recognized Belasis's Scopus."[1] His face grew sharp and suspicious. "Why were you performing it? And – which is even more to the point – where in the world did you learn such a thing? How can I do my work when I am constantly betrayed in this manner? It is astonishing to me that I have achieved any thing at all, when I am surrounded by servants who learn spells behind my back and pupils who set themselves to undo my every accomplishment!"

Childermass gave him a look of mild exasperation. "You taught it to me yourself."

"I?" cried Mr Norrell, his voice several pitches higher than usual.

"It was before you came to London, in the days when you kept

---

[1] The spell to detect magic appears in *The Instructions* by Jacques Belasis.

to your library at Hurtfew, when I used to go about the country for you buying up valuable books. You taught me the spell in case I should ever meet with any one who claimed to be a practical magician. You were afraid that there might be another magician who could . . ."

"Yes, yes," said Mr Norrell, impatiently. "I remember now. But that does not explain why you were performing it in the square yesterday morning."

"Because there was magic everywhere."

"Lucas did not notice any thing."

"It is not part of Lucas's duties to know when there is magic going on. That falls to me. It was the strangest thing I ever knew. I kept thinking that I was somewhere else entirely. I believe that for a while I was in real danger. I do not understand very well where the place was. It had some curious features – which I will describe to you in a moment – but it was certainly not England. I think it was Faerie. What sort of magic produces such an effect? And where was it coming from? Can it be that that woman was a magician?"

"Which woman?"

"The woman who shot me."

Mr Norrell made a small sound of irritation. "That bullet affected you more than I supposed," he said contemptuously. "If she had been a great magician, do you really suppose that you could have thwarted her so easily? There was no magician in the square. Certainly not that woman."

"Why? Who was she?"

Mr Norrell was silent a moment. Then he said, "Sir Walter Pole's wife. The woman I brought back from the dead."

Childermass was silent a moment. "Well, you astonish me!" he said at last. "I can think of several people who have good cause to aim a pistol at your heart, but for the life of me I cannot understand why this woman should be one of them."

"They tell me she is mad," said Mr Norrell. "She escaped the people who were set to watch her and came here to kill me – which, as I think you will agree, is proof enough of her madness." Mr Norrell's small grey eyes looked away. "After all I am known everywhere as her benefactor."

Childermass was barely listening to him. "But where did she get the pistol? Sir Walter is a sensible man. It is hard to imagine that he leaves firearms in her way."

"It was a duelling pistol – one of a pair that belongs to Sir Walter. It is kept in a locked box in a locked writing-desk in his private study. Sir Walter says that until yesterday he would have taken an oath that she knew nothing about it. As to how she contrived to get the key – both keys – that is a mystery to every one."

"It does not seem much of a mystery to me. Wives, even mad wives, have ways of getting what they want from husbands."

"But Sir Walter did not have the keys. That is the strange part of it. These pistols were the only firearms in the house and Sir Walter had some natural concerns for the security of his wife and possessions since he is so frequently away from home. The keys were in the keeping of the butler – that tall black man – I dare say you know who I mean. Sir Walter cannot understand how he came to make such a mistake. Sir Walter says he is generally the most reliable and trustworthy fellow in the world. Of course one never really knows what servants are thinking," continued Mr Norrell blithely, forgetting that he was speaking to one at that moment, "yet it can hardly be supposed that this man bears any grudge against me. I never spoke three words to him in my life. Of course," he continued, "I could prosecute Lady Pole for trying to kill me. Yesterday I was quite determined upon it. But it has been represented to me by several people that I must consider Sir Walter. Lord Liverpool and Mr Lascelles both say so, and I believe that they are right. Sir Walter has been a good friend to English magic. I should not wish to give Sir Walter any reason to regret that he has been my friend. Sir Walter has given me his solemn oath that she will be put away somewhere in the country where she will see no one and no one will see her."

Mr Norrell did not trouble to ascertain Childermass's wishes upon this point. Despite the fact that it was Childermass who was lying upon the bed sick with pain and loss of blood, and that Mr Norrell's injuries had consisted chiefly of a slight headach and a small cut upon one finger, it was clear to Mr Norrell that he was the more sinned against of the two.

"So what was the magic?" asked Childermass.

"Mine, of course!" declared Mr Norrell, angrily. "Who else's should it be? It was the magic I did to bring her back from the dead. That was what you felt and that is what Belasis's Scopus revealed. It was early in my career and I dare say there were some irregularities that may have caused it to take an odd turn and . . ."

"An odd turn?" cried Childermass, hoarsely. He was seized with a fit of coughing. When he had regained his breath, he said, "At every moment I was in danger of being transported to some realm where everything breathed magic. The sky spoke to me! Everything spoke to me! How could that have been?"

Mr Norrell raised an eyebrow. "I do not know. Perhaps you were drunk."

"And have you ever known me to be drunk in the performance of my duties?" asked Childermass, icily.

Mr Norrell shrugged defensively. "I have not the least idea what you do. It seems to me that you have been a law unto yourself from the first moment you entered my house."

"But surely the idea is not so strange when considered in the light of ancient English magic," insisted Childermass. "Have you not told me that *Aureates* regarded trees, hills, rivers and so on as living creatures with thoughts, memories and desires of their own? The *Aureates* thought that the whole world habitually worked magic of a sort."

"Some of the *Aureates* thought so, yes. It is a belief that they imbibed from their fairy-servants, who attributed some of their own extraordinary magic to their ability to talk to trees and rivers and so forth, and to form friendships and alliances with them. But there is no reason to suppose that they were right. My own magic does not rely upon any such nonsensical ideas."

"The sky spoke to me," said Childermass. "If what I saw was true, then . . ." He paused.

"Then what?" asked Mr Norrell.

In his weakened state Childermass had been thinking aloud. He had meant to say that if what he had seen was true, then everything that Strange and Norrell had ever done was child's-play and magic was a much stranger and more terrifying thing than any of them had thought of. Strange and Norrell had been merely throwing paper darts about a parlour, while real magic soared and swooped and twisted on great wings in a limitless sky far, far above them.

But then he realized that Mr Norrell was unlikely to take a very sanguine view of such ideas and so he said nothing.

Curiously, Mr Norrell seemed to guess his thoughts anyway.

"Oh!" he cried in a sudden passion. "Very well! You are there, are you? Then I advise you to go and join Strange and Murray and all the other traitors immediately! I believe you will find that their ideas suit your present frame of mind much better! I am sure that they will be very glad to have you. And you will be able to tell them all my secrets! I dare say they will pay you handsomely for it. I shall be ruined and . . ."

"Mr Norrell, calm yourself. I have no intention of taking up any new employment. You are the last master I shall ever have."

There was another short silence which perhaps allowed Mr Norrell time to reflect upon the inappropriateness of quarrelling with the man who had saved his life only yesterday. In a more reasonable tone he said, "I dare say no one has told you yet. Strange's wife is dead."

"What?"

"Dead. I had the news from Sir Walter. Apparently she went for a walk in the snow. Most ill-advised. Two days later she was dead."

Childermass felt cold. The dreary landscape was suddenly very close, just beneath the skin of England. He could almost fancy himself upon the ancient road again . . .

. . . and Arabella Strange was on the road ahead of him. Her back was turned towards him and she walked on alone into the chill, grey lands, under the magic-speaking sky . . .

"I am told," continued Mr Norrell, quite oblivious to Childermass's sudden pallor and laboured breathing, "that Lady Pole has been made very unhappy by the death of Mrs Strange. Her distress has been out of all reason. It seems they were friends. I did not know that until now. Had I had known it, I might perhaps have . . ." He paused and his face worked with some secret emotion. "But it cannot matter now – one of them is mad and the other one is dead. From all that Sir Walter can tell Lady Pole seems to consider me in some way culpable for Mrs Strange's death." He paused. Then, in case there should be any doubt about the matter, he added, "Which is nonsense, of course."

Just then the two eminent physicians whom Mr Norrell had employed to attend Childermass entered the room. They were surprized to see Mr Norrell in the room – surprized and delighted. Their smiling countenances and bowing, bobbing forms said what a very pleasing instance of the great man's condescension they thought it that he should pay this visit to his servant. They told him that they had rarely seen a household where the master was so careful of the health of his inferiors or where the servants were so attached to their master by ties, less of duty, than of respect and fond regard.

Mr Norrell was at least as susceptible to flattery as most men and he began to think that perhaps he was indeed doing something unusually virtuous. He extended his hand with the intention of patting Childermass's hand in a friendly and condescending manner. However, upon meeting Childermass's cold stare, he thought better of it, coughed and left the room.

Childermass watched him go.

All magicians lie and this one more than most, Vinculus had said.

"A black lad and a blue fella –
that ought to mean summat."

Late January 1816

S IR WALTER POLE'S carriage was travelling along a lonely
road in Yorkshire. Stephen Black rode on a white horse at
its side.

On either hand empty moors the colour of a bruise stretched up
to a dark sky that threatened snow. Grey, misshapen rocks were
strewn about, making the landscape appear still more bleak and
uncouth. Occasionally a low ray of sunlight would pierce the
clouds, illuminating for a moment a white, foaming stream, or
striking a pot-hole full of water that would suddenly become as
dazzling as a fallen silver penny.

They came to a crossroads. The coachman halted the horses and
stared gloomily at the place where, in his opinion, the fingerpost
ought to have been.

"There are no milestones," said Stephen, "nothing to say where
any of these roads might lead to."

"Always supposing they go anywhere at all," said the coachman, "which I am beginning to doubt." He took a snuff-box from
his pocket and inhaled a large pinch of it.

The footman who sat on the box beside the coachman (and who
was by far the coldest and most miserable of the three) comprehensively cursed Yorkshire, all Yorkshiremen and all Yorkshire roads.

"We ought to be travelling north or north-east, I think," said Stephen. "But I have got a little turned around on this moor. Do you have any idea which way is north?"

The coachman, to whom this question was addressed, said that all the directions looked pretty northern to him.

The footman gave a short, uncheerful laugh.

Finding that his companions were of no help, Stephen did what he always did under such circumstances; he took the whole charge of the journey upon himself. He instructed the coachman to take one road, while he took another. "If I have success, I will come and find you, or send a messenger. If you have success, deliver your charge and do not worry about me."

Stephen rode along, looking doubtfully at all the lanes and tracks he came to. Once he met with another lone rider and asked for directions, but the man proved to be a stranger to the moor like himself and had never heard of the place Stephen mentioned.

He came at last to a narrow lane that wound between two walls, built – as is the custom in that part of England – of dry stones without any mortar. He turned down the lane. On either hand a row of bare winter trees followed the line of the walls. As the first flakes of snow floated down he crossed a narrow packhorse bridge and entered a village of dour stone cottages and tumbledown walls. It was very quiet. There was scarcely more than a handful of buildings and he quickly found the one he sought. It was a long, low hall with a paved courtyard in front of it. He surveyed the low roofs, the old-fashioned casements and the moss-covered stones with an air of the deepest dissatisfaction. "Halloo!" he called. "Is there any one there?"

The snow began to fall thicker and faster. From somewhere at the side of the house two manservants came running. They were neatly and cleanly dressed, but their nervous expressions and clumsy air made Stephen wince, and wish that he had had the training of them.

For their part they stared to see a black man upon a milk-white mare in their yard. The braver of the two bobbed a sort of half-bow.

"Is this Starecross Hall?" asked Stephen.

"Yes, sir," said the courageous servant.

"I am here on business for Sir Walter Pole. Go and fetch your master."

The man ran off. A moment later the front door opened and a thin, dark person appeared.

"You are the madhouse-keeper?" inquired Stephen. "You are John Segundus?"

"Yes, indeed!" cried Mr Segundus. "Welcome! Welcome!"

Stephen dismounted and threw the reins to the servant. "This place is the very devil to find! We have been driving about this infernal moor for an hour. Can you send a man to bring her ladyship's carriage here? They took the road to the left of this one at the crossroads two miles back."

"Of course. At once," Mr Segundus assured him. "I am sorry you have had difficulties. The house is, as you see, extremely secluded, but that is one of the reasons that it suits Sir Walter. His lady is well, I hope?"

"Her ladyship is very much fatigued by the journey."

"Everything is ready for her reception. At least . . ." Mr Segundus led the way inside. "I am aware that it must be very different from what she is accustomed to . . ."

At the end of a short stone passage they came to a room which was a pleasant contrast with the bleak and sombre surroundings. It spoke nothing but comfort and welcome. It had been fitted up with paintings and pretty furniture, with soft carpets and cheerfully glowing lamps. There were footstools for her ladyship's feet if she felt weary, screens to protect her from a draught if she felt cold, and books to amuse her, should she wish to read.

"Is it not suitable?" asked Mr Segundus, anxiously. "I see by your face that it is not."

Stephen opened his mouth to tell Mr Segundus that what he

saw was quite different. He saw what her ladyship would see when she entered the room. Chairs, paintings and lamps were all quite ghostly. Behind them lay the far more substantial and solid forms of Lost-hope's bleak, grey halls and staircases.

But it was no use trying to explain any of this. The words would have changed as he spoke them; they would have turned into some nonsense about beer brewed from anger and longings for revenge; or girls whose tears turned to opals and pearls when the moon waxed and whose footprints filled with blood when the moon waned. So he contented himself with saying, "No, no. It is perfectly satisfactory. Her ladyship requires nothing more."

To many people this might have seemed a little cool – especially if they had worked as hard as Mr Segundus – but Mr Segundus made no objection. "So this is the lady whom Mr Norrell brought back from the dead?" he said.

"Yes," said Stephen.

"The single act upon which the whole restoration of English magic is founded!"

"Yes," said Stephen.

"And yet she tried to kill him! It is a very strange business altogether! Very strange!"

Stephen said nothing. These were not, in his opinion, fit subjects for the madhouse-keeper to ponder on; and it was most unlikely that he would hit upon the truth of the matter if he did.

To draw Mr Segundus's thoughts away from Lady Pole and her supposed crime, Stephen said, "Sir Walter chose this establishment himself. I do not know whose advice he took. Have you been a madhouse-keeper long?"

Mr Segundus laughed. "No, not long at all. About two weeks in fact. Lady Pole will be my first charge."

"Indeed!"

"I believe Sir Walter considers my lack of experience to be an advantage rather than otherwise! Other gentlemen in this profession are accustomed to exercise all sorts of authority over their charges and impose restraints upon them – something Sir Walter is very much opposed to in the case of his wife. But, you see, I have no such habits to break. Her ladyship will meet with nothing but kindness and respect in this house. And, apart from such little precautions as may suggest themselves to our good sense – such as keeping guns and knives out of her way – she will be treated as a guest in this house and we will strive to make her happy."

Stephen inclined his head in acceptance of these proposals. "How did you come to it?" he asked.

"The house?" asked Mr Segundus.

"No, madhouse-keeping."

"Oh! Quite by accident. Last September I had the great good fortune to meet a lady called Mrs Lennox, who has since become my benefactress. This house belongs to her. For some years she had tried to find a good tenant for it, but without success. She took a liking to me and wished to do me a kindness; so she determined upon establishing a business here and placing me in charge of it. Our first thought was a school for magicians, but . . ."

"Magicians!" exclaimed Stephen in surprize. "But what have you to do with magicians?"

"I am one myself. I have been one all my life."

"Indeed!"

Stephen looked so very much affronted by this news that Mr Segundus's natural impulse was to apologize to him – though what sort of apology one could offer for being a magician he did not know. He went on. "But Mr Norrell did not approve our plan for a school and he sent Childermass here to warn me against it. Do you know John Childermass, sir?"

"I know him by sight," said Stephen. "I have never spoken to him."

"At first Mrs Lennox and I had every intention of opposing him – Mr Norrell, I mean, not Childermass. I wrote to Mr Strange, but my letter arrived on the morning that his wife disappeared and, as I dare say you know, the poor lady died a few days later."

For a moment Stephen looked as if he were about to say something, but then he shook his head and Mr Segundus continued. "Without Mr Strange to help us, it was clear to me that we must abandon the school. I travelled up to Bath to inform Mrs Lennox. She was full of kindness and told me we would soon fix on another plan. But I confess I left her house in a very despondent frame of mind. I had not gone many steps when I saw a strange sight. In the middle of the road was a figure in tattered black rags. His sore, reddened eyes were empty of all reason and hope. He dashed his arms against the phantoms that assaulted him and cried out, entreating them to have pity on him. Poor soul! The sick in body may sometimes find respite in sleep, but I knew instinctively that this man's demons would follow him even into his dreams. I put a few coins into his hand and continued on my way. I am not aware that I thought of him particularly on the journey back, but as I stepped across the threshold of this house something very curious happened. I had what I think I must call a vision. I saw the madman in all his ravings standing in the hall – just as I had seen him in Bath – and I realized something. I realized that this house with its silence and its seclusion might be kind to persons distressed in mind. I wrote to Mrs Lennox and she approved my new plan. You said you did not know who had recommended me to Sir Walter. It was Childermass. Childermass had said he would help me if he could."

Stephen said, "It might be best, sir, if you were to avoid any mention of your profession or of the school, at least at the beginning. There is nothing in the world – in this world or any other – that would give her ladyship greater pain than to find herself in thrall to another magician."

"Thrall!" exclaimed Mr Segundus, in astonishment. "What an odd word that is! I sincerely hope that no one will ever consider themselves in thrall to me! Certainly not this lady!"

Stephen studied him for a moment. "I am sure you are a very different sort of magician from Mr Norrell," he said.

"I hope I am," said Mr Segundus, seriously.

An hour later a little commotion was heard in the yard. Stephen and Mr Segundus went out to receive her ladyship. The horses and carriage had been entirely unable to cross the packhorse bridge and Lady Pole had been obliged to walk the last fifty yards or so of her journey. She entered the courtyard of the Hall with some trepidation, glancing round at the bleak, snowy scene; and it seemed to Stephen that only the cruellest of hearts could look upon her, with all her youth, beauty and sad affliction, and not wish to offer her all the protection in their power. Inwardly he cursed Mr Norrell.

Something in her appearance seemed to startle Mr Segundus. He looked down at her left hand, but the hand was gloved. He recovered himself immediately and welcomed her to Starecross Hall.

In the drawing-room Stephen brought tea for them.

"I am told your ladyship has been greatly distressed by the death of Mrs Strange," said Mr Segundus. "May I offer my condolences?"

She turned away her head to hide her tears. "It would be more to the point to offer them to her, not me," she said. "My husband offered to write to Mr Strange and beg the favour of borrowing a picture of Mrs Strange, so that a copy might be made to console me. But what good would that do? After all, I am scarcely likely to forget her face when she and I attend the same balls and processions every night – and shall do for the rest of our lives, I presume. Stephen knows. Stephen understands."

"Ah, yes," said Mr Segundus. "Your ladyship has a horror of dancing and music, I know. Be assured that they will not be allowed here. Here we shall have nothing that is not cheerful, nothing that does not promote your happiness." He spoke to her of the books he planned they should read together and the walks they could take in spring, if her ladyship liked.

To Stephen, occupied among the tea-things, it seemed the most innocuous of conversations – except that once or twice he observed Mr Segundus glance from her ladyship to himself and back again, in a sharp, penetrating manner that both puzzled him and made him uncomfortable.

The carriage, coachman, maid and footman were all to remain at Starecross Hall with Lady Pole; Stephen, however, was to return to Harley-street. Early the next morning, while her ladyship was at breakfast, he went in to take his leave of her.

As he bowed to her, she gave a laugh half-melancholy, half-amused. "It is very ridiculous to part so, when you and I both know that we will be together again in a few hours. Do not be concerned about me, Stephen. I shall be more comfortable here. I feel I shall."

Stephen went out to the stable-yard where his horse stood waiting. He was just putting on his gloves when a voice came behind him. "I beg your pardon!"

Mr Segundus was there, as hesitant and unassuming as ever. "May I ask you something? What is the magic that surrounds you and her ladyship?" He put up his hand as if he intended to brush Stephen's face with his fingertips. "There is a red-and-white rose at your mouth. And another at hers. What does that mean?"

Stephen put his hand up to his mouth. There was nothing there. But for a moment he had some wild notion of telling Mr Segundus everything – all about his enchantment and the enchantment of the two women. He pictured Mr Segundus somehow understanding him; Mr Segundus proving to be an extraordinary magician – much greater than Strange or Norrell – who would find a way to thwart the gentleman with the thistle-down hair. But these were very fleeting fancies. A moment later Stephen's native distrust of Englishmen – and of English magicians in particular – reasserted itself.

"I do not understand you," he said quickly. He mounted his horse and rode away without another word.

The winter roads that day were some of the worst he had ever seen. The mud had been frozen into ruts and ridges as hard as iron. Fields and roads were thickly covered with white frost and an icy mist added to the general gloom.

His horse was one of the gentleman's innumerable gifts. She was a milk-white mare without so much as a single black hair anywhere. She was, besides, swift and strong, and as affectionately disposed towards Stephen as a horse can be to a man. He had named her Firenze and he doubted that the Prince Regent himself or the Duke of Wellington had a better horse. It was one of the peculiarities of his strange, enchanted life that it did not matter where he went, no one remarked upon the incongruity of a negro servant possessing the finest horse in the kingdom.

About twenty miles south of Starecross Hall he came to a small village. There was a sharp corner as the road passed between a large, elegant house and garden upon the right and a row of tumbledown stables upon the left. Just as Stephen was passing the entrance to the house, a carriage came suddenly out of the sweep and very nearly collided with him. The coachman looked round to see what had caused his horses to shy and forced him to rein them in. Seeing nothing but a black man, he lashed out at him with his whip. The blow missed Stephen but struck Firenze just above the right eye. Pained and startled, she reared up and lost her footing on the icy road.

There was a moment when everything seemed to tumble over. When Stephen was next able to comprehend what was happening, he found that he was on the ground. Firenze had fallen. He had been thrown clear, but his left foot was still caught in the stirrup and the leg was twisted in a most alarming way – he was sure it must be broken. He freed his foot and sat for a moment feeling sick and stunned. There was a sensation of something wet trickling down his face and his hands had been scraped raw by the fall. He tried to stand and found with relief that he could; the leg seemed bruised, but not broken.

Firenze lay snorting, her eyes rolling wildly. He wondered why she did not try to right herself or at least kick out. A sort of involuntary shuddering possessed her frame but apart from that she was still. Her legs were stiff and seemed to stick out at awkward angles to each other. Then it came to him: she could not move; her back was broken.

He looked at the gentleman's house, hoping that someone would come and help him. A woman appeared for a moment at a window. Stephen had a brief impression of elegant clothes and a cold, haughty expression. As soon as she had satisfied herself that the accident had produced no harm to any one or any thing belonging to her she moved away and Stephen saw no more of her.

He knelt down by Firenze and stroked her head and shoulder. From out of a saddlebag he drew a pistol, a powder flask, a ramrod and a cartridge. He loaded and primed the pistol. Then he stood and drew the hammer back to full cock.

But he found he could go no further. She had been too good a friend to him; he could not kill her. He was on the point of giving up in despair when there was a rattle in the lane behind him. Around the corner came a cart drawn by a great, shambling, placid-looking horse. It was a carrier's cart and in the cart sat the carrier himself, a big barrel-shaped man with a round, fat face. He was dressed in an ancient coat. When he saw Stephen, he reined in his horse. "Eh, lad! What's to do?"

Stephen gestured at Firenze with the pistol.

The carrier climbed down from his cart and came over to Stephen. "She was a pretty beast," he said in a kindly tone. He clapped Stephen on the shoulder and breathed sympathetic cabbage smells over him. "But, lad! Tha cannot help her now."

He looked from Stephen's face to the pistol. He reached out and gently raised the barrel until it pointed at Firenze's shuddering head. When Stephen still did not fire, he said, "Shall I do it for thee, lad?"

Stephen nodded.

The carrier took the pistol. Stephen looked away. There was a shot – a horrible sound – followed immediately by a wild cawing and the rush of wings as all the birds in the neighbourhood took flight at once. Stephen looked back. Firenze convulsed once and then was still.

"Thank you," he said to the carrier.

He heard the carrier walk away and he thought the man was gone, but in a moment he returned, nudged Stephen again and handed him a black bottle.

Stephen swallowed. It was gin of the roughest sort. He coughed.

Despite the fact that the cost of Stephen's clothes and boots could have bought the carrier's cart and horse twice over, the carrier assumed the cheerful superiority that white generally feels for black. He considered the matter and told Stephen that the first thing they must do was to arrange for the carcass to be removed. "She's a valuable beast – dead or alive. Your master won't be best pleased when he finds soom other fella has got t'horse and t'money."

"She was not my master's horse," said Stephen, "She was mine."

"Eh!" said the carrier. "Look at that!"

A raven had alighted upon Firenze's milk-white flank.

"No!" cried Stephen and moved to shoo the bird away.

But the carrier stopped him. "Nay, lad! Nay! That's lucky. I do not know when I saw a better omen!"

"Lucky!" said Stephen, "What are you talking about?"

"'Tis the sign of the old King, ain't it? A raven upon summat white. Old John's banner!"[1]

The carrier informed Stephen that he knew of a place close by where, he said, the people would for a price help Stephen make arrangements for disposing of Firenze. Stephen climbed upon the box and the carrier drove him to a farm.

The farmer had never seen a black man before and was quite

---

[1] John Uskglass's arms were the Raven-in-Flight (properly called the Raven Volant), a black raven on a white field.

astonished to find such an otherlandish creature in his yard. Despite all evidence to the contrary, he could not bring himself to believe that Stephen was speaking English. The carrier, who sympathized with the farmer in his confusion, stood beside Stephen, kindly repeating everything he said for the farmer's better understanding. But it made no difference. The farmer took no notice of either of them, but merely gaped at Stephen and made remarks about him to one of his men who stood equally entranced. The farmer wondered whether the black came off when Stephen touched things and he made other speculations of an even more impertinent and disagreeable nature. All Stephen's careful instructions concerning the disposal of Firenze's carcass went for nothing, until the farmer's wife returned from a nearby market. She was a very different sort of person. As far as she was concerned a man in good clothes with a costly horse (albeit a dead one) counted for a gentleman – let him be whatsoever colour he chose. She told Stephen of a cats-meat man who took the dead horses from the farm and who would dispose of the flesh and sell the bones and hooves for glue. She told him what the cats-meat man would pay and promised to arrange everything if she could keep one third of the money. To this Stephen agreed.

Stephen and the carrier came out of the farmyard into the lane.

"Thank you," said Stephen. "This would have been much more difficult without your help. I will pay you for your trouble, of course. But I fear I must trouble you further. I have no means of getting home. I would be very much obliged if you could take me as far as the next post-inn."

"Nay!" said the carrier. "Put th' little purse away, lad, I'll tek thee to Doncaster and it'll cost thee nowt."

In truth Stephen would have much preferred to go to the next post-inn, but the carrier seemed so pleased to have found a companion that it seemed kinder and more grateful to go with him.

The cart progressed towards Doncaster by degrees, travelling along country lanes and coming at inns and villages from odd directions, taking them by surprize. They delivered a bed-stead in this place, and a fruitcake in that place, and took up no end of oddly shaped parcels. Once they stopped at a very small cottage that stood by itself behind a high bare hedge in the middle of a wood. There they received from the hands of an ancient maid a bony, old, black-painted bird-cage containing a very small canary. The carrier informed Stephen that it had belonged to an old lady who had died and it was to be delivered to her great-niece south of Selby.

Not long after the canary had been secreted in the back of the carriage, Stephen was startled by a series of thunderous snores issuing unexpectedly from the same place. It seemed impossible that such a very loud noise should have come out of such a very small bird and Stephen concluded that there was another person in the cart, someone he had not yet been privileged to see.

The carrier produced from a basket a large pork pie and a hunk of cheese. He cut a piece off the pie with a large knife and seemed about to offer it to Stephen when he was struck by a doubt. "Do black lads eat the same as us?" he asked as if he thought they might possibly eat grass, or moonbeams.

"Yes," said Stephen.

The carrier gave Stephen the piece of pie and some cheese.

"Thank you. Does not your other passenger want something?"

"He might. When he wakes. I took him up at Ripon. He'd no money. I thowt as how he'd be someone to talk to. He were chatty enough at first but he went to sleep at Boroughbridge and he's done nowt else since."

"Very tiresome of him."

"I don't mind it. I have you to talk to now."

"He must be very tired," mused Stephen. "He has slept through the shot that finished my horse, the visit to the foolish farmer, the bed-stead and the canary – all the events of the day in fact. Where is he going?"

"Him? Nowhere. He wanders about from place to place. He is persecuted by soom famous man in London and cannot stay long anywhere – or t'oother chap's servant might catch up wi' him."

"Indeed?"

"He is blue," remarked the carrier.

"Blue?" said Stephen, mystified.

The carrier nodded.

"What? Blue with cold? Or has he been beaten?"

"Nay, lad. He is as blue as thou art black. Eh! I have a black lad and a blue fella in my cart! I niver heard o' anyone that did that before. Now if to see a black lad is good luck – which it must be, like cats – then to see a black lad and a blue fella together in one place ought to mean summat. But what?"

"Perhaps it does mean something," offered Stephen, "but not for you. Perhaps it means something for him. Or me."

"Nay, that can't be right," objected the carrier. "It's me it's happening to."

Stephen considered the unknown man's odd colour. "Does he have a disease?" he asked.

"Could be," said the carrier, unwilling to commit himself.

After they had eaten, the carrier began to nod and pretty soon he was fast asleep with the reins in his hands. The cart continued serenely along the road under the captainship of the horse – a beast of excellent sense and judgement.

It was a weary journey for Stephen. The sad exile of Lady Pole and the loss of Firenze depressed his spirits. He was glad to be relieved of the carrier's conversation for a while.

Once he heard a sort of muttering, suggesting that the blue man was waking up. At first he could not tell what the blue man was saying and then he heard very clearly, "*The nameless slave shall be king in a strange country.*"

That made him shiver; it reminded him so forcibly of the gentleman's promise to make him King of England.

It grew dark. Stephen halted the horse, got down from the box and lit the three ancient lanterns that hung about the cart. He was about to get back upon the box when a ragged, unkempt-looking person climbed suddenly out of the back and jumped down upon the icy ground to stand in front of him.

The unkempt person regarded Stephen by the lanterns' light. "Are we there yet?" he asked in a hoarse tone.

"Are we where?" asked Stephen.

The man considered this for a moment and then decided to rephrase his original question. "Where are we?" he asked.

"Nowhere. Between somewhere called Ulleskelf and another place called Thorpe Willoughby, I believe."

Though the man had asked for this information he did not seem much interested in it when it was given to him. His dirty shirt was open to the waist and Stephen could see that the carrier's description of him had been of a most misleading nature. He was not blue in the same way that Stephen was black. He was a thin, disreputable hawk of a man, whose skin in its natural state ought to have been the same colour as every other Englishman's, but it was covered in a strange patterning of blue lines, flourishes, dots and circles.

"Do you know John Childermass, the magician's servant?" he asked.

Stephen was startled – as any body would be who was asked the same question twice in two days by complete strangers. "I know him by sight. I have never spoken to him."

The man grinned and winked. "He has been looking for me for eight years. Never found me yet. I have been to look at his master's house in Yorkshire. It stands in a great park. I should have liked to steal something. When I was at his house in London I ate some pies."

It was a little disconcerting to find oneself in the company of a self-confessed thief, yet Stephen could not help but feel some sort of fellowship with someone who wished to rob the magician. After all, if it had not been for Mr Norrell Lady Pole and he would never have fallen under an enchantment. He reached into his pocket and pulled out two crown coins. "Here!" he said.

"And what is that for?" asked the man suspiciously (but he took the coins anyway).

"I am sorry for you."

"Why?"

"Because, if what I am told is true, you have no home."

The man grinned again and scratched his dirty cheek. "And if what *I* am told is true, you have no name!"

"What?"

"I have a name. It is Vinculus." He grabbed Stephen's hand. "Why do you try to pull away from me?"

"I do not," said Stephen.

"Yes, you did. Just then."

Stephen hesitated. "Your skin is marked and discoloured. I thought perhaps the marks meant you had a disease of some sort."

"That is not what my skin means," said Vinculus.

"Means?" said Stephen. "That is an odd word to use. Yet it is true – skin can mean a great deal. Mine means that any man may strike me in a public place and never fear the consequences. It means that my friends do not always like to be seen with me in the street. It means that no matter how many books I read, or languages I master, I will never be any thing but a curiosity – like a talking pig or a mathematical horse."

Vinculus grinned. "And mine means the opposite of yours. It means you will be raised up on high, Nameless King. It means your kingdom is waiting for you and your enemy shall be destroyed. It means the hour is almost come. *The nameless slave shall wear a silver crown; the nameless slave shall be a king in a strange country . . .*"

Then, keeping tight hold of Stephen's hand, Vinculus recited the whole of his prophecy. "There," he said when he was done, "now I have told it to the two magicians and I have told it to you. The first part of my task is done."

"But I am not a magician," said Stephen.

"I never said you were," answered Vinculus. Without warning he released Stephen's arm, pulled his ragged coat tight around him, plunged into the darkness beyond the glow of the lanterns and was gone.

A few days later the gentleman with the thistle-down hair expressed a sudden desire to see a wolf hunt, something he had apparently not done for several centuries.

There happened to be one going on in southern Sweden just then and so he instantly transported himself and Stephen to the place. Stephen found himself standing upon a great branch that belonged to an ancient oak in the midst of a snowy forest. From here he had an excellent view of a little clearing where a tall wooden pole had been planted in the ground. On top of the pole was an old wooden cartwheel, and on top of the cartwheel a young goat was securely tied. It bleated miserably.

A family of wolves crept out of the trees, with frost and snow clogging their fur, their gaze fixed hungrily upon the goat. No sooner had they appeared, than dogs could be heard in every part of the forest and riders could be glimpsed approaching at great speed. A pack of hounds came pouring into the clearing; the two foremost dogs leapt upon a wolf and together the three creatures became a single snapping, snarling, biting, thrashing knot of bodies, legs and teeth. The hunters galloped up and shot the wolf. The other wolves went streaming into the dark trees, and the dogs and hunters followed.

As soon as the sport waned in one place, the gentleman carried himself and Stephen through the air by magic, to wherever it was likely to be better. In this fashion they progressed from treetop to treetop, from hill to rocky outcrop. Once they travelled to the top of a church tower in a village of wooden houses, where the windows and doors were made in quaint, fairy-tale shapes and the roofs were dusted with powdery snow that glittered in the sunlight.

They were waiting in a quiet part of the wood for the hunters to appear, when a single wolf passed by their tree. He was the handsomest of his kind, with fine, dark eyes and a pelt the colour of wet slate. He looked up into the tree and addressed the gentleman in a language that sounded like the chatter of water over stones and the sighing of wind amongst bare branches and the crackle of fire consuming dead leaves.

The gentleman answered him in the same speech, then gave a careless laugh and waved him away with his hand.

The wolf bestowed one last reproachful glance upon the gentleman and ran on.

"He begs me to save him," the gentleman explained.

"Oh, could you not do it, sir? I hate to see these noble creatures die!"

"Tender-hearted Stephen!" said the gentleman, fondly. But he did not save the wolf.

Stephen was not enjoying the wolf hunt at all. True, the hunters were brave and their hounds were faithful and eager; but it was too soon after the loss of Firenze for him to take pleasure in the deaths of any creature, especially one as strong and handsome as the wolf. Thinking of Firenze reminded him that he had not yet told the gentleman about his meeting with the blue-skinned man in the cart and the prophecy. He did so now.

"Really? Well, that is most unexpected!" declared the gentleman.

"Have you heard this prophecy before, sir?"

"Yes, indeed! I know it well. All my race do. It is a prophecy of . . ." Here the gentleman said a word which Stephen did not understand.[2] "Whom you know better by his English name, John Uskglass, the Raven King. But what I do not understand is how it has survived in England. I did not think Englishmen interested themselves in such matters any more."

---

[2] Presumably the Raven King's original *Sidhe* name, which Jonathan Strange thought meant "Starling".

"The nameless slave! Well, that is me, sir, is it not? And this prophecy seems to tell how I will be a king!"

"Well, of course you are going to be a king! I have said so, and I am never wrong in these matters. But dearly as I love you, Stephen, this prophecy does not refer to you at all. Most of it is about the restoration of English magic, and the part you have just recited is not really a prophecy at all. The King is remembering how he came into his three kingdoms, one in England, one in Faerie, one in Hell. By the nameless slave he means himself. He was the nameless slave in Faerie, the little Christian child hidden in the *brugh*, brought there by a very wicked fairy who had stolen him away out of England."

Stephen felt oddly disappointed, though he did not know why he should be. After all he did not wish to be king of anywhere. He was not English; he was not African. He did not belong anywhere. Vinculus's words had briefly given him the sense of belonging to something, of being part of a pattern and of having a purpose. But it had all been illusory.

48

The Engravings

Late February–March 1816

"YOU ARE CHANGED. I am quite shocked to see you."
"Am I? You surprize me. I am perhaps a little thinner, but I am not aware of any other change."

"No, it is in your face, your air, your . . . something."

Strange smiled. Or rather he twisted something in his face and Sir Walter supposed that he was smiling. Sir Walter could not really recall what his smile had looked like before.

"It is these black clothes," said Strange. "I am like a leftover piece of the funeral, condemned to walk about the Town, frightening people into thinking of their own mortality."

They were in the Bedford coffee-house in Covent-garden, chosen by Sir Walter as a place where they had often been very merry in the past and which might therefore do something to cheer Strange's spirits. But on such an evening as this even the Bedford was somewhat deficient in cheerfulness. Outside, a cold black wind was pulling people this way and that, and driving a thick black rain into their eyes. Inside, rooms full of damp, unhappy gentlemen were producing a kind of gloomy, domesticated fog, which the waiters were attempting to dispel by putting extra shovelsful of coals on the fire and getting extra glassesful of hot spiced wine into the gentlemen.

When Sir Walter had come into the room he had discovered

Strange writing furiously in a little book. He nodded towards the book and remarked, "You have not given up magic then?"

Strange laughed.

Sir Walter took this to mean he had not – which Sir Walter was glad of, for Sir Walter thought a great deal of a man's having a profession and believed that useful, steady occupation might cure many things which other remedies could not. Only he did not quite like the laugh – a hard, bitter exclamation which he had never heard from Strange before. "It is just that you said . . ." he began.

"Oh, I said a great many things! All sorts of odd ideas crept into my brain. Excess of grief may bring on quite as fine a bout of madness as an excess of any thing else. Truth to tell, I was not quite myself for a time. Truth to tell, I was a little wild. But, as you see, that is all past now."

But – truth to tell – Sir Walter did not see at all.

It was not quite enough to say that Strange had changed. In some senses he was just what he had always been. He smiled as often as before (though it was not quite the same smile). He spoke in the same ironic, superficial tone as he had always done (while giving the impression of scarcely attending to his own words). His words and his face were what all his friends remembered – with this difference: that the man behind them seemed only to be acting a part while his thoughts and his heart were somewhere else entirely. He looked out at them all from behind the sarcastic smile and none of them knew what he was thinking. He was more like a magician than ever before. It was very curious and no one knew what to make of it, but in some ways he was more like Norrell.

He wore a mourning ring on the fourth finger of his left hand with a thin strand of brown hair inside it and Sir Walter noticed that he continually touched it and turned it upon his finger.

They ordered a good dinner consisting of a turtle, three or four beefsteaks, some gravy made with the fat of a green goose, some lampreys, escalloped oysters and a small salad of beet root.

"I am glad to be back," said Strange. "Now that I am here I intend to make as much mischief as I can. Norrell has had everything his own way for far too long."

"He is already in agonies whenever your book is mentioned. He is forever inquiring of people if they know what is in it."

"Oh, but the book is only the beginning! And besides it will not be ready for months. We are to have a new periodical. Murray wishes to bring it forward as quickly as possible. Naturally it will be a very superior production. It is to be called *The Famulus*[1] and is intended to promote *my* views on magic."

"And these are very different from Norrell's, are they?"

"But, of course! My chief idea is to examine the subject rationally without any of the restrictions and limitations that Norrell imposes upon it. I am confident that such a re-examination will rapidly open up new avenues worthy of exploration. For, when you consider the matter, what does our so-called restoration of English magic amount to? What have Norrell and I actually done? Some weaving of illusions with clouds, rain, smoke etc. – the easiest things in the world to accomplish! Bestowing life and speech upon inanimate objects – well, I grant you, that is quite sophisticated. Sending storms and bad weather to our enemies – I really cannot emphasize how simple weather-magic is. What else? Summoning up visions – well, that might be impressive if either of us could manage it with any degree of skill, but neither of us can. Now! Compare that sorry reckoning with the magic of the *Aureates*. They persuaded sycamore and oak woods to join with them against their enemies; they made wives and servants for themselves out of flowers; they transformed themselves into mice, foxes, trees, rivers, etc.; they made ships out of cobwebs, houses out of rose-bushes . . ."

"Yes, yes!" interrupted Sir Walter. "I understand that you are

[1] *Famulus*: a Latin word meaning a servant, especially the servant of a magician.

impatient to try all these different sorts of magic. But though I do not much like saying it, it seems to me that Norrell may be right. Not all these sorts of magic will suit us nowadays. Shape-changing and so on were all very well in the past. It makes a vivid incident in a story, I grant you. But surely, Strange, you would not want to practise it? A gentleman cannot change his shape. A gentleman scorns to seem any thing other than what he is. You yourself would never wish to appear in the character of a pastry-cook or a lamplighter . . ."

Strange laughed.

"Well then," said Sir Walter, "consider how much worse it would be to appear as a dog or a pig."[2]

"You are deliberately chusing low examples."

"Am I? A lion, then! Would you like to be a lion?"

"Possibly. Perhaps. Probably not. But that is not the point! I agree that shape-changing is a sort of magic which requires delicate handling, but that is not to say that some useful application might not exist. Ask the Duke of Wellington whether he would have liked to be able to turn his exploring officers into foxes or mice and have them slip about the French camps. I assure you his Grace will not be so full of qualms."

---

[2] Sir Walter is voicing a commonly-held concern. Shape-changing magic has always been regarded with suspicion. The *Aureates* generally employed it during their travels in Faerie or other lands beyond England. They were aware that shape-changing magic was particularly liable to abuses of every sort. For example in London in 1232 a nobleman's wife called Cecily de Walbrook found a handsome pewter-coloured cat scratching at her bed-chamber door. She took it in and named it Sir Loveday. It ate from her hand and slept upon her bed. What was even more remarkable, it followed her everywhere, even to church where it sat curled up in the hem of her skirts, purring. Then one day she was seen in the street with Sir Loveday by a magician called Walter de Chepe. His suspicions were immediately aroused. He approached Cecily and said, "Lady, the cat that follows you – I fear it is no cat at all." Two other magicians were fetched and Walter and the others said spells over Sir Loveday. He turned back into his true shape – that of a minor magician called Joscelin de Snitton. Shortly afterwards Joscelin was tried by the Petty Dragownes of London and sentenced to have his right hand cut off.

"I do not think you could have persuaded Colquhoun Grant to become a fox."[3]

"Oh! Grant would not have minded being a fox as long as he could have been a fox in a uniform. No, no, we need to turn our attention to the *Aureates*. A great deal more energy ought to be applied to the study of the life and magic of John Uskglass and when we . . ."

"That is the one thing you must not do. Do not even think of it."

"What are you talking about?"

"I am serious, Strange. I say nothing against the *Aureates* in general. Indeed, upon the whole, I think you are right. Englishmen take great pride in their ancient magical history – in Godbless, Stokesey, Pale and the rest. They do not like to read in their newspapers that Norrell makes light of their achievements. But you are liable to fall into the opposite mistake. Too much talk of other kings is bound to make the Government nervous. Particularly when we are liable to be overrun by Johannites at any moment."

"Johannites? Who are the Johannites?"

"What? Good Lord, Strange! Do you never look into a news-paper?"

Strange looked a little put out. "My studies take up a great deal of my time. All of it in fact. And besides, you know, in the past month I can plead distractions of a very particular nature."

"But we are not speaking of the past month. There have been Johannites in the northern counties for four years."

"Yes, but who are they?"

"They are craftsmen who creep into mills at dead of night and destroy property. They burn down factory-owners' houses. They hold pernicious meetings inciting the common people to riotous acts and they loot marketplaces."[4]

---

[3] It has already been described how Lt-Col. Colquhoun Grant's devotion to his scarlet uniform had led to his capture by the French in 1812.

[4] The common people in Northern England considered that they had suffered a great deal in recent years – and with good reason. Poverty and lack of employment had added to the general misery which the war with the French had produced. Then just when the war was over a new threat to their

"Oh, *machine-breakers*. Yes, yes, I understand you now. It is just that you misled me by that odd name. But what have machine-breakers to do with the Raven King?"

"Many of them are, or rather claim to be, his followers. They daub the Raven-in-Flight upon every wall where property is destroyed. Their captains carry letters of commission purporting to come from John Uskglass and they say that he will shortly appear to re-establish his reign in Newcastle."

"And the Government believes them?" asked Strange in astonishment.

"Of course not! We are not so ridiculous. What we fear is a great deal more mundane – in a word, revolution. John Uskglass's banner is flying everywhere in the north from Nottingham to Newcastle. Of course we have our spies and informers to tell us what these fellows are doing and thinking. Oh, I do not say that they all believe that John Uskglass is coming back. Most are as rational as you or I. But they know the power of his name among the common people. Rowley Fisher-Drake, the Member for Hampshire, has brought forward a Bill in which he proposes to make it illegal to raise the Raven-in-Flight. But we cannot forbid people to fly their own flag, the flag of their legitimate King."[5] Sir Walter sighed and poked a beefsteak upon his plate with a fork. "Other countries," he said, "have stories of kings who will return at times of great need. Only in England is it part of the constitution."

Strange waved a fork impatiently at the Minister. "But all that is politics. It is nothing to do with me. I am not going to call for the

---

[4] *cont'd* happiness had arisen – remarkable new machines which produced all sorts of goods cheaply and put them out of work. It is scarcely to be wondered at that certain individuals among them had taken to destroying the machines in an attempt to preserve their livelihoods.

[5] There could be no neater illustration than this of the curious relation in which the Government in London stood to the northern half of the Kingdom. The Government represented the King of England but the King of England was only the King of the southern half. Legally he was the steward of the northern half maintaining the rule of law until such time as John Uskglass chose to return.

re-establishment of John Uskglass's kingdom. My only wish is to examine, in a calm and rational manner, his accomplishments as a magician. How can we restore English magic until we understand what it is we are supposed to be restoring?"

"Then study the *Aureates*, but leave John Uskglass in the obscurity in which Norrell has placed him."

Strange shook his head. "Norrell has poisoned your minds against John Uskglass. Norrell has bewitched you all."

They ate in silence for a while and then Strange said, "Did I ever tell you that there is a portrait of him at Windsor Castle?"

"Who?"

"Uskglass. A fanciful scene painted upon a wall of one of the state rooms by some Italian painter. It shews Edward III and John Uskglass — warrior-king and magician-king seated side by side. It has been almost four hundred years since John Uskglass went out of England and still the English cannot quite make up their minds whether to adore him or hate him."

"Ha!" exclaimed Sir Walter. "In the north they know exactly what to think of him. They would exchange the rule of Westminster for his rule tomorrow if they could."[6]

---

[6] Naturally, at various times pretenders have arisen claiming to be John Uskglass and have attempted to take back the kingdom of Northern England. The most famous of these was a young man called Jack Pharaoh who was crowned in Durham Cathedral in 1487. He had the support of a large number of northern noblemen and also of a few fairies who remained at the King's city of Newcastle. Pharaoh was a very handsome man with a kingly bearing. He could do simple magic and his fairy supporters were quick to do more whenever he was present and to attribute it to him. He was the son of a pair of vagabond-magicians. While still a child he was seen at a fair by the Earl of Hexham who noted his striking resemblance to descriptions of John Uskglass. Hexham paid the boy's parents seven shillings for him. Pharaoh never saw them again. Hexham kept him at a secret place in Northern England where he was trained in kingly arts. In 1486 the Earl produced Pharaoh and he began his brief reign as King of Northern England. Pharaoh's main problem was that too many people knew about the deception. Pharaoh and Hexham soon quarrelled. In 1490 Hexham was murdered on Pharaoh's orders. Hexham's four sons joined with Henry VII of Southern England to attack Pharaoh and at the Battle of Worksop in 1493 Pharaoh was defeated. Pharaoh was kept in the Tower of London and executed in 1499.

A week or so later the first issue of *The Famulus* was published and, owing to the sensational nature of one of the articles, the entire run sold out within two days. Mr Murray, who was soon to publish the first volume of Strange's *The History and Practice of English Magic*, was filled with a happy anticipation of making a very large profit. The article which so thrilled the public was a description of how magicians might summon up dead people for the purposes of learning useful information from them. This shocking (but deeply interesting) subject caused such a sensation that several young ladies were reported to have fainted merely upon learning that *The Famulus* was in the house.[7] No one could imagine Mr Norrell ever approving such a publication and so every body who did not like Mr Norrell took a particular pleasure in buying a copy.

In Hanover-square Mr Lascelles read it out loud for the benefit

---

[6] *cont'd*   Other pretenders, more or less successful, were Piers Blackmore and Davey Sans-chaussures. The last pretender was known simply as the Summer King since his true identity was never discovered. He first appeared near Sunderland in May 1536 shortly after Henry VIII dissolved the monasteries. It is thought that he may have been a monk from one of the great northern abbeys – Fountains, Rievaulx or Hurtfew. The Summer King differed from Pharaoh and Blackmore in that he had no support from the northern aristocracy, nor did he attempt to gain any. His appeal was to the common people. In some ways his career was more mystical than magical. He healed the sick and taught his followers to revere nature and wild creatures – a creed which seems closer to the teachings of the twelfth-century magician, Thomas Godbless, than any thing John Uskglass ever proposed. His ragged band made no attempt to capture Newcastle or indeed to capture any thing at all. All through the summer of 1536 they wandered about Northern England, gaining supporters wherever they appeared. In September Henry VIII sent an army against them. They were not equipped to fight. Most ran away back to their homes but a few remained and fought for their King and were massacred at Pontefract. The Summer King may have been among the dead or he may have simply vanished.

[7] Consulting dead magicians may strike us as highly sensational, but it is a magical procedure with a perfectly respectable history. Martin Pale claimed to have learnt magic from Catherine of Winchester (who was a pupil of John Uskglass). Catherine of Winchester died two hundred years before Martin Pale was born. John Uskglass himself was reputed to have had conversations with Merlin, the Witch of Endor, Moses and Aaron, Joseph of Arimathea and other venerable and ancient magicians.

of Mr Norrell. "'. . . Where the magician is deficient in skill and knowledge – and this must include all modern magicians, our National Genius in such matters being sadly fallen off from what it was in former times – then he or she might be best advised to conjure up the spirit of someone who was in life a magician or had at least some talent for the art. For, if we are uncertain of the path ourselves, it is best to call on someone in possession of a little knowledge and who is able, as it were, to meet us halfway.'"

"He will undo every thing!" cried Norrell with a wild passion. "He is determined to destroy me!"

"It is certainly very aggravating," remarked Lascelles with all the calm in the world, "and after he swore to Sir Walter that he had given up magic when his wife died."

"Oh! We might all die – half of London might be swept away, but Strange will always do magic – he cannot help himself. He is too much a magician ever to stop now. And the magic that he will do is evil – and I do not know how I shall prevent him!"

"Pray, calm yourself, Mr Norrell," said Lascelles, "I am sure you will soon think of something."

"When is his book to be published?"

"Murray's advertisements say that the first volume will appear in August."

"The first volume!"

"Oh, yes! Did you not know? It will be a three-volume work. The first volume lays before the public the complete history of English magic. The second volume furnishes them with a precise understanding of its nature and the third provides the foundation for its future practice."

Mr Norrell groaned aloud, bowed his head and hid his face in his hands.

"Of course," said Lascelles thoughtfully, "as mischievous as the text undoubtedly will be, what I find even more alarming are the engravings . . ."

"Engravings?" cried Mr Norrell, aghast. "What engravings are these?"

"Oh," said Lascelles, "Strange has discovered some emigrant or other who has studied under all the best masters of Italy, France and Spain and he is paying this man a most extravagant amount of money to make the engravings."

"But what are they of? What is the subject?"

"What indeed?" said Lascelles with a yawn. "I have not the least idea." He took up *The Famulus* again and began to read silently to himself.

Mr Norrell sat for some time deep in thought, chewing at his fingernails. By and by he rang the bell and sent for Childermass.

East of the City of London lies the suburb of Spitalfields, famed far and wide as a place where wonderful silks are made. There is not now, nor ever will be, silk produced any where else in England of so fine a quality as Spitalfields silk. In the past good houses were built to accommodate the silk merchants, master-weavers and dyers who prospered from the trade. But, though the silk that comes out of the weavers' attics nowadays is every bit as remarkable as ever it was, Spitalfields itself is much fallen off. Its houses have grown dirty and shabby. The wealthy merchants have moved to Islington, Clerkenwell and (if they are very wealthy indeed) to the parish of Mary-le-bone in the west. Today Spitalfields is inhabited by the low and the poor and is much plagued with small boys, thieves and other persons inimicable to the peace of the citizens.

On a particularly gloomy day when a cold, grey rain fell in the dirty streets and pooled in the mud, a carriage came down Elder-street in Spitalfields and stopped at a tall, thin house. The coachman and footman belonging to this carriage wore deep mourning. The footman jumped down from the box, put up a black umbrella and held it up as he opened the door for Jonathan Strange to get out.

Strange paused a moment on the pavement to adjust his black

690

gloves and to cast his glance up and down Elder-street. Apart from two mongrel dogs industriously excavating a heap of refuse, the street was deserted. Yet he continued to look about him until his eye was caught by a doorway on the opposite side of the street.

It was the most unremarkable of doorways – the entrance to a merchant's warehouse or some such. Three worn stone steps led up to a massive black door of venerable construction, surmounted by a great jutting pediment. The door was much papered over with tattered playbills and notices informing the reader that upon such-and-such a day at such-and-such a tavern all the property of Mr So-and-so Esq. (Bankrupt) would be put up for sale.

"George," said Strange to the footman who held the umbrella, "do you draw?"

"I beg your pardon, sir?"

"Were you ever taught drawing? Do you understand its principles? Fore-grounds, side-screens, perspective, that sort of thing?"

"Me, sir? No, sir."

"A pity. It was part of my education. I could draw you a landscape or portrait perfectly proficient and perfectly uninteresting. Exactly like the productions of any other well-educated *amateur*. Your late mistress had none of the advantages of expensive drawing-masters that I had, yet I believe she had more talent. Her watercolours of people and children would horrify a fashionable drawing-master. He would find the figures too stiff and the colours too bright. But Mrs Strange had a genius for capturing expressions both of face and figure, for finding charm and wit in the most commonplace situations. There is something in her pictures, altogether lively and pretty which . . ." Strange broke off and was silent a moment. "What was I saying? Oh, yes. Drawing teaches habits of close observation that will always be useful. Take that doorway for instance . . ."

The footman looked at the doorway.

". . . Today is cold, dark, rainy. There is very little light and therefore no shadows. One would expect the interior of that

691

doorway to be gloomy and dim; one would not expect that shadow to be there – I mean the strong shadow going from left to right, keeping the left-hand of the doorway in utter blackness. And I believe I am right in saying that even if today were sunny and bright, a shadow would fall in the opposite direction. No, that shadow is altogether an oddity. It is not a thing that appears in Nature."

The footman looked at the coachman for some assistance, but the coachman was determined not to be drawn in and stared off into the distance. "I see, sir," said the footman.

Strange continued to regard the doorway with the same expression of thoughtful interest. Then he called out, "Childermass! Is that you?"

For a moment nothing happened and then the dark shadow which Strange objected to so strongly moved. It came away from the doorway like a wet sheet being peeled from a bed and as it did so, it changed and shrank and altered and became a man: John Childermass.

Childermass smiled his wry smile. "Well, sir, I could not expect to stay hidden from you for long."

Strange sniffed. "I have been expecting you this past week or more. Where have you been?"

"My master did not send me until yesterday."

"And how is your master?"

"Oh, poorly, sir, very poorly. He is beset with colds and headachs and tremblings in his limbs. All his usual symptoms when someone has vexed him. And no one vexes him as you do."

"I am pleased to hear it."

"By the by, sir, I have been meaning to tell you. I have some money at Hanover-square for you. Your fees from the Treasury and the Admiralty for the last quarter of 1814."

Strange opened his eyes in surprise. "And does Norrell really intend to let me have my share? I had supposed that money was gone for good."

Childermass smiled. "Mr Norrell knows nothing about it. Shall I bring the money tonight?"

"Certainly. I shall not be at home, but give it to Jeremy. Tell me, Childermass, I am curious. Does Norrell know that you go about making yourself invisible and turning yourself into shadows?"

"Oh, I have picked up a little skill here and there. I have been twenty-six years in Mr Norrell's service. I would have to be a very dull fellow to have learnt nothing at all."

"Yes, of course. But that was not what I asked. Does Norrell *know*?"

"No, sir. He suspects, but he chuses not to *know*. A magician who passes his life in a room full of books must have someone to go about the world for him. There are limits to what you can find out in a silver dish of water. You know that."

"Hmm. Well, come on, man! See what you were sent to see!"

The house had a much neglected, almost deserted air. Its windows and paint were very dirty and the shutters were all put up. Strange and Childermass waited upon the pavement while the footman knocked at the door. Strange had his umbrella and Childermass was entirely indifferent to the rain falling upon him.

Nothing happened for some time and then something made the footman look down into the area and he began a conversation with someone no one else could see. Whoever this person was, Strange's footman did not think much of them; his frown, his way of standing with both hands on his hips, the manner in which he admonished them, all betrayed the severest impatience.

After a while the door was opened by a very small, very dirty, very frightened servant-girl. Jonathan Strange, Childermass and the footman entered and, as they did so, each glanced down at her and she, poor thing, was frightened out of her wits to be looked at by so many tall, important-looking people.

Strange did not trouble to send up his name – it seemed so unlikely that they could have persuaded the little servant-girl to do it. Instead, instructing Childermass to follow him, Strange ran up the stairs and passed directly into one of the rooms. There in an obscure light made by many candles burning in a sort of fog – for the house seemed to produce its own weather – they found the engraver, M'sieur Minervois, and his assistant, M'sieur Forcalquier.

M'sieur Minervois was not a tall man; he was slight of figure. He had long hair, as fine, dark, shining and soft as a skein of brown silk. It brushed his shoulders and fell into his face whenever he stooped over his work – which was almost all the time. His eyes too were remarkable – large, soft and brown, suggesting his southern origins. M'sieur Forcalquier's looks formed a striking contrast to the extreme handsomeness of his master. He had a bony face with deep sunken eyes, a shaven head covered in pale bristles. But for all his cadaverous, almost skeletal, aspect he was of a most courteous disposition.

They were refugees from France, but the distinction between a refugee and an enemy was altogether too fine a one for the people of Spitalfields. M'sieur Minervois and M'sieur Forcalquier were known everywhere as French spies. They endured much on account of this unjust reputation: gangs of Spitalfields boys and girls thought it the best part of any holiday to lie in wait for the two Frenchmen and beat them and roll them in the dirt – an article in which Spitalfields was peculiarly rich. On other days the Frenchmen's neighbours relieved their feelings by surliness and catcalls and refusing to sell them any thing they might want or need. Strange had been of some assistance in mediating between M'sieur Minervois and his landlord and in arguing this latter gentleman into a more just understanding of M'sieur Minervois's character and situation – and by sending Jeremy Johns into all the taverns in the vicinity to drink gin and get into conversations with the natives of the place and to make it generally known that the two Frenchmen were the protégés of one of England's two magicians – "and," said Strange, raising a finger to Jeremy in instruction, "if they reply that Norrell is the greater of the two, you may let it pass – but say to them that I have a shorter temper and am altogether more sensitive to slights to my friends." M'sieur Minervois and M'sieur Forcalquier were grateful to Strange for his efforts, but, under such dismal circumstances, they had found that their best friend was brandy, taken with a strict regularity throughout the day.

They stayed shut up inside the house in Elder-street. The shutters were closed day and night against the inhospitableness of Spitalfields. They lived and worked by candlelight and had long since broken off all relations with clocks. They were rather amazed to see Strange and Childermass, being under the impression that it was the middle of the night. They had one servant – the tiny, wide-eyed orphan girl – who could not understand them and who was very much afraid of them and whose name they did not know. But in a careless, lofty way, the two men were kind to her and had given her a little room of her own with a feather-bed in it and linen sheets – so that she thought the gloomy house a very paradise. Her chief duties were to go and fetch them food and brandy and opium – which they then divided with her, keeping the brandy and opium for themselves, but giving her most of the food. She also fetched and heated water for their baths and their shaving – for both were rather vain. But they were entirely indifferent to dirt or disorder in the house, which was just as well for the little orphan knew as much of housekeeping as she did of Ancient Hebrew.

There were sheets of thick paper on every surface and inky rags. There were pewter dishes containing ancient cheese rinds and pots containing pens and pieces of charcoal. There was an elderly bunch of celery that had lived too long and too promiscuously in close companionship with the charcoal for its own good. There were engravings and drawings pinned directly on to every part of the panelling and the dark, dirty wallpaper – there was one of Strange that was particularly good.

At the back of the house in a smutty little yard there was an apple tree which had once been a country tree – until grey London had come and eaten up all its pleasant green neighbours. Once in a fit of industriousness some unknown person in the house had picked all the apples off the tree and placed them on all of the windowsills, where they had lain for several years now – becoming first old apples, then swollen corpses of apples and finally mere ghosts of apples. There was a very decided smell about the place – a compound of ink, paper, seacoals, brandy, opium, rotting apples, candles, coffee – all mingled with the unique perfume exuded by two men who work day and night in a rather confined space and who never under any circumstances can be induced to open a window.

The truth was that Minervois and Forcalquier often forgot that there were such places as Spitalfields or France upon the face of the earth. They lived for days at a time in the little universe of the engravings for Strange's book – and these were very odd things indeed.

They shewed great corridors built more of shadows than any thing else. Dark openings in the walls suggested other corridors so that the engravings appeared to be of the inside of a labyrinth or something of that sort. Some shewed broad steps leading down to dark underground canals. There were drawings of a vast dark moor, across which wound a forlorn road. The spectator appeared to be looking down on this scene from a great height. Far, far ahead on that road there was a shadow – no more than a scratch upon the road's pale surface – it was too far off to say if it were man or woman or child, or even a human person, but somehow its appearance in all that unpeopled space was most disquieting.

One picture showed the likeness of a lonely bridge that spanned some immense and misty void – perhaps the sky itself – and, though the bridge was constructed of the same massive masonry as the corridors and the canals, upon either side tiny staircases wound down, clinging to the great supports of the bridge. These staircases were frail-looking things, built with far less skill than the bridge, but there were many of them winding down through the clouds to God-knew-where.

Strange bent over these things, with a concentration to rival Minervois's own, questioning, criticizing and proposing. Strange and the two engravers spoke French to each other. To Strange's surprize Childermass understood perfectly and even addressed one or two questions to Minervois in his own language. Unfortunately, Childermass's French was so strongly accented by his native Yorkshire that Minervois did not understand and asked Strange if Childermass was Dutch.

"Of course," remarked Strange to Childermass, "they make these scenes altogether too Roman – too like the works of Palladio and Piranesi, but they cannot help that – it is their training. One can never help one's training, you know. As a magician I shall never quite be Strange – or, at least, not Strange alone – there is too much of Norrell in me."

"So this is what you saw upon the King's Roads?" said Childermass.

"Yes."

"And what is the country that the bridge crosses?"

Strange looked at Childermass ironically. "I do not know, Magician. What is your opinion?"

Childermass shrugged. "I suppose it is Faerie."

"Perhaps. But I am beginning to think that what we call Faerie is likely to be made up of many countries. One might as well say 'Elsewhere' and say as much."

"How far distant are these places?"

"Not far. I went there from Covent-garden and saw them all in the space of an hour and a half."

"Was the magic difficult?"

"No, not really."

"And will you tell me what it was?"

"With the greatest good will in the world. You need a spell of revelation – I used Doncaster. And another of dissolution to melt the mirror's surface. There are no end of dissolution spells in the books I have seen, but as far as I can tell, they are all perfectly useless so I was obliged to make my own – I can write it down for you if you wish. Finally one must set both of these spells within an overarching spell of path-finding. That is important, otherwise I do not see how you would ever get out again." Strange paused and looked at Childermass. "You follow me?"

"Perfectly, sir."

"Good." There was a little pause and then Strange said, "Is it not time, Childermass, that you left Mr Norrell's service and came to me? There need be none of this servant nonsense. You would simply be my pupil and assistant."

Childermass laughed. "Ha, ha! Thank you, sir. Thank you! But Mr Norrell and I are not done with each other. Not yet. And, besides, I think I would be a very bad pupil – worse even than you."

Strange, smiling, considered a moment. "That is a good answer," he said at last, "but not quite good enough, I am afraid. I do not believe that you can truly support Norrell's side. One magician in England! One opinion upon magic! Surely you do not agree with that? There is at least as much contrariness in your character as in mine. Why not come and be contrary with me?"

"But then I would be obliged to agree with you, sir, would I not? I do not know how it will end with you and Norrell. I have asked my cards to tell me, but the answer seems to blow this way and that. What lies ahead is too complex for the cards to explain clearly and I cannot find the right question to ask them. I tell you what I will do. I will make you a promise. If you fail and Mr Norrell wins, then I will indeed leave his service. I will take up your cause, oppose him with all my might and find arguments to vex him – and then there shall still be two magicians in England and two opinions upon magic. But, if he should fail and you win, I will do the same for you. Is that good enough?"

Strange smiled. "Yes, that is good enough. Go back to Mr Norrell and present my compliments. Tell him I hope he will be pleased with the answers I have given you. If there is any thing else he wishes to know, you will find me at home tomorrow at about four."

"Thank you, sir. You have been very frank and open."

"And why should I not? It is Norrell who likes to keep secrets, not I. I have told you nothing that is not already in my book. In a month or so, every man, woman and child in the kingdom will be able to read it and form their own opinions upon it. I really cannot see that there is any thing Norrell can do to prevent it."

49

Wildness and madness

March 1816

A FEW DAYS AFTER the visit to the engravers Strange invited Sir Walter and Lord Portishead to dinner. Both gentlemen had dined with Strange upon many occasions, but this was the first time they had entered the house in Soho-square since the death of Mrs Strange. They found it sadly changed. Strange seemed to have reverted to all his old bachelor habits. Tables and chairs were fast disappearing under piles of papers. Half-finished chapters of his book were to be found in every part of the house and in the drawing-room he had even taken to making notes upon the wallpaper.

Sir Walter started to remove a pile of books from a chair.

"No, no!" cried Strange, "Do not move those! They are in a very particular order."

"But where shall I sit?" asked Sir Walter in some perplexity.

Strange made a small sound of exasperation as if this were a most unreasonable request. Nevertheless he moved the books and only once became distracted in the process and fell to reading one of them. As soon as he had read through the passage twice and made a note of it upon the wallpaper he was able to attend to his guests again.

"I am very pleased to see you here again, my lord," he said to Portishead. "I have been asking everyone about Norrell – as much, I believe, as he has been asking about me. I hope you have a great deal to tell me."

"I thought I had already told you all about that," said Sir Walter, plaintively.

"Yes, yes. You told me where Norrell has been and whom he has been speaking to and how he is regarded by all the Ministers, but I am asking his lordship about *magic* and what you understand about magic would barely . . ."

". . . fill a square inch of wallpaper?" offered Sir Walter.

"Quite. Come, my lord. Tell me. What has Mr Norrell been doing lately?"

"Well," said Lord Portishead, "at the request of Lord Liverpool he has been working on some magic to help guard against Napoleon Buonaparte ever escaping again – and he has been studying the *Discourses upon the Kingdom of Light and the Kingdom of Darkness*. He believes he has made some discoveries."

"What is this?" cried Strange in alarm. "Something new in the *Discourses?*"[1]

"It is something he has found on page 72 of Cromford's edition. A new application of the Spell to Conjure Death. I do not understand it very well.[2] Mr Norrell seems to think that the principle might be adapted to cure diseases in men and animals – by conjuring the disease to come forth out of the body as if it were a demon."

"Oh, *that!*" exclaimed Strange in relief. "Yes, yes! I know what you mean now. I made the connexion last June. So Norrell has only just arrived there, has he? Oh, excellent!"

---

[1] Scholars of magic are always particularly excited about any new discovery concerning the great Dr Pale. He occupies an unique position in English magical history. Until the advent of Strange and Norrell he was the only noteworthy practical magician who wrote down his magic for other people to read. Naturally his books are esteemed above all others.

[2] For centuries this passage was considered an interesting curiosity, but of no practical value since no one nowadays believes that Death is a person capable of being interrogated in the manner Pale suggests.

"Many people were surprized that he did not take another pupil after you," continued Lord Portishead, "and I know that he has received a number of applications. But he has taken none of them. Indeed I do not believe he even spoke to the young men in question or answered their letters. His standards are so very exacting and no one comes up to you, sir."

Strange smiled. "Well, all that is just as I would have expected. He can scarcely bear the existence of a second magician. A third will probably be the death of him. I shall soon have the advantage of him. In the struggle to decide the character of English magic the sides will be very unevenly matched. There will only be one Norrellite magician and dozens of Strangite magicians. Or at least, as many as I can educate. I am thinking of setting up Jeremy Johns as a sort of anti-Childermass. He can go about the country seeking out all the people whom Norrell and Childermass have persuaded out of the study of magic and then he and I can persuade them back into it. I have had conversations with several young men already. Two or three are very promising. Lord Chaldecott's second son, Henry Purfois, has read a great many fourth-rate books about magic and fifth-rate biographies of magicians. It makes his conversation a little tedious, but he is scarcely to blame for that, poor fellow. Then there is William Hadley-Bright who was one of Wellington's *aides-de-camp* at Waterloo, and an odd little man called Tom Levy who is presently employed as a dancing-master in Norwich."

"A dancing-master?" frowned Sir Walter. "But is that really the sort of person whom we should be encouraging to take up magic? Surely it is a profession that ought to be reserved for gentlemen?"

"I do not see why. And besides I like Levy best. He is the first person I have met in years who regards magic as something to be enjoyed – and he is also the only one of the three who has managed to learn any practical magic. He made the window frame over there sprout branches and leaves. I dare say you were wondering why it is in that odd condition."

"To own the truth," said Sir Walter, "the room is so full of oddities that I had not even noticed."

"Of course Levy did not intend that it should remain like that," said Strange, "but after he did the magic he could not make it go back – and neither could I. I suppose I must tell Jeremy to find a carpenter to repair it."

"I am delighted you have found so many young men to suit you," said Sir Walter. "That bodes well for English magic."

"I have also had several applications from young ladies," said Strange.

"Ladies!" exclaimed Lord Portishead.

"Of course! There is no reason why women should not study magic. That is another of Norrell's fallacies."

"Hmm. They come thick and fast now," remarked Sir Walter.

"What do?"

"Norrell's fallacies."

"What do you mean by that?"

"Nothing! Nothing! Do not take offence. But I notice you do not mention taking any ladies as pupils yourself."

Strange sighed. "It is purely a matter of practicalities. That is all. A magician and his pupil must spend a great deal of time together, reading and discussing. Had Arabella not died, then I believe I might have taken female pupils. But now I would be obliged to rely upon chaperones and all sorts of tediousness that I do not have patience for at the moment. My own researches must come first."

"And what new magic are you intending to shew us, Mr Strange?" asked Lord Portishead, eagerly.

"Ah! I am glad you ask me that! I have been giving the matter a great deal of consideration. If the revival of English magic is to continue – or rather if it is not to remain under the sole direction of Gilbert Norrell – then I must learn something new. But new magic is not easily come by. I could go upon the King's Roads and try and reach those countries where magic is the general rule, rather than the exception."

"Good God!" exclaimed Sir Walter. "Not this again! Are you quite mad? I thought we had agreed that the King's Roads were far too dangerous to justify . . ."

"Yes, yes! I am well acquainted with your opinions. You lectured me long enough upon the subject. But you do not let me finish! I merely name possibilities. I shall not go upon the King's Roads. I gave my word to my . . . to Arabella that I would not."[3]

There was a pause. Strange sighed and his expression darkened. He was clearly now thinking of something – or someone – else.

Sir Walter observed quietly, "I always had the highest regard for Mrs Strange's judgement. You cannot do better than follow her advice. Strange, I sympathize – of course you wish to do new magic – any scholar would – but surely the only safe way to learn magic is from books?"

"But I do not have any books!" exclaimed Strange. "Good God! I promise to be as meek and stay-at-home as any maiden aunt if the Government will just pass a law saying Norrell must shew me his library! But as the Government will not do me this kindness, I have no choice but to increase my knowledge in any way I can."

"So what will you do?" asked Lord Portishead.

"Summon a fairy," said Strange, briskly. "I have made several attempts already."

"Did not Mr Norrell lay it down as a general rule that summoning fairies is full of hazards?" asked Sir Walter.

"There is not much that Mr Norrell does not regard as full of hazards," said Strange in tones of some irritation.

"True." Sir Walter was satisfied. After all, summoning fairies was a long-established part of English magic. All the *Aureates* had done it and all the *Argentines* had wished to.

---

[3] Most of us are naturally inclined to struggle against the restrictions our friends and family impose upon us, but if we are so unfortunate as to lose a loved one, what a difference then! Then the restriction becomes a sacred trust.

"But are you sure that it is even possible, sir?" asked Lord Portishead. "Most authorities agree that fairies hardly ever visit England any more."

"That is indeed the general opinion, yes," agreed Strange, "but I am almost certain that I was in company with one in November 1814, a month or two before Norrell and I parted."

"Were you indeed!" exclaimed Lord Portishead.

"You never mentioned this before," said Sir Walter.

"I was quite unable to mention it before," said Strange. "My position as Norrell's pupil depended upon my never breathing a word of it. Norrell would have fallen over in a blue fit at the least suggestion of such a thing."

"What did he look like, Mr Strange?" asked Lord Portishead.

"The fairy? I do not know. I did not see him. I heard him. He played music. There was someone else present who, I believe, both heard and saw him. Now, consider the advantages of dealing with such a person! No magician, living or dead, could teach me as much. Fairies are the source of everything we magicians desire. Magic is their native condition! As for the disadvantages, well, there is only the usual one – that I have almost no idea how to accomplish it. I have cast spells by the dozen, done everything I ever heard or read of, to try and get this fairy back again, but it has all been to no avail. I cannot for the life of me tell why Norrell expends so much energy in proscribing what no one can achieve. My lord, I don't suppose you know any spells for raising fairies?"

"Many," said Lord Portishead, "but I am sure you will have tried them all already, Mr Strange. We look to you, sir, to reconstruct for us all that has been lost."

"Oh!" sighed Strange. "Sometimes I think that nothing has been lost. The truth is that it is all at the library at Hurtfew."

"You said there was another person present who both saw and heard the fairy?" said Sir Walter.

"Yes."

"And I take it that this other person was not Norrell?"

"No."

"Very well then. What did this other person say?"

"He was . . . confused. He believed he was seeing an angel, but owing to his general style of living and habits of mind he did not find this quite as extraordinary as you might think. I beg your pardon but discretion forbids me to say any thing more of the circumstances."

"Yes, yes! Very well! But your companion saw the fairy. Why?"

"Oh, I know why. There was something very particular about him which enabled him to see fairies."

"Well, can you not use that somehow?"

Strange considered this. "I do not see how. It is a mere chance like one man having blue eyes and another brown." He was silent a moment, musing. "But then again perhaps not. Perhaps you are right. It is not such a very outlandish notion when you come to consider it. Think of the *Aureates*! Some of them were the fairies' near-neighbours in wildness and madness! Think of Ralph Stokesey and his fairy-servant, Col Tom Blue! When Stokesey was a young man there was scarcely any thing to chuse between them. Perhaps I am too tame, too *domestic* a magician. But how *does* one work up a little madness? I meet with mad people every day in the street, but I never thought before to wonder how they got mad. Perhaps I should go wandering on lonely moors and barren shores. That is always a popular place for lunatics – in novels and plays at any rate. Perhaps wild England will make me mad."

Strange got up and went to the drawing-room window, as if he expected to be able to survey wild England from there – although all it shewed was the very ordinary sight of Soho-square in a thick and mizzling rain. "I think you may have hit upon something, Pole."

"I?" cried Sir Walter, somewhat alarmed at where his remarks appeared to be leading, "I meant to suggest no such thing!"

"But, Mr Strange," reasoned the gentle Lord Portishead, "you cannot possibly mean this. For a man of such erudition as you possess to propose that he become a . . . a vagabond. Well, sir, it is a very shocking thought."

Strange crossed his arms and took another look at Soho-square and said, "Well, I shall not go today." And then he smiled his self-mocking smile and looked almost like his old self. "I shall wait," he said, "until it stops raining."[4]

---

[4] Even John Uskglass who had three kingdoms to rule over and all of English magic to direct was not entirely free from this tendency to go on long mysterious journeys. In 1241 he left his house in Newcastle in some mysterious fashion known only to magicians. He told a servant that he would be found asleep upon a bench in front of the fire in one day's time.

The following day the servant and members of the King's household looked for the King upon the bench in front of the fire, but he was not there. They looked for him every morning and every evening but he did not appear.

William, Earl of Lanchester, governed in his stead and many decisions were postponed "until the King shall return". But as time went on many people were inclined to doubt that this would ever happen. Then, a year and a day after his departure, the King was discovered, sleeping on the bench before the fire.

He did not seem aware that any thing untoward had happened and he told no one where he had been. No one dared ask him if he had always intended to be away so long or if something terrible had happened. William of Lanchester summoned the servant and asked him to repeat yet again the exact words that the King had said. Could it be that he had actually said he would be away for a year and a day?

Perhaps said the man. The King was generally quietly spoken. It was quite possible that he had not heard correctly.

50

The History and Practice of English Magic

April to late September 1816

STRANGE'S FRIENDS WERE glad to be assured that he did not intend to give up his comfortable houses, his good income and his servants to go and be a gypsy in the wind and the rain, but still very few of them were entirely comfortable with his new practices. They had good reason to fear that he had lost all restraint and was prepared to indulge in any and all kinds of magic. His promise to Arabella kept him from the King's Roads for the present, but all Sir Walter's warnings could not prevent him from continually talking and wondering about John Uskglass and his fairy subjects.

By the end of April, Strange's three new pupils, the Honourable Henry Purfois, William Hadley-Bright and Tom Levy, the dancing-master, had all taken lodgings near Soho-square. Every day they attended Strange's house to study magic. In the intervals between directing their magical education Strange worked at his book and performed magic on behalf of the Army and the East India Company. He had also received applications for assistance from the Corporation of Liverpool and the Society of Merchant Venturers in Bristol.

That Strange should still receive commissions from official bodies – or indeed from any one at all – so incensed Mr Norrell that he complained to Lord Liverpool, the Prime Minister, about it.

Lord Liverpool was not sympathetic. "The generals may do as they wish, Mr Norrell. The Government does not interfere in military matters, as well you know.[1] The generals have employed Mr Strange as their magician for a number of years and they see no reason to stop simply because you and he have quarrelled. As for the East India Company I am told that its officials applied to you in the first place and that you declined to help them."

Mr Norrell blinked his little eyes rapidly. "My work for the Government – my work for you, my lord – takes up so much of my time. I cannot, in conscience, neglect it for the sake of a private company."

"And believe me, Mr Norrell, we are grateful. Yet I need scarcely tell you how vital the success of the East India Company is to the prosperity of the Nation and the Company's need for a magician is immense. It has fleets of ships at the mercy of storms and bad weather; it has vast territories to administer and its armies are continually harassed by Indian princelings and bandits. Mr Strange has undertaken to controul the weather around the Cape and in the Indian Ocean and he has offered advice on the best use of magic in hostile territories. The Directors of the East India Company believe that Mr Strange's experience in the Spanish Peninsula will prove invaluable. It is yet another demonstration of Britain's sore need for more magicians. Mr Norrell, as diligent as you are, you cannot be everywhere and do everything – and no one expects that you should. I hear that Mr Strange has taken pupils. It would please me immensely to hear that you intended to do the same."

Despite Lord Liverpool's approval, the education of the three new magicians, Henry Purfois, William Hadley-Bright and Tom Levy, progressed no more smoothly than Strange's own six years before. The only difference was that whereas Strange had had

---

[1] This was not in the least true. It had been the Duke of Wellington's bitterest complaint during the Peninsular War that the Government interfered constantly.

Norrell's evasiveness to contend with, the young men were continually thwarted by Strange's low spirits and restlessness.

By early June the first volume of *The History and Practice of English Magic* was finished. Strange delivered it to Mr Murray and it surprized no one when, on the following day, he told Henry Purfois, William Hadley-Bright and Tom Levy that they must defer their magical education for a while as he had decided to go abroad.

"I think it an excellent plan!" said Sir Walter as soon as Strange told him of it. "A change of scene. A change of society. It is exactly what I would prescribe for you. Go! Go!"

"You do not think that it is too soon?" asked Strange anxiously. "I shall be leaving Norrell in possession of London so to speak."

"You think we have such short memories as that? Well, we shall make every endeavour not to forget you in the space of a few months. Besides, your book will be published soon and that will serve as a standing reminder to us all of how ill we get on without you."

"That is true. There is the book. It will take Norrell months to refute forty-six chapters and I shall be back long before he is finished."

"Where shall you go?"

"Italy, I think. The countries of southern Europe have always had a strong attraction for me. I was often struck by the appearance of the countryside when I was in Spain – or at least I believe I would have found it very striking had it not been covered in soldiers and gunsmoke."

"I hope you will write occasionally? Some token of your impressions?"

"Oh! I shall not spare you. It is the right of a traveller to vent their frustration at every minor inconvenience by writing of it to their friends. Expect long descriptions of everything."

As often happened these days, Strange's mood darkened suddenly. His light, ironic air evaporated upon the instant and he sat frowning at the coal-scuttle. "I wondered if you . . ." he said at last. "That is, I wish to ask you . . ." He made a sound of exasperation at his own hesitancy. "Would you convey a message to Lady Pole from me? I would be most grateful. Arabella was greatly attached to her ladyship and I know she would not have liked me to leave England without sending some message to Lady Pole."

"Certainly. What shall I tell her?"

"Oh! Simply give her my heartfelt wishes for her better health. Whatever you think best. It does not matter what you say. But you must say that the message is from Arabella's husband. I wish her ladyship to understand that her friend's husband has not forgotten her."

"With the greatest goodwill," said Sir Walter. "Thank you."

Strange had half-expected that Sir Walter would invite him to speak to Lady Pole himself, but Sir Walter did not. No one even knew whether her ladyship was still at the house in Harley-street. There was a rumour circulating the Town that Sir Walter had sent her to the country.

Strange was not alone in wishing to go abroad. It had suddenly become very fashionable. For far too long the British had been confined to their own island by the war with Buonaparte. For far too long they had been forced to satisfy their desire to look upon new scenes and curious people by visits to the Scottish Highlands or the English Lakes or the Derbyshire Peak. But now the war was over they could go to the Continent and see mountains and shores of quite a different character. They could view for themselves those celebrated works of art which hitherto they had only seen in books of engravings. Some went abroad hoping to find that it was cheaper to live on the Continent than at home. Some went to avoid debts or scandal and some, like Strange, went to find a tranquillity that eluded them in England.

Jonathan Strange to John Segundus

Bruxelles
Jun. 12th, 1816.

I am, as far as I can tell, about a month behind Lord Byron.[2] In every town we stop at we discover innkeepers, postillions, officials, burghers, potboys and all kinds and sorts of ladies whose brains still seem somewhat deranged from their brief exposure to his lordship. And though my companions are careful to tell people that I am that dreadful being, an English magician, I am clearly nothing in comparison to an English poet and everywhere I go I enjoy the reputation – quite new to me, I assure you – of the quiet, good Englishman, who makes no noise and is no trouble to any one . . .

It was a queer summer that year. Or rather it was no summer at all. Winter had extended its lease into August. The sun was scarcely seen. Thick grey clouds covered the sky; bitter winds blew through towns and withered crops; storms of rain and hail, enlivened by occasional displays of thunder and lightning, fell upon every part of Europe. In many ways it was worse than winter: the long hours of daylight denied people the consolation of darkness which would have hidden all these miseries for a while.

London was half empty. Parliament was dissolved and the Members of Parliament had all gone to their country houses, the better to stare at the rain. In London Mr John Murray, the publisher, sat in his house in Albermarle-street. At other times Mr Murray's rooms were the liveliest in London – full of poets, essayists, reviewers and all the great literary men of the kingdom. But the great literary men of the kingdom had gone to the country. The rain pattered upon the window and the wind moaned in the chimney. Mr Murray heaped more coals upon the fire and then sat down at his desk to begin reading that day's letters. He picked

---

[2] Lord Byron left England in April 1816 in the face of mounting debts, accusations of cruelty to his wife and rumours that he had seduced his sister.

each letter up and held it close to his left eye (the right being quite blind and useless).

It so happened that on this particular day there were two from Geneva in Swisserland. The first was from Lord Byron complaining of Jonathan Strange and the second was from Strange complaining of Byron. The two men had met at Mr Murray's house a handful of times, but until now they had never got acquainted. Strange had visited Byron at Geneva a couple of weeks before. The meeting had not been a success.

Strange (who was just now in a mood to place the highest value upon matrimony and all that he had lost in Arabella) was unsettled by Byron's domestic arrangements. "I found his lordship at his pretty villa upon the shores of the lake. He was not alone. There was another poet called Shelley, Mrs Shelley and another young woman – a girl really – who called herself Mrs Clairmont and whose relationship to the two men I did not understand. If you know, do not tell me. Also present was an odd young man who talked nonsense the entire time – a Mr Polidori."

Lord Byron, on the other hand, took exception to Strange's mode of dress. "He wore half-mourning. His wife died at Christmas, did she not? But perhaps he thinks black makes him look more mysterious and wizardly."

Having taken an immediate dislike to each other, they had progressed smoothly to quarrelling about politics. Strange wrote: "I do not quite know how it happened, but we immediately fell to talking of the battle of Waterloo – an unhappy subject since I am the Duke of Wellington's magician and they all hate Wellington and idolize Buonaparte. Mrs Clairmont, with all the impertinence of eighteen, asked me if I was not ashamed to be an instrument in the fall of so sublime a man. No, said I."

Byron wrote: "He is a great partisan for the Duke of W. I hope for your sake, my dear Murray, that his book is more interesting than he is."

Strange finished: "People have such odd notions about magicians. They wanted me to tell them about *vampyres*."

Mr Murray was sorry to find that his two authors could not agree better, but he reflected that it probably could not be helped since both men were famous for quarrelling: Strange with Norrell, and Byron with practically everybody.[3]

When he had finished reading his letters, Mr Murray thought he would go downstairs to the bookshop. He had printed a very large number of copies of Jonathan Strange's book and he was anxious to know how it was selling. The shop was kept by a man called Shackleton who looked exactly as you would wish a bookseller to look. He would never have done for any other sort of shopman – certainly not for a haberdasher or milliner who must be smarter than his customers – but for a bookseller he was perfect. He appeared to be of no particular age. He was thin and dusty and spotted finely all over with ink. He had an air of learning tinged with abstraction. His nose was adorned with spectacles; there was a quill pen stuck behind his ear and a half-unravelled wig upon his head.

"Shackleton, how many of Mr Strange's book have we sold today?" demanded Mr Murray.

"Sixty or seventy copies, I should think."

"Excellent!" said Mr Murray.

Shackleton frowned and pushed his spectacles further up his nose. "Yes, you would think so, would you not?"

"What do you mean?"

---

[3] Despite the seeming lack of sympathy between the two men, something about Strange must have impressed Byron. His next poem, *Manfred*, begun in September or October of the same year, was about a magician. Certainly Manfred does not greatly resemble Jonathan Strange (or at least not the respectable Strange whom Byron so disliked). He much more resembles Byron with his self-obsession, his self-loathing, his lofty disdain for his fellow men, his hints of impossible tragedies and his mysterious longings. Nevertheless Manfred is a magician who passes his time in summoning up spirits of the air, earth, water and fire to talk to him. It was as if Byron, having met a magician who disappointed him, created one more to his liking.

Shackleton took the pen from behind his ear "A great many people have come twice and bought a copy both times."

"Even better! At this rate we shall overtake Lord Byron's *Corsair*! At this rate we shall need a second printing by the end of next week!" Then, observing that Shackleton's frown did not grow any less, Mr Murray added, "Well, what is wrong with that? I dare say they want them as presents for their friends."

Shackleton shook his head so that all the loose hairs of his wig jiggled about. "It is queer. I have never known it happen before."

The shop door opened and a young man entered. He was small in stature and slight in build. His features were regular and, truth to tell, he would have been quite handsome had it not been for his rather unfortunate manner. He was one of those people whose ideas are too lively to be confined in their brains and spill out into the world to the consternation of passers-by. He talked to himself and the expression of his face changed constantly. Within the space of a single moment he looked surprized, insulted, resolute and angry – emotions which were presumably the consequences of the energetic conversations he was holding with the ideal people inside his head.

Shops, particularly London shops, are often troubled with lunatics and Mr Murray and Shackleton were immediately upon their guard. Nor were their suspicions at all allayed when the young man fixed Shackleton with a piercing look of his bright blue eyes and cried, "This is treating your customers well! This is gentility!" He turned to Mr Murray and addressed him thus, "Be advised by me, sir! Do not buy your books here. They are liars and thieves!"

"Liars and thieves?" said Mr Murray. "No, you are mistaken, sir. I am sure we can convince you that you are."

"Ha!" cried the young man and gave Mr Murray a shrewd look to shew he had now understood that Mr Murray was not, as he had first supposed, a fellow customer.

"I am the proprietor," explained Mr Murray hurriedly. "We

do not rob people here. Tell me what the matter is and I will be glad to serve you in any way I can. I am quite sure it is all a misunderstanding."

But the young man was not in the least mollified by Mr Murray's polite words. He cried, "Do you deny, sir, that this establishment employs a rascally cheat of magician – a magician called Strange?"

Mr Murray began to say something of Strange being one of his authors, but the young man could not wait to hear him. "Do you deny, sir, that Mr Strange has put a spell upon his books to make them disappear so that a man must buy another? And then another!" He wagged a finger at Shackleton and looked sly. "You are going to say you don't remember me!"

"No, sir, I am not. I remember you very well. You were one of the first gentlemen to buy a copy of *The History and Practice of English Magic* and then you came back about a week later for another."

The young man opened his eyes very wide. "I was obliged to buy another!" he cried indignantly. "The first one disappeared!"

"Disappeared?" asked Mr Murray, puzzled. "If you have lost your book, Mr . . . er, then I am sorry for it, but I do not quite understand how any blame can attach to the bookseller."

"My name, sir, is Green. And I did not lose my book. It disappeared. Twice." Mr Green sighed deeply, as a man will who finds he has to deal with fools and feeble-minded idiots. "I took the first book home," he explained, "and I placed it upon the table, on top of a box in which I keep my razors and shaving things." Mr Green mimed putting the book on top of the box. "I put the newspaper on top of the book and my brass candlestick and an egg on top of that."

"An egg?" said Mr Murray.

"A hard-boiled egg! But when I turned around – not ten minutes later! – the newspaper was directly on top of the box and the book was gone! Yet the egg and the candlestick were just where they had always been. So a week later I came back and bought another copy – just as your shopman says. I took it home. I put it on the mantelpiece with *Cooper's Dictionary of Practical Surgery* and stood the teapot on top. But it so happened that when I made the tea I dislodged both books and they fell into the basket where the dirty washing is put. On Monday, Jack Boot – my servant – put the dirty linen into the basket. On Tuesday the washerwoman came to take the dirty linen away, but when the bedsheets were lifted away, *Cooper's Dictionary of Practical Surgery* was there at the bottom of the basket but *The History and Practice of English Magic* was gone!"

These speeches, suggesting some slight eccentricities in the regulation of Mr Green's household, seemed to offer hope of an explanation.

"Could you not have mistook the place where you put it?" offered Mr Shackleton.

"Perhaps the laundress took it away with your sheets?" suggested Mr Murray.

"No, no!" declared Mr Green.

"Could someone have borrowed it? Or moved it?" suggested Shackleton.

Mr Green looked amazed at this suggestion. "Who?" he demanded.

"I . . . I have no idea. Mrs Green? Your servant?"

"There is no Mrs Green! I live alone! Except for Jack Boot and Jack Boot cannot read!"

"A friend, then?"

Mr Green seemed about to deny that he had ever had any friends.

Mr Murray sighed. "Shackleton, give Mr Green another copy and his money for the second book." To Mr Green he said, "I am glad you like it so well to buy another copy."

"Like it!" cried Mr Green, more astonished than ever. "I have not the least idea whether I like it or not! I never had a chance to open it."

After he had gone, Mr Murray lingered in the shop a while

making jokes about linen-baskets and hard-boiled eggs, but Mr Shackleton (who was generally as fond of a joke as any one) refused to be entertained. He looked thoughtful and anxious and insisted several times that there was something queer going on.

Half an hour later Mr Murray was in his room upstairs gazing at his bookcase. He looked up and saw Shackleton.

"He is back," said Shackleton.

"What?"

"Green. He has lost his book again. He had it in his right-hand pocket, but by the time he reached Great Pulteney-street it was gone. Of course I told him that London is full of thieves, but you must admit . . ."

"Yes, yes! Never mind that now!" interrupted Mr Murray. "My own copy is gone! Look! I put it here, between d'Israeli's *Flim-Flams* and Miss Austen's *Emma*. You can see the space where it stood. What is happening, Shackleton?"

"Magic," said Shackleton, firmly. "I have been thinking about it and I believe Green is right. There is some sort of spell operating upon the books, and upon us."

"A spell!" Mr Murray opened his eyes wide. "Yes, I suppose it must be. I have never experienced magic at first hand before. I do not think that I shall be in any great hurry to do so again. It is most eerie and unpleasant. How in the world is a man to know what to do when nothing behaves as it should?"

"Well," said Shackleton, "if I were you I would begin by consulting with the other booksellers and discover if their books are disappearing too, then at least we will know if the problem is a general one or confined to us."

This seemed like good advice. So leaving the shop in charge of the office-boy, Mr Murray and Shackleton put on their hats and went out into the wind and rain. The nearest bookseller was Edwards and Skittering in Piccadilly. When they got there they were obliged to step aside to make way for a footman in blue livery. He was carrying a large pile of books out of the shop.

Mr Murray had scarcely time to think that both footman and livery looked familiar before the man was gone.

Inside they found Mr Edwards deep in conversation with John Childermass. As Murray and Shackleton came in, Mr Edwards looked round with a guilty expression, but Childermass was just as usual. "Ah, Mr Murray!" he said. "I am glad to see you, sir. This spares me a walk in the rain."

"What is happening?" demanded Mr Murray. "What are you doing?"

"Doing? Mr Norrell is purchasing some books. That is all."

"Ha! If your master means to suppress Mr Strange's book by buying up all the copies, then he will be disappointed. Mr Norrell is a rich man but he must come to the end of his fortune at last and I can print books as fast as he can buy them."

"No,' said Childermass. "You can't."

Mr Murray turned to Mr Edwards. "Robert, Robert! Why do you let them tyrannize over you in this fashion?"

Poor Mr Edwards looked most unhappy. "I am sorry, Mr Murray, but the books were all disappearing. I have had to give more than thirty people their money back. I stood to lose a great deal. But now Mr Norrell has offered to buy up my entire stock of Strange's book and pay me a fair price for them, and so I . . ."

"Fair?" cried Shackleton, quite unable to bear this. "Fair? What is fair about it, I should like to know? Who do you suppose is making the books disappear in the first place?"

"Quite!" agreed Mr Murray. Turning to Childermass, he said, "You will not attempt to deny that all this is Norrell's doing?"

"No, no. Upon the contrary Mr Norrell is eager to declare himself responsible. He has a whole list of reasons and will be glad to tell them to any one who will listen."

"And what are these reasons?" asked Mr Murray, coldly.

"Oh, the usual sort of thing, I expect," said Childermass, looking, for the first time, slightly evasive. "A letter is being prepared which tells you all about it."

"And you think that will satisfy me, do you? A letter of apology?"

"Apology? I doubt you will get much in the way of an apology."

"I intend to speak to my attorney," said Mr Murray, "this very afternoon."

"Of course you do. We should not expect any thing less. But be that as it may, it is not Mr Norrell's intention that you should lose money by this. As soon as you are able to give me an account of all that you have spent in the publication of Mr Strange's book, I am authorized to give you a banker's draft for the full amount."

This was unexpected. Mr Murray was torn between his desire to return Childermass a very rude answer and his consciousness that Norrell was depriving him of a great deal of money and ought in fairness to pay him.

Shackleton poked Mr Murray discreetly in the arm to warn him not to do any thing rash.

"What of my profit?" asked Mr Murray, trying to gain a little time.

"Oh, you wish that to be taken into consideration, do you? That is only fair, I suppose. Let me speak to Mr Norrell." With that Childermass bowed and walked out of the shop.

There was no reason for Mr Murray and Shackleton to remain any longer. As soon as they were out in the street again, Mr Murray turned to Shackleton and said, "Go down to Thames-street . . ." (This was the warehouse where Mr Murray kept his stock.) ". . . and find out if any of Mr Strange's books are left. Do not allow Jackson to put you off with a short answer. Make him shew them to you. Tell him I need him to count them and that he must send me the reckoning within the hour."

When Mr Murray arrived back at Albermarle-street he found three young men loitering in his shop. They shut up their books the moment they saw him, surrounded him in an instant and began talking at once. Mr Murray naturally supposed that they must have come upon the same errand as Mr Green. As two of them were very tall and all of them were loud and indignant, he became rather nervous and signalled to the office-boy to run and fetch help. The office-boy stayed exactly where he was and watched the proceedings with an expression of unwonted interest upon his face.

Some rather violent exclamations from the young men such as, "Desperate villain!" and "Abominable scoundrel!" did little to reassure Mr Murray, but after a few moments he began to understand that it was not he whom they were abusing, but Norrell.

"I beg your pardon, gentlemen," he said, "but if it is not too much trouble, I wonder if you would do me the kindness of informing me who you are?"

The young men were surprized. They had supposed they were better known than that. They introduced themselves. They were Strange's three pupils-in-waiting, Henry Purfois, William Hadley-Bright and Tom Levy.

William Hadley-Bright and Henry Purfois were both tall and handsome, while Tom Levy was a small, slight figure with dark hair and eyes. As has already been noted, Hadley-Bright and Purfois were well-born English gentlemen, while Tom was an ex-dancing-master whose forefathers had all been Hebrew. Happily Hadley-Bright and Purfois took very little notice of such distinctions of rank and ancestry. Knowing Tom to be the most talented amongst them, they generally deferred to him in all matters of magical scholarship, and, apart from calling him by his given name (while he addressed them as Mr Purfois and Mr Hadley-Bright) and expecting him to pick up books they left behind them, they were very much inclined to treat him as an equal.

"We cannot sit about doing nothing while this villain, this monster destroys Mr Strange's great work!" declared Henry Purfois. "Give us something to do, Mr Murray! That is all we ask!"

"And if that something could involve running Mr Norrell through with a very sharp sabre, then so much the better," added William Hadley-Bright.

"Can one of you go after Strange and bring him back?" asked Mr Murray.

"Oh, certainly! Hadley-Bright is your man for that!" declared Henry Purfois. "He was one of the Duke's *aides-de-camp* at Waterloo, you know. There is nothing he likes better than dashing about on a horse at impossible speeds."

"Do you know where Mr Strange has gone?" asked Tom Levy.

"Two weeks ago he was in Geneva," said Mr Murray. "I had a letter from him this morning. He may be still there. Or he may have gone on to Italy."

The door opened and Shackleton walked in, his wig hung with drops of rain as if he had decorated it with innumerable glass beads. "All is well," he said eagerly to Mr Murray. "The books are still in their bales."

"You saw them with your own eyes?"

"Yes, indeed. I dare say it takes a good deal of magic to make ten thousand books disappear."

"I wish I could be so sanguine," said Tom Levy. "Forgive me, Mr Murray, but from all I ever heard of Mr Norrell once he has set himself a task he works tirelessly at it until it is accomplished. I do not believe we have time to wait for Mr Strange to come back."

Shackleton looked surprized to hear any one pronounce with such confidence upon magical matters.

Mr Murray hastily introduced Strange's three pupils. "How much time do you think we have?" he asked Tom.

"A day? Two at the most? Certainly not enough time to find Mr Strange and bring him back. I think, Mr Murray, that you must put this into our hands and we must try a spell or two to counteract Norrell's magic."

"Are there such spells?" asked Mr Murray, eyeing the novice-magicians doubtfully.

"Oh, hundreds!" said Henry Purfois.

"Do you know any of them?" asked Mr Murray.

"We know *of* them," said William Hadley-Bright. "We could probably put a fairly decent one together. What an excellent thing it would be if Mr Strange came back from the Continent and we had saved his book! That would rather make him open his eyes, I think!"

"What about Pale's Invisible What-D'ye-Call-It and Thingumajig?" asked Henry Purfois.

"I know what you mean," said William Hadley-Bright.

"A really remarkable procedure of Dr Pale's," Henry Purfois informed Mr Murray. "It turns a spell around and inflicts it upon its maker. Mr Norrell's own books would go blank or disappear! Which is, after all, no more than he deserves."

"I am not sure Mr Strange would be so delighted if he came back and found we had destroyed England's foremost magical library," said Tom. "Besides in order to perform Pale's Invisible Reflection and Protection we would have to construct a Quiliphon."

"A what?" said Mr Murray.

"A Quiliphon," said William Hadley-Bright. "Dr Pale's works are full of such machines for doing magic. I believe that in appearance it is something between a trumpet and a toasting fork . . ."

". . . and there are four metal globes on top that go round and round," added Henry Purfois.

"I see," said Mr Murray.

"Building a Quiliphon would take too long," said Tom, firmly. "I suggest we turn our attention to De Chepe's Prophylaxis.[4] That

---

[4] Walter De Chepe was an early thirteenth-century London magician. His procedure, Prophylaxis, protects a person, city or object from magic spells. Supposedly it closely follows a piece of fairy magic. It is reputed to be very strong. Indeed the only problem with this spell is its remarkable efficacy. Sometimes objects become impervious to human or fairy agency of any sort whether magical or not. Thus if Strange's students had succeeded in casting the spell over one of Strange's books, it is quite possible that no one would have been able to pick up the book or turn its pages.

In 1280 the citizens of Bristol ordered the town's magicians to cast de Chepe's Prophylaxis over the whole town to protect it from the magic spells of its enemies. Unfortunately so successful was the magic that everyone in the town, all the animals and all the ships in the harbour became living statues. No one could move; water stopped flowing within the boundaries; even the flames in the hearth were frozen. Bristol remained like this for a whole month until John Uskglass came from his house in Newcastle to put matters right.

is very quick to implement and, correctly done, should hold off Norrell's magic for a while – long enough to get a message to Mr Strange."

Just then the door opened and an untidy-looking fellow in a leather apron entered the shop. He was somewhat discomfited to find the eyes of all the room upon him. He made a little bobbing bow, handed a piece of paper to Shackleton and quickly made his escape.

"What is it, Shackleton?" asked Mr Murray.

"A message from Thames-street. They have looked inside the books. They are all blank – not a word left upon any of the pages. I am sorry, Mr Murray, but *The History and Practice of English Magic* is gone."

William Hadley-Bright stuck his hands in his pockets and gave a low whistle.

As the hours progressed it became clear that not a single copy of Strange's book remained in circulation. William Hadley-Bright and Henry Purfois were all for calling Mr Norrell out, until it was represented to them that Mr Norrell was an elderly gentleman who rarely took exercise and had never been seen with a sword or a pistol in his hand. There were no circumstances under which it would be fair or honourable for two men in the prime of life (one of them a soldier) to challenge him to a duel. Hadley-Bright and Purfois accepted this with a good grace, but Purfois could not help looking hopefully about the room for a person of equal decrepitude to Mr Norrell. He gazed speculatively at Shackleton.

Other friends of Strange appeared to condole with Mr Murray and give vent to some of the fury they felt at what Mr Norrell had done. Lord Portishead arrived and gave an account of the letter he had sent to Mr Norrell breaking off their friendship and the letter he had sent to Lascelles resigning as editor of *The Friends of English Magic* and cancelling his subscription.

"Henceforth, gentlemen," he told Strange's pupils, "I consider myself as belonging solely to your party."

Strange's pupils assured his lordship he had done the right thing and would never regret it.

At seven o'clock Childermass arrived. He walked into the crowded room with as much composure as if he were walking into church. "Well, how much have you lost, Mr Murray?" he asked. He took out his memorandum book and picked up a quill from Mr Murray's desk and dipped it in the ink.

"Put your book away again, Mr Childermass," said Mr Murray. "I do not want your money."

"Indeed? Be careful, sir, how you let these gentlemen influence you. Some of them are young and have no responsibilities . . ." Childermass gave a cool glance to Strange's three pupils and to the several officers in uniform who stood about the room. "And others are rich and a hundred pounds more or less is nothing to them." Childermass looked at Lord Portishead. "But you, Mr Murray, are a man of business and business ought to be your first consideration."

"Ha!" Mr Murray crossed his arms and looked triumphantly at Childermass with his one good eye. "You think I am in desperate need of the money – but, you see, I am not. Offers of loans from Mr Strange's friends have been arriving all evening. I believe I might set up a whole new business if I chose! But I desire you will take a message to Mr Norrell. It is this. He will pay in the end – but upon our terms, not his. We intend to make him pay for the new edition. He shall pay for the advertisements for his rival's book. That will give him greater pain than any thing else could, I believe."

"Oh, indeed! If it ever happens," said Childermass, drily. He turned towards the door. Then he paused and, staring for a moment at the carpet, seemed to debate something within himself. "I will tell you this," he said. "The book is not destroyed however it may seem at present. I have dealt my cards and asked them if there are any copies left. It seems that two remain. Strange has one and Norrell the other."

* * *

For the next month London talked of little else but the astonishing thing that Mr Norrell had done, but as to whether it were the wickedness of Strange's book or the spitefulness of Mr Norrell which was most to blame, London was divided. People who had bought copies were furious at the loss of their books and Mr Norrell did not help matters by sending his servants to their houses with a guinea (the cost of the book) and the letter in which he explained his reasons for making their books disappear. A great many people found themselves more insulted than ever and some of them immediately summoned their attorneys to begin proceedings against Mr Norrell.[5]

In September the Ministers returned from the country to London and naturally Mr Norrell's extraordinary actions formed one of the main topics of conversation at their first meeting.

"When we first employed Mr Norrell to do magic on our behalf," said one, "we had no idea of permitting him to intrude his spells into people's houses and alter their possessions. In some ways it is a pity that we do not have that magical court he is always proposing. What is it called?"

---

[5] The letter contained two implications which were considered particularly offensive: first, that the purchasers were not clever enough to understand Strange's book; and second, that they did not possess the moral judgement to decide for themselves if the magic Strange was describing was good or wicked.

The Norrellites had fully expected that the destruction of Strange's book would be controversial and they were prepared to receive a great deal of criticism, however the harm done to their own cause by the letter was entirely unintentional. Mr Norrell had been supposed to shew the letter to Mr Lascelles before it was sent out. If Lascelles had seen it, then the language and expressions would have undergone considerable modification and presumably have been less offensive to the recipients.

Unfortunately, there was a misunderstanding. Mr Norrell asked Childermass if Lascelles had made his amendments. Childermass thought they were speaking of an article for *The Friends of English Magic* and said that he had. And so the letter went out uncorrected. Lascelles was furious and accused Childermass of having purposely encouraged Mr Norrell to damage his own cause. Childermass vehemently denied doing any such thing.

From this time on relations between Lascelles and Childermass (never good) worsened rapidly and soon Lascelles was hinting to Mr Norrell that Childermass had Strangite sympathies and was secretly working to betray his master.

"The Cinque Dragownes," said Sir Walter Pole.

"I presume he must be guilty of some magical crime or other?"

"Oh, certainly! But I have not the least idea what. John Childermass probably knows, but I very much doubt that he would tell us."

"It does not matter. There are several suits against him in the common courts for theft."

"Theft!" said another Minister in surprise. "I find it very shocking that a man who has done the country such service should be prosecuted for such a low crime!"

"Why?" asked the first. "He has brought it upon himself."

"The problem is," said Sir Walter, "that the moment he is asked to defend himself he will respond by saying something about the nature of English magic. And no one is competent to argue that subject except Strange. I think we must be patient. I think we must wait until Strange comes back."

"Which raises another question," said another Minister. "There are only two magicians in England. How can we decide between them? Who can say which of them is right and which is wrong?"

The Ministers looked at each other in perplexity.

Only Lord Liverpool, the Prime Minister, was unperturbed. "We will know them as we know other men," he declared, "by the fruits that they bear."[6]

There was a pause for the Ministers to reflect that the fruits Mr Norrell was currently bearing were not very promising: arrogance, theft and malice.

It was agreed that the Home Secretary should speak to Mr Lascelles privately and ask that he would convey to Mr Norrell the extreme displeasure of the Prime Minister and all the Ministers at what Mr Norrell had done.

There seemed no more to be said, but the Ministers were unable to leave the subject without indulging in a little gossip. They had

---

[6] "Wherefore by their fruits ye shall know them." St Matthew, 7,16.

all heard how Lord Portishead had severed himself from Mr Norrell. But Sir Walter was able to tell them how Childermass – who up to this moment had seemed like his master's shadow – had distanced himself from Mr Norrell's interests and spoken to Strange's assembled friends as an independent person, assuring them that the book was not destroyed. Sir Walter sighed deeply. "I cannot help thinking that in many ways this is a worse sign than all the rest. Norrell never was a good judge of men, and now the best of his friends are deserting him – Strange is gone, John Murray and now Portishead. If Childermass and Norrell quarrel there will only be Henry Lascelles left."

Strange's friends all sat down that evening and wrote him letters full of indignation. The letters would take two weeks to reach Italy, but Strange moved about so much that it might be another two weeks before they found him. At first Strange's friends felt confident that the instant he read them he would immediately set out for England in a blaze of anger, ready to contend with Norrell in the courts and the newspapers. But in September they received news which made them think that perhaps they would have to wait a while after all.

As long as Strange had been travelling towards Italy he had seemed generally to be in good spirits. His letters had been full of cheerful nonsense. But as soon as he arrived there his mood changed. For the first time since Arabella's death he had no work to do and nothing to distract him from his widowed state. Nothing he saw pleased him and for some weeks it seemed that he could only find any relief for his misery in continual change of scene.[7] In

---

[7] ". . . I cannot tell you any thing of Piacenza," Strange wrote to Henry Woodhope, "as I did not stay long enough to see it. I arrived in the evening. After dinner I thought I would walk about for a half hour, but on entering the main piazza, I was immediately struck by a tall urn standing upon a pedestal with its long, black shadow trailing upon the stones. Two or three strands of ivy or some other creeping plant emerged from the neck of the urn but they were quite dead. I cannot say why, but this seemed to me so deeply melancholy that I could not bear it. It was like an allegory of loss, death and misery. I returned to the inn, went immediately to bed and in the morning left for Turin."

early September he reached Genoa. Liking this place a little better than other Italian towns he had seen, he stayed almost a week. During this time an English family arrived at the hotel where he was staying. Though he had previously declared to Sir Walter his intention of avoiding the society of Englishmen while he was abroad, Strange struck up an acquaintance with this family. In no time at all he was writing letters back to England full of praise for the manners, cleverness and kindness of the Greysteels. At the end of the week he travelled to Bologna, but finding no pleasure there he very soon returned to Genoa to remain with the Greysteels until the end of the month when they all planned to travel together to Venice.

Naturally, Strange's friends were very glad that he had found some agreeable company, but what intrigued them most were several references in Strange's letters to the daughter of the family, who was young and unmarried and in whose society Strange seemed to take a particular pleasure. The same interesting idea occurred to several of his friends at once: what if he were to marry again? A pretty young wife would cure his gloomy spirits better than any thing else could, and best of all she would distract him from that dark, unsettling magic he seemed so set upon.

There were more thorns in Mr Norrell's side than Strange. A gentleman called Knight had begun a school for magicians in Henrietta-street in Covent-garden. Mr Knight was not a practical magician, nor did he pretend to be. His advertisement offered young gentlemen: "a thorough Education in Theoretical Magic and English Magical History upon the same principles which guided our Foremost Magician, Mr Norrell, in teaching his Illustrious Pupil, Jonathan Strange." Mr Lascelles had written Mr Knight an angry letter in which he declared that Mr Knight's school could not possibly be based upon the principles mentioned since these were known only to Mr Norrell and Mr Strange. Lascelles threatened Mr Knight with exposure as a fraud if he did not immediately dismantle his school.

Mr Knight had written a polite letter back in which he begged to differ. He said that, upon the contrary, Mr Norrell's system of education was well known. He directed Mr Lascelles's attention to page 47 of *The Friends of English Magic* from the Autumn of 1810 in which Lord Portishead had declared that the only basis for training up more magicians approved by Mr Norrell was that devised by Francis Sutton-Grove. Mr Knight (who declared himself a sincere admirer of Mr Norrell's) had bought a copy of Sutton-Grove's *De Generibus Artium Magicarum Anglorum* and studied it. He took the opportunity to wonder whether Mr Norrell would do him the honour of becoming the school's Visiting Tutor and giving lectures and so forth. He had intended to tutor four young men, but he had been so overpowered by applications that he had been obliged to rent another house to accommodate them and hire more teachers to teach them. Other schools were being proposed in Bath, Chester and Newcastle.

Almost worse than the schools were the shops. Several establishments in London had begun to sell magical philtres, magic mirrors and silver basins which, the manufacturers claimed, had been specially constructed for seeing visions in. Mr Norrell had done what he could to halt the trade, with diatribes against them in *The Friends of English Magic*. He had persuaded the editors of all the other magical publications over which he had any influence to publish articles explaining that there never ever had been any such thing as magical mirrors, and that the magic performed by magicians using mirrors (which were in any case only a few sorts and hardly any that Mr Norrell approved) were performed using ordinary mirrors. Nevertheless the magical articles continued to sell out as fast as the shopkeepers could put them on the shelves and some shopkeepers were considering whether they ought not to give up their other business and devote their whole shop to magical accoutrements.

51

A family by the name of Greysteel

October to November 1816

Campo Santa Maria Zobenigo, Venice
Jonathan Strange to Sir Walter Pole   Oct. 16th, 1816.

We left *terra firma* at Mestre. There were two gondolas. Miss Greysteel and her aunt were to go in one, and the doctor and I were to go in the other. But whether there was some obscurity in my Italian when I explained it to the *gondolieri* or whether the distribution of Miss Greysteel's boxes and trunks dictated another arrangement I do not know, but matters did not fall out as we had planned. The first gondola glided out across the lagoon with all the Greysteels inside it, while I still stood upon the shore. Dr Greysteel stuck his head out and roared his apologies, like the good fellow that he is, before his sister – who I think is a little nervous of the water – pulled him back in again. It was the most trivial incident yet somehow it unnerved me and for some moments afterwards I was prey to the most morbid fears and imaginings. I looked at my gondola. Much has been said, I know, about the funereal appearance of these contraptions – which are something between a coffin and a boat. But I was struck by quite another idea. I thought how much they resembled the black-painted, black-curtained conjuring boxes of my childhood – the sort of boxes into which quack-sorcerers would put country people's handkerchiefs and coins and lockets. Sometimes these articles could never be got back – for which the sorcerer was always very sorry – "but fairy-spirits, Sir, is very giddy, wexatious creatures." And all the nursemaids and kitchenmaids I ever knew when I was a child, always had an aunt, who knew a woman, whose first cousin's boy had been put into just such a box, and had never been seen again. Standing on the quayside at Mestre I had a horrible notion that when the Greysteels got to Venice they would open up the gondola that should have conveyed me there and find nothing inside. This idea took hold of me so strongly that for some minutes I forgot to think of any thing else and there were actual tears standing in my eyes – which I think may serve to shew how nervous I have become. It is quite ridiculous for a man to begin to be afraid that he is about to disappear. It was towards evening and our two gondolas were as black as night and quite as melancholy. Yet the sky was the coldest, palest blue imaginable. There was no wind or hardly any, and the sea was nothing but the sky's mirror. There were immeasurable spaces of still cold light above us and immeasurable spaces of still cold light beneath. But the city ahead of us received no illumination either from sky or lagoon, and appeared like a vast collection of shadow-towers and shadow-pinnacles, all pierced with tiny lights and set upon the shining water. As we entered Venice the water became crowded with scraps and rubbish – splinters of wood and hay, orange peels and cabbage stalks. I looked down and saw a ghostly hand for a moment – it was only a moment – but I quite believed that there was a woman beneath the dirty water, trying to find her way back to the light. Of course it was only a white glove, but the fright, while it lasted, was very great. But you are not to worry about me. I am very well occupied, working on the second volume of *The History and Practice* and when I am not working I am generally with the Greysteels, who are just such a set of people as you yourself would like – cheerful, independent, and well-informed. I confess to being a little fretful that I have heard nothing as yet of how the first volume was received. I am tolerably certain of its being a great triumph – I *know* that when he read it, N. fell down on the floor in a jealous fit and foamed at the mouth – but I cannot help wishing that someone would write and tell me so.

Campo Santa Maria Zobenigo, Venice
Jonathan Strange to John Murray   Oct. 27th, 1816.

. . . from eight separate persons of what Norrell has done. Oh, I *could* be angry. I *could*, I dare say, wear out both my pen and myself in a long tirade – but to what end? I do not *chuse* to be governed any longer by this impudent little man. I shall return to London in the early spring, as I planned, and we shall have a new edition. We shall have lawyers. I have my friends, just as he has his. Let him say in court (if he dares) why he thinks that Englishmen have become children and may not know the things that their forefathers knew. And if he dares to use magic against me again, then we shall have some counter-magic and then we shall finally see who is the Greatest Magician of the Age. And I think, Mr Murray, that you will be best advised to print a great many more copies than before – this has been one of Norrell's most notorious acts of magic and I am sure that people will like to see the book that forced him to it. By the by when you print the new edition we shall have corrections – there are some horrible blunders. Chapters six and forty-two are particularly bad . . .

Harley-street, London
Sir Walter Pole to Jonathan Strange   Oct. 1st, 1816.

. . . a bookseller in St Paul's Churchyard, Titus Watkins, has printed up a very nonsensical book and is selling it as Strange's lost *History and Practice of English Magic*. Lord Portishead says some of it is copied out of Absalom[1] and some of it is nonsense. Portishead wonders which you will find the most insulting – the Absalom part or the nonsense. Like a good fellow, Portishead contradicts this imposition wherever he goes, but a great many people have already been taken in and Watkins has certainly made money. I am glad you like Miss Greysteel so much . . .

Campo Santa Maria Zobenigo, Venice
Jonathan Strange to John Murray Nov. 16th., 1816.

My dear Murray,
You will be pleased, I think, to hear that some good at least has come from the destruction of *The History and Practice of English Magic* – I have made up my quarrel with Lord Byron. His lordship knows nothing of the great controversies which are rending English magic in two and frankly cares less. But he has the greatest respect for books. He informs me that he is constantly on guard lest your over-cautious pen, Mr Murray, should alter some of his own poems and render some of the more *surprizing* words a little more respectable. When he heard that a whole book had been magicked out of existence by the author's enemy, his indignation was scarcely to be described. He sent me a long letter, vilifying Norrell in the liveliest terms. Of all the letters I received upon that sad occasion, this is my favourite. No Englishman alive can equal his lordship for an insult. He arrived in Venice about a week ago and we met at Florian's.[2] I confess to being a little anxious lest he should bring that insolent young person, Mrs Clairmont, but happily she was nowhere to beseen. Apparently he dismissed her some time ago. Our new friendly relations have been sealed by the discovery that we share a fondness for billiards; I play when I am thinking about magic and he plays when he is hatching his poems . . .

---

[1] *The Tree of Learning* by Gregory Absalom (1507–99)
[2] A famous café on the San Marco Piazza.

The sunlight was as cold and clear as the note struck by a knife on a fine wine-glass. In such a light the walls of the Church of Santa Maria Formosa were as white as shells or bones – and the shadows on the paving stones were as blue as the sea.

The door to the church opened and a little party came out into the campo. These ladies and gentlemen were visitors to the city of Venice who had been looking at the interior of the church, its altars and objects of interest, and now that they had got out of it, they were inclined to be talkative and filled up the water-lapped silence of the place with loud, cheerful conversation. They were excessively pleased with the Campo Santa Maria Formosa. They thought the façades of the houses very magnificent – they could not praise them highly enough. But the sad decay, which build-ings, bridges and church all displayed, seemed to charm them even more. They were Englishmen and, to them, the decline of other nations was the most natural thing in the world. They belonged to a race blessed with so sensitive an appreciation of its own talents (and so doubtful an opinion of any body else's) that they would not have been at all surprised to learn that the Venetians them-selves had been entirely ignorant of the merits of their own city – until Englishmen had come to tell them it was delightful.

One lady, having got to the end of her raptures, began to speak of the weather to the other lady.

"You know, it is a very odd thing, my dear, but when we were in the church, while you and Mr Strange were looking at the pictures, I just popped my head out of the door and I thought then that it was raining and I was very much afraid that you would get wet."

"No, aunt. See, the stones are perfectly dry. There is not a spot of rain upon them."

"Well then, my dear, I hope that you are not inconvenienced by this wind. It is a little sharp about the ears. We can always ask Mr Strange and papa to walk a little faster if you do not like it."

"Thank you, aunt, but I am perfectly comfortable. I like this breeze – I like the smell of the sea – it clears the brain, the senses – every thing. But perhaps, aunt, *you* do not like it."

"Oh no, my dear. I never mind any such thing. I am quite hardy. I only think of you."

"I know you do, aunt," said the young lady. The young lady was perhaps aware that the sunlight and breeze which shewed Venice to so much advantage, made its canals so blue and its marble so mystically bright, did as much – or almost as much – for her. Nothing could so well draw attention to the translucency of Miss Greysteel's complexion, as the rapid progression across it of sunlight and shadow. Nothing could be so becoming to her white muslin gown as the breeze which blew it about.

"Ah," said the aunt, "now papa is showing Mr Strange some new thing or other. Flora, my dear, would not you like to see?"

"I have seen enough. You go, aunt."

So the aunt hurried away to the other end of the campo and Miss Greysteel walked slowly on to the little white bridge that stood just by the church, fretfully poking the point of her white parasol between the white paving stones and murmuring to herself, "I have seen enough. Oh, I have seen *quite* enough!" The repetition of this mysterious exclamation did not appear to afford her spirits much relief – indeed it only served to make her more melancholy, and to make her sigh more frequently.

"You are very quiet today," said Strange suddenly. She was startled. She had not known he was so close by.

"Am I? I was not aware of it." But she then gave her attention to the view and was silent for several moments. Strange leant back against the bridge, folded his arms and looked very intently at her.

"Quiet," he repeated, "and a little sad, I think. And so, you know, I must talk to you."

This made her smile in spite of herself. "Must you?" she said. But then the very act of smiling and of speaking to him seemed to give her pain and so she sighed and looked away again.

"Indeed. Because, whenever *I* am melancholy you talk to me of cheerful things and cure my low spirits and so I must now do the same for *you*. That is what friendship is."

"Openness and honesty, Mr Strange. Those are the best foundations for friendship, I think."

"Oh! You think me secretive. I see by your face that you do. You may be right, but I . . . That is . . . No, I dare say you are right. It is not, I suppose, a profession that encourages . . ."

Miss Greysteel interrupted him. "I did not mean a fling at your profession. Not at all. All professions have their different sorts of discretion. *That*, I think, is quite understood."

"Then I do not understand you."

"It is no matter. We should rejoin my aunt and papa."

"No, wait, Miss Greysteel, it will not do. Who else will put me right, when I am going wrong, if not you? Tell me – whom do you think I deceive?"

Miss Greysteel was silent a moment and then, with some reluctance, said, "Your friend of last night, perhaps?"

"My friend of last night! What do you mean?"

Miss Greysteel looked very unhappy. "The young woman in the gondola who was so anxious to speak to you and so unwilling – for a full half hour – that any one else should."

"Ah!" Strange smiled and shook his head. "No, you have run away with a wrong idea. She is not my friend. She is Lord Byron's."

"Oh! . . ." Miss Greysteel reddened a little. "She seemed rather an agitated young person."

"She is not best pleased with his lordship's behaviour." Strange shrugged. "Who is? She wished to discover if I were able to influence his lordship and I was at some pains to persuade her that there is not now, nor ever was, I think, magic enough in England to do that."

"You are offended."

"Not in the least. Now I believe we are closer to that good understanding which you require for friendship. Will you shake hands with me?"

"With the greatest goodwill," she said.

"Flora? Mr Strange?" cried Dr Greysteel, striding up to them. "What is this?"

Miss Greysteel was a little confused. It was of the greatest importance to her that her aunt and father should have a good opinion of Mr Strange. She did not want them to know that she herself had suspected him of wrongdoing. She feigned not to have heard her father's question and began to speak energetically of some paintings in the Scuola di Giorgio degli Schiavoni that she had a great desire to see. "It is really no distance. We could go now. You will come with us, I hope?" she said to Strange.

Strange smiled ruefully at her. "I have work to do."

"Your book?" asked Dr Greysteel.

"Not today. I am working to uncover the magic which will bring forth a fairy-spirit to be my assistant. I have lost count of how many times I have tried – and how many ways. And never, of course, with the least success. But such is the predicament of the modern magician! Spells which were once taken for granted by every minor sorcerer in England are now so elusive that we despair of ever getting them back. Martin Pale had twenty-eight fairy servants. I would count myself fortunate to have one."

"Fairies!" exclaimed Aunt Greysteel. "But by all accounts they are very mischievous creatures! Are you quite certain, Mr Strange, that you really wish to burden yourself with such a troublesome companion?"

"My dear aunt!" said Miss Greysteel. "Mr Strange knows what he is doing."

But Aunt Greysteel was concerned and to illustrate her point she began to speak of a river that flowed through the village in Derbyshire where she and Dr Greysteel had grown up. It had been enchanted by fairies long ago and as a consequence had shrunk from a noble torrent to a gentle brook and, though this had happened centuries and centuries ago, the local population still remembered and resented it. They still talked of the workshops they might have set up and the industries they might have founded if only the river had been strong enough to supply the power.[3]

Strange listened politely and when she had finished he said, "Oh, to be sure! Fairies are naturally full of wickedness and exceedingly difficult to control. Were I successful, I should certainly have to take care whom my fairy – or fairies – associated with." He cast a glance at Miss Greysteel. "Nevertheless their power and knowledge are such that a magician cannot lightly dispense with their help – not unless he is Gilbert Norrell. Every fairy that ever drew breath has more magic in his head, hands and heart than could be contained in the greatest library of magical books that ever existed."[4]

"Has he indeed?" said Aunt Greysteel. "Well, that is remarkable."

Dr Greysteel and Aunt Greysteel wished Strange success with his magic and Miss Greysteel reminded him that he had promised to go with her one day soon to look at a pianoforte which they had heard was for hire from an antiquarian who lived near the Campo San Angelo. Then the Greysteels went on to the rest of the day's pleasures while Strange returned to his lodgings near Santa Maria Zobenigo.

Most English gentlemen who come to Italy nowadays write poems or descriptions of their tour, or they make sketches. Italians

---

[3] Aunt Greysteel is probably speaking of the Derwent. Long ago, when John Uskglass was still a captive child in Faerie, a king in Faerie foretold that if he came to adulthood, then all the old fairy kingdoms would fall. The king sent his servants into England to bring back an iron knife to kill him. The knife was forged by a blacksmith on the banks of the Derwent and the waters of the Derwent were used to cool the hot metal. However, the attempt to kill John Uskglass failed and the king and his clan were destroyed by the boy-magician. When John Uskglass entered England and established his kingdom, his fairy-followers went in search of the blacksmith. They killed him and his family, destroyed his house and laid magic spells upon the Derwent to punish it for its part in making the wicked knife.

[4] The views Strange is expressing at this point are wildly optimistic and romantic. English magical literature is full of examples of fairies whose powers were weak or who were stupid or ignorant.

who wish to rent apartments to these gentlemen are well advised to provide them with rooms where they can pursue these occupations. Strange's landlord, for example, had set aside a shadowy little chamber at the top of his house for his tenant's use. It contained an ancient table with four carved gryphons to serve for its legs; there was a sea-captain's chair, a painted wooden cupboard such as one might find in a church and a wooden figure two or three feet tall, which stood upon a pillar. It represented a smiling man holding something round and red in his hand, which might have been an apple, might have been a pomegranate or might have been a red ball. It was difficult to imagine quite where this gentleman could have come from: he was a little too cheerful for a saint in a church and not quite comical enough for a coffee-house sign.

Strange had found the cupboard to be damp and full of mildew and so he had abandoned it and placed his books and papers in heaps about the floor. But he had made a sort of friend of the wooden figure and, as he worked, he constantly addressed remarks to it, such as, "What is your opinion?" and "Doncaster or Belasis? What do you suggest?"[5] and "Well? Do you see him? I do not,"

---

[5] Jacques Belasis was reputed to have created an excellent spell for summoning fairy-spirits. Unfortunately the only copy of Belasis's masterpiece, *The Instructions*, was at the library at Hurtfew and Strange had never seen it. All he knew of it were vague descriptions in later histories and so it must be assumed that Strange was re-creating this magic and had only the flimsiest notion of what he was aiming at.

By contrast, the spell commonly attributed to the Master of Doncaster is very well known and appears in a number of widely available works. The identity of the Master of Doncaster is not known. His existence is deduced from a handful of references in *Argentine* histories to thirteenth-century magicians acquiring spells and magic "from Doncaster". Moreover, it is far from clear that all the magic attributed to the Master of Doncaster is the work of one man. This has led magio-historians to postulate a second magician, even more shadowy than the first, the Pseudo-Master of Doncaster. If, as has been convincingly argued, the Master of Doncaster was really John Uskglass, then it is logical to assume that the spell of summoning was created by the Pseudo-Master. It seems highly unlikely that John Uskglass would have had any need of a spell to summon fairies. His court was, after all, full of them.

and once in tones of extreme exasperation, "Oh! Be quiet, will you?"

He took out a paper on which he had scribbled a spell. He moved his lips as magicians do when they are reciting magic words. When he had finished, he glanced about the room as though he half-expected to find another person there. But whomever it was that he hoped to see, he did not see them. He sighed, crumpled the spell into a ball and threw it at the little wooden figure. Then he took another sheet of paper – made some notes – consulted a book – retrieved the first piece of paper from the floor – smoothed it out – studied it for half an hour, pulling at his hair all the while – crumpled it up again and threw it out the window.

A bell had begun to toll somewhere. It was a sad and lonely sound which made the hearer think of wild forlorn places, dark skies and emptiness. Some of these ideas must have occurred to Strange because he became distracted and stopped what he was doing and glanced out of the window as though to reassure himself that Venice had not suddenly become an empty, silent ruin. But the scene outside was the usual one of bustle and animation. Sunlight shone on blue water. The campo was crowded with people: there were Venetian ladies coming to Santa Maria Zobenigo, Austrian soldiers strolling about arm-in-arm and looking at everything, shopkeepers trying to sell them things, urchins fighting and begging, cats going about their secret business.

Strange returned to his work. He took off his coat and rolled up the sleeve of his shirt. Next he left the room and returned with a knife and a small white basin. He used the knife to let some blood from his arm. He put the basin on the table and peered into it to see if he had got enough, but the loss of blood must have affected him more than he supposed because in a moment of faintness he knocked the table and the bowl fell upon the floor. He cursed in Italian (a good cursing language) and looked around for something to wipe up the blood.

It so happened that there was some white cloth lying bundled up on top of the table. It was a nightshirt which Arabella had sewn in the early years of their marriage. Without realizing what it was, Strange reached out for it. He had almost grasped it, when Stephen Black stept out of the shadows and handed him a rag. Stephen accompanied the action with that faint half-bow that is second nature to a well-trained servant. Strange took the rag and mopped up the blood (somewhat ineffectually), but of Stephen's presence in the room he appeared to know nothing at all. Stephen picked up the nightshirt, shook out the creases, carefully folded it up and placed it neatly on a stool in the corner.

Strange threw himself back into his chair, caught the damaged part of his arm upon the edge of the table, swore again and covered his face with his hands.

"What in the world is he trying to do?" asked Stephen Black in a hushed tone.

"Oh, he is attempting to summon me!" declared the gentleman with the thistle-down hair. "He wishes to ask me all sorts of questions about magic! But there is no need to whisper, my dear Stephen. He can neither see nor hear you. They are so ridiculous, these English magicians! They do everything in such a roundabout way. I tell you, Stephen, watching this fellow try to do magic is like watching a man sit down to eat his dinner with his coat on backwards, a blindfold round his eyes and a bucket over his head! When did you ever see *me* perform such nonsensical tricks? Draw forth my own blood or scribble words on paper? Whenever I wish to do something, I simply speak to the air – or to the stones – or to the sunlight – or the sea – or to whatever it is and politely request them to help me. And then, since my alliances with these powerful spirits were set in place thousands of years ago, they are only too glad to do whatever I ask."

"I see," said Stephen. "But, though the magician is ignorant, he has still succeeded. After all, you are here, sir, are you not?"

"Yes, I dare say," said the gentleman in an irritated tone. "But that does not detract from the fact that the magic that brought me here is clumsy and inelegant! Besides what does it profit him? Nothing! I do not chuse to shew myself to him and he knows no magic to counteract that. Stephen! Quick! Turn the pages of that book! There is no breeze in the room and it will perplex him beyond any thing. Ha! See how he stares! He half-suspects that we are here, but he cannot see us. Ha, ha! How angry he is becoming! Give his neck a sharp pinch! He will think it is a mosquito!"

52

The old lady of Cannaregio

End of November 1816

SOME TIME BEFORE he had left England Dr Greysteel had received a letter from a friend in Scotland, begging that, if he were to get as far as Venice, he would pay a visit to a certain old lady who lived there. It would be, said the Scottish friend, an act of charity, since this old lady, once rich, was now poor. Dr Greysteel thought he remembered hearing once that she was of some odd, mixed parentage – as it might be half-Scottish, half-Spanish or perhaps half-Irish, half-Hebrew.

Dr Greysteel had always intended to visit her, but what with inns and carriages, sudden removals and changes of plan, he had discovered, on arriving at Venice, that he could no longer lay his hand on the letter and no longer retained a very clear impression of its contents. Nor had he any note of her name – nothing but a little scrap of paper with the direction where she might be found.

Aunt Greysteel said that under such very difficult circumstances as these, they would do best to send the old lady a letter informing her of their intention to call upon her. Though, to be sure, she added, it would look very odd that they did not know her name – doubtless she would think them a sad, negligent sort of people. Dr Greysteel looked uncomfortable, and sniffed and fidgeted a good deal, but he could think of no better plan and so they wrote the note forthwith and gave it to their landlady, so that she might deliver it to the old lady straightaway.

Then came the first odd part of the business, for the landlady studied the direction, frowned and then – for reasons which Dr Greysteel did not entirely comprehend – sent it to her brother-in-law on the island of Giudecca.

Some days later this same brother-in-law – an elegant little Venetian lawyer – waited upon Dr Greysteel. He informed Dr Greysteel that he had sent the note, just as Dr Greysteel had requested, but Dr Greysteel should know that the lady lived in that part of the city which was called Cannaregio, in the Ghetto – where the Jews lived. The letter had been delivered into the hands of a venerable Hebrew gentleman. There had been no reply. How did Dr Greysteel wish to proceed? The little Venetian lawyer was happy to serve Dr Greysteel in any way he could.

In the late afternoon Miss Greysteel, Aunt Greysteel, Dr Greysteel and the lawyer (whose name was Signor Tosetti), glided through the city in a gondola – through that part of the city which is called St Mark's where they saw men and women preparing for the night's pleasures – past the landing of Santa Maria Zobenigo, where Miss Greysteel turned back to gaze at a little candlelit window, which might have belonged to Jonathan Strange – past the Rialto where Aunt Greysteel began to tut and sigh and wish very much that she saw more shoes upon the children's feet.

They left the gondola at the Ghetto Nuovo. Though all the houses of Venice are strange and old, those of the Ghetto seemed particularly so – as if queerness and ancientness were two of the commodities this mercantile people dealt in and they had constructed their houses out of them. Though all the streets of Venice are melancholy, these streets had a melancholy that was quite distinct – as if Jewish sadness and Gentile sadness were made up according to different recipes. Yet the houses were very plain and the door upon which Signor Tosetti knocked was black enough and humble enough to have done for any Quaker meeting-house in England.

The door was opened by a manservant who let them into the house and into a dark chamber panelled with dried-out, ancient-looking wood that smelt of nothing so much as the sea.

There was a door in this chamber that was open a little. From where he stood Dr Greysteel could see ancient, battered-looking books in thin leather bindings, silver candlesticks that had sprouted more branches than English candlesticks generally do, mysterious-looking boxes of polished wood – all of which Dr Greysteel took to be connected with the Hebrew gentleman's religion. Hung upon the wall was a doll or puppet as tall and broad as a man, with huge hands and feet, but dressed like a woman, with its head sunk upon its breast so that its face could not be seen.

The manservant went through this door to speak to his master. Dr Greysteel whispered to his sister that the servant was decent-looking enough. Yes, said Aunt Greysteel, except that he wore no coat. Aunt Greysteel said that she had often noticed that male servants were always liable to present themselves in their shirt-sleeves and that it was often the case that if their masters were single gentlemen then nothing would be done to correct this bad habit. Aunt Greysteel did not know why this should be. Aunt Greysteel supposed that the Hebrew gentleman was a widower.

"Oh!" said Dr Greysteel, peeping through the half-open door-way. "We have interrupted him at his dinner."

The venerable Hebrew gentleman wore a long, dusty black coat and had a great beard of curly grey and white hairs and a black skullcap on top of his head. He was seated at a long table upon which was laid a spotless white linen cloth and he had tucked a generous portion of this into the neck of his black robe to serve him as a napkin.

Aunt Greysteel was very shocked that Dr Greysteel should be spying through chinks in doorways and attempted to make him stop by poking at him with her umbrella. But Dr Greysteel had come to Italy to see everything he could and saw no reason to make an exception of Hebrew gentlemen in their private apartments.

This particular Hebrew gentleman did not seem inclined to interrupt his dinner to wait upon an unknown English family; he appeared to be instructing the manservant in what to say to them.

The servant came back and spoke to Signor Tosetti and when he had finished Signor Tosetti bowed low to Aunt Greysteel and explained that the name of the lady they sought was Delgado and that she lived at the very top of the house. Signor Tosetti was a little annoyed that none of the Hebrew gentleman's servants seemed willing to shew them the way and announce their arrival, but, as he said, their party was one of bold adventurers and doubtless they could find their way to the top of a staircase.

Dr Greysteel and Signor Tosetti took a candle each. The staircase wound up into the shadows. They passed many doors which, although rather grand, had a queer, stunted look about them – for in order to accommodate all the people, the houses in the Ghetto had been built as tall and with as many storeys as the householders had dared – and to compensate for this all the ceilings were rather low. At first they heard people talking behind these doors and at one they heard a man singing a sad song in an unknown language. Then they came to doors that stood open shewing only darkness; a cold, stale draught came from each. The last door, however, was closed. They knocked, but no one answered. They called out they were come to wait upon Mrs Delgado. Still no reply. And then, because Aunt Greysteel said that it was foolish to come so far and just go away again, they pushed open the door and went inside.

The room – which was scarcely more than an attic – had all the wretchedness that old age and extreme poverty could give it. It contained nothing that was not broken, chipped or ragged. Every colour in the room had faded, or darkened, or done what it must until it was grey. There was one little window that was open to the evening air and shewed the moon, although it was a little surprizing that the moon with her clean white face and fingers should condescend to make an appearance in that dirty little room.

Yet this was not what made Dr Greysteel look so alarmed, made him pull at his neckcloth, redden and go pale alternately, and draw great breaths of air. If there was one thing which Dr Greysteel disliked more than another, it was cats – and the room was full of cats.

In the midst of the cats sat a very thin person on a dusty, wooden chair. It was lucky, as Signor Tosetti had said, that the Greysteels were all bold adventurers, for the sight of Mrs Delgado might well have been a little shocking to nervous persons. For though she sat very upright – one would almost have said that she was poised, waiting for something – she bore so many of the signs and disfigurings of extreme old age that she was losing her resemblance to other human beings and began instead to resemble other orders of living creatures. Her arms lay in her lap, so extravagantly spotted with brown that they were like two fish. Her skin was the white, almost transparent skin of the extremely old, as fine and wrinkled as a spider's web, with veins of knotted blue.

She did not rise at their entrance, nor make any sign that she had noticed them at all. But perhaps she did not hear them. For, though the room was silent, the silence of half a hundred cats is a peculiar thing, like fifty individual silences all piled one on top of another.

So the Greysteels and Signor Tosetti, practical people, sat down in the terrible little room and Aunt Greysteel, with her kind smile and solicitous wishes that every one should be made comfortable and easy, began their addresses to the old lady.

"I hope, my dear Mrs Delgado, that you will forgive this intrusion, but my niece and I wished to do ourselves the honour of waiting upon you." Aunt Greysteel paused in case the old lady wished to make a reply, but the old lady said nothing. "What an airy situation you have here, ma'am! A dear friend of mine – a Miss Whilesmith – lodges in a little room at the top of a house in

749

Queen's square in Bath – a room much like your own, Mrs Delgado – and she declares that in summer she would not exchange it for the best house in the city – for she catches the breezes that nobody else gets and is perfectly cool when great people stifle in their rich apartments. And she has everything so neat and tidy and just to hand, whenever she wants it. And her only complaint is that the girl from the second back pair is always putting hot kettles on the staircase – which, as you know Mrs Delgado – can be so very displeasing if you chance to strike your foot against one of them. Do you suffer much inconvenience from the staircase, ma'am?"

There was a silence. Or rather some moments passed filled with nothing but the breathing of fifty cats.

Dr Greysteel dabbed at his sweating brow with his handkerchief and shifted about inside his clothes. "We are here, ma'am," he began, "at the particular request of Mr John McKean of Aberdeenshire. He wishes to be remembered to you. He hopes that you are well and sends every good wish for your future health."

Dr Greysteel spoke rather louder than usual, for he had begun to suspect that the old lady was deaf. This had no other effect, however, than to disturb the cats, many of which began to stalk around the room, brushing against each other and sending up sparks into the twilight air. A black cat dropped from somewhere or other on to the back of Dr Greysteel's chair and walked it as if it were a tightrope.

Dr Greysteel took a moment to recover himself and then said, "May we take back some report of your health and situation to Mr McKean, ma'am?"

But the old lady said nothing.

Miss Greysteel was next. "I am glad, ma'am," she said, "to see you so well provided with good friends. They must be a great comfort to you. That little honey-coloured puss at your feet – what an elegant form she has! And such a dainty way of washing her face! What do you call her?"

But the old lady did not answer.

So, prompted by a glance from Dr Greysteel, the little Venetian lawyer began to relate much of what had already been said, but this time in Italian. The only difference was that now the old lady no longer troubled to look at them, but fixed her gaze upon a great grey cat, which was, in its turn, looking at a white cat, which was, in *its* turn staring at the moon.

"Tell her that I have brought her money," said Dr Greysteel to the lawyer. "Tell her it is a gift made to her on behalf of John McKean. Tell her she must not thank me . . ." Dr Greysteel waved his hand vigorously as if a reputation for generous deeds and benevolent actions were a little like a mosquito and he hoped in this way to prevent one from landing on him.

"Mr Tosetti," said Aunt Greysteel, "you are not well. You are pale, sir. Will you have a glass of water? I am sure that Mrs Delgado could furnish you with a glass of water."

"No, Madamina Greysteel, I am not ill. I am . . ." Signor Tosetti looked round the room to find the word he wanted. "Fearful," he whispered.

"Fearful?" whispered Dr Greysteel. "Why? What of?"

"Ah, Signor Dottore, this is a terrible place!" returned the other in a whisper, and his eyes wandered in a kind of horror first to where one of the cats was licking its paw, in preparation to washing its face, and then back to the old lady, as if in expectation of seeing her perform the same action.

Miss Greysteel whispered that in their concern to shew Mrs Delgado attention they had come in too great a number and arrived too suddenly at her door. Clearly they were the first visitors she had had in years. Was it any wonder her wits seemed temporarily to be wandering? It was too severe a trial!

"Oh, Flora!" whispered Aunt Greysteel. "Only think! To pass years and years without society of any kind!"

To be all whispering together in such a small room – for the old lady was not three feet distant from any of them – appeared to Dr

Greysteel to be very ridiculous and, from not knowing what else to do, he became rather irritable with his companions, so that his sister and daughter judged it best to go.

Aunt Greysteel insisted on taking a long and fond farewell of the old lady, telling her that they would all return when she was feeling better – which Aunt Greysteel hoped would be soon.

Just as they passed through the door, they looked back. At that moment a new cat appeared upon the sill of the window with a stiff, spiky something in its mouth – a thing remarkably like a dead bird. The old lady made a little joyous sound and sprang with surprizing energy out of her chair. It was the oddest sound in all the world and bore not the slightest resemblance to human speech. It made Signor Tosetti, in his turn, cry out in alarm and pull the door shut, and hide whatever it was that the old lady was about to do next.[1]

---

[1] Signor Tosetti later confessed to the Greysteels that he believed he knew who the old lady of Cannaregio was. He had heard her story often as he went about the city, but until he had seen her with his own eyes he had dismissed it as a mere fable, a tale to frighten the young and foolish.

It seems her father had been a Jew, and her mother was descended from half the races of Europe. As a child she had learnt several languages and spoke them all perfectly. There was nothing she could not make herself mistress of if she chose. She learnt for the pleasure of it. At sixteen she spoke – not only French, Italian and German – which are part of any lady's commonplace accomplishments – but all the languages of the civilized (and uncivilized) world. She spoke the language of the Scottish Highlands (which is like singing). She spoke Basque, which is a language which rarely makes any impression upon the brains of any other race, so that a man may hear it as often and as long as he likes, but never afterwards be able to recall a single syllable of it. She even learnt the language of a strange country which, Signor Tosetti had been told, some people believed still existed, although no one in the world could say where it was. (The name of this country was Wales.)

She travelled through the world and appeared before kings and queens; archdukes and archduchesses; princes and bishops; Grafs and Grafins, and to each and every one of these important people she spoke in the language he or she had learnt as a child and every one of them proclaimed her a wonder.

And at last she came to Venice.

But this lady had never learnt to moderate her behaviour in any thing. Her appetite for learning was matched by her appetite in other things and she had married a man who was the same. This lady and her husband came at

753

[1] *cont'd* *Carnevale* and never went away again. All their wealth they gambled away in the *Ridottos*. All their health they lost in other pleasures. And one morning, when all of Venice's canals were silver and rose-coloured with the dawn, the husband lay down upon the wet stones of the Fondamenta dei Mori and died and there was nothing anyone could do to save him. And the wife would perhaps have done as well to do the same – for she had no money and nowhere to go. But the Jews remembered that she had some claim to their charity, being in a manner of speaking a Jewess herself (though she had never before acknowledged it) or perhaps they felt for her as a suffering creature (for the Jews have endured much in Venice). However it was, they gave her shelter in the Ghetto. There are different stories of what happened next, but what they all agree upon is that she lived among the Jews, but she was not one of them. She lived quite alone and whether the fault was hers or whether the fault was theirs I do not know. And a great deal of time went by and she did not speak to a living soul and a great wind of madness howled through her and overturned all her languages. And she forgot Italian, forgot English, forgot Latin, forgot Basque, forgot Welsh, forgot every thing in the world except Cat – and that, it is said, she spoke marvellously well.

53

A little dead grey mouse

End of November 1816

THE FOLLOWING EVENING in a room where Venetian
gloom and Venetian magnificence mingled in a highly
romantic and satisfactory manner, the Greysteels and
Strange sat down to dinner together. The floor was of cracked,
worn marble, all the colours of a Venetian winter. Aunt Greysteel's head, in its neat white cap, was set off by the vast, dark door
that loomed in the distance behind her. The door was surmounted
by dim carvings and resembled nothing so much as some funerary
monument wreathed in dreary shadows. On the plaster walls,
were the ghosts of frescoes painted in the ghosts of colours, all
glorifying some ancient Venetian family whose last heir had
drowned long ago. The present owners were as poor as church
mice and had not been able to repair their house for many years. It
was raining outside and, what was more surprizing, inside too;
from somewhere in the room came the disagreeable sound of large
quantities of water dripping liberally upon floor and furniture. But
the Greysteels were not to be made gloomy, nor put off a very good
dinner, by such trifles as these. They had banished the funereal
shadows with a good blaze of candlelight and were masking the
sound of dripping water with laughter and conversation. They
were generally bestowing a cheerful Englishness on that part of the
room where they sat.

"But I do not understand," said Strange, "Who takes care of the old woman?"

Dr Greysteel said, "The Jewish gentleman – who seems a very charitable old person – provides her with a place to live, and his servants put dishes of food for her at the foot of the stairs."

"But as to how the food is conveyed to her," exclaimed Miss Greysteel, "no one knows for certain. Signor Tosetti believes that her cats carry it up to her."

"Such nonsense!" declared Dr Greysteel. "Whoever heard of cats doing anything useful!"

"Except for staring at one in a supercilious manner," said Strange. "That has a sort of moral usefulness, I suppose, in making one feel uncomfortable and encouraging sober reflection upon one's imperfections."

The Greysteels' odd adventure had supplied a subject of conversation since they had sat down to dinner. "Flora, my dear," said Aunt Greysteel, "Mr Strange will begin to think we cannot talk of any thing else."

"Oh! Do not trouble upon my account," said Strange. "It is curious and we magicians collect curiosities, you know."

"Could you cure her by magic, Mr Strange?" asked Miss Greysteel.

"Cure madness? No. Though it is not for want of trying. I was once asked to visit a mad old gentleman to see what I could do for him and I believe I cast stronger spells upon that occasion than upon any other, but at the end of my visit he was just as mad as ever."

"But there might be recipes for curing madness, might there not?" asked Miss Greysteel eagerly. "I dare say the *Aureate* magicians might have had one." Miss Greysteel had begun to interest herself in magical history and her conversation these days was full of words like *Aureate* and *Argentine*.

"Possibly," said Strange, "but if so, then the prescription has been lost for hundreds of years."

"And if it were a thousand years, then I am sure that it need be no impediment to *you*. You have related to us dozens of examples of spells which were thought to be lost and which you have been able to recover."

"True, but generally I had some idea of how to begin. I never heard of a single instance of an *Aureate* magician curing madness. Their attitude towards madness seems to have been quite different from ours. They regarded madmen as seers and prophets and listened to their ramblings with the closest attention."

"How strange! Why?"

"Mr Norrell believed it was something to do with the sympathy which fairies feel for madmen – that and the fact that madmen can perceive fairy-spirits when no one else can." Strange paused. "You say this old woman is very mad?" he said.

"Oh, yes! I believe so."

In the drawing-room after dinner Dr Greysteel fell soundly asleep in his chair. Aunt Greysteel nodded in hers, waking every now and then to apologize for her sleepiness and then promptly falling asleep again. So Miss Greysteel was able to enjoy a tête-a-tête with Strange for the rest of the evening. She had a great deal to say to him. On his recommendation she had recently been reading Lord Portishead's *A Child's History of the Raven King* and she wished to ask him about it. However, he seemed distracted and several times she had the disagreeable impression that he was not attending to her.

The following day the Greysteels visited the Arsenal and were full of admiration for its gloom and vastness, they idled away an hour or two in curiosity shops (where the shopkeepers seemed nearly as quaint and old-fashioned as the curiosities themselves), and they ate ices at a pastry-cook's near the Church of San Stefano. To all the pleasures of the day Strange had been invited, but early in the morning Aunt Greysteel had received a short note presenting his compliments and thanks, but he had come quite by accident upon a new line of inquiry and dare not leave it, ". . . and scholars, madam, as you know by the example of your own brother, are the most selfish beings in creation and think that devotion to their researches excuses any thing . . ." Nor did he appear the next day when they visited the Scuola di Santa Maria della Carità. Nor the following one when they went by gondola to Torcello, a lonely, reed-choked island shrouded in grey mists where the first Venetian city had been raised, been magnificent, been deserted and finally crumbled away, all long, long ago.

But, though Strange was shut away in his rooms near Santa Maria Zobenigo, doing magic, Dr Greysteel was spared the anguish of missing him greatly by the frequency with which his name was mentioned among them. If the Greysteels walked by the Rialto – and if the sight of that bridge drew Dr Greysteel on to talk of Shylock, Shakespeare and the condition of the modern theatre, then Dr Greysteel was sure to have the benefit of Strange's opinions upon all these subjects – for Miss Greysteel knew them all and could argue for them quite as well as for her own. If, in a little curiosity shop, the Greysteels were struck by a painting of a quaint dancing bear, then it only served as an opportunity for Miss Greysteel to tell her father of an acquaintance of Mr Strange who had a stuffed brown bear in a glass case. If the Greysteels ate mutton, then Miss Greysteel was sure to be reminded of an occasion, of which Mr Strange had told her, when he had eaten mutton at Lyme Regis.

On the evening of the third day Dr Greysteel sent Strange a message proposing that the two of them should take a coffee and a glass of Italian spirit together. They met at Florian's a little after six o'clock.

"I am glad to see you," said Dr Greysteel, "but you look pale. Are you remembering to eat? To sleep? To take exercise?"

"I believe I ate something today," said Strange, "although I really cannot recall what it was."

They talked for a while of indifferent matters, but Strange was distracted. Several times he answered Dr Greysteel almost at random. Then, swallowing the last of his *grappa*, he took out his pocket-watch and said, "I hope you will forgive my hurrying away. I have an engagement. And so, good night."

Dr Greysteel was a little surprized at this and he could not help but wonder what sort of an engagement it might be. A man might behave badly any where in the world, but it seemed to Dr Greysteel that in Venice he might behave worse and do so more frequently. No other city in the world was so bent upon providing opportunities for every sort of mischief and Dr Greysteel happened to be particularly concerned at this period that Strange should have a character beyond reproach. So he inquired with as careless an air as he could manage whether the appointment was with Lord Byron?

"No, indeed. To own the truth," Strange narrowed his eyes and grew confidential, "I believe I may have found someone to aid me."

"Your fairy?"

"No. Another human being. I have high hopes of this colla-boration. Yet at the same time I am not quite sure how the other person will greet my proposals. You will understand that under such circumstances I have no desire to keep them waiting."

"No, indeed!" exclaimed Dr Greysteel. "Go! Go!"

Strange walked away and became one of the many black figures on the piazza, all with black faces and no expressions, hurrying across the face of moon-coloured Venice. The moon itself was set among great architectural clouds so that there appeared to be another moon-lit city in the sky, whose grandeur rivalled Venice and whose great palaces and streets were crumbling and falling into ruins, as if some spirit in a whimsical mood had set it there to mock the other's slow decline.

Meanwhile, Aunt Greysteel and Miss Greysteel had taken advantage of the doctor's absence to return to the terrible little room at the top of the house in the Ghetto. They had come in secret, having an idea that Dr Greysteel, and perhaps even Mr

Strange, might try to prevent them going, or else insist upon accompanying them – and they had no wish for male companionship upon this occasion.

"They will want to be talking about it," said Aunt Greysteel, "they will be trying to guess how she came to this sad condition. But what good will that do? How does that help her?"

Miss Greysteel had brought some candles and a candlestick. She lit the candle so that they could see what they were doing. Then, out of their baskets they took a nice savoury dish of veal fricassee that filled the stale, desperate room with a good smell, some fresh white rolls, some apples and a warm shawl. Aunt Greysteel placed the plate of veal fricassee before Mrs Delgado, but she found that Mrs Delgado's fingers and fingernails were as curved and stiff as claws, and she could not coax them round the handles of the knife and fork.

"Well, my dear," said Aunt Greysteel at last, "she shews great interest in it, and I am sure it will do her good. But I think we will leave her to eat it in whatever way she thinks best."

They went down into the street. As soon as they were outside Aunt Greysteel exclaimed, "Oh, Flora! Did you see? She had her supper already prepared. There was a little china saucer – quite a pretty saucer – rather like my tea-service with rosebuds and forget-me-nots – and she had laid a mouse in it – a little dead grey mouse!"

Miss Greysteel looked thoughtful. "I dare say a head of chicory – boiled and dressed with a sauce, as they prepare it here – looks a little like a mouse."

"Oh my dear!" said Aunt Greysteel. "You know it was nothing of the sort . . ."

They were walking through the Ghetto Vecchio towards Cannaregio canal when Miss Greysteel turned suddenly away into the shadows and disappeared from sight.

"Flora! What is the matter?" cried Aunt Greysteel. "What do you see? Do not linger, my love. It is so very dark here among the houses. Dearest! Flora!"

Miss Greysteel moved back into the light as quickly as she had gone away. "It is nothing, aunt," she said. "Do not be startled. It is only that I thought I heard someone say my name and I went to see. I thought it was someone I knew. But there is no one there."

At the *Fondamenta* their gondola was waiting for them. The oarsman handed them in and then, with slow strokes, moved away. Aunt Greysteel made herself snug under the covering in the centre of the boat. Rain began to patter upon the canvas. "Perhaps when we get home we shall find Mr Strange with papa," she said.

"Perhaps," said Miss Greysteel.

"Or maybe he has gone to play billiards with Lord Byron again," said Aunt Greysteel. "It is odd that they should be friends. They seem such very different gentlemen."

"Oh, indeed! Though Mr Strange told me that he found Lord Byron a great deal less agreeable when he met him in Swisserland. His lordship was with some other poetical people who claimed all his attention and whose company he clearly preferred to that of any one else. Mr Strange says that he was barely civil."

"Well, that is very bad. But not at all surprising. Should not you be afraid to look at him, my love? Lord Byron, I mean. I think that perhaps I might – a little."

"No, I should not be afraid."

"Well, my love, that is because you are more clear-headed and steady than other people. Indeed I do not know what there is in the world that you would be afraid of."

"Oh! I do not think it is because of any extraordinary courage on my part. As to extraordinary virtue – I cannot tell. I was never yet much tempted to do any thing very bad. It is only that Lord Byron could never have any power over me or sway the least of my thoughts or actions. I am quite safe from him. But that is not to say that there might not be someone in the world – I do not say that I have seen him yet – whom I would be a little afraid to look at sometimes – for fear that he might be looking sad – or lost – or thoughtful, or – what, you know, might seem worst of all – brooding on some private anger or hurt and so not knowing or caring if I looked at him at all."

In the little attic at the top of the house in the Ghetto, Miss Greysteel's candles guttered and went out. The moon shone down into the nightmare apartment and the old lady of Cannaregio began to devour the veal fricassee which the Greysteel ladies had brought her.

She was about to swallow the last bite when an English voice suddenly said, "Unfortunately, my friends did not stay to perform the introductions and it is always an awkward business, is it not, madam, when two people are left together in a room to get acquainted? My name is Strange. Yours, madam, though you do not know it, is Delgado, and I am delighted to meet you."

Strange was leaning against the windowsill with his arms crossed, looking intently at her.

She, on the other hand, took as little notice of him as she had of Aunt Greysteel or Miss Greysteel or any of her visitors of the last few days. She took as little notice of him as a cat takes of any body who does not interest it.

"Let me first assure you," said Strange, "that I am not one of those tiresome visitors who have no real purpose for their visit and nothing to say for themselves. I have a proposal to make to you, Mrs Delgado. It is our excellent fortune, madam, that you and I should meet at this time. I am able to give you your heart's desire and in return you shall give me mine."

Mrs Delgado made no sign that she had heard any of this. She had turned her attention to the saucer with the dead mouse and her ancient mouth gaped to devour it.

"Really, madam!" cried Strange. "I must insist that you put off your dinner for a moment and attend to what I am saying." He leant forward and removed the saucer. For the first time Mrs Delgado seemed to know he was there. She made a little mew of displeasure and looked resentfully at him.

"I want you to teach me how to be mad. The idea is so simple, I wonder I did not think of it before."

Mrs Delgado growled very low.

"Oh! You question the wisdom of my proceedings? You are probably right. To wish madness upon oneself is very rash. My tutor, my wife and my friends would all be angry if they knew any thing of it." He paused. The sardonic expression disappeared from his face and the light tone disappeared from his voice. "But I have cast off my tutor, my wife is dead and I am separated from my friends by twenty miles of chill water and the best part of a continent. For the first time since I took up this odd profession, I am not obliged to consult any one else. Now, how to begin? You must give me something – something to serve as a symbol and vessel of your madness." He glanced around the room. "Unfortunately, you do not appear to possess any thing, except your gown . . ." He looked down at the saucer which he held in his hand. ". . . and this mouse. I believe I prefer the mouse."

Strange began to say a spell. There was a burst of silver lights in the room. It was something between white flames and the glittering effect which fireworks produce. For a moment it hung in the air between Mrs Delgado and Strange. Then Strange made a gesture as if he intended to throw it at her; the light flew towards her and, just for a moment, she was bathed in a silver radiance. Suddenly Mrs Delgado was nowhere to be seen and in her place was a solemn, sulky girl in an old-fashioned gown. Then the girl too disappeared to be replaced by a beautiful young woman with a wilful expression. She was followed swiftly by an older woman of imperious bearing but with a glint of impending madness in her eyes. All the women Mrs Delgado had ever been flickered for an instant in the chair. Then all of them disappeared.

On the chair was only a heap of crumpled silk. Out of it stepped a little grey cat. The cat jumped daintily down, sprang up on the windowsill and vanished into the darkness.

"Well, that worked," said Strange. He picked up the half-rotten dead mouse by its tail. Instantly he became interesting to several of the cats who mewed and purred and rubbed themselves against his legs to attract his attention.

He grimaced. "And what was John Uskglass forced to endure, I wonder, in order to forge English magic?"

He wondered if he would notice any difference. Would he find, after he had done the spell, that he was trying to guess if he were mad now? Would he stand about, trying to think mad thoughts to discover if any of them seemed more natural? He took a last look around at the world, opened his mouth and gingerly lowered the mouse into it . . .

It was like plunging beneath a waterfall or having two thousand trumpets sound in one's ear. Everything he thought before, everything he knew, everything he had been was swept away in a great flood of confused emotion and sensation. The world was made again in flame-like colours that were impossible to bear. It was shot through with new fears, new desires, new hatreds. He was surrounded by great presences. Some had wicked mouths full of teeth and huge, burning eyes. There was a thing like a horribly crippled spider that reared up beside him. It was full of malice. He had something in his mouth and the taste of it was unspeakable. Unable to think, unable to know, he found from God-knows-where the presence of mind to spit it out. Someone screamed . . .

He found that he was lying on his back staring up into a confusion of darkness, roof beams and moonlight. A shadowy face appeared and peered into his own face in an unnerving manner. Its breath was warm, damp and malodorous. He had no recollection of lying down, but then he did not have much recollection of any thing. He wondered vaguely if he were in London or Shropshire. There was the queerest sensation all over his body as if several cats were walking on him at once. After a moment he raised his head and found that this was indeed the case.

He sat up and the cats leapt away. The full moon shone down

through a broken window. Then, mounting from recollection to recollection, he began to piece the evening together. He remembered the spell by which he had transformed the old woman, his plan to bring madness upon himself in order to see the fairy. At first it seemed to him so distant that he thought he must be remembering events that had happened, oh!, perhaps a month or so ago. Yet here he was in the room and he found by his pocket-watch that scarcely any time had passed at all.

He managed to rescue the mouse. By luck his arm had fallen upon it and kept it safe from the cats. He tucked it into his pocket and left the room hurriedly. He did not want to remain there a moment longer; the room had been nightmarish to begin with – now it seemed to him a place of untold horror.

He met several people on the stairs, but they took not a scrap of notice of him. He had previously cast a spell over the inhabitants of the house and they were quite convinced that they saw him every day, that he frequented these rooms regularly, and that nothing was more natural than that he should be there. But if any one had asked them who he was, they would have been quite unable to say.

He walked back to his lodgings at Santa Maria Zobenigo. The old woman's madness still seemed to infect him. People he passed in the street were strangely changed; their expressions seemed ferocious and unintelligible, and even their gait was lumbering and ugly. "Well one thing is clear," he thought, "the old woman was very mad indeed. I could not possibly summon the fairy in that condition."

The next day he rose early and immediately after breakfast began the process of reducing the flesh and guts of the mouse to a powder, according to various well-known principles of magic. The bones he preserved intact. Then he turned the powder into a tincture. This had two advantages. First (and by no means least), it was considerably less repulsive to swallow a few drops of tincture than to put a dead mouse in his mouth. Secondly, he believed that in this way he might be able to regulate the degree of madness he imposed upon himself.

By five o'clock he had a darkish brown liquid, which smelt chiefly of the brandy he had used to make the tincture. He decanted it into a bottle. Then he carefully counted fourteen drops into a glass of brandy and drank it.

After a few minutes he looked out of the window and into the Campo Santa Maria Zobenigo. People were walking up and down. The backs of their heads were hollowed out; their faces were nothing but thin masks at the front. Within each hollow a candle was burning. This was so plain to him now, that he wondered he had never noticed it before. He imagined what would happen if he went down into the street and blew some of the candles out. It made him laugh to think of it. He laughed so much that he could no longer stand. His laughter echoed round and round the house. Some small remaining shred of reason warned him that he ought not to let the landlord and his family know what he was doing so he went to bed and muffled the sound of his laughter in the pillows, kicking his legs from time to time with the sheer hilarity of the idea.

Next morning he awoke in bed, fully dressed and with his boots still on. Apart from the dull, greasy feeling that generally results from sleeping in one's clothes, he believed he was much as usual. He washed, shaved and put on fresh clothes. Then he went out to take something to eat and drink. There was a little coffee-house he liked on the corner of the Calle de la Cortesia and the Campo San Angelo. All seemed well until the waiter approached his table and put the cup of coffee down upon it. Strange looked up and saw a glint in the man's eye like a tiny candle-flame. He found he could no longer recall whether people had candles in their heads or not. He knew that there was a world of difference between these two notions: one was sane and the other was not, but he could not for the life of him remember which was which.

This was a little unsettling.

"The only problem with the tincture," he thought, "is that it is really quite difficult to judge when the effects have worn off. I had not thought of that before. I suppose I ought to wait a day or two before trying it again."

But at midday his impatience got the better of him. He felt better. He was inclining to the view that people did *not* have candles in their heads. "And anyway," he thought, "it does not much matter which it is. The question has no relevance to my present undertaking." He put nine drops of the tincture into a glass of Vin Santo and drank it down.

Immediately he became convinced that all the cupboards in the house were full of pineapples. He was certain that there were other pineapples under his bed and under the table. He was so alarmed by this thought that he felt hot and cold all over and was obliged to sit down on the floor. All the houses and *palazzi* in the city were full of pineapples and outside in the streets people were carrying pineapples, hidden under their clothes. He could smell the pine-apples everywhere – a smell both sweet and sharp.

Some time later there was a knock at his door. He was surprized to find it was now evening and the room was quite dark. The knock sounded again. The landlord was at the door. The landlord began to talk, but Strange could not understand him. This was because the man had a pineapple in his mouth. How he had managed to cram the whole thing in there, Strange could not imagine. Green, spiky leaves emerged slowly out of his mouth and then were sucked back in again as he spoke. Strange wondered if perhaps he ought to go and fetch a knife or a hook and try and fish the pineapple out, in case the landlord should choke. But at the same time he did not care much about it. "After all," he thought with some irritation, "it is his own fault. He put it there."

The next day in the coffee-house on the corner of the Calle de la Cortesia one of the waiters was cutting up a pineapple. Strange, huddled over his coffee, shuddered to see it.

He had discovered that it was easier – far easier than any one could have supposed – to make oneself mad, but like all magic it was full of obstacles and frustrations. Even if he succeeded in summoning the fairy (which did not seem very likely), he would be in no condition to talk to him. Every book he had ever read on the subject urged magicians to be on their guard when dealing with fairies. Just when he needed all his wits, he would have scarcely any wits at all.

"How am I supposed to impress him with the superiority of my magicianship if all I can do is babble about pineapples and candles?" he thought.

He spent the day pacing up and down his room, breaking off every now and then to scribble notes upon bits of paper. When evening came he wrote down a spell for summoning fairies and put it on the table. Then he put four drops of tincture into a glass of water and swallowed it.

This time the tincture affected him quite differently. He was not assailed by any peculiar beliefs or fears. Indeed in many ways he felt better than he had in a long time: cooler, calmer, less troubled. He found that he no longer cared very much about magic. Doors slammed in his mind and he went wandering off into rooms and hallways inside himself that he had not visited in years. For the first ten minutes or so he became the man he had been at twenty or twenty-two; after that he was someone else entirely – someone he had always had the power to be, but for various reasons had never actually become.

His first desire after taking the tincture was to go to a *Ridotto*. It seemed ridiculous that he should have been in Venice since the beginning of October and never visited one. But on examining his pocket-watch he discovered that it was only eight o'clock. "That is much too early," he remarked to no one in particular. He was feeling talkative and looked round for someone to confide in. For lack of any one better, he settled upon the little wooden figure in the corner. "There will be no one worth seeing for three or four hours yet," he told it.

To fill the time he thought he might go and find Miss Greysteel. "But I suppose her aunt and father will be there." He made a small sound of irritation. "Dull! Dull! Dull! Why do pretty women always have such herds of relatives?" He looked at himself in a mirror. "Dear God! This neckcloth looks as if it was tied by a ploughman."

He spent the next half hour tying and re-tying the neckcloth until he was satisfied with it. Then he discovered that his finger-nails were longer than he liked and not particularly clean. He went to look for a pair of scissars to cut them with.

The scissars were on the table. And something else besides. "What have we here?" he asked. "Papers! Papers with magic spells on them!" This struck him as highly amusing. "You know, it is the queerest thing," he told the little wooden figure, "but I know the fellow who wrote this! His name is Jonathan Strange – and now that I think about it, I think these books belong to him." He read a little further. "Ha! You will never guess what idiocy he is engaged in now! Casting spells to summon fairies! Ha! Ha! He tells himself he is doing it to get himself a fairy-servant and further the cause of English magic. But really he is only doing it to terrify Gilbert Norrell! He has come hundreds of miles to the most luxurious city in the world and all he cares about is what some old man in London thinks! How ridiculous!"

He put the piece of paper down again in disgust and picked up the scissars. He turned and just avoided striking his head against something. "What in the world . . . ?" he began.

A black ribbon hung from the ceiling. At the end of it were a few tiny bones, a phial of some dark liquid – blood perhaps – and a piece of paper with writing on it, all tied up together. The length of the ribbon was such that a person moving about the room was almost certain to knock against it sooner or later. Strange shook his head in disbelief at other people's stupidity. Leaning against the table, he began to cut his nails.

Several minutes passed. "He had a wife, you know," he remarked to the little wooden figure. He brought his hand near to the candlelight to examine his nails. "Arabella Woodhope. The most charming girl in all the world. But dead. Dead, dead, dead." He picked up a nail-buffer from the table and began to polish his nails with it. "In fact, now that I come to think of it, was I not in love with her myself? I think I must have been. She had the sweetest way of saying my name and smiling at the same time, and every time she did so, my heart turned over." He laughed. "You know, it is really very ridiculous, but I cannot actually remember what my name is. Laurence? Arthur? Frank? I wish Arabella were here. She would know. And she would tell me too! She is not one of those women who tease one and insist upon making a game of everything long after it has ceased to be amusing. By God, I wish she were here! There is an ache here." He tapped his heart. "And something hot and hard inside here." He tapped his forehead. "But half an hour's conversation with Arabella would put both right, I am sure. Perhaps I ought to summon this fellow's fairy and ask him to bring her here. Fairies can summon the dead, can they not?" He picked up the spell from the table and read it again. "There is nothing to this. It is the simplest thing in the world."

He rattled off the words of the spell and then, because it seemed important to do so, he went back to shining his nails.

In the shadows by the painted cupboard there was a person in a leaf-green coat – a person with hair the colour of thistle-down – a person with an amused, superior sort of smile upon his face.

Strange was still intent upon his nails.

The gentleman with the thistle-down hair walked very rapidly over to where Strange stood and put out his hand to pull Strange's hair. But before he could do so, Strange looked directly at him and said, "I don't suppose that you happen to have such a thing as a pinch of snuff, do you?"

The gentleman with the thistle-down hair froze.

"I have looked in every pocket of this damned coat," continued Strange, perfectly unaware of the gentleman's astonishment, "but there is not a snuff box anywhere. I cannot imagine what I was thinking of to come out without one. Kendal Brown is what I generally take, if you have it."

As he spoke he fished in his pockets again. But he had forgotten about the little bone-and-blood posy that hung from the ceiling and as he moved, he knocked his head against it. The posy swung back, swung forward again and struck him fairly in the middle of his forehead.

54

A little box, the colour of heartache

1st and 2nd December 1816

THERE WAS A kind of snap in the air, followed immediately by a faint breeze and a new freshness, as if some stale odour had suddenly been swept from the room.

Strange blinked two or three times.

His first thought upon coming to himself was that his whole elaborate scheme had worked; here was someone – without a doubt a fairy – standing before him. His second thought was to wonder what in the world he had been doing. He pulled out his pocket-watch and examined it; almost an hour had passed since he had drunk the tincture.

"I beg your pardon," he said, "I know it is an odd question, but have I asked any thing of you yet?"

"Snuff," said the gentleman with the thistle-down hair.

"Snuff?"

"You asked me for a pinch of snuff."

"When?"

"What?"

"When did I ask you for snuff?"

"A moment ago."

"Ah! Ah. Good. Well, you need not trouble yourself. I do not need it now."

The gentleman with the thistle-down hair bowed.

Strange was conscious that his confusion shewed in his face. He remembered all the stern warnings he had read against letting members of this tricksy race suspect that they know more than oneself. So he covered up his perplexity with sarcastic looks. Then, remembering that it is generally considered even more perilous to appear superior and so make the fairy-spirit angry, he covered up his sarcasm with a smile. Finally he went back to looking puzzled.

He did not notice that the gentleman was at least as uncomfortable as himself.

"I have summoned you here," he said, "because I have long desired one of your race to aid me and instruct me in magic." He had rehearsed this little pronouncement several times and was pleased to find that it sounded both confident and dignified. Unfortunately he immediately spoilt the effect by adding anxiously, "Did I mention that before?"

The gentleman said nothing.

"My name is Jonathan Strange. Perhaps you have heard of me? I am at a most interesting point in my career. I believe it is no exaggeration to say that the entire future of English magic depends upon my actions in the coming months. Agree to help me and your name will be as famous as those of Col Tom Blue and Master Witcherley!"[1]

"Tut!" declared the gentleman in disgust. "Low persons!"

"Really?" said Strange. "I had no idea." He pressed on. "It was your . . ." He paused to find the right phrase. ". . . *kind attentions* to the King of England that first brought you to my notice. Such power! Such inventiveness! English magic today lacks spirit! It lacks fire and energy! I cannot tell you how bored I am of the same dull spells to solve the same dull problems. The glimpse I had of your magic proved to me that it is quite different. You could surprize me. And I long to be surprized!"

---

[1] Col Tom Blue was of course the most famous servant of Ralph Stokesey; Master Witcherley assisted Martin Pale.

The gentleman raised one perfect fairy eye-brow, as if he would not object in the least to surprizing Jonathan Strange.

Strange continued excitedly. "Oh! and I may as well tell you immediately that there is an old person in London called Norrell – a magician of sorts – who will be driven into fits of rage the moment he learns that you have allied yourself to me. He will do his best to thwart us but I dare say you and I will be more than a match for him."

The gentleman appeared to have stopped listening. He was glancing about the room, fixing his gaze first upon one object, then upon another.

"Is there something in the room which displeases you?" asked Strange. "I beg you will tell me if that is the case. I dare say your magical sensibilities are much finer than my own. But even in my case there are certain things which can disrupt my ability to do magic – I believe it is so with all magicians. A salt-cellar, a rowan-tree, a fragment of the consecrated host – these all make me feel decidedly unsettled. I do not say I *cannot* do magic in their presence, but I always need to take them into account in my spells. If there is something here you dislike, you have only to say so and I shall be happy to remove it."

The gentleman stared at him a moment as if he had not the least idea what Strange was talking about. Then suddenly he exclaimed, "My magical sensibilities, yes! How clever of you! My magical sensibilities are, as you suppose, quite tremendous! And just now they inform me that you have recently acquired an object of great power! A ring of disenchantment? An urn of visibility? Something of that nature? My congratulations! Shew me the object and I shall immediately instruct you as to its history and proper use!"

"Actually no," said Strange, surprised. "I have nothing of that sort."

The gentleman frowned. He looked hard, first at a chamber-pot half-hidden under the table, then at a mourning-ring that contained a miniature of an angel painted on ivory, and finally at a painted pottery jar that had once contained candied peaches and plums. "Perhaps you have come upon it by accident?" he asked. "Such objects can be very powerful even if the magician has no idea that they are present."

"I really do not think so," said Strange. "That jar, for instance, was purchased in Genoa from a confectioner's. And there were dozens in the shop, just the same. I cannot see why one would be magical and the others not."

"No, indeed," agreed the gentleman. "And really there does not seem to be any thing here apart from the usual objects. I mean," he added quickly, "the objects that I would expect to find in the apartments of a magician of your genius."

There was a short pause.

"You make no reply to my offer," said Strange. "You are undecided until you know more of me. That is just as it should be. In a day or two I will do myself the honour of soliciting your company again and we shall talk some more."

"It has been a most interesting conversation!" said the gentleman.

"The first of many, I hope," said Strange, politely, and bowed.

The gentleman bowed in return.

Then Strange released the gentleman from the spell of summoning and he promptly disappeared.

Strange's excitement was immense. He supposed he ought to sit down and make sober, scholarly notes of what he had seen, but it was difficult to keep from dancing, laughing and clapping his hands. He actually performed several figures of a country-dance, and if the carved wooden figure had not been attached by its feet to a wooden pillar he would certainly have made it his partner and whirled about the room with it.

When the dancing fit left him he was sorely tempted to write to Norrell. In fact he did sit down and begin a letter full of triumph and steeped in sarcasm. ("You will no doubt be *delighted* to learn . . .") But then he thought better of it. "It will only provoke him to make my house disappear, or something. Ha! How furious he will be when I arrive back in England. I must publish the news immediately I return. I shall not wait for the next issue of *The Famulus*. That would take much too long. Murray will complain but I cannot help that. *The Times* would be best. I wonder what he meant by all that nonsense about rings of power and chamber-pots? I suppose he was trying to account for my success in summoning him."

Upon the whole he could not have been more pleased with himself if he had conjured up John Uskglass himself and had half an hour of civil conversation with him. The only unsettling part of the business was the memory – returning to him in scraps and fragments – of the form his madness had taken this time. "I think I turned into Lascelles or Drawlight! How perfectly horrible!"

The next morning Stephen Black had business to conduct for Sir Walter. He paid a visit to a banker in Lombard-street; he spoke to a portrait-painter in Little-Britain; he delivered instructions to a woman in Fetter-lane about a gown for Lady Pole. His next appointment was at the office of an attorney. A soft, heavy snow was falling. All around him were the customary sounds of the City: the snorting and stamping of the horses, the rattle of the carriages, the cries of the street-vendors, the slamming of doors and the padding of feet through the snow.

He was standing at the corner of Fleet-street and Mitre-court. He had just taken out his pocket-watch (a present from the gentleman with the thistle-down hair), when every sound ceased as if it had been cut off with a knife. For a moment it seemed he must have been struck deaf. But almost before he could feel any alarm he looked round and realized that this was not the only peculiarity. The street was suddenly empty. There were no people, no cats, no dogs, no horses, no birds. Everyone was gone.

And the snow! That was the oddest thing of all. It hung, suspended in the air, in huge, soft white flakes, as big as sovereigns.

"Magic!" he thought in disgust.

He walked a little way down Mitre-court, looking in the windows of the shops. Lamps were still lit; goods were lying heaped or scattered over the counters – silks, tobacco, sheet-music; fires were still burning in the hearths but their flames were frozen. He looked back and discovered that he had made a sort of tunnel through the three-dimensional lace-work of snow. It was, of all the strange things he had seen in his life, the strangest.

From out of nowhere a furious voice cried, "I thought myself quite safe from him! What tricks can he be using?" The gentleman with the thistle-down hair suddenly appeared immediately before Stephen, with blazing face and glittering eyes.

The shock was so great that for a moment Stephen feared he would drop down in a swoon. But he was well aware how highly the gentleman prized coolness and composure, so he hid his fright as best he could and gasped, "Safe from whom, sir?"

"Why, the magician, Stephen! The magician! I thought that he must have acquired some potent object that would reveal my presence to him. But I could not see any thing in his rooms and he swore that he had nothing of the sort. Just to be sure I have circled the globe in the past hour and examined every ring of power, every magical chalice and quern. But none of them are missing. They are all exactly where I thought they were."

From this rather incomplete explanation Stephen deduced that the magician must have succeeded in summoning and speaking to the gentle-man with the thistle-down hair. "But surely, sir," he said, "there was a time when you wished to aid the magicians and do magic with them and gain their gratitude. That is how you came to rescue Lady Pole, is it not? Perhaps you will find you like it better than you think."

"Oh, perhaps! But I really do not think so. I tell you, Stephen, apart from the inconvenience of having him summon me whenever he chuses, it was the dreariest half hour I have spent in many a long age. I have never heard any one talk so much! He is quite the most conceited person I have ever met. People like that who must be continually talking themselves and have no time to listen to any one else are quite disgusting to me."

"Oh, indeed, sir! It is most vexatious. And I dare say that, since you will be busy with the magician, we will have to put off making me King of England?"

The gentleman said something very fierce in his own language – presumably a curse. "I believe you are right – and that makes me angrier than all the rest put together!" He thought for a moment. "But then again, it may not be so bad as we fear. These English magicians are generally very stupid. They usually want the same things. The poor ones desire an unending supply of turnips or porridge; the rich ones want yet more riches, or power over the whole world; and the young ones want the love of some princess or queen. As soon as he asks for one of those things, I will grant it to him. It is sure to bring a world of trouble on his head. It always does. He will become distracted and then you and I can pursue our plan to make you King of England! Oh, Stephen! How glad I am that I came to you! I always hear better sense from you than from anyone else!" Upon the instant the gentleman's anger evaporated and he was full of delight. The sun actually appeared from behind a cloud and all the strange, suspended fall of snow glittered and blazed around them (though whether this was the gentleman's doing or no, Stephen could not tell).

He was about to point out that he had not actually suggested any thing, but in that instant the gentleman disappeared. All the people, horses, carriages, cats and dogs immediately reappeared, and Stephen walked straight into a fat woman in a purple pelisse.

Strange rose from his bed in excellent spirits. He had slept for eight hours without interruption. For the first time in weeks he had not got up in the middle of the night to do magic. As a reward to himself for his success in summoning the fairy, he decided that today should be a holiday. Shortly after ten o'clock, he presented himself at the *palazzo* where the Greysteels were staying and found the family at their breakfast. He accepted their invitation to sit down, ate some hot rolls, drank some coffee and told Miss Greysteel and Aunt Greysteel that he was entirely at their service.

Aunt Greysteel was happy to give up her share of the favour to her niece. Miss Greysteel and Strange passed the forenoon in reading books about magic together. These were books that he had lent to her or that she had bought upon his recommendation. They were Portishead's *A Child's History of the Raven King*, Hickman's *Life of Martin Pale* and Hether-Gray's *The Anatomy of a Minotaur*. Strange had read them when he first began to study magic and he was amused to discover how simple, almost innocent, they seemed to him now. It was the most agreeable thing in the world to read them to Miss Greysteel, and answer her questions, and listen to her opinions upon them – eager, intelligent and, it seemed to him, slightly over-serious.

At one o'clock, after a light repast of cold meat, Aunt Greysteel declared that they had all sat still long enough and she proposed a walk. "I dare say, Mr Strange, that you will be glad of the fresh air. Scholars often neglect exercise."

"We are very sad fellows, madam," agreed Strange, cheerfully.

It was a fine day. They wandered through the narrow streets and alleys and chanced upon a happy succession of intriguing objects: a carving of a dog with a bone in its mouth; a shrine to a saint that none of them recognized; a set of windows whose curtains seemed at first to be made of heavy swags of the most exquisite lace, but which were found upon closer examination to be only spiders' webs – vast, intermingling spiders' webs which permeated every part of the room inside. They had no guide to tell them about these things; there was no one standing near whom they could ask; and so they entertained themselves by making up their own explanations.

Just before twilight they entered a chilly, stony, little square with a well at its centre. It was a curiously blank and empty place.

The ground was paved with ancient stones. The walls were pierced with surprizingly few windows. It was as if the houses had all been offended by something the square had done and had resolutely turned their backs and looked the other way. There was one tiny shop that appeared to sell nothing but Turkish Delight of an infinite number of varieties and colours. It was closed, but Miss Greysteel and Aunt Greysteel peered into the window and wondered aloud when it might open and whether they would be able to find their way back to it.

Strange walked about. He was thinking of nothing in particular. The air was very cold – pleasantly so – and overhead the first star of evening appeared. He became aware of a peculiar scraping sound behind him and he turned to see what was making it.

In the darkest corner of the little square something was standing – a thing the like of which he had never seen before. It was black – so black that it might have been composed of the surrounding darkness. Its head or top took the form of an old-fashioned sedan chair, such as one might occasionally see conveying a dowager about Bath. It had windows with black curtains pulled across. But beneath the windows it dwindled into the body and legs of a great black bird. It wore a tall black hat and carried a thin, black walking-stick. It had no eyes, yet Strange could tell it was looking at him. It was scraping the tip of the walking-stick across the paving stones with a horrible jerking motion.

He supposed he ought to feel afraid. He supposed that he ought perhaps to do some magic to try and fend it off. Spells of dispersal, spells of dismissal, spells of protection flowed through his brain but he somehow failed to catch hold of any of them. Although the thing reeked of evil and malevolence, he had a strong sense that it was no danger to himself or any one else just at present. It seemed more like a sign of evil-yet-to-come.

He was just beginning to wonder how the Greysteels bore with this sudden appearance of horror in their midst when something shifted in his brain; the thing was no longer there. In its place stood the stout form of Dr Greysteel – Dr Greysteel in black clothes, Dr Greysteel with a walking-stick in his hand.

"Well?" called out Dr Greysteel.

"I . . . I beg your pardon!" Strange called back. "Did you speak? I was thinking of . . . of something else."

"I asked you if you intended to dine with us tonight!"

Strange stared at him.

"What is the matter? Are you sick?" asked Dr Greysteel. He looked rather probingly at Strange as if he saw something in the magician's face or manner he did not like.

"I am perfectly well, I assure you," said Strange. "And I will dine with you gladly. I should like nothing better. Only I have promised Lord Byron that I will play billiards with him at four."

"We should find a gondola to take us back," said Dr Greysteel. "I believe Louisa is more tired than she admits to." (He meant Aunt Greysteel.) "Where do you meet his lordship? Where shall we tell the fellow to take you?"

"Thank you," said Strange, "but I shall walk. Your sister was right. I am in need of fresh air and exercise."

Miss Greysteel was a little disappointed to find that Strange was not to return with them. The two ladies and the magician took a somewhat prolonged leave of each other and reminded each other several times that they were all to meet again in a few hours, until Dr Greysteel began to lose patience with them all.

The Greysteels walked off in the direction of the *Rio*. Strange followed at a distance. Despite his cheerful assurances to Dr Greysteel, he was feeling badly shaken. He tried to persuade himself that the apparition had been nothing more than a trick of the light, but it would not do. He was obliged to admit to himself that what it most resembled was a return of the old lady's madness.

"It is really most aggravating! The effects of the tincture seemed to have worn off entirely! Well, pray God, I do not need to drink any more of it. If this fairy refuses to serve me, I shall simply have to find another way of summoning someone else."

He emerged from the alley into the clearer light of the *Rio* and saw that the Greysteels had found a gondola and that someone – a gentleman – was helping Miss Greysteel into it. He thought at first that it was a stranger, but then he saw that this person had a head of shining thistle-down hair. He hurried to meet him.

"What a beautiful young woman!" said the gentleman, as the gondola pulled away from the quayside. His eyes sparkled with brilliance. "And she dances most delightfully, I expect?"

"Dances?" said Strange. "I do not know. We were supposed to attend a ball together in Genoa, but she had the toothach and we did not go. I am surprized to see you. I had not expected that you would come until I summoned you again."

"Ah, but I have been thinking about your proposal that we do magic together! And I now perceive it to be an excellent plan!"

"I am pleased to hear it," said Strange, suppressing a smile. "But tell me something. I have been trying to summon you for weeks. Why did you not come before?"

"Oh! That is easily explained!" declared the gentleman, and he began a long story about a cousin of his who was very wicked and very jealous of all his talents and virtues; who hated all English magicians; and who had somehow contrived to distort Strange's magic so that the gentleman had not known of the summons until last night. It was an exceedingly complicated tale and Strange did not believe a word of it. But he thought it prudent to look as if he did and so he bowed his acceptance.

"And to shew you how sensible I am of the honour you do me," finished up the gentleman, "I will bring you any thing you desire."

"Any thing?" repeated Strange, with a sharp look. "And this offer is – if I understand correctly – in the nature of a binding agreement. You cannot deny me something once I have named it?"

"Nor would I wish to!"

"And I can ask for riches, dominion over all the world? That sort of thing?"

"Exactly!" said the gentleman with a delighted air. He raised his hands to begin.

"Well, I do not want any of those things. What I chiefly want is information. Who was the last English magician you dealt with?"

A moment's pause.

"Oh, you do not want to hear about that!" declared the gentleman. "I assure you it is very dull. Now, come! There must be something you desire above all else? A kingdom of your own? A beautiful companion? Princess Pauline Borghese is a most delightful woman and I can have her here in the twinkling of an eye!"

Strange opened his mouth to speak and then stopt a moment. "Pauline Borghese, you say? I saw a picture of her in Paris."[2] Then, recollecting himself, he continued, "But I am not interested in that just at present. Tell me about magic. How would I go about turning myself into a bear? Or a fox? What are the names of the three magical rivers that flow through the Kingdom of Agrace?[3] Ralph Stokesey thought that these rivers influenced events in England; is that true? There is mention in *The Language of Birds* of a group of spells that are cast by manipulating colours; what can you tell me about that? What do the stones in the Doncaster Squares represent?"

The gentleman threw up his hands in mock surprize. "So many questions!" He laughed; it was clearly meant to be a merry, carefree laugh, but it sounded a little forced.

"Well then, tell me the answer to one of them. Any one you like."

The gentleman only smiled pleasantly.

Strange stared at him in undisguised vexation. Apparently the offer did not extend to knowledge, only objects. "And if I wanted to give myself a present, I would go and buy something!" thought

---

[2] This lady was the most beautiful and tempestuous of Napoleon Buonaparte's sisters, much given to taking lovers and posing, unclothed, for statues of herself.

[3] Agrace is the name sometimes given to John Uskglass's third Kingdom. This Kingdom was thought to lie on the far side of Hell.

Strange. "If I wanted to see Pauline Borghese, I would simply go to her and introduce myself. I do not need magic for that! How in the world do I . . ." A thought struck him. Out loud he said, "Bring me something that you gained from your last dealings with an English magician!"

"What?" said the gentleman, startled. "No, you do not want that! It is worthless, utterly worthless! Think again!"

Clearly he was much perturbed by Strange's request – though Strange could not tell why he should be. "Perhaps," he thought, "the magician gave him something valuable and he is loath to give it up. No matter. Once I have seen what it is, and learnt what I can from it I shall give it back to him. That ought to persuade him of my good intentions."

He smiled politely: "A binding agreement, I think you said? I shall expect it – whatever it is – later this evening!"

At eight o'clock he dined with the Greysteels in their gloomy dining-hall.

Miss Greysteel asked him about Lord Byron.

"Oh!" said Strange. "He does not intend to return to England. He can write poems anywhere. Whereas in my own case, English magic was shaped by England – just as England herself was shaped by magic. The two go together. You cannot separate them."

"You mean," said Miss Greysteel, frowning a little, "that English minds and history and so forth were shaped by magic. You are speaking metaphorically."

"No, I was speaking quite literally. This city, for example, was built in the common way . . ."

"Oh!" interrupted Dr Greysteel, laughing. "How like a magician that sounds! The slight edge of contempt when he speaks of things being done in the common way!"

"I do not think that I intended any disrespect. I assure you I have the greatest regard for things done in the common way. No, my point was merely that the boundaries of England – its very shape was determined by magic."

Dr Greysteel sniffed. "I am not sure of this. Give me an example."

"Very well. There once was a very fine town stood on the coast of Yorkshire whose citizens began to wonder why it was that their King, John Uskglass, should require taxes from them. Surely, they argued, so great a magician could conjure up all the gold he wanted from the air. Now there is no harm in wondering, but these foolish people did not stop there. They refused to pay and began to plot with the King's enemies. A man is best advised to consider carefully before he quarrels with a magician and still more with a king. But when these two characters are combined in one person, Why! then the peril is multiplied a hundred times. First a wind came out of the north and blew through the town. As the wind touched the beasts of the town they grew old and died – cows, pigs, fowls and sheep – even the cats and dogs. As the wind touched the town itself houses became ruins before the very eyes of the unhappy householders. Tools broke, pots shattered, wood warped and split, brick and stone crumbled into dust. Stone images in the church wore away as if with extreme age, until, it was said, every face of every statue appeared to be screaming. The wind whipped up the sea into strange, menacing shapes. The townspeople, very wisely, began to run from the town and when they reached the higher ground they looked back and were just in time to see the remains of the town slip slowly under the cold, grey waves."

Dr Greysteel smiled. "Let the government be who they may – Whigs, Tories, emperors or magicians – they take it very ill when people do not pay their taxes. And shall you include these tales in your next book?"

"Oh, certainly. I am not one of those miserly authors who measure out their words to the last quarter ounce. I have very liberal ideas of authorship. Anyone who cares to pay Mr Murray their guinea will find that I have thrown the doors of my warehouse wide open and that all my learning is up for sale. My readers may stroll about and chuse at their leisure."

Miss Greysteel gave this tale a moment or two of serious consideration. "He was certainly provoked," she said at last, "but it was still the act of a tyrant."

Somewhere in the shadows footsteps were approaching.

"What is it, Frank?" asked Dr Greysteel.

Frank, Dr Greysteel's servant, emerged from the gloom.

"We have found a letter and a little box, sir. Both for Mr Strange." Frank looked troubled.

"Well, do not stand and gape so. Here is Mr Strange, sat just at your elbow. Give him his letter and his little box."

Frank's expression and attitude all declared him to be tussling with some great perplexity. His scowl suggested that he believed himself to be quite out of his depth. He made one last attempt to communicate his vexation to his master. "We found the letter and the little box on the floor just inside the door, sir, but the door was locked and bolted!"

"Then someone must have unlocked and unbolted it, Frank. Do not be making mysteries," said Dr Greysteel.

So Frank gave the letter and box to Strange and wandered away into the darkness again, muttering to himself and inquiring of the chairs and tables he met on the way what sort of blockhead they took him for.

Aunt Greysteel leaned over and politely entreated Mr Strange to use no ceremony – he was with friends and should read his letter directly. This was very kind of her, but a little superfluous, since Strange had already opened the paper and was reading his letter.

"Oh, aunt!" cried Miss Greysteel, picking up the little box which Frank had placed on the table. "See, how beautiful!"

The box was small and oblong and apparently made of silver and porcelain. It was a beautiful shade of blue, but then again not exactly blue, it was more like lilac. But then again, not exactly lilac either, since it had a tinge of grey in it. To be more precise, it was the colour of heartache. But fortunately neither Miss Greysteel nor Aunt Greysteel had ever been much troubled by heartache and so they did not recognize it.

"It is certainly very pretty," said her aunt. "Is it Italian, Mr Strange?"

"Mmm?" said Strange. He glanced up. "I do not know."

"Is there anything inside?" asked Aunt Greysteel.

"Yes, I believe so," said Miss Greysteel, beginning to open it.

"Flora!" cried Dr Greysteel and shook his head sharply at his daughter. He had an idea that the box might be a present which Strange intended to give to Flora. He did not like this idea, but Dr Greysteel did not think himself competent to judge the sorts of behaviour in which a man like Strange – a fashionable man of the world – might consider himself licensed to indulge.

Strange, with his nose still deep in the letter, saw and heard none of this. He took up the little box and opened it.

"Is there any thing inside, Mr Strange?" asked Aunt Greysteel.

Strange shut the box quickly again. "No, madam, nothing at all." He put the box in his pocket and immediately summoned Frank and asked for a glass of water.

He left the Greysteels very soon after dinner and went straight to the coffee-house on the corner of the Calle de la Cortesia. The first glimpse of the contents of the box had been very shocking and he had a strong desire to be among people when he opened it again.

The waiter brought his brandy. He took a sip and opened the box.

At first he supposed that the fairy had sent him a replica of a small, white, amputated finger, made of wax or some such material and very lifelike. It was so pale, so drained of blood, that it seemed almost to be tinged with green, with a suggestion of pink in the grooves around the fingernail. He wondered that any one should labour so long to produce any thing quite so horrible.

But the moment he touched it he realized it was not wax at all. It was icy cold, and yet the skin moved in the same way as the skin moved upon his own finger and the muscles could be detected beneath the skin, both by touch and sight. It was, without a doubt, a human finger. From the size of it he thought it was probably a child's finger or perhaps the smallest finger of a woman with rather delicate hands.

"But why would the magician give him a finger?" he wondered. "Perhaps it was the magician's finger? But I do not see how that can be, unless the magician were either a child or a woman." It occurred to him that he had heard something about a finger once, but for the moment he could not remember what it was. Oddly enough although he did not remember *what* he had been told, he thought he remembered *who* had told him. It had been Drawlight. ". . . which explains why I did not pay a great deal of attention. But why would Drawlight have been talking of magic? He knew little and cared less."

He drank some more brandy. "I thought that if I had a fairy to explain everything to me, then all the mysteries would become clear. But all that has happened is that I have acquired another mystery!"

He fell to musing upon the various stories he had heard concerning the great English magicians and their fairy-servants. Martin Pale with Master Witcherley, Master Fallowthought and all the rest. Thomas Godbless with Dick-come-Tuesday; Meraud with Coleman Gray; and most famous of all, Ralph Stokesey and Col Tom Blue.

When Stokesey first saw Col Tom Blue, he was a wild, unruly person – the last fairy in the world to ally himself to an English magician. So Stokesey had followed him into Faerie, to Col Tom Blue's own castle[4] and had gone about invisibly and discovered many interesting things.[5] Strange was not so naive as to suppose

---

[4] *Brugh*, the ancient *Sidhe* word for the homes of the fairies, is usually translated as castle or mansion, but in fact means the interior of a barrow or hollow hill.

[5] Stokesey summoned Col Tom Blue to his house in Exeter. When the fairy refused for the third time to serve him, Stokesey made himself invisible and

that the story as it had come down to children and magio-historians was an accurate description of what had happened. "Yet there is probably some truth in it somewhere," he thought. "Perhaps Stokesey managed to penetrate Col Tom Blue's castle and that proved to Col Tom Blue that he was a magician to be reckoned with. There is no reason that I could not do something similar. After all this fairy knows nothing of my skills or achievements. If I were to pay him an unexpected visit, it would prove to him the extent of my power."

---

[5] *cont'd*   followed Col Tom Blue out of the town. Col Tom Blue walked along a fairy road and soon arrived in a place that was not England. There was a low brown hill by a pool of still water. In answer to Col Tom Blue's command a door opened in the hillside and he went inside. Stokesey went after him.

In the centre of the hill Stokesey found an enchanted hall where everyone was dancing. He waited until one of the dancers came close. Then he rolled a magic apple towards her and she picked it up. Naturally it was the best and most beautiful apple in all the worlds that ever were. As soon as the fairy woman had eaten it, she desired nothing so much as another one just the same. She looked around, but saw no one. "Who sent me that apple?" she asked. "The East Wind," whispered Stokesey. On the next night Stokesey again followed Col Tom Blue inside the hill. He watched the dancers and again he rolled an apple towards the woman. When she asked who had sent it to her, he replied that it was the East Wind. On the third night he kept the apple in his hand. The fairy woman left the other dancers and looked round. "East Wind! East Wind!" she whispered. "Where is my apple?" "Tell me where Col Tom Blue sleeps," whispered Stokesey, "and I will give you the apple." So she told him: deep in the ground, on the northernmost edge of the *brugh*.

On the following nights Stokesey impersonated the West Wind, the North Wind and the South Wind and he used his apples to persuade other inhabitants of the mound to give him information about Col Tom Blue. From a shepherd he learnt what animals guarded Col Tom Blue while he slept – a wild she-pig and an even wilder he-goat. From Col Tom Blue's nurse he learnt what Col Tom Blue held in his hand while he slept – a very particular and important pebble. And from a kitchen-boy he learnt what three words Col Tom Blue said every morning upon waking.

In this way Stokesey learnt enough to gain power over Col Tom Blue. But before he could use his new knowledge, Col Tom Blue came to him and said he had reconsidered: he believed he would like to serve Stokesey after all.

What had happened was this: Col Tom Blue had discovered that the East Wind, the West Wind, the North Wind and the South Wind had all been asking questions about him. He had no idea what he could have done to offend these important personages, but he was seriously alarmed. An alliance with a powerful and learned English magician suddenly seemed a great deal more attractive.

He thought back to the misty, snowy day at Windsor when he and the King had almost stumbled into Faerie, lured by the gentleman's magic. He thought of the wood and the tiny lights within it that had suggested an ancient house. The King's Roads could certainly take him there, but – leaving aside his promise to Arabella – he had no desire to find the gentleman by magic he had already done. He wanted this to be something new and startling. When he next saw the gentleman he wanted to be full of the confidence and exhilaration that a successful new spell always bestowed on him.

"Faerie is never very far away," he thought, "and there are a thousand ways of getting there. Surely I ought to be able to find one of them?"

There was a spell he knew of that could make a path between any two beings the magician named. It was an old spell – just a step away from fairy magic. The paths it would make could certainly cross the boundaries between worlds. Strange had never used it before and he had no idea of what the path would like look or how he would follow it. Still he believed he could do it. He muttered the words to himself, made a few gestures, and named himself and the gentleman as the two beings between whom the path should be drawn.

There was a shift as sometimes happened at the start of magic. It was as if an invisible door had opened and closed, leaving him upon the other side of it. Or as if all the buildings in the city had turned round and everything was now facing in another direction. The magic appeared to have worked perfectly – something had certainly happened – but he could see no result. He considered what to do next.

"It is probably only a matter of perception – and I know how to cure that." He paused. "It is vexatious. I had much rather not use it again, but still, once more is not likely to hurt."

He reached into the breast of his coat and brought out the tincture of madness. The waiter brought him a glass of water and he carefully tipped in one tiny drop. He drank it down.

He looked around and perceived for the first time the line of glittering light which began at his foot, crossed the tiled floor of the coffee-house and led out of the door. It was very like those lines which he had often made to appear upon the silver dish of water. He found that if he looked directly at it, it disappeared. But if he kept it in the corner of his eye he could see it very well.

He paid the waiter and stepped out into the street. "Well," he said, "that is truly remarkable."

55

The second shall see his dearest possession in his enemy's hand

Night of 2nd/3rd December 1816

I T WAS AS if that fate which had always seemed to threaten the city of Venice had overtaken her in an instant; but instead of being drowned in water, she was drowned in trees. Dark, ghostly trees crowded the alleys and squares, and filled the canals. Walls were no obstacle to them. Their branches pierced stone and glass. Their roots plunged deep beneath paving stones. Statues and pillars were sheathed in ivy. It was suddenly – to Strange's senses at any rate – a great deal quieter and darker. Trailing beards of mistletoe hid lamps and candles and the dense canopy of branches blocked out the moon.

Yet none of Venice's inhabitants appeared to notice the least change. Strange had often read how men and women could be cheerfully oblivious to magic going on around them, but never before had he seen an example of it. A baker's apprentice was carrying a tray of bread on his head. As Strange watched, the man neatly circumvented all the trees he did not know were there and ducking this way and that to avoid branches which would have poked his eye out. A man and a woman dressed for the ballroom or the *Ridotto*, with cloaks and masks, came down the Salizzada San Moisè together, arm in arm, heads together, whispering. A great tree stood in their way. They parted quite naturally, passed one on each side of the tree and joined arms again on the other side.

Strange followed the line of glittering light down an alley to the quayside. The trees went on where the city stopped, and the line of light led through the trees.

He did not much care for the idea of stepping into the sea. At Venice there is no gently sloping beach to lead one inch by inch into the water; the stone world of the city ends at the quayside and the Adriatic begins immediately. Strange had no notion how deep the water might be just here, but he was tolerably certain that it was deep enough to drown in. All he could do was hope that the glittering path which led him through the wood would also prevent him from drowning.

Yet at the same time it pleased his vanity to think how much better suited he was to this adventure than Norrell. "He could never be persuaded to step into the sea. He hates getting wet. Who was it that said a magician needs the subtlety of a Jesuit, the daring of a soldier and the wits of a thief? I believe it was meant for an insult, but it has some truth in it."

He stepped off the quayside.

Instantly the sea became more ethereal and dreamlike, and the wood became more solid. Soon the sea was scarcely more than a faint silver shimmer among the dark trees and a salty tang mingling with the usual scents of a night-time wood.

"I am," thought Strange, "the first English magician to enter Faerie in almost three hundred years."[1] He felt excessively pleased at the thought and rather wished there were someone there to see him do it and be astonished. He realized how tired he was of books and silence, how he longed for the times when to be a magician meant journeys into places no Englishman had ever seen. For the first time since Waterloo he was actually doing something. Then it

---

[1] The last English magician to enter Faerie willingly before Strange was Dr Martin Pale. He made many journeys there. The last was probably some time in the 1550s.

occurred to him that, rather than congratulating himself, he ought to be looking about him and seeing if there were any thing he could learn. He applied himself to studying his surroundings.

The wood was not quite an English wood, though it was very like it. The trees were a little too ancient, a little too vast and a little too fantastic in shape. Strange had the strong impression that they possessed fully formed characters, with loves, hates and desires of their own. They looked as if they were accustomed to being treated equally with men and women, and expected to be consulted in matters that concerned them.

"This," he thought, "is just as I would have expected, but it ought to stand as a warning to me of how different this world is from my own. The people I meet here are sure to ask me questions. They will want to trick me." He began to imagine the sorts of questions they might ask him and to prepare a variety of clever answers. He felt no fear; a dragon might appear for all he cared. He had come so far in the last two days; he felt as if there was nothing he could not do if he tried.

After twenty minutes or so of walking the glittering line led him to the house. He recognized it immediately; its image had been so sharp and clear before him that day in Windsor. Yet at the same time it was different. In Windsor it had appeared bright and welcoming. Now he was struck by its overwhelming air of poverty and desolation. The windows were many, but very small and most of them were dark. It was much bigger than he expected – far larger than any earthly dwelling. "The Czar of Russia may have a house as large as this," he thought, "or perhaps the Pope in Rome. I do not know. I have never been to those places."

It was surrounded by a high wall. The glittering line seemed to stop at the wall. He could not see any opening. He muttered Ormskirk's Spell of Revelation, followed immediately by Taille-mache's Shield, a charm to ensure safe passage through enchanted places. His luck held and immediately a mean little gate appeared. He passed through it and found himself in a wide grey courtyard.

It was full of bones that glimmered whitely in the starlight. Some skeletons were clad in rusting armour; the weapons that had destroyed them were still tangled with their ribs or poking out of an eye-socket.

Strange had seen the battlefields of Badajoz and Waterloo; he was scarcely perturbed by a few ancient skeletons. Still it was interesting. He felt as if he really were in Faerie now.

Despite the dilapidation of the house he had the strongest suspicion that there was something magical about its appearance. He tried Ormskirk's Revelation again. Immediately the house shifted and changed and he could see that it was only partly built of stone. Some of what had appeared to be walls, buttresses and towers was now revealed as a great mound of earth – a hillside in fact.

"*It is a brugh!*" he thought in great excitement.[2]

He passed under a low doorway and found himself immediately in a vast room filled with people dancing. The dancers were dressed in the finest clothes imaginable, but the room itself seemed in the very worst state of repair. Indeed at one end, part of a wall had collapsed and lay in a heap of rubble. The furnishings were few and shabby, the candles were of the poorest sort and there was only one fiddler and one piper to provide the music.

No one appeared to be paying Strange the least attention and so he stood among the people near the wall and watched the dance. In many ways the entertainment here was less foreign to him than, say, a *conversazione*[3] in Venice. The manners of the guests seemed more English and the dance itself was very like the country dances that are enjoyed by ladies and gentlemen from Newcastle to Penzance every week of the year.

It occurred to him that once upon a time he had been fond of dancing, and so had Arabella. But after the war in Spain he had hardly danced with her – or indeed with any one else. Wherever he

---

[2] See Chapter 54, footnote 4.
[3] Italian party.

had gone in London – whether to a ballroom or Government office – there had always been too many people to talk to about magic. He wondered if Arabella had danced with other people. He wondered if he had asked her. "Though if I did think to ask her," he thought with a sigh, "I clearly did not listen to her answers – I cannot remember any thing about it."

"Good God, sir! What are you doing here?"

Strange turned to see who spoke. The one thing he was not prepared for was that the first person he should meet should be Sir Walter Pole's butler. He could not remember the fellow's name, though he had heard Sir Walter speak it a hundred times. Simon? Samuel?

The man grasped Strange by the arm and shook him. He seemed highly agitated. "For God's sake, sir, what are you doing here? Don't you know that he hates you?"

Strange opened his mouth to deliver one of the clever ripostes but then hesitated. Who hated him? Norrell?

In the complexity of the dance the man was whisked away. Strange looked for him again and caught sight of him on the other side of the room. The man glared furiously at Strange as if he were angry at him for not leaving.

"How odd," thought Strange. "And yet of course they would do that. They would do the thing you least expected. Probably it is not Pole's butler at all. Probably it is only a fairy in his likeness. Or a magical illusion." He began to look around for his own fairy.

"Stephen! Stephen!"

"I am here, sir!" Stephen turned and found the gentleman with the thistle-down hair at his elbow.

"The magician is here! He is here! What can he want?"

"I do not know, sir."

"Oh! He has come here to destroy me! I know he has!"

Stephen was astonished. For a long time he had imagined that the gentleman was proof against any injury. Yet here he was in a condition of the utmost anxiety and fright.

"But why would he want to do that, sir?" asked Stephen in a soothing tone. "I think it far more likely that he has come here to rescue . . . to take home his wife. Perhaps we should release Mrs Strange from her enchantment and permit her to return home with her husband? And Lady Pole too. Let Mrs Strange and Lady Pole return to England with the magician, sir. I am sure that will be enough to mollify his anger against you. I am sure I can persuade him."

"What? What are you talking about? Mrs Strange? No, no, Stephen! You are quite mistaken! Indeed you are! He has not so much as mentioned our dear Mrs Strange. You and I, Stephen, know how to appreciate the society of such a woman. He does not. He has forgotten all about her. He has a new sweetheart now – a bewitching young woman whose lovely presence I hope one day will add lustre to our own balls! There is naught so fickle as an Englishman! Oh, believe me! He has come to destroy me! From the moment he asked me for Lady Pole's finger I knew that he was far, far cleverer than I had ever guessed before. Advise me, Stephen. You have lived among these Englishmen for years. What ought I to do? How can I protect myself? How can I punish such wickedness?"

Through all the dullness and heaviness of his enchantment Stephen struggled to think clearly. A great crisis was upon him, he was sure of it. Never before had the gentleman asked for his help so openly. Surely he ought to be able to turn the situation to his advantage? But how? And he knew from long experience that none of the gentleman's moods lasted long; he was the most mercurial being in the world. The smallest word could turn his fear into a blazing rage and hatred – if Stephen misspoke now, then far from freeing himself and the others, he might goad the gentleman into destroying them all. He gazed about the room in search of inspiration.

"What shall I do, Stephen?" moaned the gentleman. "What shall I do?"

Something caught Stephen's eye. Beneath a black arch stood a familiar figure: a fairy woman who habitually wore a black veil that went from the crown of her head to the tips of her fingers. She never joined in the dancing; she half-walked, half-floated among the dancers and the standers-by. Stephen had never seen her speak to any one, but when she passed by there was a faint smell of graveyards, earth and charnel houses. He could never look upon her without feeling a shiver of apprehension, but whether she was malignant, cursed, or both, he did not know.

"There are people in this world," he began, "whose lives are nothing but a burden to them. A black veil stands between them and the world. They are utterly alone. They are like shadows in the night, shut off from joy and love and all gentle human emotions, unable even to give comfort to each other. Their days are full of nothing but darkness, misery and solitude. You know whom I mean, sir. I . . . I do not speak of blame . . ." The gentleman was gazing at him with fierce intensity. "But I am sure we can turn the magician's wrath away from you, if you will only release . . ."

"Ah!" exclaimed the gentleman and his eyes widened with understanding. He held up his hand as a sign for Stephen to be silent.

Stephen was certain that he had gone too far. "Forgive me," he whispered.

"Forgive?" said the gentleman in a tone of surprize. "Why, there is nothing to forgive! It is long centuries since any one spoke to me with such forthrightness and I honour you for it! Darkness, yes! Darkness, misery and solitude!" He turned upon his heel and walked away into the crowd.

Strange was enjoying himself immensely. The eerie contradictions of the ball did not disturb him in the least; they were just what he would have expected. Despite the poverty of the great hall, it was still in part an illusion. His magician's eye perceived that at least part of the room was beneath the earth.

A little way off a fairy woman was regarding him steadily. She was dressed in a gown the colour of a winter sunset and carried a delicate, glittering fan strung with something which might have been crystal beads – but which more resembled frost upon leaves and the fragile pendants of ice that hang from twigs.

A dance was at that moment starting up. No one appeared to claim the fairy woman's hand, so upon an impulse Strange smiled and bowed and said, "There is scarcely any one here who knows me. So we cannot be introduced. Nevertheless, madam, I should be greatly honoured if you would dance with me."

She did not answer him or smile in return, but she took his proffered hand and allowed him to lead her to the dance. They took their places in the set and stood for a moment without saying a word.

"You are wrong to say no one knows you," she said suddenly. "I know you. You are one of the two magicians who is destined to return magic to England." Then she said, as if reciting a prophecy or something that was commonly known, "*And the name of one shall be Fearfulness. And the name of the other shall be Arrogance* . . . Well, clearly you are not Fearfulness, so I suppose you must be Arrogance."

This was not very polite.

"That is indeed my destiny," Strange agreed. "And an excellent one it is!"

"Oh, you think so, do you?" she said, giving him a sideways look. "Then why haven't you done it yet?"

Strange smiled. "And what makes you think, madam, that I have not?"

"Because you are standing here."

"I do not understand."

"Did not you listen to the prophecy when it was told to you?"

"The prophecy, madam?"

"Yes, the prophecy of . . ." She finished by saying a name, but it was in her own language and Strange could not make it out.[4]

"I beg your pardon?"

"The prophecy of the King."

Strange thought back to Vinculus climbing out from under the winter hedge with bits of dry, brown grass and empty seed pods stuck to his clothes; he remembered Vinculus reciting something in the winter lane. But what Vinculus had said he had no idea. He had had no notion of becoming a magician just then and had not paid any attention. "I believe there was a prophecy of some sort, madam," he said, "but to own the truth it was long ago and I do not remember. What does the prophecy say we must do? – the other magician and I?"

"Fail."

Strange blinked in surprise. "I . . . I do not think . . . Fail? No, madam, no. It is too late for that. Already we are the most successful magicians since Martin Pale."

She said nothing.

Was it too late to fail? wondered Strange. He thought of Mr Norrell in the house in Hanover-square, of Mr Norrell at Hurtfew Abbey, of Mr Norrell complimented by all the Ministers and politely attended to by the Prince Regent. It was perhaps a little ironic that he of all people should take comfort from Norrell's success, but at that moment nothing in the world seemed so solid, so unassailable. The fairy woman was mistaken.

For the next few minutes they were occupied in going down the dance. When they had resumed their places in the set, she said, "You are certainly very bold to come here, Magician."

"Why? What ought I to fear, madam?"

She laughed. "How many English magicians do you suppose have left their bones lying in this *brugh*? Beneath these stars?"

---

[4] Presumably John Uskglass's *Sidhe* name.

"I have not the least idea."

"Forty-seven."

Strange began to feel a little less comfortable.

"Not counting Peter Porkiss, but he was no magician. He was only a *cowan*."[5]

"Indeed."

"Do not pretend that you know what I mean," she said sharply. "When it is as plain as Pandemonium that you do not."

Strange was once again perplexed what to reply. She seemed so bent upon being displeased. But then again, he thought, what was so unusual about it? In Bath and London and all the cities of Europe ladies pretended to scold the men they meant to attract. For all he knew she was just the same. He decided to treat her severe manner as a kind of flirtation and see if that soothed her. So he laughed lightly and said, "It seems you know a great deal of what has passed in this *brugh*, madam." It gave him a little thrill of excitement to say the word, a word so ancient and romantic.

She shrugged. "I have been a visitor here for four thousand years."[6]

"I should be very glad to talk you about it whenever you are at liberty."

"Say rather when *you* are next at liberty! Then I shall have no objection to answering any of your questions."

"You are very kind."

"Not at all. A hundred years from tonight then?"

"I . . . I beg your pardon?"

---

[5] A particular problem in mediaeval England was the great abundance of *cowans*. It is a term (now obsolete) properly applied to any unqualified or failed craftsmen, but here has special application to magicians.

[6] Several authorities have noted that long-lived fairies have a tendency to call any substantial period of time "four thousand years". The fairy lady simply means she has known the *brugh* time out of mind, before any one troubled to reckon up time into years, centuries and millennia. Many fairies, when asked, will say they are four thousand years old; they mean they do not know their age; they are older than human civilization – or possibly than humankind.

But she seemed to feel she had talked enough and he could get nothing more from her but the most commonplace remarks upon the ball and their fellow-dancers.

The dance ended; they parted. It had been the oddest and most unsettling conversation of Strange's life. Why in the world should she think that magic had not yet been restored to England? And what was all that nonsense about a hundred years? He consoled himself with the thought that a woman who passed much of her life in an echoing mansion in a deep, dark wood was unlikely to be very well informed upon events in the wider worlds.

He rejoined the watchers by the wall. The course of the next dance brought a particularly lovely woman close to him. He was struck by the contrast between the beauty of her face and the deep, settled unhappiness of her expression. As she raised her hand to join hands with her partner, he saw that her little finger was missing.

"Curious!" he thought and touched the pocket of his coat where the box of silver and porcelain lay. "Perhaps . . ." But he could not conceive any sequence of events which would result in a magician giving the fairy a finger belonging to someone in the fairy's own household. It made no sense. "Perhaps the two things are not connected at all," he thought.

But the woman's hand was so small and white. He was sure that the finger in his pocket would fit it perfectly. He was full of curiosity and determined to go and speak to her and ask her how she had lost her finger.

The dance had ended. She was speaking to another lady, who had her back to him.

"I beg your pardon . . ." he began.

Instantly the other lady turned. It was Arabella.

She was dressed in a white gown with an overdress of pale blue net and diamonds. It glittered like frost and snow, and was far prettier than any gown she had possessed when she lived in England. In her hair were sprays of some tiny, star-like blossoms and there was a black velvet ribbon tied around her throat.

She gazed at him with an odd expression – an expression in which surprize was mixed with wariness, delight with disbelief. "Jonathan! Look, my love!" she said to her companion. "It is Jonathan!"

"Arabella . . ." he began. He did not know what he meant to say. He held out his hands to her; but she did not take them. Without appearing to know what she did, she withdrew slightly and joined her hands with those of the unknown woman, as if this was now the person to whom she went for comfort and support.

The unknown woman looked at Strange in obedience to Arabella's request. "He looks as most men do," she remarked, coldly. And then, as if she felt the meeting were now concluded, "Come," she said. She tried to lead Arabella away.

"Oh, but wait!" said Arabella softly. "I think that he must have come to help us! Do not you think he might have?"

"Perhaps," said the unknown woman in a doubtful tone. She stared at Strange again. "No. I do not think so. I believe he came for another reason entirely."

"I know that you have warned me against false hopes," said Arabella, "and I have tried to do as you advise. But he is here! I was sure he would not forget me so soon."

"Forget you!" exclaimed Strange. "No, indeed! Arabella, I . . ."

"*Did* you come here to help us?" asked the unknown woman, suddenly addressing Strange directly.

"What?" said Strange. "No, I . . . You must understood that until now I did not know . . . Which is to say, I do not quite understand . . ."

The unknown woman made a small sound of exasperation. "Did you or did you not come here to help us? It is a simple enough question I should think."

"No," said Strange. "Arabella, speak to me, I beg you. Tell me what has . . ."

"There? You see?" said the unknown woman to Arabella. "Now let you and me find a corner where we can be peaceful together. I believe I saw an unoccupied bench near the door."

But Arabella would not be persuaded to walk away just yet. She continued to gaze at Strange in the same odd way; it was as if she were looking at a picture of him, rather than the flesh-and-blood man. She said, "I know you do not put a great deal of faith in what men can do, but . . ."

"I put no faith in them at all," interrupted the unknown woman. "I know what it is to waste years and years upon vain hopes of help from this person or that. No hope at all is better than ceaseless disappointment!"

Strange's patience was gone. "You will forgive my interrupting you, madam," he said to the unknown woman, "though I observe you have done nothing but interrupt since I joined you! I fear I must insist on a minute's private conversation with my wife! Perhaps if you will have the goodness to retire a pace or two . . ."

But neither she nor Arabella was attending to him. They were directing their gaze a little to his right. The gentleman with thistle-down hair was just at his shoulder.

Stephen pushed through the crowd of dancers. His conversation with the gentleman had been most unnerving. Something had been decided upon, but the more Stephen thought about it, the more he realized he had not the least idea what it was. "It is still not too late," he muttered as forced his way through. "It is not still too late." Part of him – the cold, uncaring, enchanted half – wondered what he meant by that. Not too late to save himself? To save Lady Pole and Mrs Strange? The magician?

Never had the lines of dancers seemed so long, so like a fence barring his way. On the other side of the room he thought he saw a head of gleaming, thistle-down hair. "Sir!" he cried. "Wait! I must speak with you again!"

The light changed. The sounds of music, dancing and conversation were swept away. Stephen looked around, expecting to find himself in a new city or upon another continent. But he was still in the great hall of Lost-hope. It was empty; the dancers and musicians were gone. Three people remained: Stephen himself and, some way off, the magician and the gentleman with the thistle-down hair.

The magician called out his wife's name. He hastened towards a dark door as if he intended to dash off into the house in search of her.

"Wait!" cried the gentleman with the thistle-down hair. The magician turned and Stephen saw that his face was black with anger, that his mouth was working as if a spell were about to explode out of him.

The gentleman with the thistle-down hair raised his hands. *The great hall was filled with a flock of birds. In the blink of an eye they were there; in the blink of an eye they were gone.*

The birds had struck Stephen with their wings. They had knocked the breath out of him. When he recovered enough to lift his head, he saw that the gentleman with the thistle-down hair had raised his hands a second time.

The great hall was full of spinning leaves. Winter-dry and brown they were, turning in a wind that had come out of nowhere. In the blink of an eye they were there; in the blink of an eye they were gone.

The magician was staring wildly. He did not seem to know what to do in the face of such overwhelming magic. "He is lost," thought Stephen.

The gentleman with the thistle-down hair raised his hands a third time. *The great hall was full of rain – not a rain of water, a rain of blood. In the blink of an eye it was there; in the blink of an eye it was gone.*

The magic ended. In that instant the magician disappeared and the gentleman with the thistle-down hair dropped to the floor, like a man in a swoon.

"Where is the magician, sir?" cried Stephen, rushing to kneel beside him. "What has happened?"

"I have sent him back to Altinum's sea colony,"[7] he said in a hoarse whisper. He tried to smile, but seemed quite unable. "I have done it, Stephen! I have done what you advised! It has taken all my strength. My old alliances have been stretched to their utmost limit. But I have changed the world! Oh! I have dealt him such a blow! Darkness, misery and solitude! He will not hurt us any more!" He attempted a triumphant laugh, but it turned into a fit of coughing and retching. When it was done he took Stephen's hand. "Do not be concerned about me, Stephen. I am a little tired, that is all. You are a person of remarkable vision and penetration. Henceforth you and I are no longer friends: we are brothers! You have helped me defeat my enemy and in return I shall find your name. I shall make you King!" His voice faded to nothing.

"Tell me what you have done!" whispered Stephen.

But the gentleman closed his eyes.

Stephen remained kneeling in the ballroom, grasping the gentleman's hand. The tallow candles went out; the shadows closed about them.

---

[7] Meaning Venice: Altinum was the city on Italy's eastern coast whence came the first inhabitants of Venice.

56

The Black Tower

3rd/4th December 1816

D R GREYSTEEL WAS asleep and dreaming. In his dream someone was calling for him and something was required of him. He was anxious to oblige whoever it was and so he went to this place and that, searching for them; but he did not find them and still they called his name. Finally he opened his eyes.

"Who's there?" he asked.

"It's me, sir. Frank, sir."

"What's the matter?"

"Mr Strange is here. He wants to speak to you, sir."

"Is something wrong?"

"He don't say, sir. But, I think there must be."

"Where is he, Frank?"

"He won't come in, sir. He won't be persuaded. He's outside, sir."

Dr Greysteel lowered his legs out of the bed and drew in his breath sharply. "It's cold, Frank!" he said.

"Yes, sir." Frank helped Dr Greysteel on with his dressing-gown and slippers. They padded through numerous dark rooms, across acres of dark marble floors. In the vestibule a lamp was burning. Frank pulled back the great iron double doors and then he picked up the lamp and went outside. Dr Greysteel followed him.

A flight of stone steps descended into darkness. Only the smell of the sea, the lap of water against stone and a certain occasional glitter and shifting-about of the darkness gave the observer to understand that at the bottom of the steps there was a canal. A few houses round about had lamps burning in windows or upon balconies. Beyond this all was silence and darkness.

"There is no one here!" cried Dr Greysteel. "Where is Mr Strange?"

For answer Frank pointed off to the right. A lamp bloomed suddenly under a bridge and by its light Dr Greysteel saw a gondola, waiting. The *gondoliero* poled his boat towards them. As it approached, Dr Greysteel could see there was a passenger. Despite all that Frank had said, it took a moment or two for Dr Greysteel to recognize him. "Strange!" he cried. "Good God! What has happened? I did not know you! My . . . my . . . my dear friend." Dr Greysteel's tongue stumbled, trying to find a suitable word. He had grown accustomed in the last few weeks to the idea that he and Strange would soon stand in a much closer relationship. "Come inside! Frank, quick! Fetch a glass of wine for Mr Strange!"

"No!" cried Strange in a hoarse, unfamiliar voice. He spoke urgently in Italian to the *gondoliero*. His Italian was considerably more fluent than Dr Greysteel's and Dr Greysteel did not understand him, but the meaning soon became clear when the *gondoliero* began to move his boat away.

"I cannot come inside!" cried Strange. "Do not ask me!

"Very well, but tell me what has happened."

"I am cursed!"

"Cursed? No! Do not say so."

"But I do say so. I have been wrong from start to finish! I told this fellow to take me a little way off. It is not safe for me to be too close to your house. Dr Greysteel! You must send your daughter away!"

"Flora! Why?"

"There is someone nearby who means her harm!"

"Good God!"

809

Strange's eyes grew wider. "There is someone who means to bind her to a life of ceaseless misery! Slavery and subjugation to a wild spirit! An ancient prison built as much of cold enchantments as of stone and earth. Wicked, wicked! And then again, perhaps not so wicked after all – for what does he do but follow his nature? How can he help himself?"

Neither Dr Greysteel nor Frank could make any thing of this.

"You are ill, sir," said Dr Greysteel. "You have a fever. Come inside. Frank can make you a soothing drink to take away these evil thoughts. Come inside, Mr Strange." He drew away slightly from the steps so that Strange might approach, but Strange took no notice.

"I thought . . ." began Strange, and then stopt immediately. He paused so long it seemed he had forgotten what he was going to say, but then he began again. "I thought," he began again, "that Norrell had only lied to me. But I was wrong. Quite wrong. He has lied to everybody. He has lied to us all." Then he spoke to the *gondoliero* and the gondola moved away into the darkness.

"Wait! Wait!" cried Dr Greysteel, but it was gone. He stared into the darkness, hoping that Strange would reappear, but he did not.

"Should I go after him, sir?" asked Frank.

"We do not know where he has gone."

"I dare say he has gone home, sir. I can follow him on foot."

"And say what to him, Frank? He would not listen to us just now. No, let us go inside. There is Flora to consider."

But once inside Dr Greysteel stood helpless, quite at a loss to know what to do next. He suddenly looked as old as his years. Frank took him gently by the arm and led him down a dark stone staircase into the kitchen.

It was a very small kitchen to service so many large marble rooms upstairs. In daylight it was a dank, gloomy place. There was only one window. It was high up on the wall, just above the level of the water outside, and it was covered by a heavy iron grille. This meant that most of the room was below the level of the canal. Yet after their encounter with Strange, it seemed a warm and friendly place. Frank lit more candles and stirred the fire into life. Then he filled a kettle to make them both some tea.

Dr Greysteel, seated in a homely kitchen chair, stared into the fire, lost in thought. "When he spoke of someone meaning harm to Flora . . ." he said at last.

Frank nodded as if he knew what came next.

". . . I could not help thinking he meant himself, Frank," said Dr Greysteel. "He fears he will do something to hurt her and so he comes to warn me."

"That's it, sir!" agreed Frank. "He comes here to warn us. Which shews that he is a good man at heart."

"He is a good man," said Dr Greysteel, earnestly. "But something has happened. It is this magic, Frank. It must be. It is a very queer profession and I cannot help wishing he were something else – a soldier or a clergyman or a lawyer! What will we tell Flora, Frank? She will not want to go – you may be sure of that! She will not want to leave him. Especially when . . . when he is sick. What can I tell her? I ought to go with her. But then who will remain in Venice to take care of Mr Strange?"

"You and I will stay here and help the magician, sir. But send Miss Flora away with her aunt."

"Yes, Frank! That's it! That's what we shall do!"

"Tho' I must say, sir," added Frank, "that Miss Flora scarcely needs people to take care of her. She is not like other young ladies." Frank had lived long enough with the Greysteels to catch the family habit of regarding Miss Greysteel as someone of exceptional abilities and intelligence.

Feeling that they had done all that they could for the present, Dr Greysteel and Frank went back to bed.

But it is one thing to form plans in the middle of the night, it is quite another to carry them out in the broad light of day. As Dr Greysteel had predicted, Flora objected in the strongest terms to being sent away from Venice and from Jonathan Strange. She did not understand. Why must she go?

Because, said Dr Greysteel, he was ill.

All the more reason to stay then, she said. He would need someone to nurse him.

Dr Greysteel tried to imply that Strange's illness was contagious, but he was, by principle and inclination, an honest man. He had had little practice at lying and he did it badly. Flora did not believe him.

Aunt Greysteel scarcely understood the change of plan any better than her niece. Dr Greysteel could not stand against their united opposition and so he was obliged to take his sister into his confidence and tell her what had happened during the night. Unfortunately he had no talent for conveying atmospheres. The peculiar chill of Strange's words was entirely absent from his explanation. Aunt Greysteel understood only that Strange had been incoherent. She naturally concluded that he had been drunk. This, though very bad, was not unusual among gentlemen and seemed no reason for them all to remove to another city.

"After all, Lancelot," she said, "I have known *you* very much the worse for wine. There was the time we dined with Mr Sixsmith and you insisted upon saying good night to all the chickens. You went out into the yard and pulled them one by one out of the henhouse and they all escaped and ran about and half of them were eaten by the fox. I never saw Antoinette so angry with you." (Antoinette was the Doctor's late wife.)

This was an old story and very demeaning. Dr Greysteel listened with mounting exasperation. "For God's sake, Louisa! I am a physician! I know drunkenness when I see it!"

So Frank was brought in. He remembered much more precisely what Strange had said. The visions he conjured up of Flora shut away in prison for all eternity were quite enough to terrify her aunt. In a very short space of time Aunt Greysteel was as eager as any one else to send Flora away from Venice. However she insisted upon one thing – something which had never occurred to Dr Greysteel and Frank: she insisted that they tell Flora the truth.

It cost Flora Greysteel a great deal of pain to hear that Strange had lost his reason. She thought at first they must be mistaken, and even when they had persuaded her that it might be true, she was still certain there was no necessity for her to leave Venice; she was sure he would never hurt her. But she could now see that her father and aunt believed otherwise and that they would never be comfortable until she went. Most reluctantly she agreed to leave.

Shortly after the departure of the two ladies, Dr Greysteel was sitting in one of the *palazzo*'s chill marble rooms. He was comforting himself with a glass of brandy and trying to find the courage to go and look for Strange, when Frank entered the room and said something about a black tower.

"What?" said Dr Greysteel. He was in no mood to be puzzling out Frank's eccentricities.

"Come to the window and I will shew you, sir."

Dr Greysteel got up and went to the window.

Something was standing in the centre of Venice. It could best be described as a black tower of impossible vastness. The base of it seemed to cover several acres. It rose up out of the city into the sky and the top of it could not be seen. From a distance its colour was uniformly black and its texture smooth. But there were moments when it seemed almost translucent, as if it were made of black smoke. One caught glimpses of buildings behind – or possibly even *within* – it.

It was the most mysterious thing Dr Greysteel had ever seen. "Where can it have come from, Frank? And what has happened to the houses that were there before?"

Before these or any other questions could be answered, there was a loud, official-sounding knock upon the door. Frank went to answer it. He returned a moment later with a small crowd of people, none of whom Dr Greysteel had ever seen before. Two of them were priests, and there were three or four young men of

813

military bearing who all wore brightly coloured uniforms decorated with an extravagant amount of gold lace and braid. The most handsome of the young men stepped forward. His uniform was the most splendid of all and he had long yellow moustaches. He explained that he was Colonel Wenzel von Ottenfeld, secretary to the Austrian Governor of the city. He introduced his companions; the officers were Austrian like himself, but the priests were Venetian. This in itself was enough to cause Dr Greysteel some surprize; the Venetians hated the Austrians and the two races were hardly ever seen in each other's company.

"You are the Sir Doctor?" said Colonel von Ottenfeld. "The friend of the *Hexenmeister*[1] of the Great Vellinton?"

Dr Greysteel agreed that he was.

"Ah! Sir Doctor! We are beggars under your feet today!" Von Ottenfeld put on a melancholy expression which was much enhanced by his long, drooping moustaches.

Dr Greysteel said he was astonished to hear it.

"We come today. We ask your . . ." Von Ottenfeld frowned and snapped his fingers. "*Vermittlung. Wir bitten um Ihre Vermittlung. Wie kann man das sagen?*" There was some discussion how this word ought to be translated. One of the Italian priests suggested "intercession".

"Yes, yes," agreed von Ottenfeld, eagerly. "We ask your intercession from us to the *Hexenmeister* of the Great Vellinton. Sir Doctor, we esteem very much the *Hexenmeister* of the Great Vellinton. But now the *Hexenmeister* of the Great Vellinton has done something. What calamity! The people of Venice are afraid. Many must leave their houses and go away!"

"Ah!" said Dr Greysteel, knowingly. He thought for a moment and comprehension dawned. "Oh! You think Mr Strange has something to do with this Black Tower."

"No!" declared von Ottenfeld. "It is not a Tower. It is the Night! What calamity!"

---

[1] German for magician.

"I beg your pardon?" said Dr Greysteel and looked to Frank for help. Frank shrugged.

One of the priests, whose English was a little more robust, explained that when the sun had risen that morning, it had risen in every part of the city except one – the parish of Santa Maria Zobenigo, which was where Strange lived. There, Night continued to reign.

"Why does the *Hexenmeister* of the Great Vellinton this?" asked von Ottenfeld, "We do not know. We beg you go, Sir Doctor. Ask him, please, for the sun to come back to Santa Maria Zobenigo? Ask him, respectfully, to do no more magic in Venice?"

"Of course I will go," said Dr Greysteel. "It is a most distressing situation. And, though I am quite sure that Mr Strange has not done this deliberately – that it will prove to be all a mistake – I will gladly help in any way I can."

"Ah!" said the priest with the good English, anxiously, and put up his hand, as if he feared that Dr Greysteel would rush out to Santa Maria Zobenigo upon the instant. "But you will take your servant, please? You will not go alone?"

Snow was falling thickly. All of Venice's sad colours had become shades of grey and black. St Mark's Piazza was a faint grey etching of itself done on white paper. It was quite deserted. Dr Greysteel and Frank stumped through the snow together. Dr Greysteel carried a lantern and Frank held a black umbrella over the Doctor's head.

Beyond the Piazza rose up the Black Pillar of Night; they passed beneath the arch of the Atrio and between the silent houses. The Darkness began halfway across a little bridge. It was the eeriest thing in the world to see how the flakes of snow, falling aslant, were sucked suddenly into it, as if it were a living thing that ate them up with greedy lips.

They took one last look at the silent white city and stepped into the Darkness.

The alleys were deserted. The inhabitants of the parish had fled to relatives and friends in other parts of the city. But the cats of Venice – who are as contrary a set of creatures as the cats of any other city – had flocked to Santa Maria Zobenigo to dance and hunt and play in the Endless Night which seemed to them to be a sort of high holiday. In the Darkness cats brushed past Dr Greysteel and Frank; and several times Dr Greysteel caught sight of glowing eyes watching him from a doorway.

When they reached the house where Strange lodged it was quiet. They knocked and called out, but no one came. Finding the door was unlocked, they pushed it open. The house was dark. They found the staircase and went up to Strange's room at the top of the house where he did magic.

After all that had happened they were rather expecting something remarkable, to find Strange in conversation with a demon or haunted by horrible apparitions. It was somewhat disconcerting that the scene which presented itself was so ordinary. The room looked as it had upon numerous occasions. It was lit by a generous number of candles and an iron stove gave out a welcome heat. Strange was at the table, bending over his silver dish with a pure white light radiating up into his face. He did not look up. A clock ticked quietly in the corner. Books, papers and writing things were thickly scattered over every surface as usual. Strange passed the tip of his finger over the surface of the water and struck it twice very gently. Then he turned and wrote something in a book.

"Strange," said Dr Greysteel.

Strange glanced up. He did not look so frantic as he had the night before, but his eyes had the same haunted look. He regarded the doctor for a long moment without any sign of recognition. "Greysteel," he murmured at last. "What are you doing here?"

"I have come to see how you are. I am concerned about you."

Strange made no reply to this. He turned back to his silver dish and made a few gestures over it. But immediately he seemed dissatisfied with what he had done. He took a glass and poured some water into it. Then he took a tiny bottle and carefully tipped two drops of liquid into the glass.

Dr Greysteel watched him. There was no label upon the bottle; the liquid was amber-coloured; it could have been any thing.

Strange observed Dr Greysteel's eyes upon him. "I suppose you are going to say I ought not to take this. Well, you may spare yourself the trouble!" He drank it down in one draught. "You will not say so when you know the reason!"

"No, no," said Dr Greysteel in his most placating tone – the one he employed for his most difficult patients. "I assure you I was going to say nothing of the kind. I only wish to know if you are in pain? Or ill? I thought last night that you were. Perhaps I can advise . . ." He stopped. He smelt something. It was quite overpowering – a dry, musty scent mixed with something rank and animal; and the curious thing was that he recognized it. Suddenly he could smell the room where the old woman lived: the mad old woman with all the cats.

"My wife is alive," said Strange. His voice was hoarse and thick. "Ha! There! You did not know that!"

Dr Greysteel turned cold. If there was any thing Strange could have said to alarm him even more, this was probably it.

"They told me she was dead!" continued Strange. "They told me that they had buried her! I cannot believe I was so taken in! She was enchanted! She was stolen from me! And that is why I need this!" He waved the little bottle of amber-coloured liquid in the doctor's face.

Dr Greysteel and Frank took a step or two backwards. Frank muttered in the doctor's ear. "All is well, sir. All is well. I shall not let him harm you. I have the measure of him. Do not fear."

"I cannot go back to the house," said Strange. "He has expelled me and he will not let me go back. The trees will not let me pass. I have tried spells of disenchantment, but they do not work. They do not work . . ."

"Have you been doing magic since last night?" asked Dr Greysteel.

"What? Yes!"

"I am very sorry to hear it. You should rest. I dare say you do not remember very much of last night . . ."

"Ha!" exclaimed Strange with bitterest irony. "I shall never forget the smallest detail!"

"Is that so? Is that so?" said Dr Greysteel in the same soothing tone. "Well, I cannot conceal from you that your appearance alarmed me. You were not yourself. It was the consequence, I am sure, of overwork. Perhaps if I . . ."

"Forgive me, Dr Greysteel, but, as I have just explained, my wife is *enchanted*; she is a prisoner beneath the earth. Much as I would like to continue this conversation, I have far more pressing matters to attend to!"

"Very well. Calm yourself. Our presence here distresses you. We will go away again and come back tomorrow. But before we go, I must say this: the Governor sent a delegation to me this morning. He respectfully requests that you refrain from performing magic for the present . . ."

"Not do magic!" Strange laughed – a cold, hard, humourless sound. "You ask me to stop now? Quite impossible! What did God make me a magician for, if not for this?" He returned to his silver dish and began to draw signs in the air, just above the surface of the water.

"Then at least free the parish from this Unnatural Night. Do that at least, for me? For friendship's sake? For Flora's sake?"

Strange paused in the middle of a gesture. "What are you talking about? What Unnatural Night? What is unnatural about it?"

"For God's sake, Strange! It is almost noon!"

For a moment Strange said nothing. He looked at the black window, at the darkness in the room and finally at Dr Greysteel. "I had not the least idea," he whispered, aghast. "Believe me! This is not my doing!"

"Whose is it then?"

Strange did not reply; he stared vacantly about the room.

Dr Greysteel feared it would only vex him to be questioned more about the Darkness, and so he simply asked, "Can you bring the daylight back?"

"I . . . I do not know."

Dr Greysteel told Strange that they would come again the next day and he took the opportunity once more to recommend sleep as an excellent remedy.

Strange was not listening, but, just as Dr Greysteel and Frank were leaving, he took hold of the doctor's arm and whispered, "May I ask you something?"

Dr Greysteel nodded.

"Are you not afraid that it will go out?"

"What will go out?" asked Dr Greysteel.

"The candle." Strange gestured to Dr Greysteel's forehead. "The candle inside your head."

Outside, the Darkness seemed eerier than ever. Dr Greysteel and Frank made their way silently through the night streets. When they reached the daylight at the western extremity of St Mark's Piazza, both breathed a great sigh of relief.

Dr Greysteel said, "I am determined to say nothing to the Governor about the overturn of his reason. God knows what the Austrians might do. They might send soldiers to arrest him – or worse! I shall simply say that he is unable to banish the Night just now, but that he means no harm to the city – for I am quite certain he does not – and that I am sure of persuading him to set matters right very soon."

The next day when the sun rose Darkness still covered the parish of Santa Maria Zobenigo. At half past eight Frank went out to buy milk and fish. The pretty, dark-eyed peasant-girl who sold milk from the milk-barge in the San Lorenzo-canal liked Frank and always had a word and a smile for him. This morning she handed him up his jug of milk and asked, "*Hai sentito che lo stregone inglese è pazzo?*" (Have you heard that the English magician is mad?)

In the fish-market by the Grand Canal a fisherman sold Frank three mullet, but then almost neglected to take the money because his attention was given to the argument he was conducting with his neighbour as to whether the English magician had gone mad because he was a magician, or because he was English. On the way home two pale-faced nuns scrubbing the marble steps of a church wished Frank a good morning and told him that they intended to say prayers for the poor, mad English magician. Then just as he was almost at the house-door, a white cat stepped out from under a gondola seat, sprang on to the quayside and gave him a look. He waited for it to say something about Jonathan Strange, but it did not.

"How in God's name did this happen?" asked Dr Greysteel, sitting up in bed. "Do you think Mr Strange went out and spoke to someone?"

Frank did not know. Out he went again and made some inquiries. It seemed that Strange had not yet stirred from the room at the top of the house in Santa Maria Zobenigo; but Lord Byron (who was the one person in all the city who treated the appearance of Eternal Night as a sort of entertainment) had visited him at about five o'clock the previous evening and had found him still doing magic and raving about candles, pineapples, dances that went on for centuries and dark woods that filled the streets of Venice. Byron had gone home and told his mistress, his landlord and his valet; and, as these were all sociable people much given to spending their evenings among large groups of talkative friends, the number of people who knew by morning was quite remarkable.

"Lord Byron! Of course!" cried Dr Greysteel. "I forgot all about him! I must go and warn him to be discreet."

"I think it's a little late for that, sir," said Frank.

Dr Greysteel was obliged to admit the truth of this. Nevertheless he felt he should like to consult someone. And who better than Strange's other friend? So that evening he dressed carefully and went in his gondola to the house of the Countess Albrizzi. The Countess was a clever Greek lady of mature years, who had published some books upon sculpture; but her chief delight was to give *conversazioni* where all sorts of fashionable and learned people could meet each other. Strange had attended one or two, but until tonight Dr Greysteel had never troubled about them.

He was shewn to a large room on the *piano nobile*. It was richly decorated with marble floors, wonderful statues, and painted walls and ceilings. At one end of the room the ladies sat in a semi-circle around the Countess. The men stood at the other end. From the moment he entered the room Dr Greysteel felt the eyes of the other guests upon him. More than one person was pointing him out to his neighbour. There was little doubt but that they were talking of Strange and the Darkness.

A small, handsome man was standing by the window. He had dark, curly hair and a full, soft, red mouth. It was a mouth which would have been striking upon a woman, but on a man it was simply extraordinary. With his small stature, carefully chosen clothes and dark hair and eyes, he had a little of the look of Christopher Drawlight – but only if Drawlight had been fearfully clever. Dr Greysteel went up to him directly, and said, "Lord Byron?"

The man turned to see who spoke. He did not look best pleased to be addressed by a dull, stout, middle-aged Englishman. Yet he could not deny who he was. "Yes?"

"My name is Greysteel. I am a friend of Mr Strange."

"Ah!" said his lordship. "The physician with the beautiful daughter!"

Dr Greysteel, in his turn, was not best pleased to hear his daughter spoken of in such terms by one of the most notorious rakes in Europe, yet he could not deny that Flora was beautiful. Putting it aside for the moment, he said, "I have been to see Strange. All my worst fears are confirmed. His reason is quite overturned."

"Oh, quite!" agreed Byron. "I was with him again a few hours ago and could not get him to talk of any thing but his dead wife and how she is not really dead, but merely enchanted. And now he shrouds himself in Darkness and works Black Magic! There is something rather admirable in all this, do you not agree?"

"Admirable?" said the doctor sharply. "Say pitiable rather! But do you think he made the Darkness? He told me quite plainly that he had not."

"But of course he made it!" declared Byron. "A Black World to match his Black Spirits! Who would not blot out the sun sometimes? The difference is that when one is a magician, one can actually do it."

Dr Greysteel considered this. "You may be right," he conceded. "Perhaps he created the Darkness and then forgot about it. I do not think he always remembers what he has said or done. I have found that he retains very little impression of my earlier conversations with him."

"Ah. Well. Quite," said his lordship, as if there was nothing very surprizing in this and that he too would be glad to forget the doctor's conversation just as soon as he could. "Were you aware that he has written to his brother-in-law?"

"No, I did not know that."

"He has instructed the fellow to come to Venice to see his dead sister."

"Do you think he will come?" asked Dr Greysteel.

"I have not the least idea!" Lord Byron's tone implied that it was somewhat presumptuous of Dr Greysteel to expect the Greatest Poet of the Age to interest himself in such matters. There was a moment or two of silence and then he added in a more natural tone, "To own the truth, I believe he will not come. Strange shewed me the letter. It was full of disjointed ramblings and reasonings that none but a madman – or a magician! – could understand."

"It is a very bitter thing," said Dr Greysteel. "Very bitter indeed! Only the day before yesterday we were walking with him. He was in such cheerful spirits! To have gone from complete sanity to complete madness in the space of one night, I cannot understand it. I wonder if there might not be some physical cause. Some infection perhaps?"

"Nonsense!" declared Byron. "The causes of his madness are purely metaphysical. They lie in the vast chasm between that which one is, and that which one desires to become, between the soul and the flesh. Forgive me, Dr Greysteel, but this is a matter of which I have experience. Of this I can speak with authority."

"But . . ." Dr Greysteel frowned and paused to collect his thoughts. "But the period of intense frustration appeared to be over. His work was going well."

"All I can tell you is this. Before this peculiar obsession with his dead wife, he was full of quite another matter: John Uskglass. You must have observed that? Now I know very little of English magicians. They have always seemed to me a parcel of dull, dusty old men – except for John Uskglass. He is quite another matter! The magician who tamed the Otherlanders![2] The only magician to defeat Death! The magician whom Lucifer himself was forced to treat as an equal! Now, whenever Strange compares himself to this sublime being – as he must from time to time – he sees himself for what he truly is: a plodding, earth-bound mediocrity! All his achievements – so praised up in the desolate little isle[3] – crumble to dust before him! That will bring on as fine a bout of despair as you could wish to see. *This is to be mortal, And seek the things beyond mortality*." Lord Byron paused for a moment, as if committing the last remark to memory in case he should want to put it in a poem. "I myself was touched with something of the same melancholia when I was in the Swiss mountains in September. I wandered about, hearing avalanches every five minutes – as if God was bent upon my destruction! I was full of regrets and immortal longings.

---

[2] A somewhat poetical name for fairies.

[3] Lord Byron is speaking of Great Britain.

Several times I was sorely tempted to blow my brains out – and I would have done it too, but for the recollection of the pleasure it would give my mother-in-law."

Lord Byron might shoot himself any day of the week for all that Dr Greysteel cared. But Strange was another matter. "You think him capable of self-destruction?" he asked, anxiously.

"Oh, certainly!"

"But what is to be done?"

"Done?" echoed his lordship, slightly perplexed. "Why would you want to do any thing?" Then, feeling that they had talked long enough about someone else, his lordship turned the conversation to himself. "Upon the whole I am glad that you and I have met, Dr Greysteel. I brought a physician with me from England, but I was obliged to dismiss him at Genova. Now I fear my teeth are coming loose. Look!"[4] Byron opened his mouth wide and displayed his teeth to Dr Greysteel.

Dr Greysteel gently tugged on a large, white tooth. "They seem very sound and firm to me," he said.

"Oh! Do you think so? But not for long, I fear. I grow old. I wither. I can feel it." Byron sighed. Then, struck by a more cheerful thought, he added, "You know, this crisis with Strange could not have come at a better time. I am by chance writing a poem about a magician who wrestles with the Ineffable Spirits who rule his destiny. Of course, as a model for my magician Strange is far from perfect – he lacks the true heroic nature; for that I shall be obliged to put in something of myself."

A lovely young Italian girl passed by. Byron tilted his head to a very odd angle, half-closed his eyes and composed his features to suggest that he was about to expire from chronic indigestion. Dr Greysteel could only suppose that he was treating the young woman to the Byronic profile and the Byronic expression.

---

[4] See Byron's letter to Augusta Leigh, October 28th, 1816.

57

The Black Letters[1]

December 1816

Santa Maria Zobenigo, Venice
Jonathan Strange to the Reverend Henry Woodhope Dec. 3rd, 1816.

My dear Henry,
You must prepare yourself for wonderful news. *I have seen
Arabella.* I have seen her and spoken to her. Is that not glorious?
Is that not the best of all possible news? You will not believe me.
You will not understand it. Be assured it was not a dream. It
was not drunkenness, or madness, or opium. Consider: you have
only to accept that last Christmas at Clun we were half-
enchanted, and all becomes believable, all becomes possible.
It is ironic, is it not, that I of all people did not recognize magic
when it wrapped itself about me? In my own defence I may say
that it was of a quite unexpected nature and came from a

---

[1] Strange's later Venetian letters (in particular his letters to Henry Woodhope) have been known by this name since their publication in London in
January 1817. Lawyers and magical scholars will doubtless continue to argue
over whether or not the publication was legal. Certainly Strange never gave
his permission and Henry Woodhope has always maintained that neither did
he. Henry Woodhope also said that the published letters had been altered and
added to, presumably by Henry Lascelles and Gilbert Norrell. In his *The Life
of Jonathan Strange* John Segundus published what he and Woodhope claimed
were the originals. It is these versions which are reprinted here.

quarter I could never have foreseen. Yet to my shame other people were quicker-witted than me. John Hyde knew that something was wrong and tried to warn me, but I did not listen to him. Even you, Henry, told me quite plainly that I was too taken up with my books, that I neglected my responsibilities and my wife. I resented your advice and on several occasions gave you a rude answer. I am sorry for it now and humbly beg your pardon. Blame me as much as you want. You cannot think me half so much at fault as I think myself. But to come to the point of all this. I need you to come here to Venice. Arabella is in a place not very far distant from here, but she cannot leave it and I cannot go there – at least [several lines expunged]. My friends here in Venice are well-meaning souls, but they plague me with questions. I have no servant and there is something here which makes it hard for me to go about the city unobserved. Of this I shall say no more. My dear, good Henry, please do not make difficulties. Come straightaway to Venice. Your reward will be Arabella safe and well and restored to us. For what other reason has God made me the Greatest Magician of the Age if not for this?

Your brother,

S

Santa Maria Zobenigo, Venice

Jonathan Strange to the Reverend Henry Woodhope Dec. 6th, 1816.

My dear Henry,

I have been somewhat troubled in my conscience since I wrote to you last. You know that I have never lied to you, but I confess that I have not told you enough for you to form an accurate opinion of how matters stand with Arabella at present. She is not dead but . . . [12 lines crossed out and indecipherable] . . . under the earth, within the hill which they call the *brugh*. Alive, yet not alive – not dead either – *enchanted*. It has been their habit since time immemorial to steal away Christian men and women and make servants of them, or force them – as in this case – to take part in their dreary pastimes: their dances, their feasts, their long, empty celebrations of dust and nothingness. Among all the reproaches which I heap on my own head the bitterest by far is that I have betrayed her – she whom my first duty was to protect.

Santa Maria Zobenigo, Venice
*Jonathan Strange to the Reverend Henry Woodhope*Dec. 15th, 1816.

My dear Henry,
It grieves me to tell you that I now have better grounds for the uneasiness I told you of in my last letter.[2] I have done everything I can think of to break the bars of her black prison, but without success. There is no spell that I know of that can make the smallest dent in such ancient magic. For aught I know there is no such spell in the whole English canon. Stories of magicians freeing captives from Faerie are few and far between. I cannot now recall a single one. Somewhere in one of his books Martin Pale describes how fairies can grow tired of their human guests and expel them without warning from the *brugh*; the poor captives find themselves back home, but hundreds of years after they left it. Perhaps that is what will happen. Arabella will return to England long after you and I are dead. That thought freezes my blood. I cannot disguise from you that there is a black mood upon me. Time and I have quarrelled. All hours are midnight now. I had a clock and a watch, but I destroyed them both. I could not bear the way they mocked me. I do not

---

[2] This letter has never been found. It is probable that Strange never sent it. According to Lord Byron (letter to John Murray, Dec. 31st, 1816.) Strange would often write long letters to his friends and then destroy them. Strange confessed to Byron that he quickly became confused as to which he had and had not sent.

sleep. I *cannot* eat. I take wine – and something else. Now at times I become a little wild. I shake and laugh and weep for a time – I cannot say *what* time; perhaps an hour, perhaps a day. But enough of that. Madness is the key. I believe I am the first English magician to understand that. Norrell was right – he said we do not need fairies to help us. He said that madmen and fairies have much in common, but I did not understand the implications then, and neither did he. Henry, you cannot conceive of how desperately I need you here. Why do you not come? Are you ill? I have received no replies to my letters, but this may mean that you are already on the road to Venice and this letter may perhaps never reach you.

"Darkness, misery and solitude!" cried the gentleman in high glee. "That is what I have inflicted upon him and that is what he must suffer for the next hundred years! Oh! How cast down he is! I have won! I have won!" He clapped his hands and his eyes glittered.

In Strange's room in the parish of Santa Maria Zobenigo three candles were burning: one upon the desk, one upon the top of the little painted cupboard and one in a wall-sconce by the door. An observer of the scene might have supposed them to be the only lights in all the world. From Strange's window nothing could be seen but night and silence. Strange, unshaven, with red-rimmed eyes and wild hair, was doing magic.

Stephen stared at him with mingled pity and horror.

"And yet he is not so solitary as I would like," remarked the gentleman, in a displeased tone. "There is someone with him."

There was indeed. A small, dark man in expensive clothes was leaning against the little painted cupboard, watching Strange with an appearance of great interest and enjoyment. From time to time he would take out a little notebook and scribble in it.

"That is Lord Byron," said Stephen.

"And who is he?"

"A very wicked gentleman, sir. A poet. He quarrelled with his wife and seduced his sister."

"Really? Perhaps I will kill him."

"Oh, do not do that, sir! True, his sins are very great, and he has been more or less driven out of England, but even so . . ."

"Oh! I do not care about his crimes against other people! I care about his crimes against *me*! He ought not to be here. Ah, Stephen, Stephen! Do not look so stricken. Why should you care what becomes of one wicked Englishman? I tell you what I will do: because of the great love I bear you, I will not kill him now. He may have another, oh!, another five years of life! But at the end of that he must die!"[3]

"Thank you, sir," said Stephen, gratefully. "You are all generosity."

Suddenly Strange raised his head and cried out, "I know you are there! You can hide from me if you wish, but it is too late! I know you are there!"

"Who are you talking to?" Byron asked him.

Strange frowned. "I am being watched. Spied upon!"

"Are you indeed? And do you know by whom?"

"By a fairy and a butler!"

"A butler, eh?" said his lordship, laughing. "Well, one may say what one likes about imps and goblins, but butlers are the worst of them!"

"What?" said Strange.

The gentleman with the thistle-down hair was looking anxiously about the room. "Stephen! Can you see my little box anywhere?"

"Little box, sir?"

"Yes, yes! You know what I mean! The little box containing dear Lady Pole's finger!"

"I do not see it, sir. But surely the little box does not matter any more? Now that you have defeated the magician?"

---

[3] Byron died of a chill five years later in Greece.

"Oh, there it is!" cried the gentleman. "See? You had put your hand down upon the table and accidentally hidden it from my view."

Stephen moved his hand away. After a moment he said, "You do not pick it up, sir."

To this remark the gentleman made no reply. Instead, he immediately returned to abusing the magician and glorying in his own victory.

"It is not his any more!" thought Stephen, with a thrill of excitement. "He may not take it! It belongs to the magician now! Perhaps the magician can use it somehow to free Lady Pole!" Stephen watched and waited to see what the magician would do. But at the end of half an hour he was forced to admit that the signs were scarcely hopeful. Strange strode about the room, muttering magic spells to himself and looking entirely deranged; Lord Byron questioned him about what he was doing and the answers that Strange gave were wild and incomprehensible (though quite to the taste of Lord Byron). And, as for the little box, Strange never once looked at it. For all that Stephen could tell, he had forgotten all about it.

58

Henry Woodhope pays a visit

December 1816

"YOU HAVE DONE quite right in coming to me, Mr Woodhope. I have made a careful study of Mr Strange's Venetian correspondence and, aside from the general horror of which you rightly speak, there is much in these letters which is hidden from the layman. I think I may say without vanity that, at this moment, I am the only man in England who is capable of understanding them."

It was twilight, three days before Christmas. In the library at Hanover-square the candles and lamps had not yet been lit. It was that curious time of day when the sky is bright and full of colour, but all the streets are dim and shadowy. Upon the table there was a vase of flowers, but in the fading light it appeared to be a black vase of black flowers.

Mr Norrell sat by the window with Strange's letters in his hands. Lascelles sat by the fire, regarding Henry Woodhope coolly.

"I confess to having been in a condition of some distress ever since I first received these letters," said Henry Woodhope to Mr Norrell. "I have not known whom to turn to for help. To be truthful I have no interest in magic. I have not followed the fashionable quarrels about the subject. But everyone says that you are England's greatest magician – and you were once Mr Strange's tutor. I shall be very grateful to you, sir, for any advice you are able to give me."

Mr Norrell nodded. "You must not blame Mr Strange," he said. "The magical profession is a dangerous one. There is no other which so lays a man open to the perils of vanity. Politics and Law are harmless in comparison. You should understand, Mr Woodhope, that I tried very hard to keep him with me, to guide him. But his genius – which makes us all admire him – is the very thing which leads his reason astray. These letters shew that he has strayed much further than I could ever have supposed."

"Strayed? Then you do not believe this queer tale of my sister being alive?"

"Not a word of it, sir, not a word of it. It is all his own unhappy imaginings."

"Ah!" Henry Woodhope sat silent for a moment as if he were deciding upon the relative degrees of disappointment and relief that he felt. He said, "And what of Mr Strange's curious complaint that Time has stopt? Can you make any thing of this, sir?"

Lascelles said, "We understand from our correspondents in Italy that for some weeks Mr Strange has been surrounded by Perpetual Darkness. Whether he has done this deliberately or whether it is a spell gone wrong we do not know. There is also the possibility that he has offended some Great Power and that this is the result. What is certain is that some action upon Mr Strange's part has caused a disturbance in the Natural Order of Things."

"I see," said Henry Woodhope.

Lascelles looked at him rather severely. "It is something which Mr Norrell has striven hard all his life to avoid."

"Ah," said Henry. He turned to Mr Norrell. "But what should I do, sir? Ought I to go to him as he begs me to?"

Mr Norrell sniffed. "The most important question is, I believe, how soon we may contrive to bring him back to England, where his friends may care for him and bring to a rapid end the delusions that beset him."

"Perhaps if you were to write to him, sir?"

"Ah, no. I fear my little stock of influence with Mr Strange all ran out some years ago. It was the war in Spain that did the mischief. Before he went to the Peninsula he was very content to stay with me and learn all I could teach him, but afterwards . . ." Mr Norrell sighed. "No, we must rely upon you, Mr Woodhope. You must make him come home and, since I suspect that your going to Venice could only prolong his stay in that city and persuade him that one person at least gives credit to his imaginings, then I most strongly urge you not to go."

"Well, sir, I must confess that it makes me very glad to hear you say so. I shall certainly do as you advise. If you could pass me my letters I shall trouble you no longer."

"Mr Woodhope," said Lascelles. "Do not be in such a hurry, I beg you! Our conversation is by no means concluded. Mr Norrell has answered all your questions candidly and without reservation. Now you must return the favour."

Henry Woodhope frowned and looked puzzled. "Mr Norrell has relieved me of a great deal of anxiety. If there is any way in which I can serve Mr Norrell, then, of course, I shall be very happy. But I do not quite understand . . ."

"Perhaps I do not make myself clear," said Lascelles, "I mean of course that Mr Norrell requires your help so that he may help Mr Strange. Is there any thing else you can tell us of Mr Strange's Italian tour? What was he like before he fell into this sad condition? Was he in good spirits?"

"No!" said Henry indignantly, as though he thought some insult was implied in the question. "My sister's death weighed very heavily on him! At least at first it did. At first he seemed very unhappy. But when he reached Genoa everything changed." He paused. "He writes no word of it now, but before his letters were full of praise for a young lady – one of the party he is travelling with. And I could not help suspecting that he was thinking of marrying again."

"A second marriage!" exclaimed Lascelles, "And so soon after the death of your sister? Dear me! How very shocking! How very distressing for you."

Henry nodded unhappily.

There was a little pause and then Lascelles said, "I hope he gave no sign of this fondness for the society of other ladies before? I mean when Mrs Strange was alive. It would have caused her great unhappiness."

"No! No, of course not!" cried Henry.

"I beg your pardon if I have offended you. I certainly meant no disrespect to your sister – a most charming woman. But such things are not uncommon, you know. Particularly among men of a certain stamp of mind." Lascelles reached over to the table where Strange's letters to Henry Woodhope lay. He poked at them with one finger until he found the one he wanted. "In this letter," he said, running his eye over it, "Mr Strange has written, 'Jeremy has told me that you did not do what I asked. But it is no matter. Jeremy has done it and the outcome is exactly as I imagined.' " Lascelles put down the letter and smiled pleasantly at Mr Woodhope. "What did Mr Strange ask you to do that you did not do? Who is Jeremy and what was the outcome?"

"Mr Strange . . . Mr Strange asked me to exhume my sister's coffin." Henry looked down. "Well, of course, I would not. So Strange wrote to his servant, a man called Jeremy Johns. A very arrogant fellow!"

"And Johns exhumed the body?"

"Yes. He has a friend in Clun who is a gravedigger. They did it together. I can scarcely describe my feelings when I discovered what this person had done."

"Yes, quite. But what did they discover?"

"What ought they to discover but my poor sister's corpse? However they chose to say they did not. They chose to put about a ridiculous tale."

"What did they say?"

"I do not repeat servants' tittle-tattle."

"Of course you do not. But Mr Norrell desires that you put aside this excellent principle for a moment and speak openly and candidly – as he has spoken to you."

Henry bit his lip. "They said the coffin contained a log of black wood."

"No body?" said Lascelles.

"No body," said Henry.

Lascelles looked at Mr Norrell. Mr Norrell looked down at his hands in his lap.

"But what has my sister's death to do with any thing?" asked Henry with a frown. He turned to Mr Norrell. "I understood from what you said before that there was nothing extraordinary about my sister's death. I thought you said no magic had taken place?"

"Oh! Upon the contrary!" declared Lascelles. "Certainly there was some magic taking place. There can be no doubt about that! The question is whose was it?"

"I beg your pardon?" asked Henry.

"Of course it is too deep for me!" said Lascelles. "It is a matter which only Mr Norrell can deal with."

Henry looked in confusion from one to the other.

"Who is with Strange now?" asked Lascelles. "He has servants, I suppose?"

"No. No servants of his own. He is attended, I believe, by his landlord's servants. His friends in Venice are an English family. They seem a very odd set of people, very much addicted to travelling, the females as much as the gentleman."

"Name?"

"Greystone or Greyfield. I do not remember exactly."

"And where are they from, these people called Greystone or Greyfield?"

"I do not know. I do not believe Strange ever told me. The gentleman was a ship's doctor, I believe, and his wife – who is dead – was French."

Lascelles nodded. The room was now so dim that Henry Woodhope could not see the faces of the other two men.

"You look pale and tired, Mr Woodhope," remarked Mr Lascelles. "Perhaps the London air does not agree with you?"

"I do not sleep very well. Since these letters began to arrive I have dreamt of nothing but horrors."

Lascelles nodded. "Sometimes a man may know things in his heart that he will not whisper in the open air, even to himself. You are very fond of Mr Strange, are you not?"

Henry Woodhope might perhaps be excused for looking a little puzzled at this since he had not the least idea what Lascelles was talking about, but all he said was, "Thank you for your advice, Mr Norrell. I will certainly do as you suggest and now, I wonder if I might take back my letters?"

"Ah! Well, as to that," said Lascelles, "Mr Norrell wonders if he might borrow them for a time? He believes there is still much to learn from them." Henry Woodhope looked as if he was about to protest, so Lascelles added in a somewhat reproachful tone, "He is only thinking of Mr Strange! It is all for the good of Mr Strange."

So Henry Woodhope left the letters in the possession of Mr Norrell and Lascelles.

When he was gone Lascelles said, "Our next step must be to send someone to Venice."

"Yes, indeed!" agreed Mr Norrell. "I should dearly love to know the truth of the matter."

"Ah, yes, well." Lascelles gave a short, contemptuous laugh. "*Truth* . . ."

Mr Norrell blinked his little eyes rapidly at Lascelles, but Lascelles did not explain what he meant. "I do not know who we can send," continued Mr Norrell. "Italy is a very great distance. The journey takes almost two weeks, I understand. I could not spare Childermass for half so long."

"Hmm," said Lascelles, "I was not necessarily thinking of Childermass. Indeed there are several arguments against sending

Childermass. You yourself have often suspected him of Strangite sympathies. It appears to me highly undesirable that the two of them should be alone together in a foreign country where they can plot against us. No, I know whom we can send."

The next day Lascelles's servants went out into various parts of London. Some of the places they visited were highly disreputable like the slums and rookeries of St Giles, Seven Dials and Saffron-hill; others were grand and patrician like Golden-square, St James's and Mayfair. They gathered up a strange miscellany of persons: tailors, glove-makers, hat-makers, cobblers, money-lenders (a great many of these), bailiffs and sponging-house-keepers; and they brought them all back to Lascelles's house in Bruton-street. When they were assembled in the kitchen (the master of the house having no intention of receiving such people in the drawing-room) Lascelles came down and paid each of them a sum of money on behalf of someone else. It was, he told them with a cold smile, an act of charity. After all if a man cannot be charitable at Christmas, when can he be?

Three days later, on St Stephen's Day, the Duke of Wellington appeared suddenly in London. For the past year or so his Grace had been living in Paris, where he was in charge of the Allied Army of Occupation. Indeed it would scarcely be an exaggeration to say that at present the Duke of Wellington ruled France. Now the question had arisen whether the Allied Army ought to remain in France or go to its various homes (which was what the French wanted). All that day the Duke was closeted with the Foreign Secretary, Lord Castlereagh, to discuss this important matter and in the evening he dined with the Ministers at a house in Grosvenor-square.

They had scarcely begun to eat when the conversation lapsed (a rare thing among so many politicians). The Ministers seemed to be waiting for someone to say something. The Prime Minister, Lord Liverpool, cleared his throat a little nervously and said, "We do not think you will have heard, but it is reported from Italy that Strange has gone mad."

The Duke paused for a moment with his spoon halfway to his mouth. He glanced round at them all and then continued eating his soup.

"You do not appear very much disturbed at the news," said Lord Liverpool.

His Grace dabbed at his lips with his napkin. "No," he said. "I am not."

"Will you give us your reasons?" asked Sir Walter Pole.

"Mr Strange is eccentric," said the Duke. "He might seem mad to the people around him. I dare say they are not used to magicians."

The Ministers did not appear to find this quite as convincing an argument as Wellington intended they should. They offered him examples of Strange's madness: his insistence that his wife was not dead, his curious belief that people had candles in their heads and the even odder circumstance that it was no longer possible to transport pineapples into Venice.

"The watermen who carry fruit from the mainland to the city say that the pineapples fly out of their boats as if they had been fired out of a cannon," said Lord Sidmouth, a small, dried-up-looking person. "Of course they carry other sorts of fruit as well – apples and pears and so on. None of these occasion the least disturbance, but several people have been injured by the flying pineapples. Why the magician should have taken such a dislike to this particular fruit, no one knows."

The Duke was not impressed. "None of this proves any thing. I assure you, he did much more eccentric things in the Peninsula. But if he is indeed mad, then he has some reason for being so. If you will take my advice, gentlemen, you will not worry about it."

There was a short silence while the Ministers puzzled this out.

"You mean to say he might have become mad *deliberately*?" said one in an incredulous tone.

"Nothing is more likely," said the Duke.

"But why?" asked another.

"I have not the least idea. In the Peninsula we learnt not to question him. Sooner or later it would become clear that all his incomprehensible and startling actions were part of his magic. Keep him to his task, but shew no surprize at any thing he does. That, my lords, is the way to manage a magician."

"Ah, but you have not heard all yet," said the First Lord of the Admiralty eagerly. "There is worse. It is reported that he is surrounded by Constant Darkness. The Natural Order of Things is overturned and a whole parish in the city of Venice has been plunged into Ceaseless Night!"

Lord Sidmouth declared, "Even you, your Grace, with all your partiality for this man must admit that a Shroud of Eternal Darkness does not bode well. Whatever the good this man has done for the country, we cannot pretend that a Shroud of Eternal Darkness bodes well."

Lord Liverpool sighed. "I am very sorry this has happened. One could always speak to Strange as if he were an ordinary person. I had hoped that he would interpret Norrell's actions for us. But now it seems we must first find someone to interpret Strange."

"We could ask Mr Norrell," suggested Lord Sidmouth.

"I do not think we can expect an impartial judgement from that quarter," said Sir Walter Pole.

"So what ought we to do?" asked the First Lord of the Admiralty.

"We shall send a letter to the Austrians," said the Duke of Wellington with his customary decisiveness. "A letter reminding them of the warm interest that the Prince Regent and the British Government will always feel in Mr Strange's welfare; reminding them of the great debt owed by all Europe to Mr Strange's gallantry and magicianship during the late wars. Reminding them of our great displeasure were we to learn that any harm had come to him."

"Ah!" said Lord Liverpool. "But that is where you and I differ, your Grace. It seems to me that if harm does come to Strange, it will not come from the Austrians. It is far more likely to come from Strange himself."

In the middle of January a bookseller named Titus Watkins published a book called *The Black Letters* which purported to be letters from Strange to Henry Woodhope. It was rumoured that Mr Norrell had paid all the expences of the edition. Henry Woodhope swore that he had never given his permission for the letters to be published. He also said that some of them had been changed. References to Norrell's dealings with Lady Pole had been removed and other things had been put in, many of which seemed to suggest that Strange had murdered his wife by magic.

At about the same time one of Lord Byron's friends – a man called Scrope Davies – caused a sensation when he let it be known that he intended to prosecute Mr Norrell upon Lord Byron's account for attempting to acquire Lord Byron's private correspondence by means of magic. Scrope Davies went to a lawyer in Lincoln's Inn and swore an affidavit in which he stated the following. He had recently received several letters from Byron in which his lordship referred to the Pillar of Constant Darkness which covered the Parish of Mary Sobendigo [sic] in Venice, and to the madness of Jonathan Strange. Scrope Davies had placed the letters on his dressing-table in his rooms in Jermyn-street, St James's. One evening – he thought the 7th of January – he was dressing to go to his club. He had just picked up a hairbrush when he happened to notice that the letters were skipping about like dry leaves caught in a breeze. But there was no breeze to account for the movement and at first he was puzzled. He picked up the letters and saw that the handwriting on the pages was behaving strangely too. The pen-strokes were coming unhitched from their moorings and lashing about like clothes-lines in a high wind. It suddenly came to him that the letters must be under the influence of magic spells. He was a gambler by profession and, like all successful gamblers, he was quick-witted and cool-headed. He quickly placed the letters inside a Bible, in the pages of St Mark's Gospel. He told some friends afterwards that, though he was entirely ignorant of magical theory, it had seemed to him that nothing was so likely to foil an unfriendly spell as Holy Writ. He was right; the letters remained in his possession and unaltered. It was a favourite joke afterwards in all the gentlemen's clubs that the most extraordinary aspect of the whole business was not that Mr Norrell should have tried to acquire the letters, but that Scrope Davies – a notorious rake and drunk – should possess a *Bible*.

59

Leucrocuta, the Wolf of the Evening

January 1817

O N A MORNING in the middle of January Dr Greysteel stepped out of his street-door and stood a moment to straighten his gloves. Looking up, he happened to observe a small man who was sheltering from the wind in the doorway opposite.

All doorways in Venice are picturesque – and sometimes the people who linger in them are too. This fellow was rather small and, despite his evident poverty, he seemed to possess a strong degree of foppishness. His clothes were exceedingly worn and shabby-looking, but he had tried to improve them by shining whatever could be shone and brushing what could not. He had whitened his old, yellowing gloves with so much chalk that he had left little chalky fingerprints upon the door beside him. At first glance he appeared to be wearing the proper equipment of a fop – namely a long watch-chain, a bunch of watch-seals and a lorgnette; but a moment's further observation shewed that he had no watch-chain, only a gaudy gold ribbon which he had carefully arranged to hang from a buttonhole. Likewise his watch seals proved to be nothing of the sort; they were a bunch of tin hearts, crosses and talismans of the Virgin – the sort that Italian pedlars sell for a frank or two. But it was his lorgnette which was best of all – all fops and dandies love lorgnettes. They employ them to stare quizzically at those less fashionable than themselves. Presumably this odd little man felt naked without one and so he had hung a large kitchen spoon in its place.

Dr Greysteel took careful note of these eccentricities so that he might amuse a friend with them. Then he remembered that his only friend in the city was Strange, and Strange no longer cared about such things.

Suddenly the little man left the doorway and came up to Dr Greysteel. He put his head on one side and said in English, "You are Dr Greyfield?"

Dr Greysteel was surprised to be addressed by him and did not immediately reply.

"You are Dr Greyfield? The friend of the magician?"

"Yes," said Dr Greysteel, in a wondering tone. "But my name is Greysteel, sir, not Greyfield."

"A thousand apologies, my dear Doctor! Some stupid person has misinformed me of your name! I am quite mortified. You are, I assure you, the last person in the world to whom I should wish to give offence! My respect for the medical profession is boundless! And now you stand there in all the dignity of poultices and pulse-taking and you say to yourself, 'Who is this odd creature that dares to address me in the street, as if I were a common person?' Permit me to introduce myself! I come from London – from Mr Strange's friends who, when they heard how far his wits had become deranged, were thrown into such fits of anxiety that they took the liberty of dispatching me to come and find out how he is!"

"Hmm!" said Dr Greysteel. "Frankly I could have wished them more anxious. I first wrote to them at the beginning of December – six weeks ago, sir! Six weeks ago!"

"Oh, quite! Very shocking, is it not? They are the idlest creatures in the world! They think of nothing but their own convenience! While you remain here in Venice – the magician's one true friend!" He paused. "That is correct, is it not?" he asked in quite a different voice. "He has no friends but you?"

843

"Well, there is Lord Byron . . ." began Dr Greysteel.

"Byron!" exclaimed the little man. "Really? Dear me! Mad, *and* a friend of Lord Byron!" He sounded as if he did not know which was worse. "Oh! My dear Dr Greysteel. I have a thousand questions to ask you! Is there somewhere you and I can talk privately?"

Dr Greysteel's street-door was just behind them, but his distaste for the little man was growing every moment. Anxious as he was to help Strange and Strange's friends, he had no wish to invite the fellow into his house. So he muttered something about his servant being in town on an errand just now. There was a little coffee-house a few streets away; why did they not go there?

The little man was all smiling acquiescence.

They set off for the coffee-house. Their way lay by the side of a canal. The little man was upon Dr Greysteel's right hand, closest to the water. He was talking and Dr Greysteel was looking around. The doctor's eyes happened to be directed towards the canal and he saw how, without warning, a wave appeared – a single wave. This was odd enough in itself, but what followed was even more surprizing. The wave rushed towards them and slopped over the stone rim of the canal and, as it did so, it changed shape; watery fingers reached out towards the little man's foot as if they were trying to pull him in. The moment the water touched him, he leapt back with an oath, but he did not appear to notice that any thing unusual had occurred and Dr Greysteel said nothing of what he had seen.

The interior of the coffee-house was a welcome refuge from the chill, damp, January air. It was warm and smoky – a little gloomy perhaps, but the gloom was a comfortable one. The brown-painted walls and ceiling were darkened with age and tobacco smoke, but they were also made cheerful by the glitter of wine bottles, the gleam of pewter tankards, and the sparkle of highly varnished pottery and gold-framed mirrors. A damp, indolent spaniel lay on the tiles in front of stove. It shook its head and sneezed when the tip of Dr Greysteel's cane accidentally brushed its ear.

"I ought to warn you," said Dr Greysteel after the waiter had brought coffee and brandy, "that there are all sorts of rumours circulating in the town concerning Mr Strange. People say he has summoned witches and made a servant for himself out of fire. You will know not to be taken in by such nonsense, but it is as well to be prepared. You will find him sadly changed. It would be foolish to pretend otherwise. But he is still the same at heart. All his excellent qualities, all his merits are just what they always were. Of that I have no doubt."

"Indeed? But tell me, is it true he has eaten his shoes? Is it true that he has turned several people into glass and then thrown stones at them?"

"Eaten his shoes?" exclaimed Dr Greysteel. "Who told you that?"

"Oh! Several people – Mrs Kendal-Blair, Lord Pope, Sir Galahad Denehey, the Miss Underhills . . ." The little man rattled off a long list of names of English, Irish and Scottish ladies and gentlemen who were currently residing in Venice and the surrounding towns.

Dr Greysteel was astounded. Why would Strange's friends wish to consult with these people in preference to himself? "But did you not hear what I just said? This is exactly the sort of foolish nonsense I am talking about!"

The little man laughed pleasantly. "Patience! Patience, my dear Doctor! My brain is not so quick as yours. While you have been sharpening yours up with anatomy and chemistry, mine has languished in idleness." He rattled on a while about how he had never applied himself to any regular course of study and how his teachers had despaired of him and how his talents did not lie in that direction at all.

But Dr Greysteel no longer troubled to listen to him. He was thinking. It occurred to him that a while ago the little man had begged to introduce himself, yet somehow he had neglected actually to do it. Dr Greysteel was about to ask him his name when the little man asked a question that swept everything else from his mind.

"You have a daughter, do you not?"

"I beg your pardon?"

The little man, apparently thinking Dr Greysteel was deaf, repeated the question a little louder.

"Yes, I have, but . . ." said Dr Greysteel.

"And they say that you have sent her out of the city?"

"They! Who are they? What has my daughter to do with any thing?"

"Oh! Only that they say she went immediately after the magician went mad. It seems to shew that you were fearful of some harm coming to her!"

"I suppose you got this from Mrs Kendal-Blair and so forth," said Dr Greysteel. "They are nothing but a pack of fools."

"Oh, I dare say! But *did* you send your daughter away?"

Dr Greysteel said nothing.

The little man put his head first on one side and then on the other. He smiled the smile of someone who knows a secret and is preparing to astound the world with it. "You know, of course," he said, "that Strange murdered his wife?"

"What?" Dr Greysteel was silent a moment. A kind of laugh burst out of him. "I do not believe it!"

"Oh! But you must believe it," said the little man, leaning forward. His eyes glittered with excitement. "It is what everybody knows! The lady's own brother – a most respectable man – a clergyman – a Mr Woodhope – was there when the lady died and saw with his own eyes."

"What did he see?"

"All sorts of suspicious circumstances. The lady was bewitched. She was entirely enchanted and scarcely knew what she did from morning to night. And no one could explain it. It was all her husband's doing. Of course he will try to use his magic to evade punishment, but Mr Norrell, who is *devoured*, quite *devoured* with pity for the poor lady, will thwart him. Mr Norrell is determined that Strange shall be brought to justice for his crimes."

Dr Greysteel shook his head. "Nothing you say shall make me believe this slander. Strange is an honourable man!"

"Oh, quite! And yet the practice of magic has destroyed stronger minds than his. Magic in the wrong hands can lead to the annihilation of every good quality, the magnification of every bad one. He defied his master – the most patient, wise, noble, good . . ."

The little man, trailing adjectives, seemed no longer to remember what he meant to say; he was distracted by Dr Greysteel's penetrating observation of him.

Dr Greysteel sniffed. "It is a curious thing," he said slowly. "You say that you are sent by Mr Strange's friends, yet you have neglected to tell me who these friends are. It is certainly a very particular sort of friend that voices it everywhere that a man is a murderer."

The little man said nothing.

"Was it Sir Walter Pole, perhaps?"

"No," said the little man in a considering tone, "not Sir Walter."

"Mr Strange's pupils, then? I have forgot their names."

"Everybody always does. They are the most unmemorable men in the world."

"Was it them?"

"No."

"Mr Norrell?"

The little man was silent.

"What is your name?" asked Dr Greysteel.

The little man tipped his head one way and then another. But finding no way of avoiding such a direct question, he replied, "Drawlight."

"Oh, ho, ho! Here's a pretty accuser! Yes, indeed, your word will carry a great deal of weight against an honest man, against the Duke of Wellington's own magician! Christopher Drawlight! Famed throughout England as a liar, a thief and a scoundrel!"

Drawlight blushed and blinked at the doctor resentfully. "It suits you to say so!" he hissed. "Strange is a rich man and you intended to marry your daughter to him! Where is the honour in that, my dear Doctor? Where is the honour in that?"

Dr Greysteel made a sound of mixed exasperation and anger. He rose from his seat. "I shall visit every English family in the Veneto. I shall warn them not to speak to you! I am going now. I wish you no good morning! I take no leave of you!" And so saying, he flung some coins upon the table and left.

The last part of this exchange had been loud and angry. The waiters and coffee-house people looked curiously at Drawlight as he sat alone. He waited until there seemed little chance of meeting the doctor in the street and then he too left the coffee-house. As he passed along the streets, the water in the canals stirred in the oddest way. Waves appeared and followed him, occasionally making little darts and forays at his feet, slopping over the brim of the canal. But he observed none of this.

Dr Greysteel was as good as his word. He paid visits to all the British families in the city and warned them not speak to Drawlight. Drawlight did not care. He turned his attention to the servants, waiters and *gondolieri*. He knew from experience that this class of person often knew a great deal more than the masters they served; and if they did not, why!, he was able to rectify that situation by telling them something himself. Soon a great many people knew that Strange had murdered his wife; that he had tried to marry Miss Greysteel by force in the Cathedral of Saint Mark and had only been prevented by the arrival of a troop of Austrian soldiers; and that he had agreed with Lord Byron that they should hold their future wives and mistresses in common. Drawlight told any lie about Strange that occurred to him, but his powers of invention were not great and he was glad to seize upon any little half-rumour, any half-formed thought in the minds of his informers.

A *gondoliero* introduced him to a draper's wife, Marianna Segati – Byron's mistress. Through an interpreter, Drawlight paid her a world of compliments and told her scandalous secrets about great ladies in London, who, he assured her, were nowhere near as pretty as herself. She told him that, according to Lord Byron, Strange kept to his room, drinking wine and brandy, and doing magic spells. None of this was very interesting, but she did tell Drawlight the little she knew about the magician in Lord Byron's poem; how he consorted with wicked spirits and defied the gods and all humankind. Drawlight conscientiously added these fictions to his edifice of lies.

But of all the inhabitants of Venice the one Drawlight desired most as a confidant was Frank. Dr Greysteel's insults had rankled with him and he had soon determined that the best revenge would be to make a traitor of his manservant. So he sent Frank a letter inviting him to a little wine-shop in San Polo. Somewhat to his surprize, Frank agreed to come.

At the appointed hour Frank arrived. Drawlight ordered a jug of rough red wine and poured them both a tumblerful.

"Frank?" he began in a soft, wistful sort of voice. "I spoke to your master the other day – as I dare say you know. He seems a very stern sort of old fellow – not at all kind. I hope you are happy in your situation, Frank? I only mention it because a dear friend of mine, whose name is Lascelles, was saying only the other day how hard it is to find good servants in London and if only someone would help him to a good manservant he believed he would pay almost any money."

"Oh!" said Frank.

"Do you think you might like to live in London, Frank?"

Frank drew circles on the table with some spilt wine in a considering sort of way. "I might," he said.

"Because," continued Drawlight, eagerly. "if you were able to do me one or two little services, then I would be able to tell my friend of your helpfulness and I am sure he would say immediately that you were the man for him!"

"What sort of services?" asked Frank.

"Oh! Well, the first is the easiest thing in the world! Indeed the moment I tell you what it is, you will be eager to do it – even if there were no reward at all. You see, Frank, I fear something quite horrible will soon happen to your master and his daughter. The magician means them a world of harm. I tried to warn your master, but he is so stubborn he would not listen to me. I can scarcely sleep for thinking of it. I curse my stupidity that I could not explain myself better. But they trust you, Frank. You could drop a few hints – not to your master, but to his sister and daughter – about Strange's wickedness, and put them on their guard." Then Drawlight explained about the murder of Arabella Strange and the pact with Byron to hold their women in common.

Frank nodded warily.

"We need to be on our guard against the magician," said Drawlight. "The others are all taken in by his lies and deceit – your master in particular. So it is vital that you and I gather up all the intelligence we can so that we can reveal his wicked plans to the world. Now, tell me Frank, is there any thing you have observed, any word the magician let fall accidentally, any thing at all that has excited your suspicions?"

"Well, now that you mention it," said Frank, scratching his head, "There is one thing."

"Really?"

"I have not told any one else about this. Not even my master."

"Excellent!" smiled Drawlight.

"Only I cannot explain it very well. 'Tis easier to shew you."

"Oh, certainly! Where do we go?"

"Just come outside. You can see it from here."

So Frank and Drawlight went outside, and Drawlight looked

about him. It was the most commonplace Venetian scene imaginable. There was a canal just before them and on the other side a tawny-coloured church. A servant was plucking some pigeons in front of an open door; their dirty feathers were scattered in a greyish, whitish circle in front of her. Everywhere was a jumble of buildings, statues, lines of washing and flowerpots. And in the distance towered the sheer, smooth face of the Darkness.

"Well, perhaps not exactly here," admitted Frank. "The buildings get in the way. Take a few steps forward and you will see it perfectly."

Drawlight took a few steps forward. "Here?" he asked, still looking about him.

"Yes, just there," said Frank. And he kicked him into the canal.

A resounding splash.

Frank lingered a little longer to shout out some reflections upon Drawlight's moral character, calling him a lying, underhand scoundrel; a low dog; a venomous, cowardly blackguard; a snake; and a swine. These remarks certainly relieved Frank's feelings, but they were rather lost upon Drawlight who was by this time under the water and could not hear them.

The water had hit him like a blow, stinging his whole body and knocking the breath out of him. He fell through murky depths. He could not swim and was certain he would drown. But he had not been in the water more than a few seconds when he felt himself plucked up by a strong current and borne away at great speed. By some accident the action of water brought him to the surface every now and then and he was able to snatch a breath. Moment after moment he continued in a state of the most abject terror, quite unable to save himself. Once the racing water bore him up high and for an instant he saw the sunlit quayside (a place he did not recognize); he saw white, foaming water dashing at the stones, soaking people and houses; he saw people's shocked faces. He understood that he had not been driven out to sea, as he had supposed, but even then it did not occur to him that the current was in any way *unnatural*. Sometimes it carried him on vigorously in one direction; sometimes all was confusion and he was certain that his end was upon him. Then suddenly the water seemed to grow tired of him; the motion ceased upon the instant and he was thrown up on to some stone steps. He was vaguely aware of cold air and buildings around him.

He drew in great, shuddering, body-racking breaths of air and, just as it became easier to breathe, he vomited up quantities of cold salt water. Then for a long time he simply lay there with his eyes closed, as a man might lie upon a lover's breast. He had no thought of any thing at all. If any desires remained in him, then they were simply to lie there for ever. Much later he became aware, firstly, that the stones were probably very dirty and, secondly, that he was fearfully cold. He began to wonder why it was so quiet and why no one came to help him.

He sat up and opened his eyes.

Darkness was all around him. Was he in a tunnel? A cellar? Under the earth! Any of these would have been quite horrible since he had not the least idea how he had got there or how he was going to get out again. But then he felt a thin, chill wind upon his cheek; he looked up and saw the white, winter stars. Night!

"No, no, no!" he pleaded. He shrank back against the stones of the quay, whimpering.

The buildings were dark and utterly silent. The only live, bright things were the stars. Their constellations looked to Drawlight like gigantic, glittering letters – letters in an unknown alphabet. For all he knew the magician had formed the stars into these letters and used them to write a spell against him. All that could be seen in any direction was black Night, stars and silence. There was no light in any of the houses and, if what Drawlight had been told was true, there were no people in any of the houses. Unless, of course, the magician was there.

With great reluctance he stood up and looked around. Nearby was a little bridge. On the other side of the bridge an alley disappeared between the high walls of dark houses. He could go that way or he could chuse the pavement by the side of the canal. It was frosted with starlight and looked particularly eerie and exposed. He chose the alley and darkness.

He crossed the bridge and passed between the houses. Almost immediately the alley opened out into a square. Several other alleys led away from the square. Which way should he go? He thought of all the black shadows he would have to pass, all the silent doorways. Suppose he never got out! He felt sick and faint with fear.

There was a church in the square. Even by starlight its façade was a monstrous thing. It bulged with pillars and bristled with statues. Angels with outspread wings held trumpets to their lips; a shadowy figure held out its arms beneath a stone canopy; blind faces gazed down at Drawlight from dark arches.

"How do I know the magician is not there?" he thought. He began to examine each black figure in turn to see if it was Jonathan Strange. Once he had begun, it was difficult to stop; he fancied that if he looked away for a moment one of the figures would move. He had almost persuaded himself that it was safe to walk away from the church when something caught his eye – the merest possible irregularity in the deep blackness of the doorway. He looked closer. There was something – or someone – lying on the steps. A man. He lay stretched out upon the stones as if in a swoon, face down, with his arm thrown over his head.

For several moments – oh! but it seemed like an eternity! – Drawlight waited to see what would happen.

Nothing happened.

Then it came to him in an instant: the magician was dead! Perhaps in his madness he had killed himself! The sense of joy and relief was overwhelming. In his excitement he laughed out loud – an extraordinary sound in all the silence. The dark figure in the

dark doorway did not stir. He drew closer until he was leaning over the figure. There was no sound of breathing. He wished that he had a stick to poke it.

Without warning, the figure turned over.

Drawlight gave a little yelp of fright.

Silence. Then, "I know you!" whispered Strange.

Drawlight tried to laugh. He had always employed laughter as a means to placate his victims. Laughter was a soothing thing, was it not? All friends together? But all that came out of his mouth was a queer braying sound.

Strange stood up and took a few steps towards Drawlight. Drawlight backed away. In the starlight Drawlight could see the magician more clearly. He could begin to trace the features of the man he had known. Strange's feet were bare. His coat and shirt hung open and he had clearly not shaved in days.

"I know you," whispered Strange again. "You are . . . You are . . ." He moved his hands through the empty air as if tracing magical symbols. "You are a Leucrocuta!"

"A Loo . . . ?" echoed Drawlight.

"You are the Wolf of the Evening! You prey upon men and women! Your father was a hyena and your mother a lioness! You have the body of a lion; your hooves are cloven. You cannot look behind you. You have one long tooth and no gums. Yet you can take human shape and lure men to you with a human voice!"

"No, no!" pleaded Drawlight. He wanted to say more; he wanted to say that he was none of those things, that Strange was quite mistaken, but his mouth was too dry and weak from terror; it was no longer able to form the words.

"And now," said Strange calmly, "I shall return you to your proper form!" He raised his hands. "Abracadabra!" he cried.

Drawlight fell to the ground, screaming over and over again; and Strange burst into such peals of laughter – eerie, mad laughter – that he bent double and staggered about the square.

Eventually the fear of one man and the hilarity of the other subsided; Drawlight realized that he had *not* been transformed into the horrible, nightmare creature; and Strange grew calmer, almost severe.

"Leucrocuta," he whispered, "stand up."

Still whimpering, Drawlight got to his feet.

"Leucrocuta, why did you come here? No, wait! I know this." Strange snapped his fingers. "I brought you here. Leucrocuta, tell me: why do you spy on me? What have I ever done that is secret? Why did you not come here and ask me? I would have told you everything!"

"They made me do it. Lascelles and Norrell. Lascelles paid my debts so I could leave the King's Bench.[1] I have always been your friend." Drawlight faltered slightly; it seemed unlikely that even a madman would believe this.

Strange raised his head, as if he gave Drawlight a defiant look, but in the Darkness Drawlight could not see his expression. "I have been mad, Leucrocuta!" he hissed. "Did they tell you that? Well, it is true. I have been mad and I will be so again. But since you came to this city I have refrained from . . . I have refrained from certain spells, so that when I saw you I would be in my right mind. My old mind. So that I would know you, and I would know what I meant to say to you. I have learnt many things in the Darkness, Leucrocuta, and one of them is this: I cannot do this alone. I have brought you here to help me."

"Have you? I am glad! I will do any thing! Thank you! Thank you!" But as he spoke Drawlight wondered how long Strange meant to keep him there; the thought turned his heart to water.

"What is . . . What is . . .." Strange appeared to be having difficulty catching hold of his thoughts. He trawled his hands through the air. "What is the name of Pole's wife?"

"Lady Pole?"

"Yes, but I mean . . . her other names?"

---

[1] The prison where Drawlight was imprisoned for debt in November 1814.

"Emma Wintertowne?"

"Yes, that is it. Emma Wintertowne. Where is she? Now?"

"They have taken her to a madhouse in Yorkshire. It is supposed to be a great secret, but I found it out. I knew a man in the King's Bench whose son's sweetheart is a mantua-maker and she knew all about it because she was employed to make Lady Pole's Yorkshire clothes – it is very cold in Yorkshire. They have taken her to a place called Star-something – Lady Pole I mean, not the mantua-maker. Stare-something. Wait! I will tell you! I know this, I swear! Starecross Hall in Yorkshire."

"Starecross? I know that name."

"Yes, yes, you do! Because the tenant is a friend of yours. He was once a magician in Newcastle or York or one of those northern places – only I do not know his name. It seems that Mr Norrell did him an unkindness once – or maybe twice. So when Lady Pole became mad, Childermass thought to mend matters a little by recommending him as a madhouse-keeper to Sir Walter."

There was a silence. Drawlight wondered how much Strange had understood. Then Strange said, "Emma Wintertowne is not mad. She appears mad. But that is Norrell's fault. He summoned a fairy to raise her from the dead and in exchange he gave the fairy all sorts of rights over her. This same fairy threatened the liberty of the King of England and has enchanted at least two more of His Majesty's subjects, one of them my wife!" He paused. "Your first task, Leucrocuta, is to tell John Childermass what I have just told you and to deliver this to him."

Strange took something out of a pocket of his coat and handed it to Drawlight. It appeared to be a small box like a snuff box, except it was a little longer and narrower than snuff boxes usually are. Drawlight took it and put it in his own pocket.

Strange gave a long sigh. The effort of speaking coherently seemed to exhaust him. "Your second task is . . . Your second task is to take a message to all the magicians in England. Do you understand me?"

"Oh, yes! But . . ."

"But what?"

"But there is only one."

"What?"

"There is only one magician, sir. Now that you are here, only one magician remains in England."

Strange seemed to consider this for a moment. "My pupils," he said. "My pupils are magicians. All the men and women who ever wanted to be Norrell's pupils are magicians. Childermass is another. Segundus another. Honeyfoot. The subscribers to the magical journals. The members of the old societies. England is full of magicians. Hundreds! Thousands perhaps! Norrell refused them. Norrell denied them. Norrell silenced them. But they are magicians nonetheless. Tell them this." He passed his hand across his forehead and breathed hard for a moment. "Tree speaks to stone; stone speaks to water. It is not so hard as we have supposed. Tell them to read what is written in the sky. Tell them to ask the rain! All of John Uskglass's old alliances are still in place. I am sending messengers to remind the stones and the sky and the rain of their ancient promises. Tell them . . ." But again Strange could not find the words he wanted. He drew something in the air with a gesture. "I cannot explain it," he said. "Leucrocuta, do you understand?"

"Yes. Oh, yes!" said Drawlight, though he had not the least idea what Strange was talking about.

"Good. Now repeat to me the messages I have given you. Tell them back to me."

Drawlight did so. Long years of collecting and repeating malicious gossip about his acquaintance had made him adept at remembering names and facts. He had the first message perfectly, but the second had descended to a few garbled sentences about magicians standing in the rain, looking at stones.

"I will shew you," said Strange, "and then you will understand. Leucrocuta, if you perform these three tasks, I shall take no revenge on you. I shall not harm you. Deliver these three messages and you may return to your night-hunts, to your devouring of men and women."

"Thank you! Thank you!" breathed Drawlight, gratefully, until a horrible realization gripped him. "Three! But, sir, you only gave me two!"

"Three messages, Leucrocuta," said Strange, wearily. "You must deliver three messages."

"Yes, but you have not told me what the third is!"

Strange made no reply. He turned away, muttering to himself.

In spite of all his terror, Drawlight had a great desire to get hold of the magician and shake him. He might have done it too, if he thought it would do any good. Tears of self-pity began to trickle down his face. Now Strange would kill him for not performing the third task and it was not his fault.

"Leucrocuta," said Strange, suddenly returning. "Bring me a drink of water!"

Drawlight looked around. In the middle of the square there was a well. He went over to it and found a horrible old iron cup attached to the stones by a length of rusting chain. He pushed aside the well-cover, drew up a pail of water and dipped the cup into the water. He hated touching it. Curiously, after everything that had happened to him that day it was the iron cup he hated the most. All of his life he had loved beautiful things, but now everything that surrounded him was horrible. It was the magicians' fault. How he hated them!

"Sir? Lord Magician?" he called out. "You will have to come here to drink." He shewed the iron chain by way of an explanation.

Strange came forward, but he did not take the proffered cup. Instead he took a tiny phial out of his pocket and handed it to Drawlight. "Put six drops in the water," he said.

Drawlight took out the stopper. His hand was trembling so

much that he feared he would pour the whole thing on the ground. Strange did not appear to notice; Drawlight shook in some drops.

Strange took the cup and drank the water down. The cup fell from his hand. Drawlight was aware – he did not know how exactly – that Strange was changed. Against the starry sky the black shape of his figure sagged and his head drooped. Drawlight wondered if he were drunk. But how could a few drops of any thing make a man drunk? Besides he did not smell of strong liquor; he smelt like a man who had not washed himself or his linen for some weeks; and there was another smell too – one that had not been there a minute ago – a smell like old age and half a hundred cats.

Drawlight had the strangest feeling. It was something he had felt before when magic was about to happen. Invisible doors seemed to be opening all around him; winds blew on him from far away, bringing scents of woods, moors and bogs. Images flew unbidden into his mind. The houses around him were no longer empty. He could see inside them as if the walls had been removed. Each dark room contained – not a person exactly – a Being, an Ancient Spirit. One contained a Fire; another a Stone; yet another a Shower of Rain; yet another a Flock of Birds; yet another a Hillside; yet another a Small Creature with Dark and Fiery Thoughts; and on and on.

"What are they?" he whispered, in amazement. He realized that all the hairs on his head were standing on end as if he had been electrified. Then a new, different sensation took him: it was a sensation not unlike falling, and yet he remained standing. It was as if his mind had fallen down.

He thought he stood upon an English hillside. Rain was falling; it twisted in the air like grey ghosts. Rain fell upon him and he grew thin as rain. Rain washed away thought, washed away memory, all the good and the bad. He no longer knew his name. Everything was washed away like mud from a stone. Rain filled him up with thoughts and memories of its own. Silver lines of water covered the hillside, like intricate lace, like the veins of an arm.

Forgetting that he was, or ever had been, a man, he became the lines of water. He fell into the earth with the rain.

He thought he lay beneath the earth, beneath England. Long ages passed; cold and rain seeped through him; stones shifted within him. In the Silence and the Dark he grew vast. He became the earth; he became England. A star looked down on him and spoke to him. A stone asked him a question and he answered it in its own language. A river curled at his side; hills budded beneath his fingers. He opened his mouth and breathed out spring . . .

He thought he was pressed into a thicket in a dark wood in winter. The trees went on for ever, dark pillars separated by thin, white slices of winter light. He looked down. Young saplings pierced him through and through; they grew up through his body, through his feet and hands. His eye-lids would no longer close because twigs had grown up through them. Insects scuttled in and out of his ears; spiders built nests and webs in his mouth. He realized he had been entwined in the wood for years and years. He knew the wood and the wood knew him. There was no saying any longer what was wood and what was man.

All was silent. Snow fell. He screamed . . .

Blackness.

Like rising up from beneath dark waters, Drawlight came to himself. Who it was that released him – whether Strange, or the wood, or England itself – he did not know, but he felt its contempt as it cast him back into his own mind. The Ancient Spirits withdrew from him. His thoughts and sensations shrank to those of a Man. He was dizzy and reeling from the memory of what he had endured. He examined his hands and rubbed the places on his body where the trees had pierced him. They seemed whole enough; oh, but they hurt! He whimpered and looked around for Strange.

The magician was a little way off, crouching by a wall, muttering magic to himself. He struck the wall once; the stones bulged, changed shape, became a raven; the raven opened its wings and, with a loud caw, flew up towards the night sky. He struck the wall again: another raven emerged from the wall and flew away. Then another and another, and on and on, thick and fast they came until all the stars above were blotted out by black wings.

Strange raised his hand to strike again . . .

"Lord Magician," gasped Drawlight. "You have not told me what the third message is."

Strange looked round. Without warning he seized Drawlight's coat and pulled him close. Drawlight could feel Strange's stinking breath on his face and for the first time he could see his face. Starlight shone on fierce, wild eyes, from which all humanity and reason had fled.

"Tell Norrell I am coming!" hissed Strange. "Now, go!"

Drawlight did not need to be told twice. He sped away through the darkness. Ravens seemed to pursue him. He could not see them, but he heard the beating of their wings and felt the currents in the air that those wings created. Halfway across a bridge he tumbled without warning into dazzling light. Instantly he was surrounded by the sound of birdsong and of people talking. Men and women were walking and talking and going about their everyday pursuits. Here was no terrible magic – only the everyday world – the wonderful, beautiful everyday world.

Drawlight's clothes were still drenched in sea-water and the weather was cruelly cold. He was in a part of the city he did not recognize. No one offered to help him and for a long time he walked about, lost and exhausted. Eventually he happened upon a square he knew and was able to make his way back to the little tavern where he rented a room. By the time he reached it, he was weak and shivering. He undressed and rinsed the salt from his body as best he could. Then he lay down on his little bed.

For the next two days he lay in a fever. His dreams were unspeakable things, filled with Darkness, Magic and the Long, Cold Ages of the Earth. And all the time he slept he was filled with dread lest he wake to find himself under the earth or crucified by a winter wood.

By the middle of the third day he was recovered enough to get up and go to the harbour. There he found an English ship bound for Portsmouth. He shewed the captain the letters and papers Lascelles had given him, promising a large fee to the ship that bore him back to England and signed by two of the most famous bankers in Europe.

By the fifth day he was on a ship bound for England.

A thin, cold mist lay upon London, mimicking – or so it seemed – the thin, cold character of Stephen's existence. Lately his enchantment weighed upon him more heavily than ever. Joy, affection and peace were all strangers to him now. The only emotions that pierced the clouds of magic around his heart were of the bitterest sort – anger, resentment and frustration. The division and estrangement between him and his English friends grew ever deeper. The gentleman might be a fiend, but when he spoke of the pride and self-importance of Englishmen, Stephen found it hard to deny the justice of what he said. Even Lost-hope, dreary as it was, was sometimes a welcome refuge from English arrogance and English malice; there at least Stephen had never needed to apologize for being what he was; there he had only ever been treated as an honoured guest.

On this particular winter's day Stephen was in Sir Walter Pole's stables in the Harley-street mews. Sir Walter had recently purchased a pair of very fine greyhounds, much to the delight of his male servants, who idled away a large part of every day in visiting the dogs and admiring them and talking with varying degrees of knowledge and understanding of their likely prowess in the field. Stephen knew he ought to check this bad habit, but he found he did not really care enough to do it. Today when Robert, the footman, had invited him to come and see the dogs, Stephen, far from scolding him, had put on his hat and coat and gone with him.

Now he watched Robert and the grooms fussing over the dogs. He felt as if he was on the other side of a thick and dirty pane of glass.

Suddenly each man straightened himself and filed out of the stables. Stephen shivered. Experience had taught him that such unnatural behaviour invariably announced the arrival of the gentleman with the thistle-down hair.

Now here he was, lighting up the cramped, dark stables with the brilliance of his silver hair, and the glitter of his blue eyes, and the brightness of his green coat; full of loud talk and laughter; never doubting for a moment that Stephen was as delighted to see him as he was to see Stephen. He was as pleased with the dogs as the servants had been, and called on Stephen to admire them with him. He spoke to them in his own language and the dogs leapt up and barked joyously, seeming more enamoured of him than any one they had ever seen before.

The gentleman said, "I am reminded of an occasion in 1413 when I came south to visit the new King of Southern England. The King, a gracious and valiant person, introduced me to his court, telling them of my many marvellous accomplishments, extensive kingdoms, chivalrous character etc., etc. However one of his noblemen chose not to attend to this instructive and elevating speech. Instead he and his followers stood gossiping and laughing together. I was – as you may imagine – much offended by this treatment and determined to teach them better manners! The next day these wicked men were hunting hares near Hatfield Forest. Coming upon them all unawares, I had the happy notion of turning the men into hares and the hares into men. First the hounds tore their masters to pieces, and then the hares – now in the shape of men – found themselves able to inflict a terrible revenge upon the hounds who had chased and harried them." The gentleman paused to receive Stephen's praises for this feat, but before Stephen could utter a word, the gentleman exclaimed, "Oh! Did you feel that?"

"Feel what, sir?" asked Stephen.

"All the doors shook!"

Stephen glanced at the stable doors.

"No, not those doors!" said the gentleman. "I mean the doors between England and everywhere else! Someone is trying to open them. Someone spoke to the Sky and it was not me! Someone is giving instructions to the Stones and Rivers and it is not me! Who is doing that? Who is it? Come!"

The gentleman seized Stephen's arm and they seemed to rise up in the air, as if they were suddenly stood upon a mountain or a very high tower. Harley-street mews disappeared and a new scene presented itself to Stephen's eyes – and then another, and then another. Here was a port with a crowd of masts as thick as a forest – it seemed to fly away beneath their feet and was immediately replaced by a grey, winter sea and ships in full sail bending to the wind – next came a city with spires and splendid bridges. Curiously there was scarcely any sensation of movement. It felt more as if the world was flying towards Stephen and the gentleman, while they remained still. Now came snow-covered mountains with tiny people toiling up them – next a glassy lake with dark peaks all around it – then a level country with tiny towns and rivers spread across it like a child's toy.

There was something ahead of them. At first it looked like a black line that cut the sky in half. But as they drew nearer, it became a Black Pillar that reached up from the earth and had no end.

Stephen and the gentleman came to rest high above Venice (as to what they might be resting *upon*, Stephen was determined not to consider). The sun was setting and the streets and buildings beneath them were dark, but the sea and sky were full of light in which shades of rose, milky-blue, topaz and pearl were all blended harmoniously together. The city seemed to float in a radiant void.

For the most part the Black Pillar was as smooth as obsidian, but, just above the level of the house-roofs, twists and spirals of darkness were billowing out from it and drifting away through the air. What they could be, Stephen could not imagine.

"Is it smoke, sir? Is the tower on fire?" asked Stephen.

The gentleman did not reply, but as they drew closer Stephen saw that it was not smoke. A dark multitude was flying out of the Tower. They were ravens. Thousands upon thousands of ravens. They were leaving Venice and flying back in the direction Stephen and the gentleman had come.

One flock wheeled towards them. The air was suddenly tumultuous with the beating of a thousand wings, and loud with a thrumming, drumming noise. Clouds of dust and grit flew into Stephen's eyes, nose and throat. He bent low and cupped his hand over his nose to shut out the stench.

When they were gone, he asked in amazement, "What are they, sir?"

"Creatures the magician has made," said the gentleman. "He is sending them back to England with instructions for the Sky and the Earth and the Rivers and the Hills. He is calling up all the King's old allies. Soon they will attend to English magicians, rather than to me!" He gave a great howl of mingled anger and despair. "I have punished him in ways that I never punished my enemies before! Yet still he works against me! Why does he not resign himself to his fate? Why does he not despair?"

"I never heard that he lacked courage, sir," said Stephen. "By all accounts he did many brave things in the Peninsula."

"Courage? What are you talking about? This is not courage! This is malice, pure and simple! We have been negligent, Stephen! We have let the English magicians get the advantage of us. We must find a way to defeat them! We must redouble our efforts to make you King!"

60

Tempest and lies

February 1817

AUNT GREYSTEEL HAD rented a house in Padua within sight of the fruit market. It was very convenient for everywhere and only eighty sechinis a quarter (which comes to about 38 guineas). Aunt Greysteel was very well pleased with her bargain. But it sometimes happens that when one acts quickly and with great resolve, all the indecisiveness and doubt comes afterwards, when it is too late. So it was in this case: Aunt Greysteel and Flora had not been living in the house a week, when Aunt Greysteel began to find fault with it and began to wonder if, in fact, she ought to have taken it at all. Although ancient and pretty, its gothic windows were rather small and several of them were fenced about with stone balconies; in other words it was inclined to be dark. This would never have been a problem before, but just at present Flora's spirits required support, and (thought Aunt Greysteel) gloom and shadows – be they ever so picturesque – might not in fact be the best thing for her. There were moreover some stone ladies who stood about the courtyard and who had, in the course of the years, acquired veils and cloaks of ivy. It was no exaggeration to say that these ladies were in imminent danger of disappearing altogether and every time Aunt Greysteel's eye fell upon them, she was put in mind of Jonathan Strange's poor wife, who had died so young and so mysteriously, and whose unhappy fate seemed to have driven her husband mad. Aunt Greysteel hoped that no such melancholy notions occurred to Flora.

But the bargain had been made and the house had been taken, so Aunt Greysteel set about making it as cheerful and bright as she could. She had never squandered candles or lamp oil in her life, but in her endeavour to raise Flora's spirits she put all questions of expence aside. There was a particularly gloomy spot on the stairs, where a step turned in an odd way that no one could possibly have predicted, and lest any one should tumble down and break their neck, Aunt Greysteel insisted upon a lamp being placed upon a shelf just above the step. The lamp burnt day and night and was a continual affront to Bonifazia, the elderly Italian maid who came with the house and who was an even more economical person than Aunt Greysteel herself.

Bonifazia was an excellent servant, but much inclined to criticism and long explanations of why the instructions she had just been given were wrong or impossible to carry out. She was aided in her work by a slow, put-upon sort of young man called Minichello, who greeted any order with a low, grumbling murmur of dialect words, quite impossible to comprehend. Bonifazia treated Minichello with such familiar contempt that Aunt Greysteel supposed they must be related, though she had yet to obtain any precise information upon this point.

So what with the arrangements for the house, the daily battles with Bonifazia and all the discoveries, pleasant or otherwise, attendant upon a sojourn in a new town, Aunt Greysteel's days were full of interesting occupation; but her chief and most sacred duty at this time was to try and find amusement for Flora. Flora had fallen into habits of quiet and solitude. If her aunt spoke to her she answered cheerfully enough, but few indeed were the conversations that she began. In Venice Flora had been the chief instigator of all their pleasures; now she simply fell in with whatever projects of exploration Aunt Greysteel proposed. She preferred those occupations that require no companion. She walked alone, read alone, sat alone in the sitting-room or in the ray of faint sunshine which sometimes penetrated the little courtyard at about one o'clock. She was less open-hearted and confiding than before; it was as if someone – not necessarily Jonathan Strange – had disappointed her and she was determined to be more independent in future.

In the first week in February there was a great storm in Padua. It happened at about the middle of the day. The storm came very suddenly out of the east (from the direction of Venice and the sea). The old men who frequented the town's coffee-houses said that there had been no sign of it moments before. But other people were not much inclined to take any notice of this; after all it was winter and storms must be expected.

First a great wind blew through the town. It was no respecter of doors or windows, this wind. It seemed to find out chinks that no one knew existed and it blew almost as fiercely within the houses as without. Aunt Greysteel and Flora were together in a little sitting-room on the first floor. The window-panes began to rattle and some crystals that hung from a chandelier began to jingle. Then the pages of a letter that Aunt Greysteel was writing escaped from beneath her hand and went flying about the room. Outside the window, the skies darkened and it became as black as night; sheets of blinding rain began to descend.

Bonifazia and Minichello entered the sitting-room. They came under the pretext of finding out Aunt Greysteel's wishes concerning the storm, but in truth Bonifazia wanted to join with Aunt Greysteel in exclamations of astonishment at the violence of the wind and rain (and a fine duet they made of it too, albeit in different languages). Minichello came presumably because Bonifazia did; he regarded the storm gloomily, as if he suspected it of having been arranged on purpose to make work for him.

Aunt Greysteel, Bonifazia and Minichello were all at the window and saw how the first stroke of lightning turned the whole familiar scene into something quite Gothic and disturbing, full of pallid, unearthly glare and unexpected shadows. This was followed by a crack of thunder that shook the whole room. Bonifazia murmured appeals to the Virgin and several saints. Aunt Greysteel, who was equally alarmed, might well have been glad of the same refuge, but as a member of the communion of the Church of England, she could only exclaim, "Dear me!" and, "Upon my word!" and "Lord bless me!" – none of which gave her much comfort.

"Flora, my love," she called out in a voice that quavered slightly, "I hope you are not frightened. It is a very horrid storm."

Flora came to the window and took her aunt's hand and told her that it was sure to be over very soon. Another stroke of lightning illuminated the town. Flora dropped her aunt's hand, undid the window-fastening and stepped eagerly out on to the balcony.

"Flora!" exclaimed Aunt Greysteel.

She was leaning into the howling darkness with both hands upon the balustrade, quite oblivious of the rain that soaked her gown or of the wind that pulled at her hair.

"My love! Flora! Flora! Come out of the rain!"

Flora turned and said something to her aunt, but what it was they could not hear.

Minichello followed her on to the balcony and, with a surprizing delicacy (though without relinquishing for a moment his native gloominess), he managed to herd her inside again, using his large, flat hands to guide her, in the same way shepherds use hurdles to direct sheep.

"Can you not see?" exclaimed Flora. "There is someone there! There, at the corner! Can you tell who it is? I thought . . ." She fell silent abruptly and whatever it was that she thought, she did not say.

"Well, my love, I hope you are mistaken. I pity any one who is in the street at this moment. I hope they will find some shelter as soon as they can. Oh, Flora! How wet you are!"

Bonifazia fetched towels and then she and Aunt Greysteel immediately set about drying Flora's gown, turning her round and round between them, and sometimes trying to give her a turn in contrary directions. At the same time both were giving Minichello urgent instructions, Aunt Greysteel in stumbling, yet insistent Italian, and Bonifazia in rapid Veneto dialect. The instructions, like the turns, may well have been at odds with each other, because Minichello did nothing, except regard them with a baleful expression.

Flora gazed over the bowed heads of the two women into the street. Another stroke of lightning. She stiffened, as if she had been electrified, and the next moment she wriggled out of the clutches of aunt and maid, and ran out of the room.

They had no time to wonder where she was going. The next half hour was one of titanic domestic struggle: of Minichello trying to close shutters in the teeth of the storm; of Bonifazia stumbling about in the dark, looking for candles; of Aunt Greysteel discovering that the Italian word she had been using to mean "shutter" actually meant "parchment". Each of them in turn lost his or her temper. Nor did Aunt Greysteel feel that the situation was much improved when all the bells in the town began to ring at once, in accordance with the belief that bells (being blessed objects) can dispel storms and thunder (which are clearly works of the Devil).

At last the house was secured – or very nearly. Aunt Greysteel left Bonifazia and Minichello to complete the work and, forgetting that she had seen Flora leave the sitting-room, she returned thither with a candle for her niece. Flora was not there, but Aunt Greysteel observed that Minichello still had not closed the shutters in that room.

She mounted the stairs to Flora's bed-chamber: Flora was not there either. Nor was she in the little dining-parlour, nor in Aunt Greysteel's own bed-chamber, nor in the other, smaller sitting-room which they sometimes used after dinner. The kitchen, the vestibule and the gardener's room were tried next; she was not in any of those places.

Aunt Greysteel began to be seriously frightened. A cruel little voice whispered in her ear that whatever mysterious fate had befallen Jonathan Strange's wife, it had begun when she had disappeared very unexpectedly in bad weather.

"But that was snow, not rain," she told herself. As she went about the house, looking for Flora, she kept repeating to herself, "Snow, not rain. Snow, not rain." Then she thought, "Perhaps she was in the sitting-room all along. It was so dark and she is so quiet, I may well not have perceived her."

She returned to the room. Another stroke of lightning gave it an unnatural aspect. The walls became white and ghastly; the furniture and other objects became grey, as if they had all been turned to stone. With a horrible jolt, Aunt Greysteel realized that there was indeed a second person in the room – a woman, *but not Flora* – a woman in a dark, old-fashioned gown, standing with a candle in a candlestick, looking at her – a woman whose face was entirely in shadow, whose features could not be seen.

Aunt Greysteel grew cold all over.

There was a crack of thunder: then pitch-black darkness, except for the two candle flames. But somehow the unknown woman's candle seemed to illuminate nothing at all. Queerer still the room seemed to have grown larger in some mysterious way; the woman and her candle were strangely distant from Aunt Greysteel.

Aunt Greysteel cried out, "Who is there?"

No one answered.

"Of course," she thought, "she is Italian. I must ask her again in Italian. Perhaps she has wandered into the wrong house in the confusion of the storm." But try as she might, she could not at that moment think of a single Italian word.

Another flash of lightning. There was the woman, standing just as she had been before, facing Aunt Greysteel. "It is the ghost of Jonathan Strange's wife!" she thought. She took a step forward, and so did the unknown woman. Suddenly realization and relief came upon her in equal measures; "It is a mirror! Oh! How foolish! How foolish! To be afraid of my own reflection!" She was so relieved she almost laughed out loud, but then she paused; it had not been foolish to be frightened, not foolish at all; *there had been no mirror in that corner until now.*

The next flash of lightning shewed the mirror to her. It was ugly and much too large for the room; she knew she had never seen it before in her life.

She hurried out of the room. She felt she would be able to think more clearly away from the sight of the baleful mirror. She was halfway up the stairs when some sounds that seemed to originate in Flora's bed-chamber made her open the door and look inside.

There was Flora. She had lit the candles they had placed for her and was in the middle of pulling her gown over her head. The gown was sopping wet. Her petticoat and stockings were no better. Her shoes were tumbled on the floor at the side of the bed; they were quite soaked and spoilt with rain.

Flora looked at her aunt with an expression in which guilt, embarrassment, defiance and several other things more difficult of interpretation were mixed together. "Nothing! Nothing!" she cried.

This, presumably, was the answer to some question she expected her aunt to put to her, but all that Aunt Greysteel said was: "Oh, my dear! Where have you been? Whatever made you go out in such weather?"

"I . . . I went out to buy some embroidery silk."

Aunt Greysteel must have looked a good deal astonished at this, because Flora added doubtfully, "I did not think the rain would last so long."

"Well, my love, I must say I think you acted rather foolishly, but you must have been a good deal frightened! Was it that that made you cry?"

"Cry! No, no! You are mistaken, aunt. I have not been crying. It is rain, that is all."

"But you are . . ." Aunt Greysteel stopped. She had been going to say, *you are crying now*, but Flora shook her head and turned away. For some reason she had wrapped her shawl into a bundle and Aunt Greysteel could not help thinking that if she had not done that the shawl would have given her some protection from the rain and she would not now be so wet. From out of the bundle she took a little bottle half full of an amber-coloured liquid. She opened a drawer, and put it inside.

"Flora! Something very peculiar has happened. I do not know quite how to tell you, but there is a mirror . . ."

"Yes, I know," said Flora, quickly. "It belongs to me."

"Belongs to you!" Aunt Greysteel was more perplexed than ever. A pause of some moments' duration. "Where did you buy it?" she asked. It was all she could think of to say.

"I do not remember exactly. It must have been delivered just now."

"But surely no one would deliver any thing in the middle of a storm! And even if any body had been so foolish as to do such a thing, they would have knocked upon the door – and not done it in this strange, secret way."

To these very reasonable arguments Flora made no reply.

Aunt Greysteel was not sorry to let the subject drop. She was quite sick of storms and frights and unexpected mirrors. The question of *why* the mirror had appeared was now resolved and so, for the present, she put aside the question of *how* it had appeared. She was glad to fall back upon the more soothing subjects of Flora's gown and Flora's shoes and the likelihood of Flora's catching cold and the necessity for Flora drying herself immediately and putting on her dressing-gown and coming and sitting by the fire in the sitting-room and eating something hot.

When they were both in the sitting-room again, Aunt Greysteel said, "See! The storm is almost passed. It seems to be going back towards the coast. How odd! I thought that was the direction it came from. I suppose your embroidery silks were ruined by the rain along with everything else."

"Embroidery silks?" said Flora. Then, remembering, "Oh! I did not get so far as the shop. It was, as you say, a foolish undertaking."

"Well, we can go out later and get whatever you need. How sorry I am for the poor market people! Everything on the stalls will have been spoilt. Bonifazia is making your gruel, my love. I wonder if I told her to use the new milk?"

"I do not remember, aunt."

"I had better go and just mention it."

"I can go, aunt," said Flora, proposing to stand up.

But her aunt would not hear of it. Flora must remain exactly where she was, at the fire-side, with her feet upon a footstool.

It was becoming lighter by the moment. Before proceeding to the kitchen, Aunt Greysteel surveyed the mirror. It was very large and ornate; the sort of mirror, in fact, that is made on the island of Murano in the Venetian Lagoon. "I confess I am surprized at you liking this mirror, Flora. It has so many scrolls and curlicues and glass flowers. Generally you prefer simple things."

Flora sighed and said she supposed she had acquired a taste for what was sumptuous and elaborate since she had been in Italy.

"Was it expensive?" asked Aunt Greysteel. "It looks expensive."

"No. Not expensive at all."

"Well, that is something, is it not?"

Aunt Greysteel went down the stairs to the kitchen. She was feeling a good deal recovered, and felt confident that the train of shocks and alarms of which the morning seemed to have been composed was now at an end. But in this she was quite wrong.

Standing in the kitchen with Bonifazia and Minichello were two men she had never seen before. Bonifazia did not appear to have begun making Flora's gruel. She had not even fetched the oatmeal and milk out of the pantry.

The moment Bonifazia laid eyes upon Aunt Greysteel, she took her by the arm and unleashed a flood of eager dialect words upon her. She was speaking of the storm – that much was clear – and saying it was evil, but beyond that Aunt Greysteel understood very little. To her absolute astonishment it was Minichello who helped her comprehend it. In a very reasonable counterfeit of the English language he said, "The magician Engliss makes it. The magician Engliss makes the *tempesta*."

"I beg your pardon?"

With frequent interruptions from Bonifazia and the two men, Minichello informed her that in the midst of the storm several people had looked up and seen a cleft in the black clouds. But what they had seen through the cleft had astonished and terrified them; it had not been the clear azure they were expecting, but a black, midnight sky full of stars. The storm had not been natural at all; it had been contrived in order to hide the approach of Strange's Pillar of Darkness.

This news was soon known all over the town and the citizens were greatly disturbed by it. Until now the Pillar of Darkness had been a horror confined to Venice, which seemed – to the Paduans at least – a natural setting for horrors. Now it was clear that Strange had stayed in Venice by choice rather than enchantment. Any city in Italy – any city in the world might suddenly find itself visited by Eternal Darkness. This was bad enough, but for Aunt Greysteel it was much worse; to all her fear of Strange was added the unwelcome conviction that Flora had lied. She debated with herself whether it was more likely that her niece had lied because she was under the influence of a spell, or because her attachment to Strange had weakened her principles. She did not know which would be worse.

She wrote to her brother in Venice, begging him to come. In the meantime she determined to say nothing. For the rest of the day she observed Flora closely. Flora was much as usual, except that there sometimes seemed to be a tinge of penitence in her behaviour to her aunt, where no tinge ought to have been.

At one o'clock on the next day – some hours before Aunt Greysteel's letter could have reached him – Dr Greysteel arrived with Frank from Venice. They told her that it had been no secret in Venice when Strange left the parish of Santa Maria Zobenigo and went to *terrafirma*. The Pillar of Darkness had been seen from many parts of the city, moving across the face of the sea. Its surface had flickered and twists and spirals of Darkness had darted in and out, so that it appeared to be made of black flames. How Strange had contrived to cross over the water – whether he had travelled in a boat, or whether his passage had been purely magical – was not known. The storm by which he had tried to hide his approach had not been conjured up until he got to Strà, eight miles from Padua.

"I tell you, Louisa," said Dr Greysteel, "I would not exchange with him now upon any consideration. Everyone fled at his approach. From Mestre to Strà he could not have seen another living creature – nothing but silent streets and abandoned fields. Henceforth the world is an empty place to him."

A few moments before, Aunt Greysteel had been thinking of Strange with no very tender feelings, but the picture that her brother conjured up was so shocking that tears started into her eyes. "And where is he now?" she asked in a softened tone.

"He has gone back to his rooms in Santa Maria Zobenigo," said Dr Greysteel. "All is just as it was. As soon as we heard he had been in Padua, I guessed what his object was. We came as soon as we could. How is Flora?"

Flora was in the drawing-room. She had been expecting her father – indeed she seemed relieved that the interview had come at last. Dr Greysteel had scarcely got out his first question when she burst forth with her confession. It was the release of an overcharged heart. Her tears fell abundantly and she admitted that she had seen Strange. She had seen him in the street below and known that he was waiting for her and so she had run out of the house to meet him.

"I will tell you everything, I promise," she said. "But not yet. I have done nothing wrong. I mean . . ." She blushed. ". . . apart from the falsehoods I told my aunt – for which I am very sorry. But these secrets are not mine to tell."

"But why must there be secrets at all, Flora?" asked her father. "Does that not tell you that there is something wrong? People whose intentions are honourable do not have secrets. They act openly."

"Yes, I suppose . . . Oh, but that does not apply to magicians! Mr Strange has enemies – that terrible old man in London and others besides! But you must not scold me for doing wrong. I have tried so hard to do good and I believe I have! You see, there is a sort of magic which he has been practising and which is destroying him – and yesterday I persuaded him to give it up! He made me a promise to abandon it completely."

"But, Flora!" said her father, sadly. "This distresses me more than all the rest. That you should regard yourself as entitled to exact promises from him is something which requires explanation. Surely you must see that? My dear, are you engaged to him?"

"No, papa!" Another burst of tears. It took a great many caresses from her aunt to restore her to tolerable calm. When she could speak again, she said, "There is no engagement. It is true that I was attached to him once. But that is all over and done with. You must not suspect me of it! It was for friendship's sake that I asked him to promise me. And for his wife's sake. He thinks he is doing it for her, but I know that she would not want him to do magic so destructive of his health and reason – whatever the object, however desperate the circumstances! She is no longer able to guide his actions – and so it fell to me to speak on her behalf."

Dr Greysteel was silent. "Flora," he said after a minute or two, "you forget, my dear, that I have seen him often in Venice. He is in no condition to keep promises. He will not even remember what promise he has made."

"Oh! But he will! I have arranged matters so that he must!"

A fresh return of tears seemed to shew that she was not quite as free of love as she claimed. But she had said enough to make her father and aunt a little easier in their minds. They were convinced that her attachment to Jonathan Strange must come to a natural close sooner or later. As Aunt Greysteel said later that evening, Flora was not the sort of girl to spend years in longing for an impossible love; she was too rational a creature.

Now that they were all together again Dr Greysteel and Aunt Greysteel were eager to continue their travels. Aunt Greysteel wished to go to Rome to see the ancient buildings and artefacts which they had heard were so remarkable. But Flora no longer had any interest in remains or works of art. She was happiest, she said, where she was. Most of the time she would not even leave the house unless absolutely forced to it. When they proposed a walk or a visit to a church with a Renaissance altarpiece, she declined to accompany them. She would complain that it was raining or that the streets were wet – all of which was true; there was a great deal of rain in Padua that winter, but the rain had never troubled her before.

Her aunt and father were patient, though Dr Greysteel in particular thought it a little hard. He had not come to Italy to sit quietly in an apartment half the size of the rooms in his own comfortable house in Wiltshire. In private he grumbled that it was perfectly possible to read novels or embroider in Wiltshire (these were now Flora's favourite pursuits) and a good deal cheaper too, but Aunt Greysteel scolded him and made him hush. If this was the way in which Flora intended to grieve for Jonathan Strange, then they must let her.

Flora did propose one expedition, but that was of a most peculiar sort. After Dr Greysteel had been in Padua about a week she announced that she had a great desire to be upon the sea.

Did she mean a sea-voyage, they asked. There was no reason why they should not go to Rome or Naples by sea.

But she did not mean a sea-voyage. She did not wish to leave Padua. No, what she would like would be to go out in a yacht or other sort of boat. Only for an hour or two, perhaps less. But she would like to go immediately. The next day they repaired to a small fishing village.

The village had no particular advantages of situation, prospect, architecture or history – in fact it had very little to recommend it at all, other than its proximity to Padua. Dr Greysteel inquired in the little wine-shop and at the priest's house until he heard of two steady fellows who would be willing to take them out upon the water. The men had no objection to taking Dr Greysteel's money, but they were obliged to point out that there was nothing to see; there would have been nothing to see even in good weather. But it was not good weather; it was raining – hard enough to make an excursion on the water most uncomfortable, not quite hard enough to dispel the heavy, grey mist.

"Are you sure, my love, that this is what you want?" asked Aunt Greysteel. "It is a dismal spot and the boat smells very strongly of fish."

"I am quite sure, Aunt," said Flora and climbed into the boat and settled herself at one end. Her aunt and father followed her. The mystified fishermen sailed out until all that could be seen in any direction was a shifting mass of grey water confined by walls of dull, grey mist. The fishermen looked expectantly at Dr Greysteel. He, in turn, looked questioningly at Flora.

Flora took no notice of any of them. She was seated, leaning against the side of the boat in a pensive attitude. Her right arm was stretched out over the water.

"There it is again!" cried Dr Greysteel.

"There is what again?" asked Aunt Greysteel, irritably.

"That smell of cats and mustiness! A smell like the old woman's room. The old woman we visited in Cannaregio. Is there a cat on board?"

The question was absurd. Every part of the fishing-boat was visible from every other part; there was no cat.

"Is any thing the matter, my love?" asked Aunt Greysteel. There was something in Flora's posture she did not quite like. "Are you ill?"

"No, Aunt," said Flora, straightening herself and adjusting her umbrella. "I am well. We can go back now if you wish."

For a moment Aunt Greysteel saw a little bottle floating upon the waves, a little bottle with no stopper. Then it sank beneath the water and was gone for ever.

This peculiar expedition was the last time for many weeks that Flora would shew any inclination to go out. Sometimes Aunt Greysteel would try to persuade her to sit in a chair by the window so that she could see what was going on in the street. In an Italian street there is often something amusing going on. But Flora was greatly attached to a chair in a shadowy corner, beneath the eerie mirror; and she acquired a peculiar habit of comparing the picture of the room as it was contained in the mirror and the room as it really was. She might, for example, suddenly become interested in a shawl that was thrown across a chair and look at its reflection and say, "That shawl looks different in the mirror."

"Does it?" Aunt Greysteel would say, puzzled.

"Yes. It looks brown in the mirror, whereas in truth it is blue. Do not you think so?"

"Well, my dear, I am sure you are right, but it looks just the same to me."

"No," Flora would say, with a sigh, "you are right."

61

Tree speaks to Stone;
Stone speaks to Water

January–February 1817

W HEN MR NORRELL had destroyed Strange's book, public opinion in England had been very much against him and very much in favour of Strange. Comparisons were made, both publicly and privately, between the two magicians. Strange was open, courageous and energetic, whereas secrecy seemed to be the beginning and end of Mr Norrell's character. Nor was it forgotten how, when Strange was in the Peninsula in the service of his country, Norrell had bought up all the books of magic in the Duke of Roxburghe's library so that no one else could read them. But by the middle of January the newspapers were full of reports of Strange's madness, descriptions of the Black Tower and speculations concerning the magic which held him there. An Englishman called Lister had been at Mestre on the Italian coast on the day Strange had left Venice and gone to Padua. Mr Lister had witnessed the passage of the Pillar of Darkness over the sea and sent back an account to England; three weeks later accounts appeared in several London newspapers of how it had glided silently over the face of the waters. In the space of a few short months Strange had become a symbol of horror to his countrymen: a damned creature – scarcely human.

But Strange's sudden fall from grace did little to benefit Mr

Norrell. He received no new commissions from the Government and, worse yet, commissions from other sources were cancelled. In early January the Dean of St Paul's Cathedral had inquired whether Mr Norrell might be able to discover the burial place of a certain dead young woman. The young woman's brother wished to erect a new monument to all the members of his family. This entailed moving the young woman's coffin, but the Dean and Chapter were most embarrassed to discover that her burial place had been written down wrongly and they did not know where she was. Mr Norrell had assured him that it would be the easiest thing in the world to find her. As soon as the Dean informed him of the young lady's name and one or two other details he would do the magic. But the Dean did not send Mr Norrell her name. Instead an awkwardly phrased letter had arrived in which the Dean made many elaborate apologies and said how he had recently been struck by the inappropriateness of clergymen employing magicians.

Lascelles and Norrell agreed that the situation was a worrying one.

"It will be difficult to sustain the restoration of English magic if no new magic is done," said Lascelles. "At this crisis it is imperative that we bring your name and achievements continually before the public."

Lascelles wrote articles for the newspapers and he denounced Strange in all the magical journals. He also took the opportunity to review the magic that Mr Norrell had done in the past ten years and suggest improvements. He decided that he and Mr Norrell should go down to Brighton to look at the wall of spells that Mr Norrell and Jonathan Strange had cast around Britain's coast. It had occupied the greater part of Mr Norrell's time for the past two years and had cost the Government a vast sum of money.

So on a particularly icy, windy day in February they stood together at Brighton and contemplated a wide stretch of featureless grey sea.

"It is invisible," said Lascelles.

"Invisible, yes!" agreed Mr Norrell, eagerly, "But no less efficacious for that! It will protect the cliffs from erosion, people's houses from storm, livestock from being swept away and it will capsize any enemies of Britain who attempt to land."

"But could you not have placed beacons at regular intervals to remind people that the magic wall is there? Burning flames hovering mysteriously over the face of the waters? Pillars shaped out of sea-water? Something of that sort?"

"Oh!" said Mr Norrell. "To be sure! I could create the magical illusions you mention. They are not at all difficult to do, but you must understand that they would be purely ornamental. They would not strengthen the magic in any way whatsoever. They would have no practical effect."

"Their effect," said Lascelles, severely, "would be to stand as a constant reminder to every onlooker of the works of the great Mr Norrell. They would let the British people know that you are still the Defender of the Nation, eternally vigilant, watching over them while they go about their business. It would be worth ten, twenty articles in the Reviews."

"Indeed?" said Mr Norrell. He promised that in future he would always bear in mind the necessity of doing magic to excite the public imagination.

They stayed that night in the Old Ship Tavern and the following morning they returned to London. As a rule Mr Norrell detested long journeys. Though his carriage was a most superior example of the carriage-makers' art with everything in the way of iron springs and thick-padded seats, still he felt every bump and dent in the road. After half an hour or so, he would begin to suffer from pains in his back and aches in his head and queasinesses in his stomach. But upon this particular morning he scarcely gave any thought to his back or his stomach at all. From the first moment of setting off from the Old Ship he was in a curiously nervous condition, beset by unexpected ideas and half-formed fears.

Through the carriage glass he saw great numbers of large black birds – whether ravens or crows he did not know, and in his magician's heart he was sure that they meant something. Against the pale winter sky they wheeled and turned, and spread their wings like black hands; and as they did so each one became a living embodiment of the Raven-in-Flight: John Uskglass's banner. Mr Norrell asked Lascelles if he thought the birds were more numerous than usual, but Lascelles said he did not know. After the birds the next thing to haunt Mr Norrell's imagination were the wide, cold puddles that were thickly strewn across every field. As the carriage passed along the road each puddle became a silver mirror for the blank, winter sky. To a magician there is very little difference between a mirror and a door. England seemed to be wearing thin before his eyes. He felt as if he might pass through any of those mirror-doors and find himself in one of the other worlds which once bordered upon England. Worse still, he was beginning to think that other people might do it. The Sussex landscape began to look uncomfortably like the England described in the old ballad:

> *This land is all too shallow*
> *It is painted on the sky*
> *And trembles like the wind-shook rain*
> *When the Raven King passed by*[1]

For the first time in his life Mr Norrell began to feel that perhaps there was too much magic in England.

When they reached Hanover-square Mr Norrell and Lascelles went immediately to the library. Childermass was there, seated at a desk. A pile of letters lay in front of him and he was reading one of them. He looked up when Mr Norrell entered the room. "Good! You are back! Read this."

---

[1] See Chapter 3, footnote 1.

"Why? What is it?"

"It is from a man called Traquair. A young man in Nottinghamshire has saved a child's life by magic and Traquair was a witness to it."

"Really, Mr Childermass!" said Lascelles, with a sigh. "I thought you knew better than to trouble your master with such nonsense." He glanced at the pile of opened letters; one had a large seal displaying someone's arms. He stared at it for several moments before he realized that he knew it well and snatched it up. "Mr Norrell!" he cried. "We have a summons from Lord Liverpool!"

"At last!" exclaimed Mr Norrell. "What does he say?"

Lascelles took a moment to read the letter. "Only that he begs the favour of our attendance at Fife House upon a matter of the utmost urgency!" He thought rapidly. "It is probably the Johannites. Liverpool ought to have requested your assistance years ago to deal with the Johannites. I am glad he realizes it at last. And as for you," he said, turning upon Childermass, "are you quite mad? Or do you have some game of your own to play? You chatter on about false claims of magic, while a letter from the Prime Minister of England lies unattended on the desk!"

"Lord Liverpool can wait," said Childermass to Mr Norrell. "Believe me when I tell you that you need to know the contents of this letter!"

Lascelles gave a snort of exasperation.

Mr Norrell looked from one to the other. He was entirely at a loss. For years he had been accustomed to rely upon both of them, and their quarrels (which were becoming increasingly frequent) unnerved him completely. He might have stood there, unable to chuse between them, for some time, had not Childermass decided matters by seizing his arm and pulling him bodily into a small, panelled ante-chamber which led off the library. Childermass shut the door with a bang and leant on it.

"Listen to me. This magic happened at a grand house in Nottinghamshire. The grown-ups were talking in the drawing-

887

room; the servants were busy and a little girl wandered off into the garden. She climbed a high wall that borders a kitchen-garden and walked along the top of it. But the wall was covered in ice and she tumbled down and fell through the roof of a hot-house. The glass broke and pierced her in many places. A servant heard her screaming. There was no surgeon nearer than ten miles away. One of the party, a young man called Joseph Abney, saved her by magic. He drew the shards of glass out of her and mended the broken bones with Martin Pale's Restoration and Rectification,[2] and he stopped the flow of blood using a spell which he claimed was Teilo's Hand."[3]

"Ridiculous!" declared Mr Norrell. "Teilo's Hand has been lost for hundreds of years and Pale's Restoration and Rectification is a very difficult procedure. This young man would have had to study for years and years . . ."

"Yes, I know – and he admits that he has hardly studied at all. He barely knew the names of the spells, let alone their execution. Yet Traquair said that he performed the spells fluidly, without hesitation. Traquair and the other people who were present spoke to him and asked him what he was doing – the girl's father was much alarmed to see Abney perform magic upon her – but, so far as they could tell, Abney did not hear them. Afterwards he was like a man coming out of a dream. All he could say was: 'Tree speaks to stone; stone speaks to water.' He seemed to think that the trees and the sky had told him what to do."

"Mystical nonsense!"

"Perhaps. And yet I do not think so. Since we came to London I have read hundreds of letters from people who think they can do magic and are mistaken. But this is different. This is true. I would

---

[2] Restoration and Rectification was a spell which reversed the effects of a recent calamity.

[3] Teilo's Hand was an ancient fairy spell which halted all sorts of things: rain, fire, wind, coursing water or blood. It presumably was named after the fairy who had first taught it to an English magician.

stake money upon it. Besides there are other letters here from people who have tried spells – and the spells have worked. But what I do not understand is . . ."

But at that moment the door against which Childermass was leaning was subject to a great rattling and shaking. A blow hit it and Childermass was thrown away from the door and against Mr Norrell. The door opened to reveal Lucas and, behind him, Davey the coachman.

"Oh!" said Lucas, somewhat surprised. "I beg your pardon, sir. I did not know you were here. Mr Lascelles said the door had jammed shut, and Davey and I were trying to free it. The carriage is ready, sir, to take you to Lord Liverpool."

"Come, Mr Norrell!" cried Lascelles from within the library. "Lord Liverpool is waiting!"

Mr Norrell cast a worried glance at Childermass and went.

The journey to Fife House was not a very pleasant one for Mr Norrell: Lascelles was full of spite towards Childermass and lost no time in venting it.

"Forgive me for saying so, Mr Norrell," he said, "but you have no one but yourself to blame. Sometimes it seems like wisdom to allow an intelligent servant a certain degree of independence – but one always regrets it in the end. That villain has grown in insolence until he thinks nothing of contradicting you and insulting your friends. My father whipped men for less – a great deal less, I assure you. And I should like, oh! I should like . . ." Lascelles twitched and fidgeted, and threw himself back upon the cushions. In a moment he said in a calmer tone, "I advise you to consider, sir, if your need of him is really as great as you think? How many of his sympathies are with Strange, I wonder? Yes, that is the real question, is it not?" He looked out of the glass at the bleak, grey buildings. "We are here. Mr Norrell, I beg that you will remember what I told you. Whatever the difficulties of the magic which his lordship requires, do not dwell upon them. A long explanation will not make them grow any less."

Mr Norrell and Lascelles found Lord Liverpool in his study, standing by the table where he conducted a great deal of his business. With him was Lord Sidmouth, the Home Secretary. They fixed Mr Norrell with solemn looks.

Lord Liverpool said, "I have here letters from the Lord Lieutenants of Lincolnshire, Yorkshire, Somerset, Cornwall, Warwickshire and Cumbria . . ." (Lascelles could scarcely refrain from giving a sigh of pleasure at the magic and the money that seemed to be in prospect.) ". . . all complaining of the magic that has recently occurred in those counties!"

Mr Norrell blinked his little eyes rapidly. "I beg your pardon?"

Lascelles said quickly, "Mr Norrell knows nothing of any magic done in those places."

Lord Liverpool gave him a cool look as if he did not believe him. There was a pile of papers on the table. Lord Liverpool picked one up at random. "Four days ago in the town of Stamford," he said, "a Quaker girl and her friend were telling each other secrets. They heard a noise and discovered their younger brothers listening at the door. Full of indignation, they chased the boys into the garden. There they joined hands and recited a charm. The boys' ears leapt off their heads and flew away. It was not until the boys had made a solemn oath never to do such a thing ever again, that the ears could be coaxed back out of the bare rose-bushes – which was where they had alighted – and persuaded to return to the boys' heads."

Mr Norrell was more perplexed than ever. "I am, of course, sorry that these badly behaved young women have been studying magic. That members of the Female Sex should study magic at all is, I may say, a thing I am very much opposed to. But I do not quite see . . ."

"Mr Norrell," said Lord Liverpool, "these girls were *thirteen*. Their parents are adamant that they have never so much as seen a magical text. There are no magicians in Stamford, no magic books of any kind."

Mr Norrell opened his mouth to say something, realized he was quite at a loss and fell silent.

Lascelles said, "This is very odd. What explanation did the girls give?"

"The girls told their parents that they looked down and saw the spell written upon the path in grey pebbles. They said the stones told them what to do. Other people have since examined the path; there are indeed some grey pebbles, but they form no symbols, no mystical writing. They are ordinary grey pebbles."

"And you say that there have been other instances of magic, in other places besides Stamford?" said Mr Norrell.

"Many other instances and many other places – mostly, but by no means solely, in the north, and almost all within the past two weeks. Seventeen fairy roads have opened up in Yorkshire. Of course the roads have existed since the reign of the Raven King, but it is centuries since they actually led anywhere and the local inhabitants allowed them to become overgrown. Now without warning they are clear again. The weeds are gone and the inhabitants report that they can see strange destinations at the end of them – places no one has ever seen before."

"Has any one . . . ?" Mr Norrell paused and licked his lips. "Has any one come down the roads?"

"Not yet," said Lord Liverpool. "But presumably it is only a matter of time."

Lord Sidmouth had been impatient to speak for some moments. "This is worst of all!" he declared in a passion, "It is one thing to change Spain by magic, Mr Norrell, but this is England! Suddenly we border upon places no one knows any thing about – places no one has ever even heard of! I can scarcely describe my feelings at this juncture. It is not treason exactly – I do not think there is even a name for what you have done!"

"But I did not do it!" said Mr Norrell in a tone of desperation.

"Why would I? I detest fairy roads! I have said so upon many occasions." He turned to Lord Liverpool. "I appeal to your lordship's memory. Have I ever given you reason to suppose that I approve of fairies or their magic? Have I not censured and condemned them at every turn?"

This was the first thing that Mr Norrell had said that seemed in any way to mollify the Prime Minister. He inclined his head slightly. "But if it is not your doing, whose is it?"

This question seemed to strike at some particularly vulnerable spot in Mr Norrell's soul. He stood, eyes staring, mouth opening and closing, entirely unable to answer.

Lascelles, however, was in complete command of himself. He had not the least idea in the world whose magic it was, nor did he care. But he did know precisely what answer would serve his and Mr Norrell's interest best. "Frankly I am surprised that your lordship need put the question," he said, coolly. "Surely the wickedness of the magic proclaims its author; it is Strange."

"Strange!" Lord Liverpool blinked. "But Strange is in Venice!"

"Mr Norrell believes that Strange is no longer the master of his own desires," said Lascelles. "He has done all sorts of wicked magic; he has trafficked with creatures that are enemies of Great Britain, of Christianity, of Mankind itself! This catastrophe may be some sort of experiment of his, which has gone awry. Or it may be that he has done it deliberately. I feel it only right to remind your lordship that Mr Norrell has warned the Government on several occasions of the great danger to the Nation from Strange's present researches. We have sent your lordship urgent messages, but we have received no replies. Fortunately for us all Mr Norrell is what he always was: firm and resolute and watchful." As he spoke, Lascelles's glance fell upon Mr Norrell, who was at the moment the very picture of everything which was dismayed, defeated and impotent.

Lord Liverpool turned to Mr Norrell. "Is this your opinion also, sir?"

Mr Norrell was lost in thought, murmuring over and over, "This is my doing. This is my doing." Although he spoke to himself, it was just loud enough for everyone else in the room to hear.

Lascelles's eyes widened; but he was master of himself in an instant. "It is only natural that you feel that now, sir," he said quickly, "but in a while you will realize that nothing could be further from the truth. When you taught Mr Strange magic, you could not have known that it would end like this. No one could have known."

Lord Liverpool looked more than a little irritated at this attempt to make Mr Norrell appear in the character of a victim. For years and years Mr Norrell had set himself up as the chief magician in England and if magic had been done in England then Lord Liverpool considered him partly responsible at least. "I ask you again, Mr Norrell. Answer me plainly, if you please. Is it your opinion that this was done by Strange?"

Mr Norrell looked at each gentleman in turn. "Yes," he said in a frightened voice.

Lord Liverpool gave him a long, hard look. Then he said, "The matter shall not rest here, Mr Norrell. But whether it is Strange or not, one thing is clear. Great Britain already has a mad King; a mad magician would be the outside of enough. You have repeatedly asked for commissions; well, here is one. Prevent your pupil from returning to England!"

"But . . ." began Mr Norrell. Then he caught sight of Lascelles's warning glance and fell silent.

Mr Norrell and Lascelles returned to Hanover-square. Mr Norrell went immediately to the library. Childermass was working at the table as before.

"Quick!" cried Mr Norrell, "I need a spell which no longer works!"

Childermass shrugged. "There are thousands. Chauntlucet;[4] Daedalus's Rose;[5] the Unrobed Ladies;[6] Stokesey's Vitrification[7] . . ."

"Stokesey's Vitrification! Yes! I have a description of that!"

Mr Norrell rushed to a shelf and pulled out a book. He searched for a page, found it and looked hurriedly around the room. On a table near the fireside stood a vase of mistletoe, ivy, red-berried holly and some sprays of a winter-flowering shrub. He fixed his eye upon the vase and began to mutter to himself.

All the shadows in the room did something odd, something not easy to describe or explain. It was as if they all turned and faced another way. Even when they were motionless again Childermass and Lascelles would have been hard pressed to say whether they were the same as they had been or not.

Something fell out of the vase and shattered upon the table with a tinkling sound.

Lascelles went over to the table and examined it. One of the branches of holly had been turned into glass. The glass branch had been too heavy for the vase and so it had toppled out; two or three unbroken holly leaves lay on the table.

"That spell has not worked for almost four hundred years," said Mr Norrell. "Watershippe specifically mentions it in *A Faire Wood*

---

[4] Chauntlucet: a mysterious and ancient spell which encourages the moon to sing. The song the moon knows is apparently very beautiful and can cure leprosy or madness in any who hear it.

[5] Daedalus's Rose: a fairly complicated procedure devised by Martin Pale for preserving emotions, vices and virtues in amber or honey or beeswax. When the preserving medium is warmed, the imprisoned qualities are released. The Rose has – or rather had – a huge number of applications. It could be used to dispense courage to oneself or inflict cowardice on one's enemy; it could provoke love, lust, nobility of purpose, anger, jealousy, ambition, self-sacrifice, etc., etc.

[6] Like many spells with unusual names, the Unrobed Ladies was a great deal less exciting than it sounded. The ladies of the title were only a kind of woodland flower which was used in a spell to bind a fairy's powers. The flower was required to be stripped of leaves and petals – hence the "unrobing".

[7] Stokesey's Vitrification turns objects – and people – to glass.

Withering as one of the spells which worked in his youth and was entirely ineffective by the time he was twenty!"

"Your superior skill . . ." began Lascelles.

"My superior skill has nothing to do with it!" snapped Mr Norrell. "I cannot do magic that is not there. Magic is returning to England. Strange has found a way to bring it back."

"Then I was right, was I not?" said Lascelles. "And our first task is to prevent him returning to England. Succeed in that and Lord Liverpool will forgive a great many other things."

Mr Norrell thought for a moment. "I can prevent him arriving by sea," he said.

"Excellent!" said Lascelles. Then something in the way Mr Norrell had phrased this last statement gave him pause. "Well, he is scarcely likely to come any other way. He cannot fly!" He gave a light laugh at the idea. Then another thought struck him. "Can he?"

Childermass shrugged.

"I do not know what Strange might be capable of by now," said Mr Norrell. "But I was not thinking of that. I was thinking of the King's Roads."

"I thought the King's Roads led to Faerie," said Lascelles.

"Yes, they do. But not only Faerie. The King's Roads lead everywhere. Heaven. Hell. The Houses of Parliament . . . They were built by magic. Every mirror, every puddle, every shadow in England is a gate to those roads. I cannot set a lock upon all of them. No body could. It would be a monstrous task! If Strange comes by the King's Roads then I know nothing to prevent him."

"But . . ." began Lascelles.

"I cannot prevent him!" cried Mr Norrell, wringing his hands. "Do not ask me! But . . ." He made a great effort to calm himself. ". . . I *can* be ready to receive him. The Greatest Magician of the Age. Well, soon we shall see, shall we not?"

"If he comes to England," said Lascelles, "where will he go first?"

"Hurtfew Abbey," said Childermass. "Where else?"

Mr Norrell and Lascelles were both about to answer him, but at that moment Lucas entered the room with a silver tray upon which lay a letter. He offered it to Lascelles. Lascelles broke the seal and read it rapidly.

"Drawlight is back," he said. "Wait for me here. I will return within a day."

62

I came to them in a cry that broke the silence of a winter wood

Early February 1817

FIRST LIGHT IN early February: a crossroads in the middle of a wood. The space between the trees was misty and indistinct; the darkness of the trees seeped into it. Neither of the two roads was of any importance. They were rutted and ill-maintained; one was scarcely more than a cart-track. It was an out-of-the-way place, marked on no map. It did not even have a name.

Drawlight was waiting at the crossroads. There was no horse standing nearby, no groom with a trap or cart, nothing to explain how he had come there. Yet clearly he had been standing at the crossroads for some time; his coat-sleeves were white with frost. A faint click behind him made him spin round. But there was nothing: only the same stretch of silent trees.

"No, no," he muttered to himself. "It was nothing. A dry leaf fell – that is all." There was a sharp snap, as ice cracked wood or stone. He stared again, with eyes addled by fear. "It was only a dry leaf," he murmured.

There was a new sound. For a moment he was all in a panic, uncertain where it was coming from; until he recognized it for what it was: horses' hooves. He peered up the road. A dim, grey smudge in the mist shewed where a horse and rider were approaching.

"He is here at last. He is here," muttered Drawlight and hastened forward. "Where have you been?" he cried. "I have been waiting here for hours."

"So?" said Lascelles's voice. "You have nothing else to do."

"Oh! But you are wrong! You could not be more wrong. You must take me to London as quickly as possible!"

"All in good time." Lascelles emerged from the mist and reined in his horse. His fine clothes and hat were beaded with a silvery dusting of dew.

Drawlight regarded him for a moment and then, with something of his old character, said sulkily, "How nicely you are dressed! But really, you know, it is not very clever of you to parade your wealth like that. Are not you afraid of robbers? This is a very horrid spot. I dare say there are all sorts of desperate characters close at hand."

"You are probably right. But you see I have my pistols with me, and am quite as desperate as any of them."

Drawlight was struck by a sudden thought. "Where is the other horse?" he asked.

"What?"

"The other horse! The one that is to take me to London! Oh, Lascelles, you noodlehead! How am I to get to London without a horse?"

Lascelles laughed. "I would have thought you would be glad to avoid it. Your debts may have been paid off – *I* have paid them – but London is still full of people who hate you and will do you an ill turn if they can."

Drawlight stared as if he had understood none of this. In a shrill, excited voice, he cried, "But I have instructions from the magician! He has given me messages to deliver to all sorts of people! I must begin immediately! I must not delay a single hour!"

Lascelles frowned. "Are you drunk? Are you dreaming? Norrell has not asked you to do any thing. If he had tasks for you, he would convey them through me, and besides . . ."

"Not Norrell. Strange!"

Lascelles sat stock still upon his horse. The horse shifted and fidgeted, but Lascelles moved not at all. Then, in a softer, more dangerous voice, he said, "What in the world are you talking about? Strange? How dare you talk to me of Strange? I advise you to think very carefully before you speak again. I am already seriously displeased. Your instructions were quite plain, I think. You were to remain at Venice until Strange left. But here you are. And there he is."

"I could not help it! I had to leave! You do not understand. I saw him and he told me . . ."

Lascelles held up his hand. "I have no wish to conduct this conversation in the open. We will go a little way into the trees."

"Into the trees!" The little colour that was left in Drawlight's face drained away. "Oh, no! Not for the world! I will not go there! Do not ask me!"

"What do you mean?" Lascelles looked round, a little less comfortable than before. "Has Strange set the trees to spy on us?"

"No, no. That is not it. I cannot explain it. They are waiting for me. They know me! I cannot go in there!" Drawlight had no words for what had happened to him. He held out his arms for a moment as if he thought he could shew Lascelles the rivers that had curled about his feet, the trees that had pierced him, the stones that had been his heart and lungs and guts.

Lascelles raised his riding-whip. "I have no idea what you are talking about." He urged his horse at Drawlight and flourished the whip. Poor Drawlight had never possessed the least physical courage and he was driven, whimpering, into the trees. A briar caught the edge of his sleeve and he screamed.

"Oh, do be quiet!" said Lascelles. "Any one would think there is murder going on."

They walked on until they came to a small clearing. Lascelles got down from his horse and tethered him to a tree. He removed the two pistols from the saddle-holsters and stuck them in the pockets of his great coat. Then he turned to Drawlight. "So you actually saw Strange? Good. Excellent, in fact. I was sure you were too cowardly to face him."

"I thought he would change me into something horrible."

Lascelles surveyed Drawlight's stained clothing and haunted face with some distaste. "Are you sure he did not do it?"

"What?" said Drawlight.

"Why did you not simply kill him? There, in the Darkness? You were alone, I presume? No one would have known."

"Oh, yes. That is very likely, is it not? He is tall and clever and quick and cruel. I am none of those things."

"I would have done it," said Lascelles.

"Would you? Well then, you are very welcome to go to Venice and try."

"Where is he now?"

"In the Darkness – in Venice – but he is coming to England."

"He said so?"

"Yes, I told you – I have messages: one for Childermass, one for Norrell and one for all the magicians in England."

"And what are they?"

"I am to tell Childermass that Lady Pole was not raised from the dead in the way Norrell said – he had a fairy to help him and the fairy has done things – wrong things – and I am to give Childermass a little box. That is the first message. And I am to tell Norrell that Strange is coming back. That is the third message."

Lascelles considered. "This little box, what does it contain?"

"I do not know."

"Why? Is it sealed shut in some way? By magic?"

Drawlight shut his eyes and shook his head. "I do not know that either."

Lascelles laughed out loud. "You do not mean to tell me that you have had a box in your possession for weeks and not tried to open it? You of all people? Why, when you used to come to my house, I never dared leave you alone for a moment. My letters

900

would have been read; my business would have been common knowledge by the next morning."

Drawlight's glance sank to the ground. He seemed to shrink inside his clothes. He grew, if it were possible, several degrees more miserable. One might have supposed that he was ashamed to hear his past sins described, but it was not that. "I am afraid," he whispered.

Lascelles made a sound of exasperation. "Where is the box?" he cried. "Give it to me!"

Drawlight reached into a pocket of his coat and brought out something wrapped in a dirty handkerchief. The handkerchief was tied into many wonderfully complicated knots to guard against the box coming open of its own accord. Drawlight gave it to Lascelles.

With a series of grimaces, expressive of extreme distaste, Lascelles set himself to undo the knots. When he had done so, he opened the box.

A moment's silence.

"You are a fool," said Lascelles and shut the box with a snap and put it in his own pocket.

"Oh! But I have to . . ." began Drawlight, reaching out ineffectually.

"You said that there were three messages. What is the other one?"

"I do not think you will understand it."

"What? You understand it, yet I will not? You must have grown a great deal cleverer in Italy."

"That is not what I meant."

"Then what do you mean? Tell me quickly. I am growing bored of this conversation."

"Strange said that tree speaks to stone. Stone speaks to water. He said magicians can learn magic from woods and stones and such. He said John Uskglass's old alliances still held."

"John Uskglass, John Uskglass! How sick I am of that name!

Yet they all rattle on about him nowadays. Even Norrell. I cannot understand why; his day was done four hundred years ago."

Drawlight held out his hand again. "Give me back my box. I must . . ."

"What the devil is the matter with you? Do not you understand? Your messages will never be delivered – except for the one to Norrell and that I shall deliver myself."

A howl of anguish burst from Drawlight. "Please, please! Do not make me fail him! You do not understand. He will kill me! Or worse!"

Lascelles spread his arms and glanced around, as if asking the wood to bear witness how ridiculous this was. "Do you honestly believe that I would allow you to destroy Norrell? Which is to say destroy *me*?"

"It is not my fault! It is not my fault! I dare not disobey him!"

"Worm, what will you do between two such men as Strange and me? You will be crushed."

Drawlight made a little sound, like a whimper of fear. He gazed at Lascelles with strange, addled eyes. He seemed about to say something. Then, with surprizing speed, he turned and fled through the trees.

Lascelles did not trouble to follow him. He simply raised one of the pistols, aimed it and fired.

The bullet struck Drawlight in the thigh, producing, for one instant, a red, wet flowering of blood and flesh in the white and grey woods. Drawlight screamed and fell with a crash into a patch of briars. He tried to crawl away but his leg was quite useless and, besides, the briars were catching at his clothes; he could not pull free of them. He turned his head to see Lascelles advance upon him; fear and pain rendered his features entirely unrecognizable.

Lascelles fired the second pistol.

The left side of Drawlight's head burst open, like an egg or an orange. He convulsed several times and was still.

Although there was no one there to see, and although his blood was pounding in his ears, in his chest, in his everything, Lascelles would not permit himself to appear in the least disturbed: that, he felt, would not have been the behaviour of a gentleman.

He had a valet who was much addicted to accounts of murders and hangings in *The Newgate Calendar* and *The Malefactor's Register*. Sometimes Lascelles would amuse himself by picking up one of these volumes. A prominent characteristic of these histories was that the murderer, however bold he was during the act of murder, would soon afterwards be overcome with emotion, leading him to act in strange, irrational ways that were always his undoing. Lascelles doubted there was much truth in these accounts, but for safety's sake he examined himself for signs of remorse or horror. He found none. Indeed his chief thought was that there was one less ugly thing in the world. "Really," he said to himself, "if he had known three or four years ago that it would come to this, he would have begged me to do it."

There was a rustling sound. To Lascelles's surprise he saw that a small shoot was poking out of Drawlight's right eye (the left one had been destroyed by the pistol blast). Strands of ivy were winding themselves about his neck and chest. A holly shoot had pierced his hand; a young birch had shot up through his foot; a hawthorn had sprung up through his belly. He looked as if he been crucified upon the wood itself. But the trees did not stop there; they kept growing. A tangle of bronze and scarlet stems blotted out his ruined face, and his limbs and body decayed as plants and other living things took strength from them. Within a short space of time nothing of Christopher Drawlight remained. The trees, the stones and the earth had taken him inside themselves, but in their shape it was possible still to discern something of the man he had once been.

"That briar was his arm, I think," mused Lascelles. "That stone . . . his heart perhaps? It is small enough and hard enough." He laughed. "That is the ridiculous thing about Strange's magic," he said to no one at all. "Sooner or later it all works against him." He mounted on his horse and rode back towards the road.

903

63

The first shall bury his heart in a dark wood beneath the snow, yet still feel its ache

Mid February 1817

MORE THAN TWENTY-EIGHT hours had passed since Lascelles had left Hanover-square and Mr Norrell was half frantic. He had promised Lascelles they would wait for him, but now he feared they would arrive at Hurtfew Abbey to find Strange in possession of the library.

No one in the house at Hanover-square was permitted to go to bed that night and by morning everyone was tired and wretched.

"But why do we wait at all?" asked Childermass. "What good do you suppose *he* will be when Strange comes?"

"I place great reliance on Mr Lascelles. You know I do. He is my only adviser now."

"You still have me," said Childermass.

Mr Norrell blinked his small eyes rapidly. They seemed to be half a sentence away from, *but you are only a servant.* Mr Norrell said nothing.

Childermass seemed to understand him anyway. He made a small sound of disgust and walked off.

At six o'clock in the evening the library door was thrown open and Lascelles walked in. He looked as he had never looked before: his hair was dishevelled, his neckcloth was stained with dust and sweat, and there were mud-splashes on his greatcoat and boots.

"We were right, Mr Norrell!" he cried. "Strange is coming!"

"When?" said Mr Norrell, turning pale.

"I do not know. He has not been so kind as to furnish us with those details, but we should leave for Hurtfew Abbey as soon as possible!"

"We can go immediately. All is in readiness. So you actually saw Drawlight? Is he here?" Mr Norrell leant sideways to see if he could catch a glimpse of Drawlight behind Lascelles.

"No, I did not see him. I waited for him, but he never came. But do not fear, sir!" (Mr Norrell was on the point of interrupting.) "He has sent a letter. We have all the intelligence we need."

"A letter! May I see it?"

"Of course! But there will be time enough for that on the journey. We must be off. You need not delay on my account. My wants are few and what I do not have, I can very easily do without." (This was perhaps a little surprizing. Lascelles's wants had never been few before. They had been numerous and complicated.) "Come, come, Mr Norrell. Rouse yourself. Strange is coming!" He strode out of the room again. Mr Norrell heard later from Lucas that he had not even asked for water to wash or for any thing to drink. He had simply gone to the carriage, thrown himself into a corner and waited.

By eight o'clock they were on their way to Yorkshire. Mr Norrell and Lascelles were inside the carriage; Lucas and Davey were upon the box; Childermass was on horseback. At the Islington tollgate Lucas paid the keeper. There was a smell of snow in the air.

Mr Norrell gazed idly at a shop window ablaze with lamplight. It was a superior sort of shop with an uncluttered interior and elegant modern chairs for the customers to sit upon; in fact it was so very refined an establishment that it was by no means clear what it sold. A heap of brightly coloured somethings lay tossed upon a chair, but whether they were shawls or materials for gowns or something else entirely, Mr Norrell could not tell. There were three women in the shop. One was a customer – a smart, stylish person in a spencer like a Hussar's uniform, complete with fur trim and frogging. On her head was a little Russian fur cap; she kept touching the back of it as if she feared it would fall off. The shopkeeper was more discreetly dressed in a plain dark gown, and there was besides a little assistant who looked on respectfully and bobbed a nervous little curtsey whenever any one chanced to look at her. The customer and the shopkeeper were not engaged in business; they were talking together with a great deal of animation and laughter. It was a scene as far removed from Mr Norrell's usual interests as it was possible to be, yet it went to his heart in a way he could not understand. He thought fleetingly of Mrs Strange and Lady Pole. Then something flew between him and the cheerful scene – something like a piece of the darkness made solid. He thought that it was a raven.

The toll was paid. Davey shook the reins and the carriage moved on towards the Archway.

Snow began to fall. A sleety wind buffeted the sides of the carriage and made it rock from side to side; it penetrated every chink and crack, and chilled shoulders, noses and feet. Mr Norrell was not made any more comfortable by the fact that Lascelles appeared to be in a very odd mood. He was excited, almost elated, though Mr Norrell could not tell why he should be. When the wind howled, he laughed, as if he suspected it of trying to frighten him and wished to shew it that it was mistaken.

When he saw that Mr Norrell was observing him, he said, "I have been thinking. This is the merest nothing! You and I, sir, will soon get the better of Strange and his tricks. What a pack of old women the Ministers are! They disgust me! All this alarm over one lunatic! It makes me laugh to think of it. Of course Liverpool and Sidmouth are the very worst of them! For years they have hardly dared put their noses out of their front doors for fear of Buonaparte and now Strange has sent them into fits merely by going insane."

"Oh, but you are wrong!" declared Mr Norrell. "Indeed, you

are! The threat from Strange is immense – Buonaparte was nothing to it – but you have not told me what Drawlight said. I should very much like to see his letter. I will tell Davey to stop at the Angel in Hadley and then . . ."

"But I do not have it. I left it at Bruton-street."

"Oh! But . . ."

Lascelles laughed. "Mr Norrell! Do not concern yourself! Do I not tell you that it does not matter? I recall it exactly."

"What does it say?"

"That Strange is mad and imprisoned in Eternal Darkness – all of which we knew before – and . . ."

"What form does his madness take?" asked Mr Norrell.

The merest pause.

"Talking nonsense mostly. But then he did that before, did he not?" Lascelles laughed. Catching sight of Mr Norrell's expression, he continued more soberly, "He babbles about trees, and stones, and John Uskglass, and," (glancing round for inspiration), "invisible coaches. And oh, yes! This will amuse you! He has stolen fingers off the hands of several Venetian maidens. Stolen them clean away! Keeps the stolen fingers in little boxes!"

"Fingers!" said Mr Norrell in alarm. This seemed to suggest some unpleasant associations to him. He thought for a moment but could make nothing of it. "Did Drawlight describe the Darkness? Did he say any thing that might help us understand it?"

"No. He saw Strange, and Strange gave him a message for you. He says that he is coming. That is the substance of the letter."

They fell into silence. Mr Norrell began to doze without intending to; but several times in his dreams he heard Lascelles whispering to himself in the darkness.

At midnight they changed horses at the Haycock Inn at Wansford. Lascelles and Mr Norrell waited in the public parlour, a large, plain apartment with wood-panelled walls, a sanded floor and two great fireplaces.

The door opened and Childermass walked in. He went straight

to Lascelles and addressed him in the following words: "Lucas says there is a letter from Drawlight telling what he has seen in Venice."

Lascelles half-turned his head, but he did not look at Childermass.

"May I see it?" asked Childermass.

"I left it at Bruton-street," said Lascelles.

Childermass looked a little surprized. "Very well then," he said. "Lucas can fetch it. We will hire a horse for him here. He will catch up with us again before we reach Hurtfew."

Lascelles smiled. "I said Bruton-street, did I not? But do you know? — I do not think it is there. I believe I left it at the inn, the one in Chatham where I waited for Drawlight. They will have thrown it away." He turned back to the fire.

Childermass scowled at him for a moment or two. Then he strode out of the room.

A manservant came to say that hot water, towels and other necessaries had been set out in two bed-chambers so that Mr Norrell and Lascelles might refresh themselves. "And it's a blindman's holiday in the passage-way, gentlemen," he said cheerfully, "so I've lit you a candle each."

Mr Norrell took his candle and made his way along the passageway (which was indeed very dark). Suddenly Childermass appeared and seized his arm. "What in the world were you thinking of?" he hissed. "To leave London without that letter?"

"But he says he remembers what it contains," pleaded Mr Norrell.

"Oh! And you believe him, do you?"

Mr Norrell made no reply. He went into the room that had been made ready. He washed his hands and face and, as he did so, he caught a glimpse in the mirror of the bed behind him. It was heavy, old fashioned and — as often happens at inns — much too large for the room. Four carved mahogany columns, a high dark canopy and bunches of black ostrich feathers at each corner all

contrived to give it a funereal look. It was as if someone had brought him into the room and shewn him his own tomb. He began to have the strangest feeling – the same feeling he had had at the tollgate, watching the three women – the feeling that something was coming to an end and that all his choices had now been made. He had taken a road in his youth, but the road did not lead where he had supposed; he was going home, but home had become something monstrous. In the half-dark, standing by the black bed, he remembered why he had always feared the darkness as a child: the darkness belonged to John Uskglass.

> For always and for always
> I pray remember me
> Upon the moors, beneath the stars
> With the King's wild company

He hurried from the room, back to the warmth and lights of the public parlour.

A little after six o'clock a grey dawn came up that was scarcely any dawn at all. White snow fell through a grey sky on to a grey and white world. Davey was so liberally coated in snow that one might have supposed that someone had ordered a wax-works model of him and the plaster mould was being prepared.

All that day a succession of post-horses laboured to bring the carriage through snow and wind. A succession of inns provided hot drinks and a brief respite from the weather. Davey and Childermass – who, as coachman and rider, were undoubtedly the most exhausted of the party – derived the least benefit from these halts; they were generally in the stables arguing with the innkeeper about the horses. At Grantham the innkeeper infuriated Childermass by proposing to rent them a stone-blind horse. Childermass swore he would not take it; the innkeeper on the other hand swore it was the best horse he had. There was very little choice and they ended by hiring it. Davey said afterwards that it was an excellent beast, hard-working and all the more obedient to his instructions since it had no other means of knowing where to go or what to do. Davey himself lasted as far as the Newcastle Arms at Tuxford and there they were obliged to leave him. He had driven more than a hundred and thirty miles and was, said Childermass, so tired he could barely speak. Childermass hired a postillion and they travelled on.

An hour or so before sunset the snow ceased and the skies cleared. Long blue-black shadows overlaid the bare fields. Five miles out of Doncaster they passed the inn that is called the Red House (by reason of its painted walls). In the low winter sun it blazed like a house of fire. The carriage went on a little way and then halted.

"Why are we stopping?" cried Mr Norrell from within.

Lucas leant down from the box and said something in reply, but the wind carried his voice away and Mr Norrell did not hear what it was.

Childermass had left the highway and was riding across a field. The field was filled with ravens. As he passed, they flew up with a great croaking and cawing. On the far side of the field was an ancient hedge with an opening and two tall holly-trees, one on each side. The opening led into another road or lane, bounded by hedges. Childermass halted there and looked first one way and then the other. He hesitated. Then he shook his reins and the horse trotted between the trees, into the lane and out of sight.

"He has gone into the fairy road!" cried Mr Norrell in alarm.

"Oh!" said Lascelles. "Is that what it is?"

"Yes, indeed!" said Mr Norrell. "That is one of the more famous ones. It is reputed to have joined Doncaster to Newcastle by way of two fairy citadels."

They waited.

After about twenty minutes Lucas climbed down from the box. "How long ought we to stay here, sir?" he asked.

Mr Norrell shook his head. "No Englishman has stept over the boundaries into Faerie since Martin Pale three hundred years ago. It is perfectly possible that he will never come out again. Perhaps . . ."

Just then Childermass reappeared and galloped back across the field.

"Well, it is true," he told Mr Norrell. "The paths to Faerie are open again."

"What did you see?" asked Mr Norrell.

"The road goes on a little way and then leads into a wood of thorn trees. At the entrance to the wood there is a statue of a woman with her hands outstretched. In one hand she holds a stone eye and in the other a stone heart. As for the wood itself . . ." Childermass made a gesture, perhaps expressive of his inability to describe what he had seen, or perhaps of his powerlessness in the face of it. "Corpses hang from every tree. Some might have died as recently as yesterday. Others are no more than age-old skeletons dressed in rusting armour. I came to a high tower built of rough-hewn stones. The walls were pierced with a few tiny windows. There was a light at one of them and the shadow of someone looking out. Beneath the tower was a clearing with a brook running through it. A young man was standing there. He looked pale and sickly, with dead eyes, and he wore a British uniform. He told me he was the Champion of the Castle of the Plucked Eye and Heart. He had sworn to protect the Lady of the Castle by challenging any one who approached with the intent of harming or insulting her. I asked him if he had killed all the men I had seen. He said he had killed some of them and hung them upon the thorns – as his predecessor had done before him. I asked him how the Lady intended to reward him for his service. He said he did not know. He had never seen her or spoken to her. She remained in the Castle of the Plucked Eye and Heart; he stayed between the brook and the thorn trees. He asked me if I intended to fight him. I reminded him that I had neither insulted nor harmed his lady. I told him I was a servant and bound to return to my master who was at that moment waiting for me. Then I turned my horse and rode back."

"What?" cried Lascelles. "A man offers to fight you and you run away. Have you no honour at all? No shame? A sickly face, dead eyes, an unknown person at the window!" He gave a snort of derision. "These are nothing but excuses for your cowardice!"

Childermass flinched as if he had been struck and seemed about to return a sharp answer, but he was interrupted by Mr Norrell. "Upon the contrary! Childermass did well to leave as soon as he could. There is always more magic in such a place than appears at first sight. Some fairies delight in combat and death. I do not know why. They are prepared to go to great lengths to secure such pleasures for themselves."

"Please, Mr Lascelles," said Childermass, "if the place has a strong appeal for you, then go! Do not stay upon our account."

Lascelles looked thoughtfully at the field and the gap in the hedge. But he did not move.

"You do not like the ravens perhaps?" said Childermass in a quietly mocking tone.

"No one likes them!" declared Mr Norrell. "Why are they here? What do they mean?"

Childermass shrugged. "Some people think that they are part of the Darkness that envelops Strange, and which, for some reason, he has made incarnate and sent back to England. Other people think that they portend the return of John Uskglass."

"John Uskglass. Of course," said Lascelles. "The first and last resort of vulgar minds. Whenever any thing happens, it must be because of John Uskglass! I think, Mr Norrell, it is time for another article in *The Friends* reviling that gentleman. What shall we say? That he was unChristian? UnEnglish? Demonic? Somewhere I believe I have a list of the Saints and Archbishops who denounced him. I could easily work that up."

Mr Norrell looked uncomfortable. He glanced nervously at the Tuxford postillion.

"If I were you, Mr Lascelles," said Childermass, softly, "I would speak more guardedly. You are in the north now. In John Uskglass's own country. Our towns and cities and abbeys were built by him. Our laws were made by him. He is in our minds and hearts and speech. Were it summer you would see a carpet of tiny flowers beneath every hedgerow, of a bluish-white colour. We call them John's Farthings. When the weather is contrary and we have warm weather in winter or it rains in summer the country people say that John Uskglass is in love again and neglects his business.[1] And when we are sure of something we say it is as safe as a pebble in John Uskglass's pocket."

Lascelles laughed. "Far be it from me, Mr Childermass, to disparage your quaint country sayings. But surely it is one thing to pay lip-service to one's history and quite another to talk of bringing back a King who numbered Lucifer himself among his allies and overlords? No one wants that, do they? I mean apart from a few Johannites and madmen?"

"I am a North Englishman, Mr Lascelles," said Childermass. "Nothing would please me better than that my King should come home. It is what I have wished for all my life."

It was nearly midnight when they arrived at Hurtfew Abbey. There was no sign of Strange. Lascelles went to bed, but Mr Norrell walked about the house, examining the condition of certain spells that had long been in place.

Next morning at breakfast Lascelles said, "I have been wondering if there were ever magical duels in the past? Struggles between two magicians? – that sort of thing."

---

[1] It has often been observed that the Northern English, though never wavering in their loyalty to John Uskglass, do not always treat him with the respect he commands in the south. In fact Uskglass's subjects take a particular delight in stories and ballads that shew him at a decided disadvantage, *c.f.* the tale of John Uskglass and the Charcoal Burner of Ullswater or the tale of the Hag and the Sorceress. There are many versions of the latter (some of them quite vulgar); it tells how Uskglass almost lost his heart, his kingdoms and his power to a common Cornish witch.

Mr Norrell sighed. "It is difficult to know. Ralph Stokesey seems to have fought two or three magicians by magic – one a very powerful Scottish magician, the Magician of Athodel.[2] Catherine of Winchester was once driven to send a young magician to Granada by magic. He kept disturbing her with inconvenient proposals of marriage when she wanted to study and Granada was the furthest place she could think of at the time. Then there is the curious tale of the Cumbrian charcoal-burner . . ."[3]

"And did such duels ever end in the death of one of the magicians?"

"What?" Mr Norrell stared at him, horror-struck. "No! That is to say, I do not know. I do not think so."

Lascelles smiled. "Yet the magic must exist surely? If you gave your mind to it, I dare say you could think of a half a dozen spells that would do the trick. It would be like a common duel with pistols or swords. There would be no question of a prosecution afterwards. Besides, the victor's friends and servants would be perfectly justified in helping him shroud the matter in all possible secrecy."

Mr Norrell was silent. Then he said, "It will not come to that."

Lascelles laughed. "My dear Mr Norrell! What else can it possibly come to?"

Curiously, Lascelles had never been to Hurtfew Abbey before. Whenever, in days gone by, Drawlight had gone to stay there,

---

[2] Like John Uskglass, the Magician of Athodel ruled his own island or kingdom. Athodel seems to have been one of the Western Isles of Scotland. But either it has sunk or else it is, as some people think, invisible. Some Scottish historians like to see Athodel as evidence of the superiority of Scottish magic over English; John Uskglass's kingdom, they argue, has fallen and is in the hands of the Southern English, whereas Athodel remains independent. Since Athodel is both invisible and inaccessible this is a difficult proposition to prove or disprove.

[3] In the tale of John Uskglass and the Charcoal Burner of Ullswater, Uskglass engages in a contest of magic with a poor charcoal-burner and loses. It bears similarities to other old stories in which a great ruler is outwitted by one of his humblest subjects and, because of this, many scholars have argued that it has no historical basis.

Lascelles had always contrived to have a previous engagement. A sojourn at a country house in Yorkshire was Lascelles's idea of purgatory. At best he fancied Hurtfew must be like its owner – dusty, old-fashioned and given to long, dull silences; at worst he pictured a rain-lashed farmhouse upon a dark, dreary moor. He was surprized to find that it was none of these things. There was nothing of the Gothic about it. The house was modern, elegant and comfortable and the servants were far from the uncouth farmhands of his imagination. In fact they were the same servants who waited upon Mr Norrell in Hanover-square. They were London-trained and well acquainted with all Lascelles's preferences.

But any magician's house has its oddities, and Hurtfew Abbey – at first sight so commodious and elegant – seemed to have been constructed upon a plan so extremely muddle-headed, that it was quite impossible to go from one side of the house to the other without getting lost. Later that morning Lascelles was informed by Lucas that he must on no account attempt to go to the library alone, but only in the company of Mr Norrell or Childermass. It was, said Lucas, the first rule of the house.

Naturally, Lascelles had no intention of obeying such a prohibition, delivered to him by a servant. He examined the eastern part of the house and found the usual arrangement of morning-room, dining-room, drawing-room – but no library. He concluded that the library must lie in the unexplored, western part. He set off and immediately found himself back in the room he had just left. Thinking he must have taken a wrong turn, he tried again. This time he arrived at one of the sculleries where a small, unclean, sniffling maid first wiped her nose on the back of her hand and then used that same hand to wash the cooking pots. No matter which path he chose, it returned him immediately to either morning-room or the scullery. He grew very sick of the sight of the little maid, and she did not seem exactly overjoyed to see him. But though he wasted an entire morning on this fruitless endeavour it never occurred to him to attribute his failure to any thing other than a peculiarity of Yorkshire architecture.

For the next three days Mr Norrell kept to the library as much as he could. Whenever he saw Lascelles he was sure to hear some fresh complaint about Childermass; while Childermass kept harassing him with demands that he search for Drawlight's letter by magic. In the end he found it easier to avoid them both.

Nor did he divulge to either of them something he had discovered which worried him a great deal. Ever since he and Strange had parted he had been in the habit of summoning up visions to try and discover what Strange was doing. But he had never succeeded. One night, about four weeks ago, he had not been able to sleep. He had got up and performed the magic. The vision had not been very distinct, but he had seen a magician in the darkness, doing magic. He had congratulated himself on penetrating Strange's counterspells at last; until it occurred to him that he was looking at a vision of himself in his own library. He had tried again. He had varied the spells. He named Strange in different ways. It did not matter. He was forced to conclude that English magic could no longer tell the difference between himself and Strange.

Letters arrived from Lord Liverpool and the Ministers with angry descriptions of more magic which no one could explain. Mr Norrell wrote back, promising his earliest attention to these matters just as soon as Strange had been defeated.

On the third evening after their arrival Mr Norrell, Lascelles and Childermass were gathered together in the drawing-room. Lascelles was eating an orange. He had a little pearl-handled fruit knife with a jagged blade, which he used to cut the peel. Childermass was laying out his cards upon a little table. He had been reading the cards for the past two hours. It was a measure of how far Mr Norrell was distracted by the present situation that he made not the slightest objection. Lascelles, on the other hand, was driven half-mad by those cards. He was certain that one of the subjects of all those layings-out and turnings-over was himself. In this he was perfectly correct.

"How I detest this inactivity!" he said, abruptly. "What can Strange be waiting for, do you suppose? We do not even know for certain that he will come."

"He will come," said Childermass.

"And how do you know that?" asked Lascelles. "Because you have told him to?"

Childermass did not respond. Something he had seen in the cards had claimed his attention. His glance flickered over them. Suddenly he rose from the table. "Mr Lascelles! You have a message for me!"

"I?" said Lascelles, in surprize.

"Yes, sir."

"What do you mean?"

"I mean that someone has recently given you a message for me. The cards say so. I would be grateful if you would deliver it to me."

Lascelles gave a snort of contempt. "I am not any body's messenger – yours least of all!"

Childermass ignored this. "Who is the message from?" he asked.

Lascelles said nothing. He went back to his knife and his orange.

"Very well," said Childermass and he sat down and laid out the cards again.

Mr Norrell, in a state of great apprehension, watched them. His hand fluttered up towards the bell-cord, but after a moment's consideration he changed his mind and went in search of a servant himself. Lucas was in the dining-room, laying the table. Mr Norrell told him what was going on. "Can not something be done to separate them?" he asked. "They might be cooler in a while. Has no message come for Mr Lascelles? Is there nothing that needs Childermass's attention? Can you not invent something? What about dinner? Can it be ready?"

Lucas shook his head. "There is no message. Mr Childermass will do as he pleases – he always does. And you ordered dinner for half-past nine, sir. You know you did."

"I wish Mr Strange were here," said Mr Norrell, miserably. "He would know what to say to them. He would know what to do."

Lucas touched his master's arm as if trying to rouse him. "Mr Norrell? We are trying to prevent Mr Strange from coming here – if you remember, sir?"

Mr Norrell looked at him in some irritation. "Yes, yes! I know that! But still."

Mr Norrell and Lucas returned to the drawing-room together. Childermass was turning over his last card. Lascelles was staring with great determination at a newspaper.

"What do the cards say?" said Mr Norrell to Childermass.

Mr Norrell asked the question, but Childermass spoke his answer to Lascelles. "They say that you are a liar and a thief. They say that there is more than a message. You have been given something – an object – something of great value. It is meant for me and yet you retain it."

A short silence.

Lascelles said coldly, "Mr Norrell, how long do you intend that I shall be insulted in this manner?"

"I ask you for the last time, Mr Lascelles," said Childermass, "will you give me what is mine?"

"How dare you address a gentleman in such a fashion?" asked Lascelles.

"And is it the act of a gentleman to steal from me?" replied Childermass.

Lascelles turned a dead white. "Apologize!" he hissed. "Apologize to me or I swear, you whoreson, you dregs of every Yorkshire gutter, I will teach you better manners."

Childermass shrugged. "Better a whoreson than a thief!"

With a cry of rage, Lascelles seized him and thrust him against the wall so hard that Childermass's feet actually left the ground. He shook Childermass and the paintings on the wall rattled in their frames.

Curiously, Childermass seemed defenceless against Lascelles. His arms had somehow got pinned against Lascelles's body and though he struggled hard, he seemed unable to free them. It was over in a moment. Childermass nodded briefly at Lascelles as if to say Lascelles had won.

But Lascelles did not release him. Instead, he leant hard against him, keeping him trapped against the wall. Then he reached down and picked up the pearl-handled knife with the jagged edge. He drew the blade slowly across Childermass's face, cutting him from eye to mouth.

Lucas let out a cry, but Childermass said nothing at all. He somehow freed his left hand and raised it. It was closed in a tight fist. They remained like that for a moment – a tableau – then Childermass dropped his hand.

Lascelles smiled broadly. He let Childermass go and turned to Mr Norrell. In a calm, quiet voice he addressed him thus: "I will not suffer any excuses to be made for this person. I have been insulted. If this person were of a rank to be noticed by me, I should certainly call him out. He knows it. His inferior condition protects him. If I am to remain another moment in this house, if I am to continue as your friend and adviser, then this person must leave your service this minute! After tonight I can never hear his name spoken by you or any of your servants again on pain of dismissal. I hope, sir, that this is sufficiently plain?"

Lucas took the opportunity to hand Childermass a surreptitious napkin.

"Well, sir," said Childermass to Mr Norrell, wiping the blood from his face, "which of us is it to be?"

A long moment of silence. Then in a hoarse voice quite unlike his usual tone, Mr Norrell said, "You must go."

"Goodbye, Mr Norrell," said Childermass, bowing. "You have

made the wrong choice, sir – as usual!" He gathered up his cards and left.

He went up to his bare little attic bedroom and lit the candle which stood upon a table. There was a cracked, cheap looking-glass hanging on the wall. He examined his face. The cut was ugly. His neckcloth and the right shoulder of his shirt were soaked in blood. He washed the wound as best he could. Then he washed and dried his hands.

Carefully he took something out of his coat-pocket. It was a box, the colour of heartache, about the size of a snuff box but a little longer. He whispered to himself, "A man cannot help his training."[4]

He opened it. For a moment or two he looked thoughtful; he scratched his head and then cursed because he had very nearly dropt blood into it. He snapped it shut and put it in his pocket.

It did not take long to collect his possessions. There was a mahogany case containing a pair of pistols, a small purse of money, a razor, a comb, a toothbrush, a bit of soap, some clothes (all as ancient as the ones he was wearing) and a small parcel of books, including a Bible, *A Child's History of the Raven King* by Lord Portishead and a copy of Paris Ormskirk's *Revelations of Thirty-Six Other Worlds*. Mr Norrell had paid Childermass well for years, but what he did with his money no one knew. As Davey and Lucas had often remarked to each other, he certainly did not spend it.

Childermass packed everything into a battered valise. There was a dish of apples upon the table. He wrapped them in a cloth and added them to the valise. Then, holding the napkin to his face, he went downstairs. He was in the stable-yard before he remembered that his pen, ink and memorandum book were still in the drawing-room. He had put them on a side-table while he read his

---

[4] At the engravers' house in Spitalfields in the early spring of 1816, Strange had told Childermass, "One can never help one's training, you know . . ."

Childermass had had several careers before he became Mr Norrell's servant and adviser. His first was as a highly talented child pick-pocket. His mother, Black Joan, had once managed a small pack of dirty, ragged child-thieves that had worked the towns of the East Riding in the late 1770s.

cards. "Well, it is too late to go back," he thought. "I shall have to buy others."

There was a party waiting for him in the stables: Davey, Lucas, the grooms and several of the manservants who had managed to slip away from the house. "What are you all doing here?" he asked, in surprise. "Holding a prayer meeting?"

The men glanced at each other.

"We saddled Brewer for you, Mr Childermass," said Davey. Brewer was Childermass's horse, a big, unhandsome stallion.

"Thank you, Davey."

"Why did you let him do it, sir?" asked Lucas. "Why did you let him cut you?"

"Don't fret about it, lad. It's of no consequence."

"I brought bandages. Let me bind up your face."

"Lucas, I need my wits tonight and I cannot think if I am all over bandages."

"But it will leave a terrible scar if the lips of the wound are not closed."

"Let it. No one will complain if I am less beautiful than I was. Just give me another clout[5] to staunch the flow. This one is soaked through. Now, lads, when Strange comes . . ." He sighed. "I do not know what to tell you. I have no advice. But if you get a chance to help them, then do it."

"What?" asked one manservant. "Help Mr Norrell and Mr Lascelles?"

"No, you blockhead! Help Mr Norrell and Mr Strange. Lucas, tell Lucy, Hannah and Dido that I said goodbye and wished them well – and good, obedient husbands when they want them." (These were three housemaids who were particular favourites of Childermass.)

Davey grinned. "And you yourself willing to do the job, sir?" he said.

---

[5] A Yorkshire word meaning "cloth".

Childermass laughed – then flinched at the pain in his face. "Well, for Hannah perhaps," he said. "Goodbye, lads."

He shook hands with all of them and was a little taken aback when Davey, who for all his strength and size was as sentimental as a schoolgirl, insisted on embracing him and actually shed tears. Lucas gave him a bottle of Mr Norrell's best claret as a parting gift.

Childermass led Brewer out of the stables. The moon had risen. He had no difficulty in following the sweep out of the pleasure-grounds into the park. He was just crossing over the bridge when the sudden realization came upon him that there was magic going on. It was as if a thousand trumpets had sounded in his ear or a dazzling light had shone out of the darkness. The world was entirely different from what it had been a moment before, but what that difference was he could not at first make out. He looked round.

Directly above the park and house there was a patch of night-sky shoved in where it did not belong. The constellations were broken. New stars hung there – stars that Childermass had never seen before. They were, presumably, the stars of Strange's Eternal Darkness.

He took one last look at Hurtfew Abbey and galloped away.

All the clocks began to strike at the same moment. This in itself was extraordinary enough. For fifteen years Lucas had been trying to persuade the clocks of Hurtfew to tell the hour together and they had never done so until this moment. But what o'clock it might be was hard to say. The clocks struck on and on, long past twelve, telling the time of a strange, new era.

"What in the world is that hideous sound?" asked Lascelles.

Mr Norrell stood up. He rubbed his hands together – with him always a sign of great nervousness and strain. "Strange is here," said, quickly. He spoke a word. The clocks were silent.

The door burst open. Mr Norrell and Mr Lascelles turned with faces all alarm, in full expectation of seeing Strange standing there. But it was only Lucas and two of the other servants.

"Mr Norrell!" began Lucas. "I think . . ."

"Yes, yes! I know! Go to the store-room at the foot of the kitchen-stairs. In the chest under the window you will find lead chains, lead padlocks and lead keys. Bring them here! Quickly!"

"And I will go and fetch a pair of pistols," declared Lascelles.

"They will do no good," said Mr Norrell.

"Oh! You would be surprized how many problems a pair of pistols can solve!"

They returned within five minutes. There was Lucas, looking reluctant and unhappy, holding the chains and locks; Lascelles with his pistols; and four or five more manservants.

"Where do you suppose he is?" asked Lascelles.

"In the library. Where else?" said Mr Norrell. "Come."

They left the drawing-room and entered the dining-room. From here they passed into a short corridor which contained an inlaid ebony sideboard, the marble statue of a centaur and its foal, and a painting of Salome carrying St John's head on a silver platter. There were two doors ahead of them. The one on the right had an unfamiliar look to Lascelles, as if he had never seen it before. Mr Norrell led them through it and they immediately found themselves – back in the drawing-room.

"Wait," said Mr Norrell in confusion. He looked behind him. "I must have . . . No. Wait. I have it now! Come!"

Once again they passed through the dining-room into the corridor. This time they went through the door upon the left. It too led straight back to the drawing-room.

Mr Norrell gave a loud, despairing cry. "He has broken my labyrinth and woven another against me!"

"In some ways, sir," remarked Lascelles, "I could have wished that you had not taught him so well."

"Oh! I never taught him to do this – and you may be sure that he never learnt it from any one else! Either the Devil taught him or he learnt it this very night in my house. This is the genius of my enemy! Lock a door against him and all that happens is that he learns first how to pick a lock and second how to build a better one against you!"

Lucas and the other servants lit more candles as if light could somehow help them see through Strange's spells and help them distinguish reality from magic. Soon each of the three apartments was ablaze with light. Candlesticks and candelabras were crowded upon every surface, but it only served to confuse them more. They went from dining-room to drawing-room, from drawing-room to corridor – "Like foxes in a stopt earth," said Lascelles. But, try as they might, they could not leave the three apartments.

Time passed. It was impossible to say how much. The clocks had all turned to midnight. Every window shewed the black of Eternal Night and the unknown stars.

Mr Norrell stopt walking. He closed his eyes. His face was as dark and tight as a fist. He stood quite still and only his lips moved slightly. Then he opened his eyes briefly and said, "Follow me." Closing his eyes again, he walked. It was as if he were following the plan of an entirely different house that had somehow got wedged inside his own. The turns he took, the rights and lefts, made a new path – one he had never taken before.

After three or four minutes he opened his eyes. There before him was the corridor he had been searching for – the one with the floor of stone flags – and at the end of it the tall shadowy shape of the library door.

"Now, we shall see what he is doing!" he cried. "Lucas, keep the lead chains and locks ready. There is no better prophylactic against magic than lead. We will bind his hands and that will hinder him a little. Mr Lascelles, how quickly do you suppose we might get a letter to one of the Ministers?" He was a little surprized that none of them made any reply and so he turned.

He was quite alone.

A little way off he heard Lascelles say something; his cold, languid voice was unmistakable. He heard one of the other servants reply and then Lucas. But gradually all the noise grew less. The sounds of the servants rushing from room to room were gone. There was silence.

64

Two versions of Lady Pole

Mid February 1817

"WELL!" SAID LASCELLES. "That was unexpected!"
He and the servants were gathered at the north
wall of the dining-room – a wall through which Mr
Norrell had just walked, with all the composure in the world.

Lascelles put out his hand and touched it; it was perfectly solid.
He pressed it hard; it did not move.

"Did he mean to do that, do you think?" wondered one of the
servants.

"I do not think it much matters what he meant," said Lucas.
"He has gone to be with Mr Strange now."

"Which is as much as to say he has gone to the Devil!" added
Lascelles.

"What will happen now?" asked another servant.

No one answered him. Images of magical battles flitted through
the minds of everyone present: Mr Norrell hurling mystical
cannonballs at Strange; Strange calling up devils to come and
carry Mr Norrell away. They listened for sounds of a struggle.
There were none.

A shout came from the next room. One of the servants had
opened the drawing-room door and found the breakfast-room on
the other side of it. Beyond the breakfast-room was Mr Norrell's
sitting-room, and beyond that, his dressing-room. The old

sequence of rooms was suddenly re-established; the labyrinth was broken.

The relief of this discovery was very great. The servants immediately abandoned Lascelles and went down to the kitchen, the natural refuge and solace of their class. Lascelles – just as naturally – sat down in solitary state in Mr Norrell's sitting-room. He had some idea of staying there until Mr Norrell returned. Or if Mr Norrell never came back, of waiting for Strange and then shooting him. "After all," he thought, "what can a magician do against a lead ball? Between the pistol firing and his heart exploding, there is no time for magic."

But such thoughts as these provided only a temporary comfort. The house was too silent, the darkness too magical. He was too aware of the servants gathered together sociably in one place, and the two magicians doing God-knew-what in another place, and himself, alone, in a third place. There was an old longcase clock that stood in one corner of the room, a last remnant of Mr Norrell's childhood home in York. This clock had, like all the others in the house, turned to midnight when Strange arrived. But it had not done so willingly; it protested very volubly against such an unexpected turn of events. Its ticking was all askew; it seemed to be drunk – or possibly in a fever – and from time to time it made a sound that was remarkably like an indrawn breath; and every time it did so Lascelles thought that Strange had entered the room and was about to say something.

He got up and followed the servants to the kitchen.

The kitchen at Hurtfew Abbey was very much like the undercroft of a great church, full of classical angles and classical gloom. In the centre of the room was a huge number of tallow candles and gathered there was every servant that Lascelles had ever seen at Hurtfew, and a great many that he had not. He leant against a pillar at the top of a flight of steps.

Lucas glanced up at him. He said, "We have been discussing what to do, sir. We shall leave within the half hour. We can do Mr

928

Norrell no good by staying here and may do ourselves some harm. That is our intention, sir, but if you have another opinion I shall be glad to hear it."

"My opinion!" exclaimed Lascelles. He looked all amazement, and only part of it was feigned. "This is the first time I was ever asked my *opinion* by a footman. Thank you, but I believe I shall decline my share of this . . ." He thought for a moment, before settling upon the most offensive word in his vocabulary. ". . . *democracy.*"

"As you wish, sir," said Lucas, mildly.

"It must be daylight in England by now," said one of the maids, looking longingly at the windows set high in the walls.

"This is England, silly girl!" declared Lascelles.

"No, sir. Begging your pardon," said Lucas, "but it is not. England is a natural place. Davey, how long to turn the horses out?"

"Oh!" cried Lascelles. "You are all very bold, I must say, to discuss your thievery in front of me! What? You think I shall not speak out against you? On the contrary I shall see you all hanged!"

Some of the servants nervously eyed the pistols in Lascelles's hands. Lucas, however, ignored him.

The servants soon agreed that those among them who had relations or friends in the neighbourhood would go to them. The rest would be dispatched with the horses to the various farms which stood upon Mr Norrell's estate.

"So, you see, sir," said Lucas to Lascelles, "nobody is stealing. Nobody is a thief. All of Mr Norrell's property is to remain on Mr Norrell's land – and we will take as good care of his horses as if they were still in his stables, but it would be a wicked cruelty to leave any creature in this Perpetual Darkness."

Sometime later the servants left Hurtfew (there was no saying exactly how much later it was – their pocket-watches, like the clocks, had all turned to midnight). With baskets and valises slung over their arms and knapsacks on their backs, they led the horses by the halter. There were also two donkeys and a goat who had always lived in the stables because the horses found him agreeable company. Lascelles followed at a distance; he had no desire to appear part of this rag-tag and bobtail procession, but neither did he want to be left alone in the house.

Ten yards short of the river they walked out of the Darkness into the Dawn. There was a sudden rush of scents upon the air – scents of frost, winter earth and the nearby river. The colours and shapes of the park seemed simplified, as if England had been made afresh during the night. To the poor servants, who had been in some doubt whether they would ever see any thing but Dark and stars again, the sight was an exceedingly welcome one.

Their watches had started up again and they found by a general consultation that it was a quarter to eight.

But the alarms of that night were not quite over yet. Two bridges now led across the river where only one had been before.

Lascelles came hurrying up. "What is that?" he demanded, pointing at the new bridge.

An old servant – a man with a beard like a miniature white cloud stuck to the end of his chin – said that it was a fairy bridge. He had seen it in his youth. It had been built long ago, when John Uskglass still ruled Yorkshire. It had fallen into disrepair and been dismantled in the time of Mr Norrell's uncle.

"And yet here it is, back again," said Lucas with a shudder.

"And what lies on the other side?" asked Lascelles.

The old servant said that it had led to Northallerton once upon a time, by way of various queer places.

"Does it meet up with the road we saw near the Red House?" asked Lascelles.

The old servant shook his head. He did not know.

Lucas was losing patience. He wished to be away.

"Fairy roads are not like Christian roads," he said. "Often they do not go where they are supposed to at all. But what does it matter? Nobody here is going to put so much as a foot upon the wicked thing."

"Thank you," said Lascelles, "but I believe I shall make up my own mind upon that point." He hesitated a moment and then strode forward on to the fairy bridge.

Several of the servants called out to him to come back.

"Oh, let him go!" cried Lucas, tightening his hold upon a basket which contained his cat. "Let him be damned if he wishes! I am sure no one could deserve it more." He threw Lascelles one last, hearty look of dislike and followed the others into the Park.

Behind them the Black Pillar rose up into the grey Yorkshire sky and the end of it could not be seen.

Twenty miles away Childermass was crossing over the packhorse bridge that led into Starecross village. He rode through the village to the Hall and dismounted.

"Hey! Hey!" He banged on the door with his whip. He shouted some more and gave the door a few vigorous kicks.

Two servants appeared. They had been alarmed enough by all the shouting and banging, but when they held up their candle and found that its author was a wild-eyed, cutthroat-looking person with a slit in his face and his shirt all bloody, they were not in the least reassured.

"Do not stand there gawping!" he told them. "Go fetch master! He knows me!"

Ten minutes more brought Mr Segundus in a dressing-gown. Childermass, waiting impatiently just within the door, saw that as he came along the passage his eyes were closed and the servant led him by the hand. It looked for all the world as if he had gone blind. The servant placed him just before Childermass. He opened his eyes.

"Good Lord, Mr Childermass!" he cried. "What happened to your face?"

"Someone mistook it for an orange. And you, sir? What has happened to you? Have you been ill?"

"No, not ill." Mr Segundus looked embarrassed. "It is living in constant proximity to strong magic. I had not realized before how weakening that can be. To a person who is susceptible to it, I mean. The servants feel no effects whatsoever, I am glad to say."

There was a queer insubstantiality about him. He looked as if he were painted on the air. The merest draught from a gap in the casement took his hair and made little corkscrews and curlicues of it, as if it weighed nothing at all.

"I suppose that is what you have come about," he continued. "But you should tell Mr Norrell that I have done nothing but study the occurrences that presented themselves. I confess I have made a few notes, but really he has nothing to complain about."

"What magic?" asked Childermass. "What are you talking about? And you need not concern yourself any longer about Mr Norrell. He has problems of his own and knows nothing of my being here. What have you been doing, Mr Segundus?"

"Only watching and recording – as a magician should." Mr Segundus leant forward eagerly. "And I have come to some surprizing conclusions concerning Lady Pole's illness!"

"Oh?"

"In my opinion it is not madness at all. It is magic!" Mr Segundus waited for Childermass to be amazed. He looked a little disappointed when Childermass simply nodded.

"I have something that belongs to her ladyship," said Childermass. "Something she has long missed. So I beg that you will do me the kindness of taking me to her."

"Oh, but . . ."

"I mean her no harm, Mr Segundus. And I believe I may be able to do her some good. I swear it by Bird and Book. By Bird and Book."[1]

---

[1] This is an old Northern English oath. John Uskglass's arms shewed a Raven-in-Flight upon a white field (Argent, Raven Volant); those of his Chancellor, William Lanchester, shewed the same with the addition of an open book (Argent, Raven Volant above an open book).

For much of the thirteenth century John Uskglass devoted himself to scholarship and magic, abandoning the business of government to Lanchester. Lanchester's arms were displayed in all the great courts of law and upon many important legal documents. Consequently, the people fell into the habit of swearing by Bird and Book, the elements of those arms.

"I cannot take you to her," said Mr Segundus. He put up his hand to forestall Childermass's objection. "I do not mean that I am unwilling. I mean I *cannot*. Charles will take us." He indicated the servant at his side.

This seemed rather eccentric, but Childermass was in no mood to argue about it. Mr Segundus grasped Charles's arm and closed his eyes.

Behind the stone-and-oak passages of Starecross Hall, a vision of another house leapt up. Childermass saw high corridors that stretched away into unthinkable distances. It was as if two transparencies had been put into a magic lantern at the same time, so that one picture overlaid the other. The impression of walking through both houses at once rapidly brought on a sensation akin to sea-sickness. Confusion mounted in his mind and, had he been alone, he would soon have been at a loss to know which way to go. He could not tell whether he was walking or falling, whether he climbed one step, or mounted a staircase of impossible length. Sometimes he seemed to be skimming across an acre of stone flags, while at the same time he was scarcely moving at all. His head spun and he felt sick.

"Stop! Stop!" he cried and sank to the ground with his eyes closed.

"It affects you badly," said Mr Segundus. "Worse even than me. Close your eyes and take hold of my arm. Charles will lead us both."

They walked on, eyes closed. Charles guided them round a right-hand turning and up a staircase. At the top of the staircase there was a murmured conversation between Mr Segundus and someone. Charles drew Childermass forward. Childermass had the impression of entering a room. It smelt of clean linen and dried roses.

"This is the person you wish me to see?" said a woman's voice. There was something odd about it, as if it were coming from two places at once, as if there were an echo. "But I know this person! He is the magician's servant! He is . . ."

"I am the person your ladyship shot," said Childermass and he opened his eyes.

He saw not one woman, but two – or perhaps it would be more accurate to say he saw the same woman doubled. Both sat in the same posture, looking up at him. They occupied the same space, so that he had the same giddy feeling in looking at her as he had had walking through the corridors.

One version of Lady Pole sat in the house in Yorkshire; she wore an ivory-coloured morning dress and regarded him with calm indifference. The other version was fainter – more ghostly. She sat in the gloomy, labyrinthine house, dressed in a blood-red evening gown. There were jewels or stars in her dark hair and she regarded him with fury and hatred.

Mr Segundus pulled Childermass to the right. "Stand just here!" he said, excitedly. "Now close one eye! Can you see it? Observe! A red-and-white rose where her mouth ought to be."

"The magic affects us differently," said Childermass. "I see something very strange, but I do not see that."

"You are very bold to come here," said both versions of Lady Pole, addressing Childermass, "considering who you are and whom you represent."

"I am not here on Mr Norrell's business. To own the truth I am not entirely sure who it is I represent. I think it is Jonathan Strange. It is my belief that he sent me a message – and I think it was about your ladyship. But the messenger was prevented from reaching me and the message was lost. Do you know, your ladyship, what Mr Strange might have wished to tell me about you?"

"Yes," said both versions of Lady Pole.

"Will you tell me what it is?"

"If I speak," they said, "I shall speak nothing but madness."

Childermass shrugged his shoulders. "I have passed twenty years in the society of magicians. I am accustomed to it. Speak."

So she (or they) began. Immediately Mr Segundus took a memorandum book out of a pocket of his night-gown and began to scribble notes. But, in Childermass's eyes, the two versions of Lady Pole were no longer speaking as one. The Lady Pole who sat in Starecross Hall told a tale about a child who lived near Carlisle,[2] but the woman in the blood-red gown seemed to be telling quite a different story. She wore a fierce expression and emphasized her words with passionate gestures – but what she said Childermass could not tell; the whimsical tale of the Cumbrian child drowned it out.

"There! You see!" exclaimed Mr Segundus, as he finished scribbling his notes. "This is what makes them think her mad – these odd stories and tales. But I have made a list of all that she has told me and I have begun to find correspondences between them and ancient fairy lore. I am sure that if you and I were to make inquiries we would discover some reference to a set of fairies who had some close connexion with songbirds. They may not have been songbird-herds. That, you will agree, sounds a little too much like settled occupation for such a feckless race – but they may have pursued a particular sort of magic related to songbirds. And it may have suited one of their number to tell an impressionable child that she was a songbird-herd."

"Perhaps," said Childermass, not much interested. "But that was not what she meant to tell us. And I have remembered the magical significance of roses. They stand for silence. That

---

[2] One autumn morning the Cumbrian child went out into her grandmother's garden. In a forgotten corner she discovered a house about the height and largeness of a bee-skep, built of spiders' webs stiffened and whitened with hoar-frost. Inside the lacy house was a tiny person who at times appeared immeasurably old and at other times no older than the child herself. The little person told the Cumbrian child that she was a songbird-herd and that for ages past it had been her task to watch over the fieldfares, redwings and mistle-thrushes in that part of Cumbria. All winter the Cumbrian child and the songbird-herd played together and the progress of their friendship was not in the least impeded by the difference in their sizes. In fact the songbird-herd generally did away with this obstacle by making herself as large as the Cumbrian child – or sometimes by making them both as small as birds, or beetles, or snowflakes. The songbird-herd introduced the Cumbrian child to many odd and interesting persons, some of whom lived in houses even more eccentric and delightful than the songbird-herd's own.

is why you see a red-and-white rose – it is a muffling spell."

"A muffling spell!" said Mr Segundus, in amazement. "Yes, yes! I see that! I have read about such things. But how do we break it?"

From his coat-pocket Childermass took a little box, the colour of heartache. "Your ladyship," he said, "give me your left hand."

She laid her white hand in Childermass's lined, brown one. Childermass opened the box, took out the finger and laid it against the empty place.

Nothing happened.

"We must find Mr Strange," said Mr Segundus. "Or Mr Norrell. They may be able to mend it!"

"No," said Childermass. "There is no need. Not now. You and I are two magicians, Mr Segundus. And England is full of magic. How many years' study do we have between us? We must know something to the point. What about Pale's Restoration and Rectification?"

"I know the form of it," said Mr Segundus. "But I have never been a *practical* magician."

"And you never will be, if you do not try. Do the magic, Mr Segundus."

So Mr Segundus did the magic.[3]

The finger flowed into the hand, making a seamless whole. In the same instant the impression of endless, dreary corridors surrounding them disappeared; the two women before Childermass's eyes resolved themselves into one.

Lady Pole rose slowly from her chair. Her eyes went rapidly this way and that, like someone who was seeing the world anew.

---

[3] Like most of Martin Pale's magic, Restoration and Rectification involves the use of a tool or key made specifically for the purpose. In this case the key is a small cross-like object made of two thin pieces of metal. The four arms of the cross represent past state and future state, wholeness (or wellness) and incompleteness (or sickness). As he later reported in *The Modern Magician*, Mr Segundus used a spoon and a bodkin from Lady Pole's dressing-case which Lady Pole's maid tied together with a ribbon.

Everyone in the room could see she was changed. There was animation and fire in every feature. Her eyes glowed with a furious light. She raised both arms; her hands were clenched in tight fists, as if she intended to bring them down upon someone's head.

"I have been *enchanted*!" she burst out. "Bargained away for the sake of a wicked man's career!"

"Good God!" cried Mr Segundus. "My dear Lady Pole . . ."

"Compose yourself, Mr Segundus!" said Childermass. "We have no time for trivialities. Let her speak!"

"I have been dead within and almost-dead without!" Tears started from her eyes and she struck her own breast with her clenched hand. "And not only me! Others suffer even now! – Mrs Strange and my husband's servant, Stephen Black!"

She recounted the cold, ghostly balls she had endured, the dreary processions she had been forced to take part in and the strange handicap that would not allow her and Stephen Black to speak of their predicament.

Mr Segundus and the servants heard each new revelation with mounting horror; Childermass sat and listened with impassive expression.

"We must write to the editors of the newspapers!" cried Lady Pole. "I am determined upon public exposure!"

"Exposure of whom?" asked Mr Segundus.

"The magicians, of course! Strange and Norrell!"

"Mr Strange?" faltered Mr Segundus. "No, no, you are mistaken! My dear Lady Pole, take a moment to consider what you are saying. I have not a word to say for Mr Norrell – his crimes against you are monstrous! But Mr Strange has done no harm – not knowingly at any rate. Surely he is more sinned against than sinning?"

"Oh!" cried Lady Pole. "Upon the contrary! I consider him by far the worse of the two. By his negligence and cold, masculine magic he has betrayed the best of women, the most excellent of wives!"

Childermass stood up.

"Where are you going?" asked Mr Segundus.

"To find Strange and Norrell," said Childermass.

"Why?" cried Lady Pole, rounding on him. "To warn them? So that they can prepare themselves against a woman's vengeance? Oh, how these men protect one another!"

"No, I am going to offer them my assistance to free Mrs Strange and Stephen Black."

Lascelles walked on. The path entered a wood. At the entrance to the wood was the statue of the woman holding the plucked eye and heart – just as Childermass had described. Corpses hung from the thorn-trees in various states of decay. Snow lay on the ground and it was very quiet.

After a while he came to the tower. He had imagined it to be a fanciful, otherlandish sort of place; "But really," he thought, "it is very plain, like the castles of the Scottish border country."

High in the tower was a single window glowing with candlelight and the shadow of someone watching. Lascelles noticed something else too, something that Childermass had either not seen, or else had not troubled to report: the trees were full of serpent-like creatures. They had heavy, sagging forms. One was in the process of swallowing whole a fresh, meaty-looking corpse.

Between the trees and the brook was the pale young man. His eyes were empty and there was a slight dew upon his brow. His uniform was, thought Lascelles, that of the 11th Light Dragoons.

Lascelles addressed him thus: "One of our countrymen approached you a few days ago. He spoke to you. You challenged him. Then he ran away. He was a dark, ill-favoured fellow. A person of despicable habits and base origins."

If the pale young man recognized Childermass from this description, he shewed no sign of it. In a dead voice he said, "I am the Champion of the Castle of the Plucked Eye and Heart. I offer challenges to . . ."

"Yes, yes!" cried Lascelles, impatiently. "I do not care about that. I have come here to fight. To erase the stain upon England's honour that was made by that fellow's cowardice."

The figure at the window leaned forward eagerly.

The pale young man said nothing.

Lascelles made a sound of exasperation. "Very well! Believe that I mean this woman all sorts of harm if it pleases you. It matters not one whit to me! Pistols?"

The pale young man shrugged.

There being no seconds to act for them, Lascelles told the young man that they would stand at twenty paces and he measured the ground himself.

They had taken their positions and were about to fire, when something occurred to Lascelles. "Wait!" he cried. "What is your name?"

The young man stared dully at him. "I do not remember," he said.

They both fired their pistols at the same time. Lascelles had the impression that, at the last moment, the young man turned his pistol and deliberately fired wide. Lascelles did not care: if the young man was a coward then so much the worse for him. His own ball flew with pleasing exactitude to pierce the young man's breast. He watched him die with the same intense interest and sense of satisfaction that he had felt when he had killed Drawlight.

He hung the body upon the nearest thorn-tree. Then he amused himself by taking shots at the decaying bodies and the serpents. He had not been engaged in this pleasant occupation for more than an hour when he heard the sounds of hooves upon the woodland path. From the opposite direction, from Faerie rather than England, a dark figure upon a dark horse was approaching.

Lascelles spun round. "I am the Champion of the Castle of the Plucked Eye and Heart," he began . . .

65

The ashes, the pearls,
the counterpane and the kiss

Mid February 1817

A s LUCAS AND the others were leaving Hurtfew Abbey,
Stephen was dressing in his bed-chamber at the top of the
house in Harley-street.

London is a city with more than its fair share of eccentricities,
but of all the surprizing places it contained at this time the most
extraordinary was undoubtedly Stephen's bed-chamber. It was
full of things that were precious, rare or wonderful. If the Cabinet,
or the gentlemen who direct the Bank of England, had been
somehow able to acquire the contents of Stephen's bed-chamber
their cares would have all been over. They could have paid off
Britain's debts and built London anew with the change. Thanks to
the gentleman with the thistle-down hair Stephen possessed crown
jewels from who-knew-what kingdoms, and embroidered robes
that had once belonged to Coptic popes. The flowerpots upon his
windowsill contained no flowers, but only ruby-and-pearl crosses,
carved jewels and the insignia of long-dead military orders. Inside
his small cupboard was a piece of the ceiling of the Sistine Chapel
and the thigh-bone of a Basque saint. St Christopher's hat hung
upon a peg behind the door and a marble statue of Lorenzo de
Medici by Michael Angel (which had stood, until recently, upon
the great man's tomb in Florence) occupied most of the floor.

Stephen was shaving himself in a little mirror balanced upon Lorenzo de Medici's knee when the gentleman appeared at his shoulder.

"The magician has returned to England!" he cried. "I saw him last night in the King's Roads, with the Darkness wrapped about him like a mystical cloak! What does he want? What can he be planning? Oh! This will be the end of me, Stephen! I feel it! He means me great harm!"

Stephen felt a chill. The gentleman was always at his most dangerous in this mood of agitation and alarm.

"We should kill him!" said the gentleman.

"Kill him? Oh no, sir!"

"Why not? We could be rid of him for ever! I could bind his arms, eyes and tongue with magic, and you could stab him through the heart!"

Stephen thought rapidly. "But his return may have nothing to do with you at all, sir," he offered. "Consider how many enemies he has in England – human enemies, I mean. Perhaps he has come back to continue his quarrel with one of them."

The gentleman looked doubtful. Any reasoning that did not contain a reference to himself was always difficult for him to follow. "I do not think *that* very likely," he said.

"Oh, but yes!" said Stephen, beginning to feel upon surer ground. "There have been terrible things written about him in the newspapers and the magical journals. There is a rumour that he killed his wife. Many people believe it. Were it not for his present situation, he would very likely have been arrested by now. And it is common knowledge that the other magician is the author of all these lies and half-truths. Probably, Strange has come to take revenge upon his master."

The gentleman stared at Stephen for a moment or two. Then he laughed, his spirits as elevated as moments before they had been the reverse. "We have nothing to fear Stephen!" he cried, in delight. "The magicians have quarrelled and hate each other! Yet they are nothing without one another. How glad that makes me! How happy I am to have you to advise me! And it so happens that I intend to give you a wonderful present today – something you have long desired!"

"Indeed, sir?" said Stephen with a sigh. "That will be most delightful."

"Yet we ought to kill someone," said the gentleman, immediately reverting to his former subject. "I have been quite put out of temper this morning and someone ought to die for it. What do you say to the old magician? – Oh, but wait! That would oblige the younger one, which I do not want to do! What about Lady Pole's husband? He is tall and arrogant and treats you like a servant!"

"But I *am* a servant, sir."

"Or the King of England! Yes, that is an excellent plan! Let you and I go immediately to the King of England. Then you can put him to death and be King in his place! Do you have the orb, crown and sceptre that I gave you?"

"But the laws of Great Britain do not allow . . ." began Stephen.

"The laws of Great Britain! Pish tush! What nonsense! I thought you would have understood by now that the laws of Great Britain are nothing but a flimsy testament to the idle wishes and dreams of mankind. According to the ancient laws by which my race conducts itself, a king is most commonly succeeded by the person who killed him."

"But, sir! Remember how much you liked the old gentleman when you met him?"

"Hmm, that is true. But in a matter of such importance I am willing to put aside my personal feelings. The difficulty is that we have too many enemies, Stephen! There are too many wicked persons in England! I know! I shall ask some of my allies to tell us who is our greatest enemy of all. We must be careful. We must be cunning. We must frame our question with exactitude.[1] I shall ask

---

[1] It is all very well in fairy-tales to ask, "Who is the fairest of them all?" But in reality no magic, fairy or human, could ever be persuaded to answer such an imprecise question.

the North Wind and the Dawn to bring us immediately into the presence of the one person in England whose existence is the greatest threat to me! And then we can kill him, whoever he is. You observe, Stephen, that I make reference to my own life, but I consider your fate and mine as bound so closely together that there is scarcely any difference between us. Whosoever is a danger to me, is a danger to you also! Now take up your crown and orb and sceptre and say a last farewell to the scenes of your slavery! It may be that you shall never see them again!"

"But . . ." began Stephen.

It was too late. The gentleman raised his long, white hands and gave a sort of flourish.

Stephen expected to be brought before one or other of the magicians – possibly both. Instead the gentleman and he found themselves upon a wide, empty moor covered in snow. More snow was falling. On one side the ground rose up to meet the heavy, slate-coloured sky; on the other was a misty view of far-away, white hills. In all that desolate landscape there was only one tree – a twisted hawthorn not far from where they stood. It was, thought Stephen, very like the country around Starecross Hall.

"Well, that is very odd!" said the gentleman. "I do not see any body at all, do you?"

"No, sir. No one," said Stephen, in relief. "Let us return to London."

"I cannot understand . . . Oh, but wait! Here is someone!"

Half a mile or so away there seemed to be a road or track of some sort. A horse and cart were coming slowly along it. When the cart drew level with the hawthorn tree, it stopped and someone got out. This person began to stump across the moor towards them.

"Excellent!" cried the gentleman. "Now we shall see our wickedest and most powerful enemy! Put on your crown, Stephen! Let him tremble before our power and majesty! Excellent! Raise your sceptre! Yes, yes! Hold forth your orb! How handsome you look! How regal! Now, Stephen, since we have a little time before he arrives . . ." The gentleman gazed at the little figure in the distance labouring across the snowy moor. ". . . I have something else to tell you. What is the date today?"

"The fifteenth of February, sir. St Anthony's Day."

"Ha! A dreary saint indeed! Well, in future the people of England will have something better to celebrate on the fifteenth of February than the life of a monk who keeps the rain off people and finds their lost thimbles!"[2]

"Will they indeed, sir? And what is that?"

"The Naming of Stephen Black!"

"I beg your pardon, sir?"

"I told you, Stephen, that I would find your true name!"

"What! Did my mother really name me, sir?"

"Yes, indeed! It is all just as I supposed! – which is scarcely surprizing since I am rarely wrong in such matters. She named you with a name in her own tongue. With a name she had heard often among her own people when she was a young girl. She named you, but she did not tell the name to a single soul. She did not even whisper it into your infant ear. She had no time because Death stole upon her and took her unawares."

A picture rose up in Stephen's mind – the dark, fusty hold of the ship – his mother, worn out by the pains of childbirth, surrounded by strangers – himself a tiny infant. Did she even speak the language of the other people on board? He had no way of knowing. How alone she must have felt! He would have given a great deal at that moment to be able to reach out and comfort her, but all the years of his life lay between them. He felt his heart harden another degree against the English. Only a few minutes ago he had struggled to persuade the gentleman not to kill Strange, but why should he care what became of one Englishman? Why should he care what became of any of that cold, callous race?

---

[2] St Anthony of Padua. Several of his miracles involve preserving from rain congregations to whom he was preaching, or maid-servants with whom he was friendly. He also helps people find things they have lost.

With a sigh, he put these thoughts aside and discovered that the gentleman was still talking.

". . . It is a most edifying tale and demonstrates to perfection all those qualities for which I am especially famed; namely self-sacrifice, devoted friendship, nobility of purpose, perceptiveness, ingenuity and courageousness."

"I beg your pardon, sir?"

"The story of my finding your name, Stephen, which I am now going to relate! Know then that your mother died in the hold of a ship, the *Penlaw*,[3] that was sailing from Jamaica to Liverpool. And then," he added in a matter-of-fact tone, "the English sailors stripped her body and flung it into the sea."

"Ah!" breathed Stephen.

"Now, as you may imagine, this made the task of recovering your name extremely difficult. After thirty or forty years, all that was left of your mother was four things: her screams in childbirth, which had sunk into the planks of the ship; her bones, which was all that was left of her, once the flesh and softer parts had been devoured by fishes . . ."

"Ah!" exclaimed Stephen again.

". . . her gown of rose-coloured cotton which had passed into the possession of a sailor; and a kiss which the captain of the ship had stolen from her, two days earlier. Now," said the gentleman (who was clearly enjoying himself immensely), "you will observe with what cleverness and finesse I traced the passage of each part of her through the world, until I was able to recover them and so divine your glorious name! The *Penlaw* sailed on to Liverpool where the wicked grandfather of Lady Pole's wicked husband disembarked with his servant – who carried your own infant person in his arms. On the *Penlaw*'s next voyage, which was to Leith in Scotland, it met with a storm and was wrecked. Various spars and bits of broken hull were cast up upon the rocky shore,

---

[3] Penlaw is the name of the place in Northumbria where John Uskglass and his fairy army first appeared in England.

including the planks that contained your mother's screams. These were taken by a very poor man to make a roof and walls for his house. I found the house very easily. It stood upon a windy promontory, overlooking a stormy sea. Inside, several generations of the poor man's family were living in the utmost poverty and degradation. Now, you should know, Stephen, that wood has a stubborn, proud nature; it does not readily tell what it knows – even to its friends. It is always easier to deal with the ashes of the wood, rather than wood itself. So I burnt the poor man's house to the ground, placed the ashes in a bottle and continued on my way."

"Burnt, sir! I hope no one was hurt!"

"Well, some people were. The strong, young men were able to run out of the conflagration in time, but the older, enfeebled members of the family, the women and infants were all burnt to death."

"Oh!"

"Next I traced the history of her bones. I believe I mentioned before that she was cast into the ocean where, due to the movement of the waters and the importunate interference of the fishes, the body became bones, the bones became dust, and the dust was very soon transformed by a bed of oysters into several handfuls of the most beautiful pearls. In time the pearls were harvested and sold to a jeweller in Paris, who created a necklace of five perfect strands. This he sold to a beautiful French Comtesse. Seven years later the Comtesse was guillotined and her jewels, gowns and personal possessions became the property of a Revolutionary official. This wicked man was, until quite recently, the mayor of a small town in the Loire valley. Late at night he would wait until all his servants had gone to bed and then, in the privacy of his bed-chamber, he would put on the Comtesse's jewels and gowns and other finery and parade up and down in front of a large mirror. Here I found him one night, looking, I may say, very ridiculous. I strangled him upon the spot – using the pearl necklace."

"Oh!" said Stephen.

"I took the pearls, let the miserable corpse fall to the ground and passed on. Next I turned my attention to your mother's pretty rose-coloured gown. The sailor who had acquired it, kept it among his things for a year or two until he happened to find himself in a cold, miserable little hamlet on the eastern coast of America called Piper's Grave. There he met a tall, thin woman and, wishing to impress her, he gave her the gown as a present. The gown did not fit this woman (your mother, Stephen, had a sweetly rounded, feminine figure), but she liked the colour and so she cut it up and sewed the pieces into a counterpane with some other cheap materials. The rest of this woman's history is not very interesting – she married several husbands and buried them all, and by the time I found her she was old and withered. I plucked the counter-pane off her bed as she slept."

"You did not kill her, did you, sir?" asked Stephen, anxiously.

"No, Stephen. Why would I? Of course it was a bitter night with four feet of snow and a raging north wind outside. She may have died of the cold. I do not know. So we come at last to the kiss and the captain who stole it from her."

"Did you kill him, sir?"

"No, Stephen – though I would certainly have done so to punish him for his insult to your esteemed mother, but he was hanged in the town of Valletta twenty-nine years ago. Fortunately he had kissed a great many other young women before he died and the virtue and strength of your mother's kiss had been conveyed to them. So all I had to do was to find them and extract what was left of your mother's kiss."

"And how did you do that, sir?" asked Stephen, though he feared that he knew the answer all too well.

"Oh! It is easy enough once the women are dead."

"So many people dead, just to find my name," sighed Stephen.

"And I would gladly have killed twice that number – nay, a hundred times – nay, a hundred thousand times or more! – so great is the love I bear you, Stephen. With the ashes that were her screams and the pearls that were her bones and the counterpane that was her gown and the magical essence of her kiss, I was able to divine your name – which I, your truest friend and most noble benefactor, will now . . . Oh, but here is our enemy! As soon as we have killed him, I will bestow your name upon you. Beware, Stephen! There will probably be a magical combat of some sort. I dare say I shall have to take on different forms – cockatrices, raw head and bloody bones, rains of fire, etc., etc. You may wish to stand back a little!"

The unknown person drew closer. He was as thin as a Banbury cheese, with a hawk-like, disreputable-looking face. His coat and shirt were in rags and his boots were broken and full of holes.

"Well!" said the gentleman after a moment. "I could not be more astonished! Have you ever seen this person before, Stephen?"

"Yes, sir. I must confess that I have. This is the man I told you about. The one with the strange disfiguration who told me the prophecy. His name is Vinculus."

"Good day to you, King!" said Vinculus to Stephen. "Did I not tell you the hour was almost come? And now it has! The rain shall make a door for you and you shall go through it! The stones shall make a throne for you and you shall sit upon it!" He surveyed Stephen with a mysterious satisfaction, as if the crown, orb and sceptre were somehow all his doing.

Stephen said to the gentleman, "Perhaps the Venerable Beings to whom you applied are mistaken, sir. Perhaps they have brought us to the wrong person."

"Nothing seems more likely," agreed the gentleman. "This vagabond is scarcely any threat to any one. To me least of all. But as the North Wind and the Dawn have taken the trouble to point him out to us, it would be most disrespectful to them not to kill him."

Vinculus seemed curiously unmoved by this proposal. He gave a laugh. "Try if you can do it, Fairy! You will discover that I am very hard to kill!"

"Are you indeed?" said the gentleman. "For I must confess that it looks to me as if nothing would be easier! But then you see I am very adept at killing all sorts of things! I have slain dragons, drowned armies and persuaded the earthquakes and tempests to devour cities! You are a man. You are all alone – as all men are. I am surrounded by ancient friends and allies. Rogue, what do you have to counter that?"

Vinculus thrust out his dirty chin at the gentleman in a gesture of the utmost contempt. "A book!" he said.

It was an odd thing to say. Stephen could not help thinking that if Vinculus had indeed possessed a book he would have been well advised to sell it and buy a better coat.

The gentleman turned his head to gaze with sudden intensity at a distant line of white hills. "Oh!" he exclaimed with as much violence as if he had been struck. "Oh! They have stolen her from me! Thieves! Thieves! English thieves!"

"Who, sir?"

"Lady Pole! Someone has broken the enchantment!"

"The magic of Englishmen, Fairy!" cried Vinculus. "The magic of Englishmen is coming back!"

"Now you see their arrogance, Stephen!" cried the gentleman, spinning round to bestow a look of vivid fury upon Vinculus. "Now you see the malice of our enemies! Stephen, procure me some rope!"

"Rope, sir? There is none for miles around, I am sure. Let you and I . . ."

"No rope, Fairy!" jeered Vinculus.

But something was happening in the air above them. The lines of sleet and snow were somehow twisting together. They snaked across the sky towards Stephen. Without warning a length of strong rope fell into his hand.

"There!" cried the gentleman, triumphantly. "Stephen, look!

Here is a tree! One tree in all this desolate waste, exactly where we need it! But England has always been my friend. She has always served me well. Throw the rope over a branch and let us hang this rogue!"

Stephen hesitated, uncertain for the moment how to prevent this new disaster. The rope in his hand seemed to grow impatient with him; it jumped away and divided itself neatly into two lengths. One snaked across the ground to Vinculus and trussed him tight and the other quickly formed itself into a well-made noose and hung itself neatly over a branch.

The gentleman was in high glee, his spirits quite restored at the prospect of a hanging. "Do you dance, rogue?" he asked Vinculus. "I shall teach you some new steps!"

Everything took on the character of a nightmare. Events happened quickly and seamlessly, and Stephen never found the right moment to intervene or the right words to say. As for Vinculus himself, he behaved very oddly throughout his entire execution. He never appeared to understand what was happening to him. He said not another word, but he did make several exclamations of exasperation as if he was being put to some serious inconvenience and it was putting him out of temper.

Without any appearance of exertion the gentleman took hold of Vinculus and placed him beneath the noose. The noose draped itself about his neck and hoisted him abruptly into the air; at the same time the other rope unwound itself from his body and folded itself neatly on the ground.

Vinculus kicked his feet uselessly in the empty air; his body jerked and spun. For all his boast of being hard to kill, his neck broke very easily – the snapping sound could be clearly heard on the empty moor. A jerk or two more and he was finished.

Stephen – forgetting that he had determined to hate all Englishmen – covered his face with his hands and wept.

The gentleman danced round and sang to himself, as a child will when something has pleased it particularly; and when he was done he said in a conversational tone, "Well, that was disappointing! He did not struggle at all. I wonder who he was?"

"I told you, sir," said Stephen, wiping his eyes. "He is the man who told me that prophecy. He has a strange disfiguration upon his body. Like writing."

The gentleman pulled off Vinculus's coat, shirt and neckcloth. "Yes, there it is!" he said in mild surprize. He scratched with one nail at a little circle on Vinculus's right shoulder to see if it would come off. Finding it did not, he lost interest.

"Now!" he said. "Let us go and cast a spell upon Lady Pole."

"A spell, sir!" said Stephen. "But why would we wish to do that?"

"Oh! So that she will die within a month or two. It is – apart from any thing else – very traditional. It is very rare that any one released from an enchantment is permitted to live long – certainly not if I have enchanted them! Lady Pole is not far away and the magicians must be taught that they may not oppose us with impunity! Come, Stephen!"

66

Jonathan Strange and Mr Norrell

Mid February 1817

MR NORRELL TURNED and looked back along the
corridor which had once led from the library to the
rest of the house. If he had had any confidence that it
could take him back to Lascelles and the servants, he would have
gone down it. But he was quite certain that Strange's magic would
simply return him to this spot.

There was a sound from within the library and he gave a start of
terror. He waited, but no one appeared. After a moment he
realized that he knew what the sound was. He had heard it a
thousand times before – it was the sound of Strange exclaiming in
exasperation over some passage in a book. It was such a very
familiar sound – and so closely connected in Mr Norrell's mind
with the happiest period of his existence – that it gave him the
courage to open the door and go inside.

The first thing that struck him was the immense quantity of
candles. The room was full of light. Strange had not troubled to
find candlesticks; he had simply stuck the candles to tables or to
bookshelves. He had even stuck them to piles of books. The library
was in imminent danger of catching fire. There were books
everywhere – scattered over tables, tumbled on the floor. Many
had been laid face-down on the floor, so that Strange should not
lose his place.

Strange was standing at the far end of the room. He was a much thinner person than Mr Norrell remembered. He had shaved himself with no extraordinary degree of perfection and his hair was ragged. He did not look up at Mr Norrell's approach.

"Seven people from Norwich in 1124," he said, reading from the book in his hand. "Four from Aysgarth in Yorkshire at Christmas in 1151, twenty-three at Exeter in 1201, one from Hathersage in Derbyshire in 1243 – all enchanted and stolen away into Faerie. It was a problem he never solved."

He spoke with such calm that Mr Norrell – who was rather expecting to be blasted with a bolt of magic at any moment – looked round to see if someone else was in the room. "I beg your pardon?" he asked.

"John Uskglass," said Strange, still not troubling to turn around. "He could not prevent fairies stealing away Christian men and women. Why should I suppose that I might be capable of something he was not?" He read a little further. "I like your labyrinth," he said conversationally. "Did you use Hickman?"

"What? No. De Chepe."

"De Chepe! Really?" For the first time Strange looked directly at his master. "I had always supposed him to be a very minor scholar without an original thought in his head."

"He was never much to the taste of people who like the showier sorts of magic," said Mr Norrell, nervously, uncertain of how long this civil mood of Strange's might last. "He was interested in labyrinths, magical pathways, spells which may be effected by following certain steps and turns – things of that sort. There is a long description of his magic in Belasis's *Instructions* . . ." He paused. ". . . which you have never seen. The only copy is here. It is on the third shelf by the window." He pointed and discovered that the shelf had been emptied. "Or it might be on the floor," he offered. "In that pile."

"I shall look in a moment," Strange assured him.

"Your own labyrinth was quite remarkable," said Mr Norrell. "I have been half the night trying to escape it."

"Oh, I did what I usually do in such circumstances," said Strange, carelessly. "I copied you and added some refinements. How long has it been?"

"I beg your pardon?"

"How long have I been in the Darkness?"

"Since the beginning of December."

"And what month is it now?"

"February."

"Three months!" exclaimed Strange. "Three months! I thought it had been years!"

Mr Norrell had imagined this conversation many times. Each time he had pictured Strange angry and vengeful, and himself putting forth powerful arguments of self-justification. Now that they had finally met, Strange's unconcern was utterly bewildering. The distant pains Mr Norrell had long felt in his small, shrivelled soul awakened. They grew claws and rent at him. His hands began to shake.

"I have been your enemy!" he burst out. "I destroyed your book – all except my own copy! I have slandered your name and plotted against you! Lascelles and Drawlight have told everyone that you murdered your wife! I have let them believe it!"

"Yes," said Strange.

"But these are terrible crimes! Why are you not angry?"

Strange seemed to concede that this was a reasonable question. He thought for a moment. "I suppose it is because I have been many things since last we met. I have been trees and rivers and hills and stones. I have spoken to stars and earth and wind. One cannot be the conduit through which all English magic flows and still be oneself. I would have been angry, you say?"

Mr Norrell nodded.

Strange smiled his old, ironic smile. "Then be comforted! I dare say I shall be so again. In time."

"And you have done all this just to thwart me?" asked Mr Norrell.

"To thwart you?" said Strange, in astonishment. "No! I have done this to save my wife!"

There was a short silence during which time Mr Norrell found it impossible to meet Strange's eye. "What do you want from me?" he asked in a low voice.

"Only what I have always wanted – your help."

"To break the enchantments?"

"Yes."

Mr Norrell considered this for a moment. "The hundredth anniversary of an enchantment is often most auspicious," he said. "There are several rites and procedures . . ."

"Thank you," said Strange, with more than a tinge of his old sarcastic manner, "but I believe I was hoping for something a little more immediate in its effect."

"The death of the enchanter puts an end to all such contracts and enchantments, but . . ."

"Ah, yes! Quite!" interrupted Strange, eagerly. "The death of the enchanter! I thought of it often in Venice. With all of English magic at my disposal there were so many ways I could have killed him. Sent him hurtling down from great heights. Burned him with bolts of lightning. Raised up mountains and crushed him beneath them. Had it been my freedom at stake, I would have certainly attempted it. But it was not my freedom – it was Arabella's – and if I had tried and failed – if I had been killed – then her fate would have been sealed forever. So I set to thinking some more. And I thought how there was one man in all the world – in all the worlds that ever were – who would know how to defeat my enemy. One man who could advise me what I ought to do. I realized the time had come to speak to him."

Mr Norrell looked more alarmed than ever. "Oh! But I must tell you that I no longer regard myself as your superior. My reading has been a great deal more extensive than yours, it is true, and I will give you what help I can, but I can offer you no security that I will be any more successful than you."

Strange frowned. "What? What are you talking about? I do not mean you! I mean John Uskglass. I want your help in summoning John Uskglass."

Mr Norrell breathed hard. The very air seemed to quiver as if a deep note had been sounded. He was aware, to an almost painful degree, of the darkness surrounding them, of the new stars above them and of the silence of the stopt clocks. It was one Great Black Moment going on for ever, pressing down upon him, suffocating him. And in that Moment it cost no effort to believe that John Uskglass was near – a mere spell away; the deep shadows in the far corners of the room were the folds of his robe; the smoke from the guttering candles was the raven mantling of his helm.

Strange, however, seemed oppressed by no such immortal fears. He leant forward a little, with an eager half-smile. "Come, Mr Norrell," he whispered. "It is very dull working for Lord Liverpool. You must feel it so? Let other magicians cast protection spells over cliffs and beaches. There will be plenty of them to do it soon! Let you and me do something extraordinary!"

Another silence.

"You are afraid," said Strange, drawing back displeased.

"Afraid!" burst out Norrell. "Of course I am afraid! It would be madness – absolute madness – to be any thing else! But that is not my objection. It will not work. Whatever you hope to gain by it, it will not work. Even if we succeeded in bringing him forth – which we might very well do, you and I together – he will not help you in the way you imagine. Kings do not satisfy idle curiosity – this King least of all."

"You call it idle curiosity . . . ?" began Strange.

"No, no!" said Norrell, interrupting hastily. "*I* do not. I merely represent to you how it will appear to *him*. What will he care about two lost women? You are thinking of John Uskglass as if he were an ordinary man. I mean a man like you or me. He was brought up and educated in Faerie. The ways of the *brugh* were natural to him – and most *brughs* contained captive Christians – he was one himself. It will not seem so extraordinary to him. He will not understand."

"Then I will explain it to him. Mr Norrell, I have changed England to save my wife. I have changed the world. I shall not flinch from summoning up one man; let him be as tremendous as he may. Come, sir! There is very little sense in arguing about it. The first thing is to bring him here. How do we begin?"

Mr Norrell sighed. "It is not like summoning any one else. There are difficulties peculiar to any magic involving John Usk-glass."

"Such as?"

"Well, for one thing we do not know what to call him. Spells of summoning require the magician to be most particular about names. None of the names by which we call John Uskglass were really his own. He was, as the histories tell, stolen away into Faerie, before he could be christened – and so he became the nameless child in the *brugh*. 'The nameless slave' was one of the ways in which he referred to himself. Of course the fairies gave him a name after their own fashion, but he cast that off when he returned to England. As for all his titles – the Raven King, the Black King, the King of the North – these are what other people called him, not what he called himself."

"Yes, yes!" declared Strange, impatiently. "I know all that! But surely John Uskglass was his true name?"

"Oh! By no means. That was the name of a young Norman aristocrat who died, I believe, in the summer of 1097. The King – our John Uskglass – claimed that man as his father, but many people have disputed whether they were really related at all. I do not suppose that this muddle of names and titles is accidental. The King knew that he would always draw the eyes of other magicians to him and so he protected himself from the nuisance of their magic by deliberately confusing their spells."

"So what ought I to do?" Strange snapped his fingers. "Advise me!"

Mr Norrell blinked his small eyes. He was unaccustomed to think so rapidly. "If we use an ordinary English spell of summoning – and I strongly advise that we do, as they cannot be bettered – then we can make the elements of the spell do the work of identification for us. We will need an envoy, a path and a handsel.[1] If we chuse tools that already know the King, and know him well, then it will not matter that we cannot name him properly, they will find him, bring him and bind him, without our help! Do you see?"

In spite of all his terror, he was growing more animated at the prospect of magic – new magic! – to be performed with Mr Strange.

"No," said Strange. "I do not see at all."

"This house is built upon the King's land, with stones from the King's abbey. A river runs by it – not more than two hundred yards from this room; that river has often borne the King in his royal barge upon its waters. In my kitchen-garden are a pear-tree and an apple-tree – the direct descendants of some pips spat out by the King when he sat one summer's evening in the Abbot's garden. Let the old abbey stones be our envoy; let the river be our path; let next year's apples and pears from those trees be our handsel. Then we may name him simply 'The King'. These stones, this river, those trees know none other!"

"Good," said Strange. "And what spell do you recommend? Are there any in Belasis?"

"Yes, three."

"Are they worth trying?"

"No, not really." Mr Norrell opened a drawer and drew out a piece of paper. "This is the best I know. I am not in the habit of

---

[1] These are the customary three elements of a traditional English summoning spell. The envoy finds the person summoned, the path brings him to the summoner and the handsel (or gift) binds him to come.

using summoning spells – but if I were, this is the one I would use."
He passed it to Strange.

It was covered with Mr Norrell's small, meticulous handwriting. At the top was written, "Mr Strange's spell of summoning."

"It is the one you used to summon Maria Absalom,"[2] explained Norrell. "I have made some amendments. I have omitted the *florilegium* which you copied word for word from Ormskirk. I have, as you know, no opinion of *florilegia* in general and this one seems particularly nonsensical. I have added an epitome of preservation and deliverance, and a skimmer of supplication – though I doubt that either will help us much in this case."[3]

"It is as much your work as mine now," observed Strange. There was no trace of rivalry or resentment in his voice.

"No, no," said Norrell. "All the fabric of it is yours. I have merely neatened the edges."

"Good! Then we are ready, are we not?"

"There is one more thing."

"What is it?"

"There are certain precautions that are necessary to secure Mrs Strange's safety," explained Mr Norrell.

---

[2] At the Shadow House in July 1809, Mr Segundus, Mr Honeyfoot and Henry Woodhope being present.

[3] "*Florilegium*", "epitome" and "skimmer" are all terms for parts of spells.

In the thirteenth and fourteenth centuries fairies in England were fond of adding to their magic, exhortations to random collections of Christian saints. Fairies were baffled by Christian doctrine, but they were greatly attracted to saints, whom they saw as powerful magical beings whose patronage it was useful to have. These exhortations were called *florilegia* (lit. cullings or gatherings of flowers) and fairies taught them to their Christian masters. When the Protestant religion took hold in England and saints fell out of favour, *florilegia* degenerated into meaningless collections of magical words and bits of other spells, thrown in by the magician in the hope that some of them might take effect.

An epitome is a highly condensed form of a spell inserted within another spell to strengthen or enlarge it. In this case an epitome of preservation and deliverance is intended to protect the magician from the person summoned. A skimmer is a sprinkling of words or charms (from a dialect word of Northern English, meaning to brighten or sparkle). A skimmer of supplication encourages the person summoned to aid the magician.

Strange cast a glance at him as if he thought it a little late in the day for Mr Norrell to be thinking of Arabella's safety, but Mr Norrell had hurried to a bookshelf and was busy delving in a large volume and did not notice.

"The spell is written in Chaston's *Liber Novus*. Ah, yes! Here it is! We must build a magical road and make a door so that Mrs Strange may come safely out of Faerie. Otherwise she might be trapped there for ever. It might take us centuries to find her."

"Oh, that!" said Strange. "I have done it already. And appointed a doorkeeper to meet her when she comes out. All is in readiness."

He took the merest stub of a candle, placed it in a candlestick and lit it.[4] Then he began to recite the spell. He named the abbey-stones as the envoy sent to seek the King. He named the river as the path the King was to come. He named next year's apples and pears from Mr Norrell's trees as the handsel the King was to receive. He named the moment of the flame's dying as the time when the King was to appear.

The candle guttered and went out . . .

. . . and in that moment . . .

. . . in that moment the room was full of ravens. Black wings filled the air like great hands gesturing, filled Strange's vision like a tumult of black flames. He was struck at from every side by wings and claws. The cawing and the croaking were deafening. Ravens battered walls, battered windows, battered Strange himself. He covered his head with his hands and fell to the floor. The din and strife of wings continued a little while longer.

Then, in the blink of an eye, they were gone and the room was silent.

---

[4] The last element of a successful summoning spell is temporal. The magician must somehow convey to the summoned person *when* he is meant to appear, otherwise (as Strange once observed) the summoned person might appear at any time and feel he had fulfilled his obligations. A candle stub is a very convenient device: the magician instructs the person summoned to appear when the flame goes out.

The candles had all been extinguished. Strange rolled on to his back, but for some moments he could do nothing but stare into the Darkness. "Mr Norrell?" he said at last.

No one answered.

In the pitch-black darkness he got to his feet. He succeeded in finding one of the library desks and felt about until his hand met with an upturned candle. He took his tinderbox from his pocket and lit it.

Raising it above his head, he saw that the room was in the last extremes of chaos and disorder. Not a book remained upon a shelf. Tables and library steps had been overturned. Several fine chairs had been reduced to firewood. A thick drift of raven feathers covered everything, as if a black snow had fallen.

Norrell was half-lying, half-sitting on the floor, his back against a desk. His eyes were open, but blank-looking. Strange passed the candle before his face. "Mr Norrell?" he said again.

In a dazed whisper, Norrell said, "I believe we may assume that we have his attention."

"I believe you are right, sir. Do you know what happened?"

Still in a whisper Norrell said, "The books all turned into ravens. I had my eye upon Hugh Pontifex's *The Fountain of the Heart* and I saw it change. He used it often, you know – that chaos of black birds. I have been reading about it since I was a boy. That I should live to see it, Mr Strange! That I should live to see it! It has a name in the *Sidhe* language, the language of his childhood, but the name is lost."[5] He suddenly seized Strange's hand. "Are the books safe?"

Strange picked up one from the floor. He shook the raven feathers off it and glanced at the title: *Seven Doors and Forty-two Keys* by Piers Russinol. He opened it and began to read at random. "*. . . and there you will find a strange country like a chessboard, where alternates barren rock with fruitful orchards, wastes of thorns with fields of*

---

[5] The chaos of ravens and wind is also described in the tale of the Newcastle glovemaker's child (Chapter 39, footnote 1).

bearded corn, water meadows with deserts. And in this country, the god of magicians, Thrice-Great Hermes, has set a guard upon every gate and every bridge: in one place a ram, in another place serpent . . . Does that sound right?" he asked doubtfully.

Mr Norrell nodded. He took out his pocket handkerchief and dabbed the blood from his face with it.

The two magicians sat upon the floor amid the books and feathers, and for a little while they said nothing at all. The world had shrunk to the breadth of a candle's light.

Finally, Strange said, "How near to us must he be in order to do magic like that?"

"John Uskglass? For aught I know he can do magic like that from a hundred worlds away – from the heart of Hell."

"Still it is worth trying to find out, is it not?"

"Is it?" asked Norrell.

"Well, for example, if we found he was close by, we could . . ." Strange considered a moment. "We could go to him."

"Very well," sighed Norrell. He did not sound or look very hopeful.

The first – and indeed only – requirement for spells of location is a silver dish of water. At Hurtfew Abbey Mr Norrell's dish had stood upon a little table in the corner of the room, but the table had been destroyed by the violence of the ravens and the dish was nowhere to be seen. They searched for a while and eventually found it in the fireplace, upside-down beneath a mess of raven feathers and damp, torn pages from books.

"We need water," said Norrell. "I always made Lucas get it from the river. Water that has travelled rapidly is best for location magic – and Hurtfew's river is quick-flowing even in summer. I will fetch it."

But Mr Norrell was not much in the habit of doing any thing for himself and it was a little while before he was out of the house. He stood on the lawn and stared up at stars he had never seen before. He did not feel as if he were inside a Pillar of Darkness in the middle of Yorkshire; he felt more as if the rest of the world had fallen away and he and Strange were left alone upon a solitary island or promontory. The idea distressed him a great deal less than one might have supposed. He had never much cared for the world and he bore its loss philosophically.

At the river's edge he knelt down among the frozen grasses to fill the dish with water. The unknown stars shone up at him from the depths. He stood up again (a little dizzy from the unaccustomed exertion) – and immediately he had an overwhelming sense of magic going on – much stronger than he had ever felt it before. If any one had asked him to describe what was happening, he would have said that all of Yorkshire was turning itself inside out. For a moment he could not think which direction the house lay in. He turned, stumbled and walked straight into Mr Strange, who for some reason was standing directly behind him. "I thought you were going to remain in the library!" he said in surprise.

Strange glared at him. "I did remain in the library! One moment I was reading Goubert's *Gatekeeper of Apollo*. The next moment I was here!"

"You did not follow me?" asked Norrell.

"No, of course not! What is happening? And what in God's name is taking you so long?"

"I could not find my greatcoat," said Norrell, humbly. "I did not know where Lucas had put it."

Strange raised one eye-brow, sighed and said, "I presume you experienced the same as me? Just before I was plucked up and brought here, there was a sensation like winds and waters and flames, all mixed together?"

"Yes," said Norrell.

"And a faint odour, as of wild herbs and mountainsides?"

"Yes," said Norrell.

"Fairy magic?"

"Oh!" said Norrell. "Undoubtedly! This is part of the same spell that keeps you here in Eternal Darkness." He looked around. "How extensive is it?"

"What?"

"The Darkness."

"Well, it is hard for me to know exactly since it moves around with me. But other people have told me that it is the size of the parish in Venice where I lived. Say half an acre?"

"Half an acre! Stay here!" Mr Norrell put the silver dish of water down upon the frozen ground. He walked off in the direction of the bridge. Soon all that was visible of him was his grey wig. In the starlight it resembled nothing so much as a little stone tortoise waddling away.

The world gave another twist and suddenly the two magicians were standing together on the bridge over the river at Hurtfew.

"What in the world . . . ?" began Strange.

"You see?" said Norrell, grimly. "The spell will not allow us to move too far from one another. It has gripped me too. I dare say there was some regrettable impreciseness in the fairy's magic. He has been careless. I dare say he named you as the English magician – or some such vague term. Consequently, his spell – meant only for you – now entraps any English magician who stumbles into it!"

"Ah!" said Strange. He said nothing more. There did not seem any thing to say.

Mr Norrell turned towards the house. "If nothing else, Mr Strange," he said, "this is an excellent illustration of the need for great preciseness about names in spells!"

Behind him Strange raised his eyes heavenward.

In the library they placed the silver dish of water on a table between them.

It was very odd but the discovery that he was now imprisoned in Eternal Darkness with Strange seemed to have raised Mr Norrell's spirits rather than otherwise. Cheerfully he reminded Strange that they still had not found a way to name John Uskglass and that this

was certain to be a great obstacle in finding him – by magic or any other means.

Strange, with his head propped up on his hands, stared at him gloomily. "Just try John Uskglass," he said.

So Norrell did the magic, naming John Uskglass as the person they sought. He divided the surface of the water into quarters with lines of glittering light. He gave each quarter a name: Heaven, Hell, Earth and Faerie. Instantly a speck of bluish light shone in the quarter that represented Earth.

"There!" said Strange, leaping up triumphantly. "You see, sir! Things are not always as difficult as you suppose."

Norrell tapped the surface of the quarter; the divisions disappeared. He redrew them, naming them afresh: "England, Scotland, Ireland, Elsewhere." The speck of light appeared in England. He tapped the quarter, redrew the divisions and examined the result. And on and on, he went, refining the magic. The speck glowed steadily.

He made a soft sound of exclamation.

"What is it?" asked Strange.

In a tone of wonder, Norrell said, "I think we may have succeeded after all! It says he is here. In Yorkshire!"

67

The hawthorn tree

February 1817

CHILDERMASS WAS CROSSING a lonely moorland. In the middle of the moor a misshapen hawthorn tree stood all alone and from the tree a man was hanging. He had been stripped of his coat and shirt, revealing in death what he had doubtless kept hidden during his life: that his skin bore a strange deformation. His chest, back and arms were covered with intricate blue marks, marks so dense that he was more blue than white.

As he rode up to the tree, Childermass wondered if the murderer had written upon the body as a joke. When he had been a sailor he had heard tales of countries where criminals's confessions were written on to their bodies by various horrible means before they were killed. From a distance the marks looked very like writing, but as he got closer he saw that they were beneath the skin.

He got down from his horse and swung the body round until it was facing him. The face was purple and swollen; the eyes were bulging and filled with blood. He studied it until he could discern in the distorted features a face he knew. "Vinculus," he said.

Taking out his pocket-knife, he cut the body down. Then he pulled off Vinculus's breeches and boots, and surveyed the body: the corpse of a forked animal on a barren, winter moor.

The strange marks covered every inch of skin – the only exceptions were his face, hands, private parts and the soles of his feet. He looked like a blue man wearing white gloves and a white mask. The more Childermass looked at him, the more he felt that the marks meant something. "This is the King's Letters," he said at last. "This is Robert Findhelm's book."

Just then it started to snow with a flurry of sharp, icy flakes. The wind blew harder.

Childermass thought of Strange and Norrell twenty miles away and he laughed out loud. What did it matter who read the books at Hurtfew? The most precious book of all lay naked and dead in the snow and the wind.

"So," he said, "it has fallen to me, has it? 'The greatest glory and the greatest burden given to any man in this Age.'"

At present the burden was more obvious than the glory. The book was in a most inconvenient form. He had no idea how long Vinculus had been dead or how soon he might begin to rot. What to do? He could take his chances and throw the body over his horse. But a freshly hanged corpse would be difficult to explain to any one he met on the road. He could hide the body and go and fetch a horse and cart. How long would it take? And supposing that in the meantime someone found the body and took it. There were doctors in York who would pay money for corpses and no questions asked.

"I could cast a spell of concealment," he thought.

A spell of concealment would certainly hide it from human eyes, but there were dogs, foxes and crows to consider. They could not be deceived by any magic Childermass knew. The book had been eaten once already. He had no wish to risk it happening a second time.

The obvious thing was to make a copy, but his memorandum book, pen and ink were lying upon the table in the drawing-room in the Darkness of Hurtfew Abbey. So what then? He could scratch a copy on to the frozen earth with a stick – but that was no better than what he had already. If only there had been some trees, he might have been able to strip the bark and burn some wood and write upon the bark with the ashes. But there was only this one twisted hawthorn.

He looked at his pocket-knife. Perhaps he ought to copy the book on to his own body? There were several things in favour of this plan. First, who was to say that the positioning upon Vinculus's body did not carry some meaning with it? The closer to the head, the more important the text? Any thing was possible. Second, it would make the book both secret and secure. He would not have to worry about any one stealing it. Whether he intended to shew it to Strange or Norrell, he had not yet decided.

But the writing upon Vinculus's body was both dense and intricate. Even if he were able to force his knife to mimic all those delicate dots, circles and flourishes exactly – which he doubted – he would have to cut quite deep to make the marks permanent.

He took off his greatcoat and his ordinary coat. He undid the wrist of his shirt and rolled up his sleeve. As an experiment, he cut one of the symbols on the inside of Vinculus's arm into the same place upon his own arm. The result was not promising. There was so much blood that it was difficult to see what he was doing and the pain made him feel faint.

"I can afford to lose some blood in this cause, but there is so much writing – it would surely kill me. Besides, how in the world could I copy what is written on his back? I will put him over my horse and if any one challenges me – well, I will fire at them if needs be. That is a plan. It is not a very good plan, but it is a plan." He put on his coat and his greatcoat again.

Brewer had wandered off a little way and was cropping at some dry grasses, which the wind had exposed. Childermass walked over to him. Out of his valise he took a length of strong rope and the box containing his pistols. He rammed a ball into each pistol and primed them with powder.

He turned back to make sure that all was right with the body. Someone – a man – was bending over it. He shoved the pistols into the pockets of his greatcoat and began to run, calling out.

The man wore black boots and a black travelling coat. He was half-stooping, half-kneeling on the snowy ground beside Vinculus. For a brief moment Childermass thought it was Strange – but this man was not quite so tall and was somewhat slighter in figure. His dark clothes were clearly expensive and looked fashionable. Yet his straight, dark hair was longer than any fashionable gentleman would have worn it; it gave him something of the look of a Methodist preacher or a Romantic poet. "I know him," thought Childermass. "He is a magician. I know him well. Why can I not think what his name is?"

Out loud he said, "The body is mine, sir! Leave it be!"

The man looked up. "Yours, John Childermass?" he said with a mildly ironic air, "I thought it was mine."

It was a curious thing but despite his clothes and his air of cool authority, his speech sounded uncouth – even to Childermass's ears. His accent was northern – of that there was no doubt – but Childermass did not recognize it. It might have been Northumbrian, but it was tinged with something else – the speech of the cold countries that lie over the North Sea and – which seemed more extraordinary still – there was more than a hint of French in his pronunciation.

"Well, you are mistaken." Childermass raised his pistols. "I will fire upon you, if I have to, sir. But I would much rather not. Leave the body to me and go on your way."

The man said nothing. He regarded Childermass a moment longer and then, as if he had become bored with him, turned back to his examination of the body.

Childermass looked round for a horse or a carriage – some indication of how the man had got here. There was nothing. In all the wide moor there were only the two men, the horse, the corpse and the hawthorn tree.

"Yet there must be a carriage somewhere," he thought. "There is not so much as a spot of mud on his coat and none on his boots. He looks as if he has just come fresh from his valet. Where are his servants?"

This was a discomfiting thought. Childermass doubted he would have much difficulty in overpowering this pale, thin, poetical-looking person, but a coachman and two or three stout footmen would be another matter entirely.

"Does the land hereabouts belong to you, sir?" he asked.

"Yes."

"And where is your horse? Where is your carriage? Where are your servants?"

"I have no horse, John Childermass. I have no carriage. And only one of my servants is here."

"Where?"

Without troubling to look up, the man raised his arm and pointed a thin, pale finger.

Childermass looked behind him in confusion. There was no one there. Just the wind blowing across the snowy tussocks. What did he mean? Was it the wind or the snow? He had heard of mediaeval magicians who claimed these and other natural forces as servants. Then comprehension dawned on him. "What? No, sir, you are mistaken! I am not your servant!"

"You boasted of it, not three days ago," said the man.

There was only one person who had any claim to be Childermass's master. Was this, in some mysterious fashion, Norrell? An aspect of Norrell? In the past, magicians had sometimes appeared in different forms according to the qualities which made up their character. Childermass tried to think what part of Gilbert Norrell's character might suddenly manifest as a pale, handsome man with a peculiar accent and an air of great authority. He reflected that strange things had happened recently, but nothing as queer as that. "Sir!" he cried. "I have warned you! Let the body be!"

The man bent closer to Vinculus's corpse. He plucked something out of his own mouth – a tiny pearl of light faintly tinged with rose and silver. He placed it in Vinculus's mouth. The corpse shivered. It was not like the shudder of a sick man, nor yet like the shiver of a healthy one; it was like the shiver of a bare birch wood as spring breathes upon it.

"Move away from the body, sir!" cried Childermass. "I will not ask you again!"

The man did not even trouble to look up. He passed the tip of his finger over the body as if he were writing upon it.

Childermass aimed the right-hand pistol somewhat wide of the man's left shoulder, intending to frighten him away. The pistol fired perfectly; a cloud of smoke and a smell of gunpowder rose from the pan; sparks and more smoke disgorged from the barrel.

But the lead refused to fly. It hung in the air as if in a dream. It twisted, swelled and changed shape. Suddenly it put forth wings, turned into a lapwing and flew away. In the same instant Childermass's mind grew as quiet and fixed as a stone.

The man moved his finger over Vinculus and all the patterns and symbols flowed and swirled as if they had been written upon water. He did this for a while and when he was satisfied, he stopped and stood up.

"You are wrong," he said to Childermass. "He is not dead." He came and stood directly before Childermass. With as little ceremony as a parent who cleans something from a child's face, the man licked his finger and daubed a sort of symbol on each of Childermass's eye-lids, on his lips and over his heart. Then he gave Childermass's left hand a knock, so that the pistol fell to the ground. He drew another symbol on Childermass's palm. He turned and seemed about to depart, but glancing back and apparently as an afterthought, he made a final gesture over the cut in Childermass's face.

The wind shook the falling snow and made it spin and twist about. Brewer made a sound as if something had disturbed him. Briefly, the snow and the shadows seemed to form a picture of a thin, dark man in a greatcoat and boots. The next moment the illusion was gone.

* * *

Childermass blinked. "Where am I wandering to?" he asked himself irritably. "And what am I doing talking to myself? This is no time to be wool-gathering!" There was a smell of gunpowder. One of his pistols lay in the snow. When he picked it up it was still warm as if he had recently discharged it. That was odd, but he had no time to be properly surprized because a sound made him look up.

Vinculus was getting up off the ground. He did it clumsily, in jerks, like something new-born that has not yet discovered what its limbs are for. He stood for a moment, his body swaying and his head twitching from side to side. Then he opened his mouth and screamed at Childermass. But the sound that came out of his mouth was no sound at all; it was the emptied skin of sound without flesh or bones.

It was, without a doubt, the strangest thing Childermass had ever seen: a naked blue man with blood-engorged eyes, silently screaming in the middle of a snow-covered moor. It was such a very extraordinary situation that for some moments he was at a loss to know what to do. He wondered if he ought to try the spell called Gilles de Marston's Restoration of Flown Tranquillity, but on further consideration, he thought of something better. He took out the claret that Lucas had given him and shewed it to Vinculus. Vinculus grew calmer and fixed his gaze upon it.

A quarter of an hour later they were seated together on a tussock beneath the hawthorn, breakfasting on the claret and a handful of apples. Vinculus had put on his shirt and breeches and was wrapped in a blanket that belonged to Brewer. He had recovered from his hanging with surprizing rapidity. His eyes were still blood-shot, but they were less alarming to look at than before. His speech was hoarse and liable to be interrupted at any moment by fits of violent coughing, but it was comprehensible.

"Someone tried to hang you," Childermass told him. "I do not know who or why. Luckily I found you in time and cut you down." As he said this, he felt a faint question disturb his thoughts.

In his mind's eye he saw Vinculus, dead on the ground, and a thin, white hand, pointing. Who had that been? The memory slipped away from him. "So tell me," he continued, "how does a man become a book? I know that your father was given the book by Robert Findhelm and that he was supposed to take the book to a man in the Derbyshire hills."

"The last man in England who could read the King's letters," croaked Vinculus.

"But your father did not deliver the book. Instead he ate it in the drinking contest in Sheffield."

Vinculus took another drink from the bottle and wiped his mouth with the back of his hand. "Four years later I was born and the King's Letters were written on my infant body. When I was seventeen, I went to look for the man in the Derbyshire hills – he lived just long enough for me to find him out. That was a night indeed! A starlit, summer night, when the King's Book and the last Reader of the King's Letters met and drank wine together! We sat upon the brow of the hill at Bretton, looking out over England, and he read England's destiny from me."

"And that was the prophecy which you told to Strange and Norrell?"

Vinculus, who had been seized with a fit of coughing, nodded. When he was able to speak again, he added, "And also to the nameless slave."

"Who?" said Childermass with a frown. "Who is that?"

"A man," replied Vinculus. "It has been part of my task to bear his story. He began as a slave. Will soon be a king. His true name was denied him at his birth."

Childermass pondered this description for a moment or two. "You mean John Uskglass?" he said.

Vinculus made a noise of exasperation. "If I meant John Uskglass, I would say so! No, no. He is not a magician at all. He is a man like any other." He thought for a moment. "But black," he added.

"I have never heard of him," said Childermass.

Vinculus looked at him with amusement. "Of course not. You have lived your life in the Mayfair magician's pocket. You only know what he knows."

"So?" said Childermass, stung. "That is not so very trifling, is it? Norrell is a clever man – and Strange another. They have their faults, as other men do, but their achievements are still remarkable. Make no mistake; I am John Uskglass's man. Or would be, if he were here. But you must admit that the restoration of English magic is their work, not his."

"Their work!" scoffed Vinculus. "Theirs? Do you still not understand? They *are* the spell John Uskglass is doing. That is all they have ever been. And he is doing it now!"

68

"Yes."

February 1817

IN THE SILVER dish of water the speck of light flickered and disappeared.

"What!" cried Strange. "What has happened? Quickly, Mr Norrell!"

Norrell tapped the water's surface, redrew the lines of light and whispered a few words, but the water in the dish remained dark and still. "He is gone," he said.

Strange closed his eyes.

"It is very odd," continued Norrell, in a tone of wonder. "What do you suppose he was doing in Yorkshire?"

"Oh!" cried Strange. "I dare say he came here on purpose to make me mad!" With a cry of mingled rage and self-pity he demanded, "Why will he not attend to me? After everything I have done, why does he not care enough to look at me? To speak to me?"

"He is an old magician and an old king," answered Norrell briefly. "Two things that are not easily impressed."

"All magicians long to astonish their masters. I have certainly astonished *you*. I wanted to do the same to him."

"But your real purpose is to free Mrs Strange from the enchantment," Norrell reminded him.

"Yes, yes. That is right," said Strange, irritably. "Of course it is. Only . . ." He did not finish his thought.

There was a silence and then Norrell, who had been looking thoughtful, said, "You mentioned magicians always wishing to impress their masters. I am reminded of something which happened in 1156 . . ."

Strange sighed.

". . . In that year John Uskglass suffered some strange malady – as he did from time to time. When he recovered, a celebration was held at his house in Newcastle. Kings and queens brought presents of immense value and splendour – gold, rubies, ivory, rare spices. Magicians brought magical things – clouds of revelation, singing trees, keys to mystical doors and so on – each one trying to outdo the other. The King thanked them all in the same grave manner. Last of all came the magician, Thomas Godbless. His hands were empty. He had no gift. He lifted his head and said, 'Lord, I bring you the trees and hills. I bring you the wind and the rain.' The kings and queens, the great lords and ladies and the other magicians were amazed at his impudence. It appeared to them as if he had done nothing at all. But for the first time since he had been ill, the King smiled."

Strange considered this. "Well," he said. "I am afraid I am with the kings and queens. I can make nothing of it. Where did you get this tale?"

"It is in Belasis's *Instructions*. In my youth I studied the *Instructions* with a passionate devotion and I found this passage particularly intriguing. I concluded that Godbless had somehow persuaded the trees and the hills and so on to greet John Uskglass in some mystical fashion, to bow down before him as it were. I was pleased to have understood something that Belasis had not, but I thought no more about it – I had no use for such magic. Years later I discovered a spell in Lanchester's *The Language of Birds*. Lanchester got it from an older book, now lost. He admitted that he did not know what it was for, but I believe it is the spell Godbless used – or one very like it. If you are serious in your intention of talking to John Uskglass, suppose we cast it now? Suppose we ask England to greet him?"

"What will that achieve?" asked Strange.

"Achieve? Nothing! At least, nothing directly. But it will remind John Uskglass of the bonds between him and England. And it will shew a sort of respectfulness on our part, which is surely more in keeping with the behaviour a king expects from his subjects."

Strange shrugged. "Well," he said. "I have nothing better to suggest. Where is your copy of *The Language of Birds*?"

He looked about the room. Every book lay where it had fallen the moment it had ceased to be a raven. "How many books are there?" he asked.

"Four or five thousand," said Norrell.

The magicians took a candle each and began to search.

The gentleman with the thistle-down hair strode rapidly along the walled lane which led to the village of Starecross. Stephen stumbled after him, on his way from one death to another.

England seemed to him to be nothing but horrors and misery now. The very shapes of the trees were like frozen screams. A bunch of dry leaves hung from a branch and rattled in the wind – that was Vinculus upon the hawthorn tree. The corpse of a rabbit ripped apart by a fox lay upon the path – that was Lady Pole, soon to be killed by the gentleman.

Death upon death, horror upon horror; and there was nothing Stephen could do to prevent any of it.

At Starecross Hall Lady Pole was seated at a desk in her sitting-room, writing furiously. The desk was scattered with sheets of paper, all covered with handwriting.

There was a knock and Mr Segundus entered the room. "I beg your pardon!" he said. "Might I inquire? Do you write to Sir Walter?"

She shook her head. "These letters are to Lord Liverpool and the editor of *The Times*!"

"Indeed?" said Mr Segundus. "Well, I have, in fact, just

finished a letter of my own – to Sir Walter – but nothing, I am sure, will delight him so much as a line or two in your ladyship's own hand, assuring him that you are well and disenchanted."

"But your own letter will do that. I am sorry, Mr Segundus, but while my dear Mrs Strange and poor Stephen remain in the power of that wicked spirit, I can spare no thought for any thing else! You must send these letters off straight away! And when they are done I shall write to the Archbishop of Canterbury and the Prince Regent!"

"You do not think perhaps that Sir Walter is the proper person to apply to such exalted gentlemen? Surely . . . ?"

"No, indeed!" she cried, all indignation. "I have no notion of asking people to perform services for me which I can do perfectly well for myself. I do not intend to go, in the space of one hour, from the helplessness of enchantment to another sort of helplessness! Besides, Sir Walter will not be able to explain half so well as me the true hideousness of Mr Norrell's crimes!"

Just then another person entered the room – Mr Segundus's manservant, Charles, who came to say that something very odd was happening in the village. The tall black man – the person who had originally brought her ladyship to Starecross – had appeared with a silver diadem upon his head, and with him was a gentleman with thistle-down hair, wearing a bright green coat.

"Stephen! Stephen and the enchanter!" cried Lady Pole. "Quickly, Mr Segundus! Summon up all your powers! We depend upon you to defeat him! You must free Stephen as you freed me!"

"Defeat a fairy!" exclaimed Mr Segundus in horror. "Oh, but no! I could not. It would take a far greater magician . . ."

"Nonsense!" she cried, with shining eyes. "Remember what Childermass told you. Your years of study have prepared you! You have simply to try!"

"But I do not know . . ." he began, helplessly.

But it did not much matter what he knew. The moment she

finished speaking she ran from the room – and, since he considered himself bound to protect her, he was obliged to run after her.

At Hurtfew the two magicians had found *The Language of Birds* – it lay open on the table at the page where the fairy spell was printed. But the problem of finding a name for John Uskglass remained. Norrell sat crouched over the silver dish of water doing location spells. They had already run through all the titles and names they could think of, and the location spell did not recognize a single one. The water in the silver dish remained dark and featureless.

"What of his fairy name?" said Strange.

"That is lost," replied Norrell.

"Did we try the King of the North yet?"

"Yes."

"Oh." Strange thought for a moment and then said, "What was that curious appellation you mentioned before? Something you said he called himself? The nameless something?"

"The nameless slave?"

"Yes. Try that."

Norrell looked very doubtful. But he cast the spell for the nameless slave. Instantly a speck of bluish light appeared. He proceeded and the nameless slave proved to be in Yorkshire – in very much the same place where John Uskglass had appeared before.

"There!" exclaimed Strange, triumphantly. "All our anxiety was quite needless. He is still here."

"But I do not think that is the same person," interrupted Norrell. "It looks different somehow."

"Mr Norrell, do not be fanciful, I beg you! Who else could it be? How many nameless slaves can there possibly be in Yorkshire?"

This was so very reasonable a question that Mr Norrell offered no further objections.

"And now for the magic itself," said Strange. He picked up the book and began to recite the spell. He addressed the trees of

England; the hills of England; the sunlight, water, birds, earth and stones. He addressed them all, one after the other, and exhorted them to place themselves in the hands of the nameless slave.

Stephen and the gentleman came to the packhorse bridge that led into Starecross.

The village was quiet; there was hardly any one to be seen. In a doorway a girl in a print-gown and woollen shawl was tipping milk from wooden pails into cheese-vats. A man in gaiters and a broad-brimmed hat came down a lane at the side of the house; a dog trotted at his side. When the man and the dog rounded the corner, the girl and the man greeted each other smilingly and the dog barked his pleasure. It was the sort of simple, domestic scene that would ordinarily have delighted Stephen, but in his present mood he could only feel a chill; if the man had reached out and struck the girl – or strangled her – he would have felt no surprise.

The gentleman was already on the packhorse bridge. Stephen followed him and . . .

. . . and everything changed. The sun came out from behind a cloud; it shone through the winter trees; hundreds of small, bright patches of sunlight appeared. The world became a kind of puzzle or labyrinth. It was like the superstition which says that one must not walk upon lines between flag stones – or the strange magic called the Doncaster Squares which is performed upon a board like a chessboard. Suddenly everything had meaning. Stephen hardly dared take another step. If he did so – if, for example, he stepped into *that* shadow or *that* spot of light, then the world might be forever altered.

"Wait!" he thought, wildly. "I am not ready for this! I have not considered. I do not know what to do!"

But it was too late. He looked up.

The bare branches against the sky were a writing and, though he did not want to, he could read it. He saw that it was a question put to him by the trees.

"Yes," he answered them.

Their age and their knowledge belonged to him.

Beyond the trees was a high, snow-covered ridge, like a line drawn across the sky. Its shadow was blue upon the snow before it. It embodied all kinds of cold and hardness. It hailed Stephen as a King it had long missed. At a word from Stephen it would tumble down and crush his enemies. It asked Stephen a question.

"Yes," he told it.

Its scorn and strength were his for the taking.

The black beck beneath the packhorse bridge sang its question to him.

"Yes," he said.

The earth said . . .

"Yes," he said.

The rooks and magpies and redwings and chaffinches said . . .

"Yes," he said.

The stones said . . .

"Yes," said Stephen. "Yes. Yes. Yes."

Now all of England lay cupped in his black palm. All Englishmen were at his mercy. Now every insult could be revenged. Now every injury to his poor mother could be paid back a thousand-fold. All of England could be laid waste in a moment. He could bring houses crashing down upon the occupants' heads. He could command hills to fall and valleys to close their lips. He could summon up centaurs, snuff out stars, steal the moon from the sky. Now. Now. Now.

Now came Lady Pole and Mr Segundus, running down from the Hall in the pale winter sunlight. Lady Pole looked at the gentleman with eyes ablaze with hatred. Poor Mr Segundus was all confusion and dismay.

The gentleman turned to Stephen and said something. Stephen could not hear him: the hills and the trees spoke too loud. But, "Yes," he said.

The gentleman laughed gaily and raised his hands to cast spells on Lady Pole.

Stephen closed his eyes. He spoke a word to the stones of the packhorse bridge.

Yes, said the stones. The bridge reared up like a raging horse and cast the gentleman into the beck.

Stephen spoke a word to the beck.

Yes, said the beck. It grasped the gentleman in a grip of iron and bore him swiftly away.

Stephen was aware that Lady Pole spoke to him, that she tried to catch hold of his arm; he saw Mr Segundus's pale, astonished face, saw him say something; but he had no time to answer them. Who knew how long the world would consent to obey him? He leapt down from the bridge and ran along the bank.

The trees seemed to greet him as he ran past; they spoke of old alliances and reminded him of times gone by. The sunlight called him King and spoke its pleasure at finding him here. He had no time to tell them he was not the person they imagined.

He came to a place where the land rose steeply upon either side of the beck – a deep dale in the moor, a place where millstones were quarried. Scattered around the sides of the dale were great, round, hewn stones, each of them half the height of a man.

The surface of the beck seethed and boiled where the gentleman was imprisoned. Stephen knelt upon a flat stone and leant over the water. "I am sorry," he said. "You intended nothing but kindness, I know."

The gentleman's hair streamed out like silver snakes in the dark water. His face was a terrible sight. In his fury and hatred he began to lose his resemblance to humankind: his eyes grew further apart, there was fur upon his face and his lips rolled back from his teeth in a snarl.

A voice inside Stephen's mind said: "If you kill me, you will never know your name!"

"I am the nameless slave," said Stephen. "That is all I have ever been – and today I am content to be nothing more."

He spoke a word to the millstones. They flew up in the air and flung themselves down upon the gentleman. He spoke to the boulders and rocks; they did the same. The gentleman was old beyond telling, and very strong. Long after his bones and flesh must have been crushed to pieces, Stephen could feel whatever was left of him struggling to bind itself back together by magic. So Stephen spoke to the stony shoulders of the dale and asked them to help him. Earth and rock crumbled; it heaped itself on top of the millstones and the rocks until there was a hill standing there as high as the sides of the dale.

For years Stephen had felt as if a pane of dirty, grey glass hung between him and the world; the moment that the last spark of the gentleman's life was extinguished, the pane shattered. Stephen stood a moment, gasping for breath.

But his allies and servants were growing doubtful. There was a question in the minds of the hills and the trees. They began to know that he was not the person they had taken him for – that all this was borrowed glory.

One by one he felt them withdraw. As the last one left him, he fell, empty and insensible, to the ground.

In Padua the Greysteels had already breakfasted and were gathered together in the little sitting-room on the first floor. They were not in the best of spirits this morning. There had been a disagreement. Dr Greysteel had taken to smoking a pipe indoors – a thing to which Flora and Aunt Greysteel were very much opposed. Aunt Greysteel had tried to argue him out of it, but Dr Greysteel had proved stubborn. Pipe-smoking was a pastime he was particularly fond of and he felt that he ought to be permitted an indulgence or two, to make up for their never going anywhere any more. Aunt Greysteel said that he ought to smoke his pipe outside. Dr Greysteel replied that he could not because it was raining. It was difficult to smoke a pipe in the rain – the rain made the tobacco wet.

So he was smoking the pipe and Aunt Greysteel was coughing; and Flora, who was disposed to blame herself, glanced at each from time to time with an unhappy expression. Things had gone on like this for about an hour when Dr Greysteel happened to look up and exclaimed in amazement, "My head is black! Completely black!"

"Well, what do you expect if you smoke a pipe?" replied his sister.

"Papa," asked Flora, putting down her work in alarm, "what do you mean?"

Dr Greysteel was staring at the mirror – the very same mirror which had so mysteriously appeared when day had turned to night and Strange had come to Padua. Flora went and stood behind his chair, so that she could see what he saw. Her exclamation of surprize brought Aunt Greysteel to join her.

Where Dr Greysteel's head ought to have been in the mirror was a dark spot that moved and changed shape. The spot grew in size until gradually it began to resemble a figure fleeing down an immense corridor towards them. The figure drew closer, and they could see it was a woman. Several times she looked back as she ran, as if in fear of something behind her.

"What has frightened her to make her run like that?" wondered Aunt Greysteel. "Lancelot, can you see any thing? Does any one chase after her? Oh, poor lady! Lancelot, is there any thing you can do?"

Dr Greysteel went to the mirror, placed his hand upon it and pushed, but the surface was as hard and smooth as mirrors usually are. He hesitated for a moment, as though debating with himself whether to try a more violent approach.

"Be careful, papa!" cried Flora in alarm. "You must not break it!"

The woman within the mirror drew nearer. For a moment she appeared directly behind it and they could see the elaborate embroidery and beading of her gown; then she mounted up upon

985

the frame as on a step. The surface of the mirror became softer, like a dense cloud or mist. Flora hastened to push a chair against the wall so that the lady might more easily descend. Three pairs of hands were raised to catch her, to pull her away from whatever it was that frightened her.

She was perhaps thirty or thirty-two years of age. She was dressed in a gown the colour of autumn, but she was breathless and a little disordered from running. With a frantic look she surveyed the unknown room, the unknown faces, the unfamiliar look of everything. "Is this Faerie?" she asked.

"No, madam," answered Flora.

"Is it England?"

"No, madam." Tears began to course down Flora's face. She put her hand on her breast to steady herself. "This is Padua. In Italy. My name is Flora Greysteel. It is a name quite unknown to you, but I have waited for you here at your husband's desire. I promised him I would meet you here."

"Is Jonathan here?"

"No, madam."

"You are Arabella Strange," said Dr Greysteel in amazement.

"Yes," she said.

"Oh, my dear!" exclaimed Aunt Greysteel, one hand flying to cover her mouth and the other to her heart. "Oh, my dear!" Then both hands fluttered around Arabella's face and shoulders. "Oh, my dear!" she exclaimed for the third time. She burst into tears and embraced Arabella.

Stephen awoke. He was lying on the frozen ground in a narrow dale. The sunlight was gone. It was grey and cold. The dale was choked with a great wall of millstones and boulders and earth – an eerie tomb. The wall had dammed the beck, but a little water still seeped through and was now spreading across the ground. Stephen's crown, sceptre and orb lay a little distance away in pools of dirty water. Wearily he stood up.

In the distance he could hear someone calling, "Stephen! Stephen!" He thought it was Lady Pole.

"I cast off the name of my captivity," he said. "It is gone." He picked up the crown, the sceptre and orb, and began to walk.

He had no notion of where he was going. He had killed the gentleman and he had allowed the gentleman to kill Vinculus. He could never go home – if home it had been in the first place. What would an English judge and jury say to a black man who was a murderer twice over? Stephen had done with England and England had done with him. He walked on.

After a while it seemed to him that the landscape was no longer as English as it had been. The trees that now surrounded him were immense, ancient things, their boughs twice the thickness of a man's body and curved into strange, fantastical shapes. Though it was winter and the briars were bare, a few roses still bloomed here, blood-red and snow-white.

England lay behind him. He did not regret it. He did not look back. He walked on.

He came to a long, low hill, and in the middle of the hill was an opening. It was more like a mouth than a door, yet it did not have an evil look. Someone was standing there, just within the opening, waiting for him. "I know this place," he thought. "It is Lost-hope! But how can that be?"

It was not simply that the house had become a hill, everything seemed to have undergone a revolution. The wood was suddenly possessed of a spirit of freshness, of innocence. The trees no longer threatened the traveller. Between their branches were glints of a serene winter sky of coldest blue. Here and there shone the pure light of a star – though whether they were stars of morning or stars of evening he could no longer remember. He looked around for the ancient bones and rusting armour – those ghastly emblems of the gentleman's bloodthirsty nature. To his surprize he found that they were everywhere – beneath his feet, stuffed into hollows of the tree roots, tangled up with briars and brambles. But they were in a far more advanced state of decay than he remembered; they were moss-covered, rust-eaten and crumbling into dust. In a little while nothing would be left of them.

The figure within the opening was a familiar one; he had often attended the balls and processions at Lost-hope. But he too was changed; his features had become more fairy-like; his eyes more glittering; his eye-brows more extravagant. His hair curled tightly like the fleece of a young lamb or like young ferns in spring, and there was a light dusting of fur upon his face. He looked older, yet at the same time more innocent. "Welcome!" he cried.

"Is this truly Lost-hope?" asked the person who had once been Stephen Black.

"Yes, grandfather."

"But I do not understand. Lost-hope was a great mansion. This is . . ." The person who had once been Stephen Black paused. "I do not have a word for what this is."

"This is a *brugh*, grandfather! This is the world beneath the hill. Lost-hope is changing! The old King is dead. The new King approaches! And at his approach the world sheds its sorrow. The sins of the old King dissolve like morning mist! The world assumes the character of the new. His virtues fill up the wood and the wold!"

"The new King?" The person who had once been Stephen Black looked down at his own hands. In one was the sceptre and in the other the orb.

The fairy smiled at him, as if wondering why he should be surprized. "The changes you wrought here far surpass any thing you did in England."

They passed through the opening into a great hall. The new King sat down upon an ancient throne. A crowd of people came and gathered around him. Some faces he knew, others were unfamiliar to him, but he suspected that this was because he had never seen them as they truly were before. For a long time he was silent.

"This house," he told them at last, "is disordered and dirty. Its inhabitants have idled away their days in pointless pleasures and in celebrations of past cruelties – things that ought not to be remembered, let alone celebrated. I have often observed it and often regretted it. All these faults, I shall in time set right."[1]

The moment the spell took effect a great wind blew through Hurtfew. Doors banged in the Darkness; black curtains billowed out in black rooms; black papers were swept from black tables and made to dance. A bell – taken from the original Abbey long ago and since forgotten – rang frantically in a little turret above the stables.

In the library, visions appeared in mirrors and clock-faces. The wind blew the curtains apart and visions appeared in the windows too. They followed thick and fast upon one another, almost too rapid to comprehend. Mr Norrell saw some that seemed familiar: the shattered branch of holly in his own library at Hanover-square; a raven flying in front of St Paul's Cathedral so that for a moment it was the living embodiment of the Raven-in-Flight; the great black bed in the inn at Wansford. But others were entirely strange to him: a hawthorn tree; a man crucified upon a thicket; a crude wall of stones in a narrow valley; an unstoppered bottle floating on a wave.

Then all the visions disappeared, except for one. It filled one of the tall library windows, but what it was a vision *of*, Mr Norrell was at a loss to know. It resembled a large, perfectly round, black stone of almost impossible brilliance and glossiness, set into a thin ring of rough stone and mounted upon what appeared to be a

---

[1] A surprizing number of kings and princes of Faerie have been human. John Uskglass, Stephen Black and Alessandro Simonelli are just three. Fairies are, by and large, irredeemably indolent. Though they are fond of high rank, honours and riches, they detest the hard work of government.

black hillside. Mr Norrell thought of it as a hillside because it bore some resemblance to a moor where the heather is all burnt and charred – except that this hillside was not the black of burnt things, it was the black of wet silk or well-shone leather. Suddenly the stone did something – it moved or spun. The movement was almost too quick to grasp but Mr Norrell was left with the sickening impression that it had blinked.

The wind died away. The bell above the stable ceased to ring.

Mr Norrell breathed a long sigh of relief that it was over. Strange was standing with his arms crossed, deep in thought, staring at the floor.

"What did you make of that?" asked Mr Norrell. "The last was by far the worst. I thought for a moment it was an eye."

"It was an eye," said Strange.

"But what could it belong to? Some horror or monster, I suppose! Most unsettling!"

"It was monstrous," agreed Strange. "Though not quite in the way you imagine. It was a raven's eye."

"A raven's eye! But it filled the whole window!"

"Yes. Either the raven was immensely large or . . ."

"Or?" quavered Mr Norrell.

Strange gave a short, uncheerful laugh. "Or we were ridiculously small! Pleasant, is it not, to see oneself as others see one? I said I wanted John Uskglass to look at me and I think, for a moment he did. Or at least one of his lieutenants did. And in that moment you and I were smaller than a raven's eye and presumably as insignificant. Speaking of John Uskglass, I do not suppose that we know where he is?"

Mr Norrell sat down at the silver dish and began to work. After five minutes or so of patient labour, he said, "Mr Strange! There is no sign of John Uskglass – nothing at all. But I have looked for Lady Pole and Mrs Strange. Lady Pole is in Yorkshire and Mrs Strange is in Italy. There is no shadow of their presence in Faerie. Both are completely disenchanted!"

There was a silence. Strange turned away abruptly.

"It is more than a little odd," continued Mr Norrell in a tone of wonder. "We have done everything we set out to do, but *how* we did it, I do not pretend to understand. I can only suppose that John Uskglass simply saw what was amiss and stretched out his hand to put it right! Unfortunately, his obligingness did not extend to freeing us from the Darkness. That remains."

Mr Norrell paused. This then was his destiny! – a destiny full of fear, horror and desolation! He sat patiently for a few moments in expectation of falling prey to some or all of these terrible emotions, but was forced to conclude that he felt none of them. Indeed, what seemed remarkable to him now were the long years he had spent in London, away from his library, at the beck and call of the Ministers and the Admirals. He wondered how he had borne it.

"I am glad I did not recognize the raven's eye for what it was," he said cheerfully, "or I believe I would have been a good deal frightened!"

"Indeed, sir," said Strange hoarsely. "You were fortunate there! And I believe I am cured of wanting to be looked at! Henceforth John Uskglass is welcome to ignore me for as long as he pleases."

"Oh, indeed!" agreed Mr Norrell. "You know, Mr Strange, you really should try to rid yourself of the habit of wishing for things. It is a dangerous thing in a magician!" He began a long and not particularly interesting story about a fourteenth-century magician in Lancashire who had often made idle wishes and had caused no end of inconvenience in the village where he lived, accidentally turning the cows into clouds and the cooking pots into ships, and causing the villagers to speak in colours rather than words – and other such signs of magical chaos.

At first Strange barely answered him and such replies as he made were random and illogical. But gradually he appeared to listen with more attention, and he spoke in his usual manner.

Mr Norrell had many talents, but penetration into the hearts of men and women was not one of them. Strange did not speak of the restoration of his wife, so Mr Norrell imagined that it could not have affected him very deeply.

69

Strangites and Norrellites

February–spring 1817

CHILDERMASS RODE AND Vinculus walked at his side. All around them was spread the wide expanse of snow-covered moor, appearing, with all its various hummocks and hills, like a vast feather mattress. Something of the sort may have occurred to Vinculus because he was describing in great detail the soft, pillowy bed he intended to sleep in that night and the very large dinner he intended to eat before he retired there. There was no doubt that he expected Childermass to pay for these luxuries, and it would not have been particularly surprizing if Childermass had had a word or two to say about them, but Childermass said nothing. His mind was wholly taken up with the problem of whether or not he ought to shew Vinculus to Strange and Norrell. Certainly there was no one in England better qualified to examine Vinculus; but, on the other hand, Childermass could not quite predict how the magicians would act when faced with a man who was also a book. Childermass scratched his cheek. There was a faint, well-healed scar upon it – the merest silvery line upon his brown face.

Vinculus had stopped talking and was standing in the road. His blanket had fallen from him and he was eagerly pushing back the sleeves of his coat.

"What is it?" asked Childermass. "What is the matter?"

"I have changed!" said Vinculus. "Look!" He took off his coat and opened his shirt. "The words are different! On my arms! On my chest! Everywhere! This is not what I said before!" Despite the cold, he began to undress. Then, when he was quite naked again, he celebrated his transformation by dancing about gleefully like a blue-skinned devil.

Childermass dismounted from his horse with feelings of panic and desperation. He had succeeded in preserving John Uskglass's book from death and destruction; and then, just when it seemed secure, the book itself had defeated him by changing.

"We must get to an inn as soon as we can!" he declared. "We must get paper and ink! We must make a record of exactly what was written upon you before. You must search every corner of your memory!"

Vinculus stared at him as if he thought he must have taken leave of his senses. "Why?" he asked.

"Because it is John Uskglass's magic! John Uskglass's thoughts! The only record any one ever had of them. We must preserve every scrap we can!"

Vinculus remained unenlightened. "Why?" he asked again. "John Uskglass did not think it worth preserving."

"But why should you change all of a sudden? There is no rhyme or reason in it!"

"There is every sort of reason," said Vinculus. "I was a Prophecy before; but the things that I foretold have come to pass. So it is just as well I have changed – or I would have become a History! A dry-as-dust History!"

"So what are you now?"

Vinculus shrugged his shoulders. "Perhaps I am a Receipt-Book! Perhaps I am a Novel! Perhaps I am a Collection of Sermons!" He was excessively diverted by these thoughts and cackled to himself and capered about some more.

"I hope you are what you have always been – a Book of Magic. But what are you saying? Vinculus, do you mean to tell me that you never learnt these letters?"

"I am a Book," said Vinculus, stopping in mid-caper. "I am *the* Book. It is the task of the Book to bear the words. Which I do. It is the task of the Reader to know what they say."

"But the last Reader is dead!"

Vinculus shrugged as if that were none of his concern.

"You must know something!" cried Childermass, growing almost wild with exasperation. He seized Vinculus's arm. "What about this? This symbol like a horned circle with a line through it. It occurs over and over again. What does it mean?"

Vinculus pulled his arm away again. "It means last Tuesday," he said. "It means three pigs, one of 'em wearing a straw hat! It means Sally went a-dancing in the moon's shadow and lost a little rosy purse!" He grinned and wagged a finger at Childermass. "I know what you are doing! You hope to be the next Reader!"

"Perhaps," said Childermass. "Though I cannot, for the life of me, tell how I shall begin. Yet I cannot see that any one else has a better claim to be the next Reader. But whatever else happens, I shall not let you out of my sight again. Henceforth, Vinculus, you and I shall be each other's shadow."

Vinculus's mood soured upon the instant. Gloomily he dressed himself again.

Spring returned to England. Birds followed ploughs. Stones were warmed by the sun. Rains and winds grew softer, and were fragranced with the scents of earth and growing things. Woods were tinged with a colour so soft, so subtle that it could scarcely be said to be a colour at all. It was more the *idea* of a colour – as if the trees were dreaming green dreams or thinking green thoughts.

Spring returned to England, but Strange and Norrell did not. The Pillar of Darkness covered Hurtfew Abbey and Norrell did not come out of it. People speculated upon the probability of Strange having killed Norrell, or Norrell having killed Strange, the different degrees to which each deserved it, and whether or not someone ought to go and find out.

But before any one could reach a conclusion concerning these interesting questions the Darkness disappeared – taking Hurtfew Abbey with it. House, park, bridge and part of the river were all gone. Roads that used to lead to Hurtfew now led back upon themselves or to dull corners of fields and copses that no one wished to visit. The house in Hanover-square and both Strange's houses – the one in Soho-square and his home in Clun[1] – suffered the same queer fate. In London the only creature in the world who could still find the house in Soho-square was Jeremy Johns' cat, Bullfinch. Indeed, Bullfinch did not appear to be aware that the house was in any way changed and he continued to go there whenever he wished, slipping between number 30 and number 32, and everyone who saw him do it agreed that it was the oddest sight in the world.[2]

Lord Liverpool and the other Ministers said a great deal publicly about their regret at Strange and Norrell's disappearance, but privately they were glad to be relieved of such a peculiar problem. Neither Strange nor Norrell had proved as respectable as they once had seemed. Both had indulged in, if not Black Magic, then certainly magic of a darker hue than seemed desirable or legitimate. Instead, the Ministers turned their attention to the great number of new magicians who had suddenly sprung up.

[1] For years afterwards the people of Clun said that if you stood, slightly upon tiptoes, close by a particular tree in winter at full moon and craned your neck to look between the branches of another tree, then it was possible still to see Ashfair in the distance. In the moonlight and snow the house looked very eerie, lost and lonely. In time, however, the trees grew differently and Ashfair was seen no more.

[2] This is by no means unusual as the following passage from *The Modern Magician* (Autumn, 1812) shews. "Where is Pale's house? Where Stokesey's? Why has no one ever seen them? Pale's house was in Warwick. The very street was known. Stokesey's house faced the cathedral in Exeter. Where is the Raven King's castle in Newcastle? Every one who saw it proclaimed it to be the first house for beauty and splendour in all the world – but has any one ever seen it in the Modern Age? No. Is there any record of it being destroyed? No. It simply disappeared. All these houses exist somewhere, but when the magician goes away or dies, they disappear. *He* may enter and leave as he pleases, but no one else may find them."

These magicians had performed scarcely any magic and were largely uneducated; nevertheless they promised to be every bit as quarrelsome as Strange and Norrell themselves, and some means of regulating them would quickly have to be found. Suddenly Mr Norrell's plans for reviving the Court of Cinque Dragownes (which had seemed so irrelevant before) were found to be of the utmost pertinence.[3]

In the second week of March a paragraph appeared in the *York Chronicle*, addressed to former members of the Learned Society of York Magicians, and also to any one who might wish to become a member of that society. It invited them to come to the Old Starre Inn on the following Wednesday (this being the day upon which the society had traditionally met).

This curious announcement offended at least as many of the former members of the York society as it pleased. Placed as it was in a newspaper, it could be read by everyone who possessed a penny. Furthermore the author (who was not named) appeared to have taken it upon himself to invite people to join the York society – something which he clearly had no right to do, whoever he was.

When the interesting evening came the former members arrived at the Old Starre to find fifty or so magicians (or would-be magicians) assembled in the Long Room. The most comfortable seats were all taken and the former members (who included Mr Segundus, Mr Honeyfoot and Dr Foxcastle) were obliged to take their places upon a little dais some distance from the fireplaces. The situation had this advantage however: they had an excellent view of the new magicians.

It was not a sight calculated to bring joy to the bosoms of the former members. The assembly was made up of the most mis-

---

[3] Many of the new magicians applied to Lord Liverpool and the Ministers for permission to go and find Strange and Norrell. Some gentlemen were so thoughtful as to append lists of equipment, both magical and mundane, which they thought they might need and which they hoped that the Government would be kind enough to supply. One, a man called Beech in Plymouth, asked for the loan of the Inniskilling Dragoons.

cellaneous people. ("With scarcely," observed Dr Foxcastle, "a gentleman among them.") There were two farmers and several shopkeepers. There was a pale-faced young man with light-coloured hair and an excitable manner, who was telling his neighbours that he was quite certain the announcement had been placed in the newspaper by Jonathan Strange himself and Strange would doubtless arrive at any moment to teach them all magic! There was also a clergyman – which was rather more promising. He was a clean-shaven, sober-looking person of fifty or sixty in black clothes. He was accompanied by a dog, as grey-haired and respectable as himself, and a young, striking-looking, female person in a red velvet gown. This seemed rather less respectable. She had dark hair and a fierce expression.

"Mr Taylor," said Dr Foxcastle to an acolyte of his, "perhaps you would be so good as to go and give that gentleman a hint that we do not bring members of our family to these meetings."

Mr Taylor scurried away.

From where they sat the former members of the York Society observed that the clean-shaven clergyman was more flinty than his quiet face suggested and that he returned Mr Taylor quite a sharp answer.

Mr Taylor came back with the following message. "Mr Redruth begs the society's pardon but he is not a magician at all. He has a great deal of interest in magic, but no skill. It is his daughter who is the magician. He has one son and three daughters and he says they are all magicians. The others did not wish to attend the meeting. He says that they have no wish to consort with other magicians, preferring to pursue their studies privately at home without distractions."

There was a pause while the former members tried, and failed, to make any sense of this.

"Perhaps his dog is a magician too," said Dr Foxcastle and the former members of the society laughed.

It soon became clear that the newcomers fell into two distinct parties. Miss Redruth, the young lady in the red velvet gown, was one of the first to speak. Her voice was low and rather hurried. She was not used to speaking in public and not all of the magicians caught her words, but her delivery was very passionate. The burden of what she had to say seemed to be that Jonathan Strange was everything! Gilbert Norrell nothing! Strange would soon be vindicated and Norrell universally reviled! Magic would be freed from the shackles that Gilbert Norrell had placed upon it! These observations, together with various references to Strange's lost masterpiece, *The History and Practice of English Magic*, drew angry responses from several other magicians to the effect that Strange's book was full of wicked magic and Strange himself was a murderer. He had certainly murdered his wife[4] and had probably murdered Norrell too.

The discussion was growing yet more heated when it was interrupted by the arrival of two men. Neither looked in the least respectable. Both had long, ragged hair and wore ancient coats. However, while one seemed to be nothing more or less than a vagabond, the other was considerably neater in his appearance and had about him an air of business – almost, one might say, of authority.

The vagabonding fellow did not even trouble to look at the York society; he simply sat down upon the floor and demanded gin and hot water. The other strode to the centre of the room and regarded them all with a wry smile. He bowed in the direction of Miss Redruth and addressed the magicians with the following words.

"Gentlemen! Madam! Some of you may remember me. I was with you ten years ago when Mr Norrell did the magic in York Cathedral. My name is John Childermass. I was, until last month, the servant of Gilbert Norrell. And this," he indicated the man sitting on the floor, "is Vinculus, a some-time street sorcerer of London."

Childermass got no further. Everyone began speaking at once. The former members of the York Society were dismayed to find

---

[4] This slander was not entirely discredited until Arabella Strange herself returned to England in early June 1817.

that they had left their comfortable firesides to come here and be lectured by a servant. But while these gentlemen were unburdening themselves of their indignation, most of the newcomers were affected quite differently. They were all either Strangites or Norrellites; but not one of them had ever laid eyes on his hero and to be seated in such proximity to a person who had actually known and spoken to him wound them up to an unprecedented pitch of excitement.

Childermass was not in the least discomfited by the uproar. He simply waited until it was quiet enough for him to speak and then he said, "I have come to tell you that the agreement with Gilbert Norrell is void. Null and void, gentlemen. You are magicians once more, if you wish to be."

One of the new magicians shouted out to know if Strange were coming. Another wished to know if Norrell were coming.

"No, gentlemen," said Childermass. "They are not. You must make do with me. I do not think Strange and Norrell will be seen again in England. At least not in this generation."

"Why?" asked Mr Segundus. "Where have they gone?"

Childermass smiled. "Wherever magicians used to go. Behind the sky. On the other side of the rain."

One of the Norrellites remarked that Jonathan Strange was wise to remove himself from England. Otherwise he would have certainly been hanged.

The excitable young man with the light-coloured hair retorted spitefully that the whole pack of Norrellites would soon find themselves at a grave disadvantage. Surely the first principle of Norrellite magic was that everything must be based upon books? And how were they going to do that when the books had all disappeared with Hurtfew Abbey?[5]

---

[5] There are very few modern magicians who do not declare themselves to be either Strangite or Norrellite, the only notable exception being John Childermass himself. Whenever he is asked he claims to be in some degree both. As this is like claiming to be both Whig and Tory at the same time, no one understands what he means.

"You do not need the library at Hurtfew, gentlemen," said Childermass. "Nor yet the library in Hanover-square. I have brought you something much better. A book Norrell long desired, but never saw. A book Strange did not even know existed. I have brought you John Uskglass's book."

More shouting. More uproar. In the midst of all of which Miss Redruth appeared to be making a speech in defence of John Uskglass, whom she insisted upon calling his Grace, the King, as if he were at any moment about to enter Newcastle and resume the government of Northern England.

"Wait!" cried Dr Foxcastle, his loud, important voice gradually overpowering first those nearest him, and then the rest of the assembly. "I see no book in this rogue's hands! Where is it? This is a trick, gentlemen! He wants our money, I'll be bound. Well, sir?" (This to Childermass.) "What do you say? Bring out your book – if indeed it exists!"

"On the contrary, sir," said Childermass, with his long, dark, one-sided grin. "I want nothing of yours. Vinculus! Stand up!"

In the house in Padua the first concern of the Greysteels and their servants was to make Mrs Strange as comfortable as they could; and each had his or her own way of doing it. Dr Greysteel's comfort chiefly took a philosophical form. He searched his memory for examples from history of people – particularly ladies – who had triumphed over adverse circumstances, often with the help of their friends. Minichello and Frank, the two manservants, ran to open doors for her – often whether she wanted to go through them or not. Bonifazia, the maid, preferred to treat a year's sojourn in Faerie as if it had been rather a severe sort of cold and brought her strengthening cordials throughout the day. Aunt Greysteel sent all over the town for the best wines and the rarest delicacies; and she purchased the softest, down-filled cushions and pillows, as if she hoped that by laying her head on them Arabella might be induced to forget all that had happened to her. But of all the various sorts of consolation that were offered her, that which seemed to suit Arabella best was Flora's company and Flora's conversation.

One morning they were sitting together at their needlework. Arabella put down her work with a gesture of impatience and went to the window. "There is a spirit of restlessness upon me," she said.

"It is to be expected," said Flora, gently. "Be patient. In time your spirits will be what they were before."

"Will they?" said Arabella, with a sigh. "Truth to own, I really do not remember what I was like before."

"Then I will tell you. You were always cheerful – tho' often left to your own devices. You were hardly ever out of temper – tho' often severely provoked. Your every speech was remarkable for its wit and genius – tho' you got no credit for it and almost always received a flat contradiction."

Arabella laughed. "Good Heavens! What a prodigy I was! But," she said with a wry look, "I am not inclined to put much trust in this portrait, since you never saw me."

"Mr Strange told me. Those are his words."

"Oh!" said Arabella. She turned her face away.

Flora cast her eyes down and said softly, "When he returns, he will do more to restore you to yourself than any one else could. You will be happy again." She glanced up.

Arabella was silent for a moment. She said, "I am not sure that we will see each other again."

Flora took up her needlework again. After a moment she said, "It is very odd that he should have gone back to his old master at last."

"Is it? There seems nothing very extraordinary in it to me. I never thought the quarrel would last as long as it did. I thought they would have been friends again by the end of the first month."

"You quite astonish me!" said Flora. "When Mr Strange was with us he did not have a good word to say for Mr Norrell – and Mr Norrell has published the most dreadful things about Mr Strange in the magical journals."

"Oh, I dare say!" said Arabella, entirely unimpressed. "But that was just their nonsense! They are both as stubborn as Old Scratch. I have no cause to love Mr Norrell – far from it. But I know this about him: he is a magician first and everything else second – and Jonathan is the same. Books and magic are all either of them really cares about. No one else understands the subject as they do – and so, you see, it is only natural that they should like to be together."

As the weeks went by Arabella smiled and laughed more often. She became interested in everything that concerned her new friends. Her days were taken up with sociable meals, errands and the pleasant obligations of friendship – small domestic matters with which her sore mind and wounded spirit were glad to refresh themselves. Of her absent husband she thought very little, except to be grateful for his consideration in placing her with the Greysteels.

There happened to be a young Irish captain in Padua just then and several people were of the opinion that he admired Flora – though Flora said that he did not. He had led a company of cavalry into the teeth of the severest gunfire at Waterloo; yet his courage all seemed to desert him where Flora was concerned. He could not look at her without blushing and was most alarmed whenever she entered a room. Generally he found it easier to apply to Mrs Strange for intelligence of when Flora might be walking in the Prato della Valle (a beautiful garden at the heart of the city) or when she might next visit the Baxters (some mutual friends); and Arabella was always glad to help him.

But there were some consequences of her captivity which she could not easily shake off. She was accustomed to dancing all night, and sleep did not come easily to her. Sometimes at night she could still hear a mournful fiddle and a pipe playing fairy tunes, compelling her to dance – though it was the last thing in the world that she wanted to do.

"Talk to me," she would say to Flora and Aunt Greysteel. "Talk to me and I think I can master it."

Then one or both of them would sit up with her and talk to her of everything they could think of. But sometimes Arabella found that the impulse to movement – any sort of movement – was too strong to be denied, and then she would take to pacing the bed-chamber she shared with Flora; and on several occasions Dr Greysteel and Frank kindly sacrificed their own sleep to walk with her in the night-streets of Padua.

On one such night in April they were strolling about near to the Cathedral; Arabella and Dr Greysteel were speaking of their departure for England which had been arranged for the following month. Arabella found the prospect of being amongst all her English friends again a little daunting and Dr Greysteel was reassuring her. Suddenly Frank gave an exclamation of surprize and pointed upwards.

The stars were shifting and changing; in the patch of sky above them were new constellations. A little further on was an ancient-looking stone arch. There was nothing exactly unusual in this; Padua is a city full of intriguing doorways, arches and arcades. But this arch was not like the others. Padua is built of mediaeval bricks and consequently many of its streets are a pleasing pink-gold colour. This arch was built of dour, dark northern stones and upon each side was a statue of John Uskglass, his face half-hidden by a cap with raven wings. Just within the arch a tall figure was standing.

Arabella hesitated. "You will not go far?" she said to Dr Greysteel.

"Frank and I shall be here," Dr Greysteel told her. "We shall not move from this spot. You have only to call us."

She went on alone. The person within the doorway was reading. He looked up as she approached, with the old, dear expression of not quite remembering where he was or what he had do with the world outside his book.

"You have not brought a thunderstorm with you this time," she said.

"Oh, you heard about that, did you?" Strange gave a slightly self-conscious laugh. "That was a little overdone perhaps. Not altogether in the best of taste. I believe I spent too much time in Lord Byron's society when I was in Venice. I caught something of his style."

They walked on a little and at every moment new patterns of stars appeared above their heads.

"You look well, Arabella," he said. "I feared . . . What did I fear? Oh! a thousand different things. I feared you would not speak to me. But here you are. I am very glad to see you."

"And now your thousand fears can be laid to rest," she said. "At least as far as they concern me. Have you found any thing yet to dispel the Darkness?"

"No, not yet. Though, to own the truth, we have been so busy recently – some new conjectures concerning naiads – that we have scarcely had time to apply ourselves seriously to the problem. But there are one or two things in Goubert's *Gatekeeper of Apollo* which look promising. We are optimistic."

"I am glad. I am miserable when I think of you suffering."

"Do not be miserable, I beg you. Apart from any thing else, I do not suffer. A little perhaps at first, but not now. And Norrell and I are hardly the first English magicians to labour under an enchantment. Robert Dymoke fell foul of a fairy in the twelfth century and thereafter could not speak but only sing – which, I am sure, is not so pleasant as it sounds. And there was a fourteenth-century magician who had a silver foot – which must have been very disagreeable. Besides who is to say that the Darkness may not be of advantage to us? We intend to go out of England and are likely to meet with all sorts of tricksy persons. An English magician is an impressive thing. Two English magicians are, I suppose, twice as impressive – but when those two English magicians are shrouded in an Impenetrable Darkness – ah, well! That, I should think, is enough to strike terror into the heart of any one short of a demi-god!"

"Where will you go?"

"Oh, there are plenty of places. This world is only one among so many, and it does not do for a magician to become too – what shall I say? – too *parochial*."

"But will Mr Norrell like it?" she asked, doubtfully. "He was never fond of travelling – not even as far as Portsmouth."

"Ah! But that is one of the advantages of our particular mode of travel. He need never leave the house if he does not wish it. The world – all worlds – will come to us." He paused and looked about him. "I had better not go further. Norrell is a little way off. For various reasons to do with the enchantment, it is best that we do not stray very far from each other. Arabella," he said, with a degree of seriousness unusual to him, "it hurt me more than I could bear to think of you under the earth. I would have done any thing – any thing at all – to fetch you safely out."

She took his hands and her eyes were shining. "And you did it," she whispered. They looked at each other for a long moment, and in that moment all was as it used to be – it was as if they had never parted; but she did not offer to go into the Darkness with him and he did not ask her.

"One day," he said, "I shall find the right spell and banish the Darkness. And on that day I will come to you."

"Yes. On that day. I will wait until then."

He nodded and seemed about to depart, but then he hesitated. "Bell," he said, "do not wear black. Do not be a widow. Be happy. That is how I wish to think of you."

"I promise. And how shall I think of you?"

He considered a moment and then laughed. "Think of me with my nose in a book!"

They kissed once. Then he turned upon his heel and disappeared into the Darkness.

ACKNOWLEDGEMENTS

Thanks are first due to the immensely wonderful, much-missed Giles Gordon. I was proud to say he was my agent. I still am.

And special thanks to Jonny Geller for everything since Giles has been gone.

For encouragement when this book began: Geoff Ryman, Alison Paice (also much missed), and Tinch Minter and her writing group, especially Julian Hall.

For encouragement along the way: my parents Janet and Stuart, Patrick and Teresa Nielsen Hayden, Ellen Datlow, Terri Windling and Neil Gaiman whose generosity to other writers never ceases to amaze me.

For everyone who helped with languages: Stuart Clarke, Samantha Evans, Patrick Marcel and Giorgia Grilli. For help with knotty problems of Napoleonic military and naval history: Nicholas Blake (needless to say, the remaining errors are entirely my responsibility). For immensely perceptive comments and suggestions: Antonia Till. For writing books that were continually helpful: Elizabeth Longford (*Wellington*) and Christopher Hibbert and Ben Weinreb (*The London Encyclopedia*).

To Jonathan Whiteland, who cheerfully gives his time and expertise so that Macs can run and books be written.

And, above all, to Colin who did everything else so I could write, who never complained, and without whom it is most unlikely this book would ever have seen the light of day.

A NOTE ON THE AUTHOR

Susanna Clarke lives in Cambridge.
This is her first novel.

A NOTE ON THE TYPE

The original punches of the types cut by John Baskerville of Birmingham were sold by Baskerville's widow to Beaumarchais and descended through various French foundaries to Beberny & Peignot. Some of the material survives and is now at the Cambridge University Press. Baskerville has been called the first of the transitional romans in England. Compared with Caslon there is more differentiation of thick and thin strokes, the serifs on lower-case letters are more nearly horizontal and the stress nearer the vertical.

Visit www.jonathanstrange.com to read Jonathan Strange and Mr Norrell's own reactions to Susanna Clarke's novel as well as their views on the author. You'll also find Susanna Clarke's short story, 'The Duke of Wellington Misplaces His Horse', an interview, e-cards, a readers' guide and many other magical things . . .

ENGLAND
HISTORY OF A
NATION

ENGLAND
HISTORY OF A NATION

DAVID ROSS

GEDDES &
GROSSET

For Will and Chris

Published 2005 by Geddes & Grosset,
David Dale House, New Lanark, ML11 9DJ, Scotland
Copyright © David Ross 2005

ISBN 1 84205 319 1

Printed and bound in Finland

Contents

Fact Windows

Foreword

English history is a vast and complicated story, made more so since 1707 by the question of where 'English' ends and 'British' begins. A history of England, no matter how long, has to be a matter of selection and focus. The long sweep of time from the first anonymous occupants of a nameless landscape to the regional government proposals of New Labour is a daunting, but also an exhilarating thing to contemplate. The descendants of those first settlers – enormously increased in numbers, added to by the ceaseless immigration of a great variety of peoples – still live in England. Continuity and change, opposing but also complementary forces, underlie the sequence of events. The pull of these two great forces is also seen in the growth of English society and the evolution of English government. Conservatism (with a small 'c') has always been a great latent power in English life. But so has been the urge to question, to do things differently. Change has often been made in the name of restoring the past, as in 1660, but that can never be quite achieved. Defenders of the old ways have often, like the Duke of Wellington, found themselves reluctant proposers of reform. Though often a source of division and destruction, this two-way pull has been, in the long term, fruitful for England and, because England has at various times been highly influential in world affairs, of concern and value to the rest of the world.

For some historians, the island position of the English is a defining factor in forming their attitude to the rest of the world and to the continent of Europe in particular. Others have remarked that the English Channel was always a less formidable barrier than the Alps. What is really important is the sense of England's resources. The country is best seen as a little continent in itself. For many centuries it was self-sufficient in the essentials of life. It has wide fertile plains, rolling grassy uplands, a long coastline, and hills that hide long, remote valleys. There are lakes, fenlands and bare mountains. It has rivers broad and slow enough for navigation, and once had great forests. Its capital was a trading town before the Romans came, and grew to be the world's most populous city. And a population of correspondingly varied attitude and outlook occupied its 50,397 square miles (130,478 sq km). To the north and the west were other countries, smaller in population, different in outlook, wilder in landscape and poorer in resources. Scotland, Ireland, Wales defined themselves in conflict with England, but unlike them, that small continent, with its variety of human habitats and possibilities for human experience, could be an all-in-all for its people. Nothing, and nowhere else were needed. (And in the twentieth century, as in the nineteenth, the moments of 'standing alone' were those when the English felt most distinctly themselves.) Such variety within a small compass explains why the English as a nation can seem so elusive, a 'secret people' in G.K. Chesterton's words. There is no single English type, but rather a whole range of them, often with conflicting characteristics. It is as English to put on a red coat and hunt foxes as it is to hold up a placard and block the road in protest against blood sports. All this has made for an independent-minded, versatile and creative people, though not, perhaps, one that finds it easy to adjust to membership of a large supranational union. In this respect England is again different from its British neighbour-nations. The roots and the development of English distinctiveness are the basic theme of this book.

> Smile at us, pay us, pass us; but do not quite forget;
> For we are the people of England, that never has spoken yet.
> There is many a fat farmer that drinks less cheerfully,
> There is many a free French peasant who is richer and sadder than we.
> There are no folk in the whole world so helpless or so wise.
> There is hunger in our bellies, there is laughter in our eyes;
> You laugh at us and love us, both mugs and eyes are wet:
> Only you do not know us. For we have not spoken yet.

> G.K. Chesterton, 'The Secret People' (1915)

CHAPTER ONE

England in the Third Millennium

A SENSE OF IDENTITY

Out of every thousand inhabitants of Great Britain, 860 are English. England is by far the most populous constituent part of the United Kingdom. In the national census carried out in the summer of 2001, its population for the first time exceeded 49 million, an increase of 5.8 per cent on the previous census ten years earlier. By way of comparison, France and Italy have around 57 million people, Germany has 80 million, Spain and Poland both have around 38 million. A hundred years earlier, the 1901 census put the population of England at a little over 32.5 million. In the twentieth century the population grew by 50 per cent. This was quite modest compared with the nineteenth century, during which the population had more than tripled.

Around the year 2000, it became a common thing in England to wonder – in print, or on television or the radio, or just in thinking aloud – what kind of country was England, as it entered the third millennium of the Common Era. What kind of country did it want to be? How did it see itself? This internal debate was partly brought on by the British difficulty in establishing a coherent and positive role within the European Union, a difficulty exacerbated not only by the Atlantic pull of its relationship with the United States of America, but also by a historic sense of detachment from the European arena. Other factors were the establishment of a separate parliament in Scotland, and of an assembly in Wales, and a new attempt at a power-sharing executive in Northern Ireland. Scotland and Wales, ancient national communities, integral parts of Great Britain along with England, both acquired forums in which they could arrange their own internal affairs and express their own sense of identity. They became political entities once again. England, politically speaking, was a non-entity. It had no forum in which strictly English internal matters could be decided by elected English members only, or in which a specifically English sense of identity could be expressed. Of course it continued to house the body still sometimes referred to as 'the mother of parliaments' – the parliament of the United Kingdom of Great Britain and Northern Ireland – but this, with Welsh, Scottish and Northern Irish members, was not an exclusively English institution.

In one sense, this did not matter. After all, England contributed more than

ENGLISH-BRITISH

The interlacing of British and English goes back far before 1707 or 1603. The Anglo-Saxons, having supplanted the Britons, quite deliberately assumed a British political identity. Their most powerful kings were called Bretwalda, 'ruler of Britain'. Later, the Arthurian legends managed to thoroughly confuse the notions of England and Britain. By the arrival of James I in 1603, it was easy contemplate a united Great Britain, though impossible to make it a political reality at that time. From 1707 England willingly invested a large part of its identity in the concept of 'Britishness' required by a multinational United Kingdom and even more by a worldwide British Empire. To separate what is English from what is British is sometimes like trying to peel the surface off a bowl of water, and it has been a problem for historians. When he published his *English History, 1914–1945*, in 1965, A.J.P. Taylor felt obliged to explain why he had not called it 'British History': 'Where the Welsh, the Scotch, the Irish, or the British overseas have the same history as the English,' he wrote, 'my book includes them also; where they have a different history, it does not.' In other words, he chose to pretend that England and Britain were one and the same thing. He was not alone in this approach, which makes a subtle but real distortion of what England was and is. Since the tenth century, England has always been the largest and most populous part of Great Britain, but has also remained a distinct entity within Britain, and to treat it as anything else does less than justice to a remarkable nation in its own right. (*See also* 'Heroes and historians'.)

five-sixths of the population of the United Kingdom: inevitably the vast bulk of domestic legislation was made with England in view. More than five out of six MPs sat for English constituencies. In other ways, it did matter. Many people felt that England's lack of its own parliament was a hindrance to the country's well-being. No one could dispute the fact that England was a distinct country. Its legal system, its established church, its educational system, quite apart from the sense of identity of nearly fifty million people, all testified to that. The Labour government, re-elected in 2001, embarked on controversial plans to establish regional assemblies based on certain major provincial cities. The English, who perhaps even more than most peoples have looked on governmental initiatives with some suspicion and scepticism, and realising that from the parish level to that of the European Parliament, they would then elect, live under and pay for five separate tiers of administration, responded with indifference at best. Apart from a brief interval in the Second World War, regions had never played a part in the history of English economic or political life. In all their history, perhaps the greatest triumph of the English was to form and foster the concept of their own united Englishness, which combined in one nation an originally diverse and mutually hostile group of peoples from Cornwall to Northumbria. They created a single and remarkable nation. To subdivide this hard-won and long-retained national entity into a set of semi-devolved regions on a mixture of historic, demographic and politically convenient bases, and make them both meaningful and inspiring to the population, seemed a task which even angels might find difficult. And yet, there were good reasons for establishing a new start, a new way of looking at England, a new framework on which English abilities and potential might flower.

IMPERIAL PROFIT AND LOSS

The twentieth century, for England, had an overriding theme which was not an easy one to cope with. In 1900 the English capital had been the focus of a great empire. By 2000 the British Empire was reduced to a few geographical specks. During a hundred years that encompassed two world wars and many lesser ones, and despite its association with victory in both of the former, the mantle of empire was tugged away, slipped off, or willingly and ceremoniously discarded. England, the last self-confessed imperial nation, was reduced to itself, to its place within the British scheme of things; and to a new alignment in political and economic union with the European nations from which it had stood aloof yet linked, independent yet involved, for centuries.

England was not impoverished by the loss of empire; in fact the residual gains in terms of new population elements and cultural variety are likely to provide it with

The Houses of Parliament, Westminster, London

stimulus and energy for a long time to come. And through the twentieth century, the gains in wealth, comfort and security for almost all its people were spectacular. But there was one important loss. The possession of an empire was England's answer to an ideology, its 'Big Idea'. Having an ideology, whether it is Marxism-Leninism, or *Liberté Egalité Fraternité*, or the vision of creating a united, war-free Europe, enables the people of a country to feel that it exists within a larger ambience, that it is making positive progress. The British Empire in its final form gave that sense to England: at one and the same time a *raison d'être*, a mission, a distraction from everyday tedium, and an object of satisfactory contemplation. Without the empire, there was nothing. England had no other ideology and indeed prided itself on the fact. It had Christianity, of an increasingly nominal sort, which in the twentieth century was far from being, or sustaining, a national ideology. It was one of the founding countries of capitalism, but the temple of Capital was very firmly centred on the western shores of the Atlantic, from where its globalising tendency threatened the spirit of Englishness as it did all other historic identities. What was now the driving spirit of England? The answer was far from clear.

THE ECONOMIC REVOLUTION

In other ways, too, England seemed to be at the end of an era. In 1900 it could still claim to be the workshop of the world, and the world's chief carrier of goods. During the 1920s and 1930s, this dominance began to be eroded. From the 1950s on, the heavy smoke-stack industries that had sustained the role crumbled and largely disappeared. Social observers wrote about a 'post-industrial society'. Year by year, manufacturing became a smaller constituent of the gross national product. Much of English industry was foreign-owned. Even in the first years of the twentieth century, the playwright George Bernard Shaw had prophesied that England would soon live solely by producing chocolate creams; in the 1960s, gloomier prophets talked about economic and social collapse; in the early 2000s, economic commentators were still worried by the continuing decline in manufacturing industry as a sector of the economy. Some social observers were concerned about the growth of a 'museum culture': wherever an industry was lost, its memory was preserved in hygienically restored and painted factory buildings, with waxworks, press-button machines, and opportunities for schoolchildren to dress up in period costume. Their effect was seen as devaluing the present and future as compared to the past. But for communities whose landmarks and livelihoods – however grim in the first case and insufficient in the second – had been ripped out, the museums were perhaps a necessary part of coming to terms with a new world whose landmarks seemed more insubstantial and transient.

In 2003, however, it seemed that the economic demise of England had been greatly exaggerated. Unemployment was very low, despite a labour force larger than ever before, and in which women outnumbered men. The population accepted and took for granted a level of domestic comfort, leisure entertainment and international mobility which would have seemed a vision of Paradise to their great-grandparents. School education and hospital care were free; medical aid was heavily subsidised; a minimum wage was enforced by law. If this state of affairs was accepted as right and normal, it was also greatly valued –

never more so than when it was seen to be under threat. There was still serious concern about the still-reducing part played in the economy by manufacturing industry; and about the extremely low level of investment in manufacturing. The discovery and exploitation of oil and natural gas under the North Sea had come at the most opportune possible moment in the late 1960s, but the reserves were being quickly depleted. But forecasters of doom had always been present.

THE BLAIR ERA

In 2001 the English electorate returned the New Labour government of Tony Blair to power with a majority as overwhelming as the one it gained in 1997. It was the first time that the Labour Party had won successive major victories, and though the turnout to vote was the lowest since 1918, it was generally accepted that the government had been given a mandate to continue with the programme of reform and improvement of public services that it had initiated in 1997. There was unanimous agreement that health and education were the prime areas for reform, with trans-port close behind. Particularly on transport, there was less agree-ment on what should be done. Having proclaimed its intention to reduce the national dependence on the private car, with conse-quent traffic jams and daily hold-ups, the government by 2003 was beginning to re-examine aban-doned plans for new roads. England's first toll motorway, owned by an Australian company which saw it rather too obviously as a licence to print money, opened in 2003. Ministerial incompetence, unlucky accidents, and the inheritance of a fractured and run-down railway industry all combined to delay the provision of an effective nationwide railway system. A large building pro-gramme of new schools and hospitals was however beginning

Tony Blair

to change the public perception of education and health provision, from shabby buildings and under-funded services, to new and shiny buildings with adequate support. The government's favoured funding method, the Private Finance Initiative, an attempt to combine state and private investment, was widely criticised from the left. But New Labour was committed to finding a 'third way' to maintain the country's economic progress and improve its basic facilities without resorting to the state corporatism of 'Old Labour' or the deregulated market forces of Thatcherism. This redefining of the political middle ground also had the effect of leaving the Conservatives, still with a large potential constituency in the country, searching for an effective means of re-presenting themselves and renewing their appeal to an electorate more volatile than ever before.

Underlying the whole diverse set of programmes, and helping to preserve a favourable public attitude, was the economic stability of the years between 1997 and 2003 which established New Labour's reputation for economic prudence and ability to run the economy. Though in early 2003 financial observers were concerned about the decline in industrial output, the degree of personal debt, the high price of houses, and the continuing low level of stock markets, there was also a realisation that for several years the British economy had performed better than those of the other major EU countries. The Blair government, anxious to maintain its financial reputation, was delaying over the moment to recommend subordinating the Bank of England to the European Central Bank and joining the single European currency. This decision would have to be approved by a referendum. To the European countries who had pledged themselves to the single currency, such a 'wait until it works to our benefit' approach was somewhat galling. It was hardly in the spirit of the team games which England had taught to the rest of the world. British diplomacy, sidelined in Europe by the strength of the French–German relationship, seemed to be an echo of the US State Department. Perhaps the best interests of Britain lay in this uncomfortable and often unconvincing posture. To sceptical Europeans, Britain seemed to be awaiting the arrival of the new member countries of the EU in 2004 in order to try to create its own bloc against the dominant French–German relationship, as if it were still pursuing its self-appointed historical task, as in the eighteenth and nineteenth centuries, of regulating the 'balance of power' in Europe.

In the first term of the Blair government, the 'Big Idea' was reform of basic services, but once this was under way, it became a nuts-and-bolts issue, its speed and provisions often criticised. A half-baked attempt to ban virtually the only remaining English blood-sport, foxhunting, which was practised by a tiny minority of people, was far short of a crusade. In New Labour's second term, the sudden shock of 11 September 2001, revealing international terrorism on an unprecedentedly organised and massively damaging scale, and delivering as great a psychological buffet as the surprise Japanese attack on Pearl Harbor in 1941, caused the American government to proclaim a war on terrorism and to identify a number of 'rogue states'. No government attached itself to this campaign with greater speed and commitment than the British. In 2001 American and British air assaults ousted the Taleban regime from Afghanistan, a country whose intractability had twice given imperial Britain a bloody nose in the nineteenth century. Far more controversially, the British government joined with the Americans in the bombardment and invasion of Iraq in March 2003, with no mandate from the United Nations, and to widespread international protests, and a sharp division of opinion among EU states. The government's claim, that the action was necessary because of Iraq's possessions of weapons of mass destruction, did not appear to be supported by evidence. The 'Big Idea' of the war on terror floundered amid accusations of bad faith and a sense that the American superpower and its British ally were importing a dangerous new principle into international affairs, that of the pre-emptive attack on a country posing a potential threat. The largest popular demonstration ever seen in London had gathered on 14 February 2003 to protest against war in Iraq. New Labour had promised an ethical foreign policy – the debate on whether it was pursuing one raised echoes that went back to Gladstone's premiership in the nineteenth century.

In June 2003 Blair demonstrated that his government had not lost a capacity

---

THE LORD CHANCELLOR

This functionary was originally the person who kept charge of the king's correspondence and thus was at the centre of affairs of the kingdom. Partly because it required a high degree of literacy, and of awareness of the international situation and historical events, the holder, invariably until the fourteenth century, and often afterwards until the sixteenth, was a churchman. As a close and confidential official, the chancellor's status and responsibilities grew with the development of royal government and became particularly concerned with the administration of justice. In modern times the chancellor's role, redefined and enlarged in the 1880s and again in the 1970s, came increasingly under fire because of its overlapping responsibilities. He was the 'speaker' of the House of Lords. He was a cabinet minister, with a political role in framing legislation. He was the head of the legal profession, with overall supervision of the court system and the power to appoint judges. He was also a judge himself, at the head of the Judicial Committee of the House of Lords, in effect Britain's national court of last appeal. In the British order of precedence, he was the leading non-royal figure after the archbishop of Canterbury: senior to the prime minister, whose office was a mere three hundred years old. The anomalous nature of this combined role had been apparent for a long time, but it had been accepted by all – save its critics – as one of the numerous aspects of English public life which could not be said to fit within a popular democracy but which had survived as part of the system.

to surprise and innovate at home when, without warning, it was announced that the office of Lord Chancellor, the oldest in English political history, was to be abolished forthwith, and to be replaced in its various functions by a Speaker in the House of Lords and the heads of a commission to appoint judges, and of a new supreme court. After much criticism of the government's hesitancy and delay in reforming the House of Lords, this major constitutional change swept home affairs for a time back into the foreground of politics.

CHAPTER TWO

Pre-England

PREHISTORIC ENGLAND

If we allow three human generations to a hundred years, then just a little more than two hundred of them will take us back far before the nineteenth century, seventy centuries, to around 5000 BC, when the inhabitants of southern England were setting up great monumental structures which still exist today. England had had human occupants for a long time before that. Its oldest known human remains go back to the Middle Pleistocene era, 200,000 years ago: skull bones of that era found at Swanscombe in the Thames Valley have been identified as those of a sub-species of *Homo sapiens*, a user of stone hand-axes and other implements. Caves in Somerset, Devon, Derbyshire and Kent have shown traces of occupancy from the mid-Palaeolithic period, some 35,000–40,000 years BC, perhaps left by Neanderthal man, the species which was supplanted by our own. Our own sub-species, *Homo sapiens sapiens*, has been traced back for about 35,000 years in Europe, though no skeletal evidence from so far back is found in England. The most southerly part of England, south of the Thames and the Bristol Channel, was never covered even by the furthest advance of ice sheets in the ice ages, though the landscape would have been a sub-arctic tundra, inhospitable to settlement. At that time, the English Channel had not yet been formed and Great Britain formed an extension of the continental land-mass. Though there were great rivers to cross, settlers from east and south were able to come on dry land until around 6000 BC, when rising sea levels formed the North Sea and the English Channel as we know them. In geological terms, the Channel is a very recent stretch of sea. Inhabitants on both sides, across many generations, had ample time to adapt to the changes in their landscape, though ultimately, twenty-one miles of still-widening salt water confirmed the existence of Europe's largest island. As with all islands, its cut-off state would encourage the development of species not known on the continent; hand-in-hand with those developments would grow an insular state of mind among the human inhabitants. But prehistoric Europeans were too enterprising to allow a narrow sea to be a barrier, and there was uninterrupted trading and contact, and also immigration, or even invasion, by boat.

From the Upper Palaeolithic period through the Mesolithic and Neolithic periods (Old, Middle and New Stone Ages) there is a continuous record of human activity, particularly in the south and east. The people were hunters and

Stonehenge on Salisbury Plain in Wiltshire

fishers, living on lake verges in temporary or transportable dwellings. As the Palaeolithic period merged slowly into the Mesolithic, the range of human activity began to develop, with the domestication of animals, the start of farming techniques and eventually the use of pottery and more specialised tools. Monumental grave mounds were built in the form of long barrows. It was during the fourth millennium BC that farming began to be practised in England, and this coincides with permanent settlements and a change in burial practice to megalithic tombs. Henge monuments, like the earliest erections at Stonehenge, belong to this era.

CELTS IN BRITAIN

As the use of bronze and then iron in tool- and weapon-making became known, the transition comes from the Stone Ages to a period which marks the start of our own 'Common Era' or AD era. By this time, the inhabitants of England were speakers of a language known to be part of the Celtic group. At this time, the Celtic languages were spoken over a great extent of central and western Europe. The language of England has been given the name Brittonic, to correspond with the people's own name for the land which was Prydein, 'Britain'. The origins of the Celtic languages are still not fully understood. In other parts of the British Isles, a different branch of the same group was spoken: this was Goidelic, a

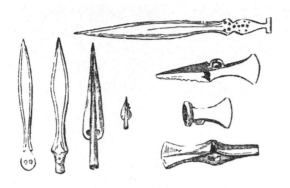

Bronze Age weapons   *Bronze Age shield*

precursor of present-day Gaelic in Ireland and Scotland. It is generally agreed among language scholars that the Brittonic speech reached Britain from the continent, probably in the fifth century BC. The means by which it reached and spread are uncertain, though various theories have been made at different times. The enforcement of a new language by invaders – often characterised as tall, red-haired, and 'aristocratic' – with iron weapons was a popular theory until the mid-twentieth century. Then most scholars dropped it in favour of the concept of a more subtle and slow advance, brought about by trading and social contacts with richer and more advanced cultures, perhaps including the transmission of religious beliefs and practices; and not related to large-scale invasion or compulsory change.

By the first century BC, Celtic languages were spoken by a wide range of European peoples, many of whom were descendants of the early inhabitants of the land, people whose original languages, with the exception of Basque, are almost completely unknown. It is likely that the majority of the inhabitants of Britain at that time were the direct descendants of Stone Age settlers, though undoubtedly there were also communities of more recent arrivals; and perhaps in some or many cases, these more recent settlers had established a political dominance over the 'aboriginal' inhabitants. This does not imply that their language also took over: a thousand years or so later, the Normans established political control, but their language failed to establish itself against that of the majority population. From around 1000 BC another significant change in the social order became apparent, with the building of hill-forts on many prominent sites. Prior to that, the most imposing constructions were those made to house the dead or to enable religious rituals of which we know nothing, other that the stone circles and other megalithic monuments were raised by people who could measure the seasonal movements of the sun and had other quite precise astronomical knowledge.

The first known foreign explorers to reach the British archipelago were Greeks, from the western Greek colonial city of Massilia (now Marseilles). Around 330 BC the navigator, Pytheas, made his way into the North Sea, and reached what he referred to as 'Thule', possibly Norway. In the ancient world, the British Isles were known only for a single product, tin, which was mined from very early times in Cornwall, and an established trading route conveyed the rare and valuable ore across the south-western peninsula and over the sea to Gaul. When the Romans reached the north coast of Gaul, they already knew a lot about the great island and its inhabitants, from spies, informers, traders and tribes who wanted to have them as allies. Their own invasion of northern Gaul had been responsible for the movement into Britain of large numbers of refugees belonging to a big tribe, the Belgae, from their territory in what is now north-east France and Flanders.

THE ROMANS AND BRITANNIA

The Roman general, Julius Caesar, decided to make a reconnaissance expedition into the island, which he called Britannia. This was in 55 BC. It was not prompted by mere curiosity; there was close contact between the inhabitants of Britain and those of Gaul, and this included military help against the Romans. Caesar himself reported that some British tribes, hard-pressed by their neighbours, had offered to surrender to Roman rule in order to obtain Roman support. His landing was opposed at first, but the Britons surrendered, only to attack again. Caesar returned to Gaul with his forces, but the Romans considered it a great victory. A year later he returned with a more substantial expedition, five legions and two thousand cavalry, on six hundred specially constructed ships. This time the Romans remained for two months. The Britons of the south-east united against them under a single commander, Cassivellaunus, but in the only battle, they were defeated, and they resorted to harassing tactics as the Romans pressed inland, fording the Thames and entering Essex. But British unity did not last, and Caesar stormed Cassivellaunus's base. The British leader made peace, hostages were given and an annual tribute was to be paid to Rome. Caesar returned satisfied. Britannia was not colonised, or annexed to Rome, but it acknowledged Roman supremacy.

Almost ninety years went by, with Britannia still beyond the limit of the Roman Empire, but linked through a steady pattern of trading and diplomatic contacts. Some British tribal leaders made alliances with the Romans, while others remained aloof. In 43 AD, under the reign of the emperor, Claudius, the Romans made the decisive move to reduce Britannia to an imperial province. Four legions were landed, at Richborough in Kent, and met little resistance as they pushed northwards to capture Camulodunum, now Colchester, centre of the strong kingdom that had until a short time before been ruled by Cunobelinus. The emperor himself made a brief visit to this remote and exotic new addition to the Roman world. His general, Aulus Plautius, extended Roman rule over the south-east regions, from the Wash to Southampton Water. But the further the invaders went from the south-east, the more fierce and hostile were the native inhabitants. In the south-west, and west of the Severn, and north of the Trent, only hard fighting and military occupation secured the Roman position. In 61 a rebellion broke out in a region they had thought pacified, when the East Anglian Iceni tribe rose, under its queen, Boudicca, and attacked and destroyed the Roman camp-towns of Camulodunum, Verulamium (St Albans) and Londinium (London). Boudicca, who had no son, had claimed to rule after the death of her husband; the Romans refused this and whipped her and her daughters. The governor, Suetonius Paulinus, who had been campaigning in north-west Wales against the tribe of Ordovices, hastily returned and defeated the Iceni, with heavy and drastic reprisals. Boudicca killed herself. The British tribes had certainly not lived in a state of mutual peace, but the organised terror of Roman colonial warfare was a new and horrifying experience for them. If the Roman army brought civilisation in its wake, it first prepared the ground by burning, rape, plunder, extortion and mass killings.

It was with a campaign of virtual genocide that the governor, Agricola, appointed to Britain in 78 and in charge until 85, smashed the Ordovices and established control of the great tribe of the Brigantes, whose territory lay right across the country north of the Humber. Three great legionary fortresses were set up to sustain Roman rule, at Eboracum (York), Deva (Chester) and Isca (Caerleon); each placed to give quick access to the still doubtful hill districts. For three hundred years the country would be Romano-British, though most of the garrison soldiers were not Roman or even Italian, but from eastern Europe: present-day Romania and the Adriatic coastal states. Many of them settled after long service, and veterans' colonies were set up at Lincoln, Colchester and Gloucester. Roman life and influence was strongest in the towns, and the countryside retained its Brittonic speech and Celtic lifestyle. The Romans had however eradicated, or tried very hard to eradicate, their druidical religion, whose great centre had been the island of Anglesey. The druids, priests, counsellors, prophets and lore-masters, had been seen as the prime source of anti-Roman agitation, and a torrent of propaganda was turned on them, as well as military force. Though worship of the Celtic gods and nature spirits certainly continued, and the Romans were not hostile to the local gods, the campaign against the druids and their cult may have helped to create a religious vacuum from which Christianity would later benefit.

PAX ROMANA

The Romans changed the map of eastern England with a vast work of reclamation in the Fens, which until the first century AD had formed an indeterminate region of shallow sea and tidal marsh, completely uninhabitable save for a few island sites. The new land was let out to native farmers, and the canalised rivers formed communication links into the interior of the country, traversed by barges carrying agricultural produce. The legions also built the best roads England was to see for a millennium and a half: well-founded, stone-surfaced routes linking the main settlements and often running straight for many miles, though bending to ease the gradients where hills and steep slopes had to be tackled. Unlike the prehistoric trackways, which followed the dry chalk and limestone ridges, the Roman roads struck across country to link the key military depots to one another, and a host of Streets, Strattons and Strettons remain in place names to mark their way-stations, just as -chester names mark their *castra*, or fortified settlements.

The countryside these roads traversed was still inhabited by the British tribes. The conquest had changed their lives to some degree; they had to pay taxes and could be recruited into Roman auxiliary forces. They became familiar with the concept of coinage and markets, and with the methods of Roman local administration. The empire was not extended in the interests of peace but of commerce and profit: the Pax Romana was necessary in order to ensure that provinces got on with the task of enriching Rome and the aristocratic, mercantile and military family groups at the apex of its social pyramid. Romans took over the iron and lead mines and salt-workings and extended them. Quarries were opened up. In the south, large estates dominated by villas – the typical Roman farm plus country house complex – were established, sometimes on a palatial scale, and occupied by

A road in Northumbria built on a Roman road

A stretch of Hadrian's Wall

leaders of the Romanised Britons as well as by wealthy colonists. Cereal growing was their main activity, to supply the demands of the army garrisons and the growing towns. The enforced peace made it easier for country people to concentrate on farm work. Livestock rearing was also of great importance, not only for meat but for all the essential by-products of the animals, from wool and horn to leather and glue. The Romans introduced various new crops, including the cabbage, turnip, carrot and celery, as well as rye, oats and flax. But they also brought the rose, violet and lily, among other flowers. The Romano-British population ate better under Roman rule than in earlier days.

In 122 Emperor Hadrian included Britannia in one of his perpetual tours of the vast Roman Empire. The northern part of the province was by no means secure either from Caledonian invasion or from internal uprising. It was Hadrian who defined the limits of the Roman province of Britannia and instigated the construction of a massive wall, crossing the breadth of the country from the Tyne Estuary to the southern shore of the Solway Firth. Despite later Roman attempts to conquer northwards, this was to remain the outermost boundary of the empire. In the mid-second century, there was a serious revolt among the Brigantes, and after this had been crushed, their *civitas*, or administrative state, was broken up and their territory largely taken into imperial control. The old tribal structure of pre-Roman Britain was destroyed in terms of political power, though its traditions and language lived on.

The third century and the first decades of the fourth were a time of relative stability and prosperity. Military activity was focused on attempts to suppress the warrior peoples of Caledonia. Roman troops could gain fighting experience in the badlands north of Hadrian's Wall, and massive expeditions were launched from the legionary headquarters at York under Emperor Septimius Severus in 208–9 and Emperor Constantius in 306. Between these imperial visitations, the provincial government was pulled to and fro by the rivalries of would-be military rulers of north-west Europe. From 260 it had been divided into two provinces, Britannia Superior, with its military centres at Chester and Caerleon to the south; and Britannia Inferior, with its headquarters at York, forming the northern province. Britannia was wealthy, its internal stability secured by its three legionary centres, its prosperity sustained by the new urban culture developed under Roman rule. The towns of Roman Britain were mostly very small, but they were true urban nuclei, trading centres, homes of craftsmen, shopkeepers and merchants, with public facilities like bath-houses, and with their own local government.

A legal distinction was applied between native peoples and Roman citizens, but this came to an end in 212, in the reign of the emperor, Caracalla, when all free-born inhabitants of the empire were granted the rights and status of Roman citizens. In Britannia as elsewhere, this still left a substantial population of slaves who were the property of their masters and had no civic rights. This was not a Roman innovation; the British tribes were long familiar with the practice of slave-ownership, though it is impossible to gauge its extent or its contribution to the economy. In the south, towns grew as open places, at fords, road junctions, or close to an old tribal centre, as with Dorchester and the adjacent hill-fort of Maiden Castle. Some were manufacturing places, like the pottery centre of Durobrivae (Water Newton) on the River Nene. As a port and commercial

Earthworks at Maiden Castle, the largest Iron Age hill-fort in Europe

centre, London was probably already the largest town, and a centre of civilian administration. Latin was the language of these urban communities, though everyone save transient Roman administrators must also have spoken Brittonic. The town councils were manned by decurions, citizens whose wealth and status qualified them – often reluctantly – for leadership. Tax collection, and the making-up of any arrears in the assessment, were prime aspects of their responsibility.

BRITANNIA IN THE LATER EMPIRE

If Britannia within its bounds was fairly secure, the same cannot be said of the world beyond. The state of the Roman Empire was like that of a huge, roughly assembled raft afloat on the ocean. When storms arose, partial break-up always threatened; communication from the centre was extremely difficult, and the captains of different sections fought each other for authority over as much of the heaving surface as they could effectively control. With the resumption of calm, the central commander would gradually re-establish overall authority, though each time it would be over a rather different structure, and with a somewhat different system of management. For a time, from 260, Britannia formed part of a 'Gallic empire' until the emperor, Aurelian, restored Roman control in 274. Again, between 287 and 296, breakaway leaders, Carausius and his assassin and successor Allectus, ruled until an imperial army under the Caesar Constantius came to reinstate central authority. Allectus appears to have been the first ruler in Britain to import foreign troops, Franks in this case, to bolster his own forces.

These power struggles had an important effect on the borders of the Roman provinces. To sustain their bids for power, the would-be emperors drew troops away from the legionary garrisons. In 296 Hadrian's Wall, left undefended by Allectus, was stormed from the north: a foretaste of what would later happen on a larger scale. Around 312 the number of provinces was increased to four: Britannia Prima and Maxima Caesariensis from the old Upper Britain; and Britannia Secunda and Flavia Caesariensis from Lower Britain. London, Cirencester, York and Lincoln were the respective capitals. These political and administrative changes reveal a firm governmental control but also a change to more intensive civilian rule compared to the old military division.

Although some historians characterised Britannia as a 'backward' province, this does not seem to have been the case. The Wall to the north and the coastline long kept it free from the invasions and warfare that plagued and finally wrecked the much greater and richer province of Gaul from the later decades of the third century. Town fortifications seem to have begun in Britannia in the late second century, originally in the form of earthworks. By the late third century, these were being replaced by walls. At this time, too, a new danger to the integrity

27

of the provinces was recognised, with the institution of the forts of the 'Saxon Shore'. Across the southern stretches of the North Sea there were portentous movements of peoples taking place. Frankish and Saxon pirates were raiding at sea and on land. The whole immensely long northern frontier of the empire was slowly crumbling under pressure from the Germanic and Slavonic peoples.

From 350 began the process, ultimately disastrous to Britannia, of imperial usurpers drawing troops away from the provinces to help their own ambitions on the European mainland. This also introduced a form of recurrent civil war, since the victor, like Emperor Constantius II in 353, would severely punish a 'rebellious' province that had, whether under duress or not, supported a usurper. The unrest and resentment brought about by this policy encouraged an alliance of Picts and Scots (the latter still one of the peoples of Ireland) to invade the north. They were forced back by elite units of the Roman army, sent over under the command of Lupicinus, the senior general of the western emperor, Julian. But, when Julian became sole emperor and focused his attention eastwards on Persia, the attacks from north and west resumed with greater intensity. A large-scale invasion took place in 367, with Saxons seemingly acting in conjunction with the Picts and Scots. These were plundering expeditions rather than conquering raids. The British provinces, once so secure, were in great disarray. The barbarian invaders were reaching as far as London, and the imperial forces were too depleted to withstand them. Emperor Valentinian sent the military count, Theodosius, to repeat what had been done by Lupicinus. Landing at Richborough (by this time a major coastal fortress) he secured London and moved rapidly against the roving war-bands. By 369 he had largely restored the order and morale of the provinces. The accounts of his campaign refer to a fifth province, Valentia, probably in the area around Carlisle, a strategic district south of the Wall. Theodosius sought to make a lasting disposition, and his campaign secured a few years of relative peace. Ironically, it was an army revolt that launched a new stage of disorder, when in 383 the army in Britain proclaimed its general, Magnus Maximus, as emperor. Invading Gaul with his army, Magnus defeated the western emperor, Gratian, and ruled until 388 when he was defeated in northern Italy by the eastern emperor, Theodosius the Great, son of the count who had reclaimed Britannia.

THE LAST DAYS OF ROMAN RULE

Theodosius was the last man to be sole ruler of the whole Roman Empire in both its eastern and western sections, with Constantinople and Rome as capitals. His son, Honorius, became western emperor in 395, and his twenty-eight year reign saw its collapse and dissolution. In Britain, where barbarian raids again resumed, there was one final backlash by the empire, when Honorius' general, Flavius

Stilicho – not a Roman but a Vandal in imperial service – made or sent a shock expedition in 398, defeating Saxons, Picts and Scots. But Stilicho, faced with irruptions on every side, fatally disabled the defences of Britannia in 401–2 by withdrawing garrison troops to fight elsewhere. The rump of troops stationed on the island, aware of their own inability to cope, elected a succession of obscure figures as their chief or 'emperor'; the last of these took the name Constantine III and attempted to join up with the Roman forces in Gaul and head off the vast numbers of Vandals, Alans and Suevians who had crossed the frozen Rhine at the end of 406, and were spreading into Gaul, and who, it was feared, would cross the Straits of Dover into Britain. Constantine III was successful for a time, but in 411 was defeated and executed by Honorius.

The death-throes of the western empire went on for some time, but already Roman government and rule in Britain were, if not non-existent, at least wholly ineffective. Town development had ceased decades before. Army deserters, self-liberated slaves, escaped criminals, ruined shopkeepers wandered in bands, raiding villas, seeking food, wine, buried treasures. In response to the anarchy which had settled on the land, a contemporary writer, Zosimus, recorded that the inhabitants of Britain revolted from Roman rule and expelled their Roman governors: 'The Britons took up arms and, braving danger for their own independence, freed their cities from the barbarians threatening them.'

Thus ended almost four centuries of Roman imperial rule, a time-span equivalent to that from the Union of the Crowns to the present day. For the moment, the Picts, Scots and Saxons were held at bay. The Britons were in control of their land, as they had been until Claudius' invasion. But they were not the same people as in AD 43 . This was especially true of those who by family and wealth were the natural leaders of the society: they were by now inescapably Romano-British. Christian, civilised, used to generations of peace and good order, accustomed to defer to the agents of their world's superpower, they faced a profoundly uncertain future.

HERESY

One of the first British clerics to be known by name, Pelagius (corresponding to Morgan, 'sea-born'), lived in the late fourth and early fifth centuries, spending his adult life in Italy and North Africa. His fame is due to his notoriety as a heretic. Pelagius rejected the concepts of original sin and predestination, preferring to focus on humanity's free will and innate capacity for good. A number of texts are ascribed to him, including *On the Trinity* and *On the Pauline Epistles*. He was condemned by a synod at Carthage in 416, and banished from Rome in 418, but Pelagianism was often revived in other forms. It was strongly held in Britain, and the Gaulish bishop Germanus' two visits to Britain in 429 and 436 were undertaken to dispute with the British Pelagians and restore the orthodox doctrines.

CHAPTER THREE

Angles, Jutes, Saxons and Britons

BELEAGUERED BRITONS

Estimates of the Celtic-speaking population of the British provinces around the year 411 hover about the million mark. A great Celtic nation might have been in the making, but the Britons were not to be left on their own to create one. On all sides they were surrounded by hostile peoples who had come to regard the former provinces as a treasure trove. Raiders came from Ireland, from Caledonia, from across the North Sea and the Channel, time and time again. The Britons did not yield tamely. A century of crowded, chaotic and almost unrecorded events followed the Roman power vacuum. What were later to be known as 'the Dark Ages' had arrived. Through those years, two long-term facts became clear. One was that the Britons were not a people with a natural tendency to unity. Despite their common language and their long experience of central government, the old tribal structure still pervaded their attitudes. Mutual hostility and shifting alliances among themselves weakened their capacity to fight back. The other deeply ominous trend was that the invaders from across the North Sea were not coming merely to raid, or to offer their services as mercenaries. They were intent on settling in the fertile lands of south-east and east Britain, and claiming them as their own.

They were no more united than were the defenders of the land. Long identi-fied as three great groups, the Angles, Jutes and Saxons, they spilled across from a great swathe of the north-west European coastlands. Their coming was part of a vast migratory movement from northern Europe, lasting for more than two hundred years, which brought Germanic peoples all through the shattered western empire, through Spain and into North Africa. They had never been under Roman rule and were wholly pagan in their religion. Archaeologists and historians, attempting to trace them back to firm districts of origin, have found it a difficult task. The Saxons emerge into recorded history in northern Germany, the province of Holstein and the lands to the south of it. The Angles appear to have occupied present-day Denmark. The Jutes have been harder to pin down, though modern scholars consider their territory to have lain to the east of the River Rhine rather than in present-day Jutland. Particularly between Angles and Saxons, there was a close kinship of language and tradition. The

Jutes occupied Kent, though its name still perpetuated the old Celtic tribe of Cantii, and they had many traditions in common with the Franks who spread into the north of Gaul and gave their name to France.

A strong tradition links the invasion with the internal disunity of the British people. In the middle of the fifth century a war-leader emerged whose name is unknown but whose title, Vortigern, means great chief. To sustain his efforts, either against Picts and Scots, or other Britons, he obtained the services of continental mercenaries under the leadership of two chiefs, Hengist and Horsa. This was in 449. By 455 Hengist and Vortigern were at war with each other. Oisc, son of Hengist, is recorded as the first King of Kent. In 477 a Saxon warlord, Aelle, landed on the south coast and established a bridgehead which was progressively enlarged into Sussex, land of the South Saxons. Further west, in 495, another group landed to form the nucleus of the kingdom of Wessex. The name of its leader, Cerdic, is believed to be British, which suggests that even at this stage there was intermarriage between ruling families of the Saxons and Britons, perhaps as a result of peace treaties or territorial negotiations. Other groups sailed up the Thames and Humber estuaries, and into the Wash, and moved inland by river and land, establishing the kingdom of Mercia, its name meaning 'border-land'. Although little detail of events is known, the expansion of all these proto-kingdoms was achieved against fierce opposition. The Romano-British tradition produced the leader, Ambrosius Aurelianus, who appears have successfully fought the invaders, perhaps in the Somerset marshes. At some point early in the fifth century, there was a battle whose fame was long preserved in Celtic Britain, the fight at Mount Badon, a site now unknown – a British victory which deterred further expansion of the Anglo-Saxon kingdoms for about fifty years. For a time there was even a reverse of the occupation process, with groups of the invaders returning to Europe and settling Frisia on the Dutch coastal fringe, a move which brought about the close resemblance between the Frisian tongue and Old English. But in the west, there was also a loss of population, as British Celtic speakers, either displaced or fearing displacement or an even worse fate, migrated into Armorica and gave their name to the Celtic state of Brittany.

But the Anglo-Saxon conquest was interrupted, not halted. By 550 the encroachment was again in full swing. A decisive battle was fought at Dyrham, near the Roman ruins of Aquae Sulis (Bath), in 577 when Ceawlin, King of Wessex, and Cuthwine defeated the Britons and cut off the Britons of the south-western peninsula. By now the new kingdoms were large enough to share boundaries and regions of debatable land, and the long rivalry between Wessex and Mercia was well established before the end of the sixth century. The West Saxons fought the Jutes. By the turn of the sixth century, most of lowland England was divided into a mosaic of Anglo-Saxon kingdoms, and statelets dominated by warlords. In the north-east, two Anglian states were fighting for land and existence: Deira, based on York, and Bernicia, based on the fortified rock of Bamburgh. From 588 these were fused into a single Northumbrian kingdom under the rule of Aethelfrith. The Northumbrians forced their way across into Celtic Cumbria and cut off the Britons north of the old Roman Wall from those to the south. Another crucial battle, at Chester, destroyed the army of the northern Welsh peoples. By 613, the Britons survived as a political entity only in Dumnonia (Devon and Cornwall, whose last king was resisting the West Saxons around 710), Wales, and in the kingdom of Strathclyde.

ANGLO-SAXON INFLUENCE

How far the Britons survived as an element of the population in the conquered lands is not clear. The Anglo-Saxons were much greater in number than the Romans who conquered before them or the later Normans. Mass graves have been found with beheaded bodies, but these may have been from reprisals or executions, rather than ethnic massacres. Bede records the slaughter, at Aethelfrith's orders, of the monks of Bangor who had come out to urge on the Britons at Chester. Many Britons must have fled westwards in fear of death or slavery; the Anglo-Saxon word for 'Briton' also meant 'slave'. Few Brittonic words were adopted into the Anglo-Saxons' language, and though many river and hill names remained Brittonic, and the names of Roman city-sites were preserved, the invaders bestowed their own names on their settlements. The culture and religion of the Britons were both eclipsed. Christianity was preserved in Wales, in Ireland, and among the Picts and Scots, but Germanic deities of war and fertility were worshipped in England, with their feasts and sacrifices duly observed. There is evidence of British survival in some place names like Bretby (Britons' town) or the many Waltons (strangers' town) as well as in some preserved laws of Wessex from around 700 which deal with British landholders. Generally speaking, it is likely that the proportion of Britons in the population of Anglo-Saxon England increased towards the west and south-west.

Although the Jutish people of Kent were set apart, culturally at least, there was little to distinguish Angles from Saxons, especially after a few generations in the new country. It is of interest that the new inhabitants' own ultimate name should come from the Angles, while the neighbours knew them as Saxons (still perpetuated in 'Sassenach'); also that the name of Britain did not fall from use. Kings competing for overlordship referred to themselves as Bretwalda, 'ruler of Britain'. The ambiguities that still exist between 'England' and 'Britain' go back even before the beginnings of the nation, when the Anglo-Saxon kings of Mercia bore the style of Rex Brittonum, 'King of the Britons'.

For two hundred years the Anglo-Saxon kingdoms would struggle among one another. The driving force was not any ideal of national unity but the desire of an individual king or dynasty to extend power by forcing neighbouring kings into submission, or to outface the ambitions of another. They were a somewhat grim and austere people, who lived according to a violent code and who celebrated warfare and the warrior's life. Their society was an aristocratic one, with a king at its head; veneration of royal descent was already deeply ingrained, and poets obligingly traced back the royal descent to Woden or another divine figure. Kings were not immune from deposition or assassination, but for each one knifed or strangled, a replacement, also of royal blood, was always available.

THE COMING OF CHRISTIANITY

In 597, with considerable trepidation, but urged on by his formidable and demanding superior in Rome, an Italian bishop, Augustine, landed in Kent with a small party of fellow-missionaries. His task, set by Pope Gregory the Great, was to convert the inhabitants to the Christian religion, and to establish a church within the ambit of Roman control. The Franks were already Christian,

and Bertha, wife of the Kentish king, Ethelbert, was a Frankish princess; diplomacy had already ensured that Augustine would not be turned away or martyred. At this time, too, the Kentish king was the most powerful monarch in the country. Ethelbert accepted the new faith and Augustine became the first Archbishop of Canterbury. But he failed to accomplish Gregory's desire to establish London and York as twin metropolises of the church. To many of the Anglo-Saxons, the religion that preached peace and universal brotherhood was a contemptible thing.

Relations between the Canterbury mission and the long-established Celtic church were uncertain or hostile; an early meeting between Augustine and a

St Augustine

group of Welsh bishops was wrecked when the archbishop received his visitors sitting down. For a time the candle of Christianity flickered perilously. In 625, Paulinus, one of Augustine's first companions, accompanied a Kentish princess to Northumbria, where she was to marry the king, Edwin. He had killed Aethelfrith and exiled that ruler's sons. Edwin converted to Christianity, but in 632 he was killed in battle against Cadwallon, King of Gwynedd, in alliance with a Mercian noble, Penda. Paulinus and the queen fled back to the south. Under Oswald, a son of Aethelfrith, who had learned his Christianity in exile on Iona, the Northumbrian forces were regrouped, and Cadwallon was defeated and killed in 633. Oswald sent to Iona for a bishop to teach Christianity to his pagan kingdom, and the saintly Aidan came and established his base on Lindisfarne. The example of the bishop and the energy of the king established the new religion with great success, and missionary monks of the Celtic church spread far and wide across England while the Roman settlement at Canterbury was still struggling to expand its work. Irish and Northumbrian monks established Christianity in East Anglia, Essex, Sussex and Wessex (where a European missionary, Birinus, linked to neither York nor Canterbury, also worked, and became the first bishop at Dorchester on Thames), and finally, around the mid-seventh century, in the great heathen kingdom of Mercia.

Baptism and the acceptance of the Creed were the necessary conditions for conversion to Christianity. When a king took the new religion it was politic or compulsory for his people to do so too. For Anglo-Saxon kings, the church offered valuable support. It had to do so, in order to induce men who considered themselves god-descended to forsake their lofty pedigrees and join the human ranks of sinners. Instead it offered them the consecration of Christian kingship, a special role under God. Perhaps more important, it brought them into an international context in which they shared the prestige of greater kings like the Frankish monarchs and even that of the far-off emperor in Constantinople. The people did not forget their ancient beliefs or superstitions and there is no doubt that pagan traditions persisted for many centuries, and indeed some have never died out. Churchmen would fight a constant battle against charms, omen-reading, nature-worship, and rituals aimed at promoting fertility, witchcraft and sorcery. But through the latter half of the seventh century an internal struggle went on in the church itself. The Northumbrian church, from its first base on Lindisfarne, was established on the Celtic model by its first bishop, St Aidan. But by the middle of the seventh century it had shaken off its Celtic aspects and conformed to the rule and doctrines of Rome, as expounded by the papally appointed incumbents of the recently established bishopric of Canterbury. Northumbria's up-and-coming clerics, like the redoubtable Wilfred, founder of Ripon Cathedral and Hexham Abbey, and the scholarly, book-collecting Benedict Biscop, founder of the monasteries at Monkwear-

BEDE

'I was born on the lands of this monastery, and on reaching seven years of age, my family entrusted me first to the most reverend Abbot Benedict, and later to Abbot Ceolfrid for my education. I have spent all the remainder of my life in this monastery, and devoted myself entirely to the study of the scriptures. And while I have observed the regular discipline and sung the choir offices daily in church, my chief delight has always been in study, teaching, and writing.'

As he himself tells us, Bede, born in 672 or 673, and living until 735, was presented to the monastery of Monkwearmouth on the Tyne as a child oblate. He was to become the greatest scholar of his time not only in England but in Europe. In 682 he moved to the new monastery of Jarrow and was ordained as a priest in 703. Always first and foremost a churchman of strong piety, his range of study and interest was enormous and testifies to the scope of the library assembled by Benedict Biscop at Monkwearmouth. Latin, Greek, Hebrew, astronomy, chronology, medicine, all featured.

What distinguishes Bede from all other writers of the time is his adoption of a scholarly method. His primary interest was in explaining the teachings of the Bible and relating them to the Christian life, but it was based on a precise understanding of grammar both in the classical languages and in Old English. His interest in numbers and dates led him to develop an efficient system of chronological record. His separation of recorded time into the eras BC and AD has lasted into modern times.

Bede was the author of numerous works, and letters of his have also been preserved. His most famous book is the great *Ecclesiastical History of the English People*, written in Latin, dedicated to 'the most glorious king Ceolwulf' of Northumbria, and completed in 731. With the later *Anglo-Saxon Chronicle*, it is one of the foundation stones of the English historical tradition. His concern is to record the advent of Christianity in Anglo-Saxon England, but in doing so he gives a great variety of details, and many intriguing hints, about life in Great Britain in the seventh and eighth centuries. An important aspect of Bede's text is the way in which he consistently refers to the English as a single people – the influence of his writing undoubtedly played a part in the acceptance of the idea of national unity.

mouth and Jarrow, were by then Anglians, not Scots. They had visited and studied in Rome and were convinced supporters of papal authority and the international church. At the Synod of Whitby in 664, called by King Oswiu of Northumbria, Wilfred had won the crucial debate with the Ionan bishop, Colman, over the central issues of the dating of Easter and the form of a monk's tonsure.

To a secular age these seem minor matters, but the Celtic churchmen, with a long tradition not merely of independence, but of maintaining the faith when it had all but collapsed elsewhere, saw the abandonment of these practices as a rejection of two hundred years of devoted labour. Such things were far from being considered trivial, and Wilfred's remark, borrowed from the headquarters briefing of a Lateran missive, and quoted in Bede's *History of the English Church*, was both insulting and wounding: 'The only people who are stupid enough to disagree with the whole world are these Scots and their obstinate adherents the Picts and the Britons, who inhabit only a portion of these two islands in the remote ocean' (Bede iii, 25). (Wilfred appears, incidentally, to have been the first Englishman to identify and patronise what much later was called 'the Celtic fringe'.) At the same time as the Northumbrian church was being 'romanised' from within, the papal foundation at Canterbury gained impetus and authority with the arrival in 669 of a new archbishop, the Greek monk Theodore of Tarsus and his chief lieutenant, the African abbot Hadrian. Already aged sixty-six, Theodore served for twenty-one years, during which he firmly established the metropolitan authority of Canterbury, and in 672 he summoned the first Council of the English Church, at Hertford. He set out a diocesan structure which remained the basis of future development, and despite firm insistence on conformity with Rome, was able to at least partly reconcile the division between the 'Celtic' and the 'Roman' elements in the church.

THE RISE OF MERCIA

In 632, when Penda became King of Mercia, it was still a pagan state and he remained a resolute heathen until his death. Soon he was a deadly rival of his former ally, Oswald of Northumbria. War between the two ended in the defeat and death of Oswald. Mercian power expanded steadily and sub-rulers acknowledged Penda's overlordship from the lands of the Hwicce people (a name still seen in Wychwood) north-east of Hereford, to East Anglia. Penda was defeated and killed by Oswald's brother and successor, Oswiu, but the rise of Mercian power was only briefly checked. Its expansion was aided by the shattering defeat of a Northumbrian invasion of Pictland, north of the Firth of Tay, in 685. This marked the end of Northumbrian imperial expansion, though it remained a unified kingdom and was the centre of remarkable achievements in stone carving, manuscript illumination, and scholarship.

With Northumbria no longer a serious threat, the rulers of Mercia confronted the only two powers large and aggressive enough to challenge their dominance: the Britons to the west, and the West Saxons to the south. Wessex in the mid-seventh century was not a major power but under the rule of Caedwalla, from 685, and his successor Ine, from 688 to 726, its frontiers were pushed out to south, east and west. London, a great prize, as the main trading centre, and formerly in the kingdom of Essex, came under the control of Wessex, and Sussex acknowledged Ine's overlordship. But the Wessex expansion did not survive Ine's reign. The eighth century was to be the great century of Mercia, ruled for most of its duration by only two men, Ethelbald from 716 to 757, and Offa from 757 to 796. Despotic leaders whose first law was the maintenance of their own power, they were still something more than warlords – to maintain a kingdom, to establish suzerainty over vassal states, to create their own kingly style, it was necessary to have a structure of laws, taxes, commercial tolls, land-division and town management. Offa – his name recalling a legendary hero of the Angles from the pre-invasion times – published a code of laws, and corresponded with the Pope and with Emperor Charlemagne. He was undisputed overlord of England south of the Humber, but he found perpetual trouble on his western flank, where the Britons of Wales resisted the Mercians' encroachment into their borderlands.

Two great invasions of South Wales failed to crush them. Late in his reign he had the great earthwork built which is still known as Offa's Dyke, a 120-mile rampart from the Wye estuary to that of the Dee. It did not mark a precise border but was a line of control and defence; the frontier between Britons and Angles would long remain an indecisive one, subject to the vagaries of war and politics.

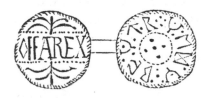

A silver penny of Offa, King of Mercia

Ethelbald and Offa were Christian, although religion was not allowed to interfere with their conduct as autocratic rulers. Offa was perhaps the first English king to realise and put to use the potential strength of the church in securing and glorifying his own position. Pope Gregory's original plan had envisaged two provinces of the church, based on London and York. Now, although London was under his control, Offa successfully petitioned the Pope to make his diocesan centre of Lichfield into the seat of a third archbishopric, which was achieved in 786, with a consequent reduction in Canterbury's domain. Great endowments were made to the church in Mercia, and, for the first time, the tenants of church estates paid their land revenues and other dues to the church instead of the king. The ability to make this large concession is a clear indication of the Mercian kingdom's wealth, sustained, among other things, by tolls on foreign trade and by tribute payments from the vassal kingdoms. There are indications that the power of Mercia caused some anxiety to Charlemagne in his newly consolidated and fragile European empire. It had not been forgotten that, in the later years of the Roman empire, powerful leaders from the great island had sought to exercise control in Gaul and even beyond. A unified England was to be feared. In his later years Offa used the style Rex Anglorum, 'king of the English': a king was still the leader of a people rather than the supreme lord of a defined country.

It may have seemed natural that the power established in the centre of the country should gradually extend its control to the boundaries. But much depended on the resource and ruthlessness of individual kings. Mercia's hegemony did not survive Offa's death, and the Lichfield archbishopric was terminated in 803, but it still took over twenty years for Egbert, King of Wessex, to establish himself as an overlord, and then not on Offa's scale. The battle of Ellandun, near Swindon, marked the end of Mercian ascendancy and by 829 the Northumbrians accepted Egbert's overlordship. The last Celtic redoubt of England, in Cornwall, was conquered by Egbert, though it remained a restive province for some time.

TERROR OF THE NORSEMEN

But even as this last piece of the Anglo-Saxon jigsaw was put into place, two hundred years after their first incursions, the invaders-turned-settlers found themselves assailed from the sea. The first Viking raids, from around 790, were no more than that, hit-and-run attacks by seaborne pirates finding rich and undefended targets close to shore, such as the monastery of Lindisfarne. Their paganism added a sinister aspect to what even by the standards of the time was appalling brutality. With little space in their ships to take slaves, they killed males indiscriminately but carried off girls and women. Within a very few years it was obvious that a profoundly unsettling new element had entered into the world of Anglo-Saxons, Britons, Picts and Scots. Perceived at first as nothing more than a harassment, the Norsemen became a very serious threat to all the established kingdoms of the British Isles. Early in the ninth century they were ceasing to be sporadic external raiders, and forming a new, strong and enduring element in the regional power-structure. There is a hard historical irony in their resemblance to the Angles and Saxons themselves of a few generations back. Like these, the Vikings were pagan. They came from the same part of northern Europe. Their language and their customs were in many ways similar to those of the Anglo-Saxons. But the Vikings were harsher, more extreme in their idolisation of violence and their warrior cult. There is ample evidence that they were found to be utterly terrifying.

The West Saxons found the lately conquered Cornish allying with Norsemen to reclaim their territory, and Egbert defeated them at Hingston Down, near Plymouth, in 838. Other Norse groups raided into Mercia and Northumbria. Nowhere in England was very far from the sea, or from a navigable river, and nowhere could feel safe from a sudden devastating raid. In the reign of Egbert's successor, Aethelwulf, Norse armies felt secure enough to winter in England in 850 and 854, choosing the defensible sites of the Isles of Thanet and Sheppey. Local resistance was often strong, including a naval battle, the first to be recorded in English history, off Sandwich in Kent, when a fleet of raiders was beaten back in 851. Larger-scale resistance was rare or non-existent, and the overlordship of the Wessex kings was a meaningless dignity when Wessex could not even defend itself against the marauders. In 864 they stormed and burned down its capital, Winchester. So far, the Viking raids had been opportunistic, led by many war-chiefs who owed allegiance to no one and whose success depended on securing plunder on the largest scale. Around 865, their campaigning took a different turn, and it became clear that they were fighting to gain and hold the land. Under two leaders of high rank, Ivar 'the Boneless' and his brother, Halfdan, an army landed in East Anglia. Over the next ten years, a vast extent of eastern England was brought under Norse rule. Northumbria was first to be subjugated, and its old Roman-British-Saxon capital became the Viking town of Jorvik. Eastern Mercia was overrun, and in 869 East Anglia and Essex were added. The pious Anglian king, Edmund, killed by the victors, was buried by his people where Bury St Edmunds now stands. The Norsemen now turned inland and forced their way up the line of the Thames and along the Downs. The conquest of Mercia was completed.

ALFRED THE GREAT

In 871, the fourth and youngest son of Aethelwulf, Alfred, had become King of Wessex, a much-assailed and reduced kingdom. He bribed the Norsemen to stop their further advance westward; instead they swept north. By 876, they returned. Under Alfred, the West Saxons put up a fierce resistance but they were gradually driven back until, at the lowest point of his fortunes, Alfred took refuge at Athelney in the Somerset marshes in the spring of 878. From here he rallied his forces to defeat the Danish leader, Guthrum, at the battle of Edington in May of that year. This was followed up by Guthrum's surrender and promise to adopt Christianity, set out in the Treaty of Wedmore.

Only one English king has ever been dubbed 'the Great'. Though he never ruled more than Wessex, Kent and part of Mercia, Alfred earned this description not only through his prowess and steadfastness as a military leader but also by his statesmanship, scholarship and care for his nation. Unlike previous kings such as Offa, he was a man of culture who thought deeply about moral issues. The national tradition of England stems from his success, for otherwise, whatever country ultimately emerged from Viking conquest, it would have had another name and perhaps its destiny set on other paths. His arrest of the Norsemen's progress made it possible for his successors to regain for the Anglo-Saxons what had been lost to the invaders. Although it is the *Anglo-Saxon Chronicle*, the history of national events founded by Alfred himself, that says so, there is no reason to doubt its comment that: 'all the English people submitted to Alfred except those who were under the power of the Danes.' To those who feared conquest, and to those already conquered, the King of Wessex offered the only real hope.

While he had peace, Alfred prepared for war, renewing his army and creating

Alfred the Great

a fleet to guard the coasts, and building fortifications round his main towns. War duly recurred in 886 and 892, with new Danish invasions, and the Danish kingdoms of eastern England coming to their support. Between 892 and 896, there was again open warfare as a further effort was made to make England a wholly Viking country; it was a bitter campaign and in the end the raiders turned away to find easier pickings in northern Europe. England was left a divided country. North of a line from London to Chester were kingdoms of the Norsemen, East Anglia, the land of the 'Five Boroughs' of Lincoln, Nottingham, Derby, Leicester and Stamford, ruled by independent earls, and the kingdom of Jorvik – more than half of the country in overall extent. This was the Danelaw, a great swathe of the country where the Norse imprint would remain for centuries to come, long after the establishment of a unified state. Place names, local dialect words, even regional accents, reveal the long period of occupation and colonisation and the slow commingling of the Norse and Anglo-Saxon populations.

ALFRED'S SUCCESSORS

The frontier was not a natural one and was inevitably transgressed. The Anglo-Saxons did not remain united. When Alfred's son, Edward, succeeded him in 899, a disaffected cousin joined the Danes and invaded Wessex, causing three years of warfare. Inheritance was always likely to cause trouble in cases like this, where the grown sons of Alfred's elder brother had at least as much claim to the kingship as the son of Alfred. The right of a king's eldest son to inherit was still far from being accepted practice. Western Mercia had been under a sub-king, whose widow was Edward's sister, Aethelflaed, 'Lady of Mercia'; and brother and sister operated a co-ordinated policy, responding to incursions from the Danelaw by attacking and annexing territory. The last Danish King of East Anglia was killed in battle in 921. By Edward's death in 924, the realm he had inherited had been greatly enlarged to encompass all the country south of the Humber. His son, Athelstan, first secured York as a sub-kingdom and then took it over. This was empire-building on a scale not seen before. The princes and chiefs of Wales also acknowledged his power by the payment of a large annual tribute. Cornwall, whose British population was again restive under English rule, was invaded and forcibly pacified. For the first time since Britannia was a single Roman province, one man could claim to be master of all England, and Athelstan's prestige was such that his numerous sisters were sought as brides by great European potentates, even Emperor Otto I. It was in support of one of his European alliances that Athelstan sent the first English force to intervene in continental power politics, in 939. Within Great Britain, Athelstan had made the Kings of Strathclyde and of the Scots acknowledge his supremacy in 927. Ten years later, they combined with Irish Vikings to attack him. But at the unidentified site of Brunanburh, Athelstan soundly defeated them. His assemblage of kingdoms and statelets barely lasted for his lifetime, however. By 939 the Vikings under Olaf Guthfrithson had retaken York and in the following year re-established a Viking kingdom around it. Though Athelstan's successors, Edmund and Eadred, fought to regain the English hold, a further Viking revival took place in 947 under Erik Bloodaxe, expelled as the King of Norway, but accepted as king at York. It was not a straightforward business. The Dublin and York Viking kingdoms fought one another, and there was much changing of sides. Erik was ousted, then reinstated. But in 954 he was killed, apparently on Stainmoor, on the border of the Viking kingdom and the Strathclyde sub-kingdom of Cumbria.

ORGANISATION AT THE END OF THE FIRST MILLENNIUM

The circumstances of Erik Bloodaxe's last stand are unclear, but his fate put an end to Norse ambitions in England for more than a generation. During this time Anglo-Saxon kings of the Wessex line continued to rule, though in great areas of the Danelaw, a semi-independence was preserved by earls with their own armed retainers, courts, markets and coinages. They did not rebel, but though they engaged in trade, nor did they integrate. Outside these islands of self-rule, a growing trend towards national unification can be seen at work. This was aided by the development of the language, with the West Saxon form of Old English spreading both in speech and written use, and gradually forming a standard across most of the country, though poetry, which was almost entirely oral at that time, preserved more regional variations. The kings kept the style and titles of their greater predecessors, and maintained a dominant position with regard to their neighbour kings. In one famous account, King

Edgar, on his coronation in 973, was rowed on the River Dee by the Kings of Scotland, Strathclyde, and Man, and by Welsh princes. Most of the country south of the Mersey–Humber line had been 'shired': divided into the administrative regions which would survive with little change until the 1970s. The older shires, like Sussex and Kent, were based on former kingdoms; some later ones, like Shropshire, ignored old divisions to place previously separate groups, in this case the Wreocensaetan, 'men of the Wrekin', and the Magonsaetan to the south, under the same administration. Each was administered by a shire-reeve, the later sheriff, whose tasks included collecting dues owed to the king and the church, calling out the local *fyrd*, or militia, and supervising justice. Shires, or groups of shires, were headed by an ealdorman, a royally appointed leader of noble descent if not actually related to the king, whose duty it was to maintain the shire's defences and to lead its army. Perhaps the most famous of these is Byrhtnoth, Ealdorman of Essex, who led his men against a Danish raid in 991 and whose death, with that of his loyal *thegns*, is celebrated in the old English poem 'The Battle of Maldon'. The thegns themselves were of noble birth, retainers either to the king or an ealdorman, or sometimes to a particularly wealthy member of their own ranks. Thegn meant literally 'one who serves'; in earlier Old English history they were known as *gesith*, 'companion'. The reward for their service was a grant of land, on which they would build their hall and which would be parcelled out in strips to the *ceorls*, men of the peasant class, who worked the land. The smallest subdivision of territory was the hide (Old English *hid*), a plot of land sufficient to support the ceorl and his household through the year. Ceorl later became 'churl', with a somewhat pejorative sense, but in pre-Conquest England he was a free man, who took part in the regular moots and courts of his 'hundred', the local grouping of hides. He paid his dues, was liable for military service, and could own slaves. In the Anglo-Saxon justice system, his life, and his oath, had a set value. This was his *wergild*, or man-price, of 200 shillings. If he was killed, this was the price to be exacted from the slayer, or his family. It compares with 1,200 shillings for a thegn. These values also applied to oaths and statements; a thegn's oath far outclassed a ceorl's.

In the subsequent history of England, despite radical changes in government and in the social structure of the country, and despite the slow decline in status of the ceorl, the independent status, direct relationship to the king, and sheer importance in the national scheme of things of this very substantial cadre of ceorls, was to have a long and powerful influence. Although the earliest descriptions relate to the Kentish ceorls, who may have been of higher status than their West or South Saxon counterparts, Sir Frank Stenton, in *Anglo-Saxon England*, was in no doubt that both shared the same essential rights and duties: 'The basis of Kentish society in Aethelberht's time was obviously the free peasant

THE TRIBAL HIDAGE

Except in Jutish Kent, the hide (Old English *hid*) formed the basis of social organisation. It originally denoted the amount of land which would support the household of a free family and its dependants, and varied in size from 40 to 120 acres (16 to 48 ha). Hyde or hide occur in many place names, such as Hyde in Cheshire, and Piddletrenthide, a district of thirty hides by the River Piddle in Dorset. As time went on, many families owned more than one hide, while others were reduced to less, a 'yardland' or quarter-hide. In the seventh century, the various kingdoms of the country were able to be divided into regions comprising a certain number of hides, and each with a royal *tun* or depot-farm where the king's dues could be collected by his reeves, in the form of grain, honey, fish – whatever range of produce the area could provide. The 'Tribal Hidage', known from a tenth-century copy of an earlier document, is the oldest known regional list of this kind, setting out names of peoples and assigning their number of hides. Originally compiled in eighth-century Mercia, it is most detailed in its information on the West Midlands. Its function was to help assess the dues payable by subject provinces, though it also served to indicate their potential military manpower. In Kent, the basic land-unit was the *sulung*, or ploughland for eight oxen, larger than a hide, but the status of the Kentish ceorl was also correspondingly greater.

landholder, without claim to nobility, but subject to no lord below the king. He was an independent person with many rights . . . The West Saxon evidence points in the same direction . . . In Wessex as in Kent, the free peasant formed the basis of society' (p. 277). Although the Norman Conquest imposed a change of structure, in which the free peasant lost his independence, the sense of self-respect and of reliance (often critical but invariably loyal in spirit) on the crown that was engendered among the 'common people' during the Anglo-Saxon period endured as a force in English life for centuries.

But through the decades towards the eleventh century, the status of the ceorl was already gradually changing in a process of steady decline. Several factors brought this about. Warfare and foreign raids made the position of peasant settlements insecure. Army service could result in death or disablement. Bad weather and epidemic illness could wreck a year's harvest. Excessive demand from the thegn could reduce a family to beggary. Local quarrels and feuds, and the haphazard application of laws which used trial by ordeal to determine guilt or innocence, and whose penalties were death or mutilation, meant that a man without a protector was vulnerable to the bully, the busybody and the bad-mouther. Even though the population – it is reasonable to suppose – was growing, and the product of the land was increasing, the demand of kings for service in building walls, ships, bridges was also growing. The bribes or Danegeld paid to deflect invasion by Aethelred Unraed required large amounts of gold and silver. All demands came ultimately to rest on the lowest, largest, and most productive section of society. But a separate social process also worked against them. It was easier for the thegns to increase their power and authority than it was for the ceorls to retain or increase theirs.

Long before the arrival of the Normans and the institution of the 'feudal system' the trend was growing for the king to cede his rights in a particular village or district to an ealdorman, a thegn or a bishop or abbot. The new lord would be the recipient of dues and services. If the community should fail to provide the food-rent, the landholder could take steps to secure his rights. Usually this resulted in his becoming the landowner. Sir Frank Stenton notes in his *Anglo-Saxon England* that although this was an economic reorganisation, 'in most cases it seems to have formed part of a wider revolution in which the individual peasant surrendered their holdings to the lord of the village and received them back from his hands, acknowledging themselves to be his men, and placing themselves under his protection' (p. 472). The consolidation of aristocratic power itself reflects the greater distinction of the kingship, now that there was only one king, instead of many. The petty kings and sub-kings of earlier times were replaced by ealdormen and the king's thegns, men who attended on him and sat in his *Witanagemot* or Council.

Larger towns, fortified by Alfred under his 'burghal system', had their own administration headed by a port-reeve. They were royal property, and the burgesses paid a fixed rent to the king, though the ealdorman was often entitled to a one-third share of the proceeds of market tolls, fines and other town income. Property speculation in the towns started early and many abbeys owned town houses. Though Winchester, Wessex's capital, and Alfred's burial-place, was the heart of the kingdom, and Norwich, York, Chester, Canterbury and Lincoln were all considerable places, the cosmopolitan port of London, part-Danish, part-English, not wholly attached to any region, was already by far the greatest town and the place of most economic importance. Tolls levied on its trade in wine, fish, wool, coal, wood and a host of other commodities made up a large element of the royal revenue.

THE POWER OF THE CHURCH

By the mid-tenth century, the church was a formidable power in the land, the wealthiest single institution, though its riches were divided among many abbeys and the bishoprics. Kings and magnates continued to make endowments. It was not as yet organised into parishes but its activities were centred on large churches or minsters, their name preserved in many place names, from where a small corps of itinerant priests served a wide area. In many places, an open-air cross served as the meeting place for religious observance. From around the year 950 emerges the first of a long succession of religious leaders who would also act as secular advisers to English kings – and sometimes fall

Winchester Cathedral, once at the heart of Alfred's Wessex

foul of them. Dunstan, abbot of the great monastery of Glastonbury, was, like most senior churchmen, a member of the nobility, in fact a relative of the king, but there is no reason to doubt his piety any more than his ability (*see* p.46).

On the anointing of Eadwig as king in 956, it was Dunstan and the Bishop of Lichfield who forced the young king back to the solemn feast when he had withdrawn to dally with a noblewoman and her daughter – or so legend later told. Dunstan was certainly exiled. But Eadwig was an unpopular and inadequate king and before his death in 959, the Mercians and Northumbrians had rejected him for his brother, Edgar, who reunited the realm on acceding to the crown of Wessex. Dunstan was recalled and made Archbishop of Canterbury. One historian called him Edgar's 'prime minister' but Dunstan was more concerned with church than state affairs, and the uneventfulness of Edgar's sixteen-year reign suggests that the king himself was a strong as well as a fortunate one. Edgar's policy towards the Danelaw was astute and benevolent, confirming their autonomy in local affairs. It may have been in his reign that the territory of Lothian, which had long been Anglian-inhabited but dominated by the Scots, was ceded to the King of Scots, with profound long-term consequences for that still-Celtic kingdom. Dunstan, with the active support of Oswald, Archbishop of York, and Ethelwold, Bishop of Winchester, introduced to the English church the reformed Benedictine rule that had given a fresh impulse to monasticism and religious life through much of northern Europe.

45

St Dunstan

ROUGH JUSTICE

Strongly religious as the Anglo-Saxons were by now, theirs was not a society which brought Christianity far into the practices of daily life. Violence was endemic. Free men carried weapons and were prepared to use them. Although fines and compensation payments were the most common judgements, many crimes were punishable by violent means. Floggings, branding, the slitting of noses and cropping of ears were routine minor punishments. Moneyers whose coins were of adulterated metal had a hand cut off. Hangings were frequent, drownings and beheadings were also resorted to. Imprisonment was rare and probably only employed in the case of high-ranking persons. Where a defendant's guilt was disputable, the 'judgement of God' was resorted to, in one of three forms. In the ordeal by water, if he floated, he was guilty (swimming was an unusual skill). Inside the church, he might be required to carry a pound weight of glowing iron for nine feet, or to take a stone out of boiling water. If the resultant injuries had not healed within three days, he was guilty. There are some signs of a more humanitarian attitude. Archbishop Wulfstan of York, drawing up laws in the time of King Cnut, wrote: 'Christian men shall not be condemned to death for all too little; but one shall determine lenient punishment for the benefit of the people, and not destroy for a little matter God's own handiwork.' King Athelstan raised the age at which a young thief might be hanged from twelve to fifteen. One social institution which the church long struggled to control was that of marriage. In the earlier centuries of the Anglo-Saxons, divorce and remarriage were easy to arrange. An early Kentish law states: 'If a freeman lie with the wife of a freeman, he shall pay . . . wergild, and get another wife with his own money and bring her to the other man's home.' Such a law does not appear to set a high or independent status on the woman, but in Anglo-Saxon society, a woman had greater freedom than was to be the case after the Norman Conquest. She could hold land in her own right and dispose of it as she pleased. She could appear as a compurgator (oath-taker) in court, and an eleventh-century law states that: 'No woman or maiden shall ever be forced to marry one whom she dislikes, nor be sold for money.' (This of course relates only to free-born women). In fact the practice of arranged marriages, at least in property-owning families, would continue for several hundred years.

THE CROWNING OF AETHELRED

The influence that could be exercised by highly placed women is shown in what was considered to be one of the greatest crimes in the Anglo-Saxons' history. King Edgar left two sons, by successive wives; and the elder, Edward, became king in 975. On 18 March 978, while visiting Aelfthryth, his stepmother, he was suddenly attacked and killed at Corfe in Dorset by the retainers of her son, Aethelred, a boy of around ten. Aethelred was crowned king. Edward had been far from saintly but the treacherous circumstances of his death caused him to be considered a martyr and eventually a saint. Aethelred's reign, which was to last thirty-eight years, thus began under a dark cloud. Whether his inadequacy as a king caused the Scandinavians to renew their attacks, or whether their attacks exposed his incapacity for effective rule, is now impossible to tell. But he failed to maintain the peace of Edgar's years. His name has passed on in history as Aethelred Unraed, 'the ill-counselled'. Even without raids from outside, he was unable to keep his ealdormen loyal and at peace.

PAYING OFF THE DANE

From the early tenth century, the Norsemen had established an independent state in the north of France, with its capital at Rouen. Still conscious of their Nordic origins, the Normans allowed their ports to be used by the raiders into

England. This caused deep resentment and hostility in England, and in 990–91, the Pope felt compelled to mediate. The diplomatic settlement did not affect the raids, which became heavier, and Aethelred's treasury was depleted by vast sums paid to buy them off. Unlike Alfred, however, he was not buying time to build up his defences. The position steadily deteriorated through the 990s, until the Vikings were undisputed masters of the seas around England and their war-bands were able to pass the winters encamped in England. Only their own disunity prevented them from overrunning the whole country; the Witan, in desperation, resorted to paying one war-band to hold off another. Individual efforts, like that of Byrhtnoth and his men at Maldon, were made in vain. For reasons now unclear, when Aethelred did take action, he struck north, into Cumbria, in 1000–1, while a Viking army, again based in Normandy, was harrying his south coast. By now a widower, in that year he married Emma, daughter of Duke Richard II of Normandy. In a desperate stroke, apparently fearing treachery, he ordered a massacre of the Danes in English service, on 13 November 1002. The extent of this is hard to gauge. But one prominent victim was Gunnhild, sister of King Swein of Denmark, living as a hostage in England. This brought about a state of war. Between 1003 and 1006, successive armies stormed across England from Norfolk to Wiltshire, until a vast tribute of £36,000 was paid. In 1007–9, Aethelred's government attempted to strengthen the defences. An associate of the king, Eadric Streona, was made Ealdorman of Mercia, and a fleet of over a hundred ships, with armour for its crews, was assembled. Dissension and suspicions of treachery set the fleet at war with itself and it counted for nothing when in 1009 a new onslaught came, of Danes and Norsemen from the great war-camp at Jómsburg at the mouth of the Vistula. In 1011 they took Canterbury and Archbishop Aelfheah (St Alphege), refusing to sanction a separate ransom for himself, was killed by their troops in 1012. The Council found £48,000 from a country sliding fast towards economic ruin to pay off the invaders once more. Nine hundred years later Rudyard Kipling made the point in 'What Dane-geld Means':

> . . . we've proved it again and again,
> That if once you have paid him the Dane-geld,
> You never get rid of the Dane.

Inevitably, in the following year the Danes returned. After the years of raids and blackmail, Swein was now aiming for complete conquest. The Danelaw accepted him as king, and with the submission of Danish England, he used it as a base to push westwards and south. Only London, where his ex-lieutenant, Thorkell the Tall, had allied himself with Aethelred, was sufficiently well-defended to resist him effectively. But when Swein's triumph was clear, London too submitted. Aethelred fled to his wife's country of Normandy. Over the next three years events moved with great speed. Swein died in February 1013. Aethelred was briefly restored, under conditions which his leading men forced him to accept, but in 1016 he died. Swein's son, Cnut, and Aethelred's son, Edmund 'Ironside', a man of greater mettle than his father, disputed the throne, while Eadric Streona played a double game, finally betraying Edmund in the last of four great battles, at Ashingdon in Essex. A truce in 1016 divided the country: Edmund kept Wessex and part of Mercia, while Cnut held the Danelaw and the North, and also controlled London. Only six weeks later Edmund died, and Cnut was acclaimed by the Witan as the King of all England.

THE STRUGGLE FOR THE ENGLISH CROWN

England's was Cnut's first throne, though in due course he ruled Denmark and Norway also. His eighteen-year reign once again showed how the personal qualities of the king were crucial to the welfare, or otherwise, of the country. Setting aside a dubious marriage to an Englishwoman, Aelfgifu, he took Aethelred's widow, Emma, as his wife, and in a great assembly at Oxford it was accepted that 'Edgar's laws' should be observed. The English-Danish population lived at peace and the prosperity of the country was restored. On Cnut's death in 1035, two sons, Harold 'Harefoot', his son by Aelfgifu, and Harthacnut, his son by Emma, disputed the great multi-state inheritance. Harthacnut was accepted as king in Denmark; in England, the half-English Harold was favoured, except by one extremely powerful magnate, Earl Godwine of Wessex, an English warrior who had risen in Cnut's service, who was forced to submit. But Harold died in 1038

and Harthacnut came to England as king. His reign too was brief: he died in 1042. The house of Cnut was at an end, and with it, for a time, Scandinavian ambitions and claims fell into the background. English leaders now invited from Normandy, Edward, the surviving son of Aethelred Unraed, a man of middle age, who had been removed from England while still an infant. Pious and mild, his sobriquet is 'the Confessor', though the image of a king perpetually at prayer is exaggerated.

Edward was able to assert

The Great Seal of Edward the Confessor

himself against the might of Earl Godwine, whose daughter Edith he had married. Godwine, his sons and his nephew, also earls, controlled almost all the country apart from Northumbria, where the Danish earl, Siward, ruled, and Mercia, where the English Leofric was earl. Godwine was anti-Norman; the king, brought up at the Norman court, had Norman tastes and friends. In 1051 Edward forced Godwine to flee the country, but the earl's popularity and power were such that he was able to return in 1052. In the following year Godwine died and his son Harold assumed the earldom of Wessex. No less than his father, Harold was a forceful promoter of the family ambitions. It was believed that the childless king had proposed the English crown to the son of his old protector, William, Duke of Normandy, who made a state visit during the winter of 1051–52. To the Godwinsons, this was the opposite policy to that of their father. There were a number of Scandinavian claimants of the crown, including the powerful Harold Hardrada, King of Norway, but the strongest claim was that of Edward, son of Edmund Ironside, who had been sent for his own safety to Hungary at the time of his father's death. Edward returned in 1056 but died before reaching London. Harold in Wessex and his brother Tostig, Earl of Northumbria after Siward's death in 1055, were the most powerful men in England, along with Aelfgar, Earl of Mercia. But Aelfgar was surrounded by Godwinson earldoms. He allied himself with Gruffud ap Llewelyn, King of Gwynedd and Powys and aspirant to rule all of Wales; and perhaps also with Harold Hardrada, in a rebellion which was put down with great difficulty by Harold and his forces in 1058. Harold and Tostig invaded south and north Wales and Gruffud was defeated and killed; Wales remained a conglomerate of petty kingdoms.

Edward, who had come from Hungary only to die, left an infant son. As Edward the Confessor increased in frailty, two great men, the rulers of Normandy and Norway, like hawks at opposite ends of a rich meadow, awaited their opportunity to acquire a kingdom. But a third already felt himself to be all but master of the land. He was not of royal descent, but Duke William was widely known to be of illegitimate birth; and though Harold Hardrada might be

---

LADY GODIVA

Godgifu was the wife of Earl Leofric of Mercia. Her death is recorded in 1080, twenty-three years after her husband's. She and Leofric dedicated several churches, but nothing else from her own time is known of this Anglo-Saxon noblewoman. The thirteenth-century chronicler Roger of Wendover preserved a story or memory of her as a benefactor of the people. In 1040 the earl had imposed severe new taxes, which greatly oppressed the Mercians. When his wife asked for the taxes to be reduced, he said he would do so, if she would ride naked through the streets of Coventry. She did, and the taxes were abated. Whatever grain of truth underlies the legend, the nude parade is most unlikely to be part of it.

a descendant of King Harold Fairhair, his immediate ancestry was of no special distinction. Harold Godwinson, the only English claimant, may have been moved by English patriotism as well as by personal ambition. Controversy has long surrounded his presence at William's court at Rouen in 1064. Norman sources later insisted that he had then solemnly sworn to be William's vassal on William's assuming the kingship of England. It was said that William bore at Hastings the holy relics on which Harold had perjured himself two years before. In the nature of things, there is no evidence from Harold's side. Whatever the nature of his oath to William, it did not stop him from accepting the crown on the death of Edward on 5 January 1066.

It was a time of crisis, caused originally by trouble in the north, where Tostig, Harold's brother, had been ejected as earl by the Northumbrians, and replaced by a Mercian nobleman, Morcar. Tostig was forced to flee but was planning a return to seize his earldom. No one doubted that Hardrada and William would both try to enforce their claims, and the choice or acceptance of Harold as king by the Witan may have been influenced by the fear of seeing England turned into a battleground between the northern and southern contenders.

Partly because of raids on the south coast by Tostig, Harold's military preparations were directed against the expected invasion from Normandy. But it was the King of Norway, with Tostig as his ally, who moved first. The invasion was opposed by the brothers , Edwin and Morcar, Earls of Mercia and Northumbria, but they were defeated on 20 September, and Hardrada prepared for his

The coronation of Harold (Bayeux Tapestry scene)

advance southwards. On 25 September he was taken by surprise by the advance of Harold's army, and at Stamford Bridge on the Derwent, he was defeated and killed, along with Tostig and a host of others. Only 24 ships returned to Norway, though more than 300 had set off. Three days later, the Duke of Normandy's forces landed at Pevensey Bay. With the same speed with which he had marched on Yorkshire, Harold returned to the south. The very rapidity of his response prevented him from mustering a full force, and neither Edwin nor Morcar joined him. His strength has been estimated as around 7,000 men at most, with William's army, composed of Normans, Bretons and French mercenaries, somewhat smaller, but having elements of archers and cavalry which the English army did not possess. On 14 October, aware of Harold's approach, William ordered his men to advance. The battle of Hastings was fought all day, and even after Harold's death some of the English fought on, in the manner praised and prescribed in their old heroic battle songs, giving their lives to avenge that of their fallen king.

CHAPTER FOUR

Norman England

THE IMPOSITION OF NORMAN RULE

The closest parallel in history to William's invasion was that of the Romans a thousand years before: a small group imposing government on a much larger one. But much had changed in that time. His army was smaller, but he was familiar with the people, the southern part of the country, and its methods of government. His aims and his methods were quite different. The Romans needed no justification or sanction for their assumption of control; William had already secured the support of the Pope and hastened to have himself formally crowned and consecrated with the Anglo-Saxon ceremonial. Edward the Confessor's promise and Harold's oath-breaking were vital elements in Norman propaganda. The new king had no ancestral claim, and was not of any royal descent himself. His rule might have been a transient thing, lasting only his own lifetime, or less. Every year from 1067 until 1071 there was an English uprising against him. All failed, and the kingdom passed on his death in 1087 to his second son, William Rufus, with his elder son, Robert, becoming Duke of Normandy. In those twenty years, Anglo-Saxon England became, irreversibly, Norman England.

This was made possible by a combination of policy, advanced military skill, and the social system evolved by the Normans. The policy was for the king to establish his own men at all strategic places in the country. Land and wealth was what they had supported him for, and they seized their chance readily. Without delay they built castles for themselves, at first only timber structures

---

HEREWARD THE WAKE

The inhabitants of the swamplands and islands of the East Anglian fens put up a long resistance to the Normans. In 1070 the Danish king, Swein, invaded the Humber region and made contact with English resistance fighters whose leading figure was a Lincolnshire thegn named Hereward. From a base on the Isle of Ely, and with the help of the Danes, he made a successful raid on Peterborough. But a pact between William I and Swein left the East Anglians on their own. Hereward's redoubt on Ely was joined for a time by other opponents of the Normans, including Morcar, the former Earl of Northumbria. In 1071 royal forces besieged Ely; Hereward and some of his men cut their way out, and passed out of history into legend. His by-name, 'the Wake' seems only to have been applied from the thirteenth century.

The remains of Colchester Castle as they appeared in the nineteenth century.
The largest Norman castle in Europe, Colchester Castle was constructed over
the massive vaults of the ruined Roman Temple of Claudius.

on artificial or natural mounds, with a wooden outer fence. In time, stone castles, such as Colchester above, would replace them on an ever-more substantial scale.

The castle was scarcely known in England until the advent of the Normans, and such as already existed were probably built by Normans invited in by Edward the Confessor. English magnates had lived in relatively unprotected halls. From the castle, the new lord could dominate his tract of land, with his own detachment of mounted soldiers and archers to ensure his security. Men could also be sent swiftly to the aid of another Norman lord, if summoned. By this means, some ten thousand incomers from Normandy, Brittany and Flanders were able to exercise rule over a country of at least a million people, with its own well-established traditions, its laws, its aristocracy and its armed men. English resistance and mutual mistrust meant that the king soon replaced such English lords as Morcar of Northumbria, who had at first submitted but later rebelled, with more reliable Normans. Like the Romans before him, William, finding the north a restive and dangerous province, carried out a campaign of devastation and terror in 1069. Even the Danelaw, always ready to acknowledge a Scandinavian overlord, did not welcome the Normans, whose speech was now Old French rather than Old Norse. The form of social organisation which underlay Norman government was what later generations called the 'feudal system'. Already the structure of English society had been moving towards the concentrated power of landowners and regional magnates at the expense of the free ceorls and the lower ranks of thegns.

THE FEUDAL SYSTEM

The introduction of feudalism nevertheless made fundamental changes to English life. Up till now ownership, service, legal rights and duties had formed a confused, varied and widely overlapping pattern, reflecting local and regional traditions, obligations and arrangements that went back to the first Anglo-Saxon settlements. One writer refers to the Norman aristocracy as a 'kleptocracy', a ruling class of thieves: twenty years on from the Conquest they had emerged as owners of virtually all the land. The principles of land tenure were made clear and universal. All land was held of the king. Thus from William I on, the king was always the King of England, rather than (as the Anglo-Saxon monarchs had in effect been) King of the English. Under him were some six hundred tenants-in-chief. They owed the king specific military service; even if they were bishops or abbots, their own vassals would include a specified number of knights. Under them was a broadening structure of tenants and sub-tenants, bound in a structure of mutual obligation.

It was never a fixed and definitive system, but like all human arrangements, was adapted to individual circumstances and tended through time towards a greater complexity which ultimately began to break up through its own rigidity and the problems caused by rivals claiming the kingship. Although it worked as an economic system, with the manor and the market as the sources of production and exchange, its origin was as a military hierarchy, with a moral element firmly cemented into it. This was the oath of fealty, a sacred tie, which, though it bound the swearer to his lord, also bound the superior in duty of care to his vassal. Neglect of this could allow the vassal to forsake his own oath, if he were strong or bold enough to do so. One consequence of feudalism was the disappearance of slavery, though the lowest-rated and largest social group, the villeins who worked the land, were not free: unable to leave their villages, unable to become landowners, unable to marry without the lord's consent, they were also compelled to put in a fixed amount of work on the lord's own land in addition to paying rents in cash and in kind. If they grew corn on their own holding, they paid to have it ground at the mill controlled by the lord. Their position would become gradually more oppressive until the great plagues of the fourteenth century brought about drastic change in the countryside.

MAINTAINING THE GRIP ON POWER

A further consequence of Norman rule was the beginning of the long involvement of England with the dynastic disputes and territorial wars fought out in France, Burgundy and the Low Countries. Later in his reign William I set the pattern of an absentee king, struggling to maintain or extend his holdings in

The Great Seal of William the Conqueror   *William the Conqueror*

France. After two hundred years of engagement with the Nordic powers, the crucial relationships of the Anglo-Norman state and its successors were now with the shifting power-bases and rich fiefdoms in the lands across the Channel.

The insecurity of a self-imposed monarchy, the distractions of possessions outside England, and the extreme energy and rapacity of some of his barons, like William's own half-brother Odo of Bayeux, were among the pressures that began a centralisation of royal power and a series of measures that increased the king's control over events which an Anglo-Saxon king might have left to the shire-reeve or the ealdorman. Only on the outer fringes, to north and west, where they acted as defenders against Welsh and Scots, were the Norman barons set no boundaries for expansion and freed to an extent from royal control, creating the 'Marcher earldoms' and leading to the 'March law' of later centuries. Overruling all other considerations of feudal loyalty was fealty to the king. Through the royally appointed sheriffs, a solemn oath of loyalty to the king was made by the entire adult male population, twice a year. If any baron should rebel, this oath overrode feudal allegiance and did not allow his vassals to follow him. And, apart from the frontier areas, William took good care that his earls and barons were allotted scattered parcels of land, across several counties, rather than great centralised holdings which might make independent power-bases. The greatest token of Norman efficiency and control was seen in the compilation of 'Domesday Book', between 1086 and 1090: this thorough, detailed inventory of land ownership, land use, owners' rights and local courts and markets in the entire country south of the River Tyne was a unique achievement in western Europe. The purpose was still military; the king wanted to

An extract from the Domesday Book

know the country's resources in order to raise men and money against the possibility of Danish invasion, or war in defence of Normandy.

A TROUBLED SUCCESSION

William II, 'Rufus', with a heavy hand kept, and consolidated what his father had won. In his reign the final form of the kingdom was achieved, with the taking of Cumbria from the Scots. The northern border now ran from Esk to Tweed. In the west he encouraged the Marcher lords to push into Wales and claim the territory of Cymric princes. In classic Norman fashion, castles were begun which would eventually become massive fortifications. William II was killed in a hunting accident in the New Forest and his brother Henry succeeded him. Henry invaded Normandy and seized the duchy from his brother, Robert. But with no surviving son, serious difficulties arose on Henry's death in December 1135. He had designated his daughter, Matilda, as heir, but his nephew, Stephen, younger son of the Count of Blois, and wealthiest of the Anglo-Norman nobles, sped to England and, with considerable support, had himself crowned king and also confirmed as Duke of Normandy. Matilda, married as a child to the Holy Roman Emperor Henry V, was now married to another powerful magnate, Geoffrey Plantagenet, Count of Anjou. In her cause, the Angevin army invaded first Normandy, then, in 1139, England; and civil war broke out between the followers of the two claimants. For a time Stephen was held captive, but Matilda failed to gain the loyalty of London and could not consolidate her position. Stephen was exchanged for her half-brother, Robert of Gloucester, and Matilda eventually retreated to Normandy. Stephen, after his own son's death, accepted the right to inherit of her son Henry, who as Henry II became the first of the Plantagenet line to rule England, in 1154. Now more than ever the English king was also embroiled in continental strife. Henry II had married Eleanor, heiress of Aquitaine, whose marriage to King Louis VII of France had been annulled a short time before. Now Henry controlled more of France than did Louis, his feudal suzerain for the French lands. Stephen's troubles and personal inadequacy as a ruler had encouraged the kind of baronial independence that William I had feared, but Henry, despite his frequent campaigns in France and three rebellions by his sons, backed by their mother, re-established the centralising tendency of royal rule in England. The barons were restored to their place under royal command and Henry's government made many reforms in law, taxation and the control of trade. Scotland, which in the previous anarchy had reclaimed Cumbria and Northumbria, was forced back, and three expeditions into Wales were followed by a balance of power between the Marcher lords and the Welsh princes. In 1171, for the first time, the futures of England and Ireland became intermeshed, when Henry II landed there with an army, in order to exert control over the conquest of the Norman-Welsh knights under 'Strongbow', Earl of Pembroke, who had launched their

---

HEROES AND HISTORIANS

The twelfth and thirteenth centuries were a golden age for the 'chroniclers' – part historians, part story-tellers, part propagandists – who, with access to many ancient documents now lost, and drawing on spoken accounts passed on in the oral tradition, wrote a wide range of histories, biographies, genealogies and accounts of great deeds. Ignoring the scholarly example of Bede, they were often credulous and inventive. But their concept of history was as something to show the reader a moral, or to glorify the present state by linking it to past greatness – or the opposite: to show how things had sunk down.

The medieval English looked backwards with a remarkably inclusive view. The Normans had no history; but there were the great Anglo-Saxon exemplars like Athelstan and Alfred the Great. And before the Anglo-Saxons? Geoffrey of Monmouth (c.1100–55), a churchman, based for a considerable part of his life in Oxford, has been described as 'the inventor of British history'. He wrote the *Historia Regum Britanniae,* 'History of the Kings of Britain'; claiming to have taken information from a 'very ancient book written in the British [Welsh] language'. Geoffrey gave a major role to a figure who would otherwise scarcely rate a footnote in history, King Arthur, the great hero of Britain, with his wizard-counsellor Merlin. His book marks the start of a torrent of Arthurian literature, and gives European literature (and pre-Raphaelite English painting) one of its greatest themes. He also enlarged on the myth that Britain was founded by one Brutus, a Trojan hero, escaping from the sack of Troy. Thus the English could look back with satisfaction on a splendidly heroic past going right back to the Greek epics, even though the precise connections with these early phases and figures might be shrouded in mystery.

Despite some scepticism even at the time the first copies were circulated, it was not until the sixteenth century that the facts of Geoffrey's account were seriously questioned. Polydore Vergil, an Italian humanist commissioned by Henry VII to write a history of England, which was published in 1534, caused outrage by dismissing the Brutus legend. But even two hundred years later the historical existence of Brutus and Arthur still influenced wishful thinkers.

own freelance invasion in 1168 at the urging of the Irish King of Leinster, Dermot MacMurrough. This was not an act of imperialism but of prudent kingship – Henry was aware of the possible danger from a rival kingdom to the west.

THE MURDER OF THOMAS BECKET

In later history, Henry II's reign has been overshadowed by a single act, one murder among many; the death of an overbearing, over-proud subject at the hands of the king's own men might not have been a momentous event. But this one was the Archbishop of Canterbury, Thomas Becket, struck down on 29 December 1170 in the chancel of his own cathedral.

Henry's relations with the church, whose prestige under the papacy of St Bernard was at a great height, had begun well. Becket, from the London merchant class, was Henry's Chancellor before also becoming primate: a prince of the church who enjoyed its pomp and ceremony and yet possessed also a strong ascetic streak. As archbishop he resigned his chancellorship and began a policy of opposition to Henry. The king, who had reformed secular justice, was opposed to the extent that the church had become a power within the state, its own courts treating all misdemeanours by the clergy, even murder, with indulgence, and equally opposed to its habit of referring and appealing to Rome. William I had refused to do homage to the Pope for his kingship of England; Henry II retained the same desire to keep the papal authority within bounds. Becket resisted every clause of the king's proposed reforms. Between king and archbishop, once close colleagues, there was no longer any understanding; Becket removed himself to Flanders and from there peppered the country with proclamations and excommunications of those who opposed him. In the wider international sphere, the Pope and Emperor Frederick

Canterbury Cathedral

ROBIN HOOD

The traditional English folk-hero, independent, resourceful, anti-authority, robber of the rich and giver to the poor, dwelling in the greenwood and capable of splitting a willow wand at a hundred paces with his mighty bow – Robin Hood was never a single individual. First mentioned in the late fourteenth century *Vision of Piers Plowman*, he was gradually woven into a sequence of legends, along with his 'merry men' and, of course, Maid Marian. The source of the free woodlanders may go back to pre-Christian notions of nature spirits and green men, and of the 'wild hunt' associated with the Norse god Woden. But the English forests, much vaster in extent than they are now, undoubtedly harboured many gangs of rebel or broken men at different times, sometimes preying on neighbouring villagers and sometimes sustained by them. Their lives and ideals are unlikely to correspond closely to the Robin Hood tales, composed in ballad form and first published in 1490, when Wynkyn de Worde issued the *Lytel Geste of Robin Hood*. The mythology of Robin Hood both reflects and sustains some important aspects of English self-perception. (*See also* 'Forests'.)

Barbarossa were moving into conflict and the Pope was wary of alienating so powerful a figure as Henry. For five years there was a stand-off. Late in 1170 an uneasy truce was confected and Becket returned, not in any conciliatory mood. His assassination soon followed. If it was not at the king's direct order, there was no doubt that it was ultimately the king's responsibility.

In 1174, with Becket already a martyr-saint, Henry II did penance at the shrine and allowed the monks to scourge him. His Irish expedition perhaps also was designed in part to draw attention away from Canterbury. He left the church to run its own courts and to make appeals to Rome. But the English church did not produce another Becket, and in the long-drawn-out struggle between emperors

The Great Seal of Richard I   *Richard I*

and Popes, Ghibellines and Guelphs, England remained largely peripheral. Henry II's sons, Henry 'the young king', Richard, and John, fought against their father and one another. Henry put his contumacious queen in prison, outfaced his sons and their supporters; and for a time had all Scotland under his subjection with the capture of its king, William, at Alnwick. The Aquitaine-Anjou inheritance was under severe pressure from King Philip Augustus of France, but Henry II left the realm of England under firm government. The successive reigns of his sons Richard I, 'Coeur de Lion', and John, almost destroyed it.

KING JOHN AND MAGNA CARTA

Richard, beguiled by the glamour and prizes of Crusade, departed for Palestine, and on his return was intercepted in Austria and held to ransom by the emperor, Henry VI. Despite a rebellion by his brother, John, the ransom was paid and he returned, only to leave again for Normandy to campaign for his French possessions.

Government was maintained and the absence of Richard proved less damaging to the country than the presence of John, who became king after Richard died in France of wounds in 1199. However bad various Edwards or Henrys might be, their names survived to be re-used; but England has only ever had one King John. The third son of Henry II, he was nicknamed 'Lackland', and later 'Softsword', when he failed to defend Normandy and Anjou against Philip Augustus in 1204. Heavy taxation to provide a war-chest, and the resistance of the Gascons to the French, enabled him to hold Gascony and most of Poitou. A bitter dispute with the powerful Pope Innocent III, over the appointment of an archbishop of Canterbury resulted in the entire country being placed under a papal interdict for five years; John was excommunicated in 1209. Most of the bishops left the country, but the lower clergy had nowhere to go, and remained, saying mass outside their churches while all church property was assumed by the crown.

In 1213, John suddenly overturned his own policy, and that of Henry II, by agreeing that England should be a papal fief, its king owing his throne to the Pope. His aim was to obtain Innocent's support in a war against his old enemy Philip Augustus. But his war on France was a disastrous failure and the English barons rose against him, supported by the citizens of London. Magna Carta, their charter of grievance and reform, sixty-two clauses long, was sealed by an unwilling and unrepentant king on 17 June 1215. The barons' subsequent attempt to enforce it led to a split in their own ranks, and warfare followed between those who sided with the king and those who, standing four-square for the Charter, declared John deposed, and invited Louis, son of Philip Augustus, to assume the throne of England.

King John

The signing of the Magna Carta

John's death in 1216, while on campaign in East Anglia, rescued the country from a civil war that was complicated by the invasion of Louis. His French troops and John's foreign mercenaries ravaged much of the south. In this critical juncture the country rallied round John's nine-year-old son, who became Henry III, under the benevolent tutelage of William the Marshal, Earl of Pembroke, as regent, and Hubert de

Burgh as Justiciar. Magna Carta was reissued at the same time as the boy was crowned. The invading French fought on until September 1217, when Louis was finally bought off and his English supporters assured of amnesty. Henry III's reign would last for fifty-six years, longer than the average life-span of his subjects.

THE REIGN OF HENRY III

During the half-century of his personal rule, western Europe experienced, on the whole, a state of peace compared with times before and times to come. Henry III himself disrupted this on two occasions with abortive efforts to regain lost territories in France; but military energies were focused on crusading wars in the East. The king himself had the instincts of a Plantagenet autocrat but neither the will nor political skills of a Henry II; the pious builder of Westminster Abbey was that rarity for the papacy, a king of England who adhered to the papal line, who obeyed the papal orders, and who was willing to impose punitive taxes on his people to help finance papal policies. More damagingly to the national church, he allowed the sale of high ecclesiastical offices to absentee foreigners who paid the Pope for their titles and the rents that went with them. On behalf of the numerous foreign relatives of his queen, Eleanor of Provence, and their hangers-on, he was crudely nepotistic, providing them with posts and titles under the crown.

This influx of high-placed and greedy foreigners to feed at the royal and ecclesiastical trough was widely resented. In England, as elsewhere in Europe, a sense of national identity was gradually developing during the thirteenth century. It was still common to find great men who owned land in several different countries and owed feudal allegiance to more than one king or duke. The church had not yet given up its mighty effort to become a single supranational institution, above the rule of kings. French was still the official language of court and law in England. Latin was the international language of learning, diplomacy and liturgy. The English language had no official status. A resident of England, asked to define his identity at this time, would have done so in terms of who his lord was, or perhaps, in terms of his parish or village. Fully three-quarters of the English people were still of the villein class, in a state of semi-servitude, their opportunities and movements restricted to the places where they had been born and by the dictates of the lord of the manor. The change in thinking was brought about by a number of separate elements, which did not have much to do with one another. In England the sea barrier round so much of the country helped to promote a sense of separateness. The emergence of a university at Oxford, first founded in 1167 by scholars who had come from Paris, followed by that of Cambridge in 1209, among Europe's earliest, helped to create a social group of 'clerks', educated men who were greatly influenced by the part-secular, part-religious communities in which their formative years were spent (the student community of Oxford numbered around 1,300 in the 1330s – a considerable figure). The Inns of Court, already established as the centre of legal education, and the cathedral and monastery schools, also housed communities of teachers and students. A sense of history and tradition was strong, though much of it was founded on the myths spun by Geoffrey of Monmouth and those who embroidered his stories. Throughout the country, except in Celtic Cornwall and parts of the Welsh Marches and Celtic Cumbria, there was a single vernacular language. The speech of the Anglo-Saxons evolved with remarkable speed over some three hundred years from the Norman Conquest to the time of Henry III, and proved to be highly assimilative in grammar and vocabulary. Possibly the fact that it was little used as a written language during this time helped to accelerate the speed of its development. Instead of declining into a group of rural dialects, its use extended upwards in society. London, with its ever-rising population, attracting migrants from all over the country, played an increasingly important part in the evolution of a national language.

FORESTS

Wood was the most basic natural resource of pre-industrial England, used for building houses, ships and every kind of artefact from wagons to gallows, and with vast amounts consumed in fires for warmth and cooking. Woodland management began in Anglo-Saxon times: Domesday Book records woods by area and sometimes by their value in fattening pigs. In medieval times, planting and coppicing were practised by monasteries, manors and village communities. Woodland was probably lost to agriculture rather than to wasteful use or lack of replanting to maintain supplies. The rights to use of wood were closely observed. But of all woodlands, those most subject to stringent laws were the royal forests.

Anglo-Saxon kings may have enjoyed wide hunting rights, but the concept of the royal forest as a vast game preserve came with William I in 1066, and undoubtedly added to the grievances of the Anglo-Saxon population. His Nova Foresta or 'New' Forest was only one of a large number. The Normans introduced the fallow deer and the rabbit to England, and deer and wild boar were 'the king's beasts'. Wild boar were once common, though hunted to extinction in the seventeenth century, by which time the royal forests were much reduced in size. But in the thirteenth century, as much as a quarter of the country was demarcated as royal forest. Henry II, an ardent huntsman, made large extensions. By his day, however, the forests were also a source of royal income as well as pleasure (and helping to stock the larder). Although individuals might hold land in the royal forests, the rights of hunting and tree-cutting were restricted to the king and 'forest law' prescribed severe penalties for poaching the king's deer or cutting down trees. Henry III's Forest Charter of 1217 began a gradual retrenchment, and over the centuries the royal forests were gradually reduced in size and number. Charles I was the last king to take extensive supplies of venison from his forests, and the era of enclosures in the later eighteenth century reduced many of them. Today, elements of old forest law are still kept up in the Forests of Dean, Ashdown, Epping, and in the New Forest.

THE DUTIES OF THE KING
AND THE POWER OF THE LAW

The two great formative forces in the emergence of a distinctively English nation were the kingship and the law. On islands, living forms frequently develop in a way different to their relatives on the mainland, even a close mainland. Both of these institutions assumed their own form in England, and they were intimately linked with each other. Monarchy, already a tradition so ancient that it merged into myth and legend, was venerated and unchallenged as the form of government. A king was expected to rule and govern, to levy specific tolls and taxes, to wage war, to ensure that justice was done, to keep civil peace, to reward his servants, and to be seen to do all these things, as well as to maintain the splendid lifestyle that went with such supremacy and responsibility. A king who failed in these respects might eventually be challenged, as John had been and Henry III was to be, without any urge to destroy or replace kingship itself. To achieve this, without appearing to be merely rebellious and disloyal, it was vital to show in what respects the king had failed, and in what respects he should act differently. This was the importance of Magna Carta and such later agreements as the Provisions of Oxford, enforced on Henry III by Simon de Montfort and other barons in 1258. They made it possible to judge the king by his performance. But alongside such contentious agreements, and far more firmly rooted in the life of the nation, was the law. By the mid-thirteenth century, a substantial treatise on *The Laws and Customs of England*, credited to the cleric and judge, Henry Bracton, a Devonshire man, not a Londoner or court figure, had been compiled. Henry II had been responsible for a great step forward in extending the role of royal justices both on circuit through the country and in the early stages of what later became the 'King's Bench' and the 'Court of Common Pleas'. Jury trial was coming to replace the outmoded methods of trial, by ordeal and the Norman-introduced trial by battle. The church had already detached itself from the ugly business of the ordeal, which now was staged out in the open. Juries served other local purposes too, including tax assessment and the inspection of weapons and other military gear. Thus the Common Law grew, with the king as its guarantor, but yet it was independent of the king, and for him to fail in his responsibility towards it was a major failing.

CHAPTER FIVE

A State Built on Wool

WELSH ANNEXATION AND SCOTTISH RESISTANCE

Under pressure from certain barons, chief among them the energetic and unbending Simon de Montfort, Earl of Leicester, Henry III's ineffectual rule crumbled. But the barons were unable to provide cohesive government. De Montfort went beyond his colleagues in zeal to curb royal power, and civil warfare resulted. His defeat and death at the battle of Evesham in the 'Barons' War' in 1265 did not put an end to his faction. In 1272, however, Henry died and another lengthy reign began, of a very different stamp, under his son Edward I.

Thorough and determined in everything he did, and not untouched by the reformist thoughts which sparked off the Barons' War, he embarked on a complete examination and reorganisation of local government, resulting in a series of statutes published over several years and covering almost every aspect of the law. Edward was a strict legalist, but found a perpetual problem in suppressing corruption among his officials, who by tradition used their functions and powers for personal gain. In 1275 he imposed the 'Great Customs', a duty on wool exports, which by this time were the country's major revenue earner. In two campaigns between 1276 and 1283 he accomplished the conquest of Wales, dividing it into shires and bringing English laws into effect. His massive castles at Caernarvon, Harlech and many other places still stand as memorials to the military science of the time and the unrelenting efforts of the king. He was first to take over the title of Prince of Wales for his eldest son.

A heavy reverse came with the French invasion of Edward's duchy of Aquitaine in 1294. The costs of war in France meant a

The reverse of the Great Seal of Edward I

severe extra tax burden for the English people. Edward also strove to promote a union of England and Scotland through the marriage of his son and the girl heir to the Scottish crown; when she died in 1290, he set out to impose himself as overlord of the Scottish realm, with considerable success until the Scots found a leader in William Wallace, and after Wallace's capture and execution in London, the guerrilla-style campaigns of Robert Bruce gradually won the country back. It was on yet another expedition to subdue the Scots that Edward died in 1307.

AN EMERGING PARLIAMENT

The emergence of the parliament of England as a power in the land is generally traced back to Edward's reign. The enormous cost of his war campaigns, and the need to justify them to the taxpayers, made him call numerous parliaments,

JEWS

England's first Jewish immigrants came in the years following the Norman Conquest. They settled in London and the bigger towns, where 'Jews' houses', some of them still surviving, were distinguished by being built of stone rather than wood or wattle and daub. They exercised the function of moneylending at interest, a primitive form of banking, which at that time was considered un-Christian, though necessary. The equipping of royal expeditions and the building of baronial castles were funded by the Jews, but both the requirement to repay, and the hostility of Christians, greatly intensified during the crusading centuries, made them vulnerable. At various times in the Middle Ages the small English Jewish communities were violently attacked, and accused of loathsome crimes, but they survived under the protection of the kings – who maintained an 'exchequer of the Jews' to help them collect what they were owed – until in 1290 Edward I ordered the expulsion of all Jews in England, confiscating their fixed property but allowing them to take cash and movable items. Conveniently, 'usurious Christians', Flemings and Italians, were by then available to lend large sums of money.

Jews began to return to England in the seventeenth century, a process legitimised by Oliver Cromwell during the Commonwealth: the 'People of the Book' were regarded with respect by the Old Testament-reading Puritans, but the decision was also prompted by the belief that the Jews must be converted before the Day of Judgement (much anticipated at the time) could come. Like other non-Anglicans their opportunities in public life were restricted by the Test and Corporation Acts, but these constraints were removed in 1858.

The nineteenth century also saw the rise of the eccentric 'British Israelite' notion, that the British people were descended from the ancient 'lost' tribes of the Jews: a theory regarded with some bewilderment by the Jews themselves. With the advent of the Russian pogroms in the late nineteenth century, many Jewish refugees arrived, mostly poor or destitute, settling in London's East End. A smaller but intellectually influential influx came from Nazi Germany and Austria during the 1930s. The census of 2001 put Britain's Jewish community at a little over 250,000, but many others have merged into the secular mode of English life.

with representatives from shires and boroughs to supplement the lords. He was not the first to call a parliament; it grew out of the Great Council from 1265, when Simon de Montfort was first to call on the chief towns each to send two representatives in addition to two knights from each shire. This was because de Montfort could rely on towns for support, and for a long time to come parliament was in effect a tool of the king, or the king's government, summoned when it was needed, expected to assent to requests for funds and taxes, and dissolved when its assent was given. It was not remotely a governing body. Authority rested with the king and his immediate council, and parliament was meant to apply this authority on a local basis throughout the land when the members returned to their homes. But a precedent was set in Edward's reign when parliament refused to discuss supply, i.e. money to support royal policy, until certain grievances had been resolved. Its origins in the Great Council, however had been as a court of justice, a function and title it still retains as the High Court of Parliament.

The lords, the church, the towns – these were the three estates which combined to form parliament, for the reason that they controlled the country's wealth. From the lords and the church also came the members of the king's immediate Council and the royal household. The king's Council was the origin of what would later be the House of Lords. Under the feudal system, a lordship was not a hereditary benefit, but reverted to the king on the holder's death; by the fourteenth century it was becoming more common for an eldest son to inherit an earldom or baronage, just as it was by now accepted that the eldest son of the king should succeed to the throne. But in England, unlike the countries of Europe, the concept and social distinctions of 'nobility' did not apply to the children of a lord, but only to the lord himself, by virtue of the office he held under the king; this remained the case from 1387, when for the first time hereditary peerages began to be awarded. The children of an earl had no more privileges under the law than any yeoman tenant on the earl's estates. This was a vital source of England's eventual two-house parliament, and equally important, of the growth of the 'country gentry' as a locally controlling element throughout much of the kingdom.

As knights and village squires, as managers of their own estates and of whatever rights went along with these, of market tolls, proceeds from court fines, fishing or mineral rights, the country gentry had a community of interest with the merchants and traders of the towns. By the time of Edward I's death, the country knights and the town burgesses were already identified as the 'Community', whose interests were not necessarily identical to those of lords and church. In the reign of Edward II, which afforded plenty of opportunity for discontent and concern for the national welfare, they formed the custom of meeting together during the course of a parliament, to discuss their own concerns. By the middle of the fourteenth century this gathering had become sufficiently formal to have its own clerk to record proceedings and its 'speaker' to report its views and present its claims to the full parliament. In this way, without formal statute or charter, the House of Commons began its emergence as a separate if still junior chamber to the House of Lords.

FRIENDS, FAVOURITES – AND MURDER

Edward II, disinclined to action, and from 1314 with the stigma of England's defeat by the Scots at Bannockburn to live down, was like Henry III hemmed in by a reformist group of barons, the 'Lords Ordainers', led by the Earl of Warwick, who in 1312 captured and summarily executed the king's close friend and virtual co-ruler, Piers Gaveston. In 1322, with a new and stronger right-hand man, Hugh Despenser, Edward reasserted royal control over a country which was slipping into baronial anarchy, but Scottish raids, a French invasion of Gascony, and the barons' resentment against Despenser's personal empire-building, wrecked everything. His queen, Isabella, sister of the King of France, went to Paris to negotiate a peace, but once there, she stayed, and became the mistress of Roger Mortimer, an exiled magnate of the Welsh marches and bitter opponent of Despenser. Isabella and Mortimer landed in England with an army of Dutch mercenaries in 1326 and Edward II, deserted by everyone, became their prisoner. He was compelled to abdicate in favour of his fourteen-year-old son Edward III, and in 1327 he was murdered in Berkeley Castle.

For three years, Roger Mortimer, his status confirmed as Earl of March, was the de facto ruler of England. He acquired vast estates in the Marches and south Wales, made inglorious peace treaties with Scotland and France, and for a time held off opposition until in 1330 the eighteen-year-old king finally shook off his mother's control and with the aid of the Earl of Lancaster arrested Mortimer and had him hanged at Tyburn like a common thief. Isabella went into secluded retirement.

An effigy of Edward II in Gloucester Cathedral

EDWARD III: A MILITARY KING

Edward III was determined to be a military king who would restore the Planta-genet prestige and fortunes. Scotland was to be subjugated as a vassal state; Gascony was to be reclaimed – and, as grandson of King Philip the Fair of France, he aspired to the French throne. Allied to the Netherlands and the Austro-German 'Holy Roman Empire', he embarked on the war with France which would continue, with inter-missions, as the 'Hundred Years War', and which, despite some famous English victories, would end in the complete eradication of English rule in France with the sole exception of the town of Calais, and would in turn precipi-tate the internal upheavals of the 'Wars of the Roses'.

The Great Seal of Edward III

As ever, warfare and the subsi-dising of continental allies was vastly expensive. In 1340–41 the king's demands for money pro-voked a political crisis, in which Edward was forced to back down in the face of the united opposition of Lords and Commons. So far, apart from the naval victory of Sluys, the war had not gone well. But after the renewal of relations between king and parliament, and with the adoption of shorter campaigns not reliant on allies, the course of warfare swung in England's favour. On 26 August 1346, with his son, the Black Prince, Edward won the shattering victory of Crécy over the French. Later that year King David II of Scotland was captured in battle at Neville's Cross and began an eleven-year imprisonment.

THE BLACK DEATH

But from 1348, for a time the true ruler not only of England but of all Britain and western Europe was a bacillus, later known as *Pasteurella pestis*, spread by the flea-infested black rat. The interwoven diseases caused by this tiny organ-ism, bubonic plague, pneumonic plague and septicaemic plague, collectively known as the Black Death, advanced inexorably across the country from ports on the south coast during the summer of that year. Its cause undetectable, its symptoms untreatable, it was the greatest natural disaster ever to befall

THE ARCHERS

Archery does not seem to have been practised in Celtic England; it was probably first introduced by the Romans. The Anglo-Saxons used the bow and arrow, but archery was used against them to greater effect by Norsemen and Normans. The Welsh took to it more enthusiastically than the English, and medieval English commanders, recognising its power, looked in Wales for men both to train English archers and to serve with them. Edward I made great use of archers, but most of his were Welsh mercenaries. Even among the 3,700 archers who won the victory at Crécy in 1346, around 1,700 were Welsh. Training of archers began early in life, and king Edward III made archery supreme to all other sports in order to maintain the supply. The work of an archer was demanding. The longbow, preferably made of Spanish yew, was as tall as he was, and required a pull of up to 100 lbs (45 kg) to send the shaft, 28 inches (71 cm) long, a distance of 250 yards (227 m). At his belt he carried twenty-four arrows. The men at Crécy could thus fire a lethal storm of nearly 90,000 arrows in a very short space of time. By Henry VIII's day, archery was becoming old-fashioned as a means of doing battle, but it remained a highly popular sport, and of course, a valuable silent weapon for the deer poacher. Over 3,000 archers came to participate in a two-day championship meet at Shoreditch in 1583. Unsurprisingly in a country where conservative values were cherished, some tacticians even in the eighteenth century were arguing the case for putting bowmen as well as, or instead of, musketeers in the firing line.

Longbow archers

England. The human tolls of floods, storms and wars were far less than the death-count of this silent and irresistible invasion. Town and country were equally at risk. In London, with some seventy thousand inhabitants, around a third of the population perished; and this was probably the case with the rest of the country. In a population generally supposed to be around four million persons in 1348, something like 1,300,000 perished by 1350. A second outbreak, in 1361, decimated, or more than decimated, the reduced population, and there would be four lesser epidemics before the end of the century.

Our modern view of the fourteenth century as a time of universal, if often naive religious belief, might presuppose a collapse of national morale in the face of what could only be considered a divinely ordained catastrophe. But there is little evidence of this, and, on the contrary, the resilience of European communities in the face of the Black Death was as strong as it was in both earlier and later disasters on a less vast scale. Perhaps the main victim of popular opinion was the church, which, as intermediary between the people and God, had totally failed to predict or prevent the onset of God's wrath. During the plague outbreaks, many people sought protection in th e remedies of quack doctors or country superstition rather than in prayer. The church itself lost a high proportion, between a third and a half, of its priests. In his history of these events, *The Black Death*, Philip Ziegler notes that: 'The villagers observed with interest that the parish priest was just as likely, indeed more likely, to die of the plague than his parishioners' (p. 228). As with a tidal wave or volcanic eruption, those who survived were more likely to congratulate themselves and dedicate themselves to the business of living (and procreation) than to spend time in considering the spiritual implications of what had happened.

THE CHANGING FACE OF ENGLAND

Historians are agreed that the estimated four million of 1348 constituted 'overpopulation' in the sense that the working population was greater than required for the available amount of work, as generated by the economic and social system. There was surplus labour available, wages fell, and there was privation and hunger where too-large family groups had use of too-small plots of land within the manor. The consequence of the plague was to reverse this situation. Many manors were untenanted, fields were left to revert to wilderness, and the wages of rural workers rose sharply as they found their services in demand, while agricultural prices fell and the cost of manufactured articles rose sharply. Larger estates were often rented off in small units. Struggling to oppose a sense of universal social upheaval, government with its limited resources found it impossible to cope, though ordinances were made in 1349 and 1351 to prevent workers, even those who were not villeins, to change masters. The degree of moral and religious change is hard to assess, but government certainly did not collapse, vacant posts were replaced; there was intermittent warfare both in Brittany and Gascony, and at sea, from 1347 to 1354, before full-scale Anglo-French hostilities broke out again in the latter year. At Poitiers in 1356, Edward the Black Prince (the reason for the by-name is unclear; perhaps he fought in black armour) captured the French King Jean, though the war continued. Edward III failed in a bid to take Reims and be crowned King of France there. But in 1360 the Treaty of Brétigny confirmed his triumph. Aquitaine and all the old Plantagenet lands were restored to him, and in consideration of this he renounced his claim to the French crown. The Kings of France and Scotland were released against huge ransoms. With peace at home, victory abroad, a popular king and an heir-apparent of similar mould, the affairs of England were at a high point. The decline was rapid. France, much larger, richer and more populous than England, with its own new spirit of national identity, continued to fight for its western provinces. The Black Prince fell ill and died.

The king himself declined into senility, surrounded by a court of spongers and self-seekers typified by his mistress, Alice Perrers, and managed by his third son, John of Gaunt, Duke of Lancaster. This was profoundly resented by successive parliaments, culminating in the new process of impeachment of incompetent or corrupt officials introduced by the 'Good Parliament' of 1376. This exasperation was felt by a wide range of people across the country, a broad section of the community which had seen its wealth rise and was not disposed to see it taxed away by an incompetent and self-indulgent government. Cloth manufacture was the basis of that wealth. In earlier times, English wool was exported to Flanders to be made into fine cloth. Now, partly through the arrival of Flemish weavers, following Edward III's Flemish alliance, and partly through English adoption of the Flemings' techniques, a cloth industry arose in many parts of the country, from Westmorland to Somerset, and from Yorkshire to the Cotswolds. The interdependence of weaver and sheep farmer did much to develop the internal economy and to foster a sense of national cohesion. A class of middlemen and wholesalers managed the trade, so that the activities of small farmers and cottage-based weavers culminated in a substantial industry which not only catered for the home market but quickly became a large export trade, which in turn benefited the seaports and the shipbuilding industry.

An effigy of Edward the Black Prince in Canterbury Cathedral

LOLLARDS

This uncomplimentary name, given by their enemies, came from a Dutch word meaning 'mumbler'. The Lollards were Christians who believed that the business of the church was to encourage people to live a Christ-like life of evangelical witness and poverty. Not all Lollards adhered to the poverty aspect. Similar doctrines were emerging elsewhere in Europe at this time; John Wyclif, who lived from around 1330 to 1384, was their great English spokesman. A doctor of divinity of Oxford University, Wyclif was no hedge-priest, and John of Gaunt acted as his unofficial patron and protector. Central to Wyclif's belief was the concept of the Elect, who alone were in a state of grace and who did not require the aid of the church to mediate between themselves and God. It was for the benefit of his fellow-Elect that Wyclif embarked on a translation of the Bible into English, which was completed by others during the 1390s. By 1379 his views had moved to a denial of transubstantiation of the bread eaten at the communion service, a position too extreme to be respectable. He retired to his country rectory at Lutterworth but was not persecuted. This fate awaited a number of his followers. Under Henry IV in 1401, an Act of Parliament, *De Heretico Comburendo*, authorised the burning of obstinate heretics, and a number of Lollards suffered this penalty, the most famous being Sir John Oldcastle, hanged and burned in 1417; as with many other Lollards, there was an element of social subversiveness in his beliefs that attracted the wrath of civil as well as church authority. Wyclif's most important influence was on the Czech reformer Johann Hus, who based much of his teaching directly on Wyclif. In Britain, Lollardy declined into a semi-underground movement, among craftspeople of town and country, and survived as such to add its contribution to the spirit of Protestantism and Puritanism in the sixteenth century.

REVOLTS, TRUCES AND PARLEYS

In 1377 the ten-year-old son of the Black Prince succeeded to the crown as Richard II. The tutelage of his uncle, John of Gaunt, was a dubious advantage when the discontents of the country peasantry erupted into open revolt in June 1381: the duke was identified with misgovernment and military disaster. Poll taxes, a tax levied on every adult inhabitant, were among the prime causes of the revolt, though it had many roots. For a few days a peasant army, drawn mostly from Kent and Essex, controlled London. John of Gaunt's Savoy Palace was wrecked and the Chancellor and Treasurer were both summarily executed. The fourteen-year-old king boldly faced the rebels. Wat Tyler, at the head of the Kentish rebels, was wounded in a scuffle with the Lord Mayor of London and subsequently executed. Richard promised concessions, including the abolition of serfdom, and promptly revoked them when the countrymen dispersed. Troubles continued in the provinces, and John of Gaunt fled to Scotland, but neither the uprisings, nor the repression that followed, reached the scale and savagery of similar revolts in at the time in Europe, like the French 'Jacquerie'.

Through the reign of Richard II, three powers were in contention. The king himself, increasingly despotic and erratic, regarded by many as a spoilt child who had failed to grow up, with a court party of promoted favourites and opportunist earls, was one. The magnates of the kingdom, with the church leaders, formed another; for a time in 1388–89, as the 'Lords Appellant' they held the king in check. Parliament, with the lords closely linked to the Appellants, was the third force. Richard finally overreached himself by claiming for the crown the vast estates of Lancaster, on the death of John of Gaunt. John's heir, Henry of Lancaster, known from his Lincolnshire birthplace as Bolingbroke, was already in exile. Richard was childless; his presumptive heir had been Roger Mortimer, fourth Earl of March, who was killed in Ireland in 1398, leaving a family of young children. In 1399 Henry, with a tiny army but many promises of support, landed on the Humber estuary. Richard, who had been campaigning in Ireland, returned to face him. Truces and parleys followed, but it was plain that Henry had the upper hand. Richard II was imprisoned, and compelled to abdicate, while Henry was proclaimed as king, both by inheritance and right of conquest. Parliament had proposed that Richard be confined for life, but his murder in 1400 was inevitable, in order to remove a potential source of revanchist rebellion. He was the last in the direct line of the Plantagenets. Henry IV was the first Lancastrian King of England and his, and his heirs', occupation of the throne was not to go unchallenged. Through Mortimer's eldest son, the boy Earl of March, and his heirs, the hopes and challenges of the Yorkists would be mounted.

CHAUCER'S ENGLAND

This was the age of Chaucer's England – the first era in which we gain a picture of English life written in the English language. Geoffrey Chaucer, London wine merchant, member of parliament, royal diplomat, for even his own generation above all a poet – 'first finder of our fair language', said his younger contemporary Thomas Hoccleve – was the leading light in the first great age of English literature. Among his works, *The Canterbury Tales* has always enjoyed the greatest popular acclaim, but this collection of verse stories and linking passages, veering from high literary modes to crude folk humour, shot through with sardonic and satirical vision, is not intended as a realistic or complete portrayal of English life.

Chaucer was a member of the 'establishment' of his time, and though he recognised many of the ills of society, from brigandage to the decline in faith and holiness of the clergy, he was not a reformer in social or religious matters. Though his adult life coincided with English defeat abroad and dissension at home, it reveals, behind the troubled foreground of an ungovernable king and scheming barons, the steady rise of a strong English culture based on language, identity, tradition and an accepted moderate, tolerant, and humane view of life. Such a culture also required a sound economic basis, which may have been stronger in London and the south-east, and around the bigger towns, than in the country as a whole.

Many events still to come would test or question that moderation and tolerance. Violence was endemic at all levels of society. Henry IV would approve of the burning of heretics. Englishmen in positions of power could be as grasping, harsh and relentless as any Italian *condottiere* or iron-fisted Teutonic knight. An English army could wreck and raze and commit rape and looting in a captured foreign city as readily as any other. But the roots of a more measured and self-disciplined approach went very deep. They lay above all in respect for the law and in the feeling that the law was everyone's possession. It was a remedy for those who were offended against, and a warning to those who offended. The king, as ever, was its guarantor, but if the king went beyond the law, he could be made to retract, or he could be removed.

The sharpest challenge to Henry IV came from Wales, where Owain Glyndwr, proclaimed as Prince of Wales, maintained a successful revolt against English suzerainty and oppressive colonial rule for several years and allied himself with the semi-independent Percy Earls of Northumberland and the Marcher lord, Roger Mortimer, to divide England in three. In 1405 he led a Welsh and French

VILLAGE NAMES

Most of the villages of England are Anglo-Saxon in origin. Imported custom, the need for security, and the agricultural system all encouraged the grouping of houses. Naming of these settlements followed various forms, often based on the name of a leading individual or a tribal group. Gillingham meant homestead of the Gyllingas: Gylla's people. Godalming meant the people or dependents of Godhelm. The locality took on their name when they settled down in it. Names of this kind often shed light on settlement patterns, as with Englefield in Berkshire, indicating a community of Angles in territory that was primarily West Saxon. The many -borough places derive from Old English *burh*, 'fortified place', and the even more frequent -ton names mostly come from *tun*, 'farmstead'. Names ending in -ham need careful tracing to either Old English *ham*, 'homestead', or *hamm*, 'enclosure' and also 'water-meadow'. A host of natural landscape features also play a role in place names; the Anglo-Saxons had many specific words for landforms which nowadays are simply regarded as hills and valleys (or dales in the areas where Scandinavian influence was strong).

After the arrival of the Normans, a new proprietorial element came in, and the familiar combination of place and family in two-part names arose, adding the name of the lord of the manor. Most of these names reached their final form in the thirteenth and fourteenth centuries, and continued even when the lord's name altered. They had some use in distinguishing the many Newtons, Cliftons, Ashtons, Eastons, Westons and so on from one another; as with Charlton Mackrell and Charlton Musgrove in Somerset (Charl- is from *ceorl*). Some of the double names are found in Domesday Book, like Holme Lacy in Herefordshire and Kingston Bagpuize in Oxfordshire.

army into England, but, with Henry holding aloof and avoiding battle, he withdrew again. By 1408, the Welsh threat had receded, and a rival Prince of Wales, the future Henry V, was re-establishing English control. From then, Wales was effectively brought into English political control, though never assimilated culturally.

FRANCE GAINED AND LOST

In 1413 Henry IV, long suffering from ill health, died and his son became Henry V. His tavern-haunting youth as 'Prince Hal' was the stuff of later legend. He was a pious, militant and ambitious figure whose impatience to rule was apparent from 1410.

Crushing a plot to replace him as king with Edmund Mortimer, Earl of March (who was not involved and served him faithfully), he invaded France in 1415, pursuing his claim to the French crown. The capture of Harfleur and the lucky but decisive victory of Agincourt on 25 October 1415 heralded a chain of victories which once again brought English international prestige to a high point. As master of Normandy and most of northern France, Henry was accepted as heir by King Charles VI, and in 1420 he married Catherine of Valois, Charles's daughter. What might have resulted remains a permanent question: aged only thirty-five, Henry was killed by that scourge of all armies on campaign, dysentery. His widow, Catherine, was to play a surprising part in the future of the English monarchy. But the immediate effect of Henry's untimely death was the succession of his infant son, less than a year old, as Henry VI, and a long and factious regency. On the death of Charles VI, the baby was also proclaimed King

of France. In France, his uncle, the Duke of Bedford, acted as his regent; in England his uncle, the Duke of Gloucester, and his great-uncle, Henry Beaufort, Bishop of Winchester and later a cardinal, were bitter rivals for control of affairs.

It was clear from the beginning that Henry VI's kingship of France was not to be taken for granted. The son of Charles VI intended to become Charles VII. Until 1429, the English, in alliance with the Duke of Burgundy, maintained their hold,

Parliament in the time of Henry V

A doorway in King's College, Cambridge

consolidated by the crushing defeat of a French–Scottish army at Verneuil in 1424. In 1428 the siege of Orleans, held for Charles, began. Against all apparent odds, the siege was raised by a French army led and inspired by an illiterate peasant girl, Joan of Arc. She swept on through English-occupied territory to take Reims and witness the coronation of Charles VII in its cathedral. Her failure to take Paris, her capture, her trial as a witch, and her burning at Rouen in 1431 under the auspices of Norman clerics and the English army, did not put an end to Joan's achievement or her legend. The French were firmly in the ascendant. In 1431, Henry VI was brought to Paris to be crowned, but few were impressed; warfare went on with intermittent fruitless peace negotiations. Burgundy dropped its alliance. In 1437 Henry VI was deemed to have come of age, but was to remain very much under the influence of his Beaufort relations (descendants of John of Gaunt) and a dominating French wife, Queen Margaret. The 'royal saint', in John Milton's words, who founded King's College, Cambridge, and Eton College, and preferred reading to hunting, has also been castigated by historians as the king who lost the French lands. After the battle of Castillon in 1453, England was left holding only Calais.

THE WARS OF THE ROSES

A more warlike figure might still have failed to prevent this; but Henry VI's inadequacy was fatal in his inability to contain and control Richard, heir to the Earl of March, and now Duke of York, who, until the birth of a crown prince in 1453, was next in line to the throne. A Yorkist faction grew up and Richard took up arms in his own cause first in 1452 and more effectively in 1455. Allied with the Earl of Warwick, he rebelled again in 1459 but was forced to flee to Ireland. Warwick however took Henry VI prisoner in 1460 and York returned to press his claim. He was killed fighting pro-Lancastrian forces at Wakefield in that year. Warfare continued, and in February 1461 Warwick was defeated and Henry VI was released. The Yorkists then proclaimed Richard of York's son, Edward, as King Edward IV. He had just defeated a Lancastrian force under Jasper Tudor, Earl of Pembroke, at Mortimer's Cross in the Welsh Marches, and confirmed his throne with a victory over the northern Lancastrians at Towton, Yorkshire. Henry VI and Margaret took refuge at the court of Scotland.

Always more of a dynastic power struggle than a real civil war, the 'Wars of the Roses' as they were later named were partly a result of the loss of the French lands, which was seen by all classes in England as a national humiliation and caused intense controversy. There were no more French campaigns, or Crusades, to divert military energy. But the seeds of these wars lay in the contested claims to the throne which had existed since 1400. Even if Henry VI had been strong enough to have the Duke of York killed, the existence of divided loyalties and the opportunities for bold men to profit from a change of ruler would still have promoted conflict. The Earl of Warwick, 'Kingmaker' to later historians, was a prime example. Having assisted Edward IV to the throne, he turned against the king when in 1469 Edward announced his marriage to Elizabeth Woodville, widow of a Lancastrian stalwart, with two children, five brothers and seven sisters all eager to benefit from their sudden social elevation. The furore was so great that Edward briefly fled the country in late 1470, but returned, buttressed by Burgundian forces, and first by diplomacy, then by force of arms, retrieved his position. Warwick, having gone full circle and pledged his loyalty to Henry VI, whom he released from the Tower of London, was defeated and killed at the battle of Barnet on Easter Sunday, 1471. A further battle at Tewkesbury, in which Henry VI's son Edward was killed, confirmed the re-establishment of Edward IV. Edward had learned the lesson that Henry VI had shunned; on 24 April that year, Henry was murdered. Until his sudden death in April 1483, Edward IV reigned unchallenged. His elder son, aged thirteen, was duly proclaimed as Edward V.

THE PRINCES IN THE TOWER

The boy was being brought to London for his coronation, in the charge of his mother's brother, Earl Rivers, when the cavalcade was halted by a more powerful uncle, his father's brother, Richard, Duke of Gloucester. Rivers was arrested and Gloucester took possession of the king and was appointed Protector, as normal in a period of a king's minority. But on 26 June 1483, Gloucester announced the deposition of Edward, and his own accession to the throne as Richard III. The excuse was that it had been found the young king and his brother were of illegitimate birth. Even if this were so, his elder brother, George, Duke of Clarence, executed by Edward IV after many betrayals, had sons whose claim

The Tower of London

would outweigh his own. The young king and his brother disappeared in the Tower; their fate was never revealed, but Richard was undoubtedly responsible for their murder.

The sense of apparent ease with which, at the right time, a strong hand could reach out and seize the crown, had mastered everything Richard possessed by way of loyalty, morality and political common sense. His crime was an ancient one: these were hardly the first children to be sacrificed to a kinsman's greedy ambition – what was modern was the reaction. In a country that venerated kingship, this was seen as usurpation of the crudest sort; in a country that still held a strong Lancastrian party, this was confirmation that the Yorkists would flout everything sacred to keep power. But Yorkist supporters too turned against him. Few would fight for imprisoned or executed Woodvilles, but Richard had Lord Hastings, Edward IV's loyal chamberlain, killed, as well as many Lancastrian sympathisers.

CHAPTER SIX

Tudor England

THE HOUSE OF TUDOR

To counter the Gloucester coup, it was necessary to have a claimant to the throne whose case would be sufficiently convincing. Edward IV had had a daughter, Elizabeth, but no one sought in these circumstances to propose a queen in her own right. But among the Lancastrian nobility was Henry, Earl of Richmond, son of Edmund Tudor, Earl of Richmond, and of Margaret Beaufort. His grandfather was a Welshman from a prominent Anglesey family, Owen Tudor, who had come to London and eventually obtained the post of wardrobe master in the household of Henry V's widow, Catherine of Valois. Later he secretly married the dowager queen, and they had two sons, whom Henry VI accepted as members of the nobility, according them the titles of Earls of Richmond and Pembroke. The Beauforts were the children of John of Gaunt and his mistress, Catherine Swynford, whom he had married near the end of his life: an act of parliament had expressly excluded them from the royal line of succession. Henry Tudor's was not the strongest of claims, but no Lancastrian had a better one. After an abortive attempt to invade England in December 1483, he landed at Milford Haven, in Wales, in 1485. In Wales his Tudor ancestry helped him to increase his army, and in the battle of Bosworth, 22 August 1485, he defeated Richard III, who was killed.

With Henry VII, the House of Tudor assumed the monarchy of England. He duly married Elizabeth of York, and the long, damaging rivalry was brought to

The Great Seal of Henry VII

Henry VII

A Perkin Warbeck groat (silver coin)

an end, though discontented Yorkists, encouraged for their own reasons by the Irish Earl of Kildare and the King of Scots, produced two challengers for the throne. First was Lambert Simnel, pretending to be Edward, son of the Duke of Clarence. On his capture, Henry with contemptuous clemency sent him to work as a kitchen boy. A more serious threat was Perkin Warbeck, who also pretended to be Edward before finding a stronger role as Richard, the younger of the princes murdered at the behest of Richard III. After two failed invasion attempts he was captured and imprisoned in the Tower of London. Further intrigues and escape attempts brought about his execution, along with that of the real Edward, whom Henry had also got locked up in the Tower.

Provident, generous in spirit though careful with the royal funds, Henry VII did much to foster a sense of national renewal after the fractured decades that had gone before. His personal style was domestic rather than grandiose and he did not greatly impress his subjects. The rule of law was gradually reimposed on a country which had grown used to the retinues of great men fighting out their disputes, and where brigandage was rife. Gaps in the system remained; corruption and bribery of officials were still common, and Henry's efficient and self-enriching collectors of dues and fines were deeply loathed. Becoming more financially grasping in later life, he introduced the practice of selling high offices, including the chief justiceship of the Court of Common Pleas and the post of speaker of the House of Commons. Predecessor kings had based a military foreign policy on conquest of French domains, but Henry VII pursued a steady, often devious and essentially commercial foreign policy of avoiding – if possible – warfare and encouraging the great and vital English cloth trade with the Netherlands, by now under Spanish dominion.

Henry's eldest son, Arthur, died before him and it was his second son who succeeded, uncontested, as Henry VIII in 1509. At the start of his reign he married Catherine, daughter of the King of Aragon, the widow of his brother Arthur. Only one child of the union survived, the future Queen Mary. The historian Sir Keith Feiling wrote that Henry, 'if greatness can be irrespective of virtue, must be held a great man'.

For many reasons, including the development at this time of portraiture, and of printing, and not least his chequered matrimonial career, Henry VIII impressed his memory on subsequent generations almost as deeply as he dominated his own.

The Great Seal of Henry VIII   *Henry VIII*

RENAISSANCE IN ENGLAND

In the course of Henry's thirty-eight-year reign, England was to experience profound changes. In previous generations, revolutionary change had meant little more than a change of person at the very top, and a consequent redistribution of power among the magnates. The nature of the institutions of the country – the royal household, parliament, church, law – were not greatly affected by such changes. They followed their own paths of progress or decline. The nature of the kingship itself had altered little from feudal times. It took more than the abounding self-confidence, undoubted intelligence, and ruthless ambition of one man to achieve radical changes within one generation. But imperceptibly, through the later decades of the fifteenth century, there had grown a change of attitude within the educated community of Europe and of England. If a date could be assigned to it, it might be the fall of Constantinople to the Turks in 1453, after which a flood of refugee scholars and clerics streamed into western Europe, bringing in their luggage a host of manuscripts and commentaries which generated not only a revival of interest in the literature and philosophy of ancient Greece and Rome but also a new wave of interest in mysticism, magic and the occult.

For a time, until the conquest of Moorish Granada in 1492, European Christendom was hemmed in by Islam to east and west. Crusades were proposed, but the papacy, by this time a territorial power as well as a religious one, was embroiled in the power politics of Italy and Europe and had lost the spiritual authority of the great medieval popes. The rediscovery of pagan Latin and Greek writers, the emergence of a challenging intellectual attitude to the church, the realisation that there was a vast unknown world to explore beyond the oceans, all combined to foster a spirit of enquiry different to what had existed before. It was centred on the individual, the man or woman who could

Erasmus, the leading scholar of the Renaissance in north-west Europe

bring knowledge and experience to bear on any question, and resolve it. England, on the north-west periphery, was not immune to this change in intellectual life.

Universities and their scholars were still an international community based on teaching in Latin. The German invention of printing with movable type in 1455 was brought to England by William Caxton in 1476. From then, reading could not be confined to the monastery or college: books could be read at home, and hidden away, if they were on forbidden topics. Apart from some crumbled and half-buried remnants, and the remains of Hadrian's Wall close to the remote and dangerous northern frontier, the English had no great monuments of antiquity to contemplate and emulate as had the Italians, the French and the Spanish; their language had evolved from a barbarian speech, not from a classical tongue; they had no line of descent to trace back to Virgil, Aristotle or Homer. But the spirit which led to the Renaissance and the Reformation empowered them just as it empowered men like Michelangelo in Italy, Erasmus in Holland, and Martin Luther in Germany.

It brought Sir Thomas More to write his *Utopia*, in 1516, an exploration of how classical humanist ideals, lacking divine revelation, could be reconciled with the divinely inspired but degenerate Christianity of his day. In Utopia, gold was used to make chamber pots, and military glory was contemptible.

DEFENDER OF THE FAITH AND DESTROYER OF THE MONASTERIES

Henry VIII, supreme individualist, made his own pattern out of the traditional and novel elements of his world. Patron of new music, new art, new architecture, he also relished hunting and horsemanship. Far from averse to military glory, he launched several wars against France; at first in alliance with the papacy, though these campaigns brought him no gains and vast expenditures. Through his generals he was more successful against Scotland, inflicting the crushing defeats of Flodden in 1513, when James IV was killed, and Solway Moss in 1542, which precipitated the death of James V. But his policy of over-lordship or union was a failure, and Scotland remained the ally of France.

He was at first a strenuous defender of Catholic orthodoxy and wrote a book against the teachings of Luther; the Pope rewarded him with the title 'Defender of the Faith'. His alienation from the papacy began in 1527, when he began to seek a divorce from Catherine. The Pope's reluctance to grant this was based in part on the fact that Catherine had a powerful supporter in her nephew, the Holy Roman Emperor, and in part on Henry's insistence that the dispensation allowing him to marry his brother's widow should be admitted, against all Vatican practice, as an error. By 1527, with no annulment, the king took matters into his own hands. He dismissed his chancellor, Cardinal Wolsey, in 1529 and appointed Sir Thomas More instead. For long, he had held to the notion of the kingship as something more than the position of a supreme feudal lord; now he elaborated the idea of himself as supreme head of the church in England. Wolsey's former associate, Thomas Cromwell, became his chief agent in procuring parliamentary support. A series of acts of parliament traces his steps to the final Act of Supremacy in 1534. More and Bishop Fisher of Canterbury were beheaded for their refusal to accept either this or the legitimacy of Henry's marriage to Anne Boleyn, already pregnant with his second daughter, the future Elizabeth I.

PRINTING

By 1450 the use of movable type had been invented or at least developed to full effectiveness by Johannes Gutenberg in Germany. An Englishman in the trading community of Bruges in Flanders, William Caxton (*c*.1420–91), born in Kent, acquired the skills of this intensely exciting new technology and, first in Bruges, then London, became the first printer of books in English. Already over fifty when he set up his printing shop, he was not only printer and publisher, but also himself a translator. His first publication was a history of the Trojan War, in 1471; the second was *The Game and Playe of the Chesse*. *The Canterbury Tales* and *Chronicles of England* followed among a stream of other works. Not only books but pamphlets, single-sheet poems, news-sheets and advertisements were turned out. Caxton's enterprise brought printing to England early, and the circulation of texts of all kinds in multiple copies heralded significant changes in English life. Literacy was encouraged. The transmission of accurate information was made much easier. The spread of printed texts through the country began to standardise the English language, which at that time still had quite wide regional variations. In the decades before printing, manuscript copying had already become quite a substantial industry, but manuscripts could preserve regional variations in a way in which print did not; and Caxton's choices had a strong influence on later written English.

Hampton Court Palace, relinquished to Henry VIII by Cardinal Wolsey in 1528

With Cromwell as a highly efficient manager, and Thomas Cranmer as a compliant though piously evangelical archbishop of Canterbury, Henry used his authority to dissolve or close down the abbeys, nunneries and friaries of England. The monastic life was not highly regarded by Cranmer, who had taken a wife. In many of the monasteries, the number of monks was much smaller than in their high days of the twelfth and thirteenth centuries, and few maintained the old rigour. Most abbeys owed allegiance to a parent house in France, and many abbots were foreigners or absentees. But if they had few residents, and little influence, the abbeys still had great wealth in property and treasure. The new, unblushingly named Court of Augmentation of the King's Revenue acquired some £200,000, a colossal sum, by the end of the dissolutions in November 1539. For the first time in English history, the king was richer than the church. The vast windfall was soon dissipated in the military campaigns of the 1540s and on the need to share much of the proceeds with territorial magnates on whose support Henry, who had no standing army, was reliant. Their aid was vital in breaking a rebellion in Lincolnshire in 1536 and a more substantial one, the Pilgrimage of Grace, in Yorkshire in 1539, both seeking restitution of traditional religion together with elements of political reform.

In 1536 Anne Boleyn was executed and Henry married Jane Seymour, who bore him a son and died a few days afterwards. She was succeeded by a diplomatic marriage to Anne, daughter of the Duke of Cleves in Flanders; this was a failure in all respects and was annulled in 1540. A brief marriage to Catherine Howard followed before she was executed for adultery (an activity Henry permitted only to himself), and the king's sixth wife, Catherine Parr, survived her tempestuous husband.

Despite his increasing megalomania and despotic tendencies, Henry VIII was not a tyrant. He ruled with the general consent and with no standing army to back up his authority, and his personal flamboyance and the ostentation of palaces like the now-vanished Nonsuch were seen as suitably kingly by most of his people. Parliament was a vital part of his governmental procedure, and he summoned it far more regularly than his father had.

In an address to parliament in 1543, he said: 'we at no time stand so high in our estate royal as in the time of Parliament, when we as head and you as members are conjoined and knit together in one body politic.' In many aspects of church reform he was a conservative: his church never abandoned the Mass, and Archbishop Cranmer had to send his wife away. His 'Six Articles' of 1539 confirmed most aspects of basic Catholic worship, though destruction of relics, statues and shrines went on, and the Bible in English was ordered to be placed in every parish church. Its text was not merely to be expounded by the priest-hood, but to be available to anyone who could read. Cromwell, architect of the Cleves alliance, was dispensed with in 1540, executed in macabre symmetry with six Lutherans, and six Romanists who denied the royal supremacy. Perse-cutions and burnings of adherents to both extremes went on, though on a rela-tively small scale. The constant tension between Cranmer and Stephen Gardiner, Bishop of Winchester and leader of the Catholic tendency, which Henry tolerated, was typical of a wider and deepening divide in the population, between those who either accepted Henry's church, or harked back to papal supremacy; and those who were in sympathy with the Lutheran and Calvinist Reformation.

Despite the monastic funds, Henry's military campaigns of the 1540s were so expensive that heavy taxation and forced loans from wealthy merchants were imposed. The currency was debased, with the silver coin being reduced to one part silver to two parts alloy; the king who had inherited full coffers would die with his Exchequer almost bankrupt. With Scotland an independent Catholic kingdom, and Ireland a part-colonised Catholic nation, Henry felt a strong necessity to safeguard his church by extending it throughout the British Isles. Only in Wales was this policy successful; a statute of union annexed Wales to England, completed its division into shires, finishing off the old Marcher lord-ships, and allowing for twenty-four Welsh members to attend the Westminster parliament. In Ireland, though he had himself named as king, rather than 'Lord of Ireland' like his predecessors, his control was limited to the English 'pale' around Dublin. At his death, the Scottish war was still being fought. Although the Catholic tendency had seemed to gain ground in his later years, he left his son to be educated by Protestants and with the Protestant camp in the majority in the regency Council. Tormented by ulcers in the legs, he died in January 1547.

A SENSE OF NATIONALISM

Partly because we still live with aspects of the England that Henry VIII presided over or created, we feel that we 'know' him and subsequent monarchs while his predecessors occupy a more remote place in our minds. Serfdom and villeinage had become virtually non-existent by his time, except in certain specific areas and activities, including coal and salt mining. Great men were building houses for themselves rather than castles. The days of earls and barons possessed of semi-independent power in the north and west were now past. The basis of England's foreign policy moved from a futile acquisitiveness in Europe to a new sense of nationalism, and so to the concept of seeking to maintain a balance of power there, among the kings of France and Spain, the

The Henri Grace Dieu, *built for the English fleet at the command of Henry VIII*

emperor, and the papacy: England's security lay in none of these achieving dominance over the others. One of its bases lay in control of the narrow seas, and to this reign the Royal Navy owes its origins, as did Trinity House, for long the authority in charge of lights, pilotage and coastal navigation.

Henry's navy not only had, for the first time, specialised fighting ships owned by the crown, but also warships of a new design. Hitherto, warships had been built for hand-to-hand fighting at close quarters; the new ships were longer and more manoeuvrable, carrying guns in rows along the sides, and capable of destroying an enemy from long range; these floating gun platforms would transform naval warfare. Henry's death, however, occurred in a period of deep uncertainty and flux, in which living standards were falling, where the pattern and outcome of events was far from clear; and the new king was a rather sickly boy of nine.

EDWARD VI: PLOT AND COUNTER-PLOT

In traditional manner, a Council of Regency was formed, and a Protector of the Realm was appointed, the Duke of Somerset, brother of the king's mother, Jane Seymour. An unusual figure in the English nobility, he was a successful general and also a convinced religious ideologue who sought to extend the Protestant Reformation well beyond the point at which Henry VIII had stopped. In other ways he continued his old master's methods, including warfare in Scotland and a continued debasement of the coinage. Popular unrest, perhaps increased by the sense that Somerset was sympathetic to the poor, made for almost permanent crisis in East Anglia and the south-west, the Scottish policy collapsed when the young Queen Mary was sent to France to marry its Dauphin rather than Edward VI, and Somerset was ousted from the Protectorship by the Earl of Warwick in October 1549. As Lord President of the Council, Warwick (Duke of Northumberland from 1551) established some reforming policies, including a restoration of the coinage. He was a superficial Protestant, but family ambition seems to have underlain his attempt, when Edward VI was clearly destined for an early death, to put forward Lady Jane Grey as heir to the throne. Although Edward was in agreement, it was in contravention of Henry VIII's will, which had named his daughters Mary and Elizabeth as heirs after Edward. Northumberland married his son to Lady Jane and when Edward VI died on 6 July 1553, he and his Council proclaimed Queen Jane. But the plot was not wholehearted enough to imprison or do away with the Tudor princesses. Mary, whose mother Catherine of Aragon had always had much popular sympathy, was escorted to London by the gentry of East Anglia; and Northumberland, despite a sudden re-conversion to Catholicism, was beheaded.

MARY I AND CATHOLIC RESURGENCE

During the populist risings – in which religious protest played a part – and aristocratic plottings of Edward VI's short reign, steady progress was being made by determined men in the Protestant interest. Although the suppression of chantry chapels – often rich endowed foundations – by Somerset was mainly to get hold of their wealth, the policy of image-breaking and destruction of relics and religious art went on apace. More constructively, Cranmer produced his great Prayer Book which was to form one of the strongest pillars of the later Anglican church. But Mary's assumption of rule brought the Protestant Revolution to a grinding halt, and then forced it into reverse.

She had never renounced her Catholicism. The half-Spanish Mary, with many friends, advisers and relatives from her mother's country, set out on a policy which was as bold as her father's but far more foolhardy. It was to unmake his church, and to restore England's obedience to the Pope. She desired too, to give the church back what property and wealth it had lost. But here she met a major obstacle. Most of that property had been sold or presented by the crown to members of the English nobility, who had no intention of giving any of it up. Buoyed up only by those who shared her own views, dubiously supported even by those who, like Cranmer's old opponent, Stephen Gardiner, now at last enjoyed power and authority, but believed England could be Catholic without being papal, and increasingly resented and finally loathed by those who held to the nationalist–Protestant view that Henry VIII had helped to create and had benefited from, Mary underlined her whole policy by enthusiastically becoming the wife of the heir to the Spanish throne, who became Philip II of Spain in

The Great Seal of Mary I

1556. Until Mary's death, England was an instrument of Spanish foreign policy. This led directly to the loss of Calais, in the course of a Spanish-led war with France: it had been England's last small foothold on the European continent. Parliament, and a Kentish revolt under Sir Thomas Wyatt, had opposed her Spanish marriage. From 1555 to 1558, some three hundred people were burned to death for promoting Protestant beliefs. They included the ex-Archbishop Cranmer, the influential preacher Hugh Latimer, and Nicholas Ridley,

The burning of Anne Askew and other martyrs from Foxe's Book of Martyrs

Bishop of Rochester: in the deaths of such men as these the Anglican church found the baptism of fire which greatly enhanced its later identity and spiritual authority. Cancer of the stomach killed Mary at the age of forty-two; had she lived as long as her half-sister and successor, many things might have been very different.

CONCORD AND COMPROMISE

Elizabeth, the twenty-five-year-old daughter of Anne Boleyn, was very different in her own way. Her mother's family too had inclined towards religious reform. Henry VIII's will prevailed without question and though in the eyes of traditional Catholics she was a bastard and so debarred from the throne, her accession was uncontested and greeted with general relief. It was hardly to be expected that she would continue Mary's policy. At the time of the Wyatt rebellion she had been imprisoned for a time in the Tower of London, and then lived under virtual house arrest. In these respects as well as in an excellent scholastic education, she was well-trained for the practice of monarchy, which she would exercise for forty-four years. As her coronation motto she took the word 'Concord'.

It is mildly piquant that Elizabeth and the man who for almost all her reign was

---

THE *BOOK OF MARTYRS*

No book, other than the Bible and the Prayer Book, was so influential for so long as Foxe's *Acts and Monuments*, first published in 1563 and reprinted in countless editions, popularly known as the *Book of Marytrs*. This was the visceral text of Anglican Protestantism. Its author, John Foxe (1517–87), was an Anglican clergyman from Boston, Lincolnshire. Adhering to the more extreme Protestant wing of Anglicanism, he was a man of personal tolerance, and his friendships extended from the anti-Trinitarian Joan Bocher (burned in the reign of Edward VI) to the religiously conservative Duke of Norfolk (executed in the reign of Elizabeth I), whose tutor he had once been. His great work, begun in exile during Mary I's reign, was to collect and collate the stories of anti-Catholic martyrs. The book, telling their stories, and illustrated with woodcuts showing all manner of hideous executions, was enormously successful. Foxe worked on a number of revised and enlarged editions, and criticism and counter-shots from the papal side merely increased its success. It was a key contribution in creating the basic climate of hostility to the Roman Catholic church and the Pope which continued in English life through the seventeenth and eighteenth centuries.

---

her chief minister, William Cecil, both possessed Welsh ancestors and Welsh names in Tewdwr and Seisyllt. Both thoroughly English in spirit and feeling, they were indirect beneficiaries of the great and gentle absorptiveness which English society already displayed. The Cecils, to be the country's most enduring political dynasty, rose to ultimate grandee-status from a modest role in Lincolnshire in the service of one of Henry VII's Welsh supporters who had been rewarded with land there. In 1558 the queen and her counsellor were at the helm of a country which was great in no one's eyes, lately dominated by Spain, still impoverished from the financial mismanagement of earlier decades, a peripheral force in European power politics, and socially very much divided on the religious issue. Philip II's hopes of marrying Elizabeth helped to shelter England from either French or Spanish attack during the early years of the reign, and the queen and her government were able to address themselves to the essential business of religious settlement and of economic restoration.

In the church, on the benches of the law courts, and in many other offices, persons appointed under Mary continued to discharge their functions, and not all adapted to the views of the new regime. In fact when in 1559, after three months' hard debate, the Act of Supremacy was passed by parliament, restoring the royal governorship of the church and making Cranmer's Prayer Book the only legal form of worship, the bishops, with one exception, opposed it and were deprived of their posts. The great majority of the parish clergy, around seven out of eight thousand, accepted the changes. For the older ones, it was their fourth change: the 'Vicar of Bray' of the next century had many predecessors in this one. Although a Puritan tendency remained on the one hand, and a Catholic one on the other, the settlement of 1559 was satisfactory to the great majority of the people and their clerics; most historians believe that the evangelical Cecil had managed a somewhat more Protestant form than the queen herself would have liked. But by this time the Counter-Reformation had been launched by the Pope, and a clear stand had to be taken between the positions of Rome and Geneva (and, soon, Edinburgh). The first Elizabethan Archbishop of Canterbury, Matthew Parker, shared all of Cecil's instincts and steered a firm middle way between the two opposed extremes which would each subject the monarch to the control of God, as interpreted by his clerics. Thirty-nine Articles spelled out the essential beliefs of the church, and were accepted by Convocation, its own parliament, in 1563.

Readers of this book will by now be familiar with the two crucial aspects of English society. One was veneration of the idea of monarchy. Linked to this was the belief that the monarch should be free to pursue his – and, more lately, her – own course of policy. Such a course would not necessarily be accepted tamely, or by everyone. Parliament petitioned Mary against her Spanish marriage. Wyatt led an armed revolt against it. Up and down the country, Protestants quietly ignored Mary's ban, and Catholics ignored Elizabeth's wherever they were strong enough in numbers. But the principle and the practice are both generally clear. The other vital aspect was the acceptance that the law checked, and in some respects governed, the monarch. The ultimate expression of that law lay with parliament.

NO WEAK AND FEEBLE WOMAN

The reign of Elizabeth I shows, not quite for the first time – her grandfather Henry VII had shown the way – but in a manner which made a deep impression on the English people, how these two ideas, in combination, could result in the monarch and her counsellors on the one hand, and parliament on the other, working together in the interest of the survival and prosperity of the nation as a whole. The queen's vanity, played up to by courtiers and sycophants, her avoidance of difficult decisions, her highly successful 'Gloriana' mythology screening her failures and lackings, has led to a campaign of detraction by some modern historians. But there is every reason to consider her one of the country's most successful, as well as remarkable, monarchs, in the execution over many years of a job which was fraught from beginning to end with difficult choices, dangerous decisions and intense pressures from many conflicting quarters. Not every act of her government was admirable or calculated to enhance the national interest. Compared to her successors, however, she was a paragon, who understood and respected the scope and the limitations of power and who never lost a deep sense of involvement with the people over whom circumstances had placed her as sovereign. She gave them

Elizabeth I

the necessary regal flamboyance but at the same time something more: a joltingly demotic popular touch which told them that, like them, she was 'mere English'. No previous monarch, male or female, could have adopted this tone to a parliamentary delegation: 'Though I be a woman, I have as good a courage answerable to this place as ever my father had. I am your anointed queen. I will never be by violence constrained to do anything. I thank God that I am endued with such qualities that if I were turned out of the realm in my petticoat, I were able to live in any place in Christendom.'

The parliamentarians, not for the first or last time, were trying to discover the answer to a troubling question: what plans, if any, the queen had for marriage, or the succession. For a long time it was assumed that she would marry; the only question was, who? After the refusal of Philip II, various royal continentals entered a claim; Cecil was afraid she would marry her court favourite, Robert Dudley, Earl of Leicester, son of the ambitious Northumberland. In the end she married no one and allowed the cult of the Virgin Queen to grow around her.

AN AGE OF DISCOVERY

An important early achievement of her government was the reform of the currency, which was completed by 1561, with all the adulterated coins called in and a new silver coinage minted. With a currency that could be trusted, business confidence among the small but economically very important and politically influential merchant class was restored. Helped by peace, international trading went into a phase of rapid growth. Confirmation of freedom from papal decisions also meant that English sailors could ignore the Pope's division of the New World between Spain and Portugal. First revealed to western Europe by Christopher Columbus in 1492, the Americas were by now a source of fabulous wealth in gold, silver and delicious, exotic foodstuffs. If an Englishman could grab some of the plunder by force, then he would. The line between merchant venturers and buccaneers was often too finely drawn to be visible. The population was growing rapidly, with the most informed estimates putting the total at

3.01 million in 1551, and 4.1 million in 1601: an increase of a third in two generations. But trade was also growing fast, agriculture was prosperous and becoming more commercial, towns were becoming more populous and city markets were becoming larger, more varied in their goods and commodities and more sophisticated in their forms of dealing. England was still a small country measured against France and Spain, but among the smaller countries of Europe, it was one of the most influential, especially when after 1559, it was confirmed as a Protestant state.

At this time, it may be noted, no one in England had ever eaten, or even heard of, a potato. No one had chewed or smoked tobacco. Tea and coffee were equally unknown. Oranges were exotic rarities and tropical fruits unseen. Silk was a rare and highly expensive import, as was virtually every other high quality fabric and such luxury items as fine china and glassware. These were accessible only to the wealthiest. The country's main imports were wine, manufactured cloth, timber, pig iron and furs. Its exports were corn, wool, coarse cloth and coal. The 'balance of payments' was probably weighted slightly in favour of imports over exports. For the majority of the population, the large increase in numbers brought a steady drop in living standards. It was a young population; schooling was minimal or non-existent for the majority; and it was expected that a child would work. A larger labour market depressed wages and led to unemployment and a growing drift from the country into the towns, especially London. With the increase in the value of land, the tenant farmer was put at a serious disadvantage. Such practices as the enclosure of common lands by land-lords, which reduced the amount of grazing for tenants' flocks, had been going on to some extent even in the previous century, but now became more wide-spread. Dispossessed peasant farmers sought unoccupied 'wilderness' ground to squat on and cultivate; but no ground lacked an owner, and there were frequent local disturbances over land rights. Between 1550 and 1610, the cost of living, as expressed in necessary purchases, almost doubled, while earnings appear to have fallen by about 20 per cent in the same period. The wage rate used in this example is that of building craftsmen in southern England, a group who might have been supposed to flourish at a time when towns were growing fast and an era of country house building was beginning. There were elements here of an explosive situation both in town and country, but deprivation and discontent never reached the point of a widespread or national outbreak of anger and frustration.

MANAGEMENT AND CONTROL

One factor in population growth was immigration. In the Netherlands, the eighty-year-long struggle to free the Dutch provinces from Spanish rule had begun in 1566. In France there was fierce conflict between the Protestants, known as Huguenots, and Catholics. Refugees from these troubles began to make their way into England, and in most cases they brought skills and trades which added to the country's resources, and depleted those of their countries of origin. Cecil's government, keen to extend copper, lead and zinc mining, encouraged the immigration of miners from Saxony and Thuringia. England's economic and industrial rise was partly owed to the distractions of the Netherlands and the decline, for a time, of their great trading and manufacturing cities.

Elizabethan England was thus a far from peaceful, prosperous and united country. Internal stresses and external pressures were a permanent aspect of life for the queen and her government. The ministry of Cecil shows clearly how far the role of central government had spread into the management of the country. He was no revolutionary; his instincts were conservative and his nature cautious. But from Whitehall Palace he surveyed, not the old England of territorial lords exercising feudal privileges, but the gradually evolving new England – a land of shires administered through royally appointed and monitored officials and local justices of the peace, and each with a lord lieutenant as the queen's representative, responsible for raising the local militia; an aristocracy subservient to the crown; and a church which was a department of state. Such a country required a far more intensive pattern of legislation and control than ever before, and a greater prescriptiveness was noticeable in the actions of government. A new law required people to eat fish twice a week. This was not on dietary grounds but to support a growing fishing industry which in turn provided a stream of experienced seamen for the Royal Navy and for merchant shipping. Reaching out to the Newfoundland Banks, the fishing industry also provided a link with the toehold settlements in the north of the New World. In 1563 the Statute of Labourers set out the pattern of work and reward for artisans and craftsmen, enforcing seven-year apprenticeships and giving special advantages to skilled crafts. Wages were to be fixed on a local basis by the justices of the peace, with the Council ready to step in if there was serious complaint. A new Poor Law in 1563 established a uniform parish rate to provide funds for paupers.

Council brought its decisions as proposals to parliament, and parliament usually passed them as laws, in the queen's name. But the Council's activities went further. Political insecurity, and the need to exercise wide control, meant that it employed an extensive network of spies and informants, controlled by Sir Francis Walsingham, Principal Secretary from 1573. Cecil's executive was very well informed of what went on, particularly among the more suspect or dangerous sections of society, including the diehard Catholics who had never accepted Elizabeth's rule as legitimate and who found the Act of Supremacy intolerable.

MARY, QUEEN OF SCOTS

For them, a new focus was presented in 1568, when Mary, the deposed Queen of Scots, fled from defeat by her country's Calvinist government to seek safety in England. The Scottish queen was a Catholic, who had been compelled to abdicate in favour of her baby son, James VI. By her descent from Margaret Tudor, sister of Henry VIII and wife of James IV of Scotland, she was Elizabeth's closest living relative. Her French relations had already proclaimed her as Queen of England when Mary I died. Mary was nine years younger than Elizabeth, who at thirty-five was nearing the end of her child-bearing potential. The spectre of another Catholic Queen Mary caused great alarm to Elizabeth's Council. The two women never met, and for nineteen years Mary was kept in confinement, nominally on the grounds of implication in the murder of her second husband, Lord Darnley. In 1569 the Earls of Westmorland and Northumberland attempted a pro-Catholic rebellion which was speedily put down, but it was the first of a number of plots which eventually would cost Mary her life. In 1570 the Pope proclaimed Elizabeth a heretic and formally deposed her. It was more than a futile gesture, as it enabled her opponents to plan legally, in their terms, for her assassination. The official reaction to this open threat to the queen was the encouragement of the anti-papal, anti-Catholic feeling that would come to run deep in the English population. In 1584–85, an Act of Parliament made any Englishman ordained priest by papal authority after 1559 to be automatically guilty of treason. A hundred and forty-six priests were executed between 1584 and 1603.

THREATS FROM ABROAD AND THREATS AT HOME

Slowly, through a series of minor crises, acts of piracy, sporadic peace negotiations, diplomatic initiatives and failures over a period of fifteen years from 1571, England and Spain moved closer to an ultimate confrontation. If Philip II's desire to eliminate Europe's strongest Protestant haven was his main driving force, the permanent irritation at England's penetration and harassment of his Spanish–Portuguese empire cannot have been far behind. Francis Drake, the most successful of the buccaneer-merchant-explorers, completed his circumnavigation of the globe between 1577 and 1580 and in an act of deliberate provocation to Spain, the queen knighted him in 1581 on the deck of his ship, the *Golden Hind*. London merchants' money had subsidised his voyage and it triumphantly symbolised the opening of the world to English enterprise. The killing of the Dutch leader, William the Silent, by Spanish agents in 1584, sharpened the anxiety of the English government. In May 1585, the Spanish seized all English shipping in the harbours of Spain and Portugal, and the Earl of Leicester was sent to Holland with an army to support the insurgent Dutch against their Spanish rulers. This military expedition was an ignominious failure and Leicester was recalled, though he did not lose the queen's favour. In 1587 a naval expedition under Drake destroyed the Spanish fleet at Cadiz.

Sir Francis Drake

Madrid's invasion plans, already well advanced, had to be put back for a year.

In February 1587, in the wake of a further assassination plot against the queen, organised by Anthony Babington, a Derbyshire landowner, Mary of Scotland was beheaded. Only a muted protest came from north of the border, but the act made war with Spain inevitable, which is perhaps why Elizabeth both wished and un-wished it in a way that has always been discreditable to her own reputation.

THE SPANISH ARMADA

The grand strategy of the Spanish Armada was well founded. England possessed no standing army and its local militias were inexperienced and formed of small separate units without a central command. The Spanish army, 22,000 strong, if

THE *GOLDEN HIND*

First named *Pelican*, after the emblem of her main financial backer, the merchant Sir Christopher Hatton, she was renamed by her captain, Francis Drake, at the Magellan Straits in August 1578. She was a typical ship of galleon type, with a burden of around 150 tonnes, and well-armed with eighteen guns on two decks. Around eighty crew were squeezed into her small hull. The *Golden Hind* was the first English vessel to circumnavigate the globe, between 1577 and 1580, returning with substantial plundered treasure. In 1583 she was used in Sir Humphry Gilbert's transatlantic expedition to Labrador. Queen Elizabeth I ordered the ship to be preserved at Deptford on the Thames, but the shed to house her was never completed. By 1660, there was virtually nothing left of the historic craft, though replicas have been built in recent times.

The Spanish Armada being attacked by the English Fleet

it could be landed, was assured of conquest, and, with England mastered, the Dutch revolt would soon be ended. Prevention of a landing was all-important to the English, and the Spanish plan for the fleet to sail up-Channel and make a union with the Duke of Parma's forces invading from Flanders gave them their opportunity. It was not a short battle: from 21 to 29 July, 1588, the Spanish fought their way towards the Flemish coast and the English fought to bar their passage. Half the English fleet of 105 ships were merchant vessels, but the key to victory was held in the heavily gunned fighting galleons, new or rebuilt, designed to be sailed closer to the wind, to turn faster, and to mount a more destructive broadside, than any other ships of the time. By the time the Armada reached Calais it was battered but not broken, but was forced to wait for the land forces in Flanders. On the night of 7 August, the English sent eight fire-ships drifting towards the close-packed Spanish fleet, forcing many ships to cut their cables and disperse. A close-range battle ensued off the coast at Grave-lines, with a tactical victory for the English, and a change in the wind sent the Armada vessels northwards into the North Sea.

For some time it was not clear what had happened, and their return was anxiously awaited by an English fleet desperately short of ammunition. But the south-westerly wind prevailed and the damaged ships were sent round the north of Scotland and the west of Ireland, succumbing as they went to leaks and storms. Only half returned to Spain. It was a close thing, and desperate days were spent in assembling London volunteers and arming them with bows and arrows, in anticipation of invasion. But the Armada was in no state to turn back and resume its task.

THE LAST YEARS OF ELIZABETH

England was saved from Spanish conquest, and the struggle in the Netherlands continued, with English subsidies sent to support the Dutch rebels and the French Protestants, and small-scale military expeditions. These were sometimes repaid in kind, as when the Spanish attacked and destroyed Penzance. Warfare broke out in Ireland. Only one old embattled frontier was at peace: James VI of Scotland, anticipating the English crown, and in receipt of an English pension, did his best to prevent border raids and gave no help to France or Spain. In Elizabeth's latter years, neither English diplomacy nor English arms achieved much success, though the country's mercantile development continued. Cecil, ennobled as Lord Burghley, died in 1598; his son Robert, later Earl of Salisbury, was made Secretary of State in 1596 and pursued the same careful policies as his father. The queen's increasing age, her refusal to name any successor, her hostility to the increasingly Puritanical tone of her parliaments, the old-fashioned atmosphere of her court in a country with a large youthful population, and a sense of lack of economic opportunity at home (if not abroad) made her last ten years a decade of decline. A disastrous decision appointed her cousin and court favourite, Robert Devereux, Earl of Essex, as Lord Lieutenant in Ireland in 1599, to counter the rising led by Hugh O'Neill. Instead of gaining victory, or even fighting seriously, Essex signed a truce, and his relations with the queen never recovered. Always a bitter rival of Robert Cecil, in 1601 he attempted a political coup to 'rescue' the queen from her Cecil-dominated Council, and on its immediate collapse he was executed for treason. A more sensible royal decision was the removal of various unpopular trade monopolies in that same year. The welcome this was given brought the queen to say to her parliamentarians, with whom she had often been at odds: 'Though God hath raised me high, yet this I

ENGLISH QUALITIES

The qualities that a nation recognises in itself are not always the same as those detected by others. The notion of 'perfidious Albion' certainly did not originate on the English side of the Channel. By the end of Elizabeth I's reign, certain characteristics, which were to be seen as typical, both at home and abroad, were exemplified by some leading figures of the time. There was coolness, with Sir Francis Drake finishing his game of bowls before sailing against the Armada. There was courtesy, with Sir Walter Raleigh casting his cloak over a puddle for the queen to walk dry-shod. There was hot-blooded courage, with Sir Richard Grenville in the *Revenge* refusing to flee before overpowering Spanish strength. There was gallantry, with the dying Sir Philip Sidney refusing water in favour of a wounded soldier at Zutphen. All these qualities were united in the idealised persona of the English gentleman. He might be a sportsman or a scholar, but these basic qualities were what he was expected to aspire to.

count the glory of my crown, that I have reigned with your loves.' To the end, she was a past mistress in the art of self-presentation, but there is no reason to suppose that she did not fully believe her own words.

The Puritan strain of parliament reflected a strong trend in the country at large. Stimulated by the long warfare with Spain and France, which promoted an anti-Catholic spirit, encouraged by the establishment of a Calvinist church in Scotland, the English church found in many of its clergy and adherents a powerful trend to accentuate its own differences to Catholicism. Elizabeth was opposed to the Puritan trend both on religious grounds and because it represented a growing threat to her governorship of the church. But though she clung to her supremacy, she was unable to undo or otherwise deal with the fact that in 'her' church, depending on the views of the parish priest and his patron the lord or squire, the form of worship might be anything from virtually the old Catholic Mass to the service prescribed by the Calvinist capital, Geneva. The queen's management left much to be desired. Many parishes had no priest; the queen left bishoprics vacant while their revenues went to the crown; and though the Church of England contained both saintly and spiritual men, like Richard Hooker, whose writings *On the Laws of Ecclesiastical Polity* did much to spell out the philosophical basis of Anglicanism, it was administered in a thoroughly materialistic spirit by officials and clergy whose prime aim was to make money from it and resist any change which imperilled their wealth and prospects. Any attempts through parliament to change things were vetoed by the queen. When Parker's successor as archbishop of Canterbury, Edmund Grindal, refused to curb Calvinist sermons and the use of Calvin's catechism, he was suspended and placed under house arrest in 1577. His successor, John Whitgift, was able to combine Calvinist sympathies with a strong disciplinarian approach. Backed by the Lord Chancellor, Sir Christopher Hatton, through his Court of High Commission he enforced the clergy's adherence to the Thirty-nine Articles, but he also permitted a number of reformed practices to continue. Puritanism was to a large extent accommodated, but it had already taken many forms, some of them quite extreme. For those who believed that religion was an individual faith, a matter between the person and God, the concept of a state church was intolerable. Separatist congregations were set up, but their denial of the royal supremacy was opposed with as much vigour as the papists'; and after a number of arrests and executions, many of the congregationalists fled to Holland.

CHAPTER SEVEN

Stuart England: Civil War and Commonwealth

THE STUART DYNASTY

The death of Queen Elizabeth, on 24 March 1603, was perceived as the end of an era, though in fact all the problems of her later years passed on unchanged and unresolved. But there was a new king, and a new dynasty. James Stuart, King of Scots, a sound Protestant and firm opponent of church rule in secular matters, was the choice of the Council as well as that of the old queen, and an attempt, known as the 'Main Plot', to substitute his first cousin, Arabella Stuart, never had a chance of success. James I installed himself as rapidly as possible, and in the twenty-two years of his English reign, made only one short return to Scotland. The opportunity which he himself perceived, and promoted, to form a united kingdom of Great Britain, fell on stony ground. Parliament could see little prospect of benefit in a union with Scotland and believed, mistakenly, that the old military threat from the north had been finally ended with the Union of the Crowns.

The kingdom which James inherited at the age of thirty-seven was very different to the one which he had reigned over since his babyhood. Despite

The Great Seal of James I

James I

their sharing a language, there had been little or no intercourse between England and Scotland. Edinburgh was as foreign a capital as Lisbon or Copenhagen. His new metropolis was the largest in Europe, a cosmopolitan warren, a seaport trading with the world, a centre of international commerce and exchange conscious of the fact that huge opportunities still lay ahead. Plague raged through it in 1603, killing almost 40,000 people, a tenth of the population, but nothing could quench its terrible vitality. Instead of the fractious, independent-minded ministers of the Scottish Kirk, often disrespectful to royalty and parading their loyalty to a higher king, James had Whitgift's Anglican church, a loyal department of the state, with its structure of bishoprics and himself as its supreme head.

SHAKESPEARE AND ENGLISH CULTURE

His court was very much larger, grander, more opulent and ceremonious – in fact James's more informal ways upset the gravitas of Tudor grandees. He came to England at a high point in artistic culture. In the course of Elizabeth's reign, there had been a great leap in the imaginative life. English drama had developed from something relatively crude and traditional, still showing its origins in medieval mummery, into a sophisticated entertainment which mingled, at its best, great poetry, dramatic action, exciting stories and a sharp awareness of contemporary politics and social life. During Essex's brief attempt to hijack the government in 1601, William Shakespeare's play *Richard II* had been performed – a play which openly discussed the possibility of replacing a king. London had purpose-built theatres and two theatre companies.

The Globe Theatre, London

Though it is often now referred to as 'Shakespeare's England', the great playwright, much respected and admired as he was, certainly did not dominate it in any way. His work characterises England's spirit: in its exploration of what is most human and individual in us; its insistence on the dangers and ultimate failure of despotism; its expression of our subordination to a fate which we cannot direct or control but which by suffering, learning, understanding, we can still transcend. Shakespeare's underlying ideas retain their interest because they are still the fundamental themes of our own era five hundred years after him. But they retain their vitality and resonance because they are set down in magnificent poetry, infused with humour ranging from crudity to high subtlety, and presented in a context of vivid dramatic action, in a totality which no other dramatist has yet exceeded. In other ways he reflected his time, being a shrewd courtier and businessman, unlike his stormy fellow-dramatist Christopher Marlowe, killed in a tavern brawl, whose curtailed career foreshadows that of many later English poets. In modern England, such a man would undoubtedly be Lord Shakespeare, with a string of honorary degrees and other social distinctions; in Jacobean England, despite great and appreciated service with the King's Company, he retired, plain Mr Shakespeare, to his home town of Stratford-upon-Avon. Politics and warfare could make lords; the time of the artist was not yet come. Music was an important auxiliary in the English drama and at a high point in its own right. Church and secular music was composed in great quantity and widely admired throughout Europe. Singing was a national pastime, accompanying work as well as leisure.

A SCIENTIFIC LORD CHANCELLOR

In the time of Francis Bacon (1561–1626), science was not known as such, but was a part of philosophy. When William Harvey, Bacon's doctor and himself the discoverer of how blood circulates in the body, said of Bacon, 'He writes philosophy like a Lord Chancellor', he set down the success and limitations of this remarkable man, who never managed to ingratiate himself with Elizabeth I but succeeded with James I, whose Lord Chancellor he became in 1618. In 1621 it took either the receipt of bribes on a very large scale, or very powerful enemies, for a Lord Chancellor to be impeached. In Bacon's case it was the enemies; his acceptance of 'gifts' was entirely typical of his times and there is no evidence that it affected his judgements. His trial ended his political career. But it is as a pioneer of English science, and an engaging essayist, that he is now remembered. Bacon's scientific interest was personal and deep, bringing him no rewards at the time. Although his iconoclastic attitude to Aristotle and medieval philosophers was partly motivated by a mistaken view that there was a lost deeper, older knowledge, what most impressed the next generation was his focus on establishing facts and on experiment. His conception that all ideas are ultimately the product of sensation or feeling was taken up and explored far more intensively by John Locke. The spread of scientific investigation and the founding of the Royal Society can be directly linked to Bacon's influence.

THE REACH OF PARLIAMENT

The quirky, clever new king undoubtedly relished the more spacious airs of England, though he preferred the formal pageantry and political correctness of the musical masque to the rough-and-tumble of the stage play. Well educated and intelligent like his Tudor predecessors, he was more self-consciously intellectual. Inheriting the kingship of England had obsessed him for most of his adult life and though he could do little positive to obtain it, he made very sure that he did nothing to upset his chance. Royal government was something he had pondered over and written a book about, *Basilikon Doron*, 'The Gift of Kingship', as a primer for his elder son, Henry. James's view was that a king ruled by divine right, and that to oppose his will was a sin in God's eyes as well as an offence against the state. Naturally, in such a scheme of things, bishops and a church hierarchy played an essential role. The Church of England fitted James's view to satisfaction, though he stored up national disaster by refusing even to consider any extension of tolerance towards Puritan practice. The parliament of England did not fit so well. The single-house Scottish Parliament was a simple organism compared to England's two houses, which had a far wider range of interest, authority and self-confidence.

The economy of England, if not the largest, was probably the most advanced and complex in Europe. Still strongly based upon the cloth trade, still with a predominantly agricultural base, it showed aspects of developing industrialisation in shipyards, cannon-foundries, brickworks and ironworks. The range of trades was greater, incorporating glaziers, plumbers and other skilled crafts whose work added to the amenities of wealthy homes, churches and places of assembly like guild halls. The developing skills in medicine and surgery required new and specialist instruments. New imports were coming in from west and east, including tobacco (against the use of which the new king wrote a book) and chocolate. To control and protect trading in far-off places, new businesses had been created, the Muscovy Company and the Levant Company, respectively granted monopolies on trade with Russia and the eastern Mediterranean. The regulation of this diverse activity had become the joint concern of the Council and of parliament, with some men being members of both bodies, as Sir Francis Walsingham had been. Parliament retained its composition of knights of the shires and burgesses of the towns in the Commons, and lords and bishops in the upper house. The prime function of parliament remained 'supply', the granting and securing of the royal finances, and its strength lay in its capacity to refuse supply until its grievances were attended to. In internal matters it had grown much more powerful during Elizabeth's reign; in foreign affairs it still had little to say.

James I never really understood the operations and management of parliament and law in England. Both institutions had evolved in what had already become a characteristically English manner, in that neither was quite what it appeared to be. The problem was not that James was an outsider: many outsiders both then and later quickly got the hang of how things worked and integrated themselves into it. The stubborn Stuart doctrine of divine right, adhered to single-mindedly by James and even more so by his successor Charles I, prevented them from doing what Elizabeth and her executive had done, to work as part of the system, albeit the controlling one; to know when to make concessions, or to retreat, with grace and so reap a reward of popularity that could be used to achieve some other goal. To James, parliament was his, summoned by him, to carry out his requests and wishes. The law was also his, to support his policies and maintain his state and dignity. That parliament should feel able to question, challenge, refuse, was intensely disagreeable. That the law should elude him, and could be used by opponents against him, was equally unpalatable. In 1610 the judges declared that the king could not by proclamation 'create any offence which was not an offence before', and further, that: 'the King hath no prerogative but that which the law of the land allows him.' Nevertheless, James was mentally flexible and shrewd enough to accept these things as realities. There was still a great deal a king of England could do. Previous experience and his own taste in religion made him bear down hard on

Bates   R. Winter C. Wright J. Wright Percy   Fawkes   Catesby   T. Winter

The Gunpowder Plot conspirators (from a contemporary print)

Puritans and mitigate the laws against Catholics. But anti-Catholicism had gone very deep and popular reaction forced him to reimpose the penal laws, resulting in the dangerous moment of the 'Gunpowder Plot' of 1605, when a Catholic conspiracy to blow up king and parliament together came within a few hours of success before information was leaked and Guy Fawkes was apprehended in the cellars.

   This in turn reinforced the anti-Catholic prejudices and laws. James's policy of peaceful relations with Spain, though opposed by diehards, was a sensible one and brought dividends in trade. Salisbury's death in 1612 removed his most efficient and respected counsellor; from then on James was excessively influenced by his own court favourites. Between 1614 and 1621 he did not summon parliament at all.

TROUBLE FROM ABROAD

To some indignation in England, the now independent Dutch provinces, all their trading instincts and creative urges set free like a released spring in a great flush of national effort, behaved in a way that showed little regard for their former helpers. Despite a continuing alliance with England, Dutch merchant venturers established colonies and trading stations and organised themselves to keep English traders out. Dutch fishermen considered the North Sea their own and fought off English vessels. Having made peace with Spain, and aware that France had no fleet, the English government allowed the navy to run down, and while its merchant fleet grew, England was no longer capable of enforcing control even of its own coastline. Vulnerable places on the south coast were open to raids from pirates. English mariners had to fight their own battles on the high seas and in far-off anchorages against the Dutch, French and Spanish, as well as pirates of every breed. Despite these difficulties, English colonies were successfully established in Virginia (where Jamestown became the first permanent English settlement in 1607), Bermuda and Barbados. From 1620, the private enterprise of non-conforming Puritans established the New England colonies. James I had no foreign ambitions and a principled objection to warfare that some historians have falsely attributed to personal cowardice. He liked to offer his authority and detached status to arbitrate in the disputes of other nations. But his attempts to stave off what was to become the Thirty Years War, which would devastate much of central Europe, were a humiliating failure. Religious divisions and power politics erupted in 1618 when the Protestant Bohemians rose up against Catholic Austrian rule. Acceptance of the Bohemian crown by a German prince, the Elector Palatine, who was married to James's daughter Elizabeth, widened the war until, from the extreme ends of Europe, Spanish and Swedish armies fought across German principalities and Austrian duchies, assisted by hosts of mercenaries from England, Scotland and Ireland.

England played a peripheral part in this great struggle. James's prime concern was to retrieve the fortunes of the Elector Palatine, now a refugee in England; but the chosen method employed by his court favourite, George Villiers, promoted to Duke of Buckingham, was nonsensical. With the dubious bait of a marriage between Charles (crown prince following the early death of Henry) and the Spanish Infanta, he hoped to persuade the aggressively Catholic Philip IV of Spain to restore a militant Protestant prince in the middle of a ferocious religious war. Furthermore, English national sentiment and his own alliances with Protestant states forced James to make a show of entering the war against the Austrian emperor, Spain's ally. A parliament was called in 1621, and voted him large supplies for this purpose, but when it began investigating abuses and corruption, and called for the marriage of Charles to a Protestant princess, the king dissolved it. A marriage with the Catholic Princess Henrietta Maria of France, was arranged for Charles in 1624.

CHARLES I: RELIGIOUS DIVISIONS AND CONFLICT WITH PARLIAMENT

Buckingham had been cultivating the friendship and support of the crown prince since 1622, and when James I died in February 1625, King Charles I maintained the favourite as chief minister. There were many reasons for Buckingham to have opponents and enemies. He was a social upstart, he was a

The Great Seal of Charles I

Charles I

corrupt counsellor who sold official posts and peerages, he encouraged the king's hostility to parliament, he was an incompetent politician and an inept general. Almost his only useful contribution was, as Lord High Admiral, to develop the use of frigates for the royal navy.

Buckingham's continued role played a large part in parliament's reserved attitude to Charles I at the start of his kingship: instead of granting the king 'tunnage and poundage' (the proceeds of import and export duties) for life, or an extended period, it gave him only one year. War had been declared on Spain in 1624, and Charles extended hostilities to France in 1626. Such campaigns as there were, including an attempt to replicate Drake's old success at Cadiz, and an expedition led by Buckingham against the Île de Ré in France, were failures. Buckingham, defended by the king against parliamentary impeachment, was assassinated by a disgruntled officer in 1628.

The intermingling of religion and politics that prevailed through the seventeenth century and beyond may be puzzling to a twenty-first-century generation which has seen religion in England marginalised to an extent that would have astounded its nineteenth-century ancestors and horrified those of the seventeenth. But it is of great importance to present times. Much of modern political thought and attitudes stem from the religious divisions and splits of the time of James I and Charles I. Quite apart from doctrinal questions, there was a clear separation between two sorts of organisation. One, the traditional Catholic one, perpetuated in the structure of the Anglican church, was of a top-down religion, in which the accepted tenets were preserved and applied by the priesthood, and worship was expressed through the priest. Its form corresponded

---

QUAKERS

George Fox (1624–91) was born in Leicestershire and later apprenticed to a general merchant. Around the age of twenty-one, he began to experience a sense of 'inner light', leading to his conclusion in 1646 that contact with the divine comes from a voice within the individual soul. He advocated simplicity of dress, speech and manner, and regarded the panoply and ministry of the church as irrelevant. He preached his belief up and down the country, often interrupting conventional church services, and travelled to Ireland, the Netherlands and America to spread it. The movement he started, first called 'Friends of the Truth' and – long after Fox's death – 'The Religious Society of Friends', was best known to outsiders as the 'Quakers', so called from the tremblings of religious ardour that some members experienced during their assemblies. Quakers' refusal to take oaths and their objection to hierarchies of all kinds, resulted in much official hostility and persecution, and Fox himself was in and out of prison. By 1656 there were around a thousand Quakers in prison, which suggests that their overall numbers were much greater. The Friends' undemanding charity eventually won them public respect. Though their numbers were never very large, they founded a number of very successful schools and were prominent among the early industrialists. (*See also* 'Rights of Way'.)

with the structure of society in general, with the two coming together in the person and role of the monarch as supreme governor of the church and head of state. During the reign of Charles I, encouraged by William Laud, Archbishop of Canterbury, some of its supporters formed the Arminian movement, anti-Calvinist and seeking to preserve or reinstate the ceremonious and priestly aspects of church procedure. The other was a religion with no hierarchy of priests and bishops. Its truths and teachings were the possession of the whole congregation and the minister enjoyed no greater communion with God than any other member. The congregation ruled itself through elected members and gave a voice to everyone. Though some of the members were wealthy people, the great majority were not. The austerity of the Puritan life suited their purses as well as their principles.

Of fundamental importance in the growth of this new kind of church was the existence of the Bible in English. Long desired by the Lollards, sponsored by Henry VIII for his own reasons, the opening of the sacred texts to everyone (for those who could not read could be read to) had a far more profound effect on English life than all the writings of the greatest minds of the age. Reading the Bible, pondering its many messages, encouraged independent thought. There was ample evidence, in the history of the Israelites, of the overthrow of proud and wicked kings and of the relationship of an entire people to their God. It was by an entirely natural process that such emphasis on individual understanding extended from religion into other areas of life, and coloured politics with religious views and attitudes. Beneath its apparent monolithic structure of episcopal control, the Anglican church was deeply imbued with Puritan ideas and ideals. Naturally, the members of parliament, especially in the House of Commons, all of them self-declared Anglicans, shared the same spectrum of views and attitudes. But those of a Puritan persuasion also had the opportunity to express them and to try, within established law and custom, to make them influence law and policy.

Between 1625 and 1629 Charles I summoned, and rapidly dissolved, three parliaments. The history of these shows a diametric opposition of views between the members and the king. The parliaments disliked the king's minister, his Catholic queen, his foreign policy, his unsuccessful wars, and the Arminianism they detected in his religious views. Having failed to grant the king sufficient supplies, they opposed his own alternative methods of raising funds, which included forced loans from the wealthy and the imposition of taxes without parliamentary consent. They also opposed the royal policy of arbitrary arrest and imposing martial law upon the civilian population. A 'Petition of Right' was drawn up by parliament, enumerating its claims and grievances, and reluctantly accepted by the king as a means of gaining supply. But Charles, fully imbued with his father's doctrine of divine right, and far more obstinate than

---

FREEDOMS

Among the many controversies marking Charles I's personal rule was that of Licensing, a royal measure intended to control and censor all forms of publication, and so prevent the spreading of subversive ideas in religion and politics. Pamphlets and broadsheets were the only kind of 'broadcasting' available and were essential tools in presenting a case to the whole nation. On the opposing side, the debate was taken up by John Milton (1608–74), the future author of *Paradise Lost*. Already a poet of some note, he was a political radical in the 1640s, and his 1644 pamphlet, *Areopagitica: A Speech for the Liberty of Unlicensed Printing*, was the first reasoned argument for the freedom of the press. Milton's thesis was that the normal law – including laws against blasphemy and defamation – was the only protection needed:

'For books are not absolutely dead things, but doe contain a potencie of life in them to be as active as that soule was whose progeny they are; nay they do preserve as in a violl the purest efficacie and extraction of that living intellect that bred them. I know they are as lively, and as vigorously productive, as those fabulous Dragons teeth; and being sown up and down, may chance to spring up armed men. And yet on the other hand unless warinesse be us'd, as good almost kill a Man as kill a good Book; who kills a Man kills a reasonable creature, God's image; but hee who destroyes a good Booke, kills reason it selfe, kills the Image of God, as it were in the eye. Many a man lives a burden to the earth; but a good Booke is the pretious life-blood of a master spirit, imbalm'd and treasur'd up on purpose to a life beyond life.'

Pamphlet warfare was not always conducted in such majestic language; it often descended to scurrility and abuse, but through the seventeenth and early eighteenth centuries, it provided a constant debate on a host of issues, and helped to form basic English views on ethics, church and state in the nineteenth and twentieth centuries.

James, did not feel himself bound by such a document, merely because he had signed it when nothing else would do. By 1629, after tumult in the Commons, when the doors were locked and the Speaker held down in his chair to prevent an adjournment of the proceedings, it was clear to Charles that he could not govern with parliament. For eleven years, he ruled without it.

A KING BY DIVINE RIGHT

The years of royal autocracy were generally peaceful. With its restricted ability to impose taxes, Charles's administration had to be careful and it could not afford foreign gestures or adventures. It was also, for its era, notably uncorrupt, once Buckingham was gone. Unlike his father, Charles did not sell peerages or baronetcies. If the judges were his judges, the bishops his bishops, he was doing no more than following his own philosophy. His most notable servant, Thomas Wentworth, President of the Council of the North and then Lieutenant of Ireland, had been until 1628 one of his most outspoken parliamentary critics. Three other prominent members of parliament were kept, in violation of parliamentary privilege, in the Tower of London where one, Sir John Eliot, died.

Some valuable public works were undertaken, including a partial draining of the Fen country. But the money-raising recourses of the Council aroused resentment: monopoly corporations were set up to control everyday commodities like salt and soap, and prices were pushed high to achieve profits for the businessmen who had paid dearly for their monopoly rights. Customs duties were steadily raised. From 1634 to 1639 the Council issued writs for 'ship money'; this tax had originally only been levied on certain ports but it was now extended to the whole country. There was a real need to enlarge the navy but this point was overshadowed by the perceived illegality of the tax, famously challenged by a Buckinghamshire landowner, John Hampden, in 1636. Hampden's case was rejected by the judges but only by their reliance on the king's supremacy to the law.

Many whose opinions were far from Puritan or anti-royal felt threatened by the direction in which English political life was moving. Despotic monarchies prevailed over much of Europe at this time, the beginning of the age of Louis XIV. It seemed that despite two hundred years of parliamentary tradition, England might go the same way. This tendency in the administration was summed up in the single word 'thorough' which Wentworth, now made a baron, used to define his method of bringing Ireland into the modern Carolean era. Ireland was a fractious composition of old Gaelic chieftaincies, Anglo-Irish lordships, mostly Catholic, and English domains in the Dublin hinterland, made even more volatile by the 'plantation' of Ulster, during James I's reign, with thousands of southern Scots and northern English, many of them from the pacified Border region. They formed a Presbyterian enclave hostile both to the Catholicism of the Irish and the Anglicanism of the English. Wentworth was remarkably successful in reducing the anarchic state of Ireland and in reforming its administration and economy. For the first time since it went under English rule, it contributed to English revenues rather than drew on them. Like the men who would impose control over India in the next century, Wentworth was none too scrupulous in his methods – his defenders claim he could not afford to be – and also made a very large personal profit.

SCOTLAND REVOLTS

The unravelling of Charles I's royal autocracy began in an unexpected place. Of his old kingdom, James I had boasted that he ruled Scotland from Whitehall with his pen. Charles, just old enough to have been born there, revisited it only once, for a belated coronation in 1633. Archbishop Laud, who accompanied him, was shocked to find just how different the organisation of the church was there. To him and to the king, the notion of two different official forms of Christianity in the king's realms flew across all their conceptions of a royal church. In 1637 a new Prayer Book for Scotland was produced by Laud, supplanting that of John Knox. The result was riot, defiance, and, in 1638, the signing of a National Covenant, proclaiming both loyalty to the king and to true religion. There was no doubt which came first. By the time Charles realised the depth of feeling, and began to make concessions, it was too late. The Kirk abolished its bishops and reverted to its old presbyterian form. Charles mustered an army to restore the Scots to discipline. The Scots mustered an army that was altogether more formidable than the ill-trained royal levies, and a peace was patched up, though it was plainly not going to last.

The king brought back his strong man, Wentworth, from Ireland, and raised him to Earl of Strafford. Successful revolution in Scotland was creating huge excitement, particularly among those who opposed both the Arminian tendency and the concept of personal rule by the king. Strafford's view was clear: the Scots must be forced into conformity. To achieve this, a parliament would have to be called to provide funds and support for a proper military campaign. Summoned in April 1640, the 'Short Parliament' in its three weeks of life proved to be far less concerned about the threat of a Scottish invasion than it was about the accumulated grievances of the past eleven years. The exasperated king dissolved it, and, with his Council, set about forming an army and raising money to finance it from an increasingly restive and resistant population. Meanwhile the church's Convocation, packed with Arminian clergy, issued dire threats of vengeance in the next world on those who took up arms against their king. The royal army advanced to Newburn on the Tyne, and was rapidly dispersed by the invading Scots, many of whom were veterans of the Thirty Years War. With a hostile army in the land, no funds, no army (though Strafford had left a substantial force under arms in Ireland, which he urged the king to use), and little support among a mutinous people, the king was compelled to summon parliament once again. This was to become known as the 'Long Parliament'. Called into being by the king, it proceeded to demolish the foundations of his personal rule. The Scottish army, encamped in the north and subsidised at £850 a day, was the guarantor that the parliament would not be dissolved by royal order. Names that would soon ring out on battlefields participated in its work, including the quiet but influential member for Huntingdon, Oliver Cromwell. Strafford, seen as parliament's great enemy, was impeached for treason and put on trial in March 1641. Of all the crimes or misdemeanours that might be laid at Strafford's door, this was the least plausible, but it showed that his prosecutors were aiming high, as high as they dared. They wanted his head. But if the king's chief agent were convicted of treason, what of the king? Strafford defended himself with logic, skill and energy, and the trial collapsed. Instead parliament passed a Bill of Attainder against him and

113

sent it to the king for signature, along with another bill specifying that this parliament could not be dissolved except by its own consent. Charles, his back still to the wall, had no option but to sign them, and Strafford was beheaded two days later. 'Put not your trust in princes' has come down as the ex-parliamentarian's last words.

PARLIAMENT GAINS THE UPPER HAND

In all the furore of activity, the House of Commons was taking the lead, driven in its turn by the pent-up energy and frustration of John Pym, William Prynne (whose ears had been cropped off by Laud's courts), Hampden and other leaders of the Puritan tendency, the 'root-and-branch' reformist party. Most members of the House of Lords tried to moderate the more extreme measures being proposed in the Commons, including the abolition of bishops, and a number of prominent members of the Commons also adopted a moderate tone. With the king's acceptance of regular parliaments and of parliament's right to control taxes, they felt their aims had been achieved. But the reformists were hungry for more, including the impeachment of Archbishop Laud, and parliamentary approval of the king's choice of ministers and high officials. They also suspected the king of duplicity and saw how he was making efforts to build up pro-royalist support, beginning with Scotland, where he accepted the religious reforms and made other concessions which England had not obtained.

In October 1641, news of a rebellion in Ireland, under Catholic leadership, brought anti-Catholic feeling to new heights, whipped on by hysterical

John Pym

speeches and propaganda. It was falsely claimed that Charles had authorised the massacre of Protestant settlers which accompanied the rising in Ulster. Pym made use of this in introducing the 'Grand Remonstrance', an appeal to public opinion which attacked all the obstacles to reform, such as 'bishops and recreant lords' as well as the king. Put to the vote, the Remonstrance was carried by a majority of seven: narrow enough, when Pym also had the London mob vociferously behind him and ready to intimidate half-hearted members. To Charles's more extreme advisers, Pym was 'King Pym' and must be stopped. Deadlock existed between king and parliament on which should raise a militia force to counter the Irish rising. Each mistrusted the intentions of the other. Rumours of plots and counter plots on both sides, created by a storm of paper in a war of pamphlets, destroyed any confidence and left many people in a state of perplexity about what was really going on, and unsure whom to believe or trust. This artificial climate of suspicion and tension endured into 1642, while attitudes hardened both on the religious and political issues. Perhaps in anticipation of attempts to impeach the queen, Charles's attorney-general impeached five members of the Commons and one peer, and on 4 January, with a large force of soldiers, the king came himself to the House of Commons to arrest them. Forewarned, they had taken refuge in London, which became almost on the instant an openly insurgent city. The king left for the north, where he would still find loyal support.

In April he was refused entry to the city of Hull, where an arsenal of weapons was stored. Opposing authorities were now publicly asserted. Parliament set about raising a militia. The king forbade any mustering of troops except with his assent. No one could mediate in this dispute. By July, opposing bands of royalist and parliamentary supporters were already fighting. On 20 August, at Nottingham, the king raised his standard and called on all who supported him to join the ranks. With both sides protesting that they were defending England's ancient rights, laws and customs, the Civil Wars began.

THE CIVIL WARS

The old caricature of battles between dashing, long-haired Cavaliers and dour, determined Roundheads, as two supposed English archetypes, completely fails to describe the movement of events between 1642, when the king's opponents wished only to establish controls over his power, and 1649, when the king was executed for alleged treachery against his own country. Beginning as a constitutional war, exacerbated by religious dispute, its ending was dominated by struggles between different religious factions. A war that was not based on dynasty or territory was a new experience for the English people. Indeed, if the parliamentary forces had been able to sponsor an alternative royal candidate, like a Henry of Lancaster, to challenge a Richard III, the outcome would have been different. But Charles I's two sons remained loyal to their father.

At the start, the royalists' great asset was the king himself. He was still king of the whole nation and could command a strong traditional loyalty across the population. Whilst naturally his allies included the Catholics and Arminian Anglicans, the spectrum of support went beyond this and included many moderate Anglicans who felt that it was their duty to support a consecrated king. For many people it was a hard decision, and large numbers took no part at all. In some areas, farmers and peasants banded together as 'clubmen' to oppose the arrival of armed bands of either side, whose appearance meant forced requisitions and billeting at best. The royalist troops based in Oxford gained an ugly reputation for looting. Most of the nobility rallied to the king, and he had strong support in the West Country and the north. After the indecisive first battle at Edgehill in October 1642, the royal cause prevailed in 1643, with a series of victories which gained them the important city of Bristol and enabled the king to threaten London from the Midlands and the west. But the prospect of a royal hammer-blow was hampered by the unwillingness of his best army, from Cornwall, to venture too far east while the parliament still held Plymouth; and the need to secure the great houses and castles of his baronial allies with garrisons against parliamentary attacks. Meanwhile, the parliamentary side was slowly learning what war meant and how to wage it. An alliance, the Solemn League and Covenant, was made with the Scottish Protestants, at the price of a religious settlement 'according to the Word of God and the example of the best reformed churches'. The Scots appear to have been so sure that they exemplified the latter that they did not trouble to have it spelled out: a source of problems to come. The king in turn arranged a truce with the Irish Catholic Confederacy, enabling some of the troops engaged there to fight in England, supported by detachments from the rebels whom they had lately been fighting. This arrival of Catholic forces raised the heat among parliamentary supporters, though in the event the Irish army was quickly defeated at Nantwich by Sir Thomas Fairfax's army and many of its Protestant members deserted to the parliamentary side. On 2 July, at Marston Moor, close to York, two royal armies under the Marquis of Newcastle and Charles's nephew, Prince Rupert, were defeated by Sir Thomas Fairfax and Oliver Cromwell, backed up by a substantial Scottish contingent. The whole north was secured for parliament. But in the south-west, a parliamentary army under the Earl of Essex was defeated at Lostwithiel in Cornwall, and the Earl of Manchester's poor generalship lost the chance of a victory at Newbury on 27 October.

From his headquarters at Oxford, Charles still commanded a great swathe of the country. In the winter of 1643–44, he returned a truculent answer to a parliamentary overture on peace negotiation, and the feelings of his supporters were sharpened by the parliament's execution of the elderly Archbishop Laud, whom it had been holding in prison. Attitudes had hardened on both sides. Both reformed their armies and command structures, but parliament did so more thoroughly. A 'self-denying ordinance' forbade members of parliament also to be commanders in the field. By irresistible demand from the ranks of the army, one exception was made to this: the Lieutenant General of Cavalry, Oliver Cromwell. Parliament's 'new model' army, with Fairfax as general and Cromwell as his deputy, though it consisted of conscripts as much as volunteers, was paid, trained, disciplined, and instilled, from its leaders down, with a will to win. 'Ironsides' was Rupert's nickname for Cromwell; it soon spread to his troopers. On 14 June 1645, with Charles I leading his troops, the royal army suffered a decisive defeat at Naseby. A push to the west followed and the royalists of Cornwall surrendered in March 1646. As the parliamentary forces set about besieging Oxford, the king slipped out and in April gave himself up to the Scottish army which was encamped at Newark.

PARLIAMENT DIVIDED: THE ARMY GAINS CONTROL

This brought about an end to hostilities and a whole new set of uncertainties. Charles had surrendered his person but not his cause. For nine months the Scots held him while negotiations went on. The Scots wanted to see the Solemn League and Covenant implemented. When it was finally plain that Charles would never agree to this, they washed their hands of him. Claiming and receiving the arrears of £400,000 which they were owed under the treaty with parliament, they handed over the king to his English opponents, and withdrew beyond the Tweed. It was the parliamentarians' turn to find that the captive king was a master of argument, delay, hair-splitting definition, petty complaint and endless amendments and new proposals to every settlement draft. It was in his interest to buy time, to hope that something would turn up to restore his fortune. His captors were not united. The heat and zeal of the campaigns had seen two broad groupings emerge, the Presbyterians and the Independents. Both were 'Puritan', but the Presbyterians wanted to impose a state church on the Scottish model, which everyone must join. The Independents covered a variety of sects, each fiercely cherishing its own quirks of belief and practice. Their own small numbers, if nothing else, made them in favour of toleration and people's freedom to worship as they wished (so long as it was Protestant in form). Some of them believed that the Day of Judgement was about to happen. Many of them believed that equality in the sight of God should be matched by equality in society, and that all ranks and titles should be abolished. Parliament – still the Long Parliament – had a Presbyterian majority among its members. In open war, the rift between Presbyterians and Independents could be forgotten; in peace negotiations, it could not be ignored and Charles adroitly exploited it to prolong the debate and split the opposition. While negotiations were going on, the Presbyterian party, ignoring the fact that their majority in parliament was not matched by a majority in the country, or, more crucially, in the army, made dispensations which brought hostility from all sides. Prominent campaigners for the king were heavily fined and frequently forced to sell off their land to friends of parliament. A great mass of the middle ground population were angered by the suppression of Anglican worship, the forbidding of the Prayer Book, and the ousting of some two thousand parish clergy. The Independents were enraged by such measures as life imprisonment for Baptists, and the prohibition of lay-men from preaching. These issues were brought to climax by an ordinance for disbandment of the army, apart from a few regiments retained to subdue Ireland. The war was won, and the cost of a standing army was very great; there were growing complaints about the level of taxation required. But the soldiers' pay was in arrears, and the new model army was imbued with the spirit of the Independents. The army refused to stand down, and at its head, looming larger than Fairfax, his nominal superior, was Oliver Cromwell, now the most powerful man in England.

Cromwell, backed by his able son-in-law, Henry Ireton, took possession of the king and brought the army to London, scaring away enough Presbyterian members of the Commons to produce an Independent majority. He was prepared to negotiate a settlement with Charles, the 'Heads of the Proposals' of September 1647, but the king was still playing his waiting game and the army was less conciliatory in spirit than Cromwell. On 11 November, Charles escaped and reached the Isle of Wight, where the governor held him at Caris-brooke Castle. For a few months Charles maintained a pretence at negotiation, until in April 1648 a long-planned royalist uprising broke out, supported by a further invasion from Scotland, of a different colouring to those which had come in 1639 and 1643. From Kent to Berwick, men came out in arms for the

Oliver Cromwell

king. It was Charles's last gambit. By August, Fairfax and Cromwell's regulars had smashed the royalists. The army was now in indisputable control of the country. When the Long Parliament met again on 6 December 1648, Colonel Thomas Pride seized 137 members, all Presbyteri-ans, placing 41 under arrest and warning the rest not to reappear. Sixty Independents now formed the House of Commons, a 'Rump' even less representative of the country than the previous assembly. It proceeded to take momen-tous decisions, passing a bill to arrange the trial of the king, and voting that 'to levy war against the Parliament and realm of England was treason'. A special High Court was convened to try the king. No judge would sit in it, and Fairfax would have none of it, but Cromwell, backed by the army, pressed on. Denying the legitimacy of the proceedings, Charles refused to plead. He was found guilty, sentenced to death, and beheaded in front of a great, silent crowd in Whitehall on 30 January 1649.

ENGLAND LOSES A KING – AND BECOMES A COMMONWEALTH

England was proclaimed to be a 'Commonwealth', under the government of the House of Commons and a Council of State, with Cromwell as its chairman. The House of Lords was abolished.

Such events encouraged the extreme democrats among the army rank and file, 'Levellers' and 'Diggers' who demanded annual parliaments and social equality, but their disjointed attempt at a coup was forcibly put down by Cromwell, who did not share these aspirations. Ireland, still in a state of revolt, and Scotland, which had proclaimed Charles II as its king, were to be incorporated into the Commonwealth, which claimed all the dominions of the executed king. Cromwell took an army to Ireland and commenced the subjection of the country, which Ireton completed in 1650. Cromwell meanwhile turned on the Scots, but in 1651 the Scots brought war into England, when Charles II accompanied an invading army. The hope was to arouse English support, but little was forthcoming, and Cromwell defeated them at Worcester on 3 September 1651. Charles II fled abroad. With the 'crowning mercy' of Worcester, the Civil Wars were ended, and England faced a new era.

The Great Seal of the Commonwealth: front

The Great Seal of the Commonwealth: reverse

The lowest point of English estimation of Oliver Cromwell came at the restoration of the kingdom in 1660, when his decayed corpse was exhumed, dismembered and abused. His old admirers kept their heads down. The highest point was when he was offered the crown, in 1656. But the stock of the great king-slayer has generally been high, in a deeply monarchic country. This is partly owed to his personal qualities of honesty and sincerity, but mostly to the fact that his rule was successful. The Commonwealth was born in the immediate aftermath of shock, large-scale bloodshed and bitter division. Civil war, disrupted trade and bad harvests had made the late 1640s a grim time. When Cromwell died, his state had unified England, Wales and Scotland as a single entity, was united, prosperous, at peace, and had made itself respected abroad. At first his energies were absorbed in the subjection of Ireland and Scotland. In Ireland, where, in sacking Drogheda and Wexford, he permitted his troops to run amuck in a way he never did in Great Britain, he earned loathing. From January 1649, England was under the control of the 'Rump Parliament', watched over with increasing irritation and impatience by the army. The Rump's main object seemed to be its own preservation, and in this it was aided by the military leaders, whose principles demanded a general election and a new representative parliament, but who shrank from the prospect of the Anglican-royalist dominated assembly that was likely to result. On 20 April 1653, Cromwell took matters into his own hands. After a few blunt home-truths – 'Do you think to sit here till Doomsday come?' quoted a balladist – he brought a troop of soldiers into parliament, dissolved the Rump and sent the members home. From then on, though he attempted various forms of quasi-parliamentary government, his own presence at the head of affairs was the consistent and driving element in national life. The 'Barebone's parliament', composed of nominated members, one of whom, Praise-God Barbon, gave it its name, had a brief life in 1653.

In December of that year Cromwell assumed the title of Lord Protector. In September 1654 the first all-British parliament met, with English, Welsh, Scottish and Irish members; by Cromwell's own constitutional document, the Instrument of Government, he could not dissolve it for five months, but he did not wait a day longer. Its offence was to discuss the lord protector's role, rather than to govern as he wished it to. For eighteen months he ruled on his own, then in late 1655 he divided England into twelve military districts, each governed by a major-general with wide powers. This reminder that the army – paid for by substantial and efficiently collected taxes – was still in command caused widespread protest. Still experimenting, Cromwell called a third parliament in September 1656; by now his experience had taught him that only a partial reversion to traditional forms would bring long-term stability, and he planned a new Upper House. It was this parliament that offered him the crown. Though he refused it, in the knowledge that acceptance would split the army and bring more strife, the protectorship in its last phase was hardly distinguishable from a monarchy; it was even made hereditary.

ENGLAND UNDER THE COMMONWEALTH

A famous later comment by Lord Macaulay said that the Puritans abolished bear-baiting, not because it gave pain to the bears, but because it gave pleasure to the spectators. With varying degrees of success, Cromwell's administration sought to curb the 'sinful' pleasures of old England, from maypole dancing to madrigal singing. It was easy enough to close a theatre: much more difficult to stop traditional seasonal fun and games in every village, vestiges of paganism though they might be.

But the Commonwealth allowed a wider range of religious practice than previous governments. The official religion of the state was severely Puritan. Everyone paid tithes to this nameless church, which occupied the place of Anglican Christianity without its liturgy. But no one was compelled to attend, or to swear to its tenets. Provided it was done discreetly, Anglicans, Anabaptists, even Catholics, were able to worship according to their own rituals or lack of them. Cromwell, who had stabled his horses and billeted troopers in some of the country's great cathedrals, had a wide tolerance of religious expression as long as it stayed outside of politics. During his rule, Jews were admitted to England for the first time since Edward I had expelled them in 1290; their arrival, along with the continuing inflow of Huguenots, played its part in the accelerating growth of London as the world's greatest trading city, overtaking Amsterdam.

The Commonwealth was an expensive state to administer. There had never been a standing army before; now it was 50,000 strong. The strength and size of the navy were also greatly increased. These were costs on top of the normal costs of government. But wealth was increasing. The restoration of peace encouraged the resumption of trade and manufacture. Evidence of this wealth can be seen in the foundation and enlargement of schools and the building of almshouses and hospitals. London, the seaport towns, the cloth towns, the mining and manufacturing districts (still small but densely populated) had always backed the parliamentary cause, and the rewards of peace were theirs to work for. Whatever else the Protectorate prohibited, it did not prohibit trade, enterprise, profit or education. Economic strength extended outwards. The Rump had begun a war against the Dutch in 1652, a new stage in the established struggle over control of the North Sea, of dominance in sea-trading, and in the establishment of colonies. Parliament and then the Commonwealth found an admiral in Robert Blake to rival the great Dutchman, Van Tromp. In 1649 Blake destroyed the fleet created by Prince Rupert and in doing so brought

English naval power into the Mediterranean. Defeated by Van Tromp off Dungeness in 1652, he won a victory off Portland in 1654, and in a further victory off Texel, won by another general-at-sea, George Monck, Van Tromp was killed.

By 1654, the revitalised navy had established the position of mastery in the narrow seas which it was very rarely to lose again. When Cromwell made peace with Holland in 1654, Dutch concessions benefited English trade. In 1655 war was declared on Spain, and an English naval expedition captured Jamaica but failed to take Hispaniola, its prime objective. At Tenerife, Blake destroyed the Spanish fleet in April 1657. In the Commonwealth's dual foreign policy of protection and extension of English trade, and Cromwell's ambition to form a Protestant League, it was on the whole English interests that won. A treaty with France – where the Edict of Nantes still extended toleration to Protestantism – and joint attacks on the remaining Spanish holdings in the Low Countries, won the possession of Dunkirk. The Commonwealth, whose first envoys had been insulted and even murdered with impunity in European capitals, had made itself into a significant force in world affairs.

THE RESTORATION OF THE MONARCHY

The death of the Protector, in his fifty-ninth year, threw all his achievement into disarray. His son Richard, aged thirty-eight, named as his successor, was well-intentioned but not of his father's calibre, and had not grown up with the training, expectations and advice of an heir-apparent. Nor could he command the historic obedience given to a king.

At first he was backed by the army, but soon it was plain that the army commanders had conflicting views about the way forward. People who

The Great Seal of Richard Cromwell

Richard Cromwell

supported, or were working for, the accession of Charles II were pleased to see the army begin to disintegrate into factions, some supporting a return to the republican ideals of 1649, some looking for a generalissimo-figure to assume control. The parliament called by Richard was equally riven by contrary opinions, with many royalist sympathisers. He dissolved it in April 1659 and resigned his post, retiring to obscure country life. Casting about with a degree of desperation for a national authority with some claim to legitimacy, a military committee recalled the surviving members of the Rump Parliament so ignominiously dismissed by Oliver Cromwell. Forty duly appeared, to be blown hither and thither in their discussions by pressure from different generals, until one of the two most determined soldiers, John Lambert, forced its dissolution. While royalist demonstrations and local risings became more frequent, the other soldier, George Monck, commanding in Scotland, crossed into England with his army. Already in communication with Charles II and his advisers, he destroyed Lambert's efforts to resist his advance, and took control of London. Here he summoned, not the residue of the Rump again, but all the surviving members of the Long Parliament, as it was before Pride's purge. Monck was now in open negotiation with the exiled court at Brussels, but it was in the end this 'Convention Parliament' which, in May 1660, formally invited Charles, Prince of Wales and already King of Scotland, to assume his father's English crown.

CHAPTER EIGHT

Restoration and Revolution

A RESTORATION IN MANY SENSES

Charles accepted the invitation with alacrity, and would probably have agreed to greater limitations on his powers and income than the parliament required. In any case, the first elected parliament of the new reign, the 'Cavalier Parliament', restored every royal prerogative that Charles I had possessed, as if the previous two decades had never been. The crumbling of the Commonwealth might have been a foreign military conquest, such was the ardour and anti-Puritan vehemence, and the spirit of reconciliation that was fostered at the start was soon dissipated. A visitor to London in 1658 and 1662 would have seen enough change to make him or her shy of making generalisations about English life and character. In London, the lax morals of the royal court and its pleasures in entertainments of all kinds, high and low, spilled over into the tavern, coffee house, brothel, cockpit and theatre life of London in the area between Soho and

ROYAL MISTRESSES

King Charles II, with his eleven children by different women, none of them his wife, was not unusual in his extra-marital affairs. Among the kings of England, it was more unusual not to have a mistress. The few since William I who remained faithful to their wives included Edward I, George III, George V and George VI. Royal marriages were almost always arranged affairs, the product of state politics and international relations. Beyond the desired production of an heir, they were not supposed to be affairs of the heart. Their political aspect might be allowed to weigh against the sanctity of the marriage vow. In the seventeenth and eighteenth centuries, the mistresses of Charles II and the Georges I and II, usually advanced to the rank of duchess, sometimes played overt political roles. Melusine von der Schulenburg, Duchess of Kendal, mistress of George I (who had locked up his wife when she in turn took a lover) was deeply involved in two financial scandals, one of them the South Sea Bubble. Later, such relationships were more discreet, or at any rate kept apart from public business.

It seems also that the English did not disapprove of a lusty king. In this a faint echo of the very earliest kind of kingship can perhaps still be discerned, when the king, reigning for only a year, enacted the fertility rites which were meant to ensure good crops and new births in the following year. In those primitive times, the king's own blood contributed to the fertility ceremony each autumn, and a new king then was chosen; as the readers of Sir James Frazer's vast pioneer work in cultural anthropology, *The Golden Bough* (1890–1915) learned to their fascination. The reigning queens, it may be noted by contrast, were either chaste, as with Elizabeth I, or faithful wives in every other case.

Covent Garden. Elsewhere in the country, the contrast was less sharp; a tipping of the scales away from Puritan decorum rather than a wholesale descent into Cavalier debauchery.

Charles II, no less than his father and grandfather, believed firmly in the divine right of kings. In his case the belief was tempered by his famous wish not to go on his travels again, and by a sense of what was possible, but he pushed his personal rule as far as he dared. He did not want to alienate the wealthy Puritans, and though royal and church lands that had been sold off under the Commonwealth were now reclaimed, royalists' land that had been sold, often at a knock-down price, to individuals was not allowed to be reclaimed. In time the first fulsome, adulatory tone of parliament changed to notes of criticism and complaint, and there were long periods when it was not summoned. All the circumstances of the Restoration helped to suggest that the Puritan element in England was a minority and that an Anglican–royalist attitude typified the majority.

Broadly speaking, this perception was correct, but it glossed over a considerable range of views within that majority, both about religion and about sovereignty and government. It also had a tendency to ignore the facts that the minority was a large and growing one and that, just as had been the case in 1641, it formed a majority in a number of vital places and regions, including the ever-swelling city of London and the country's main seaports and manufacturing districts. Even more than before, it controlled most of the country's wealth. Meanwhile, even an Anglican–royalist parliament remained a firmly Protestant one, and Charles's growing difficulties with it were partly caused by

The Great Seal of Charles II

Charles II

the conflict between the desire of parliament to see the country allied with Protestant powers, and the policy of the king, which was to cultivate friendly relations with France. Two secret aspects underwrote Charles's later foreign policy: a series of financial subsidies from France directly to the royal purse; and his own long dalliance with Roman Catholicism. He used his possible conversion as a bait to keep up his French income, though he did not take the final step until he was on his deathbed. Though court indiscretion, and the difficulties of concealing large amounts of cash, eventually made these into rather open secrets, the king was not directly challenged on these issues.

DISSENT, PLAGUE AND FIRE

The public controversies of his reign were primarily sparked off by religious disputes. The Cavalier Parliament, which was not finally dissolved until 1679, passed a series of acts against Non-conformists, of which the most important was the Act of Uniformity of 1662, following which some two thousand parish clergy resigned or were ejected, most of them taking their congregations into independent worship. Added to the existing Independents, these 'Dissenters' made a formidable element in English society. Excluded from the grammar schools and the two universities, they set up their own schools and academies, with an equally high standard of teaching. In 1673 the Test Act, requiring candidates for public office to subscribe to the tenets of the Anglican church, effectively barred them from holding any official or legal post, though the rigour of

London during the Great Fire from the Bankside, Southwark

its application varied. Such measures caused intense resentment and also embarrassed Charles, who wished to repeal the strong anti-Catholic laws, but who could scarcely extend to Catholics what was being refused to independent Protestants. The polyphiloprogenitive king fathered at least seventeen children, but none of them by his wife, the Portuguese Catherine of Braganza, and in 1669 his brother and heir-presumptive, James, Duke of York, declared himself a Catholic. The ravages of the Great Plague in 1665 and the destruction of much of the city of London in the Great Fire of 1666 occurred at the same time as – in a second Dutch war from 1665 to 1667 – the Dutch fleet under Admiral de Ruyter demonstrated that the English navy seemed less effective than in Cromwell's day. De Ruyter took his ships, with impunity, right into the Medway. These events destroyed any lingering notion that Restoration England was a special favourite of Divine Providence.

WHIGS AND TORIES

Suspicion of the Duke of York, and anti-Catholic feeling, reached fever-point in 1678 with revelations made by one Titus Oates, a Catholic convert of low character who claimed to be in possession of the details of a plot to assassinate Charles II and put the Duke of York on the throne. Plots were endemic, and generally of little real threat; it is quite likely that Oates had been on the periphery of something genuine, but his ability to sustain the part for more than four years of gradually more detailed revelations shows a sort of neurosis in English life at this time. It was only in 1684 that York, to save his own reputation and his claim to the throne, used the law to confront Oates, won a libel case, and discredited the informer. Much political energy was taken up by the Exclusionist movement, which wanted to debar York from the crown, and allow Charles's illegitimate son, the Duke of Monmouth, or the king's niece, Mary, wife of the Dutch Prince William of Orange, to inherit instead. In the ebbs, flows and eddies of political manoeuvring that resulted, something of long-term significance was taking shape: the emergence of two groups that eventually became recognisable political parties.

Neither was founded in a formal way but gradually coalesced into loose but lasting alliances, and both acquired names bestowed by their enemies: the Whigs so-called from the Scottish Whiggamores, ultra-Protestant cattle lifters; the Tories from Irish Catholic bandits. Led by the Earl of Shaftesbury, the Whigs were first to emerge; they were closely identified with exclusion – a temporary issue – but also shared the view that royal power should not be allowed to grow too great. The Tories grew out of the pro-York party, as the supporters of legitimate and traditional royal privilege. Shaftesbury, outfaced by the king and discredited by his links with Oates, fled into exile. The Whigs were caught at a

127

severe disadvantage, made worse by the discovery of a plot to assassinate the king as he passed Rye House on his way to the races at Newmarket in 1683; two party leaders were executed and one killed himself. But the Whiggish tendency would revive, with plenty to oppose in the following reign.

JAMES II AND THE COUNTER-REFORMATION

Strengthened by the Whig debacle, Charles II was developing a style of royal autocracy when he died, unexpectedly, of an apoplectic fit in February 1685. His younger brother, James, succeeded as the first Catholic English monarch since Mary Tudor. This in itself would have been a serious trial for both the king and his countrymen, the majority of whom had long been accustomed to regard 'popery' as anti-English, dangerous to the state, and unnecessary in the practice of Christianity. A king of exceptional qualities might perhaps have found a means of keeping his crown in such circumstances. The times were not favourable to religious tolerance. In 1685, Louis XIV had revoked the Edict of Nantes, which had allowed Protestant freedom of worship; there was religious war in France, and once again Huguenots were seeking refuge in England. James easily survived the first crisis: an invasion by the Duke of Monmouth, who hoped that the country would rise for him as a Protestant king, was crushed at the battle of Sedgemoor on 6 July 1685, and a simultaneous effort by the Earl of Argyll in Scotland was also a failure.

So-called 'absolute' monarchies, where the king or emperor exercised the

The Great Seal of James II

James II

power of the state with little constraint by other institutions, were strongly established in France, Spain, Austria, the Papal States of Italy, and Russia at this time – the divine right assumed by the Stuarts, and which was the firm credo of James II, was not a strange or unusual doctrine in seventeenth-century Europe. Absolutism was not exclusively linked with Catholicism or Orthodoxy. Sweden, Denmark and Prussia, Protestant states, were ruled by authoritarian kings. The promotion of the Counter-Reformation, and the rise of the Jesuits, had revived the vigour and missionary spirit of Catholicism. James II was not trying to put the clock back. He had some reason to feel that his policy was both modern and reformist. But within three years it collapsed utterly.

The vindictive repression after Sedgemoor, when Chief Justice Jeffreys carried out his 'Bloody Assizes' with hundreds of executions and transportations to the colonies, shocked all but the most rabidly anti-Protestant. James was fifty-two; his brother had died at fifty-five. He pressed on with the appointment of Catholics to civil and military posts. Declarations of Indulgence in 1687 and 1688 relieved the constraints on both Catholics and Independents. After circumventing the Test Act by royal dispensations, he set about an attempt to repeal it, which brought parliament and the bishops against him. The birth of a crown prince in 1688 removed the likelihood that the Protestant Mary would inherit the crown after James. The king had estranged his original supporters, the Anglican Tories, and his attempts to show balance in his reforms by giving freedom of worship to the Protestant sects fooled nobody, since it was evident that his aim was to put Catholics in all positions of power, and that in due course the force of law would fall once again on the Independents.

WILLIAM OF ORANGE

Events in England were being closely studied from Holland by Whig exiles and by their host, William, Prince of Orange, head of state of the United Provinces of the Netherlands. As a grandson of Charles I and husband of James II's daughter, Mary, he had a more than neighbourly interest in the government of the three kingdoms of the British Isles. William's prime concern was to create a system of alliances to protect the United Provinces from the imperial ambitions of Louis XIV of France. In this aim, the wealth, strategic position, naval power, and army of England were assets of supreme importance. William could only view James II's pro-Catholic policy with alarm, and the pregnancy of James's queen promised to effectively sideline his chances of ever wielding those powers. During 1688, increasingly close exchanges between various English politicians and William's court at Amsterdam produced an understanding. In May, William informed his English allies that, if invited by some of the leading men of the kingdom, he would invade in September. In June, James II proclaimed his second Declaration of Indulgence, which was resisted by the Archbishop of Canterbury and six other bishops. Put on trial for seditious libel, they were acquitted amid scenes of popular rejoicing. Ignoring such signs, as well as warnings from France, and the advice of his own chief minister, the Earl of Sunderland, James intensified his efforts and was by now plainly ruling with no intention of convening a parliament. In June seven men signed an invitation to William of Orange. They were two bishops, the Tory Earl of Danby, the formerly

The Great Seal of William and Mary

Catholic Earl of Shrewsbury, the Whig Earl of Cavendish, and Henry Sidney and Edward Russell, both related to Whig notables who had been executed after the Rye House Plot. Behind those names stood a formidable if temporary alliance of other leading Whigs and Tories. Unfortunately for James II, who placed strong reliance on his army, it eventually included John Churchill, his most able soldier, whom he appointed Lieutenant General to resist William's invasion.

James at last realised that William of Orange had the resources as well as the will to invade. His attempts to conciliate his opponents were too late and too transparently opportunist to have any effect. The invasion came, after one false start, on 5 November 1688. With a large army of 24,000 men, William of Orange landed at Torbay, favoured by a gale that kept the English fleet at anchor. His announced aim was to restore parliamentary government and uphold the laws of England; also to investigate the legitimacy of the infant crown prince. James had 40,000 men under arms but even as he and his forces marched west, defections began on an increasingly large scale. Not only Churchill but his son in law, Prince George of Denmark, husband of the future Queen Anne, deserted him. The king returned to London and sent his wife and son to France. He tried to escape himself and although he was caught and sent back, he was finally allowed to flee to France on 23 December 1688, while his son-in-law's forces occupied an unresisting London.

THE STUARTS IN EXILE

It was not the first time that a reigning king had made a tactical retreat abroad. But James II was no Edward IV, and no supporting group was in a position to

William and Mary

enforce his return. The long exile of the Stuarts had begun. It lasted until 'Henry IX' died in Rome in 1807, a pensioner of the English crown, and Jacobitism would play a part in politics for another sixty years. But from December 1688 the divine right of kings was a dead letter in England. By education and his own philosophy, William of Orange was a believer in constitutional monarchy. A 'Convention' rather than a parliament, was summoned and met in January 1689. Intensive discussion took place – although there was almost universal agreement that James should stay away, his status was another matter. Was he to be deposed, or had he by his flight already abdicated? It was clear that he had no intention of formally renouncing his crown. William, as canny as a supreme card player, made his own terms known. He would not be a regent to the absent James, nor would he serve as a secondary consort to his own wife. The House of Lords swallowed its reservations, the House of Commons acclaimed it, and the 'Glorious Revolution' was accomplished. William and Mary were declared joint sovereigns, with the survivor to reign alone, and to be succeeded either by a child born to Mary or, if none, then by her sister, Anne, and her heirs. A Bill of Rights was drawn up, whose main provision excluded any Catholic from becoming king or queen.

THE 'GLORIOUS REVOLUTION'

It was a strange revolution, and the English took some pride in its strangeness. In England (though not in Scotland or Ireland) it was almost bloodless, especially by comparison with the bloody aftermath of Monmouth's rebellion. And after it, apart from the provisions of the Bill of Rights, virtually nothing appeared to have changed. No grand new constitutional settlement was enacted, binding the king or extending the role of parliament; the question of sovereignty was not addressed. But from then on it was accepted that the monarch of England ruled through parliament, that parliament made law and that the king was under, not above, the law. The Test Acts and Corporation Acts, excluding Non-conformists from holding public office, remained in place. But by dint of 'occasional conformity' or by simply ignoring the Acts, many Dissenters became justices and councillors.

The joint sovereigns (though the dominant partner was always William) had to fight Jacobite armies to secure their crowns in Scotland and Ireland. England remained at peace though by no means tranquil as William, seeking to instil a sense of moderation into the bitterness of the Whig–Tory dispute, which had speedily resumed, outraged the expectations of the Whigs in 1689 by appointing a Tory ministry under Danby, who had managed much of Charles II's secret diplomacy. A Toleration Act in the same year removed discrimination against most dissenting sects. In July 1690 the defeat of James II and his French allies by William III at the battle of the Boyne in Ireland confirmed the new situation. But any dissatisfied politician or courtier could always find a friendly ear at the Jacobite court of St Germain, in France, and a succession of plots or suspected plots helped to maintain an atmosphere of tension and particularly to disrupt and discredit the Tories. Meanwhile, William had his long-desired control of England's resources to deploy in his war with France, and used it to the full in an intense involvement with foreign policy, centring on negotiations with France over the breaking up of the Spanish empire and the contested succession to the Spanish throne. As in centuries long past, an English army was used to fight for the king's continental interests, but now it was an army whose funding was voted, and whose management was jealously watched, by an English parliament; though William's parliaments could no more control his foreign policy than any predecessor could have done. From this time, France became more and more the great rival and enemy state, a fact which in itself demonstrates the increase in English power through the seventeenth century. The wars with France would be fought on virtually a world scale, at a cost and with a deployment of resources that would have taken the breath away of an Elizabethan or Jacobean minister.

In the years since the Civil Wars, the English people had become accustomed to the existence of a permanent army in the country: something unknown previously. From Tudor times, the Yeoman Warders of the Tower formed a small royal guard, and armies were raised only to deal with specific situations. The new army's red coats were a legacy of Cromwell's Ironsides but it was essentially made up of foot-soldiers, armed with musket and bayonet. Under the command of John Churchill, made Earl of Marlborough after 1688, it became a force to be reckoned with. Churchill, whose allegiance was to the Princess Anne more than to William and Mary, had an often strained relationship with the king, but in 1700 he was put in charge of British forces in the Netherlands and commissioned to form an anti-French alliance, as the War of the Spanish Succession loomed.

Smallpox was still rife throughout the country; Queen Mary II died of it in 1694. William III died in 1702, of complications following a riding accident, and England acquired its third reigning queen, Anne. Her seventeen pregnancies failed to provide a surviving heir. In France, James II had died in 1701, but his son, Anne's half-brother, James, the 'Old Pretender' as he became known, was fourteen years old and in good health. Much speculation hung around what would happen if this boy should become a Protestant. Meanwhile in 1701, parliament had passed the Act of Succession, providing that if Anne had no heir, the next in line should be Sophia, wife of the Elector of Hanover (a granddaughter of James I) and her heirs.

ENGLAND IN THE SEVENTEENTH CENTURY

In the course of the seventeenth century, England underwent revolution, counter-revolution and revolution again. Through the storms and confusions of these events, a wayward and uncertain progression can be traced. At the beginning of the century, a new king arrived to rule a country still in many respects linked to the Middle Ages, and determined to set up a royal autocracy. At the end of the century, another king from elsewhere reigned as a parliamentary monarch. Parliament had appointed him, and though he, not parliament, made policy, it was within the limitations of laws made by and enforceable by parliament. England was very far from being a parliamentary democracy, and the next hundred years would show less progress in politics; but a genuine revolution had been achieved.

And yet, much remained the same. The social structure was not overturned. The royal Council was filled largely by lords, either descendants of the old landed families or new appointments (but the elasticity and absorptiveness of the English nobility was nothing new). The country gentry, mostly Anglican and Tory in their sympathies, exercised control over local events. Liberty, Equality, Fraternity – the watchwords of revolutions still to come – were not ideas of the seventeenth century, except among groups like the Levellers, who had no influence on the wider population. The economic structure of life was not overturned, though it became larger and more complex. Manufacturing, distribution of goods, importing and exporting of goods and raw materials, all became steadily more important through the century and vastly increased the national wealth. But its distribution was uneven. If society can be represented as a pyramid with a broad base, ever-narrowing to a peak, then its wealth could be represented by a similar pyramid, only with its position reversed. The bulk of the wealth was at the disposal of a small minority of the population. As landowners, farmers, exploiters of forests and minerals, factory-owners, merchants and traders, they considered themselves legitimate proprietors and no government would dispute their basic rights. The structure of the church was not overturned. At the end of the century, as at the beginning, bishops ruled it and Cranmer's Prayer Book, with only minor alterations, defined its liturgy. The two universities were still closed to Non-conformists. But a vigorous structure of Non-conformist education, theological teaching, and worship now existed alongside the Church of England.

A REVOLUTION IN IDEAS

In *A Short History of Scientific Ideas*, Charles Singer called the seventeenth 'the Insurgent Century', since it was during those hundred years that the work of new generations of scientists and thinkers overturned the old view of the universe that had prevailed since the time of Aristotle. The great progenitors of the revolution in thought were an Italian, Galileo Galilei, and a Frenchman, René Descartes. New ways of measurement and analysis, new ways of organising thought, were taken up with enthusiasm in England, but equally so in Denmark, Sweden, Germany and Scotland. England was among the first countries to grant official support to the new kind of learning, with the granting of a charter by Charles II, in 1662, to the Royal Society for the Promotion of Natural Knowledge – the oldest such body to be in continuous existence. 'Nullius in verba' was its motto: 'Nothing in words', which is to say, trust evidence, not belief or hearsay. English scientists were responsible for such fundamental discoveries as the circulation of the blood (William Harvey in 1616) and Boyle's Law (1662, though Robert Boyle might be described as Anglo-Irish) and many others, with the prime achievement in the work of Sir Isaac Newton, whose *Philosophiae Naturalis Principia Mathematica*, 'Mathematical Principles of Natural Philosophy', was published in 1687 and defined the basic workings of the universe until it was partially supplanted by Albert Einstein's General Theory of Relativity in 1915. England shared in the intellectual revolution. In 1600 almost everyone in the country believed that the earth was placed at the centre of the universe, that the sun went round it, and that the stars were fixed in an outer sphere which defined the limits of the physical world. In 1700, it was common knowledge that the earth moved round the sun, that the solar system was only a small part of an unimaginably vast universe, and that mathematically proven universal laws governed the movements of planets and pebbles with equal effect.

The development of the scientific attitude had an effect in England, setting in motion a slow process of secularisation and materialism, and a swifter process of industrial growth. Yet it was not unique to England and cannot account for the unique cohabitation of a ruling monarch and an ultimately controlling parliament which emerged from the Revolution Settlement of 1688 and which dominated national life for almost a century and a half. The sources lie else-where. Through the travails of English political history, a distrust of extremist views and respect for a balance between strongly opposing attitudes emerged. Perhaps the country's geographical detachment played a part: through the Middle Ages it was possible to watch from England as the spiritual power of the papacy and the political power of the Holy Roman Empire struggled for supremacy in Europe. In England there was a temperamental preference for solutions rather than for abstract speculation. Implicit in the old English vener-ation of kingship was a sense of national consent in this form of government. This consensus was fractured by the religious disputes which began with the Lollards. The Church of England saw its own beginnings in a search for moder-ation: the Preface to its Authorised Version of the Bible begins: 'It hath been the wisdom of the Church of England, ever since the compiling of her public liturgy, to keep the mean between two extremes.' Its failure to commend itself to the whole nation resulted in the three-way pull between Anglicanism, Catholicism and the Independent Protestant sects. No monarch could bestride these three horses, though Charles II maintained a successful illusion of doing so: his father and brother paid the penalties of not even trying. Civil war, a self-inflicted experience which the nation thoroughly detested, was a result. From 1658 onwards, the desire to find a working compromise was very strong.

Before 1688, the most important English books on political philosophy had come from the royalist camp. Sir Robert Filmer had written *Patriarcha: or the Nat-ural Power of Kings*, a defence of the divine right thesis, in Charles I's time, though it was only published in 1680. Far more influential, and more constructively con-troversial in the long run, was Thomas Hobbes's *Leviathan*, published in 1651. Hobbes's view of human life in its natural state was that it was 'solitary, poor, nasty, brutish and short'. A social agreement was needed in any human com-munity to accept a ruler, in order to promote peace; and absolute obedience must be given to that ruler while he had the power to protect his subjects. Hobbes made no concessions with regard to tyranny: a horror of anarchy seems to under-lie his writing and though the sovereign is expected to have the good of the peo-ple in mind, this is not a necessity. Firm and stable government is everything.

A SOCIAL CONTRACT

The prime statement on the philosophy of liberalism that came to underlie public life in England was published after the Glorious Revolution, not before it. But the philosopher John Locke wrote his two *Treatises of Government* during the turbulent years from 1678, and there is no doubt that his ideas were widely discussed through the next decade. Educated as a medical doctor, he came from a parliamentary background and was personal physician to the Whig Earl of Shaftesbury, but his influence as a philosopher has made his a greater name than his patron's. His starting point, the 'state of nature', is totally different to Hobbes's: 'Men living together according to reason, without a common superior on earth, with authority to judge between them, is properly the state of nature.' Locke held that most people are naturally good, but that government is necessary because some are bad and even good people might fall out with one another. Government is thus the creation of the people for the people's benefit. But because a government might fall out with one or more individuals, it should not be all-powerful, or it becomes accuser, judge and jury. This was to lead, in England and America, to the separation of the law system from the executive. With a strength of statement that would be echoed by several generations of Whig/Liberal politicians to come, Locke spelt out what he considered the chief business of government: 'The great and chief end of men uniting into commonwealths, and putting themselves under government, is the preservation of their property.' It was not a doctrine likely to find favour with those who had no property, but for the magnates and landowners of England, it had a powerful appeal. The final points of Locke's second treatise to be relevant here are his insistence on the separation of the executive (the monarch and the royal advisers) and the legislature (the parliament). Implicit in this is the series of 'checks and balances' that must exist in a smooth-running state in order to prevent clashes and deal with disagreements. Locke also said that some disputes might be unresolvable by any judge under Heaven. This implied the possibility of further civil war, or revolution; but, even if the great philosopher allowed for it, English statesmen and monarchs would generally shrink from trying to put matters to such a test again.

The concept of a 'social contract' underlying community life was strong in Locke's time, and later, though it was also accepted that in literal terms it was a fiction, or at best a figurative expression, to describe the beginnings of a civilised society. The science of social anthropology had yet to be invented. But the England of the Glorious Revolution illustrates the notion of a social contract in operation more clearly than any other society of its time. Royal autocracy and military dictatorship had both been tried, and failed. To prevent the country from tearing itself apart, the parliamentary monarchy, with all its flaws and fudges, and despite its lack of legitimacy in the eyes of many Tories, was essential, and accepted by all but the most narrow-minded extremists.

CHAPTER NINE

Union, Hanoverian Kings and Whig Rule

A STRONG AND PROUD NATION

During the reign of Queen Anne, from 1702 to 1714, particularly its early years, acceptance of the new system was encouraged by a sharp rise in England's international prestige. A series of victories by English–Dutch armies under the command of Marlborough (made a duke by his old patroness) at Blenheim, Ramillies, Oudenarde and Malplaquet between 1704 and 1709, showed that the balance of power in Europe had changed. Pride and gratitude were reflected in the gifts bestowed on the duke, including the building of a huge and opulent mansion, Blenheim Palace.

Fire-ravaged London was being rebuilt under the supervision of Sir Christopher Wren, and a new and vast St Paul's was rising above the Thames, with an Anglican dome whose scale surpassed that of Michelangelo's St Peter's in Rome.

St Paul's Cathedral

In natural philosophy Newton had made England supreme. Fire and water had been harnessed in a new way, and from 1698, Thomas Savery's atmospheric steam engines, improved by Thomas Newcomen in 1705 and 1711, marked the opening of a new industrial age. It was a self-confident society, more mature than that of the Restoration, and more united.

The Atlantic had ceased to be a vast unknown and had become a network of trading routes to a string of colonial ports from Nova Scotia to the West Indies. In addition to the exchange of manufactured goods for the products of the New World, a new and lucrative business was growing fast in the acquisition of black African tribespeople and their transportation and

East India House, London, 1726

sale as slaves on the sugar plantations. The East India Company, its charter going back to 1600, was re-established and enlarged in 1708; its fleet of heavily armed merchant ships was a navy in itself.

With so much money in the country, and the government's need to borrow vast amounts to pay for the war, new ways of running the nation's economy were found. The Bank of England was established with government backing in 1694 by William Paterson, a Scot.

UNION WITH SCOTLAND

Whilst England had grown more prosperous under Stuart rule – though not as a direct result of it – Scotland, deprived of the presence of a monarch and riven even more by religious warfare, and by the Jacobite–Orange issue, had seen a decline. Sharing a king had not made English merchants generous to their Scottish rivals, and new Acts of Trade and Navigation reserved English imports and exports for English ships, while England's wars closed off Scotland's markets in France and Spain. In 1695, Scotland's somewhat rudimentary parliament and small trading community had heavily backed a colonial trading venture to the East Indies, the Company of Scotland, which was aborted by English opposition. Instead, the aggrieved Scots set up a short-lived, doomed colony, the Darien Scheme, in what is now Panama.

Mercantile England cared nothing for Scotland, but political England, concerned to maintain the Protestant succession, was aware of a problem. Scotland's parliament had welcomed William and Mary, and Anne after them, but it was not bound by the English parliament's Act of Succession. After Anne, the Scots could choose their own monarch, and no one knew this better than the Old Pretender. To the queen's advisers, a political union seemed essential. Between 1703 and 1706, Anglo-Scottish relations reached such a low point that war seemed a real possibility, with each parliament passing hostile acts. Three crewmen of an English ship, the *Worcester*, were hanged at Leith on doubtful evidence for piracy against a Darien vessel. It was against this inflamed and dangerous background that after a failed attempt in 1702, serious negotiations for union began in 1706. In March 1707 the English parliament approved the Treaty of Union, which the Scottish parliament had already passed.

NEWTON'S APPLE

Rather surprisingly, as most anecdotes about great men turn out to be invented or distorted, the story that Newton's epoch-making explanation of the law of gravity was inspired by a falling apple seems to be true. His friend, Dr William Stukeley, made this report:

'On 15 April 1726 I paid a visit to Sir Isaac at his lodgings in Orbels Buildings in Kensington, dined with him, and spent the whole day with him . . . After dinner, the weather being warm, we went into the garden and drank tea, under the shade of some apple trees, only he and myself. Amidst other discourse, he told me he was just in the same situation as when, formerly, the notion of gravitation came into his mind. It was occasioned by the fall of an apple, as he sat in a contemplative mood. Why should that apple always fall perpendicularly to the ground, thought he to himself? Why should it not go sideways or upwards, but constantly to the earth's centre? Assuredly the reason is, that the earth draws it. There must be a drawing power in matter: and the sum of the drawing power in the matter of the earth must be in the earth's centre, not in any side of the earth . . . And thus by degrees he began to apply this property of gravitation to the motion of the earth and of the heavenly bodies, to consider their distances, their magnitudes and their periodical revolutions; to find out that this property, conjointly with a progressive motion impressed on them at the beginning, perfectly solved their circular courses, kept the planets from falling on one another, or dropping all together into one centre; and thus he unfolded the universe.'

Statue of Newton

Parliament House and Square, Edinburgh

It was a full, incorporating union, not a federal one, as some had argued for, and, in a sense, at that moment, the realm of England ceased to be, as did that of Scotland. In their place was a new, single entity, the United Kingdom of Great Britain. Until recently, historians made little of this momentous event, which was seen mainly as an extension of the English state. Its repercussions were much more evident in Scotland than in England. The influence of union on England was slower and more subtle, and its full extent has yet to be investigated. But in the spring of 1707, practically nothing seemed different in England. There were no noticeable changes beyond a new flag, which combined the crosses of St George and St Andrew, and the arrival in London of forty-five Scottish members of the Commons, and sixteen of the Lords. Strongly anti-Jacobite, they allied themselves naturally with the Whigs. Parliament was now the 'Parliament of Great Britain', but national English institutions remained in the law and the church. The economic and political weight of Scotland was too slight to affect the course of government policy, and though 'British' replaced English as an adjective, whenever officials (and later historians) remembered, it was a continuing English policy that was pursued.

GAINS ABROAD AND PLOTS AT HOME

That policy meant continuance of the war in Europe, with Britain, the Netherlands and the Austrian–German states (still the Holy Roman Empire) fighting

The Great Seal of Anne after the Union: front

The Great Seal of Anne after the Union: reverse

the French and Spanish (except the Catalans) in the Netherlands, Italy and Spain. Domestic politics were overshadowed by the question of the succession, with Anne keeping at arms' length both the expectant Hanoverians and the hopeful Stuarts. For most of her reign her chief minister was Lord Godolphin, an administrator rather than a politician, whose natural Toryism was deflected by his support for the war, and consequent need to ally himself with the Whigs, who at this time were the 'war party'. But old issues remained hot, and Godolphin's ministry was sacked in 1710 after it had prosecuted a Tory clergyman, Dr Sacheverell, for sedition, following two violent sermons on 'False Brethren in Church and State'. The Sacheverell case provoked a national outcry, and Anne called on the leader of the Tories, Robert Harley, to form a new cabinet, at the same time discharging her long-time friend, favourite and adviser, Sarah, Duchess of Marlborough, who went most reluctantly. Harley was determined to stop the war, and recalled the Duke of Marlborough; whose reputation as a military victor was now dimmed by the revelation of the vast personal profits he had made from his position as commander in chief of the Grand Alliance. The

---

JOHN BULL

'John Bull', the personification of the bluff, straightforward, no-nonsense Englishman, was the creation of a Scot. Dr John Arbuthnot (1667–1735) was one of many Scottish medical men who settled in England; his interest in politics and literature took him into London literary circles, and in 1712 he wrote, as part of a set of satires against the Duke of Marlborough, *The Famous History of John Bull*: 'John Bull was in the main an honest plain-dealing fellow, choleric, bold, and of a very inconstant temper . . . he was very apt to quarrel with his best friends, especially if they pretended to govern him. If you flattered him, you might lead him as a child.'

---

war was resolved for Britain in 1713 by the Treaty of Utrecht, which gave Britain possession of Gibraltar, as well as of Newfoundland and Nova Scotia from French Canada.

The queen's health was failing by this time, and the question of succession became dominant. Intrigues and speculation were rife. For the Tories, it was important to ascertain whether the son of James II would renounce his Catholicism for the Church of England; if he had done so, many or all would have supported him as a Protestant king with the strongest claim. The Whigs were closely allied with the Hanoverian court. For both parties, there was profit as well as principle to be reckoned with: political power meant the opportunity to reward oneself and one's allies with lucrative positions and contracts. A Hanoverian monarch would unquestionably put in a Whig administration. The refusal of James Stuart to change his religion split the Tories. Harley would not support James, but his colleague, Henry St John, Viscount Bolingbroke, led a faction which was willing to install James as king, and thus themselves as his government. A crafty politician, Bolingbroke outmanoeuvred Harley and was appointed chief minister. But the queen died before he could put his programme into effect, and the Whig grandees, thoroughly alarmed, acted quickly, using their majority on the larger Privy Council to compel Bolingbroke's cabinet to follow the law as already enacted, and summon the Elector Georg Ludwig of Hanover to receive the crown as George I.

The triumph of the Whigs was complete. George's inability to speak English, and his preference for living in Hanover have often been criticised, but they contributed to the establishment of parliamentary government. Personal rivalry and animosity among the Whig leaders made up for the lack of serious Tory

The Great Seal of George I

George I

THE 'KING'S EVIL'

An earnest of the English belief that kings were different to the common run of human-ity was found in the long-standing tradition – from the time of Edward the Confessor to that of Queen Anne – that the touch of the king's or queen's hand could cure the condi-tion of scrofula, the 'King's Evil', a form of tuberculosis, resulting in swellings and abscesses of the neck glands. Among the last people to be presented for 'touching' was Samuel Johnson, aged three, in 1712. By the mid-eighteenth century, medical progress had reduced scrofula to just another disease. The long belief in the royal touch may be wondered at, but superstition and hope have always played a large part in the treatment of all kinds of ailment.

---

opposition in both houses of parliament. Their ascendancy was further con-firmed by the failure of a Jacobite rising in 1715. While this was most serious in Scotland, it had been hoped by the Jacobite court, now joined by Bolingbroke, that Wales and the West Country would also rise up. Pre-emptive troop move-ments and arrests of Jacobite sympathisers ensured that the Duke of Ormonde's landing in Devon was brief and unsupported. Though Jacobite sympathisers ral-lied in Northumberland and Lancashire, the regular forces quickly defeated them. Some thirty leading conspirators were beheaded or hanged, but the gov-ernment resisted any more vindictive actions, and many prominent exiles, even Bolingbroke, returned and were pardoned over the next few years.

THE SOUTH SEA BUBBLE

In 1716 the Whigs extended the life of a parliament from three to seven years. War with Spain, caused by its breach of the Treaty of Utrecht, went on between 1718 and 1720, marked chiefly by a naval victory in the Mediterranean. The Whig government, for all its divisions, was generally in favour of business and enterprise, and in a host of different ways, trade and industry continued to develop. Simultaneously, with the government's tightening up of coastal secu-rity and the protection of legitimate import–export business, which supplied vital and steadily growing customs revenues, there grew up a hidden economy based on smuggling. This was often done on a large scale, and connived at by prominent citizens. The consumption of tea was increasing dramatically, as was that of French wine and brandy, and Dutch gin. Quite apart from the steady growth of factories, mines and honest trading companies, there were opportu-nities, irresistible to some, to make quick fortunes illegally or semi-legally. The most dramatic instance of this came in the scandal known as the South Sea Bubble. The South Sea Trading Company had been founded in 1710 to trade with Spanish America and the known Pacific lands (the Dutchman Abel Tasman had reached Australia in 1644).

South Sea House

It was not exactly a flourishing concern, despite its monopoly of the slave trade to Spanish America, but it had substantial reserves, and in 1713 its directors put an ambitious and tempting proposal to the government. For a payment of seven and a half million pounds, they would take over management of £31 million of the national debt. Their plan was to offer shares in the Company to the creditors, instead of payment of interest and eventual repayment of the capital sums. A leading Whig politician, Sir Robert Walpole, protested and proposed an alternative scheme in which the Bank of England would take control. The cabinet, led by the Earls of Stanhope and Sunderland, accepted the scheme, which was approved by parliament. For a time it worked, with the value of South Sea shares soaring and creditors and new investors clamouring to buy. The enthusiasm prompted opportunist or crooked businessmen to set up a range of other companies, most of them destined for rapid oblivion. A mania for investment raged though the spring and early summer of 1720, until it became clear that the prospects of the South Sea Company could not remotely sustain the hugely inflated value of the shares. Their price collapsed even faster than it had gone up, the other bubble companies went with it, and thousands of people were left poorer, or ruined, and all feeling cheated and looking for vengeance on those responsible. The Stanhope–Sunderland ministry collapsed and it later became clear that bribery had played a large part in their support of the scheme. The opposing faction of Whigs, led by Walpole and his brother-in-law, Lord Townshend, were called in by King George to replace their discredited colleagues.

THE WALPOLE GOVERNMENT

For twenty-one years, Sir Robert Walpole was First Lord of the Treasury, establishing this post as that of 'Prime Minister', which it has remained ever since. He was the first chief minister to sit as a member of the House of Commons, a precedent which showed how much the authority and status of that house had increased, though the Lords remained the senior chamber, with full power to veto any legislative proposal of which they disapproved. Walpole's supremacy survived the death of George I in 1727 and the accession of George II, a tetchy, military-minded monarch who inherited his father's preoccupation with the affairs of Hanover.

Walpole's long ministry generally maintained peace with the rest of the world up to 1740, though there were two short trade-related wars with the declining power of Spain, and the growth of business, industry and population were also kept up. After the years of European war, the lack of foreign military campaigns helped to keep taxation at a low level. 'Improvement' was a buzz-word of the times, and improved, science-based methods were transforming agriculture. New crops were introduced, and Townshend, a leading pioneer on his own lands, where he introduced regular four-year crop rotation, was known as 'Turnip' Townshend for his sponsorship of this new vegetable, which at first was so exotic it was consumed as a dessert. During the 1730s, the deplorable state of roadways was taken in hand – a sign of the demands of distributive trade – with the formation of turnpike trusts, in which locally raised capital paid for road-building which was then repaid by tolls.

The Walpole government can also be accused of many shortcomings, not all of which can be excused as being 'of the time'. Preservation of his own position was his primary aim, and any initiative that was likely

King George II

to risk it was quickly withdrawn, like his plan of 1733 to reform and extend the excise system, abolishing duty at the ports but imposing it instead through retailers. This was widely opposed and Walpole dropped it. He brought forward no other bills of a reformist nature. He preferred colleagues of less brain and ambition than himself, and substituted the more subservient Duke of Newcastle for Townshend in 1730. If Newcastle and his colleagues profited from their posts, the same was true of the prime minister himself. Bribery, whether with jobs or money, was Walpole's way of dealing with opposition. Patronage was the accepted way of staffing the civil service and rewarding supporters. No one would have expected Walpole to do anything other than put loyal Whigs in office, but he rarely chose men of independent spirit or exceptional energy. Nor did he tackle any of the injustices or inequalities in English life.

As long as he dominated the Commons, Walpole did not mind whether

The House of Commons in the time of Sir Robert Walpole

large areas of the country were unrepresented while rotten boroughs continued to provide large numbers of MPs. The increasingly archaic Test and Corporations Acts, excluding all but signed-up Anglicans from public office, continued in force. Walpole's grip on events began to shake in 1739, when he gave in to a public and parliamentary demand for war on Spain, the so-called 'War of Jenkins' Ear', brought on by the humiliation of an English captain by Spanish coastguards in 1731. A strong opposition group led by Whigs whom he had sacked or ignored began to subject him to fierce attack in parliament. A motion for his dismissal was defeated in 1740, but the general election of 1741, though it returned a Whig majority, did not provide enough pro-Walpole members. Against George II's wishes, he resigned in February 1742, accepting a peerage but playing no further part in public life. He had a large country house, art collection and fortune. His departure from office set another precedent: it was not because he lad lost the favour of the king who had appointed him, but because he could not command a majority in the House of Commons.

Walpole's achievement is remarkable. In opposition to him were two large segments of the population, including the Tories and the Dissenters. The Tories, sidelined by the hostility of both George I and George II and still susceptible to the charge of Jacobitism and therefore treachery, were in a weak position. The majority of them, even if they believed in the restoration of the Stuarts, did not pursue their belief to the point of civil war, as the events of 1745 would show; not least because most of them were also Anglicans who had no commitment – rather hostility – to Catholicism or the papacy. They might fume, and complain, and the grander ones keep in touch with St Germain, but they were powerless. The docility of the Dissenters is less easy to explain, though 'occasional conformity' no doubt played a part. In other respects, they were left alone to pursue their religion and their social avocations. Their academies continued to flourish, and many also sent their sons to the Scottish universities, where Non-conformity was no bar to entry. As many of them were employers and workers in business, manufacturing and trading, the low taxes and general laisser-faire policy of the government were popular. And of course, however little a Whig government did for them, they could be certain that a Tory government would be definitely against them.

THE JACOBITE RISINGS

It was under the shadow of, and in opposition to, a new European war that Walpole resigned. The petty war with Spain became part of a new, wider war caused by opposition to the Archduchess Maria Theresa becoming Empress of Austria. Participation in the War of the Austrian Succession was enthusiastically backed by a new member of the cabinet, Lord Carteret, and by George II (who became the last king to lead the army in battle, at the victory of Dettingen, in 1743), but it proved an unpopular war, and a new cabinet was formed in 1744 under Henry Pelham, younger brother of the Duke of Newcastle. This became known as the 'Broad-Bottom' ministry, representing a wider range of the Whigs than Walpole had included. While the continental war was going on, with most of the British army abroad, the 'Young Pretender', Prince Charles Edward Stuart, arrived in Scotland with a handful of men, and successfully raised an army. Capturing the city of Edinburgh, and defeating the regular forces at Prestonpans, he proceeded to invade England in the winter of 1745–46. This unexpected stroke caused some panic among the London public, but the government kept its nerve, summoned back regiments from Flanders, and called out the militias, though with only limited success. The Tory squires were in no hurry to ride to the rescue of George II and his Whigs. But nor did they join the Rising. Lancashire, once seen as a stronghold of the Jacobite cause, raised a few cheers as they went by but contributed nothing. The prince's expectations of a flood of recruits were revealed as sheer fantasy, and at Derby, on 6 December, his commanders forced him to order a retreat. Gazed at by English burghers and countryfolk like a visitation from another epoch of the world, the tartan-clad, Gaelic-speaking Highlanders made their way northwards again, with two government armies forming up in pursuit. Despite two further victories over government troops, the rising met its end at Culloden on 16 April 1746. The young Duke of Cumberland, in command, won the plaudits of a relieved government and capital city, though his large-scale campaign of repression after the battle showed an unhappy return to the kind of murderous vindictiveness that stained James II's name after Sedgemoor.

THE RISE OF WILLIAM PITT

The Forty-Five was Jacobitism's last throw. Further schemes were no more than dreams and occasional scares. England's rejection was final and overwhelming, and the Hanoverian dynasty could feel secure. The war in Europe went on inconclusively until it ended in the Treaty of Aachen, in 1748, leaving the colonial rivalry between Britain and France still a burning issue. There had been fighting in North America and in India, where the French from their base at Pondicherry had conquered the British colony of Madras. But the treaty stipulated the return of conquered territory, which was done with an ill grace. The Pelham government remained in office for a further eight years, largely content to keep a steady ship without embarking on reform or warfare. A new member of this administration was William Pitt, a vocal opponent of Walpole who as a result had won the lasting hostility of George II. As Paymaster of the Forces from

1746, he occupied a post which traditionally enabled its holder to become very rich. Pitt's ostentatious refusal to profit from government office, untypical of his generation, won him public respect. It was also plain that in a government of dull and pedestrian figures, he was a man of ideas and ability. Pelham's government had few dynamic ideas and the historian, Sir Charles Oman, went so far as to describe him and his brother, Newcastle, as imbeciles. This was an absurd exaggeration. His main achievement was to bring some reform to the management of that sensitive subject, the National Debt, by instituting the Consolidated Fund, soon known as 'consols', paying interest at 3 per cent rather than the previous 4 per cent, and saving the Treasury something of the order of £500,000 a year. Another useful aspect of national housekeeping included the reformation of the calendar in 1752, somewhat belatedly compared to other European countries, when eleven days were omitted, so that 2 September was followed by 14 September, in order to establish the more accurate Gregorian calendar. The beginnings of a London police force were made with the formation of the Bow Street Runners, attached to the magistrates' court. But the Pelham–Newcastle ministry took little account of the changing situation, and gathering tensions, both at home and abroad.

A PROSPEROUS COUNTRY

Around the mid-century, an English government might well feel a certain complacency. Great Britain was united, and in general both prosperous and busy. Ireland was at peace under its now-established 'Protestant Ascendancy'. The thirteen North American colonies, their population around two million, had developed rapidly both as sources of supply and purchasing markets for English products: a surge in transatlantic trade was driving the growth of Liverpool and Bristol, and promoting the building of western harbours from Whitehaven to Watchet. The West Indian colonies had brought the plantation system to a point where bulk production of sugar was possible at a cheap price, through the use of slave labour. By-products, like molasses and rum (issued daily in the Navy from 1745), became widely available. In India, there were important British settlements at Madras, Bombay and Calcutta. The East India Company was poised for expansion. London, main port for the Indies, was the world's metropolis. For its most distinguished man of letters, Samuel Johnson, 'the man who is tired of London is tired of life.' Food prices were low and wages were stable. Pelham's government reduced the size of the Royal Navy, and kept the strength of the army at around 20,000 men. Reduced strength of the forces kept their cost down, and land tax was reduced by half.

This was the kind of government that the English liked. The national aversion to taxation was long established and had both supported, and been sustained by, the growing power of parliament. Central government was not expected, or wanted, to exercise too much control over people's lives. The rule of law, nationally applied by judges and magistrates, was the arbiter of rights and wrongs, but individual gentlemen would still resort to duels, sometimes formal, sometimes deadly, to settle personal enmities. Local and parochial management was strong, whether applied by borough councils, merchant corporations, or a combination of squire and parson. Health, schooling and the welfare of the elderly, were not concerns of government. Charitable bodies set up and maintained schools, hospitals and almshouses, and sometimes the bequest of a single wealthy individual created a new one, like John Harrison's London Hospital in 1740. Richer municipalities might do things on their own account; by 1750 Newcastle upon Tyne had its own public library. In most places, traditional boards and bodies going back to Tudor times if not earlier, kept up local customs and social structures. With little or no policing, there was ample opportunity for illegalities of various kinds. Though the Revenue Service was perhaps the most vigorous arm of government, its own activity proves the degree to which the smuggling industry flourished. Roads were not wholly safe; the celebrated Dick Turpin, hanged in 1739, was by no means the last of the highwaymen.

RICH MAN, POOR MAN

Around seven million people lived in England in 1750. London accounted for perhaps 700,000 of them. Next largest was Bristol, with 100,000 in the city and surrounding area. Norwich had 50,000. Manchester, already a conurbation with Salford, had 45,000, Liverpool 35,000, Birmingham 30,000. Hull, Sheffield and Newcastle had about 20,000 inhabitants; Leeds, Nottingham and Chester around 15,000 each. Few if any other places exceeded 10,000 people. The population was largely rural, reflecting the nature of the main industries of the time: farming, cloth-making, even mining were all cottage- and village-based. Almost whatever their origin, individuals of exceptional ability or ambition could achieve wealth, prestige and even high rank within English society. Such opportunities for upward mobility were not new, and had always been an element of the English way of doing things. But these were exceptions in a largely static structure. At its head, of course, was the monarch and his family. The monarchy was buttressed by the nobility, in a now-established gradation of ranks from dukes to marquesses, earls, viscounts and barons. Some of these aristocrats traced their titles back to the Plantagenets, and some still owned and controlled great tracts of the country. Others were more recent. The Duke of Newcastle was one of the largest landowners in England, but he had acquired his title in 1715 for backing the Hanoverian succession.

More than ever, the English nobility was one of office rather than of ancestry, though many lords who played little or no part in the affairs of the state still exercised great power and influence within their own districts. The creation of new peerages meant that there was a substantial network of relationships between the nobility and the politically active families of the wealthy merchant and country gentry class. This numerous but heterogeneous group encompassed the smaller country landowners, the 'squires', the rich burgesses and aldermen of cities and towns, the clergy, the lawyers, the doctors, the army and naval officers, government officials, as well as a more socially indistinct group of emergent professions, such as architects, journalists

The Duke of Newcastle

and technicians. These were joined by an even more dubious collection of poets, actors, impresarios, musicians, painters and craftsmen, whose links ranged between the royal court and Grub Street. Below the gentry and its associates the social layers were increasingly larger. Tenant farmers, shopkeepers, skilled craftsmen and local functionaries from poor-house managers to beadles, were considered a superior group to the assistants, journeymen, farm labourers, quarrymen, soldiers, seamen, packmen, and domestic servants who formed by far the largest group. At the bottom of the whole hierarchy were the paupers, beggars, and a special category, still in a form of serfdom, the miners of coal and salt, hereditary performers of arduous tasks, not allowed to leave their hovel-villages, the most oppressed section of the community, for whom 'social mobility' would have been a phrase empty of meaning.

GRUB STREET

Grub Street, nowadays a synonym for the lower reaches of literature and politico-literary journalism, was an actual street in the City of London until 1830. It was well known as a haunt of literary hacks. Samuel Johnson's *Dictionary of the English Language*, published in 1755, observed that it was 'much inhabited by writers of small histories, dictionaries, and temporary poems; whence any mean production is called *grub street*.' Johnson himself lived just off Fleet Street. His inclusion of dictionary writers is of a piece with his definition of a lexicographer as 'a harmless drudge.'

Unlike the more rigidly defined society of France, with its greater extremes of power and repression, and a much larger population, this society had within it a considerable capacity for adaptation to change. Such inherent elasticity was to be of great benefit, for turbulent times were ahead, at home and abroad. Problems would arise where there was least chance of adaptation and rapid reform, in the more fixed aspects of this social structure, through which individuals could move, but which preserved national institutions and attitudes in all their ancient and archaic rigidity.

There were gross anomalies and injustices in English life. The rapidly growing urban centres of Birmingham and Manchester were still, technically, villages. Their local government was of the kind intended to deal with agricultural communities in the Middle Ages. They had no municipal structure and returned no members to parliament. Other areas were seriously underrepresented. Certain places in Cornwall and Yorkshire that were no more than place names returned two members, their seats in the gift of the lord of the manor. Electorates even in real places were very small, consisting of those adult males who were owners of freehold property. Only the four London seats, with around ten thousand electors, had anything remotely resembling a modern electorate. Where elections were contested, bribery was the accepted way of gaining a majority. Since the vote was open and public, there was no chance of the electors making their choice a private matter. Even among the most privileged, there were big differences. The Bishop of Durham commanded revenues of £8,000 a year; his colleague of Oxford only £500 (still a princely sum compared with the £20 plus board of a skilled tradesman in London, or the country schoolmaster of Oliver Goldsmith's 'Deserted Village', 'passing rich on forty pounds a year'). The law was framed and administered in order to bear down heavily on the non-propertied classes. Over 160 crimes and offences were punishable by the death penalty, which, if often avoided or commuted, was also often used, and inflicted in public. The severity of the law may have been in proportion to the lack of policing and detection, but its application was often seen to be casual and self-interested. To quote Goldsmith again:

> And hungry judges soon the sentence sign,
> And wretches hang, that jurymen may dine.

But Thomas Parker, Lord Macclesfield, the Lord Chancellor, who was impeached in 1725 on charges of selling law posts and embezzlement of the funds held in Chancery on behalf of children and minors, was imprisoned in the Tower for six weeks and fined £30,000, though it was known that he had misappropriated a great deal more than this. He was allowed to retain several official positions. At this time, a teenage boy who stole Parker's handkerchief could have been hanged.

CULTURAL VIGOUR

A society possessing the wealth and confidence of eighteenth-century England, and embracing such a range of contrasts and contradictions, might be expected to have a vibrant cultural life. The polemical, political and devotional strains that typified seventeenth-century writing gradually merged into a much wider stream of literature. An urbane tone was set from the founding of the weekly *Spectator* by Joseph Addison and Richard Steele in 1711, which produced a quintessential English type in the engaging, easy-going country squire, Sir Roger de Coverley. A new kind of realism arose in the social novels of Samuel Richardson and the picaresque adventures of Henry Fielding's Tom Jones, of 1749. As a magistrate himself, and brother to Sir John Fielding, the founder of the detective system, Fielding was well acquainted with the colourful, vicious criminal subculture that flourished on prostitution, smuggling and theft.

An important literary monument was Samuel Johnson's *Dictionary of the English Language* (1755), not the first but the most magisterial work of its kind. But the qualities of the age flashed out most in satirical writing. John Gay's *Beggars' Opera* of 1728 took as its target the sleazy life of Walpole's London, but Jonathan Swift, though he flayed the government and individual targets, made the whole human race his victim in *Gulliver's Travels* (1726). The later decades of

Samuel Johnson

the century were less rich in quality, perhaps, but what typified the time was a torrent of information books, handbooks, and guides on everything from sex (*The Oeconomy of Love*) to fertilising the soil. Though one of the century's later writers of genius was William Blake, with a spiritual vision and ardour of a unique sort, it was not an era of spiritual distinction, but a worldly age which enjoyed the new comforts of modern life and set store by good manners and social correctness. These were summed up in Lord Chesterfield's *Letters to His Son*, published in 1774 and described by Johnson as 'teaching the morals of a whore, and the manners of a dancing master'. Religious passion was most strongly expressed by John Wesley and his brother, Charles, both Anglican priests, who developed, at first within the church, the 'Methodist' movement. For more than forty years from 1738, through open-air sermons, the Wesleys took evangelical Christianity to the people throughout the country in a manner to which the established church was scarcely accustomed. After John's death in 1791, the Methodists and Anglicans went their separate ways.

A POWER ON LAND AND AT SEA

The peace confirmed in 1748 at Aachen did not last for very long. Hostilities soon resumed in India, where Robert Clive, son of a Shropshire squire and a captain in the East India Company's army, captured Arcot from the French in 1750, and, following the French tactic of using Indian troops, proceeded to regain the whole region of the Carnatic in the following year.

Clive of India

War in North America resumed with a French attempt to take control of the lands to the west of the English colonies. By 1756, Britain and France were at war across the world. Not for the last time, it opened disastrously for Britain, with a weak government, a run-down army and navy, and a confused notion of what to do. Minorca, then a British possession, was captured by the French, and a British naval squadron, under Admiral Byng, sent to relieve the besieged troops, turned away from the larger French fleet without a battle. Minorca was lost, the French were gaining ground in Canada, and the English colony at Calcutta was captured by the Nawab of Bengal. His confinement of 146 prisoners in the 'Black Hole' where all but twenty-three perished of suffocation overnight entered the English imagination and licensed an equally vindictive policy against Indian prisoners.

In November 1756 the Newcastle government resigned. Admiral Byng was court-martialled and shot, despite the protests of William Pitt. Pitt, who had argued long and loud for a strong navy, could not now be ignored, but the enmity of George II ensured some squalid political infighting before a strong ministry was formed, in which Pitt directed the war effort and all that went with it, while Newcastle did what he was best at, keeping parliament in line by an adroit mixture of emollience, patronage and hints of benefits to come. Pitt's distrust of land campaigns was justified by the failure of a military expedition led by the Duke of Cumberland, sent to protect the Hanover principality from French invasion.

By 1758, the tide of events began to run in Britain's favour. With the power of France and Austria against him, and only Prussia as an ally (though a formidable one under Frederick the Great) Pitt had the strategic vision to see that world war must be waged, and the nerve and will to sustain it. With a more sophisticated financial system available to him than his predecessors had, he financed the expansion and equipping of the army, the building of a series of new warships, and the subsidising of Prussia, by huge loans. Victory would make repayment easy; defeat was not to be contemplated. Under the command of Prince Frederick of Brunswick, a British–Prussian army held the French back at Minden, in 1759.

In that same year British supremacy at sea was established by victories at Lagos and Quiberon Bay. On 13 September, an English army led by General James Wolfe stormed Quebec, both he and his great French rival, Montcalm, being killed in the battle. The French fell back on Montreal, but were compelled to surrender in 1760, and their great colony of New France came under the Union flag. In India, the redoubtable and unscrupulous Clive recovered Calcutta, and by a combination of intrigue and the robust military tactics employed at the battle of Plassey, where his 3,000 men put to flight a force estimated at 50,000, gained the great realm of Bengal as a dependency of the British East India Company. By 1760, all French possessions in India had been taken over. Making war in areas of the globe remote from Britain was a nerve-racking business. Fleets and armies were dispatched into the unknown, and a long silence ensued. Though the situation on the ground or at sea could change with dramatic speed in the course of a day's battle, news took a long time to reach either side. During the eighteenth century, the Admiralty commissioned numbers of a new type of ship, the fast cutter, specially to carry dispatches, but even so, it could take three months for news of victory or defeat, or a plea for reinforcements, to come from India. Pitt and his advisers had to be patient, while officers in command often found that the orders they set off with had little relevance to the situation they found on arrival.

CHAPTER TEN

Loss and Gain of Empire

GEORGE III AND THE TORY ASCENDANCY

The remarkable string of triumphs achieved under the Newcastle–Pitt government did not result in universal adulation. Indeed, from 25 October 1760, a prime critic moved into a crucial position, when George II died and his grandson became King George III, at the age of twenty-two. Newcastle was sixty-seven, a politician of great experience if not of great reputation; Pitt was fifty-two, at the height of his powers and renown, a hero to the American colonists, who renamed the French Fort Duquesne as Pittsburg, as well as to the British public.

King George III

George had no direct experience of public affairs at all. The first Hanoverian monarch to have a strong sense of his role as British king, he was earnest, pious, well-intentioned, with an abounding sense of his own ability to be right, and determined to exercise every power which the constitutional arrangements allowed him. His tutor in regal matters and world affairs was a Scottish peer, Lord Bute, who was a Tory in sympathies, and encouraged the young George's antipathy to the party which, in one faction or another, had been in power for so long that few of its members could remember being in opposition. The leading Whigs had long been accustomed to governing with the acquiescence of the king being taken almost for granted, and by the time they understood George III better, he had formed his own following from among the nobility and courtiers. Many of these were essentially Tories, happy to support a young king who could say, 'I glory in the name of Briton.' With these 'King's Friends' began the political comeback of the Tories, shorn by now of any lingering taint of Jacobite sympathy, and keen to promote a royally led government that would cut the arrogant Whig leaders down to size. They became the peace party, complaining of the vast cost of the war and arguing that, with all that had been gained, it was time to bring hostilities to an end.

At the king's insistence, Bute joined the ministry in 1761, as Secretary of State. Peace negotiations were long drawn out, through hagglings over how much France was willing to concede, and intercepted dispatches from France to Spain revealed that France was playing a double game. Pitt was for war on Spain, but finding the cabinet virtually united against him, resigned in October 1761. In 1762 Newcastle also resigned, and the government, now headed by Bute, though it cut back on Pitt's expenditure, felt obliged to declare war on Spain. Henry Fox, like Newcastle a Whig politician of the old school, a wealthy man of affairs who saw political office as a means of personal enrichment and ennoblement (he duly became Lord Holland), managed the House of Commons, and a peace treaty with France was eventually completed in February 1763, ending what was known as the Seven Years War. The terms of the Treaty of Paris could not fail to be of great benefit to Great Britain, but the Duke of Choiseul, Louis XV's minister, saved a great deal for France.

RURAL UPHEAVAL: THE ENCLOSURE MOVEMENT

Political and social life at home began to reflect the tumult abroad. Political controversy over the Treaty of Paris, over the appointment of Bute, over the sidelining of Pitt (now Lord Chatham but still very much in politics) was joined by social and economic agitation in the country. The main cause of this was the sudden acceleration of a process that had been going on, accompanied by local protests and riots, all through the seventeenth century. Enclosure of common land was a consequence of the changes in agricultural practice. In Tudor times, with the expansion of sheep-farming, many formerly cultivated fields had been transferred to pasture, but the overall form of farming had not changed greatly. Around the nucleus of a village or hamlet was a spread of common land on which each villager could graze an agreed number of animals. Cultivated ground was divided into a great many small strips, each allocated to a villager, whose patches might be widely separated. Management of the system was entrusted to the manorial court, dominated by squire and parson, but also with elected village officers. The court apportioned the strips of land and ensured that each villager contributed to the basic tasks, like keeping ditches clear, and pollarding riverside willow trees.

It was an ancient system, suited to a stable population and to an economy which combined the self-sufficiency in food of peasant agriculture with such localised cottage industries as weaving cloth, basket-making and wood-cutting. These brought a modest amount of cash into circulation. Milling of corn was done on a local basis, with the miller paid in cash or kind, or both. Now this time-honoured system was breaking up under stresses of different kinds. The new, scientific idea of agriculture, based on crop rotation and the careful breeding of animals, was totally unsuited to the old open strip-fields. It needed larger fields, and enclosed fields so that indiscriminate breeding was made impossible. A growing urban population needed assured supplies of flour and meat, and improved communication by road and waterways made this possible at increasingly low cost. A drift of population away from the country areas towards towns and cities was reducing the cohesion and effectiveness of the village community. The lure was an improved way of life, in a larger community whose economy was based on production to sell, and with money as the basis; and with the greater interests and excitements generated by larger numbers of people living together. The increased use of new commodities and goods, spreading downwards from the wealthy class, made them cheaper. Country folk might brew their own ale and make their own cider, but tea and tobacco had to be brought in and paid for.

Ownership of the parish land was based on tradition, with allocation often unchanged through generations. To the bewilderment of many of the villagers, it was now possible for the local gentry to apply for a private Act of Enclosure from parliament. Commissioners then arrived to examine the ground and apportion it among those who could present a valid claim. Inevitably the prime beneficiaries were those who already owned or controlled the largest areas. The cost of the exercise was borne by all, which meant that those who emerged with the smallest shares, and had no cash reserves, were forced almost immediately to mortgage or sell their tiny holding. Country banks grew or were founded on the lucrative business of funding enclosure and land purchase. An energetic promoter of the process emerged in the person of Arthur Young, author of *Six Weeks' Tour Through the Southern Counties of England and Wales* (1768) and many subsequent pamphlets, who traversed the country over thirty years, and was appointed Secretary to the newly formed Board of Agriculture in 1794. During that period, around two and a half million acres of open fields were enclosed. Another million and a half were enclosed in the following forty years, and in addition, great areas regarded as 'waste' were reclaimed and enclosed. Farm production increased dramatically throughout these decades. It was at this time that the English landscape, seen as traditional in modern times, took shape: it is actually a relatively recent one, totally unlike the much older and longer-established fieldscape which it replaced. Thousands of miles of hedgerow were laid; roads were straightened; farmhouses and barnyards were built in the open country, and many rural villages went into decline or were completely abandoned. The family farm, of around a hundred acres or less, became the standard, with a solid Georgian farmhouse and a few hovels for its labourers. Whereas in the old days, farmers had had to kill most of their young animals at the onset of winter, as there was no means of feeding them, now larger buildings and the provision of winter feed enabled herds to be kept and built up.

THE HIGH AND THE LOWLY

As the new rural economy developed, the peasantry of England disappeared. In their place there were tenant farmers, who employed labourers. Some of these workers were hired on a permanent basis but most were reliant on seasonal employment. The economic basis of life for many cottage-dwelling families was reduced, often to below subsistence level. 'The first ingredient in the happiness of a people is that the gentry should reside on their native soil, and spend their rents among those from whom they receive them,' observed Lord George Bentinck, himself the descendant of one of William III's leading followers, and most of the gentry, even those who possessed a town house in London or a regional social centre like York or Bath, lived primarily on their estates. Great houses in classical style overlooked wide landscaped grounds, beyond which the enclosed fields extended towards the next stately demesne.

But below the rural prosperity was an underclass which did not share in it. The old form of the village, with its mixture of agriculture and cottage industry, was becoming increasingly unsustainable. For one or two generations the rural crafts would continue – leatherwork, basket-weaving, wagon-building, tanning, milling, brewing, shoemaking, tailoring, and of course cloth-weaving – on a steadily diminishing basis. Meanwhile, the population was entering a phase of growth. With schooling non-existent or minimal for most children, this produced a large increase in the unskilled labour market within the space of a few years. It also expanded the market for food, cloth, housing and other basic necessities. But not everyone could or would migrate to the towns, and a substantial landless underclass remained in country areas. The profits of the tenant farmers went into house-building, home comforts and luxuries, higher rents, education of their children, investment in new equipment: they did not percolate downwards to the labourers and their families who lived in a state verging on destitution. And yet the workers were necessary: farming was still a labour-intensive business, particularly at seed-time and harvest-time.

The traditional means of looking after the poor, sick and old was based on the parish, with each one supposed to look after its own. Strenuous efforts were made by the locally elected overseers to keep the parish poor to a minimum: vagrants were chased off, and when incoming workers were needed, they were given short-term contracts of less than the year's duration that would entitle them to benefits if they lost their employment. Their children were hired out as contract labour by these parish boards, especially those close to towns where child labour was preferred in many occupations because it was cheap. An Act of 1723 empowered parishes to set up workhouses for paupers, but relatively few did so; and a further Act of 1782 restricted the workhouses to the old, the sick, and to orphan or abandoned children. The parish was required to find work for its able-bodied poor. The farmers employed them, when they were needed, at wages less than it cost to feed a family. In 1795, a year of bad harvest, with food shortage exacerbated by lack of imports due to the war, there was desperation in many areas. The 'Speenhamland' Act in that year, named after a Berkshire parish whose magistrates made a regular practice of what had been a sporadic one in other places, allowed parishes to levy a rate in order to make up the wages of the poorest to a subsistence level. In such conditions, petty theft was all too likely to occur, and was consequently looked out for and punished severely. Rural villages had no prisons and small towns only had one or two cells attached to the court-house for prisoners awaiting trial: exposure in the stocks or whippings were awarded by local magistrates for trivial crimes; transportation to the plantations of the Indies or (from 1787) to penal colonies in Australia and the South Pacific was the sentence of the circuit judge, often as an alternative to hanging.

MIGRATION TO THE TOWNS

Changes in the countryside speeded up the movement of population to the towns and cities. Factories – a new development – needed large numbers of workers and their owners were actively advertising for labour. The

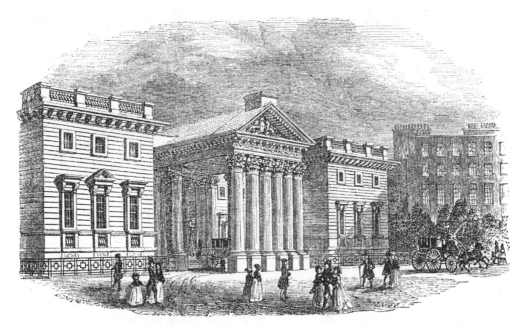

Carlton House – one of London's great Georgian houses

transformation of English society from a predominantly rural to an urban and industrial one was well under way in the early years of George III's sixty-year reign; by the king's death in 1820, a majority people were living in towns.

The concentration of relatively large numbers of people in built-up areas was not a new phenomenon – London had for long been a large city. But London had been unique, and the rapid growth of many towns caused problems for the government. Some of these, like Liverpool and Wakefield, were old corporations but others, like Bradford, Huddersfield or Walsall, were former villages. Even the older places struggled to adjust their small-scale local government to the new conditions, while the new places had no charters or civic structure at all, and simply spread across the landscape, enriching the landowner with rents and leases, and centred on a coal pit, or mill. A new kind of industrialist arose in the building contractor, employer of a large labour force and capable of putting up large-scale buildings and of constructing whole streets at a time, rather than single houses. The development of large urban areas destroyed the old pattern of social cohesion, based on the working family within a village unit, and with ancient links to the county and especially the parish. Now there were large, and growing, groups of workers employed for pay, requiring a different scale of shop-keeping, of entertainment, and of management both in an industrial and a political sense.

Groups of workers, living in close proximity, had a potential to organise in their own interests. The absence of squire and vicar encouraged a social attitude less deferential to the role of the gentry, while the authoritarian regime of the factory caused resentment, especially when business went down, and pay-cuts and lay-offs were instantly implemented. Cheap alcohol, especially gin and ale, was the great palliative of this early epoch of industrialisation. Hard work, typically twelve hours a day, and hard drinking (wages were paid in a public house owned or leased out by the factory or mine owner) helped to maintain a degree of social order if not tranquillity. Food prices were the issue most likely to flash into riot and disturbance. To the eyes of most gentlefolk of England, the new industrial population was an undifferentiated, brutish mass, which needed to be kept in order. Local militias were reformed and trained as much with an eye on the new townships as on the prospect of a French invasion. But in close-packed communities, ideas could circulate quickly and take root.

INDUSTRIAL ADVANCES

The growth of industry was beyond the comprehension, let alone the control, of the government. The energy and acumen of individual entrepreneurs and inventors drove the process on, new inventions often building on what had gone before. Technology was not always home-grown: silk-making machinery was brought to Norwich from Italy in 1718. In 1733 John Kay's invention of the fly shuttle doubled the productivity of the weaver. Things speeded up in the 1770s with Richard Arkwright's patenting of a horse-driven spinning frame – water-powered from 1771. Arkwright was the prototype English industrialist, rising from a humble background to factory-ownership, a knighthood, and the sheriffdom of Derbyshire. In the mid-1770s, James Hargreaves's spinning jenny enabled the spinner to produce several threads at once. The Lancashire cotton industry, still cottage-based, rose to prominence on the use of these machines, and from being a fabric of limited production and use, it was produced in increasingly large quantities. A partnership of profound importance began in 1775, when the Scot James Watt, whose invention of the condenser created the modern steam engine, set up an engine-building factory with Matthew Boulton, in Soho, Birmingham. The engines were at first used only in mining, as Newcomen's atmospheric steam engines had been, but the first steam-powered cotton spinning machine was built in 1785.

In 1740 Benjamin Huntsman, son of German immigrants, began the production of crucible steel in Sheffield. Coalbrookdale, on the Severn, had been a centre of progress in the iron industry since Abraham Darby began using coking coal for smelting in 1709. In 1779 his grandson completed the world's first cast-iron bridge there, dramatically bestriding the Severn Gorge in a single arch. By that time England was producing 68,000 tons of pig iron a year, a modest

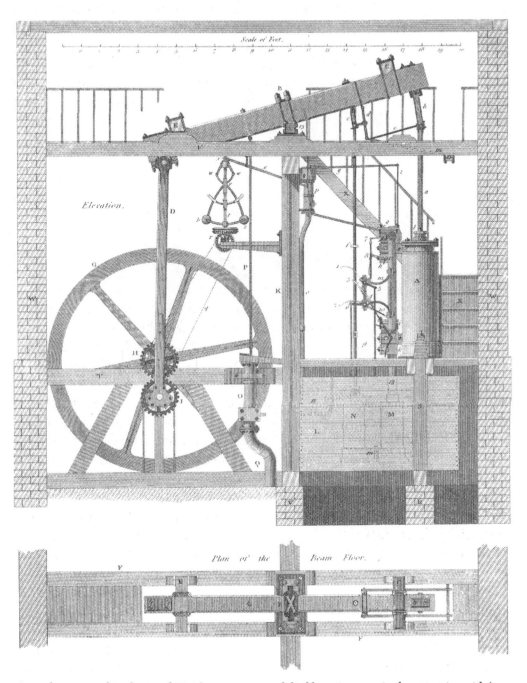

An early version of Boulton and Watt's steam-powered double-acting rotative beam engine with 'sun and planet' gearing c.1798

The cast-iron bridge over the Severn at Coalbrookdale (Ironbridge)

amount by future standards but already more than the rest of the world put together. Staffordshire was already a pottery-making district when Josiah Wedgwood opened his first factory in 1759; ten years later his new Etruria works was involved both in mass production and in luxury porcelain items. Also in 1759, work began on the Bridgewater Canal, the first independent navigation cut in England, from the Duke of Bridgewater's coal mine at Worsley to the Mersey at Salford. The expanding canal network quickly reduced the price of coal and other raw materials and thus aided the growth as well as well as the efficiency of industry.

THE FINANCE INDUSTRY

A few independent institutions were established to support and exploit the new developments. From 1692, Edward Lloyd's coffee house in the city of London had been a centre for ship-broking and marine insurance, and he had started a commercial journal of record, *Lloyd's News*. From 1726 this was re-established as *Lloyd's Lists*, and Lloyd's Register of Shipping was begun at the same time. For over two hundred years, until the organisation's downfall and reform in the 1990s, Lloyd's underwriters would make large annual profits

THE LUNAR SOCIETY

The town of Birmingham was growing fast in size and importance in the second half of the eighteenth century. It was at the heart of what would for a time become the Black Country, a great concentration of workshops and small factories, mostly involved with metal working. In and around it there lived a number of remarkable men, industrialists and philosophers, keenly interested both in mechanical invention and in exploring more fundamental aspects of scientific knowledge. In 1766 the Lunar Society was founded, to enable them to present and discuss their ideas. The name came from the fact that they met monthly at the time of the full moon, so that their journeys would have some illumination. They met in the house of Matthew Boulton, who in 1775 set up a business with James Watt to build steam engines. Other members included Joseph Priestley, the discoverer of oxygen; Erasmus Darwin, botanist; Richard Lovell Edgeworth, author and inventor; Thomas Day, author and educationist; and Josiah Wedgwood, who had set up his own pottery business in 1759. Sharing an interest in dissenting religion, often of a unitarian or deistic sort, as well as a firm belief in the value of education, and a liberal attitude to issues such as slavery, they were influential precursors of Liberalism and Utilitarianism.

from an ever-enlarging insurance business in which shipping became merely a part. The Bank of England had a monopoly of all business operations that used the joint-stock principle – the South Sea Bubble was not forgotten – but the Stock Exchange began business in 1773, and local banks, like that begun by the ironware-making Sampson Lloyd in Birmingham in 1765, helped to finance expansion, many of them going bust in the process.

A CONTROLLING MONARCH

George III's government, in its early years, was a spectator of the changes that were recasting the economy, rearranging the landscape, and altering even the spirit of the country. Henry Fox retired with his peerage. Bute, out of his depth and shocked by the extent of press and public vituperation against him, resigned in 1763. A new ministry, headed by Pitt's brother-in-law, George Grenville, took over. The main task confronting it was restoration of the national finances after the war. But other problems distracted it, not least the king himself. George's determination to be an active king, combined with his need to rely on Whig politicians, produced a constitutional hiatus for twenty years. In the words of the nineteenth-century writer Walter Bagehot, 'Throughout the greater part of his life George III was a kind of consecrated obstruction.' During this time the restless and frequently irritated monarch tried various combinations of parliamentarians in order to govern the country in the way he thought most appropriate. None satisfied him. This was inevitable, as even the most conservative of Whigs believed in cabinet government, under a prime minister, dependent on majority support in the House of

Commons, and with the monarch playing an important but not controlling part, while the king was striving to return to the pre-Walpole era, when the prime minister was appointed to carry out the king's will, and the cabinet was there to serve him.

'NO TAXATION WITHOUT REPRESENTATION'

In the 1760s, there was little real sense of party difference. In one sense everybody was a Whig; in another sense, Whiggism meant little more than adherence to the constitutional triangle of king, cabinet and parliament. The Whigs were not a unified party but a loose coalition of groups, known as 'interests' or 'connexions', each with its own leader. Pitt, now the Earl of Chatham, naturally a critic of the peace settlement, and with his own 'connexion', was kept firmly on the sidelines by the king's determination to exclude him from government. Successive administrations were called into being by the king and dismissed again, while in general elections, the Whig control of the great majority of seats remained unchanged. Two great issues now began to emerge, at first unseen as such by the government; but then, both were new, brought about by new ideas. Grenville's financial policy included new taxes, always an unpopular move. A tax on cider infuriated the south-western counties, where, as it happened, Tory members were prominent. More controversial still was a proposal to extend certain taxes to the North American colonies. These were intended to help pay for the ten thousand British troops stationed there. The Seven Years War, fought in North America, had shown the need for a British garrison to supplement the local militias raised by colonists. The imposition of taxes aroused a storm of resentment in the thirteen colonies, which for the first time began to see the desirability of co-operating in their own common interest. Their slogan, 'No taxation without representation', was actually borrowed from William Pitt, and no British parliamentarian could seriously oppose such a principle. On the other hand, the question of representation was not easy to resolve. The thirteen colonies had a combined population greater than Scotland's. Most were strongholds of religious independence and had constitutions of their own which varied greatly but usually took little or no account of a hereditary nobility and an established church. For George III and his advisers, the irruption of a phalanx of American colonial members of parliament, even if practicable, would have been intolerable. With hindsight, the progress to American independence might seem inevitable, but in 1765, when Grenville's government resigned, the colonies were not united, the majority of their citizens were loyal to the king and identified their security and future with that of Great Britain, which was also by far their major trading customer and source of supply.

'WILKES AND LIBERTY'

The other issue was far closer to home. When Lord Bute was made prime minister, a Whig member of parliament, John Wilkes, hitherto unknown except as a prominent debauchee even in an age of rakes, became his most vocal and effective opponent. Wilkes, son of a rich London distiller, made adroit use of Bute's patronage of incoming Scots to foment a mixture of anti-Scottish and anti-government feeling. The London-based Scottish novelist, Tobias Smollett, had started a weekly paper, *The Briton*, in support of Bute; Wilkes craftily set up a mirror-image, *The North Briton*, which regularly and savagely satirised the court and government. When the government arrested and prosecuted him for seditious libel, he successfully pleaded that his privilege as a member of parliament had been infringed. The government had used a general warrant, which allowed the arrest of persons without specifically naming them, and this was rejected as illegal by the Lord Chief Justice.

Among the more democratically inclined Whigs, and especially in London, Wilkes became identified with the concept of the free-speaking, common Englishman, and 'Wilkes and Liberty' became something of a slogan. Wilkes's publishing of the obscene poem 'An Essay on Woman' was raised against him, and the Commons passed a bill to establish that libel was not covered by parliamentary privilege. A Bute supporter fought a duel with Wilkes, who was wounded. He fled to France and, having failed to appear for trial, was formally declared an outlaw and expelled from the House of Commons. But Wilkes, no longer representing his constituency of Aylesbury, still had a large constituency behind him, that of public opinion. Then as now, the 'average Englishman' was impossible to define. But interest in politics and current affairs was growing at a dramatic rate. In part it reflected a variety of shades of opinion among relatively small though influential groups: nuclei of ideas and attitudes which spread out and affected a wider and less vocal and responsive public.

Between 1769 and 1777 the number of daily newspapers printed in London – their circulation very limited – rose from seven to seventeen, and a large number of journals and a host of pamphlets supplemented them. The new coffee-house culture also stimulated discussion. Outside of parliament, a debate was going on, fuelled from several different sources, including the writings of the French thinker, Jean-Jacques Rousseau, whose attacks on human inequality and human institutions at the expense of human beings – 'Man is born free but everywhere he is in chains' – were profoundly influential. The intensity of this debate was comparable to the excitement of the 1640s, when the common people had first known the heady experience of having the country's future in their hands. But this time, religion played a vastly smaller part. Politics was at the core, and though its roots went back to Levellers and Lollards

Lord North

in a long tradition of opposition to established ideas, it was in the 1760s that modern English radicalism was born.

Badgered by the king, and with the instinct of oligarchs to resist pressure from below, the short-lived governments of Lord Rockingham, Pitt (by this time Earl of Chatham and a sick man), and the Duke of Grafton came and went. It was not until 1770 that George III at last found a prime minister of congenial views and with the ability to control the House of Commons, in Lord North (the 'Lord' was a courtesy title for most of his life: he sat in the Commons), who would survive in the post for more than ten years.

THE IRREPRESSIBLE WILKES

In 1768 the unputdownable Wilkes returned, despite having been exiled, and stood for parliament again, failing to get a London seat but winning Middlesex. Eventually standing trial, he was sentenced to twenty-two months' jail and a fine of £1,000. Even before his trial, popular demonstrations in his support had resulted in the 'Massacre of St George's Fields' when the Scots Guards fired on the London crowd, killing six, and creating a mood of dangerous resentment. Radicalism was discovering that entrenched interests did not give way easily. In February 1769, the government again expelled Wilkes from the Commons. At a by-election, he was re-elected. He was expelled. At another by-election, he was again re-elected, only to be once again expelled by the vote of the House. These farcical proceedings helped to reduce the authority of parliament and of Grafton's government, and 'Wilkes and Liberty' took on a new tone of anger. At a fourth by-election, Wilkes, still a prisoner, was again returned by a large majority, but the House of Commons re-expelled him and declared his opponent elected. There were demonstrations, mass meetings, strikes, petitions – every form of extra-parliamentary agitation short of civil uprising. The Wilkites were however only really strong in London. They had a reform programme, which included shorter parliaments, exclusion of office-holders and 'placemen' from parliament, and 'a fair and equal representation of the people in Parliament', but succeeded only in obtaining political control of the capital, of which Wilkes himself became Lord Mayor in 1774. Finally accepted as a member of parliament in that year, he found himself and his twelve supporters hopelessly outnumbered by the pensioners, placemen, knights of the shires, Scots who had not forgiven the gibes of the *North Briton*, and the 'King's Friends'. His attempt to introduce a Reform Bill got nowhere. Almost sixty years would elapse before reform became a real political issue. But radicalism was well established, to the alarm of government, which soon began to use the powers of the state against it, including spies and *agents provocateurs*. Wilkes's influence gradually declined, and though he remained a reformer, he grew less radical in his later years. But one important victory survived from his campaigns: the right of the press to report the proceedings of parliament. Up to that time, debates had been private, and jealously kept so, but from now the words of members were open to public scrutiny.

Wilkes's supporters were predominantly from among the artisans, and weavers, hatters, hat-dyers, joiners, watermen, tailors and glass-grinders were among the groups who went on strike in his support. A business recession, partly caused by disturbances in America, and high food prices caused by poor harvests, exacerbated the mood of protest. But neither his temper nor theirs led to insurrection, and despite the riots, shootings and sense of disaffection in 1769–70, revolution did not seem likely, except to a few of the more alarmist government supporters. The governments were not totally deaf and blind to what was going on. The hated cider tax was repealed, and the Spitalfields Act established a fixed wage for weavers. Instead of revolution, the country received Lord North, a politician who did not believe in party at all, and who considered himself and his ministers responsible to the king.

WAR WITH THE AMERICAN COLONISTS

Though North is inevitably associated with the loss of the American colonies, their alienation had begun earlier. Some of the colonies, like Massachusetts, had been founded by men and women who had felt forced to leave England and their descendants had not forgotten the fact. Pennsylvania had been a 'holy experiment' in social and religious freedom. The spirit of the colonists did not fit well with the attitudes of the governors and military men sent out from England for short terms of office. In 1766, at Pitt's urging the stamp tax had been repealed, but Charles Townshend, Chancellor of the Exchequer in the last cabinet before North's, applied taxes to American imports of lead, paper, glass, painters' colours and tea, causing furious protest. North repealed all these, except the tax on tea. This was not enough to placate the colonists, especially as the duty was kept not for the revenue it generated but to maintain the principle that parliament could tax the colonies. In 1773 the East India Company was in financial trouble, which the government tried to resolve by giving it the monopoly on tea supply to America. This offended the American merchants and led to smuggling and Company ships being turned back, and to the celebrated Boston Tea Party, when colonists disguised as Indians threw part of a cargo into

Boston Harbour. Heavy-handed British action to obtain compensation from Massachusetts, and then to annul its constitution, led to the Continental Congress of September 1755: the colonies found unity in opposition, and British attempts to divide them failed. Fighting began on 19 April 1775, at Lexington, though the American Declaration of Independence was not made until 4 July 1776.

This was a war quite different to any later colonial wars. English principles, English pronouncements, the words of English philosophers like John Locke, were turned against the London government and its apologists by the rebel colonists. But the war was not waged in any apologetic spirit by the British, and majority public opinion in England was firmly on the government side, with only those of strong radical sympathies against it. The final 'olive branch petition' from the Congress was ignored, and an army of 20,000 men was mustered. Many were German mercenaries from Hesse and Hanover. Whilst the British armies could win battles, they were not equipped to deal with a mobile enemy spread across a vast countryside, nor, after victory, to hold down a hostile, well-organised and resourceful population. In October 1777 General Burgoyne, with an over-extended army, surrendered at Saratoga. Soon after this news was known, France, under Louis XVI, recognised American independence and declared war on Great Britain. Just before his death, in 1778, Chatham made his last speech in parliament, urging the House of Lords to make a reconciliation with America, but the king's policy was to fight on all fronts, and North was his obedient servant. By 1780 Spain had also declared war, and war was declared against Holland, which refused to allow its merchant ships to be searched for American supplies. Russia and the Scandinavian countries adopted a posture of 'armed neutrality' for the same reason. Britain was again involved in international conflict. Colonial empires, and control of the vital sea-routes, were still the great prizes, and the French fleet had been re-established as a formidable force.

CONFLICT ON ALL FRONTS

An invasion of the southern states, where many colonists were opposed to the northern-led war, was at first brilliantly successful, and under Lord Cornwallis, Georgia and Carolina were restored to British rule. But a push northwards into Virginia led to Cornwallis's army being cut off on the Yorktown peninsula, and the British ships intended to relieve them were beaten off by a French fleet. In October 1781, Cornwallis was forced to surrender to General George Washington. Britain still had substantial forces in North America, but the demands of war on many fronts fatally weakened the Royal Navy's ability to maintain supremacy at sea, outnumbered as it was by hostile fleets. American and French ships appeared off the English coast, and as many as three thousand British merchant ships were captured or sunk. France was capturing West Indian colonies, and British control of India was gravely threatened; Spain was in Florida. Invasion seemed probable.

North's government appeared scarcely in control of events at home, when a savage ten-day burst of rioting in London, stirred up by the Scottish Lord George Gordon and aimed at the Catholic population, broke out on 2 June 1780. Spurred on by war with Catholic France, it was a protest against the Relief Act of 1778, which had removed some of the penal legislation against Catholics, but was fomented by the sense that things were going badly for England in the war. An unusual contrast to the relative mildness of protest in England, this caused some 700 deaths and huge destruction of property. It was faced down not by the government but by the king, who personally ordered in some 12,000 troops. Against the use of musketry and cavalry charges, the rioters dispersed. Twenty-five people were subsequently executed.

In Ireland, whose parliament was both unrepresentative of the majority of the population, and subordinate to the final judgement of Westminster and White-hall, there was a swift upsurge of national feeling, resulting in the demand for parliamentary independence, backed up by a nationwide organisation of armed volunteers. Profiting from a pro-law-and-order reaction against the Gordon riots, North won a general election in 1780, though his majority in the Commons was reduced, but dissatisfaction and anger ran deep through the country. The Association movement, headed by Christopher Wyvill, a Yorkshire squire, organised mass meetings and petitions in an extra-parliamentary campaign for political and economic reform. Within parliament, a 'Chathamite' member, John Dunning, successfully proposed a motion that the influence of the crown 'has increased, is increasing, and ought to be diminished'. North and his cabinet struggled on, at the urging of the king, floundering in domestic strife and a catalogue of losses in the war. The position of the king now was the precise reverse of that when he had acceded: his policy had led to a war that was even more financially ruinous than the Seven Years War, and with none of the military glory and potentially lucrative conquests. A new generation of able young politicians had entered the Commons, including William Pitt, younger son of the Earl of Chatham, and were intensely hostile to the American war. To the fury and despair of George III, Lord North finally resigned in March 1782.

A NEW GENERATION OF PARLIAMENTARIANS

The king had no options left. The Whig notables were ready and waiting to assume political power, though as before they were not a united group. Lord Rockingham became prime minister and his faction included Charles James Fox, thirty-three-year-old son of Henry Fox. The other powerful figure, destined

William Pitt, the Younger

to become premier after Rockingham's death in that same year, was Lord Shelburne, among whose followers was the younger Pitt, aged twenty-three. Pitt and Fox, both reformers, both intensely ambitious, both of great ability, uneasy allies at present, would determine the future course of British politics. From now on, that course would be based on the supremacy of parliament. As the historian, G.M. Trevelyan, noted, this may actually have served to preserve the principle of monarchy: 'If the personal government of George III and of his children after him had been protracted into the next century, the democratic and Reform movements of the new era, finding themselves opposed by the King as their chief source of conservative resistance, must have become anti-royalist and very probably republican.'

Ironically for the king, the long string of defeats and humiliations now began to end. An important naval victory in the West Indies, under Admiral Rodney, stemmed the French and Spanish incursions in April 1782. In September the three-year-long siege of Gibraltar, key to the Mediterranean, was finally beaten off. There was much business for the new government, which speedily passed an Economic Reform Bill, reducing the power of government to exercise what was traditionally known as 'patronage' but what was in fact bribery in the awarding of sinecures, official positions providing large salaries and requiring no work. When Shelburne took over in July his government was weakened by the defection of almost half of the Whig supporters, including Fox, to ally themselves with the Tories. This was not the result of differences of policy or principle, but of personal, almost tribal hostilities within the Whig party. Shelburne, daring or desperate, made William Pitt Chancellor of the Exchequer and leader of the House of Commons. Sir Charles Oman observed: 'The younger Pitt was the most remarkable man of his age. He had inherited from his father high principles, an enthusiastic belief in the future of England, and a sympathy for the cause of reform. He had been reared as a Whig, but had no sympathies for the old parliamentary jobbing and corruption of the party. His personal integrity was as great as that of his father, and his hatred of intrigue and bribery even greater . . . As Chatham had believed himself the destined saviour of England from the dangers of foreign war, so it was his son's aim and end to deliver

England from internal faction, and to build up a great constitutional party which should combine loyalty to the crown with progressive and democratic legislation. This party, as Pitt imagined, would consist of the more enlightened Whigs . . . That it would ever grow to be known as the "Tory" party, would at this moment have been beyond his comprehension.' This is perhaps to read from Pitt's final record rather than give a portrait of his views and aspirations at the time when he first took up office. Pitt was a politician and like all successful politicians had a very good grasp of how to retain power and keep the opposition on the defensive.

Shelburne's government survived long enough to concede the claim of American independence, and to negotiate the terms on which the war with France, Spain and Holland might end. These inevitably included British concessions: Spain received Florida, France was back in India, though the Dutch were forced to accept British trade in the East Indies. Hostility to this acceptance of defeat brought a Fox–North coalition to power in parliament. The old jobber and the young reformer getting into political bed together made a field day for satirists and cartoonists.

STRUGGLE FOR CONTROL OF INDIA

As with the swing of a mighty pendulum, the focus of attention moved from the lost empire of America (and the fate of its numerous pro-British loyalists) to the recently gained and precariously held territories of India. (In passing, it may be noted that Captain James Cook had landed at Botany Bay in 1770 and claimed the southern continent for Great Britain.) In India, not only French attacks but also the rising of Indian rulers against European occupation had made the situation critical. But there were other issues. The Indian 'factories' and forts were set up and maintained by the East India Company, an independent body which only approached the government when it was in trouble. English feelings were strong against the 'nabobs' who made huge personal fortunes and came back to establish themselves in grand style as landowners. A Regulating Act in

Warren Hastings

173

EDMUND BURKE

One of the many Irishmen who have been assimilated into English politics and culture, Burke (1729–97) came to study law in London at the age of twenty-one, but quickly became involved in literature and politics. Though in and out of parliament, and rarely holding any government post, his published work in analysing and commenting on public affairs underlies much of subsequent English politics. His greatest period was as a member of the Whig opposition to Lord North's government of 1770–82, when he pleaded for conciliation with America and condemned the abuses of government. In 1780 his support for relaxation of trade sanctions against Ireland, and for relaxation of the anti-Catholic laws, cost him his seat at Bristol, to whose electors he addressed a magisterial reproach setting out the duties of an MP as an independent representative, not a delegate, of his constituents. He was an early and influential opponent of the French Revolution. His crucial part in the eventually unsuccessful prosecution of Warren Hastings damaged his later reputation, though here too there were abuses of power to be challenged; perhaps from his Irish background, Burke had an unusual appreciation, for the time, of the rights of native peoples. His later support of Pitt, together with his anti-Jacobin sentiments, have identified him with conservatism, though he infused it with a spirit of tolerance and concern for justice. An orator of passion and brilliance, he is endlessly quotable. One of his most memorable, and most often misquoted phrases, is this: 'When bad men combine, the good must associate; or else they will fall, one by one, an unpitied sacrifice in a contemptible struggle' (*Thoughts on the Cause of the Present Discontents*, 1770).

1773 had established partial government control and the post of governor general, first given to Warren Hastings, an experienced Company man, who maintained Company rule for ten years against internal and external attacks. His position was more like that of a medieval king than a modern administrator, and his methods, though they worked successfully, were open to criticism.

But political rivalries in London, and personal jealousies, prompted the India Bill drawn up by Fox and Edmund Burke, which would have replaced the Company's rule by that of a commission of seven persons appointed by parliament (and nobody doubted that the seven would be loyal supporters of Fox and Lord North, who knew no other system than 'jobbery'). Opposition to the India Bill united George III and William Pitt, and when the House of Lords, under intense personal pressure from the king – who made it known that: 'Whoever voted for the bill was not only not His Majesty's friend, but would be considered as his enemy' – rejected it, and the ministry fell, George offered Pitt the post of prime minister.

PITT'S ADMINISTRATION

Pitt accepted, though his small group of reformist Whig supporters consorted oddly with the 'King's Friends' in parliament. But he moved speedily to hold a general election in early 1784. The magic of his own name, and the public distaste for the all-too-apparent cynicism of the Fox–North alliance, won him a large majority. Reformists, even radicals, might have drawn a deep breath and hoped for great things now. In the initial stage, Pitt did indeed introduce a bill for parliamentary reform, but it was decisively rejected. The rotten boroughs remained; electors' votes continued to be bought; the expanding cities continued to have little or no representation. Pitt made no further effort to reform parliament, and opposed three attempts, backed by Fox, to repeal the Test and Corporation Acts: the long-term links between the Dissenters and the Whigs, later the Liberals, began here. Substantial opportunities for patronage still remained, and Pitt used them all, including the creation of over ninety new peerages in England, largely to reward his supporters and pack them into the House of Lords. Although his government was to have a lasting effect in many ways, constitutional reform was not one of them. His alliance with the king made him – as his former allies pointed out – the leader of the Tories, and it was he who formed them into a political party with a solid basis in the country's business life as well as among the country squires. It became the party of conservatism and often of reactionary and anti-liberal views, but under occasional leaders of exceptional quality and originality, like Pitt himself, it would also be a party of significant reform. The king accepted actions and decisions of Pitt's which would have caused explosions before: but the alternative to Pitt was Fox, and George III detested Fox as a politician and a man. While Pitt's rigorous morality looked forward to the nineteenth-century ideal, Fox's private life was much more akin to that of the old rakes. Furthermore, he was a drinking crony of the Prince of Wales, heir to the throne, who had none of George III's piety, earnestness or domestic respectability.

Pitt concentrated on economic and trade matters. The national debt was tackled, customs duties were rationalised and new measures were taken to reduce if not prevent smuggling. Having benefited from Adam Smith's pioneering work on economics, *The Wealth of Nations*, published in 1776, he would have liberalised trade laws if the pressure of mercantile interest had not forced him to maintain them against Ireland and to create new Navigation Acts to restrict access to American shipping. In 1784 he oversaw the passing of a Government of India Act which brought parliamentary control over British India, but he did not prevent the vindictive, long-drawn-out and ultimately futile prosecution of Warren Hastings for misgovernment, in which Edmund Burke played a major part. A Canada Act in 1790 provided for a large degree of self-rule in this colony with its great French province of Quebec, and assured its continuance under the British crown. His economic housekeeping was greatly assisted by industrial growth. Between 1780 and 1800, exports almost doubled. Textiles were the largest element, comprising almost 60 per cent of exports by value, but coal output doubled in the same period, and the production of iron rose by the same amount. Investment in machinery was growing at an even faster rate, and though this was the great age of water-power, steam engines were becoming increasingly common. In the 1790s, the Cornish engineer, Richard Trevithick, developed a compact, high-pressure steam engine, cheaper and more versatile than the cumbrous low-pressure Watt engines. Machines produced more, faster, cheaper, and the English textile industry offered goods of standard quality and wide variety at a lower price than any other country could match.

REVOLUTION IN FRANCE

In 1788 Pitt's government faltered when George III suffered his first bout of insanity. The Prince of Wales expected to be appointed regent, and to bring in a new government formed from his Whig associates, but the king recovered, and the government survived. Already at this time there was plenty of news of unrest in France. England had always been open to ideas from abroad, and without them would have possessed a far narrower and shallower culture. But foreign influences were usually slow and gradual in permeating through the structures of English society and the layered membranes of English tradition. In July 1789, however, the news of the French Revolution rushed through the country like a gust of cold, invigorating air. The radically minded welcomed this confirmation of their own beliefs: 'Bliss was it in that dawn to be alive,' wrote William Wordsworth (who did not dream, at that moment, of his own later incarnation as a conservative-minded poet laureate to the youthful Queen Victoria), 'but to be young was very heaven.' Like many others he went to France to share in the sense of a new order emerging.

William Wordsworth

Charles James Fox proclaimed his admiration of the revolutionaries. And even the more conservatively inclined felt it was good that France had shaken off a despotic royal government in favour of a constitutional monarchy.

CHAPTER ELEVEN

'They Will Not Come by Sea'

WAR WITH FRANCE

As it became clear that France's revolution was not taking the same kind of course as England's 'glorious' event of 1688, the initial enthusiasm began to disappear. Mob rule, wild proclamations, the flight and arrest of the king in 1791, all caused many English sympathisers to fall silent, while Burke had already published a strong and influential condemnation in 1790. A new stream of refugees, Catholic and royalist, began to flow in from France. With proclamation of the French Republic, only a few extreme radicals on the fringe of the Whig party, and the even fewer republicans in England were left in support. When King Louis XVI was guillotined on 21 January 1793, and the Convention appealed to all nations to overthrow monarchy, the British government was already, though belatedly, preparing for war.

France was already at war with Austria and Prussia, and declared war on

The execution of Louis XVI

Britain on 8 February. Seeing France hemmed in by hostile powers, Pitt antici-pated a short campaign. This was not to be – after the series of revolutionary governments had managed to survive the first year of war, the 'Directory' government was accepted by other European states, and Prussia and Spain withdrew from hostilities. Holland, where a British army under the Duke of York had been routed, was turned into a French dependency, with its powerful navy now at the disposal of France. By the end of 1795, the original coalition was reduced to Britain, Austria and Sardinia. By the end of 1797, Britain stood alone to face the power of France, Spain and Holland.

It seemed to be an English tradition to begin a war badly. The army was always small, and there were no land frontiers to sweep across: troops had to be transported by ship, a logistical nightmare, especially when the destination was the other side of the Atlantic, or India. Poor strategy and technical incompe-tence were displayed. The defeat in Flanders and the failure to defend Toulon and its royalists, and the dispatch of a large army to the West Indies where far greater numbers perished through fever than through battle, contributed to a sense of gloom about the prospects of the war. The defeat of the French in India, the gains of West Indian islands and of the Dutch colony of the Cape of Good Hope, seemed remote compared to the threat from continental Europe.

THE PRE-WAR MOOD FOR REFORM

At the start of the war, French propaganda – perhaps even belief – declared that 50,000 English republicans were ready to join their cause. Nobody in England believed this. But the ideas and first success of the Revolution had built on and reinspired the strong spirit of radicalism already present in England. Constitu-tional societies had been formed throughout the country, and discussed univer-sal suffrage and how to achieve real democracy. Their members were by no means only from the artisan and shopkeeping classes; Charles Grey, a future earl and prime minister, was a founder member of the Society of the Friends of the People, committed to parliamentary reform and a wider electorate. Thomas Paine's *The Rights of Man*, published in 1791, argued the case against Burke's hostile *Reflections upon the Revolution in France*, and was far more widely read. Paine, born in Thetford, Norfolk, had spent time in America and France, and was a convinced republican, considering government as a 'necessary evil' which should be based on reason and the natural equality of all humans. As radical reformists became more confident, vocal and numerous, and calls for abolition of monarchy and social rank, and for taxation of the rich, grew louder and more frequent, advocates and opponents of the revolution sometimes abandoned argument for fights and riots. Loyalist Associations were formed. 'Church and king' mobs in Birmingham wrecked dissenting chapels and drove the scientist and revolutionary sympathiser Joseph Priestley to flee to America in the summer of 1791. Until the outbreak of war, Pitt's government felt able to contain the situation, and an important step in the direction of liberalism was taken in 1792 by an act of parliament – promoted by Fox – which left it to juries, not to judges, to decide whether a libel had been committed. The French appeal for 'natural law' and the overthrow of monarchies, and the opening of hostilities, brought a sudden hardening of the government's attitude.

THE RESPONSE TO WAR: REPRESSION

In an atmosphere of panic and fear of a revolutionary movement in Great Britain, Pitt's government began to clamp down on internal opposition. In parliament, a large majority of the Whigs joined them, their fear for existing rights of property far greater than their commitment to reform. Only a rump were left, devoid of any influence in affairs and easily labelled as anti-British and traitorous. In 1794 the government suspended habeas corpus, enabling its officers to arrest anyone without giving a cause, and claimed a revolutionary plot was being hatched, but could produce no evidence of it. A number of leading radicals were arrested and prosecuted for treason, to be acquitted by juries. Coincidentally, food prices were rising sharply after bad harvests, and this, as always, provoked sharp public reaction. 'Bread and no war' became a popular slogan for a time. Parliament passed legislation forbidding public meetings of more than fifty people, unless authorised by a magistrate, and limiting the right to write or speak on treasonable topics. In any case the bloodbath of the Terror period in France, and the steady decline of the initial idealism of the Revolution, caused many radical sympathisers to moderate or abandon their views. The number of government spies and paid informants increased enormously, and a new bureaucracy arose to digest their reports and arrange their payments.

However, the greatest hazard to national security was the government's own doing. Like his father, Pitt was well aware that in any war, control of the sea was vital to Britain. The new ships of the line being built for the Royal Navy were the best in the world in terms of hull design and of armament; command of the seas kept officers and men trained and ready for action – the navy itself was the supreme weapon at the government's disposal. The ignored element was the sailors – not the officers who came from the gentry, but the thousands of men required to work the ships and guns. At nineteen shillings a month, seamen's pay had not changed for more than a hundred years. It was paid late, sometimes by years. Prize money from captured ships enriched admirals and captains but not ordinary seamen. Their food was bad and inadequate. It was well known that the purser of a man-of-war could make £1,000 a year from his post. Even in

179

a home anchorage, seamen were usually kept on board, as desertion was all too likely. Discipline was maintained by flogging of any recalcitrants. Few volunteered for service at sea, and the only way of crewing the ships was by use of the Impress Service, the naval press gang. In 1792 the fleet had 16,000 men; in 1802 it would have 135,000. The extraordinary complacency of the Admiralty officials who administered this corrupt, inefficient and inhuman system sheds some light on more general social attitudes of the time. Numerous officers had warned of the dangers and had been ignored.

1797: CRISIS IN THE NAVY AND AT HOME

The naval victory of St Vincent against Spain in February 1797 perhaps encouraged their complacency. The mutinies of April–June 1797 which began at Spithead and spread to the squadrons stationed at the Nore and Yarmouth were the direct result of long oppression and exploitation of the crewmen, and of the resentment of pressed men, although cries of treachery immediately arose. Red flags were displayed, and Pitt was hanged in effigy. A rise in pay and some other concessions quickly pacified the Spithead fleet, but the North Sea fleet, intended to hold the Dutch navy at bay, was stiffened by a spirit of political reform. For a few days in June things looked dangerous. From the Nore, mutineers blockaded the Thames estuary and looted some merchant vessels, but reproaches from the Channel fleet men, a shift in the early public sympathy, lack of provisions, and a tough line from the government, broke the mutiny. Even the fleet off Cadiz was affected. Its commander, Admiral Jervis, the victor of St Vincent (a harsh disciplinarian greatly disliked by the seamen), bombarded the Spanish port in order, as he put it, 'to divert the animal from these damnable doctrines which letters from England have produced'. He also instructed his captains to forbid men to speak Irish together. Meanwhile Admiral Duncan was blockading the Dutch with two ships. But by October, his again-united fleet destroyed the Dutch navy in the battle of Camperdown. Confidence in the navy was restored. Jervis, as Lord St Vincent, was eventually able to say to the House of Lords in 1803: 'I do not say the French will not come. I only say, they will not come by sea.'

The naval crisis, French military successes, food shortages and consequent profiteering, and a general rise in prices, made 1797 a year of profound anxieties. A French attempt to invade Ireland at the end of 1796 had been defeated by bad weather, and other attempts at invasion there or in England were expected. The government, with a huge majority in parliament, continued to pass laws that restricted freedom. Believers in liberty were forced into silence. The economic crisis and lack of confidence in the future caused the wealthy members to convert their paper money into gold – these were days

---

RIGHTS OF WAY

The old phrase, 'the king's highway', meant just what it said. The roads used by the people to get from place to place belonged to nobody, except the king. His owner-ship was the guarantee of freedom to use them. It did not extend to maintenance. Until the eighteenth century, the idea of a national road system had little value: long-distance traffic went by river and sea whenever possible. The old scattered field system encour-aged the development of local parish paths, many of which were lost after enclosure, but many others still remain as rights of way: an estimated 140,000 miles in total. Enclosure also encouraged the re-aligning of roadways, though the number of right-angle bends on country roads shows also that directness was not of major importance, and speed even less so. In the later eighteenth century, the growth of the turnpike trusts, providing stretches of maintained road for the price of a toll, helped to build a national road system. The trusts, with other local bodies, were eventually merged into the new county councils from 1888 and the use of roads became free again. Numerous bridge tolls remained. The toll notice for the celebrated bridge over the Severn Gorge, the first iron bridge in the world (1779), sturdily underlined where the 'king's highway' came to a temporary hiatus: 'N.B. This Bridge being private property, every Officer or Soldier, whether on duty or not, is liable to pay toll for passing over, as well as any baggage-waggon, Mail-coach or the Royal Family.' Its builders, the Darbys, were Quakers and no respecters of rank for its own sake.

---

in which the Bank of England's promise to pay the bearer 'on demand' meant exactly what it said. The resultant run on the banks made many country banks bankrupt and the Bank of England's gold reserves were so low that the government had to allow it to refuse cash payments of more than £1. Paper money only was in circulation until 1819. Yet the demand for war material, ships, guns, uniforms, wagons, shells, ropes, provisions, was enormous and growing, and every producer and distributor was doing well out of the war, so long as the government's money could be trusted. It was not an auspi-cious year for Grey and Fox to promote a bill for extending the electorate, which was defeated by a huge majority, and Fox effectively removed himself from public life for the next four years. During that time, the country was a one-party state, and a repressive home policy was steadily intensified.

NO FREEDOM FOR WORKERS

From quite early in the century, groups of workers in a single trade and place had begun to organise themselves in 'trade clubs' of a largely social nature. These had sometimes also acted protectively, as when the Spitalfields silk-weavers, with Wilkes's support, obtained an act of parliament in 1773 to reg-ulate their earnings. In theory, local magistrates had power to set local wage rates, but such an arrangement, going back to the days of Queen Elizabeth, was quite unable to cope with the vastly greater number of trades, the consolidation of work in factories, and the rise of the mill owner and factory proprietors. New machinery and methods meant that, instead of semi-independent workers like the weavers, more people were being employed in single workforces. For groups such as these to organise themselves was seen as a dangerous threat to established order. Among the most prominent opponents of such combinations was William Wilberforce, the friend of Charles James Fox and already an ardent campaigner against slavery, who was the moving spirit of the Combination Act of 1799, slightly amended in 1800, which made trade unions illegal. Any working man who combined with another to gain an increase in wages, or a decrease in working hours, was liable, for a first offence, to three months in jail, or two months' hard labour. Although employers' combinations were also declared illegal, there were no sanctions against them, and they flourished quite openly. These acts showed a government beginning to come to grips with the new phenomenon of industrial England. Possibly the spirit of the times, the nation at war, the fear of revolution, helped to make the response such a heavy-handed one. But it is very much of a piece with the way in which the Admiralty regarded the sailors, as expendable, unworthy of serious consideration, a mass to kept under control rather than individual citizens with rights. In both cases the desire and opportunity to make as large profits as possible distorted the vision of those in charge. Parliament of course represented only the proprietors, and the total eclipse of the radical fringe of the Whigs merely intensified its attitude. A long, slow, difficult learning curve lay ahead of both employers and employees, with parliament usually the last to master any of the painful lessons, and the agents of the law in no doubt about their responsibilities in the matter. In 1810 the typesetters on *The Times* newspaper were brought to court for combining, and sentenced to periods varying from nine months to two years for what the judge called 'a most wicked conspiracy' against 'the very employers who give you bread'.

THE THREAT OF INVASION AND
IRISH UPRISINGS

In 1795 and 1797 there were sporadic peace negotiations, with Pitt's government accepting the resurgent power of France and prepared to concede much of what Britain had gained in the fighting. The developing imperial spirit created in France by the victories of Napoleon Bonaparte killed any chance of mutual compromise. In 1798 only constant command of the Channel and its approaches prevented invasion by the Armée d'Angleterre, and blockading squadrons cruised permanently off the Texel, Brest, Ferrol, Cadiz, Cartagena

The battle of the Nile

and Toulon. To confront the rising star of one of history's greatest generals, England, from the unlikely background of a Norfolk country rectory, produced one of history's greatest admirals. In a bold night attack, a French fleet was shattered by Horatio Nelson at the battle of the Nile.

But on land Bonaparte remained invincible. Trouble erupted in India when Tippu, Sultan of Mysore, rose up against British control. The strategy and tactics of two Wellesleys, the Marquis, who was governor general, and Sir Arthur, a professional soldier who was governor of Mysore, defeated him, but warfare went on in India for another ten years. In Ireland, where the establishment of an independent parliament in 1782 had not altered the overwhelming political dominance of the Anglican–Tory squirearchy, there had for several years been fears of French invasion to back up an uprising for real self-government. In 1796 only bad weather had prevented a large-scale invasion; the defeat of the Dutch fleet had stopped another in 1797, but in 1798 the 'Great Rebellion' erupted without any French participation until too few forces arrived, too late. The uprising, though put down after two weeks of fierce fighting and further disturbances afterwards, led to the maintenance of a substantial army in Ireland.

In the course of 1799, Pitt's diplomacy had brought Russia and Austria into coalition with Great Britain, and while Bonaparte's army was still in Egypt,

Napoleon Bonaparte crossing the Alps

without means of returning, substantial victories were won against the French in Europe. By the end of the year, Bonaparte had returned, and become First Consul of France. Under his generalship and after a dramatic crossing of the Alps, the Austrians were crushed at Marengo and Hohenlinden in 1800, and the Russians withdrew from the coalition.

The British war effort was by now at full pitch, despite the need to fight on several fronts and to protect a vulnerable rear in Ireland. Lord Wellesley was engaged on the venture of bringing all India under British rule. An army of 20,000 men was sent to Egypt and forced the surrender of the French army there in early 1801. The French aim was to counter the British blockade by closing off all trade and access between Britain and Europe. Russia, Denmark and Sweden formed a league of 'Armed Neutrality' as a form of passive hostility to Britain. It was in response to this that the naval battle of Copenhagen was fought in April 1801, the second of Nelson's great victories won by unorthodox, and in this case disobedient, tactics. Denmark left the League, and shortly afterwards Russia, under a new tsar, Alexander I, renewed its alliance with Britain.

The affairs of Ireland, or more correctly at this time, of England-in-Ireland, would have a powerful and distorting effect on British politics throughout the nineteenth century and into the twentieth. Following the escapes of 1796–97 and the short but bloody rising of 1798, Pitt's government had resolved on the policy of completing British union by bringing the kingdom of Ireland into full parliamentary union with England and Scotland. By dint of diplomacy, promises, machinations and bribes, this was achieved in 1800. A hundred members of the Commons, four bishops, and twenty-eight peers expanded the parliament at Westminster, and the union flag assumed its present aspect, with the diagonal red cross of St Patrick integrated with those of St George and St Andrew. This might have been a triumph for Pitt, but it also brought about his downfall. Among the promises had been that of lifting the laws still in place restricting the rights of Roman Catholics. The good understanding between Pitt and George III that had gone on for sixteen years foundered on this. Claiming that to give his assent would be a breach of his coronation oath, the king absolutely refused. Pitt consequently resigned in March 1801, to the chagrin and dismay of many who were not Catholics, but with his departure from power, Fox and his associates again began to take an interest in active politics. Meanwhile the king requested Henry Addington, 'a vapid nonentity' in Sir Charles Oman's words, to form a government.

A BRIEF INTERLUDE

On 25 March 1802 a peace agreement was signed with France, Spain and Holland, in the Treaty of Amiens. Addington has been criticised for having conceded too much, though there was no position of victory to dictate from. Ceylon and Trinidad were gained from Holland and Spain, but conquered French colonies, including those in India, were restored. Britain recognised Bonaparte's Consular regime. Among the wealthier and more cultured, there was great relief that once again the 'Grand Tour' through Europe could be safely undertaken, and a string of 'milords', antiquarians, and youthful aristocrats or plutocrats with their tutors set off on the way to Paris, Florence, Rome and Naples. The peace was brief, however. On 12 May 1803, war was declared on France, following increasingly hostile remarks and actions by the First Consul. Around ten thousand British citizens were caught by the announcement and impounded in France for the eleven-year duration of the war.

THE PRINCIPAL PROTAGONISTS

For the first time in a foreign war, the nation had a single individual on whom to focus its sense of hostility and fear. Not since one half of the English had reviled Cromwell as regicide and wrecker had there been such concentration of spleen. Bonaparte was the great bogeyman, finding his way even into the nursery:

> Baby, baby, naughty baby,
> Hush, you squalling thing, I say;
> Hush your crying, or it may be
> Bonaparte shall pass this way.

The Corsican Ogre was described as a pervert, a brigand, a murderer, as incestuous, atheistic, and identified by some as the Beast of the Apocalypse. Government propaganda encouraged this, though much of it was spontaneous, caused by reluctant acceptance of renewed war and anger with the man seen as the cause of it. Income tax, which had been imposed to help pay for the war in 1799 and had been lifted with the Treaty of Amiens, was promptly reimposed. 'There had suddenly blazed up in the breasts of millions a fierce, unenquiring, unappeasable detestation of the individual,' wrote a contemporary, General Bunbury. No doubt Napoleon's assumption of absolute power had a lot to do with this attitude, in a country which prized the principle of hereditary monarchy. By this time George III, aged sixty-four in 1802, was far from well, and his bouts of insanity were increasing in frequency. To most of the English he was 'the good old king', his responsibility for the American debacle forgotten or forgiven in the light of his personification of traditional values. Across the Channel, everything was being turned topsy-turvy from the administrative system to that of weights and measures. Fear of Napoleon was perhaps as much the fear of change – change imposed by decree from above – as of military conquest. Change was endemic in English society, but it was happening from within, from a widespread mass of individual efforts that were rapidly linking themselves and being linked into a national system of industry. In 1804, the year in which Bonaparte was crowned as Emperor of France, Richard Trevithick built and ran the world's first railway locomotive.

As with the Whigs in the previous century, the sense of an assured Tory majority in parliament began to lead to factions and splits within the ruling party. The Whigs, out of power and influence while the king lived or was deemed capable of performing his role, were restive at the thought that at any time he might be removed from the scene. Their political patron, the Prince of Wales, was even more restlessly aware of these contingencies. Infighting among Tory leaders saw the ailing Pitt restored to the premiership in 1804; he had hoped to prosecute the war with a coalition government including the Whig George Grenville who had served as Foreign Secretary in his first government, and even Fox; but the continuing dispute with the Whigs over Catholic emancipation prevented that, and he presided over a divided Tory party.

WAR BY LAND AND SEA

In 1803–04 the threat of invasion was a national preoccupation. Pursuing the policy of 1801, Napoleon sought to impose the 'Continental System', closing off every European port to British trade. The entire coastline from Jutland to the Adriatic was under his control, with the exception of Gibraltar. Active preparations for an invasion were going on along the Flemish coastline, while an army 160,000 strong drilled in readiness. Defensive Martello towers, named for a prototype at Mortella in Corsica, were built along the south and east coasts and other fortifications were made or reinforced. The depleted Royal Navy was placed at full stretch in a resumption of the blockade policy, while ships were also needed to support the war in the colonies and on the high seas. Between the regular army and militia volunteers, Britain had about 175,000 men under arms, nothing like enough to face the military might of France, with a much greater population. To divert invasion and to enforce victory, a coalition with other powers was essential, and the Pitt government set about the business of assembling one. In the summer of 1805 Russia and Austria were again brought into alliance, along with Sweden, but Napoleon's military genius destroyed the coalition at Ulm and Austerlitz.

Despite the resumption of war within Europe, including two futile British ventures in southern Italy and Pomerania, Napoleon did not remove his attention from the plan to invade England. His huge fleet of landing craft and gunboats needed the protection of men of war, and a clever strategy was devised to break the Channel blockade. The French battle squadrons at Toulon, Brest and Rochefort were instructed to break out and make for the West Indies. Their arrival there would undoubtedly draw a massive British response. The breakouts were uncoordinated and led to fruitless naval chases across the Atlantic and round the coast of Spain during most of 1805. By the end of August, having learned that the bulk of his navy had failed to make the Channel and was anchored with the Spanish fleet at Cadiz, the emperor suspended his invasion plans; the Armée d'Angleterre became the Grande Armée and turned its attentions on Britain's coalition partners. The Combined Fleet at Cadiz was later given new orders, to enter the Mediterranean in support of the army in southern Italy. On 19 October Admiral Villeneuve led a combined French and Spanish fleet out of Cadiz, to be met by the waiting British under Nelson and Collingwood. With the prospect of invasion now removed, Nelson was not, as Admiral Jellicoe was to feel himself in 1915, the only man who could lose the war in a day; but he was profoundly aware that the battle must be decisive. He wanted, not 'honourable victory', but 'to bring Bonaparte to his marrow-bones; numbers only can annihilate'. The numbers were relatively even. On 21 October the twenty-nine French and Spanish ships of the line were attacked by twenty-seven British ships. Nelson's battle plan was a new one in naval tactics, to break through the enemy's line in two places, destroying the ships in the middle and rear before turning on those of the vanguard. Though not without risk, it was fully vindicated by a victory which left only ten ships of the Combined Fleet to struggle back to Cadiz, but, for the British, it was gravely marred by the death of Nelson himself. The victory at Trafalgar sealed British mastery not only of the seas off Europe but of the world's sea-lanes. Despite some embarrassments at the hands of the United States in 1812–13, this supremacy would not be seriously challenged until the rise of imperial Germany.

HERO OF TRAFALGAR

The English attitude towards Lord Nelson was something completely new, and was felt at the time to be extraordinary. To a modern reader it is instantly recognisable: this smallish, battle-scarred man, bereft of an eye and an arm, had star quality in abundance. He knew it in himself; it was one aspect of his energy, perception and drive. The heightened atmosphere of the time, with the population and politicians (if not the admirals) still believing in the possibility of invasion, made him, already the victor of the Nile and of Copenhagen, the focus of public hopes and fears.

There were scenes of almost religious adulation as he left Portsmouth to assume command of the fleet off Cadiz: 'I had their huzzas before,' he said to his flag-captain, Hardy, 'I have their hearts now.' When he reached the fleet,

Horatio Nelson

according to Rear-Admiral Codrington, 'a sort of general joy was the consequence of his arrival'. The expression of emotion on the news of his death and at the solemn state funeral, unrivalled as a spectacle until that of the queen-empress, Victoria, in 1902, was equally strong. The only other figure of the war to command a similar degree of public excitement and veneration – though not, of course, in England – was the Emperor of France, Napoleon.

The Nelson factor shows a sense of national self-awareness different to any previous form. There had been popular and charismatic figures in national life before. There had been moments of crisis – the time of the Spanish Armada in 1588 is perhaps the closest parallel, when national expectations were keyed up and a chain of beacons blazed from the south coast to Skiddaw to spread the news of victory. Communications in 1805 were not much faster than they had been in the late sixteenth century: it was sixteen days after the battle that Lieutenant Lapenotiere arrived in London with Collingwood's dispatches to the Admiralty. No journalists sailed on HMS *Victory* to give on-the-spot reporting. The difference was made by the scale of the war and every community's sense of involvement in it. About one in fifteen of all able-bodied men were in the armed forces; even a parish of a thousand people would have over twenty; and by 1803 there were also 347,000 men organised in volunteer forces. In former times, the war-chest was filled by the wealthy; now, income tax and high prices reminded everyone that the war was being paid for directly by everybody who earned money. The war was being directed by an elected government, answerable to a parliament whose debates were published for all to read, not a remote and secret royal council.

THE SUCCESSORS OF PITT

William Pitt made a brief but memorable speech to the Lord Mayor's Banquet that year, when he was hailed somewhat prematurely as the saviour of Europe (a Europe then firmly in the grip of Napoleon): 'England has saved herself by her own exertions, and will, I trust, save Europe by her example.' Ten gruelling years of war still lay ahead, but Pitt himself died in January 1806. The social repression, the climate of spying and informing, the judicial bullying, the hangings and transportations that characterised the domestic policy of his war government have clouded the reputation of one who began as a reformer, and whose peace-time government laid much of the foundation of the modern constitutional monarchy with a sovereign parliament which nevertheless acknowledges the unique status of the king or queen.

Pitt was succeeded as prime minister by William Grenville, who formed a coalition ministry 'of all the talents', including Fox, who was Foreign Secretary. This government achieved one of the ailing Fox's great aims, which he had once shared with Pitt, and which had long been campaigned for by William Wilberforce, the abolition of slavery within British dominions.

Fox died in September 1806. A new generation of politicians had emerged, occupying a spectrum of views from the reactionary conservatism of Lord Sidmouth, who had been premier as Mr Addington and who would be a repressive Home Secretary between 1812 and 1822, to the somewhat more liberal George Canning, the nearest thing to a political heir of Pitt. But the balance of successive governments was towards a socially intolerant and anti-reformist

A medal struck to celebrate the abolition of slavery

policy at home, and dogged if uninspired and uninspiring conduct of the war abroad. Though Whigs or Whiggish figures occasionally served in them, these ministries were Tory-led and dominated by Tory ideas. Even when George III became permanently incapable in 1811, and the nine-year regency began, the conditions attached to the Prince Regent's position and his own drift towards Toryism stopped his predilection for the old and by now almost extinct rakish element of the Whig tradition. As regent and king, George IV is remembered chiefly for his squalid personal life, which brought the royal family, if not the monarchy, into extreme disrepute, and as the figurehead of the 'regency' period in which social affectation and a preoccupation with superficial etiquette cloaked a low standard of ethical and moral behaviour. His brother, the Duke of York (and Commander in Chief of the army) was revealed by a discarded mistress to have profited personally by selling officers' commissions.

NAPOLEON ON THE DEFENSIVE

With invasion of England not an immediate prospect, Bonaparte's imperial government determined on a full implementation of the Continental System, shutting off every continental harbour to trade from Britain. As Britain was the entrepot for most transoceanic goods, the result of this was to cut off France and its allies and conquered territories from sugar, tea, coffee and chocolate as well as the machine-made textiles and other manufactured articles from British factories. A huge smuggling industry grew up and the French government was obliged to license merchants to trade with the enemy. International relations with neutral countries, particularly the United States of America, were soured by British arrests and inspections of their ships on the high seas, to prevent them from trading with blockaded France. Many American ships had British naval deserters among their crews, and these, if recognised, were summarily hauled off and reintroduced to the naval regime they had fled from. Meanwhile a new front of war had opened up in the Iberian peninsula. In 1807 the French invaded Portugal and in 1808 the conflict widened dramatically when Napoleon had installed his brother, Joseph, as King of Spain, causing a national uprising in protest. A small British force, commanded by Sir Arthur Wellesley, landed in Portugal in June 1808 and inflicted a defeat on the French, led by Marshal Junot. The arrival of a senior British general, Dalrymple, prevented

---

THE BEAU

The life of George Brummell (1778–1840) illustrates the vital aspects of upper-class Regency England. Absorptive and elastic despite an apparently rigid caste structure, the small world of aristocracy and fashion could also be mercilessly excluding. Born the son of a well-off but not rich government official, schooled at Eton, 'Beau' Brummell devoted his life to creating a personal style. The type of the leisurely, cultured dilettante was long established; a predecessor was 'Beau Nash' of Bath in the early 1700s. In 1712 Alexander Pope's *The Rape of the Lock* mocked:

> Sir Plume, of amber snuff-box justly vain,
> And the nice conduct of a clouded cane.

The style had been perfected by Horace Walpole (a son of the premier) in the previous generation. But Brummell made no contribution to literature or aesthetics. His art was to create himself. For a time he was the social arbiter of London society, an intimate friend of the Prince Regent. Anyone 'cut' by Brummell became a social outcast. Even when the Prince Regent became king and dropped his old friend, Brummell maintained his position. In a celebrated but apocryphal encounter, he is said to have been walking with one lord, while the king came towards them walking with another lord. King and Beau ignored each other, but while the king spoke to Brummell's companion, Brummell asked the other: 'Who's your fat friend?'

Naturally, Brummell did not work. His income came from a modest inheritance and from successful gambling at the card table. But it could not maintain his position, and his bubble burst in May 1816, when he fled to France, leaving huge debts of between £40,000 and £50,000, mostly to London tradesmen who catered to high society. Never able to return, he lived first at Calais, then at Caen. By the late 1830s he was an impoverished, pathetic and forgotten figure, suffering from premature senility and finally taken to the sanatorium of the Sisters of Charity to die.

His career prefigures that of a range of other originals, in the nineteenth and twentieth centuries, who emerged to shine brightly in English society and then make an inglorious or disgraced exit. Oscar Wilde, Horatio Bottomley, Robert Maxwell, in their various ways are prime examples, all 'outsiders' combining aspects of genius and fatality. Somehow the conditions of English life provide a Big Top for such social or financial tightrope walkers to show off their funambulistic skills – but there is no safety net. A country rich in cautionary proverbs also enjoys watching the spectacular risk-taker. (*See also* 'Horatio Bottomley'.)

Wellesley, whose Indian campaigns made him a mere 'sepoy general' to Whig critics of the government's strategy, from following up his victory. Although Junot conceded possession of Portugal, there was a court of inquiry, Dalrymple was relieved of his command, and Wellesley returned to lead the army. Meanwhile Napoleon himself, with the Grande Armée, had established firm control of Spain. For six years, under two able generals, Sir John Moore who was killed at Corunna in January 1809, and Wellesley, elevated in title to Viscount Wellington (though he said he would have preferred to receive reinforcements), a British force that never exceeded 30,000, with the aid of Portuguese and Spanish militias and irregulars, harassed, held at bay, and inflicted defeats on the French imperial troops, who numbered around 200,000. The government was embarrassed by the Walcheren expedition, an abortive British invasion of Flanders under Pitt's brother, Lord Chatham, in mid-1809, when 11,000 out of 40,000 men went down with marsh fever. In 1809–10 Wellington held the army of Marshal Masséna at the fortified lines he had had built at Torres Vedras, protecting Lisbon, until the French were forced to retreat.

The Continental System was a severe test of endurance on both sides. From 1807, Russia had been in alliance with France, but the combination of the British blockade and the self-imposed sanctions against British imports created enormous dissatisfaction and unrest. The alliance collapsed, and Napoleon declared war on Russia. In June 1812 he invaded with an army of 600,000 men. By January 1813 he was back in Germany with a remnant of barely 60,000. The Prussians rose against him and he was obliged to draw troops from Spain, where in 1812 Wellington had already won a string of significant victories. By the end of 1813 Wellington had defeated Marshals Marmont, Jourdan and Soult, and the French were driven from Spain. In October 1813, the Austrians, Prussians and Russians won a decisive victory at Leipzig. After these events, the Allies began conferring on a peace settlement. In April 1814, with the Austrians, Russians and Prussians victorious to the east, and with the British advancing from the south-west, where Wellington had defeated Soult at Toulouse, Napoleon was forced to abdicate.

A SECOND AMERICAN WAR

The stresses of the Continental System led in 1812 to a second American war. The British blockade policy had long infuriated the Americans, who had developed their own export trade but who were also Britain's biggest export market. The ministry, headed by Spencer Perceval from 1809, did little to placate the Americans, despite much agitation from British commercial and industrial interests, and they finally declared war on Britain in 1812. Invasions of Canada were beaten back three times, but British naval pride received a severe jolting by a number of frigate actions in which individual British vessels were captured by Americans. Perceval was shot dead in the House of Commons on 11 May 1812; as his assassin was a bankrupt who blamed the government for his losses, the prime minister himself fell victim to the effects of his government's policy. With the end of war in Europe, substantial reinforcements were sent to the United States. Washington was burned down in 1814, but British armies were held off in New York State and beaten at New Orleans. As the original cause of the war was now effectively removed, peace was signed on 24 December 1814, though relations between Britain and the United States remained difficult for much of the nineteenth century.

WATERLOO

After less than a year's exile to the island of Elba, and while the Congress of Vienna was still discussing the post-war dispensation in Europe, Napoleon Bonaparte landed again in France, on 1 March 1815. There the Bourbon dynasty had been reinstated in the person of the elderly Louis XVIII, who fled the country when it became clear that the ex-emperor had won over the army. Napoleon promised a liberal constitution and asked for peace with the countries of Europe. A strong section of Whig opinion, hostile to the restoration of the old regime in France, was in favour of negotiation, but the ministry, headed by Lord Liverpool, joined with the continental powers, Prussia, Austria and Russia, in declaring war. British and Prussian forces were mustered to converge in Belgium to make an invasion from the north. Napoleon, with his old speed and resolution, set out to strike first, before the allied force could be effectively merged. In mid-June 1815, he drove the Prussian army, under the veteran Marshal Blücher, off its planned course in two hard battles. Wellington, made a duke for his Peninsular War triumphs, at the head of a combined army of 67,000 British, Dutch and German troops, was forced to retreat to keep in contact with the Prussians.

Napoleon believed that the Prussians were in retreat to Germany and sent 33,000 men under Marshal Grouchy in pursuit. In fact the Prussians were regrouping not far from the position taken up by Wellington at Waterloo. On 18 June the Grande Armée, 74,000 strong, was ranged against the allied force in a day-long battle which was, as Wellington remarked after eventual victory, 'the nearest run thing you ever saw in your life'. The arrival of the Prussians after some five hours of intensive bombardment and cavalry and infantry charges enabled Wellington to regroup his centre which had been broken by successive attacks by Marshal Ney. A final push from the French side failed to break through, and at sunset, Wellington ordered a general advance which resulted in the disintegration of the French formations; Napoleon left the field, and the battle ended in a rout. On 6 July Wellington and Blücher entered Paris. Napoleon, having abdicated for the second time, fled across France to Rochefort, where he surrendered to the Royal Navy. HMS *Bellerophon* took him first to Plymouth, then to the permanent exile of St Helena.

THE AFTERMATH OF THE WARS

Louis XVIII returned to Paris, and the Congress of Vienna resumed its sessions. The leading British representative was the Foreign Secretary, Lord Castlereagh. It was twenty-six years since the French Revolution had begun. Castlereagh's brief and his own personal mission were to ensure that there would be a balance of power in Europe to prevent a Napoleonic-style hegemony in the future. The victorious powers, in the words of Norman Davies in *Europe: A History*, 'resolved their differences by compensating the disgruntled at the expense of the defeated'. But France, largely at Britain's urging, escaped heavy reparation: it lost very little land, retaining its frontiers as they had been in 1790, and was made to pay an indemnity of 700 million francs, while an army under Wellington's command was to occupy certain key fortresses for five years. The effect of the Congress of Vienna was to confirm the position of the old-established monarchies and empires, most of them both reactionary and despotic. 'Republics are out of fashion,' commented the Russian tsar.

In the minds of all the chief delegates, reform and revolution were virtually synonymous. The example of France was there to show how reform could get out of hand and create a monster: hundreds of thousands of lives had been lost, the warring nations had come perilously close to financial bankruptcy, social disruption and political chaos. All the carnage, dangers, horrors and evils of the war could be traced back, by the tradition-minded, to those fatal three words that had inflamed the Parisians: 'Liberty, Equality, Brotherhood!' There was no one at Vienna who cared to examine the causes of the French Revolution or to consider whether Britain had striven so painfully for more than twenty years merely in order to return Louis XVIII to the throne of his forebears. Compared to the tsar and the Austrian chancellor, Count Metternich, Liverpool and Castlereagh were almost libertarians. But they, with the solid backing of Wellington, the 'Iron Duke' who was an admired and respected national figure though not a beloved national superstar as Nelson had been, were united in the view that to concede political or social reform was to invite the worst excesses of revolution. They had successfully managed the war, but now they were to find that the peace was equally demanding and difficult, and in some ways more so. 'You cannot mend the roof while the gale is blowing,' an opponent of reform had said in the 1790s, but now the gale had ceased.

CHAPTER TWELVE

Resistance and Reform

THE NEED FOR REFORM

> I met Murder on the way –
> He had a mask like Castlereagh,
> Very smooth he looked, yet grim,
> Seven bloodhounds followed him.

The voices of reform in England were many and various, and their tone was equally diverse. They included the poetic protest of Percy Bysshe Shelley in 'The Mask of Anarchy', from which the lines above are quoted, and the derisive satire of his friend, Lord Byron, in 'Don Juan', comparing the gifts lavished on the Duke of Wellington after Waterloo with the hunger of unemployed ex-soldiers:

> And I shall be delighted to learn who,
> Save you and yours, have gain'd by Waterloo?

They also included the robust plain prose of William Cobbett, a journalist of genius whose radical sentiments sprang from an old-style Tory patriotism and whose journal *The Political Register* was (unlike Shelley's poems at the time) widely read. Corruption in politics and public life was Cobbett's main target, and his appeal was aimed not at a small highbrow public but at the 'free-born Englishman' whose worth and independence were being eroded by the evils of the time: industrialisation, the philosophy of utilitarianism, and the rich, self-perpetuating, self-rewarding oligarchy which controlled the Houses of Parliament. Between 1816 and 1820, the *Register* was reputed to sell over 40,000 copies a week and its contents were read by, or read to, up to

Lord Byron

Lord Liverpool

ten times that number. After the years of war there was both demand for and expectation of change.

For Lord Liverpool's government, there were a number of issues to address. One was the colossal cost of the war. The national debt was around £860 million in 1816; in *The Common People* G.D.H. Cole and Raymond Postgate reckoned that 'each citizen of the country owed his fellow-citizens nearly £45' – this was at a time when agricultural wages were falling from a wartime high of sixteen shillings a week to a level of eight or nine shillings, less than £24 a year. On this basis the involuntary 'debt' was more than two years' wages. And, as these authors point out, it was chiefly from the poor that the government was to claim the funds. Income tax, which, although widely dodged, was collected from the wealthier citizens, was abolished immediately after the war's end.

The government needed to raise £31,500,000 each year simply to pay interest on the national debt. Tea, sugar, beer, soap and candles were all heavily taxed. Another important concern was corn prices. The prices of most commodities fell after the war. But in 1815, at the urging of the strong farming interests represented in parliament, a Corn Law was passed, forbidding the import of corn unless the price rose above £4 a quarter (or £3 10s. in the case of wheat from Canada). The result of this was to keep the price of bread artificially high at a time of plummeting wages and high unemployment.

A further issue for the government was law and order. Over three hundred thousand men returned from the army to civilian life to find that a slump in demand both at home and abroad had drastically reduced industrial production. There were few jobs to be found, and wages were very low. Factory owners preferred to employ women and children, who were cheaper and more controllable. The government did not see unemployment as a matter for its attention, but it was concerned about the unemployed as a source of public disturbance. There was already industrial trouble for another reason. The invention of the power loom had placed the thousands of cottage-based hand-loom weavers at an increasingly severe disadvantage. Factory production did not monopolise the industry but left a varying, marginal amount of work for the hand-loom weavers. In a period of slump, this meant destitution for the weaving households, whose numbers had greatly increased through immigration from Ireland.

Competition for work in a declining market led to a breakdown in the traditional system of apprentice and journeyman. From 1811 the 'Luddite' movement arose in Cheshire, Lancashire, Nottinghamshire and Yorkshire. It was not a campaign against new machinery as such, at least not in its initial stage: the machines of employers who broke the rules were smashed. The machine breakers, supposedly led by the elusive 'Ned Ludd', appeared to be well organised and had the passive support of their fellow-workers.

TIGHTENING THE GRIP

Faced with such a raft of problems, the response of the government was to behave as if there was still a war going on. The machinery of surveillance, informers and *agents provocateurs* was expanded. The law of habeas corpus was suspended in 1817–18 and supposed or actual revolutionaries put in jail without trial. 'Gagging Acts' forbade public meetings except those licensed by magistrates, and magistrates were instructed to use 'the utmost severity' in dealing with any subversive behaviour. Local yeomanry troops were called out to clear the streets of angry people in the new manufacturing towns. In early 1817, the 'Blanketeers' March' to London of unemployed Lancashire weavers, intending to present petitions to the Prince Regent, was harassed and stopped by military action, and a few 'rebel' weavers from Derbyshire, marching on Nottingham, were caught by soldiers: four were hanged, others transported or imprisoned. In August 1819, the reformist campaigner Henry Hunt was addressing a meeting of some 80,000 people at St Peter's Fields, Manchester, when mounted yeomanry and regular cavalry attacked the gathering. Eleven people were killed and many injured by horses' hooves and sabre cuts. 'Peterloo' by the standards of some other governments was a small-scale event, but it reverberated deeply among English workers. The government rushed further legislation into being, the 'Six Acts'. Among the provisions were heavy penalties for seditious or blasphemous journalism, and an extension of the tax on newspapers to all periodical publications – an attempt to stamp out the reformist press, which was largely defied, at the expense of numerous jail sentences and fines. The unmasking of the 'Cato Street Conspiracy' of 1820, in which a band of extremist reformers plotted to assassinate the cabinet, lent some justification to the government's crackdown.

Restoration of the gold standard, in 1819, was the main element in economic policy, and, like most aspects of the Liverpool government's thinking, it betrayed a yearning for the old days before 1792, when Pitt had presided over a prosperous and peaceful country. Like all such nostalgic views, it omitted any sight of the problems that Pitt had ignored or failed to resolve, almost all of which, in a more modern guise, remained, and now demanded

---

THE *ROCKET*

The Rainhill trials of October 1829, held to determine whether any steam locomotive could satisfy the conditions laid down by the Liverpool and Manchester Railway, attracted interested parties from as far away as the United States and Russia. Many people believed that fixed engines and cable haulage were the only answer to climbing gradients on railways. The *Rocket* proved them wrong. Built by George and Robert Stephenson, its working parts anxiously tweaked and twiddled right up to starting time, it triumphantly satisfied the requirements, won the £500 prize, and generated an order for eight more of its kind to operate the new line. England had already begun to export locomotives, but the success of the *Rocket* brought a surge in demand from Europe and North America. The steam locomotive literally opened the path for an enormous range of industries and social activities.

---

action. From 1820, as economic recovery gradually began, and the panic sense of an imminent revolt decreased, the government began taking some account of these.

PHILOSOPHERS AND SCIENTISTS

If government was relatively devoid of original ideas, it was not because these were lacking in the country beyond Whitehall. The first official census of the population, in 1801, had established it at eight million. By 1821 it had increased by half as much again. This was partly due to the stream of economic migrants from Ireland, but also to a much increased birth rate and to a steady increase in the survival rate of babies and infants, though this varied widely from place to place. The average life span was getting longer. Influenced by Thomas Malthus's *Essay on the Principle of Population*, of 1798 and 1807, administrators believed that population tended to increase to a point where food supplies would be insufficient, unless preventive checking was undertaken. Inability to conceive of such measures meant a degree of official fatalism in the face of food shortages. A key sentence in Malthus's thesis was this: '. . . as the provisions of the country must, in consequence of the increased population, be distributed to every man in smaller proportions, it is evident that the labour of those who are not supported by parish assistance will purchase a smaller quantity of provisions than before and consequently more of them must be driven to ask for support.' David Ricardo's *Political Economy* of 1817 argued against such protectionism as Corn Laws and in favour of free international trade. Jeremy Bentham, social analyst and advocate of legal and prison reform, and the 'philosophic radical' James Mill believed that society functioned on abstract principles and that social action should be aimed at 'the greatest good of the greatest number': this utilitarianism, developed by Mill's son, John Stuart

Mill, and the public health reformer Sir Edwin Chadwick, would have a great impact on English life.

Lord Brougham, later to be lord chancellor, was a founder of the Society for the Diffusion of Useful Knowledge, which published a vast amount of inexpensive works on economics and industry, generally intended to encourage workers to accept the benefits that technology would, eventually, bring. Prison reform, especially for women and children, was taken up by an ardent campaigner, Elizabeth Fry, from 1813. She was a Quaker, and religious Dissenters had long been associated with reform movements of various kinds; Wilberforce, perhaps the best known, was still campaigning for an end to slavery in the world. Working men's institutes and mechanics' libraries were being founded, their aim usually that of intellectual improvement. In 1824 George Birkbeck founded the London Mechanics' Institute, now Birkbeck College; and London University was established in 1828 – unlike the two old universities, it was open to Dissenters.

Scientific discoveries were transforming human understanding of the world.

MORAL ARITHMETIC

At its most extreme, the utilitarian view reduced life literally to a 'felicific calculus' or 'moral arithmetic' and believed that the benefits of every thought and action could be evaluated. There were few out-and-out utilitarians, but the basic idea was widely held. For many, it was linked with the materialist, scientific view of the universe. Others saw in it the hand of God, setting out universal laws. Either way, there was not much humanity in this philosophy, which bolstered the development of an unbridled capitalism. Part of the great popular appeal that Carlyle and Ruskin had was in their sustained opposition to the notion that people were no more than economic units or pawns moved by impersonal forces. The author of *Utilitarianism* (1830), Carlyle's friend John Stuart Mill (1806–73), tempered the austerity of Bentham's ideas by allowing for social feelings and the varying quality of 'pleasure' in the felicific calculus. In the process he accepted that social life and social progress, while still having a utilitarian basis, were not reducible to formulas. Mill's many writings synthesised most of the intellectual ideas of the century and made him its most important writer on society, its nature and its organisation. His own reaction against the arid utilitarian education forced on him by his Scottish father enabled him to appreciate some of the values of the evangelicals as well as the importance of Samuel Taylor Coleridge's ideas. To intellectuals of the time, Coleridge was more significant as a critic and social commentator than as the inspired poet of *The Ancient Mariner* and *Kubla Khan*. His insistence on spiritual values and on the role of the state in nourishing a national culture were deeply influential.

Although the culture of the nineteenth century can be sometimes seen as formed of great monolithic blocks of thought: utilitarianism, Christian evangelicalism, scientific evolutionism, socialism, there was nothing immutable about any of them. There was a great deal of overlap. Discussion and controversy often became highly intense, and were reflected in the spiritual crises and moments of profound uncertainty and doubt frequently experienced by the greatest thinkers of the age.

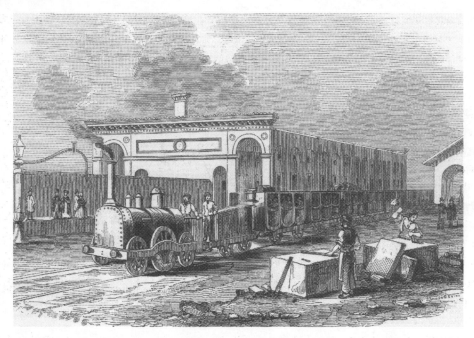

Cambridge Station, 1845

In 1830, Charles Lyell's *Principles of Geology* placed the assumption of a seven-day Creation in the realm of myth or metaphor; and the general, long-held belief in the age of the earth being around 4,000 years ceased to be intellectually supportable. Newton's law of gravity had seemed, if anything, to reinforce the notion of a Creator, but geology and other discoveries in chemistry and physics encouraged a mechanistic view of the universe. Technical progress was speeding up. In 1825, the world's first public railway to be operated by locomotives was opened, between Stockton and Darlington; by 1830 when the first trunk line, between Liverpool and Manchester, was inaugurated, the steam locomotive had been greatly improved by the Northumbrian engineers led by George Stephenson. In a great many fields, new ideas, improvements and reforms were under way. The government could hardly remain impervious to the permanent and increasing shower of ideas and initiatives, or be unaware of the bricks and mortar of new institutions that were assuming a role in the national life.

THE ENGLAND OF GEORGE IV

An older institution was immersed in scandal in 1820 when George IV finally became king and his long-estranged wife, now Queen Caroline, returned from residence abroad. The king tried to get parliament to pass a divorce bill and remove her as queen, but popular uproar prevented this. She was forcibly kept away from his coronation in 1821, but her death soon after removed the possibility of a constitutional crisis. With no direct heir, and the prospect of one of the king's brothers, all discredited in one way or another, eventually succeeding, the monarchy remained at a low ebb in national esteem and political influence.

It was caution, conservative-mindedness, and a certain reluctance to interfere with the business of the country beyond preserving internal peace and law, that typified the government, rather than an active policy

King George IV

of repression and determination to stifle every call for reform. Compared to most other countries in Europe, Britain even at this time was a beacon-state of individual liberty, of freedom to speak, write and publish, where an elected parliament could remove the government from power, and where the likelihood of revolutionary violence and bloodshed on a large scale was remote. England benefited from the arrival of many gifted individuals from the autocratic German states whose skills and enterprise helped sustain the growth of industry. Although 1830 is often associated with the start of political reform, the process began before that. It was plain that the changed demographic pattern, with new cities and conurbations growing as fast as speculative builders could throw up terraces of shoddy houses, with railway tracks spreading across the country, with factories now employing hundreds or even thousands of people, had to be confronted, and changes made to cope with an entirely new situation. The novelty was part of the problem. Nobody knew how to administer a new and ever-growing city like Bradford or Birmingham. London had evolved: these had leapt into being. And so much had already happened, or was already under way – how could legislation control new developments when previous things had simply been allowed to happen? A government that could move very fast with the 'Six Acts' when social unrest seemed to threaten property and owners' rights, was timid, reluctant and slow when faced with the need to control and place limits on what the property owners, mine owners and factory proprietors could do. And – unlike the great bulk of the working population – these owners were solidly represented in both houses of parliament, with even those who accepted some need for change being anxious to maintain their position and their dividends.

CAUTIOUS REFORMS

From 1823 Liverpool had ministers in his team who were prepared to address some of the apparent problems. Among them was Sir Robert Peel, whose father had first introduced Factory Acts which dealt with at least the worst aspects of child exploitation in factory and mine work. As Home Secretary, Peel achieved, among other law reforms, the abolition of the death penalty for over a hundred offences, thereby doing justice a service, as juries had tended not to convict anyone who ran the risk of hanging for shoplifting or picking pockets.

As President of the Board of Trade and then Colonial Secretary, William Huskisson played an important part in promoting freer trade, with a substantial relaxation of the restrictive Navigation Laws, though substantial advantages of 'Imperial Preference' were extended to the colonies. The Corn Law was amended three times, with the price falling, to the fury of what William Cobbett dubbed 'the agriculturasses'. Excise duties were reformed, abolished in the case of salt tax; and a huge consolidating Tariff Bill in 1825 repealed over a thousand old and obsolete statutes. In 1824–25 the 'Six Acts' and the anti-trade union Combination Acts were repealed.

George Canning

George Canning, now Foreign Secretary, distanced himself from the autocratic regimes of Europe and supported the independence of Greece from Turkey and that of the Spanish South American colonies. He was prepared to act boldly, and in 1827 British, French and Russian warships, under British command, destroyed the Turkish fleet at Navarino. In 1827 Canning was briefly prime minister, with a cabinet combining the liberal Tories and a number of Whigs, but he died that same year; he was succeeded briefly by Lord Goderich, then by an arch-conservative, the Duke of Wellington.

Wellington was fifty-eight. He had already been a powerful source of resistance to previous policy, especially Canning's espousal of foreign liberalism. British foreign policy went into reverse. But Wellington too had to retain the confidence of the House of Commons. Although Whig members were the moving spirits of the legislation, his ministry saw through the repeal of the old Test and Corporation Acts, finally giving Dissenters the same civil rights as Anglicans. This was in 1828 and in 1829 it was followed by the far more contentious Catholic Emancipation Act. Since Pitt's failure to achieve it in 1800, the question of full civil rights for Catholics – a tiny minority in England but a large majority in Ireland – had dogged successive governments, with its supporters and opponents equally adamant. The duke's natural supporters in the Tory party, all of them opponents of emancipation, were outraged by what they saw as treachery and deception when Wellington and Peel colluded with the Whigs and Radicals to pass the measure, obtaining the king's extremely

King William IV

reluctant assent. For a time, politics were thrown into a state of flux, and there was no clear governing or opposing party. The death in 1830 of George IV and the accession of his brother, the sixty-five-year-old Duke of Clarence, as William IV, led to a general election.

Reforms in other areas of public life inevitably put the unreformed state of parliament into the spotlight. The rotten boroughs, the limited electorate, the open bribery of electors – the continuing existence of all this seemed increasingly indefensible, and though Wellington pledged himself to defend Britain's 'perfect constitution', almost every constituency with a genuine choice returned a reformist member.

THE REFORM ACT OF 1832

Lord Grey, a conservative Whig but a long-time supporter of parliamentary reform, was appointed premier after Wellington's inevitable defeat in the new House, and a Reform Bill was introduced. There were still enough supporters of the old ways to block the bill, and in 1831 a new election was called, giving Grey a comfortable majority in the Commons, but the House of Lords rejected the bill. In the unwritten constitution of the country, they were entitled to do so: only on financial bills was the supremacy of the Commons accepted. But the spectacle of the unelected House rejecting reform of the elected one provoked a storm of protest up and down the land. It was a year of cholera epidemics in towns and countryside, and of economic depression, with unrest almost on the scale of 1819 in some areas, notably Kent, where unemployed farm workers formed gangs under the supposed leadership of 'Captain Swing' and fired hayricks and destroyed agricultural machinery. The Grey government acted against them with unhesitating severity. Agitation for reform combined with protest against the price of corn and the inadequacy of poor relief, and to some observers it seemed that anarchy loomed, with the two houses of parliament locked in immovable opposition. Introducing a new Reform Bill, Grey steered a careful course. His course of last resort was to create fifty new peers, supporters of reform. This would need the king's consent, which was somewhat uncertain; Wellington and other diehards considered military action to prevent the scheme. In May 1832, in the face of an extraordinary effort by the Tories to hijack the bill and put it through in modified form as a Tory measure, Grey resigned. For five days Wellington considered the possibility of forming a government, but Peel would not support him, his party was deeply divided between 'Ultras' and 'Waverers', and he finally yielded to the king's pressure and the force of public opinion. Grey accepted reappointment, and on 4 June 1832, with most 'Ultras' abstaining, the Reform Bill was passed by the Lords and became law. Though the rotten boroughs were abolished and the new towns and cities gained members of parliament, the extent of reform was otherwise not very great. But these fifteen stormy months had created the political nation. The popular leaders who had argued for universal suffrage felt that their cause was advancing. The Whig Party by making itself the party of reform was – whatever its less reformist leading figures might think – committed to further steps. The Tories, riven by these events, subsided into opposition but, under Peel's leadership, would eventually reinvent and regenerate their party. What 1832 showed was that in Great Britain, politics was strong enough, and capable enough, to initiate major reform of the state without recourse to revolution or civil war. There were few other countries of which this could be said.

CHAPTER THIRTEEN

Victorian England

THE CLASS STRUCTURE

> The rich man in his castle,
> The poor man at his gate;
> God made them, high or lowly,
> And ordered their estate.

These lines, now usually omitted, from the popular children's hymn 'All Things Bright and Beautiful' were penned in 1848 by Cecil Frances Alexander, wife of the Anglican Archbishop of Dublin. They serve to show that inequalities and social gulfs not merely existed but were taken for granted as part of the established scheme of things, at least by those on the comfortable side of the gate. In fact social mobility was much greater than such lines suggest. The old resilience in English society, which could be seen in much earlier times, was still there in the nineteenth century. A commoner, even someone born in poverty, could make his way by talent and good luck to the peak of society. Benjamin Disraeli was a prime example. Where once the church had been the means of ascent, now politics, commerce and industry all made occupancy of the castle possible to those who started with few material advantages. The success of the English upper class was in its absorption of such individuals. They assumed its habits, styles and attitudes, and if in the first generation they might be regarded as 'new money' and social upstarts, their children would blend in, by marriage and association, to maintain the social order. This was common ground between Whigs and Tories in politics; if the Whiggish interest tended to come from industry and trade, and the Tory interest from land, there was still a great deal of overlap between the two.

One of the consequences of the Reform Act was the consolidation of England's class structure. A simple breakdown into aristocracy, upper class, middle class and working class does not tackle the complex ordering of the social hierarchy. Its most numerous group was of course that of the workers, becoming ever more numerous as the population was on its way to doubling by mid-century, to double again by 1900. But the working class had its own strata and demarcations, of skilled labour and unskilled, of foremen and journeymen; of house owners and renters, of those in fixed employment and itinerants who sought seasonal work. Workers comprised men, women and children over the

'DICKENSIAN'

The vividness of the descriptions of English life penned by Charles Dickens (1812–70) have made his name part of the language, even if he might not have relished its association with the antiquated and inefficient. Probably the most widely read of all nineteenth-century novelists, his whirlwind activity also encompassed millions of words of journalism and public readings of his own works. The process of reform had already begun before Dickens grew up, but his contribution to its continuing momentum was immense. His short but searing time as a working child, aged twelve, in a London blacking factory, gave him a sense of experience and insight which never left him. Dickens felt an urgent need for reform in the law, in schools, in prisons, in the care of children, in working conditions, in the relationship between the classes. His genius was not to condemn the defects and shortcomings of society directly, but to expose them, and make them both laughable and intolerable, through stories which engaged people's emotion and interest in a new way. The serial publishing of most of his novels, episode by episode, heightened public suspense, sometimes almost to fever point, as with the lingering demise of Little Nell in *The Old Curiosity Shop*. Satire, sentiment, and shock were among the tools Dickens used to show the middle classes the essential individuality and humanity of the working masses, but he was a novelist first and foremost, and this gave him his power to move and influence his readers.

Charles Dickens

age of ten, and the greatest number were at the bottom end of the wage scale. Even if male and over twenty-one, they had no vote: the Reform Act's provision was that an elector must be a 'Ten Pound Householder' in a borough, and a 'Forty Shilling Freeholder' in the country constituencies. Hardly anyone of the working class could fit that requirement; indeed, to do so would place him in the lower reaches of the next socio-economic group. The lowest stratum of those actually working was found in the countryside, among the rural labourers, where a steadily dropping demand for workers – 18 per cent of the working population in 1851, down to 11 per cent by 1871 – helped to keep wage levels low. Until the 1870s these were also among the least organised of any working-class group, with no trade union and no bargaining power to increase their wages or improve their often scandalously bad housing. Picturesque enough from the outside, the countryman's cottage, in the various regional building styles which existed prior to the mass-producing industrial brickworks, was dark, damp and insanitary inside. In towns and cities, the unskilled workers were the lowest-paid. If they were male, they had some hopes of progressing towards the more skilled and better-paid trades, but for women workers there was scant chance of this. They remained as basic machine-minders. These groups also had little negotiating power. With no special skills to offer, they were easily replaceable, especially as the continuing drift of population from agricultural counties like Norfolk and Lincoln into the cities created a permanent supply of fresh labour. Skilled workers – miners, ironworkers, bricklayers, riveters, carpenters, engine-men, plasterers, glaziers and a host of other trades, some very recent – were in a stronger position to claim and hold out for higher wage scales.

WORK, TRADES AND PROFESSIONS

For the working class, a range of new work opportunities arose. Between the censuses of 1851 and 1871, the number of persons employed in domestic service increased from 900,000 to 1,500,000. This in turn reflected another important change, the rise of the professional 'middle' class. In the same period, the number of professional workers rose from 272,000 to 684,000 and continued to rise steadily. These were the teachers, ministers, engineers, industrial designers, accountants, lawyers, borough and county officials, army and navy officers, clerks, factory managers – a largely urban group, living in bigger terraced houses or separate 'villas', and employing at the very least a cook and a parlour-maid. Within this range there was again a definite hierarchy. In the London and North Western Railway's new town of Crewe, built from the 1840s on a greenfield site around the new engine works, the chief mechanical engineer and a junior draughtsman were both of the middle class but a gulf of status and income separated them. On the other hand, one of those junior draughtsmen would eventually rise to the height of command: there was no substitute for the skills they learned on the job. Heredity, considered adequate for the control of vast estates (though of course the question of ownership was all-important here, and all great landowners employed land agents), was of scant value in engineering. Even among famous father-and-son engineers like the Stephensons, the Brunels and the Trevithicks, or scientific clans like the Darwins and Huxleys, individual ability was what counted. Between the 'upper' reaches of the working class and the 'lower' reaches of the middle class there was a broad area of interpenetration. Family groups often spread across both. The Stephensons, though more prominent than most, were quite typical. George Stephenson, born in 1781, the son of a mine worker and first employed

George Stephenson

as cowherd while still a small boy, became the country's leading engineer and railway builder, a man consulted with some deference by parliamentarians and dukes. His son, Robert, an equally gifted engineer (heredity works sometimes) became a wealthy member of the professional class. George's brother, Jemmy, remained an engine driver on the Stockton and Darlington Railway.

For the expanding middle class, new work opportunities were being created by the continuing stream of inventions and technical improvements begun in England or imported from elsewhere, and the increasing number and size of commercial companies. Great Britain was entering its later nineteenth-century phase as the 'workshop of the world', and not only the workshop but the carrier. British shipbuilding developed enormously. Whereas once it had been spread around the coast, dependent on using accessible timber, now it was metal-based and in England concentrated primarily on the Tyne, Thames and Mersey estuaries. The merchant marine and the vast extension of foreign commerce provided a further range of employment. In India and Africa, the small cadres of British colonial administrators would be complemented by the often youthful managers of plantations, harbours, railways, sawmills and mines. The concept of empire was ingrained into the English people at least as much by commerce as by conquest, military occupation, pomp and ceremony.

SS *GREAT BRITAIN*

Isambard Kingdom Brunel (1806–59), son of an immigrant French engineer, has a special place among English engineers because of the grand scale of his conceptions. His railway, the Great Western, was built to a gauge of 7ft (2,140 mm), compared to Stephenson's standard 56.5 in (1,435 mm). The *Great Britain*, designed by Brunel and launched at Bristol in 1843, was the biggest iron ship yet built, at 3,270 tonnes, and the first to be intended for deep-sea voyages. The wrought iron plates of the hull were made at Coalbrookdale on the River Severn. Determined to be at the technological forefront, Brunel changed his design from paddle propulsion to make this the first iron ship driven by a screw propellor. In 1886, with engines removed, it was converted into a storage hulk at Port Stanley, Falkland Islands, and in 1970 was towed back to Bristol for restoration.

THE EDUCATION GAP

Within this great burgeoning of population, industry, activity and national wealth, there was a hidden flaw. England, which had produced the steam engine and Brunel's iron ship, and which had nurtured the intellectual explosions caused by the science of geology and – in 1859 – of Charles Darwin's *On the Origin of Species by Means of Natural Selection*, the England that was among the most literate countries in the world, was falling behind in a crucial field. Education was not something that government considered to be among its responsibilities. It was not in the English tradition for a government to compel parents to send their children to school, or to set standards of attainment either in the old subjects or the new ones. While more centralised

Isambard Kingdom Brunel

regimes in Europe and Russia established technical universities and national qualification systems, the English way was to allow things to happen through a mixture of individual initiatives and the gradually evolving practices of different crafts. This remains the case in medicine even today. Engineers in England began as apprentices, either 'premium' ones whose fathers paid for them to enter the business, or ordinary apprentices who were paid a tiny amount. They learned on the shop floor. The Institution of Civil Engineers, founded in 1818, and that of Mechanical Engineers, in 1848, did not at first set out national standards. The universities, old and new, were more concerned with the humanities, law and divinity than with the sciences and technology, unlike those of the United States, where professors taught commerce, science and technology. In the later decades of the nineteenth century, it was increasingly evident that England was ceasing to be the prime nursery of new technology. If inspiration and application were what got the 'Industrial Revolution' going, technical education was vital in order to maintain it. But technical education in England lagged behind that of other industrialised countries, and as a result the engineer and technician never gained the social respect accorded to doctors and lawyers. In one way the result of this can be seen in Admiral Beatty's words at the battle of Jutland in 1915: 'There seems to be something wrong with our bloody ships today.' Brilliant men, like Sir Charles Parsons, who developed the high-speed steam turbine in 1884, could always break through, but the system did not encourage innovation.

THE GROWTH OF GOVERNMENT

This determined non-intervention in certain aspects of national life was characteristic of the English approach to government, and as such had its positive side as well as a negative effect. Government did not regard it as necessary to tell people how to run their lives, their businesses or their communities. The role of government, around the time of Queen Victoria's accession, was to maintain certain basic structures – the established church, the currency, the common law; to keep domestic peace and order, and to conduct a foreign policy in the best interests of the country.

In the realm of administration, the story of the nineteenth century is of how government, usually reluctantly, at least at first, found itself intervening more and more in every area of national life, until by the end of the century the scale, organisation and involvement of government and government agencies would have staggered and shocked politicians of the era of Canning and the Duke of Wellington.

The first and largest reason for this revolution was the growth and concentration of the population. Immigration from Ireland, Scotland and Europe added numbers to the increased birth rate. Despite the epidemics of cholera and typhus that swept through the close-packed and insanitary towns, and the endemic tuberculosis, the average life span was increasing; despite a horrendous rate of infant and child mortality, more children survived into adulthood. By mid-century, Liverpool, Manchester and Birmingham were all around the half-million mark, and London's population was well over three million. Private enterprise had funded the enormous growth of these places, building hundreds of thousands of houses, often the notorious 'back-to-back' dwellings. Hundreds of thousands of coal-burning stoves and fireplaces added their contribution of smoke and soot to that of the factory stacks. Water supplies consisted of one standpipe for every street or group of streets, fed from a river or pond likely to be polluted by human sewage and industrial effluent. Water had to be paid for and the pipe was often turned on only for a limited period. Domestic sewage systems and refuse collections were non-existent in these places. Even when they had gained one or two members of parliament in 1832, the new cities had no form of administration that could cope with their size and their problems. The streets were unlit and unpoliced. The old parish structure was weakened at both extremes: in some places a parish might have expanded from three thousand to thirty thousand people; in others the population had dwindled from three thousand to a few hundred, mostly elderly and infirm.

Municipal reform began in 1835 with an act providing for local government in the larger towns, elected by all who paid rates, or local taxes. From then on, new functions were continually added to the business of local government, which eventually became responsible for police, elementary schools, water, lighting, urban transport, provision of housing in many cases, and were large employers of labour in their own right. In 1833 a Factory Act had been passed, limiting the number of hours to be worked by children; most significantly, it also provided for inspection to ensure the act was implemented. This was objected to as an infringement of the liberties of the factory owners, but it launched a succession of further social welfare legislation which ended with the abolition of child labour and the institution of universal primary education, in 1882. Also in 1833, slavery, as distinct from the already-abolished slave trading, was abolished throughout the British Empire. The vast sum of twenty million pounds was paid in compensation to the colonial slave owners.

CONSERVATIVES, RADICALS AND THE PROBLEM OF THE POOR

While Whigs tended to dominate the new urban councils, the parliamentary Whigs were running out of steam. Apart from the tiny radical element, they were not out-and-out reformers. With a profound respect for property rights and for the purpose of business as making money, they had little appetite for adventurous legislation. Yet it was plain that other matters required active government, not least management of the economy. Here the Whigs had few answers; in 1834–35 there was a short-lived Tory administration under Sir Robert Peel, whose reforming of the party as the Conservative Party had incorporated the necessity of a degree of further political reform; then in 1841 a general election returned a Conservative

Sir Robert Peel

majority and Peel succeeded the conservative Whig Lord Melbourne as the country's first reformist Conservative premier.

Peel, whose 'Tamworth Manifesto' of 1834 had spelled out his principle of conserving what was worth preserving, was to make a number of substantial and enduring reforms and policy changes in his term of office between 1841 and 1846. But both he and the Whigs were in accord on one matter, that political and social agitation among the workers must not be allowed to get out of hand.

For the radicals outside parliament, the various reforms accomplished since 1832 merely indicated the huge distance there was still to go. There was a sense of impatience among them, and a new disaffection with and distrust of national politics. Seen from outside, the seven eighths of the population that formed the workers might appear as a rabble, a potential mob, requiring the discipline of the factory hooter, the foreman's stick and the policeman's truncheon, with the musket and bayonet of the infantry and the judge's sentence of transportation or death as a final resort. Seen from within, there was capacity for organisation, not merely on a local, but on a regional and even a national scale. Trade unions were legal bodies.

In 1834 a project appeared for a Grand National Consolidated Trades Union, which would bring the whole working people to unite in a general strike, followed by a peaceful reform of society on an egalitarian basis. Improbable as it was, it attracted the usual official alarm, and six farm labourers were arrested in Tolpuddle, in rural Dorset, for swearing new members into a Lodge which was intending to join the 'Consolidated'. Their sentence of seven years' transportation aroused widespread anger and sympathy for the 'Martyrs', but the great plan collapsed.

A new Poor Law was passed in 1834, following the report of a board of commissioners, who were shocked to find that in some parish poorhouses, the inmates were kept in 'sluggish sensual indolence'. The union workhouse, so called because it served several parishes, was instituted with the express purpose of being as unpleasant as possible whilst keeping the inmates in a state of physical health. Men and women were strictly segregated, even if married. The harsh and retributive Poor Law was the other side of the reform coin, devised and put in action by the same people who fought against urban squalor and disease.

In a country supposedly dedicated to pragmatic solutions, this was the uncompromising theory of utilitarianism put into practice, with Edwin Chadwick and its other advocates believing that by making conditions for the poor almost intolerable, they would encourage them to find work and that wages would rise as a result, thereby procuring the greatest good of the greatest number. This did happen in those areas where the 'Speenhamland' payments

A soup kitchen at Spitalfields in east London

had been subsidising wages. But in many areas that system was not being applied. Unfortunately, too, the philosophy took no account of the real-life effects of a slump in trade and manufacture, which always resulted in large-scale laying off of workers. This duly took place in the period of industrial depression between 1837 and 1842, and often during such times it was only soup kitchens which kept many workers and their families from starvation.

THE CHARTIST MOVEMENT AND THE ANTI-CORN LAW LEAGUE

It was against this background that in 1837, the leaders of radical groups in London combined to draw up a list of six points which they considered essential to the political and social health of the nation, and framed them in a petition to the House of Commons. They were: a vote for every adult male; electoral districts of equal size; a secret ballot in elections; annual parliaments; salaries for members of parliament; and abolition of the requirement for any MP to be a property owner. Five of these eventually became law and are seen as basic aspects of modern democracy; and most people will feel grateful to be spared an annual parliamentary election. In 1837, however, they met entrenched and indignant opposition. In 1838 the six points were formed into 'the People's Charter', and the Chartist movement received its name. Hundreds of local Chartist groups were formed, and hopes were high for a time. As in 1819, a Whig government set out to clamp down, using every means at its disposal, including infiltrators and paid informants. Chartism comprised a great number of disparate interest groups, all of whom subscribed to the six principles but whose further agendas, and methods of achieving them, ranged from the wholly legal to violence and assassination. The popular strength of Chartism is seen in the fact that the original petition, when presented in its massive entirety to parliament in 1839, was signed by 3,317,702 persons. The original leaders were overshadowed by a fiery orator from Ireland, Feargus O'Connor, who was neither an organiser nor a conspirator, and while Chartism remained a prime aspiration among the radical-minded, the heady hopes of 1838 were blown away by the abortive affray at Newport, Monmouthshire, anticipated and stamped out by the authorities in 1839. After that, despite strikes and demonstrations in different English cities, Chartism was wrecked. A second petition was rejected by parliament in 1842 and strikes in Staffordshire and Lancashire led to riots and disorder. While hardship bit deeply into the lives of the English, the government formed by Peel itself resigned – on the young Queen Victoria's refusal to admit some grand Tory dames to the exclusive, influential and wholly Whig circle of Women of the Bedchamber. For two years Melbourne returned to lead a doddering ministry that could not cope with Chartist and anti-Corn Law protest. The Anti-Corn Law League had grown very quickly from its foundation in 1838. Although cheaper corn prices were its great proclaimed aim, in fact it was a free trade movement supported by manufacturing interests,

THE PENNY POST

As the scale of commerce between companies grew in the 1830s, and with the population becoming both larger and more mobile, the need for a proper postal system became pressing. Post had been not only very expensive, but paid for by the recipient. The privilege granted to MPs, of sending their mail free, was widely abused on behalf of their friends. This was just the kind of problem for a utilitarian solution, and a utilitarian was ready, in the person of Rowland Hill (1795–1879), a Kidderminster-born educationist with a keen interest in inventions and current affairs, and a member of the Society for the Diffusion of Useful Knowledge. From 1835 he conceived and promoted the idea of a national flat-rate postage charge, of one penny, using adhesive stamps, and his *Post-office Reform* was published in 1837. The technology was available; the railways were offering a rapid transport system; his problem was to convince the Post Office. In 1840, the flat-rate penny post was introduced. From 1846 to 1864, Hill was secretary first to the Postmaster General, then to the Post Office, and initiated further innovations, including parcel post, to provide Victorian Britain with the most efficient postal service in the world.

The 'May 2nd Penny Black' – the first known posting of any stamp in the world

chiefly the cotton makers of Lancashire. Its leaders, John Bright and Richard Cobden, both emerged from the factory owners, and their 'liberal' radicalism which encompassed free trade had little to do with the popular radicalism of the Chartists.

The backers of the League had little interest in industrial reform; the freedom they wanted was manufacturers' freedom from government controls and tariffs. It has been described as the first important middle-class movement in politics, though its impact was largely confined to the textile-producing districts in the north, and it was identified in particular with the city of Manchester. In 1841 a general election returned Peel and the Conservatives with a majority of ninety.

CONSERVATIVE 'FIRST AID'

Action was badly needed. The budget deficit had climbed year by year for five years; wages had fallen but corn prices had steadily risen; around one-eleventh of the population were paupers by the government's own definition; millions of people lived in a potentially rebellious frame of mind, deprived both of

Richard Cobden, one of the leaders of the Anti-Corn Law League

adequate livelihood and political power. Peel for the first time introduced income tax outside wartime, at first for a year only, at 7d. in the pound (2.9 per cent) on incomes exceeding £150 a year. Duties and tariffs were cut back on a wide range of products. The policy succeeded, or at any rate the depression in trade went away, and the factories and mills began to operate at full stretch again. The country's underlying wealth was seen in the extraordinary 'railway mania' of 1846–47 when, in a fit of passion unseen since the forgotten episode of the 'South Sea Bubble', shares in hundreds of new railway schemes were put on the market, sold and resold at ever higher prices, until the eventual and inevitable moment when it was realised that things had gone too far. The resultant collapse left a few sharp operators very rich but many middle-class families lost heavily in the speculation, and, once again, joint-stock companies were left with a bad name. Peel also brought down the price of corn, though he stopped short of abolishing protection, something his party was unlikely to agree to. Income tax was renewed for three years in 1845 (and has remained ever since) and a further range of tariffs was abolished. Industrial reform excluded women and boys of under ten from underground work in coal mines. There were other slight industrial reforms, an extension of the detested Poor Law, and a horribly revealing commission of investigation into the sanitation of towns, which would result in a substantial clean-up.

Peel's policy defined what many later Tory governments would aim for, with varying success: to provide conservative government which would produce lower living costs for the mass of the working population, and improve the dividends, rents and earnings of the higher paid and those who lived on their incomes without the necessity of work. On the whole, he was successful. Though the decade of the 1840s was remembered as the 'Hungry Forties', and many things were as bad at the end as at the beginning, much had improved. The people worst affected were those in industries left behind by mechanisation or by fashion, like the hand-loom weavers and the cottage-based hosiery knitters. Social mobility took a new meaning with the construction of a national railway network, and William Gladstone, President of the Board of Trade, was long remembered for the provision in 1844 of the 'parliamentary train', costing a penny a mile, which the grudging railway companies were compelled to operate on all their lines at least once a day, so that even the poorest could ride. The railway companies much preferred first-class passengers and freight trains to the 'Great Unwashed' (a description first coined in 1833). And railway haulage brought the price of household coal in London right down, in the process also making the Tyne keels and collier brigs obsolete. As the first really big domestic business concerns, the railway companies dominated commercial life through the nineteenth century.

EMPIRE AND WORLD POWER

By this time, Great Britain was the world's superpower. Though the import, not to say the value, of this may have been lost on those confined in the union-houses or working seventy-two-hour weeks in factories, there is no doubt that the imperial ethos was well ingrained. Pride played its part in this: the old strains of 'Rule Britannia!' from 1740 remained popular and everyone remembered, with the Prussians' role forgotten, that Britain had beaten 'Boney' in 1815. There were few people who did not have a relative, or an acquaintance, in the army, or working as a merchant seaman, or employed in some capacity in one of the colonies. The products of these colonies came in a steady flow – teak as well as tea, copra as well as coffee – and in enormous variety to feed the more sophisticated demands of social life and of manufacturing industry. The territory claimed by James Cook, of convenience for several decades as a dumping ground for convicts, was the vast land of Australia, becoming disenchanted with its allotted role but with unlimited potential. Skilful management and the provision of 'responsible government' had kept Canada as a colony. In India, British dominance was firm. From Delhi, Bombay, Calcutta, Madras, a relatively small group of administrators and soldiers exercised control over the old princely states and vast tribal territories. Africa was in some ways a special source of interest and pride – Britain had stopped the transatlantic slave trade, even if slave-taking was

David Livingstone

still practised by Arab traders, and the churches took a special interest in that vast and still largely uncharted continent, characterised by the work of David Livingstone, ex-millhand, now a doctor, a missionary, an explorer, a reporter, and a national hero.

As ever, the strong threads that bound this British Empire together and to the metropolis, the deterrent to potential antagonists, was the fleet. The Royal Navy was the largest in the world, not one fleet but several, with stations in the Mediterranean, the Far East, the Cape, and the West Indies. But it was in quantity, rather than in quality, that it was superior to any enemy. In 1848, the Admiralty, a deeply conservative body, was still launching wooden warships driven by sail. The example of France, constructing iron-hulled, steam-powered warships, finally pushed the reluctant sea-lords towards steam power and the different formations and battle plans that it both needed and allowed for. Possession of the empire was of tremendous importance. Although the population of Great Britain had grown and was growing vastly, the same was true of other countries – France, Germany, not least the United States of America – and these too had hurled themselves into the technological era, and news of inventions and industrial progress poured from them as much as from England. But the empire turned Europe's great island into a world power: for a time, the world power. Events would show the limitations, as well as the extent, of that geopolitical strength. In the disposition of Europe, Great Britain remained one of four large powers, with France, Austria and Russia. Germany by 1850 had not yet been welded into a fifth. The Ottoman Empire with its territories in south-east Europe was seen as a primarily Asiatic power. But no other country had the worldwide military reach that Britain possessed.

THE END OF A TORY ERA AND THE DAWN OF LIBERALISM

The domestic policies of Peel's government were not such as to appeal to the old landed and moneyed interest which formed a substantial part of the Conservative Party in parliament. But whereas the land and its representatives had historically been the strongest element in the country, by the late 1840s it was plain that, in economic and social terms, England's strength lay chiefly in manufacturing, in mining and in commerce; and the needs of a largely urban population could not be ignored. In May 1846, in the teeth of opposition from his own side, and with Whig support, Peel abolished the Corn Laws. Among his most vocal opponents was a young Tory member, the novelist Benjamin Disraeli, who, as so often among British politicians of that time, combined what nowadays seem to be opposing views, reactionary in some respects, progressive in others. But the rigidity of party lines and the demarcation of party views had yet to be established, let alone enforced. Peel resigned, never to hold office again: 'Thank God I am relieved from the trammels of such a party,' he wrote. The Conservatives split into Peelite and Protectionist factions, the former gradually merging with the Whigs, who were beginning to drop their ancient name and refer to themselves as Liberals. Gladstone was a member of this group. For most of the next thirty years the Liberals, bolstered by their permanent large majorities in Scotland and Wales, and – usually – by the Irish members, would be the governing party at Westminster.

The integration of Ireland into the United Kingdom remained a contentious subject. Agitation for the restoration of an Irish parliament had been strong in the 1830s. For a time it was dimmed by the appalling events of the Great Famine of 1845–49, when the successive failure of the Irish potato crop over several years caused death, disease and misery on a scale unprecedented since the years of the Black Death. The strict Whig principles of the new government of Lord John Russell from 1846, of non-intervention and economic self-help, had to go by the board, though neither official nor the extensive voluntary help of Quaker and church groups could cope with the extent of the catastrophe, and the £9.5 million that the government spent on relief measures was contrasted with the £20 million recently given to compensate the slave owners. From 1849, the movement for Irish separatism resumed.

In 1848, a year of insurrection and revolution across Europe, a third Chartist

---

MARX AND ENGLAND

Karl Marx came with his family to London in 1849 as a political refugee. He had already written the *Communist Manifesto* in 1848, and spent the next years largely in the reading room of the British Museum, researching and writing his most famous work, *Capital*, and other studies of political economy. He was already a close friend of Friedrich Engels, his financial benefactor, scion of a German cotton-manufacturing family, who was the firm's Manchester agent and who had already (1844) written *The Condition of the Working Class in England*, an analysis of industrialisation's effects which was heavily based on the 'Blue Books' of government inquiries and commissions into industrial life. It was not published in English translation until 1892. England, as the world's most industrialised society, was both Marx's great example and his despair. The English working class, so numerous, so much the majority, so exploited, yet seemed so unwilling to move into the revolutionary phase which Marxist doctrine saw as inevitable. Once the workers had thrown away their chains, socialism would displace capitalism, and the state, with all its powers, would wither away in a perfect society in which each gave according to his ability and received according to his needs. Marx lived in relative obscurity in London until his death in 1883: the causes, and small occasional outbreaks, of the class struggle he predicted lay all around him, but the great conflagration had to wait for Lenin and Russia in 1917.

petition was presented to parliament; the six points were still being sought. Despite government fears and precautions, the revolutionary spirit did not catch hold. There were demonstrations and confrontations with the police in Liverpool, Ashton-under-Lyne, Leicester and other places, but efficient police spying ensured the arrest of a group who hoped to emulate in London the successful Paris revolt which had re-established a republic in France. Chartism as a movement disappeared, though its principles did not. Its legacy included a far sharper self-awareness in the working class; one of its remaining activists, George Harney, wrote angrily in his journal *The Red Republican*: 'Every proletarian who does not see and feel that he belongs to an enslaved and degraded class is a fool.' In publications like this, the fundamentals of politics were far more actively discussed than in the establishment newspapers and journals. *The Red Republican* would publish the first English version of the Communist Manifesto in 1850.

SCANDALS, INJUSTICES AND REMEDIES

The governing Liberals, however, were not committed to further reforms; indeed their most eminent economist, Nassau Senior, arguing against reduction of the working day to ten hours, advanced the view that it was in the 'the last hour' that profits were made, and any reduction would bankrupt industry. Such views, akin to the advice of quarrying companies' doctors that slate and stone dust were beneficial to the workers' lungs, may be charitably ascribed to the undeveloped state of their respective sciences. However, by this time proper scientific methods were well established and those who argued for the status quo were choosing their evidence in a highly selective way. Only individual persistence by such figures as Lord Shaftesbury, the most vocal and successful opponent of excessive exploitation of children and women, or gross scandals, like the starvation of paupers at Andover – which caused the replacement of the Poor Law Commissioners by a ministerial Board in 1847 – could achieve even minor reforms. Perhaps the most significant was the Public Health Act of 1848, long pressed for by Chadwick and his associates, establishing a central directorate of public health and enabling municipalities to set up their own boards.

Meanwhile, workers, particularly those in skilled trades, began to turn again to trade unions, of which little had been heard since the Tolpuddle case. Like the original 'combinations' of the previous century, these were more concerned to work out local agreements on wages and terms than to influence political events. In 1844 the Equitable Pioneers of Rochdale founded what was to grow into the Co-operative movement. Though it would eventually have a political arm, its initial purpose was economic, to give its members good food at market prices, and to share the profits in the 'dividend'. The adulteration of food was a serious problem. 'Sanding the sugar' and watering down the beer were ancient complaints, often half-jokes, but the inclusion of alum in bread and of red and white lead as colouring agents in confectionery were harmful to life. Again, through the energy of individuals – in this case doctors using their journal, *The Lancet* – the government was forced into legislation with an Adulteration Act in 1860, though it was not until 1875 that official analysis and prosecution of offenders were regularised. Time and again, against its instincts, but forced by the needs of a complex, mass society, the government found itself compelled to pass laws, to set up agencies, to appoint commissions of inquiry and investigation, to provide for preventive measures and prosecutions. In 1876 the scandal of 'floating coffins', exposed by Samuel Plimsoll, produced the Merchant Shipping Act and the 'Plimsoll line', preventing the overloading of cargo ships. Government pressure forced the unwilling railway companies to install automatic brakes on passenger trains in 1889: the technology had been available since 1876. Unsurprisingly, the later nineteenth century was a wonderful time for lawyers and the various specialisations of their profession.

VICTORIA AND ALBERT

In 1850, the head of state for thirteen years had been Queen Victoria. She was still only thirty-one, and had been married for ten of those years to Prince Albert of Saxe-Coburg-Gotha, her first cousin, the same age as herself, and a highly influential husband, who was awarded the title of Prince Consort in

Queen Victoria

Prince Albert

THE GREAT EXHIBITION, 1851

This celebrated event of 1851, the first 'World's Fair' (full title, The Great Exhibition of the Works of All Nations), was the brainchild of Henry Cole, a leading member of the Royal Society of Arts, and keenly supported by Albert, Queen Victoria's consort. It was set up in Hyde Park, London, in the first industrial prefabricated building in architectural history, the iron and glass 'Crystal Palace' designed by Joseph Paxton. Despite the name, it was intended to display British supremacy in all walks of life, and over half the exhibits came from Great Britain and its empire. But the range of exhibits from other states reflected the success and fruits of free trade and did a great deal to broaden the British people's awareness of the rest of the world. Like all such events to follow, it was denounced as extravagance, by Charles Dickens, Thomas Carlyle and John Ruskin, among others, and for its concentration on material objects. But it was a triumphant success with the general public. The railways ran thousands of cheap excursions from the provinces, and around six million visitors came, many from across the Channel and the Atlantic. It was said that while those who bought expensive tickets came to be seen, the 'shilling visitors' came to learn. A large profit was made, and used to buy the ground in South Kensington on which now stand the Natural History, Science, and Victoria and Albert Museums.

1857. The only previous royal husband had been Prince George of Denmark, husband of Queen Anne. But George was unambitious, indolent and stupid, and Albert was none of these things.

The young queen had at first been greatly influenced by Lord Melbourne and so had strong Whiggish sympathies (as Peel had discovered), but she accepted Albert's vision of the monarchy as being above party. It is likely that the prince, more familiar with German monarchies than the British one, had not anticipated the degree to which that would remove the monarchy from effective involvement in government; but his advice in this case was timely and this attitude, combined with the rectitude of the young couple's domestic life, repaired the rackety reputation bequeathed by the Hanover kings and restored respect for the monarch as well as for the idea of monarchy. Republicanism, though preached by many of the more thoroughgoing radicals, had very few active supporters. The queen certainly did not feel detached from events, not hesitating to give her prime ministers the benefit of her opinions, and her direct influence was apparent sometimes, as when

Lord Melbourne

Lord Palmerston as Liberal Foreign Secretary accepted the 1851 coup d'état by which Bonaparte's nephew became Emperor Napoleon III of France, and was dismissed from his office as a result.

THE CRIMEAN WAR

Palmerston was however back in office in 1852 as Home Secretary, after a brief interval in which Lord Derby had led a Tory ministry. Aged sixty-seven, he remained full of the bullish energy which had characterised his previous actions. No other politician, except perhaps Disraeli, so obviously enjoyed playing the imperial games which Britain's naval supremacy allowed. In 1850 he had blockaded Athens until the Greek government paid a debt owed to a Gibraltarian British subject known as Don Pacifico. In March 1854 the British and French governments, acting in coalition for the first time, declared war on Russia, which had invaded the decrepit Ottoman Empire, and an army and fleet were sent to the Black Sea, eventually combining with the French before the fortress of Sebastopol. Palmerston, the main advocate of the war, benefited by his lack of direct involvement in its disastrous first years. A generation of comparative peace meant that the administration had to relearn, at the expense of the fighting troops and seamen, the business of directing and supplying a war; worse, the generals did not know how to fight one. No Wellington emerged in the Crimea, though there were bold individual commanders in the cases of Sir Colin Campbell and his 'Thin Red Line', and the more idiotic bravery of Lord Lucan and the unnecessary 'Charge of the Light Brigade'. Alfred

---

CONSTITUTION

In 1867 the journalist and social observer Walter Bagehot (1826–77), editor of *The Economist*, published *The English Constitution*, a book which caused some stir. At the time, Queen Victoria's retreat from public life had made the monarchy unpopular and republicanism was widely discussed. Bagehot advanced the startling view that Britain was already a 'disguised republic' in which the monarch had the right to be consulted, to encourage, and to warn – but not to govern. The queen 'must sign her own death warrant if the two Houses unanimously send it up to her'. More seriously, he distinguished between the 'dignified' parts of government, which excite and preserve the excitement and reverence of the population, and the 'efficient parts – those by which it, in fact, works and rules'. Bagehot's analysis placed cabinet government at the heart of the efficient aspect, emphasising its secrecy in discussion and decision-making. He also recognised the genuine cultural roots of the pomp and ceremony of official life: though these theatrical shows served to obscure such realities as the 'despotic power' of the middle classes, and to hold the masses in check, they were also felt to belong to the whole nation. The relevance and accuracy of his views, on the situation both then and now, are still argued over.

The Crimean War – the 'Charge of the Light Brigade' in October 1854

Tennyson, recently appointed poet laureate after Wordsworth's death, captured the public estimation of what had happened:

> Was there a man dismayed?
> Not though the soldier knew
> Some one had blundered:
> Their's not to make reply,
> Their's not to reason why,
> Their's but to do and die:
> Into the valley of Death
> Rode the six hundred.

In January 1855, the British commander, Lord Raglan, had to report that he had 13,000 soldiers sick and only 11,000 capable of action. Newspaper reports enlarged on the horrific details of neglect and incompetence behind this situation. The prime minister, Lord Aberdeen, resigned, and Palmerston bounced into office, adding his own vigour to the general realisation that victory must be planned for, provided for and fought for. In March 1856 the Peace of Paris finally confirmed the British and French victory, though the benefits of the war were unclear. More clear, perhaps, was the curious English indifference to the army which a later poet, Rudyard Kipling, would also comment on. Although

Florence Nightingale

the case for army reform was abundantly clear, nothing was done about it for another twelve years. Whilst no one questioned the need for, and permanence of, the Royal Navy, possession of an army seemed like an encumbrance unless there actually was a war to be waged. The war also produced a national heroine in the person of Florence Nightingale, the reverse of the conventional picture of the vapid middle-class Victorian woman with nothing to do: 'What is my business in this world?' she had wondered, before becoming superintendent of the Hospital for Invalid Gentlewomen in London in 1853. She found out when asked to lead a group of nurses to the Crimea in 1854. In a few months of hectic and strenuous activity as much against the 'fossils' in control as against the appalling conditions, she and her team brought the death rate among the fever-stricken troops down from 42 per cent to 2 per cent. She invented in the process the profession of nursing and the modern hospital, which she would spend the rest of a long life developing and defending against the aggressive self-protection of the male medical establishment.

THE INDIAN MUTINY

Palmerston was to remain prime minister for another ten years, apart from another short-lived minority Conservative administration led by Derby and

The Indian Mutiny – the Storming of Delhi, 1857

Disraeli. Two minor imperialist wars during this period, against China in the promotion of British and French mercantile interests, and against Persian expansion in Afghanistan, were overshadowed by the shock of the Indian 'Mutiny' in 1857.

Consolidation and extension of British suzerainty and direct rule over the many Indian states had continued under successive governors general from the time of the Napoleonic Wars. The run of events had been marked by a substantial defeat of British troops and British interests in Afghanistan in 1839–40, but by 1857 the entire subcontinent was under British rule, though with many resentments and dangerous areas. The English language, British justice, British prisons, British trains, could not cover up the fact that a disparate and often mutually hostile mosaic of peoples and religions was held together by British arms. But there were some 40,000 European troops stationed there, compared to 230,000 Indian. The famous cause of the Bengal army's mutiny, the ignorant or uncaring greasing in England of cartridges with beef fat – product of the Hindus' sacred animal – was a spark which ignited a host of resentments and opportunist uprisings. Their lack of central purpose and leadership enabled the British to fight a series of separate campaigns, while many areas, like the Punjab, remained quiescent. Atrocities to the civilian population were committed on both sides, with the British press naturally giving lurid preference to the carnage of the well at

Cawnpore, into which British women and children had been thrown, dead or alive, and similar horrors. By the end of 1858, British control was reasserted, and government was finally transferred fully from the East India Company to the crown, with the appointment of a Secretary of State.

Palmerston, though he was no friend to autocratic governments and treated the regime of Napoleon III with reserve verging on hostility, was no reformist at home. 'We cannot go on legislating for ever' was one of his dictums. In this respect as in some others he harked back to a more limited and leisured view of government than was possible in the Britain of the 1850s and 1860s. Despite short term fluctu-

William Gladstone

ations, the economy was continuing to expand. Gladstone, as Chancellor of the Exchequer, continued with a policy oriented toward free trade. In 1860, linked with a French treaty for corresponding action there, he reduced or abolished tax on a range of French imports and extended this to the same articles and goods from all countries. Only tea and sugar continued to be stiffly taxed, and income tax was 2.4 per cent. The increases in revenue more than compensated for the reduction in duty. Gladstone's star was rising. By 1865 income tax was down to 1.6 per cent and the tea duty was halved. But in that year, the cotton industry was in acute crisis. The outbreak of the American Civil War in 1861 interrupted the supplies of cotton and tobacco as well as all other goods from the United States. British trade benefited in other ways from the Americans' distraction, however. With a succession of Gladstonian budgets showing an economic surplus, free trade seemed to be the key to economic success. On Palmerston's death in 1865, Gladstone was the natural leader of the Liberals.

THE CHURCH IN VICTORIAN ENGLAND

If one considers the institutions of England alone, within the wider British context – the church, or churches, the law, and education – an interesting perspective on reform comes into view. The Church of England was as much a department of state as it had been in the previous centuries; its bishops were appointed by the queen, its supreme governor, on the advice of her prime minister. Tithes were due to it from all parishioners, whether or not they were baptised into it or attended its services. All bishops were members of the House of Lords. But the most notable thing about the church was its quiescence and lack of involvement in any of the great issues of the time. Gone were the days when archbishops were also first ministers, or risked burning, or sent others to be condemned to that fate. In 1836 payment of actual tithes was replaced by a fixed charge based on corn prices, and the boundaries of dioceses were redrawn to reduce the glaring discrepancies in size and income. The Wesleyans had organised themselves into a separate church. The evangelical trend which had been strong in the late eighteenth and early nineteenth centuries, giving passion to such men as Wilberforce, and which had resulted in the formation of Bible Societies and widespread missionary activity at home and abroad, had subsided.

From Oxford University, always a stronghold of high churchmanship since the time of Charles I, arose a new trend. The Oxford movement, or Tractarians, so-called from their published 'Tracts for the Times', whose leading names were William Keble and Edward Pusey, put a revived emphasis on ceremonial, the sacraments, and the priestly and apostolic tradition. Such ideas, if pursued logically, were not consistent with a state-governed church, and the religious and intellectual communities were stirred in mid-century by the reception of some leading Anglicans, most notably John Henry Newman and Henry Manning, into the Roman Catholic church (both were to become cardinals). Another side of the Church of England was shown in the work of a few Christian Socialist clergymen, of whom Charles Kingsley was the most prominent example. Passionately hostile to the ideas of Newman, they believed in the engagement of the church with the huge social problems of the time. Their trust was in divine providence rather than social agitation, but books like Kingsley's still-read *The Water Babies* (1863) and F.D. Maurice's establishment of the Working Men's College in 1854 helped to promote the process of social reform.

The established church was a lopsided presence in national life. With a strong and honoured place at the upper levels of government and at court, and its buildings at the centre of every town and village, its direct influence on the lives of most people was slight. The chapel at the edge of the community or in the suburbs was often a more vibrant place than the parish church. In 1850, the Roman Catholic church set up its own episcopal structure in England, as it was now free to do, and though there were growls and protests from Anglican and Non-conformist quarters, there were no riots. But the extension of elected local government, and its growing range of responsibilities,

ATHEISM

Charles Bradlaugh (1833–91) was the first professed atheist in English public life. Radical and republican in his politics, he edited a magazine, *The National Reformer*, which was a vehicle for his own ideas. Not a revolutionary, he was elected to parliament for Northampton in 1880. As an atheist, he claimed the right to affirm his loyalty rather than take the prescribed oath which invoked the deity. As a result he was refused permission to take his seat, and forcibly ejected by ten policemen. He was re-elected three times before he was finally allowed to make an affirmation, and represent his constituency, in 1886. Public avowal of atheism in the nineteenth century was rare: belief in God was almost universal, however expressed. It needed an element of personal flamboyance to carry off a reputation for atheism, and in the orthodox nineteenth-century mind it was automatically linked with immorality. Bradlaugh's support of birth control was seen as further evidence of his bad character. The careful and discreet agnosticism of Thomas Huxley, Darwin and many other scientists was far more common than paraded atheism. But the Darwinian and other discoveries inevitably encouraged a materialist view of the universe.

tended to sideline the involvement of church in community; instead there was the involvement of the community – at least of the congregation – in the church. The census of 1851 yielded information which both damaged and distressed both the established and Non-conformist churches: just over half the population of England did not attend church at all.

EDUCATION FOR ALL

One aspect of community life which the churches did control, or heavily influence, was education. Once a prime purpose of education had been to produce priests, and virtually all schools above the level of the dame-school teaching basic literacy were run by clergymen, whether Anglican or Dissenting. Religious education naturally was a large element in the curriculum. From Tudor times the sons of the upper classes had been sent away to school – a privilege they shared with the more fortunate orphans who were brought up in charitable foundations. These schools were notorious for brutality and bullying, and a process of gradual and uneven reform began under Thomas Arnold at Rugby School in 1828: the ethos of self-reliance, team spirit, competitiveness, sportsmanship, responsibility and conformity would influence other schools and certain national institutions, especially the army. The universities of Oxford and Cambridge were open only to committed male Anglicans; all their teachers had taken holy orders. Non-conformists wishing to educate their sons beyond grammar school level still sent them to Dissenting academies, where they were well taught but could not receive university degrees, or to one of the four Scottish universities.

Partly through fear of stirring up religious controversy, of stepping into church preserves, and spending money, the government avoided the matter of national education as much as possible until 1869. But from 1833 grants had been paid from central funds to help maintain church schools, at first only £20,000 a year, but by 1860 it was closer to £1 million. In the 1860s, such children as went to school normally left it at the age of eleven, to begin work. Two million children under eleven, it was estimated, were receiving no education at all. England was lagging far behind other countries in this respect. The United States and Prussia, with universal education, were seen to be moving into leading positions in the industrial and technological fields. France, Austria and Russia had much better technical education facilities. To institute a state education service in England was almost a revolutionary move, but from the radical section of the community there was an insistent demand; and even conservative Liberals like Robert Lowe, resistant to further political reform, could see the need. The Education Act of 1870 brought the state into education, though further acts would complete the process and universal free elementary education was only established in 1891. School boards were set up, with authority to compel attendance. The resultant great increase in the number of schools was significant in providing, for the first time, a large number of jobs for educated women. School education for girls led to the demand for higher education also, and the universities with varying degrees of reluctance – far greater among the old ones than the new ones – gradually opened their doors to female undergraduates. The faculties of medicine, law, and, of course, divinity, were the last bastions to fall.

LEGAL REFORMS AND SOCIAL CHANGES

While the legal profession had readily adapted and enlarged itself to take account of all the opportunities offered by a technological and highly organised society, from patent law to labour law, and in the interpretation of an unprecedented and ever-increasing amount of legislation dealing with industry, trade, and the rights and duties of municipalities and new public bodies, the basic structure of the courts long remained unaltered. Ridiculed in the novels of Charles Dickens, reviled by Utilitarian-minded modernisers, it was only in 1873, with the Judicature Act promoted by Roundell Palmer, later Lord Selbourne, as Lord Chancellor, that the archaic and confused structure was regularised, with the establishment of a supreme court, a court of appeal, and the high court with its separate divisions dealing with criminal and civil matters.

Reform, or modernisation, often seemed like two steps forward, and one step back. Nothing was accomplished without vehement criticism and angry opposition from vested interests or established opinion. A large body of radical and

Non-conformist opinion was infuriated by the insistence of the Education Secretary of 1870, William Forster, on maintaining church schools, which meant that in many places they were obliged to send their children to be taught the Anglican form of worship and not their own, and also to pay for it. When finally under Edward Cardwell as Secretary for War, the army was reformed and the purchase of commissions abolished, another roar of protest went up. The institution of a secret ballot in 1871 was denounced by its opponents as 'unmanly' – an Englishman should be unafraid to declare his interests (the Chartists had known very well how the open ballot led to bribery and bullying).

Benjamin Disraeli

In the 1870s, people could still look back to the era of their grandparents, the time of Pitt, whose England seemed a simpler, kinder, less demanding place. Much was forgotten, or edited out of this picture, but it had great allure. On the other the hand, the onward course of modernisation was leading to – what? There were people in England who discussed how an ideal workers' republic might be established, with ownership and social inequality abolished. Gladstone clung to a deeply held orthodox Anglican view of a state and church in harmony. Disraeli, his great rival from the later 1860s, developed the concept of an empire, benevolently led but firmly administered. Few people were out-and-out reformers or reactionaries.

The most widely read men of ideas, Thomas Carlyle and John Ruskin, reflected the contrary pulls and trends of thought. Carlyle had declared in 1829 that the machine age had arrived, for good or ill. But he idealised the hero-figure or great man in an age when political power was slowly passing to the masses. Ruskin abominated railways and all manifestations of the mechanical age, and preached a return to medieval standards of linked craftsmanship and spirituality. But he also accepted the need for social reform and attempted a practical as well as philosophical programme of improvement of working men's lives.

For everyone, however, the essential implicit message of the times was hammered home by the experience of daily life, by the business reports in the

A Victorian holiday scene – the beach at Brighton, 1859

newspapers, by the observation or reports of what was going on in other countries. There was no going back. More and more labour-saving machines were being invented and manufactured. Gas lighting, piped sewage, clean water supply, all set national standards that everyone wanted to attain. The taste for holidays, outings, better quality food and drink, was easily acquired and led to greater demand. Thomas Cook started the first travel agency by organising a temperance outing, by train, from Leicester to Loughborough in 1841.

In the prosperity of the 1870s, with wages rising and workers in a position to negotiate through trade unions, these developing tastes could be met. There was a distinct, though unplanned, aspect to modernisation, and that was a steady levelling up of some aspects of social life. Occasional events marked it clearly. The abolition of stamp duty on newspapers in 1851 ceased to make them the bulletin board of the wealthy, or the politically active, and encouraged the spread of a regional and national press. The *Daily Telegraph* became the leading Liberal paper from 1855. Another marker was the provision in 1872 by the Midland Railway of third-class carriages on all its express trains. In 1875 it abolished second-class travel and provided padded seats in third-class. This 'pampering of the working classes', learned from the USA, was grudgingly followed by its competitors. Great social gulfs remained, and the structure of classes existed as before. Deference to rank was expected, and even the most modest middle-class households had their domestic servants. But universal education, the mass production of cheap clothing in fashionable designs, and the increasing ability of the working class to purchase items that once were impossible luxuries, from oranges to clocks, from carpets to china dishes, were beginning to blur the edges of social distinction.

POLITICS AND POWER IN THE LATE NINETEENTH CENTURY

From 1865, both political parties sought to identify themselves with reform. To do otherwise would have meant extinction. But both approached the matter cautiously and with reservations. Among the Liberals, the pressure came from the junior ranks. It was being taught to the Conservatives by their effective leader, Benjamin Disraeli, who would take over from Lord Derby in 1869; with Derby's acquiescence he convinced the party that it had to move with the tide. In 1866 the Conservatives came to power, having successfully opposed a modest Liberal bill for electoral reform, and passed a far more sweeping act of parliament that brought virtually all adult males into the electorate apart from the low-income farm labourers. Despite this the Liberals were returned to power in 1868, with Gladstone as premier, and bound to keep up the momentum.

Against a background of falling prices, until the mid-1890s, and a modest rising trend in wages, the sense of national prosperity continued. The great exception was agriculture, suffering both from lower prices and from new and heavy competition from American wheat and Australian lamb and wool. The large steam cargo ship, with refrigeration, transformed the international food trade. The incomes of farmers and landowners fell, and the farm workers suffered correspondingly. In 1872 the National Agricultural Labourers' Union was founded by Joseph Arch, and many from this least organisable section of the working class went on strike in 1874. An influential section of the Conservative Party demanded protection for British agriculture, and 'Protection' joined 'Ireland', 'Free Trade', 'Imperialism', 'Retrenchment' and 'Reform' as battle-cries in the parliaments which saw Gladstone in power to 1874, Disraeli from 1874 to 1880, Gladstone again from 1880 to 1885 and briefly in 1886, a Conservative administration under Lord Salisbury to 1892, and Gladstone's final premiership from then to his retirement in 1894.

Both parties could claim commitment to reform. Though the Liberals would have liked to call it their own cause, Disraeli was too adroit a politician to allow that to happen, and his 1874 administration passed useful legislation on housing, food and drugs. Retrenchment was a Liberal cause, reflecting the old Whig concern to keep down taxes and government interference. Whilst this was a popular theme, it also offered a stick to the Tories. They accused the Liberals of neglecting the navy, and of hazarding Britain's position in the world by penny-pinching policies. There was certainly a strong anti-war and anti-colonialist strain among the more radical members. The Liberals accused the Tories of imperialism, by which they meant adventurism and arrogance in diplomacy and foreign affairs. The Tories however gloried in their own definition of imperialism, which meant preserving, enlarging and profiting from the empire. Always good at sensing and flattering public opinion (in this respect perhaps the first modern British politician), Disraeli made a shrewd move in having Queen Victoria proclaimed Empress of India in 1876. It cost nothing, but was a grand gesture which also, in the British public's opinion, reminded the Germans (Wilhelm I had been proclaimed Emperor in 1871), Austrians and Russians who had the biggest empire of the lot. More expensive was his strategic purchase of the Egyptian Khedive's shares in the Suez Canal, built by the

---

'CHINESE' GORDON AND THE MAHDI

The Mahdi, like Tippu Sultan before him and President Kruger of the Boers after him, was one of those far-off alien figures who not only disturbed the councils of empire but became English household names of menace and dread through their ability to defeat British armies. The Mahdi Mohammed Ahmed, rising against British-backed Egyptian rule of the Sudan, defeated the army of Egypt in 1883. Gladstone's Liberal government was not disposed to have an imperial adventure in the Sudan and General 'Chinese' Gordon (his nickname referring to distinguished service in China), a previous governor of the Sudan, had been sent out to take charge of evacuating the British garrisons. Gordon, a thoroughgoing imperialist with a sense of divine mission as great in its way as the Mahdi's (a messianic Muslim title), decided to stay and hold Khartoum against the rebels whom his prime minister saw as freedom fighters. He was trapped in a five-month siege, his small force vastly outnumbered. Gordon's self-inflicted plight aroused a storm of sympathetic concern at home from the queen down, but not in Gladstone. A relief expedition was reluctantly authorised, slow in its formation and despatch, and on 26 January 1885 the Mahdi stormed the city and killed Gordon and his men. Two days later the relieving force arrived. The Mahdi survived and Sudan remained under rebel rule until General Kitchener's victory at Omdurman in 1898 restored British imperial control.

Gordon became a symbolic victim of the great imperial ideal, with the knife-edge margin of time increasing the drama of his death. It was not until Lytton Strachey's hostile analysis of his character and motives in his celebrated 'debunking' study, *Eminent Victorians* (1918), that the whole episode was re-examined to uncover the tangle of contrary ideas, personal ambitions and animosities, failures of contact between government and army, and conflicting interests within the government, that underlay just one episode in the story of the British Empire.

French in 1869. The $4 million price brought the strategic waterway under British control.

'Empire' as a cause increasingly meant Africa, whose vast, thinly populated extent, potential wealth and perceived need to be rescued by a European form of civilisation from paganism, disease and slavery all offered prospects of colonial empire, not least to Belgium and Germany, while France was establishing its political dominance all along the north. British interest in African acquisitions fluctuated depending on which party was in government, but both had to tackle the problems of southern Africa. The original Dutch colony of the Cape of Good Hope had been under British rule since the Napoleonic wars. From 1835, many of the Dutch-speaking Afrikaners or 'Boers' had moved northwards to found independent republics, which coalesced into the Orange Free State. In 1880–81 the first Boer War ended with British defeat and concessions from the Liberal government, but the settlement was uneasy and made even more so by the discovery of large deposits of diamonds and gold, which brought an influx of European prospectors and adventurers. North of the Boer republics, the British South Africa Company, founded by Cecil Rhodes in 1887, was establishing what would later be Rhodesia and now Zimbabwe.

DISRAELI, GLADSTONE AND
IRISH HOME RULE

The years from around 1865 to 1881, when Disraeli died, have been stamped with the image of the opposition of himself and Gladstone, like two giants dominating the arena. Disraeli's Jewish and literary-bohemian background, his humour, his sense of occasion and feeling for public opinion, and his ability to charm the cantankerous old Queen Victoria make him a fascinating figure, but in the historical perspective the contribution of Gladstone is vastly greater. Without Disraeli, little would have changed; without Gladstone, the history of the British state and English nation would have been very different. He was responsible for the Treasury in its modern form, and his governments broke down most of the barriers denying opportunity to talent and ability. In his progression, untypical then and later, from youthful high Toryism to a mature Liberalism that occasionally verged on radicalism, he was impelled by a moral seriousness which even his many detractors admitted. For Gladstone, politics without a strong moral passion was nothing, which is why he despised Palmerston and Disraeli, and why, despite being a high Anglican, he was greatly admired by Non-conformists. One of Gladstone's legacies was the notion that British foreign policy ought to be conducted on an ethical basis; a hook on which numerous later governments have dangled uncomfortably, notably in 1956, and as recently as 2003. His principles made it possible for him to change his mind, if he saw good reason, and this turned him in the direction of Irish home rule, something he had earlier opposed. Of all the causes that prompted political slogans, it was Ireland which had the most devastating effect on British politics.

Gladstone's conversion to the concept of home rule, with a restored Irish parliament, was taken up with the same moral zeal as his other causes. He had already brought about the disestablishment of the Church of Ireland, in 1868, without serious opposition. But many senior members of his own party were opposed to home rule. Considerations of national security, property rights, and the protests of the unionist Irish, mostly in the province of Ulster, who foresaw themselves permanently outnumbered by a Catholic majority, all played a part. These objections were also held strongly by most Conservatives. From 1883 a bombing campaign funded by the American Clan na Gael spread alarms in England about Fenian terrorism, but also promoted a reluctance to yield to violence. Gladstone's Home Rule Bill of 1886 was rejected by the Commons and split his party into two hostile factions. A Conservative government followed until 1892, when Gladstone, now aged eighty-four, again introduced an Irish Home Rule Bill. In 1893 it passed the Commons but was heavily defeated by the House of Lords. That ended the matter, for parliament, for almost twenty years. The 'Grand Old Man' retired from politics with his final cause unsecured, and his party broken in two – Liberals and Liberal Unionists, the latter increasingly allied to the Conservatives.

THE FRANCHISE AND THE TRADE UNIONS

By 1885, all adult men had the vote and the country was organised into single-member constituencies. In 1888, elected county councils replaced the former system of management by justices of the peace and local boards. In 1891, elementary education was made completely free. Though the secondary education system remained largely voluntary and paid for, there was a wide extension of university foundations, including those of Birmingham, Liverpool, Leeds, Sheffield and Bristol. An ever-increasing expectancy, deplored by Gladstone, of 'constructive' administration meant that government began to extend into many areas it had hitherto ignored. The Board of Agriculture was formed in 1889 and ten years later the Board of Education followed. Nobody had dreamed of controlling horse transport, but the arrival of the motor car led quickly to a national registration scheme. Between 1891 and 1911 the number of persons in government employment, 'civil servants', doubled. In his *English History, 1914–1945*, A.J.P. Taylor wrote: 'Until August 1914 a sensible, law-abiding Englishman could pass through life and hardly notice the existence of the state, beyond the post office and the policeman.' Nevertheless, before the turn of the century many were deploring the extent of government involvement with everyday life.

Others actively sought to increase it. The working classes in the 1880s and 1890s were a much more organised as well as numerically overwhelming group. The 1.5 million or so who had joined a trade union by 1892 had a wide influence among those who had not yet become members. The trade union organisers and political thinkers who led or reflected working-class opinion and aspiration knew very well that every inch of progress they had made had been made possible by government action, even if that action had been slow, reluctant and partial, prompted by pressure, agitation and political rivalry rather than by any enthusiasm to see the workers in a position to choose who governed them. After some precarious and difficult times in the 1860s, the unions felt on safer ground with Gladstone's Trade Unions Act of 1871, which gave them legal status and freed them from being sued for restraint of trade if they took industrial action. A simultaneous Criminal Law Amendment Act however made picketing illegal and made it easy for employers' lawyers to claim intimidation if a strike was called or even discussed; this was amended largely in the unions' favour by the Conservative government in 1875. In 1874 the first working men to be MPs were elected, Alexander Macdonald for Stafford, and Thomas Burt for Morpeth, both miners, elected on a 'Trade Union' ticket and with union financial support. Despite the violent scenes and riots which accompanied many strikes and lock-outs, there was no revolutionary movement among the workers, and no real fear of it among the middle and upper classes. English republicans and anarchists were tiny groups whose shadows loomed large because of the portentous nature of their ideas, and their links with shadowy foreign organisations in countries where the prospect of revolution was much more substantial. The trade unions had achieved a great deal within the law and they were thoroughly respectable bodies. They wanted more, not less, government in order to improve the security and prospects of their members and their families and their own organisations, which were fiercely opposed by most employers and employers' confederations. In the main, they saw the Liberal Party, personified by Joseph Chamberlain, from 1880 its leading radical and 'constructive' figure, as the one most likely to bring this about; another early working-class MP was Joseph Arch, returned as Liberal member for North-west Norfolk in 1885. At this time members of parliament were still unsalaried, which meant that only someone with private wealth or some other form of financial backing could become an MP.

THE BIRTH OF LABOUR AND THE WOMEN'S SUFFRAGE MOVEMENT

The Liberal split over Irish home rule, which saw Chamberlain – a Unionist – in alliance with Lord Salisbury's Conservative government from 1887 was one of the factors which encouraged the development of a new political movement. A Labour Representation League had been formed in London in 1869. 'Labour' then simply meant workers, not any political theory, but through the later decades of the century the concepts underlying a socialist form of government were being worked out, by clubs and groups of which the most influential was the Fabian Society, founded in 1884. The Fabians were an intellectual group; they aimed to reform opinion. Meanwhile some union activists had come to the realisation that neither of the existing political parties was ever going to put the interest of the workers first. Three Independent Labour members were elected to parliament in 1892, and the formation of the Independent Labour Party followed, in Bradford, in 1893.

Suffragettes chain themselves to railings outside 10 Downing Street, 1908

At much the same time, ignored or opposed by most, though not all, of the supporters of democracy and workers' rights, the campaign for women's suffrage, which had existed in a small way for twenty years or more, began to take the form of an organised and widely supported movement. Seventy-three members of parliament had supported John Stuart Mill's attempt to secure votes for women in 1867, but since then the cause had gone into abeyance. A new generation of university-educated women, brought up to discuss all manner of new ideas, was chafing against the refusal of the legal and medical professions to admit them, and their exclusion from public life seemed more and more intolerable. Local women's suffrage groups and societies were formed, but no political party or movement took on their cause. Some of the most vocal opponents were women in leading society positions.

THE BEGINNINGS OF IMPERIAL DECLINE

Neither of these developments seemed of great importance to the leaders of political and social life in the 1890s. The great issues were in foreign policy: the rise of imperial Germany, the division of Africa, the South African question; and in trade, where the Conservatives were beginning to promote imperial preference and tariff reform against the old-standing Liberal doctrine of free trade. Public opinion followed their priorities. The period from 1895 to the end of the century, under Salisbury's Conservative–Liberal Unionist government, marked the high point of British imperialism. The occasions of Queen Victoria's golden jubilee in 1887 and diamond jubilee ten years later were made national celebrations, with great pomp and ceremony. The aged queen-empress, whose long seclusion from public life, following Prince Albert's early death in 1861, had aroused strong anti-monarchic feeling in the later 1860s, was now ensconced as a venerated symbol of British unity and power. The quirks and oddities of her court were forgotten or ignored. One-fourth of the entire human race were the subjects of this diminutive but regal old person, invariably clad in black bombazine, in whose name all the official business of nation and empire was carried out. The granddaughter of George III would survive into the first year of the twentieth century. Like George, she had an heir whose judgement she distrusted and whose habits she deplored: the Prince of Wales had a taste for gambling, ladies and congenial company which was highly reminiscent of George IV and his brothers. It was during this time that German and American steel production overtook that of Great Britain. The long-established industrial lead was slipping away, but business was expanding, wages rising, earning power was high, unemployment was low – in the high noon of empire, Britain seemed unassailable.

Tension in South Africa remained high between the two Boer states and the British colonies, exacerbated by the policies of Cecil Rhodes, who was hungry for a showdown with the Boers. As Colonial Secretary, Joseph Chamberlain was an enthusiastic advocate of a new war. The second Boer War of 1899–1902 was of more significance than other colonial wars. It cost Great Britain £200 million and consumed 20,000 British lives, but as Sir Keith Feiling wrote in *A History of England*: 'It cut much deeper, for by it British imperialism was judged, in some

British Lancers at Modderfontein on 17 September 1901 during the Second Boer War. Outnumbered by 150 to 400, they refused to surrender and few survived.

respects found wanting, and transformed; while it made part also of an alteration of balances within Britain and of the causes of the world war.' The tempered language of a scholarly historian cannot conceal how the war cut through much of the bombast and complacency of British attitudes and revealed the armed forces to be of lesser quality than their own estimation had suggested.

Though the war produced its heroes and heroic moments, it also found Britain engaged in actions like the gathering of Boer non-combatants, women and children into 'concentration camps', where thousands died, and which certainly did not fall within any kind of ethical policy. Altogether, for the historically minded, there were parallels to be drawn with that other war fought against determined farmers, the American War of Independence. But the deployment of massive resources ensured that Britain emerged as victor in the Boer War. Germany had encouraged the Boers and now emerged openly as a power determined to challenge the pretensions of the British Empire: that in itself was enough to make it a patriotic English war. But although the majority of the population supported the war, and the Tories won a 'khaki' election in 1902, opposition had also been vocal. The new Liberal leader, Sir Henry Campbell-Bannerman, had condemned the barbarity of the campaigns, and though anti-war candidates had a hard time in the 1902 election, the sense of a war at first ill-fought, and at last ill-won, helped to provide a constructive attitude to the Boers (though not to the Africans: the blessing of the eventual apartheid state that would prevail until 1994 was given now), and also to set further army reforms in motion. Perhaps the best thing to emerge from the war was the Boy Scout and Girl Guide movement, soon to become an international force for youthful goodwill, created by General (later Lord) Baden-Powell, the hero of the long siege of Mafeking, from exercises and drills he devised for the young soldiers under his command.

CHAPTER FOURTEEN

Empire and Economics

VOLUNTARY AND SPORTING ASSOCIATIONS

'We shall wag our own tails.'
(A Carpenters' delegate at the
Trades Union Congress, 1902)

The publication of *Scouting for Boys* and the formation of local scout groups from 1908 hardly seems a defining moment in English history – nor was it such. The movement was largely middle-class, entirely non-political, and led to nothing except a great deal of enjoyment for the great majority of those who took part. But it showed how much society had changed. A hundred – even fifty – years earlier, such a development would have been unthinkable. Any form of national movement had arisen from or been driven by self-interest; this was something new and selfless. It also treated children, hitherto a scarcely regarded section of the community, as important in their own right. Though it remained largely a middle-class movement, scouting was important in the way its ethos of service and team spirit permeated the national attitude, and in its wide extension of the principle of voluntary service given by adults in the interest of society as a whole.

The earlier founding of the National Lifeboat Institution and that in 1938 of the Women's Voluntary Service showed the same general sense that a person should 'do one's bit', however modest; and that not all beneficent activity should be left to the

Sir Robert Baden-Powell, founder of the scouting movement

state to run. Both these organisations were to include 'Royal' in their titles, and this accolade given to worthy independent bodies reveals the way in which the monarchic idea could both confer distinction and receive a degree of reflected lustre in return. It implied a relationship between people and king or queen quite separate and different from that between people and parliament or government, and demonstrated the extent to which England remained a country strongly committed to the idea of local initiative and effort, and to the institution of kingship.

Ease of transport, quick communication by the electric telegraph, a thriving local and national press, and a modicum of disposable income for all but the very poor, encouraged the formation of a host of societies and organisations. In the latter part of the nineteenth century, sports had become codified and governing bodies were elected. Ball games, which had been played in a disorderly way with local rules for hundreds of years, were organised on a national and competitive basis. Association football soon overtook the older-established cricket as the most popular sport both for participation and watching. With the county championship established from 1873, cricket remained a popular game, though its export was confined to colonial territories with a strong expatriate British community. From the 1870s, football was already becoming a mass spectator sport. The Cup competition began in 1871, the League in 1888. By then, most large towns had their own soccer club, or more than one. League sides often grew out of clubs for boys or youths: the chance of founding by a Catholic priest for Catholic youth, as with Everton FC, determined the later affiliations of certain clubs. The club system, eventually taken up by almost

Aston Villa versus Blackburn Rovers, 1910

every other nation, showed a remarkable capacity for organisation on a national basis. By the early twentieth century, organised sport was in effect a major industry, with professional players (their leagues strictly segregated from amateur 'gentlemen's'), its own newspapers and a widespread though illegal gambling underworld.

PLAY UP AND PLAY THE GAME

English amateurism, which went arm-in-arm with voluntarism, was an elusive and complex aspect of life. Nobody wanted the railways to be operated by amateur signalmen, or to be chloroformed by an amateur anaesthetist. Nor were such things likely – professional standards were set and maintained across the range of responsible activities. Since 1854, candidates for most government service (though not the 'diplomatic') were appointed on merit after competitive examination. Competitiveness ran quite deep in all sorts of ways, whether in horse racing, or in municipalities vying to build a more sumptuous town hall, or in railway companies building new and uneconomic lines merely to prevent a rival from gaining a little extra traffic. In military and naval life, drill, ceremonial and 'spit-and-polish' could easily become an obsession, and obedience to orders a priority over common sense, as when Vice-Admiral Tryon's faulty order in the course of manoeuvres caused the collision and sinking of two battleships in June 1893. Some unease was detectable around the end of the nineteenth century – a feeling that behind the brilliant façade of the 'top nation' all was not well. 'It is beginning to be hinted that we are a nation of amateurs,' said Lord Rosebery, a former Liberal prime minister, to a student audience in 1900, while the Boer War was going badly. Though England had pioneered the utilisation of electricity with Michael Faraday, it was in the United States that electric lighting had been invented, and in Germany that the electric locomotive had first appeared. The cutting edge of industrial progress was no longer to be found in England. In 1902 Albert Einstein began publishing the papers on physics which would overturn the Newtonian concept of the universe. That the rest of the industrialised world should catch up with England was inevitable, but England did not seem to be keeping pace. The decades of the nineteenth century had fostered an English yen for a kind of effortless superiority, which deplored trying too hard, or struggling to succeed. Being too clever was equally bad: the ideal was high accomplishment performed with modesty and rounded off with self-deprecation. When there was a price to pay, it was paid without demur, whether it was the rough and common 'private of the Buffs' executed for refusing to 'kow-tow' to a Chinese official, or the gallant young Indian Army officer whose courage brought him to a lonely death at the hands of a rebel band.

The arch-bard of this spirit was Sir Henry Newbolt, and his most famous lines, from 'Vitae Lampada', are still appreciatively quoted:

> There's a breathless hush in the Close to-night –
> Ten to make and the match to win –
> A bumping pitch and a blinding light,
> An hour to play and the last man in.
> And it's not for the sake of a ribbon'd coat
> Or the selfish hope of a season's fame,
> But his Captain's hand on his shoulder smote –
> 'Play up! play up! and play the game.'

The schools, particularly the public schools, whose number and influence grew greatly in the later nineteenth century, were the nursery of this viewpoint, but they themselves reflected the expectations and attitudes of the wealthy parents who sent their sons (and eventually their daughters) away to be educated. The education was a largely classical one, based on Greek, Latin and history, with few concessions to the sciences. At its best it turned out able scholars and administrators, imbued with humane values, and a sense of team spirit. But it was an education for future judges, clergymen and administrators, not for scientists or engineers. A manufacturing background, and even more a manufacturing future, had little social prestige. This came from the conversion of industrial wealth into the ownership of a country house and broad acres, and the adoption of a career or style of life far removed from the steam, soot and smoke of the nineteenth-century factory.

There are other reasons for the aversion to industry, including a reluctance to deal with the industrial workers and their representatives. Unlike those who

---

HMS *DREADNOUGHT*

The Royal Navy, though as conservative an institution as any other, was shaken up by the forceful and unconventional mind of Admiral Lord Fisher (1841–1920), appointed First Sea Lord (operational head of the navy) in 1904. Fisher had served on the RN's first steam-powered ironclad, HMS *Warrior*, in 1863 and had long been interested in the technical side, especially in gunnery and torpedoes. As Admiral of the Mediterranean fleet, he taught the feasibility of long-range gunnery. As Second Sea Lord in 1902, he developed a programme of technical training and examination, to the discomfiture of many officers. In 1904, he initiated and supervised the design of a 'super-battleship' armed with ten 12-inch (305mm) heavy guns. The prototype was HMS *Dreadnought*, launched at Portsmouth Dockyard in October 1906. Powered by steam turbines and driven by quadruple screws, the design confirmed Britain's naval superiority but also led to an arms race with Germany; each country building battleships in an attempt to outgun the other.

Sheffield, 1879

worked in domestic service, they were not biddable, and long experience had taught them that confrontation and straight talk got better results than deference and acceptance of what they were told. The enforced and automatic obedience of the troops, the hushed respect of the servants' hall, were much easier to cope with.

THE NEW MONEY-MAKERS

As the wealth resulting from mining, quarrying, manufacturing, exporting and importing increased, there was an increasingly wide appreciation of the fact that – quite apart from making things – money in large amounts could be made to generate even more money. London had always been a centre of trade, and this was not a new discovery – it had fuelled the South Sea Bubble and the Railway Mania, when anyone who could borrow a hundred pounds could buy shares, watch their value rise, sell for five hundred pounds, and repeat the exhilarating experience on a greater scale until it ended in riches – or bankruptcy and a large collection of worthless share certificates. Financial houses like that of the Baring family, founded in 1762, played a vital part in supporting international trade and overseas investment. With immigrant families playing a substantial part, London's importance as a centre of stable international banking and insurance grew through the nineteenth century. The old City of London between St Paul's Cathedral and the Tower was gradually losing its population and their multifarious trades as these were pushed out beyond its boundaries by the building of new office blocks, staffed by workers who lived in the outer suburbs and came in by train to new termini built at the edge of the City, or into its heart on the underground railway. The stock exchange, the merchant banks, the other commodity exchanges that grew up, all were more congenial places than the factory floor, where social life could play a part. If many of those who were 'something in the City' were dilettantes, there were many more who were strongly motivated towards money-making. It was also understood that without some degree of self-regulation and accepted practice, the whole system could crash. Close-knit networks of families and their connections helped to maintain the system, despite some spectacular failures caused by crookedness and incompetence. The invisible earnings of the City institutions served to compensate for the increasing deficit on materials, goods and products. Despite being the 'workshop of the world', and a major coal exporter up to 1914, the value of Britain's imports had become greater than that of exports, by as much as £134 million in 1911.

THE SOCIAL IMBALANCE

A visitor to England in the reign of King Edward VII, between 1901 and 1910, might well have felt that the country was run by an oligarchy – a government by the few: in this case a combination of the aristocracy with the richest manufacturers and bankers.

THE SOUTH POLE

Captain Robert Falcon Scott of the Royal Navy had been commander of the *Discovery*, home ship of the British Antarctic Expedition of 1901–04, and he was appointed leader of a further Royal Geographical Society expedition in 1910 which aimed to be the first to reach the South Pole. It was a large and well-provided expedition. Exceptionally cold and snowy conditions hampered its progress, and some of its innovations, like motor tractors, were of little assistance. Scott and four of the eleven-man party persevered by 'man-hauling' their loaded sledges across the ice-cap, reaching the Pole on 18 January 1912, only to find that the Norwegian explorer Roald Amundsen, using dogs for haulage, had reached the uttermost south a month before them. Scott and his companions died of hunger, cold and fatigue on their return journey. The discovery of their frozen bodies, and of Scott's diaries, in November 1912, created a legend of heroic endurance. Only much later were the methods, skills and management of the expedition held up to question. But Scott of the Antarctic's legacy of British grit, of seeing things through to the bitter end, was, like that of Gordon of Khartoum, a valuable and sustaining example in the world war that was shortly to break out.

King Edward VII

Often all three were combined in the same person or family. Political life revolved around the London and country houses of famous hostesses like Lady Londonderry. The governing class followed a social routine of the seasons that was set by the court, and marked by major sporting occasions like the Ascot Races, and a lengthy summer break in country or Scottish or Irish estates. There was not a united approach to politics, and if the Liberals remained irreparably split on the question of Irish home rule, the Conservatives, in government until 1905, were to be perplexed and divided by the campaign for tariff protection and imperial preference driven with great energy by Joseph Chamberlain. The power of employers in the land had been confirmed by the Taff Vale Railway case in 1901, when the House of Lords, as supreme court, held the railway workers' union liable for the company's loss of earnings during an unofficial strike; the union lost the huge sum of £50,000, but the wider implications of the judgement seemed to undo all the earlier union reforms.

But the political power of the oligarchy was based upon the sufferance of the voters. In the first decades of the twentieth century, Britain was not a democracy, in that half the adult population had no vote, but almost half did possess the vote, and were beginning to understand the power which it put in their hands. Trade union membership in the early 1900s had already passed three million, nearly all men. The heavy defeat of the Tories in the 1905 general election was more due to fears about high prices from tariff reform than the Taff Vale judgement, but the incoming Liberal government found itself under immediate and irresistible pressure to clarify and reform trade union law, in favour of legitimate union activity. Twenty-nine Labour members were elected to parliament in that year. The more astute politicians among Liberals and Conservatives realised that the earth was moving beneath their feet, but both parties were too firmly linked to property ownership –

particularly in England – and neither could undo its own history. The
rise of the Labour Party, hesitant
and unsure as it was, continued
until in 1923 it was the second-
largest party in parliament and a
somewhat anxious King George V
invited its parliamentary leader,
James Ramsay MacDonald, to form
a government.

AVERTING CONSTITUTIONAL CRISES

The most astute member of the 1905
government was David Lloyd George,
prominent on the radical and Non-
conformist side of the party, and the
first Welshman to become a household name in England since Owen
Tudor was revealed as the husband of
the widowed Queen Catherine
around 1428.

His closest ally was Winston
Churchill, son of the Tory politician
Lord Randolph Churchill. A senior
figure to them was H.H. Asquith,
who took over as premier on the
death of Campbell-Bannerman in
1908. These men were the driving
force behind the Old Age Pensions
Act of 1908, the National Insurance
Act of 1911, and the 'People's
Budget' of 1909 which imposed
higher death duties (these had been
first introduced by the Liberals in
1895) and a 'super-tax' on incomes
over £5,000 (the salary level of a
bishop). These were the high points

James Ramsay MacDonald

David Lloyd George

249

of a string of reforms which produced ever-greater anger in the overwhelmingly Conservative House of Lords. A number of government measures were vetoed by the unelected chamber, culminating in rejection of the Budget. A great political storm erupted over this, and the crisis between the two houses went on for almost two years, prolonged by the death of Edward VII in 1910 and the accession of his son as George V. Both kings accepted the supremacy of the House of Commons and were willing, with certain delays and checks, to name enough new peers to ensure the will of the Commons was not thwarted. Two general elections maintained the Liberal majority, supported by Irish and Labour members, and the Lords finally accepted Asquith's Parliament Act in August 1911. This removed their control over bills certified by the Speaker as money bills, and replaced their veto on all other bills by a two-year delay, after which a disputed bill would still become law. A parliament's life was reduced from seven to five years. This legislation confirmed the role of the Lords for the rest of the century. A few very old men who had been Chartists in their youth might have smiled wryly as they reflected on the contentious 'six points' of sixty years before and how much – and how little – had been achieved.

The constitutional storm was intensified by other political events. From 1903, concern about German ambitions had already brought about alliances with France and Russia. There was a strong popular demand to enlarge the navy, prompted by the German warship building programme. Under Admiral Fisher as First Sea Lord, the navy had been modernised, and the dreadnought warship design had been completed in 1906: it made other capital ships out of date but it was soon being copied. Under Richard Haldane, as Secretary for War, the Cardwell army reforms were greatly extended, and an efficient central organisation and supply system were put in place.

Another great issue was the renewed Irish question. The eighty-four Irish Nationalist members were an essential part of the Liberal government's majority after the general election of December 1910, but their price for support in the battle with the Lords was a new Home Rule Bill. Bringing a new dimension into the raging constitutional debate, this inflamed matters further. The protests of Unionists in Ulster were taken up by Andrew Bonar Law, the Conservative leader, whose speeches strayed on occasion towards backing armed resistance; and for the first time since the Commonwealth, officers of the army attempted to force the hand of politicians by threatening to resign their commissions if instructed to take action against the Protestant-Unionist inhabitants of Ulster. Here there were at least some of the makings of the kind of right-wing coup familiar in many other countries where democracy had been deemed to go too far. But the British oligarchy was not united in its views, and had no history of overthrowing lawful government – it had always been the lawful government. The king carried out his above-politics role with great common sense and steadiness. And on 4 August 1914, when German forces entered Belgium on the way to invade France, and Great Britain was committed to war on the continent, the domestic threat passed. The Irish question was shelved by agreement of all the political parties, while the long-awaited conflict – which no one expected to last for more than a few months – was tackled.

THE RESPONSE TO WAR WITH GERMANY

While the army and navy moved into rehearsed action, it was very quickly plain that far more fighting men were needed. In the course of 1914 recruiting stations were set up and over three million volunteers appeared. Such an unprecedented number underlined the general understanding that this was a war on a scale not previously known, and that, in the judgement of the people, it was a just war, waged on behalf of small nations against larger ones; liberty against oppression. That sense of justice and necessity survived, though sorely tried, for more than four years, and through the deaths of over 900,000 men – a tenth of the war's overall toll of life – and the wounding of two million more.

There was no invasion threat, but, for the first time since John Paul Jones had fired his cannons off Flamborough Head in 1779, England experienced foreign raids. Ominously for the future, these came from the air, as zeppelin airships, and, later, aircraft attacked Scarborough and other coastal towns. Air raids focused attention on aircraft technology and the Royal Flying Corps, with sixty-three planes in 1914, became the Royal Air Force in 1917, a third armed service. But for the great majority, the war was happening elsewhere, though made immediate and compelling by virtually every family having members in the forces, by the illustrated daily news reports in the national press, and by the still-new technique of cinematograph films.

As had not happened since the early years of the nineteenth century, the country's producing and manufacturing capacity was pushed towards its maximum potential. But the Britain of 1914 had three times the population of 1814 and a vastly greater range of industry. Little of this industry had been geared towards war production, however. The government faced three major and immediate tasks. There was the actual direction of the war, in conjunction with the French on the western front and in liaison with other allied powers including the Russian and Japanese Empires. There was the supply of armament, munitions and other war materials from uniforms to stretchers, required by armies and fleets. And there was the need to feed the population. For decades now Britain had been reliant on imported wheat and beef, in addition to home produce. A fourth task might be added – the need to maintain public support and resolution. G.M. Trevelyan's *History of England* sums up the reason: 'Since the "lower orders" had developed into an enfranchised and partially educated democracy, only persuasion could effect what repression had accomplished in the days of the Luddites. In the struggle with Jacobin France, the war-time specific was Combination Acts to suppress Trade Unions; in the struggle with Germany it was the raising of wages to an unprecedented height, and inducing leaders of the Labour Party to enter the Coalition cabinet. The hardships of war did not, as a hundred years before, fall with their greatest force on the fortunes of the wage-earner.'

Almost unanimous support for the war did not mean any other sort of unanimity. Among craft workers there was resentment against the arrival of unskilled, untrained, and often female additions to the labour force. Conflict between employers and employers' groups and the trade unions would be endemic through the war; the former groups pressing for relaxation of union rules and demarcations; the latter resisting such demands and also demanding a full share for the workers in the profits brought by full order books and enormous government contracts. Women workers were of course nothing new, but they were concentrated in certain industries, especially the cloth and garment trades; the railway signalwoman or female lathe operator in an engineering shop was a new phenomenon.

In July 1915 Christabel Pankhurst, leader of the suffragettes, led a procession in London demanding, not votes, but 'the right to serve'. By 1916 almost 800,000 women were working in engineering and a further 250,000 were working on the land, where farmers were encouraged to get as much ground under crops as possible. There was a great deal of suspicion of profiteering by large companies, and in 1915 an 'excess profits' tax was introduced, of 50 per cent of any increase on a company's pre-war profits; A.J.P. Taylor noted that this contributed a quarter of the total wartime tax revenue. Income tax also rose, to 20 per cent, and the threshold of liability was lowered. But wages also went up, and, with prices of essential items largely held under control, savings increased substantially during the war period.

To achieve its tasks the government was accorded powers by parliament which went far beyond anything that had gone before, in war or peace. The Defence of the Realm Act provided heavy penalties for even casual remarks which seemed to undermine the war effort. Coal mines, railways, and merchant shipping were taken under state control and managed by government-appointed industrialists with no prior links to parliament. The Ministry of Munitions, headed by Lloyd George from 1915 until he became prime minister, was turned into a power-centre of a type previously unknown in England. But production of armaments shot up dramatically.

THE CONDUCT OF THE WAR

Where the government was least successful was in the first of its tasks – managing the actual business of waging war. The dedication and courage of what was at first a largely volunteer army was never in question. But the story of the conduct of strategy is a tragic catalogue of incompetence, indecision, personal animosities and staff infighting. But the British were no worse in these respects than their French allies or their German opponents. Generals trained in colonial wars found themselves controlling a battle-front hundreds of miles long, in a bloody stalemate that lasted four years and in which any attack was fated to gain only a mile or two of ground at the cost of tens of thousands of lives. The western front was too vast and its fate too crucial to be left to the generals; its military and logistical aspects too complex to be influenced by the politicians. Military disasters caused increasing criticism of Asquith's Liberal government, which had been in power on the declaration of war. In May 1915 he made a coalition with the Conservatives, but continuing military failures, the lack of munitions, and a sense that Asquith was not pursuing the war with enough ardour and determination, led to political crisis. The year 1916 saw the battle of Jutland, in which the Grand Fleet succeeded in driving the German High Seas Fleet permanently back into port, but, rather than achieving a Nelson-style annihilation, itself suffered more losses than the enemy. And, by the end of 1916, German submarines were sinking 300,000 tons of British shipping every month.

1916 was the year in which volunteering dried up and – despite the reservations or opposition of many Liberal and Labour politicians – compulsory conscription for men into the armed forces was introduced. The maximum age was forty-one, later increased to fifty. It was the year of the Easter Rising in Dublin, with the threat of German invasion of Ireland. Lord Kitchener, Secretary of State for War, esteemed by the general public, at least, as a vital member of the war cabinet, was killed in the mining of HMS *Hampshire* in that year.

In the face of mounting criticism Asquith resigned, expecting to be reappointed, as the only statesman capable of leading a national coalition. But Lloyd George's energy, combined with political skills in winning the backing of Conservative, Labour and dissatisfied Liberal MPs, had made him the man of the moment. The Tory leader, Bonar Law, would not form a government unless Asquith joined it, and Asquith refused to play second fiddle after leading the orchestra. On 6 December 1916 Lloyd George became prime minister. The Clerk to the Privy Council compared the result as being 'the substitution of dynamite for a damp squib'.

The most important of Lloyd George's victories was won against the British Admiralty. In 1917, with no progress on the western front, German submarines

The British front in Flanders, 1917

were winning a sea war, sinking British ships at a terrifying rate, over 600,000 tons in April alone. With extraordinary blinkeredness, the Admiralty announced it could see no solution to the problem. Convoys, the obvious means, were discounted because 'merchant captains could not keep station'. Lloyd George overruled Sir Edward Carson, political head of the Admiralty, and the admirals, and compelled the introduction of convoys. Following this, losses fell dramatically. But at one point, food stocks had dwindled to a forecast level of six weeks' supply. With the success of the convoy system, and the American entry into the war on the Allied side, it was possible to foresee victory, even though Russia, in the throes of revolution, made a separate peace with Germany, releasing battle-hardened divisions to the western front.

THE SOCIAL AFTERMATH

Another novel feature of this war was that it accelerated social reform on the home front. Again this had much to do with the government's awareness that the entire working population must both will the war and see progress from it. Education was reformed, and works and factory conditions improved with such innovations as works canteens providing subsidised meals. Such 'concessions', as was obvious to such far-sighted Quaker-commercial reformers as Seebohm

Rowntree, in charge of the Welfare Department of the Munitions Ministry, were also instrumental in maintaining or improving workers' productivity. Plans were made for state housing schemes, built to approved standards. A Ministry of Health was introduced.

In anticipation of victory, Lloyd George proclaimed his intention of making Great Britain 'a land fit for heroes to live in' – a piece of phrase-making that would later dog him when the reality fell far behind the rhetoric. Although hostilities ended in November 1918, the government did not give up its special powers until 1921. The spirit of idealism and unity of 1914 had changed by 1919 under the effects of war and of events elsewhere. The Russian, German and Austrian Empires had collapsed and were replaced with 'peoples' regimes'. A brimstone-whiff of revolution in Britain was also in the air – or at least in the ultra-sensitive nostrils of the government. A new Franchise Act in 1917 extended voting rights to all adult men and to women over thirty, adding over ten million names to the electoral register, and Lloyd George won his reward with a large majority after the 'coupon election' of 1918: the coupon was the coalition ticket, opposed by a rump of Asquithian Liberals and by the now well-organised Labour Party. But, as the heroes came marching home, and as the industrial workers contemplated a return to peace-time conditions, many felt that the way forward was being shown by the soviets and workers' councils that had appeared in other countries, and that the four-year holocaust should not have been endured merely to see the clock put back to 1914, or even earlier. The activists were few in number, though industrial discontent drew out large crowds to hear and cheer. Demonstrations were firmly suppressed by use of wartime powers. The corporate state that had been created was returned to its owners, the joint-stock companies, to meet the war-strengthened trade unions in an industrial climate that was fast heading for a slump. De-control of the coal mines was swiftly followed by disputes; the owners had already announced wage cuts, and a lockout of the workers ensued. Through the twenties, the miners would be the vanguard of workers' organisation and protest, driven by the run-down state of their own industry. The mine owners, facing a slump in demand and heavy competition from America, Germany, Poland (and the rapidly growing petroleum industry) saw no remedy other than to cut down their labour costs.

A NATION OF CONSUMERS

In such a country as England, instant large-scale social change is rare. A long history, a strong sense of the past, a feeling in each generation that the previous one was in some way better, more blessed, more distinctively English – all these promote a cautious and considering attitude to the new. Change, when

---

HORATIO BOTTOMLEY

Brought up in an orphanage in the East End of London, Bottomley (1860–1933), became an errand boy, then a solicitor's clerk and graduated to shorthand writer in the high court. Discovering he had great journalistic skills, he started a local paper, the *Hackney Hansard*, the first in a series of businesses that made him a multi-millionaire. Possessed of boundless self-confidence and the con man's ability to keep just ahead of the game, Bottomley was an arch-populist, adept at identifying popular causes, good or bad, and pushing them to the limit. By the time he was thirty he had set up around fifty companies, but concern about his business dealings led to a succession of fraud charges and bankruptcy petitions, which he successfully avoided. In 1906 he started a picture magazine, *John Bull*, and became an MP until 1911, when he did go bankrupt. *John Bull* promoted a coarse and jingoistic nationalism during the First World War, along with virulent anti-Germanism. The fruits of patriotism enabled Bottomley to pay off his debts and in 1918 he was re-elected to parliament. However in 1922 he was prosecuted for fraud and this time sent to jail for five years. After that his popular appeal and esteem vanished, and he died in poverty. His rags-to-riches and back again story acquired a legendary quality. In an invented episode, a former acquaintance, on a prison visit, saw Bottomley in the mail-bag workshop with needle and thread. 'Sewing, Bottomley?' he asked. 'No, reaping,' was the supposed answer.

---

it occurs, is often disguised, or disclaimed by those who are introducing it. Whether salutary or not, change is often unwelcome. But some changes were embraced quickly. The Liverpool and Manchester Railway, the world's first steam-powered passenger line, sold 400,000 tickets between its two terminal cities in its first year: an increase of some ten-fold on the previous volume of travel between these places. Cigarettes, mass-produced and packaged from 1880s, caught on very fast. The cinema – the world's first purpose-built one opened at Colne, Lancashire in 1908 – quickly became immensely popular. A common link between all three is that they involved discretionary expenditure. Nobody had to buy cigarettes or cinema tickets, but they did, in huge numbers. Another important link is choice: soon after the Liverpool and Manchester line, other railways opened. People could choose which brand of cigarette they smoked, and what kind of film, or which film stars, they liked, or where they could go. Not suddenly in a rush, but quite stealthily, and by the 1920s quite definitely, the English people had become consumers.

There had been shops for a long time. Adam Smith and Napoleon Bonaparte had both commented on the shopkeeping propensities of the English. But shops in the past had been take-what-we-have places where flour, grains and sugar were kept in sacks, and other commodities in large jars and boxes. Now shops had labelled, branded goods in attractive small packages – and the wider the choice, the more customers they had. The political party which best understood this process was the Conservative Party, which with its protectionist and tariff reform views had won the support of much of industry and business. In the new democracy, it also needed wide popular support, and this came from the section of the community best able to exercise its consuming choice, and keen to extend the range of its possessions, from radios to motor cars, the professional middle class. Its policies made it the natural ally of the farmers, and many farm and rural workers voted with their employers in the interest of their industry, rather than taking the same political side as urban workers. One of the most remarkable features of English political life, for over three hundred years, has been the ability of the 'conservative tendency' to regroup and reform itself, to revitalise itself periodically and to reappear as a force in national life.

Side by side with consumerism, however, the English people retained an element of belief in the involvement of the state in some basic aspects of life. For the great majority of the population, it was the government which provided schooling, and which provided the modest but often vital payments of old age pensions and national insurance. It was the government which was appointing district medical officers and health boards. Many people still remembered the times before these advances. Government on a local basis supplied water, sewerage, often public transport. For many things to which the working class or its representatives still aspired, such as secondary education for all, free hospitals and medical treatment, and further improvements to working conditions, it was the government which would have to be the provider. And the government most likely to provide would be a Labour one. Despite the writings of political philosophers on both sides, the Labour–Tory divide which would typify twentieth-century politics arose from these two concepts: choice plus the ability to choose; and central management by the state. Both could bring social and economic progress and many people saw the way forward as a combination of the two.

There was a broad middle ground in English politics, and 'floating voters' often decided election results. The party which lost out was the Liberals, who lost much of their radical support to Labour when it became clear that the Labour Party was a serious political force, and found themselves squeezed between the forces of consumerism and centralism. Split between Asquithian 'Squiffites' and Lloyd-Georgists, bereft of the financial base given to the other parties by business and the trade unions, the Liberal Party never disappeared but, while always promising revival, it remained peripheral in national politics.

ENGLISH VOICES AND AMERICAN INFLUENCE

Two arms of technological progress reached far into the creative and receptive aspects of English culture in the 1920s – these were radio and the cinema. In 1922 the British Broadcasting Company (later Corporation) was established, with a single studio in London. Although recorded sound went back to the invention of the phonograph in the USA in 1877, the transmission of 'live' news and music and the projection of moving pictures on a big screen were revolutionary changes in the fields of entertainment, news-gathering and information.

The BBC revealed much of England to itself, including the way everyone sounded. The new corporation, conscious of its responsibilities, encouraged a certain form of pronunciation that became known as 'BBC English', a rather artificial, clipped, precise form that seemed to distance the newsreader from the news. Eventually, the BBC lost its fear of regional accents, but radio's very existence raised the question of how English should be spoken, and what was 'correct' usage. The written language had long been the same from Northumberland to Cornwall, and literary experiments like those of the nineteenth-century poet. William Barnes, who wrote in Dorset dialect, were rare. Now the growth of a national radio network began to exert a standardising effect on English speech, which was also encouraged by the extension of school education to a minimum leaving age of fourteen. Local dialect forms were dropped by the young. Instead, and to the irritation of the old, they picked up or formed new phrases and expressions. Many of these came from the cinema, and therefore from the United States. American culture had arrived.

The American involvement in the Great War and the American participation in the Versailles peace negotiations had made the British people aware that there was now an English-speaking nation that was more populous, wealthier and stronger than Great Britain. The following decade showed it to have an industrial, scientific and commercial dynamism greater than that of any other nation, and a mixed, vibrant, unabashedly modern culture. American movies showed a luxurious lifestyle with domestic accessories which even the better-off English did not possess. American music, jazz and blues, discordant to conservative ears, attracted the young and began to influence progressive composers. Two expatriate Americans, Ezra Pound and T.S. Eliot, compelled a reassessment of how English poetry should be conceived and written.

British visitors to Europe found new things happening there too – in music, art and drama especially, but also in popular culture: the comedy, wit and satire of club and café. In many ways British culture still seemed rooted in a pre-war mode, but one major change was highly visible. For the first time in history, English women showed their legs, even their knees, in public, as hemlines rose. Curiously, for a woman to wear trousers was seen as much more outrageous than for her to wear a short skirt. Even though many women were ousted from their wartime jobs, this was the decade of female emancipation. By the end of it, all women had the vote. They were accepted, grudgingly or not, in all professions save the clergy. The first woman to take a seat in parliament, Lady Astor, was elected for Plymouth in 1919.

GENERAL STRIKE AND GREAT DEPRESSION

These developments and trends, though noted and commented on at the time, were often overshadowed by more immediate events. Political and economic conditions in the 1920s were often precarious. The rise of American economic power, the rapid industrialisation of Japan, the economic ruin of Germany, the sovietisation of Russia, and the running down of war economies created a new set of international conditions which no single government was able to cope with. Lloyd George's artificial coalition with the Conservatives collapsed in autumn 1922 and was followed briefly by a Conservative administration under Stanley Baldwin, before its fall opened the way to the first Labour government in 1923. Both the hopes and fears engendered by this

The 1926 General Strike – the Guards returning from Hackney and the London Docks after the General Strike

turned out to be grossly exaggerated. Even if it had dramatic plans, its MPs were still outnumbered by combined Liberals and Tories. But though Ramsay MacDonald had no such programme, it lasted hardly a year, destroyed by suspicion of communist sympathies and plots. Baldwin returned to power. By now the *fait accompli* of independence for twenty-six Irish counties as a 'free state' was done, and the Irish Nationalist phalanx was no longer a force in the Westminster parliament. In an attempt to revert to a pre-war financial system which was impossible to resurrect, Winston Churchill, as Chancellor of the Exchequer (and now a Conservative), restored the gold standard in 1925, backing the pound sterling with the Bank of England's reserves, and the value of sterling rose, reducing British exports in an already depressed world trading system. High unemployment and falling wages produced the brief General Strike of May 1926, built on the combining of miners and railway workers. The strike was a failure, and membership of trade unions went into rapid decline; the miners held out for six bitter months before returning to work for longer hours and no increase in pay.

Although the Baldwin government produced a number of reforms, extending the responsibility of county and borough councils, as well as the abolition of the Poor Law, made redundant by centrally administered pension and national insurance schemes, it could do little to alleviate economic problems which stemmed from the barriers and imbalances of international trading.

In the elections of June 1929 Labour was the largest party, though without an overall majority, and MacDonald formed his second government. In October, the entire capitalist system was shaken to its roots by the Wall Street crash in the USA. The drop in share values and the consequent lack of confidence, the calling in of debts, the cancellation of investment, the cutting back in trade and production resulted in the five years of the Great Depression. Unemployment in Great Britain, which had been about one million, rose rapidly as output fell and businesses cut back or closed down. A flood of cheap imports from other countries came in – for those who still had an income, this was a time of acquisition, not hardship – while sterling's value held exports down. By 1931 the apparent insolubility of the Depression led to a political crisis. Only two men had made bold proposals to take the country out of slump. Lloyd George in 1929 had published his 'Orange Book' proposing a large programme of public works and investment; in 1930 a minor member of the Labour government, Sir Oswald Mosley, had proposed an even more radical 'national plan' which the government rejected. Both of these schemes resembled the 'New Deal' by which the United States hauled itself out of the Depression. By Easter 1931 almost three million people were unemployed. The modest improvements made to unemployment benefit, 'the dole', by the government had not been intended to cater for such a huge number, almost a quarter of the working population. Government spending was increasing dramatically. Cuts were envisaged, including a 10 per cent reduction in the already small dole. Angry resistance within the Labour Party to this prompted MacDonald to a bold stroke of another kind – bypassing the opposition in his own party, he resigned as prime minister only to re-emerge immediately as premier of a National government in alliance with the Conservatives and a small section of the Liberals. This government, formed to preserve the stability of the pound and 'save the nation', called a general election in October 1931. It won an overwhelming majority, with 558 supporters in the Commons, of whom 417 were Conservatives. A tiny opposition consisted of only forty-nine Labour members and a small assortment of the fragmented Liberals. Ten per cent cuts in all official salaries and the dole were duly implemented. New tariffs and imperial preference for colonial produce marked the end of free trade, but had little impact on the economic situation.

FASCISM, DEPRESSION AND ABDICATION

Heavy industry, transport and agriculture bore the great brunt of the Depression. Coal and iron towns became sumps of social and industrial decay, with unemployment often close to 90 per cent. Thousand of tons of shipping were laid up, many of the vessels being old-fashioned coal-burners that would never steam again. Modernisation of the railways, reduced to four major companies since 1923, was drastically slowed down. The drift from the land continued. Also badly hit were the mass-market clothing factories and shops. The East End of London, always the repository of the most recent immigrants and the poorest and most exploited workers, as well as the tough Cockney working class of the docks, railways and factories, suffered as badly as northern coal towns like Wigan or cotton towns like Salford. In 1932 Sir Oswald Mosley formed the British Union of Fascists, on the model of fascist parties in Italy. Uniforms, calls for national discipline and an invoking of anti-Semitic feeling aroused some support and there were parades and fights with left-wing and Jewish groups. But the most notable thing about British fascism, as with organised British communism at the same time, was how small these movements were. They had shock value, but few people in Britain felt that the regimes of Mussolini and Hitler offered a suitable model; of Stalin's Russia less was known, but the first expectations of communism bringing an early new dawn for the workers had long before vanished. The stability of the British state, even if it went with a somewhat stodgy way of life and the least appetising cookery in Europe, began to feel something of value rather than something to be taken for granted, even to those who lived there. To many in other countries, it was again a beacon of freedom – if it could be reached. In the 1930s Britain benefited from a stream of refugees who brought distinction to intellectual life, like Sigmund Freud and the architectural historian, Nikolaus Pevsner, and many others less prominent.

Like outbreaks of plague, the industrial selectiveness of the Depression marked off one place or region from another. 'Hunger marches' pioneered by Jarrow on Tyneside brought unemployed workers through affluent southern counties to Westminster where the National government, having saved the pound, was hoping the nation would save itself. MacDonald had been succeeded by Baldwin as premier in 1935, but the prime political figure was Neville Chamberlain, Chancellor of the Exchequer, who would become prime minister in 1937. The few government schemes designed to counter the slump had little effect; to designate somewhere as a 'special area' was rather like defining it as a plague zone. But throughout, three-quarters of the population, or more, remained in employment. The new light industries, cars, aircraft, household goods, machine tools, became steadily more important, often sited on new-style trading estates away from the old, grimy smokestack centres. Road transport was more important to them than rail. Electricity and gas were their preferred power sources. It was not until 1937, with rising demand for iron and steel and other metals, that some revitalisation really began in heavy industry. But a dual legacy of the slump would remain, in a partly run-down and obsolescent industrial base, and in the memories of a large number of electors who felt that what was now perceived as a Conservative rather than a 'National' government, should have done more.

'Something must be done' was indeed the only remembered phrase from the public life of the Prince of Wales, briefly King Edward VIII in 1936, uttered when visiting the slump-struck Merthyr Tydfil in Wales. His desire to marry a

---

KEYNESIANISM

John Maynard Keynes (1883–1946) was the most influential economist of the twentieth century, though many of his ideas and doctrines would be challenged by other economists, especially the neoclassical school of the later twentieth century, and by events. His most important book was *The General Theory of Employment, Interest and Money* (1936), which set out the basis of modern macro- (i.e. large-scale) economics. Keynes took issue with the long-standing belief that cycles of expansion and depression were inherent and unpreventable in a modern economy. He identified the key problem as a decline in consumers' and producers' confidence about future prospects, and argued that government spending, even if it meant a deficit in the public accounts, was the way to re-create confidence and demand, and to level out the boom–slump sequence. Post-war governments would operate on a Keynesian basis until the end of the 1970s, when the simultaneous occurrence of rising unemployment and monetary inflation did not seem to allow for a Keynesian solution. A neoclassical return to letting markets find their own level, while retaining a right control on money supply, followed in the 1980s.

Edward VIII and his brothers in 1936 – from left to right, the Duke of Kent, Edward VIII, the Duke of York, the Duke of Gloucester

twice-divorced American lady, Mrs Wallis Simpson, and to remain king-emperor, was frustrated by Baldwin. He chose the lady, and abdicated with the title of Duke of Windsor in December 1936. By a collusion of press owners unimaginable nowadays, the affair was entirely screened from British public knowledge until December, when some newspapers and politicians, including Winston Churchill, supported the idea of a morganatic marriage, with Wallis not receiving the status of queen. The abdication, and accession of Edward's brother as King George VI, all organised behind the scenes, powerfully evoked the notion of the English 'Establishment' at work. The coronation ceremony of 1937 was deliberately grandiose, but the episode revealed how completely the monarchy had become a matter of ceremonial and status, hedged about by protocol and advice. (The ghost of George IV, who had entered a form of marriage with a Mrs Fitzherbert in 1785, and whose union with her lasted well past his official marriage to Princess Caroline of Brunswick in 1795, might well have chuckled hollowly.)

THE FAILURE OF APPEASEMENT

Winston Churchill in the 1930s was a supporter of forlorn causes. Almost uniquely among senior English politicians, he was a bellicose figure, always ready to take up a martial standpoint, even as Home Secretary in 1910, sending armed troops against rioting miners. He had served as a cavalry officer in the Boer War, and, demoted from the Admiralty when his Unionist enemies joined the government in 1915, went off to command an army brigade until Lloyd George brought him back to run the Ministry of Munitions. In the 1930s he was seen as a maverick figure, one whose time was past rather than to come, and his transitions from Conservative to Liberal and back again were regarded as signs of unreliability (to a party man, of course, they were just that). His reading of the threat to Europe from Nazi Germany was correct, but British politicians, temperamentally opposed to war, were prepared to go to great lengths to avoid it. Neville Chamberlain's visits to Hitler were earnest and sincere but he failed or refused to see they were regarded by his host as signs of weakness. With hindsight he and his supporters were labelled as appeasers of tyranny, but it was they rather than Churchill who were following the traditional British form of diplomacy. All the correct formalities, guards of honour, ceremonials, signed documents, assurances and handshakes concealed from Chamberlain that in Hitler and Mussolini he was dealing with the leaders of adventurist and gangster regimes that had inserted themselves into the formal structures of their countries. Despite the appeasement policy, however, from 1935 the running down of the armed services was ended. New fighter planes were designed, with 240 a month being built in 1938, and anti-aircraft defences began to be worked on.

In the course of 1938 events began to shake both the government itself and the popular approval in which it had basked. The Foreign Secretary, Anthony Eden, resigned over the government's acceptance of Italy's invasion of Abyssinia (now Ethiopia), and the First Lord of the Admiralty, Duff Cooper, resigned over Chamberlain's Munich Agreement. This apparent accord with Hitler was described by Chamberlain in a phrase of Disraeli's, as 'peace for our time' – one of those phrases which become a millstone round the neck of its utterer. A practical politician, of a far from Gladstonian outlook, Chamberlain described the German invasion of Czechoslovakia as 'a quarrel in a far-away country between people of whom we know nothing' – an odd phrase for the leading politician of an imperial power, but showing a lofty detachment from Europe. Less than six months later he signed a treaty committing Britain to the defence of Poland. What happened in between was the collapse of Czechoslovakia, the German occupation of Prague, and a realisation by the British people that appeasement was not only a practical failure but had also been inspired by motives that hardly fitted British self-perception: unwillingness to face a bully and fear of attack (the prospect of mass destruction from the air created a real sense of terror). Chamberlain and his ministers had been fooled; Churchill had been right. Public opinion pushed the government into a corner; when Germany invaded Poland on 1 September 1939, delaying tactics were no longer possible. After two days of hesitation, war was declared on 3 September.

CHAPTER FIFTEEN

World War II

AN UNCERTAIN START

Unlike 1914, there was no sudden engagement of forces. The period known as the 'phoney war' began. Its main feature was the evacuation, from cities to country areas, of a million and a half children – a bewildering and sometimes traumatic experience both for the evacuees and those on whom they were billeted, as many memoirs testify. Evelyn Waugh's novel *Put Out More Flags* gives a satirical account of the confrontations. Though many returned home, to be moved out again when the bombs actually began to fall, the campaign was generally felt to be necessary. Less sympathy was extended to those families rich enough to send their children across the Atlantic to the USA or Canada. A small army of four divisions was ferried over to northern France. The enforced self-destruction of the German battleship *Graf Spee* at Montevideo displayed the worldwide reach of the Royal Navy, but a daring U-boat attack within the anchorage of Scapa Flow, sinking HMS *Royal Oak*, also demonstrated the deficiency of British defences.

In Whitehall, events were still presided over by Chamberlain and the government of appeasement, with Churchill now included as First Lord of the Admiralty. Events speeded up in early 1940 as vague and ill-formed plans for occupation of northern Norway were pre-empted by Germany's invasion of Denmark and Norway in April 1940, rapidly followed by the invasion of the Netherlands and Belgium. The Royal Navy, it was clear, did not even control the North Sea. The brief campaign centred on Narvik was a humiliating failure. As A.J.P. Taylor observed, 'it was a nice twist that a campaign, directed largely by Churchill, should bring Chamberlain down and raise Churchill up.' But it was apparent that Churchill had the will to wage war and Chamberlain did not. When around a hundred members of his own party voted against him or abstained in the vote following a debate on the Norwegian campaign, Chamberlain resigned. Unlike Lloyd George, who had actively plotted his course to the premiership in 1916, Churchill remained aloof. Chamberlain, King George VI, and the Labour leader, Clement Attlee, would have liked to see Lord Halifax, the Foreign Secretary, assume command of a coalition government. But when Churchill mutely refused to serve under Halifax, he, backed by his small but vociferous 'war party' among Conservative MPs and with strong support from the powerful press magnate Lord Beaverbrook, was the inevitable choice. On 10 May Churchill was asked by the king to form a government. Labour and Liberal members joined it, with Attlee as deputy premier. Although Labour was a small party in parliamentary terms, following the rout of 1935, it was a mass party in the country and its close relationship with the trade unions was a vital asset in a country which, with the collapse of France in June 1940, now found itself facing all-out war and the imminent likelihood of massive air attack and invasion. Labour's long opposition to the European dictatorships also earned it public approval.

BLOOD, TOIL, TEARS AND SWEAT

Churchill had spent much of the 1930s reading and writing history, and the example of the elder and younger Pitts was not lost on him. His wartime speeches, relayed to the country and the world via the BBC, orotund, defiant, uncompromising, rallied the nation to great efforts and to great endurance.

The retreat of the expeditionary force, the loss of its equipment, and the rescue under gunfire of most of its survivors – 200,000 men plus 139,000 French troops – from Dunkirk by the legendary fleet of 860 'little ships' consisting of everything from naval destroyers to railway steamers and fishing trawlers, was a remarkable achievement but the opposite of a military triumph. Once again the British had entered a war in disastrous fashion. Yet the 'Dunkirk spirit' showed a united resolve and the understanding that if the war was to be won, it had to be everybody's war. World War II was different to World War I in that there was no great gulf of experience and understanding between the fighting troops and the civilian population. Though many volunteered for service, it was essentially a conscript war from the first, with people waiting their turn to be called up. A nationwide organisation of Local Defence Volunteers, later the Home Guard, was also speedily formed, reaching a million members, though so short of equipment that some paraded with pitchforks. Beaverbrook, appointed as Minister of Aircraft Production, took a barnstorming

Winston Churchill

approach to the task, backed at first by the trade unionist Ernest Bevin as Minister of Labour. Boy Scouts gathered surplus pots and pans. People sacrificed their iron garden railings. Much of this was a propaganda exercise but the increase in fighter aircraft production was real – and vital.

From August 1940, the air onslaught began in ferocious earnest. Fifty-five fighter squadrons, mostly based on hastily rolled out new airfields in south-east and eastern England, were matched against the Luftwaffe. Their commander, Air Marshal Hugh Dowding, occupied the uncomfortable position that Admiral Jellicoe had had in 1915 – he was the man who could lose the war, if not in a day, then in a very short period of time. Between mid-August and mid-September the battle of Britain was fought in the air above Kent and Sussex, the 'dogfights' watched with fascinated apprehension by spectators on the ground.

Air superiority was a necessary preliminary to a German invasion, and despite anxious days in early September when British losses seemed to be escalating, the necessary control of the skies was never achieved. On 17 September Hitler suspended invasion plans. But though the island was not invaded, it was not inviolate. From August 1940 both Britain and Germany began the night-time bombing of cities and towns. The 'Blitz' on London and other large industrial cities and seaports went on intensively until May 1941. Coventry, Birmingham, Plymouth and Southampton were among those which suffered most. It resulted

Battle of Britain – RAF crew next to a Spitfire, 1940

The remains of Coventry Cathedral following an air raid, 1940

in the deaths of around 30,000 people and damage or destruction of more than three and a half million houses. The House of Commons was destroyed. Buckingham Palace was hit. Throughout the war the king and his family set a sterling and greatly admired example – they did not leave their home, were reputed to 'eat spam off a gold plate', and a line was painted on the baths to limit the use of hot water.

The German hope that bombing of civilian targets would reduce morale was not borne out. Half-wrecked shops took pride in putting up a 'Business as Usual' notice, and the inconveniences, the 'blackout', shortages, cancelled trains, power cuts, queues, sleeping in underground stations and in damp, chilly air raid shelters, were borne with a grumbling stoicism. 'England can take it' was the consistent message.

THE REACH OF THE STATE AND SOCIAL LEGISLATION

State interference in most aspects of life was even more extensive than it had been in 1914–18. Regional government, of a type very different to that late r proposed in 2002, operated efficiently, with regional controllers who had authority to co-ordinate the work of regional offices of the various ministries.

269

HURRICANES AND SPITFIRES

In the 1930s there were numerous British aircraft builders. With the gradual acceptance of the need to rearm, from the mid-1930s, new designs began to emerge. The events of 1940 were to give lasting fame to the two fighter airrcraft designs of this period, the Hurricane, designed by Sydney Camm and his team at Hawker, and the Spitfire, designed by R.J. Mitchell at Supermarine. As that company's name suggests, it was originally concerned with seaplanes, and the Spitfire design emerged from Mitchell's fast seaplanes that won the international Schneider speed trophy in the 1920s. Britain's first mono-wing fighters, the Hurricane prototype appeared in November 1935, the Spitfire in March 1936. Mitchell's original fighter design was turned down by the Air Ministry; the quality of his revised 'Type 300' was such that the officials rewrote their own specification around it. Both planes used the Rolls-Royce 'Merlin' engine, which was steadily enlarged in power output. Adjustment to these fast and relatively more sophisticated planes was not easy for pilots: 36 of the 306 Mark 1 Spitfires were written off in training accidents. In the summer of 1940 these were the main weapons of defence against the German attempts to take command of the air. Hurricanes, more numerous at the time, shot down more German aircraft than all other aircraft and weapons combined. They remained in service until 1947. The Spitfire, whose numbers with variant types eventually reached over 22,500, had a longer career, flying its last operational mission in Malaya in January 1954, and some remained in service until 1967.

But this was non-elective government, dispensed with after the war, when power returned to the counties and boroughs. Other controllers of various kinds were put in charge of key industries or the production of vital materials, though the most basic industry, coal, was left largely in the hands of its owners and declined in efficiency and production throughout the war, until from 1943 it became necessary to draft some conscripts, the 'Bevin boys', to the mines, to help maintain coal supplies. 'Austerity' standards were set for many products and rationing was instituted for clothes as well as food. All this bred a culture of petty officialdom and semi-official snooping, which was both intensified and alleviated by the fact that almost everyone, to a modest extent, did a bit of buying or selling on the 'black market'. This extended from the farmer's wife not declaring all her eggs, to the criminal element's bulk thefts and resale of petrol and other goods. Much fell off the backs of army lorries. Political life was low-key; the coalition parties had agreed an electoral pact in by-elections, and the life of the 1935 parliament was extended. Local council elections were suspended. But below the surface, political discussion was universal and intense, aided by so many people being in camps, and large workforces. Army education classes helped to pass the troops' enforced spells of leisure but also created forums of debate. With the declarations of war by Germany on Russia, and, following the Japanese attack, also on America, most people believed that ultimate victory was inevitable even if it must still be battled for; and there was great speculation about the dispositions of the post-war

Women producing component parts for Spitfires

world, and of Britain within it. The political compromise of the coalition, plus the fact that the great majority of MPs were Conservatives, ruled out any significant legislative changes except those needed for the war effort and acknowledged as temporary.

One by-product of the war effort was an improvement in the health and nourishment of the nation's children. School meals were provided, as were cheap milk, vitamin supplements and cod liver oil. Urban slum diseases like rickets were virtually eliminated. Most government thinking about post-war reconstruction was vague, but an exception was the report on the Future of Social Insurance and Allied Services, produced by Sir William Beveridge. This was the most important document on civilian life to be produced in the twentieth century. With wide experience of social administration, economics and politics, Beveridge stretched his brief to the utmost to provide what was in effect the blueprint of the post-war 'welfare state'. His report, published in 1942, envisaged the slaying of the five giants of 'want, disease, ignorance, squalor and idleness' through a cradle-to-grave social system encompassing free health care, family allowances, unemployment benefit at a decent subsistence level, universal secondary education, and the whole thing to be paid for by a combination of state funding and individual payments generated by full employment. Half a million copies of the report were sold and it created a storm of interest. To the generation which had lived through the Great Depression and was now fighting a war, Sir William's mandarin prose and voluminous statistics seemed to be a guide to the promised land. To the government it was something of an embarrassment, dealt with by long and slow consideration.

In September 1944 a white paper proposed a considerably watered down version of Beveridge's proposals. Even so, under a Conservative premier and Conservative-dominated cabinet, it incorporated the revolutionary notion that the government was responsible for maintaining employment at a sufficient level, and for taking steps to cope with what were seen as cyclic variations of boom and slump in commerce and industry. No government, including those recently headed by Baldwin and Chamberlain, had ever accepted that this was part of its task. The main enduring piece of wartime social legislation was the Education Act produced by R.A. Butler in 1944, providing for free secondary education for all children, with the leaving age raised to fifteen, and three types of school, grammar, technical and modern, with entry determined by an 'eleven-plus' examination.

A CHANGED WORLD ORDER

American entry into the war brought a new familiarity for the English with a nation they had previously known largely through the distorting medium of the cinema film. Through 1942 and 1943, large numbers of US servicemen were stationed in England, in anticipation of a new landing in Europe, and their ample stocks of cigarettes, nylon stockings (nylon was first produced in 1938) and chewing gum became forms of alternative currency for all ages. For the leaders of politics and the war campaigns, it also brought the reality that Great Britain, having stood alone in 1940, was now the junior partner in an American-led alliance. By now certain generals, especially Bernard Montgomery, victor at El Alamein in 1942, were household names, but it was an American general, Dwight D. Eisenhower, who assumed supreme command of Operation Overlord, the planned landings in Normandy.

As the war, now truly a world war, expanded, another truth became ever more evident, so deeply unpalatable that many politicians could not accept it or closed their eyes to it. Great Britain was no longer capable of sustaining an imperial role. The Japanese capture of the fortress of Singapore on 15 February 1942 confirmed that Britain could not hold its great Far East stations; the sinking of HMS *Prince of Wales* and *Repulse* by Japanese aircraft had shown two months earlier that the long reach of the Royal Navy meant nothing without air power on a scale that Britain could not provide. The Indian nationalist leader Mahatma Gandhi put his finger bluntly on a sore point when, offered Indian independence after the war, he refused to accept 'post-dated cheques on a bankrupt empire'.

VICTORY

On 6 June 1944 the Normandy landings began, and a vast allied army moved into the series of battles that would take them through, not without damaging setbacks and heavy resistance, to the German border and beyond. Around the same time, Londoners learned to dread the approach of the flying bomb, and over 6,000 people were killed by these before it was found they could be quite easily shot down by fighter planes. No defence was found against the V2 rockets, of which over 1,000 were fired at London. Only the eradication of their launch sites, and

General Montgomery

the eventual land victory, saved the situation. On 8 May 1945, Churchill was able to announce the surrender of Germany and Italy to the House of Commons. There were cheers, laughter, tears and dancing in the streets.

CHAPTER SIXTEEN

The Atlantic Europeans

THE CHANGED FACE OF BRITAIN

Post-war reality began for Britain on 2 September 1945. The day of Japan's formal surrender was also the day on which the American Lend-Lease programme, which had supplied a vast amount of materials in the later part of the war, was abruptly terminated. On 26 July the first general election for ten years had returned a massive Labour majority and a government pledged to implement state ownership of coal, transport, iron and steel-making, power, telecommunications and civil aviation, and to bring about the 'welfare state'. The circumstances could hardly have been less auspicious. Expectations ran high, but the country was practically bankrupt. The fruits of victory began to seem ashen when rationing not only was continued but sometimes extended. British export trade was down by almost two-thirds, and the size of the merchant fleet was reduced by almost one-third. The war effort had drained the nation's finances: the government was in debt to the tune of £4,198,000,000, and its expenditure rate was running at five times the pre-war level. Yet the co-victor could scarcely present itself in line with the shattered, defeated nations for American aid whilst also insisting on its status as a great power and its role

---

THE FESTIVAL OF BRITAIN, 1951

A hundred years after the Great Exhibition, to mark the spirit of post-war recovery, the 1951 Festival of Britain was held on the south bank of the Thames, in London. Mounted with a curious but effective mixture of pomp-and-circumstance and off-beat quirkiness, it held up a mirror to a rather more introverted country than that of 1851. With India recently proclaimed as an independent republic, the theme of empire was muted. This was a time whose transitional aspect is more apparent now: when adjacent pavilions could show new jet engines and new steam locomotives; when groups of neighbours crowded round black-and-white television sets in darkened rooms; when the flat cap was still the universal headwear of the working man; when Football League teams looked for players in their own home towns; but when the motor car was already becoming the most common means of transport, and the individual dress style of the 'Teddy boys' was heralding the dramatic shift towards a youth-oriented culture. The Festival of Britain helped to stimulate new approaches in architecture and design, notably in the use of more lightweight but strong materials, moving away from traditional British solidity to a 'modern' functionality. The Royal Festival Hall is the only remaining structure from the Festival.

---

in reshaping the post-war world. But the employment level remained high, although the workforce had expanded by three million, and there was no repeat of the post-war slump of the 1920s.

Attlee's government pressed ahead with an unprecedented programme of industrial and social change, against the sustained opposition of not only the owners of nationalised businesses, whether steelworks or medical practices, but almost the entire industrial and commercial community. The lines of this battleground were blurred, and the eventual result was a compromise. A socialist and egalitarian Britain did not develop. But much had changed. Domestic servants had disappeared from all but the wealthiest homes, leaving a distaste for working in 'service' that was long traceable in British life. Social divisions became increasingly fluid and though the majority of citizens would still consider themselves to be 'working class', it was a working class with a sense of confidence, and money to spend. The consequences of this became more apparent in the early 1950s, when it combined with another radical change. This was the beginning of what became known as 'youth culture'. The age-group between sixteen and thirty had not contributed a great deal to social life in previous decades. It was an in-between group, expected gradually to identify itself with the values and practices of its elders. But now it began to assert its own identity and spending power, and to generate its own fashions, starting with the 'Teddy boy' style. The great reversal of creative direction and flow now got under way. Fashions, which had always begun in upper class circles and worked their way down, now went the other way. Trends, especially in music, which had been passed on to the young, were now increasingly passed on by the young. In all this, American influence was strong but most of the new upsurge of popular culture, like 'Skiffle' music, and the later, colossally successful Beatles and Rolling Stones, was home-grown.

ENLARGING GOVERNMENT

For almost thirty years, through an alternation of Labour and Conservative governments, there was a broad acceptance of the principles so heavily endorsed in 1945. This consensus was often obscured by set-piece disputes like the denationalisation, renationalisation and re-denationalisation of the steel industry by successive governments, but both parties practised a degree of government control of the economy which would have been unthinkable to the Conservative politicians of the 1930s; both were committed to programmes of improvement in housing, school-building, railway modernisation and road-building. Certain industries, including the coal mines and the railways, remained in public ownership until the 1980s.

By this time it was normal for people to expect the government to do something about any issue on which they felt strongly, from animal welfare to youthful graffitists. The era of the parliamentary lobbyist and the pressure group had come. Governments generally responded. Eventually the questions of government intrusion into matters previously left to individual decision or social agreement, and of the size, range and cost of government activity, became an issue in themselves. At successive elections, political parties promised less central government and more devolution of power to local bodies. In power, this did not happen. A kind of natural law says that more legislation leads inevitably to yet more legislation, so the role of government and administration gets larger.

EMPIRE, COMMONWEALTH AND IMMIGRATION

The concept of the British Commonwealth, first developed in the time of King George V, replaced that of the British Empire. George VI was the last Emperor of India, but his daughter Elizabeth II who acceded on his death in 1952, was still Queen of Canada, Australia, and New Zealand as independent states, as well as of African and West Indian colonies. Imperialist reactions had not quite disappeared. In reply to the Egyptian government's intended takeover of the Suez Canal in 1956, Britain, with France and Israel, launched an invasion of the canal zone. In the face of United Nations censure and strong American opposition, the operation ended in ignominious withdrawal, with Anthony Eden, then premier, suffering a collapse in his reputation for integrity. The imperial legacy affected England in various other ways. The expansion of the jobs market in the early 1950s brought a recruitment drive for workers from Jamaica to work in London's transport system; and job opportunities and higher wages in the English textile towns brought immigrants from Bengal, beginning the growth of England's black and Asian communities which by the end of the century would form about 10 per cent, and the fastest-growing part, of the total population. They followed the classic path of immigrant workers, congregating in areas of poorer housing and taking on the least desirable and lowest-paid tasks. An element of colour prejudice arose, but most politicians shunned the implications of a multi-racial society until the Conservative, Enoch Powell, made it an issue in 1968. Powell did not seem to be preaching harmony, but governments were compelled to take action to prevent social discrimination on grounds of race or skin colour.

'Britain will be honoured by historians more for the way in which she disposed of an empire than for the way in which she acquired it' – hopeful

---

THE *EMPIRE WINDRUSH*

Launched in Germany as the *Monte Rosa* in 1930, this ship was handed over to Britain as part of war reparations in 1945 and used as a troopship, being renamed *Empire Windrush* in January 1947. In 1948, in the course of a voyage from Australia to England, it put in at Kingston, Jamaica, to pick up servicemen on leave. With vacant space, passages to London were advertised at a special price of £28 and 10 shillings. Just under five hundred young men took advantage of this. About a quarter of these had places waiting in the Royal Air Force, the others were going on speculation, but it was known there were jobs available in Britain. The docking of the ship at Tilbury on 22 June 1948 attracted a great deal of publicity, some of it hostile. More than two hundred of the new colonists were at first accommodated in the Clapham Common Deep Shelter, built against air raids. Most of the voyagers expected to stay only a few years, but the arrival of the *Empire Windrush*'s passengers, the harbingers of many more from the West Indies, India, Pakistan and Africa, is now seen as a seminal event, beginning the still-evolving formation of a multi-cultural, multi-ethnic Britain.

---

words from Lord Harlech, British ambassador to the USA, in the *New York Times*, 28 October 1962. The withdrawal from empire created few ripples in English life, largely because the process began to be seen as inevitable, and had little or no adverse effect on economic life. The bloodbath between Muslims and Hindus that marked the emergence of Pakistan, the tensions between Greeks and Turks in Cyprus, the civil wars of Nigeria all remained matters for the newly independent states to resolve if they could. There was some indignation in Britain when in 2003 the prime minister of Zimbabwe, the erstwhile Southern Rhodesia, was still blaming the old colonial power for the troubles of his country.

RELATIONSHIPS WITH AMERICA AND EUROPE

The centres of concern for foreign policy were now the United States, which had pulled so sharply on the rein at the time of the Suez invasion, and the resurgent Europe, where a firm alliance between France and the new Federal Republic of Germany had become the basis of a new dynamism reflected in a prosperity which overtook that of Great Britain. Britain, like France, had acquired the technology of nuclear fission and possessed hydrogen bombs and nuclear warheads. These were seen as the guarantors of a permanent seat in the United Nations' Security Council and of acceptance as a great power. The cultivation of the 'special relationship' with the USA, begun by Winston Churchill and followed enthusiastically by every prime minister since, had its origin in wartime necessity. Its continuance was due to the Cold War with

---

'BAN THE BOMB'

Pacifism has a long and honourable tradition in England, which has never been a militaristic country and whose bouts of jingoistic war-fever, as in the late 1890s, and again in 1914–15, have been brief. This did not make life any easier for conscientious objectors in times of conscription, and many went to prison, and suffered abuse and physical attacks. In the 1950s, Britain's development of the hydrogen bomb resulted in a new form of non-violent protest, the Campaign for Nuclear Disarmament, whose leading figures were a Church of England priest, Canon John Collins, and an atheist, the eminent philosopher Bertrand Russell. CND initiated a series of annual marches from the nuclear weapons research centre at Aldermaston to London, as well as other demonstrations. This was the first time that a movement had arisen in protest against the manufacture and deployment of a particular weapon. Despite a huge popular following in the 1960s, CND did not persuade either Labour or Conservative governments to abandon the 'independent deterrent', or to forbid American nuclear bases in Britain; but its new tradition of anti-military protest survived into demonstrations against the wars in Vietnam and Iraq.

Russia, in which Britain and the USA could perceive mutual usefulness, and they formed the main axis of the NATO military alliance. The collapse of the Soviet Union in 1990 and the emergence of the USA as an unchallenged world superpower seemed to remove that necessity along with the purpose of NATO. The USA did not require a front-line radar base and rocket launching site. Britain did not need the backup of American intercontinental ballistic missiles.

But if strategy, and the desire to play a world role drew British interests across the Atlantic, the bread-and-butter issues of trade were increasingly dependent on Europe. The countries of Europe were Britain's main export market, not the Commonwealth, not the USA. Europe was only twenty-one miles away at its nearest point, and Britain for centuries had sought to be an arbiter in European affairs. Now western Europe was recreating itself in the European Economic Community. At first, Britain attempted to create an alternative market bloc, recruiting a number of smaller countries into the European Free Trade Association, but this was not a success. When Britain, under a Conservative government, sought to join the EEC in 1963, the application was vetoed by France. Ten years later, another Conservative government, under Edward Heath, made a successful application, and this was tested by a referendum – an unprecedented occurrence in British politics – in 1975. The issue was fiercely contested, with the question of British sovereignty lying at its heart, but two-thirds of those voting approved entry. Every English constituency recorded a majority in favour. It was a pivotal moment, and even though successive governments, sometimes while braying their desire to be in the European 'fast lane', persisted in watering down or resisting European proposals, it defined the future course of British politics and economic life. The agreement to build the Channel Tunnel, linking England to France for the first time since the Holocene era, and its completion in 1994, was an earnest of this.

THE BACKGROUND OF THATCHERISM

But entry into the Common Market did not result in sudden prosperity. The quadrupling of oil prices in the mid-1970s caused a surge in manufacturing and transport costs, and set off a ten-year period of monetary inflation in which the earning power of the pound sterling fell dramatically. In 1976 the danger of a collapse of the pound forced the Labour government of James Callaghan to seek a loan of $3.9 billion from the International Monetary Fund and impose heavy cuts in public spending. Price rises and wage demands on an unprecedented scale were accompanied by a severe rise in unemployment, reaching over two million by 1980 and three million by 1983. The commitment of government to manage the economy stalled with the economy itself. Industrial unrest erupted on a wide scale with fears of a return to the depths of 1932. A 'winter of discontent' in 1978–79 helped to oust the Labour government and brought in the Conservatives under Margaret Thatcher, the first woman prime minister in British history, and a politician convinced about what needed to be done. 'Thatcherism' was more an attitude of non-compromise and non-conformity with received opinion than a coherent strategy, but for the first time since 1945, a new political philosophy emerged. Armed with the subversive ideas of Sir Keith Joseph's Centre for Policy Studies, she set about knocking down the already shaky structure of a mixed state-capitalist economy. Market forces, not government provision, were now to drive the nation forward, on the rails of monetarism – stabilising the economy by tight control of the money supply. This in turn required a continued decrease in government spending. Thus the unemployment of the 1980s was not, like that of the 1930s, the result of laissez-faire economics but of a determined policy.

THE THATCHER YEARS

Mrs Thatcher's mettle was tested by the Argentinian occupation of the Falkland Islands, one of the residual fragments of the empire, in April 1982. A variegated armada of warships and merchant vessels was dispatched to the South Atlantic to restore British possession. The war was not without its risks and the Argentinians' French-made Exocet missiles sank or heavily damaged several British ships. Under controversial circumstances the nuclear submarine HMS

Margaret Thatcher visiting Ronald Reagan at the White House, 1983

Conqueror torpedoed and sank the Argentinian battleship *General Belgrano*. But the islands were retaken and Mrs Thatcher's prestige reached a high point. Though inevitably seen by some as a last twitch of British imperialism, the Falklands campaign was more than that. It was generally accepted as just and necessary. Argentina was a dictatorship; it had invaded illegally. The task of ousting its troops, no more and no less, had to be faced.

The 'Iron Lady's' second term of office, from 1985, pushed forward the doctrine of privatisation – nationalised or part state-owned industries were broken up and sold to become private companies. Councils which since 1945 had built thousands of houses and flats to rent, were compelled to sell them. Harold Macmillan, Tory prime minister from 1957 to 1963, later Lord Stockton, an elder statesman, protested in typical terms and to no avail about 'selling off the family silver'. Deregulation was an important element in the Thatcherist onslaught. Bus services competed at minimal fares on busy routes until only the one with the deepest pockets survived; then the fares went up. Mrs Thatcher found a new equivalent to the Argentine leader, Galtieri, in the leader of the mine workers, Arthur Scargill, who took his members out on a long, bitter and sometimes violent strike in 1984–85. The events of this campaign, with 'flying pickets' concentrating on certain sites, and massed police assembled in response, had some of the characteristics of civil warfare. Many civil libertarians were worried by the forceful role played by the police. Thatcherism was hostile to trade unions and a number of laws were passed to limit their activities, notably that of 'secondary picketing'. Union membership slumped from 13 million in

---

CARPET-BAGGERS

This originally American phrase gained wider currency in the 1990s, when the movement to convert mutual businesses, like friendly societies and building societies, into limited companies was at its height. Mutual businesses were owned by the totality of their members, as borrowers or savers, or both; and the conversion to company status brought a financial windfall, usually of around £1,500, to individual members. Many people opened small accounts with targeted societies in order to share in the hand-out – these were the carpet-baggers. Several large building societies converted themselves into banks, while others made a virtue of continuing to be mutual, and made provisions to deter carpet-bagging.

The building societies began in the nineteenth century; as *The Common People* notes, the name was always a misnomer: 'For the Building Society never builds; it merely advances money to enable its clients to buy their houses on the hire-purchase system.' Their effect – backed up by the Thatcher government's drive on the sale of council-owned houses in the 1980s – was to make England a nation of home-owners to a much greater degree than other industrialised countries. The vast amounts of capital located with the building societies, and the sensitivity of mortgage borrowers to rises in interest rates, contributed to the Blair government's perceived difficulties in achieving Britain's economic convergence with the other large EU countries and thus joining in the single European currency and accepting the financial rule of the European Central Bank.

1980 to under 7 million in 1999. In the end the miners had to yield against a government that had almost the whole press, and most public opinion, on its side. The government's hope of creating a nation of shareholders, with people buying shares in privatised utilities like British Gas and British Telecom, did not materialise. But a stock exchange boom did, and many people became extremely rich.

Mrs Thatcher won a third consecutive election in 1987, helped by the economic recovery of the 'boom'. Then in October 1987 the stock market crashed. The pound came under pressure on foreign exchanges, and interest rates went up to 15 per cent, a penal rate for those who had bought houses at inflated prices during the boom years and now faced much larger mortgage payments. The government's attempt to replace the out-of-date rating system for local taxation by a community charge based on individuals rather than property proved to be a disaster. Mrs Thatcher's implacable opposition to closer integration within the European Community also alienated the strong pro-Europe wing of the Tory party. The policy of reducing direct taxation and keeping down government spending had led both to a huge deficit in the balance of payments, and to a visible deterioration in the quality of schools, hospitals and public transport. Population groups whose lack of purchasing power put them beyond the interest of market forces, like pensioners and many working mothers, were protesting about their neglect. In 1990 opposition within her party and her cabinet to Mrs Thatcher resulted in a successful challenge to her leadership, and she resigned.

SOCIAL LIBERALISATION AND THE EROSION OF CLASS DISTINCTIONS

Within English society, there were trends which some regarded as progressive and liberalising, and which others saw as a pattern of moral and social decline. What was indisputable was a greater openness about matters previously considered taboo in public discussion. A failed prosecution in 1960 of D.H. Lawrence's novel of four decades earlier, *Lady Chatterley's Lover*, also cleared the way for many less literary and more sexually explicit works to be published. Homosexuality, always an element in private life, its practice almost always subject to extreme penalties, was legalised in 1967 ten years after the publication of the Wolfenden Report which recommended its decriminalisation. The official censorship of plays was dropped in 1968, though a law against blasphemy remained. Sexual mores generally were relaxed, and related matters discussed in public often in great detail. Abortion, once illegal except under special circumstances, was legalised, and the contraceptive pill radically changed birth-control methods. Divorce, which had been frowned on and made difficult by both church and state, was made very much easier to obtain, and the divorce rate increased dramatically.

Those who deplored these trends often demanded that the government give a moral lead; Harold Macmillan, as premier, responded that that was a matter for the bishops. The church, however, was an institution on the sidelines and the only bishops to be noticed were those who advocated a new theology which seemed far from the Thirty-nine Articles of Anglicanism. The Church of England sponsored a new translation of the Bible and a new Prayer Book, intended to reflect modern language and modern life, but they did not seem likely to enjoy the respect and longevity accorded to their predecessors. In 1994, in response to long tapping at the door, the church also finally admitted women to the priesthood. The Non-conformist churches had had women ministers for some time before. In part it was a response to the decline in male candidates for the clergy; now in religion as in medicine, it seemed likely that women would eventually outnumber men. By the end of the century, with civil weddings allowed to happen virtually anywhere, and with cremation the increasingly favoured method of disposal of the dead, many of the population would never enter a church at all.

Though in the census of 2001, 71.7 per cent of the population described themselves as Christian, religious observance seemed to be moving towards something like the cult of the pre-Christian Roman Empire, a matter of forms and ceremonies, presided over the by the leaders of society and not of much account to the population other than some pious country folk. Many would not even avail themselves of the formality of civil marriage. In 2001, there were over three million households consisting of a co-habiting couple or a one-parent family (many of these involving a divorced rather than an unmarried parent), compared to seven million conventional family households. The enormous growth in the number of unmarried mothers, together with the great increase in divorces, made the one-parent family socially acceptable among all classes. The stigma attached to 'illegitimate' birth disappeared. This dramatic change in the social composition of England had occurred within a period of hardly more than thirty years. Though it was inevitably treated as a 'breaking down' of social forms and traditional practice, it was not yet clear what new kinds of bonds and structures were being formed within this unscripted and entirely spontaneous trend, and to what extent it would change the concept or sense of 'Englishness'.

The concept of 'class' itself suffered some erosion in the storm. At the end of the twentieth century, the terms upper, middle and working class still had some relevance to life in England. Everyone knew what they meant. But the words had little practical significance except perhaps for a small section of the 'upper class' and for the declining numbers who still considered themselves to be 'working class'. Almost everyone else was in the middle, a vast group which could be split, fragmented, analysed in any way the observer could desire, but whose subdivisions all had too much in common to be truly separate from one another in the way of the former class distinctions. Time seemed to be running out for the few remaining social-revolutionary class warriors: the system itself was likely to expire first. Economic divisions were wide but increasingly unrelated to class. A small group, the directors of large companies and employees of some financial trading companies, aroused envy and hostility by their very large salaries and pay-offs; a culture of mutual self-provision, as effective as anything seen in the eighteenth century, was rampant among remuneration committees and non-executive directors. The social commentator, Will Hutton, railed against 'an opted-out overclass, uncommitted and disconnected from the aspirations and moral judgements of their fellow-citizens' (*The Stakeholding Society*, 1999). Another high-earning small group attracted more public favour, even if it could be short-lived or invasive: these were the stars of sport and screen, who (often willingly) paid the price of public revelations of their private lives in return for the opulent lifestyle of the super-rich. But whereas the lifestyle of the wealthy had once been completely different from that of the rest of the population, now the difference was of cost and degree. Mass travel to sun-baked beaches offered everyone what had been the experience of only the very rich, or very adventurous, before the era of the wide-bodied jet plane. Class was no barrier to power, wealth or status: and to attain any one or more of these, only a very moderate ability was sometimes necessary.

ENGLAND AT THE TURN OF THE MILLENNIUM

Mrs Thatcher's successor in 1990 was a compromise-figure, John Major, whose low-key style was very different but who was a faithful Thatcherite in policy. British involvement in the American-led Gulf War of 1991 helped Major to election victory in 1992, but the chaotic period ensuing, when the value of sterling crashed, interest rates were briefly pushed up to absurd levels and Britain pulled out of the Exchange Rate Mechanism system, destroyed faith in his government and also shattered Conservative morale. By 1995, after eighteen consecutive years in power, and faced by the efficient and aggressive ranks of New Labour under Tony Blair, the Conservatives went down to a defeat even greater than that of 1945. Indeed, in the last years of the twentieth century, the Conservatives lost their reputation as the party that was sensible with the country's money, and instead became identified with 'boom-and-bust' management; and the Labour Party, previously hampered by a 'tax-and-spend' label, became seen as the home of financial rectitude. To achieve this, it had a plan, in which a central part was the control of monetary inflation. In a theatrical but effective gesture in 1997 the Chancellor of the Exchequer, Gordon Brown, handed control of interest rates, hitherto a government responsibility, to the Bank of

---

AN OMELETTE AND A GLASS OF WINE

Although royal Tudor cooks could roast a pigeon inside a hen inside a goose inside a swan, the art of cooking was never closely associated with England. 'Thirty religions, and only one sauce,' the Italian Francesco Carraciolo was said to have remarked in the eighteenth century. Little changed in this respect until the 1950s. In the first year of that decade Elizabeth David (1913–92) published *Mediterranean Cookery*, and later *French Country Cooking*. Her evocative prose found an echo in a nation once again able to travel to the continent, and, with the advent of the package tour, soon doing so in unprecedented numbers. Olive oil, previously regarded as a medical aid for external use, began to be used, and the English discovered what other nations already knew about herbs and garlic. Over the next fifty years, Italian, Indian, Chinese and Thai food were also discovered and appreciated, in restaurants and in home cooking. By the end of the century, the café with pavement seats was a normal sight in British high streets, and an eclectic range of food had brought dramatic changes in eating habits. Big changes also took place in drinking habits: the restricted hours for public drinking introduced in the First World War were largely abandoned; and Britain took to wine-drinking on a scale unprecedented in any country that was not itself a wine-producer.

England. The rest of the plan involved continuance of its Conservative predecessor's spending cuts and limitations, until the government's accumulated 'war-chest' eventually began to be dispensed, under such rigorous controls that many projects were delayed. Although the Labour Party and the trade unions remained in alliance, the unions were disappointed to find that much of the legislation of the Thatcher years, against secondary and sympathy strikes, was going to remain in force. The government was at pains to show that it was not hostile to the business world while also, in fields such as overseas aid, showing a more positive commitment to help the underdeveloped countries than any of its predecessors. On both sides of the old political divide, observers could tot up plus and minus marks, depending on their points of view, while the New Labour government itself, again more than any before it, tried to subject every area it controlled, from primary schools to police forces, from ambulances to air traffic controllers, to a regime of targets, assessments, rewards and penalties. This attempt to make the country, in a popular current phrase, 'get its act together' was pursued with impressive vigour, even if it was found vexing and sometimes counter-productive in the workplace. As Great Britain, certainly not yet New Britain, came to celebrate the end of a millennium, the government's own effort to address the occasion, the exhibition-cum-spectacle staged in the vastly expensive Greenwich 'Millennium' Dome, was awarded a very moderate mark by the people. There was no 'Festival of Britain' spirit. Those who remembered World War II were old age pensioners by now, and feeling themselves a neglected and unappreciated section of society. With no great recent national struggle to look back on, but only the political and social legacy of fifty-five years of relative peace, defined by 'post-' words: post-imperial, post-industrial, post-modern – it was still unclear what the 'pre-' word, or words, might be, that would signify Britain's, and England-within-Britain's, direction and significance in the twenty-first century.

A Chronology of Events in England

55 BC

- Roman exploratory expedition lands on south coast.

54 BC

- Second Roman expedition penetrates past the Thames.

AD 43

- Roman invasion begins, under Aulus Plautius; British resistance under Caractacus.
- Founding of Colchester: oldest Romano-British town, and colony of Britannia.

50

- Defeat of Caractacus.

51

- Capture of Caractacus.

61

- Uprising of the Iceni tribe under Queen Boudicca is suppressed by Romans; death by suicide of Boudicca.

74

- Conquest of the Brigantes by Petilius Cerialis.

78

- Agricola, Roman governor, begins campaign of conquest.

85

- Roman colony at Lincoln founded around this time.

98

- Roman colony of Gloucester founded around this time.

122

- Roman Emperor Hadrian visits Britannia.

126

- Completion of Hadrian's Wall as northern boundary.

196

- Albinus proclaims himself emperor in Britain; killed at Lyons in 197.

211

- Emperor Septimius Severus dies at York.

212

- All free inhabitants of Britannia are eligible to be Roman citizens.

286

- Carausius proclaims himself emperor.

293

- Allectus proclaimed emperor after assassination of Carausius; is himself murdered. Constantius restores imperial rule.

304

- St Alban becomes first Christian martyr in Britain.

306

- Constantius, western emperor, dies at York; Constantine is hailed there as emperor.

312

- Number of provinces in Britannia increased to four, around this time.

314

- British bishops attend synod at Arles.

367

- Pictish invasions past Hadrian's Wall.

369

- Theodosius effects restoration of central power; establishes Valentia as a fifth province.

383

- Revolt of Magnus Maximus; he becomes Emperor of Britain and Gaul (to 388).

398

- Stilicho's expedition against the Picts and Scots.

405

- Missionary work of St Patrick begins.

407

- Roman army in Britain declares Constantine emperor (to 411).

410

- Legions withdrawn from Britain.

411

- Pelagius, heretical theologian, active around this time.

446

- 'Groans of the Britons': unsuccessful appeal to Aetius, minister of Valentinian III, for protection.

449

- Invasions by Germanic tribes: Angles, Jutes, Saxons, settlements begin. Emergence of Vortigern as British leader.

477

- South Saxons under Aelle begin settling.

495

- West Saxons under Cerdic begin settling.

516

- Battle of Mount Badon stems Anglo-Saxon settlement for a time.

526

- East and Middle Saxons settling around this time.

546

- Kingdom of Bernicia founded by Ida.

547

- Around now, Gildas writes his *De Excidio Britanniae*.

560

- Kingdom of Deira founded by Aella.

577

- Battle of Dyrham: West Saxons defeat the British.

588

- Bernicia and Deira joined as Northumbria under Aethelric.

597

- Augustine sent by Pope Gregory on mission to Kentish court; he becomes first Archbishop of Canterbury.

603

- Battle of Degsastan: Northumbrians defeat Scots.

604

- Death of St Augustine.

613

- Battle of Chester: Northumbrians defeat Britons of North Wales.

627

- Edwin, King of Northumbria, adopts Christianity.

628

- Mercians under Penda defeat West Saxons at Cirencester.

633

- Mercians with British allies defeat Northumbrians.

634

- Oswald defeats Britons; re-establishes Northumbrian kingdom.

635

- St Aidan called from Iona to Lindisfarne.

642

- Oswald defeated and killed in battle with Mercians under Penda, at Oswestry.

655

- Battle of the Winwaed: Penda defeated and killed by Northumbrians under Oswiu.

659

- Mercian power restored under Wulfhere.

664

- Synod of Whitby approves the Roman ritual.

669

- Theodore of Tarsus becomes Archbishop of Canterbury; organises English church.

671

- Ecgfrith becomes King of Northumbria.

672

- First synod of English clergy, at Hertford.

680

- Caedmon, first known poet in English, lives around this time.

685
- Northumbrians defeated by Picts at Nechtansmere; death of Ecgfrith.

687
- Death of St Cuthbert, Bishop of Lindisfarne.

688
- Ine becomes King of Wessex.

709
- Death of St Wilfred, Bishop of York.

715
- *Beowulf*, Old English narrative poem, composed around this time.

716
- Ethelbald becomes King of Mercia.

731
- Bede completes his *Ecclesiastical History of the English People*.

733
- Ethelbald of Mercia becomes Overlord of Wessex.

735
- Death of Bede.

752
- Battle of Burford: Cuthred of Wessex defeats Ethelbald.

757
- Offa becomes King of Mercia.

777
- Offa defeats West Saxons under Cynewulf.

784
- Offa's Dyke built around this time.

786
- Offa has Lichfield made the seat of an archbishop (to 803).

787
- First annual offering of 'Peter's pence' to the Pope.

793
- First recorded Viking raids, on Lindisfarne.

796
- Offa makes commercial treaty with Charlemagne.
- Death of Offa.

802
- Egbert becomes King of Wessex.

825
- Egbert conquers Cornwall; becomes Overlord of Mercia, Kent and Essex around this time.

829
- Battle of Ellandun: Egbert conquers Mercia.

838
- Egbert defeats alliance of Cornish and Danes.

839
- Death of Egbert; Aethelwulf becomes King of Wessex.

851
- Aethelwulf defeats Danes at Ockley.

855
- Danes winter in Sheppey.

862
- Death of St Swithin, Bishop of Winchester.

864
- Danes destroy Winchester, capital of Wessex.

866
- 'Great Army' of Danes lands in East Anglia.

867
- Danes take York; Northumbrian kingdom overthrown.

869
- Danish conquest of East Anglia; death of its king, Edmund.

871
- Danes invade Wessex. Death of Aethelred, King of Wessex; succeeded by Alfred.

874
- Danes overthrow the kingdom of Mercia.

878
- Danes under Guthrum invade Wessex; battle of Chippenham, King Alfred forced to take refuge; later defeats Guthrum at battle of Ethandun, or Edlington.
- Treaty of Wedmore establishes truce for fifteen years; Guthrum adopts Christianity.
- Division of the country between English and Danish dominion.

886
- Alfred takes control of London.

891
- Compilation of the *Anglo-Saxon Chronicle* begins (to 1154).

893
- Danish invasion defeated at Farnham and Benfleet.

899
- Death of Alfred the Great; succession of Edward the Elder.

902
- Edward the Elder defeats Northumbrian Danes at battle of the Holme.

911
- Danish invasion defeated by Edward the Elder at Wednesfield.

916
- Edward the Elder and Aethelflaed, Lady of Mercia, gain eastern Mercia.
- Edward defeats Danes at Tempsford and Maldon.

921
- East Anglia recovered.

924

- Death of Edward the Elder; succeeded briefly by Elfward, then Athelstan.

926

- Athelstan takes control of Northumbria.

937

- Athelstan defeats combination of Scots, Britons and Vikings at Brunanburh.

939

- Death of Athelstan; accession of Edmund I.

943

- Around this time, Dunstan becomes Abbot of Glastonbury.

946

- Murder of Edmund I; Eadred becomes king.

947

- Erik Bloodaxe becomes king at York.

954

- Death of Erik Bloodaxe; Northumbria becomes an Anglo-Saxon earldom.

955

- Death of Eadred; accession of Eadwig.

956

- Exile of Dunstan.

957

- Division of rule between Eadwig and Edgar.

959

- Death of Eadwig; Edgar becomes sole king.

960

- Dunstan is made Archbishop of Canterbury and begins ecclesiastical reforms.

970

- The *Exeter Book*, compilation of Old English poems and riddles, is compiled around this time.

975

- Death of Edgar; accession of Edward ('the Martyr').

978

- Murder of Edward; accession of Aethelred Unraed, aged ten.

980

- Viking attacks on Southampton, Thanet and Chester.
- First payments of Danegeld by Aethelred's government.

991

- English defeat at Maldon is commemorated in the poem *The Battle of Maldon*.

993

- Danes sack Bamburgh.

1000

- Widespread anticipation of Day of Judgement on 1 January is not realised.

1002
- Massacre of Danes in England on St Brice's Day (13 November).

1007
- First levying of ship money.

1011
- Danes capture Canterbury.

1012
- Killing of Archbishop Aelfheah (St Alphege) by Danes.

1013
- Swein Forkbeard invades England for the third time; Aethelred flees to Normandy; Danish rule established.

1014
- Death of Swein; Cnut succeeds him. Return of Aethelred.

1016
- Death of Aethelred; his son, Edmund Ironside, chosen as king by the Saxons; continued fighting with Danes under Cnut. Partition of kingdom arranged, but Edmund's death leaves Cnut as sole king.

1018
- Battle of Carham confirms Scottish possession of Lothian.

1035
- Death of Cnut; English kingdom divided between Harold Harefoot and Harthacnut.
- William, illegitimate son of Duke Robert, becomes Duke of Normandy.

1038
- Death of Harold Harefoot; Harthacnut becomes king.

1042
- Death of Harthacnut; accession of Edward the Confessor, son of Aethelred.

1045
- Edward marries Edith, daughter of Earl Godwine of Wessex.

1051
- Exile of Earl Godwine.

1052
- Return of Earl Godwine.

1053
- Death of Earl Godwine; his son, Harold Godwinson, is Earl of Wessex.

1065
- Consecration of Westminster Abbey.

1066
- Death of King Edward the Confessor.
- Harold Godwinson claims throne; defeats Harold Hardrada at Stamford Bridge.
- William of Normandy invades and defeats Harold at Hastings; is crowned as king.

1067
- William I begins building of Tower of London.

1068
- Anti-Norman revolts crushed.

1069
- Danish invasion; William I devastates the north after anti-Norman uprising.

1070
- Hereward the Wake active in anti-Norman raids.

1072
- William I invades Scotland.

1079
- Foundation of Newcastle upon Tyne.

1086
- Compilation of Domesday Book, to 1090.

1087
- Death of William I; accession of William II, 'Rufus'.

1092
- William II annexes Cumbria.

1097
- Westminster Hall erected.

1100
- William II killed in New Forest; accession of Henry I.

1109
- War with France (to 1113).

1110
- The pipe-roll system of exchequer records introduced.

1123
- The chronicler Orderic Vitalis begins

his *Historia Ecclesiae* ('History of the Church').

1135
- Death of Henry I; crown is claimed by Stephen of Blois.

1138
- Civil war between supporters of Stephen and Matilda; Scots supporting Matilda defeated at battle of the Standard.

1141
- Capture of Stephen.

1142
- Stephen exchanged for Robert of Gloucester.

1147
- Matilda leaves England.

1153
- Treaty of Wallingford accepts Henry Plantagenet of Anjou as heir to the throne.

1154
- Death of Stephen; accession of Henry II, first Angevin or Plantagenet king.
- Nicholas Breakspear elected as Pope Hadrian IV.

1155
- Henry II extends the royal forests.

1157
- Thomas Becket appointed Chancellor.

1162

- Thomas Becket appointed Archbishop of Canterbury.

1165

- 'Constitutions of Clarendon' set limits to church's jurisdiction.
- Becket leaves the country.

1166

- System of travelling judges, 'justices in eyre' set up, under Assize of Clarendon; towns and counties instructed to erect jails.

1167

- Foundation of Oxford University.

1170

- Becket returns; is assassinated in Canterbury Cathedral.

1171

- Henry II makes an expedition to assert control of Ireland.

1172

- Henry II is reconciled with the papacy.

1174

- Henry II's penance for Becket's murder, at Canterbury.
- Battle of Alnwick, King William 'the Lion' of Scotland captured.

1176

- Building of Old London Bridge (demolished in 1832).

1184

- Assize of Woodstock regulates management of royal forests.

1185

- Earthquake damages Lincoln Cathedral.

1188

- Henry II's sons, Richard and John, ally against him, with Philip II of France.
- Tax levied for the first time on personal property, to pay for Third Crusade.

1189

- Death of Henry II; accession of Richard I, 'Coeur de Lion'.
- First recorded Mayor of London, Henry Fitzaylwin.

1190

- Persecutions of English Jews.
- Capture of Richard I by Duke of Austria.

1193

- Hubert Walter, Archbishop of Canterbury, is appointed Justiciar during imprisonment of Richard I by the Holy Roman Emperor.

1194

- Release and return of Richard I.

1196

- Richard I makes war on France.

1199

- Death of Richard I; accession of John.
- Foundation of Liverpool.

1202
- War in France.

1204
- War in France; English possessions north of the Loire are lost.

1205
- Dispute between King John and Pope Innocent III over appointment of an archbishop of Canterbury.

1208
- Pope places England under interdict.

1209
- King John excommunicated.
- Invasion of Scotland; peace made with William the Lion.
- Establishment of Cambridge University.

1212
- War with France; the French fleet is largely destroyed.

1213
- King John submits to the Pope.
- Foundation of St Thomas's Hospital, London.

1214
- War in France; French naval defeat at Damme, but land victory at Bouvines.

1215
- Barons of England force John to accept their charter, Magna Carta.
- War breaks out between baronial groups in support of and opposition to King John.

1216
- A group of barons invite Prince Louis of France to become king; he lands in England.
- Death of John; accession of Henry III.

1219
- Hubert de Burgh appointed Justiciar.

1222
- St George's Day (23 April) established as a national holiday.

1231
- Charter granted to Cambridge University.

1234
- Nobles rebel against Henry III's patronage of foreigners, especially French.

1235
- Matthew Paris, chronicler, works on *Chronica Maiora* at St Albans Abbey.

1236
- Henry III marries Eleanor of Provence; influx of French courtiers.

1238
- Consecration of Peterborough Cathedral.

1247
- Foundation of Bethlehem Hospital, London, by Simon Fitzmary.

1248
- Simon de Montfort appointed Seneschal of Gascony.
- Charter granted to Oxford University.

1250
- *The Harrowing of Hell*: oldest known dramatic work in English.

1255
- Henry III accepts crown of Sicily for his son, Edmund.

1256
- Simon de Montfort heads a group of barons protesting against Henry III's rule.

1258
- Henry III holds a Council at Oxford; the 'Provisions of Oxford' are imposed by the barons on Henry III.
- Consecration of Salisbury Cathedral.

1259
- Treaty of Paris defines English possessions in France.

1263
- Henry III renounces Provisions of Oxford.

1264
- Barons' War breaks out. Simon de Montfort defeats Henry III at battle of Lewes (14 May).
- The Mise of Amiens: Louis IX of Frances arbitrates in favour of Henry III.

1265
- Simon de Montfort defeated and killed at battle of Evesham.

1272
- Death of Henry III; accession of Edward I.

1275
- First Statute of Westminster.

1276
- Edward I invades Wales.

1283
- Edward I proclaims the annexation of Wales to England.

1285
- Justices of the peace installed for the first time.

1290
- Treaty of Birgham with Scotland provides for marriage of Margaret, 'Maid of Norway' and Edward of Caernarvon.
- Jews are expelled from England.

1294
- Death of Roger Bacon, philosopher and early scientist.

1295
- Edward I invades France.

1296
- Edward I invades Scotland, removes John Balliol from kingship and proclaims himself Lord of Scotland.

1297
- English army defeated at Stirling (11 September).

1298
- Edward I defeats Scots under William Wallace at battle of Falkirk (22 July).

1301

- Inauguration of Edward of Caernarvon as first English Prince of Wales.

1303

- Avoirdupois weight measurement system introduced.

1307

- Death of Edward I on his way to invade Scotland. Accession of Edward II.

1308

- Edward II marries Princess Isabella of France. He is forced to exile his controversial favourite, Piers Gaveston.

1310

- The Lords Ordainers assume control of government from Edward II.

1312

- Piers Gaveston (returned to England) is executed.

1314

- Edward II is defeated by Robert I of Scotland at battle of Bannockburn (24 June).

1321

- Edward II forced by barons to exile his favourites, the Despensers.

1322

- Edward II defeats Thomas of Lancaster at Boroughbridge.
- Recall of the Despensers.

1326

- Queen Isabella goes to Paris; becomes mistress of Roger Mortimer. They invade England and attack the Despensers.

1327

- Edward II deposed by Isabella and Mortimer (January) and murdered (21 September). Edward III accedes, with effective power held by Isabella and Mortimer.

1328

- England acknowledges Scottish independence in Treaty of Edinburgh–Northampton.

1330

- Assertion of power by Edward III: execution of Roger Mortimer.

1332

- First recorded division of parliament into separate Houses of Lords and Commons.

1333

- Edward III defeats an invading Scottish army at Halidon Hill (19 July).

1335

- Edward III invades Scotland.
- Internal free trade established in England.

1337

- Beginning of the Hundred Years War with France.

1340

- Naval victory over France at battle of Sluys (24 June).

1345

- Completion of building at York Minster.

1346

- Edward III defeats French at battle of Crécy (26 August); siege of Calais begins (August).
- David II of Scotland invades England; defeated and captured at battle of Neville's Cross (17 October).

1347

- Naval victory over French at battle of Crotoye; English conquer Calais.

1348

- First appearance of the Black Death in England, with enormous death toll and economic and social disruption.
- Truce with France until 1350.
- Around this time Edward III founds the Order of the Garter, oldest English order of chivalry.

1349

- Death of William of Occam or Ockham, philosopher and propounder of 'Occam's Razor'.

1350

- New invasion of France by Edward III.

1351

- Statute of Labourers attempts to regulate wages and prices after the disruption of the Black Death.

1352

- Death of Laurence Minot, patriotic poet.

1353

- The Statute of Praemunire is passed, to limit papal claims in England.

1356

- Edward III defeats the French at battle of Poitiers (19 September); King Jean of France captured.
- Edward III invades Scotland in the 'Burnt Candlemas'.

1360

- Treaty of Brétigny with France: Edward II renounces claim to French throne but holds Calais, Guienne, Gascony and Poitou.

1362

- *Piers Plowman*, poem attributed to William Langland.
- English replaces Norman French as language of parliament and the law courts.

1364

- Warfare with France resumes.

1367

- Construction of Exeter Cathedral completed.
- The Black Prince defeats French and rebel Spanish at battle of Navarrette (3 April).

1372

- English fleet defeated by Spanish at La Rochelle.

1376

- Death of the Black Prince.
- The 'Good Parliament' is convened.

1377

- Death of Edward III and accession of Richard II, with John of Gaunt, Duke of Lancaster, as regent.
- First of a series of poll taxes imposed.
- John Wyclif, intellectual leader of the Lollards, summoned before Bishop of London.
- Post of Speaker of House of Commons is first recorded.

1381

- First Navigation Act to protect maritime trade.
- Peasants revolt against poll tax, under leadership of Wat Tyler; he is killed by Mayor of London.
- Execution of John Ball, peasant leader.

1382

- Wyclif's teachings condemned by a church council in London; his Bible translation completed around this time.

1384

- Death of John Wyclif.

1386

- Treaty of Windsor establishes alliance with Portugal.

1387

- Barons opposing the policies of Richard II, the 'Lords Appellant', defeat Richard and assume control of government.

- French and Castilian invasion fleet defeated off Margate.
- Geoffrey Chaucer begins writing *The Canterbury Tales*.

1388

- Scots win battle of Otterburn (Chevy Chase, 15 August) in Douglas–Percy war.
- Associates of Richard II condemned to death by 'Merciless Parliament'.
- Around this time, Wyclif's later version of the Bible is completed by his followers.

1389

- Richard II reassumes control of government.

1396

- Richard II campaigns in Ireland.

1397

- Richard II acts against the 'Lords Appellant'.
- Dick Whittington is elected Mayor of London.

1399

- Death of John of Gaunt; Richard II refuses to allow Henry of Lancaster to inherit. Henry invades England and forces Richard's abdication; he becomes Henry IV by consent of parliament.

1400

- Richard II dies in prison.
- Welsh revolt under Owain Glyndwr, proclaimed as Prince of Wales.
- Death of Geoffrey Chaucer.

1401

- A new statute, De Heretico Comburendo, allows for the burning to death of heretics. William Sawtrey is the first victim.

1402

- Scots defeated at battle of Homildon Hill.

1403

- Henry Percy ('Hotspur') joins Glyndwr in revolt; he is killed in battle of Shrewsbury (21 July).

1405

- Further insurrection against Henry IV led by Archbishop Scrope of York and the Earl of Nottingham. Scrope executed.

1406

- James, crown prince of Scotland, captured at sea on his way to France and imprisoned in London.

1408

- Death of John Gower, poet.

1411

- Construction of the Guildhall, city of London, begins.

1413

- Death of Henry IV; accession of Henry V.

1415

- Henry V invades France and wins battle of Agincourt (25 October).

1417

- Sir John Oldcastle, prominent Lollard, burned as a heretic.
- Caen captured by Henry V.

1418

- English besiege Rouen.

1419

- English capture Rouen.

1420

- Treaty of Troyes recognises Henry V as heir to the King of France.

1421

- Scots and French defeat English at Baugé, France.

1422

- Death of Henry V; the infant Henry VI becomes king. John of Lancaster and Humphrey of Gloucester head regency council.

1424

- English defeat the French at battle of Verneuil (17 August).

1428

- Siege of Orleans begins.

1429

- The French, led by Joan of Arc, defeat the English at battle of Patay and raise the siege of Orleans (7 May).

1431

- Joan of Arc is condemned as a witch and burned at Rouen.

1436

- The French regain Paris.

1437

- Henry VI assumes government.

1441

- Henry VI founds King's College, Cambridge.

1448

- The French regain Anjou and Maine.

1450

- Rebellion in Kent led by Jack Cade; he is killed by Sheriff of Kent.
- The French regain Normandy.

1453

- Final battle of the Hundred Years War, at Castillon.
- English lose Bordeaux to French (19 October).
- First battle in Wars of the Roses, at Stamford Bridge (August).

1454

- Richard, Duke of York, made Protector during Henry VI's mental illness.

1455

- Dismissal and rebellion of York; Yorkists win battle of St Albans (22 May).

1460

- Battle of Northampton (10 July): Yorkists under Earl of Warwick defeat Henry VI. Battle of Wakefield (30 December): Lancastrians defeat Yorkists. Death of the Duke of York.

1461

- Yorkist victory at battle of Mortimer's Cross (2 February); Lancastrian victory at second battle of St Albans (17 February). Henry VI is deposed and flees to Edinburgh. Lancastrian victory at battle of Ferrybridge (28 March); Yorkist victory at battle of Towton (29 March) results in proclamation of Edward IV as king.

1464

- Return of Henry VI; battles of Hedgeley Moor (25 April) and Hexham (15 May) are Yorkist victories.

1465

- Henry VI imprisoned.

1469

- Battle of Edgecote (26 July): Edward IV defeated by Earl of Warwick.

1470

- Restoration of Henry VI.
- Edward IV is victorious at battle of Empingham (12 March).

1471

- Yorkists victorious at battles of Barnet (14 April) and Tewkesbury (4 May).
- Edward IV reclaims throne; Henry VI is imprisoned and murdered.

1475

- Edward IV invades France.
- First book to be printed in English is *Recuyell of the Histories of Troye*, by William Caxton's press in Bruges.

1482

- England permanently gains Berwick-upon-Tweed from Scotland.

1483

- Death of Edward IV and accession of twelve-year-old Edward V – assassinated with his brother in the Tower of London by order of his uncle, the Duke of Gloucester, who becomes king as Richard III.
- Rebellion against Richard III by Duke of Buckingham is put down.

1484

- Council of the North established in attempt to give stable government to the region.
- Bail for defendants in law courts is introduced.

1485

- Richard III is defeated and killed at battle of Bosworth (22 August); Henry VII becomes king as first Tudor monarch.
- Formation of Yeomen of the Guard as royal bodyguard.
- Caxton prints Sir Thomas Malory's *Morte d'Arthur*.

1486

- Marriage of Henry VII and Elizabeth, daughter of Edward IV, ends Wars of the Roses.

1487

- Lambert Simnel's revolt.
- Battle of Stoke (16 June) won by royal forces.

1495

- Morality play of *Everyman* composed around now.
- Completion of building at Canterbury Cathedral.

1496

- Failure of Perkin Warbeck's first invasion.
- Magnus Intercursus: important trade treaty with the Netherlands.

1497

- Perkin Warbeck captured after failed invasion of Cornwall, and imprisoned.
- John Cabot's expedition to Labrador, Newfoundland and South Carolina.

1498

- Desiderius Erasmus, celebrated humanist, visits Oxford.

1499

- Perkin Warbeck is hanged.

1503

- Marriage of Margaret Tudor, daughter of Henry VII, to James IV of Scotland – this makes possible the accession of James I in 1603.

1509

- Death of Henry VII; accession of Henry VIII.
- Marriage of Henry VIII and Catherine of Aragon.

1510

- Erasmus lectures on Greek at Oxford University.

1512
- Foundation of the Admiralty.

1513
- Henry VIII invades France; defeats French at battle of Guinegate.
- Invading Scottish army is defeated at Flodden (9 September).

1514
- Henry VIII grants a charter to Trinity House.

1515
- Cardinal Wolsey appointed Lord Chancellor.

1516
- Sir Thomas More publishes *Utopia*.

1517
- Foundation of the Royal College of Physicians, by Thomas Linacre.

1520
- Henry VIII confers with François I of France at the 'Field of the Cloth of Gold'.

1521
- Henry VIII receives papal title of Defender of the Faith for his refutation of Martin Luther.

1523
- English invasion of France under Duke of Suffolk.

1525
- William Tyndale completes his English version of the New Testament.

1526
- Building of Fountains Abbey completed.

1528
- England and France declare war on the Holy Roman Empire.

1529
- Peace of Cambrai between England and France and the Holy Roman Empire.
- Henry VIII seeks a divorce from Catherine of Aragon; dismissal of Wolsey. More becomes Lord Chancellor.

1530
- Death of Wolsey.

1532
- More resigns as Lord Chancellor.
- 'Submission of the Clergy' to Henry VIII.

1533
- Henry VIII marries Anne Boleyn; he is excommunicated by the Pope.
- Thomas Cromwell appointed as the king's chief minister.

1534
- The Act of Supremacy severs the Anglican church from papal control; Henry VIII becomes Supreme Governor of the Church of England.
- Peter's Pence annual offering to the Pope is abolished.

1535
- Execution of Sir Thomas More.
- Publication of Miles Coverdale's Bible in English.

- Thomas Cromwell appointed Vicar-General.

1536

- First act for dissolution of monasteries.
- Execution of Anne Boleyn for adultery (19 May); Henry VIII marries Jane Seymour (30 May).
- Insurrection in the north, known as the Pilgrimage of Grace, is suppressed; further uprising in Lincolnshire also put down.

1537

- Execution of Robert Aske and John Pickering, leaders of the Pilgrimage of Grace.
- Death of Jane Seymour in childbirth.

1539

- 'Six Articles' Act against heresy.

1540

- Anne of Cleves married to and divorced by Henry VIII. He marries Katharine Howard.
- Execution of Thomas Cromwell.

1541

- Execution of Margaret Pole, Countess of Salisbury.

1542

- Scottish army defeated at battle of Solway Moss (14 December).
- Katharine Howard executed for adultery.

1543

- Henry VIII marries Catherine Parr.

1544

- English army invades Scotland in the 'Rough Wooing'.

1545

- New ship *Mary Rose* sinks in the Solent (raised 1982)

1546

- Anne Askew tortured and burned as a heretic in London.

1547

- Death of Henry VIII; accession of Edward VI; Earl of Hertford (made Duke of Somerset) is Protector.
- Somerset repeals heresy laws.
- English victory over Scots at battle of Pinkie (10 September).
- English replaces Latin in church services.

1549

- First Book of Common Prayer sanctioned by parliament.
- Act of Uniformity makes the Catholic Mass illegal.
- Rebellion in eastern counties under Robert Kett against land enclosures is put down; Kett hanged.
- Rebellion under Earl of Arundel is put down.
- Somerset imprisoned; Earl of Warwick (made Duke of Northumberland) becomes Protector.
- France declares war on England.

1550

- French fleet besieging Jersey is defeated; peace is made with France.

1552

- Somerset is executed.
- Second Act of Uniformity.
- Second Book of Common Prayer published.

1553

- Death of Edward VI; Lady Jane Grey is proclaimed as queen by Northumberland, but Mary Tudor is acclaimed and accedes to the throne. Execution of Northumberland.

1554

- Mary I announces her intention to marry Philip, heir to the Spanish throne; Sir Thomas Wyatt leads a failed rebellion in Kent.
- Execution of Lady Jane Grey and her husband.
- Cardinal Pole arrives in England; parliament votes to restore Catholic religion.

1555

- Burnings of Protestant heretics, including Bishops Latimer and Ridley.
- Muscovy Company founded, to trade with Russia.

1556

- Thomas Cranmer, Archbishop of Canterbury, burned for heresy; Cardinal Pole is made Archbishop of Canterbury.

1557

- England declares war on France, in support of Spain.

1558

- England loses Calais, its last French possession.
- Death of Mary I; accession of Elizabeth.

1559

- Colloquy of Westminster.
- Treaty of Cateau-Cambresis between the Holy Roman Empire, France and England.
- Third Act of Uniformity and new Act of Supremacy, confirming independence of the Anglican church with the queen as its supreme governor.
- New Book of Common Prayer published.
- John Foxe completes his *Book of Martyrs*.

1560

- English army sent to assist Protestant cause in Scotland.
- Treaty of Edinburgh makes peace between England and Scotland.

1562

- English troops sent to France to assist the Huguenots.

1563

- Convocation of the Church of England agrees on the Thirty-nine Articles.
- London is infested by plague.

1564

- First punishments of Puritans.

1566

- First organised Lord Mayor's Show in London.

1568
- Mary I of Scotland flees to England and is imprisoned.

1569
- Spanish treasure ships seized at Falmouth and Southampton.

1571
- The Thirty-nine Articles are formally enacted by parliament.
- First anti-Catholic penal legislation.
- The Royal Exchange is founded by Sir Thomas Gresham.

1572
- Alliance between France and England.
- Execution of Earl of Northumberland as a rebel.

1576
- First permanent theatre opens in London.

1577
- Drake embarks on voyage round the world.
- Discovery of the siphon principle by William Welwood.

1578
- Publication of Holinshed's *Chronicles*, one of Shakespeare's story sources.

1579
- Publication of Edmund Spenser's *The Shepherd's Calendar* and Thomas Lyly's *Euphues*.

1580
- Drake returns following first English

circumnavigation of the earth (26 September).

1581
- Execution of Edmund Campion, Catholic priest.
- Knighting of Sir Francis Drake aboard the *Golden Hind*.
- The Levant Company founded, for trading to eastern Mediterranean.

1583
- Newfoundland claimed for England by Sir Humphrey Gilbert (drowned on his return voyage).
- Foundation of Cambridge University Press.

1584
- An association is formed for the protection of Queen Elizabeth I.

1585
- Drake campaigns in the West Indies; captures Cartagena.
- An army under the Earl of Leicester is sent to support the Dutch revolt against Spanish rule.
- Court of Star Chamber orders closure of provincial printing offices.
- Foundation of Oxford University Press.

1586
- Leicester is made Governor of the Dutch United Provinces.
- Battle of Zutphen; death of Sir Philip Sidney.
- Babington plot against Elizabeth I is discovered and suppressed; Anthony Babington executed.

1587

- Mary I of Scotland is executed following her trial for treason.
- Drake's Cadiz expedition destroys the Spanish fleet (19 April).
- Sir Walter Raleigh's second expedition to the New World.
- John Davis names the Davis Strait, Greenland.
- Potatoes are introduced from North America.

1588

- Spanish invasion fleet, or Armada, is defeated in the Channel (July), and shattered by storms on its return voyage.
- 'Martin Marprelate' Puritan tracts are published.
- English merchants buy The Gambia from Portuguese.
- Death of the Earl of Leicester.

1589

- Drake's expedition against Portugal is a failure.

1591

- Spanish naval victory over England at the Azores.

1593

- Anti-Puritan statute causes many to flee to Holland; acts promulgated also against Catholics.
- Death of Christopher Marlowe, playwright, in a tavern brawl (30 May).

1594

- First performances of Shakespeare plays: *Comedy of Errors* and *Titus Andronicus*.

1596

- Triple Alliance made between England, United Provinces and France.
- English expedition captures Cadiz.
- Sir Robert Cecil is made Secretary of State.
- Spenser's *The Faerie Queene* is published.
- Death of Sir Francis Drake (28 January).
- Sir John Harington invents the water closet.

1597

- Publication of Richard Hooker's *The Ecclesiastical Polity*.

1598

- The Bodleian Library, Oxford, founded by Sir Thomas Bodley.

1599

- Earl of Essex is made Lord Lieutenant of Ireland; is disgraced upon his return.

1600

- Foundation of the East India Company, for trading to the Far East.
- William Gilbert publishes *De Magnete*, on the earth's magnetism.

1601

- Rebellion of the Earl of Essex in London: he is executed.
- Poor Law Act is passed.

1602

- First performance of Shakespeare's *Hamlet*.

1603
- Death of Elizabeth I; accession of James I (James VI of Scotland).

1604
- Hampton Court Conference of Clergy.
- Peace is made between England, Spain and the Netherlands.

1605
- Discovery of the 'Gunpowder Plot' to blow up king and parliament (5 November).

1606
- Execution of Guy Fawkes (31 January).
- The London Company is chartered to establish colonies in Virginia.

1607
- Parliament rejects proposal for union with Scotland.
- First permanent English settlement in Virginia at Jamestown.

1609
- English Baptist church first established, in Amsterdam.
- Settlement of Bermuda.

1610
- James I dissolves parliament in constitutional struggle.
- Publication of Douai Bible, first Catholic translation in English.
- Hudson Bay is named after Henry Hudson.

1611
- Publication of the Authorised 'King James' version of the Bible.

- Title of 'Baronet' is established.

1612
- English factory (trading point) established at Surat, India.

1615
- England sends an ambassador, Sir Thomas Roe, to court of Great Mogul in India.
- Sir William Harvey discovers the circulation of the blood.

1616
- Rise to power of Duke of Buckingham, favourite of James I.
- Baffin Bay is discovered by William Baffin.
- Ben Jonson is made first poet laureate.
- John Rolfe brings his Indian bride, Pocahontas, to England.
- Death of William Shakespeare.

1617
- Decimal notation is introduced by Henry Briggs.

1618
- Sir Walter Raleigh is executed for treason.

1620
- The Pilgrim Fathers leave for New England in the *Mayflower* (6 September).
- Francis Bacon publishes *Novum Organum*, a scientific work.
- Dud Dudley patents coking process.
- Around this time, horse racing begins at Epsom.

1621

- Parliament produces Protestation of Rights: is dissolved by the king.
- Francis Bacon, Lord Chancellor, convicted of bribe taking.

1623

- Abolition of the right of sanctuary for criminals.

1624

- Monopoly Act passed to protect patents.

1625

- Death of James I; accession of Charles I.
- Parliament grants Charles I tunnage and poundage for one year only.
- Treaty of Southampton between England and the United Provinces.
- Failure of naval expedition to Cadiz.
- Barbados claimed for England.
- Nicholas Lanier is first Master of the King's Musick.

1627

- Duke of Buckingham impeached by parliament.
- Forced loans to the king result in arrest of Sir John Eliot and others.
- Unsuccessful siege of Île de Ré in support of French Protestants.

1628

- The Petition of Right is passed by parliament and receives royal assent.
- Assassination of the Duke of Buckingham.
- Sir William Harvey publishes *De Motu Cordis*, on the work of the heart.

1629

- Charles I dissolves parliament for eleven years.
- Peace established with France.

1631

- Death of John Donne, poet and clergyman.
- New Hampshire founded by John Mason.

1632

- Sir John Eliot dies in prison.

1633

- Sir Thomas Wentworth (Earl of Strafford) appointed Lord Deputy in Ireland.
- William Laud becomes Archbishop of Canterbury.
- Death of George Herbert, poet.

1634

- Charles I demands ship money tax.
- Settlement of Maryland in America.

1635

- First settlements in Connecticut, America.

1636

- John Hampden leads refusal to pay ship money.
- First settlements in Rhode Island.

1637

- Judges condemn John Hampden.

1638

- English settle in British Honduras (Belize).

1639

- First Bishops' War.
- Act of Toleration.

1640

- The 'Short Parliament' sits April–May.
- Second Bishops' War.
- First meeting of 'Long Parliament' (November): not finally dissolved until 1660.
- Archbishop Laud impeached.

1641

- Trial and execution of Strafford.
- Charles I attempts to raise help in Scotland.
- Court of Star Chamber abolished by parliament.
- Grand Remonstrance against Charles I published by parliament.

1642

- Charles I attempts to seize five members of the House of Commons.
- Civil War begins (22 August).
- Battle of Edgehill (23 October): indecisive result.
- Closure of theatres.

1643

- Bishops abolished by parliament.
- Solemn League and Covenant agreed between parliament and Scottish Protestants.
- Civil War: royalist victories at battle of Stratton (16 May), Chalgrove Field, where John Hampden is killed (18 June), Adwalton Moor (30 June), Lansdowne (5 July), Roundway Down (13 July); royalists take Bristol; battle of Newbury (20 September) is indecisive.

- Death of John Pym, parliamentary leader.

1644

- Scottish army enters England in support of parliamen
- Civil War: parliamentary victories at battles of Alresford (29 March), and Selby (11 April); royalists win at Cropredy Bridge (29 June); major parliamentary victory at Marston Moor (2 July); parliamentary army under Earl of Essex surrenders at Lostwithiel (2 September); parliamentary forces win second battle of Newbury (27 October).

1645

- Archbishop Laud executed.
- New Model Army organised under Sir Thomas Fairfax and Oliver Cromwell.
- Civil War: battle of Naseby (14 June) is a parliamentary victory; also Langport (10 July) and Rowton Heath (24 September).
- The Self-Denying Ordinance prevents parliamentary leaders from leading the army.
- Parliament retakes Bristol.

1646

- Charles I surrenders to the Scottish army at Newark.

1647

- Charles I is handed over to parliament; is later carried off by the army.
- 'Heads of the Proposals' prepared as possible settlement.
- Charles I escapes to Isle of Wight.
- Foundation of the Society of Friends by George Fox.

1648
- Cromwell defeats royalist Scottish army at Preston.
- Parliament is 'purged' by Thomas Pride; only the Rump remains.

1649
- Execution of Charles I (30 January).
- Republican regime of the Commonwealth is instituted.
- Rump Parliament abolishes the monarchy and House of Lords.
- Cromwell crushes dissent among the Levellers.
- Cromwell campaigns in Ireland.

1650
- Coffee houses begin to be opened around this time.

1651
- Scottish army supporting Charles II is defeated by Cromwell at Worcester (3 September).
- Navigation Act passed in support of English traders.
- Thomas Hobbes publishes *Leviathan*.
- Foundation of the Muggletonians, one of many Puritan sects.

1652
- War with Holland: Dutch naval victory off Dungeness.
- English colonise Bengal.

1653
- Battle of Portland (18–20 February): English fleet under Blake defeats the Dutch under van Tromp.
- Cromwell dissolves the Rump Parliament (20 April).

- 'Barebone's Parliament' meets July–December: is dissolved.
- Cromwell accepts post of Protector.

1654
- End of Dutch war.

1655
- Treaty of Westminster with France.
- War with Spain: Jamaica is captured by English forces (May).

1656
- Act of Union between England and Scotland (annulled in 1660).
- Death of Oliver Cromwell (3 September); Richard Cromwell is named as Lord Protector.
- English fleet under Blake captures Spanish treasure ships and wins battle of Tenerife.
- Foundation of the Grenadier Guards.
- First recorded mention of tea in England.

1657
- New House of Lords appointed.

1658
- English and French defeat Spanish at battle of the Dunes.

1659
- The Rump Parliament is recalled.
- Richard Cromwell resigns post of Lord Protector.
- Foundation of the Coldstream Guards.
- Cheques first used in accounting.

1660

- General Monck marches from Scotland to London.
- Dissolution of the Long Parliament.
- Restoration of the monarchy with the proclaiming of Charles II (29 May).
- Election of the 'Cavalier Parliament'.
- General Letter Office established by an act of parliament.
- Sir Isaac Newton discovers the composition of light.

1661

- Savoy Conference of religious leaders fails to reach agreement.
- Corporation Act: first legislation against Dissenters.
- Foundation of the Board of Trade.
- St Helena is claimed by the East India Company.
- First use of hand-struck postage stamps.

1662

- Act of Uniformity leads to the expulsion of many Puritan clergy; the start of Non-conformism.
- England obtains Bombay and Tangier from Portugal as marriage dowry of Catherine of Braganza, Charles II's queen.
- Incorporation of the Royal Society.
- Dunkirk sold to France by Charles II.

1663

- First Drury Lane Theatre opens in London.

1664

- Conventicle Act passed against religious assemblies.
- English take New Amsterdam and change its name to New York.

- Foundation of the Royal Marines (originally the Duke of York and Albany's Maritime Regiment of Foot).

1665

- Battle of Lowestoft: naval victory over the Dutch (3 June).
- Outbreak of the Great Plague in London.

1666

- War with Holland naval battles: the Downs, English defeat (1–3 June), the Goodwins, inconclusive (1–4 July); Royal Navy victorious in battle of North Foreland (4 August).
- Great Fire of London (2–6 September) destroys much of city.
- Newton discovers the spectrum of light.

1667

- English defeat French and Dutch fleets at St Kitts (10 May); Dutch fleet in the Medway (7 June).
- Peace of Breda with the Dutch; Surinam ceded to the Netherlands.
- Publication of John Milton's *Paradise Lost*.
- Boyle's Law expounded by Robert Boyle.

1668

- Charles II establishes the 'cabal' ministry.
- Triple alliance between England, Holland and Sweden.
- John Dryden appointed poet laureate.

1669

- Building of the Sheldonian Theatre, Oxford.

1670

- Second Conventicle Act passed.
- Charles II makes a secret treaty with Louis XIV of France.
- Hudson's Bay Company is granted a royal charter.

1671

- Colonel Blood attempts to steal the crown jewels.

1672

- First Declaration of Indulgence.
- New declaration of war with Holland; Dutch fleet defeats English off Southwold (7 June).

1673

- Test Act passed to restrict Catholics from public office.
- Declaration of Indulgence cancelled by Charles II.

1674

- Peace agreement with Holland.
- Death of John Milton, poet.

1675

- Shaftesbury's parliamentary opposition marks start of the Whigs.
- Founding of the Royal Observatory at Greenwich.

1677

- Foundation of the Ashmolean Museum, Oxford: first museum in England.

1678

- Unveiling of the 'Popish Plot' by Titus Oates.

- Test Act extended to members of House of Lords.
- Beginning of Exclusion Struggle against succession of James II.

1679

- Habeas Corpus Act passed (27 May).
- First use of Tories as name for a political group.

1681

- First use of oil lighting in London streets.

1682

- Edmund Halley establishes the circuit of the comet now named after him.

1683

- The Rye House Plot against Charles II and his brother exposed: execution of Algernon Sidney and Lord Russell.
- Death of Izaak Walton, author of *The Compleat Angler*.

1684

- Newton establishes principle of the law of gravity.
- Publication of John Bunyan's *The Pilgrim's Progress*.

1685

- Death of Charles II; accession of James II.
- Duke of Monmouth mounts an abortive rebellion; loses battle of Sedgemoor (6 July), is executed (15 July).
- The Bloody Assizes in West Country: 320 rebels executed and 800 transported.

1686

- James II begins to appoint Catholics to public posts.

1687

- Second Declaration of Indulgence.
- Daniel Quare invents the repeating watch.

1688

- Seven bishops tried for sedition and acquitted.
- William of Orange invited to assume kingship; lands at Torquay (November); James II takes refuge in France.
- War with France, instigated by William of Orange.
- Lloyd's Coffee House functions as a base for insurance brokers.

1689

- William and Mary declared joint sovereigns (13 February).
- Toleration Act allows freedom of worship to Protestant Dissenters.
- Declaration of Rights (February) and Bill of Rights (October).
- First performance of Henry Purcell's *Dido and Aeneas*.

1690

- Battle of Beachy Head; French naval victory; Teignmouth is burned down.
- Publication of John Locke's *Essay Concerning Human Understanding*.

1691

- Final defeat of Jacobite campaigns in Ireland.
- Death of George Fox, Quaker leader.

1692

- Defeat of French fleet at Cape la Hogue.
- Nahum Tate becomes poet laureate.

1693

- The 'Alfred Jewel' found at Athelney: relic of Alfred the Great.

1694

- The Bank of England is founded by William Paterson.
- The National Debt is established.
- Stamp duty introduced.
- Opening of the Royal Hospital, Chelsea.

1695

- Principle of freedom of the press established, by non-renewal of Licensing Act.
- Death of Henry Purcell, composer.

1697

- Treaty of Ryswick ends war between England, its allies, and France.
- Dedication of new St Paul's Cathedral (2 December).
- First public concert hall in London opens (Hickford's Room, Haymarket).

1698

- New East India Company founded.
- Foundation of Society for the Promoting of Christian Knowledge.
- Thomas Savery builds a working steam engine.

1700

- Bonded warehouses first established.
- Completion of the first Eddystone Lighthouse (destroyed 1703).

317

- First performance of William Congreve's *The Way of the World*.
- Death of John Dryden, poet.

1701

- Act of Settlement bars Catholics from the throne of England.
- Death of James II; his son, James, will become known as the 'Old Pretender'.

1702

- Death of William III; accession of Anne, younger sister of Mary II.
- War of the Spanish Succession breaks out: naval battle of Vigo Bay, English–Dutch fleet destroys French–Spanish fleet (12 October); Marlborough captures Liège.
- First daily newspaper, the *Daily Courant*.

1703

- Methuen Treaty with Portugal.
- Death of Samuel Pepys, Admiralty official and diarist.

1704

- Aliens Act passed against Scots.
- Gibraltar captured; battle of Blenheim: English and allies under Marlborough defeat French.
- Publication of Newton's *Opticks*.
- Bath becomes a fashionable resort under Beau Nash.

1705

- Ministry of Harley and Bolingbroke.
- Thomas Newcomen develops a steam pumping engine.

1706

- Marlborough defeats French at Ramillies.
- Performances of George Farquhar's *The Beaux' Stratagem* and *The Recruiting Officer*.
- First recorded insurance company.

1707

- Act of Union between England and Scotland creates United Kingdom of Great Britain with a single parliament.
- Edward Lhuyd publishes *Archaeologica Britannica*.

1708

- Whig ministry takes over government.
- Marlborough and Prince Eugene of Savoy defeat French at Oudenarde.
- The two East India companies are combined.

1709

- First Copyright Act passed.
- Marlborough and Eugene defeat French at Malplaquet.
- Richard Steele launches *The Tatler*.
- Abraham Darby smelts iron ore by using coke.

1710

- Harley and Bolingbroke return to office.
- The impeachment of Dr Sacheverell creates a furore.
- South Sea Trading Company is set up.
- George Berkeley publishes *Treatise on the Principles of Human Knowledge*.
- Academy of Ancient Music established in London.

1711

- Dismissal of Marlborough from army command.
- Joseph Addison and Richard Steele launch *The Spectator*.
- John Shore invents the tuning fork.
- Completion of St Paul's Cathedral.
- First Ascot race meeting (11 August).

1712

- Truce with France.
- Jane Wenham is last person to be executed for witchcraft.
- Soap tax imposed.
- Alexander Pope publishes *The Rape of the Lock*.

1713

- Treaty of Utrecht ends the War of the Spanish Succession.
- South Sea Company arranges to take over the national debt.

1714

- Death of Anne; accession of George I as first Hanoverian king.
- Harley dismissed from office and long period of Whig government begins.
- Parliament offers £20,000 to discoverer of the Northwest Passage.

1715

- Bolingbroke moves to France as a Jacobite; Harley is impeached.
- Jacobite rebellion in the north is suppressed.
- Habeas Corpus suspended, and Riot Act passed, to deal with civil disturbance.
- First annual Thames race for Doggett's coat and badge.

1716

- Septennial Act sets life of a parliament at seven years.
- Founding of Royal Regiment of Artillery.

1717

- Whigs split: Stanhope's ministry begins.
- Britain, France and Holland ally against Spain.
- Inoculation against smallpox is pioneered by Lady Mary Wortley Montagu.

1718

- Austria joins the Alliance: Royal Navy under Admiral Byng defeats Spanish fleet off Cape Passaro.
- First banknotes issued by Bank of England.

1719

- Daniel Defoe publishes *Robinson Crusoe*.
- Thomas Lombe establishes a water-powered silk mill on the Derwent at Derby.
- Death of Joseph Addison, essayist; John Flamsteed, first Astronomer Royal.

1720

- Townshend and Walpole return to office.
- South Sea Bubble scandal is exposed.
- Peace is made between Quadruple Alliance and Spain.
- First recorded use of wallpaper in England.

1721

- Walpole is appointed First Lord of the Treasury: in effect is prime minister.
- First regular postal service from London to northern towns.

1722

- Habeas Corpus Act again suspended.
- Daniel Defoe publishes *Moll Flanders*.
- Thomas Guy, bookseller, founds Guy's Hospital.

1723

- Bolingbroke returns from exile.
- Death of Sir Christopher Wren, architect and rebuilder of City of London.

1724

- Jonathan Swift publishes the satirical *Drapier's Letters*.
- Three Choirs Festival, oldest music festival in England, instituted at Hereford, Gloucester and Worcester.

1725

- Order of the Bath revived by George I.
- Chiswick House built by Lord Burlington and William Kent.

1726

- War with Spain.
- Jonathan Swift publishes *Gulliver's Travels*.
- Completion of St Martin-in-the-Fields, London, by James Gibbs.

1727

- Death of George I; accession of George II.
- First Annual Act removing restrictions on Non-conformists.

- Thomas Coram establishes Foundling Hospital in London.
- Death of Sir Isaac Newton.

1728

- Publication of parliamentary debates is declared a breach of privilege.
- Alexander Pope publishes *The Dunciad* (anonymously).
- First performance of John Gay's *Beggars' Opera*.

1729

- Treaty of Seville confirms end of war with Spain.
- Death of William Congreve, playwright.

1730

- Townshend leaves government; introduces four-crop rotation on his Norfolk estate.
- John and Charles Wesley found Methodist Society at Oxford.
- Colley Cibber appointed poet laureate.

1731

- Commercial treaty with Russia.
- Spanish coastguards arrest ship *Rebecca* and cut off the ear of Jenkins, its captain.
- Prime minister first resides at 10 Downing Street.

1732

- Original Covent Garden Opera House opens.
- Christopher Pinchbeck invents the alloy of copper and zinc, named after him.

1733
- Walpole withdraws his unpopular Excise Bill.
- Alexander Pope publishes *Essay on Man*.
- John Kay invents the flying shuttle.

1734
- Lloyds List first issued.

1735
- William Hogarth completes his *Rake's Progress* paintings.
- John Harrison makes the first chronometer.
- Carpet-making begins at Kidderminster.

1736
- Army rank of field marshal is introduced.

1737
- An act of parliament confirms Lord Chamberlain as censor of plays.

1739
- War is declared on Spain, using pretext of Jenkins' ear (*see* 1731).
- George Anson's circumnavigation of the world begins (to 1744).
- John Wesley develops the Methodist Society.
- Foundation of Queen Charlotte's Lying-In Hospital, London.
- Execution of Dick Turpin, highwayman.

1740
- Thomas Arne's patriotic masque *Alfred* contains 'Rule Britannia!' (words by James Thomson).

- Samuel Richardson publishes *Pamela*.
- The London Hospital is founded by John Harrison.

1741
- Highway Act introduced for road improvement.
- Royal Military Academy established at Woolwich.
- First appearance of David Garrick on the London stage.
- First use of wrought iron in bridge construction in Wynch suspension bridge over the Tees.

1742
- Walpole resigns; succeeded by Wilmington and Carteret.
- Henry Fielding publishes *Joseph Andrews*.
- William Kent lays out Horse Guards Parade, London.

1743
- Henry Pelham becomes prime minister.
- War of the Austrian Succession: George II is last British king to lead an army in battle, at defeat of the French at Dettingen.
- First London performance of Handel's *Messiah* is a sensation.
- Hogarth completes his *Marriage à la Mode* series.

1744
- War of the Austrian Succession: British fleet defeated at battle of Toulon.
- First cotton factory in England.
- Death of Alexander Pope, poet.

1745

- Jacobite army invades from Scotland under Prince Charles Edward Stuart.
- War of the Austrian Succession: British defeated by Marshal Saxe.
- Warfare with France in North America.
- Robert Bakewell begins improvements in sheep breeding.
- Admiral Vernon introduces navy rum ration.
- Death of Dolly Pentreath, last Cornish speaker.
- Death of Robert Walpole (Earl of Orford), politician.

1746

- Jacobites retreat; win victory over government forces at Clifton Moor but ultimately defeated at Culloden in Scotland.
- France captures English settlement at Madras.
- Foundation of the Surgeons' Company – separate from old barber-surgeons.

1747

- War of the Austrian Succession: Anson and Hawke defeat French in battles of Finisterre (3 May and 2 October).

1748

- Treaty of Aix-la-Chapelle ends War of the Austrian Succession.

1749

- Publication of Henry Fielding's *Tom Jones*.

1750

- Publication of Thomas Gray's 'Elegy Written in a Country Churchyard'.
- Horace Walpole builds Strawberry Hill, first 'modern Gothic' house.

1751

- Robert Clive captures and defends Arcot, India.
- Royal Worcester porcelain works established.

1752

- War in India between British and French.
- Britain adopts the Gregorian Calendar, days 2–14 September omitted to catch up.
- Cornwall's last Stannary Parliament held at Truro.
- Establishment of Manchester Infirmary.

1753

- British Museum founded.

1754

- Newcastle's ministry begins.
- Royal Society of Arts founded.
- Death of Henry Fielding, novelist.

1755

- War in North America between British and French.
- Publication of Samuel Johnson's *Dictionary of the English Language*.

1756

- Devonshire and Pitt (later Earl of Chatham) form a ministry.
- War declared on France: beginning of the Seven Years War.

- Calcutta captured by Surajah Dowlah: 123 persons die in the 'Black Hole'.
- French capture Minorca.
- Construction of Bridgewater Canal begins.

1757

- Devonshire–Pitt ministry replaced by Newcastle–Pitt ministry.
- Clive captures Calcutta and wins battle of Plassey.
- Admiral Byng executed for failure to attack French at Minorca.

1759

- British lay siege to Quebec and capture it (13 September), with death of Generals Wolfe and Montcalm. Naval battle of Quiberon Bay: Admiral Hawke destroys French fleet.
- Samuel Johnson publishes *Rasselas, Prince of Abyssinia*.
- British Museum opens to the public.
- Opening of Kew Gardens, London.

1760

- Death of George II; accession of George III.
- Seven Years War: siege of Pondicherry, India. French capitulate at Montreal and Britain takes control of Canada.
- First banker's cheques printed by Lawrence Childs.

1761

- Lord Bute becomes prime minister.
- British take Pondicherry.
- John Harrison's fourth chronometer wins government's prize of £20,000, for determining longitude.

1762

- Havana captured.
- Introduction of cigars, from Cuba.
- John Wilkes founds *The North Briton*.

1763

- Bute resigns; Grenville forms ministry.
- Treaty of Paris ends Seven Years War.
- Imprisonment and release of Wilkes.

1764

- Expulsion of Wilkes from the House of Commons.
- Horace Walpole publishes *The Castle of Otranto*.
- House numbering is introduced in London.
- Around this time, James Hargreaves invents the spinning jenny.

1765

- Rockingham ministry formed.
- Stamp Act passed by parliament for colonial taxation.
- Opening of Sadler's Wells theatre in London.
- Thomas Percy publishes *Reliques of Ancient Ballads*.
- Launch of HMS *Victory* (still preserved) at Portsmouth.

1766

- Stamp Act repealed.
- Ministry of Chatham and Grafton.
- Isle of Man becomes a crown colony.
- Falkland Isles occupied by British.
- Oliver Goldsmith's *The Vicar of Wakefield* is published.
- Opening of Theatre Royal, Bristol.
- James Brindley begins work on the Grand Trunk Canal.
- Death of 'The Old Pretender'.

1767

- Parliament imposes tax on tea, and other duties on North America.
- Mysore War in India against Hyder Ali.
- First publication of the *Nautical Almanac*.
- Building of Royal Crescent, Bath, by John Wood.
- James Watt makes improvements to the steam engine.
- Joseph Priestley publishes *The History and Present State of Electricity*.

1768

- Retirement of Chatham; Grafton leads ministry.
- Establishment of the Royal Academy; Joshua Reynolds is first president.
- Richard Arkwright invents the water spinning frame.
- Death of Lawrence Sterne, novelist.

1769

- Anonymous *Letters of Junius* begin publication.
- Captain James Cook reaches New Zealand.

1770

- Lord North becomes prime minister.
- Spain cedes Falkland Islands to Britain.
- Foundation of the Radcliffe Observatory, Oxford.
- Edmund Burke publishes *Thoughts on the Present Discontents*.
- Cook discovers Botany Bay and claims New South Wales for Britain.
- Death by suicide of Thomas Chatterton, poet.

1771

- Parliament accepts publication of its proceedings.
- Opening of the Assembly Rooms in Bath.

1772

- Slavery declared illegal in Great Britain.
- Daniel Rutherford discovers nitrogen.

1773

- Regulating Act to control East India Company.
- Warren Hastings appointed first governor general of Bengal.
- Boston Tea Party heralds American War of Independence.
- First performance of Oliver Goldsmith's *She Stoops to Conquer*.
- Assay offices opened in Birmingham and Sheffield.

1774

- Hansard record of parliamentary proceedings is instituted by Luke Hansard.
- Warren Hastings appointed governor general of India.
- Joseph Priestley discovers the existence of oxygen.
- Death by suicide of Lord Clive, of India fame.

1775

- First Mahratta War in India.
- War of Independence begins in America: British defeated at Lexington; Americans defeated at Bunker Hill.
- Samuel Johnson publishes *A Journey to the Western Islands of Scotland*.

1776

- American colonies declare independence (4 July).
- Adam Smith publishes *The Wealth of Nations*.
- Edward Gibbon begins publication of *The Decline and Fall of the Roman Empire*.
- Sir William Chambers builds Somerset House, London, as a government archive office.
- Henry Cavendish discovers the properties of hydrogen.
- St Leger horse race first run at Doncaster.

1777

- American War of Independence: British surrender at Saratoga.
- Habeas Corpus Act suspended.
- John Howard publishes *The State of the Prisons in England and Wales*.

1778

- Roman Catholic Relief Act passed.
- France declares war on Britain.
- First performance of *A School for Scandal* by Richard Brinsley Sheridan.
- Fanny Burney publishes *Evelina*.
- Death of Lord Chatham (William Pitt); Thomas Arne, composer.

1779

- Spain declares war on Britain; siege of Gibraltar begins (to 1783).
- Completion of the world's first iron bridge, over the Severn at Coalbrookdale.
- Samuel Crompton invents the spinning mule.
- Captain Cook murdered in the Sandwich Islands.

- The Oaks horse race first run at Epsom.
- Death of David Garrick, actor; Thomas Chippendale, furniture maker.

1780

- Mahratta War continues.
- First Mysore War in India.
- American War of Independence: Americans defeated at Camden.
- Admiral Rodney defeats the Spanish fleet off Cape St Vincent.
- Britain declares war on Holland.
- Gordon riots: anti-Catholic outbreak in London leads to civil disorder.
- The Derby horse race first run at Epsom.

1781

- Mysore War: siege and capture of Mysore.
- War of American Independence: Cornwallis surrenders to Washington at Yorktown (19 October).
- William Herschel discovers existence of the planet Uranus.
- First Building Society established, in Birmingham.

1782

- Lord North resigns; second Rockingham ministry, then Shelburne becomes prime minister.
- Mahratta War ended by Treaty of Salbai.
- Mysore War continues.
- Rodney defeats French fleet at battle of the Saints.
- Death of Lord Rockingham, Whig politician.

1783

- Shelburne resigns; William Pitt the Younger becomes Britain's youngest prime minister (19 December).
- Treaty of Versailles ends War of American Independence with British acceptance of American colonies' independence.
- Newgate Prison rebuilt in London.
- Death of Lancelot 'Capability' Brown, landscape designer.

1784

- Pitt wins general election with large majority.
- India Act establishes government control of East India Company.
- Mysore War: British garrison at Mangalore surrenders to Tippu Sahib.
- First balloon ascents in England.
- Henry Cort invents the iron puddling furnace.
- Mail coaches first run between London and Bristol.
- Death of Samuel Johnson, author and lexicographer.

1785

- Pitt's parliamentary Reform Bill is defeated.
- Warren Hastings resigns and returns to England.
- Clandestine marriage of the Prince of Wales (later George IV) and Mrs Fitzherbert.
- Foundation of the *Daily Universal Register* by John Walter.
- Edmund Cartwright invents the power loom.

1786

- Pitt introduces financial reforms.

- Botany Bay becomes a penal settlement for transported convicts.
- Sir William Jones traces the existence of the Indo-European language.
- Death of George Hepplewhite, cabinetmaker.

1787

- Impeachment of Warren Hastings for corrupt conduct in India.
- Foundation of the Marylebone Cricket Club (MCC) at Lord's ground, Dorset Square.

1788

- Temporary insanity of George III.
- Trial of Warren Hastings opens.
- *Daily Universal Register* changes its name to *The Times*.
- Gibbon completes *The Decline and Fall of the Roman Empire*.
- Death of Thomas Gainsborough, painter.

1789

- Second Mysore War begins, against Tippu Sahib.
- Mutiny on HMS *Bounty* leads to an epic row-boat voyage by Captain Bligh and loyal crew members.
- Gilbert White publishes *The Natural History and Antiquities of Selborne*.
- William Blake publishes *Songs of Innocence*.
- First steam-powered cotton factory, in Manchester.

1790

- Mysore War continues.
- Burke publishes *Reflections on the Revolution in France*.
- Death of John Howard, prison reformer, in Russia, of typhus.

1791

- Mysore War: Lord Cornwallis defeats Tippu Sahib.
- Establishment of the Ordnance Survey, for mapping.
- Joseph Priestley's house in Birmingham burned down: he flees to America.
- First publication of *The Observer*, oldest Sunday newspaper.
- Thomas Paine publishes first part of *The Rights of Man*.
- James Boswell publishes *The Life of Samuel Johnson*.

1792

- Second Mysore War ends with surrender of Tippu Sahib.
- Mary Wollstonecraft publishes *The Rights of Women*.
- Coal gas lighting first introduced at Redruth, Cornwall, by William Murdoch.
- Death of Sir Joshua Reynolds, painter; Robert Adam, architect; Lord North, politician.

1793

- France declares war on Britain.
- The Board of Agriculture is established.
- Bank of England issues the first £5 notes.
- First free settlers emigrate to New South Wales.
- William Godwin publishes *Political Justice*.

1794

- Habeas Corpus Act is suspended (until 1801).
- Admiral Howe defeats French fleet in battle of the Glorious First of June.

- Ann Radcliffe publishes *Mysteries of Udolpho*.
- Death of Edward Gibbon, historian.

1795

- Britain forms Triple Alliance with Austria and Russia; Ceylon, Malacca and Cape Town taken from the Dutch.
- Speenhamland system of poor relief is extended.
- Warren Hastings's trial ends in acquittal.
- Royal Navy makes compulsory use of lime juice as preventative against scurvy.
- Joseph Bramah invents the hydraulic press.
- Death of James Boswell, Johnson's biographer.

1796

- Spain declares war on Britain.
- Edward Jenner revives anti-smallpox vaccination.

1797

- Bank of England suspends cash payments.
- Admiral Jervis defeats French fleet at battle of Cape St Vincent.
- Mutinies in the Royal Navy at Spithead and the Nore.
- Admiral Duncan defeats the Dutch fleet at Camperdown.
- Thomas Bewick publishes Volume 1 of his *British Birds*.
- Henry Cavendish calculates the mass of the earth.
- Death of Edmund Burke, political thinker; John Wilkes, libertarian.

1798

- Rebellion in Ireland is suppressed.

- Admiral Nelson destroys French fleet in battle of the Nile.
- Thomas Malthus publishes his first *Essay on the Principle of Population*.
- William Wordsworth and Samuel Taylor Coleridge publish *Lyrical Ballads*.

1799

- Income tax is introduced as a war-time measure.
- Pitt's government legislates against radical political associations and trade unions.
- Third Mysore War: Seringapatam stormed and Tippu Sahib killed.
- Foundation of the Royal Military College, Sandhurst.
- Foundation of the Royal Institution of Great Britain.

1800

- Ireland is incorporated into the United Kingdom, with representation in the Westminster parliament.
- First shipment of the Parthenon frieze ('Elgin marbles') from Athens to the British Museum.
- Company of Surgeons becomes the Royal College of Surgeons.

1801

- Pitt resigns; Addington becomes prime minister.
- Madras brought under British rule.
- British defeat French army at Aboukir, Egypt.
- Naval battle of Copenhagen won by Nelson.
- First census of Great Britain is made in June.

1802

- Treaty of Amiens brings temporary end to war with France.
- Second Mahratta War begins in India.
- First Factory Act passed, to reform work practices.

1803

- Second Mahratta War continues, with British victory at Assaye.
- War with France resumes: about 10,000 English detained in France.
- First publication of Debrett's *Peerage*.
- Opening of horse-drawn Surrey Iron Railway: first public railway.

1804

- Pitt becomes prime minister again (until 1805).
- Second Mahratta War continues.
- Foundation of Royal Society of Painters in Watercolour.
- First English savings bank set up, at Rotherham.
- Richard Trevithick builds the first steam railway locomotive.
- Death of Joseph Priestley, scientist and political thinker.

1805

- Naval battles: Cape Finisterre (22 July), French defeated by Admiral Calder; and Trafalgar (21 October), French and Spanish fleets destroyed by Nelson, who is killed in the action.
- First Trooping of the Colour ceremony.
- Sir Walter Scott publishes *The Lay of the Last Minstrel*.
- Completion of the Grand Junction Canal.

1806

- Ministry 'of all the talents' including Fox, formed after death of Pitt.
- Battle of Maida: British defeat French in Italy.
- Napoleon institutes the Continental System to stifle British trade.
- Death of William Pitt and Charles James Fox, politicians.

1807

- Portland and Perceval form ministry.
- Parliament passes a bill for abolition of the slave trade.
- Humphry Davy discovers potassium and sodium.
- Opening of the Swansea and Mumbles Railway (horse-drawn).
- First Ascot Old Cup horse race.

1808

- Napoleonic Wars spread to Iberia as Peninsular War. Sir Arthur Wellesley (later Duke of Wellington) takes command.
- Disappearance of the pigtail in male hairstyle.

1809

- Spencer Perceval becomes prime minister.
- Failed invasion of Walcheren.
- Peninsular War: British army makes successful retreat to Corunna; Wellington defeats French at Oporto and Talavera.
- Dartmoor Prison opens, at first for French prisoners of war.
- Death of Thomas Paine, libertarian radical.

1810

- Peninsular War: Wellington's army digs in behind Lines of Torres Vedras.
- Luddites active in industrial districts.

1811

- George III incapacitated by insanity: Prince of Wales becomes Prince Regent.
- Peninsular War continues.
- Mary Anning finds an ichthyosaurus fossil at Lyme Regis.
- First women's county cricket match.

1812

- Spencer Perceval assassinated in the House of Commons; Lord Liverpool becomes prime minister.
- War breaks out with the USA over maritime policy.
- Peninsular War: Wellington captures Badajoz and Salamanca and advances to Madrid.
- Publication of *Childe Harold's Pilgrimage* by Lord Byron.
- Establishment of the Gas Light and Coke Company.

1813

- Britain forms Quadruple Alliance with Austria, Prussia and Russia against France.
- Peninsular War: Wellington invades southern France from Spain.
- Jane Austen publishes *Pride and Prejudice*.
- William Hedley builds two steam locomotives at Wylam, in Northumberland.

1814

- Treaty of Paris ends war with Napoleonic France.

- American war: British burn the White House and Capitol in Washington; Treaty of Ghent ends the war.
- Gurkha War begins.
- Sir Walter Scott publishes *Waverley* (anonymously).
- MCC moves to present Lord's ground: first match there on 22 June.

1815

- First Corn Law passed to control corn price.
- Gurkha War continues.
- Return of Napoleon to France: his 'Hundred Days' end in defeat by Wellington and Blücher at Waterloo (18 June). Napoleon surrenders to the British and is transported to St Helena.
- Sir Humphry Davy invents a safety lamp for use in mines.

1816

- Gurkha War ends.
- Luddite riots in the North and Midlands.
- Death of Richard Brinsley Sheridan, playwright and politician.

1817

- Seditious Meetings Act passed; habeas corpus suspended.
- Third Mahratta War begins.
- William Hone is acquitted in a case relating to freedom of the press.
- David Ricardo publishes *Principles of Political Economy*.
- Death of Jane Austen, novelist.

1818

- Third Mahratta War ends with destruction of Mahratta power.

- Institution of Civil Engineers is founded (royal charter granted 1828).
- Mary Shelley completes *Frankenstein*.

1819

- Parliament passes the 'Six Acts' to restrict public meetings.
- Peterloo Massacre: eleven people killed by troops at radical meeting at St Peter's Fields, Manchester.
- Bank of England resumes cash payments.
- Thomas Hancock opens first vulcanised rubber factory, in London.

1820

- Death of George III; accession of George IV.
- Exposure of 'the Cato Street Conspiracy' to assassinate members of the cabinet; five executed.
- George IV's Divorce Bill fails.
- Foundation of the Royal Astronomical Society (charter received 1831).

1821

- Queen Caroline banned from George IV's coronation.
- Founding of the *Manchester Guardian*.
- Mary Anning discovers plesiosaurus remains near Lyme Regis.
- Death of John Keats, poet.

1822

- New Corn Laws passed.
- Suicide of Lord Castlereagh, Foreign Secretary.
- Death by drowning of Percy Bysshe Shelley, poet.

1823

- Foundation of *The Lancet*, medical journal.
- The Baltic Exchange established in London.
- Rugby football begins to be played at Rugby School.
- Death of Edward Jenner, pioneer of vaccination.

1824

- Abolition of Combination Laws; trade unions made legal.
- First Ashanti War in Africa.
- First Burma War.
- Founding of London Mechanics' Institute (later Birkbeck College).
- Founding of Royal Society for Prevention of Cruelty to Animals.
- Founding of the Royal National Lifeboat Institution.
- Founding of the National Gallery, London.
- Death of Lord Byron, poet.

1825

- A year of financial crisis.
- First Ashanti War ends with defeat of Ashanti.
- Opening of the Stockton and Darlington Railway: first public line worked by steam.
- Thomas Telford completes the Menai Suspension Bridge.
- Sir Stamford Raffles founds the London Zoological Society.

1826

- Riots in Lancashire against the intro-duction of power looms.

1827

- Canning becomes prime minister

briefly, then dies. Goderich becomes prime minister.
- British and allied fleets destroy the Turkish navy.
- John Clare publishes *The Shepherd's Calendar*.
- Charles Babbage invents a calculating machine.
- Death of William Blake, poet and visionary.

1828

- Wellington becomes prime minister.
- Repeal of Test and Corporation Acts.
- Foundation of University College, London.
- Opening of Regent's Park, London.
- Thomas Arnold becomes headmaster of Rugby School.

1829

- Passing of the Catholic Emancipation Act.
- Sir Robert Peel establishes the Metropolitan Police.
- Rainhill locomotive trials (October): George and Robert Stephenson's *Rocket* is winner.
- London's first omnibus service (horse-drawn) from Marylebone Road to the Bank.
- First Thames boat race between Oxford and Cambridge Universities.
- Death of Sir Humphry Davy, scientist and inventor.

1830

- Death of George IV; accession of William IV.
- Earl Grey becomes prime minister.
- Opening of Liverpool and Manchester Railway, first trunk line. William Huskisson, ex-President of the Board

of Trade, is knocked down and killed by a train.

- Founding of the Royal Geographical Society.
- Founding of the Plymouth Brethren by the Rev. John Darby.

1831

- Reform Bill passed by House of Commons; rejected by Lords.
- Founding of British Association for the Advancement of Science.
- HMS *Beagle* begins a five-year circumnavigation of the world, for survey and scientific purposes.

1832

- After resistance in the Lords, the first Reform Bill becomes law.
- Founding of Durham University.
- Death of Jeremy Bentham, political economist.

1833

- New Factory Act bans employment of children under nine years old.
- The Rev. John Keble launches the Oxford movement (Tractarians).
- Thomas Carlyle publishes *Sartor Resartus*.
- Death of William Wilberforce, anti-slavery campaigner.

1834

- Lord Melbourne becomes prime minister, then Peel is appointed.
- Poor Law system reformed; workhouses introduced.
- Tolpuddle Martyrs transported for trade union activity.
- Abolition of practice of burying suicides at crossroads.

- Houses of Parliament destroyed by fire.
- Joseph Hansom patents design of the hansom cab.
- Death of Samuel Taylor Coleridge, poet and critic; Charles Lamb, essayist.

1835

- Municipal Reform Act passed.
- Peel resigns; Melbourne again prime minister.
- Marie Tussaud founds Madame Tussaud's Waxworks, London.
- Sir Henry Rawlinson deciphers cuneiform writing.
- Isambard Kingdom Brunel begins construction of the Great Western Railway.

1836

- Chartist movement begins.
- Civil marriage is made legal.
- Appointment of the first registrar-general, Thomas Lister.

1837

- Death of William IV; accession of Victoria.
- Charles Dickens publishes *The Pickwick Papers*.
- London's first railway station opens at Euston Square with completion of London and Birmingham Railway.
- Isaac Pitman publishes *Stenographic Shorthand*.
- Rowland Hill proposes the penny post system.
- Grand National horse race first run at Liverpool.
- Death of John Constable, painter.

1838

- Richard Cobden and John Bright found the Anti-Corn Law League.
- Chartists publish *The People's Charter*.
- Grace Darling rescues survivors of the *Forfarshire* (7 September).

1839

- Peel becomes prime minister; he resigns over the 'Bedchamber' issue; Melbourne resumes office.
- Parliament rejects Chartist petition.
- First Afghan War begins.
- Indian tea first consumed in England.
- First publication of *Bradshaw's Railway Guide*.
- First Henley Regatta held.

1840

- Queen Victoria marries Prince Albert of Saxe-Coburg.
- Opium War with China begins; Afghan War continues.
- Transportation of convicts to New South Wales is ended.
- Rowland Hill introduces the penny postage system.

1841

- Melbourne resigns; Peel becomes prime minister.
- Thomas Cook founds the first travel agency.
- Foundation of the Pharmaceutical Society of Great Britain.

1842

- Afghan War continues; end of the Opium War with Treaty of Nanking.
- Blueprint process for copying of plans and drawings is introduced.
- First publication of the *Illustrated London News*.

1843

- Afghan War continues; war also in India. The British conquer Sind province.
- The McNaghten Rules formulated for the legal definition of insanity.
- William Wordsworth appointed poet laureate.
- Founding of *The Economist* magazine.
- Brunel builds the first ocean-going iron ship, SS *Great Britain*, at Bristol.

1844

- Demolition of the Fleet Prison, London.
- First Co-operative store opens in Rochdale.
- George Williams founds the Young Men's Christian Association.
- Death of John Dalton, scientist.

1845

- First Sikh War.
- Peel resigns in cabinet dispute over Corn Law repeal but is recalled as prime minister.
- Friedrich Engels writes *Conditions of the Working Class in England*.
- The Rev. John Henry Newman converts to Catholicism.
- Death of Elizabeth Fry, prison reformer.

1846

- Repeal of the Corn Laws; Lord John Russell becomes prime minister.
- End of First Sikh War.
- Owens College, Manchester (later Manchester University) founded by John Owens.
- Edward Lear publishes *The Book of Nonsense*.

1847

- Poor Law Board replaces earlier Poor Law Commission.
- Factory Act establishes ten-hour working day.
- Charlotte Brontë publishes *Jane Eyre*; Emily Brontë publishes *Wuthering Heights*; Anne Brontë publishes *Agnes Grey*.
- William Makepeace Thackeray publishes *Vanity Fair*.

1848

- Britain annexes the Orange River Territory in South Africa.
- Second Sikh War begins in India.
- Foundation of the Pre-Raphaelite Brotherhood of Artists.
- Death of George Stephenson, engineer; Lord Melbourne, politician, Emily Brontë, novelist.

1849

- Second Sikh War continues.
- Cockfighting is banned.
- Matthew Arnold publishes *Poems*.
- First publication of *Who's Who*.
- Death of Anne Brontë, novelist.

1850

- Public Library Act allows for opening of municipal libraries.
- Foundation of the Meteorological Office by James Glaisher.
- Catholic hierarchy reinstated in England.
- Alfred Tennyson publishes *In Memoriam*; he is appointed poet laureate.
- Death of Sir Robert Peel, politician; William Wordsworth, poet laureate.

1851

- Palmerston dismissed as Foreign Secretary for unauthorised recognition of French coup d'état.
- The Great Exhibition opens in Crystal Palace, London.
- George Borrow publishes *Lavengro*.
- First telegraph cable laid across English Channel.
- Death of Mary Shelley, author; J.M.W. Turner, painter.

1852

- Earl of Derby becomes prime minister.
- Great Ormond Street Children's Hospital opens.
- Last duel fought in England.
- Opening of the South Kensington Museum, London (renamed Victoria and Albert Museum, 1889).
- Death of the Duke of Wellington, soldier and politician.

1853

- Earl of Aberdeen becomes prime minister.
- Soap tax abolished.
- Humfrey Cheetham founds Cheetham's Library, Manchester.

1854

- Crimean War begins; battle of the Alma; Balaclava and the Charge of the Light Brigade; battle of Inkerman.
- Around this time, cigarettes are introduced in England.

1855

- Palmerston becomes prime minister.
- Crimean War: capture of Sebastopol.
- Abolition of Letters of Marque ends privateering.

- Victoria and Albert finish rebuilding of Balmoral Castle.
- Nathan Adler, Chief Rabbi, founds Jews' College, London.
- Last Bartholomew Fair held at West Smithfield, London.
- Stamp tax on newspapers abolished.
- Death of Charlotte Brontë, novelist.

1856

- Treaty of Paris ends Crimean War.
- The Victoria Cross is established as prime decoration for valour.
- Elizabeth Garrett Anderson qualifies as first woman doctor.
- Thomas Hughes publishes *Tom Brown's Schooldays*.
- Henry Bessemer develops the Bessemer converter for steel production.

1857

- Albert created Prince Consort.
- Indian Mutiny breaks out; massacre of Cawnpore; siege and relief of Lucknow.
- '*Arrow*' War with China, precipitated by Chinese boarding of a British-registered ship suspected of piracy.
- Britannia Royal Naval College founded at Portland.
- National Portrait Gallery founded.
- Sir Charles Hallé establishes the Hallé Orchestra in Manchester.
- First telegraph cable laid across the Atlantic.

1858

- Derby becomes prime minister.
- Public Health Board dissolved; new Public Health Act.
- Jewish Disabilities Removal Act enables Jews to stand for House of Commons.
- Indian Mutiny brought to an end at battle of Gwalior.
- Government of India transferred to the crown; office of viceroy instituted.
- Launching of Brunel's *Great Eastern*, world's largest ship.

1859

- Palmerston again prime minister.
- Military Volunteer movement arises.
- Big Ben clock and bell put into service.
- Vauxhall Gardens closes.
- William Rathbone introduces district nursing.
- Publication of Charles Darwin's *The Origin of Species*; John Stuart Mill's *On Liberty*.
- Death of Isambard Kingdom Brunel, engineer.

1860

- William Ewart Gladstone, Chancellor of the Exchequer, introduces a free trade budget.
- Richard Cobden negotiates free trade treaty with France.
- Florence Nightingale founds training school for nurses at St Thomas's Hospital.
- John Ruskin completes *Modern Painters*.
- Launch of HMS *Warrior*, first British iron-clad warship.
- Last bare-knuckle prizefight in England.

1861

- Post Office Savings Bank established.
- Thomas Graham introduces the study of colloid chemistry.

- Death of Albert, prince consort.

1862
- Land registry established.

1863
- Broadmoor Asylum for the criminal insane opened.
- World's first underground railway, the Metropolitan, opens in London.
- Formation of the Football Association.
- Death of W.M. Thackeray, novelist.

1864
- International Working Men's Association founded in London.
- Opening of Clifton Suspension Bridge, Bristol.
- *British Pharmacopoeia* first published.

1865
- Earl Russell becomes prime minister.
- William Booth founds the Salvation Army.
- Lewis Carroll publishes *Alice's Adventures in Wonderland*.
- Joseph Bazalgette completes his London drainage system.
- Death of Lord Palmerston, politician.

1866
- Russell resigns, ministry formed by Lord Derby.
- Crisis in financial markets.
- Isle of Man gains home rule.
- Founding of the Howard League for Penal Reform.
- First effective Atlantic telegraph cable laid from SS *Great Eastern*.
- Last major outbreak of cholera in England.

1867
- Second Reform Act passed, doubling electorate to over two million.
- Fenian attacks in London and Manchester.
- Thomas Barnardo founds Dr Barnardo's Homes.
- Queensberry Rules for boxing introduced.

1868
- Benjamin Disraeli becomes prime minister; followed by Gladstone after general election.
- Trades Union Congress formed.
- Last public execution held in London (26 May).
- Wilkie Collins publishes *The Moonstone*.

1869
- The Post Office is given a monopoly on telegraphic communication.
- Formation of the Labour Representation League.
- First publication of *Nature*, scientific periodical.
- Opening of the College for Women, Cambridge (renamed Girton College, 1872).

1870
- Bankruptcy Act abolishes imprisonment for debt.
- Education Act establishes primary education for all children.
- Founding of the Institute of Accountants.
- British Red Cross Society founded.
- Death of Charles Dickens, novelist.

1871
- Trade unions given legal status.

- Bank holidays introduced; first is Whit Monday.
- Society of Telegraph Engineers formed (later the Institution of Electrical Engineers).
- Oxford University abolishes religious test for admission.
- George Eliot publishes *Middlemarch*.
- Opening of the Royal Albert Hall.
- Foundation of the Rugby Union.
- Death of Sir John Herschel, astronomer.

1872
- Ballot Act establishes secret voting.
- Ship *Mary Celeste* found abandoned in mid-Atlantic.

1873
- Game of badminton introduced around this time.
- Death of Sir Edwin Landseer, painter.

1874
- Disraeli replaces Gladstone as prime minister.
- Founding of Leeds University.

1875
- Founding of Mason College in Birmingham (later Birmingham University).
- Captain Matthew Webb is first to swim the English Channel.

1876
- Queen Victoria is proclaimed Empress of India.
- Britain buys ownership of the Suez Canal.
- Founding of Bristol University.
- The Plimsoll line, devised by Samuel Plimsoll, is required as loading line on all merchant vessels.

1877
- Establishment of the Library Association.
- Red Cross forms the Ambulance Association (later St John's Ambulance Brigade).
- 'Cleopatra's Needle' obelisk transported from Egypt to London.
- Anna Sewell publishes *Black Beauty*.
- First Wimbledon Lawn Tennis Championships.

1878
- Status of outlawry is abolished.
- First Zulu War: British defeated at Isandhlwana; capture of Cetewayo.
- Second Afghan War.
- Foundation of Firth College, Sheffield (later Sheffield University).
- Three women's colleges founded in Oxford: Somerville, St Anne's and Lady Margaret Hall.
- Foundation of the *Liverpool Echo*.
- Newman is created a cardinal.

1879
- Zulu War continues: Zulus defeated at Rorke's Drift.
- William Barnes publishes *Poems of Rural Life in the Dorset Dialect*.
- George Meredith publishes *The Egoist*.

1880
- Gladstone again prime minister.
- Greenwich Mean Time established throughout the country.
- First telephone directory in England is issued.
- Founding of Amateur Athletics Association.

- Death of George Eliot, novelist.

1881
- Postal orders first introduced.
- First Boer War; Britain recognises independence of the Transvaal.
- Revolt in Egypt against British–French rule
- Opening of University College, Nottingham (later Nottingham University).
- First use of domestic electric light in England.
- First electric power station in England, at Godalming.
- Death of Benjamin Disraeli (Lord Beaconsfield), politician; Thomas Carlyle, author.

1882
- Revolt in Egypt: Britain occupies Suez Canal Zone.
- Foundation of the Society for Psychical Research.
- George Smith founds *Dictionary of National Biography*.
- Institution of 'The Ashes' in cricket.
- Death of Charles Darwin, scientist; Anthony Trollope, post office official and novelist.

1883
- Married Women's Property Act becomes law.
- Sudan Campaign: partial British withdrawal.
- Founding of the Fabian Society.
- Robert Louis Stevenson publishes *Treasure Island*.
- Death in London of Karl Marx.

1884
- Third Reform Act further expands electorate.
- Sudan Campaign: General Gordon under siege in Khartoum.
- Foundation of the National Society for the Prevention of Cruelty to Children, by the Rev. Benjamin Waugh.
- Sir Charles Parsons develops the steam turbine.

1885
- Lord Salisbury becomes prime minister.
- Sudan Campaign: death of General Gordon; relief expedition arrives a few days later.
- First performance of *The Mikado* by W.S. Gilbert and Arthur Sullivan.
- H. Rider Haggard publishes *King Solomon's Mines*.
- Professional football is legalised.

1886
- Gladstone again prime minister; resigns after defeat of Irish Home Rule Bill; Salisbury becomes prime minister.
- Cruft's Dog Show moves to London.
- Construction of Severn Tunnel completed: world's longest railway tunnel.
- Frances Hodgson Burnett publishes *Little Lord Fauntleroy*.

1887
- Trades Union Congress forms Labour Electoral Association.

1888
- County councils are established.
- 'Jack the Ripper' murders in East London.

- Formation of the Football League; first matches held on 8 September.
- Formation of the Lawn Tennis Association.

1889
- Board of Agriculture becomes a government ministry.
- Museums Association founded.
- Women's Franchise League founded by Emmeline Pankhurst.
- Jerome K. Jerome publishes *Three Men in a Boat*.
- Death of Wilkie Collins, novelist; Robert Browning, poet.

1890
- Britain cedes Heligoland to Germany.
- Opening of the first electric underground railway (City and South London).
- Death of John Henry Newman, cardinal.

1891
- Tranby Croft case: Prince of Wales gives evidence in connection with a gambling scandal.
- Completion of New Scotland Yard building, by Norman Shaw.
- First electric tramcars, in Leeds.
- National Sporting Club founded.
- Death of Thomas Cook, pioneer travel agent.

1892
- Gladstone's last term as prime minister begins.
- Foundation of Reading University, as University Extension College.
- 'Gentleman Jim' Corbett becomes first world heavyweight boxing champion.

- Death of Lord Tennyson, poet laureate.

1893
- National coal miners' strike.
- Arthur Conan Doyle publishes *The Memoirs of Sherlock Holmes*.
- Founding of Bournemouth Municipal Orchestra.

1894
- Gladstone resigns; Earl of Rosebery becomes prime minister.
- Parish, rural and urban district councils established.
- Death duties introduced in the Budget.
- Opening of the Manchester Ship Canal; also Tower Bridge, London.
- Anthony Hope publishes *The Prisoner of Zenda*.

1895
- Salisbury again prime minister: last prime minister to sit in House of Lords.
- Foundation of the National Trust for Places of Historic Interest or Natural Beauty.
- First performance of *The Importance of being Earnest* by Oscar Wilde.
- Foundation of the London Promenade Concerts, by Sir Henry Wood.
- Northern Union (later Rugby League) secedes from Rugby Union.

1896
- Conciliation Act provides for resolving industrial disputes.
- Sudan Campaign: Mahdist forces defeated by Kitchener's army.

339

- A.E. Housman publishes *A Shropshire Lad*.
- Alfred Austin becomes poet laureate.
- Locomotive Act removes need for red flag to precede motor vehicles.

1897

- Employers' Liability Act makes employers responsible for safety in workplaces.
- Opening of the Tate Gallery, London.
- Foundation of the Royal Automobile Club.
- Bram Stoker publishes *Dracula*.

1898

- Kitchener completes conquest of the Sudan.
- Robert Bridges publishes *Poetical Works*; Thomas Hardy publishes *Wessex Poems*.
- William Ramsay discovers the element xenon and inert gases krypton and neon.

1899

- London County Council established.
- Second Boer War begins.
- First 'garden city' established, at Letchworth.
- John Rylands Library founded in Manchester.
- Edward Elgar composes *The Enigma Variations*.
- National Physical Laboratory founded.

1900

- Second Boer War continues.
- Founding of the Labour representation Committee in London.
- Opening of the Wallace Collection in London.

- Death of John Ruskin, art critic; Sir Arthur Sullivan, composer; Oscar Wilde, playwright.

1901

- Death of Victoria; accession of Edward VII.
- Second Boer War continues. Sir Henry Campbell-Bannerman denounces use of concentration camps.
- Taff Vale railway case makes trade unions liable for losses incurred in strikes.
- Engineering Standards Committee established, later British Standards Institution.
- First Royal Navy submarine launched.

1902

- Salisbury reigns, Arthur Balfour becomes prime minister.
- End of Boer War with Treaty of Vereeniging.
- Death of Cecil Rhodes, imperialist.

1903

- Chamberlain resigns from government to pursue Protectionist policies.
- Emmeline and Christabel Pankhurst form Women's Social and Political Union.
- Fingerprint evidence first used in a criminal trial.
- Motor-car registration introduced.
- Death of Herbert Spencer, political economist.

1904

- Entente Cordiale signed with France.
- Licensing Act regulates drinking premises.
- First performance of *Peter Pan* by J.M. Barrie.

1905

- Campbell-Bannerman becomes prime minister
- Office of prime minister is officially recognised.
- Britannia Naval College moves to Dartmouth.
- Automobile Association founded.
- Admiral Lord Fisher introduces the 'dreadnought' warship design.
- Death of Thomas Barnardo, philanthropist.

1906

- Trades Disputes Act reverses Taff Vale decision.
- Frederick Hopkins identifies existence of vitamins.
- Opening of deep underground lines in London: Bakerloo and Piccadilly.

1907

- Inauguration of the Territorial Army.
- Boy Scout movement founded by Sir Robert Baden-Powell.
- First Isle of Man TT motorcycle races.
- Opening of Brooklands motor race-track.

1908

- Resignation of Campbell-Bannerman; H.H. Asquith becomes prime minister.
- Old Age Pensions Act approved by parliament.
- Elizabeth Garrett Anderson elected first woman mayor, at Aldeburgh.
- National Farmers' Union founded.
- Kenneth Grahame publishes *The Wind in the Willows*.
- Fourth modern Olympic Games held in London, also unofficial Winter Games.

1909

- David Lloyd George's 'People's Budget' is rejected by House of Lords: beginning of a two-year parliamentary crisis.
- Old age pensions introduced.
- Lord Lonsdale founds Lonsdale Belt boxing award.
- Death of George Meredith, poet and novelist.

1910

- Death of Edward VII; accession of George V.
- Girl Guides Association founded by Baden-Powell.
- Labour Exchanges established.
- Death of Florence Nightingale, nursing pioneer; William Holman Hunt, painter.

1911

- An act of parliament reduces powers of House of Lords.
- National Insurance Act passed.
- 'Siege of Sidney Street': police attack an Anarchist cell in London.
- English Folk Dance Society founded by Cecil Sharp.
- Charles Wilson develops the cloud chamber.
- Death of Sir William Gilbert, composer.

1912

- Coal Mines (Minimum Wage) Act establishes principle of minimum wage, after miners' strike.
- Royal Flying Corps established.
- RMS *Titanic* sinks in the Atlantic (15 April), 1,513 people lost.
- Announcement of discovery of prehistoric 'Piltdown Man': a hoax.

- Captain Scott and three of his party reach the South Pole, already reached by Roald Amundsen; they die on the return journey.
- Death of Lord Lister, pioneer of anti-septics; William Booth, Salvationist.

1913

- Sickness, unemployment and maternity benefits introduced.
- Trades Union Act allows unions to hold a political fund.
- Emily Davison, suffragette protester, killed under the king's horse during the Derby.
- Robert Bridges becomes poet laureate.
- First Chelsea Flower Show.
- Death of Alfred Austin, poet laureate.

1914

- Army officers mutiny at the Curragh Camp, Ireland.
- Royal Naval Air Service formed.
- Cub Scouts (Wolf Cubs) movement begins.
- World War I begins: Britain declares war on Germany after German invasion of Belgium; British Expeditionary Force lands in France (September).
- Mass volunteers are called for the armed forces.

1915

- Zeppelin raids on Norfolk towns.
- Asquith forms coalition government.
- Sir Douglas Haig replaces Sir John French as British supreme commander.
- Women's Institute founded.
- Death of Rupert Brooke, poet; W.G. Grace, cricketer.

1916

- Asquith resigns; Lloyd George becomes prime minister (December).
- Conscription introduced in Great Britain.
- First use of tanks in warfare.
- Battle of Jutland between British and German fleets: both sides claim victory.
- Introduction of Daylight Saving, 'British Summer Time', to lengthen working day.
- Kitchener drowned in loss of HMS *Hampshire*.
- National Savings introduced.
- Discovery of Proxima Centauri by Robert Innes.

1917

- Royal family changes name from Saxe-Coburg-Gotha to Windsor.
- Order of the British Empire founded.
- Army Tank Corps founded.

1918

- Armistice on the Western Front (11 November).
- Establishment of Royal Air Force from Royal Flying Corps.
- Huge outbreak of influenza claims thousands of lives.
- Women over thirty are given the vote.
- Lytton Strachey publishes *Eminent Victorians*.
- Death of Wilfred Owen, poet.

1919

- Widespread labour disputes.
- Nancy Astor is first woman MP to take her seat in the House of Commons (for Plymouth).
- Airship R34 makes first airship crossing of the Atlantic (5–6 July).

1920

- End of military conscription.
- Opening of Royal Air Force College, Cranfield.
- Women are admitted to degrees at Oxford University.
- Communist Party of Great Britain founded.
- Unveiling of the Cenotaph, national war memorial, in Whitehall.

1921

- Founding of the BBC as British Broadcasting Company.
- British Legion founded by Earl Haig.
- First birth control clinic in England opens in London.
- First English woman barrister qualifies.

1922

- Resignation of Lloyd George; Andrew Bonar Law forms a Conservative government after general election.
- First skywriting advertisement, over Epsom Downs.
- Radio licences introduced.
- Richmal Crompton publishes *Just William*; T.S. Eliot publishes *The Waste Land*.
- Death of Sir Ernest Shackleton, explorer; Lord Northcliffe, newspaper owner.

1923

- Bonar Law resigns and Stanley Baldwin becomes prime minister. General election returns minority Conservative government. Labour are second-largest party.
- First publication of *Radio Times*.
- First Wembley FA Cup final. The crowd invade the pitch but are controlled by Billy, the White Horse of Wembley, and his rider, PC George Scorey.

1924

- Baldwin government resigns; Ramsay MacDonald forms first Labour government.
- Affair of the 'Zinoviev letter' purporting to foment Communist revolution in Britain.
- General election returns Conservative government under Baldwin.
- British Empire Exhibition held at Wembley.
- Consecration of Liverpool Cathedral (begun 1904).
- First British appearance of a crossword, in *Sunday Express*.
- Cheltenham Gold Cup horse race first run.
- Death of E. Nesbit and Frances Hodgson Burnett, writers of children's books; Joseph Conrad, novelist.

1925

- Britain returns to the Gold Standard.
- British Summer Time made a permanent institution.
- Death of Sir Henry Rider Haggard, novelist.

1926

- General Strike (3 May–13 May); miners remain on strike until 27 November.
- John Logie Baird demonstrates television.
- T.E. Lawrence publishes *Seven Pillars of Wisdom*; A.A. Milne publishes *Winnie the Pooh*.
- First British Grand Prix run at Brooklands.

1927
- British Broadcasting Corporation receives royal charter.
- First automatic traffic lights installed.
- Greyhound racing begins at White City.
- Sir Malcolm Campbell gains world land and water speed records.
- Death of Jerome K. Jerome, author.

1928
- Women allowed to vote on exactly the same terms as men (i.e. from age twenty-one).
- Malvern Festival inaugurated.
- Alexander Fleming discovers penicillin at St Mary's Hospital, London.
- Death of Thomas Hardy, poet and novelist; Earl Haig, soldier; H.H. Asquith, politician; Emmeline Pankhurst, women's rights campaigner.

1929
- General election returns minority Labour government under MacDonald.
- Financial crisis spreads from USA.
- Poor Law system abolished.
- Ealing Film Studios start up.
- BBC makes its first experimental TV broadcast.
- Pony Club movement founded.
- Death of Lily Langtry, actress; Lord Rosebery, politician.

1930
- Unemployment rising sharply, exceeds two million.
- Youth Hostels Association founded.
- John Masefield appointed poet laureate.
- R101, world's largest airship, explodes on maiden flight, killing forty-eight people.
- Death of Arthur Balfour, politician; D.H. Lawrence, novelist; Sir Arthur Conan Doyle, author.

1931
- Economic slump deepens.
- Sir Oswald Mosley forms the New Party.
- Britain abandons the gold standard and devalues the pound sterling.
- MacDonald resigns and forms a National government; general election overwhelmingly returns National government members.
- *Highway Code* first published.
- Death of Arnold Bennett, novelist.

1932
- Mosley's party becomes the British Union of Fascists.
- Three Methodist churches unite as the Methodist Church of Great Britain and Ireland.
- New Shakespeare Memorial Theatre opens in Stratford-upon-Avon.
- George V makes first royal Christmas broadcast.
- Aldous Huxley publishes *Brave New World*.

1933
- Left-wing parties form Popular Front Against Fascism.
- Foundation of the British Film Institute in London.

1934
- Unemployment reaches over 80 per cent in some single-industry towns.
- Glyndebourne Festival Opera founded.

- Launch of RMS *Queen Mary*.
- Death of three composers: Sir Edward Elgar, Gustav Holst and Frederick Delius.

1935

- MacDonald resigns; Baldwin succeeds as prime minister in National government.
- Introduction of driving tests and 30-mile limit in built-up areas.
- Founding of Alcoholics Anonymous.
- Establishment of the British Council.
- Green Belt scheme for London is instituted.
- First practical demonstration of radar.
- Death of T.E. Lawrence, author, in motorcycle accident.

1936

- Death of George V (20 January); accession of Edward VIII, who abdicates on 10 December; George VI becomes king.
- Hunger march of unemployed from Jarrow to London.
- First 'open prison' at New Hall, Yorkshire.
- Crystal Palace destroyed by fire.
- John Maynard Keynes publishes *The General Theory of Employment, Interest and Money*.
- Death of Rudyard Kipling and G.K. Chesterton, writers.

1937

- Baldwin resigns; Neville Chamberlain becomes prime minister.
- Divorce on grounds other than adultery is made legal.
- First test of a jet engine by Sir Frank Whittle.

- Introduction of 999 telephone emergency call.
- Death of Lord Rutherford, scientist; Ramsay MacDonald, politician.

1938

- State takes over control of the coal industry.
- Women's Voluntary Service founded (made Royal, 1966).
- Launch of RMS *Queen Elizabeth*.
- Graham Greene publishes *Brighton Rock*.

1939

- Parliament passes Emergency Powers Act.
- Conscription of men introduced.
- Identity cards introduced.
- World War II begins.
- Wholesale evacuation of children from urban areas.
- First air raids.
- Anglo-Saxon treasure found in burial ship at Sutton Hoo.

1940

- Food rationing is introduced.
- Chamberlain resigns; Winston Churchill becomes prime minister.
- Local Defence Volunteers (LDV) founded; name changed to Home Guard.
- Hundreds of small ships join in evacuation of British Expeditionary Force from Dunkirk.
- Channel Islands under German occupation.
- Air war over Kent and Sussex, the battle of Britain, for control of the Channel (August–September), ends in British victory; German invasion plans cancelled.

- Heavy bombing of London and other cities (the 'Blitz') begins.
- George Medal and George Cross introduced.
- Council for Encouragement of Music and the Arts founded.
- Death of Neville Chamberlain, politician; Sir J.J. Thomson, physicist.

1941

- Heavy bombing raids on London and industrial areas.
- Clothes rationing introduced.
- Conscription of women begins.
- First flight of a British jet aircraft.
- Death of Lord Baden-Powell, founder of scouting movement; Virginia Woolf, author.

1942

- Soap rationing introduced.
- Beveridge Report on plans for post-war Britain published.
- Foundation of Oxford Committee for Famine Relief (Oxfam).
- BBC first broadcasts *Desert Island Discs*.
- First discoveries of Roman silver treasures at Mildenhall, Suffolk.

1943

- American forces arrive in England.
- Preparations begin for invasion of Occupied Europe.
- Death of Beatrice Webb, socialist thinker; Beatrix Potter, children's writer.

1944

- Allied invasion of Normandy begins on D-Day (6 June).
- Home Guard disbanded (November).

- Education Act for England and Wales extends secondary education.
- Pay As You Earn (PAYE) tax system introduced by Sir Cornelius Gregg.
- Death of Sir Edwin Lutyens, architect; Sir Henry Wood, conductor; W. Heath Robinson, illustrator.

1945

- War with Germany ends on VE Day (8 May).
- General election results in Labour government under C.R. Attlee.
- War with Japan ends on VJ Day (15 August).
- Demobilisation of armed forces begins.
- Family Allowance (later Child Benefit) introduced.
- Evelyn Waugh publishes *Brideshead Revisited*.
- Death of David Lloyd George, politician.

1946

- Bank of England brought into public ownership.
- Television licences introduced.
- Bread rationing introduced.
- New Bodleian Library opened in Oxford.
- Thirty-three football fans crushed to death at Burnden Park, Bolton.
- Death of J. Maynard Keynes, economist; John Logie Baird, inventor; H.G. Wells, author.

1947

- Coal industry brought into public ownership.
- Princess Elizabeth marries Prince Philip of Greece.
- School leaving age raised to fifteen.

- First British nuclear reactor is built, at Harwell.
- First turbo-prop engine in use (Rolls-Royce Dart).
- Extremely severe winter causes disruption and hardship.
- Death of Sidney Webb, socialist thinker; Stanley Baldwin, politician.

1948

- The National Health Service is brought into being.
- Sir Oswald Mosley revives BUF as British Union Movement.
- Plural voting abolished, only one vote per adult.
- Railways brought into public ownership as British Railways.
- Electricity companies brought into public ownership.
- First British supermarket opens in London.
- Bread rationing is ended.
- George Orwell publishes *1984*.
- Institute of Contemporary Arts founded in London.
- Fourteenth modern Olympic Games are held in London.
- First British Grand Prix to be run at Silverstone.

1949

- Clothes rationing is ended.
- Gas industry brought into public ownership.
- The Goon Show radio series begins.
- First flight of De Havilland Comet, first jet airliner.
- The Nature Conservancy Council is established.
- Death of Tommy Handley, comedian.

1950

- Labour win general election with much reduced majority.
- Stone of Destiny is removed from Westminster Abbey by Scottish nationalists.
- Korean War begins: troops sent from Britain against North Korea.
- Petrol and soap rationing ended.
- Introduction of free legal aid.
- Bertrand Russell wins Nobel Prize for Literature.
- The BBC first broadcasts *The Archers*, radio serial.
- C.S. Lewis publishes *The Lion, the Witch and the Wardrobe*.
- Death of George Orwell, author; George Bernard Shaw, playwright.

1951

- Conservatives win general election; Churchill again prime minister.
- Guy Burgess and Donald Maclean, diplomats, revealed as Soviet spies, flee to Russia.
- Festival of Britain is held, in London.
- Zebra crossings introduced for pedestrians.
- First performance of *Billy Budd*, opera by Benjamin Britten.
- First Miss World contest is held, in London.
- Death of Ernest Bevin, politician; Ivor Novello, composer.

1952

- Death of George VI; accession of Elizabeth II.
- Identity cards abolished.
- Devastating floods at Lynmouth, North Devon.
- First performance of *The Mousetrap*, by Agatha Christie.

- Tramcars abolished in London.
- Myxomatosis rabbit disease introduced to limit rabbit population.

1953
- Rationing of sweets and sugar ended.
- Amnesty granted to World War II military deserters.
- British expedition is first to reach summit of Mount Everest, though actual summiteers are Edmund Hillary (New Zealand) and Tensing Norgay (Nepal).
- Launch of Royal Yacht *Britannia*.
- Execution of John Christie, multiple murderer.
- Sir Arthur Bliss is made Master of the Queen's Musick.
- 'Double helix' structure of DNA discovered by James Watson and Francis Crick.
- Death of Queen Mary, widow of George V; Kathleen Ferrier, singer; Hilaire Belloc, author.

1954
- All food rationing ends.
- William Golding publishes *Lord of the Flies*; Kingsley Amis publishes *Lucky Jim*.
- Roger Bannister is first man to run a four-minute mile (6 May).
- Death by suicide of Alan Turing, mathematician and computer scientist.

1955
- Churchill resigns; Sir Anthony Eden becomes prime minister; Conservatives win general election.
- Execution of Ruth Ellis for murder: last woman to be hanged in England.
- Commercial television is introduced.

- The hovercraft is patented by Sir Christopher Cockerell.
- Death of Sir Alexander Fleming, scientist.

1956
- Suez Canal Zone is invaded following secret agreement between Britain, France and Israel. British forces withdrawn under UN and US pressure.
- British Railways rename third class as second class.
- Premium savings bonds first issued; winners decided by electronic sorting machine, ERNIE.
- First experimental colour transmissions.
- First performance of *Look Back in Anger* by John Osborne.
- Calder Hall atomic power station commissioned.
- Death of A.A. Milne and Sir Max Beerbohm, authors.

1957
- Eden resigns; Harold Macmillan becomes prime minister.
- John Braine publishes *Room at the Top*.
- First British hydrogen bomb tested at Christmas Island.
- Jodrell Bank radio telescope begins operations.
- Death of Dorothy L. Sayers, detective storywriter.

1958
- First women peers take their seats in House of Lords.
- Bertrand Russell and Canon John Collins found the Campaign for Nuclear Disarmament (CND).
- London Planetarium opens.

- Inauguration of Duke of Edinburgh Awards scheme.
- Last presentation of debutantes to the Queen.
- Parking meters first introduced, in Westminster.
- Race riots in Notting Hill Gate, London, and Nottingham.
- First performance of *The Birthday Party* by Harold Pinter.
- Gatwick Airport opens.
- Britain's first motorway opens (Preston bypass).
- Seven members of Manchester United Football Club killed in plane crash at Munich.
- Death of Christabel Pankhurst, women's rights campaigner; Ralph Vaughan Williams, composer; Marie Stopes, pioneer of birth control.

1959

- Conservatives win general election; Macmillan remains prime minister.
- Last flypast of Hurricane and Spitfire aircraft over London.
- Postcodes are introduced.
- London–Birmingham motorway (M1) opened.
- Death of Sir Jacob Epstein, sculptor; Sir Stanley Spencer, painter.

1960

- Launch of HMS *Dreadnought*, first British nuclear submarine.
- Introduction of Ministry of Transport (MOT) tests on older vehicles.
- First traffic wardens, in London.
- Founding of the Royal Shakespeare Company.
- Publication of unexpurgated *Lady Chatterley's Lover* by D.H. Lawrence is

followed by trial for obscenity; prosecution fails.
- First episode of *Coronation Street* shown on TV.
- Football League matches televised for first time.
- Death of Aneurin Bevan, politician; Sylvia Pankhurst, women's rights campaigner.

1961

- Farthing ceases to be legal tender.
- Oral contraceptive pill is introduced.
- First minicabs in London.
- Betting legalised: first betting shops open.
- Tamar Road Bridge opens.
- Death of Sir Thomas Beecham, conductor; Augustus John, painter; George Formby, comedian.

1962

- New Coventry Cathedral is consecrated.
- Establishment of the National Theatre; Sir Laurence Olivier is first director.
- Crick and Watson awarded the Nobel Prize for medicine and physiology.
- Thalidomide drug is withdrawn after showing it causes severe defects in unborn children.
- Death of R.H. Tawney and G.M. Trevelyan, historians; Charles Laughton, actor and director.

1963

- British application for entry to the European Economic Community is vetoed by France.
- Kim Philby, revealed as a spy, defects to Russia.
- Further spy scandal causes resignation

of John Profumo, Secretary of State for War.
- Macmillan resigns; Sir Alec Douglas Home renounces peerage to become prime minister.
- Britain, USA and Russia sign nuclear test-ban treaty.
- Britain agrees to buy Polaris ballistic missiles from USA.

1964

- Labour victory in general election: Harold Wilson becomes prime minister.
- Last two men hanged for murder in England.
- First pirate radio station, Radio Caroline.
- BBC2 TV channel begins transmission.
- Radio Manx is Britain's first licensed commercial radio station.
- Death of Ian Fleming, author of 'James Bond' novels; Lord Beaverbrook, press magnate and wartime minister.

1965

- Edward Heath becomes the first elected leader of the Conservative Party.
- Death penalty for murder is abolished.
- Opening of the Pennine Way, long-distance walkers' path.
- Motorway speed limit fixed at 70 mph.
- Opening of the Post Office Tower, London's tallest building.
- TV advertising of cigarettes is banned.
- Founding of the Confederation of British Industries (CBI).

- First use of starting stalls in horse races, at Newmarket.
- Death of Sir Winston Churchill, politician and war leader; Stan Laurel, film comedian.

1966

- Labour wins general election; Wilson remains prime minister.
- Post Office issues special Christmas stamps for the first time.
- Myra Hindley and Ian Brady sentenced to life imprisonment for the 'Moors murders' of children.
- First performance of *Rosencrantz and Guildenstern are Dead*, by Tom Stoppard.
- Launch of HMS *Resolution*, nuclear submarine with Polaris missiles.
- Gas fields discovered in the North Sea.
- John Ridgeway and Chay Blyth are first Britons to row across the Atlantic.
- World Cup football tournament held in England: England are winners.
- Death of Evelyn Waugh, novelist.

1967

- First British Ombudsman appointed.
- Parliament legalises abortion as a medical procedure.
- Steel industry is again brought into public ownership.
- Majority verdicts allowed in jury trials.
- 'Breathalyser' tests introduced for motorists.
- Consecration of new Roman Catholic cathedral in Liverpool.
- BBC2 begins broadcasting in colour.
- Radio Leicester is England's first local radio station.

- North Sea gas first pumped ashore on the Durham coast.
- Launch of liner *Queen Elizabeth II*.
- First British satellite, *Ariel III*, is launched.
- Death of John Masefield, poet laureate; Clement Attlee (Earl Attlee), politician; Vivien Leigh, actress; Arthur Ransome, children's writer.

1968

- Race Relations Act comes into force.
- Introduction of decimal coinage with the 5p and 2p coins.
- Post Office introduces two classes of mail, first and second.
- New Euston Station is opened, with electrification of West Coast main line; last steam trains run on British Railways.
- First heart transplant in Britain carried out.
- Manchester United are first English team to win the European Cup.
- Death of Tony Hancock, TV comedian, by suicide in Australia; Enid Blyton, children's writer.

1969

- Voting age is lowered from twenty-one to eighteen.
- The 50p decimal coin is introduced.
- British–French supersonic airliner Concorde makes its maiden flight.
- Death of Richmal Crompton, children's writer; Brian Jones, Rolling Stones musician.

1970

- Conservatives win general election; Edward Heath becomes prime minister.

- Britain makes third application to join the European Economic Community.
- Ten-shilling notes withdrawn from circulation.
- Germaine Greer publishes *The Female Eunuch*.
- Death of Bertrand Russell (Lord Russell), philosopher; E.M. Forster, novelist; Sir John Barbirolli, conductor of the Hallé Orchestra.

1971

- Decimal coinage in full use; abolition of old pence and shillings.
- Inauguration of the Open University.

1972

- 'Bloody Sunday' in Northern Ireland: British paratroops fire on civil rights demonstrators, killing thirteen.
- Many Ugandan Asians come to Britain after expulsion from Uganda.
- Sir John Betjeman appointed poet laureate.
- Death of the Duke of Windsor, formerly King Edward VIII; C. Day Lewis, poet laureate.

1973

- Britain joins the European Economic Community.
- Miners' strike brings 'three-day week' to conserve coal stocks.
- Value Added Tax (VAT) introduced.
- Establishment of the British Library, formerly part of the British Museum.
- Commercial radio stations begin broadcasting.
- Death of Sir Noel Coward, playwright; J.R.R. Tolkien, academic and author; W.H. Auden, poet.

1974

- Minority Labour government under Wilson after general election (March); further general election (October) produces small Labour majority.
- IRA bombs kill 21 and injure 120 in two Birmingham pubs.
- Disappearance of Lord Lucan following murder of his children's nanny and attempted murder of his wife.
- Covent Garden fruit market moves to new site at Nine Elms, London.

1975

- Conservatives elect Margaret Thatcher as first woman leader of a major political party.
- Referendum on British membership of the Common Market: majority in favour.
- Equal Pay and Sex Discrimination Acts come into force.
- Parliamentary debates broadcast for the first time.
- Domestic video recorders go on sale.
- Death of P.G. (Sir Pelham) Wodehouse, author; Sir Arthur Bliss, composer; Sir Julian Huxley, biologist.

1976

- Wilson resigns; James Callaghan becomes prime minister.
- National Exhibition Centre (NEC) opened at Birmingham.
- Richard Dawkins publishes *The Selfish Gene*.
- Death of Dame Agatha Christie, crime writer; Viscount Montgomery, soldier; Benjamin Britten (Lord Britten), composer.

1977

- Lib–Lab pact formed by Labour and Liberal parties.
- Red Rum wins the Grand National for a record third time.
- Death of Sir Charles (Charlie) Chaplin, actor; Sir Terence Rattigan, playwright.

1978

- Industrial disputes and pay freeze create 'Winter of Discontent'.
- First 'test-tube' baby, Louise Brown, is born.

1979

- Conservatives win general election; Margaret Thatcher becomes first woman prime minister.
- Sir Anthony Blunt, Surveyor of the Queen's Pictures, exposed as a Soviet spy.
- Death of Dame Gracie Fields, singer.

1980

- Post Office loses control of telephone system with formation of British Telecom.
- Special Air Service (SAS) troops storm the Iranian Embassy to release hostages.
- Modernised Book of Common Prayer is published.
- William Golding publishes *Rites of Passage*.
- Death of John Lennon, former Beatles singer, murdered in New York; Sir Alfred Hitchcock, film director; Sir Oswald Mosley, politician; Sir Cecil Beaton, photographer.

1981

- Four former Labour politicians form the Social Democratic Party.
- Peter Sutcliffe is convicted of the 'Yorkshire Ripper' murders.
- Wedding of Prince Charles and Lady Diana Spencer.
- Summer riots in Brixton, Liverpool and Manchester.
- Opening of the Humber Bridge.
- Death of Jessie Matthews, actress; Bill Shankly, football manager.

1982

- Unemployment in Britain exceeds three million for first time since the 1930s.
- Falklands War: Britain dispatches a task force to reclaim the Falkland Islands, following an Argentinian invasion (5 April). Argentinians surrender, June 14.
- *Mary Rose*, sixteenth-century warship, raised in the Solent.
- Women's Peace Camp established at US Air Force base, Greenham Common.
- Pope John Paul II makes first visit of a reigning pope to Britain.
- Channel 4 goes on the air.
- Thames Flood Barrier in use for the first time.

1983

- Conservatives win general election; Thatcher continues as prime minister.
- Wearing of front seat belts in cars is made compulsory.
- William Golding is awarded the Nobel Prize for Literature.
- Death of David Niven and Sir Ralph Richardson, actors; Sir William Walton, composer.

1984

- The European Community is established.
- IRA bomb kills five people at Conservative Party Conference hotel in Brighton.
- A woman police officer, Yvonne Fletcher, is shot dead by a gunman during the Libyan Embassy siege.
- Miners strike against large-scale closures of coalmines.
- Fire causes serious damage to York Minster.
- Ted Hughes is appointed poet laureate.
- Death of Sir John Betjeman, poet laureate; James Mason and Richard Burton, actors; Eric Morecambe, comedian; J.B. Priestley, author and wartime broadcaster.

1985

- Miners return to work after failure of year-long strike.
- Wreck of the *Titanic* is located in North Atlantic.
- 'Live Aid' charity drive raises £40 million for victims of Ethiopian famine.
- England banned from international soccer after Liverpool fans riot at Heysel Stadium, Brussels.
- Death of Sir Michael Redgrave, actor; Laura Ashley, fashion retailer; Robert Graves and Philip Larkin, poets.

1986

- Britain signs up to the Single European Act.
- Construction of Channel Tunnel begins.

- Death of Henry Moore, sculptor; Cary Grant, British-born film actor.

1987

- Conservatives returned in general election: Margaret Thatcher begins her third term as prime minister.
- Plans to introduce a Community Charge are denounced as a 'poll tax'.
- Car ferry *Herald of Free Enterprise* capsizes off Zeebrugge, with loss of 188 lives.
- Order of the Garter is opened to women.
- Stock values collapse on 'Black Monday' (19 October) in London.
- Death of Jacqueline du Pré, cellist.

1988

- Liberal and Social Democratic Parties merge to form Social and Democratic Liberal Party (SDLP).
- National Theatre becomes Royal National Theatre.
- Stephen Hawking publishes *A Brief History of Time*.
- Death of Trevor Howard, actor; Sir Frederick Ashton, choreographer; Kenneth Williams, comedian.

1989

- First televising of proceedings in the House of Commons.
- Salman Rushdie publishes *The Satanic Verses*: then threatened with death by a *fatwah* from Ayatollah Khomeini of Iran.
- Release of 'Guildford Four', wrongly convicted of IRA pub bombings in 1974.
- Disaster at Hillsborough Stadium, Sheffield: ninety-five football fans crushed to death when barriers collapse.
- Death of Lord (Laurence) Olivier, actor-director; Daphne du Maurier, novelist; Sir A.J. Ayer, philosopher.

1990

- Britain joins the Exchange Rate Mechanism (ERM) intended to stabilise European currency systems; British government rejects timetable for establishment of a single European currency.
- Margaret Thatcher resigns as prime minister and Conservative leader; John Major becomes prime minister.
- Poll tax is implemented: protests in London turn into riots.
- First Gulf War: Britain joins USA and other nations in condemning the Iraqi occupation of Kuwait.
- Channel Tunnel excavation teams meet in the middle.

1991

- The government proposes the replacement of poll tax by Council Tax, based on property values.
- First Gulf War: British units participate in 'Operation Desert Storm' to return Kuwait to its previous rule.
- Mysterious death of Robert Maxwell, newspaper publisher, revealed to have left huge debts and evidence of financial chicanery.
- Death of Dame Peggy Ashcroft, actress; Dame Margot Fonteyn, ballerina; Freddie Mercury, pop singer.

1992

- Conservatives win general election; Major remains prime minister.
- The coal industry is privatised.

- Run on the pound and financial crisis force British withdrawal from the ERM.
- Legal separation of Prince Charles and Princess Diana.
- Windsor Castle badly damaged by fire.
- Death of Robert Morley, actor; Francis Bacon, painter; Benny Hill and Frankie Howerd, comedians.

1993
- Implementation of Maastricht Treaty creates the European Union (EU).
- Single European Market inaugurated.
- Government admits to secret talk with IRA leaders.
- Betty Boothroyd becomes first woman Speaker of House of Commons.
- Police are accused of mishandling inquiry after murder of a black youth, Stephen Lawrence, in south London.
- Death of Sir William Golding, novelist; Anthony Burgess, writer; Audrey Hepburn, actress.

1994
- Tony Blair is elected leader of the Labour Party.
- National Lottery introduced.
- Sunday shopping is legalised.
- Channel Tunnel is opened for rail travel between England and France.
- Death of Peter Cushing, actor; Derek Jarman and Lindsay Anderson, film directors; John Osborne, playwright.

1995
- Major submits himself for re-election as Tory leader; wins, and continues as prime minister.
- Blair wins vote to rewrite clause four of Labour Party's constitution.

- Unemployment lowest for fifteen years.
- Nuclear power plants to be privatised.
- Frederick West, accused of multiple sexual attacks and murders in Gloucester, commits suicide in prison.
- Will Carling, English Rugby captain, is sacked after describing the game's ruling body as 'fifty-seven old farts'.
- Death of Lord (Harold) Wilson and Lord Home, politicians; Patricia Highsmith, crime writer; Jean Muir, fashion designer.

1996
- Written preliminary driving test introduced.
- IRA bomb blasts on Isle of Dogs and in central Manchester cause huge destruction; over 200 injured.
- Protesters occupy trees to delay building of Newbury bypass.
- Prince Charles and Princess Diana divorce.
- Stone of Destiny formally returned to Scotland from Westminster Abbey.
- Fire on a train blocks the Channel Tunnel.
- EU bans all export of beef from Britain, because of concerns over 'mad cow' disease.
- Euro '96 football tournament is held in England; England defeated in semifinal by Germany.
- Death of William Rushton, humorist; Bob Paisley, football manager; Marjorie Proops, journalist.

1997
- 'Sleaze' accusations and scandals damage the standing of the Major government.

- Labour victory in general election: Tony Blair becomes prime minister.
- Control of base interest rate is passed to the Bank of England.
- £2 coin is introduced.
- IRA bomb scare stops the Grand National.
- Alliance & Leicester Building Society is floated as a public company; resulting windfall for members from this and other demutualisations is estimated at over £22 billion.
- Britain's ninety-nine-year lease of Hong Kong ends; China takes over.
- Royal Yacht *Britannia* is decommissioned.
- Death of Denis Compton, cricketer; Rev. W. Awdry, children's writer; V.S. Pritchett, author.

1998

- Severe floods in central England: worst of twentieth century.
- Good Friday Agreement hailed as producing a peace process for Northern Ireland.
- Government announces end of peers' hereditary right to sit in the House of Lords.
- Violent outbreaks at the public inquiry into the 1993 Stephen Lawrence murder case.
- 'Countryside March' in London is claimed to be largest demonstration for a decade.
- Michael Owen, at eighteen, is England's youngest-ever football international.
- Death of Frank Muir, humorist; Ted Hughes, poet laureate; Enoch Powell, politician; Catherine Cookson, novelist; Sir Michael Tippett, composer.

1999

- Bomb attacks in Brixton market, London, and a gay pub in Soho, London: 2 dead and over 120 people injured.
- Farmers protest over plummeting prices for sheep and lamb.
- Millennium Dome and 'London Eye' Ferris Wheel set up.
- British Steel merges with Dutch Hoogovens, as Corus: cutbacks in staff and production are announced.
- Thirty people killed in train crash outside Paddington Station.
- Andrew Motion is appointed poet laureate.
- Manchester United win the European Cup.
- Lennox Lewis is world heavyweight champion.
- Death of Lionel Bart, composer; Basil Hume, cardinal; Dame Iris Murdoch, novelist; Lord (Donald) Soper, preacher and politician; Yehudi Menuhin (Lord Menuhin), musician; Dusty Springfield, singer.

2000

- Widespread fears of computer breakdowns at 'Y2K' are not borne out.
- Applications for political asylum reach record level.
- Post Office proposes to change its name to 'Consignia'.
- Formal lifting of the ban on homosexuals joining the armed forces.
- Ken Livingstone is elected as first Mayor of London (post of Lord Mayor of City of London is not affected).
- Fifty-eight illegal immigrants found suffocated in a lorry at Dover.
- £530 million government aid is directed to 'Super Jumbo' European

Airbus project.

- London Stock Exchange votes to turn itself into a public limited company.
- BMW sells Rover car business to the Phoenix Consortium.
- Genetically modified crops are planted at a number of test sites; Norfolk jury acquits Greenpeace campaigners of damage.
- Attendances at the Millennium Dome are judged to be disappointing.
- Fuel tax protests and roadblocks create a temporary crisis (September).
- Death of Lord Annan, academic administrator; Bernie Grant, politician; Lords Coggan and Runcie, former Archbishops of Canterbury.

2001

- Outbreak of foot and mouth disease spreads rapidly across the country from February; escalates in May: over 2,000 cases in the year, with great disruption to country life and the slaughter of millions of animals.
- Labour win general election in lowest turnout (59.4 per cent) since 1918; Blair remains prime minister.
- Emergency anti-terrorism bill following 'September 11' attack on USA; war cabinet is set up to supervise joint attack with USA on Afghanistan.
- Efforts to sell the Millennium Dome collapse.
- House of Lords votes against a ban on foxhunting.
- First fifteen appointed 'people's peers' join House of Lords.
- Racial violence flares in northern cities, culminating in Bradford in July.
- Lord (Jeffrey) Archer, Conservative politician, convicted of perjury and jailed.

- Death of Sir David Spedding, ex-head of MI6; Lords Hailsham and Longford, politicians; George Harrison, musician.

2002

- Queen Elizabeth II celebrates her golden jubilee.
- Foot and mouth disease outbreak is declared over (January).
- Severe gales and storms in the north.
- Further local referendums to determine whether mayors should be elected: so far eighteen have been held, with only six accepting the proposal.
- Freight traffic through the Channel Tunnel is suspended because of presence of illegal immigrants.
- Murder of two young girls in Soham prompts the establishment of a new Violent and Sex Offenders Register.
- The High Court rules that a mentally alert person can legally end her life by ceasing to use a vital ventilating machine.
- Collapse of ITV Digital TV scheme creates problems for many football clubs who will not now receive payments from it.
- Seven killed in Potters Bar rail crash; seventy injured.
- Consignia reverts to being Royal Mail plc.
- Fertility rates of women in England and Wales lowest since records began in 1924: 1.64 children per woman of child-bearing age.
- Death of Princess Margaret; Queen Elizabeth the Queen Mother; Lady (Barbara) Castle, politician.

2003

- Tobacco advertising is banned.
- House of Commons votes again to abolish hunting foxes with hounds.
- Largest protest demonstration ever seen in London, against war with Iraq (14 February).
- Britain participates with America in air attack on, and invasion of, Iraq; controversy follows over justification of the war. The government is accused of 'sexing up' intelligence reports about Iraq's possession of 'weapons of mass destruction'.
- Government plans for large increase of population in south-east, and publishes proposals for referendums on three northern regional parliaments by October 2004.
- The government announces the end of the lord chancellor's office, and a new supreme court, independent of government control.
- London congestion plan is introduced; drivers pay to enter central area.
- The Church of England's first overtly gay nominee for a bishopric (Reading) stands down because of wide opposition.
- Gravesend records England's highest-ever temperature, 100.6°F/38.1°C (August).
- Concorde supersonic jet is retired from regular service.
- The suicide of Dr David Kelly, a government weapons expert, intensifies the Iraqi weapons controversy; Lord Hutton is asked to inquire into the circumstances of his death.
- Michael Howard is elected Tory leader following Iain Duncan Smith's resignation.
- Britain's first toll motorway opens, around Birmingham.
- FA Cup won by Arsenal; Manchester United are Premiership champions.
- Deaths of Sir Wilfred Thesiger, explorer and writer; Lord (Roy) Jenkins, politician; Wendy Hiller, actress; Barry Sheene, motor-cycling champion; Bernard Williams, philosopher.

2004

- Lord Hutton's report severely criticises the BBC's editorial service, and though accepting that the Joint Intelligence Committee may have been 'subconsciously influenced' by government desires for a compelling dossier, exonerates the government from 'sexing up' the case. The chairman and managing director of the BBC both resign.
- A further report under Lord Butler is set up to examine the accuracy of intelligence reports leading to the invasion of Iraq.
- Multiple murderer, Dr Harold Shipman, commits suicide in prison.
- A national police Serious Organised Crime Agency (SOCA) is to be set up.
- Twenty illegal immigrant workers from China are drowned while cockling in Morecambe Bay.
- Five British prisoners released from US prison at Guantanamo Bay.
- Prime Minister Blair announces there will be a referendum on acceptance of the new EU constitution. The government provisionally signs it. European Parliament elections (June) show substantial gains for anti-Europe candidates.

- London is named a candidate city for 2012 Olympics.
- FA Cup won by Manchester United; Arsenal are Premiership Champions.

- Deaths of Alistair Cooke, broadcaster; Thom Gunn, poet; Sir Peter Ustinov, actor; Sir Alan Bullock, historian.

Bibliography

Black, J.B., *The Reign of Elizabeth*. 2nd edn, Oxford, 1959

Bury, J.B., and others, *The Cambridge Medieval History*. Cambridge, 1936–39

Clapham, J.H., *A Concise Economic History of Great Britain*. Cambridge, 1949

Clark, G. Kitson, *The Making of Victorian England*. London, 1962

Cole, G.D.H. and Postgate, Raymond, *The Common People*. London, 1938

Colley, Linda, *Britons*. London, 1992

Drabble, Margaret, *The Oxford Companion to English Literature*. Oxford, 2000

Elton, G.R., *England Under the Tudors*. 3rd edn, London, 1991

Ensor, Sir Robert, *England 1870–1914*. Oxford, 1936

Feiling, Keith, *A History of England*. London, 1952

Hill, Christopher, *Puritanism and Revolution*. London, 1958

Hutton, Will, *The Stakeholding Society*. London, 1999

Langford, Paul, *Englishness Identified*. Oxford, 2000

Marcus, G., *A Naval History of England: The Age of Nelson*. London, 1971

Poole, Austin L., *From Domesday Book to Magna Carta*. 2nd edn, Oxford, 1955

Porter, Roy, *English Society in the Eighteenth Century*. London, 1990

Salway, Peter, *Roman Britain*. Oxford, 1980

Singer, Charles, *A Short History of Scientific Ideas*. Oxford, 1959

Stenton, Sir Frank, *Anglo-Saxon England*. Oxford, 1971

Taylor, A.J.P., *English History, 1900–1945*. Oxford, 1965

Trevelyan, G.M., *History of England*. London, 1926

Whitelock, Dorothy, *The Beginnings of English Society*. London, 1952

Williams, Raymond, *Culture and Society, 1780–1950*. London, 1958

Ziegler, Philip, *The Black Death*. London, 1969

Index

INDEX